GRAPHIC SCIENCE AND DESIGN

GRAPHIC SCIENCE AND DESIGN

THIRD EDITION

THOMAS E. FRENCH
Late Professor of Engineering Drawing,
The Ohio State University

CHARLES J. VIERCK
Visiting Professor to the Graphics Division of the
Department of Mechanical Engineering,
University of Florida, Gainesville

McGRAW-HILL BOOK COMPANY

New York   St. Louis   San Francisco
Düsseldorf   London   Mexico   Panama   Sydney   Toronto

GRAPHIC SCIENCE AND DESIGN

Library of Congress Catalog Card Number: 70-118395

34567890   VHVH   798765

ISBN 07-022301-7

This book was set in Baskerville by Graphic Services, Inc., printed on
permanent paper and bound by Von Hoffman Press, Inc. The designer
was John L. Horton. The editors were Roland S. Woolson, Jr., and
Frances A. Neal. John F. Harte supervised the production.

PREFACE

Engineering education, since its very beginning, has undergone many changes in curriculum and literature, paralleling new discoveries and advancements in scientific knowledge. Recently, but especially in the last decade, analysis and appraisal of all aspects of engineering teaching has intensified because of accelerated research and development in practically all phases of science and engineering. When one considers the advances in knowledge of atomic energy, communications, space technology, electronics, and many other scientific fields, the increase in total scientific and engineering comprehension is quite astounding. This expansion has forced engineering educators to fit more and more factual information into the curriculum and authors of textbooks have continually revised their works to upgrade, modernize, and keep abreast of current practice.

One important and recent outgrowth of engineering thinking is the realization that we must give more attention to design methods and procedures in all phases of engineering instruction. The reasons for this changing attitude are numerous, but basically, as scientific and engineering knowledge increases, the application of that knowledge in the design of new devices, machines, structures, hardware, etc., becomes much more complex and involved. Until recently, design as such has been approached more or less by assuming that studying one's field intensively would almost automatically develop the ability to design. We know now that this assumption is entirely erroneous. In years past, industry bore the burden of design teaching, but now that such methods and procedures have been brought to some prominence in industrial literature, feedback to engineering education is occurring. Further, the departments of engineering graphics throughout the country are prepared to lift some of the teaching burden from major degree-giving departments and are now emerging as important centers for the teaching of design. This is because design, in an engineering sense, requires education in a number of areas closely allied to graphic methods.

First of all, a designer must have a complete command of graphic representations. This is mandatory in order to communicate design concepts to others who will prepare complete drawings and documents for construction.

Second, the designer must also have a complete command of spatial relationships and designations, both graphical and mathematical, so that his design will be precise regarding sizes, functions, and relationships of components.

Third, the designer must be familiar with the use of materials and their specifications so that strength, environmental stability, and reliability will be maintained. The study of materials and their characteristics is an active and continuing investigation because new materials are constantly being developed.

Fourth, the designer must be educated in graphical and mathematical methods so that his designs are valid from a purely scientific standpoint.

Fifth, the designer must be thoroughly versed in design methods and procedures. It is in this area that the engineering curriculum can be greatly improved. Because of emphasis on the newer aspects of engineering practice, the teaching of design as such becomes increasingly significant. Moreover, a hopeful attitude now emerges that brings design to a new foreground of engineering thinking and accomplishment.

Sixth, the designer must have experience. This comes through involvement in numerous and varied problems during the learning phases, coupled with significant guidance by accomplished and inspiring teachers.

On the basis of the foregoing conceptions, this textbook has been prepared. Chapters 1 through 8 give information on representation. Chapters 9 through 15 discuss spatial conceptions and determinations. Chapters 16 through 19 present practical elements of construction. Chapter 18 is specifically devoted to procedures and methods for the teaching of engineering design. Chapters 20 through 24 cover graphical solutions and graphical-mathematical counterparts. Finally, Chap. 25 contains a number of professional problems for discussion and accomplishment on a higher level than any problem material offered previously in any graphics text.

It is the author's conviction that with this text, the subject of graphics attains a professional standing not heretofore conceived as the role of graphics in engineering.

Even though the teaching of design in the graphics department is presently very important, this does not mean that the older conceptions of graphics teaching are any less important than formerly. Every engineer must be thoroughly familiar with graphic methods.

Bookmaking also plays an important part in the overall conception of a text. The extensive and completely functional use of color and other illustrative techniques adds greatly to the effectiveness of the book. Research on teaching methods has proved that page makeup, effective use of color, illustration placement, caption content, and some other factors aid greatly in the processes of learning and retention.

A book of such scope and completeness requires cooperation between the author and all other persons involved in bringing the work to fruition. The frank, honest, and sometimes extensive discussion with associates is highly valued. In addition, Mr. David Beal and Professors Thomas Neff and James Smith aided in the prepara-

tion of the chapter on professional problems and Professor Richard
I. Hang worked closely with the author on the preparation of the
chapter on graphical and mathematical counterparts. Also greatly
appreciated is the assistance of Esther E. Vierck in the total effort
necessary to bring this work to completion.

Chas. J. Vierck
Tequesta, Florida
November, 1969

CONTENTS

GRAPHIC SCIENCE AND DESIGN

The picture at left illustrates an important difference between the graphic language and word languages. The objects shown may seem unfamiliar and unrelated; nevertheless, they are common in hydraulic research and other phases of engineering investigation.

Study the photograph as you read the text that follows and note the difficulties that occur when an attempt is made to describe physical objects by using words alone.

A comprehensive drawing (graphic representation) of the objects would describe them clearly, concisely, and accurately to the last small detail.

Introduction

1.1. In beginning the study of graphics, you are embarking upon a rewarding educational experience and one that will be of real value in your future career. When you have become proficient in it, you will have at your command a method of communication used in all branches of technical industry, a language unequaled for accurate description of physical objects.

The importance of this graphic language can be seen by comparing it with word languages. All who attend elementary and high school study the language of their country and learn to read, write, and speak it with some degree of skill. In high school and college most students study a foreign language. These word languages are highly developed systems of communication. Nevertheless, any word language is inadequate for describing the size, shape, and relationship of physical objects. Study the photograph at the opening of this chapter and then try to describe it verbally so that someone who has not seen it can form an accurate and complete mental picture. It is almost impossible to do this. Even

3

FIG. 1.1. Try to describe in words the shape, the relative size, and the position of the objects in this picture.

a picture such as Fig. 1.1, although possibly easier to describe, presents an almost insurmountable problem. Furthermore, in trying to describe either picture, you may want to sketch all or part to make the word description more complete, or gesture to aid in explaining shape and relationship. Thus we see that a word language is often without resources for accurate and rapid communication of shape and size and the relationships of components.

Engineering is applied science, and communication of physical facts *must* be complete and accurate. Quantitative relationships are expressed mathematically. The written word completes many descriptions. But whenever machines and structures are designed, described, and built, graphic representation is necessary. Although the works of artists (or photography and other methods of reproduction) would provide pictorial representation, they cannot serve as engineering descriptions. Shaded pictorial drawings and photographs are used for special purposes, but the great bulk of engineering drawings are made in line only, with separate views arranged in a logical system of projection. To these views, dimensions and special notes giving operations and other directions for manufacture are added. This is the language of graphics, which can be defined as *the graphic representation of physical objects and relationships.*

As the foundation upon which all designing and subsequent manufacture are based, engineering graphics is one of the most important single branches of study in a technical school. Every engineering student must know how to make and how to read drawings. The subject is essential in all types of engineering practice, and should be understood by all connected with, or interested

in, technical industry. All designs and directions for manufacture are prepared by draftsmen, professional writers of the language, but even one who may never make drawings must be able to read and understand them or be professionally illiterate. Thorough training in engineering graphics is particularly important for the engineer because he is responsible for and specifies the drawings required in his work and must therefore be able to interpret every detail for correctness and completeness.

Our object is to study the language of engineering graphics so that we can write it, expressing ourselves clearly to one familiar with it, and read it readily when written by another. To do this, we must know its basic theory and composition, and be familiar with its accepted conventions and abbreviations. Since its principles are essentially the same throughout the world, a person who has been trained in the practices of one nation can readily adapt himself to the practices of another.

This language is entirely graphic and written, and is interpreted by acquiring a visual knowledge of the object represented. A student's success with it will be indicated not alone by his skill in execution, but also by his ability to interpret lines and symbols and to visualize clearly in space.

As a background for study, we shall introduce in this chapter various aspects of graphics that will be discussed at length later. It is hoped that this preview will serve as a broad perspective against which the student will see each topic, as it is studied, in relation to the whole. Since our subject is a graphic language, illustrations are helpful in presenting even this introductory material; figures are used both to clarify the text and to carry the presentation forward.

1.2.   ESSENTIALS OF DRAFTING: LINES AND LETTERING.   Drawings are made up of lines that represent the surfaces, edges, and contours of objects. Symbols, dimensional sizes, and word notes are added to these lines, collectively making a complete description. Proficiency in the methods of drawing straight lines, circles, and curves, either freehand or with instruments, and the ability to letter word statements are fundamental to writing the graphic language. Furthermore, lines are connected according to the geometry of the object represented, making it necessary to know the geometry of plane and solid figures and to understand how to combine circles, straight lines, and curves to represent separate views of many geometric combinations.

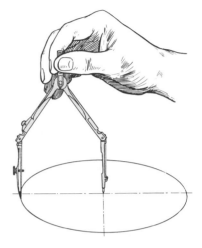

THE USE OF INSTRUMENTS.   Facility in the use of instruments makes for speed and accuracy.

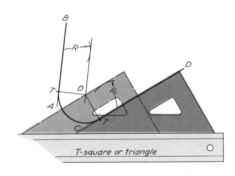

GRAPHIC GEOMETRY.   A knowledge of, and facility in, the construction of lines and geometric figures promotes efficiency.

LETTERING.   The standard lettering for engineering drawings is known as "commercial Gothic." Both vertical and inclined styles are used.

1.3.   METHODS OF EXPRESSION.   There are two fundamental methods of writing the graphic language: freehand and with instruments.

Freehand drawing is done by sketching the lines with no instruments other than pencils and erasers. It is an excellent method during the learning process because of its speed and because at this stage the study of projection is more important than exactness of delineation. Freehand drawings are much used commercially for preliminary designing and for some finished work. Instrument drawing is the standard method of expression. Most drawings are made "to scale," with instruments used to draw straight lines, circles, and curves con- cisely and accurately. Training in both freehand and instrument work is necessary for the engineer so that he will develop competence in writing the graphic language and the ability to judge work done under his direction.

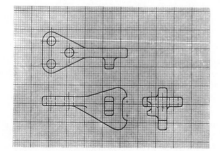

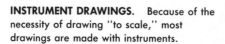

FREEHAND DRAWINGS. The freehand method is fine for early study because it provides training in technique, form, and proportion. It is used commercially for economy.

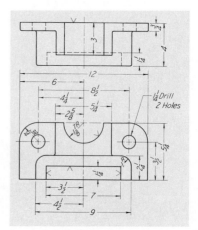

INSTRUMENT DRAWINGS. Because of the necessity of drawing "to scale," most drawings are made with instruments.

1.4. METHODS OF SHAPE DESCRIPTION. Delineation of the *shape* of a part, assembly, or structure is the primary element of graphic communication. Since there are many purposes for which drawings are made, the engineer must select, from the different methods of describing shape, the one best suited to the situation at hand. Shape is described by projection, that is, by the process of causing an image to be formed by rays of sight taken in a particular direction from an object to a picture plane.

Following projective theory, two methods of *representation* are used: orthographic views and pictorial views.

For the great bulk of engineering work, the orthographic system is used, and this method, with its variations and the necessary symbols and abbreviations, constitutes an important part of this book. In the orthographic system, separate views arranged according to the projective theory are made to show clearly all details of the object represented. The figures that follow illustrate the fundamental types of orthographic drawings and orthographic views.

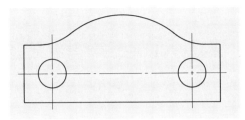

ONE-VIEW DRAWINGS.   These are used whenever views in more than one direction are unnecessary, for example, for parts made of thin material.

TWO-VIEW DRAWINGS.   Parts such as cylinders require only two views. More would duplicate the two already drawn.

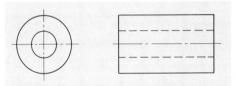

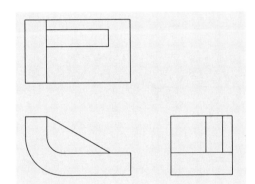

THREE-VIEW DRAWINGS.   Most objects are made up of combined geometric solids. Three views are required to represent their shape.

"Pictorial representation" designates the methods of projection resulting in a view that shows the object approximately as it would be seen by the eye. Pictorial representation is often used for presentation drawings, text, operation, and maintenance book illustrations, and some working drawings.

There are three main divisions of pictorial projection: axonometric, oblique, and perspective. Theoretically, axonometric projection is projection in which only one plane is used, the object being turned so that three faces show. The main axonometric positions are isometric, dimetric, and trimetric.

ISOMETRIC DRAWING.   This method is based on turning the object so that three mutually perpendicular edges are equally foreshortened.

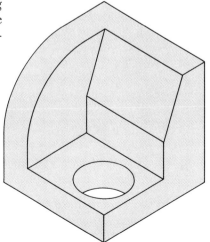

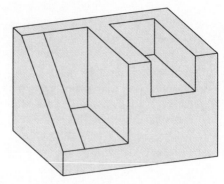

DIMETRIC DRAWING.   This method is based on turning the object so that two mutually perpendicular edges are equally foreshortened.

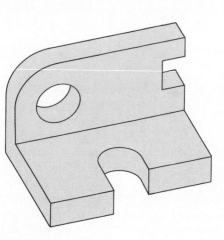

TRIMETRIC DRAWING.   This method is based on turning the object so that three mutually perpendicular edges are all unequally foreshortened.

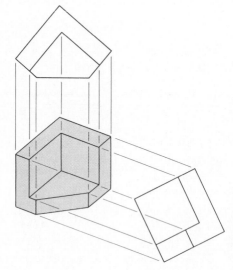

AXONOMETRIC PROJECTION FROM ORTHOGRAPHIC VIEWS. Pictorials—isometric, dimetric, or trimetric—may be obtained by projection from orthographic views. The views are located by a geometric method.

Oblique projection is a pictorial method used principally for objects with circular or curved features only on one face or on parallel faces; and for such objects the oblique is easy to draw and dimension. Perspective projection gives a result identical with what the eye or a single-lens camera would record.

OBLIQUE DRAWING.   This pictorial method is useful for portraying cylindrical parts. Projectors are oblique to the picture plane. Cavalier and cabinet drawings are specific forms.

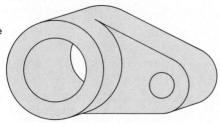

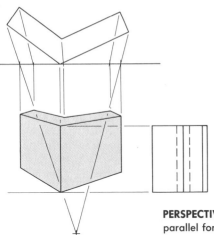

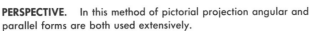

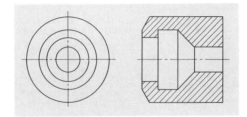

OBLIQUE PROJECTION FROM ORTHOGRAPHIC VIEWS. In this pictorial method views are arranged so that, by projection, an oblique drawing results.

PERSPECTIVE. In this method of pictorial projection angular and parallel forms are both used extensively.

SECTIONAL VIEWS. These are used to clarify the representation of objects with complicated internal detail.

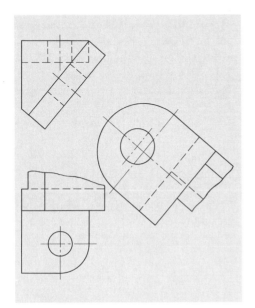

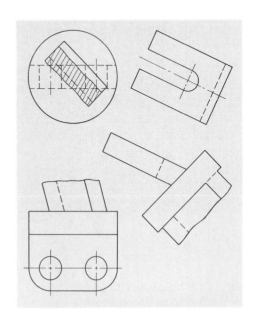

AUXILIARIES: NORMAL, POINT, AND EDGE VIEWS. Auxiliaries are used to show the *normal view* (true size and shape) of an inclined surface (at an angle to two of the planes of projection), shown at left, or of a skew surface (inclined to all three planes of projection), shown at right. Point and edge views are also frequently required.

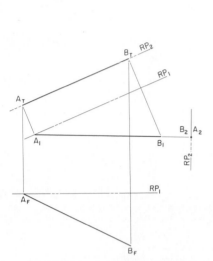

POINT, EDGE, AND NORMAL VIEWS.
These are the views needed to solve
space problems.

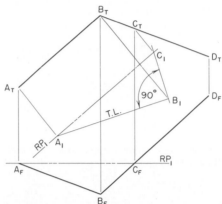

POINTS AND STRAIGHT LINES. These are
the simplest elements of space problems.

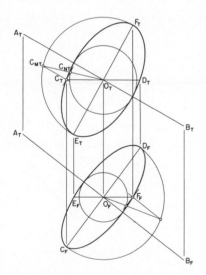

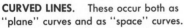

CURVED LINES. These occur both as
"plane" curves and as "space" curves.

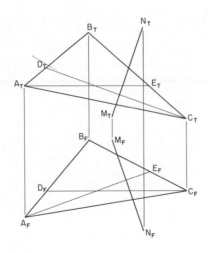

LINES AND PLANES. These elements
are fundamental to many problems.

1.5. **DESCRIPTIVE GEOMETRY.** The continuing study of auxiliaries expands to *descriptive geometry,* the application of the theory of projection to the solution of space problems. Machines and structures are made up, for the most part, of geometrical elements combined in various and sometimes complicated ways. The numerous points, lines, planes, and surfaces are combined to form basic structure, operating components, and housing. These elements of any physical object may involve parallelism, perpendicularity or angularity of lines and planes, and the relationship of these to curved or warped surfaces. Determination of position, clearances, and movement is a basic consideration. In many cases, graphic accuracy is sufficient; in others, graphics is supplemented by mathematical calculations. In either case, a graphic representation is usually necessary for a complete understanding of the space problem and a graphic analysis of the relationship of the elements before mathematical procedures are attempted.

Descriptive geometry is a powerful tool for research, design, and development. Design usually begins with the graphic stage, and there will be a correlated activity involving engineering drawing, engineering geometry, and mathematics, as they relate to the scientific aspects of the design. Engineering geometry will be employed to solve the problems of space and the relationship of the various elements, then will either solve or aid in determining stresses, and will also be invaluable in the visualization of components and the functioning of the completed product.

The following outline classifies problems in engineering geometry according to the geometric elements:

I. Fundamentals
   A. Drawing and projection (Chaps. 1 to 7)
   B. Auxiliaries: point, edge, and normal views (Chap. 8)
II. Points and lines
   A. Points and straight lines (Chap. 9)
   B. Curved lines (Chap. 10)
III. Planes: straight lines and planes (Chap. 11)
IV. Surfaces
   A. Curved and warped surfaces (Chap. 12)
V. The geometry of forces: vector geometry (Chap. 13)
VI. Intersections and developments (Chap. 14)

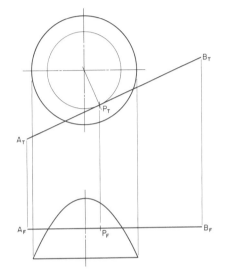

CURVED AND WARPED SURFACES.
These occur often in modern designs.

VECTOR GEOMETRY. The geometry of forces.

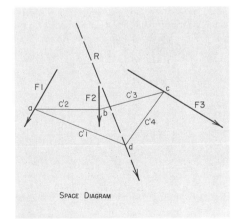

SPACE DIAGRAM

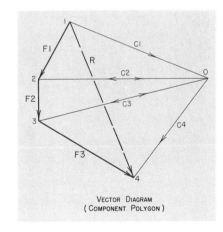

VECTOR DIAGRAM
(COMPONENT POLYGON)

INTERSECTIONS. Geometric surfaces or solids often are combined so that additional projection is needed to determine the line of intersection between the parts.

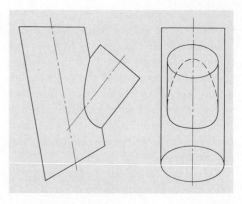

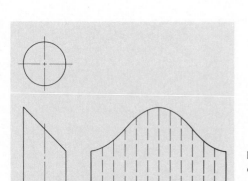

DEVELOPMENTS. These are the projections of geometric surfaces into a flat pattern.

1.6. METHODS OF SIZE DESCRIPTION. After delineation of shape, *size* is the second element of graphic communication, completing the representation of the object. Size is shown by "dimensions," which state linear distances, diameters, radii, and other necessary magnitudes.

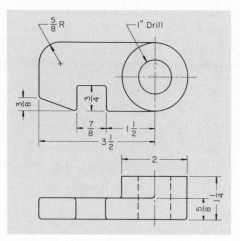

DIMENSIONING ORTHOGRAPHIC DRAWINGS. Dimensions showing the magnitude and relative position of each portion of the object are placed on the view where each dimension is most meaningful.

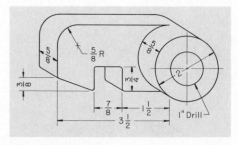

DIMENSIONING PICTORIAL DRAWINGS. The descriptions of magnitudes and positions are shown on the pictorial by dimensions placed so as to be easily readable.

1.7.   BASIC MACHINE ELEMENTS.   Many machine elements occur repeatedly in all kinds of engineering work. Familiarity with these elements is necessary so that dimensioning and specifications on the drawings will be correct. The material that follows introduces basic machine elements and shop processes, so illustrating the principles of engineering drawing laid out in the previous sections.

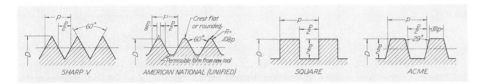

SCREW THREADS.   Screw threads are used on fasteners, on devices for making adjustments, and for the transmission of power and motion. The screw thread is the most extensively used machine element.

FASTENERS.   Bolts and screws in a wide variety of forms are used for fastenings. Familiarity with the standard sizes available and their drawing and specification is fundamental.

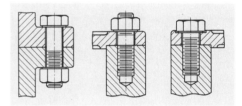

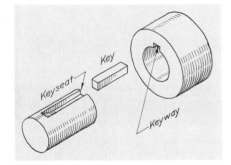

KEYS.   Keys are used to prevent cylindrical elements such as gears and pulleys from rotating on their shafts.

RIVETS.   Rivets are permanent fasteners. They are cylinders of metal with a head on one end. When placed in position, the opposite head is formed by impact.

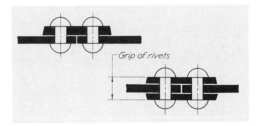

SPRINGS.   A spring is an elastic body that stores energy when deflected. Basic forms are illustrated.

Compression Spring

Torsion Spring

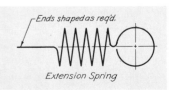

Extension Spring

DRAWINGS: SPECIFICATION FOR MANUFACTURE. To delineate a drawing properly and give accurate size description and specifications for manufacture, a knowledge of processing methods is essential.

DESIGN. Study of the fundamentals of design is mandatory for anyone participating in the creation of new products.

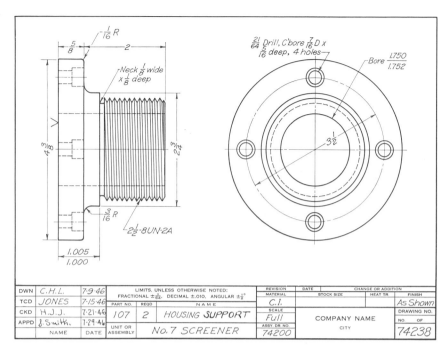

WORKING DRAWINGS.   A knowledge of the methods and procedures for making working drawings is absolutely necessary for anyone involved in the design and production of machines and structures.

DWN	C.H.L.	7-9-46		LIMITS, UNLESS OTHERWISE NOTED: FRACTIONAL $\pm\frac{1}{64}$. DECIMAL $\pm.010$. ANGULAR $\pm\frac{1}{2}°$			REVISION	DATE		CHANGE OR ADDITION	
TCD	JONES	7-15-46					MATERIAL		STOCK SIZE	HEAT TR.	FINISH
			PART NO.	REQD		NAME	C.I.				As Shown
CKD	H.J.J.	7-21-46	107	2	HOUSING SUPPORT		SCALE		COMPANY NAME		DRAWING NO.
APPD	J.Smith.	7-29-46					Full				NO. OF
	NAME	DATE	UNIT OR ASSEMBLY		No.7 SCREENER		ASSY. DR. NO. 74200		CITY		74238

1.8.   GRAPHICS.   Some writers have applied the term "graphics" to all drawing of any kind that may be necessary in engineering or scientific work. A dictionary definition for the word runs as follows: (1) the art of making drawings, as in architecture or engineering, in accordance with mathematical rules; (2) calculation of stresses, etc., from such drawings. The term "engineering graphics" as used in this text is intended to apply in part to both these definitions but is restricted in meaning to apply to the areas of activity which cannot be classified strictly as engineering drawing or engineering geometry.

There is a graphic counterpart for almost every mathematical procedure or method. One can graphically add, subtract, multiply, divide, determine powers and roots, and solve problems by algebra or calculus quite as easily as, in many cases as accurately as, and sometimes more quickly than with symbolic mathematics. Any engineer or scientist not familiar with graphic methods of calculation is approaching his job with only part of the desirable equipment.

In the research, design, and development of modern equipment, reactions, stresses, and deflections have to be calculated. The behavior characteristics of electrical currents, solids, fluids, and gases have to be known. The special properties of materials according to their internal structure play an important part in the design of machines and structures. All these problems of basic science may be handled by mathematics and by graphics. The curves obtained from research will be invaluable in predicting the behavior of materials, etc., when employed in the final product. In many cases the equation of a curve may be determined.

For any standard calculation that must be repeated again and again, a nomograph is an invaluable aid. This may be in the form of special slide rules, conversion charts, or alignment charts of a wide variety.

Problems involving rate of change may be solved easily and within the accuracy of the original data by graphic calculus. In cases where the relationship of rate of change is complex and the mathematical equation cannot be written, the graphic method is the only known method of solution.

The following lists various graphic solutions by type:

I. Charts, graphs, and diagrams (Chap. 20)
II. Graphic solutions of equations (Chap. 21)
III. Graphic solutions of empirical data (Chap. 22)
IV. Graphic calculus (Chap. 23)
V. Graphical-mathematical counterparts (Chap. 24)

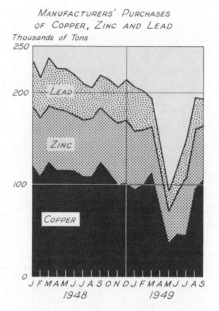

CHARTS, GRAPHS, AND DIAGRAMS.
The graphic representation of statistics.

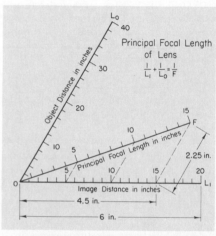

GRAPHIC SOLUTIONS OF EQUATIONS.
These promote economy in many fields.

GRAPHIC SOLUTIONS OF EMPIRICAL DATA. This technique is fundamental to research.

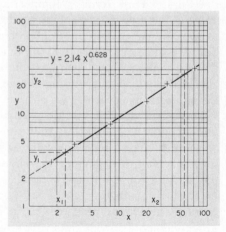

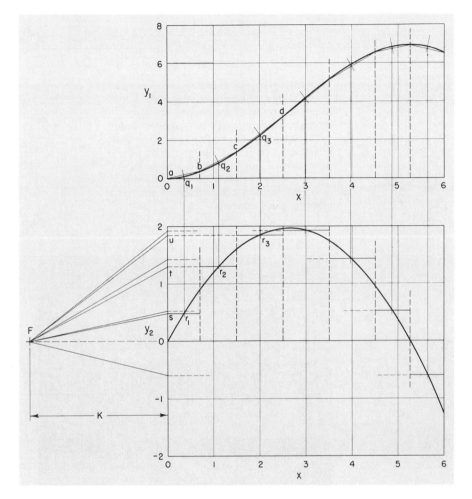

GRAPHIC CALCULUS. The determination of rates of change of variables.

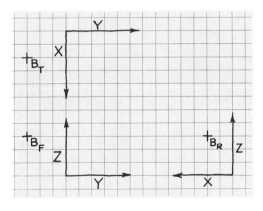

GRAPHICAL-MATHEMATICAL COUNTERPARTS.
For almost every graphic solution there is a mathematical counterpart. In modern engineering practice, especially since the invention and development of computers, graphic designs are supported by mathematical data. An understanding of graphical-mathematical counterparts is necessary before computer programming can proceed.

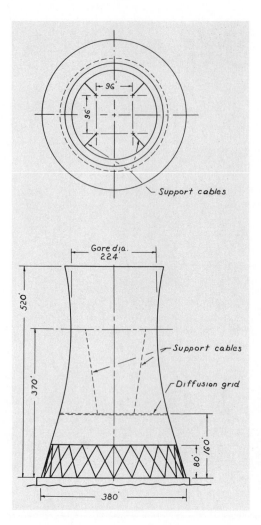

Support cables

Gore dia. 224

520'

370'

Support cables

Diffusion grid

80'

160'

380'

PROFESSIONAL PROBLEMS. Graphics as a course of study has, since its original conception as a fundamental of engineering education, progressed over a number of years to include all the subjects in this text and their correlation to mathematics, physics, chemistry, and other pure sciences. The professional problems given in this text are exercises intended to develop the ability to apply a knowledge of graphics and engineering subjects.

1.9. SPECIAL FIELDS AND PRACTICES. The methods of projection, the choice of representational type (shape description), and the accompanying size description are more or less uniform in all fields because these are the elements of which all drawings are composed. However, for most special fields certain symbols and notation, drawing, and dimensioning practices have been standardized, and a knowledge of these is necessary so that drawings in these fields will be readily and efficiently understood.

Special practices or fields include: charts, graphs, and diagrams; various portions of mechanisms and systems; welding; electrical drawing; structural and topographic practices; and commercial practices and economies. Instructions for making drawings in these fields can be found in many standard textbooks, such as "A Manual of Engineering Drawing for Students and Draftsmen," tenth edition (McGraw-Hill, New York, 1966).

1.10. TERMINOLOGY. During any course of study in engineering drawing the student must become thoroughly familiar with the terminology of design and construction. The glossary of technical, structural, architectural, and welding terms in the Appendix should be consulted as needed. Form the habit of never passing over a word without understanding its meaning completely.

1.11. APPENDIX TABLES. Many details of engineering drawing depend upon specifications for drills, bolts and screws, fits, limits, pipe sizes, symbols, and other standards. It is important to become well acquainted with this material, which is given in the Appendix.

DROPPER BOTTLE IN
BOTTLEHOLDER

QUEEZE" DROPPER TUBE

2.4. Standard bottle in
lder; Leroy pen-filler cartridge.
e cartridge is particularly
nvenient.

2.10. PENCIL POINTER. After the wood of the ordinary pencil is cut away with a pocketknife or mechanical sharpener, the lead must be formed to a long, conic point. A lance-tooth steel file, Fig. 2.3*A*, about 6 in. long is splendid for the purpose. Some prefer the standard sandpaper pencil-pointer pad, Fig. 2.3*B*.

2.11. ERASERS. The Ruby pencil eraser, Fig. 2.3*C*, large size with beveled ends, is the standard. This eraser not only removes pencil lines effectively but is better for ink than the so-called ink eraser, as it removes ink without seriously damaging the surface of paper or cloth. A good metal erasing shield, Fig. 2.3*D*, aids in getting clean erasures.

Artgum or a *soft*-rubber eraser, Fig. 2.3*E*, is useful for cleaning paper and cloth of finger marks and smears that spoil the appearance of the completed drawing.

2.12. PENHOLDERS AND PENS. The penholder should have a grip of medium size, small enough to enter the mouth of a drawing-ink bottle easily yet not so small as to cramp the fingers while in use. A size slightly larger than the diameter of a pencil is good.

An assortment of pens for lettering, grading from coarse to fine, may be chosen from those listed in Chap. 4.

A penwiper of lintless cloth or thin chamois skin should always be at hand for both lettering and ruling pens.

2.13. DRAWING INK. Drawing ink is finely ground carbon in suspension, with natural or synthetic gum added to make the mixture waterproof. Nonwaterproof ink flows more freely but smudges easily. Drawing ink diluted with distilled water or Chinese ink in stick form rubbed up

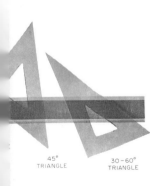

45°
TRIANGLE   30-60°
               TRIANGLE

uare and triangles. These are
ment for drawing **straight lines.**

with water on a slate slab is used in making wash drawings and for very fine line work.

Bottleholders prevent the bottle from upsetting and ruining the drawing table or floor. They are made in various patterns; one is illustrated in Fig. 2.4. As a temporary substitute, the lower half of the paper container in which the ink is sold may be fastened to the table with a thumbtack, or a strip of paper or cloth with a hole for the neck of the bottle may be tacked down over the bottle. Several companies are now supplying ink in small-necked plastic bottles or tubes, Fig. 2.4, which are squeezed to supply the ink, a drop at a time. These containers prevent spillage and protect the ink from deterioration through evaporation or contamination.

2.14. THE T SQUARE. The fixed-head T square, Fig. 2.5, is used for all ordinary work. It should be of hardwood, and the blade should be perfectly straight. The transparent-edged blade is much the best. A draftsman will have several fixed-head squares of different lengths and will find an adjustable-head square of occasional use.

2.15. TRIANGLES. Triangles, Fig. 2.5, are made of transparent celluloid (fiberloid) or other plastic material. Through internal strains they sometimes lose their accuracy. Triangles should be kept flat to prevent warping. For ordinary work a 6- or 8-in. 45° and a 10-in. 30-60° are good sizes.

2.16. SCALES. Scales, Figs. 2.6 to 2.9, are made in a variety of graduations to meet the requirements of many different kinds of work. For convenience, scales are classified according to their most common uses.

During the design stage and later when detail and assembly drawings are made for manufacture and construction, the great bulk of all drawings are made to "scale." This is done so that the sizes of components and their relationship can be studied and all features can be properly correlated into a finished product. This procedure assures good design, which includes proper strength of parts and of the whole, proper use of materials, good fastening methods, and economical assembly, as well as many other important aspects. To accomplish all this, the drawings must be made accurately with drawing instruments.

Instruments and Their Use

2.1. Since engineering drawing is entirely a graphic language, equipment is needed to record information on the drawing surface. Even for drawings made freehand, pencils, erasers, and sometimes coordinate paper or other special items are used.

The lines made on drawings are *straight* or *curved* (including circles and arcs). They are made with drawing instruments, which are the necessary tools for laying down lines on a drawing in an accurate and efficient manner. Furthermore, it is essential to learn the correct form and technique of handling the instruments in order to promote economy and to produce clean, readable drawings.

The various instruments will be described in detail later, but the opening of this chapter will serve as an introduction. To draw straight lines, the T square with its straight blade and perpendicular head, or a triangle is used to support the stroke of the pencil. To draw circles, a compass is needed. In addition to the compass, the draftsman needs dividers for spacing distances and a small bow compass for drawing small circles. To draw curved lines other than circles, a french curve is required. A scale is used for making measurements. To complete drawings in ink the draftsman will require pens for inking and an ink bottle in holder.

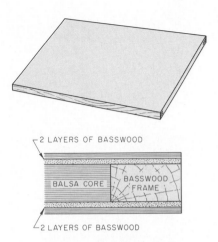

FIG. 2.1.   Drawing board. This one is light and rigid. *Courtesy of Keuffel & Esser Co.*

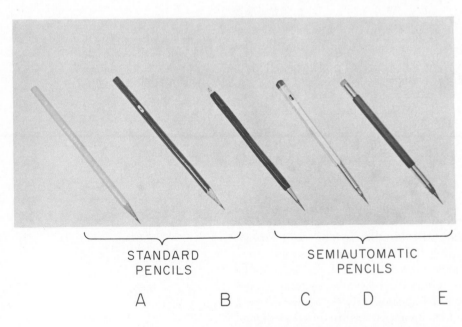

STANDARD PENCILS

SEMIAUTOMATIC PENCILS

A   B   C   D   E

FIG. 2.2.   Drafting pencils. The semiautomatics are most convenient to use.

2.2.   SELECTION OF INSTRUMENTS.   In selecting instruments and materials for drawing, secure the *best* you can afford. For one who expects to do work of professional grade, it is a mistake to buy inferior instruments. Sometimes a beginner is tempted to get cheap instruments for learning, expecting to buy better ones later. With reasonable care a set of good instruments will last a lifetime, whereas poor ones will be an annoyance from the start and worthless after short use. Since poor instruments can be difficult to distinguish from good ones, it is well to seek trustworthy advice before buying. Instruments have been greatly improved in recent years.

2.3.   DRAWING BOARDS.   The drawing surface may be the table top itself or a separate board. In either case the working surface should be made of well-seasoned clear white pine or basswood, cleated to prevent warping. The working edge must be straight and should be tested with a steel straightedge. Some boards and table tops are supplied with a hardwood edge or a steel insert on the working edge, thus ensuring a better-wearing surface. Figure 2.1 illustrates a drawing board which, because of its design and the materials of which it is made, is rigid, sturdy, and light.

2.4.   DRAWING PAPER.   Drawing paper is made in a variety of qualities and may be had in sheets or rolls. White drawing papers that will not turn yellow with age or exposure are used for finished drawings, maps, charts, and drawings for photographic reproduction. For pencil layouts and working drawings, cream or buff detail papers are preferred as they are easier on the eyes and do not show soil so quickly as white papers. In general, paper should have sufficient grain, or "tooth," to take the pencil, be agreeable to the eye, and have a hard surface not easily grooved by the pencil, with good erasing qualities. Formerly imported papers were considered the best, but American mills are now making practically all the paper used in this country. Cheap manila papers should be avoided.

2.5.   TRACING PAPER.   Tracing papers are thin papers, *natural* or *transparentized,* on which drawings are traced, in pencil or ink, and from which blueprints or similar contact prints can be made. In most drafting rooms original drawings are penciled on tracing papers, and blueprints are made directly from these drawings, a practice increasingly successful because of improvements both in papers and in printing. Tracing papers

vary widely in color, thickness, surface, etc., and the grade of pencil and the technique must be adjusted to suit the paper, but with the proper combination, good prints can be obtained from such drawings.

2.6.   TRACING CLOTH.   Finely woven cloth coated with a special starch or plastic is used for making drawings in pencil or ink. The standard tracing cloth is used for inked tracings and specially made pencil cloth for pencil drawings or tracings. Cloth is more permanent than paper as it will stand more handling. Tracing and duplicating processes are described in Chap. 13.

2.7.   DRAFTING TAPE.   The paper to be used is usually attached to the drawing board by means of Scotch drafting tape, with a short piece stuck across each corner or with tape along the entire edge of the paper. Drafting tape is not the same as masking tape (made by the same company); the latter has a heavier coating of adhesive and does not come off the drawing paper so cleanly as the former.

2.8.   THUMBTACKS.   The best thumbtacks are made with thin heads and steel points screwed into them. Cheaper ones are made by stamping. Use tacks with tapering pins of small diameter, and avoid flat-headed (often colored) map pins, as the heads are too thick and the pins rather large.

2.9.   PENCILS.   The basic instrument is the graphite lead pencil, made in various hardnesses. Each manufacturer has special methods of processing designed to make the lead strong and yet give a smooth clear line. Figure 2.2 shows five varieties of pencils. At the left are two

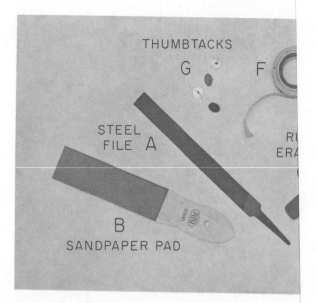

THUMBTACKS

G   F

STEEL FILE   A

R
ERA

B
SANDPAPER PAD

PLASTIC "S

FIG.
ho
Th
use
pen

ordinary pencils, with the lead set in wood. (*A*) is of American and (*B*) of foreign manufacture. Both are fine, but have the disadvantage that, in use, the wood must be cut away to expose the lead (a time-consuming job), and the pencil becomes shorter until the last portion must be discarded. Semiautomatic pencils, (*C*) to (*E*), with a chuck to clamp and hold the lead, are more convenient. (*C*) has a plastic handle and changeable tip (for indicating the grade of lead). (*D*) has an aluminum handle and indexing tip for indication of grade. (*E*) is the rather elegant Alteneder pencil with rosewood handle, hardened-steel chuck ring, and eraser. Drawing pencils are graded by numbers and letters from 6B, very soft and black, through 5B, 4B, 3B, 2B, B, and HB to F, the medium grade; then H, 2H, 3H, 4H, 5H, 6H, 7H, and 8H to 9H, the hardest. The soft (B) grades are used primarily for sketching and rendered drawings and the hard (H) grades for instrument drawings.

T SQUA

FIG. 2.5.   T s
standard equi

Mechanical Engineer's Scales. These are divided and numbered so that fractions of inches represent inches. The most common ranges are ⅛, ¼, ½, and 1 in. to the *inch*. These scales are known as the *size* scales because the designated reduction also represents the ratio of size, as, for example, *one-eighth* size. A full- and half-size scale is illustrated in Fig. 2.6. Mechanical engineer's scales are almost always "full divided," that is, the smallest divisions run throughout the entire length. They are often graduated with the marked divisions numbered from right to left, as well as from left to right, as shown in Fig. 2.6. Mechanical engineer's scales are used mostly for drawings of machine parts and small structures where the drawing size is never less than one-eighth the size of the actual object.

Civil Engineer's Scales. These are divided into decimals with 10, 20, 30, 40, 50, 60, and 80 divisions to the inch (Fig. 2.7). Such a scale is usually full divided and is sometimes numbered both from left to right and right to left. Civil engineer's scales are most used for plotting and drawing maps, although they are convenient for any work where divisions of the inch in tenths is required.

Architect's Scales. Divided into proportional feet and inches, these scales have divisions indicating ⅛, ¼, ⅜, ½, ¾, 1½, and 3 in. to the *foot* (Fig. 2.8). They are usually "open divided," that is, the units are shown along the entire length, but only the end units are subdivided into inches and fractions. These scales are much used by all engineers—mechanical, industrial, chemical, etc.—for both machine and structural drawings and are sometimes called *mechanical engineer's* scales.

A variety of special scales, made with divisions specified by the customer, are available from most instrument companies. Compared with standard scales, they are expensive.

Scales are made with various cross-sectional shapes, as shown in Fig. 2.9. The triangular form, (*A*) and (*B*), has long been favored because it carries six scales as a unit and is very stiff. However, many prefer the flat types as being easier to hold flat to a board and having a particular working scale more readily available. The "opposite-bevel" scale, (*C*) and (*D*), is easier to pick up than the "flat-bevel" scale, (*F*); moreover, it shows only one graduation at a time. The "double-bevel" scale, (*E*), in the shorter lengths is convenient as a pocket scale, but it can be had in lengths up to 24 in.

Practically all drafting scales of good quality were formerly made of boxwood, either plain or with white edges of celluloid. Although metal scales have been available for more than thirty years,

FIG. 2.6. A mechanical engineer's full- and half-size scale. Divisions are in inches to sixteenths of an inch. (The half-size scale is on the back of the full-size scale.)

FIG. 2.7. A civil engineer's scale. Divisions are 10, 20, 30, 40, 50, and 60 parts to the inch.

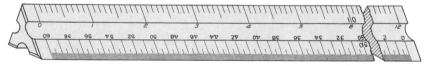

FIG. 2.8. An architect's (or mechanical engineer's) scale. Reduction in size is based on proportion of a foot.

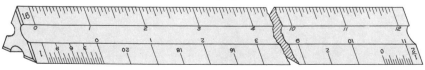

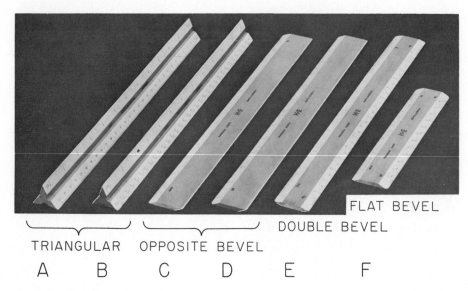

TRIANGULAR   OPPOSITE BEVEL   DOUBLE BEVEL   FLAT BEVEL

A   B   C   D   E   F

FIG. 2.9. Scale types. Flat scales are the most effective.

Both magnesium and aluminum have been used successfully. These scales have all the reading advantages of a white-edge boxwood scale together with the stability afforded by metal.

2.17. CURVES. Curved rulers, called "irregular curves" or "french curves," are used for curved lines other than circle arcs. The patterns for these curves are laid out in parts of ellipses and spirals or other mathematical curves in various combinations. For the student, one ellipse curve of the general shape of Fig. 2.10*A* or *D* and one spiral, either a logarithmic spiral (*B*) or one similar to the one used in Fig. 2.60, is sufficient. (*C*) is a useful small curve.

they were seldom used until about 1935, when drafting machines equipped with metal scales made rather important gains in popularity. Extruded medium-hard aluminum alloys are the preferred metals. The Second World War brought a period of considerable experimentation with various types of plastic for all kinds of drafting scales. Up to the present time the white-edge scale has retained a large measure of its popularity. Another type of scale is now getting considerable attention, a metal scale with a white plastic coating that carries the graduations.

2.18. THE "CASE" INSTRUMENTS. We have so far, with the exception of curves, considered only the instruments (and materials) needed for drawing straight lines. A major portion of any drawing is likely to be circles and circle arcs, and the so-called "case" instruments are used for these. The basic instruments are shown in Fig. 2.11. At the left is a divider of the "hairspring" type (with a screw for fine adjustment), used for laying off or transferring measurements. Next is the large compass with lengthening bar and pen attachment. The three "bow"

FIG. 2.10. Irregular curves. These are used for drawing curves where the radius of curvature is not constant.

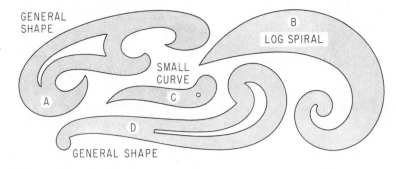

GENERAL SHAPE

B
LOG SPIRAL

SMALL CURVE

A   C

D

GENERAL SHAPE

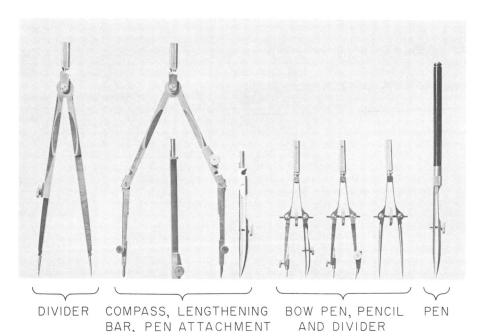

DIVIDER COMPASS, LENGTHENING BOW PEN, PENCIL PEN
              BAR, PEN ATTACHMENT   AND DIVIDER

FIG. 2.11. The basic three-bow set. Large compass and dividers; bow pen, pencil, and dividers; ruling pen.

instruments are for smaller work. They are almost always made without the conversion feature (pencil to pen). The ruling pen, at the extreme right, is used for inking straight lines. A set of instruments of the type shown in Fig. 2.11 is known as a three-bow set.

Until recently the three-bow set was considered the standard, in design and number of pieces, for all ordinary drafting work. However, the trend now is for more rigid construction and fewer pieces. The 6-in. compass in Fig. 2.12 embraces practically a whole set in one instrument. Used as shown, the instrument is a pencil compass; with pencil replaced by pen, it is used to ink circles; with steel point installed in place of pencil point, it becomes a divider; the pen point, placed in the handle provided, makes a ruling pen; and there is a small metal container for steel points and lead. Similar instruments of other manufac-

ture are shown in Figs. 2.13 and 2.14. The instrument in the central part of Fig. 2.14 is a "quick-change" design (with vernier adjustment), a great convenience when changing from a very small setting to a large one.

Figure 2.13*B* shows a quick-action bow employing special nylon nuts in which the center screw operates. The design allows the legs to be moved in or out to change the setting, after which the center screw is used for fine adjustment.

Even though it is possible to find an instrument that serves practically all purposes, it is convenient to have several instruments, thus saving the time required to convert from pencil leg to ink leg or divider points. For this reason the newer more rigid instruments are also made as separate pieces in different sizes. Figure 2.15 shows the 6-in. dividers and large 6-in. bow compass; three 3-in. bow

PENCIL COMPASS

PEN HANDLE

PEN   LEADS, POINTS

FIG. 2.12. Large bow. It performs triple service as dividers, pen, and pencil compass. Pen leg in handle makes ruling pen.

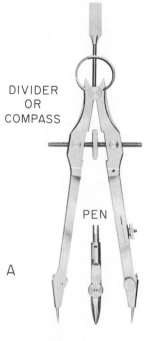

DIVIDER
OR
COMPASS

PEN

A

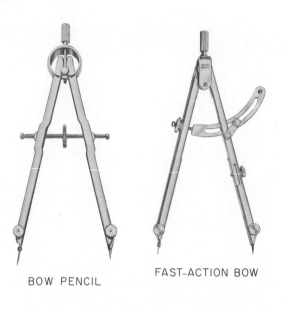

BOW PENCIL

FAST-ACTION BOW

FIG. 2.14. Three different designs of large bow instruments. All are rigid and efficient.

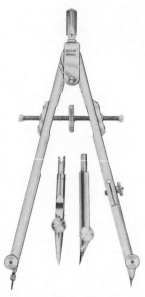

LARGE PENCIL COMPASS
WITH PEN AND
DIVIDER LEGS

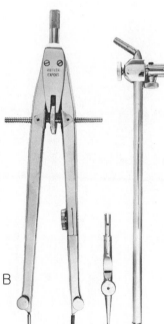

FIG. 2.13. (*A*) A very rugged bow. Serves as dividers, or pen or pencil compass. (*B*) A quick-action bow instrument, with pencil and pen legs and extension bar.

compasses, two with pencil and one with ink leg, which can also be used as dividers by changing attachments; and pen points, which are used on the 6-in. compass or in a handle (not shown) to make a ruling pen.

The standard 6-in. compass will open to only approximately 5 in. The lengthening bar of the older-type compass (Fig. 2.11) will extend the radius to about 8 in. Lengthening bars for the newer spring-bow instruments are of the beam type. The instrument in Fig. 2.16 has a center point on the beam, thus employing the pencil and pen of the instrument itself, while the compass in Fig. 2.17 uses the center point of the instrument and separate pen and pencil attachments on the beam. A standard metal beam compass for drawing circles up to 16-in. radius is shown in Fig. 2.18.

Various ruling pens are shown in Fig. 2.19. (*A*) to (*E*) are standard types. Note that (*D*) uses the compass-pen leg in a handle. (*F*) is a contour pen, (*G*) is a border pen for wide lines, (*H*) and (*I*) are "railroad" pens for double lines, and (*J*) and (*K*) are border pens with large ink capacity.

All manufacturers supply instruments made up in sets, with leather, metal, or plastic case. Figure 2.20 shows a standard three-bow combination and Fig. 2.21 a large-bow set with beam compass. The case in Fig. 2.22*A* is unique in that fillers may be removed to provide space for any combination of instruments desired.

Figure 2.22*B* shows a modern case made of plastic with a magnetic fastener. This set of instruments includes the newer technical fountain pen with several sizes of points.

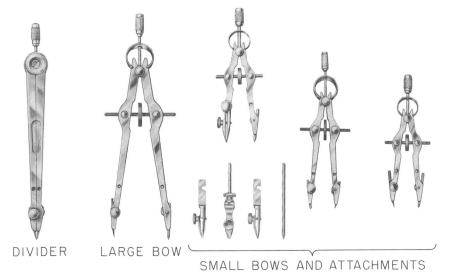

DIVIDER LARGE BOW

SMALL BOWS AND ATTACHMENTS

FIG. 2.15. A large- and small-bow set. Combines the advantages of both standard three-bow and large-bow designs.

BEAM

PENCIL ADJUSTABLE POINT

FIG. 2.16. Extender for large bow. This type extends the range of its center point, with the pen or pencil on the bow.

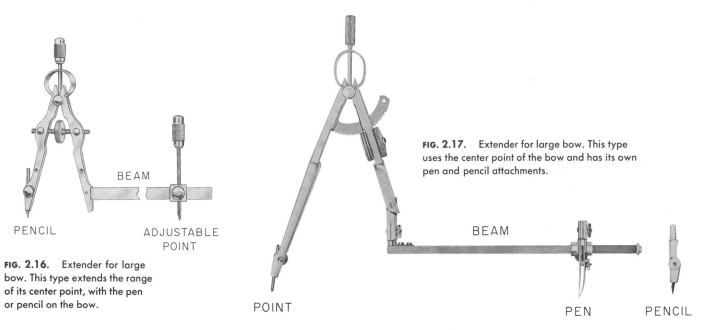

FIG. 2.17. Extender for large bow. This type uses the center point of the bow and has its own pen and pencil attachments.

BEAM

POINT PEN PENCIL

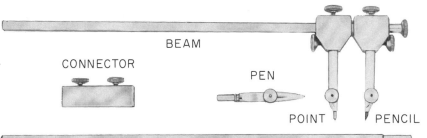

BEAM

CONNECTOR

PEN

POINT PENCIL

FIG. 2.18. A beam compass. This compass is adjustable for radii of 1 to 16 inches.

EXTENSION BEAM

2.19. LETTERING DEVICES. The Braddock-Rowe triangle and the Ames lettering instrument (Figs. 4.2*A* and *B*) are convenient devices used in drawing guide lines for lettering.

2.20. CHECK LIST OF INSTRUMENTS AND MATERIALS. Set of drawing instruments, including: 6-in. compass with fixed needle-point leg, removable pencil and pen legs, and lengthening bar; 6-in. hairspring dividers; 3½-in. bow pencil, bow pen, and bow dividers; two ruling pens; box of leads. Or large-bow set containing 6½-in. bow compass; 4½-in. bow compass; 6½-in. friction dividers and pen attachment for compass; 5½-in. ruling pen; beam compass with extension beam; box for extra leads and points

Drawing board
T square
45° and 30-60° triangles

Three mechanical engineer's scales, flat pattern, or the equivalent triangular scale
Lettering instrument or triangle
French curves
Drawing pencils, 6H, 4H, 2H, H, and F
Pocketknife or pencil sharpener
Pencil pointer (file or sandpaper)
Pencil eraser (Ruby)
Artgum or cleaning rubber
Penholder, pens for lettering, and penwiper
Bottle of drawing ink and bottleholder
Scotch drafting tape or thumbtacks
Drawing paper to suit
Tracing paper and cloth
Dustcloth or brush

To these may be added:

Civil engineer's scale
Protractor
Erasing shield
Slide rule
Six-foot steel tape
Clipboard or sketchbook
Hard Arkansas oilstone
Piece of soapstone
Cleaning powder or pad

The student should mark all his instruments and materials plainly with his initials or name as soon as they have been purchased and approved.

2.21. ADDITIONAL INSTRUMENTS. The instruments and materials described in this chapter are all that are needed for ordinary practice and are, with the exception of such supplies as paper, pencils, ink, and erasers, what a draftsman is as a rule expected to take with him into a drafting room.

FIG. 2.19. Various ruling pens. Standard pens are all-purpose instruments. Special pens (*F* to *K*) are convenient and efficient for contours, double lines, and heavy lines.

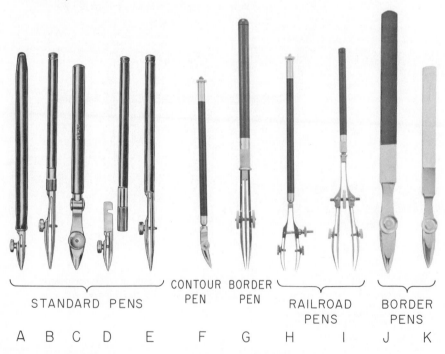

STANDARD PENS   CONTOUR PEN   BORDER PEN   RAILROAD PENS   BORDER PENS

A   B   C   D   E   F   G   H   I   J   K

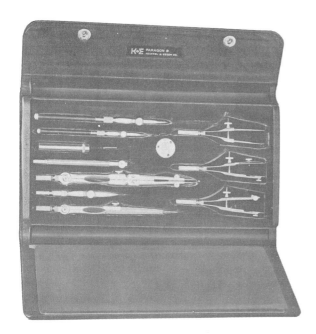

FIG. 2.20. A three-bow set, in case. It contains large dividers, large compass with extension bars and pen attachment, two ruling pens, bow pen, bow pencil, bow dividers, and bone center.

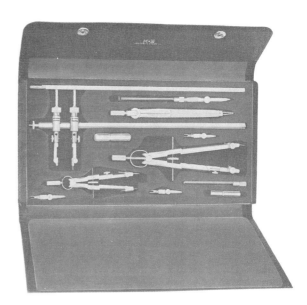

FIG. 2.21. A large-bow set, in case. It contains large- and small-bow compasses with attachments, dividers, ruling pen, and beam compass.

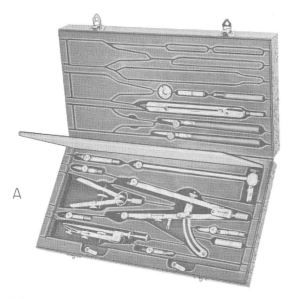

A

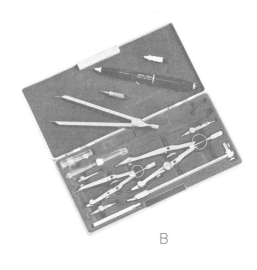

B

FIG. 2.22. (*A*) A special case which can be adapted to many combinations by removing fillers. (*B*) A set of instruments in plastic case. This set is supplied with technical fountain pen.

There are many other special instruments and devices that are not necessary in ordinary work but with which the draftsman should be familiar, as they may be convenient in special cases and are often found as a part of drafting-room equipment. Consult manufacturers' catalogues.

2.22.   THE USE OF INSTRUMENTS.   In beginning to use drawing instruments, it is important to learn to handle them correctly. Carefully read the instructions and observe strictly all details of technique.

Facility will come with continued practice, but it is essential to adhere to good form from the outset. Bad form in drawing can be traced in every instance to the formation of bad habits in the early stages of learning. Once formed, these habits are difficult to overcome.

It is best to make a few drawings solely to become familiar with the handling and feel of the instruments so that later, in working a drawing problem, you will not lose time because of faulty manipulation. Practice accurate penciling first, and do not attempt inking until you have become really proficient in penciling. With practice, the correct, skillful use of drawing instruments will become a subconscious habit.

For competence in drawing, *accuracy* and *speed* are essential, and in commercial work neither is worth much without the other. It is well to learn as a beginner that a *good* drawing can be made as quickly as a *poor* one. Erasing is expensive and most of it can be avoided. The draftsman of course erases occasionally, and a student must learn to make corrections, but in beginning to use instruments, strive for sheets without blemish or inaccuracy.

2.23.   PREPARATION FOR DRAWING.   The drawing table should be set so that the light comes from the left, and it should be adjusted to a convenient height, that is, 36 to 40 in., for use while sitting on a standard drafting stool or while standing. There is more freedom in drawing standing, especially when working on large drawings. The board, for use in this manner, should be inclined at a slope of about 1 to 8. Since it is more tiring to draw standing, many modern drafting rooms use tables so made that the board can be used in an almost vertical position and can be raised or lowered so that the draftsman can use a lower stool with swivel seat and backrest, thus working with comfort and even greater freedom than when an almost horizontal board is used.

The instruments should be placed within easy reach, on the table or on a special tray or stand which is located beside the table. The table, the board, and the instruments should be wiped with a dustcloth before starting to draw.

2.24.   THE PENCIL AND ITS USE.   The grade of pencil must be selected carefully, with reference to the surface of the paper as well as to the line quality desired. For a pencil layout on detail paper of good texture, a pencil as hard as 5H or 6H may be used, while for finished pencil drawings on the same paper, 2H, 3H, or 4H pencils give the blacker line needed. For finished pencil drawings or tracings on vellum, softer pencils, H to 3H, are employed to get printable lines. The F pencil is much used for technical sketching, and the H is popular for lettering. In every case the pencil must be hard enough not to blur or smudge but not so hard as to cut grooves in the paper under reasonable pressure.

To sharpen a pencil, cut away the wood from the unlettered end with a penknife or mechanical sharpener, as shown in Fig. 2.23 *A,* and then sharpen the lead to make a long, conic point, as at (*B*), by twirling the pencil as the lead is rubbed with long even strokes against the sandpaper pad or file or placed in a special lead sharpener.

A flat or wedge point will not wear away in use so fast as a conic point, and on that account some prefer it for straight-line work. The long, wedge point illustrated at (*C*) is made by first sharpening, as at (*A*), then making the two long cuts on opposite sides, as shown, then flattening the lead on the sandpaper pad or file, and finishing by touching the corners to make the wedge point narrower than the diameter of the lead.

Have the sandpaper pad within easy reach, and *keep the pencils sharp.* Some hang the pad or file on a cord attached to the drawing table. The professional draftsman sharpens his pencil every few minutes. After sharpening the lead, wipe off excess graphite dust before using the pencil. Form the habit of sharpening the lead as often as you might dip a writing pen into the inkwell. Most commercial and many college drafting rooms are equipped with Dexter or other pencil sharpeners to save time.

Not only must pencil lines be clean and sharp, but for pencil drawings and tracings to be blueprinted, it is absolutely necessary that all the lines of each kind be uniform, firm, and opaque. This means a careful choice of pencils and the proper use of them. The attempt to make a dark line with too hard a pencil results in cutting deep grooves in the paper. Hold the pencil firmly, yet with

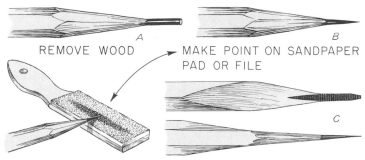

REMOVE WOOD — MAKE POINT ON SANDPAPER PAD OR FILE

WEDGE POINT FOR STRAIGHT LINES

FIG. 2.23. Sharpening the pencil. Wood is removed first, then the point is made with sandpaper or a file or special lead sharpener. For semi-automatic pencils, adjust the lead to the proper length and make the point with sandpaper or a file.

as much ease and freedom as possible.

Keep an even constant pressure on the pencil, and when using a conic point, rotate the pencil as the line is drawn so as to keep both the line and pencil sharp. Use a draftsman's brush or soft cloth occasionally to dust off excess graphite from the drawing.

Too much emphasis cannot be given to the importance of clean, careful, accurate penciling. Never entertain the thought that poor penciling can be corrected in tracing.

2.25. **PLACING THE PAPER.** Since the T-square blade is more rigid near the head than toward the outer end, the paper, if much smaller than the size of the board, should be placed close to the left edge of the board (within an inch or so) with its lower edge several inches from the bottom of the board. With the T square against the left edge of the board, square the top of the paper; hold it in this position, slipping the T square down from the edge, and put a thumbtack in each upper corner, pushing it in up to the head so that the head aids in holding the paper. Then move the T square down over the paper to smooth out possible wrinkles, and put thumbtacks in the other two corners. Drafting tape may be used instead of thumbtacks.

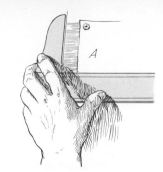

SLIDE TO POSITION

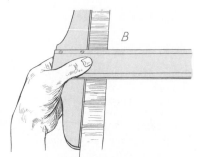

ADJUST CAREFULLY

HOLD IN POSITION
AS LINE IS DRAWN

FIG. 2.24. Manipulating the T square. The head must be firmly against the straight left edge of the board.

2.26. USE OF THE T SQUARE. The T square and the triangles have straight edges and are used for drawing straight lines. Horizontal lines are drawn with the T square, which is used with its head against the left edge of the drawing board and manipulated as follows: Holding the head of the tool, as shown in Fig. 2.24*A*, slide it along the edge of the board to a spot very near the position desired. Then, for closer adjustment, change your hold either to that shown at (*B*), in which the thumb remains on top of the T-square head and the other fingers press against the underside of the board, or, as is more usual, to that shown at (*C*), in which the fingers remain on the T square and the thumb is placed on the board.

Figure 2.25 shows the position of the hand and pencil for drawing horizontal lines. Note that the pencil is inclined in the direction the line is drawn, that is, toward the right, and also slightly away from the body so that the pencil point is as close as possible to the T-square blade.

In drawing lines, take great care to keep them accurately parallel to the guiding edge of the T square. The pencil should be held lightly, but close against the edge, and the angle should not vary during the progress of the line. Horizontal lines should always be drawn from left to right. A T-square blade can be tested for straightness by drawing a sharp line through two points and then turning the square over and with the same edge drawing another line through the points, as shown in Fig. 2.26.

2.27. USE OF THE TRIANGLES. Vertical lines are drawn with the triangle, which is set against the T square with the perpendicular edge nearest the head of the square and thus toward the light (Fig. 2.27). These lines are always drawn upward, from bottom to top.

In drawing vertical lines, the T square is held in position against the left edge of the board by the thumb and little finger of the left hand while the other fingers of this hand adjust and hold the triangle. You can be sure that the T square is in contact with the board when you hear the little double click as the two come together, and slight pressure of the thumb and little finger toward the right will maintain the position. As the line is drawn, pressure of all the fingers against the board will hold the T square and triangle firmly in position.

As in using the T square, care must be taken to keep the line accurately parallel

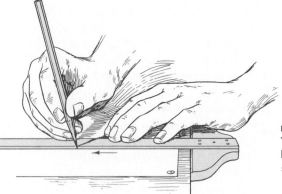

FIG. 2.25. Drawing a horizontal line. Hold the T square with the left hand; draw the line from left to right; incline the pencil in the direction of stroke, so that the pencil "slides" over the paper.

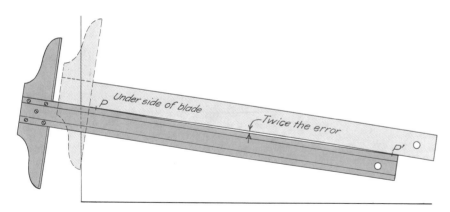

FIG. 2.26. To test a T square. Turn the T square upside down; draw the line; turn it right side up and align it with the original line; draw the second line and compare it with the first.

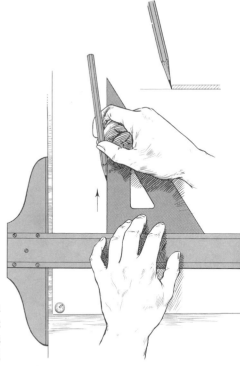

FIG. 2.27. Drawing a vertical line. With the T square and triangle in position, draw the line from bottom to top —always away from the body.

to the guiding edge. Note the position of the pencil in Fig. 2.27.

In both penciling and inking, the triangles must always be used in contact with a guiding straightedge. To ensure accuracy, never work to the extreme corner of a triangle; to avoid having to do so, keep the T square below the lower end of the line to be drawn.

With the T square against the edge of the board, lines at 45° are drawn with the standard 45° triangle, and lines at 30° and 60° with the 30-60° triangle, as shown in Fig. 2.28. With vertical and horizontal lines included, lines at increments of 45° are drawn with the 45° triangle as at (*B*), and lines at 30° increments with the 30-60° triangle as at (*A*). The two triangles are used in combination for angles of 15, 75, 105°, etc. (Fig.

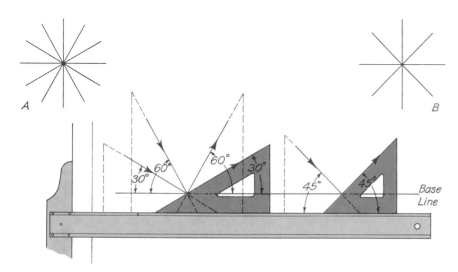

FIG. 2.28. To draw angles of 30°, 45°, 60°. Multiples of 30° are drawn with the 30-60° triangle, multiples of 45° with the 45° triangle.

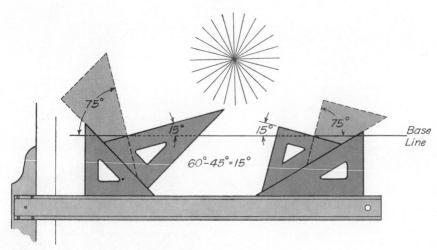

FIG. 2.29. To draw angles of 15° and 75°. Angles in increments of 15° are obtained with the two triangles in combination.

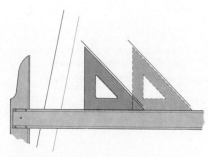

FIG. 2.30. To draw parallel lines. With the T square as a base, the triangle is aligned and then moved to the required position.

2.29). Thus any multiple of 15° is drawn directly; and a circle is divided with the 45° triangle into 8 parts, with the 30-60° triangle into 12 parts, and with both into 24 parts.

To Draw One Line Parallel to Another (*Fig. 2.30*). Adjust to the given line a triangle held against a straightedge, hold the guiding edge in position, and slide the triangle on it to the required position.

To Draw a Perpendicular to Any Line (*Fig. 2.31*). Place a triangle with one edge against the T square (or another triangle), and move the two until the hypotenuse of the triangle is coincident with the line, as at (*A*); hold the T square in position and turn the triangle,

as shown, until its other side is against the T square; the hypotenuse will then be perpendicular to the original line. Move the triangle to the required position. A quicker method is to set the triangle with its hypotenuse against the guiding edge, fit one side to the line, slide the triangle to the required point, and draw the perpendicular, as shown at (*B*).

Never attempt to draw a perpendicular to a line with only one triangle by placing one leg of the triangle along the line.

Through internal strains, triangles sometimes lose their accuracy. They may be tested by drawing a perpendicular and then reversing the triangle, as shown in Fig. 2.32.

2.28. THE LEFT-HANDED DRAFTSMAN. If you are left-handed, reverse the T square and triangles left for right as compared with the regular right-handed position. Use the head of the T square along the right edge of the board, and draw horizontal lines from right to left. Place the triangle with its vertical edge to the right, and draw vertical lines from bottom to top. The drawing table should be placed with the light coming from the right.

2.29. USE OF THE SCALE. Scale technique is governed largely by the requirements of accuracy and speed. Before a

FIG. 2.31. To draw perpendicular lines. With the T square as a base and the triangle in position *A*, the triangle is aligned, then rotated and moved to perpendicular position; for position *B*, only the triangle is moved.

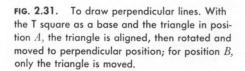

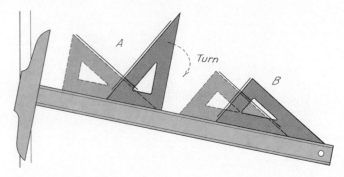

line can be drawn, its relative position must be found by scaling, and the speed with which scale measurement can be made will greatly affect the total drawing time.

Precise layouts and developments, made to scale for the workmen, must be very accurately drawn, at the expense of speed; conversely, drawings with figured dimensions need not be quite so carefully scaled, and better speed may be attained.

To make a measurement, place the scale on the drawing where the distance is to be laid off, align the scale in the direction of the measurement, and make a *light* short dash with a sharp pencil at the proper graduation mark (Fig. 2.33). In layout work where extreme accuracy is required, a "pricker," or needle point set in a wood handle, may be substituted for the pencil, and a *small* hole pricked into the paper in place of the pencil mark. It is best to start with the "zero" of the scale when setting off lengths or when measuring distances. In using an open-divided scale, inches (or fractions) are accounted for in one direction from the zero graduation while feet (or units) are recorded in the opposite direction.

Measurements should not be made on a drawing by taking distances off the scale with dividers, as this method is time-consuming and not more accurate than the regular methods.

To avoid cumulative errors, successive measurements on the same line should, if possible, be made without shifting the scale. In representing objects that are larger than can be drawn to their natural or full size, it is necessary to reduce the size of the drawing in some regular proportion, and for this purpose one of the standard mechanical engineer's, civil engineer's, or architect's scales is used. Standard scales are given in Fig. 2.34.

The first reduction is to *half size,* or to the scale of $6'' = 1'\text{-}0''$. In other words, $\frac{1}{2}$ in. on the drawing represents a distance of 1 in. on the object. Stated in terms used for the architect's scales, a

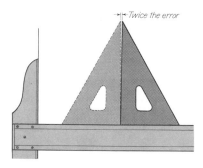

FIG. 2.32. To test a triangle for right angle. Draw a line with the triangle in each position; twice the error is produced.

FIG. 2.33. Making a measurement. Place the scale in position; the distance is marked on paper by short, light *lines.*

SCALES

MECHANICAL ENGINEER'S

$1'' = 1''$ (full size)	$\frac{1}{2}'' = 1''$ ($\frac{1}{2}$ size)
$\frac{1}{4}'' = 1''$ ($\frac{1}{4}$ size)	$\frac{1}{8}'' = 1''$ ($\frac{1}{8}$ size)

ARCHITECT'S OR MECHANICAL ENGINEER'S

$12'' = 1'\text{-}0''$ (full size)	$1'' = 1'\text{-}0''$ ($\frac{1}{12}$ size)	$\frac{1}{4}'' = 1'\text{-}0''$ ($\frac{1}{48}$ size)
$6'' = 1'\text{-}0''$ ($\frac{1}{2}$ size)	$\frac{3}{4}'' = 1'\text{-}0''$ ($\frac{1}{16}$ size)	$\frac{3}{16}'' = 1'\text{-}0''$ ($\frac{1}{64}$ size)
$3'' = 1'\text{-}0''$ ($\frac{1}{4}$ size)	$\frac{1}{2}'' = 1'\text{-}0''$ ($\frac{1}{24}$ size)	$\frac{1}{8}'' = 1'\text{-}0''$ ($\frac{1}{96}$ size)
$1\frac{1}{2}'' = 1'\text{-}0''$ ($\frac{1}{8}$ size)	$\frac{3}{8}'' = 1'\text{-}0''$ ($\frac{1}{32}$ size)	$\frac{3}{32}'' = 1'\text{-}0''$ ($\frac{1}{128}$ size)

CIVIL ENGINEER'S

10, 20, 30, 40, 50, 60, or 80 divisions to the inch representing feet, 10 ft, 100 ft, rods, miles, or any other necessary unit

FIG. 2.34. Standard scales. Special scales are available. See manufacturers' catalogues.

distance of 6 in. on the drawing represents 1 ft on the object. This scale is used even if the object is only slightly larger than could be drawn full size. If this reduction is not sufficient, the drawing is made to *quarter size,* or to the scale of $3'' = 1'\text{-}0''$. If the quarter-size scale is too large, the next reduction is *eighth size,* or $1\frac{1}{2}'' = 1'\text{-}0''$, the smallest proportion usually supplied on standard mechanical engineer's scales, but the architect's scales are used down to $\frac{3}{32}'' = 1'\text{-}0''$, as shown by the listings in Fig. 2.34.

In stating the scale used on a drawing, the information should be given in accordance with the scale used to make the drawing. If a standard mechanical engineer's scale is employed, the statement may read that the scale is (1) *full size,* (2) *half size,* (3) *quarter size,* or (4) *eighth size.* These scales may also be given as (1) $1'' = 1''$, (2) $\frac{1}{2}'' = 1''$, (3) $\frac{1}{4}'' = 1''$, or (4) $\frac{1}{8}'' = 1''$. If a standard architect's scale is used, the statement is given in terms of inches to the foot. Examples are (1) $3'' = 1'\text{-}0''$, (2) $1\frac{1}{2}'' = 1'\text{-}0''$, or (3) $1'' = 1'\text{-}0''$. In stating the scale, the first figure always refers to the drawing and the second to the object. Thus $3'' = 1'\text{-}0''$ means that 3 in. on the *drawing* represents 1 ft on the *object.*

Drawings to odd proportions, such as $9'' = 1'\text{-}0''$, $4'' = 1'\text{-}0''$, $5'' = 1'\text{-}0''$, are used only in rare cases when drawings are made for reduction and the conditions of size demand a special scale.

The terms "scale" and "size" have different meanings: The scale $\frac{1}{4}'' = 1'\text{-}0''$ is the usual one for ordinary house plans and is often called by architects the "quarter scale." This term should not be confused with the term "quarter size," as the former means $\frac{1}{4}$ in. to 1 ft and the latter $\frac{1}{4}$ in. to 1 in.

The size of a circle is generally stated by giving its diameter, while to draw it the radius is necessary. Two scales are usually supplied together on the same body, for example, half and quarter size. Therefore, in drawing to half size, it is often convenient to lay off the amount of the diameter with the quarter-size scale and use this distance as the radius.

Small pieces are often made "double size," and very small mechanisms, such as watch parts, are drawn to greatly enlarged sizes: 10 to 1, 20 to 1, 40 to 1, and 50 to 1, using special enlarging scales.

For plotting and map drawing, the civil engineer's scales of decimal parts, with 10, 20, 30, 40, 50, 60, and 80 divisions to the inch, are used. These scales are not used for machine or structural work but in certain aircraft drawings.

The important thing in drawing to scale is to think and speak of each dimension in its full size and not in the reduced (or enlarged) size it happens to be on the paper. This practice prevents confusion between *actual* and *represented* size.

2.30. READING THE SCALE. Reading the standard mechanical engineer's scales is rather simple, because the scale is plainly marked in inches, and the smaller graduations are easily recognized as the regular divisions of the inch into $\frac{1}{2}$, $\frac{1}{4}$, $\frac{1}{8}$, and $\frac{1}{16}$. Thus the scales for half size, quarter size, and eighth size are employed in exactly the same manner as a full-size scale.

The architect's scales, being open divided and to stated reductions, such as $3'' = 1'\text{-}0''$, may require some study by the beginner in order to prevent confu-

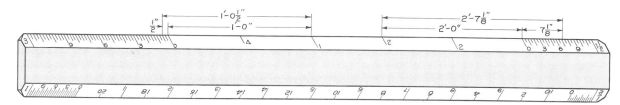

sion and mistakes. As an example, consider the scale of $3'' = 1'\text{-}0''$. This is the first reduction scale of the usual triangular scale; on it the distance of 3 in. is divided into 12 equal parts, and each of these is subdivided into eighths. This distance should be thought of not as 3 in. but as a foot divided into inches and eighths of an inch. Notice that the divisions start with the *zero* on the inside, the inches of the divided foot running to the *left* and the open divisions of feet to the *right,* so that dimensions given in feet and in inches may be read directly, as $1'\text{-}0\frac{1}{2}''$ (Fig. 2.35). On the other end will be found the scale of $1\frac{1}{2}'' = 1'\text{-}0''$, or eighth size, with the distance of $1\frac{1}{2}$ in. divided on the right of the zero into 12 parts and subdivided into quarter inches, with the foot divisions to the left of the zero coinciding with the marks of the 3-in. scale. Note again that in reading a distance in feet and inches, for example, the $2'\text{-}7\frac{1}{8}''$ distance in Fig. 2.35, feet are determined to the left of the zero and inches to the right of it. The other scales, such as $\frac{3}{4}'' = 1'\text{-}0''$ and $\frac{1}{4}'' = 1'\text{-}0''$, are divided in a similar way, the only difference being in the value of the smallest graduations. The scale of $\frac{3}{32}'' = 1'\text{-}0''$, for example, can be read only to the nearest 2 in.

2.31. "LAYING OUT" THE SHEET. The paper is usually cut somewhat larger than the desired size of the drawing and trimmed to size after the work is finished. Suppose the finished size is to be 11 by 17 in. with a ½-in. border inside. Lay the scale down on the paper close to the lower edge and measure 17 in., marking the distance with the pencil; at the same time mark ½ in. inside at each end for the border line. Use a short dash forming a continuation of the division line on the scale in laying off a dimension. Do not bore a hole with the pencil. Near the left edge mark 11- and ½-in. borderline points. Through these four marks on the left edge, draw horizontal lines with the T square; and through the points on the lower edge, draw vertical lines, using the triangle against the T square.

2.32. USE OF DIVIDERS. Dividers are used for transferring measurements and for dividing lines into any number of equal parts. Facility in their use is essential, and quick and absolute control of their manipulation must be gained. The instrument should be opened with one hand by pinching the chamfer with the thumb and second finger. This will throw it into correct position with the thumb and forefinger outside the legs and the second and third fingers inside, with the head resting just above the second joint of the forefinger (Fig. 2.36). It is thus under perfect control, with the

FIG. 2.36. Handling the dividers. The instrument is opened and adjusted with one hand.

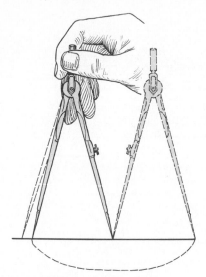

FIG. 2.37. Bisecting a line. Half is estimated; then the dividers are readjusted by estimating half the original error.

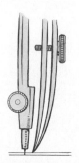

FIG. 2.38. Adjusting the needle point of a large compass. The point is adjusted to the pen; the pen is then replaced by the pencil leg and the pencil adjusted to the point.

thumb and forefinger to close it and the other two to open it. Practice this motion until you can adjust the dividers to the smallest fraction. In coming down to small divisions, the second and third fingers must be gradually slipped out from between the legs as they are closed down upon them. Notice that the little finger is not used in manipulating the dividers.

2.33. TO DIVIDE A LINE BY TRIAL. In bisecting a line, the dividers are opened at a guess to roughly half the length. This distance is stepped off on the line, holding the instrument by the handle with the thumb and forefinger. If the division is short, the leg should be thrown out to half the remainder (estimated by eye), without removing the other leg from the paper, and the line spaced again with this new setting (Fig. 2.37). If the result does not come out exactly, the operation can be repeated. With a little experience, a line can be divided rapidly in this way. Similarly, a line, either straight or curved, can be divided into any number of equal parts, say, five, by estimating the first division, stepping this lightly along the line, with the dividers held vertically by the handle, turning the instrument first in one direction and then in the other. If the last division falls

short, one-fifth of the remainder should be added by opening the dividers, keeping one point on the paper. If the last division is over, one-fifth of the excess should be taken off and the line respaced. If it is found difficult to make this small adjustment accurately with the fingers, the hairspring may be used. You will find the bow spacers more convenient than the dividers for small or numerous divisions. Avoid pricking unsightly holes in the paper. The position of a small prick point may be preserved, if necessary, by drawing a small circle around it with the pencil.

2.34. USE OF THE COMPASSES. The compasses have the same general shape as the dividers and are manipulated in a similar way. First of all, the needle should be permanently adjusted. Insert the pen in place of the pencil leg, turn the needle with the shoulder point out, and set it a trifle longer than the pen, as in Fig. 2.38; replace the pencil leg, sharpen the lead to a long bevel, as in Fig. 2.39, and adjust it to the needle point. All this is done so that the needle point will be in perfect position for using the pen; the pencil, which must be sharpened frequently, can be adjusted each time to mate in length with the needle point.

To Draw a Circle. Set the compass on

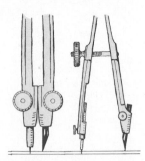

FIG. 2.39. Adjusting the pencil lead. The length is adjusted so that the instrument will be vertically centered.

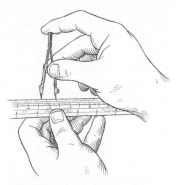

FIG. 2.40. Setting the compass to radius size. Speed and accuracy are obtained by adjusting directly on the scale.

FIG. 2.41. Guiding the needle point. For accuracy of placement, guide with the little finger.

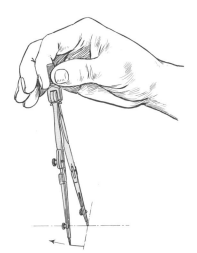

FIG. 2.42. Starting a circle. The compass is inclined in the direction of the stroke.

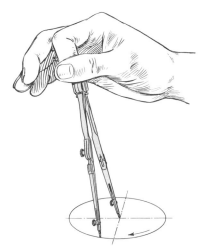

FIG. 2.43. Completing a circle. The stroke is completed by twisting the knurled handle in the fingers.

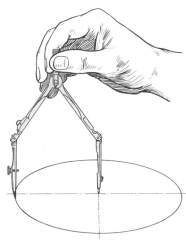

FIG. 2.44. Drawing a large circle. Knuckle joints are bent to make the legs perpendicular to the paper.

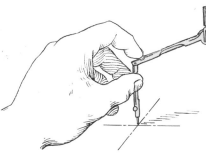

FIG. 2.45. Use of the lengthening bar. The joints must be bent to bring the legs perpendicular. Usually two hands are used because the handle is off center.

the scale, as shown in Fig. 2.40, and adjust it to the radius needed; then place the needle point at the center on the drawing, guiding it with the left hand (Fig. 2.41). Raise the fingers to the handle and draw the circle in one sweep, rolling the handle with the thumb and forefinger, inclining the compass slightly in the direction of the line (Fig. 2.42).

The position of the fingers after the rotation is shown in Fig. 2.43. The pencil line can be brightened, if necessary, by making additional turns. Circles up to perhaps 3 in. in diameter can be drawn with the legs of the compass straight, but for larger sizes, both the needle-point leg and the pencil or pen leg should be bent at the knuckle joints so as to be perpendicular to the paper (Fig. 2.44).

The 6-in. compass may be used in this way for circles up to perhaps 10 in. in diameter; larger circles are made by using the lengthening bar, as illustrated in Fig. 2.45, or the beam compass (Fig. 2.18). In drawing concentric circles, the *smallest* should always be drawn first, before the center hole has become worn.

The bow instruments are used for small circles, particularly when a number are to be made of the same diameter. To avoid wear (on side-wheel instruments), the pressure of the spring against the nut can be relieved in changing the setting by holding the points in the left hand and spinning the nut in or out with the finger. Small adjustments should be made with one hand with the needle point in position on the paper (Fig. 2.46).

FIG. 2.46. Adjusting a bow instrument. One hand only is needed. Center-wheel bows are held similarly.

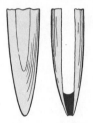

FIG. 2.47. Correct shape of pen nibs. A nicely uniform elliptical shape is best.

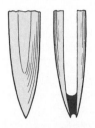

FIG. 2.48. Incorrect shape of pen nibs. This point is much too sharp. Ink will not flow well.

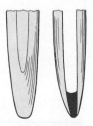

FIG. 2.49. Incorrect shape of pen nibs. This point is too flat. Ink will blob at the beginning and end of the line.

FIG. 2.50. Shape of worn pen nibs. This point needs sharpening to the shape of Fig. 2.47.

When several concentric circles are drawn, time may be saved by marking off the several radii on the paper from the scale and then setting the compass to each mark as the circles are made. In some cases it may be advantageous to measure and mark the radius on the paper instead of setting the compass directly on the scale. This method must be used whenever the radius is greater than the length of the scale.

When *extreme accuracy* is required, the compass is set, a light circle is drawn on the paper, and the diameter is checked with the scale; if the size is not satisfactory, the compass is adjusted and the operation is repeated until the size needed is obtained.

2.35. THE RULING PEN. The ruling pen is for inking straight lines and noncircular curves. Several types are illustrated in Fig. 2.19. The important feature is the shape of the blades; they should have a well-designed ink space between them, and their points should be rounded (actually elliptical in form) equally, as in Fig. 2.47. If pointed, as in Fig. 2.48, the ink will arch up as shown and will be provokingly hard to start. If rounded to a blunt point, as in Fig. 2.49, the ink will flow too freely, forming blobs and overruns at the ends of the lines. Pens in constant use become dull and worn, as illustrated in Fig. 2.50. It is easy to tell whether a pen is dull by looking for the reflection of light that travels from the side and over the end of the point when the pen is turned in the hand. If the reflection can be seen all the way, the pen is too dull. A pen in poor condition is an abomination, but a well-sharpened one is a delight to use. Every draftsman should be able to keep his pens in fine condition.

High-grade pens usually come from

the makers well sharpened. Cheaper ones often need sharpening before they can be used.

2.36. TO SHARPEN A PEN. The best stone for the purpose is a hard Arkansas knife piece. It is well to soak a new stone in oil for several days before using. The ordinary carpenter's oilstone is too coarse for drawing instruments.

The nibs must first be brought to the correct shape, as in Fig. 2.47. Screw the nibs together until they touch and, holding the pen as in drawing a line, draw it back and forth on the stone, starting the stroke with the handle at 30° or less with the stone and swinging it up past the perpendicular as the line across the stone progresses. This will bring the nibs to exactly the same shape and length, leaving them very dull. Then open them slightly, and sharpen each blade in turn, on the outside only, until the bright spot on the end has just disappeared. Hold the pen, as in Fig. 2.51, at a small angle with the stone and rub it back and forth with a slight oscillating or rocking motion to conform to the shape of the blade. A stone 3 or 4 in. long held in the left hand with the thumb and fingers gives better control than one laid on the table. Silicon carbide cloth or paper can be substituted for the stone, and for a fine job, crocus cloth may be used for finishing. A pocket magnifying glass may be helpful in examining the points. The blades should not be sharp enough to cut the paper when tested by drawing a line across it without ink. If oversharpened, the blades should again be brought to touch and a line swung very lightly across the stone as in the first operation. When tested with ink, the pen should be capable of drawing clean sharp lines down to the finest hairline. If these finest lines are ragged or broken, the pen is not

FIG. 2.51. Sharpening a pen. After bringing the point to the shape of Fig. 2.47, work down the sides by a rocking motion to conform to blade contour.

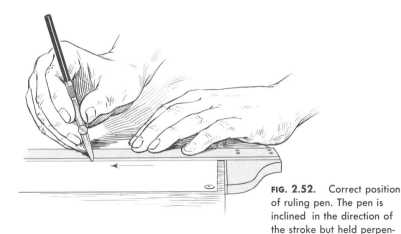

FIG. 2.52. Correct position of ruling pen. The pen is inclined in the direction of the stroke but held perpendicular to the paper, as in Fig. 2.53.

perfectly sharpened. It should not be necessary to touch the inside of the blades unless a burr has been formed, which might occur if the metal is very soft, the stone too coarse, or the pressure too heavy. To remove such a burr, or wire edge, draw a strip of detail paper between the nibs, or open the pen wide and lay the entire inner surface of the blade flat on the stone and move it with a very light touch.

2.37.   USE OF THE RULING PEN.   The ruling pen is always used in connection with a guiding edge—T square, triangle, or curve. The T square and triangle should be held in the same positions as for penciling.

To fill the pen, take it to the bottle and touch the quill filler between the nibs. Be careful not to get any ink on the outside of the blades. If the newer plastic squeeze bottle is used, place the small spout against the sides of the nibs and carefully squeeze a drop of ink *between* the nibs. Not more than 3/16 to 1/4 in. of ink should be put in; otherwise the weight of the ink will cause it to drop out in a blot. The pen should be held in the fingertips, as illustrated in Fig. 2.52, with the thumb and second finger against the sides of the nibs and the handle rest-

ing on the forefinger. Observe this hold carefully, as the tendency will be to bend the second finger to the position used when a pencil or writing pen is held. The position illustrated aids in keeping the pen at the proper angle and the nibs aligned with the ruling edge.

The pen should be held against the straightedge or guide with the blades parallel to it, the screw on the outside and the handle inclined slightly to the right and always kept in a plane passing through the line and perpendicular to the paper. The pen is thus directed by the upper edge of the guide, as illustrated in actual size in Fig. 2.53. If the pen point is thrown out from the perpendicular, it will run on one blade and make a line that is ragged on one side. If the pen is turned in from the perpendicular, the ink is likely to run under the edge of the guide and cause a blot.

A line is drawn with a steady, even arm movement, the tips of the third and fourth fingers resting on, and sliding along, the straightedge, keeping the angle of inclination constant. Just before the end of the line is reached, the two guiding fingers on the straightedge should be stopped and, without stopping the motion of the pen, the line finished with a finger movement. Short lines are

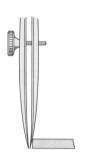

FIG. 2.53. Correct pen position. Even though the pen is inclined in the direction of the stroke, both nibs must touch the paper equally.

FIG. 2.54. Inking over pencil line. *Center ink line over original layout line.*

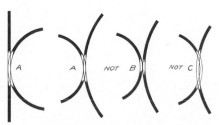

FIG. 2.55. Correct and incorrect tangents. Lines must be the width of one line at tangent point.

FIG. 2.56. The alphabet of lines for pencil drawings.

drawn with this finger movement alone. When the end of the line is reached, the pen is lifted quickly and the straightedge moved away from the line. The pressure on the paper should be light but sufficient to give a clean-cut line, and it will vary with the kind of paper and the sharpness of the pen. The pressure against the T square, however, should be only enough to guide the direction.

If the ink refuses to flow, it may be because it has dried in the extreme point of the pen. If pinching the blades slightly or touching the pen on the finger does not start it, the pen should immediately

be wiped out and fresh ink supplied. Pens must be wiped clean after using.

In inking on either paper or cloth, the full lines will be much wider than the pencil lines. You must be careful to have the center of the ink line cover the pencil line, as shown in Fig. 2.54.

Instructions in regard to the ruling pen apply also to the compass. The compass should be slightly inclined in the direction of the line and both nibs of the pen kept on the paper, bending the knuckle joints, if necessary, to effect this.

It is a universal rule in inking that *circles and circle arcs must be inked first.* It

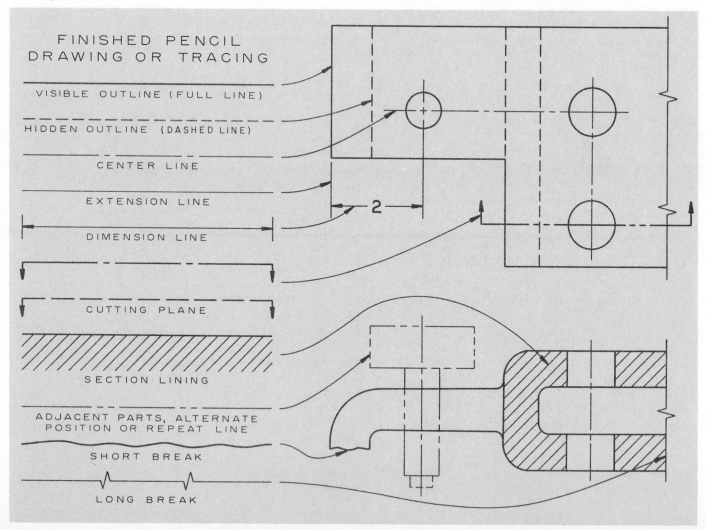

FINISHED PENCIL
DRAWING OR TRACING

VISIBLE OUTLINE (FULL LINE)

HIDDEN OUTLINE (DASHED LINE)

CENTER LINE

EXTENSION LINE

DIMENSION LINE

CUTTING PLANE

SECTION LINING

ADJACENT PARTS, ALTERNATE
POSITION OR REPEAT LINE

SHORT BREAK

LONG BREAK

is much easier to connect a straight line to a curve than a curve to a straight line.

2.38.   TANGENTS.   It should be noted particularly that two lines are tangent to each other when the center lines of the lines are tangent and not simply when the lines touch each other; thus at the point of tangency, the width will be equal to the width of a single line (Fig. 2.55). Before inking tangent lines, the point of tangency should be marked in pencil. For an arc tangent to a straight line, this point will be on a line through the center of the arc and perpendicular

to the straight line, and for two circle arcs it will be on the line joining their centers, as described in paragraphs 3.5 to 3.16.

2.39.   THE "ALPHABET OF LINES."   As the basis of drawing is the line, a set of conventional symbols covering all the lines needed for different purposes may properly be called an alphabet of lines. Figures 2.56 and 2.57 show the alphabet of lines adopted by the ANSI as applied to the following:

1. Drawings made directly or traced in pencil on tracing paper or pencil

FIG. 2.57.   The alphabet of lines for inked drawings.

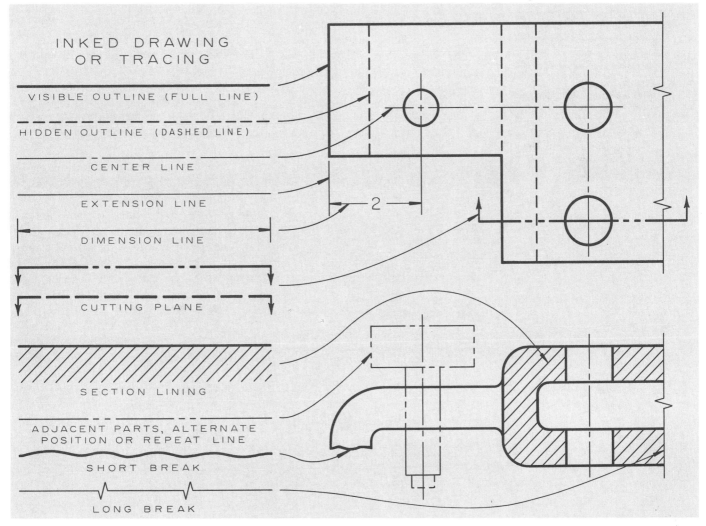

cloth, from which blueprints or other reproductions are to be made (Fig. 2.56).

2. Tracings in ink on tracing cloth or tracing paper and inked drawings on white paper for display or photoreproductions (Fig. 2.57).

The ANSI recommends three widths of lines for finished drawings: *thick* for visible outlines, cutting-plane, and short-break lines; *medium* for hidden outlines; and *thin* for section, center, extension, dimension, long-break, adjacent-part, alternate-position, and repeat lines. The actual widths of the three weights of lines, on average drawings, should be about as in Figs. 2.56 and 2.57. A convenient line gage is given in Fig. 2.58. If applied to Fig. 2.57, this gage would show the heavy lines in ink to be between 1/30 and 1/40 in., the medium lines 1/60 in., and the fine lines 1/100 in. in width. To use the line gage, draw a line about 1½ in. long in pencil or ink on a piece of the drawing paper and apply it alongside the gage. By this method a good comparison can be made. Note that the standard lines for pencil drawings are somewhat thinner than for inked drawings, the thick line being about 1/60 in., medium about 1/80 in. and thin between 1/100 and 1/150 in. Study Figs. 2.56 and 2.57 carefully and try to make your drawings conform to these standard lines. Professional appearance depends to a great extent upon the line weights used. Line widths for layout drawings are *thin* throughout because the watchword here is accuracy. Layout drawings are often traced in pencil or ink to the weights given in Figs. 2.56 and 2.57 and are then *finished* drawings.

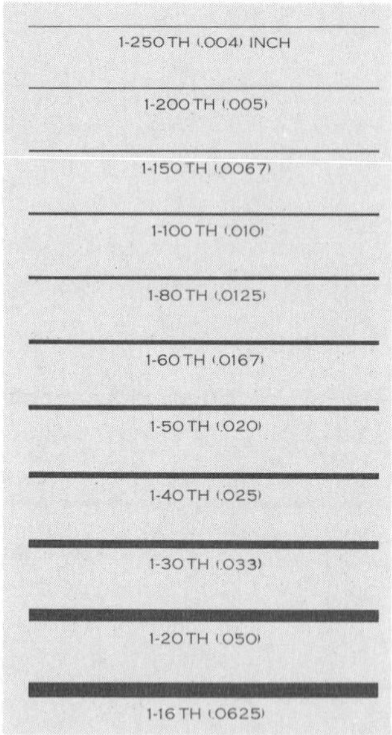
1-250 TH (.004) INCH
1-200 TH (.005)
1-150 TH (.0067)
1-100 TH (.010)
1-80 TH (.0125)
1-60 TH (.0167)
1-50 TH (.020)
1-40 TH (.025)
1-30 TH (.033)
1-20 TH (.050)
1-16 TH (.0625)

FIG. 2.58. Line gage. Draw a line on the paper to be used and apply it here to determine the width.

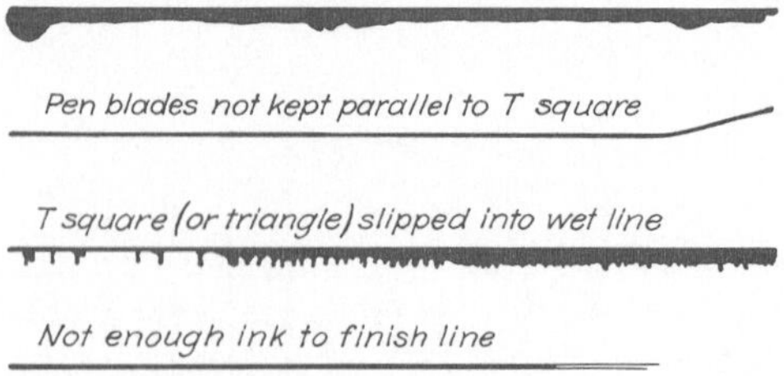
Pen pressed against T square too hard
Pen sloped away from T square
Pen too close to edge, ink ran under
Ink on outside of blade, ran under
Pen blades not kept parallel to T square
T square (or triangle) slipped into wet line
Not enough ink to finish line

FIG. 2.59. Faulty ink lines. The difficulty is indicated in each case.

2.40. LINE PRACTICE. After reading the preceding paragraphs, take a blank sheet of paper and practice making straight lines and circles in all the forms—full, dashed, etc.—shown in Figs. 2.56 and 2.57. Include starting and stopping lines, with special attention to tangents and corners.

In pencil, try to get all the lines uniform in width and color for each type. Circle arcs and straight lines should match exactly at tangent points.

In ink, proceed as for pencil practice and pay particular attention to the weight of lines and to the spacing of dashed lines and center lines.

If the inked lines appear imperfect in any way, ascertain the reason immediately. It may be the fault of the pen, the ink, the paper, or the draftsman; the probabilities are greatly in favor of the last if the faults resemble those in Fig. 2.59, which illustrates the characteristic appearance of several kinds of poor line. The correction in each case will suggest itself.

2.41. USE OF THE FRENCH CURVE. The french curve is a guiding edge for noncircular curves. When sufficient points have been determined, it is best to sketch in the line lightly in pencil, freehand and without losing the points, until it is clean, smooth, continuous, and satisfactory to the eye. Then apply the curve to it, selecting a part that will fit a portion of the line most nearly and seeing to it, particularly, that the curve is so placed that the direction in which its curvature increases is the direction in which the curvature of the line increases (Fig. 2.60). In drawing the part of the line matched by the curve, *always* stop a little short of the distance in which the guide and the line seem to coincide. After drawing this portion, shift the curve to find another place that will coincide with the continuation of the line. In shifting the curve, take care to preserve smoothness and continuity and to avoid breaks or cusps. Do this by seeing that in its successive positions the curve is always adjusted so that it coincides for a short distance with the part of the line already drawn. Thus at each junction the tangents will coincide.

If the curved line is symmetrical about an axis, marks locating this axis, after it has been matched accurately on one side, may be made in pencil on the curve and the curve then reversed. In such a case take exceptional care to avoid a "hump" at the joint.

It is often better to stop a line short of the axis on each side and close the gap afterward with another setting of the curve.

When using the curve in inking, the pen should be held perpendicular and the blades kept parallel to the edge. The inking of curves is excellent practice.

Sometimes, particularly at sharp turns, a combination of circle arcs and curves may be used: In inking a long, narrow ellipse, for example, the sharp curves may be inked by selecting a center on the major diameter by trial, draw-

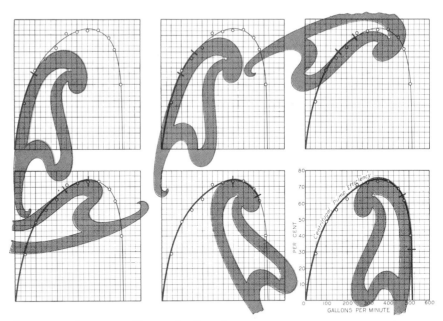

ing as much arc as will practically coincide with the ends of the ellipse, and then finishing the ellipse with the curve. The experienced draftsman will sometimes ink a curve that cannot be matched accurately by varying the distance of the pen point from the ruling edge as the line progresses.

2.42. ERASING. The erasing of pencil lines and ink lines is a necessary technique to learn. When changing some detail, a designer, working freely but lightly, uses a soft pencil eraser so as not to damage the finish of the paper. Heavier lines are best removed with a Ruby pencil eraser. If the paper has been grooved by the line, it may be rubbed over with a burnisher or even with the back of the thumbnail. In erasing an ink line, hold the paper down firmly and rub lightly and patiently, with a Ruby pencil eraser, first along the line and then across it, until the ink is removed. A triangle slipped under the

FIG. 2.60. Use of the french curve. The changing curvature of line and curve must match.

paper or cloth gives a good backing surface.

When an erasure is made close to other lines, select an opening of the best shape on the erasing shield (Fig. 2.3D) and rub through it, holding the shield down firmly, first seeing that both of its sides are clean. Wipe the eraser crumbs off the paper with a dustcloth or brush. Never scratch out a line or blot with a knife or razor blade, and use so-called ink erasers sparingly, if at all. A skilled draftsman sometimes uses a sharp blade to trim a thickened spot or overrunning end on a line.

For extensive erasing, an electric erasing machine is a great convenience. Several successful models are on the market.

2.43. CAUTIONS IN THE USE OF INSTRUMENTS. To complete this discussion of instruments, here are a few points worth noting:

NEVER use the scale as a ruler for drawing lines.

NEVER draw horizontal lines with the lower edge of the T square.

NEVER use the lower edge of the T square as a horizontal base for the triangles.

NEVER cut paper with a knife and the edge of the T square as a guide.

NEVER use the T square as a hammer.

NEVER put either end of a pencil into the mouth.

NEVER work with a dull pencil.

NEVER sharpen a pencil over the drawing board.

NEVER jab the dividers into the drawing board.

NEVER oil the joints of compasses.

NEVER use the dividers as reamers, pincers, or picks.

NEVER use a blotter on inked lines.

NEVER screw the pen adjustment past the contact point of the nibs.

NEVER leave the ink bottle uncorked.

NEVER hold the pen over the drawing while filling.

NEVER put into the drawing-ink bottle a writing pen that has been used in ordinary writing ink.

NEVER try to use the same thumbtack holes in either paper or board when putting paper down a second time.

NEVER scrub a drawing all over with an eraser after finishing. It takes the life out of the lines.

NEVER begin work without wiping off the table and instruments.

NEVER put instruments away without cleaning them. This applies with particular force to pens.

NEVER put bow instruments away without opening to relieve the spring.

NEVER work on a table cluttered with unneeded instruments or equipment.

NEVER fold a drawing or tracing.

2.44. EXERCISES IN THE USE OF INSTRUMENTS. The following problems can be used as progressive exercises for practice in using the instruments. Do them as finished pencil drawings or in pencil layout to be inked. Line work should conform to that given in the alphabet of lines (Figs. 2.56 and 2.57).

The problems in Chap. 3 afford excellent additional practice in accurate penciling.

PROBLEMS

GROUP 1.   STRAIGHT LINES

2.1.1.   An exercise for the T square, triangle, and scale. Through the center of the space draw a horizontal and a vertical line. Measuring on these lines as diameters, lay off a 4-in. square. Along the lower side and upper half of the left side measure ½-in. spaces with the scale. Draw all horizontal lines with the T square and all vertical lines with the T square and triangle.

2.1.2.   An interlacement. For T square, triangle, and dividers. Draw a 4-in. square. Divide the left side and lower side into seven equal parts with dividers. Draw horizontal and vertical lines across the square through these points. Erase the parts not needed.

2.1.3.   A street-paving intersection. For 45° triangle and scale. An exercise in starting and stopping short lines. Draw a 4-in. square. Draw its diagonals with 45° triangle. With the scale, lay off ½-in. spaces along the diagonals from their intersection. With 45° triangle, complete the figure, finishing one quarter at a time.

2.1.4.   A square pattern. For 45° triangle, dividers, and scale. Draw a 4-in. square and divide its sides into three equal parts with

dividers. With 45° triangle, draw diagonal lines connecting these points. Measure ⅜ in. on each side of these lines, and finish the pattern as shown.

2.1.5.   An acoustic pattern. For 45° triangle, T square, and scale. Draw two intersecting 45° diagonals 4 in. long, to form a field. With the scale lay off ½-in. spaces from their intersection. Add the narrow border ³⁄₁₆ in. wide. Add a second border ½ in. wide. The length of the border blocks is projected from the corners of the field blocks.

2.1.6.   Five cards. Visible and hidden lines. Five cards 1¾ by 3 in. are arranged with the bottom card in the center, the other four overlapping each other and placed so that their outside edges form a 4-in. square. Hidden lines indicate edges covered.

2.1.7.   A Maltese cross. For T square, spacers, and 45° and 30-60° triangles. Draw a 4-in. square and a 1⅜-in. square. From the corners of the inner square, draw lines to the outer square at 15° and 75°, with the two triangles in combination. Mark points with spacers ¼ in. inside each line of this outside cross, and complete the figure with triangles in combination.

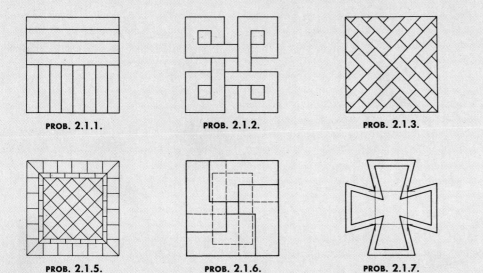

PROB. 2.1.1.   PROB. 2.1.2.   PROB. 2.1.3.   PROB. 2.1.4.

PROB. 2.1.5.   PROB. 2.1.6.   PROB. 2.1.7.

GROUP 2.   STRAIGHT LINES AND CIRCLES

2.2.1.   Insigne. For T square, triangles, scale, and compasses. Draw the 45° diagonals and the vertical and horizontal center lines of a 4-in. square. With compass, draw a ¾-in.-diameter construction circle, a 2¾-in. circle, and a 3¼-in. circle. Complete the design by adding a square and pointed star as shown.

2.2.2.   A six-point star. For compass and 30-60° triangle. Draw a 4-in. construction circle and inscribe the six-point star with the T square and 30-60° triangle. Accomplish this with four successive changes of position of the triangle.

2.2.3.   A stamping. For T square, 30-60° triangle, and compasses. In a 4-in. circle draw six diameters 30° apart. Draw a 3-in. con-struction circle to locate the centers of ⁵⁄₁₆-in.-radius circle arcs. Complete the stamping with perpendiculars to the six diameters as shown.

2.2.4.   Insignia. The device shown is a white star with a red center on a blue background. Draw a 4-in. circle and a 1¼-in. circle. Divide the large circle into five equal parts with the dividers and construct the star by connecting alternate points as shown. Red is indicated by vertical lines and blue by horizontal lines. Space these by eye approximately ¹⁄₁₆-in. apart.

2.2.5.   A 24-point star. For T square and tri-angles in combination. In a 4-in. circle draw 12 diameters 15° apart, using T square and triangles singly and in combination. With the same combinations, finish the figure as shown.

PROB. 2.2.1.

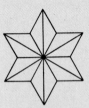

PROB. 2.2.2.

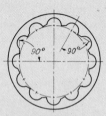

PROB. 2.2.3.

PROB. 2.2.4.

PROB. 2.2.5.

GROUP 3.   CIRCLES AND TANGENTS

2.3.1.   Concentric circles. For compass (legs straight) and scale. Draw a horizontal line through the center of a space. On it mark off radii for eight concentric circles ¼ in. apart. In drawing concentric circles, always draw the smallest first.

2.3.2.   A four-centered spiral. For accurate tangents. Draw a ⅛-in. square and extend its sides as shown. With the upper right corner as center, draw quadrants with ⅛- and ¼-in. radii. Continue with quadrants from each cor-ner in order until four turns have been drawn.

2.3.3.   A loop ornament. For bow compass.

Draw a 2-in. square, about center of space. Di-vide AE into four ¼-in. spaces with scale. With bow pencil and centers A, B, C, and D, draw four semicircles with ¼-in. radius, and so on. Complete the figure by drawing the horizontal and vertical tangents as shown.

2.3.4.   A rectilinear chart. For french curve. Draw a 4-in. field with ½-in. coordinate divi-sions. Plot points at the intersections shown, and through them sketch a smooth curve very lightly in pencil. Finish by marking each point with a ¹⁄₁₆-in. circle and drawing a smooth line with the french curve.

PROB. 2.3.1.

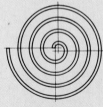

PROB. 2.3.2.

PROB. 2.3.3.

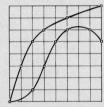

PROB. 2.3.4.

2.4.1. Scale practice.

(*a*) Measure lines *A* to *G* to the following scales: *A*, full size; *B*, ½ size; *C*, 3″ = 1′-0″; *D*, 1″ = 1′-0″; *E*, ¾″ = 1′-0″; *F*, ¼″ = 1′-0″; *G*, ³⁄₁₆″ = 1′-0″.

(*b*) Lay off distances on lines *H* to *N* as follows: *H*, 3³⁄₁₆″, full size; *I*, 7″, ½ size; *J*, 2′-6″, 1½″ = 1′-0″; *K*, 7′-5½″, ½″ = 1′-0″; *L*,

10′-11″, ⅜″ = 1′-0″; *M*, 28′-4″, ⅛″ = 1′-0″; *N*, 40′-10″, ³⁄₃₂″ = 1′-0″.

(*c*) For engineer's scale. Lay off distances on lines *H* to *N* as follows: *H*, 3.2″, full size; *I*, 27′-0″, 1″ = 10′-0″; *J*, 66′-0″, 1″ = 20′-0″; *K*, 105′-0″, 1″ = 30′-0″; *L*, 156′-0″, 1″ = 40′-0″; *M*, 183′-0″, 1″ = 50′-0″; *N*, 214′-0″, 1″ = 60′-0″.

PROB. 2.4.1.

A ├──────────────┤

B ├──────────┤

C ├────────────────┤

D ├──────────────┤

E ├──────────────┤

F ├──────────────────┤

G ├────────────────────┤

H ├────────────────────┤

I ├────────────────────┤

J ├────────────────────┤

K ├────────────────────┤

L ├────────────────────┤

M ├────────────────────┤

N ├────────────────────┤

GROUP 5. COMBINATIONS

2.5.1. A telephone dial plate. Draw double size.

2.5.2. A film-reel stamping. Draw to scale of 6″ = 1′-0″.

2.5.3. Box cover. Make a one-view drawing for rectangular stamping 3 by 4 in., corners rounded with ½-in. radius. Four holes, one in each corner, ³⁄₁₆-in. diameter, 3 and 2 in. center to center, for fasteners. Rectangular hole in center, ⅜ by 1 in., with 1-in. side parallel to 4-in. side. Two slots ¼ in. wide, 2 in. long with semicircular ends, located midway between center and 4-in. edges, with 2-in. side parallel to 4-in. side and centered between 3-in. edges.

2.5.4. Spacer. Make a one-view drawing for circular stamping 4 in. OD (outside diameter), 2 in. ID (inside diameter). Six ¼-in.-diameter holes equally spaced on 3-in.-diameter circle, with two holes on vertical center line. Two semicircular notches 180° apart made with ⅜-in. radius centered at intersections of horizontal center line and 4-in.-OD circle.

2.5.5. Blank for wheel. Make a one-view drawing for stamping 5 in. OD; center hole ½ in. in diameter; eight spokes ⅜ in. wide connecting 1½-in.-diameter center portion with ½-in. rim. Eight ¼-in.-diameter holes with centers at intersection of center lines of spokes and 4½-in. circle; ⅛-in. fillets throughout to break sharp corners.

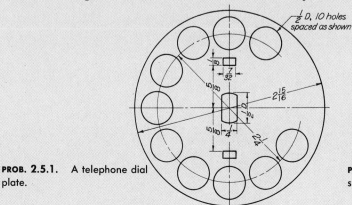

PROB. 2.5.1. A telephone dial plate.

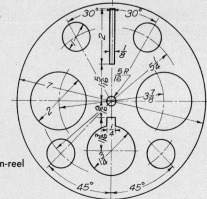

PROB. 2.5.2. A film-reel stamping.

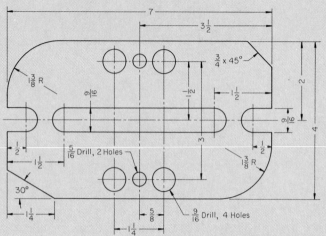

PROB. 2.5.7. Fixture base.

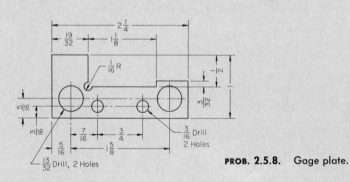

PROB. 2.5.8. Gage plate.

2.5.6. Cover plate. Make a one-view drawing for rectangular stamping 3 by 4 in., corners beveled ½-in. each way. Four holes, one in each corner, ¼-in. diameter, 3 and 2 in. center to center, for fasteners. Rectangular hole in center, ½ by 1 in. with 1-in. side parallel to 4-in. side. Two holes, ¾-in. diameter, located midway between the slot and short side of rectangle on center line through slot.

2.5.7. Drawing of fixture base. Full size. Drill sizes specify the diameter (see Glossary).

2.5.8. Drawing of gage plate. Scale, twice size. Drill sizes specify the diameter (see Glossary).

2.5.9. Drawing of milling fixture plate. Scale, twice size. Drill size specifies diameter (see Glossary).

PROB. 2.5.9. Milling fixture plate.

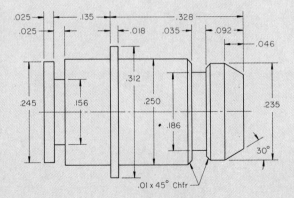

PROB. 2.5.10. Dial shaft.

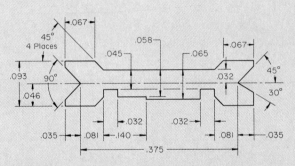

PROB. 2.5.11. Inner toggle for temperature control.

2.5.10. Drawing of dial shaft. Use decimal scale and draw 10 times size.

2.5.11. Drawing of inner toggle for temperature control. Use decimal scale and draw 10 times size.

2.5.12. Drawing of mounting surface—O control. Scale, twice size.

2.5.13. Drawing of mounting leg—O control. Scale, full size.

2.5.14. Drawing of cooling fin and tube support. Full size.

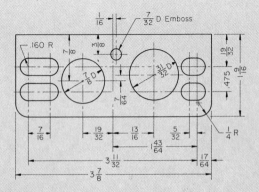

PROB. 2.5.12. Mounting surface: O control.

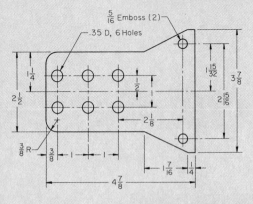

PROB. 2.5.13. Mounting leg: O control.

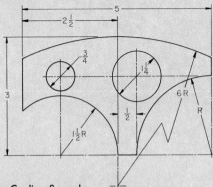

PROB. 2.5.14. Cooling fin and tube support.

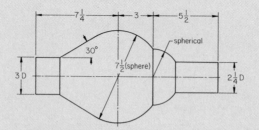

PROB. 2.5.15. Cone, sphere, and cylinder combinations.

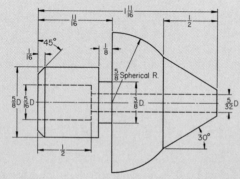

PROB. 2.5.16. Cone and ball check.

2.5.15. Drawing of cone, sphere, and cylinder combinations. Scale, half size.

2.5.16. Drawing of cone-and-ball check. Scale, four times size.

2.5.17. Drawing of bell crank. Stamped steel. Scale, full size.

2.5.18. Drawing of control plate (aircraft hydraulic system). Stamped aluminum. Scale, full size.

2.5.19. Drawing of torque disk (aircraft brake). Stamped steel. Scale, half size.

2.5.20. Drawing of brake shoe. Stamped steel with molded asbestos composition wear surface. Scale, full size.

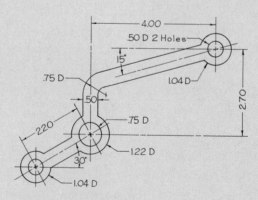

PROB. 2.5.17. Bell crank.

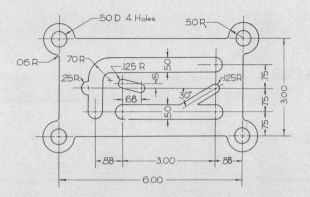

PROB. 2.5.18. Control plate.

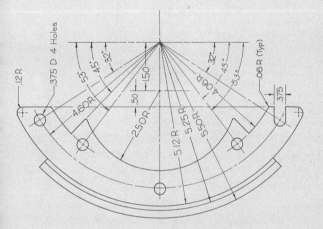

PROB. 2.5.19. Torque disk.

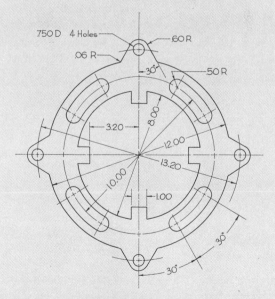

PROB. 2.5.20. Brake shoe.

In the previous chapter on instruments and their use the need for accurate drawings was stressed. This chapter discusses methods of constructing line connections, tangents, normals, divisions, curves, angles, and geometric figures—all necessary for the making of accurate, readable, reliable drawings.

Graphic Geometry

3.1. Strict interpretation of constructional geometry allows use of only the compass and an instrument for drawing straight lines, and with these the geometer, following mathematical theory, accomplishes his solutions. In engineering drawing the principles of geometry are employed constantly, but instruments are not limited to the basic two as T square, triangles, scales, curves, etc., are used to make constructions with speed and accuracy. Since there is continual application of geometric principles, the methods given in this chapter should be mastered thoroughly. It is assumed that students using this book understand the elements of plane geometry and will be able to apply their knowledge.

The constructions given here afford excellent practice in the use of instruments. Remember that the results you obtain will be only as accurate as your skill makes them. Take care in measuring and in drawing so that your work will be accurate and professional in appearance.

For easy reference, the various geometric figures are given in Fig. 3.101 at the end of this chapter.

This chapter is divided, for convenience and logical arrangement, into four parts: Line Relationships and Connections, which represent the bulk of the geometry needed in everyday work; Geometry of Straight-line Figures; Geometry of Curved Lines; and Constructions for Lofting and Large Layouts.

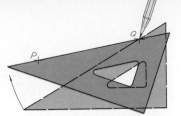

FIG. 3.1. To draw a line through two points. Use the pencil as a pivot and align the triangle or T square with the second point.

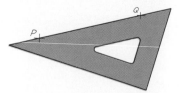

FIG. 3.2. To draw a line through two points (*alternate method*). Carefully align the triangle or T square with the points, and draw the required line.

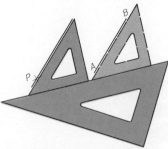

FIG. 3.3. To draw a line parallel to another. Align a triangle with the given line *AB* using a base as shown; move it to position through the given point *P* and draw the required line.

FIG. 3.4. To draw a line parallel to and a given distance from a line. Space the distance with circle arc *R;* then align a triangle on a base as shown, move to position tangent to the circle arc, and draw the required line.

LINE RELATIONSHIPS AND CONNECTIONS

3.2. TO DRAW STRAIGHT LINES (FIGS. 3.1 AND 3.2).
Straight lines are drawn by using the straight edge of the T square or one of the triangles. For short lines a triangle is more convenient. Observe the directions for technique in paragraphs 3.2, 3.3, and 3.4.

To draw a straight line through two points (Fig. 3.1), place the point of the pencil at *Q* and bring the triangle (or T square) against the point of the pencil. Then, using this point as a pivot, swing the triangle until its edge is in alignment with point *P,* and draw the line.

To draw a straight line through two points, *alternate method* (Fig. 3.2), align the triangle or T square with points *P* and *Q,* and draw the line.

3.3 TO DRAW PARALLEL LINES (FIGS. 3.3 AND 3.4).
Parallel lines may be required in any position. Parallel horizontals or verticals are most common. Horizontals are drawn with T square alone, verticals with T square and triangle. The general cases (odd angles) are shown in Figs. 3.3 and 3.4.

To draw a straight line through a point, parallel to another line (Fig. 3.3), adjust a triangle to the given line *AB,* with a second triangle as a base. Slide the aligned triangle to its position at point *P* and draw the required line.

To draw a straight line at a given distance from and parallel to another line (Fig. 3.4), draw an arc with the given distance *R* as radius and any point on the given line *AB* as center. Then adjust a triangle to line *AB,* with a second triangle as a base. Slide the aligned triangle to position tangent to the circle arc and draw the required line.

3.4. TO DRAW PERPENDICULAR LINES (FIGS. 3.5 AND 3.6).
Perpendiculars occur frequently as horizontal-to-vertical (Fig. 3.5) but also often in other positions (Fig. 3.6). Note that the construction of a perpendicular utilizes the 90° angle of a triangle.

To erect a perpendicular to a given straight line (*when the given line is horizontal, Fig. 3.5*), place a triangle on the T square as shown and draw the required perpendicular.

To erect a perpendicular to a given straight line (*general position, Fig. 3.6*), set a triangle with its hypotenuse against a guiding edge and adjust one side to the given line. Then slide the triangle so that the second side is in the position of the perpendicular and draw the required line.

3.5. TANGENTS (FIGS. 3.7 TO 3.20).
A *tangent* to a curve is a line, either straight

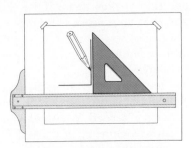

FIG. 3.5. To draw a line perpendicular to another (when the *given line* is *horizontal*). Place the triangle on the T square and draw the required line.

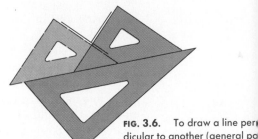

FIG. 3.6. To draw a line perpendicular to another (general position). Align a triangle with the given line as shown; slide it (on another triangle as a base) to position of perpendicular and draw the required line.

or curved, that passes through two points on the curve infinitely close together. One of the most frequent geometric operations in drafting is the drawing of tangents to circle arcs and the drawing of circle arcs tangent to straight lines or other circles. These should be constructed accurately, and on pencil drawings that are to be inked or traced the points of tangency should be located by short cross marks to show the stopping points for the ink lines. The method of finding these points is indicated in the following constructions. Note in all the following tangent constructions that the location of tangent points is based on one of these geometric facts: (1) the tangent point of a straight line and circle will lie at the intersection of a perpendicular to the straight line that passes through the circle center, and (2) the tangent point of two circles will lie on the circumferences of both circles and on a straight line connecting the circle centers. See Fig. 3.7.

3.6.   TANGENT POINTS (FIG. 3.7).
To find the point of tangency for line AB and a circle with center D, draw DC perpendicular to line AB. Point C is the tangent point.

To find the tangent point for two circles (Fig. 3.7) with centers at D and E, draw DE, joining the centers. Point P is the tangent point.

3.7.   TO DRAW A CIRCLE OF GIVEN SIZE TANGENT TO A LINE AND PASSING THROUGH A POINT (FIG. 3.8).
Draw a line AB, the given radius distance R away from and parallel to the given line. Using the given point S as center, cut line AB at O with the given radius. O is the center of the circle. Note that there are two possible positions for the circle.

3.8.   TO DRAW A CIRCLE TANGENT TO A LINE AT A POINT AND PASSING THROUGH A SECOND POINT (FIG. 3.9).
Connect the two points P and S and draw the perpendicular bisector AB (see paragraph 3.38). Draw a perpendicular to the given line at P. The point where this perpendicular intersects the line AB is the center O of the required circle.

3.9.   TO DRAW A TANGENT TO A CIRCLE AT A POINT ON THE CIRCLE (FIG. 3.10).
Given the arc ACB, draw a tangent at the point C. Arrange a triangle in combination with the T square (or another triangle) so that its hypotenuse passes through center O and point C. Holding the T square firmly in place, turn the triangle about its square corner and move it until the hypotenuse passes through C. The required tangent then lies along the hypotenuse.

3.10.   TO DRAW A TANGENT TO A CIRCLE FROM A POINT OUTSIDE (FIG. 3.11).
Given the arc ACB and point P, arrange a triangle in combination with another triangle (or T square) so that one side passes through point P and is tangent to the circle arc. Then slide the triangle until the right-angle side passes through

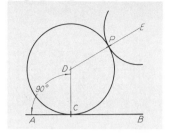

FIG. 3.7.   Tangent points. The tangent point of a straight line and circle is on the perpendicular from the circle center. The tangent point of two circles is on a line connecting their centers.

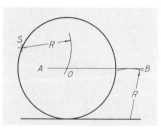

FIG. 3.8.   A circle tangent to a line and passing through a point. The circle center must be equidistant from the line and the point.

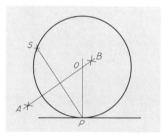

FIG. 3.9.   A circle tangent to a line at a point and passing through a second point. The circle center is at the intersection of the bisector of the chord connecting the points and the perpendicular from the point on the line tangent.

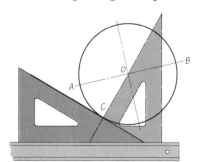

FIG. 3.10.   A tangent at a point on a circle. The tangent line must be perpendicular to the line from the point to the center of the circle.

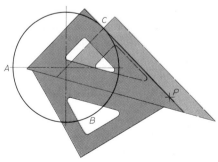

FIG. 3.11.   A tangent to a circle from a point outside. The line is drawn by alignment through the point and tangent to the circle; the tangent point is then located on the perpendicular from the circle center.

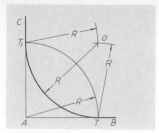

FIG. 3.12. An arc tangent at right-angle corner. The arc center must be equidistant from both lines.

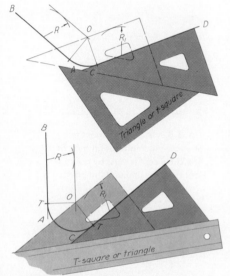

FIG. 3.13. An arc tangent to two straight lines. The arc center must be equidistant from both straight lines.

the center of the circle and mark lightly the tangent point *C*. Bring the triangle back to its original position and draw the tangent line.

3.11. TO DRAW A CIRCLE ARC OF GIVEN RADIUS TANGENT TO TWO LINES AT RIGHT ANGLES TO EACH OTHER (FIG. 3.12).

Draw an arc of radius *R*, with center at corner *A*, cutting the lines *AB* and *AC* at *T* and T_1. Then with *T* and T_1 as centers and with the same radius *R*, draw arcs intersecting at *O*, the center of the required arc.

3.12. TO DRAW AN ARC OF GIVEN RADIUS TANGENT TO TWO STRAIGHT LINES (FIG. 3.13).

Given the lines *AB* and *CD*, set the compass to radius *R*, and at any convenient point on the given lines draw the arcs *R* and R_1. With the method of Fig. 3.4, draw parallels to the given lines through the limits of the arcs. These parallels are the loci of the centers of all circles of radius *R* tangent to lines *AB* and *CD*, and their intersection at point *O* will be the center of the required arc. Find the tangent points by erecting perpendiculars, as in Fig. 3.11, to the given lines through the center *O*. The figure above shows the method for an obtuse angle, below for an acute angle.

3.13. TO DRAW A TANGENT TO TWO CIRCLES (FIG. 3.14, OPEN BELT).

Arrange a triangle in combination with a T square or triangle so that one side is in the tangent position. Move to positions 2 and 3, marking lightly the tangent points T_1 and T_2. Return to the original position and draw the tangent line. Repeat for the other side.

3.14. TO DRAW A TANGENT TO TWO CIRCLES (FIG. 3.15, CROSSED BELT).

Arrange a triangle in combination with a T square or triangle so that one side is in the tangent position. Move to positions 2 and 3, marking lightly the tangent points T_1 and T_2. Return to the original position and draw the tangent line. Repeat for the other side.

3.15. TO DRAW A CIRCLE OF RADIUS *R* TANGENT TO A GIVEN CIRCLE AND A STRAIGHT LINE (FIG. 3.16).

Let *AB* be the given line and R_1 the radius of the given circle. Draw a line *CD* parallel to *AB* at a distance *R* from it. With *O* as center and radius $R + R_1$, swing an arc intersecting *CD* at *X*, the desired center. The tangent point for *AB* will be on a perpendicular to *AB* from *X;* the tangent point for the two circles will be on a line joining their centers *X* and *O*.

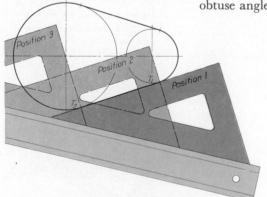

FIG. 3.14. Tangents to two circles (open belt). Tangent lines are drawn by alignment with both circles. Tangent points lie on perpendicular lines from circle centers.

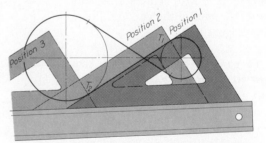

FIG. 3.15. Tangents to two circles (crossed belt). Tangent lines are drawn by alignment with both circles. Tangent points lie on perpendicular lines from circle centers.

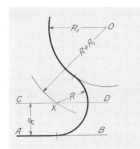

FIG. 3.16. An arc tangent to a straight line and a circle. The arc center must be equidistant from the line and the circle.

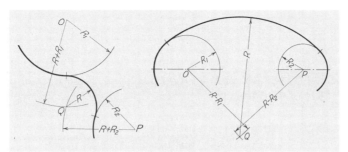

FIG. 3.17. An arc tangent to two circles. The arc center must be equidistant from both circles.

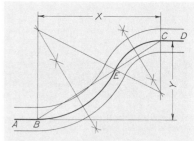

FIG. 3.18. An ogee curve. It is made of circle arcs tangent to each other and to straight lines.

3.16. TO DRAW A CIRCLE OF RADIUS R TANGENT TO TWO GIVEN CIRCLES. *First Case (Fig. 3.17, Left).* The centers of the given circles are outside the required circle. Let R_1 and R_2 be the radii of the given circles and O and P their centers. With O as center and radius $R + R_1$, describe an arc. With P as center and radius $R + R_2$, swing another arc intersecting the first arc at Q, which is the center sought. Mark the tangent points in line with OQ and QP.

Second Case (Fig. 3.17, Right). The centers of the given circles are inside the required circle. With O and P as centers and radii $R - R_1$ and $R - R_2$, describe arcs intersecting at the required center Q.

3.17. TO DRAW A REVERSE, OR OGEE, CURVE (FIG. 3.18). Given two parallel lines AB and CD, join B and C by a straight line. Erect perpendiculars at B and C. Any arcs tangent to lines AB and CD at B and C must have their centers on these perpendiculars. On the line BC assume point E, the point through which it is desired that the curve shall pass. Bisect BE and EC by perpendiculars. Any arc to pass through B and E must have its center somewhere on the perpendicular from the middle point. The intersection, therefore, of these perpendicular bisectors with the first two perpendiculars will be the centers for arcs BE and EC. This line might be the center line for

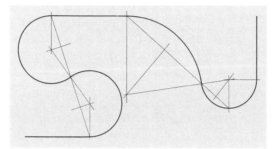

FIG. 3.19. Ogee applications. Note that the circle arcs are tangent on a line connecting the centers.

a curved road or pipe. The construction may be checked by drawing the line of centers, which *must* pass through E. Figure 3.19 illustrates the principle of reverse-curve construction in various combinations.

3.18. TO DRAW A REVERSE CURVE TANGENT TO TWO LINES AND TO A THIRD SECANT LINE AT A GIVEN POINT (FIG. 3.20). Given two lines AB and CD cut by the line EF at points E and F, draw a perpendicular JH to EF through a given point P on EF. With E as center and radius EP, intersect CD at G. Draw a perpendicular from G intersecting JH at H. With F as center and radius FP, intersect AB at K. Draw a perpendicular to AB from K intersecting JH at J. H and J will be the centers for arcs tangent to the three lines.

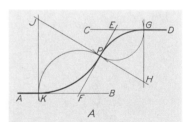
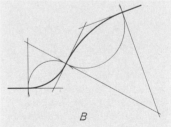
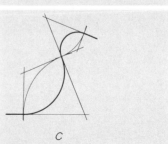

FIG. 3.20. Reverse curve tangent to three lines. Note that the arc centers must lie on a line perpendicular to the tangent line at the point of tangency.

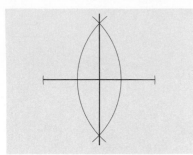

FIG. 3.21. To bisect a line (with compass). The intersections of equal arcs locate two points on the perpendicular bisector.

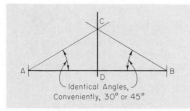

FIG. 3.22. To bisect a line (with T square and triangle). Equal angles locate one point on the perpendicular bisector.

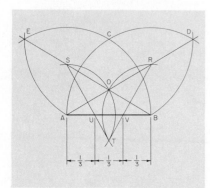

FIG. 3.23. To trisect a line (with compass). Construction is based on the geometry of an equilateral triangle.

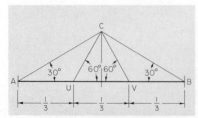

FIG. 3.24. To trisect a line (with T square and triangle). Third points are located by 30° and 60° angles.

GEOMETRY OF STRAIGHT-LINE FIGURES

3.19. TO BISECT A LINE (FIG. 3.21). *With Compass.* From the two ends of the line, swing arcs of the same radius, greater than one-half the length of the line, and draw a line through the arc intersections. This line bisects the given line and is also the *perpendicular* bisector. Many geometric problems depend upon this construction.

With T Square and Triangles (Fig. 3.22). At two points, *A* and *B,* on the line, draw lines *AC* and *BC* at equal angles with *AB.* A perpendicular *CD* to *AB* then cuts *AB* at *D,* the midpoint, and *CD* is the perpendicular bisector of *AB.*

3.20. TO TRISECT A LINE. Trisection of a line is not nearly so often needed as bisection, but will occasionally be required.

With Compasses and Straightedge (Fig. 3.23). On given line *AB* and with radius *AB,* draw two arcs of somewhat more than quarter circles, using *A* and *B* as centers. These arcs will intersect at *C.* Using the same radius *AB* and with *C* as center cut the first arcs at *D* and *E.* Then draw *DA* and *EB,* which intersect at *O.* Using *OA* (or *OB*) as radius and *A* and *B* as centers, cut *AD* and *BE* at *R* and *S.* Using *AB* as radius and *R* and *S* as centers, draw arcs to intersect at *T* and draw *RT* and *ST,* which will intersect

AB at third points *U* and *V.* You will recognize, upon analysis, that this construction is based on the geometry of an equilateral triangle inscribed in a circle, where the diameter of the circle is equal to one side of the triangle.

With T Square and Triangles (Fig. 3.24). The above construction can be accomplished with less detail by using a 30-60° triangle to obtain the needed angles. From *A* and *B* draw lines at 30° to intersect at *C.* Then at 60° to *AB* draw lines from *C* that intersect *AB* at *U* and *V,* the third points.

3.21. TO DIVIDE A LINE INTO 2, 3, 4, 6, 8, 9, 12, OR 16 PARTS (FIGS. 3.25 AND 3.26). Divisions into successive halves, 2, 4, 8, etc., are the most common. The principle of Fig. 3.22 can easily be applied to accomplish the division. As shown in Fig. 3.25, equal angles from *A* and *B* locate *C,* and the perpendicular from *C* to *AB* then gives the mid-point. Successive operations will give 4, 8, 16, etc., parts.

The principles of bisection (Fig. 3.22) and trisection (Fig. 3.24) can be combined to get 6, 9, or 12 parts. As indicated in Fig. 3.26, lines at 30° to *AB* from *A* and *B* locate *C,* and lines at 60° to *AB* from *C* locate *D* and *E,* the third points. Then 30° lines from *A* and *D* will bisect *AD* at *F,* giving sixth divisions; or trisecting by the principle of Fig. 3.24 as from *D* and *E,* giving *G* and *H,* will pro-

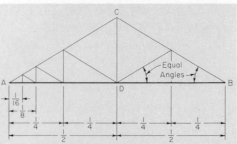

FIG. 3.25. To divide a line into 2, 4, 8, or 16 parts. Equal angles locate a point for bisection.

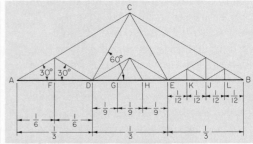

FIG. 3.26. To divide a line into 3, 6, 9, or 12 parts. The 30-60° triangle is used to obtain third points.

Graphic Geometry

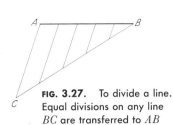

FIG. 3.27. To divide a line. Equal divisions on any line *BC* are transferred to *AB* by parallels to *AC*.

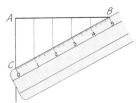

FIG. 3.28. To divide a line. Scale divisions are transferred to given line *AB*.

FIG. 3.29. To divide a line. Scale divisions divide (in this case) the vertical space.

duce ninth points; or as from *E* and *B*, the half point located at *J*, and again the half points of *EJ* and *BJ* located at *K* and *L*, give twelfth divisions of *AB*.

3.22.   TO DIVIDE A LINE INTO ANY NUMBER OF PARTS.   *First Method (Fig. 3.27)*. To divide a line *AB* into, say, five equal parts, draw any line *BC* of indefinite length. On it measure, or step off, five divisions of convenient length. Connect the last point with *A*, and using two triangles as shown in Fig. 3.3, draw lines through the points parallel to *CA* intersecting *AB*.

Second Method (Figs. 3.28 and 3.29). Draw a perpendicular *AC* from *A*. Then place a scale so that five convenient equal divisions are included between *B* and the perpendicular, as in Fig. 3.28. With a triangle and T square draw perpendiculars through the points marked, dividing the line *AB* as required. Figure 3.29 illustrates an application in laying off stair risers. This method can be used for dividing a line into any series of proportional parts.

3.23.   TO LAY OUT A GIVEN ANGLE.   *Tangent Method (Fig. 3.30)*. The trigonometric tangent of an angle of a triangle is the ratio of the length of the side opposite the angle divided by the length of the adjacent side. Thus, tan $A = Y/X$, or X tan $A = Y$. To lay out a given angle, obtain the value of the tangent from a table of natural tangents (see the Appendix), assume any convenient distance X, and multiply X by the tangent to get distance Y. Note that the angle between the sides X and Y must be a right angle.

3.24.   TO LAY OUT A GIVEN ANGLE.   *Chordal Method (Fig. 3.31)*. If the length of a chord is known for an arc of given radius and included angle, the angle can be accurately laid out. Given an angle in degrees, to lay out the angle, obtain the chord length for a 1-in. circle arc from the table in the Appendix. Select any convenient arc length R and multiply the chord length for a 1-in. arc by this distance, thus obtaining the chord length C for the radius distance selected. Lay out the chord length on the arc with compass or dividers and complete the sides of the angle.

The chord length for an angle can be had from a sine table by taking the sine of one-half the given angle and multiplying by two.

3.25.   TO LAY OUT AN ANGLE OF 45° **(FIG. 3.32).**   Angles of 45° occur often, and are normally drawn with the 45° triangle. However, for large constructions or when great accuracy is needed, the method of equal legs is valuable (tangent 45° = 1.0). With any distance *AB* on the given line, with center *B* and radius *AB* draw more than a quarter circle. Erect a perpendicular at *B* (to *AB*) which intersects the arc at point *C*. Then *CA* makes 45° with *AB*.

3.26.   TO LAY OUT ANGLES OF 30°, 60°, **90°, 120°, ETC. (FIG. 3.33).**   As with 45° angles, angles in multiples of 30° may

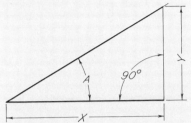

FIG. 3.30.   Angle by tangent. The proportion of *Y* to *X* is obtained from a table of natural tangents.

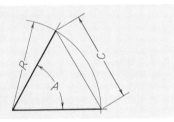

FIG. 3.31.   Angle by chord. The proportion of *C* to *R* is obtained from a table of chords.

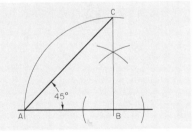

FIG. 3.32.   To lay out a 45° angle. The two legs, *AB* and *BC*, are equal and perpendicular.

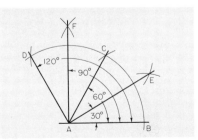

FIG. 3.33.   To construct angles in multiples of 30°. Chords equal to the radius will divide a circle into six equal parts.

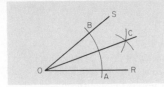

FIG. 3.34. To bisect an angle. Equal arcs from *A* and *B* locate *C* on the bisector.

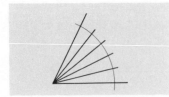

FIG. 3.35. To divide an angle into equal parts. Equal divisions (chords) are stepped off on an arc of the angle.

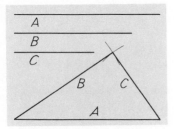

FIG. 3.36. To construct a triangle. The legs are laid off with a compass.

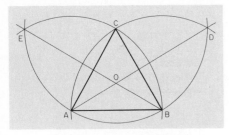

FIG. 3.37. To locate the geometric center of an equilateral triangle. Perpendicular bisectors of the sides intersect at the center.

also be needed for large constructions or when great accuracy is required. On a given line, with any convenient radius *AB*, swing an arc with *A* as center. With the same radius and *B* as center cut the original arc at *C*. The included angle *CAB* is 60° and by bisection (equal arcs from *C* and *B* to locate *E*) 30° is obtained at *CAE* and *EAB*. For 120°, *AB* laid off again from *C* to *D* gives *DAB* as 120°, and by bisecting *DAC*, 90° is given at *FAB*.

3.27. TO BISECT AN ANGLE (FIG. 3.34). Given angle *SOR*, using any convenient radius shorter than *OR* or *OS*, swing an arc with *O* as center, locating *A* and *B*. Then with the same radius or another radius longer than one-half the distance from *A* to *B*, swing arcs with *A* and *B* as centers, locating *C*. The bisector is *CO*. With repeated bisection, the angle can be divided into 4, 8, 16, 32, 64, etc., parts.

3.28. TO DIVIDE AN ANGLE (FIG. 3.35). Sometimes an angle must be divided into some number of parts, say 3, 5, 6, 7, or 9, that cannot be obtained by bisection. It is possible to trisect an angle by employing a movable scale, but this method is more complicated and not as accurate as dividing an arc with the dividers and is of no use for odd parts.

To divide an angle into, for example, 5 parts (Fig. 3.35), draw any arc across the angle as shown, and use the bow dividers to divide the arc into equal

parts. Lines through these points to the apex are the required divisions.

3.29. TO CONSTRUCT A TRIANGLE HAVING GIVEN THE THREE SIDES (FIG. 3.36). Given the lengths *A*, *B*, and *C*. Draw one side *A* in the desired position. With its ends as centers and radii *B* and *C*, draw two intersecting arcs as shown. This construction is used extensively in developments by triangulation.

3.30. TO LOCATE THE GEOMETRIC CENTER OF AN EQUILATERAL TRIANGLE (FIG. 3.37). With *A* and *B* as centers and radius *AB*, draw arcs as shown. These will intersect at *C*, the third corner. With center *C* and radius *AB* cut the original arcs at *D* and *E*. Then *AD* and *BE* intersect at *O*, the geometric center.

3.31. TO TRANSFER A POLYGON TO A NEW BASE. *By Triangulation (Fig. 3.38).* Given polygon *ABCDEF* and a new position of base *A'B'*, consider each point as the vertex of a triangle whose base is *AB*. With centers *A'* and *B'* and radii *AC* and *BC*, describe intersecting arcs locating the point *C'*. Similarly, with radii *AD* and *BD* locate *D'*. Connect *B'C'* and *C'D'* and continue the operation always using *A* and *B* as centers.

Box or Offset Method (Fig. 3.39). Enclose the polygon in a rectangular "box." Draw the box on the new base and locate the points *ABCEF* on this box. Then set point *D* by rectangular coordinates as shown.

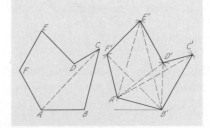

FIG. 3.38. To transfer a polygon: by triangulation. All corners are located by triangles having a common base.

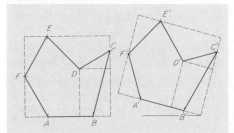

FIG. 3.39. To transfer a polygon: by "boxing." Each corner is located by its position on a rectangle.

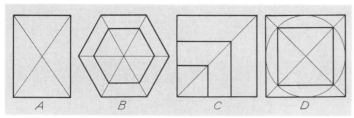

FIG. 3.40. Uses of the diagonal. The diagonals will locate the center of any regular or symmetrical geometric shape that has an even number of sides.

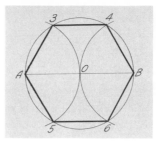

FIG. 3.41. A hexagon. Arcs equal to the radius locate all points. (Corner distance AB is known.)

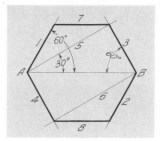

FIG. 3.42. A hexagon. The 30-60° triangle gives construction for all points. (Corner distance AB is known.)

3.32. USES OF THE DIAGONAL.

The diagonal is used in many ways to simplify construction and save drafting time. Figure 3.40 illustrates the diagonal used at (A) for locating the center of a rectangle, at (B) for enlarging or reducing a geometric shape, at (C) for producing similar figures having the same base, and at (D) for drawing inscribed or circumscribed figures.

3.33. TO CONSTRUCT A REGULAR HEXAGON, GIVEN THE DISTANCE ACROSS CORNERS.

First Method (Fig. 3.41). Draw a circle with AB as a diameter. With the same radius and A and B as centers, draw arcs intersecting the circle and connect the points.

Second Method (without Compass). Draw lines with the 30-60° triangle in the order shown in Fig. 3.42.

GIVEN THE DISTANCE ACROSS FLATS. The distance across flats is the diameter of the inscribed circle. Draw this circle, and with the 30-60° triangle draw tangents to it as in Fig. 3.43.

3.34. TO INSCRIBE A REGULAR PENTAGON IN A CIRCLE (FIG. 3.44).

Draw a diameter AB and a radius OC perpendicular to it. Bisect OB. With this point D as center and radius DC, draw arc CE. With center C and radius CE, draw arc EF. CF is a side of the pentagon. Step off this distance around the circle with dividers.

3.35. TO INSCRIBE A REGULAR OCTAGON IN A SQUARE (FIG. 3.45).

Draw the diagonals of the square. With the corners of the square as centers and a radius of half the diagonal, draw arcs intersecting the sides and connect these points.

3.36. TO CONSTRUCT A REGULAR POLYGON, GIVEN ONE SIDE (FIG. 3.46).

Let the polygon have seven sides. With the side AB as radius and A as center, draw a semicircle and divide it into seven equal parts with dividers. Through the second division from the left draw radial line A-2. Through points 3, 4, 5, and 6 extend radial lines as shown. With AB as radius and B as center, cut line A-6 at C. With C as center and the same radius, cut A-5 at D, and so on at E and F. Connect the points *or*, after A-2 is found, draw the circumscribing circle. Another method is to guess at CF and divide the circle by trial; this is more common than the geometric method because the intersections of arcs are sometimes difficult.

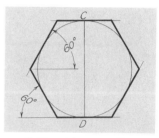

FIG. 3.43. A hexagon. Tangents drawn with the 30-60° triangle locate all points. (Across-flats distance is known.)

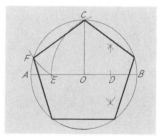

FIG. 3.44. To inscribe a regular pentagon in a circle. Arc construction locates one side; others are stepped off.

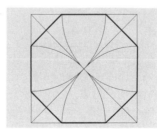

FIG. 3.45. To inscribe a regular octagon in a square. Arcs from the corners of the enclosing square locate all points.

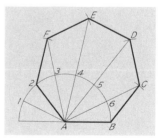

FIG. 3.46. To construct a regular polygon. Given one side, a polygon of any number of sides can be drawn by this method.

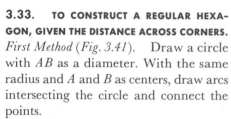

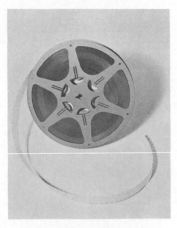

Application of circles and arcs

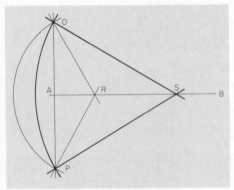

FIG. 3.47. Arc centers. The center of any arc lies on the perpendicular bisector of any chord of the arc.

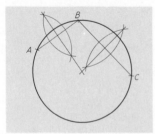

FIG. 3.48. Circle through three points. Perpendicular bisectors of chords locate the center.

GEOMETRY OF CURVED LINES

3.37. DEFINITIONS. A *curved line* is generated by a point moving in a constantly changing direction, according to some mathematical or graphic law. Curved lines are classified as single-curved or double-curved.

A *single-curved line* is a curved line having all points of the line in a plane. Single-curved lines are often called "plane curves."

A *double-curved line* is a curved line having no four consecutive points in the same plane. Double-curved lines are also known as "space curves."

We have defined (paragraph 3.5) a *tangent* to a curved line as a line, either straight or curved, that passes through two points on the curve that are infinitely close together. Note that this definition of tangency places the tangent in the plane of the curve for single-curved lines and in an instantaneous plane of the curve for double-curved lines.

A *normal* is a line (or plane) perpendicular to a tangent line of a curve at the point of tangency. A normal to a single-curved line will be a line in the plane of the curve and perpendicular to a straight line connecting two consecutive points on the curve.

3.38. ARC AND CIRCLE CENTERS (FIGS. 3.47 TO 3.50). The center of any arc must lie on the perpendicular bisector of any and all chords of the arc. Thus, in Fig. 3.47, through two points O and P, an infinite number of arcs may be drawn but all will have centers such as R and S which lie on the perpendicular bisector AB of chord OP. This construction is used in Fig. 3.9 where the circle is required to pass through points S and P.

Using the above principle, only one circle can be drawn through three points, as illustrated in Fig. 3.48. The center must lie on the perpendicular bisectors of both chords, AB and BC. Incidentally, the center will also lie on the perpendicular bisector of chord AC. This construction can be used as a check on accuracy.

Any diameter of a circle and a third point on the circumference, connected to form a triangle, will produce two chords of the circle that are perpendicular to each other. Therefore, the center of a circle may be found, as in Fig. 3.49, by selecting any two points such as A and B, drawing the perpendicular chords AC and BD and then the two diameters CB and DA, which cross at center O. Note in Fig. 3.50 that all chords connecting the diameter AB—AD and DB, AC and CB, AE and EB, AF and FB—form a right angle between the chords.

3.39. TO INSCRIBE A CIRCLE IN AN EQUILATERAL TRIANGLE (FIG. 3.51). With center A and radius AB, draw an arc as shown. With B and C as centers and radius AB, cut this arc at D and E. Then EC and DB intersect at O, the geometric center, and the radius of the subscribing circle is OG and/or OF.

3.40. TO INSCRIBE AN EQUILATERAL TRIANGLE IN A CIRCLE (FIG. 3.52). Using the radius of the circle and starting at A, the known point of orientation, step off distances AB, BC, CD, and DE. The equilateral triangle is ACE. Note that six chords equal in length to the radius will give six equally spaced points on the circumference.

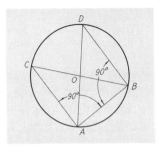

FIG. 3.49. To locate the center of a circle. Perpendicular chords to chord AB produce diameters BC and AD.

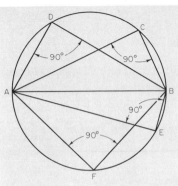

FIG. 3.50. Chords connecting a diameter. Chords from a point, connected to a diameter, form a right angle between the chords.

FIG. 3.51. To inscribe a circle in an equilateral triangle. Construction (to get perpendicular bisectors of two sides) locates the circle center.

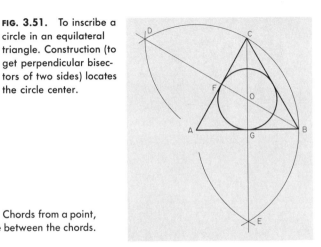

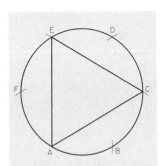

FIG. 3.52. To inscribe an equilateral triangle in a circle. By stepping off the radius twice, corners are located. Compare with Fig. 3.41.

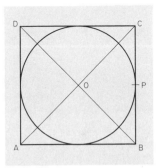

FIG. 3.53. To inscribe a circle in a square. Diagonals locate the circle center.

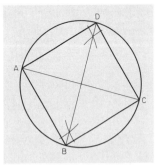

FIG. 3.54. To inscribe a square in a circle. The perpendicular bisector of one diameter locates the two corners to be found.

3.41. TO INSCRIBE A CIRCLE IN A SQUARE (FIG. 3.53).

Given the circle $ABCD$, draw diagonals AC and BD, which intersect at point O, the center. OP is the radius of the circle.

3.42. TO INSCRIBE A SQUARE IN A CIRCLE (FIG. 3.54).

From A, the known point of orientation, draw diameter AC and then erect BD, the perpendicular bisector of AC. The square is $ABCD$.

3.43. TO SCRIBE A CIRCLE IN OR ON A REGULAR POLYGON (FIG. 3.55).

Draw perpendicular bisectors of any two sides, for example PO and SO of AB and CD, giving O, the center. The inner circle radius is OF or OG and the external circle radius is OA, OB, etc.

3.44. TO LAY OFF ON A STRAIGHT LINE THE APPROXIMATE LENGTH OF A CIRCLE ARC (FIG. 3.56).

Given the arc AB. At A draw the tangent AD and the chord produced, BA. Lay off AC equal to half the chord AB. With center C and radius CB, draw an arc intersecting AD at D; then AD will be equal in length to arc AB (very nearly).[1] If the given arc is between 45° and 90°, a closer approximation will result by making AC equal to the chord of half the arc instead of half the chord of the arc.

The usual way of rectifying an arc is to set the dividers to a space small

[1] In this (Professor Rankine's) solution, the error varies as the fourth power of the subtended angle. For 60° the line will be ⅟₉₀₀ part short, while at 30° it will be only ⅟₁₄,₄₀₀ part short.

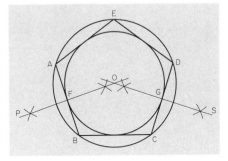

FIG. 3.55. To draw a circle on a regular polygon. Perpendicular bisectors of two sides locate the center.

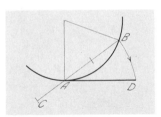

FIG. 3.56. To approximate the length of an arc. See footnote[1] for accuracy.

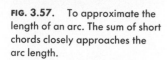

FIG. 3.57. To approximate the length of an arc. The sum of short chords closely approaches the arc length.

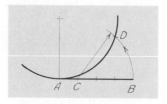

FIG. 3.58. To lay off, on an arc, a specified distance. See footnote[1] for accuracy.

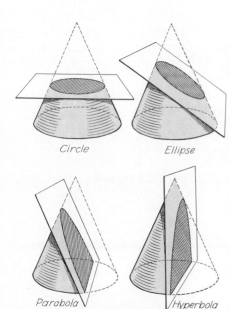

Circle   *Ellipse*

Parabola   *Hyperbola*

FIG. 3.59. The conic sections. Four plane curves are produced by "cutting" a cone.

Application of ellipse (intersection)

enough to be practically equal in length to a corresponding part of the arc. Starting at *B*, step along the arc to the point nearest *A* and without lifting the dividers step off the same number of spaces on the tangent, as shown in Fig. 3.57.

3.45.   TO LAY OFF ON A GIVEN CIRCLE THE APPROXIMATE LENGTH OF A STRAIGHT LINE (FIG. 3.58).   Given the line *AB* tangent to the circle at *A*. Lay off *AC* equal to one-fourth *AB*. With *C* as center and radius *CB*, draw an arc intersecting the circle at *D*. The line *AD* is equal in length to *AB* (very nearly).[1] If arc *AD* is greater than 60°, solve for one-half *AB*.

3.46.   PLANE CURVES: THE CONIC SECTIONS. In cutting a right-circular cone (a cone of revolution) by planes at different angles, we obtain four curves called "conic sections" (Fig. 3.59). These are the *circle,* cut by a plane perpendicular to the axis; the *ellipse,* cut by a plane making a greater angle with the axis than do the elements; the *parabola,* cut by a plane making the same angle with the axis as do the elements; the *hyperbola,* cut by a plane making a smaller angle than do the elements.

3.47.   THE ELLIPSE: MAJOR AND MINOR DIAMETERS (FIG. 3.60).   An ellipse is the plane curve generated by a point moving so that the sum of its distances from two fixed points (F_1 and F_2), called

"focuses," is a constant equal to the major axis,[2] or *major diameter, AB.*

The minor axis, or *minor diameter, DE,* is the line through the center perpendicular to the major diameter. The focuses may be determined by cutting the major diameter with an arc having its center at an end of the minor diameter and a radius equal to one-half the major diameter.

Aside from the circle, the ellipse is met with in practice much more often than any of the other conics, so it is important to be able to construct it readily. Several methods are given for its construction, both as a true ellipse and as an approximate curve made by circle arcs. In the great majority of cases when this curve is required, its major and minor diameters are known.

The mathematical equation of an ellipse with the origin of rectilinear coordinates at the center of the ellipse is $x^2/a^2 + y^2/b^2 = 1$, where *a* is the intercept on the *X* axis and *b* is the intercept on the *Y* axis.

3.48.   THE ELLIPSE: CONJUGATE DIAMETERS (FIG. 3.61).   Any line through the center of an ellipse may serve as *one of*

[2] "Major axis" and "minor axis" are the traditional terms. However, because of the confusion between these and the mathematical *X* and *Y* axes and the central axis (axis of rotation), the terms "major diameter" and "minor diameter" will be used in this discussion.

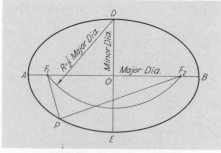

FIG. 3.60. The ellipse: major and minor diameters. These are perpendicular to each other.

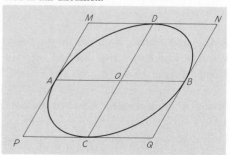

FIG. 3.61. The ellipse: conjugate diameters. Each is parallel to the tangent at the end of the other.

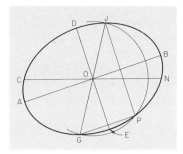

FIG. 3.62. Determination of major and minor diameters from conjugate diameters. Curve is given.

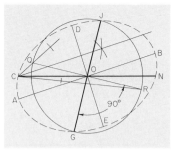

FIG. 3.63. Determination of major and minor diameters from conjugate diameters. Curve is not given.

a pair of conjugate diameters. Each of a pair of conjugate diameters is always parallel to the tangents to the curve at the extremities of the other. For example, AB and CD are a pair of conjugate diameters. AB is parallel to the tangents MN and PQ; and CD is parallel to the tangents MP and NQ. Also, each of a pair of conjugate diameters bisects all the chords parallel to the other. A given ellipse may have an unlimited number of pairs of conjugate diameters.

To Determine the Major and Minor Diameters, Given the Ellipse and a Pair of Conjugate Diameters. First Method (Fig. 3.62). The conjugate diameters are CN and JG. With center O and radius OJ, draw a semicircle intersecting the ellipse at P. The major and minor diameters will be parallel to the chords GP and JP, respectively.

Second Method: When the Curve Is Not Given (Fig. 3.63). The conjugate diameters CN and JG are given. With center O and radius OJ, describe a circle and draw the diameter QR at right angles to JG. Bisect the angle QCR. The major diameter will be parallel to this bisector and equal in length to $CR + CQ$. The length of the minor diameter will be $CR - CQ$.

3.49. ELLIPSE CONSTRUCTION: PIN-AND-STRING METHOD. This well-known method, sometimes called the "gar-dener's ellipse," is often used for large work and is based on the definition of the ellipse. Drive pins at the points D, F_1, and F_2 (Fig. 3.60), and tie an inelastic thread or cord tightly around the three pins. If the pin D is removed and a marking point moved in the loop, keeping the cord taut, it will describe a true ellipse.

3.50. ELLIPSE CONSTRUCTION: TRAMMEL METHOD FOR MAJOR AND MINOR DIAMETERS. *First Method (Fig. 3.64).* On the straight edge of a strip of paper, thin cardboard, or sheet of celluloid, mark the distance ao equal to one-half the major diameter and do equal to one-half the minor diameter. If the strip is moved, keeping a on the minor diameter and d on the major diameter, o will give points on the ellipse. This method is convenient as no construction is required, but for accurate results great care must be taken to keep the points a and d exactly on the major and minor diameters.

Second Method (Fig. 3.65). On a strip —as used in the first method—mark the distance do equal to one-half the minor diameter and oa equal to one-half the major diameter. If this strip is moved, keeping a on the minor diameter and d on the major diameter, o will give points on the ellipse. This arrangement is preferred where the ratio between the major and minor diameters is small.

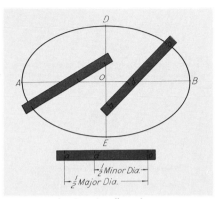

FIG. 3.64. An ellipse by trammel (first method). Points on the curve are plotted.

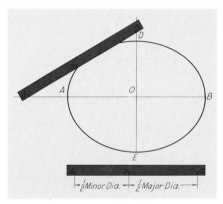

FIG. 3.65. An ellipse by trammel (second method). Points on the curve are plotted.

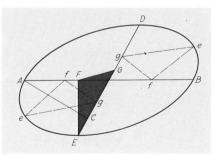

FIG. 3.66. An ellipse by triangle trammel (conjugate diameters). Points are plotted at the apex of the triangle.

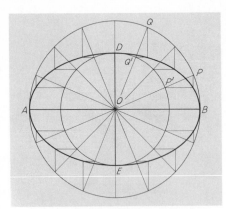

FIG. 3.67. An ellipse by concentric-circle method. Major- and minor-diameter circles and construction give points on the curve.

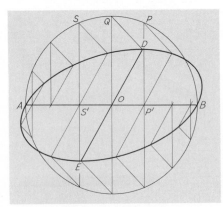

FIG. 3.68. An ellipse by circle method (conjugate diameters). After first construction, parallels plot points on the curve.

3.51. ELLIPSE CONSTRUCTION: TRIANGLE TRAMMEL FOR CONJUGATE DIAMETERS (FIG. 3.66).

The conjugate diameters *AB* and *DE* are given. Erect the perpendicular *AC* to the diameter *ED* and lay off distance *AC* from *E* to locate point *G*. Erect the perpendicular *EF* to the diameter *AB*. Transfer to a piece of paper, thin cardboard, or sheet of celluloid, and cut out the triangle *EFG*. If this triangle is moved, keeping *f* on *AB* and *g* on *ED*, *e* will give points on the ellipse. Extreme care must be taken to keep points *f* and *g* on the conjugate diameters.

3.52. ELLIPSE CONSTRUCTION: CONCENTRIC-CIRCLE METHOD FOR MAJOR AND MINOR DIAMETERS (FIG. 3.67).

This is perhaps the most accurate method for determining points on the curve. On the two principal diameters, which intersect at *O*, describe circles. From a number of points on the outer circle, as *P* and *Q*, draw radii *OP*, *OQ*, etc., intersecting the inner circle at *P′*, *Q′*, etc. From *P* and *Q* draw lines parallel to *OD*, and from *P′* and *Q′* draw lines parallel to *OB*. The intersection of the lines through *P* and *P′* gives one point on the ellipse, the intersection of the lines through *Q* and *Q′* another point, and so on. For accuracy, the points should be taken closer

together toward the major diameter. The process may be repeated in each of the four quadrants and the curve sketched in lightly freehand; or one quadrant only may be constructed and repeated in the remaining three by marking the french curve.

3.53. ELLIPSE CONSTRUCTION: CIRCLE METHOD FOR CONJUGATE DIAMETERS (FIG. 3.68).

The conjugate diameters *AB* and *DE* are given. On the conjugate diameter *AB*, describe a circle; then from a number of points, as *P*, *Q*, and *S*, draw perpendiculars as *PP′*, *QO*, and *SS′* to the diameter *AB*. From *S* and *P*, etc., draw lines parallel to *QD*, and from *S′* and *P′* draw lines parallel to *OD*. The intersection of the lines through *P* and *P′* gives one point on the ellipse, the intersection of the lines through *S* and *S′* another point, and so on.

3.54. ELLIPSE CONSTRUCTION: PARALLELOGRAM METHOD (FIGS. 3.69 AND 3.70).

This method can be used either with the major and minor diameters or with any pair of conjugate diameters. On the given diameters construct a parallelogram. Divide *AO* into any number of equal parts and *AG* into the same number of equal parts, numbering points

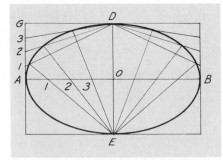

FIG. 3.69. An ellipse by parallelogram method. Points are plotted by construction through equal divisions of *AO* and *AG*.

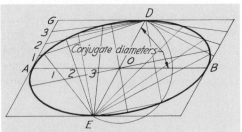

FIG. 3.70. An ellipse by parallelogram method (conjugate diameters). The constructive method of Fig. 3.69 is used, but here applied to conjugate diameters.

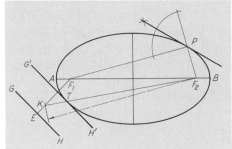

FIG. 3.71. Tangents to an ellipse at a point and parallel to a given line. Focuses are used in construction.

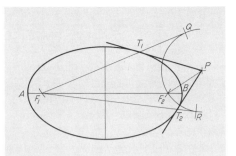

FIG. 3.72. Tangents to an ellipse from an outside point. Tangent points T_1 and T_2 are accurately located.

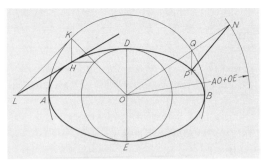

FIG. 3.73. Tangent and normal to an ellipse. The concentric-circle method is used.

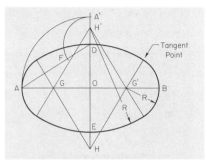

FIG. 3.74. A four-centered approximate ellipse. Four tangent circle arcs give elliptical shape.

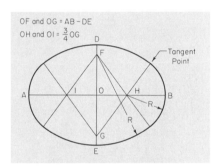

FIG. 3.75. A four-centered approximate ellipse. This method works best when major and minor diameters are nearly equal.

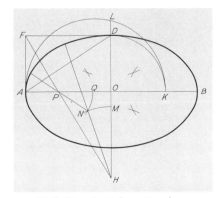

FIG. 3.76. An eight-centered approximate ellipse. This gives a much better approximation than the four-center methods but requires more construction.

from A. Through these points draw lines from D and E, as shown. Their intersections will be points on the curve.

3.55. TO DRAW A TANGENT TO AN ELLIPSE.

At a Given Point on the Curve (*Fig. 3.71*). Draw lines from the given point P to the focuses. The line bisecting the exterior angle of these focal radii is the required tangent.

Parallel to a Given Line (*Fig. 3.71*). Draw F_1E perpendicular to the given line GH. With F_2 as center and radius AB, draw an arc cutting F_1E at K. The line F_1K cuts the ellipse at the required point of tangency T, and the required tangent passes through T parallel to GH.

From a Point Outside (*Fig. 3.72*). Find the focuses F_1 and F_2. With the given point P and radius PF_2, draw the arc RF_2Q. With F_1 as center and radius AB, strike an arc cutting this arc at Q and R. Connect QF_1 and RF_1. The intersections of these lines with the ellipse at T_1 and T_2 will be the tangent points of tangents to the ellipse from P.

Concentric-circle Method (*Fig. 3.73*). When the ellipse has been constructed by the concentric-circle method (Fig. 3.67), a tangent at any point H can be drawn by dropping a perpendicular to AB from the point to the outer circle at K and drawing the auxiliary tangent KL to the outer circle, cutting the major diameter at L. From L draw the required tangent LH.

3.56. TO DRAW A NORMAL TO AN ELLIPSE (FIG. 3.73).

From point P on the curve, project a parallel to the minor diameter to intersect the major diameter circle at Q. Draw OQ extended to intersect (at N) an arc with center at O and radius $AO + OE$. NP is the required normal.

Or, normals may be drawn perpendicular to the tangents of Figs. 3.71 and 3.72.

3.57. TO DRAW A FOUR-CENTERED APPROXIMATE ELLIPSE (FIG. 3.74).

Join A and D. Lay off DF equal to $AO - DO$. This is done graphically as indicated on the figure by swinging A around to A' with O as center where now DO from OA' is DA', the required distance. With D as center, an arc from A' to the diagonal AD locates F. Bisect AF by a perpendicular crossing AO at G and intersecting DE produced (if necessary) at H. Make OG' equal to OG, and OH' equal to OH. Then G, G', H, and H' will be centers for four tangent circle arcs forming a curve *approximating* the shape of an ellipse.

Another method is shown in Fig. 3.75. This should be used only when the minor diameter is at least two-thirds the length of the major diameter.

3.58. TO DRAW AN EIGHT-CENTERED APPROXIMATE ELLIPSE (FIG. 3.76).

When a closer approximation is desired, the eight-centered ellipse, the upper half of which is known in masonry as the "five-

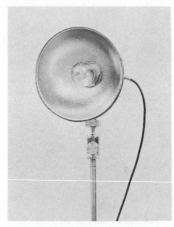

Application of the parabola

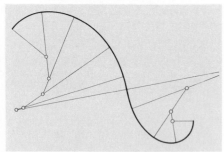

FIG. 3.77. A curve constructed with circle arcs. Note that lines through pairs of centers locate the tangent points of arcs.

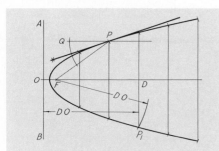

FIG. 3.78. A parabola. Points on the curve are equidistant from the focus *F* and directrix *AB*.

centered arch," may be constructed. Draw the rectangle *AFDO*. Draw the diagonal *AD* and a line from *F* perpendicular to it, intersecting the extension of the minor diameter at *H*. Lay off *OK* equal to *OD*, and, on *AK* as a diameter, draw a semicircle intersecting the extension of the minor diameter at *L*. Make *OM* equal to *LD*. With center *H* and radius *HM*, draw the arc *MN*. From *A*, along *AB*, lay off *AQ* equal to *OL*. With *P* as center and radius *PQ*, draw an arc intersecting *MN* at *N*; then *P, N*, and *H* are centers for one-quarter of the eight-centered approximate ellipse.

It should be noted that an ellipse changes its radius of curvature at every successive point and that these approximations are therefore not ellipses, but simply curves of the same general shape and, incidentally, not nearly so pleasing in appearance.

3.59.   TO DRAW ANY NONCIRCULAR CURVE (FIG. 3.77).   This may be approximated by drawing tangent circle arcs: Select a center by trial, draw as much of an arc as will practically coincide with the curve, and then, changing the center and radius, draw the next portion, remembering always that *if arcs are to be*

tangent, their centers must lie on the common normal at the point of tangency.

Curves are sometimes inked in this way in preference to using irregular curves.

3.60.   THE PARABOLA.   The parabola is a plane curve generated by a point so moving that its distance from a fixed point, called the "focus," is always equal to its distance from a straight line, called the "directrix." Among its practical applications are searchlights, parabolic reflectors, some loud-speakers, road sections, and certain bridge arches.

The mathematical equation for a parabola with the origin of rectilinear coordinates at the intercept of the curve with the X axis and the focus on the axis is $y^2 = 2px$, where p is twice the distance from the origin to the focus.

To draw a parabola when the focus F and the directrix *AB* are given (Fig. 3.78), draw the axis through F perpendicular to *AB*. Through any point D on the axis, draw a line parallel to *AB*. With the distance *DO* as radius and F as center, draw an arc intersecting the line, thus locating a point P on the curve. Repeat the operation as many times as needed.

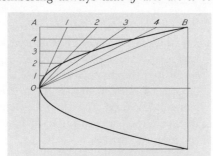

FIG. 3.79. A parabola by parallelogram method. Points are plotted by lines through equal-numbered divisions of *OA* and *AB*.

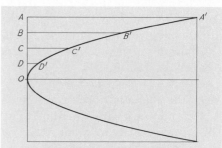

FIG. 3.80. A parabola by offset method. Offsets are proportionate to squares of divisions of *OA*.

To Draw a Tangent at Any Point P.
Draw *PQ* parallel to the axis and bisect
the angle *FPQ*.

3.61. PARABOLA CONSTRUCTION: PARALLELOGRAM METHOD.

Usually when a
parabola is required, the dimensions of
the enclosing rectangle, that is, the width
and depth of the parabola (or span and
rise), are given, as in Fig. 3.79. Divide
OA and *AB* into the same number of
equal parts. From the divisions on *AB,*
draw lines converging at *O.* From the
divisions on *OA,* draw lines parallel to
the axis. The intersections of these with
the lines from the corresponding divisions on *AB* will be points on the curve.

3.62. PARABOLA CONSTRUCTION: OFFSET METHOD (FIG. 3.80).

Given the enclosing rectangle, the parabola can be
plotted by computing the offsets from
the line *OA.* These offsets vary in length
as the square of their distances from *O.*
Thus if *OA* is divided into four parts,
DD' will be $\frac{1}{16}$ of *AA'; CC',* since it is
twice as far from *O* as *DD',* will be $\frac{4}{16}$
of *AA';* and *BB',* $\frac{9}{16}$. If *OA* had been
divided into five parts, the relations
would be $\frac{1}{25}$, $\frac{4}{25}$, $\frac{9}{25}$, and $\frac{16}{25}$, the denominator in each case being the square
of the number of divisions. This method
is the one generally used by civil engineers in drawing parabolic arches.

3.63. PARABOLA CONSTRUCTION: PARABOLIC ENVELOPE (FIG. 3.81).

This method
of drawing a pleasing curve is often
used in machine design. Divide *OA* and
OB into the same number of equal parts.
Number the divisions from *O* and *B* and
connect the corresponding numbers. The
tangent curve will be a portion of a
parabola—but a parabola whose axis is
not parallel to either coordinate.

3.64. THE HYPERBOLA.

The hyperbola
is a plane curve generated by a point
moving so that the difference of its distances from two fixed points, called the
"focuses," is a constant. (Compare this
definition with that of the ellipse.)

The mathematical equation for a
hyperbola with the center at the origin
of rectilinear coordinates and the focuses
on the *X* axis is $x^2/a^2 - y^2/b^2 = 1$,
where *a* is the distance from the center
to the *X* intercept and *b* is the corresponding *Y* value of the asymptotes, lines
that the tangents to the curve meet at
infinity.

*To Draw a Hyperbola When the Focuses
F_1 and F_2 and the Transverse Axis AB
(Constant Difference) Are Given (Fig. 3.82).*
With F_1 and F_2 as centers and any radius
greater than F_1B, as F_1P, draw arcs.
With the same centers and any radius
$F_1P - AB$, strike arcs intersecting these
arcs, giving points on the curve.

To Draw a Tangent at Any Point P.
Bisect the angle F_1PF_2.

3.65. EQUILATERAL HYPERBOLA.

The
case of the hyperbola of commonest
practical interest to the engineer is the
equilateral, or rectangular, hyperbola
referred to its asymptotes. With it, the
law $PV = c$, connecting the varying pressure and volume of a portion of steam or
gas, can be graphically presented.

*To Draw an Equilateral Hyperbola (Fig.
3.83).* Let *OA* and *OB* be the asymptotes
of the curve and *P* any point on it (this
might be the point of cutoff on an indicator diagram). Draw *PC* and *PD.* Mark
any points 1, 2, 3, etc., on *PC,* and
through these points draw a system of
lines parallel to *OA* and a second system
through the same points converging at
O. From the intersections of the lines of
the second system with *PD* extended,

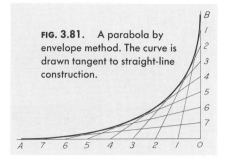

FIG. 3.81. A parabola by
envelope method. The curve is
drawn tangent to straight-line
construction.

Application of the hyperbola
(intersection)

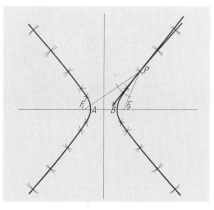

FIG. 3.82. A hyperbola. From
any point, the difference in distance to the focuses is a constant.

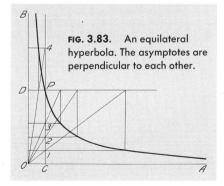

FIG. 3.83. An equilateral
hyperbola. The asymptotes are
perpendicular to each other.

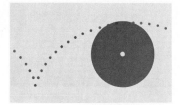

Formation of a cycloid

Application of the involute

draw perpendiculars to OA. The intersections of these perpendiculars with the corresponding lines of the first system give points on the curve.

3.66. CYCLOID CURVES. A cycloid is the curve generated by the motion of a point on the circumference of a circle rolled in a plane along a straight line. If the circle is rolled on the outside of another circle, the curve generated is called an "epicycloid"; if rolled on the inside, it is called a "hypocycloid." These curves are used in drawing the cycloid system of gear teeth.

The mathematical equation for a cycloid (parametric form) is $x = r\theta - r\sin\theta$, $y = r - r\cos\theta$, where r is the radius of a moving point and θ is the turned angle, in radians, about the center from zero position.

To Draw a Cycloid (*Fig. 3.84*). Divide the rolling circle into a convenient number of parts (say, eight), and, using these divisions, lay off on the tangent AB the rectified length of the circumference. Draw through C the line of centers CD, and project the division points up to this line by perpendiculars to AB. Using these points as centers, draw circles representing different positions of the rolling circle, and project, in order, the division

points of the original circle across to these circles. The intersections thus determined will be points on the curve. The epicycloid and hypocycloid are drawn similarly, as shown in Fig. 3.85.

3.67. THE INVOLUTE. An involute is the spiral curve traced by a point on a taut cord unwinding from around a polygon or circle. Thus the involute of any polygon can be drawn by extending its sides, as in Fig. 3.86, and, with the corners of the polygon as successive centers, drawing arcs terminating on the extended sides.

The equation of the involute of a circle (parametric form) is $x = r(\sin\theta - \theta\cos\theta)$, $y = r(\cos\theta + \theta\sin\theta)$, where r is the radius of the circle and θ is the turned angle for the tangent point.

In drawing a spiral in design, as for example of bent ironwork, the easiest way is to draw it as the involute of a square.

A circle may be conceived of as a polygon of an infinite number of sides. Thus to draw the involute of a circle (Fig. 3.87), divide it into a convenient number of parts, draw tangents at these points, lay off on these tangents the rectified lengths of the arcs from the point of tangency to the starting point, and con-

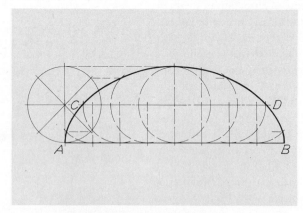

FIG. 3.84. A cycloid. A point on the circumference of a rolling wheel describes this curve.

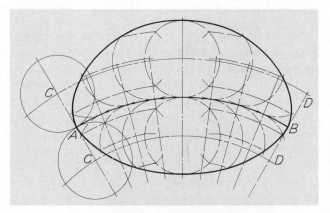

FIG. 3.85. An epicycloid and hypocycloid. Both are formed by a circle rolling on another circle.

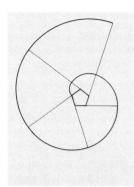

FIG. 3.86. An involute of a pentagon. A point on a cord unwound from the pentagon describes this curve.

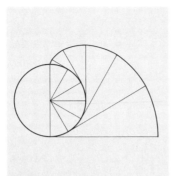

FIG. 3.87. An involute of a circle. As a taut cord is unwound from the circle, it forms a series of tangents to the circle.

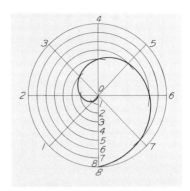

FIG. 3.88. The spiral of Archimedes. This curve increases uniformly in distance from the center as rotation (angular velocity) is constant.

nect the points by a smooth curve. The involute of the circle is the basis for the involute system of spur gearing.

3.68. THE SPIRAL OF ARCHIMEDES. The spiral of Archimedes is the plane curve generated by a point moving uniformly along a straight line while the line revolves about a fixed point with uniform angular velocity.

To Draw a Spiral of Archimedes That Makes One Turn in a Given Circle (Fig. 3.88). Divide the circle into a number of equal parts, drawing the radii and numbering them. Divide the radius 0-8 into the same number of equal parts, numbering from the center. With 0 as center, draw concentric arcs intersecting the radii of corresponding numbers, and draw a smooth curve through these intersections. The Archimedean spiral is the curve of the heart cam used for converting uniform rotary motion into uniform reciprocal motion.

The mathematical equation is $p = a\theta$ (polar form).

3.69. OTHER PLANE CURVES. The foregoing paragraphs discuss common plane curves that occur frequently in scientific work. Other curves, whenever needed, can be found in any good textbook of analytic geometry and calculus. Typical of the curves that may be met with are the catenary, cardioid, sine curve, cosine curve, logarithmic spiral, reciprocal (hyperbolic) spiral, parabolic spiral, logarithmic curve, exponential curve, and curves of velocity and acceleration.

3.70. DOUBLE-CURVED LINES. The scarcity of geometric double-curved lines, by comparison with the numerous single-curved lines, is surprising. There are only two double-curved lines, the cylindrical and the conic helix, much used in engineering work. Double-curved lines will, however, often occur as the lines of intersection between two curved solids or surfaces. These lines are not geometric but are double-curved lines of general form.

3.71. THE HELIX. The helix is a space curve generated by a point moving uniformly along a straight line while the line revolves uniformly about another line as an axis. If the moving line is parallel to the axis, it will generate a cylinder. The word "helix" alone always

Application of the helix

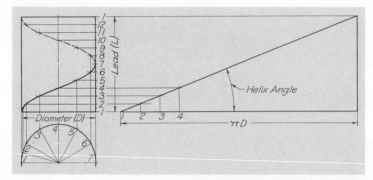

FIG. 3.89. The cylindrical helix and its development. Any point moves at a constant rate both around and along the axis.

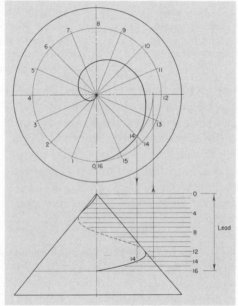

FIG. 3.90. The conic helix. A point traverses the surface of the cone while moving at a constant rate both around and along the axis.

tour elements. Divide this lead into a number of equal parts (say, 12) and the circle of the front view into the same number. Number the divisions on the top view starting at point 1 and the divisions on the front view starting at the front view of point 1. When the generating point has moved one-twelfth of the distance around the cylinder, it has also advanced one-twelfth of the lead; when halfway around the cylinder, it will have advanced one-half the lead. Thus points on the top view of the helix can be found by projecting the front views of the elements, which are points on the circular front view of the helix, to intersect lines drawn across from the corresponding divisions of the lead. If the cylinder is developed, the helix will appear on the development as a straight line inclined to the base at an angle, called the "helix angle," whose tangent is $L/\pi D$, where L is the lead and D the diameter.

3.73. TO DRAW A CONIC HELIX (FIG. 3.90). First make two views of the right-circular cone (see Chap. 5) on which the helix will be generated. Then lay out uniform angular divisions in the view showing the end view of the axis (in Fig. 3.90, the top view) and divide the lead into the same number of parts. Points can now be plotted on the curve. Each plotted point will lie on a circle cut from the cone by a plane dividing the lead and will also lie on the angular-division line. Thus, for example, to plot point 14, draw the circle diameter obtained from the front view, as shown in the top view. Point 14 in the top view then lies at the intersection of this circle and radial-division line 14. Then locate the front view by projection from the top view to plane 14 in the front view.

means a cylindrical helix. If the moving line intersects the axis at an angle less than 90°, it will generate a cone, and the curve made by the point moving on it will be a "conic helix." The distance parallel to the axis through which the point advances in one revolution is called the "lead." When the angle becomes 90°, the helix degenerates into the Archimedean spiral.

3.72. TO DRAW A CYLINDRICAL HELIX (FIG. 3.89). Draw the two views of the cylinder (see Chap. 5), and then measure the lead along one of the con-

CONSTRUCTIONS FOR LOFT-ING AND LARGE LAYOUTS

3.74. There are cases when the regular drafting instruments are impractical, either because of size limitations or when extreme accuracy is necessary. The geometric methods for common cases of parallelism, perpendicularity, and tangency are given in the following paragraphs.

3.75. **TO DRAW A LINE THROUGH A POINT AND PARALLEL TO A GIVEN LINE (FIG. 3.91).** With the given point *P* as center and a radius of sufficient length, draw an arc *CE* intersecting the given line *AB* at *C*. With *C* as center and the same radius, draw the arc *PD*. With *C* as center and radius *DP,* draw an arc intersecting *CE* at *E*. Then *EP* is the required line.

3.76. **TO DRAW A LINE PARALLEL TO ANOTHER AT A GIVEN DISTANCE.** *For Straight Lines (Fig. 3.92).* With the given distance as radius and two points on the given line as centers (as far apart as convenient), draw two arcs. A line tangent to these arcs will be the required line.

For Curved Lines (Fig. 3.93). Draw a series of arcs with centers along the line. Draw tangents to these arcs with a french curve (see Fig. 2.60).

3.77. **TO ERECT A PERPENDICULAR FROM A POINT TO A GIVEN STRAIGHT LINE (FIG. 3.94).** With point *P* as center and any convenient radius R_1, draw a circle arc intersecting the given line at *A* and *B*. With any convenient radius R_2 and with centers at *A* and *B*, draw intersecting arcs locating *Q*. The required perpendicular is *PQ,* with *S* the intersection of the perpendicular and the given line.

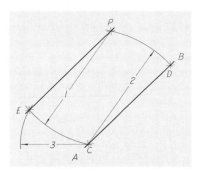

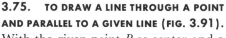

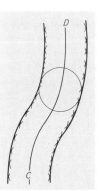

FIG. 3.91. Parallel lines. Two points determine the parallel.

FIG. 3.92. Parallel lines. The parallel is drawn tangent to a pair of arcs.

FIG. 3.93. Curved parallel lines. The curves are drawn tangent to circle arcs.

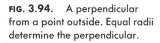

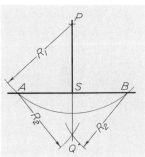

FIG. 3.94. A perpendicular from a point outside. Equal radii determine the perpendicular.

3.78. **TO ERECT A PERPENDICULAR FROM A POINT ON A GIVEN STRAIGHT LINE.** *First Method (Fig. 3.95).* With point *P* on the line as center and any convenient radius R_1, draw circle arcs to locate points *A* and *B* equidistant from *P*. With any convenient radius R_2 longer than R_1 and with centers at *A* and *B*, draw intersecting arcs locating *Q*. *PQ* is the required perpendicular.

Second Method (Fig. 3.96). With any convenient center *C* and radius *CP,* draw somewhat more than a semicircle from the intersection of the circle arc with the given line at *A*. Draw *AC* extended to meet the circle arc at *Q*. *PQ* is the required perpendicular.

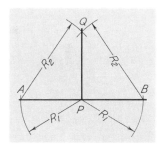

FIG. 3.95. A perpendicular from a point on a line. Equal radii determine a point on the perpendicular.

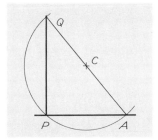

FIG. 3.96. A perpendicular from a point on a line. Geometrically, perpendicular chords of a circle produce this solution.

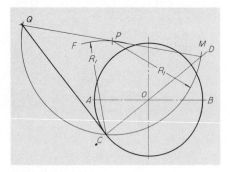

FIG. 3.97.   To draw a tangent at a point on a circle. This solution sets up two right-angle chords of a circle. One chord passes through the center of the given circle.

3.79.   TO DRAW A TANGENT TO A CIRCLE AT A POINT ON THE CIRCLE (FIG. 3.97).   Given the arc ACB and to draw a tangent at point C, draw the extended diameter CD and locate point M. Then with any convenient radius R_1, locate point P equidistant from C and M. With P as center and the same radius R_1, draw somewhat more than a semicircle and draw the line MPQ. The line QC is a tangent to the circle at point C.

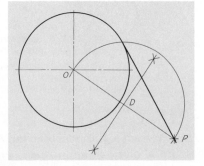

FIG. 3.98.   To draw a tangent from an outside point. Here, as in Fig. 3.97, perpendicular chords determine the solution.

3.80.   TO DRAW A TANGENT TO A CIRCLE FROM A POINT OUTSIDE (FIG. 3.98).   Connect the point P with the center of the circle O. Then draw the perpendicular bisector of OP, and with the intersection at D as center, draw a semicircle. Its intersection with the given circle is the point of tangency. Draw the tangent line from P.

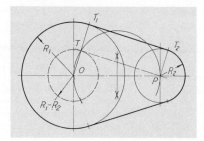

FIG. 3.99.   Tangent lines (open belt). The difference in radius of the two circles is the geometric basis. Then perpendicular chords are used.

3.81.   TO DRAW A TANGENT TO TWO CIRCLES.   *First Case: Open Belt (Fig. 3.99).* At center O draw a circle with radius $R_1 - R_2$. From P draw a tangent to this circle by the method of Fig. 3.98. Extend OT to T_1, and draw PT_2 parallel to OT_1. Join T_1 and T_2, giving the required tangent.

Second Case: Crossed Belt (Fig. 3.100). Draw OA and O_1B perpendicular to OO_1. From P, where AB crosses OO_1, locate tangents as in Fig. 3.98.

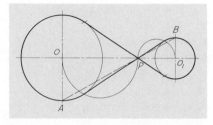

FIG. 3.100.   Tangent lines (crossed belt). A duplicate of Fig. 3.99, except for position of the tangent lines.

FIG. 3.101. Geometric shapes. These plane figures, solids, and surfaces should be studied and remembered.

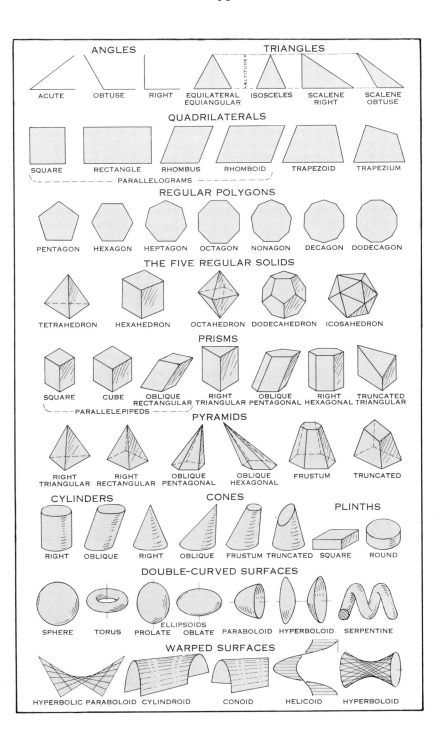

PROBLEMS

To be of value both as drawing exercises and as solutions, geometric problems must be worked accurately. Keep your pencil sharp, and use comparatively light lines. Locate a point by two intersecting lines; indicate the length of a line by short dashes across it.

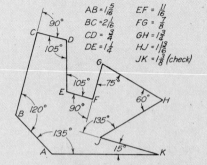

PROB. 3.1.3.   Irregular polygon.

GROUP 1.   LINES AND PLANE FIGURES

3.1.1. Near the center of the working space, draw a horizontal line 4½ in. long. Divide it into seven equal parts by the method of Fig. 3.27.

3.1.2. Draw a vertical line 1 in. from the left edge of the space and 3⅞ in. long. Divide it into parts proportional to 1, 3, 5, and 7.

3.1.3. Construct a polygon as shown in the problem illustration, drawing the horizontal line *AK* (of indefinite length) ⅜ in. above the bottom of the space. From *A* draw and measure *AB*. Proceed in the same way for the remaining sides. The angles can be obtained by proper combinations of the two triangles (see Figs. 2.28 and 2.29).

3.1.4. Draw a line *AK* making an angle of 15° with the horizontal. With this line as base, transfer the polygon of Prob. 3.1.3.

3.1.5. Draw a regular hexagon having a distance across corners of 4 in.

3.1.6. Draw a regular hexagon, distance across flats 3⅜ in.

3.1.7. Draw a regular dodecagon, distance across flats 3⅜ in.

GROUP 2.   PROBLEMS IN ACCURATE JOINING OF TANGENT LINES

3.2.1. Draw the offset swivel plate.

3.2.2. Draw two lines *AB* and *AC* making an included angle of 30°. Locate point *P*, 4 in. from *A* and ½ in. from line *AB*. Draw two circle arcs centered at point *P*, one tangent to line *AB*, the other to *AC*. Then draw two lines tangent to the opposite sides of the arcs and passing through point *A*. Locate all tangent points by construction.

3.2.3. Construct an ogee curve joining two parallel lines *AB* and *CD* as in Fig. 3.18, making *X* = 4 in., *Y* = 2½ in., and *BE* = 3 in. Consider this as the center line for a rod 1¼ in. in diameter, and draw the rod.

3.2.4. Make contour view of the bracket. In the upper ogee curve, the radii R_1 and R_2 are equal. In the lower one, R_3 is twice R_4.

3.2.5. Draw an arc of a circle having a radius of 3¹³⁄₁₆ in., with its center ½ in. from the top of the space and 1¼ in. from the left edge. Find the length of an arc of 60° by construction; compute the length arithmetically, and check the result.

3.2.6. Front view of washer. Draw half size.

3.2.7. Front view of shim. Draw full size.

3.2.8. Front view of rod guide. Draw full size.

3.2.9. Front view of a star knob. Radius of circumscribing circle, 2⅜ in. Diameter of hub, 2½ in. Diameter of hole, ¾ in. Radius at points, ⅜ in. Radius of fillets, ⅜ in. Mark tangent points in pencil.

3.2.10. Front view of sprocket. *OD,* 4¾ in. Pitch diameter, 4 in. Root diameter, 3¼ in. Bore, 1¼ in. Thickness of tooth at the pitch line is ⁹⁄₁₆ in. Splines, ¼ in. wide by ⅛ in. deep. Mark tangent points in pencil. See Glossary for terms.

3.2.11. Front view of a fan. Draw full size.

3.2.12. Front view of a level plate. Draw full size.

3.2.13. Front view of an eyelet. Draw full size.

3.2.14. Front view of a stamping. Draw full size.

3.2.15. Front view of spline lock. Draw full size.

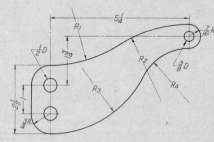

PROB. 3.2.1.   Offset swivel plate.

PROB. 3.2.4.   Bracket.

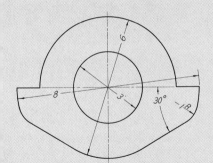

PROB. 3.2.6. Washer.

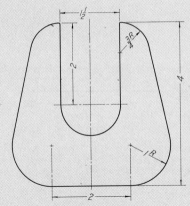

PROB. 3.2.7. Shim.

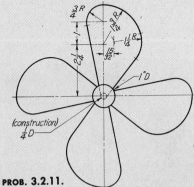

PROB. 3.2.8. Rod guide.

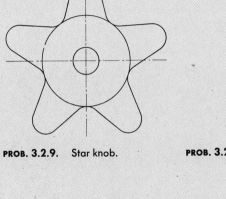

PROB. 3.2.9. Star knob.

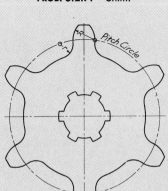

PROB. 3.2.10. Sprocket.

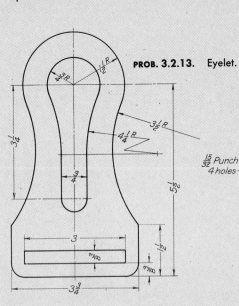

PROB. 3.2.11. Fan.

PROB. 3.2.13. Eyelet.

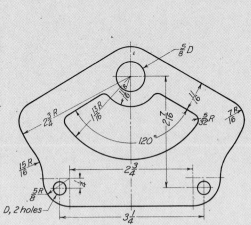

PROB. 3.2.12. Level plate.

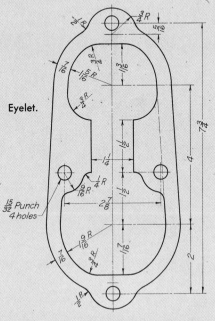

PROB. 3.2.14. Stamping.

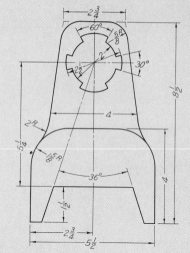

PROB. 3.2.15.   Spline lock.

3.2.16.   Front view of gage cover plate. Draw full size.

3.2.17.   Drawing of heater tube. Draw twice size.

3.2.18.   Drawing of exhaust-port contour. Draw twice size.

3.2.19.   Drawing of toggle spring for leaf switch. Use decimal scale and draw 20 times size.

3.2.20.   Drawing of pulley shaft. Draw full size.

3.2.21.   Drawing of cam for type A control. Plot cam contour from the polar coordinates given. Use decimal scale and draw five times size.

PROB. 3.2.16.
Gage cover
plate.

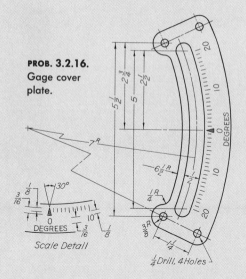

Scale Detail

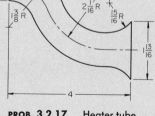

PROB. 3.2.17.   Heater tube.

PROB. 3.2.18.
Exhaust-port
contour.

DETERMINE

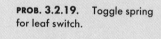

PROB. 3.2.19.   Toggle spring
for leaf switch.

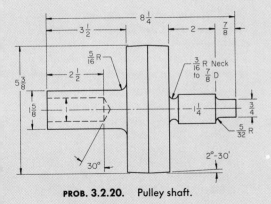

PROB. 3.2.20. Pulley shaft.

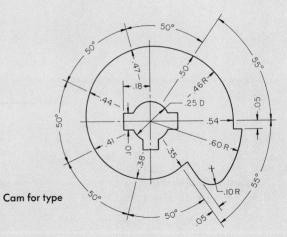

PROB. 3.2.21. Cam for type A control.

GROUP 3.   PLANE CURVES

3.3.1. The conjugate diameters of an ellipse measure 3 and 4 in., the angle between them being 60°. Construct the major and minor diameters of this ellipse and draw the ellipse.

3.3.2. Using the pin-and-string method, draw an ellipse having a major diameter of 6 in. and a minor diameter of 4¼ in.

3.3.3. Using the trammel method, draw an ellipse having a major diameter of 4½ in. and a minor diameter of 3 in.

3.3.4. Using the trammel method, draw an ellipse having a major diameter of 4½ in. and a minor diameter of 4 in.

3.3.5. Using the concentric-circle method, draw an ellipse having a major diameter of 4⅜ in. and a minor diameter of 1½ in.

3.3.6. Draw an ellipse on a major diameter of 4 in. One point on the ellipse is 1½ in. to the left of the minor diameter and ⅞ in. above the major diameter.

3.3.7. Draw an ellipse having a minor diameter of 2³⁄₁₆ in. and a distance of 3¼ in. between focuses. Draw a tangent at a point 1⅜ in. to the right of the minor diameter.

3.3.8. Draw an ellipse whose major diameter is 4 in. A tangent to the ellipse intersects the minor diameter 1¾ in. from the center, at an angle of 60°.

3.3.9. Draw a five-centered arch with a span of 5 in. and a rise of 2 in.

3.3.10. Draw an ellipse having conjugate diameters of 4¾ in. and 2¾ in., making an angle of 75° with each other. Determine the major and minor diameters.

3.3.11. Draw the major and minor diameters for an ellipse having a pair of conjugate diameters 60° apart, one horizontal and 6¼ in. long, the other 3¼ in. long.

3.3.12. Using the circle method, draw an ellipse having a pair of conjugate diameters, one making 15° with the horizontal and 6 in. long, the other making 60° with the first diameter and 2½ in. long.

3.3.13. Using the triangle-trammel method, draw an ellipse having a pair of conjugate diameters 60° apart, one horizontal and 6 in. long, the other 4 in. long.

3.3.14. Using the triangle-trammel method, draw an ellipse having a pair of conjugate diameters 45° apart, one making 15° with the horizontal and 6 in. long, the other 3 in. long.

3.3.15. Draw a parabola, axis vertical, in a rectangle 4 by 2 in.

3.3.16. Draw a parabolic arch, with 6-in. span and a 2½-in. rise, by the offset method, dividing the half span into eight equal parts.

3.3.17. Draw an equilateral hyperbola passing through a point P, ½ in. from OB and 2½ in. from OA. (Reference letters correspond to Fig. 3.83.)

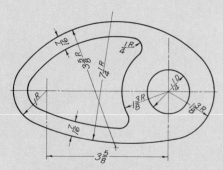

PROB. 3.3.24. Front view of cam.

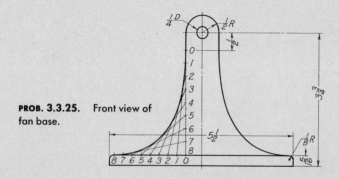

PROB. 3.3.25. Front view of fan base.

3.3.18. Draw two turns of the involute of a pentagon whose circumscribed circle is ½ in. in diameter.

3.3.19. Draw one-half turn of the involute of a circle 3¼ in. in diameter whose center is 1 in. from the left edge of the space. Compute the length of the last tangent and compare with the measured length.

3.3.20. Draw a spiral of Archimedes making one turn in a circle 4 in. in diameter.

3.3.21. Draw the cycloid formed by a rolling circle 2 in. in diameter. Use 12 divisions.

3.3.22. Draw the epicycloid formed by a 2-in.-diameter circle rolling on a 15-in.-diameter directing circle. Use 12 divisions.

3.3.23. Draw the hypocycloid formed by a 2-in.-diameter circle rolling inside a 15-in.-diameter directing circle. Use 12 divisions.

3.3.24. Front view of cam. Draw full size.

3.3.25. Front view of fan base. Draw full size.

3.3.26. Front view of trip lever. Draw half size.

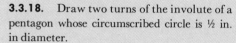

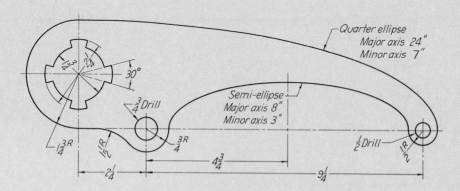

Quarter ellipse
Major axis 24″
Minor axis 7″

Semi-ellipse
Major axis 8″
Minor axis 3″

PROB. 3.3.26. Front view of trip lever.

GROUP 4. PROBLEMS FOR SLIDE RULE AND MATHEMATICAL TABLES

3.4.1.   Find the altitude of an equilateral triangle, each side of which is 4 in.

3.4.2.   Find the value of one-third of an angle of 231°4′2″.

3.4.3.   A tank is 31 in. in diameter and 4 ft 7½ in. long. Find the capacity in liters.

3.4.4.   A 4-in.-diameter cold-rolled steel bar is 96 cm long. What is the weight in pounds? In grams?

3.4.5.   A circle of 12⅝-in. diameter used as a target for optical devices is to be compared in area with a lens of 80 mm diameter. What percentage is the lens area to the target area?

3.4.6.   A guided missile is fired, hits a target 841 miles away, and during flight rises to a height of 91 miles. What are these distances in kilometers?

3.4.7.   Find one side of a square whose equivalent area is a circle of 6⅜-in. diameter. Answer in centimeters.

3.4.8.   An ellipse has a major axis of 14 in. and a minor axis of 8½ in. How far from the geometric center is each focus? What is the equivalent distance in centimeters?

3.4.9.   A certain pressure is recorded by a column of water 2 ft 4½ in. high. What is the equivalent pressure in inches of mercury?

3.4.10.   Find the area of a tract of land designated by a traverse that is an equilateral triangle each side of which is 228 ft 4 in. long. Answer in square miles. Also calculate the area in square kilometers.

3.4.11.   A square is inscribed in a circle of 4-in. diameter. What is the area of the square?

3.4.12.   An equilateral triangle is inscribed in a circle of 9⅜-in. diameter. What is the sum of the sides of the triangle? What is the circumference of the circle? What is the area of the triangle and of the circle?

3.4.13.   A round copper bar 2 in. in diameter and 4 ft long is to be balanced in weight by a cube of aluminum. What is the size of the cube?

3.4.14.   If a 2-in. round bar of steel 2 ft 6 in. long is to be replaced by a bar of bakelite, what will be the difference in weight?

3.4.15.   A circular opening 6 in. in diameter is to be replaced by a number of openings 0.70 cm in diameter. How many openings must be used in order to give an equivalent area?

3.4.16.   A 3⅛-in. cube of aluminum is to be replaced by steel. What is the percentage difference in weight?

3.4.17.   A vertical water tank 4 ft 0 in. square holds 980 gallons. What is the pressure, per square inch, on the bottom of the water tank?

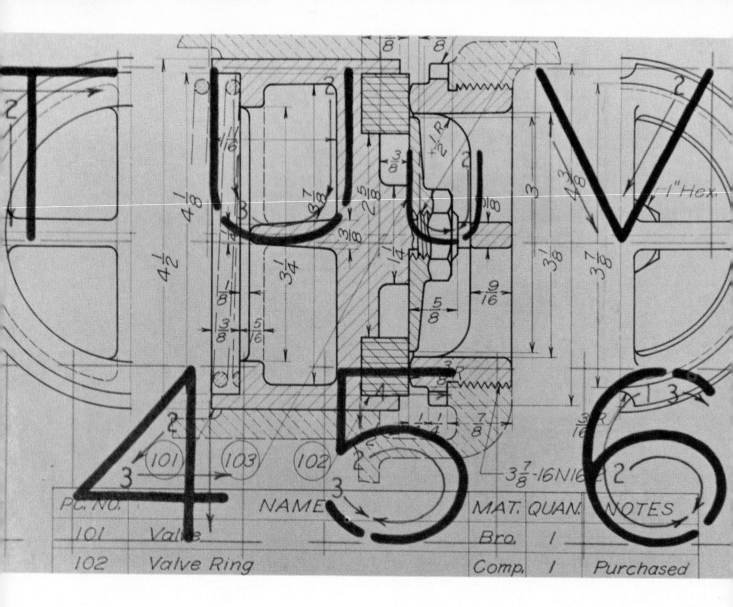

PC. NO.	NAME	MAT.	QUAN.	NOTES
101	Valve	Bro.	1	
102	Valve Ring	Comp.	1	Purchased

In the two preceding chapters, the need for accurate representation on drawings was emphasized. It is equally important that the lettered dimensions, notes, and specifications giving such details as sizes, machining methods, material specifications, finish, and other information be accurate and readable.

Lettering: Factual Drawing Supplements

4.1. Graphic representation of the shape of a part, machine, or structure gives one aspect of the information needed for its construction. To this must be added, to complete the description, figured dimensions, notes on material and finish, and a descriptive title—all lettered, freehand, in a style that is perfectly legible, uniform, and capable of rapid execution. As far as the appearance of a drawing is concerned, the lettering is the most important part. But the usefulness of a drawing, too, can be ruined by lettering done ignorantly or carelessly, because illegible figures are apt to cause mistakes in the work.

In a broad sense, lettering is a branch of design. Students of lettering fall into two general classes: those who will use letters and words to convey information on drawings, and those who will use lettering in applied design, for example, art students, artists, and craftsmen. The first group is concerned mainly with legibility and speed, the second with beauty of form and composition. In our study of engineering graphics we are concerned only with the problems of the first group. The engineering student takes up lettering as an early part of his work in drawing and continues its practice throughout his course, becoming more and more skillful and proficient.

4.2. SINGLE-STROKE LETTERING. By far the greatest amount of lettering on drawings is done in a rapid single-stroke letter, either vertical or inclined, and every engineer must have absolute command of these styles. The ability to letter well can be acquired only by continued and careful practice, but it can be acquired by anyone with normal muscular control of his fingers who will practice faithfully and intelligently and take the trouble to observe carefully the shapes of the letters, the sequence of strokes in making them, and the rules for their composition. It is not a matter of artistic talent or even of dexterity in handwriting. Many persons who write poorly letter very well.

The term "single-stroke," or "one-stroke," does not mean that the entire letter is made without lifting the pencil or pen but that the width of the stroke of the pencil or pen is the width of the stem of the letter.

4.3. GENERAL PROPORTIONS. There is no standard for the proportions of letters, but there are certain fundamental points in design and certain characteristics of individual letters that must be learned by study and observation before composition into words and sentences should be attempted. Not only do the widths of letters in any alphabet vary, from *I,* the narrowest, to *W,* the widest, but different alphabets vary as a whole. Styles narrow in their proportion of width to height are called "**COMPRESSED,**" or "**CONDENSED,**" and are used when space is limited. Styles wider than the normal are called **"EXTENDED."**

The proportion of the thickness of stem to the height varies widely, ranging from ⅓ to ¹⁄₂₀. Letters with heavy stems are called **"BOLDFACE,"** or **"BLACK-**

FACE," those with thin stems "LIGHT-FACE."

4.4. THE RULE OF STABILITY. In the construction of letters, the well-known optical illusion in which a horizontal line drawn across the middle of a rectangle appears to be below the middle must be provided for. In order to give the appearance of stability, such letters as *B, E, K, S, X,* and *Z* and the figures *3* and *8* must be drawn smaller at the top than at the bottom. To see the effect of this illusion, turn a printed page upside down and notice the appearance of the letters mentioned.

4.5. GUIDE LINES. Always draw light guide lines for both tops and bottoms of letters, using a sharp pencil. Figure 4.1 shows a method of laying off a number of equally spaced lines. Draw the first base line; then set the bow spacers to the distance wanted between base lines and step off the required number of base lines. Above the last line mark the desired height of the letters. With the same setting, step down from this upper point, thus obtaining points for the top of each line of letters.

The Braddock-Rowe triangle (Fig. 4.2*A*) and the Ames lettering instrument (Fig. 4.2*B*) are convenient devices for spacing lines of letters. In using these instruments, a sharp pencil is inserted in the proper row of countersunk holes, and the instrument, guided by a T-square blade, is drawn back and forth by the pencil, as indicated by Fig. 4.3. The holes are grouped for capitals and lower case, the numbers indicating the height of capitals in thirty-seconds of an inch; thus no. 6 spacing of the instrument means that the capitals will be ⁶⁄₃₂, or ³⁄₁₆, in. high.

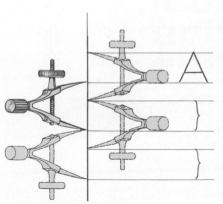

FIG. 4.1. To space guide lines. Bow dividers are spaced for the distance between base lines; this distance stepped off from capital and base lines locates successive lines of lettering.

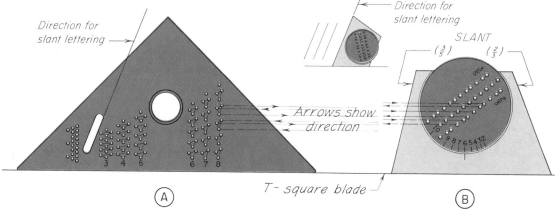

FIG. 4.2. (*A*) Braddock-Rowe triangle. Numbered sets of holes locate capital, waist (see Fig. 4.18), and base lines of successive lines of lettering. (*B*) Ames lettering instrument. A center disk, adjusted to letter-height number, gives equal spaces or 2:3 and 3:5 waist-line proportion for successive lines of lettering.

FIG. 4.3. Using the Ames lettering instrument. Lines are drawn as the pencil moves the instrument along the T square (or triangle).

4.6. LETTERING IN PENCIL. Good technique is as essential in lettering as in drawing. The quality of the lettering is important whether it appears on finished work to be reproduced by one of the printing processes or as part of a pencil drawing to be inked. In the first case, the penciling must be clean, firm, and opaque; in the second, it may be lighter. The lettering pencil should be selected carefully by trial on the paper. In one instance, the same grade may be chosen as that used for the drawing; in another, a grade or two softer may be preferred. Sharpen the pencil to a long, conic point, and then round the lead slightly on the end so that it is not so sharp as a point used for drawing.

The first requirement in lettering is the correct holding of the pencil or pen.

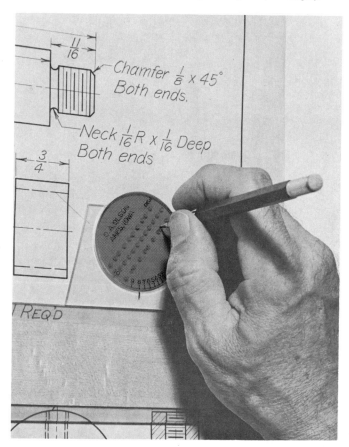

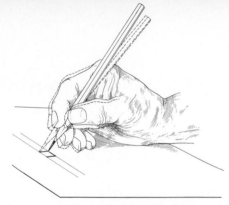

FIG. 4.4. Vertical strokes. These are made entirely by finger movement.

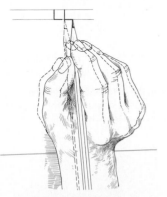

FIG. 4.5. Horizontal strokes. These are made by pivoting the whole hand at the wrist; fingers move slightly to keep the stroke perfectly horizontal.

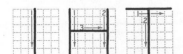

FIG. 4.6. The *I-H-T* group. Note the direction of fundamental horizontal and vertical strokes.

FIG. 4.7. The *L-E-F* group. Note the successive order of strokes.

Figure 4.4 shows the pencil held comfortably with the thumb, forefinger, and second finger on alternate flat sides and the third and fourth fingers on the paper. Vertical, slanting, and curved strokes are drawn with a steady, even, *finger* movement; horizontal strokes are made similarly but with some pivoting of the hand at the wrist (Fig. 4.5). Exert pressure that is firm and uniform but not so heavy as to cut grooves in the paper. To keep the point symmetrical, form the habit of rotating the pencil after every few strokes.

4.7. SINGLE-STROKE VERTICAL CAPITALS. The vertical, single-stroke, commercial Gothic letter is a standard for titles, reference letters, etc. As for the proportion of width to height, the general rule is that the smaller the letters are, the more extended they should be in width. A low extended letter is more legible than a high compressed one and at the same time makes a better appearance.

For proficiency in lettering it is essential to learn the form and peculiarity of each of the letters. Although lettering must be based on a careful regard for the fundamental letter forms, this is not to say that it will be without character. Individuality in lettering is often nearly as marked as in handwriting.

4.8. ORDER OF STROKES. In the following figures an alphabet of slightly extended vertical capitals has been arranged in family groups. Study the shape of each letter, with the order and direction of the strokes forming it, and practice it until its form and construction are perfectly familiar. Practice it first in pencil to large size, perhaps ⅜ in. high, then to smaller size, and finally directly in ink.

To bring out the proportions of widths to heights and the subtleties in the shapes of the letters, they are shown against a square background with its sides divided into sixths. Several of the letters in this alphabet, such as *A* and *T,* fill the square; that is, they are as wide as they are high. Others, such as *H* and *D,* are approximately five spaces wide, or their width is five-sixths of their height. *These proportions must be learned visually* so well that letters of various heights can be drawn in correct proportion without hesitation.

The I-H-T Group (Fig. 4.6). The letter *I* is the foundation stroke. You may find it difficult to keep the stems vertical. If so, draw direction lines lightly an inch or so apart to aid the eye. The *H* is nearly square (five-sixths wide), and in accordance with the rule of stability, the crossbar is just above the center. The top of the *T* is drawn first to the full width of the square, and the stem is started accurately as its middle point.

The L-E-F Group (Fig. 4.7). The *L* is made in two strokes. The first two strokes of the *E* are the same as for the *L;* the third, or upper, stroke is slightly shorter than the lower; and the last stroke is two-thirds as long as the lower and just above the middle. *F* has the same proportions as *E.*

The N-Z-X-Y Group (Fig. 4.8). The

FIG. 4.8. The *N-Z-X-Y* group. Note that *Z* and *X* are smaller at the top than at the bottom, in accordance with the rule of stability.

FIG. 4.9. The *V-A-K* group. The horizontal of *A* is one-third from the bottom; the second and third strokes of *K* are perpendicular to each other.

FIG. 4.10. The *M-W* group. *M* is one-twelfth wider than it is high; *W* is one-third wider than it is high.

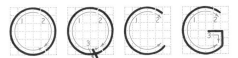

FIG. 4.11. The *O-Q-C-G* group. All are based on the circle.

FIG. 4.12. The *D-U-J* group. These are made with combinations of straight and curved strokes.

parallel sides of *N* are generally drawn first, but some prefer to make the strokes in consecutive order. *Z* and *X* are both started inside the width of the square on top and run to full width at the bottom. This throws the crossing point of the *X* slightly above the center. The junction of the *Y* strokes is at the center.

The V-A-K Group (Fig. 4.9). *V* is the same width as *A*, the full breadth of the square. The *A* bridge is one-third up from the bottom. The second stroke of *K* strikes the stem one-third up from the bottom; the third stroke branches from it in a direction starting from the top of the stem.

The M-W Group (Fig. 4.10). These are the widest letters. *M* may be made in consecutive strokes or by drawing the two vertical strokes first, as with the *N*. *W* is formed of two narrow *V*'s, each two-thirds of the square in width. Note that with all the pointed letters the width at the point is the width of the stroke.

The O-Q-C-G Group (Fig. 4.11). In this extended alphabet the letters of the *O* family are made as full circles. The *O* is made in two strokes, the left side a longer arc than the right, as the right side is harder to draw. Make the kern of the *Q* straight. A large-size *C* and *G* can be made more accurately with an extra stroke at the top, whereas in smaller letters the curve is made in one stroke (Fig. 4.19). Note that the bar on the *G* is halfway up and does not extend past the vertical stroke.

The D-U-J Group (Fig. 4.12). The top and bottom strokes of *D* must be horizontal. Failure to observe this is a common fault with beginners. In large letters *U* is formed by two parallel strokes, to which the bottom stroke is added; in smaller letters, it may be made in two strokes curved to meet at the bottom. *J* has the same construction as *U*, with the first stroke omitted.

The P-R-B Group (Fig. 4.13). With *P*, *R*, and *B*, the number of strokes depends upon the size of the letter. For large letters the horizontal lines are started and the curves added, but for smaller letters only one stroke for each lobe is needed. The middle lines of *P* and *R* are on the center line; that of *B* observes the rule of stability.

The S-8-3 Group (Fig. 4.14). The *S*, 8, and 3 are closely related in form, and the rule of stability must be observed carefully. For a large *S*, three strokes are used; for a smaller one, two strokes; and for a very small size, one stroke only is best. The *8* may be made on the *S* construction in three strokes, or in "head and body" in four strokes. A perfect *3* can be finished into an *8*.

The 0-6-9 Group (Fig. 4.15). The cipher is an ellipse five-sixths the width of the letter *O*. The backbones of the *6* and *9* have the same curve as the cipher, and the lobes are slightly less than two-thirds the height of the figure.

The 2-5-7-& Group (Fig. 4.16). The secret in making the *2* lies in getting the

FIG. 4.13. The *P-R-B* group. Note the rule of stability with regard to *R* and *B*.

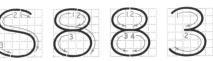

FIG. 4.14. The *S-8-3* group. A perfect *S* and *3* can be completed to a perfect *8*.

FIG. 4.15. The *0-6-9* group. The width is five-sixth of the height.

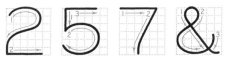

FIG. 4.16. The *2-5-7-&* group. Note the rule of stability. The width is five-sixth of the height.

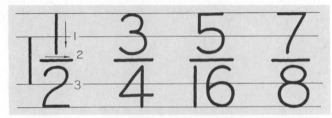

FIG. 4.17. Fractions. The total height of a fraction is twice that of the integer.

FIG. 4.18. Basic forms for lowercase letters. For standard letters, the waist-line height is two-thirds of capital height; capital line and drop line are therefore one-third above and one-third below the body of the letter.

FIG. 4.19. Single-stroke vertical capitals and lower case. Note the alternate strokes for small-size capitals and the alternate shapes for lowercase *a, g,* and *y*.

reverse curve to cross the center of the space. The bottom of *2* and the tops of *5* and *7* should be horizontal straight lines. The second stroke of *7* terminates directly below the middle of the top stroke. Its stiffness is relieved by curving it slightly at the lower end. The ampersand (&) is made in three strokes for large letters and two for smaller ones and must be carefully balanced.

The Fraction Group (*Fig. 4.17*). Fractions are always made with horizontal bar. Integers are the same height as capitals. The total fraction height is best made twice the height of the integer. The numerator and denominator will be about three-fourths the height of the integer. Be careful to leave a clear space above and below the horizontal bar. Guide lines for fractions are easily obtained with lettering instruments by using the set of uniformly spaced holes or by drawing the integer height above and below the center, the position of the horizontal bar.

4.9. VERTICAL LOWER-CASE LETTERS. The single-stroke, vertical lower-case letter is not commonly used on machine drawings but is used extensively in map drawing. It is the standard letter for hypsography in government topographic drawing. The bodies are made two-thirds the height of the capitals with the ascenders extending to the capital line and the descenders dropping the same distance below. The basic form of the letter is the combination of a circle and a straight line (Fig. 4.18). The alphabet, with some alternate shapes, is shown in Fig. 4.19, which also gives the capitals in alphabetic order.

4.10. SINGLE-STROKE INCLINED CAPITALS. Many draftsmen use the inclined, or slant, letter in preference to the upright. The order and direction of strokes are the same as in the vertical form.

After ruling the guide lines, draw slanting "direction lines" across the lettering area to aid the eye in keeping the slope uniform. These lines may be drawn with a special lettering triangle of about 67½°, or the slope of 2 to 5 may be fixed on the paper by marking two units on a horizontal line and five on a vertical line and using T square and triangle as shown in Fig. 4.20. The Braddock-Rowe

triangle and the Ames instrument (Figs. 4.2A and B) both provide for the drawing of slope lines. The form taken by the rounded letters when inclined is illustrated in Fig. 4.21, which shows that curves are sharp in all upper right-hand and lower left-hand corners and flattened in the other two corners. Take particular care with the letters that have sloping sides, such as A, V, and W. The sloping sides of these letters must be drawn so that they appear to balance about a slope guide line passing through each vertex, as in Fig. 4.22. The alphabet is given in Fig. 4.23. Study the shape of each letter carefully.

Professional appearance in lettering is due to three things: (1) keeping to a uniform slope, (2) having the letters full and well shaped, and (3) keeping them close together. The beginner invariably cramps the individual letters and spaces them too far apart.

4.11. SINGLE-STROKE, INCLINED LOWER-CASE LETTERS.

The inclined lower-case letters (Fig. 4.23) have bodies two-thirds the height of the capitals with the ascenders extending to the capital line and the descenders dropping the same distance below the base line. Among older engineers, particularly civil engineers, this letter is generally known as the "Reinhardt letter," in honor of Charles W. Reinhardt, who first systematized its construction. It is legible and effective and, after its swing has been mastered, can be made rapidly. The lower-case letter is suitable for notes and statements on drawings because it is much more easily read than all capitals, since we read words by the word shapes, and it can be done much faster.

All the letters of the Reinhardt alphabet are based on two elements, the

FIG. 4.20. Slope guide lines. The standard slope angle of 67½° (see Figs. 4.2A and B) can be approximated by a slope of 2 to 5.

FIG. 4.21. Form of curved-stroke inclined capitals. The basic shape is elliptical.

FIG. 4.22. Form of straight-stroke inclined capitals. The "center line" must be a slope line.

FIG. 4.23. Single-stroke inclined capitals and lower case. Note the alternate strokes for small-size capitals and the alternate shapes for lower case a, g, and y.

FIG. 4.24. The straight-line inclined lower-case letters. Note that the center lines of the letters follow the slope angle.

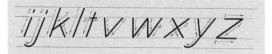

FIG. 4.25. The loop letters. Note the graceful combination of elliptical body, ascenders, and descenders.

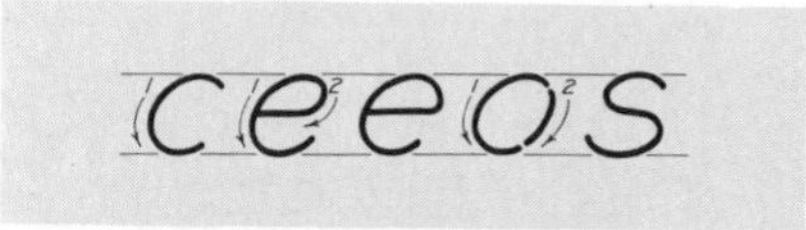

FIG. 4.26. The ellipse letters. Their formation is basically elliptical.

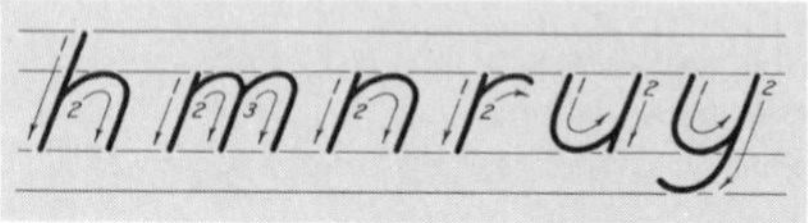

FIG. 4.27. The hook letters. They are combinations of ellipses and straight lines.

straight line and the ellipse, and have no unnecessary hooks or appendages. They may be divided into four groups, as shown in Figs. 4.24 to 4.27. The dots of *i* and *j* and the top of the *t* are on the "*t* line," halfway between the waist line and the capital line. The loop letters are made with an ellipse whose long axis is inclined about 45° in combination with a straight line. In lettering rapidly, the ellipse tends to assume a pumpkin-seed form; guard against this.

The *c*, *e*, and *o* are based on an ellipse of the shape of the capitals but not inclined quite so much as the loop-letter ellipse. In rapid small work, the *o* is often made in one stroke, as are the *e*, *v*, and *w*. The *s* is similar to the capital but, except in letters more than ⅛ in. high, is made in one stroke. In the hook-letter group, note particularly the shape of the hook.

The single-stroke letter may, if necessary, be much compressed and still be clear and legible (Fig. 4.28). It is also used sometimes in extended form.

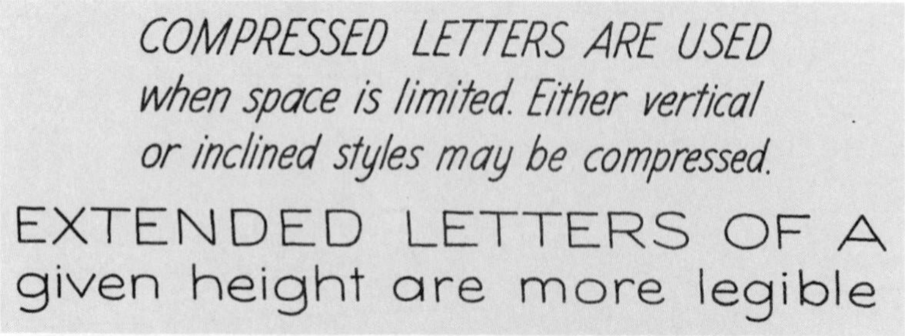

COMPRESSED LETTERS ARE USED when space is limited. Either vertical or inclined styles may be compressed.

EXTENDED LETTERS OF A given height are more legible

FIG. 4.28. Compressed and extended letters. Normal width has *O* the same in width as in height and the other letters in proportion. Wider than high for *O* is extended, narrower compressed.

4.12. FOR LEFT-HANDERS ONLY. The order and direction of strokes in the preceding alphabets have been designed for right-handed persons. The principal reason that left-handers sometimes find lettering difficult is that whereas the right-hander progresses away from the body, the left-hander progresses toward the body; consequently his pencil and hand partially hide the work he has done, making it harder to join strokes and to preserve uniformity. Also, in the case of inclined lettering, the slope direction, instead of running toward his eye, runs off into space to the left of his body, making this style so much harder for him that he is strongly advised to *use vertical letters exclusively*.

For the natural left-hander, whose writing position is the same as a right-hander except reversed left for right, a change in the sequence of strokes of some of the letters will obviate part of the difficulty caused by interference with the line of sight. Figure 4.29 gives an analyzed alphabet with an alternate for some letters. In *E* the top bar is made before the bottom bar, and *M* is drawn from left to right to avoid having strokes hidden by the pencil or pen. Horizontal portions of curves are easier to make from right to left; hence the starting points for *O*, *Q*, *C*, *G*, and *U* differ from the standard right-hand stroking. *S* is the perfect letter for the left-hander and is best made in a single smooth stroke. The figures *6* and *9* are difficult and require extra practice. In the lower-case letters *a*, *d*, *g*, and *q*, it is better to draw the straight line before the curve even though it makes spacing a little harder.

The hook-wrist left-handed writer, who pushes his strokes from top to bottom, finds vertical lettering more difficult than does the natural left-hander.

In Fig. 4.29, where alternate strokes are given for some of the letters, the hook-wrist writer will probably find the second stroking easier than the first. Some prefer to reverse *all* the strokes, drawing vertical strokes from bottom to top and horizontal strokes from right to left.

By way of encouragement it may be said that many left-handed draftsmen letter beautifully.

4.13. COMPOSITION.

Composition in lettering has to do with the selection, arrangement, and spacing of appropriate styles and sizes of letters. On engineering drawings the selection of the style is practically limited to vertical or inclined single-stroke lettering, so composition here means arrangement into pleasing and legible form. After the shapes and strokes of the individual letters have been learned, the entire practice should be on composition into words and sentences, since proper spacing of letters and words does more for the appearance of a block of lettering than the forms of the letters themselves. Letters in words are not spaced at a uniform distance from each other but are arranged so that the areas of white space (the irregular backgrounds between the letters) are approximately equal, making the spacing *appear* approximately uniform. Figure 4.30 illustrates these background shapes. Each letter is spaced with reference to its shape and the shape of the letter preceding it. Thus adjacent letters with straight sides would be spaced farther apart than those with curved sides. Sometimes combinations such as *LT* or *AV* may even overlap. Definite rules for spacing are not successful; it is a matter for the draftsman's judgment and sense of design. Figure 4.31 illustrates word composition. The sizes of letters to use in

any particular case can be determined better by sketching them lightly than by judging from the guide lines alone. A finished line of letters always looks larger than the guide lines indicate. Avoid the use of a coarse pen for small sizes and one that makes thin wiry lines for large sizes. When capitals and small capitals are used, the height of the small capitals should be about four-fifths that of the capitals.

In spacing words, a good principle is to leave the space that would be taken by an assumed letter *I* connecting the two words into one, as in Fig. 4.32. The

FIG. 4.29. Strokes for left-handers. Several alternate strokes are given. Choose the one that is most effective for you.

FIG. 4.30. Background areas. Equal areas between letters produce spacing that is visually uniform.

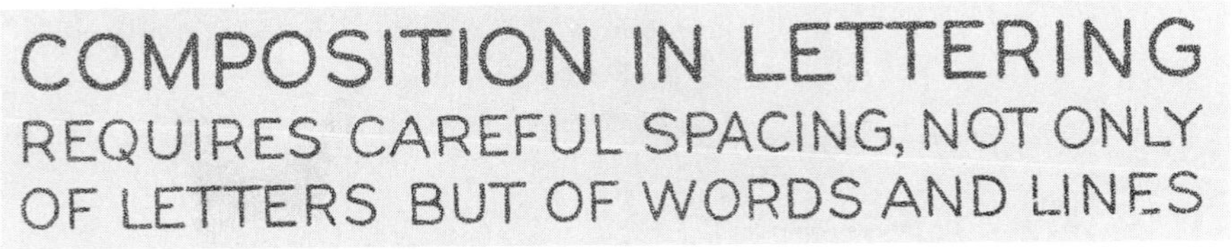

COMPOSITION IN LETTERING
REQUIRES CAREFUL SPACING, NOT ONLY
OF LETTERS BUT OF WORDS AND LINES

FIG. 4.31. Word composition. Careful spacing of letters and words and the proper emphasis of size and weight are important.

WORDSISPACEDIBYISKETCHINGIANIIIBETWEEN
WORDS SPACED BY SKETCHING AN I BETWEEN

FIG. 4.32. Word spacing. Space words so that they read naturally and do not run together (too close) or appear as separate units (too far apart).

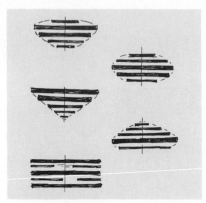

FIG. 4.33. Shapes in symmetrical composition. Design for clarity and emphasis.

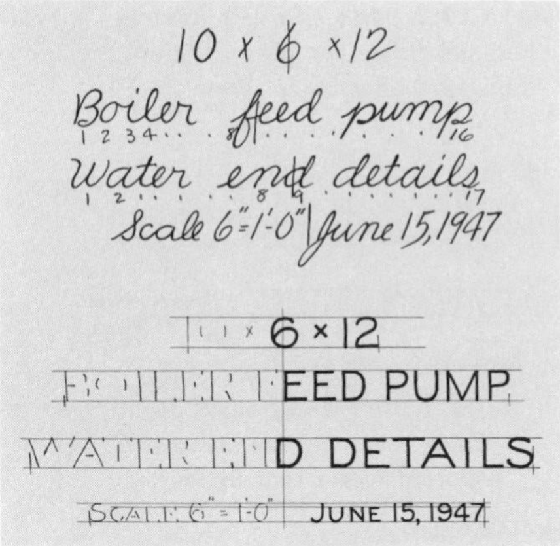

$$10 \times 6 \times 12$$
Boiler feed pump
1 2 3 4 · · 5 6 · · 7 8 9 · · · 16
Water end details
1 2 · · 3 4 5 · · 6 7 8 · 9 · 10 11 12
Scale 6"=1'-0" June 15,1947

6 × 12
BOILER FEED PUMP
WATER END DETAILS
SCALE 6"=1'-0" JUNE 15,1947

FIG. 4.34. Title composition. Sketch lightly; then when satisfactory, complete.

space would never be more than the height of the letters.

The clear distance between lines may vary from ½ to 1½ times the height of the letter but for the sake of appearance should not be exactly the same as the letter height. The instruments in Figs. 4.2 and 4.3 provide spacing that is two-thirds of the letter height. Paragraphs should always be indented.

4.14. TITLES. The most important problem in lettering composition is the design of titles. Every drawing has a descriptive title that is either all hand-lettered or filled in on a printed form. It gives necessary information concerning the drawing, and the information that is needed will vary with the different kinds of drawings (see paragraph 13.15).

The usual form of lettered title is the *symmetrical title,* which is balanced or "justified" on a vertical center line and designed with an elliptical or oval outline. Sometimes the wording necessitates a pyramid or inverted-pyramid ("bag") form. Figure 4.33 illustrates several shapes in which titles can be composed. The lower right-hand corner of the sheet is, from long custom and because of convenience in filing, the usual location for the title, and in laying out a drawing, this corner is reserved for it. The space allowed depends on the size and purpose of the drawing. On an 11- by 17-in. working drawing, the title may be about 3 in. long.

4.15. TO DRAW A TITLE. When the wording has been determined, write out the arrangement on a separate piece of paper as in Fig. 4.34 (or, better, typewrite it). Count the letters, including the word spaces, and make a mark across the middle letter or space of each line. The lines must be displayed for prominence according to their relative importance as judged from the point of view of the persons who will use the drawing. Titles are usually made in all capitals. Draw the base line for the most important line of the title and mark on it the approximate length desired. To get the letter height, divide this length by the number of letters in the line, and draw the capital line. Start at the center line, and sketch lightly the last half of the line, drawing only enough of the letters to show the space each will occupy. Lay off the length of this right half on the other side, and sketch that half, working forward or backward. When this line is satisfactory in size and spacing, draw the remainder in the same way. Study the effect, shift letters or lines if necessary, and complete in pencil. Use punctuation marks only for abbreviations.

Scratch-paper Methods. Sketch each line of the title separately on a piece of scratch paper, using guide lines of determined height. Find the middle point of each of these lines, fold the paper along the base line of the letters, fit the middle point to the center line on the drawing, and draw the final letters directly below the sketches. *Or* draw the letters along the edge of the scratch paper, using the upper or lower edge as one of the guide lines. *Or* letter the title on scratch paper, cut it apart and adjust until satisfactory, and then trace it.

LEONARDT 516 F:506 F
HUNT 512:ESTERBROOK 968
Esterbrook 1000   Spencerian No.1
Gillott 404: Gillott 303

For very fine lines Gillott 170 and 290 or Esterbrook 356 and 355

FIG. 4.35. Pen strokes, full size. These are used principally for average-size lettering on working drawings.

4.16 NOTES AND FILLED-IN TITLES. By far the principal use of lettering on engineering drawings occurs on working drawings, where the dimensions, explanatory notes, record of drawing changes, and title supplement the graphic description of the object.

Styles vary, but the trend is toward the use of capital letters exclusively. Most draftsmen are able to letter in capital letters with greater readability and fewer mistakes than in lower case. However, for some structural drawings and others where space may be at a premium, lower case is used.

On any working drawing the accuracy of the information conveyed is paramount. For this reason it is important to make the shapes of the letters precisely correct with no personal flourishes, embellishments, or peculiarities. For example, a poorly made *3* may be read as an *8* or vice versa. A poorly made *5* may be misconstrued as a *6*. Strive for a smooth, professional appearance with, above all, perfect readability. The problems of Group 5 at the end of this chapter give practice in the lettering of notes. For added practice, copy some of the information from the working drawings in Chap. 13.

4.17. LETTERING PENS. There are many steel writing pens that are adaptable to or made especially for lettering. The size of the strokes of a few popular ones is shown in full size in Fig. 4.35. Several special pens made in sets of graded sizes have been designed for single-stroke lettering; among them are those illustrated in Fig. 4.36. These are particularly useful for large work. The ink-holding reservoir of the Henry tank pen (Fig. 4.37) assists materially in maintaining uniform weight of line. A similar device can be made by bending a brass strip from a paper fastener, a piece of an-

nealed watch spring, or—perhaps best—a strip cut from a piece of shim brass into the shape shown in Fig. 4.38 and inserting it in the penholder so that the curved end just touches the pen nib.

To remove the oil film, always wet a new pen and wipe it thoroughly before using. A lettering pen well broken in by use is worth much more than a new one. It should be kept with care and never lent. A pen that has been dipped into writing ink should never be put into drawing ink. When in use, a pen should be wiped clean frequently with a cloth penwiper.

4.18. USING THE PEN. Use a penholder with cork grip (the small size) and set the pen in it firmly. Many prefer to ink a pen with the quill filler, touching the quill to the underside of the pen point, rather than dipping the pen in the ink bottle. If the pen is dipped, the surplus ink should be shaken back into the bottle or the pen touched against the neck of the bottle as it is withdrawn. Lettering with too much ink on the pen gives the results shown in Fig. 4.39.

In lettering, the penholder is held in the fingers firmly but without pinching, in the position shown in Fig. 4.40. The strokes of the letters are made with a steady, even motion and a slight, uniform pressure on the paper that will not spread the nibs of the pen.

4.19. OTHER LETTERING STYLES. This chapter has been devoted entirely to the commercial Gothic letter because this style predominates in all types of commercial drawings. However, other letter styles are used extensively on architectural drawings and on maps, in design and for display, and for decorative letters on commercial products. Some traditional letter styles and their uses are given in the Appendix.

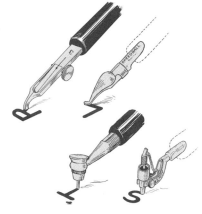

FIG. 4.36. Barch-Payzant, Speedball, Edco, and Leroy pens. These are used principally for displays, large titles, and number blocks.

FIG. 4.37. Henry tank pen. The reservoir is designed to prevent spreading of the nibs.

FIG. 4.38. Ink holder. This helps to avoid heavy flow of ink when the pen is full.

EHMNWTZ

FIG. 4.39. Too much ink. Fill the pen sparingly and often.

FIG. 4.40. Holding the pen. Note that the thumb, forefinger, and second finger make a three-point support.

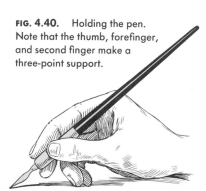

PROBLEMS

GROUP 1.   SINGLE-STROKE VERTICAL CAPITALS

4.1.1.   Large letters in pencil for careful study of the shapes of the individual letters. Starting 9/16 in. from the top border, draw guide lines for five lines of 3/8-in. letters. Draw each of the straight-line letters *I, H, T, L, E, F, N, Z, Y, V, A, M, W,* and *X,* four times in pencil only, studying carefully Figs. 4.6 to 4.10. The illustration is a full-size reproduction of a corner of this exercise.

4.1.2.   Same as Prob. 4.1.1 for the curved-line letters *O, Q, C, G, D, U, J, B, P, R,* and *S.* Study Figs. 4.11 to 4.14.

4.1.3.   Same as Prob. 4.1.1 for the figures *3, 8, 6, 9, 2, 5, 1/2, 3/4, 5/8, 7/16,* and *9/32.* Study Figs. 4.14 to 4.17.

4.1.4.   Composition. Same layout as for Prob. 4.1.1. Read paragraph 4.13 on composition; then letter the following five lines in pencil: (*a*) WORD COMPOSITION, (*b*) TOPOGRAPHIC SURVEY, (*c*) TOOLS AND EQUIPMENT, (*d*) BRONZE BUSHING, (*e*) JACK-RAFTER DETAIL.

4.1.5.   Quarter-inch vertical letters in pencil and ink. Starting 1/4 in. from the top, draw guide lines for nine lines of 1/4-in. letters. In the group order given, draw each letter four times in pencil and then four times directly in ink, as shown in the illustration.

4.1.6.   Composition. Make a three-line design of the quotation from Benjamin Lamme on the Lamme medals: "THE ENGINEER VIEWS HOPEFULLY THE HITHERTO UNATTAINABLE."

4.1.7.   One-eighth-inch vertical letters. Starting 1/4 in. from the top, draw guide lines for 18 lines of 1/8-in. letters. Make each letter and numeral eight times directly in ink. Fill the remaining lines with a portion of paragraph 4.13 on composition.

4.1.8.   Composition. Letter the following definition: "Engineering is the art and science of directing and controlling the forces and utilizing the materials of nature for the benefit of man. All engineering involves the organization of human effort to attain these ends. It also involves an appraisal of the social and economic benefits of these activities."

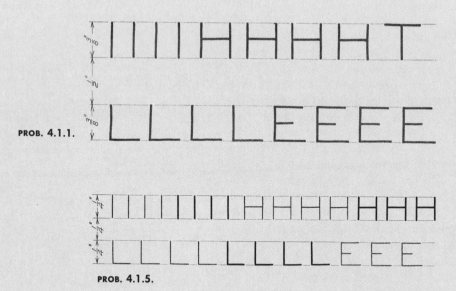

PROB. 4.1.1.

PROB. 4.1.5.

GROUP 2.   SINGLE-STROKE INCLINED CAPITALS

4.2.1 to 4.2.8.   Same spacing and specifications as for Group 1, Probs. 4.1.1 to 4.1.8, but for inclined letters. Study paragraph 4.10 and Figs. 4.20 to 4.23.

GROUP 3.   SINGLE-STROKE INCLINED LOWER CASE

4.3.1.   Large letters in pencil for use with ⅜-in. capitals. The bodies are ¼ in., the ascenders ⅛ in. above, and the descenders ⅛ in. below. Starting ⅜ in. from the top, draw guide lines for seven lines of letters. This can be done quickly by spacing ⅛ in. uniformly down the sheet and bracketing capital and base lines. Make each letter of the alphabet four times in pencil only. Study Figs. 4.23 to 4.27.

4.3.2.   Lower case for ³⁄₁₆-in. capitals. Starting ½ in. from the top, draw capital, waist, and base lines for 13 lines of letters (Braddock or Ames no. 6 spacing). Make each letter six times in pencil and then six times in ink.

4.3.3.   Composition. Same spacing as Prob. 4.3.2. Letter the opening paragraph of this chapter.

4.3.4.   Letter paragraph 4.4.

GROUP 4.   TITLES

4.4.1.   Design a title for the assembly drawing of a rear axle, drawn to the scale of 6 in. = 1 ft, as made by the Chevrolet Motor Co., Detroit. The number of the drawing is C82746. Space allowed is 3 by 5 in.

4.4.2.   Design a title for the front elevation of a powerhouse, drawn to ¼-in. scale by Burton Grant, Architect, for the Citizens Power and Light Company of Punxsutawney, Pennsylvania.

GROUP 5.   NOTES

4.5.1 to 4.5.3.   Vertical capitals. Copy each note in no. 6 (Ames or Braddock) spacing; then in no. 4 spacing.

4.5.4 to 4.5.6.   Inclined capitals. Copy in no. 5 or no. 4 spacing.

4.5.7 to 4.5.9.   Vertical lower case. Copy in no. 5 spacing.

4.5.10 to 4.5.12.   Inclined lower case. Copy in no. 4 spacing.

4.5.13.   For extra practice, select any of Probs. 4.5.1 to 4.5.12 and letter in a chosen style and size.

PAINT WITH METALLIC SEALER AND TWO COATS LACQUER AS PER CLIENT COLOR ORDER.
    PROB. 4.5.1.

THIS PRINT IS AMERICAN THIRD-ANGLE PROJECTION
    PROB. 4.5.2.

TO BE REMOVED AFTER MACHINING AND BEFORE ASSEMBLY.
    PROB. 4.5.3.

THIS HOLE IN PIECE NO. 821 ONLY. REMOVE BURR ON UPPER SIDE.
    PROB. 4.5.6.

Pivot point for high pressure bellows.
    PROB. 4.5.9.

CUTOFF BURR MUST NOT PROJECT BEYOND THIS SURFACE.
    PROB. 4.5.4.

ALTERNATE MATERIAL: 1ST. RED BRASS 85 % CU. 2ND. COMM. BRASS 90 % CU. 3RD. COMM. BRASS 95 % CU.
    PROB. 4.5.5.

Flatten ear on this side to make piece No. 51367. See detail.
    PROB. 4.5.7.

Deburring slot must be centered on 0.625 hole within ±0.001.
    PROB. 4.5.8.

Extrude to 0.082 ±.002 Dia. 3-56 Class 2 tap.
    PROB. 4.5.12.

Material: #19 Ga (0.024) C R Steel. Temper to Rockwell B-40 to 65.
    PROB. 4.5.10.

This length varies from 0.245 to 0.627. See table Ⓐ below.
    PROB. 4.5.11.

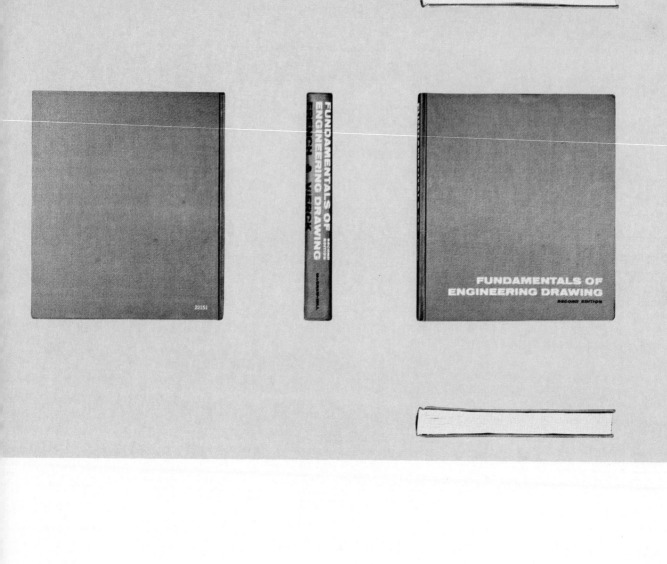

The standard method of describing the shape of an object is orthographic projection—*a system of separate views related to each other. To illustrate, study the accompanying picture while demonstrating to yourself by holding your textbook before you. The front of the book is of course obvious, and a view taken looking directly at this face will be the* front view. *Now, if the direction of observation is changed to look down upon the top of the book, this will be the* top view, *shown in green above the front view in the picture. Similarly, by looking upward at the bottom of the book, the* bottom view *will be obtained, shown in the photograph in green below the front view. Also in similar fashion look directly at the shelf stamp giving the* left side view *and then reverse this direction to look directly at the page ends, giving the* right side view, *both shown in red in the picture. It should now be obvious that looking directly at the back of the book will yield the* rear view, *shown to the left of the left side view in brown.*

The views just described are the six standard views. Orthographically, they are all related to each other by planes of projection and by projectors to be described later. These will become clearly defined and familiar as the chapter is studied.

Orthographic Drawing and Sketching

THEORY

5.1.   The previous chapters have been preparatory to the real subject of drawing as a language. Typically, engineers design and develop machines and structures and direct their construction. Furthermore, to design and then *communicate* every detail to manufacturing groups, descriptions must be prepared that show every aspect of the *shape* and *size* of each part and of the complete machine or structure. Because of this necessity, drawing is the fundamental method of communication. Only as a supplement, for notes and specifications, is the word language used.

In this chapter and Chap. 6 we are concerned with the methods of describing shape. Chapter 15 discusses size description.

Shape is described by projection, that is, by the process of causing an image to be formed by rays of sight taken in a particular direction from an object to a picture plane.[1] Methods of projection vary according to the direction in which the rays of sight are taken to the plane. When the rays are perpendicular to the plane, the projective method is *orthographic*. If the rays are at an angle to the plane, the projective method is called *oblique*. Rays taken to a particular station point result in *perspective projection*. By the methods of perspective the object is represented as it would appear to the eye.

[1] Only in *projective geometry*, a highly theoretical graphic subject, are surfaces other than a plane used.

Projective theory is the basis of background information necessary for shape representation. In engineering drawing, two fundamental methods of *shape representation* are used:

(1) *Orthographic views,* consisting of a set of two or more separate views of an object taken from different directions, generally at right angles to each other and arranged relative to each other in a definite way. Each of the views shows the shape of the object for a particular view direction and collectively the views describe the object completely. Orthographic projection *only* is used.

(2) *Pictorial views,* in which the object is oriented behind and projected upon a single plane. Either orthographic, oblique, or perspective projection is used.

Since orthographic views provide a means of describing the *exact shape* of any material object, they are used for the great bulk of engineering work.

5.2. THEORY OF ORTHOGRAPHIC PROJECTION. Let us suppose that a transparent plane has been set up between an object and the station point of an observer's eye (Fig. 5.1). The intersection of this plane with the rays formed by lines of sight from the eye to all points of the object would give a picture that is practically the same as the image formed in the eye of the observer. This is perspective projection.

If the observer would then walk backward from the station point until he reached a theoretically *infinite* distance, the rays formed by lines of sight from his eye to the object would grow longer and finally become infinite in length, parallel to each other, and perpendicular to the picture plane. The image so formed on the picture plane is what is known as "orthographic projection." See Fig. 5.2.

5.3. DEFINITION. Basically, orthographic[2] projection could be defined as any single projection made by dropping perpendiculars to a plane. However, it

[2] Literally, "right writing."

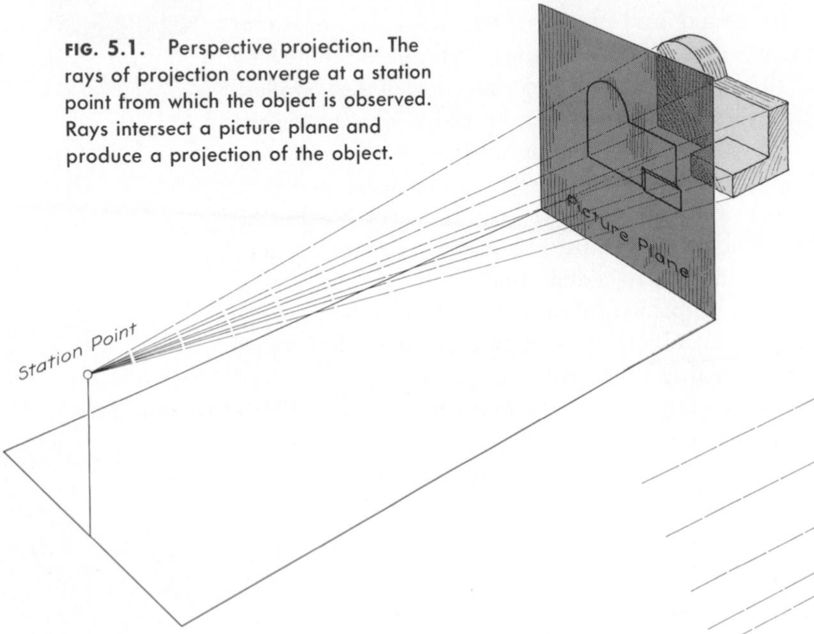

FIG. 5.1. Perspective projection. The rays of projection converge at a station point from which the object is observed. Rays intersect a picture plane and produce a projection of the object.

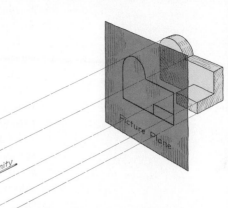

FIG. 5.2. Orthographic projection. The station point is at infinity, making the rays parallel to each other. The rays are perpendicular to the picture plane.

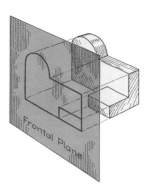

FIG. 5.3. The frontal plane of projection. This produces the front view of the object.

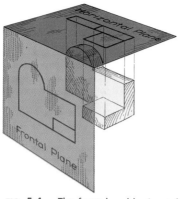

FIG. 5.4. The frontal and horizontal planes of projection. Projection on the horizontal plane produces the top view of the object. Frontal and horizontal planes are perpendicular to each other.

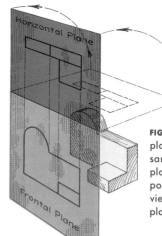

FIG. 5.5. The horizontal plane rotated into the same plane as the frontal plane. This makes it possible to draw two views of the object on a plane, the drawing paper.

has been accepted through long usage to mean the combination of two or more such views, hence the following definition: *Orthographic projection is the method of representing the exact shape of an object by dropping perpendiculars from two or more sides of the object to planes, generally at right angles to each other; collectively, the views on these planes describe the object completely.* (The term "orthogonal"[3] is sometimes used for this system of drawing.)

5.4. ORTHOGRAPHIC VIEWS. The rays from the picture plane to infinity may be discarded and the picture, or "view," thought of as being found by extending perpendiculars to the plane from all points of the object, as in Fig. 5.3. This picture, or projection on a frontal plane, shows the shape of the object when viewed from the front, but it does not tell the shape or distance from front to rear. Accordingly, more than one projection is required to describe the object.

In addition to the frontal plane, imagine another transparent plane placed horizontally above the object, as in Fig. 5.4. The projection on this plane, found by extending perpendiculars to it from the object, will give the appearance

[3] Meaning right-angled.

of the object as if viewed from directly above and will show the distance from front to rear. If this horizontal plane is now rotated into coincidence with the frontal plane, as in Fig. 5.5, the two views of the object will be in the same plane, as if on a sheet of paper. Now imagine a third plane, perpendicular to the first two (Fig. 5.6). This plane is called a "profile plane," and a third view can be projected on it. This view shows the shape of the object when viewed from the side and the distance from bottom to top and front to rear. The horizontal and profile planes are shown rotated into the same plane as the frontal plane (again thought of as the plane of the drawing paper) in Fig. 5.7. Thus related in the same plane, they give correctly the three-dimensional shape of the object.

In orthographic projection the picture planes are called "planes of projection;" and the perpendiculars, "projecting lines" or "projectors."

In looking at these theoretical projections, or views, do not think of the views as flat surfaces on the transparent planes, but try to imagine that you are looking *through* the transparent planes at the object itself.

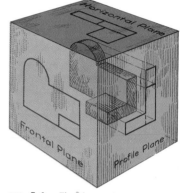

FIG. 5.6. The three planes of projection: frontal, horizontal, and profile. Each is perpendicular to the other two.

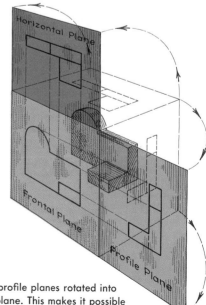

FIG. 5.7. The horizontal and profile planes rotated into the same plane as the frontal plane. This makes it possible to draw three views of the object on a plane, the drawing paper.

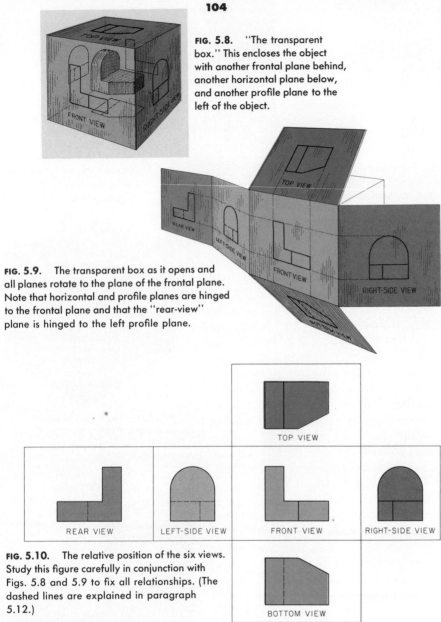

FIG. 5.8. "The transparent box." This encloses the object with another frontal plane behind, another horizontal plane below, and another profile plane to the left of the object.

FIG. 5.9. The transparent box as it opens and all planes rotate to the plane of the frontal plane. Note that horizontal and profile planes are hinged to the frontal plane and that the "rear-view" plane is hinged to the left profile plane.

FIG. 5.10. The relative position of the six views. Study this figure carefully in conjunction with Figs. 5.8 and 5.9 to fix all relationships. (The dashed lines are explained in paragraph 5.12.)

TOP VIEW

REAR VIEW · LEFT-SIDE VIEW · FRONT VIEW · RIGHT-SIDE VIEW

BOTTOM VIEW

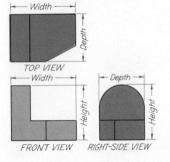

Width · *Depth*

TOP VIEW

Width · *Depth*

FRONT VIEW · RIGHT-SIDE VIEW

Height

FIG. 5.11. Top, front, and right-side views. This is the most common combination. Note that the top view is directly above and in projection (alignment) with the front view; and that the right-side view is to the right of and in projection with the front view. Observe also that *two* (and remember *which two*) space dimensions of height, width, and depth are represented in each view.

5.5. THE SIX PRINCIPAL VIEWS. Considering the matter further, we find that the object can be entirely surrounded by a set of six planes, each at right angles to the four adjacent to it, as in Fig. 5.8. On these planes, views can be obtained of the object as it is seen from the top, front, right side, left side, bottom, and rear.

Think now of the six sides, or planes, of the box as being opened up, as in Fig. 5.9, into one plane, the plane of the paper. The front is already in the plane of the paper, and the other sides are, as it were, hinged and rotated into position as shown. The projection on the frontal plane is the *front view, vertical projection,* or *front elevation;* that on the horizontal plane, the *top view, horizontal projection,* or *plan;* that on the side, or "profile," plane, the *side view, profile projection, side elevation,* or sometimes *end view* or *end elevation.* By reversing the direction of sight, a *bottom view* is obtained instead of a *top view,* or a *rear view* instead of a *front view.* In comparatively rare cases a bottom view or rear view or both may be required to show some detail of shape or construction. Figure 5.10 shows the relative position of the six views as set by the ANSI. In actual work there is rarely a time when all six principal views are needed on one drawing, but no matter how many are required, their positions relative to one another are given in Fig. 5.10 (except as noted in paragraph 5.7). All these views are principal views. Each of the six views shows two of the three dimensions of height, width, and depth.

5.6. COMBINATION OF VIEWS. The most usual combination selected from the six possible views consists of the *top, front,* and *right-side* views, as shown in Fig.

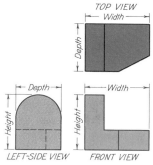

FIG. 5.12. Top, front, and left-side views. Note that the left-side view is drawn to the left of and in projection with the front view. The left-side view is preferred only when, because of the shape of the object, representation is clearer with the left-side view than with the right-side view.

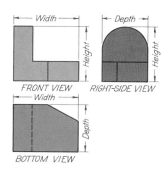

FIG. 5.13. Front, bottom, and right-side views. The bottom view is used instead of the top view only when its use gives clearer representation.

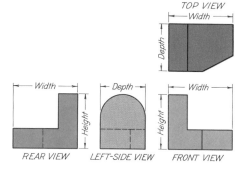

FIG. 5.14. Top, front, left-side, and rear views. The rear view is added *only* when some detail on the rear of the object is important and representation can be improved by its use.

5.11, which, in this case, best describes the shape of the given block. Sometimes the left-side view helps to describe an object more clearly than the right-side view. Figure 5.12 shows the arrangement of *top, front,* and *left-side* views for the same block. In this case the right-side view would be preferred, as it shows no hidden edges (see paragraph 5.12 on hidden features). Note that the *side view of the front face of the object is adjacent to the front view* and that the side view of any point will be the same distance from the front surface as is its distance from the front surface on the top view. The combination of *front, right-side,* and *bottom* views is shown in Fig. 5.13 and of *front, top, left-side,* and *rear* views in Fig. 5.14.

5.7. "ALTERNATE-POSITION" VIEWS. The top of the enclosing transparent box may be thought of as in a fixed position with the front, rear, and sides hinged, as in Fig. 5.15, thus bringing the sides in line with the top view and the rear view above the top view, Fig. 5.16. This

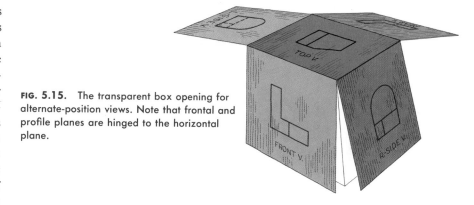

FIG. 5.15. The transparent box opening for alternate-position views. Note that frontal and profile planes are hinged to the horizontal plane.

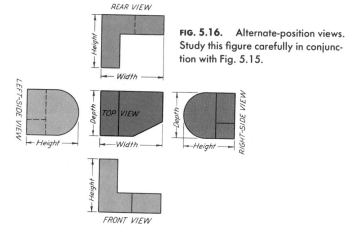

FIG. 5.16. Alternate-position views. Study this figure carefully in conjunction with Fig. 5.15.

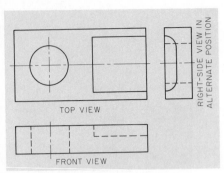

FIG. 5.17. Right-side view in alternate position. Note the saving in paper area (compared with regular position) for this broad, flat object. Compare with Fig. 5.11.

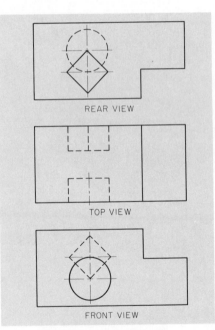

FIG. 5.18. Rear view in alternate position. This method is preferable when no left-side view is needed. Compare with Fig. 5.14.

alternate-position arrangement is of occasional use to save space on the paper in drawing a broad, flat object (Fig. 5.17). The alternate position for the rear view may be used if this arrangement makes the drawing easier to read (Fig. 5.18).

5.8. THE THREE SPACE DIMENSIONS. As all material objects, from single pieces to complicated structures, have distinct limits and are measurable by three space dimensions,[4] it is desirable for drawing purposes to define these dimensions and to fix their direction.

Height is the difference in elevation between any two points, measured as the perpendicular distance between a pair of horizontal planes that contain the points, as shown in Fig. 5.19. Edges of the object may or may not correspond with the height dimensions. Edge *AB* corresponds with the height dimension, while edge *CD* does not, but the space heights of *A* and *C* are the same, as are *B* and *D*. Height is always measured in a vertical direction and has

[4] *Space dimensions* and *dimensions of the object* should not be confused. The primary function of orthographic projection is to show the shape of the object. Size is not established until the figured dimensions and/or the scale are placed on the drawing. Space dimensions are *only* the measure of three-dimensional space.

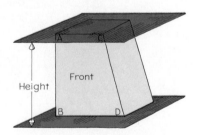

FIG. 5.19. Definition of height. This is the difference in elevation between two points.

no relationship whatever to the shape of the object.

Width is the positional distance left to right between any two points measured as the perpendicular distance between a pair of profile planes containing the points. In Fig. 5.20 the relative width between points *E* and *G* on the left and *H* and *F* on the right of an object is shown by the dimension marked "width." The object edge *EF* is parallel to the width direction and corresponds with the width dimension, but edge *GH* slopes downward from *G* to *H*, so this actual edge of the object is longer than the width separating points *G* and *H*.

Depth[5] is the positional distance front to rear between any two points measured as the perpendicular distance between two frontal planes containing the points. Figure 5.21 shows two frontal planes, one at the front of the object containing points *J* and *L*, the other at the rear containing points *K* and *M*. The relative depth separating the front and rear of the object is the perpendicular distance between the planes as shown.

Any point can be located in space by giving its height, width, and depth relative to some other known point. Figure 5.22 shows a cube with four identified corners *A*, *B*, *C*, and *D*. Assuming that

[5] As in the civil engineering sense.

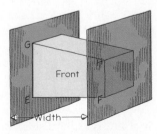

FIG. 5.20. Definition of width. This is the difference from left to right between two points.

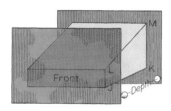

FIG. 5.21. Definition of depth. This is the difference from front to rear between two points.

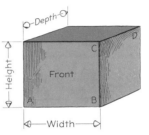

FIG. 5.22. Location of points in space. Height, width, and depth must be designated.

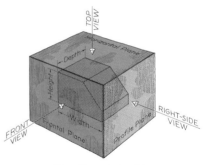

FIG. 5.23. The relationship between space directions and the planes of projection. View directions are perpendicular to their planes of projection. Height is parallel to frontal and profile planes, width is parallel to frontal and horizontal planes, and depth is parallel to horizontal and profile planes.

the plane containing points *A* and *B* is the front of the object, height, width, and depth would be as marked. Assuming also that point *A* is fixed in space, point *B* could be located from point *A* by giving the width dimension, including the statement that height and depth measurements are zero. *C* could be located from *A* by giving width, height, and zero depth. *D* could be located from *A* by giving width, height, and depth measurements.

5.9. THE RELATIONSHIP OF PLANES, VIEW DIRECTIONS, AND SPACE DIMENSIONS.

As explained in paragraphs 5.4 and 5.5, the object to be drawn may be thought of as surrounded by transparent planes upon which the actual views are projected. The three space dimensions—height, width, and depth—and the planes of projection are unchangeably oriented and connected with each other and with the view directions (Fig. 5.23). Each of the planes of projection is perpendicular, respectively, to its own view direction. Thus the frontal plane is perpendicular to the front-view direction, the horizontal plane is perpendicular to the top-view direction, and the profile plane is perpendicular to the side-view direction. The two space measurements for a view are parallel to the plane of

that view and perpendicular to the view direction. Therefore height and width are parallel to the frontal plane and perpendicular to the front-view direction; width and depth are parallel to the horizontal plane and perpendicular to the top-view direction; height and depth are parallel to the profile plane and perpendicular to the side-view direction. Note that the three planes of projection are *mutually* perpendicular, as are the three space measurements and the three view directions. Carefully study the views in Figs. 5.11 to 5.17 and note the space dimensions marked on each figure.

5.10. CLASSIFICATION OF SURFACES AND LINES.

Any object, depending upon its shape and space position, may or may not have some surfaces parallel or perpendicular to the planes of projection.

Surfaces are classified according to their space relationship with the planes of projection (Fig. 5.24). *Horizontal, frontal,* and *profile* surfaces are shown at (*A*). When a surface is inclined to two of the planes of projection (but perpendicular to the third), as at (*B*), the surface is said to be *auxiliary* or *inclined.* If the surface is at an angle to all three planes, as at (*C*), the term *oblique* or *skew* is used.

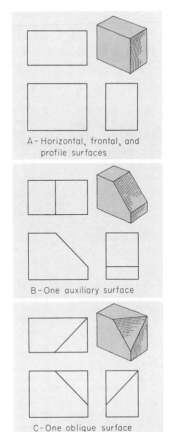

A – Horizontal, frontal, and profile surfaces

B – One auxiliary surface

C – One oblique surface

FIG. 5.24. Classification of surface positions.

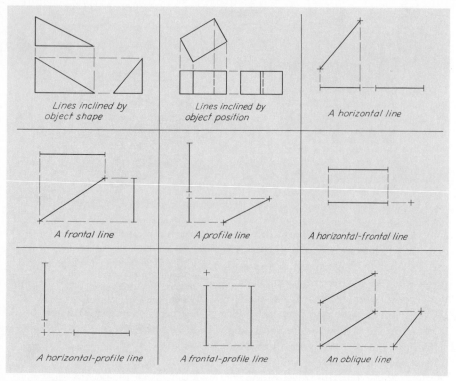

FIG. 5.25. Classification of line positions.

Lines inclined by object shape

Lines inclined by object position

A horizontal line

A frontal line

A profile line

A horizontal-frontal line

A horizontal-profile line

A frontal-profile line

An oblique line

and a *profile line* is a line in a profile plane. When a line is parallel to two planes, the line takes the name of both planes, as *horizontal-frontal, horizontal-profile,* or *frontal-profile.* A line not parallel to any plane of projection is called an *oblique* or *skew line.* Figure 5.25 shows various positions of lines.

An edge appears in true length when it is parallel to the plane of projection, as a point when it is perpendicular to the plane, and shorter than true length when it is inclined to the plane. Similarly, a surface appears in true shape when it is parallel to the plane of projection, as a line when it is perpendicular to the plane, and foreshortened when it is inclined to the plane. As an example, Fig. 5.24*A* shows an object with its faces parallel to the planes of projection; top, front, and right-side surfaces are shown in true shape; and the object edges appear either in true length or as points. The inclined surface of the object at (*B*) does not show in true shape in any of the views but appears as an edge in the front view. The front and rear edges of the inclined surface are in true length in the front view and foreshortened in the top and side views. The top and bottom edges

The edges (represented by lines) bounding a surface may, because of the shape or position of the object, also be in a simple position or inclined to the planes of projection. A line in, or parallel to, a plane of projection takes its name from the plane. Thus a *horizontal line* is a line in a horizontal plane, a *frontal line* is a line in a frontal plane,

Intersection of two surfaces

Edge view of surface
Surface Limit

LEGEND
• *Edge view of surface* ○ *Intersection of two surfaces*
△ *Surface Limit*

FIG. 5.26. What a line indicates.

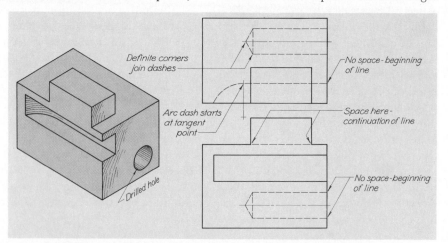

Definite corners join dashes

Arc dash starts at tangent point

Drilled hole

No space - beginning of line

Space here - continuation of line

No space - beginning of line

FIG. 5.27. Dashed-line technique. Note especially that a dashed line begins with a space when it continues in the same direction as a full line.

of the inclined surface appear in true length in top and side views and as points in the front view. The oblique (skew) surface of the object at (*C*) does not show in true shape in any of the views, but each of the bounding edges shows in true length in one view and is foreshortened in the other two views.

5.11. REPRESENTATION OF LINES.

Although uniform in appearance, the lines on a drawing may indicate three different types of directional change on the object. An *edge* view is a line showing the edge of a receding surface that is perpendicular to the plane of projection. An *intersection* is a line formed by the meeting of two surfaces when either one surface is parallel and one at an angle or both are at an angle to the plane of projection. A *surface limit* is a line that indicates the reversal of direction of a curved surface (or the series of points of reversal on a warped surface). Figure 5.26 illustrates the different line meanings, and these are further explained in paragraph 5.45.

5.12. HIDDEN FEATURES.

To describe an object completely, a drawing should contain lines representing all the edges, intersections, and surface limits of the object. *In any view there will be some parts of the object that cannot be seen from the position of the observer, as they will be covered by portions of the object closer to the observer's eye.* The edges, intersections, and surface limits of these hidden parts are indicated by a discontinuous line called a *dashed line.*[6] See the alphabet of lines

[6] The line indicating hidden features has been traditionally known as a "dotted" line. However, in this treatise the term "dashed" line will be used because it accurately describes the appearance of the line. The term "hidden line," also sometimes used, is completely inaccurate because there are no *lines* on the object, and the line indicating hidden features *is* visible on the drawing.

(Figs. 2.56 and 2.57). In Fig. 5.27 the drilled hole[7] that is visible in the right-side view is hidden in the top and front views, and therefore it is indicated in these views by a dashed line showing the hole and the shape as left by the drill point. The milled slot (see Glossary) is visible in the front and side views but is hidden in the top view.

The beginner must pay particular attention to the execution of these dashed lines. If carelessly drawn, they ruin the appearance of a drawing and make it harder to read. Dashed lines are drawn lighter than full lines, of short dashes uniform in length with the space between them very short, about one-fourth the length of the dash. It is important that they start and stop correctly. A dashed line always starts with a dash except when the dash would form a continuation of a full line; in that case a space is left, as shown in Fig. 5.27. Dashes always meet at corners. An arc must start with a dash at the tangent point except when the dash would form a continuation of a straight or curved full line. The number of dashes used in a tangent arc should be carefully judged to maintain a uniform appearance (Fig. 5.28). Study carefully all dashed lines in Figs. 5.27 and 5.29.

[7] See Glossary and Index.

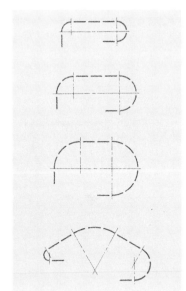

FIG. 5.28. Dashed arcs, actual size.

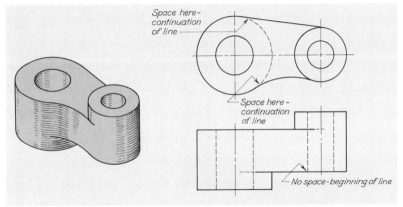

FIG. 5.29. Dashed lines and arcs. Study this figure in conjunction with Figs. 5.27 and 5.28.

FIG. 5.30. Coincident-line study. Coincident lines are caused by the existence of features of identical size or position, one behind the other.

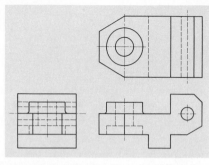

FIG. 5.31. Projection studies. Study each picture and the accompanying orthographic views and note the projection of all features.

5.13. CENTER LINES. In general, the first lines drawn in the layout of an engineering drawing are the center lines, which are the axes of symmetry for all symmetrical views or portions of views: (1) Every part with an axis, such as a cylinder or a cone, will have the axis drawn as a center line before the part is drawn. (2) Every circle will have its center at the intersection of two mutually perpendicular center lines.

The standard symbol for center lines on finished drawings is a fine line made up of alternate long and short dashes, as shown in the alphabet of lines (Figs. 2.56 and 2.57). Center lines are always extended slightly beyond the outline of the view or portion of the view to which they apply. They form the skeleton construction of the drawing; the important measurements are made and dimensions given to and from these lines. Study the center lines in Probs. 5.5.1 to 5.5.21.

5.14. PRECEDENCE OF LINES. In any view there is likely to be a coincidence of lines. Hidden portions of the object may project to coincide with visible portions. Center lines may occur where there is a visible or hidden outline of some part of the object.

Since the physical features of the object must be represented, full and dashed lines take precedence over all other lines. Since the visible outline is more prominent by space position, full lines take precedence over dashed lines. A full line could cover a dashed line, but a dashed line could not cover a full line. It is evident also that a dashed line could not occur as one of the boundary lines of a view.

When a center line and cutting-plane (explained in Chap. 8) line coincide, the one that is more important for the readability of the drawing takes precedence over the other.

Break lines (explained in Chap. 8) should be placed so that they do not spoil the readability of the over-all view.

Dimension and extension lines must always be placed so as not to coincide with other lines of the drawing.

The following list gives the order of precedence of lines:

1. Full line
2. Dashed line
3. Center line or cutting-plane line
4. Break lines
5. Dimension and extension lines
6. Crosshatch lines

Note the coincident lines in Fig. 5.30.

5.15. EXERCISES IN PROJECTION. The principal task in learning orthographic projection is to become thoroughly familiar with the theory and then to practice this theory by translating from a picture of the object to the orthographic views. Figures 5.31 and 5.32 contain a variety of objects shown by a pictorial sketch and translated into orthographic views. Study the objects and note (1) how the object is oriented in space, (2) why the orthographic views given were chosen, (3) the projection of visible features, (4) the projection of hidden features, and (5) center lines.

FIG. 5.32. Projection studies. Study each picture and the accompanying orthographic views and note the projection of all features.

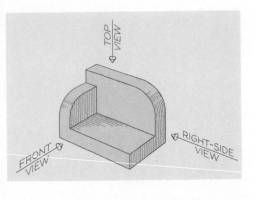

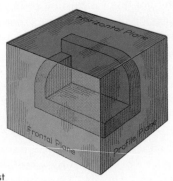

FIG. 5.33. Object orientation. Use the simplest position. It will give the clearest possible representation and be the easiest to draw.

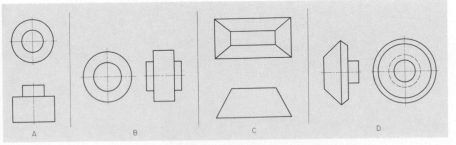

FIG. 5.34. Two-view drawings. These are sufficient for any object having a third view identical with or similar to one of the two views given.

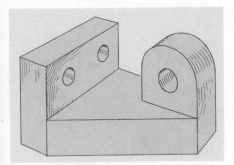

FIG. 5.35. Geometric shapes combined. Even the most complicated objects can be analyzed as combined geometric shapes.

WRITING THE GRAPHIC LANGUAGE

5.16. The major objective of a student of the graphic language is to learn orthographic drawing. In addition to an understanding of the theory of orthographic projection, several aspects of drawing are necessary preliminaries to its study. These have been discussed in the preceding chapters and include skill and facility in the use of instruments (Chap. 2), a knowledge of applied geometry (Chap. 3), and fluency in lettering (Chap. 4). In writing the graphic language, a topic we will now take up, always pay careful attention to accuracy and neatness.

5.17. OBJECT ORIENTATION. An object can, of course, be drawn in any of several possible positions. *The simplest position should be used,* with the object oriented so that the principal faces are perpendicular to the sight directions for the views and parallel to the planes of projection, as shown in Fig. 5.33. Any other position of the object, with its faces at some angle to the planes of projection, would complicate the drawing, foreshorten the object faces, and make the drawing difficult to make and to read.

5.18. SELECTION OF VIEWS. In practical work it is important to choose the combination of views that will describe the shape of an object in the best and most economical way. Often only two views are necessary. For example, a cylindrical shape, if on a vertical axis, would require only a front and top view; if on a horizontal axis, only a front and side view. Conic and pyramidal shapes can also be described in two views. Figure 5.34 illustrates two-view drawings. Some shapes will need more than the three regular views for adequate description.

Objects can be thought of as being made up of combinations of simple geometric solids, principally cylinders and rectangular prisms, and the views necessary to describe any object would be determined by the directions from which it would have to be viewed to see the characteristic contour shapes of these parts. Figure 5.35, for example, is made up of several prisms and cylinders.

If each of these simple shapes is described and its relation to the others is shown, the object will be fully represented. In the majority of cases the three regular views—top, front, and side—are sufficient to do this.

Sometimes two views are proposed as sufficient for an object on the assumption that the contour in the third direction is of the shape that would naturally be expected. In Fig. 5.36, for example, the figure at (A) would be assumed to have a uniform cross section and be a square prism. But the two views *might* be the top and front views of a wedge, as shown in three views at (B). Two views of an object, as drawn at (C), do not describe the piece at all. The object at (A) might be assumed to be square in section, but it could as easily be round, triangular, quarter-round, or of another shape, which should have been indicated by a side view. Sketch several different front views for each top view, Fig. 5.37 A to C.

With the object preferably in its functioning position and *with its principal surfaces parallel to the planes of projection,* visualize the object, mentally picturing the orthographic views one at a time to decide on the best combination. In Fig. 5.38, the arrows show the direction of observation for the six principal views of an object, and indicate the mental process of the person making the selection. He notes that the front view would show the two horizontal holes as well as the width and height of the piece, that a top view is needed to show the contour of the vertical cylinder, and that the cutout corner calls for a side view to show its shape. He notes further that the right-side view would show this cut in full lines, while the left-side view would give it in dashed lines. He ob-

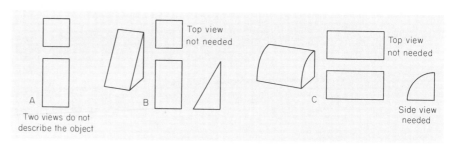

FIG. 5.36. A study of views. Two views do not describe a rectangular object (A), but a wedge shape (B) or quarter round (C) is described by two views.

serves also that neither a bottom view nor a rear view would be of any value in describing this object. Thus he has correctly chosen the front, top, and right-side views as the best combination for describing this piece. As a rule, the side view containing the fewer dashed lines is preferred. If the side views do not differ in this respect, the right-side view is preferred in standard practice.

In inventive and design work, any simple object should be visualized mentally and the view selected without a picture sketch. In complicated work, a pictorial or orthographic sketch may be used to advantage, but it should not be necessary, in any case, to sketch all possible views in order to make a selection.

FIG. 5.37. Top views given. One view does not describe an object unless some additional explanation is given. Sketch several front views for (A), (B), and (C).

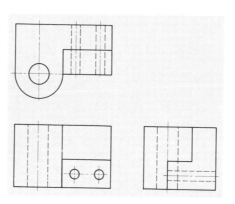

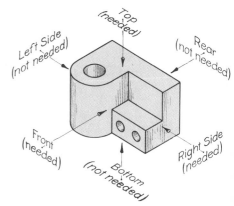

FIG. 5.38. Selection of views. A view must be drawn in each direction (top, front, side) needed to conclusively designate every feature of the object, but unnecessary views must *not* be drawn.

FIG. 5.39. Selection-of-view study.
Determine in each case (*A* to *K*) why
the views shown are the best choice.

Study the drawings in Fig. 5.39 and determine why each view was chosen.

5.19. DRAWING SIZES. Standard sizes for sheets of drawing paper, based on multiples of 8½ by 11 in. and 9 by 12 in., are specified for drawings by the ANSI. Trimmed sizes of drawing paper and cloth, with suitable border and title dimensions, are given in Fig. 19.8.

5.20. SPACING THE VIEWS. View spacing is necessary so that the drawing will be balanced within the space provided. A little preliminary measuring is necessary to locate the views. The following example describes the procedure: Suppose the piece illustrated in Fig. 5.40 is to be drawn full size on an 11- by 17-in. sheet. With an end-title strip, the working space inside the border will be 10½ by 15 in. The front view will require $7^{11}/_{16}$ in., and the side view 2¼ in. This leaves $5^{1}/_{16}$ in. to be distributed between the views and at the ends.

This preliminary planning need not be to exact dimensions, that is, small fractional values, such as $^{15}/_{64}$ in. or $^{31}/_{32}$ in., can be adjusted to ¼ and 1 in., respectively, to speed up the planning. In this case the $7^{11}/_{16}$-in. dimension can be adjusted to 7¾ in.

Locate the views graphically and quickly by measuring with your scale along the bottom border line. Starting at the lower right corner, lay off first 2¼ in. and then 7¾ in. The distance between views can now be decided upon. It is chosen by eye to separate the views without crowding, yet placing them sufficiently close together so that the drawing will read easily (in this case 1½ in.). Measure the distance; half the remain-

FIG. 5.40. Spacing the views on the paper. This is done graphically. Study the text carefully while referring to this figure and go through the steps by laying out the given object on a standard 11- × 17-in. sheet.

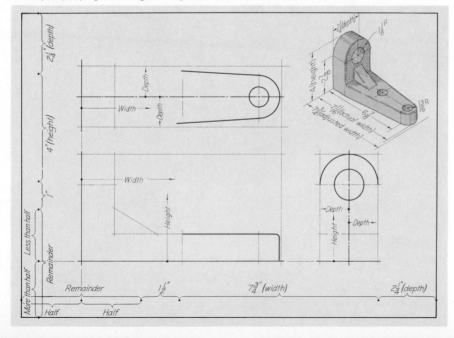

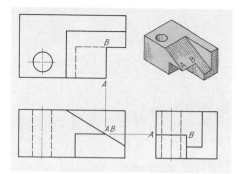

FIG. 5.41. Projection of lines. Carry all views along together. The greatest mistake possible is to try to complete one view before starting another.

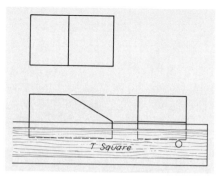

FIG. 5.42. Making a horizontal projection. This is the simplest operation in drawing. The T square provides *all* horizontal lines.

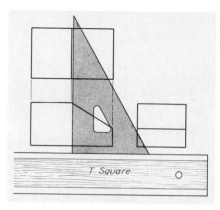

FIG. 5.43. Making a vertical projection. The 90° angle of a triangle with one leg on the horizontal T square produces the vertical.

ing distance to the left corner is the starting point of the front view. For the vertical location: the front view is 4 in. high, and the top view 2¼ in. deep. Starting at the upper left corner, lay off first 2¼ in. and then 4 in.; judge the distance between views (in this case 1 in.), and lay it off; then a point marked at less than half the remaining space will locate the front view, allowing more space at the bottom than at the top for appearance.

Block out lightly the spaces for the views, and study the over-all arrangement, because changes can easily be made at this stage. If it is satisfactory, select reference lines in each view from which the space measurements of height, width, and depth that appear in the view can be measured. The reference line may be an edge or a center line through some dominant feature, as indicated on Fig. 5.40 by the center lines in the top and side views and the medium-weight lines in all the views. The directions for height, width, and depth measurements for the views are also shown.

5.21. PROJECTING THE VIEWS. After laying out the views locate and draw the various features of the object. In doing this, carry the views *along together,* that is, *do not* attempt to complete one view before proceeding to another. Draw first the most characteristic view of a feature and then project it and draw it in the other views before going on to a second feature. As an example, the vertical hole of Fig. 5.41 should be drawn first in the top view, and then the dashed lines representing the limiting elements or portions should be projected and drawn in the front and side views.

In some cases, one view cannot be completed before a feature has been located and drawn in another view. Study the pictorial drawing in Fig. 5.41, and note from the orthographic views that the horizontal slot must be drawn on the front view before the edge *AB* on the slanting surface can be found in the top view.

Projections (horizontal) between the front and side views are made by employing the T square to draw the required horizontal line (or to locate a required point), as in Fig. 5.42.

Projections (vertical) between the front and top views are made by using the T square and a triangle as in Fig. 5.43.

Projections between the top and side views cannot be projected directly but must be measured and transferred or found by special construction. In carrying the top and side views along together, it is usual to transfer the depth measurement from one to the other with dividers, as in Fig. 5.44*A,* or with a scale, as at (*B*). Another method, used for an irregular figure, is to "miter" the points around,

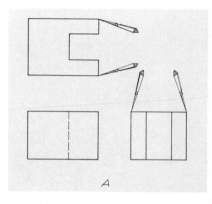

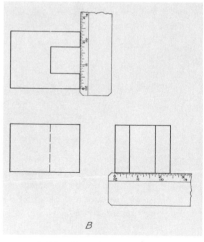

FIG. 5.44. Transferring depth measurements. Depth cannot be projected. Transfer the necessary distances with dividers, as at (*A*), or with scale, as at (*B*).

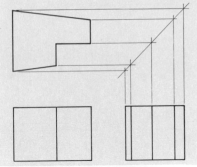

FIG. 5.45. Projecting depth measurements. A "miter line" at 45°, with horizontal and vertical projectors, transfers the depth from top to side view (or vice versa).

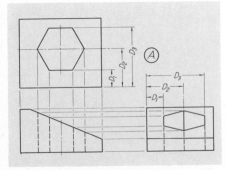

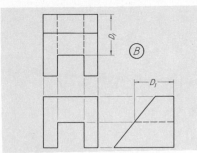

FIG. 5.46. Projections of surfaces bounded by linear edges. Depth measurements cannot be projected directly with T square and triangle. They must be transferred.

using a 45° line drawn through the point of intersection of the top and side views of the front face, extended as shown in Fig. 5.45. The method of Fig. 5.45, however, requires more time and care than the methods of Fig. 5.44 and is, therefore, not recommended.

5.22.   PROJECTIONS OF SURFACES BOUNDED BY LINEAR EDGES. In drawing projections of inclined surfaces, in some cases the corners of the bounding edges may be used, and in other cases the bounding edges themselves may be projected. In illustration of these methods Fig. 5.46A shows a vertical hexagonal hole that is laid out from specifications in the top view. Then the front view is drawn by projecting from the six corners of the hexagon and drawing the four dashed lines to complete the front view. To get the side view, a horizontal projection is made from each corner on the front view to the side view, thus locating the height of the points needed on the side view. Then measurements D_1, D_2, and D_3 taken from the top view and transferred to the side view locate all six corners in the side view. The view is completed by connecting these corners and drawing the three vertical dashed lines. The object in Fig. 5.46B shows a horizontal slot running out on an inclined surface. In the front view the

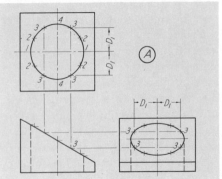

true width and height of this slot is laid out from specifications. The projection to the side view is a simple horizontal projection for the dashed line, indicating the top surface of the slot. To get the top view, the width is projected from the front view and then the position of the runout line is measured (distance D_1) and transferred to the top view.

In summary, it may be stated that, if a line appears at some angle on a view, its two ends must be projected; if a line appears parallel to its path of projection, the complete line can be projected.

5.23.   PROJECTIONS OF AN ELLIPTICAL BOUNDARY. The intersection of a cylindrical hole (or cylinder) with a slanting (inclined or skew) surface, as shown in Fig. 5.47, will be an ellipse, and some projections of this elliptical edge will appear as another ellipse. The projection can be made as shown in Fig. 5.47A by assuming a number of points on the circular view and projecting them to the edge view (front) and then to an adjacent view (side). Thus points 1 to 4 are located in the top view and projected to the front view, and the projectors are then drawn to the side view. Measurements of depth taken from the top view (as D_1) will locate the points in the side view. Draw a smooth curve through the points, using a french curve.

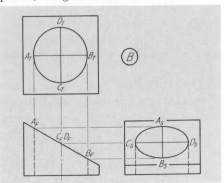

FIG. 5.47. Projection of an elliptical boundary. Points on the curve are projected to determine the curve (A), or the curve is determined by major and minor diameters (B).

For an ellipse on an inclined surface, the projection can also be made by establishing the major and minor diameters of the ellipse, as shown in Fig. 5.47B. A pair of diameters positioned so as to give the largest and smallest extent of the curve will give the required major and minor diameters. Thus, AB will project to the side view as the smaller, or minor, diameter A_sB_s, and CD will project as the larger, or major, diameter C_sD_s. The ellipse can then be drawn by one of the methods of paragraphs 3.50, 3.52, and 3.54.

If the surface intersected by the cylinder is skew, as shown in Fig. 5.48, a pair of perpendicular diameters located in the circular view will give a pair of conjugate diameters in an adjacent view. Therefore, A_TB_T and C_TD_T projected to the front view will give conjugate diameters that can be used as explained in paragraphs 3.51, 3.53, and 3.54 to draw the required ellipse.

In projecting the axes, they can be extended to the straight-line boundary of the skew surface. Thus the line 1–2 located in the front view and intersected by projection of A_TB_T from the top view locates A_FB_F. Similarly, lines 3–4 and 5–6 at the ends of the axis CD locate C_FD_F.

5.24. PROJECTIONS OF A CURVED BOUNDARY.

Any nongeometric curve (or a geometric curve not having established axes) must be projected by locating points on the curve. If the surface is in an inclined position, as in Fig. 5.49A, points may be assumed on the curve laid out from data (assumed in this case to be the top view) and projected first to the edge view (front) and then to an adjacent view (side). Measurements,

such as 1, 2, etc., from the top view transferred to the side view complete the projection. A smooth curve is then drawn through the points.

If the surface is skew, as in Fig. 5.49B, elements of the skew surface, such as $1'$-1, $2'$-2, etc., located in an adjacent view (by drawing the elements parallel to some known line of the skew surface, such as AB) make it possible to project points on the curve 1, 2, etc., to the adjacent view, as shown.

5.25. PROJECTIONS BY IDENTIFYING COR-NERS.

In projecting orthographic views or in comparing the views with a picture, it is helpful in some cases to letter (or number) the corners of the object and, with these identifying marks, to letter the corresponding points on each of the views, as in Fig. 5.50. Hidden points

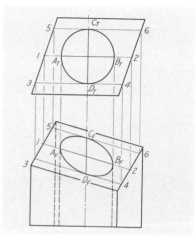

FIG. 5.48. Projection of an elliptical boundary by employing conjugate diameters. Refer to paragraph 3.53 and Fig. 3.68.

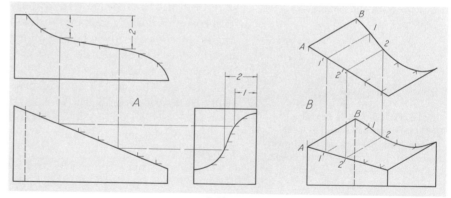

FIG. 5.49. Projection of a curved boundary. Points are plotted and a smooth curve is drawn through them.

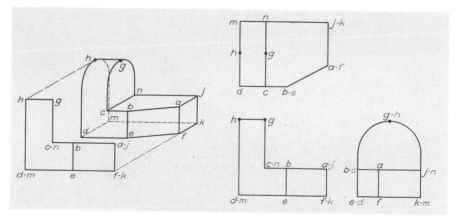

FIG. 5.50. Identified corners. Each corner is lettered (or numbered) as an aid in making projections.

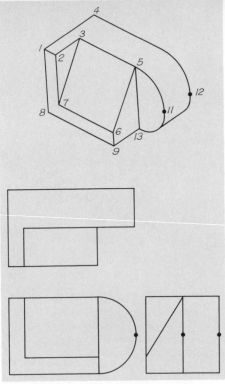

FIG. 5.51. Projection study. Number the corners of the orthographic views to correspond with the numbers on the picture.

FIG. 5.52. Stages in penciling. (*A*) block out the views; (*B*) locate center lines; (*C*) start details, drawing arcs first; (*D*) draw dominant details; (*E*) finish. See text for explanation.

directly behind visible points are lettered to the right of the letter of the visible point, and in this figure, they have been further differentiated by the use of "phantom," or dotted, letters. Study Fig. 5.51, and number or letter the corners of the three views to correspond with the pictorial view.

5.26.   ORDER OF DRAWING.   The order of working is important, as speed and accuracy depend largely upon the methods used in laying down lines. Avoid duplications of the same measurement and keep to a minimum changing from one instrument to another. Naturally, *all* measurements cannot be made with the scale at one time or *all* circles and arcs drawn without laying down the compass, but as much work as possible should be done with one instrument before shifting to another. An orderly placement of working tools on the drawing table will save time when changing instruments. The usual order of working is shown in Fig. 5.52.

1. Decide what combination of views will best describe the object. A freehand sketch will aid in choosing the views and in planning the general arrangement of the sheet.

2. Decide what scale to use, and by calculation or measurement find a suitable standard sheet size; or pick one of the standard drawing-sheet sizes and find a suitable scale.

3. Space the views on the sheet, as described in paragraph 5.20.

4. Lay off the principal dimensions, and then block in the views with light, sharp, accurate outline and center lines. Draw center lines for the axes of all symmetrical views or parts of views. Every cylindrical part will have a center line—the projection of the axis of the piece. Every circle will have two center lines intersecting at its center.

5. Draw in the details of the part, beginning with the dominant characteristic shape and progressing to the minor details, such as fillets and rounds. Carry the different views along together, projecting a characteristic shape, as shown in one view to the other views, instead of finishing one view before starting another. Use a minimum of construction and draw the lines to finished weight, if possible, as the views are carried along. *Do not make the drawing lightly and then "heavy" the lines later.*

6. Lay out and letter the title.

7. Check the drawing carefully.

5.27.   ORDER OF TRACING.   If the drawing is to be traced in ink as an exercise in the use of instruments or for a finished orthographic drawing without dimensions, the order of working is as follows:

1. Place the pencil drawing to be traced on the drawing board, carefully align it with the T square, and put thumbtacks in the two upper corners. Then place the tracing paper or cloth (dull side up) over the drawing. Holding the cloth in position, lift the tacks one at a time and replace them to hold both sheets. Then put tacks in the two lower corners.

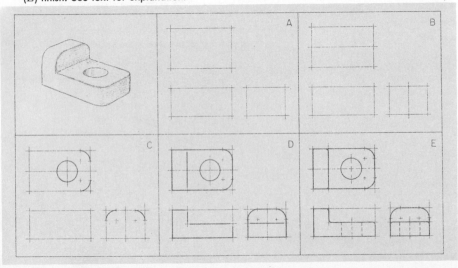

2. To remove any oily film, prepare the surface of the cloth or paper by dusting it lightly with prepared pounce or soft white chalk. *Then wipe the surface perfectly clean with a soft cloth.*

3. Carefully set the pen of the compass to the correct line width, and ink all full-line circles and circle arcs, beginning with the smallest. Correct line weights are given in Fig. 2.57.

4. Ink dashed circles and arcs in the same order as full-line circles.

5. Carefully set the ruling pen to draw a line exactly the same width as the line in the full-line circles. The best way to match the straight lines to the circles is to draw with the compass and ruling pen outside the trim line of the sheet or on another sheet of the same kind of paper and adjust the ruling pen until the lines match.

6. Ink irregular curved lines.

7. Ink straight full lines in this order: horizontal (begin at the top of the sheet and work down), vertical (from the left side of the sheet to right), and inclined (uppermost first).

8. Ink straight dashed lines in the same order. Be careful to match these lines with the lines in the dashed circles.

9. Ink center lines.

10. Crosshatch all areas representing cut surfaces.

11. Draw pencil guide lines and letter the title.

12. Ink the border.

13. Check the tracing for errors and omissions.

5.28. ORTHOGRAPHIC FREEHAND DRAWING.

Facility in making freehand orthographic drawings is an essential part of the equipment of every engineer, and since ability in sketching presupposes some mastery of other skills (as we have seen in Chaps. 1 to 4), practice should be started early. Although full proficiency in freehand drawing is synonymous with mastery of the graphic language and is gained only after acquiring a background of knowledge and skill in drawing with instruments, sketching is an excellent method for learning the fundamentals of orthographic projection and can be used by the beginner even before he has had much practice with instruments. In training, as in professional work, time can be saved by working freehand instead of with instruments, as with this method more problems can be solved in an allotted amount of time.

Although some experienced teachers advocate the making of freehand sketches before practice in the use of instruments, some knowledge of the use of instruments and especially of applied geometry is a great help because the essentials of line tangents, connections, and intersections as well as the basic geometry of the part should be well defined on a freehand drawing. Drawing freehand is, of course, an excellent exercise in accuracy of observation. Figure 5.53 is an example of a good freehand drawing.

FIG. 5.53. A freehand drawing. Note the "roughness" of lines as compared with instrument work, but that all features are concise and readable.

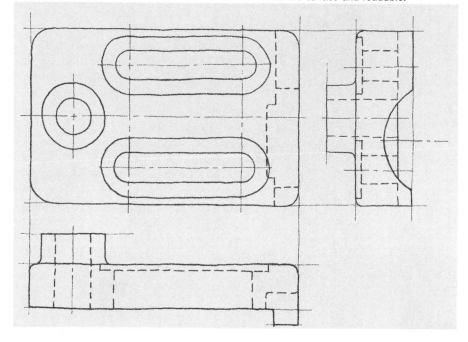

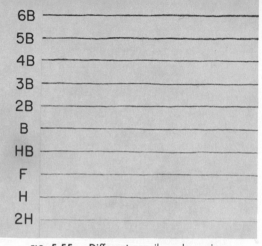

| 6B |
| 5B |
| 4B |
| 3B |
| 2B |
| B |
| HB |
| F |
| H |
| 2H |

FIG. 5.54. Different pencil grades, using medium pressure on paper of medium texture.

FIG. 5.55. Different pencil grades, using firm pressure on paper of medium texture.

5.29. LINE QUALITY FOR FREEHAND WORK. Freehand drawings are made on a wide variety of papers, ranging from inexpensive notebook or writing grades to the finer drawing and tracing papers and even pencil cloth. The surface texture—smooth, medium, or rough—combined with the grade of pencil and pressure used will govern the final result. If a bold rough effect is wanted for a scheming or idea sketch, a soft pencil and possibly rough paper would be employed. For a working sketch or for representation of an object with much small or intricate detail, a harder pencil and smoother paper would help to produce the necessary line quality.

Figure 5.54 is a photograph (reproduced about half size) showing lines made with pencils of various grades with medium pressure on paper of medium texture. Note that the 6B pencil gives a rather wide and rough line. As the hardness increases from 5B to 4B, etc., up to 2H, the line becomes progressively narrower and lighter in color. This does not mean that a wide line cannot be made with a fairly hard pencil, but with ordinary sharpening and with uniform pressure the softer grades wear down much faster than the harder grades. Unless a soft pencil such as 6B, 5B, or 4B is

sharpened after each short stroke, fine lines are impossible. Also, the harder grades such as F, H, and 2H, once sharpened, will hold their point for some time, and fairly fine lines can be obtained without much attention to the point. With ordinary pressure and normal use the soft grades give bold rough results, and the harder grades give light smooth lines.

5.30. RANGE OF PENCIL GRADES. The 6B grade is the softest pencil made and gives black, rough lines. With normal pressure, the line erases easily but is likely to leave a slight smear. The 6B, 5B, and 4B pencils should be used when a rather rough line is wanted, for example, for scheming or idea sketches, architectural renderings, and illustrations. The range from 3B to HB, inclusive, is usually employed for engineering sketches on medium-textured paper. For example, a sketch of a machine part with a normal amount of small detail can be made effectively with a 2B or B pencil. The smoothness and easy response to variations in pressure make these grades stand out as the preferred grades for a wide variety of work. However, for more critical work where there is much detail and also where the smear-

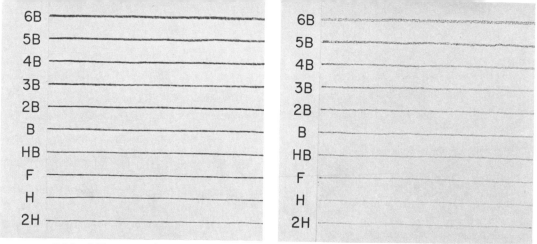

FIG. 5.56. Different pencil grades, using firm pressure on smooth paper.

FIG. 5.57. Different pencil grades, using firm pressure on rough paper.

ing of the soft grades is objectionable, the grades from F to 2H are used. For a sketch on fairly smooth paper, F or H are quite satisfactory. Grades harder than 2H are rarely used for freehand work. Incidentally, a fine pencil for ordinary writing is the 2B grade.

5.31. SHARPENING THE PENCIL. The pencil should be sharpened to a fairly long, conic point, as explained in paragraph 2.24. However, for freehand work a point not quite so sharp as for instrument drawing gives the desired line width without too much pressure. If after sharpening in the regular way the point is too fine, it can be rounded off slightly on a piece of scratch paper before use on the drawing.

5.32. PENCIL PRESSURE AND PAPER TEXTURE. The pencil grade, pressure, and paper texture all have an effect on the final result. Figure 5.54 shows the various pencil grades with medium pressure on paper of medium texture. To mark the difference in line quality obtainable by increasing the pressure, Fig. 5.55 shows the same paper but with firm pressure on the pencil. Note that the lines in Fig. 5.55 are much blacker than those in Fig. 5.54. The line quality of

Fig. 5.55 is about right for most engineering sketches. The rather firm opaque lines are preferred to the type in Fig. 5.54, especially if reproductions, either photographic or by transparency process, are to be made from the sketch.

To show the difference in line quality produced by paper texture, Fig. 5.56 shows the same firm pressure used in Fig. 5.55, but this time on smooth paper. In Fig. 5.57 the same pressure has been used on rough paper. Figure 5.58 is given to aid in comparing the effect of pressure and texture. On the left is the medium pressure on medium-textured paper; at (A), (B), and (C) firm pressure

FIG. 5.58. Comparison of different pencil pressures and paper surfaces. Medium pressure on medium paper—left column. Firm pressure on medium paper at (A), on smooth at (B), and on rough at (C).

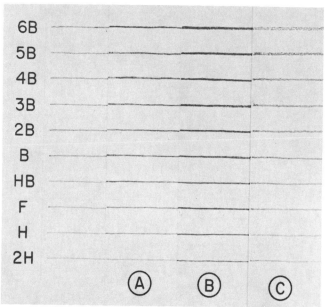

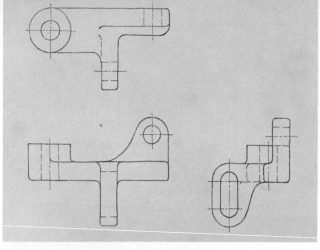

FIG. 5.59. A freehand drawing on plain paper. This drawing was made by an expert of long experience. More "roughness" or "waviness" of lines is permissible on freehand than on instrument drawings, but care should be taken to keep all details concise and readable.

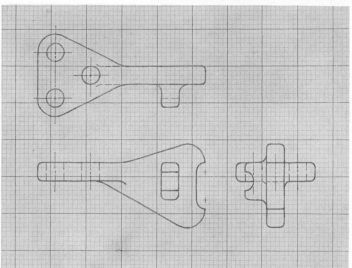

FIG. 5.60. A freehand drawing on coordinate tracing paper. The coordinates, on the back of the paper, aid greatly in making projections, in keeping the right proportions, and in drawing straight and accurate lines.

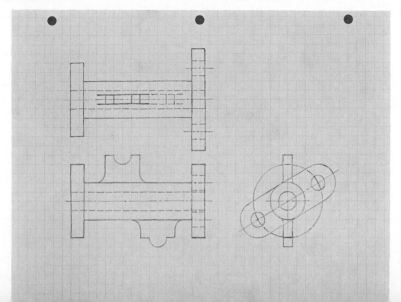

has been used but at (*A*) on medium-, at (*B*) on smooth-, and at (*C*) on rough-textured paper.

5.33. KINDS OF PAPER. *Plain and Co-ordinate.* Sketches are made for many purposes and under a variety of circumstances, and as a result on a number of different paper types and surfaces. A field engineer in reporting information to the central office may include a sketch made on notebook paper or a standard letterhead. On the other hand, a sketch made in the home office may be as important as any instrument drawing and for this reason may be made on good-quality drawing or tracing paper and filed and preserved with other drawings in a set. Figure 5.59 is an example of a sketch made on plain paper, which might be the letterhead paper of the field engineer or a piece of fine drawing or tracing paper. The principal difficulty in using plain paper is that proportions and projections must be estimated by eye. A good sketch on plain paper requires better-than-average ability and experience. Use of some variety of co-ordinate paper is a great aid in producing good results. There are many kinds of paper and coordinate divisions available, from smooth to medium texture and coordinate divisions of ⅛ or ⅒ to ½ in., printed on tracing paper or various weights of drawing paper. Usually one coordinate size on tracing paper and another (or the same) on drawing paper will supply the needs of an engineering office. Figure 5.60 is an example of a sketch on paper with coordinate divisions of ⅛ in. Figure 5.61 has divisions of ¼ in. Figure 5.62 is a sketch made on ¼-in. coordinate paper, actual size.

FIG. 5.61. A freehand drawing on coordinate notebook paper. Coordinates are ¼ in. apart.

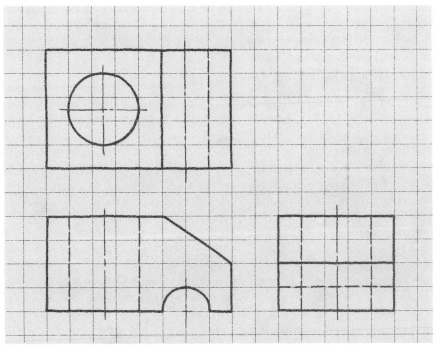

FIG. 5.62. A freehand drawing on coordinate paper (actual size). Note the bold but concise technique.

FIG. 5.63. Sketching a vertical line. Draw downward with finger movement, overlapping the strokes for long lines.

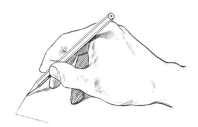

FIG. 5.64. Sketching a horizontal line. Draw from left to right with wrist pivot for short lines and forearm movement for long lines. Overlap strokes if necessary.

The paper type, tracing or regular, is another factor to be considered. Reproduction by any of the transparency methods demands the use of tracing paper. If coordinate paper is used, it may be desirable to obtain prints on which the coordinate divisions do not show. Figure 5.60 is an example of a sketch on tracing paper with the coordinate divisions printed on the back of the paper in faint purplish-blue ink. Since the divisions are on the back, erasures and corrections can be made without erasing the coordinate divisions. Normally the divisions will not reproduce, so prints give the appearance of a sketch made on plain paper. Figure 5.61 is a sketch on standard, three-hole notebook paper with ¼-in. divisions in pale blue ink.

The use of coordinate paper is a great aid in freehand drawing, and speeds up the work considerably. Projections are much easier to make on it than on plain paper, and to transfer distances from top to side view, the divisions can be counted.

5.34. TECHNIQUE. The pencil is held with freedom and not close to the point. Vertical lines are drawn downward with a finger movement in a series of overlapping strokes, the hand somewhat in the position of Fig. 5.63. Horizontal lines are drawn with the hand shifted to the position of Fig. 5.64, using a wrist motion for short lines and a forearm motion for longer ones. In drawing any straight line between two points, *keep your eyes on the point to which the line is to go rather than on the point of the pencil.* Do not try to draw the whole length of a line in a single stroke. It may be helpful to draw a very light line first, as in

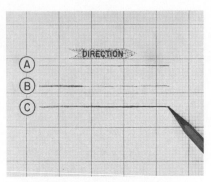

FIG. 5.65. Technique of sketching lines. (*A*) set direction with a *light* construction line; (*B*) first stroke; (*C*) complete line with a series of overlapping strokes.

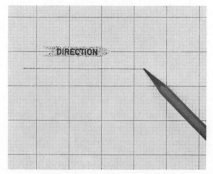

FIG. 5.66. Sketching a horizontal line. Draw from left to right.

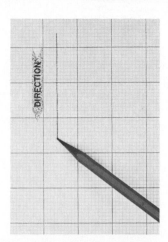

FIG. 5.67. Sketching a vertical line. Draw from top to bottom.

Fig. 5.65*A,* and then to sketch the finished line, correcting the direction of the light line and bringing the line to final width and blackness by using strokes of convenient length, as at (*B*). The finished line is shown at (*C*). Do not be disturbed by any nervous waviness. Accuracy of direction is more important than smoothness of line.

5.35. STRAIGHT LINES. Horizontal lines are drawn from left to right as in Fig. 5.66, vertical lines from top to bottom as in Fig. 5.67.

Inclined lines running downward from right to left (Fig. 5.68) are drawn with approximately the same movement as vertical lines, but the paper may be turned and the line drawn as a vertical (Fig. 5.69).

Inclined lines running downward from left to right (Fig. 5.70) are the hardest to draw because the hand is in a somewhat awkward position; for this reason, the paper should be turned and the line drawn as a horizontal, as in Fig. 5.71.

The sketch paper can easily be turned

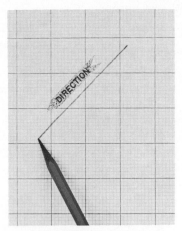

FIG. 5.68. Sketching an inclined line sloping downward from right to left. This line may be drawn in either direction, whichever is more convenient by personal preference.

in any direction to facilitate drawing the lines because there is no necessity to fasten the paper to a drawing-table top. The paper may, of course, be taped to a drawing board or attached to a clip board.

It is legitimate in freehand drawing to make long vertical or horizontal lines using the little finger as a guide along the edge of the pad or clip board. The three important things about a straight line are that it (1) be essentially straight, (2) be the right length, and (3) go in the right direction.

5.36 CIRCLES. Circles can be drawn by marking the radius on each side of the center lines. A more accurate method is to draw two diagonals in addition to the center lines and mark points equidistant from the center of the eight radii; at these points, draw short arcs perpendicular to the radii, and then complete the circle as shown in Fig. 5.72. A modification is to use a slip of paper as a trammel. Large circles can be done smoothly, after a little practice, by using the third or fourth finger as a

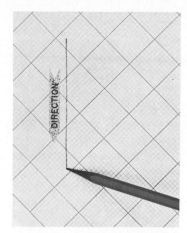

FIG. 5.69. Turning the paper to sketch an inclined line as a vertical line. This is often a great help because of the awkward position of the inclined line. An alternate turn is to the position of Fig. 5.71.

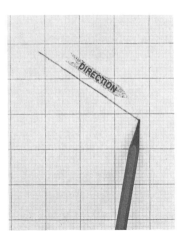

FIG. 5.70. Sketching an inclined line sloping downward from left to right. This is the most awkward position of any line. The paper should be turned as in Fig. 5.71 to aid in obtaining a smooth, accurate line.

FIG. 5.71. Paper turned to sketch an inclined line as a horizontal line. This should be done especially for the type of line shown in Fig. 5.70.

pivot, holding the pencil stationary and rotating the paper under it, or by holding two pencils and using one as a pivot about which to rotate the paper. Another way of drawing a circle is to sketch it in its circumscribing square.

5.37.   PROJECTION. In making an orthographic sketch, remember and apply the principles of projection and applied geometry. Sketches are *not* made to scale but are made to show fair proportions of objects sketched. It is legitimate, however, when coordinate paper is used, to count the spaces or rulings as a means of proportioning the views and as an aid in making projections. Take particular care to have the various details of the views in good projection from view to view. It is an inexcusable mistake to have a detail sketched to a different size on one view from that on another.

When working on plain paper, projections between the top and front views or between the front and side views are easily made by simply "sighting" between the views or using *very* light construction lines, as in Fig. 5.73. Projections between the top and

FIG. 5.72. Method of drawing freehand circles. (*A*) draw center lines; (*B*) draw diagonals; (*C*) space points on the circle with *light*, short lines (by eye); (*D*) correct and begin filling in; (*E*) finish.

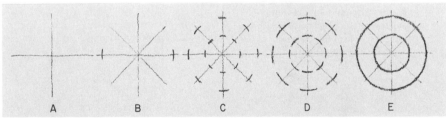

side views are laid off by judging the distance by eye, by measuring the distance by holding the finger at the correct distance from the end of the pencil and transferring to the view, or by marking the distance on a small piece of paper and transferring to the view. Note in Fig. 5.73 that distances *A, B,* and others could be transferred from the top to the side view by the methods just mentioned.

Even though freehand lines are somewhat "wavy" and not so accurate in position as ruled lines, a good freehand drawing should present the same clean appearance as a good instrument drawing.

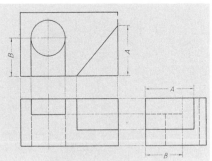

FIG. 5.73. Freehand projections. Judge the projections by eye (aided by coordinate lines if lined paper is used). Judge the measurements (*A* and *B*) by eye; or measure the distances with a pencil or by marking on a strip of paper.

5.38. **METHOD.** Practice in orthographic freehand drawing should be started by drawing the three views of a number of simple pieces, developing the technique and the ability to "write" the orthographic language, while exercising the constructive imagination in visualizing the object by looking at the three projections. Observe the following order of working:

1. Study the pictorial sketch and decide what combination of views will best describe the shape of the piece.

2. Block in the views, as in Fig. 5.74*A,* using a very light stroke of a soft pencil (2B, B, HB, or F) and spacing the views so as to give a well-balanced appearance to the drawing.

3. Build up the detail in each view, carrying the three views along together as at (*B*).

4. Brighten the outline of each view with bold strokes as at (*C*).

5. Brighten the detail with bold strokes, thus completing the full lines of the sketch as at (*D*).

6. Sketch in all dashed lines, using a stroke of medium weight and making them lighter than the full lines, as at (*E*), thus completing the shape description of the object.

7. Check the drawing carefully. Then cover the pictorial sketch and visualize the object from the three views.

After drawing a number of simple pieces freehand, try more complicated problems such as Probs. 5.2.9 to 5.2.37. Faintly ruled coordinate paper (illustrated in Fig. 5.60) may be used if desired.

5.39 **SHOP PROCESSES.** Shop processes are properly a part of dimensioning and specification for working drawings and in this text are given in Chap. 17, following dimensioning and tolerancing, screw threads and fasteners. However, in order to read the pictorial drawings (problems) to be drawn in orthographic projection, some knowledge of processing fundamentals is necessary. Therefore, Chaps. 17 and 19 should be studied, especially for a knowledge of hole processing (drilling, reaming, etc.) and for information on fillets, rounds, finished surfaces, and methods of part manufacture. Consult the Glossary for unfamiliar terms.

5.40. **DIMENSIONING SYSTEMS.** For the same reasons given in the previous paragraph, some knowledge of dimensioning systems is necessary at this time. Basically, two methods are used: fractional and decimal. These are explained in Chap. 15, paragraph 15.12. Note especially that a decimally dimensioned part is laid out with a decimal scale.

FIG. 5.74. Stages in making an orthographic freehand drawing. (*A*) block in view spaces; (*B*) locate principal features with light lines; (*C*), (*D*), and (*E*) finish progressively to final weight, working from dominant to smaller details.

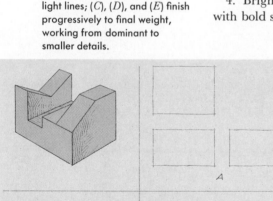
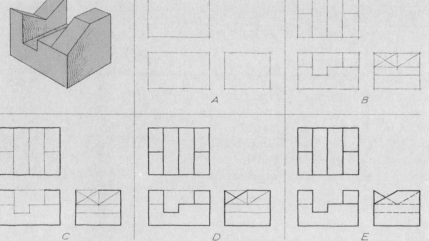

READING THE GRAPHIC LANGUAGE

5.41.   ORTHOGRAPHIC READING.   The engineer must be able to *read* and *write* the orthographic language. The necessity of learning to read is absolute because everyone connected with technical industry must be able to read a drawing without hesitation or concede technical illiteracy.

Reading the orthographic language is a mental process; a drawing is not read aloud. To describe even a simple object with words is almost impossible. Reading proficiency develops with experience, as similar conditions and shapes occur so often that a person in the field gradually acquires a background of knowledge that enables him to visualize readily the shapes shown. Experienced readers read quickly because they can draw upon their knowledge and recognize familiar shapes and combinations without hesitation. However, reading a drawing should always be done carefully and deliberately, as a whole drawing cannot be read at a glance any more than a whole page of print.

5.42.   PREREQUISITES AND DEFINITION. Before attempting to read a drawing, familiarize yourself with the principles of orthographic projection, as explained in paragraphs 5.1 to 5.14. Keep constantly in mind the arrangement of views and their projection, the space measurements of height, width, and depth, what each line represents, etc.

Visualization is the medium through which the shape information on a drawing is translated to give the reader an understanding of the object represented. The *ability to visualize* is often thought to be a "gift" that some people possess and others do not. This, however, is not true. Any person of reasonable intelligence has a visual memory, as can be seen from his ability to recall and describe scenes at home, actions at sporting events, and even details of acting and facial expression in a play or motion picture.

The ability to visualize a shape shown on a drawing is almost completely governed by a person's knowledge of the principles of orthographic projection. The common adage that "the best way to learn to read a drawing is to learn how to make one" is quite correct, because in learning to make a drawing you are forced to study and apply the principles of orthographic projection.

Reading a drawing can be defined as *the process of recognizing and applying the principles of orthographic projection to interpret the shape of an object from the orthographic views.*

5.43.   METHOD OF READING.   A drawing is read by visualizing units or details one at a time from the orthographic projection and mentally orienting and combining these details to interpret the whole object finally. The form taken in this visualization, however, may not be the same for all readers or for all drawings. Reading is primarily a reversal of the process of making drawings; and inasmuch as drawings are usually first made from a picture of the object, the beginner often attempts to carry the reversal too completely back to the pictorial. The result is that the orthographic views of an object like those shown in Fig. 5.75 are translated to the accompanying picture, with the thought of the object as positioned in space or

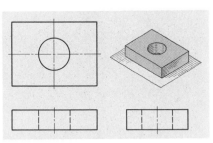

FIG. 5.75.   Orthographic views and picture. Simple objects can be visualized in pictorial form but for complex objects this is difficult.

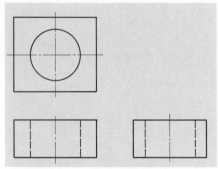

FIG. 5.76. Views to be read. Compare this drawing with Fig. 5.77.

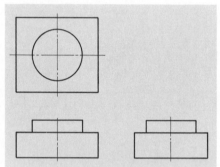

FIG. 5.77. Views to be read. Compare this drawing with Fig. 5.76.

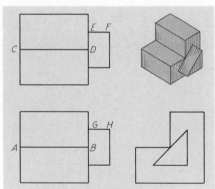

FIG. 5.78. The meaning of lines. *AB, CD,* and *EF* represent the edge views of surfaces. *GH* represents an edge. Study carefully, reading *all* views.

placed on a table or similar surface. Another will need only to recognize in the drawing the geometry of the solid, which in the case of Fig. 5.75 would be a rectangular prism so high, so wide, and so deep with a hole passing vertically through the center of it. This second reader will have read the views just as completely as the first but with much less mental effort.

To most, it is a mental impossibility (and surely unnecessary) to translate more than the simplest set of orthographic views into a complete pictorial form that can be pictured in its entirety. Actually, the reader goes through a routine pattern of procedure (listed in paragraph 5.44). Much of this is done subconsciously. For example, consider the object in Fig. 5.76. A visible circle is seen in the top view. Memory of previous projection experience indicates that this must be a hole or the end of a cylinder. The eyes rapidly shift back and forth from the top view to the front view, aligning features of the same size ("in projection"), with the mind assuming the several possibilities and finally accepting the fact that, because of the dashed lines and their extent in the front view, the circle represents a hole that extends through the prism. Following a similar pattern of analysis, the reader will find that Fig. 5.77 represents a rectangular prism surmounted by a cylinder. This thinking is done so rapidly that the reader is scarcely aware of the steps and processes involved.

The foregoing is the usual method of reading; but how does the beginner develop this ability?

First, as stated in paragraph 5.42, he must have a reasonable knowledge of the principles of orthographic projection.

Second, as described in paragraphs 5.45 and 5.46 he must acquire a complete understanding of the principles behind the meaning of lines, areas, etc., and the mental process involved in interpreting them, as these principles are applied in reading.

There is very little additional learning required. Careful study of all these items plus practice will develop the ability and confidence needed.

5.44. PROCEDURE FOR READING. The actual steps in reading are not always identical because of the wide variety of subject matter (drawings). Nevertheless, the following outline gives the basic procedure and will serve as a guide:

First, orient yourself with the views given.

Second, obtain a general idea of the over-all shape of the object. Think of each view as the object itself, visualizing yourself in front, above, and at the side, as is done in making the views. Study the dominant features and their relation to one another.

Third, start reading the simpler individual features, beginning with the most dominant and progressing to the subordinate. Look for familiar shapes or conditions that your memory retains from previous experience. Read all views of these familiar features to note the extent of holes, thickness of ribs and lugs, etc.

Fourth, read the unfamiliar or complicated features. Remember that every point, line, surface, and solid appears in every view and that you must find the projection of every detail in the given views to learn the shape.

Fifth, as the reading proceeds, note the relationship between the various portions or elements of the object. Such items as the number and spacing of holes, placement of ribs, tangency of surfaces, and the proportions of hubs, etc., should be noted and remembered.

Sixth, reread any detail or relationship not clear at the first reading.

5.45. THE MEANING OF LINES. As explained in paragraph 5.11, a line on a drawing indicates (1) the *edge of a surface,* (2) an *intersection of two surfaces,* or (3) a *surface limit.* Because a line on a view may mean any one of these three conditions, the corresponding part of another view must be consulted to determine the meaning. For example, the meaning of line *AB* on the front view of Fig. 5.78 cannot be determined until the side view is consulted. The line is then found to be the edge view of the horizontal surface of the cutout corner. Similarly, line *CD* on the top view cannot be fully understood without consulting the side view, where it is identified as the edge view of the vertical surface of the cutout corner. Lines *EF* on the top view and *GH* on the front view are identical in appearance. However, the side view shows that line *EF* represents the edge view of the rear surface of the triangular block and that line *GH* is the intersection of the front and rear surfaces of the triangular block.

The top and front views of the objects shown in Figs. 5.78 and 5.79 are identical. Nevertheless, lines *AB* and *CD* in Fig. 5.79 do not represent what they represent in Fig. 5.78 but are in Fig. 5.79 the intersection of two surfaces. Also, lines *EF* and *GH* in Fig. 5.79 are identical in appearance with those in Fig. 5.78, but in Fig. 5.79 they represent the surface limits of the circular boss.

From Figs. 5.78 and 5.79 it is readily seen that a drawing cannot be read by looking at a single view. Two views are not always enough to describe an object completely, and when three or more views are given, all must be consulted to be sure that the shape has been read correctly. To illustrate with Fig. 5.80, the front and top views show what appears to be a rectangular projection on the front of the object, but the side view shows this projection to be quarter-round. Similarly, in the front and side views the rear portion of the object appears to be a rectangular prism, but the top view shows that the two vertical rear edges are rounded.

A shape cannot be assumed from one or two views—*all the views must be read carefully.*

The several *lines* representing one feature must be read in all the views. As an exercise in reading the lines on an orthographic drawing, find *all* the lines representing the hole, triangular prism, slot, and cutoff corner in Fig. 5.81.

5.46. THE MEANING OF AREAS. The term "area" as used here means the contour limits of a surface or combination of tangent surfaces as seen in the different orthographic views. To illustrate, an area of a view as shown in

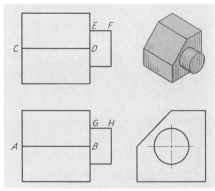

FIG. 5.79. The meaning of lines. *AB* and *CD* represent the intersection of two surfaces. *EF* and *GH* represent a curved-surface limit. Compare this drawing carefully with Fig. 5.78.

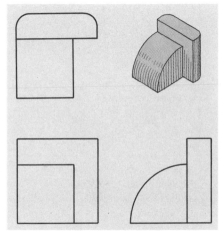

FIG. 5.80. Read all views. Read each feature by looking at all three views; then school yourself to remember all features.

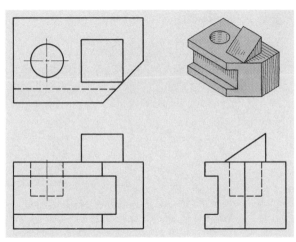

FIG. 5.81. Read all views, features, and lines. This drawing is more complex than Fig. 5.80. Read all features in all views, by reading all lines, then school yourself to remember all features.

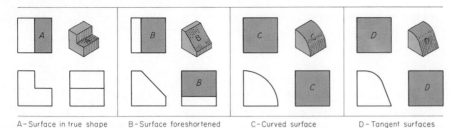

A–Surface in true shape   B–Surface foreshortened   C–Curved surface   D–Tangent surfaces

FIG. 5.82. The meaning of areas. Two views must be read to determine what an area means. Compare *A* with *B* and *C* with *D*.

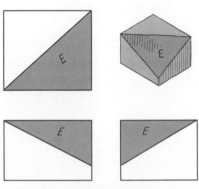

FIG. 5.83. Oblique surface. This will appear as an area in all three principal views.

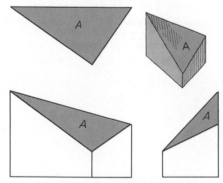

FIG. 5.84. Oblique surface. Note that area *A*, representing this surface, appears in all views as an area of similar shape formed by lines connected in the same order.

Fig. 5.82 may represent (1) a surface in true shape as at *A*, (2) a foreshortened surface as at *B*, (3) a curved surface as at *C*, or (4) a combination of tangent surfaces as at *D*.

When a surface is in an oblique position, as surface *E* of Fig. 5.83, it will appear as an area in all principal views of the surface. A study of the surfaces in Figs. 5.82, 5.83, and others will establish with the force of a rule that *a plane surface, whether it is positioned in a horizontal, frontal, profile, or an inclined or skew position, will always appear in a principal orthographic view as a line or an area.* Principal views that show a skew surface as an area in more than one view will always show it in like shape. As an example, surface *A* of Fig. 5.84 appears as a triangular area in all the principal views; the length of the edges and the angles between the edges may change, but all views show the area with the same number of sides. It should be noted that a plane surface bounded by a certain number of sides can never

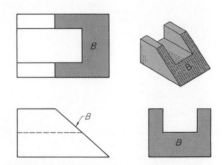

FIG. 5.85. Auxiliary surface. Note that the surface appears as an edge in the front view and as an area of similar shape in top and side views.

appear to have more or fewer sides except when the surface appears as an edge. Moreover, the sides in any view will always connect in the same sequence. For example, in Fig. 5.85 the front view shows surface *B* as an edge; the top and side views show the surface as an area having a similar shape, the same number of sides, and with the corners in the same sequence.

5.47. ADJACENT AREAS. No two adjacent areas can lie in the same plane. It is simple logic that, if two adjacent areas *did* lie in the same plane, there would be no boundary between the areas, and therefore, orthographically, the two adjacent areas would not exist. As an illustration, note that in Fig. 5.86 areas *A, B, C*, and *D* are shown in the front and side views to lie in different planes.

Further proof of these principles is given by Fig. 5.87, in which two top views are shown. By analysis of the projection between top and front views, it is seen that areas *G* and *H* shown in the top views must lie in planes *G* and *H*, respectively, shown in the front view. Also, by projection, it is seen that area *J* of top view *A* must lie in plane *H* and that area *K* must lie in plane *G*. Because areas *H* and *J* lie in plane *H*, and areas *G* and *K* lie in plane *G*, the cor-

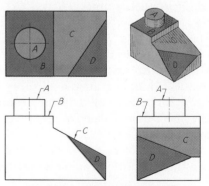

FIG. 5.86. Adjacent areas. *A, B, C*, and *D* all lie in different planes.

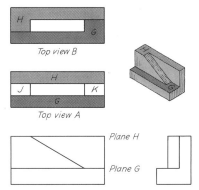

FIG. 5.87. Adjacent areas. Read all areas and note that *B* is the correct top view.

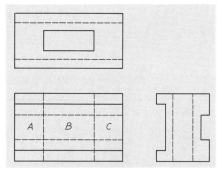

FIG. 5.88. Reading hidden areas. Read all views and note that areas *A, B,* and *C* do not represent three different surfaces.

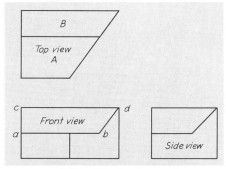

FIG. 5.89. Reading lines and areas. Read this drawing to determine how areas *A* and *B* of the top view are represented in the front and side views.

rect top view, therefore, is top view *B*.

Hidden areas may sometimes be confusing to read because the areas may overlap or even coincide with each other. For example, areas *A, B,* and *C* in Fig. 5.88 are not separate areas because they are all formed by the slot on the rear of the object. The apparent separation into separate areas is caused by the dashed lines from the rectangular hole, which is not connected with the slot in any way.

5.48. READING LINES AND AREAS.

The foregoing principles regarding the meaning of lines and areas must be used to analyze any given set of views by correlating a surface appearing in one view as a line or an area with its representation in the other views, in which it may appear as a line or an area. Study, for example, Fig. 5.89, first orienting yourself with the given views. From their arrangement, the views are evidently top, front, and right-side. An over-all inspection of the views does not reveal a familiar geometric shape, such as a hole or boss, so an analysis of the surfaces is necessary. Beginning with the trapezoidal area *A* in the top view and

then moving to the front view, note that a similar-shaped area of the same width is not shown; therefore, the front view of area *A* must appear as an edge, the line *ab*. Next, consider area *B* in the top view. It is shown as a trapezoidal area (four sides) the full width of the view. Again, going to the front view for a mating area or line, the area *abcd* is of similar shape and has the same number of sides with the corners in projection. Area *abcd,* therefore, satisfies the requirements of orthographic projection and is the front view of area *B*. The side view should be checked along with the other views to see if it agrees. Proceed in this way with additional areas, correlating them one with another and visualizing the shape of the complete object.

Memory and experience aid materially in reading any given drawing. However, every new set of views must be approached with an open mind because sometimes a shape that looks like a previously known condition will crowd the correct interpretation from the mind of the reader. For example, area *E* in Fig. 5.90 is in a vertical position. The front view in Fig. 5.91 is identical with the

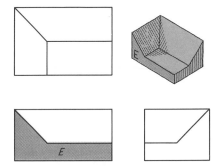

FIG. 5.90. Identical areas may have different meanings. Compare area *E* with area *F* of Fig. 5.91.

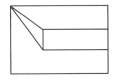
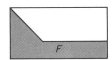

FIG. 5.91. Identical areas may have different meanings. Compare area *F* with area *E* of Fig. 5.90.

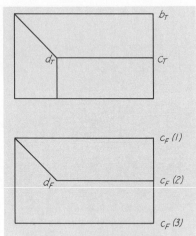

FIG. 5.92. Identification of corners. This helps to determine mating lines and areas in the views.

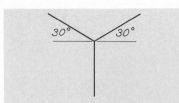

FIG. 5.93. Pictorial axes (isometric). This is the "framework" for sketching in isometric. See Fig. 5.94.

front view in Fig. 5.90, but in Fig. 5.91 the surface *F* is inclined to the rear and is not vertical.

5.49.   READING CORNERS AND EDGES. The corners and edges of areas may be numbered or lettered to identify them in making additional views or as an aid in reading some complicated shape. If there are no coincident conditions, the corners and edges are easily named by projection; that is, the top view is directly over the front view, and the side view lies on a horizontal projector to the front view. When coincident conditions are present, it may be necessary to coordinate a point with an adjacent point as shown in Fig. 5.92. Corner *c* in the front view (c_F) may be in projection with c_T at any one of the three positions marked 1, 2, 3. However, the point *c* is one end of an edge *dc,* and the front view of *c* must therefore be at position 2. An experienced reader could probably make the above observations without marking the points, but a beginner can often gain valuable experience by marking corners and edges, especially if the object he is studying has an unusual combination of surfaces.

5.50.   LEARNING TO READ BY SKETCHING. A drawing is interpreted by mentally understanding the shape of the object represented. You can prove that you have read and understood a drawing by making the object in wood or metal, by modeling it in clay, or by making a pictorial sketch of it. Sketching is the usual method. Before attempting to make a pictorial sketch, make a preliminary study of the method of procedure. Pictorial sketching may be based on a skeleton of three axes, one vertical and two at 30°,[8] representing three mutually perpendicular lines (Fig. 5.93). On these axes are marked the proportionate width, depth, and height of any rectangular figure. Circles are drawn in their circumscribing squares.

Study the views given in Fig. 5.94, following the procedure outlined in paragraph 5.44. Then with a soft pencil (F) and notebook paper make a *very light* pictorial construction sketch of the object, estimating its height, width, and depth and laying the distances off on the axes as at (*A*); sketch the rectangular box that would enclose the piece, or the

[8] Isometric position. Oblique or other pictorial methods may also be used (see Chap. 6).

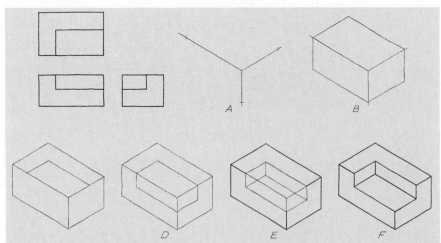

FIG. 5.94. Stages in making a pictorial sketch. (*A*) draw axes; (*B*) block in the enclosing shape; (*C*) and (*D*) draw outline of detail on top, front, and side; (*E*) and (*F*) finish by completing surfaces represented on the orthographic drawing.

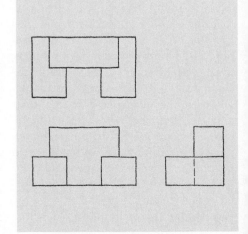

FIG. 5.95. A drawing to be read. This is the object modeled in Fig. 5.96.

block from which it could be cut (*B*). On the top face of this box sketch lightly the lines that occur on the top view of the orthographic drawing (*C*). Note that some of the lines in top views may not be in the top plane. Next sketch lightly the lines of the front view on the front face of the box or block, and if a side view is given, outline it similarly (*D*). Now begin to cut the figure from the block, strengthening the visible edges and adding the lines of intersection where faces of the object meet (*E*). Omit edges that do not appear as visible lines unless they are necessary to describe the piece. Finish the sketch, checking back to the three-view drawing. The construction lines need not be erased unless they confuse the sketch.

5.51.   PICTORIAL DRAWING AND SKETCHING.

The foregoing discussion of pictorial sketching should suffice as a guide for making rough sketches as an aid in reading a drawing. However, many experienced teachers like to correlate orthographic drawing, sketching, and reading, with pictorial drawing (which we will take up in Chap. 6). This is found helpful not only because it gives the student valuable training in understanding all methods of graphic expression but also because the making of a pictorial drawing from an othographic drawing forces the student to read the orthographic drawing.

5.52.   LEARNING TO READ BY MODELING.

Modeling the object in clay or modeling wax is another interesting, and effective aid in learning to read a drawing. It is done in much the same way as reading by pictorial sketching. Some shapes are easily modeled by cutting out from the enclosing block; others, by first

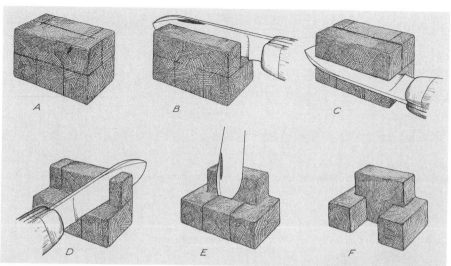

FIG. 5.96.   Stages in modeling. (*A*) score details on top, front, and side; then make cuts at (*B*), (*C*), (*D*), and (*E*) to finish as at (*F*).

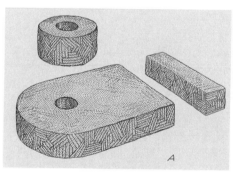

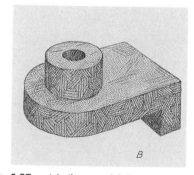

FIG. 5.97.   A built-up model. Separate pieces (*A*) are combined to make the finished model (*B*).

analyzing and dividing the object into its basic geometric shapes and then combining these shapes.

Starting with a rectangular block of clay, perhaps 1 in. square and 2 in. long, read Fig. 5.95 by cutting the figure from the solid. With the point of the knife or a scriber, scribe lightly the lines of the three views on the three corresponding faces of the block (Fig. 5.96*A*). The first cut could be as shown at (*B*) and the second as at (*C*). Successive cuts are indicated at (*D*) and (*E*), and the finished model is shown at (*F*).

Figure 5.97 illustrates the type of

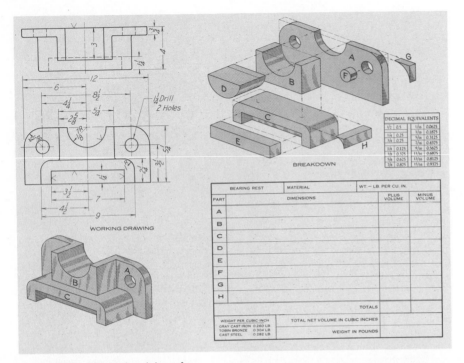

WORKING DRAWING

BREAKDOWN

DECIMAL EQUIVALENTS			
1/2	0.5	1/16	0.0625
1/4	0.25	3/16	0.1875
3/4	0.75	5/16	0.3125
		7/16	0.4375
1/8	0.125	9/16	0.5625
3/8	0.375	11/16	0.6875
5/8	0.625	13/16	0.8125
7/8	0.875	15/16	0.9375

BEARING REST		MATERIAL	WT.— LB. PER CU. IN.		
PART		DIMENSIONS		PLUS VOLUME	MINUS VOLUME
A					
B					
C					
D					
E					
F					
G					
H					
			TOTALS		
WEIGHT PER CUBIC INCH		TOTAL NET VOLUME IN CUBIC INCHES			
GRAY CAST IRON 0.260 LB TOBIN BRONZE 0.304 LB CAST STEEL 0.282 LB		WEIGHT IN POUNDS			

FIG. 5.98. Shape breakdown for volume and weight calculations. Each feature of the object is analyzed individually.

model that can be made by building up the geometric shapes of which the object is composed.

5.53. CALCULATION OF VOLUME AS AN AID IN READING.

To calculate the volume of an object, it must be broken down into its simple geometric elements and the shape of each element must be carefully analyzed before beginning computation. Thus the calculation of volume is primarily an exercise in reading a drawing. Before the computations are completed, the object has usually been visualized, but the mathematical record of the volume of each portion and the correct total volume and weight are proof that the drawing has been read and understood.

The procedure closely follows the usual steps in reading a drawing. Figure 5.98 illustrates the method.

1. Study the orthographic drawing and pick out the principal masses (*A, B,* and *C* on the breakdown and in the pictorial drawing). Pay no attention in the beginning to holes, rounds, etc., but study each principal over-all shape and its relation to the other masses of the object. Record the dimensions of each of these principal portions and indicate plus volume by placing a check mark in the plus-volume column.

2. Examine each principal mass and find the secondary masses (*D* and *E*) that must be added to or subtracted from the principal portions. Bosses, lugs, etc., must be added; cutout portions, holes, etc., subtracted. Record the dimensions of these secondary masses, being careful to indicate plus or minus volume.

3. Further limit the object to its actual shape by locating smaller details, such as holes, fillets, rounds, etc. (parts *F, G,* and *H*). Record the dimensions of these parts.

4. Compute the volume of each portion. This may be done by longhand multiplication or, more conveniently, with a slide rule. Record each volume in the proper column, plus or minus. When all unit volumes are completed, find the net volume by subtracting total minus volume from total plus volume.

5. Multiply net volume by the weight per cubic inch of metal to compute the total weight.

The calculations are simplified if all fractional dimensions are converted to decimal form. When a slide rule is used, fractions *must* be converted to decimals. A partial conversion table is given in Fig. 5.98 and a more complete one in the Appendix.

Complete volume and weight calculation not only gives training in recognition of the fundamental geometric portions of an object but also serves to teach neat and concise working methods in the recording of engineering data.

5.54. EXERCISES IN READING. Figures 5.99 and 5.100 contain a number of three-view drawings of block shapes

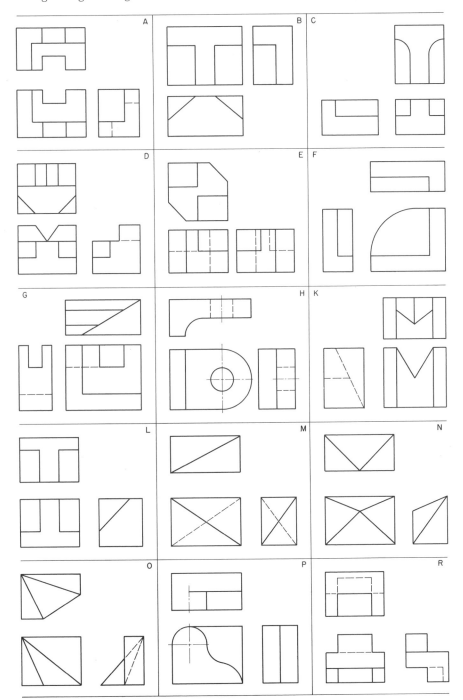

FIG. 5.99. Reading exercises. Read each drawing, (A) to (R). Make pictorial sketches or models if necessary for understanding.

made for exercises in reading orthographic projection and translating into
pictorial sketches or models. Proceed as

described in the previous paragraphs,
making sketches not less than 4 in. over-
all. Check each sketch to be sure that all

FIG. 5.100. Reading exercises. Read
each drawing, (*A*) to (*R*). Make pictorial
sketches or models if necessary for
understanding.

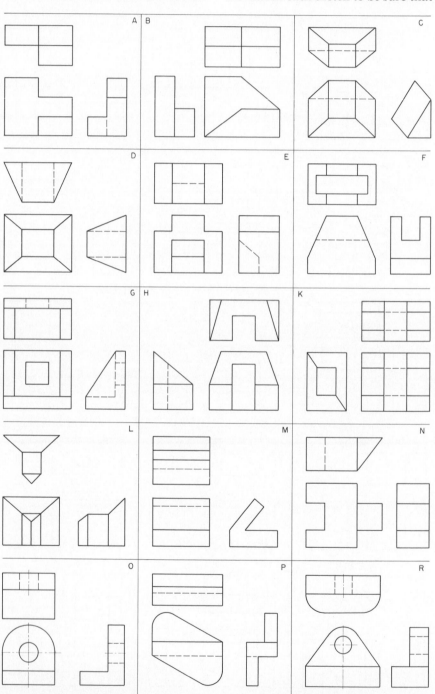

intersections are shown and that the original three-view drawing could be made from the sketch. In each drawing in Fig. 5.101 some lines have been intentionally omitted. Read the drawings and supply the missing lines.

FIG. 5.101. Missing-line exercises. Read each drawing, (A) to (R), and sketch the lines missing on the views. Check carefully. Use a model or sketch, if necessary, as an aid in locating all lines.

PROBLEMS

For practice in orthographic freehand drawing, select problems from the following group.

GROUP 1. FREEHAND PROJECTIONS FROM PICTORIAL VIEWS.

The figures for Probs. 5.1.1 to 5.1.16 contain a number of pictorial sketches of pieces of various shapes which are to be translated into three-view orthographic freehand drawings. Make the drawings of fairly large size, the front view, say, 2 to 2½ in. in length, and estimate the proportions of the different parts by eye or from the proportionate marks shown but without measuring. The problems are graduated in difficulty for selection depending on ability and experience.

Problem 5.1.16 gives a series that can be used for advanced work in freehand drawing or that can be used later on, by adding dimensions, as dimensioning studies or freehand working-drawing problems.

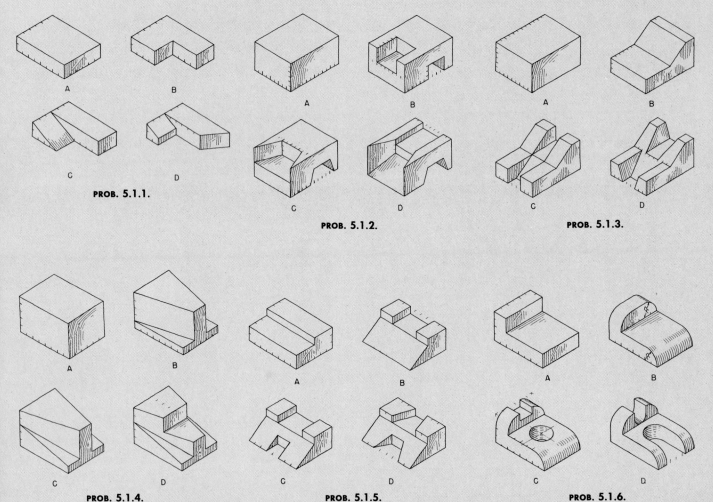

A

B

C

D

PROB. 5.1.1.

A

B

C

D

PROB. 5.1.2.

A

B

C

D

PROB. 5.1.3.

A

B

C

D

PROB. 5.1.4.

A

B

C

D

PROB. 5.1.5.

A

B

C

D

PROB. 5.1.6.

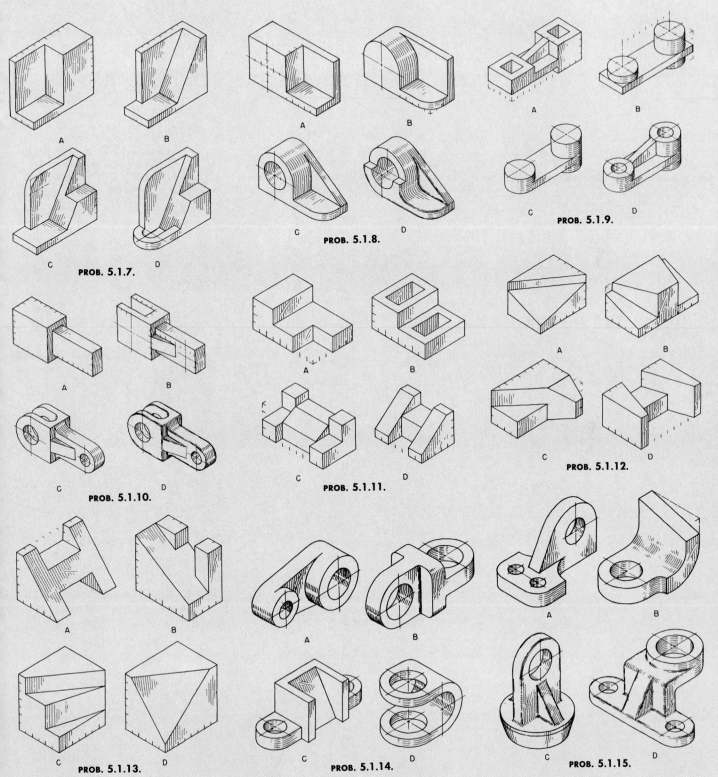

A

B

C

D

PROB. 5.1.7.

A

B

C

D

PROB. 5.1.8.

A

B

C

D

PROB. 5.1.9.

A

B

C

D

PROB. 5.1.10.

A

B

C

D

PROB. 5.1.11.

A

B

C

D

PROB. 5.1.12.

A

B

C

D

PROB. 5.1.13.

A

B

C

D

PROB. 5.1.14.

A

B

C

D

PROB. 5.1.15.

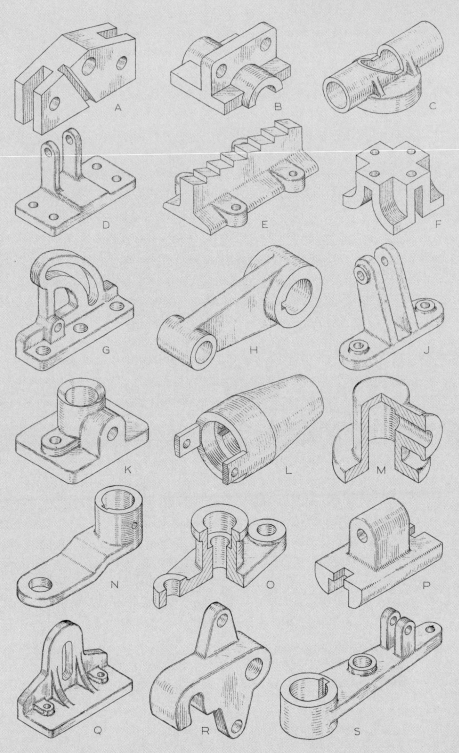

PROB. 5.1.16. Pieces to be drawn freehand in orthographic projection.

Problems

5.1.17. Make a freehand drawing of the end bracket.

5.1.18. Make a freehand drawing of the radar wave guide.

Select problems from the following groups for practice in projection drawing. Most of the problems are intended to be drawn with instruments but will give valuable training done freehand, on plain or coordinate paper.

The groups are as follows:

2. Projections from pictorial views
3. Special scales, decimal sizes, projections from photo drawings, references to Appendix material
4. Views to be supplied freehand
5. Views to be supplied
6. Views to be changed
7. Drawing from memory
8. Volume and weight calculations with slide rule

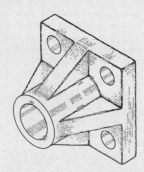

PROB. 5.1.17. End bracket.

PROB. 5.1.18. Radar wave guide.

GROUP 2. PROJECTIONS FROM PICTORIAL VIEWS

5.2.1. Draw the top, front, and right-side views of the beam support.

5.2.2. Draw the top, front, and right-side views of the vee rest.

5.2.3. Draw three views of the saddle bracket.

5.2.4. Draw three views of the wedge block.

5.2.5. Draw three views of the slotted wedge.

5.2.6. Draw three views of the pivot block.

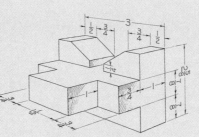

PROB. 5.2.2. Vee rest.

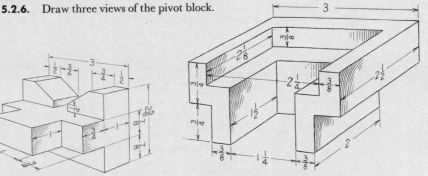

PROB. 5.2.3. Saddle bracket.

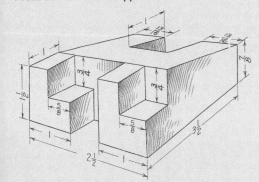

PROB. 5.2.1. Beam support.

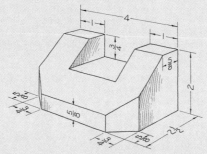

PROB. 5.2.5. Slotted wedge.

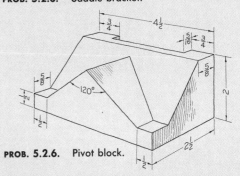

PROB. 5.2.6. Pivot block.

PROB. 5.2.4. Wedge block.

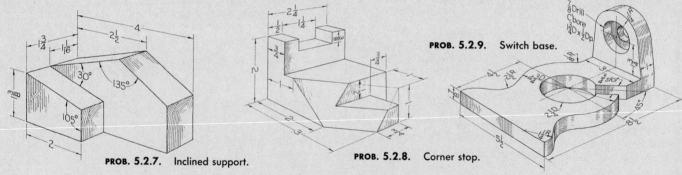

PROB. 5.2.7. Inclined support.

PROB. 5.2.8. Corner stop.

PROB. 5.2.9. Switch base.

5.2.7. Draw three views of the inclined support.

5.2.8. Draw three views of the corner stop.

5.2.9. Draw three views of the switch base.

5.2.10. Draw three views of the adjusting bracket.

5.2.11. Draw three views of the guide base.

5.2.12. Draw three views of the bearing rest.

5.2.13. Draw three views of the swivel yoke.

5.2.14. Draw three views of the truss bearing.

5.2.15. Draw three views of the sliding-pin hanger.

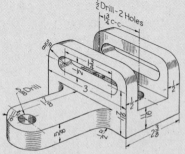

PROB. 5.2.10. Adjusting bracket.

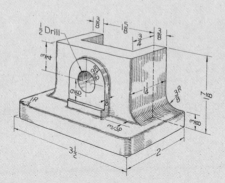

PROB. 5.2.11. Guide base.

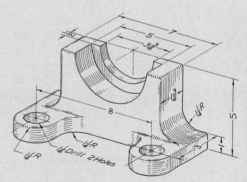

PROB. 5.2.12. Bearing rest.

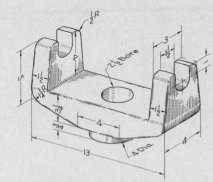

PROB. 5.2.13. Swivel yoke.

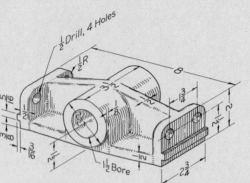

PROB. 5.2.14. Truss bearing.

PROB. 5.2.15. Sliding-pin hanger.

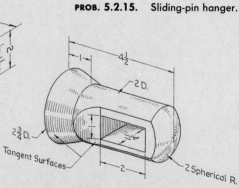

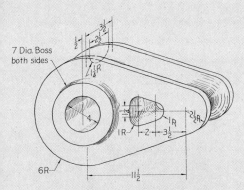

PROB. 5.2.16. Wire thimble.

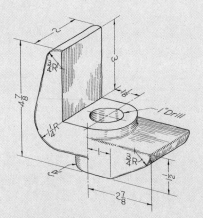

PROB. 5.2.17. Hanger jaw.

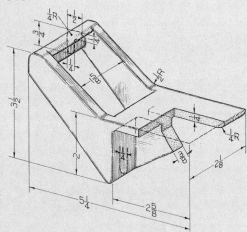

PROB. 5.2.18. Adjustable jaw.

5.2.16. Draw two views of the wire thimble.
5.2.17. Draw three views of the hanger jaw.
5.2.18. Draw three views of the adjustable jaw.
5.2.19. Draw two views of the shifter fork.
5.2.20. Draw three views of the mounting bracket.

5.2.21. Draw three views of the hinged bearing.
5.2.22. Draw two views of the clamp lever.
5.2.23. Draw three views of the bedplate stop.
5.2.24. Draw top, front, and partial side views of the spanner bracket.

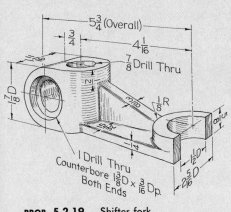

PROB. 5.2.19. Shifter fork.

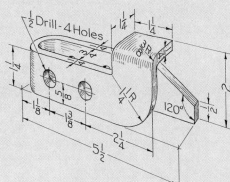

PROB. 5.2.20. Mounting bracket.

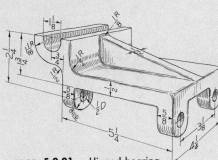

PROB. 5.2.21. Hinged bearing.

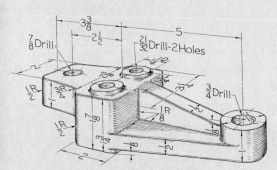

PROB. 5.2.22. Clamp lever.

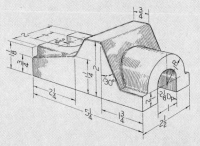

PROB. 5.2.23. Bedplate stop.

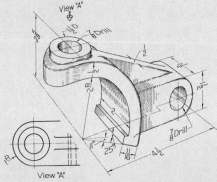

PROB. 5.2.24. Spanner bracket.

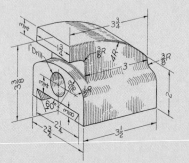

PROB. 5.2.25.   Sliding stop.

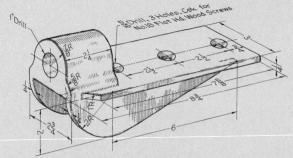

PROB. 5.2.26.   Clamp bracket.

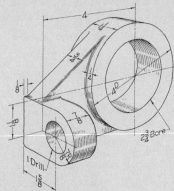

PROB. 5.2.27.   Tube hanger.

5.2.25.   Draw two views of the sliding stop.
5.2.26.   Draw three views of the clamp bracket.
5.2.27.   Draw three views of the tube hanger.
5.2.28.   Draw three views of the gage holder.
5.2.29.   Draw three views of the shaft guide.

5.2.30.   Draw three views of the clamp block.
5.2.31.   Draw three views of the offset yoke.
5.2.32.   Draw three views of the angle connector.
5.2.33.   Draw three views of the buckstay clamp.

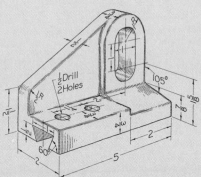

PROB. 5.2.28.   Gage holder.

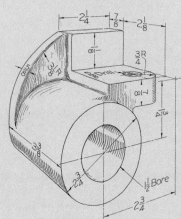

PROB. 5.2.29.   Shaft guide.

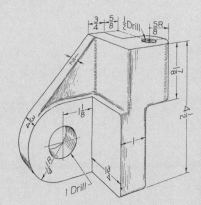

PROB. 5.2.30.   Clamp block.

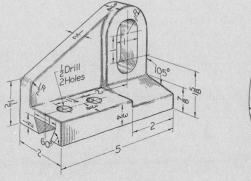

PROB. 5.2.31.   Offset yoke.

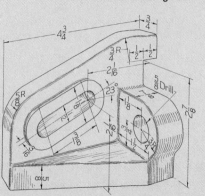

PROB. 5.2.32.   Angle connector.

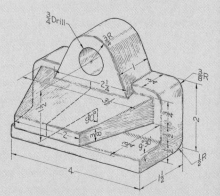

PROB. 5.2.33.   Buckstay clamp.

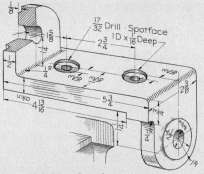

PROB. 5.2.34.   Stop base.

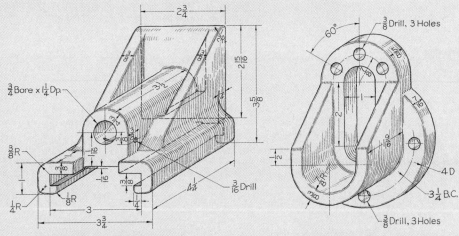

PROB. 5.2.35.   Sliding buttress.

PROB. 5.2.36.   End plate.

5.2.34.   Draw three views of the stop base.
5.2.35.   Draw three views of the sliding buttress.
5.2.36.   Draw two views of the end plate.
5.2.37.   Draw three views of the plastic switch base.
5.2.38.   Draw two views of the pawl hook.
5.2.39.   Draw three views of the step-pulley frame.

PROB. 5.2.39.   Step-pulley frame.

PROB. 5.2.37.   Switch base.

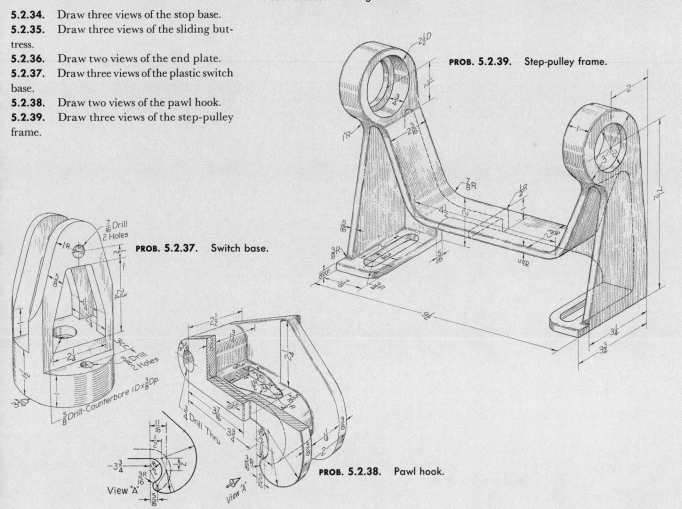

PROB. 5.2.38.   Pawl hook.

GROUP 3.   SPECIAL SCALES, DECIMAL SIZES, PROJECTIONS FROM PHOTO DRAWINGS, REFERENCES TO APPENDIX MATERIAL

The problems in this group (5.3.1 to 5.3.16) will give practice in the use of a decimal scale for layout. The projections from the photo drawings of Chap. 19 are given here not only to serve as problem material, but to acquaint the student with this form of pictorial representation. Details of photo-drawing methods are given in Chap. 22. Wood-screw and bolt sizes are given in the Appendix.

5.3.1.   Draw top, front, and right-side views.
5.3.2.   Draw top, front, and right-side views.
5.3.3.   Draw top, front, and right-side views.
5.3.4.   Draw top, front, and left-side views.
5.3.5.   Draw top, front, and right-side views.
Bend radii and setbacks are 0.10 in.
5.3.6.   Draw top, front, and right-side views.
Screw and bolt sizes are given in the Appendix. Clearance over bolt and screw diameters

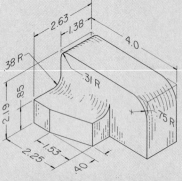

PROB. 5.3.1.   Motor mount.

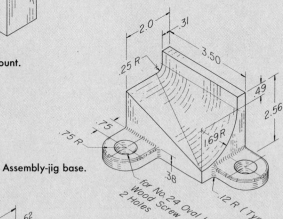

PROB. 5.3.2.   Assembly-jig base.

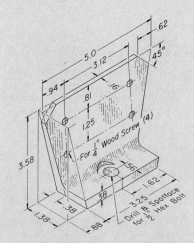

PROB. 5.3.3.   Cargo-hoist tie-down.

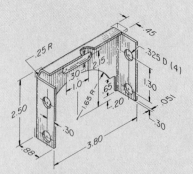

PROB. 5.3.5.   Cover bracket.

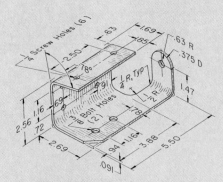

PROB. 5.3.6.   Seat-latch support.

PROB. 5.3.4.   Aileron tab-rod servo fitting.

are necessary in dimensioning but not in drawing the views.

5.3.7. Draw top, front, left-side, and right-side views. Show only *necessary* hidden detail. The 0.44D hole extends through the piece. The limit-dimensioned holes ($.75 \begin{smallmatrix} +0.005 \\ -0.002 \end{smallmatrix}$ and $\frac{.86}{.89}$) are given here as an introduction to precise methods, which will be presented in detail later. Regardless of their dimensional accuracy, features are drawn to their basic size with no more scaled accuracy than for other less accurate features.

5.3.8. Draw top and front views. See Prob. 5.3.7 for comment on limit-dimensioned holes.

5.3.9. Draw top, front, and left-side views. Bolts should have clearance. Undimensioned radii are ¼R.

5.3.10. Draw top and front views. See Prob. 5.3.7 for comment on limit-dimensioned holes.

5.3.11. Draw two views of the conveyor link, Prob. 19.6.1.

5.3.12. Draw necessary views of lift-strut pivot, Prob. 19.6.3.

5.3.13. Draw necessary views of hydro-cylinder support (right- and left-hand), Prob. 19.6.2.

5.3.14. Draw necessary views of length-adjuster tube, Prob. 19.6.4. See Chap. 16 for thread symbol.

5.3.15. Draw necessary views of third terminal, Prob. 19.6.6.

5.3.16. Select a part from the conveyor link assembly, Prob. 19.6.7, and make an orthographic drawing.

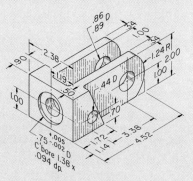

PROB. 5.3.7. Latch bracket.

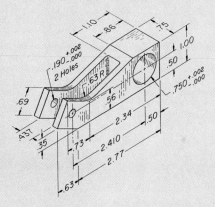

PROB. 5.3.8. Control crank.

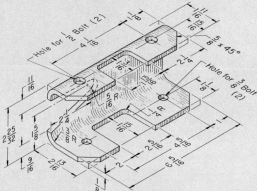

PROB. 5.3.9. Transformer mounting.

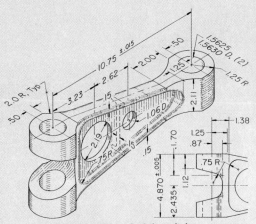

PROB. 5.3.10. Stabilizer link.

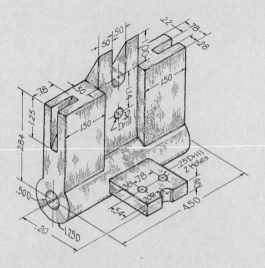

PROB. 5.3.17.   Jet-engine bracket.

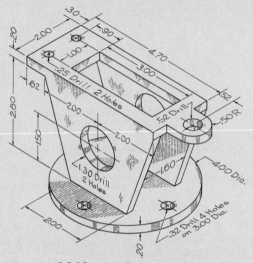

PROB. 5.3.18.   Missile gyro support.

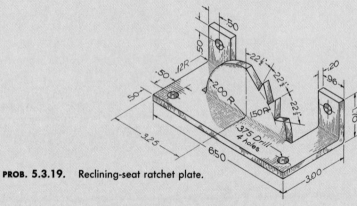

PROB. 5.3.19.   Reclining-seat ratchet plate.

5.3.17.   Make an orthographic drawing of the jet-engine bracket.

5.3.18.   Make an orthographic drawing of the missile gyro support.

5.3.19.   Make an orthographic drawing of the reclining-seat ratchet plate.

5.3.20.   Make an orthographic drawing of the rigging yoke.

5.3.21.   Make an orthographic drawing of the door bracket.

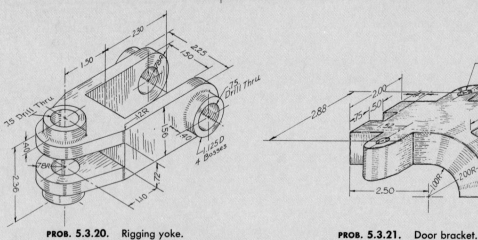

PROB. 5.3.20.   Rigging yoke.

PROB. 5.3.21.   Door bracket.

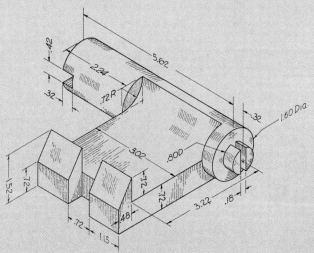

PROB. 5.3.22. Missile release pawl.

5.3.22. Make an orthographic drawing of the missile release pawl.
5.3.23. Make an orthographic drawing of the jet-engine inner-strut bracket.
5.3.24. Make an orthographic drawing of the transmission transfer fork.
5.3.25. Make an orthographic drawing of the reversing fork.

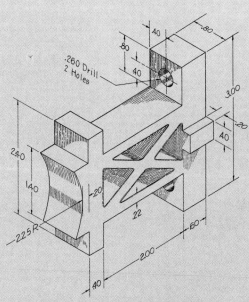

PROB. 5.3.23. Jet-engine inner-strut bracket.

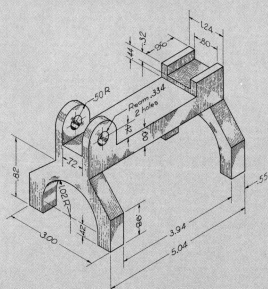

PROB. 5.3.24. Transmission transfer fork.

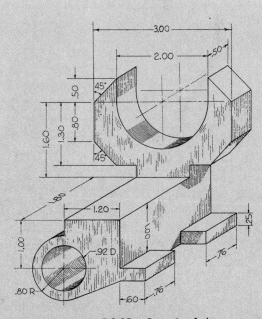

PROB. 5.3.25. Reversing fork.

GROUP 4. VIEWS TO BE SUPPLIED FREEHAND

These problems (5.4.1 to 5.4.3) will give valuable training in reading orthographic views, as well as further practice in applying the principles of orthographic projection.

Study the meaning of lines, areas, and adjacent areas. Corners or edges of the object may be numbered or lettered to aid in the reading or to aid later in the projection.

A pictorial sketch may be used, if desired, as an aid in reading the views. This sketch may be made before the views are drawn and completed or at any time during the making of the drawing. For some of the simpler objects, a clay model may be of assistance.

After the views given have been read and

drawn, project the third view or complete the views as specified in each case.

Remember that every line representing an edge view of a surface, an intersection of two surfaces, or a surface limit will have a mating projection in the other views. Be careful to represent all hidden features and pay attention to the precedence of lines.

The figures in this group contain a number of objects with two views drawn and the third to be supplied. In addition to helping to develop the ability to draw freehand this exercise will give valuable practice in reading. These problems may be worked directly in the book or on plain or coordinate paper.

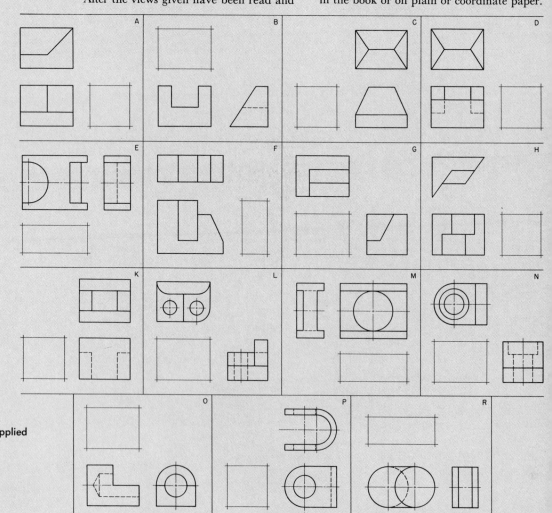

PROB. 5.4.1. Views to be supplied freehand.

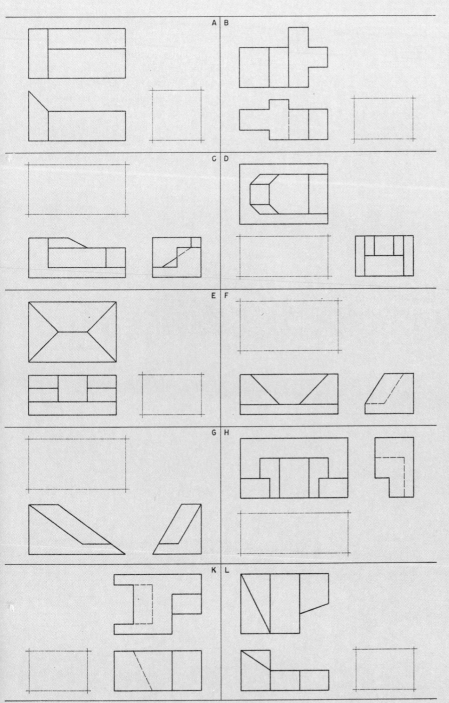

PROB. 5.4.2.   Views to be supplied freehand.

PROB. 5.4.3.   Views to be supplied freehand.

5.4.4.   Given top and front views, add side view. Find at least three solutions. Use tracing paper for the second and third solutions.

5.4.5.   Given front and side views, add top view. Find at least three solutions. Use tracing paper for the second and third solutions.

5.4.6.   Given top and front views, add side view. Find two solutions. Use tracing paper for the second solution.

5.4.7.   Given top and front views, add side view. Find at least three solutions. Use tracing paper for the second and third solutions.

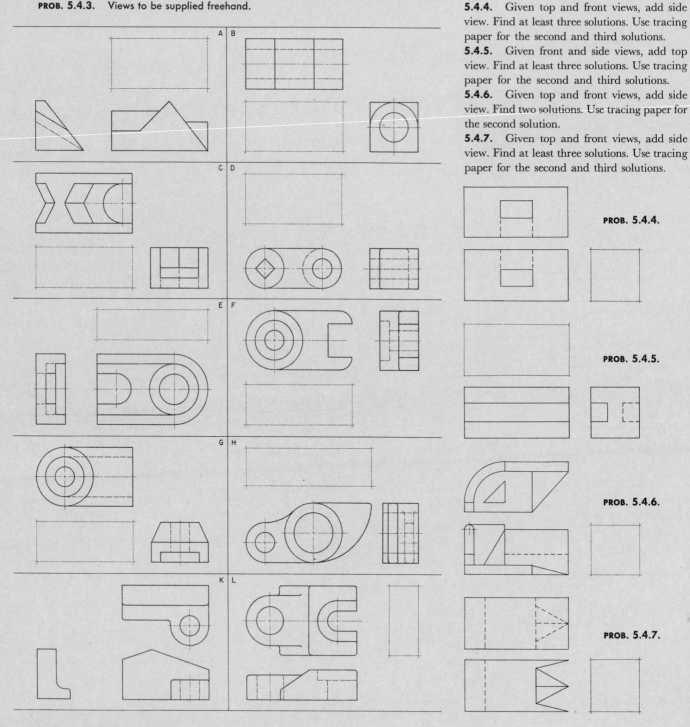

PROB. 5.4.4.

PROB. 5.4.5.

PROB. 5.4.6.

PROB. 5.4.7.

GROUP 5.   VIEWS TO BE SUPPLIED

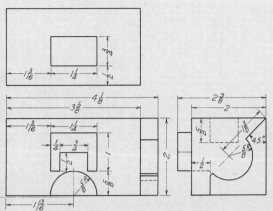

PROB. 5.5.1.   Projection study.

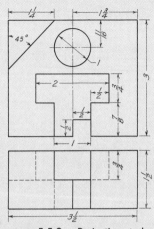

PROB. 5.5.2.   Projection study.

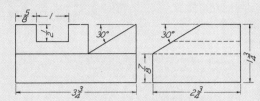

PROB. 5.5.3.   Projection study.

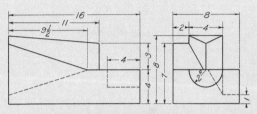

PROB. 5.5.4.   Bit-point forming die.

5.5.1.   Draw the views given, completing the top view from information given on the front and side views. Carry the views along together.

5.5.2.   Given top and front views of the block, add side view. See that dashed lines start and stop correctly.

5.5.3.   Given front and right-side views, add top view.

5.5.4.   Given front and right-side views, add top view.

5.5.5.   Given front and top views, add right-side view.

5.5.6.   Given top and front views, add right-side view.

5.5.7.   Complete the three views given.

5.5.8.   Given front and left-side views, add top view.

5.5.9.   Given front and right-side views, add top view.

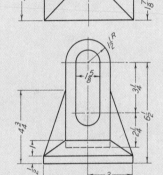

PROB. 5.5.5.   Rabbeting-plane guide.

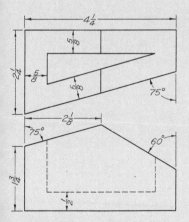

PROB. 5.5.6.   Wedge block.

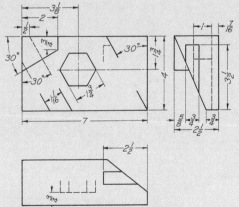

PROB. 5.5.7.   Projection study.

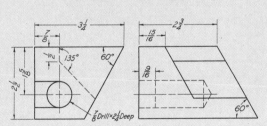

PROB. 5.5.8.   Burner-support key.

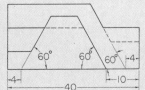
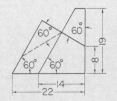

PROB. 5.5.9.   Abutment block.

5.5.10. Given front and top views, add right-side view.

5.5.11. Assume this to be the right-hand part. Draw three views of the left-hand part.

5.5.12. Given front and top views, add side view.

5.5.13. Given front and top views, add side view.

5.5.14. Given top and front views, add left-side view.

5.5.15. Given front and top views, add side view.

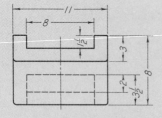

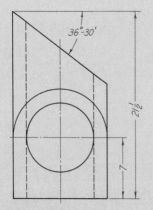

PROB. 5.5.10. Sliding port.

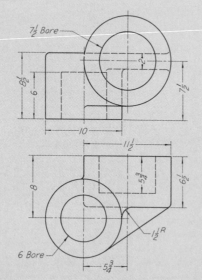

PROB. 5.5.11. Bumper support and post cap.

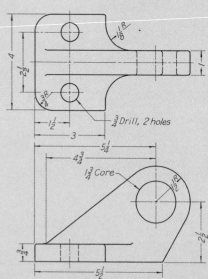

PROB. 5.5.12. Anchor bracket.

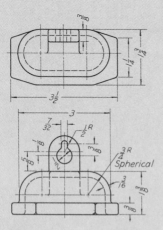

PROB. 5.5.13. Entrance head.

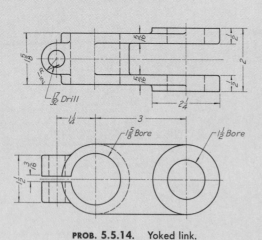

PROB. 5.5.14. Yoked link.

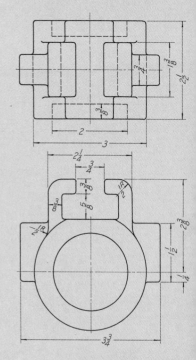

PROB. 5.5.15. Rubber-mounting bracket.

5.5.16. Given front and top views, add side view.

5.5.17. Given front and top views, add side view.

5.5.18. Given top and front views, add side view.

5.5.19. Given top and front views, add left-side view.

5.5.20. Given top and front views, add side view.

5.5.21. Given front and top views, add side view.

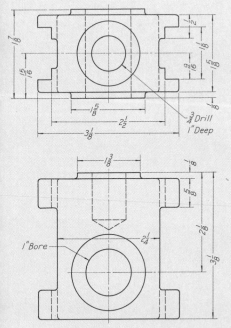

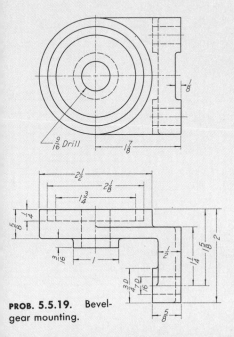

PROB. 5.5.16. Crosshead.

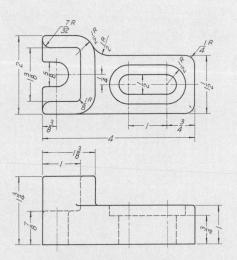

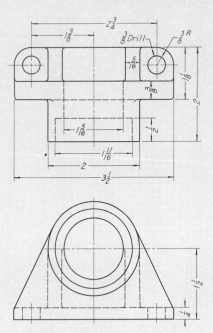

PROB. 5.5.17. Tool holder.

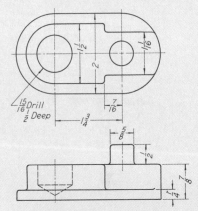

PROB. 5.5.18. Lock plate.

PROB. 5.5.19. Bevel-gear mounting.

PROB. 5.5.20. Cylinder support.

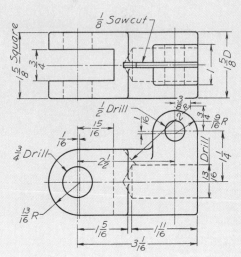

PROB. 5.5.21. Rod yoke.

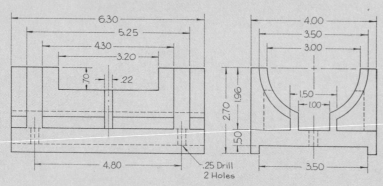

PROB. 5.5.22. Electric-motor support.

5.5.22. Given front and right-side views of electric-motor support. Add top view.

5.5.23. Given front and left-side views of master brake cylinder. Add top view.

5.5.24. Given front and right-side views of end frame for engine starter. Add top view.

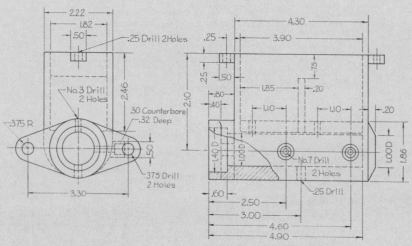

PROB. 5.5.23. Master brake cylinder.

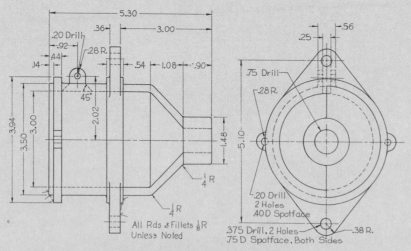

PROB. 5.5.24. End frame for engine starter.

GROUP 6. VIEWS TO BE CHANGED

These problems (5.6.1 to 5.6.6) are given to develop the ability to visualize the actual piece in space and from this mental picture to draw the required views as they would appear if the object were looked at in the directions specified.

In addition to providing training in reading orthographic views and in orthographic projection, these problems are valuable exercises in developing drawing technique. Note that all the problems given are castings containing the usual features found on such parts, that is, fillets, rounds, runouts, etc., on unfinished surfaces. Note also that sharp corners are formed by the intersection of an unfinished and finished surface or by two finished surfaces. After finishing one of these problems, check the drawing carefully to make sure that all details of construction have been represented correctly.

5.6.1. Given front and top views, new front, top, and side views are required, turning the block so that the back becomes the front and the top the bottom. The rib contour is straight.

5.6.2. Given front, left-side, and bottom views, draw front, top, and right-side views.

5.6.3. Given front, right-side, and bottom views, draw front, top, and left-side views.

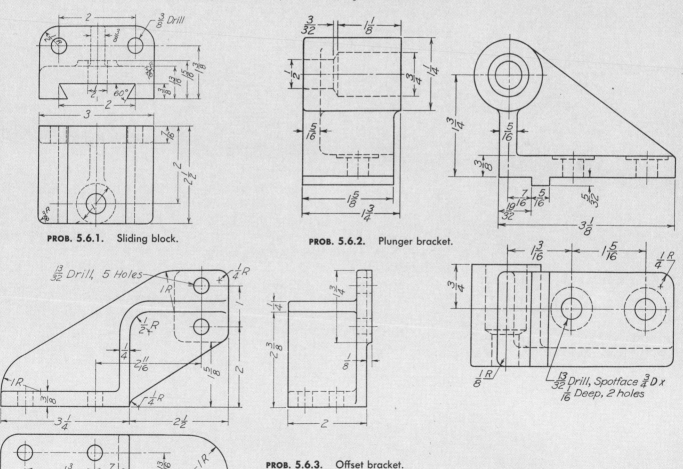

PROB. 5.6.1. Sliding block.

PROB. 5.6.2. Plunger bracket.

PROB. 5.6.3. Offset bracket.

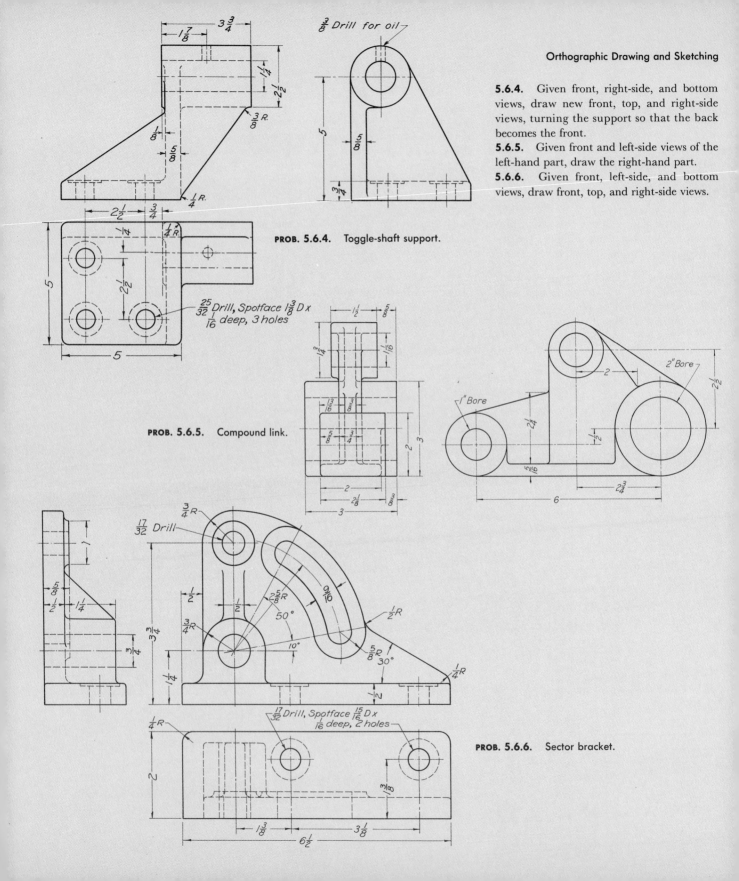

5.6.4. Given front, right-side, and bottom views, draw new front, top, and right-side views, turning the support so that the back becomes the front.

5.6.5. Given front and left-side views of the left-hand part, draw the right-hand part.

5.6.6. Given front, left-side, and bottom views, draw front, top, and right-side views.

PROB. 5.6.4. Toggle-shaft support.

$\frac{3}{8}$ Drill for oil

$\frac{25}{32}$ Drill, Spotface $1\frac{3}{8}$ D x $\frac{1}{16}$ deep, 3 holes

PROB. 5.6.5. Compound link.

1" Bore

2" Bore

PROB. 5.6.6. Sector bracket.

$\frac{17}{32}$ Drill

$\frac{17}{32}$ Drill, Spotface $\frac{15}{16}$ D x $\frac{1}{16}$ deep, 2 holes

5.6.7. Given top and front views of jet-engine hinge plate. Add right- and left-side views.

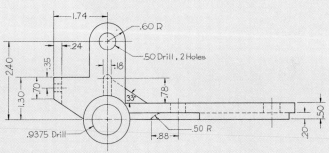

PROB. 5.6.7. Jet-engine hinge plate.

GROUP 7.   DRAWING FROM MEMORY

One of the valuable assets of an engineer is a trained memory for form and proportion. A graphic memory can be developed to a surprising degree in accuracy and power by systematic exercises in drawing from memory. It is well to begin this training as soon as you have a knowledge of orthographic projection.

Select an object not previously used; look at it with concentration for a certain time (from 5 sec to ½ min or more), close the book, and make an accurate orthographic sketch. Check with the original and correct any mistakes or omissions. Follow with several different figures. The next day, allow a 2-sec view of one of the objects, and repeat the orthographic views of the previous day.

GROUP 8.   VOLUME AND WEIGHT CALCULATIONS WITH SLIDE RULE

In calculating the weight of a piece from a drawing, the object is broken up into the geometric solids (prisms, cylinders, pyramids, or cones) of which it is composed. The volume of each of these shapes is calculated and the individual volumes are added, or subtracted, to find the total volume. The total volume multiplied by the weight of the material per unit of volume gives the weight of the object.

A table of weights of materials is given in the Appendix.

5.8.1. Find the weight of the cast-iron anchor bracket, Prob. 5.5.12.
5.8.2. Find the weight of the cast-iron bracket, Prob. 5.5.15.
5.8.3. Find the weight of the wrought-iron tool holder, Prob. 5.5.17.
5.8.4. Find the weight of the cast-steel cylinder support, Prob. 5.5.20.
5.8.5. Find the weight of the malleable-iron sliding block, Prob. 5.6.1.

Pictorial representations may be accomplished by employing any one of several methods: isometric, *where three pictorial axes are equally foreshortened;* oblique, *in which one face is shown in true shape;* dimetric, *where two pictorial axes are equally foreshortened;* trimetric, *a method having all three axes foreshortened at different rates; and* perspective, *wherein the object is represented as the eye of an observer would see it.*

The picture at left shows a portion of a modern building, an example of photographic perspective. Note the interplay of surface relationships produced by the choice of camera position.

Pictorial Drawing and Sketching

6.1   In discussing the theory of projection in Chap. 5, we noted that in perspective projection (Fig. 5.1) the object is represented as it appears to the eye. However, its lines cannot be measured directly for accurate description of the object; and in orthographic projection the object is shown, in two or more views, as it really is in form and dimensions but interpretation requires experience to visualize the object from the views. To provide a system of drawing that represents the object pictorially and in such a way that its principal lines can be measured directly, several forms of one-plane conventional or projectional picture methods have been devised in which the third dimension is taken care of either by turning the object so that its three dimensions are visible or by employing oblique projection. A knowledge of these picture methods and of perspective projection is extremely desirable as they can all be used to great advantage.

Mechanical or structural details not clear in orthographic views can be drawn pictorially or illustrated by supplementary pictorial views. Pictorial views are used advantageously in technical illustrations, Patent Office drawings, layouts, piping plans, and the like. Pictorial methods are useful also in making freehand sketches, and this is one of the most important reasons for learning them.

161

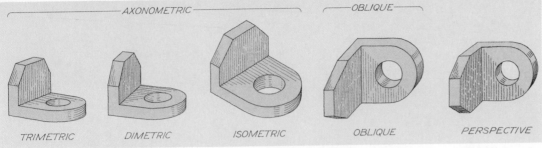

FIG. 6.1. Pictorial methods.

TRIMETRIC   DIMETRIC   ISOMETRIC   OBLIQUE   PERSPECTIVE

FIG. 6.2. The object face is parallel to the picture plane. One face only is seen in the front view.

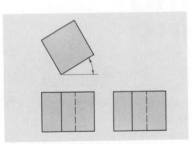

FIG. 6.3. The object is rotated about a vertical axis. Two faces are seen.

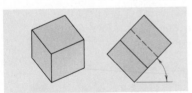

FIG. 6.4. The object is rotated about both a vertical and a profile axis. Three faces are seen.

6.2. PICTORIAL METHODS. There are three main divisions of pictorial drawing: (1) axonometric, with its divisions into trimetric, dimetric, and isometric; (2) oblique, with several variations; and (3) perspective. These methods are illustrated in Fig. 6.1.

The trimetric form gives an effect more pleasing to the eye than the other axonometric and oblique methods and allows almost unlimited freedom in orienting the object, but is difficult to draw. With the dimetric method the result is less pleasing and there is less freedom in orienting the object, but execution is easier than with trimetric. The isometric method gives a result less pleasing than dimetric or trimetric, but it is easier to draw and has the distinct advantage that it is easier to dimension. The oblique method is used principally for objects with circular or curved features only on one face or on parallel faces, and for objects of this type the oblique is easy to draw and dimension. Perspective drawing gives a result most pleasing to the eye, but it is of limited usefulness because many lines are unequally foreshortened; isometric and oblique are the forms most commonly used.

6.3. AXONOMETRIC PROJECTION. Axonometric projection is theoretically orthographic projection in which only one plane is used, the object being turned so that three faces show. Imagine a transparent vertical plane with a cube behind it, one face of the cube being parallel to the plane. The projection on the plane, that is, the front view of the cube, will be a square (Fig. 6.2). Rotate the cube about a vertical axis through any angle less than 90°, and the front view will now show two faces, both foreshortened (Fig. 6.3). From this position, tilt the cube forward (rotation axis perpendicular to profile) any amount less than 90°. Three faces will now be visible on the front view (Fig. 6.4). There can be an infinite number of axonometric positions, depending upon the angles through which the cube is rotated. Only a few of these positions are ever used for drawing. The simplest is the isometric (equal-measure) position, in which the three faces are foreshortened equally.

6.4. ISOMETRIC PROJECTION. If the cube in Fig. 6.5A is rotated about a vertical axis through 45°, as shown at (B), and then tilted forward, as at (C), until the edge RU is foreshortened equally with RS and RT, the front view of the cube in this position is said to be an "isometric projection." (The cube has been tilted forward until the body diagonal through R is perpendicular to the front plane. This makes the top face slope approximately 35°16'.[1]) The projections

[1] The only difference between rotation and auxiliary projection is that in the former the object is moved and in the latter the plane is moved or the observer is considered to have changed his viewing position. Thus an auxiliary view on a plane perpendicular to a body diagonal of the cube in position (B) would be an isometric projection, as illustrated by the dotted view.

of the three mutually perpendicular edges *RS, RT,* and *RU* meeting at the front corner *R* make equal angles, 120°, with each other and are called "isometric axes." Since the projections of parallel lines are parallel, the projections of the other edges of the cube will be, respectively, parallel to these axes. Any line parallel to an edge of the cube, whose projection is thus parallel to an isometric axis, is called an "isometric line." The planes of the faces of the cube and all planes parallel to them are called "isometric planes."

The isometric axes *RS, RT,* and *RU* are all foreshortened equally because they are at the same angle to the picture plane.

6.5.   ISOMETRIC DRAWING.

In nearly all practical use of the isometric system, this foreshortening of the lines is disregarded, and *their full lengths are laid off on the axes,* as explained in paragraph 6.6. This gives a figure of exactly the same shape but larger in the proportion of 1.23 to 1, linear, or in optical effect 1.23^3 to 1.00^3 (Fig. 6.6). Except when drawn beside the same piece in orthographic projection, the effect of increased size is usually of no consequence, and since the advantage of measuring the lines directly is of great convenience, isometric drawing is used almost exclusively rather than isometric projection.

In isometric projection the isometric lines have been foreshortened to approximately $^{81}\!/_{100}$ of their length, and an isometric scale to this proportion can be made graphically as shown in Fig. 6.7 if it is necessary to make an isometric projection by the method of isometric drawing.

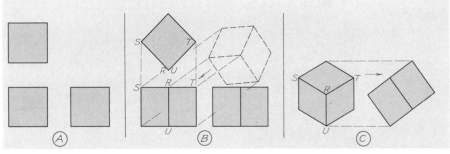

FIG. 6.8.   Isometric axes, first position. The starting point is the upper front corner.

6.6.   TO MAKE AN ISOMETRIC DRAWING.

If the object is rectangular (Fig. 6.8), start with a point representing a front corner, shown at (*A*) with heavy lines, and draw from it the three isometric axes 120° apart, one vertical (*B*), the other two with the 30° triangle. On these three lines measure the height, width, and depth of the object, as indicated at (*C*); through the points so determined draw lines parallel to the axes, completing the figure. When drawing in isometric, remember the direction of the three principal isometric planes. Hidden lines are omitted except when they are needed to describe the piece.

It is often convenient to build up an isometric drawing from the lower front corner, as illustrated in Fig. 6.9, starting from axes in what may be called the "second position." The location of the starting corner is again shown by heavy lines at (*A*), (*B*), and (*C*).

6.7.   NONISOMETRIC LINES.

Edges whose projections or drawings are not parallel to one of the isometric axes are called "nonisometric lines." The one impor-

FIG. 6.5.   The isometric cube. Rotated from position (*A*) to (*B*) then to (*C*), the three perpendicular edges are now equally foreshortened.

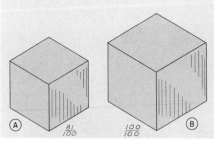

FIG. 6.6.   (*A*) isometric projection; (*B*) isometric drawing.

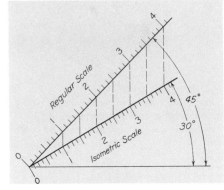

FIG. 6.7.   To make an isometric scale.

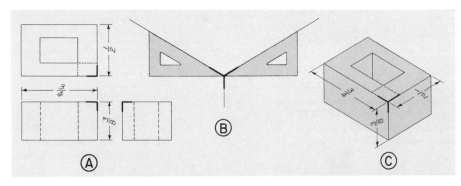

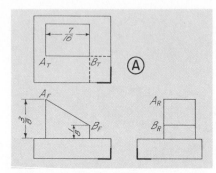

FIG. 6.9. Isometric axes, second position. The starting point is the lower front corner.

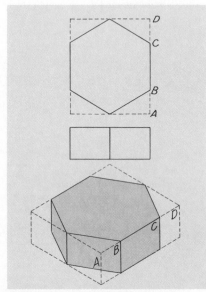

FIG. 6.10. Box construction. Points on the orthographic box are transferred to the pictorial box. Identical scale must be used.

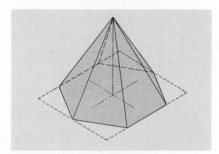

FIG. 6.11. Semibox construction. Points on the base are transferred by boxing. The altitude is located by a vertical from the base center. Identical scale must be used.

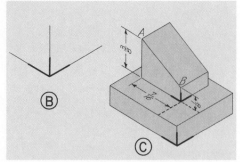

tant rule is that *measurements can be made only on the drawings of isometric lines;* conversely, measurements *cannot* be made on the drawings of *nonisometric* lines. For example, the diagonals of the face of a cube are nonisometric lines; although equal in length, their isometric drawings will not be at all of equal length on the isometric drawing of the cube. Compare the length of the diagonals on the cube in Fig. 6.6. Since a nonisometric line does not appear in the isometric drawing in its true length, the isometric view of each end of the line must be located and the isometric view of the line found by joining these two points. In Fig. 6.9, *A* and *C*, line *AB* is a nonisometric edge whose true length cannot be measured on the isometric drawing. However, the vertical distances above the base to points *A* and *B* are parallel to the vertical isometric axis. These lines can, therefore, be laid off, as shown at (*C*), to give the isometric view of line *AB*.

6.8. NONISOMETRIC LINES: BOXING METHOD. When an object contains many nonisometric lines, it is drawn by the "boxing method" or the "offset method." When the boxing method is used, the object is enclosed in a rectangular box, which is drawn around it in orthographic projection. The box is then drawn in isometric and the object located in it by its points of contact, as in Figs. 6.10 and 6.12. It should be noted that the isometric views of lines that are parallel on the object are parallel. This knowledge can often be used to save a large amount of construction, as well as to test for accuracy. Figure 6.10 might be drawn by putting the top face into isometric and drawing vertical lines equal in length to the edges downward from each corner. It is not always necessary to enclose the whole object in a rectangular "crate." The pyramid (Fig. 6.11) would have its base enclosed in a rectangle and the apex located by erecting a vertical axis from the center.

The object shown in Fig. 6.12 is composed almost entirely of nonisometric lines. In such cases the isometric drawing cannot be made without first making the orthographic views necessary for boxing. In general, the boxing method is adapted to objects that have the nonisometric lines in isometric planes.

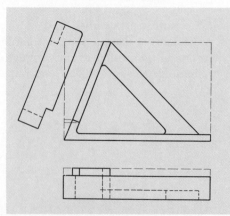
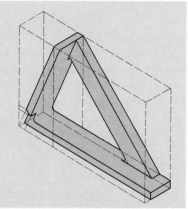

FIG. 6.12. Box construction. Points on, and offsets from, the orthographic box are transferred to the pictorial box. Identical scale must be used.

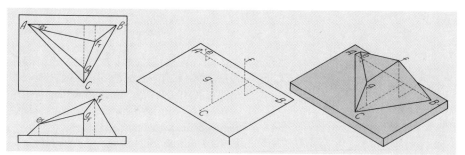

6.9. NONISOMETRIC LINES: OFFSET METHOD.

When an object is made up of planes at different angles, it is better to locate the ends of the edges by the offset method rather than by boxing. When the offset method is used, perpendiculars are extended from each point to an isometric reference plane. These perpendiculars, which are isometric lines, are located on the drawing by isometric coordinates, the dimensions being taken from the orthographic views. In Fig. 6.13, line AB is used as a base line and measurements are made from it as shown, first to locate points on the base; then verticals from these points locate e, f, and g. Figure 6.14 is another example of offset construction. Here a vertical plane is used as a reference plane. Note that, as in Fig. 6.13, the *base* of the offset is located first; then the offset distance is measured.

6.10. ANGLES IN ISOMETRIC.

The three isometric axes, referred back to the isometric cube, are mutually perpendicular but in an isometric drawing appear at 120.° to each other. For this reason, angles specified in degrees do not appear in their true size on an isometric drawing and must be laid off by coordinates that will be parallel to the isometric axes. Thus if an orthographic drawing has edges specified by angular dimensions, as in Fig. 6.15A, *a view to the same scale as the isometric drawing is* made as at (B); from this view the coordinate dimensions a, b, and c are transferred with dividers or scale to the isometric drawing.

6.11. CURVES IN ISOMETRIC.

For the reasons given in paragraphs 6.7 and 6.10, a circle or any other curve will not show in its true shape when drawn in isometric. A circle on any isometric plane will be an ellipse, and a curve will be shown as the isometric projection of the true curve.

Any curve can be drawn by plotting points on it from isometric reference lines (coordinates) that are parallel to the isometric axes, as shown in Fig. 6.16. A circle plotted in this way is shown in Fig. 6.17. Note that in both these figures coordinates a and b are parallel to the isometric axes and the coordinate distances must be obtained from an orthographic view drawn to the same scale as the isometric.

6.12. ISOMETRIC CIRCLES.

Circles occur so frequently that they are usually drawn by a four-centered approximation, which is sufficiently accurate for ordinary work. Geometrically, the center for any arc tangent to a straight line lies on a *perpendicular from the point of tangency*

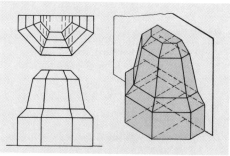

FIG. 6.14. Offset construction. All points are located on a plane or by offsets from the plane. Identical scale must be used.

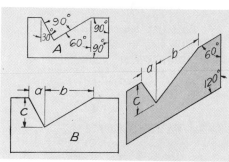

FIG. 6.15. Angles in isometric. These must be laid out by offsets from an orthographic view to the same scale.

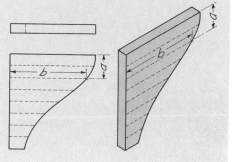

FIG. 6.16. Curves in isometric. Points are transferred from the orthographic view to the pictorial by offsets. Identical scale must be used.

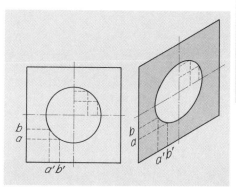

FIG. 6.17. Isometric circle, points plotted. Points are transferred from the orthographic view to the pictorial by offsets. Identical scale must be used.

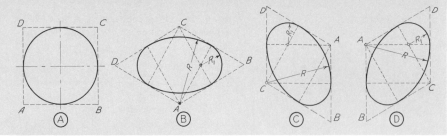

FIG. 6.18. Isometric circles, four-centered method. The ellipse is approximated by circle arcs.

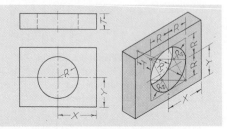

FIG. 6.19. Locating and laying out a hole in isometric. Locate the center, draw the enclosing isometric square, and then draw the circle by the method of Fig. 6.18.

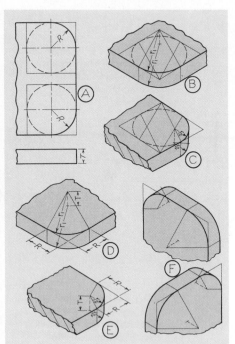

FIG. 6.20. Isometric quarter circles. The radius center lies on perpendiculars from tangent points that are the radius distance from the corner.

(Fig. 6.18A). In isometric, if perpendiculars are drawn from the middle point of each side of the circumscribing square, the intersections of these perpendiculars will be centers for arcs tangent to two sides (B). Two of these intersections will evidently fall at the corners A and C of the isometric square, as the perpendiculars are altitudes of equilateral triangles. Thus the construction at (B) to (D) can be made by simply drawing 60° lines (horizontals also at C and D) from the corners A and C and then arcs with radii R and R_1, as shown.

Figure 6.19 shows the method of locating and laying out a hole in isometric from the given orthographic views. First locate and then draw the center lines for the hole by laying out the distances X and Y, as shown. On these lines construct an isometric square with sides equal to the diameter of the hole by laying out the radius R in each direction from the intersection of the center lines. Then use the four-center method, as shown in Fig. 6.18. Should the piece be thin enough, a portion of the back

side of the hole will be visible. To determine this, drop the thickness T back on an isometric line and swing the large radius R_1 of the isometric circle with this point as center. If the arc thus drawn comes within the boundary of the isometric circle, that portion of the back will be visible. In extra-thin pieces, portions of the small arcs R_2 might be visible. This would be determined the same way.

If a true ellipse is plotted by the method of paragraph 6.11 in the same square, it will be a little longer and narrower and of much more pleasing shape than this four-center approximation, but in most drawings the difference is not sufficient to warrant the extra expenditure of time required in execution.

The isometric drawing of a *sphere* is a circle with its diameter equal to the long axis of the ellipse that is inscribed in the isometric square of a great circle of the sphere. It would thus be 1.23/1.00 of the actual diameter (the isometric *projection* of a sphere would be a circle of the actual diameter of the sphere).

6.13. ISOMETRIC CIRCLE ARCS. To draw any circle arc, draw the isometric square of its diameter in the plane of its face, with as much of the four-center

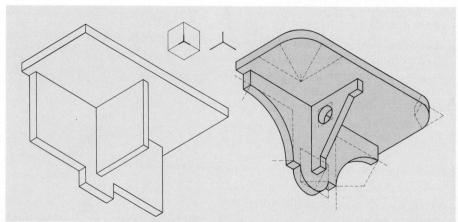

FIG. 6.21. Isometric with reversed axes. The bottom and two sides are shown. Construction methods are the same as for regular position.

6.17. Trimetric Projection

construction as is necessary to find centers for the part of the circle needed, as illustrated in Fig. 6.20. The arc occurring most frequently is the quarter circle. Note that in illustrations (*D*) and (*E*) only two construction lines are needed to find the center of a quarter circle in an isometric plane. Measure the true radius R of the circle from the corner on the two isometric lines as shown, and draw *actual* perpendiculars from these points. Their intersection will be the required center for radius R_1 or R_2 of the isometric quadrant. (*F*) illustrates the construction for the two vertical isometric planes.

6.14. REVERSED ISOMETRIC. It is often desirable to show the lower face of an object by tilting it *back* instead of *forward,* thus reversing the usual position so as to show the underside. The construction is the same as when the top is shown, but the directions of the principal isometric planes must be kept clearly in mind. Figure 6.21 shows the reference cube and the position of the axes, as well as the application of reversed-isometric construction to circle arcs. A practical use of this construction is in the representation of such architectural features as are naturally viewed from below. Figure 6.22 is an example.

Sometimes a piece is shown to better advantage with the main axis horizontal, as in Fig. 6.23.

6.15. ISOMETRIC SECTIONS. Isometric drawings are, from their pictorial nature, usually outside views, but sometimes a sectional view (see Chap. 8) is used to good advantage to show a detail of shape or interior construction. The cutting planes are taken as isometric planes, and the section lining is done in the di-

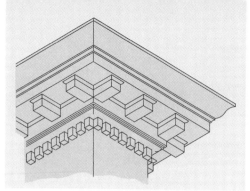

FIG. 6.22. An architectural detail on reversed axes.

rection that gives the best effect; this is, in almost all cases, the direction of the long diagonal of a square drawn on the surface. As a general rule, a half section is made by outlining the figure in full and then cutting out the front quarter, as in Fig. 6.24; for a full section, the cut face is drawn first and then the part of the object behind it is added (Fig. 6.25).

6.16. DIMETRIC PROJECTION. The reference cube can be rotated into any number of positions in which two edges are equally foreshortened, and the direction of axes and ratio of foreshortening for any one of these positions might be taken as the basis for a system of dimetric drawing. A simple dimetric position is one with the ratios 1 to 1 to ½. In this position the tangents of the angles are ⅛ and ⅞, making the angles approximately 7° and 41°. Figure 6.26 shows a drawing in this system. Dimetric is seldom used because of the difficulty of drawing circles in this projection.

6.17. TRIMETRIC PROJECTION. Any position in which all three axes are unequally foreshortened is called "trimetric." Compared with isometric and dimetric, distortion is reduced in trimetric projection, and even this effect can be lessened with some positions. However, because it is slower to execute

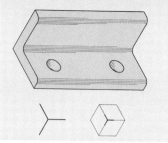

FIG. 6.23. Isometric with the main axis horizontal. It is used when the object looks more natural in this position.

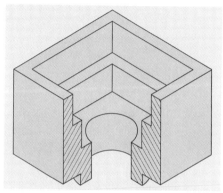

FIG. 6.24. Isometric half section. One-fourth of the object is removed to reveal interior construction.

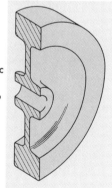

FIG. 6.25. Isometric full section. Half of object is removed to reveal object shape.

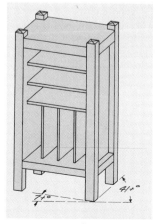

FIG. 6.26. Dimetric drawing. It is used principally for rectangular objects.

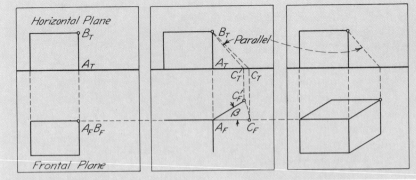

FIG. 6.27. Oblique projection. Projectors are at an oblique angle to the picture plane.

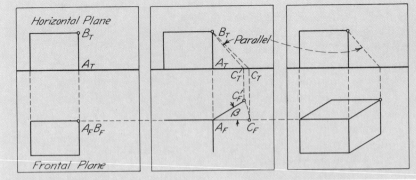

FIG. 6.28. Various oblique positions. (*A*) up, to the right at 30°; (*B*) up, to the right at 45°; (*C*) up, to the left at 45°; (*D*) down, to the right at 30°; (*E*) down, to the left at 30°.

than isometric or dimetric, it is seldom used except when done by projection. Axonometric projection from orthographic views is given in paragraph 6.26.

6.18.   OBLIQUE PROJECTION.   When the projectors make an angle other than 90° with the picture plane, the resulting projection is called "oblique." The name "cavalier projection" is given to the special and most used type of oblique projection in which the projectors make an angle of 45° with the plane of projection. Cavalier projection is often called by the general name "oblique projection," or "oblique drawing." The principle is as follows: Imagine a vertical plane with a rectangular block behind it, having its long edges parallel to the plane. Assume a system of parallel projecting lines in any direction making an angle of 45° with the picture plane (they could be parallel to any one of the elements of a 45° cone with its base in the picture plane). Then that face of the block which is parallel to the plane is projected in its true size, and the edges perpendicular to the plane are projected in their true length. Figure 6.27 illustrates the principle. The first panel shows the regular orthographic projection of a rectangular block with its front face in the frontal plane. An oblique projector from the back corner

B is the hypotenuse of a 45° right triangle of which *AB* is one side and the projection of *AB* on the plane is the other side. When this triangle is horizontal, the projection on the plane will be *AC*. If the triangle is rotated about *AB* through any angle β, *C* will revolve to *C′* and $A_F C_F{'}$ will be the oblique projection of *AB*.

6.19.   TO MAKE AN OBLIQUE DRAWING. Oblique drawing is similar to isometric drawing in that it has three axes that represent three mutually perpendicular edges and upon which measurements can be made. Two of the axes are always at right angles to each other, as they are in a plane parallel to the picture plane. The third, or depth, axis may be at any angle to the horizontal, 30° or 45° being generally used (Fig. 6.28). Oblique drawing is thus more flexible than isometric drawing. To draw a rectangular object (Fig. 6.29) start with a point representing a front corner (*A*) and draw from it the three oblique axes, one vertical, one horizontal, and one at an angle. On these three axes measure the height, width, and depth of the object. In this case the width is made up of the 2½-in. distance and the 1⁵⁄₁₆-in. radius. Locate the center of the arc, and draw it as shown. The center for the arc of the hole in the

6.21. Starting Plane

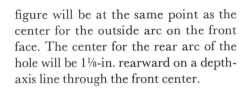

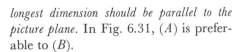

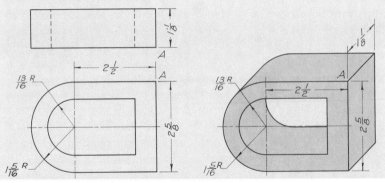

FIG. 6.29. Oblique drawing. The front face, parallel to the picture plane, is identical with an orthographic view.

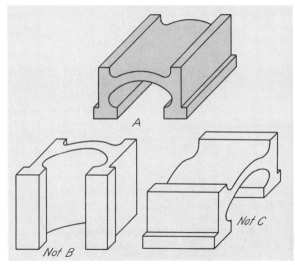

FIG. 6.30. Illustration of the first rule. Note the distortion at (*B*) and (*C*).

figure will be at the same point as the center for the outside arc on the front face. The center for the rear arc of the hole will be 1⅛-in. rearward on a depth-axis line through the front center.

6.20. OBJECT ORIENTATION FOR OBLIQUE. Any face parallel to the picture plane will evidently be projected without distortion. In this, oblique projection has an advantage over isometric that is of particular value in representing objects with circular or irregular outline.

The *first rule* for oblique projection is to *place the object with the irregular outline or contour parallel to the picture plane.* Note in Fig. 6.30 the greater distortion at (*B*) and (*C*) than at (*A*).

One of the greatest disadvantages in the use of isometric or oblique drawing is the effect of distortion produced by the lack of convergence in the receding lines—a violation of perspective. In some cases, particularly with large objects, this becomes so painful as practically to preclude the use of these methods. This is perhaps even more noticeable in oblique than in isometric and of course increases with the length of the depth dimension.

Hence the *second rule: preferably, the*

longest dimension should be parallel to the picture plane. In Fig. 6.31, (*A*) is preferable to (*B*).

In case of conflict between these two rules, *the first always takes precedence,* as the advantage of having the irregular face without distortion is greater than that gained by the second rule, as illustrated in Fig. 6.32. The first rule should be given precedence even with shapes that are not irregular if, in the draftsman's judgment, the distortion can be lessened, as in Fig. 6.33, where (*B*) is perhaps preferable to (*A*).

6.21. STARTING PLANE. Note that as long as the front of the object is in one plane parallel to the plane of projection, the front face of the oblique projection is *exactly the same as in the orthographic front view.* When the front is made up of more than one plane, take care to preserve the relationship between the planes by selecting one as the starting plane and working from it. In a piece such as the

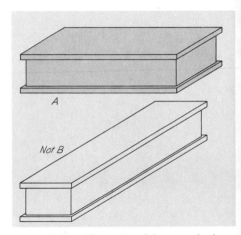

FIG. 6.31. Illustration of the second rule. Note the exaggerated depth at (*B*).

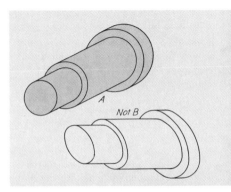

FIG. 6.32. Precedence of the first rule. (*A*), following the first rule, is easier to draw and also shows less distortion than (*B*).

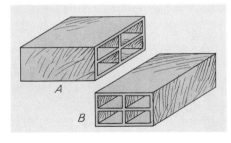

FIG. 6.33. Choice of position. (*B*) is preferable to (*A*).

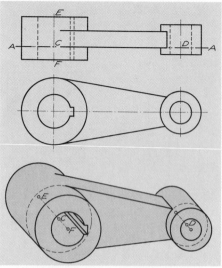

FIG. 6.34. Offsets from reference plane. Distances forward and rearward are measured from the frontal plane.

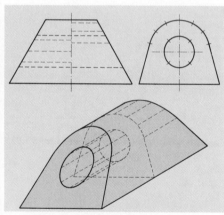

FIG. 6.35. Offsets from right section. Measurements forward and rearward are made from the frontal plane.

FIG. 6.36. Oblique circle construction. Note that the tangent points of arcs must be at the midpoints of the enclosing oblique square.

link in Fig. 6.34, the front bosses can be imagined as cut off on the plane *A-A,* and the front view, that is, the section on *A-A,* drawn as the front of the oblique projection. Then lay off depth axes through the centers *C* and *D,* the distances, for example, *CE* behind and *CF* in front of the plane *A-A.*

When an object has no face perpendicular to its base, it can be drawn in a similar way by cutting a right section and measuring offsets from it, as in Fig. 6.35. This offset method, previously illustrated in the isometric drawings in Figs. 6.13, 6.14, and 6.16, is a rapid, convenient way of drawing almost any figure; it should be studied carefully.

6.22.   **CIRCLES IN OBLIQUE.** When it is necessary to draw circles that lie on oblique faces, they can be drawn as circle arcs, with the compasses, on the same principle as the four-center isometric approximation shown in Fig. 6.18. In isometric it happens that *two of the four intersections of the perpendiculars from the middle points* of the containing square fall at the corner of the square, and advantage is taken of the fact. In oblique, the position of the corresponding points depends on the angle of the depth axis. Figure 6.36 shows three squares in oblique positions at different angles and the construction of their inscribed circles. The important point to remember is that the circle arcs *must* be tangent at the mid-points of the sides of the oblique square.

6.23.   **ARCS IN OBLIQUE.** Circle arcs representing rounded corners, etc., are

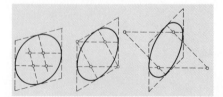

drawn in oblique by the same method given for isometric arcs in paragraph 6.13. The only difference is that the angle of the sides tangent to the arc will vary according to the angle of the depth axis chosen.

6.24.   **CABINET DRAWING.** This is a type of oblique projection in which the parallel projectors make an angle with the picture plane of such a value that distances measured parallel to the depth axis are reduced one-half that of cavalier projection. The appearance of excessive thickness that is so disagreeable in cavalier projection is entirely overcome in cabinet projection. The depth axis may be at any angle with the horizontal but is usually taken at 30° or 45°. The appearance of cavalier and cabinet drawing is shown in Fig. 6.37.

6.25.   **OTHER FORMS.** Cabinet drawing is popular because of the easy ratio, but the effect is often too thin. Other oblique drawing ratios, such as 2 to 3 or 3 to 4, may be used with pleasing effect.

6.26.   **AXONOMETRIC PROJECTION FROM ORTHOGRAPHIC VIEWS.** In making pictorial drawings of complicated parts, especially whenever curves are plotted, axonometric projection from orthographic views may give an advantage in speed and ease of drawing over axonometric projection made directly from the object. Any position—isometric, dimetric, or trimetric—may be used.

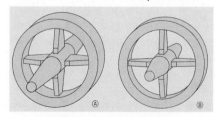

FIG. 6.37. Oblique (*A*) and cabinet drawing (*B*). Note less exaggeration of depth at (*B*).

The three axes of an axonometric drawing are *three mutually perpendicular edges* in space. If the angle of rotation and the angle of tilt of the object are known or decided upon, the three axes for the pictorial drawing and the location of the orthographic views for projection to the pictorial can easily be found. Figure 6.38 illustrates the procedure. The three orthographic views of a cube are shown at (*G*). The three mutually perpendicular edges *OA*, *OB*, and *OC* will be foreshortened differently when the cube is rotated in space for some axonometric position, but the ends of the axes *A*, *B*, and *C* will always lie on the surface of a sphere whose radius is *OA* = *OB* = *OC*, as illustrated by (*G'*). At any particular angle of tilt of the cube, the axis ends *A* and *B* will describe an ellipse, as shown, if the cube is rotated about the axis *OC*. The axis *OC* will appear foreshortened at *oc'*. Thus for any particular position of the cube in space, representing some desired axonometric position, the axes can be located and their relative amounts of foreshortening found.

Moreover, if a face of the cube is rotated about a *frontal axis perpendicular to the axis that is at right angles to the face*, an orthographic view of the face, in projection with the axonometric view, will result. Thus, the top and right-side views may be located as at (*J*) and projected as at (*K*) to give the axonometric drawing.

The drawings at (*H*), (*J*), and (*K*) illustrate the practical use of the theory of rotation just described. The actual size of the sphere is unimportant, as it is used only to establish the direction of the axes. First, the desired angle of rotation *R* and the angle of tilt *T* are decided upon and laid out as at (*H*). The minor diameter for the ellipse upon which *A* and *B* will lie is found by projecting ver-

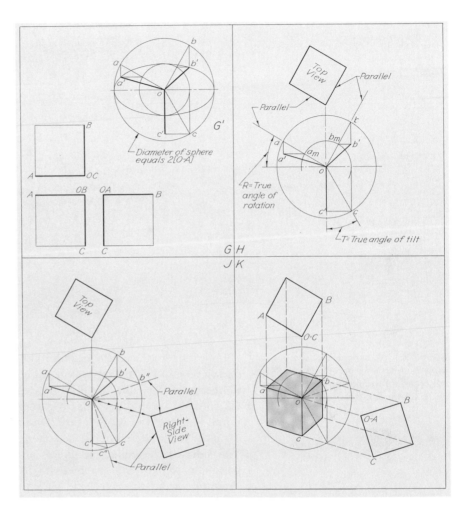

tically from *c* and drawing the circle as shown. *A* and *B* on the major-diameter circle of the ellipse will be at *a* and *b*; on the minor-diameter circle, they will be at a_m and b_m; and they are found in the axonometric position by projecting, as in the concentric-circle ellipse method, to *a'* and *b'*. The foreshortened position of *C* is found by projecting horizontally across from *c* to *c'*.

The top orthographic view of the cube (or object) will be parallel to *oa* and *ob*, and projection from the orthographic view to the axonometric will be vertical (parallel to *aa'* and *bb'*).

FIG. 6.38. Axonometric projection from orthographic views. (*G*) construction to locate axes; (*H*) location of top view; (*J*) location of side view; (*K*) projection.

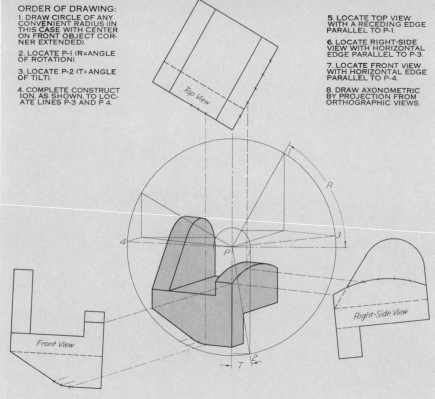

ORDER OF DRAWING:
1. DRAW CIRCLE OF ANY CONVENIENT RADIUS (IN THIS CASE WITH CENTER ON FRONT OBJECT CORNER EXTENDED).

2. LOCATE P-1 (R=ANGLE OF ROTATION).

3. LOCATE P-2 (T= ANGLE OF TILT).

4. COMPLETE CONSTRUCTION, AS SHOWN, TO LOCATE LINES P-3 AND P 4.

5. LOCATE TOP VIEW WITH A RECEDING EDGE PARALLEL TO P-1.

6. LOCATE RIGHT-SIDE VIEW WITH HORIZONTAL EDGE PARALLEL TO P-3.

7. LOCATE FRONT VIEW WITH HORIZONTAL EDGE PARALLEL TO P-4.

8. DRAW AXONOMETRIC BY PROJECTION FROM ORTHOGRAPHIC VIEWS.

FIG. 6.39. An axonometric drawing by projection from orthographic views. Note the order of drawing and refer back to Fig. 6.38 for details of construction.

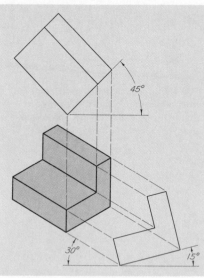

FIG. 6.40. Isometric by projection. Top view turned 45° and side view turned 15° locate views for projection to the isometric.

Projection from an orthographic right-side view would be as shown at (J). The right side of the cube, containing axes OC and OB, is found by projecting from b' and c', parallel to oa', to locate b'' and c'' on the circle representing the sphere. The sides of the cube (or object) are parallel to ob'' and oc'', as shown at (J). Projection from the right-side view to the axonometric view is in the direction of oa', as indicated.

The axonometric drawing is shown projected at (K). The dashed lines indicate the actual projectors, and the light solid lines and circles show the necessary construction just described.

One advantage of this method is that the angle of rotation and tilt can be decided upon so that the object will be shown in the best position. Figure 6.39 is an example of an axonometric drawing made by projection from orthographic views. The curved faces are plotted by projecting points as shown.

Pictorial Drawing and Sketching

6.27. ISOMETRIC PROJECTION FROM ORTHOGRAPHIC VIEWS. Isometric is, of course, a special type of axonometric projection in which all three axes are foreshortened equally. The work of finding the axes for isometric projection from orthographic views is reduced if the views are located by angle, as illustrated in Fig. 6.40.

6.28. OBLIQUE PROJECTION FROM ORTHOGRAPHIC VIEWS. In oblique projection the projectors make some oblique angle with the picture plane. The actual angle of the projectors (with horizontal and frontal planes) is not critical, and a variety of angles may be used. The making of an oblique drawing by projection from orthographic views is simple, as illustrated by Fig. 6.41. The picture plane is located, and one face of the object is made coincident with the picture plane. The front view is located at a convenient place on the paper. The angle of the projectors in the top view may be assumed (in this case 45°) and projections made to the picture plane as shown. The angle of the projectors in the front view can then be assumed (in this case 30°). Projection from the front view at the assumed angle and vertically from the picture plane, as shown, will locate the necessary lines and points for the oblique view.

Reversed axes can be obtained by projecting downward from the front view. An axis to the left can be located by changing the direction of the projectors in the top view. Any desired oblique axes can be located by altering the angles (top and front) for the projectors.

6.29. PERSPECTIVE DRAWING. Perspective drawing represents an object as it appears to an observer stationed at a particular position relative to it. The object is seen as the figure resulting when visual rays from the eye to the object are cut by a picture plane. There is a difference between an artist's use of perspective and geometric perspective. The artist often disregards true perspective since he draws the object as he sees it through his creative imagination, while geometric perspective is projected instrumentally on a plane from views or measurements of the object represented. Projected geometric perspective is, theoretically, very similar to the optical system in photography.

In a technical way, perspective is used more in architecture and in illustration than in other fields, but every engineer will find it useful to know the principles of the subject.

6.30.   FUNDAMENTAL CONCEPTS.   Imagine an observer standing on the sidewalk of a city street, as in Fig. 6.42, with the picture plane erected between him and the street scene ahead. Visual rays from his eye to the ends of lamppost A intercept a distance aa' on the picture plane. Similarly, rays from post B intercept bb', a smaller distance than aa'. This apparent diminution in the size of like objects as the distance from the objects to the eye increases agrees with our everyday experience and is the keynote of perspective drawing. It is evident from the figure that succeeding lampposts will intercept shorter distances on the picture plane than the preceding ones, and that a post at infinity would show only as a point o at the level of the observer's eye.

In Fig. 6.43 the plane of the paper is the picture plane, and the intercepts aa', bb', etc., show as the heights of the respective lampposts as they diminish in their projected size and finally disappear

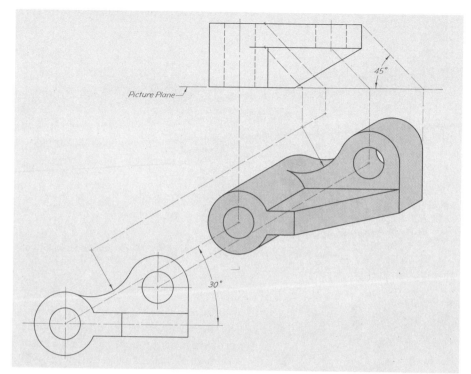

FIG. 6.41.   Oblique by projection. Projection at an angle from the top view to the picture plane and directly from the side view gives the oblique view.

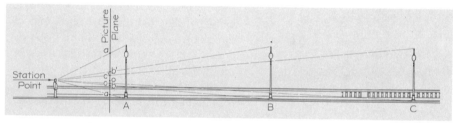

FIG. 6.42.   Theory of perspective illustrated. Rays from the objects to the observer's eye intersect the picture plane.

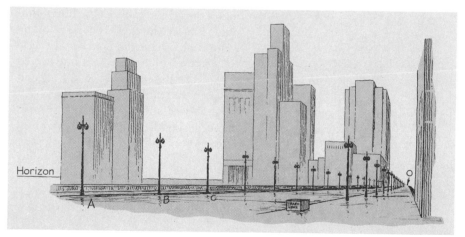

FIG. 6.43.   The perspective drawing. This is the image formed on the picture plane of Fig. 6.42.

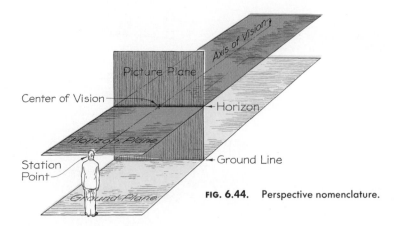

FIG. 6.44.　Perspective nomenclature.

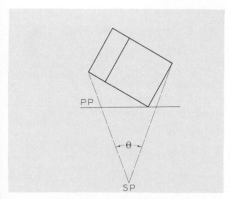

FIG. 6.45.　Lateral angle of view.

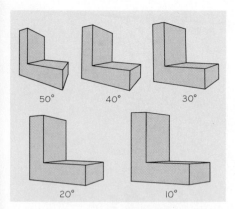

FIG. 6.46.　Comparative lateral angles of view. Angles greater than 30° give an unpleasing perspective.

the intersection of the ground plane and picture plane. The *axis of vision* is the line through the station point which is perpendicular to the picture plane. The piercing point of the axis of vision with the picture plane is the *center of vision*.

6.32.　SELECTION OF THE STATION POINT. In beginning a perspective drawing, take care in selecting the station point, as an indiscriminate choice may result in a distorted drawing. If the station point is placed to one side of the drawing, the same effect is obtained as when a theater screen is viewed from a position close to the front and well off to one side: heights are seen properly but not horizontal distances. Therefore, *the center of vision should be somewhere near the picture's center of interest.*

Wide angles of view result in a violent convergence of horizontal lines and so should be avoided. The angle of view is the included angle θ between the widest visual rays (Fig. 6.45). Figure 6.46 shows the difference in perspective foreshortening for different lateral angles of view. In general, an angle of about 20° gives the most natural picture.

The station point should be located at the point from which the object is seen to best advantage. For this reason, for large objects such as buildings, the station point is usually taken at a normal standing height of about 5 ft above the ground plane; for small objects, the best

at a point on the horizon. In a similar way the curbings and balustrade appear to converge at the same point O. Thus a system of parallel horizontal lines will vanish at a single point on the horizon, and all horizontal planes will vanish on the horizon. Verticals such as the lampposts and the edges of the buildings, being parallel to the picture plane, pierce the picture plane at an infinite distance and therefore show as vertical lines in the picture.

6.31.　DEFINITIONS AND NOMENCLATURE. Figure 6.44 illustrates perspective theory and names the points, lines, and planes used. An observer in viewing an object selects his *station point* and thereby determines the *horizon plane,* as the horizontal plane is at eye level. This horizon plane is normally above the horizontal *ground plane* upon which the object is assumed to rest. The *picture plane* is usually located between the station point and the object being viewed and is ordinarily a vertical plane perpendicular to the horizontal projection of the line of sight to the object's center of interest. The *horizon line* is the intersection of the horizon plane and picture plane, and the *ground line* is

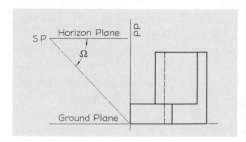

FIG. 6.47.　Elevation angle of view.

6.33. To Draw a Perspective

representation demands that the top, as well as the lateral surfaces, be seen, and the station point must be elevated accordingly. Figure 6.47 shows the angle of elevation Ω between the horizon plane and the extreme visual ray. By illustrating several different angles of elevation (Ω), Fig. 6.48 shows the effect of elevation of the station point. In general, the best picturization is obtained at an angle of about 20° to 30°.

Accordingly, *the visual rays to the object should be kept within a right-circular cone whose elements make an angle of not more than 15° with the cone axis* (total included angle of 30°).

In choosing the station point, see that its position is always offset to one side and also that it is offset vertically from the exact middle of the object, or a rather stiff and awkward perspective will result. Similarly, in locating the object with reference to the picture plane, avoid having the faces make identical angles with the picture plane, or the same stiffness will appear.

6.33. TO DRAW A PERSPECTIVE.

Perspective projection is based on the theory that visual rays from the object to the eye pierce the picture plane and form an image of the object on the plane. Thus in Fig. 6.49, the image of line YZ is formed by the piercing points y and z of the rays. Several projective methods may be used. The simplest method, basically, but the most laborious to draw is illustrated by the purely orthographic method of Fig. 6.50, in which the top and side views are drawn in orthographic. The picture plane (edge view) and the station point are located in each view. Assuming that the line YZ in Fig. 6.49 is one edge of the L-shaped block in Fig. 6.50, visual rays from Y and Z

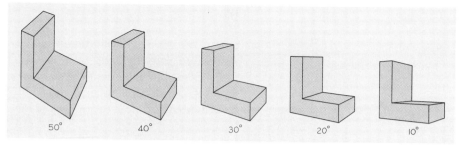

FIG. 6.48. Comparative elevation angles of view. Angles greater than 30° give an unpleasing perspective.

FIG. 6.49. Perspective of a line.

will intersect the picture plane in the top view, thus locating the perspective of the points laterally. Similarly, the intersections of the rays in the side view give the perspective heights of Y and Z. Projection from the top and side views of the picture plane gives the perspective of YZ, and a repetition of the process for the other lines will complete the drawing. Note that *any* point such as Y or Z can be located on the perspective, and thus the perspective is actually plotted, by projection, point after point.

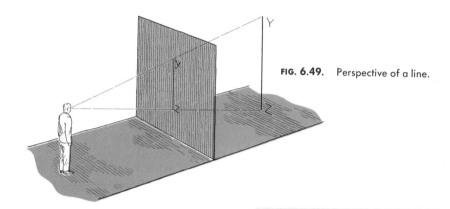

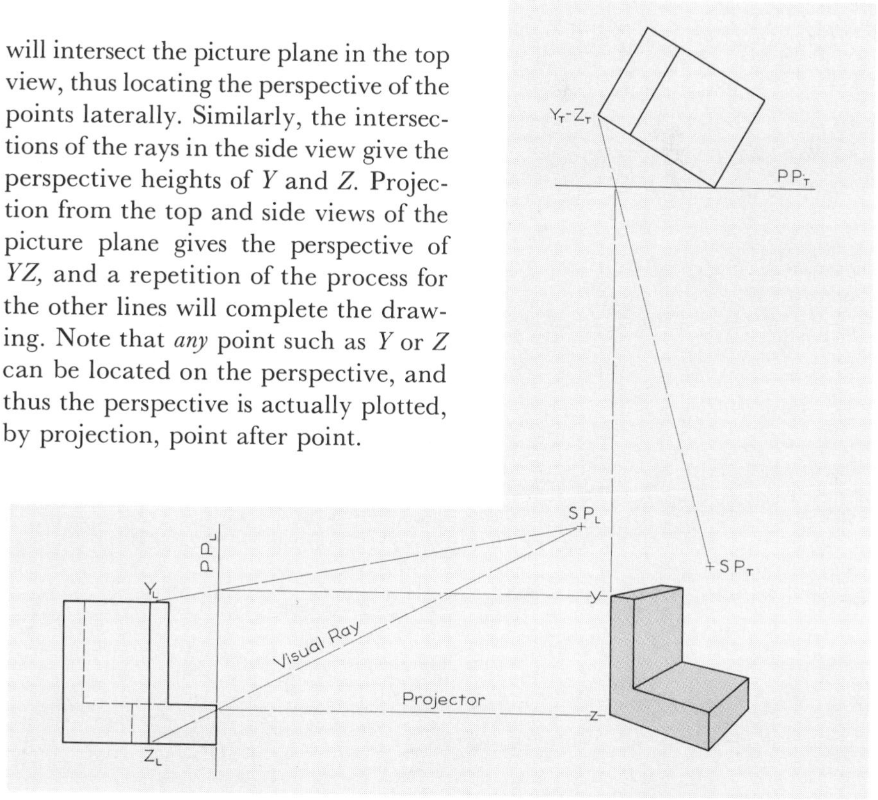

FIG. 6.50. Perspective drawing (orthographic method). Points are plotted from the intersection of rays with the picture plane.

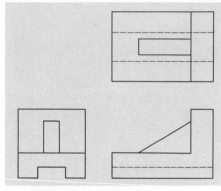

FIG. 6.51. Sliding block. This object is drawn in perspective in Fig. 6.52.

FIG. 6.52. Use of vanishing points and measuring lines. This saves time and extra construction, as compared with the orthographic method used in Fig. 6.50.

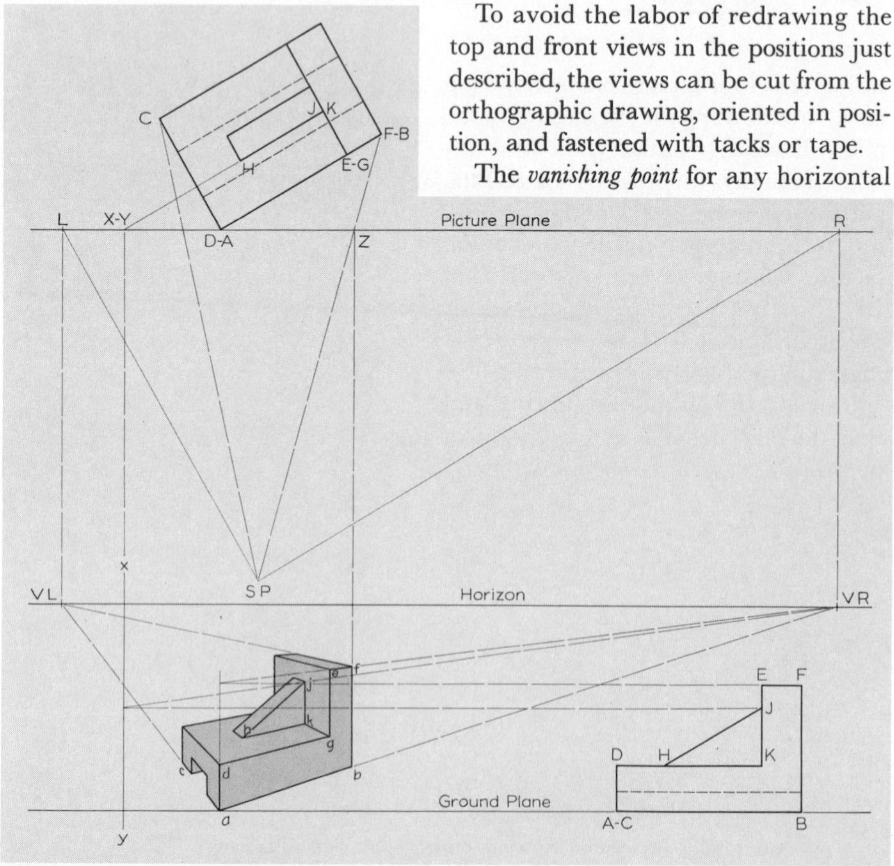

6.34. **THE USE OF VANISHING POINTS AND MEASURING LINES.** These facilitate the projections. Let it be required to make a perspective of the sliding block in Fig. 6.51. The edge view of the picture plane (plan view) is drawn (Fig. 6.52), and behind it the top view of the object is located and drawn. In this case, one side of the object is oriented at 30° to the picture plane in order to emphasize the L shape more than the end of the block. The station point is located a little to the left of center and far enough in front of the picture plane to give a good angle of view. The ground line is then drawn, and on it is placed the front view of the block from Fig. 6.51. The height of the station point is then decided—in this case, well above the block so that the top surfaces will be seen—and the horizon line is drawn at the station-point height.

To avoid the labor of redrawing the top and front views in the positions just described, the views can be cut from the orthographic drawing, oriented in position, and fastened with tacks or tape.

The *vanishing point* for any horizontal line can be found by drawing a visual ray from the station point *parallel* to the horizontal line and finding the piercing point of this visual ray with the picture plane. Thus, in Fig. 6.52, the line *SP* to *R* is parallel to the edge *AB* of the object, and *R* is the piercing point. Point *R* is then projected to the horizon line, locating *VR,* the vanishing point for *AB* and all edges parallel to *AB*. The vanishing point *VL* for *AC* and edges parallel to *AC* is found similarly, as shown.

In visualizing the location of a vanishing point, imagine that the edge, for example, *AB,* is moved to the right along the ground, still making the same angle with the picture plane; the intercept of *AB* will become less and less until, when *A* is in coincidence with *R,* the intercept will be zero. *R* then must be the top view of the vanishing point for all lines parallel to *AB*.

Point *A* lies in both the picture plane and the ground plane and will therefore be shown in the perspective at *a,* on the ground line, and in direct projection with the top view. The perspective of *AB* is determined by drawing a line from *a* to *VR* (the perspective *direction* of *AB*) and then projecting the intercept *Z* (of the visual rays *SP* to *B*) to the line, thus locating *b*.

All lines behind the picture plane are foreshortened in the picture, and only those lying in the picture plane will appear in their true length. For this reason, *all measurements must be made in the picture plane.* Since *AD* is in the picture plane, it will show in its actual height as *ad*.

A *measuring line* will be needed for any verticals such as *BF* that do not lie in the picture plane. If a vertical is brought forward to the picture plane along some established line, the true height can be measured in the picture plane. If, in Fig. 6.52, *BF* is imagined as moved forward along *ab* until *b* is in coincidence

6.35. Planes Parallel to the Picture Plane

with *a*, the true height can be measured vertically from *a*. This vertical line at *a* is then the measuring line for all heights in the vertical plane containing *a* and *b*. The height of *f* is measured from *a*, and from this height point, a vanishing line is drawn to *VR*; then from *Z* (the piercing point in the picture plane of the visual ray to *F*), *f* can be projected to the perspective.

The measuring line can also be thought of as the intersection of the picture plane with a vertical plane that contains the distance to be found. Thus *ad*, extended, is the measuring line for all heights in surface *ABFEGD*. The triangular rib in Fig. 6.52 is located by continuing surface *HJK* until it intersects the picture plane at *XY*, thereby establishing *xy* as the measuring line for all heights in *HJK*. In the figure, the height of *J* is measured on the measuring line *xy*, and *j* is found as described for *f*.

Note that heights can be measured with a scale on the measuring line or they can be projected from the front view, as indicated in Fig. 6.52.

To Make a Perspective Drawing

1. Draw the top view (edge of the picture plane).

2. Orient the object relative to the picture plane so that the object will appear to advantage, and draw the top view of the object.

3. Select a station point that will best show the shape of the object.

4. Draw the horizon and ground line.

5. Find the top view of the vanishing points for the principal horizontal edges by drawing lines parallel to the edges, through the station point, and to the picture plane.

6. Project from the top views of the vanishing points to the horizon line, thus locating the vanishing points for the perspective.

7. Draw the visual rays from the station point to the corners of the object in the top view, locating the piercing point of each ray with the picture plane.

8. Start the picture, building from the ground up and from the nearest corner to the more distant ones.

6.35. PLANES PARALLEL TO THE PICTURE PLANE. Objects with circles or other curves in a vertical plane can be oriented with their curved faces parallel to the picture plane. The curves will then appear in true shape. This method, often called "parallel perspective," is also suitable for interiors and for street vistas and similar scenes where considerable depth is to be represented.

The object in Fig. 6.53 has been

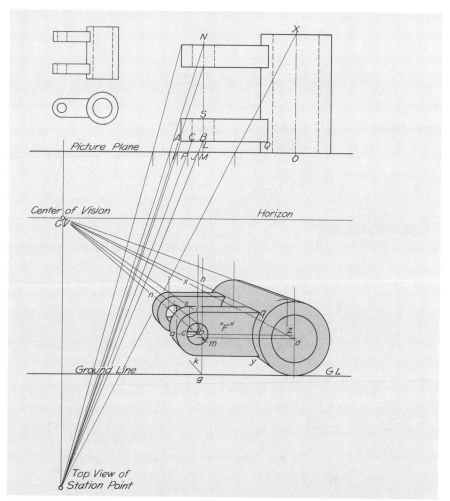

FIG. 6.53. Planes parallel to the picture plane. Compare the position of this object with that of Fig. 6.52.

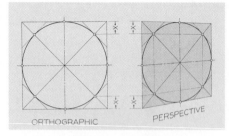

FIG. 6.54. Perspective of a circle. Points are plotted.

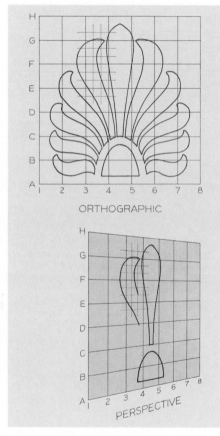

ORTHOGRAPHIC

PERSPECTIVE

FIG. 6.55. Graticulation. Points are plotted.

placed so that the planes containing the circular contours are parallel to the picture plane. The horizontal edges parallel to the picture plane will appear horizontal in the picture and will have no vanishing point. Horizontals perpendicular to the picture plane are parallel to the axis of vision and will vanish at the center of vision *CV*. Except for architectural interiors, the station point is usually located above the object and either to the right or left, yet not so far in any direction as to cause unpleasant distortion. For convenience, one face of the object is usually placed in the picture plane and is therefore not reduced in size in the perspective.

In Fig. 6.53, the end of the hub is in the picture plane; thus the center *o* is projected from *O* in the top view, and the circular edges are drawn in their true size. The center line *ox* is vanished from *o* to *CV*. To find the perspective of center line *MN*, a vertical plane is passed through *MN* intersecting the picture plane in measuring line *gh*. A horizontal line from *o* intersecting *gh* locates *m*, and *m* vanished to *CV* is the required line.

By using the two center lines from *o* and *m* as a framework, the remaining construction is simplified. A ray from the station point to *B* pierces the picture plane at *J*, which, projected to *mn*, locates *b*. The horizontal line *bz* is the center line of the front face of the nearer arm, and the intercept *IJ* gives the perspective radius *ab*. The circular hole having a radius *CB* has an intercept *PJ*, giving *cb* as the perspective radius. The arc *qy* has its center on *ox* at *z*. On drawing the tangents *lq* and *ky*, the face "*F*" is completed.

The remaining construction for the arms is exactly the same as that for "*F*."

The centers are moved back on the center lines, and the radii are found from their corresponding intercepts on the picture plane.

6.36. CIRCLES IN PERSPECTIVE. The perspective of a circle is a circle only when its plane is parallel to the picture plane; the circle appears as a straight line when its plane is receding from the station point. In all other positions the circle projects as an ellipse whose major and minor diameters are not readily determinable. The major diameter of the ellipse will be at some odd angle except when a vertical circle has its center on the horizon plane; then the major diameter will be vertical. Also, when a horizontal circle has its center directly above, below, or on the center of vision, the major diameter will be horizontal. It should be noted that in all cases the center of the circle is not coincident with the center of the ellipse representing the circle and that concentric circles are not represented by concentric ellipses. The major and minor diameters of the ellipses for concentric circles are not even parallel except in special cases.

The perspective of a circle can be plotted point by point, but the most rapid solution is had by enclosing the circle in a square, as shown in Fig. 6.54, and plotting points at the tangent points and at the intersections of the diagonals. The eight points thus determined are usually sufficient to give an accurate curve. The square, with its diagonals, is first drawn in the perspective. From the intersection of the diagonals, the vertical and horizontal center lines of the circle are established; where these center lines cross the sides of the square are four points on the curve. In the orthographic view, the measurement *X* is made, then laid out *in the picture plane* and vanished, crossing the diagonals at four additional points.

Note that the curve is tangent to the lines enclosing it and that the *direction* of the curve is established by these tangent lines; if the lines completing the circumscribing octagon are projected and drawn, the direction of the curve is established at eight points.

6.37.   GRATICULATION.   The perspectives of irregular curves can be drawn by projecting a sufficient number of points to establish the curve, but if the curve is complicated, the method of graticulation may be used to advantage. A square grid is overlaid on the orthographic view as shown in Fig. 6.55; then the grid is drawn in perspective and the outlines of the curve are transferred by inspection from the orthographic view.

6.38.   MEASURING POINTS.   It has been shown that all lines lying in the picture plane will be their own perspectives and can be scaled directly on the perspective drawing. The adaptation of this principle has an advantage in laying off a series of measurements, such as a row of pilasters, because it avoids a confusion of intercepts on the picture plane and the inaccuracies due to long projection lines.

In the measuring-points method, a surface, such as the wall between *A* and *B* in Fig. 6.56, is rotated into the picture plane for the purpose of making measurements, as shown at *AB'*. While in the picture plane, the entire surface can be laid out directly to the same scale as the top view; therefore, *ab'* and other horizontal dimensions of the surface are established along the ground line as shown. The counterrotation of the wall

to its actual position on the building and the necessary projections in the perspective are based on the principle that the rotation has been made about a vertical axis and that any point has traveled in a horizontal plane. By drawing, as usual, a line parallel to *BB'*, from the station point to the picture plane, and then projecting to the horizon, the vanishing point *MR* is found. This vanishing point is termed a *measuring point* and may be defined as the vanishing point for lines joining corresponding points of the actual and rotated positions of the face considered. The divisions on *ab'* are therefore vanished to *MR;* where this construction intersects *ab* (the perspective of *AB*), the lateral position of the pilasters, in the perspective, is determined. Heights are scaled on the vertical edge through *a,* as this edge lies in the picture plane. The perspective of the wall between *A* and *B* is completed by the regular methods previously described. For work on the end of the building, the end wall is rotated as indicated, measuring point *ML* is found, and the projections are continued as described for the front wall.

FIG. 6.56.   Use of measuring points. An edge of the object is rotated into the picture plane.

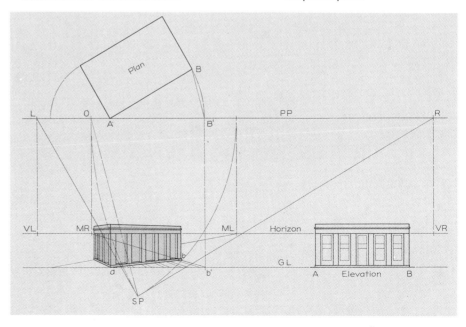

Measuring points can be more readily located if the draftsman recognizes that the triangles *ABB'* and *R O SP* are similar. Therefore, a measuring point is as far from its corresponding vanishing point as the station point is from the picture plane, measuring the latter parallel to the face concerned. *MR* can then be found by measuring the distance from the station point to *R* and laying off *RO* equal to the measurement, or by swinging an arc, with *R* as center, from the station point to *O,* as shown. The measuring point *MR* is then projected from *O.*

6.39. INCLINED LINES.

Any line that is not parallel or perpendicular to either the picture plane or the horizon plane is termed an inclined line. Any line may have a vertical plane passed through it, and if the vanishing line of the plane is found, a line in the plane will vanish at some point on the vanishing line of the plane. Vertical planes will vanish on vertical lines, just as horizontal planes vanish on a horizontal line, the horizon.

In Fig. 6.57, the points *a* to *e* have all been found by regular methods previously described. The vanishing point of the horizontal *ab* is *VR*. The vertical line through *VR* is the vanishing line of the plane of *abc* and all planes *parallel to abc*. This vanishing line is intersected by the extension of *de* at *UR*, thereby determining the vanishing point for *de* and all edges *parallel to de*.

The vanishing point for inclined lines can also be located on the theory that the vanishing point for any line can be determined by moving the line until it appears as a point, while still retaining its original angle with the picture plane. The vanishing point of *de* can therefore be located by drawing a line through the station point parallel to *DE* and finding its piercing point with the picture plane. This is done by laying out *SP T* at the angle β to *SP R* and erecting *RT* perpendicular to *SP R*. Then *RT* is the height of the vanishing point *UR* above *VR*.

If measuring points are used for the initial work on the perspective, it will be an advantage to recognize which one of the measuring points was used for determining horizontal measurements in the parallel vertical planes containing the inclined lines; at that measuring point, the angle β is laid out, above or below the horizon depending upon whether the lines slope up or down as they go into the distance. Where this construction intersects the vanishing line for the vertical planes containing the inclined lines, the vanishing point is located.

6.40. INCLINED PLANES.

An inclined plane is any plane not parallel or perpendicular to either the picture plane or the horizon plane. The vanishing line for an inclined plane can be found

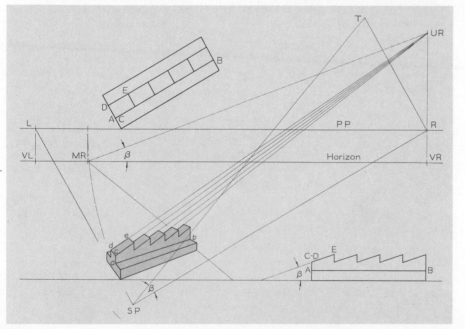

FIG. 6.57. Vanishing point of inclined lines. This simplifies construction when there are many parallel inclined lines.

by locating the vanishing points for any two systems of parallel lines in the inclined plane. To determine the vanishing line of plane *ABCD* in Fig. 6.58, the vanishing point *VL* of the horizontal edges *AD* and *BC* is one point, and the vanishing point *UR* for the inclined edges *AB* and *DC* gives a second point on the vanishing line *VL UR* for plane *ABCD*.

It is often necessary to draw the line of intersection of two inclined planes. The intersection will vanish at the point of intersection of the vanishing lines of both planes. The intersection *J* of the two vanishing lines of the roof planes in Fig. 6.58 is the vanishing point of the line of intersection of the two planes.

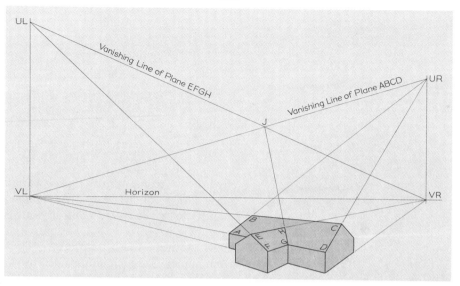

FIG. 6.58. Vanishing lines for inclined planes and vanishing point for the line of intersection of two inclined planes.

6.41. PICTORIAL SKETCHING.

The need for the engineer to be trained in freehand sketching was emphasized in Chap. 5, where the discussion referred particularly to sketching in orthographic projection. Before he can be said to have a command of the graphic language, his training in freehand drawing must include also acquiring the ability to sketch *pictorially* with skill and facility.

In designing and inventing, the first ideas come into the mind in pictorial form, and sketches made in this form preserve the ideas as visualized. From this record the preliminary orthographic design sketches are made. A pictorial sketch of an object or of some detail of construction can often be used to explain it to a client or workman who cannot read the orthographic projection intelligently. One of the best ways of reading a working drawing that is difficult to understand is to start a pictorial sketch of it. Usually before the sketch is finished, the orthographic drawing is perfectly clear. Often a pictorial sketch can be made more quickly and serve as a better record than orthographic views of the same piece. A young engineer should not be deterred by any fancied lack of "artistic ability." An engineer's sketch is a record of information, not a work of art. The one requirement is *good proportion*.

6.42. METHODS.

Although this is not a complete classification, there may be said to be three pictorial methods of sketching: axonometric, oblique, and perspective. The mechanical construction has been explained in detail.

6.43. PREREQUISITES.

It should be clearly understood at the outset that pictorial sketching means the making of a pictorial drawing *freehand*. The same construction that is used for locating points and lines and for drawing circles and arcs with instruments will be used in pictorial sketching. From this standpoint, a knowledge of the constructions already given is necessary before attempting pictorial sketching. Note in Figs. 6.69 to 6.75 that the ellipses representing holes and rounded contours have, before being drawn, been boxed

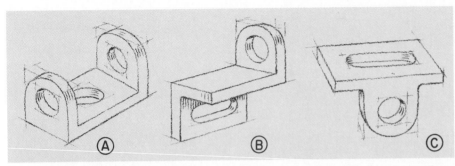

FIG. 6.59. Choice of axes and object position.

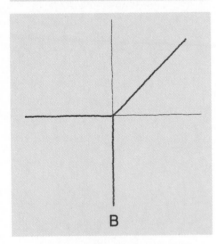

FIG. 6.60. Locating the axes. (*A*) isometric; (*B*) oblique at 45°.

in with construction lines representing the enclosing square in exactly the same manner as for an instrument drawing.

6.44. MATERIALS AND TECHNIQUE. The same materials, pencil grades, etc., used for orthographic freehand drawing, described in Chap. 5, are employed for pictorial sketching. The directions given there for drawing straight lines, circles, and arcs will apply here also.

6.45. PICTORIAL SKETCHING: CHOICE OF TYPE AND DIRECTION OF VIEW. After a clear visualization of the object, the first step is to select the type of pictorial—axonometric, oblique, or perspective—to be used.

Isometric is the simplest axonometric position, and it will serve admirably for representing most objects. Although dimetric or trimetric may be definitely advantageous for an object with some feature that is obscured or misleading in isometric, it is best to try isometric first, especially if there is doubt that another form will be superior. This is principally because proportions are easier to judge in isometric.

Oblique forms (cavalier or cabinet) may be used to advantage for cylindrical objects or for objects with a number of circular features in parallel planes. Nevertheless, a true circle, representing a circular feature parallel to the picture

plane in oblique, is much harder to sketch than an ellipse, representing the same feature in isometric, as the slightest deviation from a circle is evident, while the same deviation in an ellipse is unnoticed. Also, inherently, there is more distortion in the oblique than in axonometric forms. Therefore, especially for the sake of professional appearance, an axonometric form has the advantage.

Perspective is the best form for pictorial sketching because it is free from any distortion. A perspective is not much more difficult to sketch than an axonometric or an oblique, but attention must be paid to the convergence of the lines and to keeping good proportion. However, do not discard axonometric and oblique from consideration. As will be seen in paragraphs 6.46 and 6.47, these forms can be handled as successfully as perspective by some flattening of the axes and by converging the lines properly.

Choose carefully the *direction* in which the object is to be viewed. There are many possibilities. The object may be turned so that any lateral face will be represented on the right or the left side of the pictorial. Orient the object so that the two *principal* faces will show to advantage. Use reversed axes if necessary. Do this by mentally visualizing and turning the object in every possible position in order to arrive at the best representation for all features. Be alert to see that some feature will not be hidden by a portion in front of it. The proper choice of direction is an important factor in pictorial sketching.

Fig. 6.59 illustrates these points. At (*A*) an object is sketched in isometric; all features are clearly represented and the object appears natural in this form. At (*B*) trimetric has been used so that the slot in the lower portion is not obscured by the horizontal middle portion. At (*C*) another trimetric position has been chosen to present the semicircular ear as the definite front face of the object. For further illustration of the possibilities, study the pictorial drawings in Chap. 5.

6.46. SKETCHING THE AXES. After the type of pictorial and the position of the object have been decided upon, the first step in making the sketch is to draw the axes.

In isometric, the three axes should be located as nearly as possible 120° from one another (one vertical and two at 30° with the horizontal). Because no triangles are used in sketching, the angles must be located by judgment. Figure 6.60*A* shows a satisfactory method of judging the position of the lines. First draw a *light* horizontal and vertical and then divide both upper quadrants into thirds. The lines at the top of the lower thirds are then the two axes at 30° to the horizontal, and the third axis is the vertical. This method is simple and accurate because it is easy to estimate equal thirds of a quadrant.

In dimetric, the standard angles are 7° and 41°. For the 7° axis, again referring to Fig. 6.60*A,* draw the bisector of the 30° axis for isometric to get 15°, and then bisect again to get 7½°, which will be quite satisfactory and can be done fairly accurately. For the 41° axis, take the mid-line of the second 30° section, which is 45°, and shade it a little to approximate 41°.

In trimetric, almost any combination representing three mutually perpendicular lines is possible. However, a pronounced distortion will occur if the two transverse axes are more than 30° from

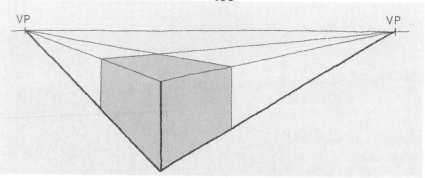

FIG. 6.61. Perspective layout with vanishing points.

the horizontal. Read the cautions in paragraph 6.47.

In oblique, the common angles are 30° and 45° although theoretically any angle is possible. To prevent violent distortion, never make the depth axis greater than 45°. To locate a 45° axis, sketch a vertical and horizontal as in Fig. 6.60*B,* and then sketch the bisector of the quadrant (see oblique positions) where the axis is wanted. For an axis at 30°, proceed as in Fig. 6.60*A* for isometric.

For perspective, as explained in paragraph 6.32, take care to have a reasonable included angle of view; otherwise a violent convergence will occur. In order to prevent difficulty, first locate two vanishing points, as in Fig. 6.61, as widely separated as the paper will allow (attach extra paper with scotch tape if necessary). Then sketch the *bottom* edges of the object (the heavier lines in Fig. 6.61) and on these sketch a rectangular shape, as shown. It will be immediately evident that the arrangement is satisfactory or that the vanishing points must be moved *or* that the base lines must be altered. Remember that the two vanishing points *must* be at the same level, the horizon.

6.47. SKETCHING THE PRINCIPAL LINES. Almost without exception, the first lines sketched should be those that box in the

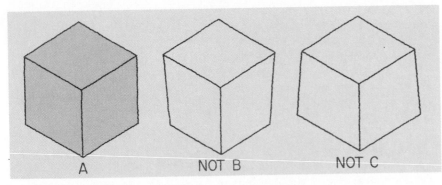

FIG. 6.62. Sketching vertical lines. These must be accurately vertical to define object shape.

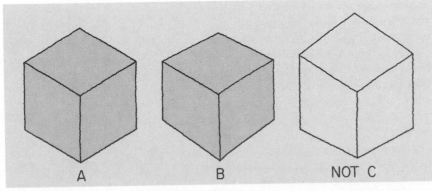

FIG. 6.63. Sketching the receding edges. These must be parallel (*A*); or converging (*B*); *never separating* (*C*).

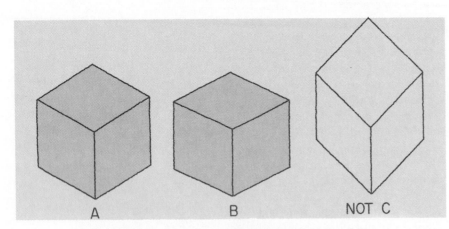

FIG. 6.64. Angle of axes. Isometric position (*A*) or flattened (*B*) gives a natural appearance. Distortion is inherent in steep axes as at (*C*).

whole object, or at least its major portion. These first lines are all-important to the success of the sketch, for early mistakes are difficult to correct later. Observe three points carefully:

1. *Verticals must be parallel to the vertical axis.* In Fig. 6.62 a cube is sketched correctly at (*A*). At (*B*) and (*C*) the same cube is sketched but at (*B*) the verticals converge downward and at (*C*), upward. It is evident that (*B*) and (*C*) do not look cubical at all, but like frustums of pyramids. This is proof that verticals *must be kept accurately vertical.* Be critical of the verticals throughout the construction—accurate verticals add a stability and crispness not attained in any other way.

2. *Transverse lines must be parallel or converging.* In Fig. 6.63 a cube is sketched at (*A*) with the transverse lines (receding right and left edges) made accurately parallel. At (*B*) these lines are made to converge as they recede. Note that (*B*) looks more natural than (*A*) because of the effect of perspective foreshortening. The monstrosity at (*C*) is produced by the separating of the receding lines as they recede. In his attempt to get the lines parallel, the beginner often makes a mistake like that at (*C*). Converge the lines deliberately, as in (*B*), to avoid the results of (*C*)!

3. *Axes must be kept flat to avoid distortion.* In Fig. 6.64 an accurate isometric sketch is shown at (*A*). At (*B*) the axes have been flattened to less than 30° with the horizontal. (*B*) possibly looks more natural than (*A*). At (*C*), however, the axes are somewhat more than 30° to the horizontal. Note the definite distortion and awkward appearance of (*C*). Therefore, especially in isometric, but also in other forms, keep the axes at their correct angle or flatter than the normal angle.

6.50. Sketching Circular Features

The foregoing three points must be kept constantly in mind. Hold your sketch at arm's length often during the work to see errors that are not so evident in the normal working position. Become critical of your own work and you will soon develop confidence and a good sense of line direction.

6.48. DIVISIONS FOR SYMMETRY. Continually in sketching, centers must be located and divisions of a face must be made into thirds, fourths, fifths, etc. Division into halves to locate a center line is the simplest and most common, and is easily accomplished by judging the mid-point along one of the sides, as indicated on the top face of the rectangular shape in Fig. 6.65. Also shown on this top face are additional divisions into quarters and eighths. Practice this to develop your judgment of equal spacings.

Division into thirds is a little harder but after short practice is readily done. The left face of Fig. 6.65 shows third divisions and one space divided in half to give a sixth point. The right face of Fig. 6.65 shows division into fifths.

Practice dividing lines or spaces into various equal units. The experience will be valuable in later work.

6.49. USES OF THE DIAGONAL. The two diagonals of a square or rectangle will locate its geometric center, as indicated on the left face of Fig. 6.66. The center is also readily located by drawing two center lines, estimating the middle of the space as shown on the top and right faces of Fig. 6.66.

The diagonals of a rectangular face can also be used to increase or decrease the rectangle symmetrically about the same center and in proportion as shown on the left face of Fig. 6.67, or with two sides coincident as shown on the right

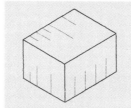

FIG. 6.65. Judging equal spaces. This can be done satisfactorily by eye.

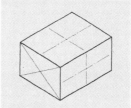

FIG. 6.66. Locating centers. Use diagonals or judge the position of center lines.

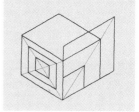

FIG. 6.67. Using diagonals to increase or decrease rectangular shapes.

face. To increase or decrease by equal units, the distance (or space) between lines must be judged as explained in paragraph 6.48.

6.50. SKETCHING CIRCULAR FEATURES. A circle in pictorial is an ellipse whose major diameter is always perpendicular to the *rotation axis*. Thus its minor diameter coincides on the drawing with the rotation axis (Fig. 6.68). These facts can be used to advantage when drawing an object principally made up of cylinders on the same axis. Note particularly from the above that *all* circles on horizontal planes are drawn as ellipses *with the major diameter horizontal* (Fig. 6.69).

Most objects, however, are made up of combinations of rectangular and circular features, and for this reason it is best to draw the enclosing pictorial square for all circular features. Figure 6.70 shows circles on all three axono-

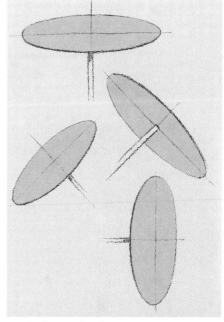

FIG. 6.68. Circles in pictorial. The major diameter of the ellipse is perpendicular to the axis of rotation.

FIG. 6.69. Circular features on horizontal planes. The major diameter of the ellipse is horizontal.

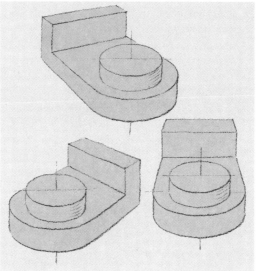

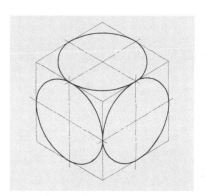

FIG. 6.70. Circles in isometric. Ellipses are tangent to the enclosing isometric squares at the mid-points of the sides.

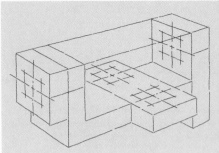

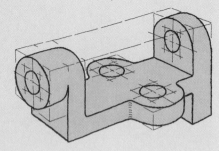

FIG. 6.71. Boxing construction for circular features. This is necessary to assure correct shape and proportion.

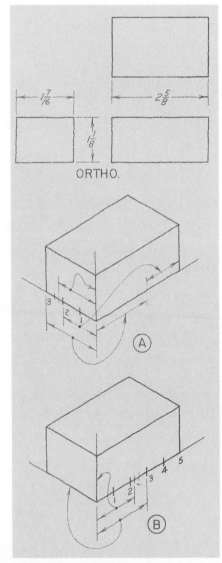

FIG. 6.72. Proportioning the distances. By dividing one side into units, all other distances are proportioned.

metric planes. Note particularly that the ellipses must be tangent to the sides of the pictorial square at the mid-points of the sides; accordingly, it is best always to draw center lines, also shown. Always sketch the enclosing pictorial square for *all* circular features because by this method the size of the ellipse and the thickness of the cylindrical portion are easily judged. Figure 6.71 illustrates the boxing of circular features. This object would be difficult to sketch without first boxing in the circular portions.

6.51. PROPORTIONING THE DISTANCES. The ability to make divisions into equal units, discussed in paragraph 6.48, is needed in proportioning distances on a sketch. The average object does not have distances that are easily divisible into even *inches, half inches,* etc., but as sketches are *not* made to scale, only to good proportions, great accuracy is not necessary. Also, most objects, dimensioned as they invariably are in various odd distances, are difficult to judge from the standpoint of one distance being ½, ⅓, ¼, etc., of another. Nevertheless, the proportioning can be done easily and quickly by the method we are about to discuss.

Figure 6.72 shows a simple rectangular object, but the distances are not multiples of any simple unit. The best way to proportion this object (and others) is to lay off on *one* axis a distance that is to represent one side of the object. This *sets the size* of the sketch. Then

divide this first side into some unit that can be used easily to proportion other distances. At (*A*) the *left* side has been laid off and divided into three parts. Each of these parts now represents *approximately* a half inch. To get the distance for the vertical axis, the last third (at the rear) has been divided in half, and again in half, so that the dimension shown is approximately 1⅛ in. Transfer this distance to the vertical axis (1) by judging by eye, (2) by measuring with the finger on the pencil, or (3) by marking the distance on a piece of scratch paper. The method to be used will suggest itself according to the relative accuracy needed. The right-axis distance is obtained similarly, by first transferring the whole left distance (representing approximately 1½ in.) and then adding two-thirds of the left distance (approx. 1 in.), which gives a total of 2½ in., close enough to the actual 2⅝ in. dimension of the object. Any side may be chosen to start the sketch. At (*B*) the right side has been laid off and divided, this time, into five parts so that again each unit is approximately ½ in. The procedure is then similar to that described for (*A*).

Remember that great accuracy is unnecessary. Do not make the proportioning a burden. It is simply a method of getting distances reasonably close to the actual distance and eliminating the need for wild guesses or extra construction on the sketch.

Figure 6.73 shows the method applied to a more complex object. The left axis has been divided into 4 parts. In this case the upper details have been located by projection upward from the left axis divisions, a method that is often used. Note the boxing of circular features, as described in paragraph 6.50. Study this figure carefully, with particular attention to the proportioning and construction.

6.52. STEPS IN MAKING A PICTORIAL SKETCH.

Because a variety of objects are sketched, the order of procedure will not always be the same, but the following will serve as a guide:

A. Visualize the shape and proportions of the object from the orthographic views, a model, or other source.
B. Mentally picture the object in space and decide the pictorial position that will best describe its shape.
C. Decide on the type of pictorial to use —axonometric, oblique, or perspective.
D. Pick a suitable paper size.
E. Then proceed as shown in Fig. 6.74.

Numbers 1 through 6 show light con-

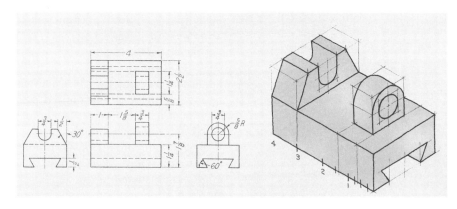

FIG. 6.73. Proportioning the distances. After one side is divided into units, distances are projected or transferred.

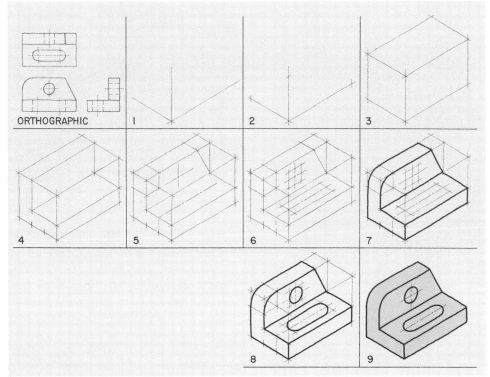

FIG. 6.74. Steps in making a pictorial sketch. Progressive layout, (1) to (6); finishing, (7) to (9).

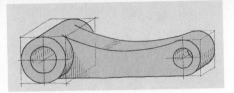

FIG. 6.75. An oblique sketch. Note boxing of circular features.

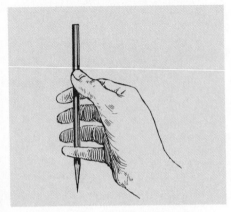

FIG. 6.76. Estimating distances and proportion.

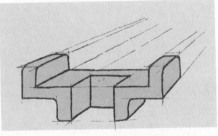

FIG. 6.77. A perspective sketch. The front face of the object is parallel to the picture plane.

struction, 7, 8, and 9 completion to final weight.

1. Sketch the axes.
2. Lay off the proportions of an enclosing rectangular box for the whole object or a principal portion of it.
3. Sketch the enclosing box.
4. Divide one axis for proportioning distances and sketch the most dominant detail of the object.
5. Proportion smaller details by reference to the divided axis and sketch the enclosing boxes, center lines, or outlines.
6. Complete the boxes for circular features. Check to be sure that all features are in good proportion and that there are no errors in representation (see paragraph 6.47). In work with light lines, corrections are easily made.
7. Start sketch to final line width. Begin with the dominant feature.
8. Sketch the smaller details.
9. Remove construction.

6.53. AXONOMETRIC SKETCHING. The methods presented thus far have been directed toward the making of axonometric sketches because they are the type most used. However, the practices given apply to oblique and perspective sketching, for which additional helps are given in the two paragraphs that follow.

6.54. OBLIQUE SKETCHING. The advantage of oblique projection in preserving one face without distortion is of particular value in sketching, as illustrated by Fig. 6.75. The painful effect of distortion in oblique drawing that is done instrumentally can be greatly lessened in sketching by foreshortening the depth axis to a pleasing proportion. By converging the lines parallel to the depth axis, the effect of perspective is obtained. This converging in axonometric or oblique is sometimes called "fake perspective."

6.55. PERSPECTIVE SKETCHING. A sketch made in perspective gives a better effect than in axonometric or oblique. For constructing a perspective drawing of a proposed structure from its plans and elevations, a knowledge of the principles of perspective drawing is required, but for making a perspective sketch from the object, you can get along by observing the ordinary phenomena of perspective which affect everything we see: the fact that objects appear proportionately smaller as their distance from the eye increases, that parallel lines appear to converge as they recede, and that horizontal lines and planes appear to "vanish" on the horizon.

In perspective sketching from the model, make the drawing simply by observation, estimating the directions and proportionate lengths of lines by sighting and measuring on the pencil held at arm's length and use your knowledge of

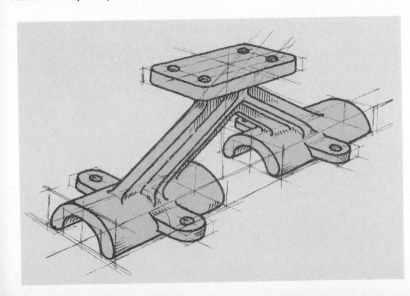

FIG. 6.78. A perspective sketch. The object is in an angular position.

perspective phenomena as a check. With the drawing board or sketch pad held in a comfortable drawing position perpendicular to the line of sight from the eye to the object, test the direction of a line by holding the pencil at arm's length parallel to the board, rotating the arm until the pencil appears to coincide with the line on the model, and then moving it parallel to this position back to the board. Estimate the apparent lengths of lines in the same way; holding the pencil in a plane perpendicular to the line of sight, mark with the thumb the length of pencil which covers the line of the model, rotate the arm with the thumb held in position until the pencil coincides with another line, and then estimate the proportion of this measurement to the second line (Fig. 6.76).

Make the sketch lightly, with free sketchy lines, and do not erase any lines until the whole sketch has been blocked in. *Do not make the mistake of getting the sketch too small.*

In starting a sketch from the object, set it in a position to give the most advantageous view, and sketch the directions of the principal lines, running them past the limits of the figure toward their vanishing points. Block in the enclosing squares for all circles and circle arcs and proceed with the figure, drawing the main outlines first and adding details later; then brighten the sketch with heavier lines.

The drawing in Fig. 6.77 shows the general appearance of a "one-point" perspective sketch before the construction lines have been erased. Figure 6.78 is an example showing the object turned at an angle to the picture plane.

6.56.   PICTORIAL ILLUSTRATION. Pictorial illustration combines any one of the regular pictorial methods with some method of shading or "rendering." In considering a specific problem, decide upon the pictorial form—axonometric, oblique, or perspective—and then choose a method of shading that is suited to the method of reproduction and the general effect desired.

6.57.   LIGHT AND SHADE. The conventional position of the light in light-and-shade drawing is the same as that used for orthographic line shading, that is, a position to the left, in front of, and above the object. Any surface or portion of a surface perpendicular to the light direction and directly illuminated by the light would receive the greatest amount of light and be lightest in tone on the drawing; any face not illuminated by the light would be "in shade" and darkest on the drawing. Other surfaces, receiving less light than the "high" light but more than a shade portion, would be intermediate in tone.

An understanding of the simple one-light method of illumination is needed at the outset, as well as some artistic appreciation for the illumination on various surfaces of the object. Figure 6.79 shows a sphere, cylinder, cone, and cube illuminated as described and shaded accordingly. Study the tone values in this illustration.

6.58.   SHADE LINES. Shade lines, by their contrast with other lines, add some effect of light and shade to the drawing. These lines used alone, without other shading, give the simplest possible shading method. Usually the best effect is obtained by using heavy lines only for the left vertical and upper horizontal edges of the dark faces (Fig. 6.80). Holes and other circular features are drawn

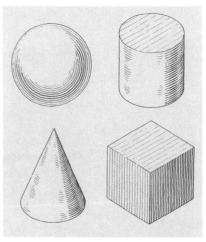

FIG. 6.79.   Light and shade. The light source is from the upper left front.

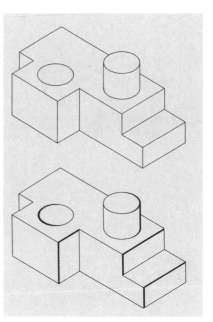

FIG. 6.80.   Outline and shade lines. The side away from the light source is drawn with heavier lines.

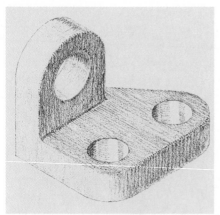

FIG. 6.81.   Continuous-tone shading.

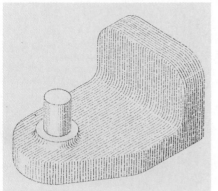

FIG. 6.82.   Line-tone shading.

with heavy lines on the shade side. Shade lines should be used sparingly as the inclusion of too many heavy lines simply adds weight to the drawing and does not give the best effect.

6.59.   PENCIL RENDERING.   There are two general methods of pencil shading—continuous tone and line tone. Continuous-tone shading is done with a fairly soft pencil with its point flattened. A medium-rough paper is best for the purpose. Start with a light, over-all tone and then build the middle tones and shade portions gradually. Figure 6.81 is an example. Clean high lights with an eraser.

Line-tone shading requires a little more skill, as the tones are produced by line spacing and weight. Light lines at wide spacing produce the lightest tone, and heavy lines at close spacing make the darkest shade. Leave high lights perfectly white. Pure black may be used

sparingly for deep shade or shadow. Figure 6.82 is an example, drawn with only a light outline.

Complete over-all shading is somewhat heavy, and a lighter, more open treatment is usually desired. To achieve this, leave light portions of the object with little or no shading, and line middle tones and shade sparingly. The few lines used strongly suggest light, shade, and surface finish (Fig. 6.83). There are many variations which can be made in this type of rendering.

6.60.   PEN-AND-INK RENDERING.   Pen-and-ink methods follow the same general pattern as work in pencil, with the exception that no continuous tone is possible. However, there are some variations not ordinarily used in pencil work. Figure 6.84 shows line techniques. As in pencil work, the common and usually the most pleasing method is the partially shaded, suggestive system.

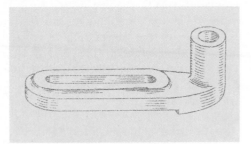

FIG. 6.83.   Line-shading technique in pencil.

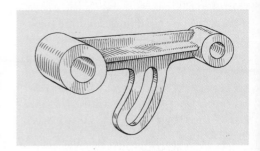

FIG. 6.84.   Line-shading technique in ink.

PROBLEMS

The following problems are intended to furnish practice (1) in the various methods of pictorial representation and (2) in reading and translating orthographic projections.

In reading a drawing, remember that a line on any view always means an edge or a change in direction of the surface of the object and always look at another view to interpret the meaning of the line.

GROUP 1. ISOMETRIC DRAWINGS

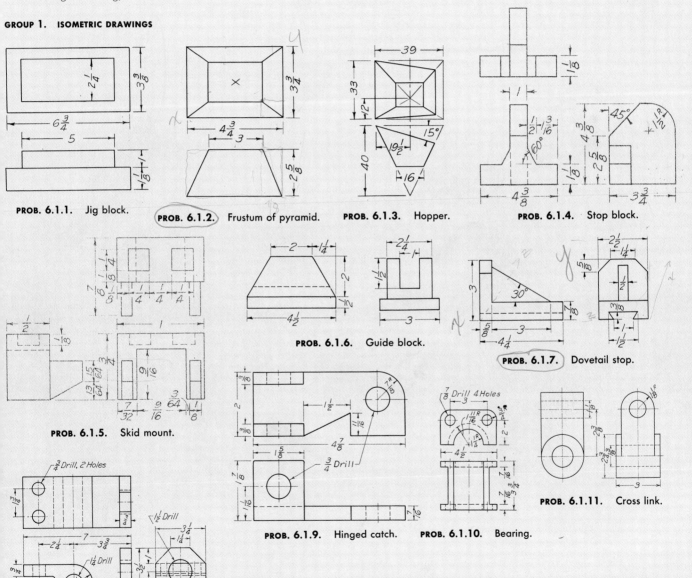

PROB. 6.1.1. Jig block.

PROB. 6.1.2. Frustum of pyramid.

PROB. 6.1.3. Hopper.

PROB. 6.1.4. Stop block.

PROB. 6.1.5. Skid mount.

PROB. 6.1.6. Guide block.

PROB. 6.1.7. Dovetail stop.

PROB. 6.1.8. Bracket.

PROB. 6.1.9. Hinged catch.

PROB. 6.1.10. Bearing.

PROB. 6.1.11. Cross link.

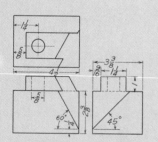

PROB. 6.1.12. Wedge block.

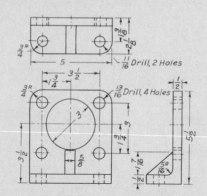

PROB. 6.1.13. Head attachment.

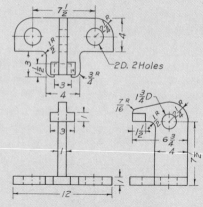

PROB. 6.1.14. Slide stop.

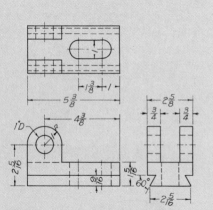

PROB. 6.1.15. Dovetail bracket.

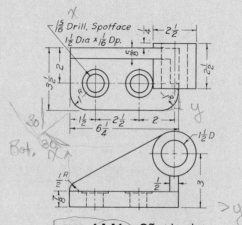

PROB. 6.1.16. Offset bracket.

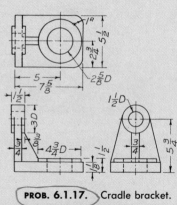

PROB. 6.1.17. Cradle bracket.

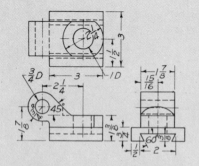

PROB. 6.1.18. Dovetail hinge.

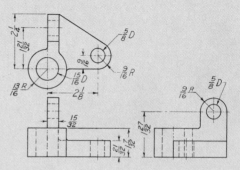

PROB. 6.1.19. Cable clip.

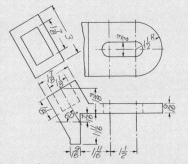

PROB. 6.1.20. Strut anchor.

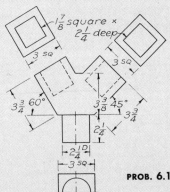

PROB. 6.1.21. Strut swivel.

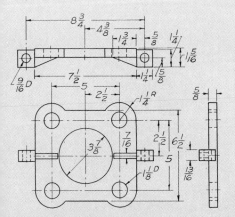

PROB. 6.1.22. Tie plate.

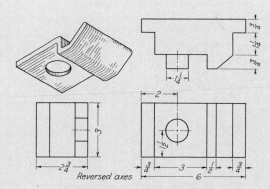

PROB. 6.1.23. Forming punch.

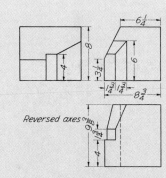

PROB. 6.1.24. Springing stone.

GROUP 2.   ISOMETRIC SECTIONS

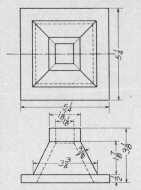

PROB. 6.2.1. Column base.

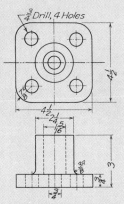

PROB. 6.2.2. Base plate.

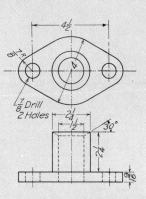

PROB. 6.2.3. Gland.

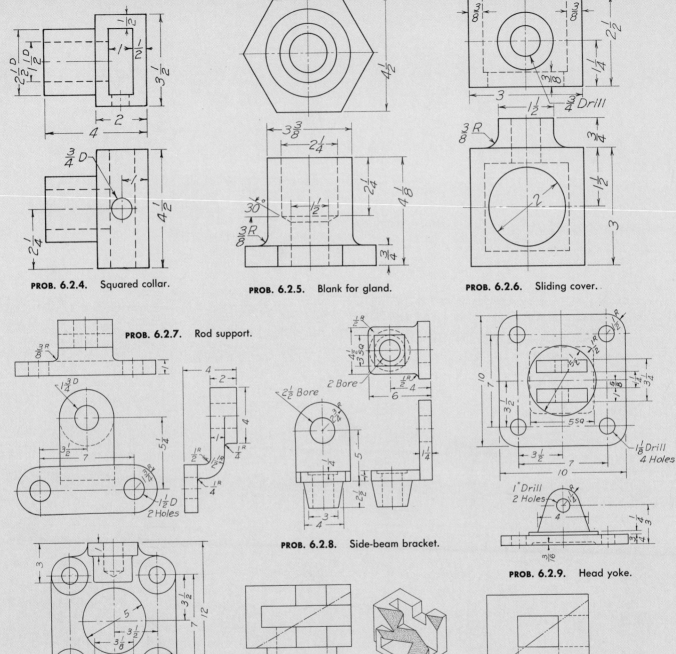

PROB. 6.2.4. Squared collar.

PROB. 6.2.5. Blank for gland.

PROB. 6.2.6. Sliding cover.

PROB. 6.2.7. Rod support.

PROB. 6.2.8. Side-beam bracket.

PROB. 6.2.9. Head yoke.

PROB. 6.2.10. Trunnion plate.

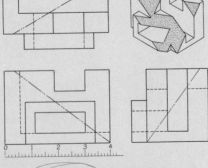

PROB. 6.2.11. Section study.

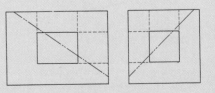

PROB. 6.2.12. Section study.

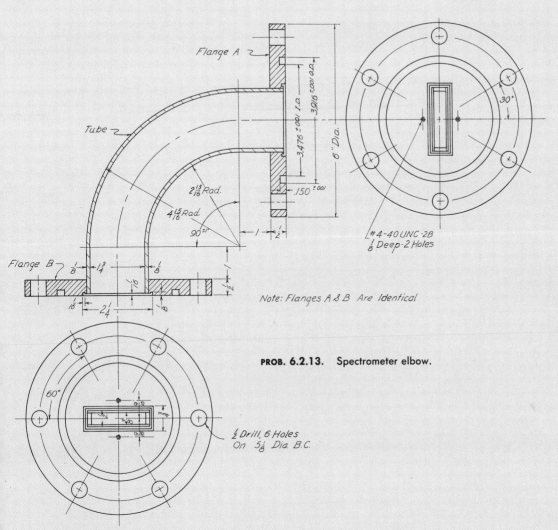

Flange A

Tube

$2\frac{13}{16}$ Rad.

$4\frac{15}{16}$ Rad.

$90°\pm1°$

3.476 ±.001 I.D.

3.9/6 ±.001 O.D.

6" Dia.

.150 ±.001

$1\frac{1}{2}$

#4-40 UNC-2B
$\frac{1}{8}$ Deep-2 Holes

30°

Flange B $\frac{1}{8}$ $1\frac{3}{4}$ $\frac{1}{8}$

$\frac{3}{16}$ $\frac{1}{2}$

$\frac{1}{16}$ $2\frac{1}{4}$ $\frac{1}{8}$

Note: Flanges A & B Are Identical

60°

$\frac{1}{2}$ Drill, 6 Holes
On $5\frac{1}{2}$ Dia. B.C.

PROB. 6.2.13. Spectrometer elbow.

GROUP 3. OBLIQUE DRAWINGS

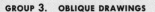

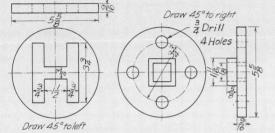

$5\frac{5}{8}$

$\frac{9}{16}$

$3\frac{1}{4}$

$\frac{3}{4}$

$\frac{3}{4}$ $\frac{1}{2}$ $\frac{3}{4}$

Draw 45° to left

PROB. 6.3.1. Letter die.

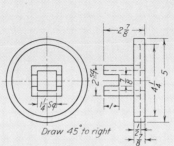

Draw 45° to right
$\frac{3}{4}$ Drill
4 Holes

$5\frac{5}{8}$

$\frac{11}{16}$

$\frac{5}{8}$

$\frac{9}{16}$

PROB. 6.3.2. Guide plate.

Draw 45° to right

$2\frac{7}{8}$

$2\frac{3}{4}$

$\frac{7}{8}$

5

$4\frac{1}{4}$

$1\frac{1}{4}$ Sq.

1

$\frac{1}{2}$

$2\frac{7}{8}$

PROB. 6.3.3. Brace base.

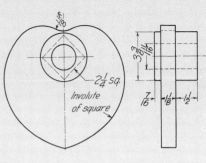

$1\frac{1}{8}$ R

$2\frac{1}{4}$ Sq.

Involute
of square

$3\frac{3}{8}$

$1\frac{1}{16}$

$\frac{7}{16}$ $\frac{1}{8}$ $1\frac{1}{2}$

Draw half size and 30° to right

PROB. 6.3.4. Heart cam.

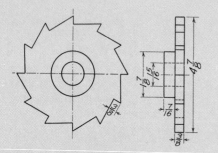

Draw 45° to left

PROB. 6.3.5.   Ratchet wheel.

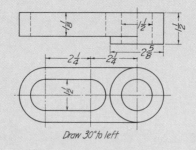

Draw 30° to left

PROB. 6.3.6.   Slotted link.

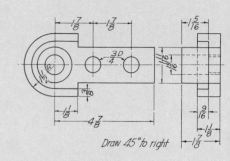

Draw 45° to right

PROB. 6.3.7.   Swivel plate.

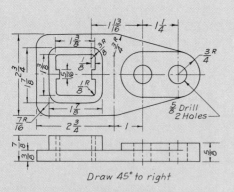

Draw 45° to right

PROB. 6.3.8.   Slide bracket.

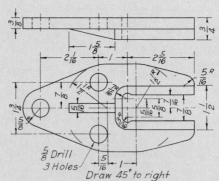

Draw 45° to right

PROB. 6.3.9.   Jaw bracket.

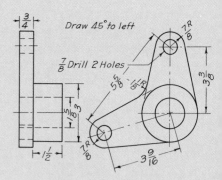

Draw 45° to left

PROB. 6.3.10.   Bell crank.

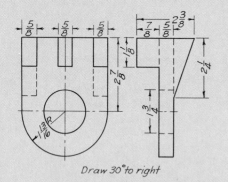

Draw 30° to right

PROB. 6.3.11.   Stop plate.

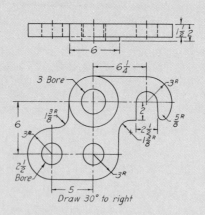

Draw 30° to right

PROB. 6.3.12.   Hook brace.

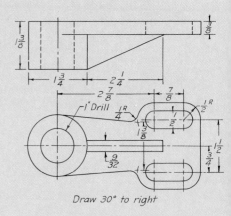

Draw 30° to right

PROB. 6.3.13.   Adjusting-rod support.

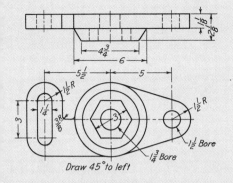

PROB. 6.3.14. Link.

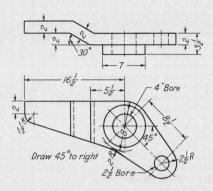

PROB. 6.3.15. Pawl.

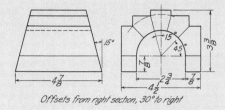

Offsets from right section, 30° to right

PROB. 6.3.16. Culvert model.

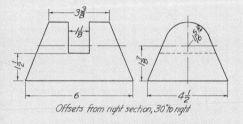

Offsets from right section, 30° to right

PROB. 6.3.17. Slotted guide.

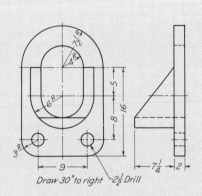

Draw 30° to right

PROB. 6.3.18. Support bracket.

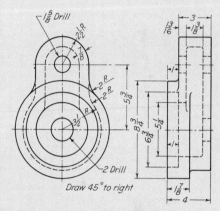

Draw 45° to right

PROB. 6.3.19. Port cover.

GROUP 4. OBLIQUE SECTIONS

6.4.1. Oblique full section of sliding cone.
6.4.1*A.* Oblique half section of sliding cone.
6.4.2. Oblique full section of conveyor-trough end.

6.4.2*A.* Oblique half section of conveyor-trough end.
6.4.3. Oblique full section of ceiling flange.
6.4.3*A.* Oblique half section of ceiling flange.

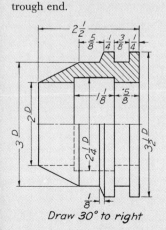

Draw 30° to right

PROB. 6.4.1. Sliding cone.

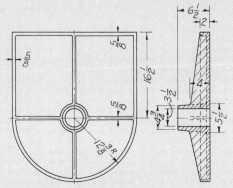

Draw 30° to right

PROB. 6.4.2. Conveyor-trough end.

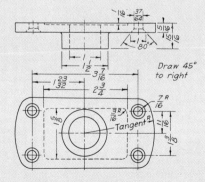

Draw 45° to right

PROB. 6.4.3. Ceiling flange.

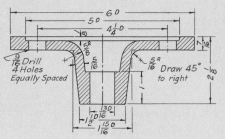

PROB. 6.4.4. Hanger flange.

6.4.4. Oblique full section of hanger flange.

6.4.4A. Oblique half section of hanger flange.

6.4.5. Oblique half section of the base plate of Prob. 6.2.2.

6.4.6. Oblique half section of the gland of Prob. 6.2.3.

6.4.7. Oblique half section of regulator level.

6.4.8. Oblique full section of anchor plate.

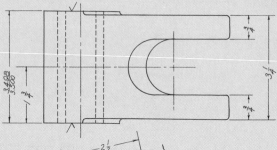

PROB. 6.4.7. Regulator level.

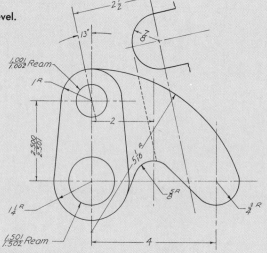

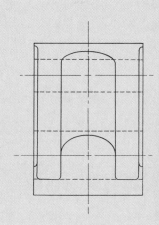

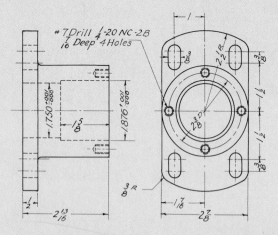

PROB. 6.4.8. Anchor plate.

6.4.9. Oblique drawing of shaft guide. Use sections, as needed, to describe the part.

6.4.10. Oblique half section of rod support. Partial sections and phantom lines can also be used to describe the part.

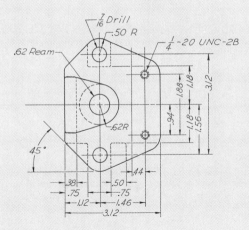

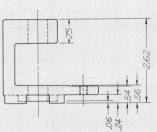

PROB. 6.4.9. Shaft guide.

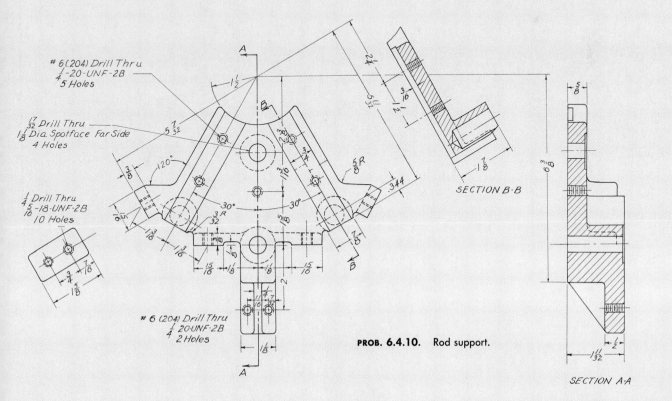

PROB. 6.4.10. Rod support.

SECTION A·A

GROUP 5.   DIMETRIC AND CABINET DRAWING

6.5.1.   Make a dimetric drawing of the jig block, Prob. 6.1.1.

6.5.2.   Make a dimetric drawing of the guide block, Prob. 6.1.6.

6.5.3.   Make a cabinet drawing of the gland, Prob. 6.2.3.

6.5.4.   Make a cabinet drawing of the ceiling flange, Prob. 6.4.3.

GROUP 6.   PERSPECTIVE DRAWINGS

The following are a variety of different objects to be drawn in perspective. A further selection can be made from the orthographic drawings in other chapters.

6.6.1.   Double wedge block.
6.6.2.   Notched holder.
6.6.3.   Crank.

6.6.4.   Corner lug.
6.6.5.   House.
6.6.6.   Church.

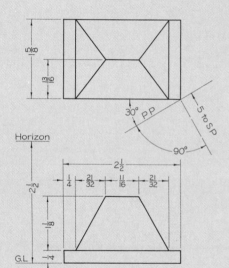

PROB. 6.6.1.   Double wedge block.

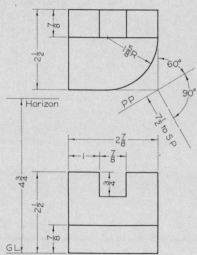

PROB. 6.6.2.   Notched holder.

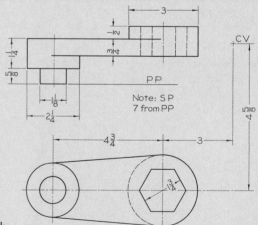

PROB. 6.6.3.   Crank.

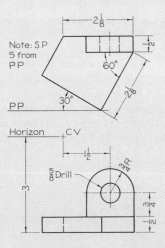

PROB. 6.6.4. Corner lug.

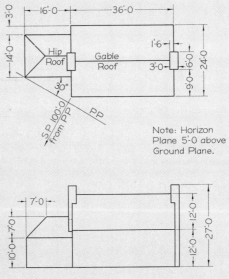

Note: Horizon
Plane 5'-0 above
Ground Plane.

PROB. 6.6.5. House.

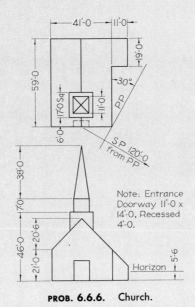

Note: Entrance
Doorway 11'-0 x
14'-0, Recessed
4'-0.

PROB. 6.6.6. Church.

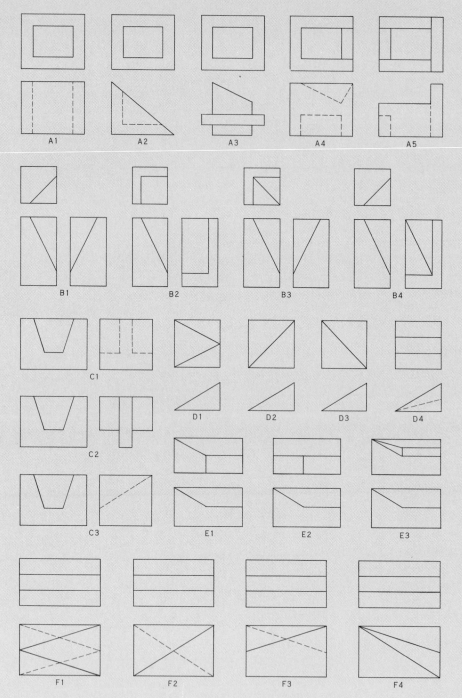

The following problems are planned to develop skill not only in pictorial sketching but also in reading orthographic drawings. Make the sketches to suitable size on 8½- by 11-in. paper, choosing the most appropriate form of representation—axonometric, oblique, or perspective—with partial, full, or half sections as needed. Small fillets and rounds may be ignored in these problems and shown as sharp corners.

PROB. 6.7.1. Objects to be sketched.

PROB. 6.7.2. Objects to be sketched.

PROB. 6.7.3.   Objects to be sketched.

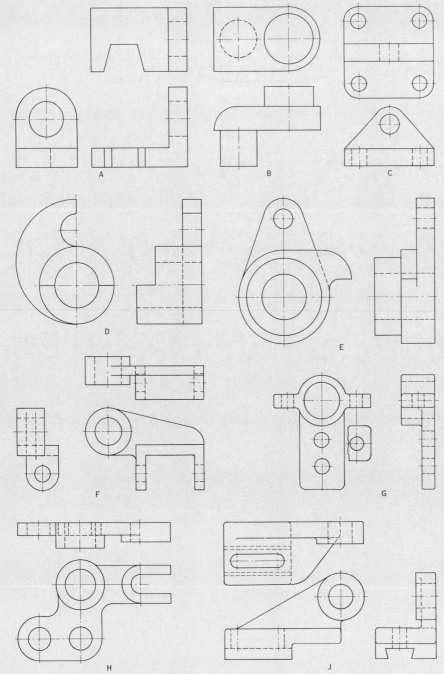

PROB. 6.7.4. Objects to be sketched.

PROB. 6.7.5.   Objects to be sketched.

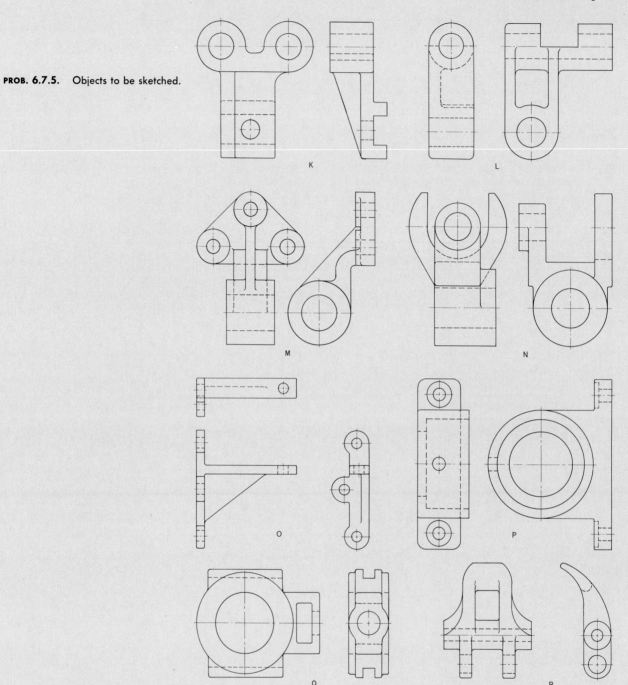

GROUP 8.   OBLIQUE SKETCHING

Select an object from Group 3 not previously drawn with instruments, and make an oblique sketch.

GROUP 9.   PERSPECTIVE SKETCHING

Select an object not previously drawn with instruments, and make a perspective sketch.

GROUP 10.   AXONOMETRIC AND OBLIQUE PROJECTION FROM ORTHOGRAPHIC VIEWS

Any of the problems given in this chapter may be used for making axonometric or oblique projections from the orthographic views by first drawing the orthographic views to suitable scale and then employing these views as described in paragraphs 6.26 to 6.28 to obtain the pictorial projection.

GROUP 11.   PICTORIAL DRAWINGS FROM MACHINE PARTS

Machine parts, either rough castings and forgings or finished parts, offer valuable practice in making pictorial drawings. Choose pieces to give practice in isometric and oblique drawing. Use the most appropriate form of representation, and employ section and half-section treatments where necessary to give clearer description.

GROUP 12.   PICTORIAL WORKING DRAWINGS

Any of the problems in this chapter offer practice in making complete pictorial working drawings. Follow the principles of dimensioning in Chap. 17. The form and placement of the dimension figures are given in paragraph 17.37.

6.12.1   Pictorial working drawing of dovetail stop, Prob. 6.1.7.

6.12.2.   Pictorial working drawing of hinged catch, Prob. 6.1.9.

6.12.3.   Pictorial working drawing of tie plate, Prob. 6.1.22.

6.12.4.   Pictorial working drawing of head yoke, Prob. 6.2.9.

6.12.5.   Pictorial working drawing of jaw bracket, Prob. 6.3.9.

6.12.6.   Pictorial working drawing of adjusting-rod support, Prob. 6.3.13.

6.12.7.   Pictorial working drawing of port cover, Prob. 6.3.19.

6.12.8.   Pictorial working drawing of ceiling flange, Prob. 6.4.3.

6.12.9. Make a pictorial working drawing of the extension block. Use any reasonable technique such as exploding the part (with note to explain), partial sections, extra views, or phantom lines to completely describe the part.

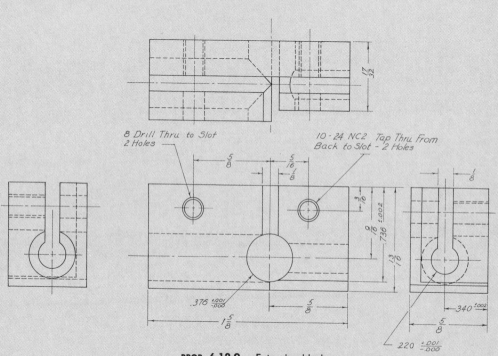

PROB. 6.12.9. Extension block.

6.12.10. Make a pictorial working drawing of the double sleeve clamp. Show the two halves as an exploded assembly.

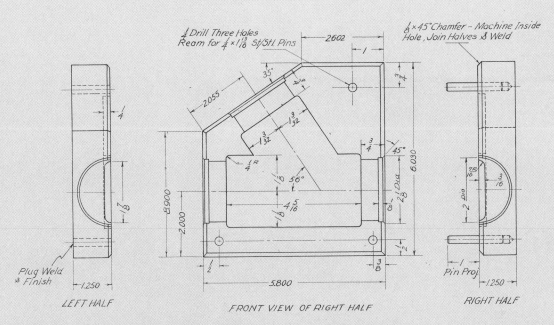

PROB. 6.12.10. Double sleeve clamp.

Sectional views are used to describe the internal shape of objects more clearly than is possible by the use of outside views alone. This is accomplished either by drawing separate sectional views depicting internal shape or, in cases where the external shape is still obvious, by making one or more of the regular views as a sectional view. The chapter describes the many types, uses, and conventional treatments.

Sectional Views and Conventional Practices

7.1. **DEFINITION.** When the interior of an object is complicated or when the component parts of a machine are drawn assembled, an attempt to show hidden portions by the customary dashed lines in regular orthographic views often results in a confusing network, as shown in Fig. 7.1 at (*A*), which is difficult to draw and almost impossible to read clearly.

In cases of this kind, to aid in describing the object, one or more views are drawn to show the object as if a portion had been cut away to reveal the interior, as at (*B*). Also, if some detail of the shape of an object is not clear, a cut taken through the portion and then turned up, or turned up and removed, as at (*C*), will describe the shape concisely and often eliminate the need for an extra complete view.

Either of these conventions is called a *section*, which is defined as an imaginary cut made through an object to expose the interior or to reveal the shape of a portion. A view in which all or a substantial portion of the view is sectioned is known as a *sectional view*.

For some simple objects where the orthographic, *unsectioned* views can be easily read, sectional views are often preferable because they show clearly and emphasize the solid portions, the voids, and the shape.

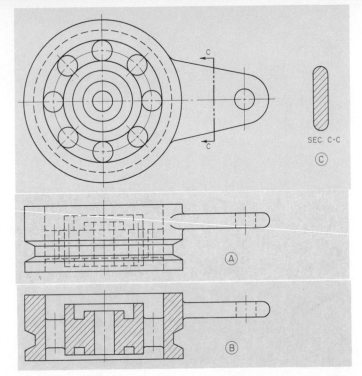

SEC. C-C

©

FIG. 7.1. Advantage of sectional views. (A) orthographic view with hidden edges indicated by dashed lines; (B) the same view but made as a section to clarify the shape; (C) cross-sectional shape of lug shown by removed section.

7.2. HOW SECTIONS ARE SHOWN. The place from which the section is taken must be identifiable on the drawing, and the solid portions and voids must be distinguished on the sectional view. The place from which the section is taken is in many cases obvious, as it is for the sectional view (B) in Fig. 7.1; the section is quite evidently taken through the center (at the center line of the top view). In such cases no further description is needed. If the place from which a section is taken is not obvious, as at (C), a *cutting plane,* directional arrows, and identification letters are used to identify it. Whenever there is any doubt,

the cutting plane (see alphabet of lines, paragraph 2.39) should be shown. A cutting plane is the imaginary medium used to show the path of cutting an object to make a section. Cutting planes for each kind of section will be discussed in the following paragraphs.

A sectional view must show which portions of the object are solid material and which are spaces. This is done by section lining, sometimes called "cross-hatching," the solid parts with lines, as shown at (B) and (C). Section-lining practice is given in paragraph 7.11, where codes for materials are also discussed.

7.3. TYPES OF SECTIONS. Although the different sections and sectional views have been named for identification and for specifying the type of view required in a drawing, the names are not shown on the drawing for the same reason that a top, front, or side view would not be so labeled—the views are easily interpreted and a workman does not require the name to read the drawing. The names are assigned by the character of the section or the amount of the *view* in section, *not* by the amount of the object removed.

7.4. FULL SECTION. A full section is one in which the cutting plane passes entirely across the object, as in Fig. 7.2, so

FIG. 7.2. Cutting planes for a full section. The plane may cut straight across (A) or change direction (B and C) to pass through features to be shown.

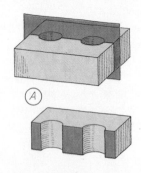

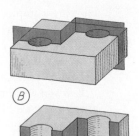

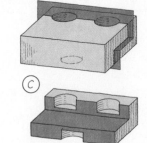

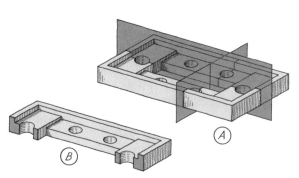

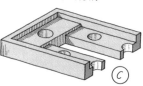

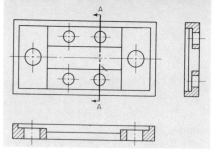

FIG. 7.3. Two cutting planes. The two planes at (A) will produce sections (B) and (C). Each section is considered separately, without reference to what has been removed for the other view.

FIG. 7.4. Full sections. This is the orthographic drawing of the object in Fig. 7.3. The cutting-plane position is obvious for the front-view section and is not identified in the top view. Section A-A (side view) has its cutting plane identified because the section might be made elsewhere.

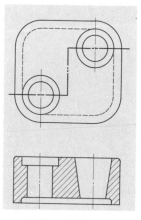

FIG. 7.5. A full section. The cutting plane is offset to pass through both principal features of the object.

that the resulting view is completely "in section." The cutting plane may pass straight through, as at (A), or be offset, changing direction forward or backward, to pass through features it would otherwise have missed, as at (B) and (C). Sometimes *two* views are drawn in section on a pair of cutting planes, as at (A) in Fig. 7.3. In such cases each view is considered separately, without reference to what has been removed for another view. Thus (B) shows the portion remaining and the cut surface for one sectional view, and (C) for the other sectional view. Figure 7.4 is the orthographic drawing of the object, with indication for sectioning, as shown in Fig. 7.3. Both the front and side views are full-sectional views.

Figure 7.5 shows a full section made on an offset cutting plane. Note that the *change in plane direction* is *not* shown on the sectional view, for the cut is purely imaginary and *no edge* is present on the object at this position.

7.5. HALF SECTION.

This is a view sometimes used for symmetrical objects in which one half is drawn in section and the other half as a regular exterior view. The cutting plane is imagined to extend halfway across, then forward, as in Fig. 7.6. A half section has the advantage of showing both the interior and exterior

of the object on one view without using dashed lines, as at (A) in Fig. 7.7. However, a half section thus made is difficult to dimension without ambiguity, and so, if needed for clarity, dashed lines may be added, as at (B).

Note particularly that a *center line* separates the exterior and interior portions on the sectional view. This is for the same reason that the change in plane direction for the offset of the cutting plane of Fig. 7.5 is not shown—no edge exists *on the object* at the center.

7.6. BROKEN-OUT SECTION.

Often an interior portion must be shown but a full or half section cannot be used because the cutting plane would remove some feature that must be included. For this condition the cutting plane is ex-

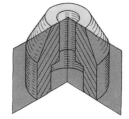

FIG. 7.6. Cutting plane for a half section. The resulting sectional view will be half in section and half an external view.

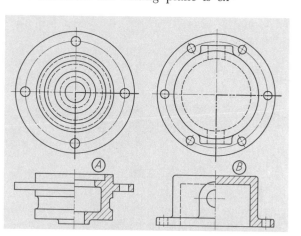

FIG. 7.7. Half sections. Dashed lines are rarely necessary (A), but may be used for clarity or to aid in dimensioning (B).

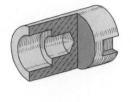
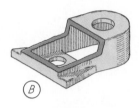

Ⓐ

Ⓑ

FIG. 7.8. Cutting planes for broken-out sections. The cutting plane extends only slightly beyond the features to be shown in section.

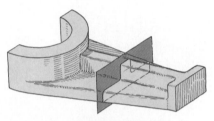

FIG. 7.9. A broken-out section. Note that a standard break line terminates the sectional portion.

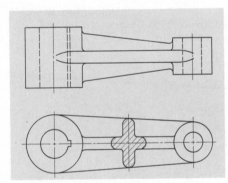

FIG. 7.10. The cutting plane for a rotated or a removed section. A slice of negligible thickness is taken.

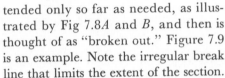

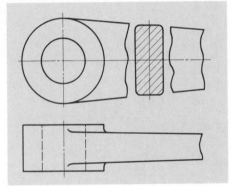

FIG. 7.11. A rotated section. The section is rotated 90° to bring it into the plane of the view.

FIG. 7.12. A rotated section with broken view. The view is broken thus whenever the view outline interferes with the section.

tended only so far as needed, as illustrated by Fig 7.8*A* and *B*, and then is thought of as "broken out." Figure 7.9 is an example. Note the irregular break line that limits the extent of the section.

7.7.   ROTATED SECTION.   As indictated in paragraph 7.1, a section may be a slice of negligible thickness used to show a shape that would otherwise be difficult to see or describe. The cutting plane for such a section is shown in Fig. 7.10. If the resulting section is then rotated 90° *onto* the view as in Fig. 7.11, the section is called a rotated section. Whenever the view outline interferes with the section, the view is broken, as in Fig. 7.12.

7.8.   REMOVED SECTIONS.   These are used for the same purpose as rotated sections, but instead of being drawn *on* the view, they are removed to some adjacent place on the paper (Fig. 7.13).

The cutting plane with reference letters should always be indicated unless the place from which the section has

been taken is obvious. Removed sections are used whenever restricted space for the section or the dimensioning of it prevents the use of an ordinary rotated section. When the shape of a piece changes gradually or is not uniform, several sections may be required (Fig. 7.14). It is often an advantage to draw the sections to larger scale than that of the main drawing in order to show dimensions more clearly. Sometimes sections are removed to a separate drawing sheet. When this is done, the section must be carefully shown on the main drawing with cutting plane and identifying letters. Often these identifying letters are made as a fraction in a circle, with the numerator a letter identifying the section and the denominator a number identifying the sheet. The sectional view is then marked with the same letters and numbers. The ANSI recommends that, if possible, a removed section be drawn in its natural projected position. This practice is followed in Fig. 7.14.

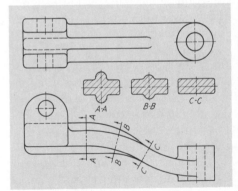

FIG. 7.13.   Removed sections. Cutting planes and mating sections must be identified.

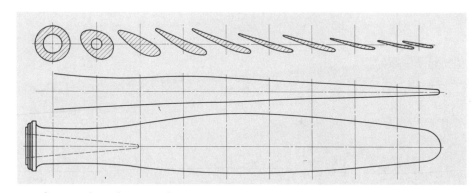

FIG. 7.14. Removed sections in projection. Identifications of cutting planes and mating sections are not needed.

7.9. AUXILIARY SECTIONS. These are sectional views conforming to all the principles of edge and normal views given in Chap. 8. The section shows the *normal* view of a cutting plane that is in a position on an inclined feature so as to reveal the interior, as shown in Fig. 7.15. The edge view of any perpendicular faces will also be seen in the normal view, as in Fig. 7.15. All types of sections —full, half, broken-out, rotated, and removed—are used on auxiliaries. Figure 7.16 shows auxiliary partial sections, which are also properly called removed sections in auxiliary position. Note in Fig. 7.16 that the two sections are normal views of their cutting planes.

7.10. ASSEMBLY SECTIONS. As the name implies, an assembly section is made up of a combination of parts. All the previ-

ously mentioned types of sections may be used to increase the clarity and readability of assembly drawings. The cutting plane for an assembly section is often offset, as in Fig. 7.17, to reveal the separate parts of a machine or structure.

The purpose of an assembly section is to reveal the interior of a machine or structure so that the separate parts can be clearly shown and identified, but the separate parts do not need to be completely described. Thus only such hidden details as are needed for part identification or dimensioning are shown. Also, the small amount of clearance between mating or moving parts is not shown because, if shown, the clearance would have to be greatly exaggerated, thus confusing the drawing. Even the clearance between a bolt and its hole, which may be as much as $\frac{1}{16}$ in., is rarely

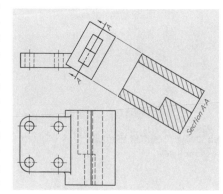

FIG. 7.15. Auxiliary section. The section is a normal view of the cutting plane.

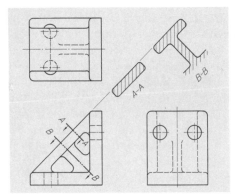

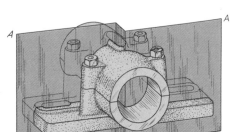

FIG. 7.16. Auxiliary sections (partial). Identifications of the cutting planes and mating sections are necessary.

FIG. 7.17. The cutting plane for an assembly section. It is often offset to pass through features to be shown in the section.

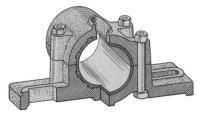

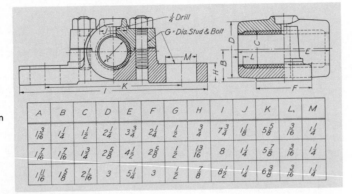

FIG. 7.18. A sectional assembly drawing. The sectional views give emphasis to construction and separate parts.

A	B	C	D	E	F	G	H	I	J	K	L	M
$1\frac{3}{16}$	$1\frac{1}{4}$	$1\frac{1}{2}$	$2\frac{1}{4}$	$3\frac{3}{4}$	$2\frac{1}{4}$	$\frac{1}{2}$	$\frac{3}{4}$	$7\frac{3}{4}$	$1\frac{1}{8}$	$5\frac{5}{8}$	$\frac{3}{16}$	$1\frac{1}{4}$
$1\frac{7}{16}$	$1\frac{7}{16}$	$1\frac{3}{4}$	$2\frac{5}{8}$	$4\frac{1}{2}$	$2\frac{5}{8}$	$\frac{1}{2}$	$\frac{13}{16}$	8	$1\frac{1}{4}$	$5\frac{7}{8}$	$\frac{3}{16}$	$1\frac{1}{4}$
$1\frac{11}{16}$	$1\frac{5}{8}$	$2\frac{1}{16}$	3	$5\frac{1}{4}$	3	$\frac{1}{2}$	$\frac{7}{8}$	$8\frac{1}{2}$	$1\frac{1}{4}$	$6\frac{3}{8}$	$\frac{3}{16}$	$1\frac{1}{4}$

FIG. 7.19. Cutting plane for a sectional view.

shown. Figure 7.18 is an example of an assembly section in tabular form with both views in half section. The component is similar to that in Fig. 7.17.

Crosshatching practice for assembly sections is explained in paragraph 7.11.

7.11. DRAWING PRACTICES FOR SECTIONAL VIEWS. In general, the rules of projection are followed in making sectional views. Figure 7.19 shows the picture of a casting intersected by a cutting plane, giving the appearance that the casting has been cut through by the plane *A-A* and the front part removed, exposing the interior. Figure 7.20 shows the drawing of the casting with the front view in section. The edge of the cutting plane is shown in the top view by the cutting-plane symbol, with reference letters and arrows to show the direction in which the view is taken. It must be understood that, in thus removing the nearer portion of the object to make the sectional view, the portion assumed to be removed is not omitted in making other views. Therefore, the top and right-side views of the object in Fig. 7.20 are full and complete, and only in the front view has part of the object been removed.

The practices recommended by the ANSI for inclusion of the cutting-plane symbol, of visible and hidden edges, and for crosshatching are as follows:

The Cutting-plane Symbol. It may be shown on the orthographic view where the cutting plane appears as an edge and may be more completely identified with reference letters along with arrows to show the direction in which the view is taken. The cutting-plane line symbol is shown in the alphabet of lines, Figs. 2.56 and 2.57. Use of the symbol is illustrated in Figs. 7.1 and 7.20. Often when the position of the section is evident, the cutting-plane symbol is omitted (Fig. 7.21). It is not always desirable to show the symbol through its entire length; so in such cases the beginning and ending of the plane is shown, as in sections *A-A* and *B-B* in Prob. 19.3.9. Removed sections usually need the cutting-plane symbol with arrows for the direction of sight and letters for the resulting sectional view (Fig. 7.16).

Unnecessary Hidden Detail. Hidden edges and surfaces are not shown unless they are needed to describe the object. Much confusion may result if all detail behind the cutting plane is drawn. In

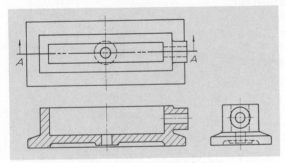

FIG. 7.20. A drawing with a sectional view. This is the same object as in Fig. 7.19.

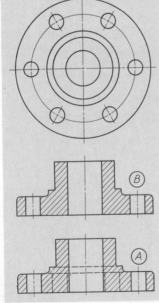

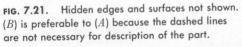

FIG. 7.21. Hidden edges and surfaces not shown. (*B*) is preferable to (*A*) because the dashed lines are not necessary for description of the part.

Fig. 7.21, (*A*) shows a sectional view with all the hidden edges and surfaces shown by dashed lines. These lines complicate the view and do not add any information. The view at (*B*) is preferred because it is simpler, less time-consuming to draw, and more easily read than the view at (*A*). The holes lie on a circular center line; and where similar details repeat, all may be assumed to be alike.

Necessary Hidden Detail. Hidden edges and surfaces are shown if necessary for the description of the object. In Fig. 7.22 view (*A*) is inadequate since it does not show the thickness of the lugs. The correct treatment is in view (*B*), where the lugs are shown by dashed lines.

Visible Detail Shown in Sectional Views. Figure 7.23 shows an object pictorially with the front half removed, thus exposing edges and surfaces behind the cutting plane. At (*A*) a sectional view of the cut surface only is shown, with the visible elements omitted. This treatment should *never* be used. The view should be drawn as at (*B*) with the visible edges and surfaces behind the cutting plane included in the sectional view.

Visible Detail Not Shown in Sectional Views. Sometimes confusion results if all visible detail behind the cutting plane is drawn, and it may be omitted if it does not aid in readability. Omission of detail should be carefully considered and may be justified as time saved in drawing. This applies mainly for assembly drawings to show how the pieces fit together rather than to give complete information for making the parts (see Fig. 7.24).

Section Lining. Wherever material has been cut by the section plane, the cut surface is indicated by section lining done with fine lines generally at 45° with the principal lines in the view and spaced uniformly to give an even tint. These lines are spaced entirely by eye except when some form of mechanical section liner is used. The pitch, or distance between lines, is governed by the size of the surface. For ordinary working drawings, it will not be much less than ¹⁄₁₆ in. and rarely more than ⅛ in. *Very* small pieces may require a spacing closer than ¹⁄₁₆ in. Take care in setting the pitch by the first two or three lines, and glance back at the first lines often

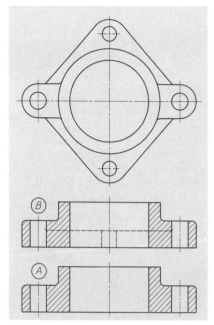

FIG. 7.22. Hidden edges and surfaces shown. (*B*) *must* be used instead of (*A*) because the dashed lines are necessary for description of the part.

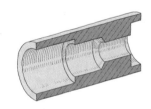

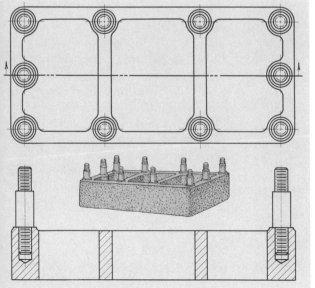

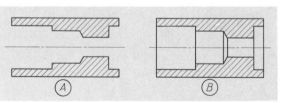

FIG. 7.23. Visible edges shown. These are the edges seen behind the plane of the section and must be shown as at (*B*).

FIG. 7.24. Omission of detail. Detail behind the plane of the section may be omitted when it does not aid in readability or when it might cause ambiguity.

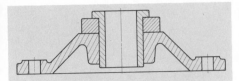

FIG. 7.25. Crosshatching of adjacent parts. Adjacent parts are crosshatched in opposite directions and/or different spacing, for emphasis. The same piece in different views or different parts of the same view should be crosshatched with identical spacing and direction (auxiliaries are a possible exception).

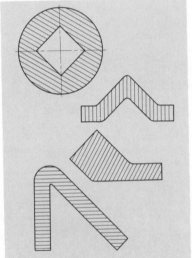

FIG. 7.26. Section-line directions for unusual shapes. Avoid crosshatch directions parallel to the view outlines.

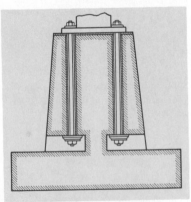

FIG. 7.27. Outline sectioning. This saves drafting time on large views or on large drawings.

to see that the pitch does not gradually increase or decrease. Nothing mars the appearance of a drawing more than poor section lining. The alphabet of lines, Figs. 2.56 and 2.57, gives the weight of crosshatch lines.

Two adjacent pieces in an assembly drawing are crosshatched in opposite directions. If three pieces adjoin, one of them may be sectioned at other than 45° (usually 30° or 60°, Fig. 7.25), or all pieces may be crosshatched at 45° by using a different pitch for each piece. If a part is so shaped that 45° sectioning runs parallel, or nearly so, to its principal outlines, another direction should be chosen (Fig. 7.26).

Large surfaces are sometimes sectioned around the edge only, as in Fig. 7.27.

Very thin sections, as of gaskets, sheet metal, or structural-steel shapes to small scale, may be shown in solid black, with white spaces between the parts where thin pieces are adjacent (Fig. 7.28).

Section lining for the same piece in different views or different parts of the same view should be identical in spacing and direction[1] (Figs. 7.18 and 7.24).

Adjacent pieces are section-lined in opposite directions and are often distinguished more clearly by varying the

[1] An exception is made for crosshatching of an auxiliary view to avoid crosshatch lines parallel or perpendicular, or nearly so, to outlines of the view.

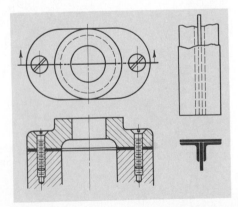

FIG. 7.28. Thin material in section (drawn solid for lack of room to crosshatch).

pitch of the section lines for each piece, using closer spacing for the smaller pieces (Figs. 7.25 and 7.29).

Code for Materials in Section. Symbolic section lining is not commonly used on ordinary working drawings, but in an assembly section it is sometimes useful to show a distinction between materials, and a recognized standard code is an obvious advantage. The USASI symbols indicating different materials are given in the Appendix. Code section lining is used only to aid in reading a drawing and is not to be taken as the official specification of the materials. Exact specifications of material for each piece always appear on the detail drawing.

7.12. CONVENTIONAL PRACTICES. All sections are conventions in that they represent an assumed imaginary cut from which, following the theory of projection rather closely, the sectional views are made. However, the strict rules of projection may be disregarded if by so doing a type of view can be drawn which more accurately depicts the shape of the object. It is impossible to illustrate all the conditions that might occur, but the following principles are recognized as good practice, resulting in clearness and readability.

7.13. PARTS NOT SECTIONED. Many machine elements, such as fasteners, pins, and shafts, have no internal construction and, in addition, are more easily recognized by their exterior views. These parts often lie in the path of the section plane, but if they are sectioned (and crosshatched), they are more difficult to read because their typical identifying features (boltheads, rivet heads,

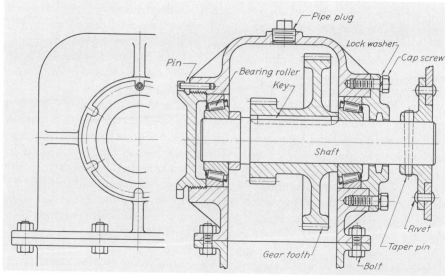

FIG. 7.29. Part of a sectional assembly. Shafts, bolts, nuts, rods, rivets, keys, and the like whose axes occur in the plane of the section are left in full (not sectioned).

chamfers on shafts, etc.) are removed. Thus features of this kind should be left in full view and *not sectioned*. To justify this treatment, the assembly is thought of as being sectioned on a particular plane, with the nonsectioned parts placed in the half holes remaining after the section is made. Figure 7.17 shows a full section made on an offset cutting plane that passes through a bolt, with the bolt in full view. Figure 7.29 shows several nonsectioned parts; it is evident that if the shaft, bolts, nuts, rivets, etc., were sectioned, the drawing would be confusing and difficult to read.

7.14. SPOKES AND ARMS IN SECTION. A basic principle for sectioning circular parts is that any element not continuous (not solid) around the axis of the part should be drawn without crosshatching in order to avoid a misleading effect. For example, consider the two pulleys in Fig. 7.30. Pulley (*A*) has a solid web connecting the hub and rim. Pulley (*B*) has four spokes. Even though the cut-

ting plane passes through two of the spokes, the sectional view of (*B*) must be made without crosshatching the spokes in order to avoid the appearance of a solid web, as in pulley (*A*).

Other machine elements treated in this manner are teeth of gears and sprockets, vanes and supporting ribs of cylindrical parts, equally spaced lugs, and similar parts.

7.15. RIBS IN SECTION. For reasons identical with those given in paragraph 7.14, when the cutting plane passes longitudinally through the center of a rib or web, as in Fig. 7.31*A*, the cross-

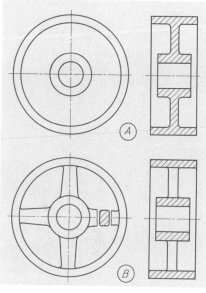

FIG. 7.30. Spokes in section. The wheel with spokes (*B*) is treated as though the cutting plane were in front of the spokes, to avoid misreading the section as a solid web line (*A*).

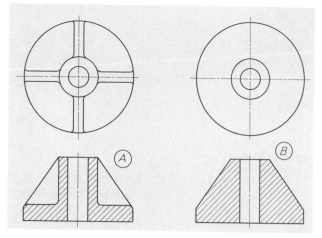

FIG. 7.31. Ribs in section. Ribs at (*A*) are treated as though the cutting plane were in front of them, to avoid misreading the section as a solid (*B*).

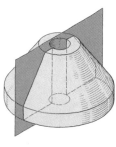

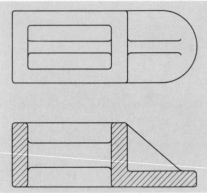

FIG. 7.32. Ribs in section. These are treated as though the cutting plane were in front of the ribs.

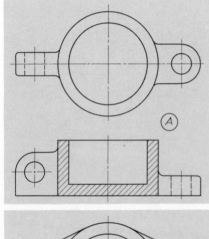

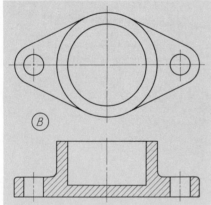

FIG. 7.33. Lugs in section. Small lugs (*A*) are treated like spokes (Fig. 7.30) and ribs (Figs. 7.31 and 7.32). Large lugs (*B*) are considered as the solid base of the part.

hatching is eliminated from the ribs as if the cutting plane were just in front of them or as if they had been temporarily removed and replaced after the section was made. A true sectional view with the ribs crosshatched gives a heavy, misleading effect suggesting a cone shape, as shown at (*B*). The same principle applies to ribs cut longitudinally on rectangular parts (Fig. 7.32). When the cutting plane cuts a rib transversely, that is, at right angles to its length or axis direction (the direction that shows its thickness), it is always crosshatched (Fig. 7.24).

7.16.   LUGS IN SECTION.   For the same reasons given in paragraphs 7.14 and 7.15, a lug or projecting ear (Fig. 7.33*A*), usually of *rectangular* cross section, is not crosshatched; note that crosshatching either of the lugs would suggest a circular flange. However, the somewhat similar condition at (*B*) should have the projecting ears crosshatched as shown because these ears *are* the base of the part.

7.17.   ALTERNATE CROSSHATCHING.   In some cases omitting the crosshatching of ribs or similar parts gives an inadequate and sometimes ambiguous treat-

ment. To illustrate, Fig. 7.34*A* shows a full section of an idler pulley. At (*B*) four ribs have been added. Note that the top surfaces of the ribs are flush with the top of the pulley. Without crosshatching, the section at (*B*) is identical with (*A*) and the ribs of (*B*) are not identified at all on the sectional view. A better treatment in this case is to use alternate crosshatching for the ribs, as at (*C*), where half (alternating) the crosshatch lines are carried through the ribs. Note that the line of demarcation between rib and solid portions is a *dashed* line.

7.18.   ALIGNED SPOKES AND ARMS.   Any part with an odd number (3, 5, 7, etc.) of spokes or ribs will give an unsymmetrical and misleading section if the principles of true projection are strictly adhered to, as illustrated by the drawing of a handwheel in Fig. 7.35. The preferred projection is shown in the second sectional view where one arm is drawn as if aligned or, in other words, the arm is rotated to the path of the vertical cutting plane and then projected to the side view. Note that neither arm should be sectioned for the reasons given in paragraph 7.14.

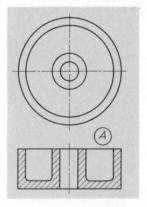 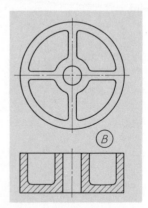 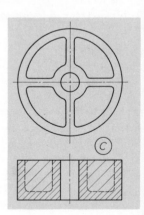

FIG. 7.34.   Alternate crosshatching. Section (*B*), with ribs flush at the top, looks like section (*A*), with no ribs. Alternate crosshatching (*C*) identifies the ribs.

This practice of alignment is well justified logically because a part with an odd number of equally spaced elements is just as symmetrical as a part with an even number and, therefore, should be shown by a symmetrical view. Moreover, the symmetrical view shows the true *relationship* of the elements, while the true projection does not.

7.19. ALIGNED RIBS, LUGS, AND HOLES. Ribs, lugs, and holes often occur in odd numbers and following the principles given in paragraph 7.18, should be aligned to show the true relationship of the elements. Figure 7.36 shows several examples of how the cutting plane may pass through a symmetrical object, permitting the removal of a portion of the object so as to better describe the shape. Note how the cutting planes may change direction so as to pass through the holes. In Fig. 7.37, true projection of the ribs would show the pair on the right foreshortened, as at (A), suggesting in the sectional view that they would not extend to the outer edge of the base. Here, again, the alignment shown at (B) gives a symmetrical section of a symmetrical part and shows the ribs in their true relationship to the basic part. To illustrate further, at (C) and (D) the lugs and holes are aligned, thus showing the holes at their true radial distance from the axis, and, incidently, eliminating some difficult projections.

In all cases of alignment, the element can be thought of as being swung around to a common cutting plane and then projected to the sectional view. Note at (C) that because an offset cutting plane is used, each hole is brought separately into position on a common cutting plane before projection to the sectional view. The cutting plane used here is similar to that of (D) in Fig. 7.36.

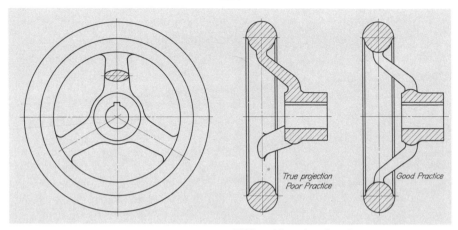

FIG. 7.35. Aligned spokes. True projection is misleading and difficult to draw. Alignment gives a symmetrical section for a symmetrical part.

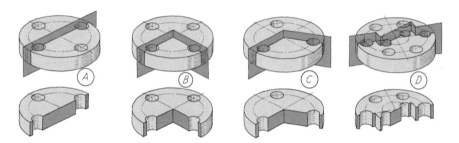

FIG. 7.36. Cutting planes for alignment of holes.

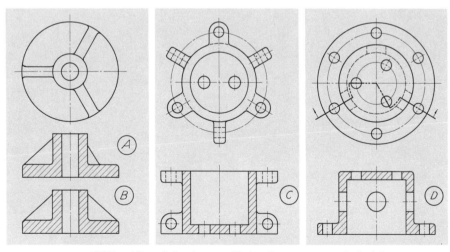

FIG. 7.37. Aligned ribs, lugs, and holes. True projection of ribs (A) is misleading. Alignment (B) gives a symmetrical section for a symmetrical part. The same is true for lugs (C) and holes (D).

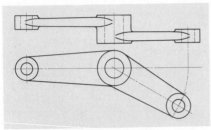

FIG. 7.38. Aligned view. This is to avoid drawing in the foreshortened position.

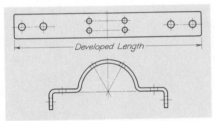

FIG. 7.39. Developed view. This part is drawn as though it were straightened out in one plane.

7.20. ALIGNMENT OF ELEMENTS IN FULL VIEWS. In full views, as well as in sectional views, certain violations of the rules of true projection are recognized as good practice because they add to the clearness of the drawing. For example, if a front view shows a hexagonal bolthead "across corners," the theoretical projection of the side view would be "across flats"; but in a working drawing, boltheads are drawn across corners in both views to show better the shape and the space needed. As another example, the slots of screw heads are always drawn at an angle of 45° in all views so that the closely spaced lines will not be confused with horizontal and vertical center lines.

Lugs or parts cast on for holding purposes and to be machined off are shown by "adjacent-part" lines (Figs 2.56 and 2.57). If such parts are in section, the section lines are dashed. "Alternate-position" lines (Figs. 2.56 and 2.57) are used to indicate the limiting positions of moving parts and to show adjacent parts that aid in locating the position or use of a piece. Note in Figs. 2.56 and

2.57 that the symbol of a long dash and two short dashes, alternating, is used to indicate adjacent parts, alternate positions, and also repeated features.

7.21. ALIGNED AND DEVELOPED VIEWS. Pieces that have elements at an angle to one another, as the lever of Fig. 7.38, may be shown straightened out or aligned in one view. Similarly, bent pieces of the type of Fig. 7.39 should have one view made as a developed view of the *blank* to be punched and formed. Extra metal must be allowed for bends.

7.22. HALF VIEWS. When space is limited, it is allowable to make the top or side view of a symmetrical piece as a half view. If the front is an exterior view, the *front* half of the top or side view would be used, as in Fig. 7.40; but if the front view is a sectional view, the *rear* half would be used, as in Fig. 7.41. Figure 7.42 shows another space-saving combination of a half view with a half section. Examples of half views occur in Probs. 19.3.6 to 19.3.8.

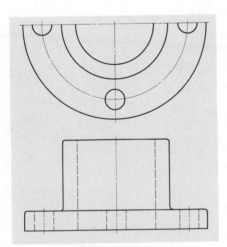

FIG. 7.40. Half view. The front half is drawn when the mating view is external.

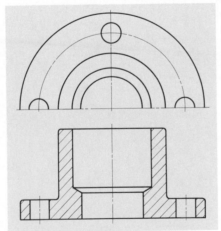

FIG. 7.41. Half view. The rear half is drawn when the mating view is a full section.

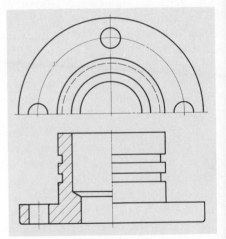

FIG. 7.42. Half view. The rear half is drawn when mating view is a half section.

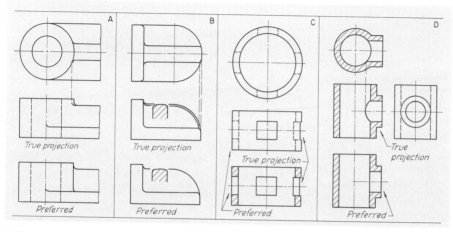

FIG. 7.43. Conventional intersections. These are used when there is a small difference as compared with true projection.

7.23. **CONVENTIONAL PRACTICES.** One statement can be made with the force of a rule: *If anything in clearness can be gained by violating a principle of projection, violate it.* This applies to full as well as sectional views. Permissible violations are not readily apparent to the reader, since when they occur the actual conditions are described in a better and usually simpler form than if they were shown in true projection.

However, some care and judgment must be used in applying conventional treatments. Persons trained in their use ordinarily understand their meaning, but workmen often do not. Some unusual convention may be more confusing than helpful, and result in greater ambiguity than true projection.

There are occasions when the true lines of intersection are of no value as aids in reading and should be ignored. Some typical examples are shown in Fig. 7.43. It must be noted, however, that in certain cases that are similar but where there is a major difference in line position when the true projection is given, as compared with conventional treatment, the true line of intersection should be shown. Compare the treatment of the similar objects in Figs. 7.43

and 7.44. It would not be good practice to conventionalize the intersections on the objects in Fig. 7.44 because the difference between true projection and the convention is too great. To develop your judgment of the use of conventional intersections, carefully study Figs. 7.43 and 7.44 and observe the difference between true projection and conventional treatment in each case.

7.24. **FILLETS AND ROUNDS.** In designing a casting, never leave sharp internal angles because of the liability of fracture at those points. The radius of the fillet depends on the thickness of the metal and other design conditions. When not dimensioned, it is left to the patternmaker. External angles may be rounded

FIG. 7.44. True intersections. These are used when there is a major difference as compared with conventional treatment.

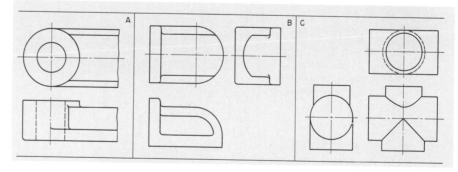

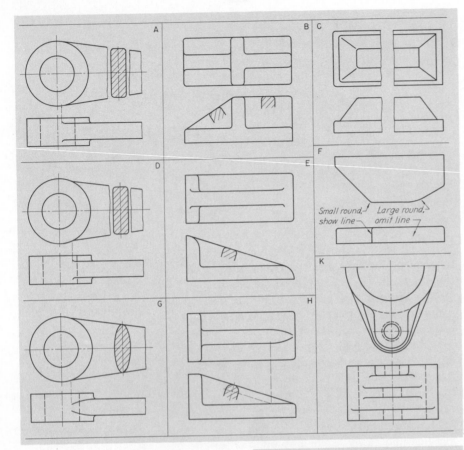

FIG. 7.45. Conventional fillets, rounds, and runouts. These are conventionalized intersections.

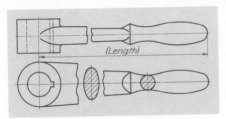

FIG. 7.46. Broken view with rotated sections. A broken view saves drawing the whole length of the part.

FIG. 7.47. Conventional breaks.

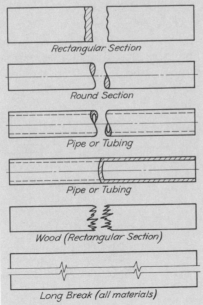

Rectangular Section

Round Section

Pipe or Tubing

Pipe or Tubing

Wood (Rectangular Section)

Long Break (all materials)

for appearance or comfort, with radii ranging from enough merely to remove the sharp edges to an amount nearly equal to the thickness of the piece. An edge made by the intersection of two unfinished surfaces of a casting should always be "broken" by a very small round. A sharp corner on a drawing indicates that one or both of the intersecting surfaces are machined. Small fillets, rounds, and "runouts" are best put in freehand, both in pencil and ink. Runouts, or "dieouts," as they are sometimes called, are conventional indications of filleted intersections where, theoretically, there would be no line because there is no abrupt change in direction. Figure 7.45 shows some conventional representations of fillets and rounds with runouts of arms and ribs intersecting other surfaces.

7.25. CONVENTIONAL BREAKS. In making the detail of a long bar or piece with a uniform cross section, it is rarely necessary to draw its whole length. It may be shown to a larger and therefore better scale by breaking out a piece, moving the ends together, and giving the true length by a dimension, as in Fig. 7.46. The shape of the cross section is indicated by a rotated section or more often by a semipictorial break line, as in Fig. 7.47.

7.26. CONVENTIONAL SYMBOLS. Engineers and draftsmen use conventional representation to indicate many details, such as screw threads, springs, pipe fittings, and electrical apparatus. These have been standardized by the ANSI, whose code for materials in section has already been referred to in paragraph 7.11.

The symbol of two crossed diagonals

is used for two distinct purposes: (1) to indicate on a shaft the position of finish for a bearing, and (2) to indicate that a certain surface (usually parallel to the picture plane) is flat. These two uses are not apt to be confused (Fig. 7.48).

Because screw threads recur constantly, the designation for them is one of the most important items under conventional symbols. Up to the time of official standardization by the ANSI, there were a dozen different thread symbols in use. Now a regular symbol

and a simplified one have been adopted for American drawings, and both are understood internationally. The symbols for indicating threads on bolts, screws, and tapped holes are given in Chap. 16.

The conventional symbols mentioned are used principally on machine drawings. Architectural drawing, because of the small scales employed, uses many conventional symbols, and topographic drawing is made up almost entirely of symbols. Electrical *diagrams* are completely symbolic.

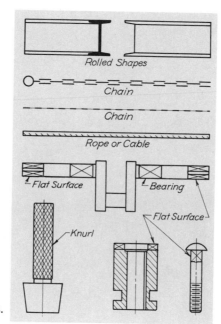

FIG. 7.48. Various symbols.

PROBLEMS

GROUP 1. SINGLE PIECES

The following problems can be used for practice in shape description only or, by adding dimensions, in making working drawings.
7.1.1. Draw the top view, and change the front and side views to sectional views as indicated.

7.1.2. Draw the top view, and make the front and two side views in section on cutting planes as indicated. Scale to suit.
7.1.3 to 7.1.5. Given the side view, draw full front and side views in section. Scale to suit.

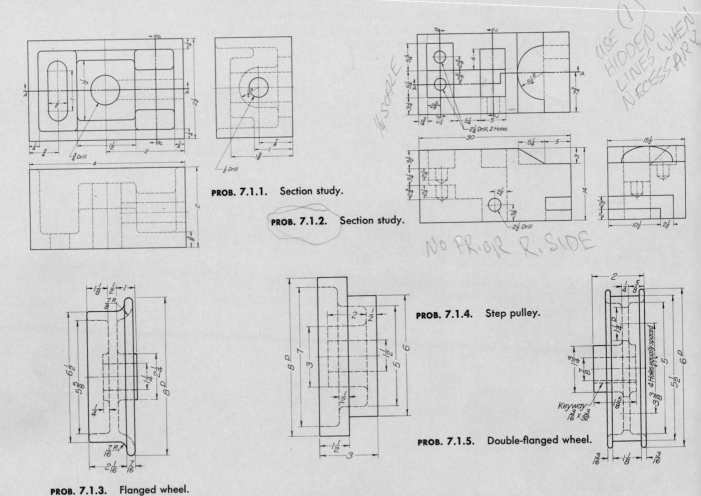

PROB. 7.1.1. Section study.

PROB. 7.1.2. Section study.

PROB. 7.1.3. Flanged wheel.

PROB. 7.1.4. Step pulley.

PROB. 7.1.5. Double-flanged wheel.

7.1.6 and 7.1.7. Change the right-side view to a full section.

7.1.8 and 7.1.9. Change the right-side view to a full section.

7.1.10. Change the right-side view to a full section.

7.1.11. Change the right-side view to a sectional view as indicated.

7.1.12 and 7.1.13. Change the front view to a full section.

7.1.14 and 7.1.15. Change the front view to a full section.

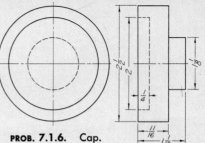

PROB. 7.1.6. Cap.

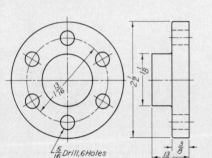

PROB. 7.1.7. Flanged cap.

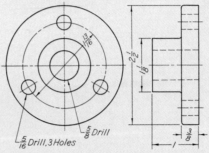

PROB. 7.1.8. Pump-rod guide.

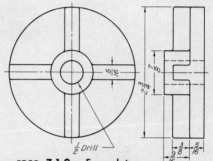

PROB. 7.1.9. Face plate.

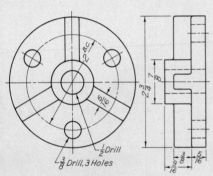

PROB. 7.1.10. Ribbed support.

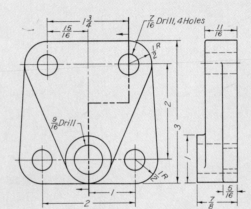

PROB. 7.1.11. Housing cover.

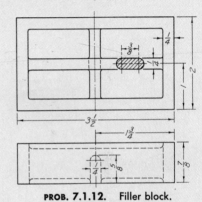

PROB. 7.1.12. Filler block.

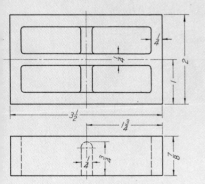

PROB. 7.1.13. Filler block.

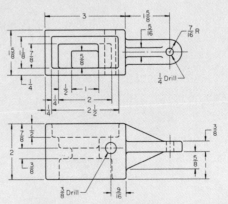

PROB. 7.1.14. Bumper body.

PROB. 7.1.15. V-belt pulley.

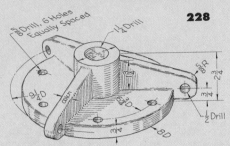

PROB. 7.1.16.   End plate.

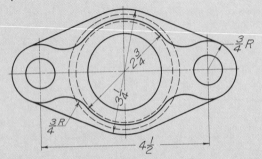

PROB. 7.1.18.   Pump flange.

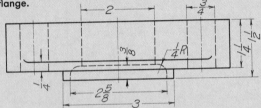

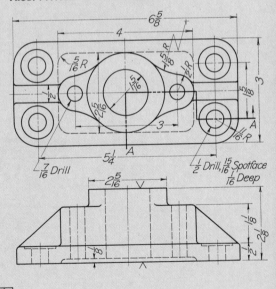

PROB. 7.1.17.   Piston cap.

7.1.16 and 7.1.17.   Select views that will best describe the piece.

7.1.18.   Draw the top view as shown in the illustration and the front view as a full section.

7.1.19.   Draw the top view as illustrated and the front view in half section on *A-A*.

7.1.20.   Draw the top view as shown, and change the front and side views to sections as indicated.

PROB. 7.1.19.   Brake-rod bracket.

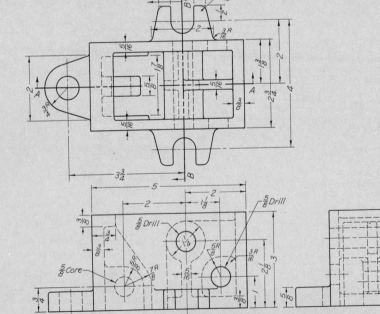

PROB. 7.1.20.   Bolted anchor block.

7.1.21. Draw the top view and sectional view (or views) to best describe the object.

7.1.22. Turn the object through 90°, and draw the given front view as the new top view; then make the new front view as section *B-B* and auxiliary section *A-A*. Refer to paragraph 7.9, for instructions on making auxiliary sections. See also Chap. 8 for the method of projection for the auxiliary section. Note in this case that the new top view, front-view section *B-B*, and auxiliary section *A-A* will completely describe the object. However, if desired, the side view may also be drawn, as shown or as an aligned view (described in paragraph 7.21).

7.1.22*A.* As an alternate for Prob. 7.1.22, draw views as follows: with the object in the position shown, draw the front view as shown, draw the left-side view as section *B-B*, and draw the new top view as an aligned view.

7.1.23. Draw the top view and front view in section.

7.1.24 and 7.1.25. Draw the views and add the sectional views indicated.

7.1.26 and 7.1.27. Draw a view and sectional view to best describe the piece.

7.1.28. Draw the top view and necessary sectional view (or views) to best describe the object.

7.1.29. Draw three views, making the side view as a section on *B-B*.

7.1.29*A.* Draw three views, making the top view as a half section on *A-A*.

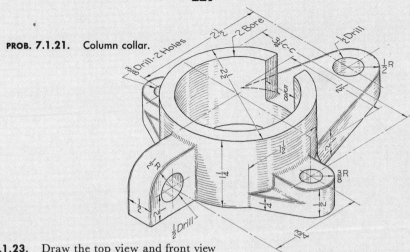

PROB. 7.1.21. Column collar.

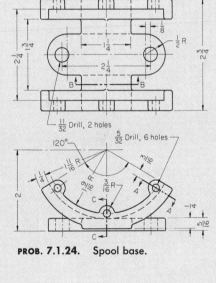

PROB. 7.1.24. Spool base.

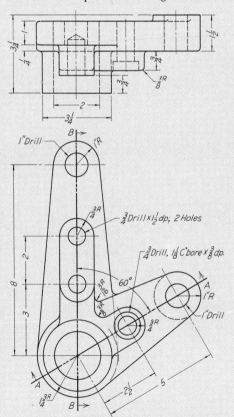

PROB. 7.1.22. Compound bell-crank.

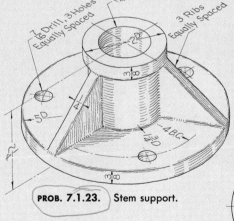

PROB. 7.1.23. Stem support.

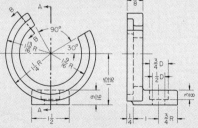

PROB. 7.1.25. Saddle collar.

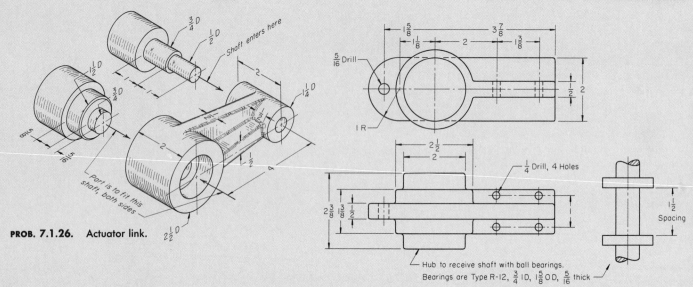

PROB. 7.1.26. Actuator link.

PROB. 7.1.27. Vibrator-drive bearing support.

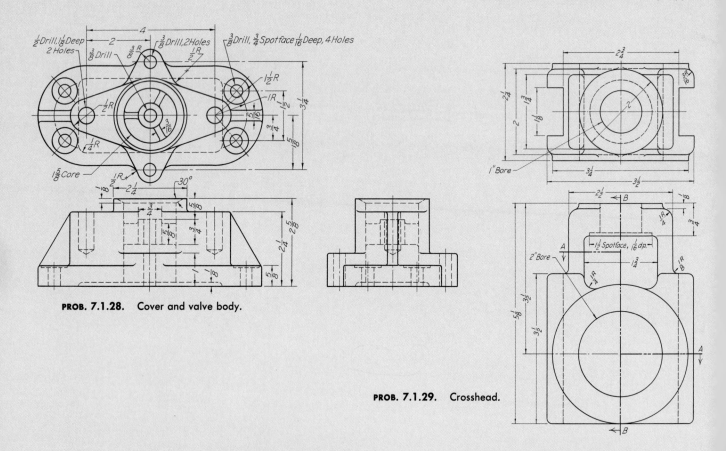

PROB. 7.1.28. Cover and valve body.

PROB. 7.1.29. Crosshead.

7.1.30. Select views that will best describe the piece.

7.1.31. Top view and front view in section, of rigging yoke, Prob. 5.3.20.

7.1.32. Three views with front view in section, of missile gyro support, Prob. 5.3.18.

7.1.33. Three views with front view in section, of end frame for engine starter, Prob. 5.5.24.

7.1.34. Three views with front view in section, of master brake cylinder, Prob. 5.5.23.

7.1.35. Choose views and sectional views that will best describe the electric-motor support, Prob. 5.5.22.

7.1.36. Choose views and sectional views that will best describe the jet-engine hinge plate, Prob. 5.6.7.

7.1.37. Two views with sectional treatment that will best describe the anchor plate, Prob. 6.4.8.

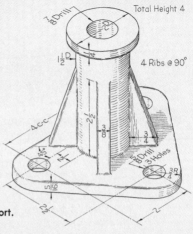

PROB. 7.1.30. Spindle support.

GROUP 2. ASSEMBLIES

7.2.1. Draw a half end view and a longitudinal view as full section.

7.2.2. Draw the top view as shown in the figure and new front view in section. Show the shape (right section) of the link with rotated or removed section. The assembly comprises a cast-steel link, two bronze bushings, steel toggle pin, steel collar, steel taper pin, and part of the cast-steel supporting lug.

7.2.3. Draw the front view and longitudinal section. The assembly comprises a cast-iron base, a bronze bushing, a bronze disk, and two steel dowel pins.

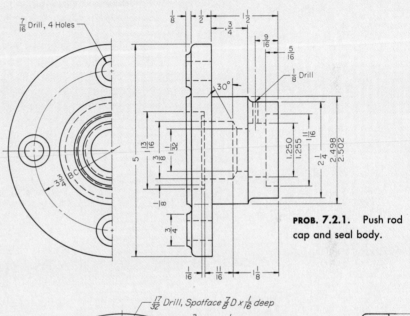

PROB. 7.2.1. Push rod cap and seal body.

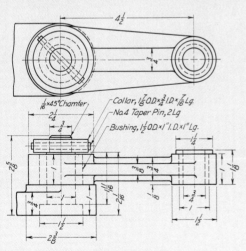

PROB. 7.2.2. Link assembly.

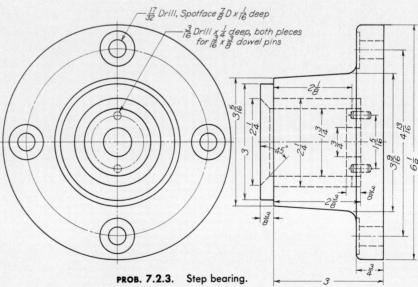

PROB. 7.2.3. Step bearing.

7.2.4. Draw two half end views and a longitudinal section. The assembly consists of cast-iron body, two bronze bushings, steel shaft, cast-iron pulley, and steel taper pin.

7.2.5. Make an assembly drawing in section. The bracket is cast iron, the wheel is cast steel, the bushing is bronze, and the pin and taper pin are steel. Scale: full size.

7.2.5*A.* Make a drawing of the bracket with one view in section. Material is cast iron. Scale: full size.

7.2.5*B.* Make a drawing of the wheel with one view in section. Material is cast steel. Scale: full size.

7.2.6. Make an assembly drawing in section. The assembly comprises two cast-iron brackets, two bronze bushings, steel shaft, cast-steel roller, and cast-iron base. The bushings are pressed into the roller, and the shaft is drilled for lubrication. Scale: full size.

7.2.6*A.* Make a drawing of the roller and

bushing assembly that gives one view in section. See Prob. 7.2.6 for materials. Scale: full size.

7.2.7. Sectional assembly of sealed shaft unit, Prob. 19.2.1.

7.2.8. Sectional assembly of crane hook, Prob. 19.2.2.

7.2.9. Sectional assembly of caster, Prob. 19.2.3.

7.2.10. Sectional assembly of antivibration mount, Prob. 19.4.1.

7.2.11. Sectional assembly of pump valve, Prob. 19.4.3.

7.2.12. Sectional assembly of boring-bar holder, Prob. 19.4.6.

7.2.13. Sectional assembly of conveyor link unit, Prob. 19.6.7.

7.2.14. Sectional assembly of pressure cell piston, Prob. 19.4.10.

7.2.15. Sectional assembly of pivot nut and adjustable screw, Prob. 19.4.11.

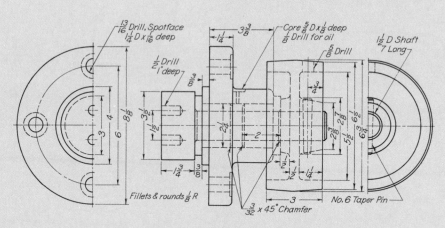

PROB. 7.2.4. Pulley-bracket assembly.

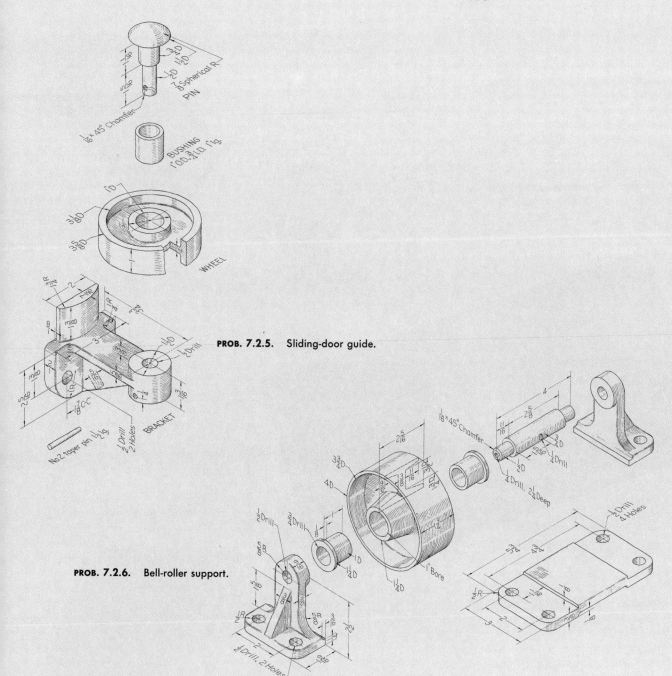

PROB. 7.2.5. Sliding-door guide.

PROB. 7.2.6. Bell-roller support.

Auxiliary views are used to obtain a "true" view of some feature of an object which occurs at an angle to the three (H, F & P) planes of projection (paragraph 8.1). This might be the end view of a line, the true length of a line, the edge view of a plane, or the normal view of a plane.

To illustrate the procedure, place your textbook on a horizontal surface at an angle to your view from the front and tilt it back so that, when viewed directly from the top and front, it will appear as in the picture. Leaving the book in this position, change your direction of observation so that you are looking directly at the shelf (library) title as indicated by the large arrow. This is the true (normal) view of the shelf title: the front and rear, upper and lower edges of the cover will appear as point views of the edges and the front and rear covers will appear as edge views. If you now open the front and rear covers to the same plane as the shelf title, both will appear as true (normal) views of the front and rear covers.

Auxiliaries: Point, Edge, and Normal Views

8.1. BASIC CONCEPTS. A plane surface is shown in true shape when the direction of view is perpendicular to the surface; for example, rectangular objects can be placed with their faces parallel to the principal planes of projection and be fully described by the principal views. In Fig. 8.1 the top, front, and right-side views show the true shape, respectively, of the top, front, and right side of the object. Note especially that the planes of projection are *parallel* to the top, front, and right side of the object and that the directions of observation are *perpendicular* to the object faces and to the planes of projection. Figure 8.2 is a pictorial of Fig. 8.1, given here to aid in visualizing the relationship of object faces, planes of projection, and view directions.

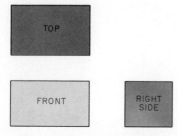

FIG. 8.1. Object faces parallel to the principal projection planes. Top, front, and side views are normal views, respectively, of top, front, and side of the object.

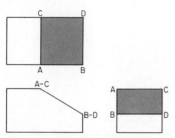

FIG. 8.3. One object face inclined to two principal planes. The inclined face does not appear in its true size and proportions in any view.

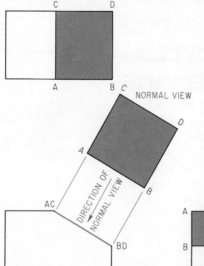

FIG. 8.5. Orthographic drawing of the object in Figs. 8.3 and 8.4. The normal view gives the true size and proportions of the inclined face.

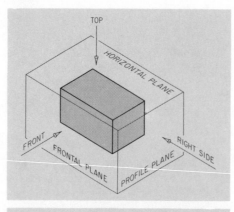

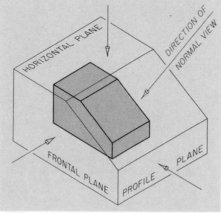

Note in Figs. 8.1 and 8.2 that each view also shows the *edge* of certain surfaces of the object. For example, the front view shows the edge of the top, bottom, and both sides of the object. For a surface to appear as an edge it must be perpendicular to the plane of projection for the view.

Sometimes an object will have one or more *inclined* surfaces whose true shape it is necessary to show, especially

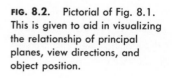

FIG. 8.2. Pictorial of Fig. 8.1. This is given to aid in visualizing the relationship of principal planes, view directions, and object position.

FIG. 8.4. Pictorial of Fig. 8.3. A view projected perpendicular to the inclined face will show it in true size and proportions.

if they are irregular in outline. Figure 8.3 shows an object with one inclined face, *ABDC*. This face is inclined to the horizontal and profile planes and perpendicular to the frontal plane. The face *ABDC* therefore appears as an edge in the front view, but none of the principal views shows the true size and shape of the surface. To show the true size and shape of *ABDC,* a view is needed that has a direction of observation perpendicular to *ABDC* and is projected on a plane parallel to *ABDC,* as shown in Fig. 8.4. This view is known as a *normal* view. The top, front, and side views of Fig. 8.1 are normal views of the top, front, and side surfaces of the object, because they *all* show the true size and shape of a surface by having the direction of observation at right angles to the surface. The dictionary defines a *normal,* in geometry, as "any perpendicular." In graphics, a plane of projection is involved as well as a direction of observation; hence, *a normal view is a projection that has the viewing direction perpendicular to, and made on a plane parallel to, the object face.*

Figure 8.5 is the orthographic counterpart of Fig. 8.4. To get the normal view of surface *ABDC,* a projection is made perpendicular to *ABDC.* This projection is made *from* the view where the surface shows as an edge, in this case, the front view and thus perpendicularity from the surface is seen in true relationship. Extra views such as the normal view of Fig. 8.5 are known as *auxiliary views* to distinguish them from the principal (top, front, side, etc.) views. However, since an auxiliary is made for the purpose of showing the true configuration of a surface, the terms *normal view* or *edge view* state positively what the view is and what it shows.

Detailed instructions for making a normal view of any surface in *any possible position* are given in the paragraphs that follow. Edge views are discussed in paragraph 8.9.

8.2. CLASSIFICATION OF SURFACES. Surfaces may occur in any of the positions shown in Fig. 8.6. At (*A*) all the surfaces are aligned with the principal planes of projection and thus each of the principal views is a normal view. At (*B*) the shaded surface is at an angle to *two* of the principal planes but perpendicular to one plane and is called an *inclined* surface. At (*C*) the shaded surface is at an angle to *all three* principal planes of projection and is known as a *skew,* or *oblique,* surface (that is, one that takes a slanting or oblique course or direction).

8.3. DIRECTIONS OF INCLINED SURFACES. Inclined surfaces may occur anywhere on an object, and because other features of the object must also be represented, the inclined surface may be in any one of the twelve positions shown in Fig. 8.7. The first column, (*B*) to (*E*), shows surfaces inclined to the front and side so that the surface may be on (*B*) the

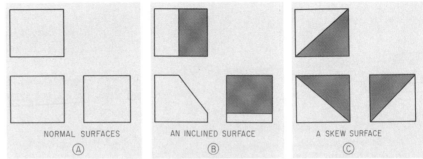

FIG. 8.6. Classification of surfaces.

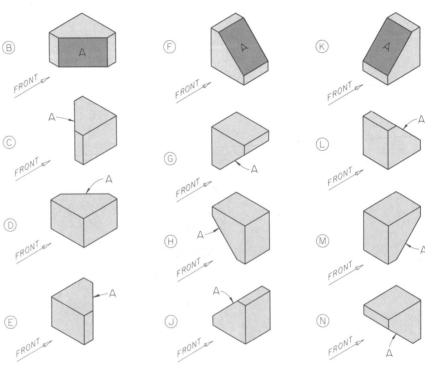

right front, (*C*) left front, (*D*) left rear, or (*E*) right rear. The second column, (*F*) to (*J*), shows surfaces inclined to the top and side, so that the surface may be on (*F*) the upper right, (*G*) lower right, (*H*) lower left, or (*J*) upper left. The third column, (*K*) to (*N*), shows surfaces inclined to the top and front, so that the surface may be on (*K*) the upper front, (*L*) upper rear, (*M*) lower rear, or (*N*) lower front.

FIG. 8.7. Inclined-surface positions. (*B*) to (*E*) are inclined to front and side; (*F*) to (*J*), to top and side; and (*K*) to (*N*), to front and top.

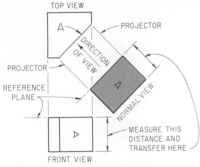

FIG. 8.8. Normal view of an inclined surface. The object is in position (B) of Fig. 8.7.

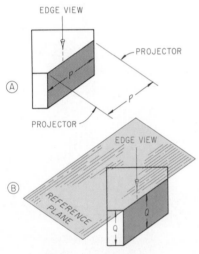

FIG. 8.9. Relationship of projectors, reference plane, and surface dimensions.

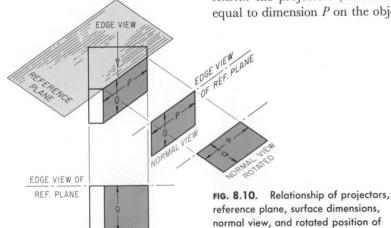

FIG. 8.10. Relationship of projectors, reference plane, surface dimensions, normal view, and rotated position of normal view.

Inclined surfaces occur at *angles* of inclination differing from those shown in Fig. 8.7 but, for general position, no other locations are possible.

8.4. THE NORMAL VIEW OF AN INCLINED SURFACE. No matter what the position of an inclined surface may be, the fundamentals of projecting a normal view of the surface are the same, as will be seen from Figs. 8.8 to 8.21.

Figure 8.8 is the orthographic drawing of the object in position (B) of Fig. 8.7. The inclined surface, identified by the letter *A*, is on the right front of the object and shows, in Fig. 8.8, as an *edge* in the top view. Because surface *A* appears as an edge in the top view, the direction of observation for the normal view is established perpendicular to the edge view, as shown. We are looking, in this case, in a horizontal direction, *directly at* surface *A*. Projectors parallel to the viewing direction (also, perpendicular to surface *A*) establish one dimension of the surface needed for the normal view. This is the *horizontal* distance from the left-front vertical edge to the right-rear vertical edge of surface *A*. Figure 8.9*A* shows that the distance *between* the projectors (dimension *P*) is equal to dimension *P* on the object.

All orthographic views have two dimensions, and to complete the normal view of surface *A*, we now need its second dimension. That dimension is, in this case, the vertical distance *Q*, shown at (*B*), which is the vertical height of surface *A* and appears in true length *on the front view* (Fig. 8.8). This distance cannot be projected but must be transferred from the front view to the normal view as shown in Fig. 8.8. In order to facilitate transferring the distance (this will apply particularly in later problems where the surface may not be rectangular), a *reference plane* (Figs. 8.9*B* and 8.10) is established on both the normal view and front view. This reference plane *must* be perpendicular to the distance to be measured and transferred; it is therefore perpendicular to the projectors between the top and front views *and in the front view,* and also perpendicular to the projectors from the top view to the normal view *and in the normal view,* as shown in Fig. 8.8. The reference plane, here, is at the *top edge* of surface *A* in both views. This can be visualized in the normal view by considering the reference plane as a hinge that will rotate the normal view 90° downward to its original position in coincidence with the top view. This is shown pictorially in Fig. 8.10 to aid in visualizing the relationship. It must be understood that the normal view, projected directly out from its original coincidence on the object, occurs in the position first shown in Fig. 8.8. To get the view into coincidence with the plane of the drawing paper, the view is rotated to the position shown in Fig. 8.10. Carefully study Figs. 8.8 to 8.10 and reread the text to fix all relationships.

The foregoing constitutes all the geometry and projection needed for drawing *any* normal view of an inclined sur-

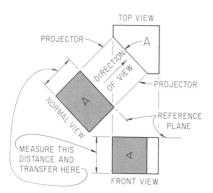

FIG. 8.11. Normal view of an inclined surface. The object is in position (*C*) of Fig. 8.7.

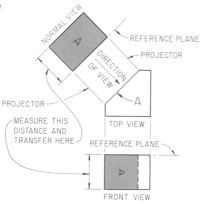

FIG. 8.12. Normal view of an inclined surface. The object is in position (*D*) of Fig. 8.7.

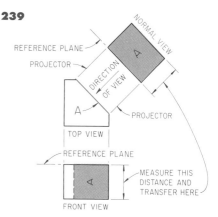

FIG. 8.13. Normal view of an inclined surface. The object is in position (*E*) of Fig. 8.7.

face. The projection will in some cases be made from a different view and the measurement transferred will be width or depth instead of height, but the fundamental relationships of the views will *be the same in every case.*

Consider the other positions of the object, (*C*) to (*E*), of Fig. 8.7. In every case the inclined surface is similarly oriented in space to that of Fig. 8.8, but turned to a different position. Figure 8.11 (position *C* of Fig. 8.7) has the inclined surface on the left front of the object. As in the first case, the direction of view must be perpendicular to the inclined face, and is seen in true relationship in the top view, where surface *A* appears as an edge. The projectors for the normal view are parallel to the viewing direction and of course perpendicular to surface *A*. The reference plane is established in the normal view perpendicular to the projectors for the normal view and in the front view perpendicular to the projectors between top and front views. The measurement of height, transferred from the front view to the normal view, completes the normal view.

Note that the reference plane will *always* appear in the two views that are in projection *with* the view that shows the inclined surface as an edge, and that

the reference plane is always perpendicular to the projectors between these pairs of views.

Figure 8.12 shows position (*D*) of Fig. 8.7. This time the inclined surface is at the left rear of the object. Figure 8.13 shows position (*E*) of Fig. 8.7. Read the explanation given for Figs. 8.8, 8.9, and 8.10 while studying these two figures (8.12 and 8.13) and note that the directions given for Figs. 8.8 to 8.10 apply equally well for Figs. 8.12 and 8.13. This shows that the actual position of the inclined surface is simply a variation.

Turning now to the second column of positions (*F* to *J*) of Fig. 8.7, note again that all these positions have the inclined surface at an angle to top and side. Then, looking at Figs. 8.14 to 8.17 inclusive (these are all similar because the inclined surface appears in every case as an edge on the front view), observe that Fig. 8.14 is position (*F*), Fig. 8.15 position (*G*), Fig. 8.16 position (*H*), and 8.17 position (*J*).

The projection of the normal view in Figs. 8.14 to 8.17 is unchanged geometrically and projectively as compared with Figs. 8.8 to 8.13. The *only* difference is that the projectors for the normal view this time emanate from the front view, where the inclined surface appears as an

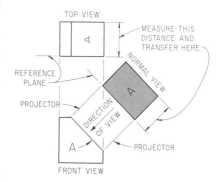

FIG. 8.14. Normal view of an inclined surface. The object is in position (*F*) of Fig. 8.7.

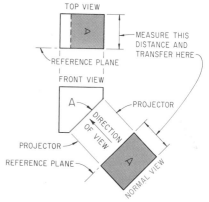

FIG. 8.15. Normal view of an inclined surface. The object is in position (*G*) of Fig. 8.7.

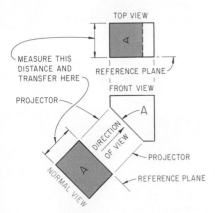

FIG. 8.16. Normal view of an inclined surface. The object is in position (*H*) of Fig. 8.7.

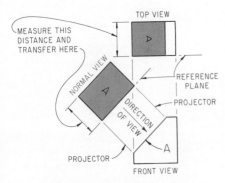

FIG. 8.17. Normal view of an inclined surface. The object is in position (*J*) of Fig. 8.7.

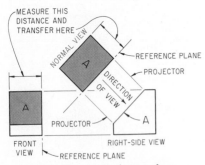

FIG. 8.18. Normal view of an inclined surface. The object is in position (*K*) of Fig. 8.7.

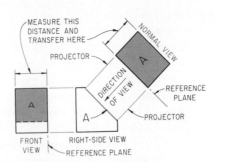

FIG. 8.19. Normal view of an inclined surface. The object is in position (*L*) of Fig. 8.7.

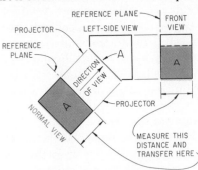

FIG. 8.20. Normal view of an inclined surface. The object is in position (*M*) of Fig. 8.7.

edge. While studying Figs. 8.14 to 8.17, consider again the principles of projection involved and the procedure followed: (1) The direction of observation for the normal view is perpendicular to the inclined surface and, on the drawing, perpendicular to the edge view of the surface. (2) The projectors for the normal view are parallel to the viewing direction, perpendicular to the inclined surface and, on the drawing, perpendicular to the edge view of the surface. (3) The projectors (or the spacing between them) determine one dimension of the normal view. (4) The second dimension for the normal view is now needed. (5) The reference plane for making the needed measurement will appear in the normal perpendicular to the projectors between edge view and normal view, and in the principal view (in projection with the edge view) perpendicular to the projectors between edge view and principal view. (6) The measurement perpendicular to the reference plane in the principal view is then transferred to the normal view, perpendicular to the reference plane, thus completing the layout of the normal view.

Figures 8.18 to 8.21 show the inclined surface positions of the third column of Fig. 8.7 (*K* to *N*), in the same order. Note that the projective system is the same as before. The only difference now

is that the edge view of the inclined surface appears in the *side* view, and because *either* side view *might* be drawn, the projectors from the edge view to the normal view will have to be drawn from whichever side view, right or left, is used. To illustrate this variation, Figs. 8.18 and 8.19 have been drawn with the right-side view and Figs. 8.20 and 8.21 with the left-side view. Note also that the reference plane, with measurements taken from it, will in these cases be in the normal view and the front view, since the front view is the view in *direct* projection with the edge view of the inclined surface.

Study Figs. 8.7 to 8.21 carefully, note the recurrence of certain principles of projection, and study the relationships of views, projectors, directions, and measurements.

8.5. NORMAL VIEWS OF INCLINED SURFACES ON PRACTICAL OBJECTS. So far we have presented only the pertinent principles of projection and the procedure for drawing a normal view, using a rectangular object for illustration. Practical objects are, of course, made up of rectangular, conic, cylindrical, and other shapes, and this is sometimes considered by the uninitiated to be a complication. However, this is not the case; a machine part is often easier to draw than a purely

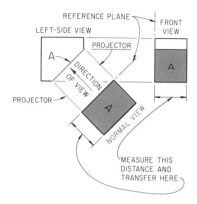

FIG. 8.21. Normal view of an inclined surface. The object is in position (N) of Fig. 8.7.

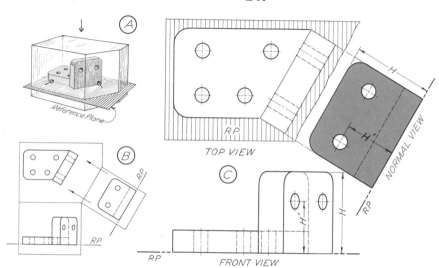

FIG. 8.22. Machine part with surface inclined to front and side. (A) planes of projection; (B) the planes opened up; (C) front, top, and normal views of the inclined surface.

geometric shape because it is more readily visualized.

Figure 8.22 shows a part with a surface inclined to front and side, about in the same position as the inclined surface in Fig. 8.8. At (A) the object is shown pictorially, surrounded by the planes of projection, and at (B) the projection planes are opened up into the plane of the paper. Note that the reference plane is placed, in this case, at the *base* of the object because this is a natural reference surface. Thus at (C) the reference plane is drawn at the base in the front and normal views, and measurements are made *upward* (dimensions H and H') to needed points. Note that the top view is the normal view of the reference plane, which appears as an edge in the front and normal views.

Figure 8.23 illustrates the procedure for drawing the normal view of an inclined surface on a machine part. Steps are as follows:

1. Draw the partial top and front views, as at (B), and locate the view direction by drawing projectors perpen-

dicular to the edge view of the inclined surface, as shown.

2. Locate the reference plane (RP) in the front view. The reference plane may be taken above, below, or through the view, and is chosen for convenience in measuring. In this case it is taken through the natural center line of the front view. The reference plane in the normal view will be perpendicular to the projectors already drawn, and is located at a convenient distance from the top view, as shown at (C).

3. As shown at (D), measure the distance (height) from the reference plane

FIG. 8.23. Stages in drawing a machine part with a surface inclined to front and side.

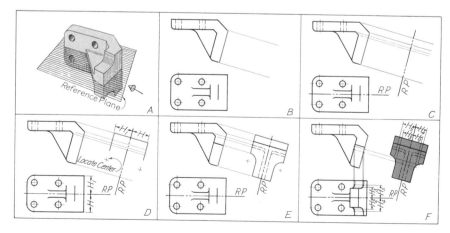

FIG. 8.24. A machine part with surfaces inclined to top and side. (*A*) planes of projection; (*B*) the planes opened up; (*C*) front, top, and normal views of the inclined surfaces.

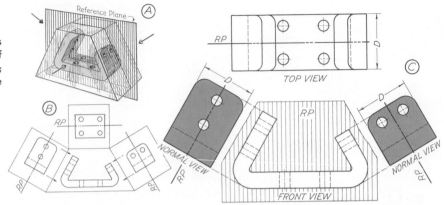

of various points needed, as, for example, *H* and H_1, and transfer these measurements with dividers or scale to the normal view, measuring from the reference plane in the normal view.

4. Complete the normal view from specifications of the rounds, etc., as shown at (*E*). Note that any measurement in the front view, made *toward* the top view, is transferred to the *normal view, toward* the top view. Note also that the front view could not be completed without using the normal view.

5. To get the front view of the circular portions, the true shape of which shows only in the normal view as circle arcs, select points in the normal view, project them back to the top view, and then to the front view. On these projectors transfer the heights H_2 and H_3 from the normal view to find the corresponding points in the front view. H_4, H_5, and others will complete the curve in the front view. Note that this procedure is exactly reversed from the operation of measuring from the front view to locate a distance in the normal view.

Figure 8.24 shows an object with *two* inclined surfaces. Note that the normal views are only partial views because the base of the object is fully described in top and front views. The reference plane is taken through the center because the object is symmetrical.

Figure 8.25 illustrates the steps in drawing the normal view of a face inclined to top and side:

1. Draw the partial top and front views, as at (*B*), and locate the view direction by drawing projectors perpendicular to the inclined surface, as shown.

2. Locate the reference plane in the top view. The reference plane may be taken in front of, through, or to the rear of the view but is here located at the rear flat surface of the object because of convenience in measuring. The reference plane in the normal view will be perpendicular to the projectors already drawn, and is located at a convenient distance from the front view, as shown at (*C*).

FIG. 8.25. Stages in drawing a machine part with a surface inclined to top and side.

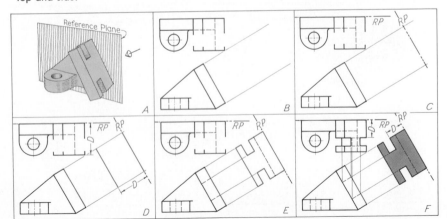

3. As shown at (*D*), measure the distance (depths) from the reference plane (of various points needed), and transfer these measurements with dividers or scale to the normal view, measuring from the reference plane in the normal view. Note that the points are in front of the reference plane in the top view and are therefore measured toward the front in the normal view.

4. From specifications, complete the normal view, as shown at (*E*).

5. Complete the drawing, as shown at (*F*). In this case the top view could have been completed before the normal view was drawn. However, it is considered better practice to lay out the normal view before completing the view that will show the surface foreshortened.

A part might also be drawn with the inclined surface on the lower or upper front or rear. Orientation of this type is shown in Fig. 8.26, where the inclined surface is on the upper front. The steps in drawing an object of this type are given in Fig. 8.27 as follows:

1. Draw the partial front, top, and right-side views, as at (*B*), and locate the normal view direction by drawing projectors perpendicular to the inclined surface, as shown.

2. Locate the reference plane in the front view. This reference plane is taken at the left side of the object, because both the vertical and inclined portions have a left surface in the same profile plane. The reference plane in the normal view will be perpendicular to the projectors already drawn, and is located at a convenient distance from the right-side view, as shown at (*C*).

3. As shown at (*D*), measure the distances (widths) from the reference plane (of various points needed), and transfer these measurements with dividers or scale to the normal view, measuring

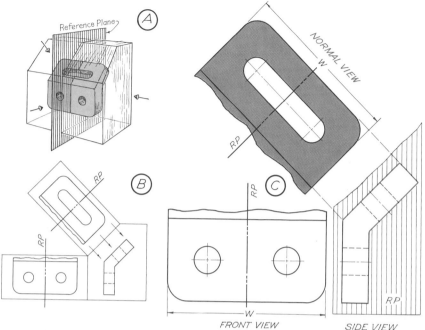

from the reference plane in the normal view. Note that points to the right of the reference plane in the front view will be measured in a direction *toward* the right-side view in the normal view.

4. From specifications of the surface contour complete the normal view (*E*).

5. Complete the right-side and front views by projecting and measuring from the normal view. As an example, one intersection of the cut corner is projected to the right-side view and from

FIG. 8.26.   A machine part with a surface inclined to top and front. (*A*) planes of projection; (*B*) the planes opened up; (*C*) front, side, and normal views of the inclined surface.

FIG. 8.27.   Stages in drawing a machine part with a surface inclined to top and front.

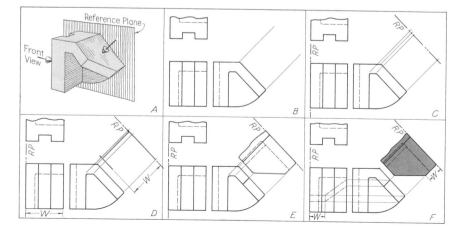

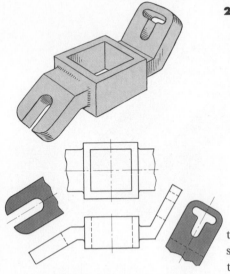

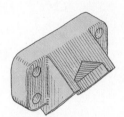

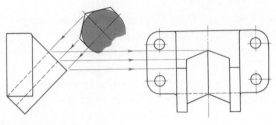

FIG. 8.29. Use of the normal view for construction of other views.

FIG. 8.28. Use of partial views.

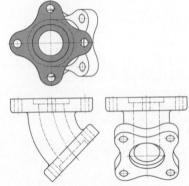

FIG. 8.30. Top, front, and right-side views of an irregular part.

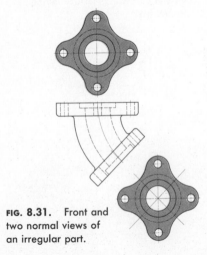

FIG. 8.31. Front and two normal views of an irregular part.

there to the front view; the other intersection is measured (distance W) from the normal view and then laid off in the front view.

8.6 PURPOSES OF NORMAL VIEWS.

In practical work the chief reason for using a normal view is to show the true shape of an inclined surface.

In a normal view, the inclined surface will be shown in its true shape, but the other faces of the object appearing in the view will be foreshortened. In practical work these foreshortened parts are usually omitted, as in Fig. 8.28. Views thus drawn are called *partial views.* The exercise of drawing the complete view, however, may aid the student in understanding the subject.

Another important use of a normal view is in the case where a principal view has a part in a foreshortened position which cannot be drawn without first constructing a normal view in its true shape from which the part can be projected back to the principal view. Figure 8.29 illustrates this procedure. Note in this figure that the view direction is set up looking along the semihexagonal slot and perpendicular to the face that is at a right angle to the slot. From the normal view showing the true semihexagonal shape, the side view and then the front view can be completed.

In most cases the normal view cannot be projected from the principal views but *must be drawn from dimensional specifications of the surface shape.*

Another practical example is the flanged 45° elbow of Fig. 8.30, a casting with an irregular inclined face, which not only cannot be shown in true shape in any of the principal views but also is difficult to draw in its foreshortened position. An easier and more practical selection of views for this piece is shown in Fig. 8.31, where normal views looking in directions perpendicular to the inclined faces show the true shape of the surfaces and allow for simplification. This is because each view can be laid out independently from specifications, and there is not even need for a reference plane, measurements, etc.

8.7. SKEW SURFACES.

In paragraph 8.2, in the classification of surfaces, the skew surface was described and illustrated. For convenience, Fig. 8.32 again shows this type of surface both pictorially and orthographically. Remember that a skew surface is one that occurs at an angle to *all* the principal planes of projection.

The normal view of a skew surface cannot (without resorting to special projective methods) be projected directly from the principal views, but must be projected from an *edge* view of the surface. Also, the edge view is almost always needed to show other features such as the angle a surface makes with its base. Thus, *two* views are required and we must first learn how to get the edge view.

8.8. DETERMINING EDGE VIEWS: NORMAL AND END VIEWS OF LINES.

The normal view of a surface shows the true length of *all* lines in the surface. To prove this, go back to Fig. 8.8 and visualize *any* line on surface A of the figure. You will find that the line shows in true length in the normal view. Any line that is parallel to one of the planes of projection will have a principal view that is the normal view. Thus in Fig. 8.33 where the lines are horizontal (A), frontal (B), and profile (C), the normal views of the lines are at (A) the top view, at (B) the front view, and at (C) the side view.

Often a line is skew to *all* the planes of projection and an extra view is required to give the normal view. To find the normal view of a surface, the direction of observation must be *perpendicular* to the surface; the same direction of observation is needed in finding the normal view of a line—the direction of observation *must* be perpendicular to the line. Thus at (D) projectors are drawn in the top view *perpendicular* to the top view of the line. The direction of view is now established perpendicular to the line, since the line could be on a surface, the top view being the *edge* view of the assumed surface. Next, the reference plane will appear perpendicular to the projectors just established for the normal view and will appear again in the front view perpendicular to the projectors between top and front views. Finally, point A is *on* the reference plane and on the projector from the top

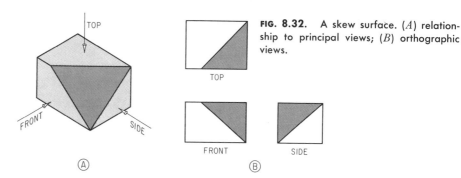

FIG. 8.32. A skew surface. (*A*) relationship to principal views; (*B*) orthographic views.

view and is thus located in the normal view. Point B, then measured from the reference plane in the front view, transferred to the normal view and laid off from the reference plane *on* the projector for point B, completes the normal view. A similar normal view can be projected from the front view as at E, or from the side view as at F. Note in both cases that the projectors for the normal view *must* be perpendicular to the line in the view the normal is projected from.

FIG. 8.33. Normal views of lines.

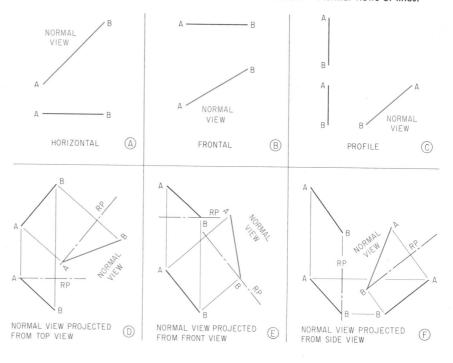

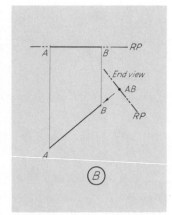

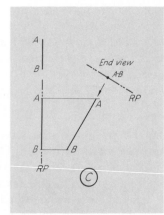

FIG. 8.34. End view of a line. (*A*) horizontal line; (*B*) frontal line; (*C*) profile line.

The key to determining the direction of observation needed to obtain the edge view of a surface is to locate a direction that will give the *end view of one line* of the surface. This is easily done if the surface contains a line that is horizontal, frontal, or profile. In Fig. 8.34*A* the line is horizontal and a view made looking in a horizontal direction that is *aligned with the line* will give the end view. Note in Fig. 8.34*A* that points *A* and *B* (the two ends of the line) are both on the same projector and that both lie on the reference plane thus giving coincidence of the two ends of the line in the end view. Also note that the end view must be projected from the

normal view of the line, in this case the top view. The end view of a frontal line is shown at (*B*); it is projected from the front (normal) view. The end view of a profile line is shown at (*C*); it is projected from the side (normal) view.

8.9.   EDGE VIEWS OF SKEW SURFACES. As stated before, the edge view of a surface is made by first obtaining the end view of any line of the surface. In Fig. 8.35 surface *ABDC* is a skew surface (at an angle to *all* principal planes). However, lines *AB* and *DC* are horizontal lines of the surface. Selecting *DC* as the key line, a projector is drawn aligned with *DC* and another projector

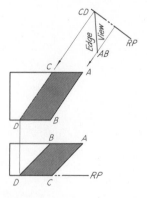

FIG. 8.35. Edge view of a skew surface. Projection is in the direction of the horizontal line *DC*.

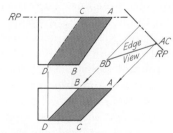

FIG. 8.36. Edge view of a skew surface. Projection is in the direction of frontal line *AC*.

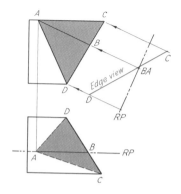

FIG. 8.37. Edge view of a skew surface. The direction of the edge view is located by the horizontal line *AB*.

(parallel) is drawn for *AB*. This establishes the direction of view for the end view of both *DC* and *AB*. The reference plane for the edge view will appear as an edge perpendicular to these projectors, and will appear again as an edge in the front view perpendicular to the projectors between top and front views. For convenience, the reference plane is placed through points *D* and *C*. Then *D* and *C* both project to the edge view on the same projector and both lie on the reference plane, giving *DC* in the edge view. *A* and *C* both project to the edge view on the same projector. The distance from the reference plane in the front view to points *A* and *C* is measured and transferred to the edge view, thus locating *AC* in the edge view. The line connecting *DC* and *AB* is the edge view of surface *ABDC*.

Figure 8.36 shows the identical surface *ABDC* of Fig. 8.35 but this time the edge view has been obtained by looking along the two frontal lines *AC* and *BD*. The edge view is projected in the direction of *AC* and *BD* from the front view because *AC* and *BD* are normal in the front view. The reference plane then located in the edge view and top view, and *AC* and *BD* located with reference to it, complete the edge view.

In Fig. 8.37 the surface *ACD* does not contain any horizontal, frontal, or profile line, and so to get an end view of one line of the surface a horizontal, frontal or profile line must be laid out on the surface. A horizontal line has been selected and is drawn at *AB* in the front view and then projected to the top view. This line (*AB*) is then normal in the top view and projectors parallel to it from *AB, C,* and *D* will establish the direction for the edge view of *ACD*. The reference plane is conveniently located through *AB* in front and edge views; then *D* and *C* are measured from the reference plane in the front view and transferred to the edge view. Note that *D* lies *above* the reference plane and *C below* and that they are transferred accordingly to the edge view. To avoid reversing a normal or edge view, remember this simple rule: if a point is on the side of the reference plane *toward* the view projected from in making an edge or normal view (the top view, in this case), the point will be transferred *toward* that same view. As an example of the rule, note in Fig. 8.37 that *D* is on the side *toward* the top view from the reference plane in both front and edge views while *C* is on the side *away* from the reference plane.

FIG. 8.38. Normal view of a skew surface. *BCDE* is a skew surface because of the position of the object.

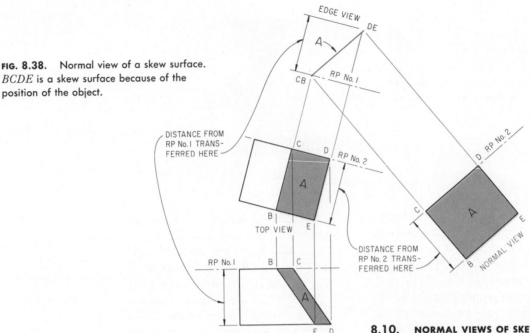

FIG. 8.39. Normal view of a skew surface. The edge view is projected in the direction of the horizontal line *CB*. The normal view is perpendicular to the edge view.

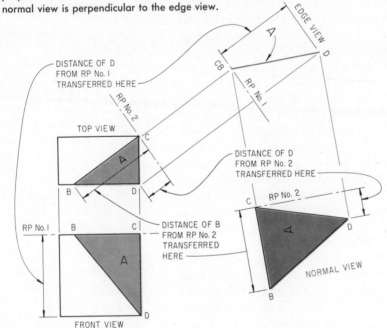

8.10. NORMAL VIEWS OF SKEW SURFACES.

A skew surface is produced by an object with an inclined surface that is turned at an angle to the principal planes, as in Fig. 8.38, or by an object with a face at an angle to three object faces, as in Figs. 8.39 and 8.40. Figure 8.38 is easier to visualize, so we will discuss it first.

Surface *BCDE* of Fig. 8.38 is a skew surface. *CB* and *DE* are horizontal lines of the surface. The edge view is obtained by looking in the direction of *CB* and *DE*, as shown in Fig. 8.38 and described in paragraph 8.9.

The normal view is made with the direction of observation perpendicular to the edge view. To draw the normal view, first draw projectors perpendicular to the edge view (Fig. 8.38), establishing the direction for the normal view. As in all earlier examples, the reference plane for the normal view (*RP* No. 2 in Fig. 8.38) is perpendicular to the projectors. The reference plane appears normal in

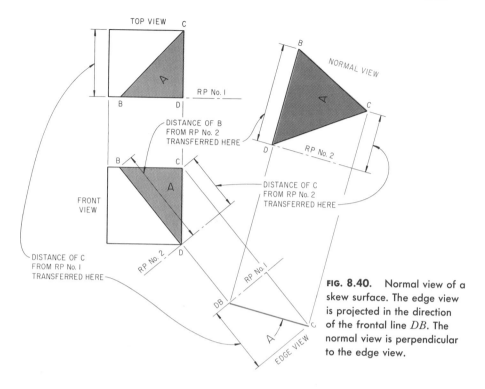

FIG. 8.40. Normal view of a skew surface. The edge view is projected in the direction of the frontal line *DB*. The normal view is perpendicular to the edge view.

the edge view and appears again as an edge in *any* other view in direct projection with the edge view. In this case therefore, the reference plane shows as an edge in the top view, and is perpendicular to the projectors between top and edge views. To prove this relationship to yourself, note that here the top view, edge view, and normal view have *exactly* the same relationship as the front view, top view, and normal view of Fig. 8.8. Finally, transfer the distance of *B* and *E* from the reference plane (No. 2) in the top view to the normal view, as shown.

Figure 8.39 is similar to 8.38 but this time the object faces are parallel to the principal planes, and surface *BCD* is skew to object faces and principal planes. Again, one line (*BC*) of the skew surface is horizontal and gives the direc-

tion for the edge view. In the edge view, *B* and *C* are on the reference plane. Point *D*, measured from reference plane No. 1 in the front view, is transferred to the edge view, as shown. Then, projectors perpendicular to the edge view give the direction for the normal view, and reference plane No. 2 is drawn in normal and top views perpendicular to the projectors connecting each with the edge view. Finally the distances of *B* and *D* from reference plane No. 2 are transferred to the normal view.

The object of Fig. 8.40 is similar to that of Fig. 8.39 but in Fig. 8.40 the frontal line (*BD*) of surface *BCD* has been used for the direction of the edge view. The edge view is therefore projected from the front view. All other constructions are the same as before and are evident from the figure.

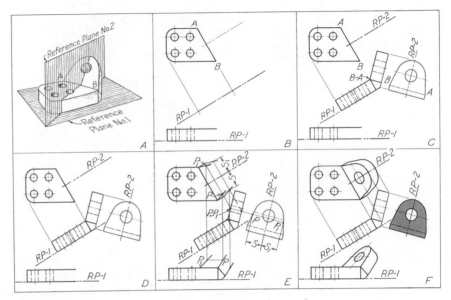

FIG. 8.41.   Stages in drawing a machine part with a skew surface.

8.11.   NORMAL VIEWS OF SKEW SURFACES ON PRACTICAL OBJECTS.   Figure 8.41 illustrates the successive steps in drawing a normal view. The pictorial illustration (*A*) shows a typical object with a skew surface. The line of intersection between the skew portion and the horizontal base is line *AB*. In order to get an edge view of the skew surface, a view may be taken looking in the direction of line *AB*, thus giving an end view of *AB*. Because *AB* is a line of the skew surface, the edge view will result. The reference plane (*RP* No. 1) for this view will be horizontal. The direction of observation for the normal view will be perpendicular to the skew surface. The reference plane (*RP* No. 2) for the normal view will be perpendicular to the edge-view direction and thus perpendicular to edge *AB*, as shown at (*A*).

At (*B*), partial top and front views are shown. The projectors and reference plane for the required edge view are also shown.

At (*C*), the edge view has been drawn. Note that line *AB* appears as a point in the edge view. The angle that the skew surface makes with the base is laid out in this view from specifications.

At (*D*), the normal view is added. The projectors for the view are perpendicular to the edge view. The reference plane is drawn perpendicular to the projectors for the normal view and at a convenient distance from the edge view. The reference plane in the top view is drawn midway between points *A* and *B* in the top view because the skew surface is symmetrical about this reference plane. The normal view is drawn from specifications of the shape. The projection back to the edge view can then be made.

The views thus completed at (*D*) describe the object, but the top and front views may be completed for illustrative purposes or as an exercise in projection. The method is illustrated at (*E*) and (*F*). Any point, say *P*, may be selected and projected back to the edge view. From this view a projector is drawn back to the top view. Then the distance *S* from the normal view is transferred to the reference plane in the top view. A number of points so located will complete the top view of the circular portion, and the straight-line portion can be projected in similar manner. The front view is found by drawing projectors to the front view for the points needed, measuring the heights from the reference plane in the edge view, and transferring these distances to the front view. Note that this procedure for completing the top and front views is the same as for drawing the views originally but in reverse order.

8.12. SPACE GEOMETRY. For an object to be described, dimensioned, and specified completely on a working drawing, some preliminary work must often be done in order to determine true relationships between lines or surfaces, to find intersections, to locate elements or tangents, to ascertain clearances, or to decide relationships affecting the design of a single part (or of parts) in a machine or structure. To do this work, one must have a knowledge of points, lines, planes, and curved and warped surfaces, combined with a complete understanding of their geometrical properties.

This branch of graphic science is variously known as "descriptive geometry," "engineering geometry," "the geometry of engineering drawing," "practical descriptive geometry," "three-dimensional descriptive geometry," and some other rather inaccurate terms. Actually, the subject is simply an expansion of orthographic projection for the solution of geometric space problems.

To solve the basic problems of space involving points, lines, planes, and surfaces, the orthographic views required are:

1. The normal view of a line

2. The end, or point, view of a line

3. The edge view of a plane

4. The normal view of a plane

With these available views, together with a knowledge of plane and solid geometry, all problems may be solved involving parallelism, perpendicularity, angularity, clearance, tangency, true length, true size and shape, distance, area, volume, location, and layout.

The four basic views described above and the various ways in which they may be obtained are the necessary equipment for problem solution.

8.13.   NORMAL, EDGE, AND POINT VIEWS.
Directions for making normal views of lines and surfaces of solid objects have been given. However, teaching experience has shown the necessity for review of projection principles for the making of normal views of planes and surfaces when theoretical lines and surfaces, instead of solid objects, are to be dealt with. This is because lines and surfaces are not visualized nearly so readily as practical objects having features such as holes, lugs, bosses, ribs, and other elements which are easily recognizable.

The term "normal" is mathematically defined as meaning "perpendicular" or "at right angles." The term is here geometrically applied to a view in which the direction of observation is perpendicular to a line or surface. For example, the normal view (true length of a line; true size of a plane) of a horizontal line or plane is shown in the top view because the view direction for the projection of the top view is perpendicular to the horizontal plane (and any line or plane lying in that plane). Similarly, the front view is the normal view of any frontal line or plane, and the side view the normal view of any profile line or plane.

The term "edge" is defined as the view of a plane wherein all lines of the plane appear as a single line; that is, the direction of observation is aligned with the plane. *The point (or end) view of a line is that view at which all points on the line appear as a single point;* in other words, the direction of observation is aligned with the line.

The student should carefully and thoroughly review paragraphs 8.1 through 8.11, and then pay particular attention to the following outline:

I. Line Positions

    A. A line may lie in two, one, or none of the principal planes of projection.

        1. A line that lies in *two* principal planes of projection will appear *normal* (showing its true length) in *two* views and is named for the planes it lies in (see Fig. 8.42). A line lying in *two* principal planes will appear as a point in the third principal plane.

        2. A line in *one* principal plane of projection will appear normal in *one* view and is named for the plane it lies in (see Fig. 8.42). A line lying in *one* principal plane of projection may be inclined to the other two principal planes. To show the end view of the line an auxiliary view is required.

        3. A line in *none* of the principal planes of projection, called a *skew line,* will not appear normal in any of the principal views. Auxiliary views are needed to show the normal and end views of a skew line.

II. Plane Positions

    A. A plane may be *parallel* to *one* of the principal planes of projection, *inclined* to *two* principal planes of projection, or *inclined* to *all three* principal planes.

        1. A plane *parallel* to *one* of the principal planes receives its name from that principal plane and will appear normal in *that* one principal view (see Fig. 8.44).

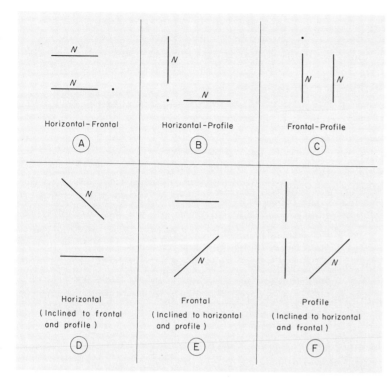

FIG. 8.42. Normal views of lines lying in *two* principal planes of projection and in *one* principal plane of projection.

2. A plane *inclined* to *one* principal plane of projection will also be inclined to another principal plane and will not appear normal in any view, but will appear as an edge in one view (see Fig. 8.44).

3. Planes described in (1) and (*A*), (*B*), and (*C*) of Fig. 8.44 are *parallel* to *one* principal plane of projection and *perpendicular* to the other two; planes described in (2) and (*D*), (*E*), and (*F*) of Fig. 8.44 are *perpendicular* to *one* of the principal planes. An auxiliary view is required to show the normal view.

4. A plane *inclined* to *all three* principal planes of projection, called a *skew plane,* will not appear normal or as an edge in any of the principal views (see Fig. 8.45). Auxiliary views are required to show the edge and normal views.

III. Viewing Directions for Normal Views
   A. Lines
   1. A horizontal-frontal line will appear normal in both the top and front views (Fig. 8.42*A*).
   2. A horizontal-profile line will appear normal in both the top and side views (Fig. 8.42*B*).
   3. A frontal-profile line will appear normal in both the front and side views (Fig. 8.42*C*).
   4. A horizontal line will appear normal in the top view (Fig. 8.42*D*).

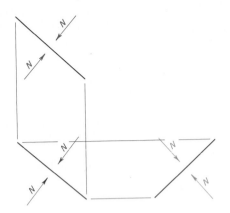

FIG. 8.43. Directions of observation to obtain the normal view of a skew line.

5. A frontal line will appear normal in the front view (Fig. 8.42*E*).
6. A profile line will appear normal in the side view (Fig. 8.42*F*).
7. A skew line (Fig. 8.43) will not appear normal in any of the principal views. An auxiliary is required to obtain the normal view. As stated at the beginning of paragraph 8.43, the normal view will be seen when the line of sight is *perpendicular* to the line. As seen in (1) through (6) and in Fig. 8.42, a line will appear normal when the view direction is perpendicular to a plane the line lies in. Further, any number of planes can be passed through a line. A plane passed through the line so that it appears as an edge in one of the principal views will indicate the direction of an auxiliary that will give the normal view of the line. In Fig. 8.46, plane *ABCD* has been assumed through line *BD*, a skew line. Plane *ABCD* appears as an edge in the front view. An auxiliary projected from the front view perpendicular to *ABCD*, and of course perpendicular to *BD*, will give the normal view of *BD*. Note that a plane through any skew line can be assumed so that it appears as an edge in any one of the principal views. Thus an auxiliary projected through the line and *perpendicular* to any principal view will give the normal view of the line (see Fig. 8.47).

B. Planes
1. A horizontal plane will appear normal in the top view (Fig. 8.44*A*).
2. A frontal plane will appear normal in the front view (Fig. 8.44*B*).

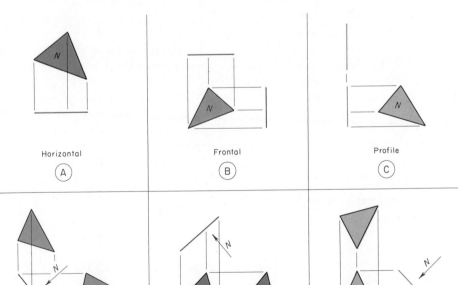

Horizontal
Ⓐ

Frontal
Ⓑ

Profile
Ⓒ

FIG. 8.44. Horizontal, frontal, profile, and inclined planes. Designation of normal view or direction of observation for normal view is indicated.

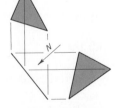

Inclined to Horizontal and Profile—
Perpendicular to Frontal
Ⓓ

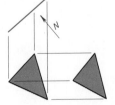

Inclined to Frontal and Profile—
Perpendicular to Horizontal
Ⓔ

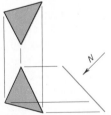

Inclined to Frontal and Horizontal—
Perpendicular to Profile
Ⓕ

3. A profile plane will appear normal in a side view (Fig. 8.44*C*).

4. A plane perpendicular to frontal will appear as an edge in the front view, and an auxiliary taken in a direction perpendicular to the edge view will give the normal view (Figs. 8.44*D* and 8.46).

5. A plane perpendicular to horizontal will appear as an edge in the top view, and an auxiliary taken perpendicular to the edge view will give the normal view (Fig. 8.44*E*).

6. A plane perpendicular to profile will appear as an edge in the side view, and an auxiliary taken perpendicular to the edge view will give the normal view (Fig. 8.44*F*).

7. A skew plane (Fig. 8.45), not being parallel or perpendicular to any of the principal planes of projection, will not appear as either an edge or normal view in any of the principal views. The normal view (refer to Fig. 8.46) must be projected from an edge view. To obtain an edge view, the direction of the view *must be along a line of the plane*. In Fig. 8.48, line *AD*, a frontal line, has been drawn on skew plane *ABC*. Line *AD*, being frontal, appears in true length in the front view. An auxiliary, projected from the front view, with the viewing direction aligned with the line *AD* of plane *ABC*, will give the *end* view of *AD* and the *edge* view of *ABC*. This direction is shown as direction *E* on Fig. 8.48. The normal view of *ABC* can now be made by making a second auxiliary in a direction *perpendicular* to the edge view of *ABC*. This direction is shown on Fig. 8.48 as direction *N*.

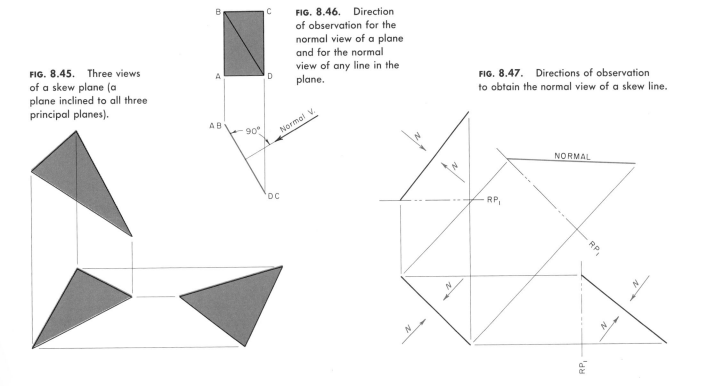

FIG. 8.45. Three views of a skew plane (a plane inclined to all three principal planes).

FIG. 8.46. Direction of observation for the normal view of a plane and for the normal view of any line in the plane.

FIG. 8.47. Directions of observation to obtain the normal view of a skew line.

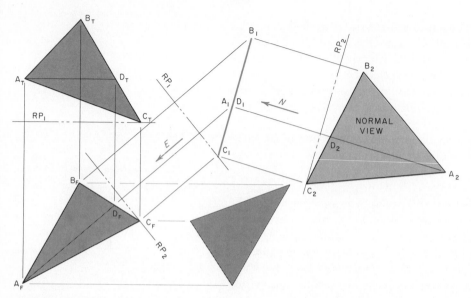

FIG. 8.48. Directions of observation to obtain the normal view of a skew plane.

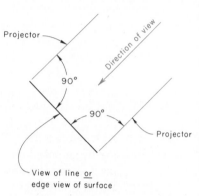

FIG. 8.49. Relationship of projectors to the principal view of a line for obtaining the normal view of the line or, from the edge view of a plane, the normal view of the plane.

IV. Projectors for Normal Views

A. General: Projectors are always parallel to the view direction.

B. Normal views of lines

    1. The projectors for the normal view of a line will be perpendicular to any view of the line (Fig. 8.49). *Note:* If the line is already in true length, the same view as had previously will result. Also, a view perpendicular to the end view of a line will result in the normal view.

C. Normal views of planes

    1. The normal view of a plane is had only when the direction of view is perpendicular to the edge view. Therefore, the projectors for the normal view of a plane will always be perpendicular to an edge view of the plane (Fig. 8.49).

V. Reference Planes

A. General: A reference plane is represented on the drawing by a line which represents the edge view of the reference plane.

    1. The view from which an auxiliary is projected will always contain the normal view of the reference plane required to construct the auxiliary view (Fig. 8.50).

B. Relationship of reference plane representation (line) to projectors

    1. Because in making an auxiliary the reference plane appears as an edge in any view in projection with the view *projected from:*

        a. The reference plane appears as an edge on the auxiliary as a line *perpendicular* to the projectors for the auxiliary (Fig. 8.51).

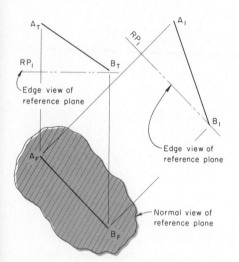

FIG. 8.50. Relationship of reference plane to projectors.

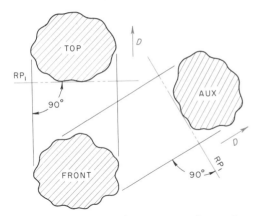

FIG. 8.51. Direction of measurement from reference plane.

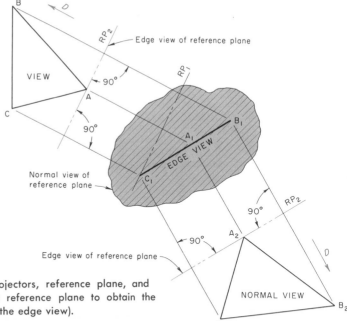

FIG 8.52. Relationship of projectors, reference plane, and direction of measurement from reference plane to obtain the normal view of a plane (having the edge view).

    b. The reference plane appears as an edge on any other view in *direct* projection with the view *projected from* in making an auxiliary (Fig. 8.51).

    c. The reference plane will appear as a line (representing the edge view of a plane) perpendicular to the projection lines connecting views. The line representing the edge view of the reference plane can *never* appear at an angle to projectors; it *must* be perpendicular (Fig. 8.51).

    d. Regardless of the view *projected from* (for example, an auxiliary projected from an edge view to obtain a normal view, as in Fig. 8.52), the reference plane will appear as an edge and will be represented by *a line perpendicular to the projectors* to the view in which the reference plane appears as a line (Fig. 8.52).

VI. Measurements from Reference Planes

    A. Measurements are *always* made perpendicular to the reference plane.

       1. On the drawing, the reference plane (edge view) is represented by a line. Therefore, the measurement will be made perpendicular to the line representing the edge view of the reference plane (Fig. 8.52).

       2. Measurements *must* be made in the same direction from both views (edge) of the reference plane. To orient the views, take the view projected from as a "central view." Then with Fig. 8.52 as an example, a measurement made in a direction away from the central view, in the view previous to the central view, will be made in a direction away from the central view for the auxiliary view. This is illustrated by the direction *D* of Figs. 8.51 and 8.52. Study this figure very carefully to

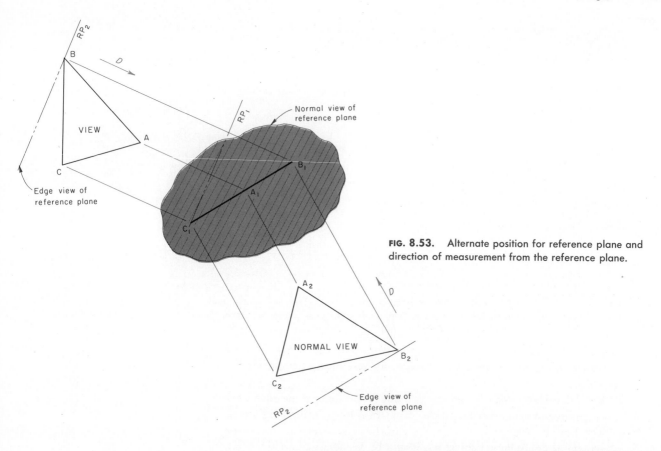

FIG. 8.53.   Alternate position for reference plane and direction of measurement from the reference plane.

confirm this fact. Refer also to Fig. 8.53, a duplicate of Fig. 8.52, except that the reference plane has been placed on the *away* side of both views which are in projection with the central view. Note that a combination of directions (one view as in Fig. 8.52 and another as in Fig. 8.53) *would make a reversal of views*. Study both Figs. 8.52 and 8.53 very carefully.

VII. Terms of Reference

Terms of reference are necessary for identification of the views and constructions needed in the solution of space problems. This is to assure accuracy of description both in the textbook and in class discussion. The following terms of reference are used in this text:

A. Lines
  1. Aligned with two principal planes
      a. Horizontal-frontal
      b. Horizontal-profile
      c. Frontal-profile
  2. Aligned with one principal plane
      a. Horizontal (inclined to frontal and profile)

   b. Frontal (inclined to horizontal and profile)
   c. Profile (inclined to horizontal and frontal)
  3. Skew (inclined to all principal planes)
 B. Planes
  1. Principal
   a. Horizontal
   b. Frontal
   c. Profile
  2. Inclined
   a. Inclined to frontal and profile (perpendicular to horizontal)
   b. Inclined to horizontal and profile (perpendicular to frontal)
   c. Inclined to horizontal and frontal (perpendicular to profile)
  3. Skew (inclined to all principal planes)
 C. Viewing directions
  1. Described as:
   a. Normal *or* perpendicular to _____ line or _____ plane
   b. Aligned with _____ line or _____ plane
 D. Projectors
  1. Always aligned with (parallel to) the viewing direction. Description the same as for viewing direction.
 E. Reference planes
  1. Horizontal ⎫
  2. Frontal   ⎬ for first auxiliary (see **VIII**, **Notation**)
  3. Profile   ⎭
  4. Others—for second auxiliary (see **VIII**, **Notation**)
 F. Auxiliary views (description)
  1. Projected from (top, front, side, rear, bottom) view.
   a. Normal view of line
   b. Point (end) view of line
   c. Edge view of plane
   d. Normal view of plane
  2. Projected from _____ auxiliary (point, edge, or normal) view. This is a second auxiliary view.
   a. Normal view of line
   b. Point (end) view of line
   c. Edge view of plane
   d. Normal view of plane
  3. Whenever more than one auxiliary is required, these are described as (*a*) the first auxiliary, (*b*) the second auxiliary, etc.

VIII. Notation

Subscripts are used to designate points, lines, and planes in the various views. In the different views a point A would be designated as follows:

Top view: A_T

Front view: A_F

Right-side view: A_R

Left-side view: A_L

Side view (not designated right or left): A_S

Rear view: A_{RE}

Bottom view: A_B

First auxiliary: A_1

Second auxiliary: A_2

First auxiliary reference plane: RP_1

Second auxiliary reference plane: RP_2

Designation of normal: N (placed on view)

Designation of edge: E (placed on view)

Designation of true length: TL (placed on view)

Rotated view (top): A_{RT}

Rotated view (front) A_{RF}

Rotated view (side) A_{RS}

Rotated view (auxiliary): A_{R1}, A_{R2}

The foregoing discussion and outline give the essential transitional information connecting paragraphs 8.1 through 8.11 (the making of point, edge, and normal views of the surfaces of practical objects) with the approach, now, to the study of space problems. Study the outline very thoroughly. Practically every difficulty encountered later can be traced back to the student's failure to understand completely the fundamentals given there.

8.14. SPECIFICATION OF A LINE. A line may be located in space by specifying *two points* on it. If the two points are located in two adjacent orthographic views, the points are fixed in space and the line passing through these two points therefore has its direction in space determined. A line is considered to be infinite in length, and the portion between any two points on it simply specifies a segment. The *space direction* (bearing and slope) and *one point* will also locate a line.

8.15. NORMAL VIEW OF A LINE. The general case is where the line is in a skew

position (not parallel to any of the three principal planes of projection). Again, as explained in paragraph 8.13, the normal view of such a line is the one observed *in a direction perpendicular to the line.* Figure 8.54 shows a line AB that is a skew line. The top and front views ($A_T B_T$ and $A_F B_F$) of Fig. 8.54A and B show that the line extends from point A in a direction downward, to the right, and toward the rear. In Fig. 8.54C, AB extends from A in a direction upward, to the right, and forward. At (A) the normal view of the line $A_1 B_1$ has been obtained by making an auxiliary view projected from the top view and taken in a direction perpendicular to the line. This line of sight perpendicular to the line may be visualized if one imagines that the observer moves around the line, looking in a horizontal direction, until his direction of observation is oriented perpendicular to the line; or one may hold a pencil in the position of the line and observe this simple phenomenon. It should also be observed that, in accordance with the theory of orthographic projection, the observer is theoretically at infinity and all points of

Normal view of a line.

the line will be equidistant from the eye. Therefore the true length of the line will be obtained. So in Fig. 8.54A the lines of projection for the auxiliary are drawn parallel to the line of sight shown, which is perpendicular to the top view of AB. The horizontal reference plane RP_1 is established in the front view through point A_F. The reference plane RP_1, for the auxiliary view, is located at some convenient distance from $A_T B_T$ and perpendicular to the lines of projection for the auxiliary view. The auxiliary view is then drawn by locating A_1 on the reference plane, measuring the distance in the front view from the reference plane to B_F, and transferring this distance to the auxiliary, thus locating B_1.

Figure 8.54B shows a normal view of AB made by employing an auxiliary view projected from the front view. Observe that this auxiliary, projected in a direction perpendicular to the front view ($A_F B_F$), will have a *viewing direction* perpendicular to line AB. Similarly, Fig. 8.54C shows the normal view of AB obtained by using an auxiliary view projected from the side view. As described before, this view must be projected perpendicular to the line in the side view to obtain the normal view.

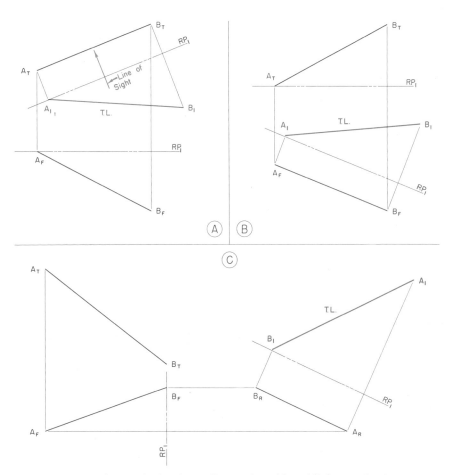

FIG. 8.54. Normal view of a line by auxiliary projected from (A) the top view, (B) the front view, and (C) the side view.

Summary

1. Draw projectors perpendicular to the line in one of the views (top, front, or side).

2. Draw a reference plane (RP_1) perpendicular to these projectors and at a convenient distance from the view projector from (top, front, or side).

3. Draw a reference plane perpendicular to the projectors between the two adjacent principal views, and in a view that is adjacent to, and in projection with, the *view the auxiliary is projected from*. (a) If the auxiliary view is projected from the top view, RP_1 will be drawn in the front view. (b) If the auxiliary view is projected from the front view, RP_1 will be drawn in either the top view or a side view. (c) If the auxiliary view is projected from the side view, RP_1 will be drawn in the front view.

4. Measure distances from the RP described in (3) and lay these distances off from the RP described in (2). Note that if a distance is measured from the reference plane in a direction away from

the view the auxiliary is projected from, that distance will be laid off in the auxiliary in a direction *away* from the *view the auxiliary is projected from.*

5. Draw the line in the auxiliary view. This is the normal view.

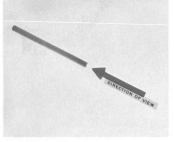

Point view of a line.

8.16. END VIEW OF A LINE. The end, or point, view of a line may be made only after the true-length, or normal, view has been drawn. To get the end view of a line, the direction of observation must be aligned with the line. In Fig. 8.55*A,* the line *AB* is a skew line; its normal view has been made as an auxiliary projected from the top view at A_1B_1. If now a second auxiliary view is made looking in the direction of A_1B_1, the end view will be obtained. The reference plane RP_2 for the end view will be perpendicular to the viewing direction for the end view. This reference plane will appear again as an edge in the top view; it will be perpendicular

to the rays of projection between the top and auxiliary views; and it is most conveniently placed through A_TB_T. Thus in the end view, the line *AB* appears on one single projector and on the reference plane and, therefore, appears as a point, the end view of the line. Figure 8.55*B* illustrates the end view obtained by a first auxiliary projected from the front view and a second auxiliary giving the end view. Study both illustrations of Fig. 8.55 carefully and note the relationships of viewing direction, projectors, and reference planes.

Summary

1. Draw a normal view (auxiliary) of the line (described in paragraph 8.15).

2. Draw a projector aligned with the auxiliary view of the line. This is the projector for the second auxiliary view.

3. Draw a line (representing the edge view of the reference plane) perpendicular to the projector for the second auxiliary (Fig. 8.55).

4. Draw a line (representing the edge view of the reference plane) perpendicular to the projectors, between the first auxiliary and the view the first auxiliary is projected from, *and in* the view the first auxiliary is projected from (Fig. 8.55).

5. The point (end) view of the line is on the single projector and the reference plane of the second auxiliary (Fig. 8.55).

8.17. SPECIFICATION OF A PLANE. As described in paragraph 8.14, a line is located in space by specifying two points on the line. If a plane is passed through a line, the plane may be rotated around the line as an axis and is therefore not fixed immovably in space. To determine

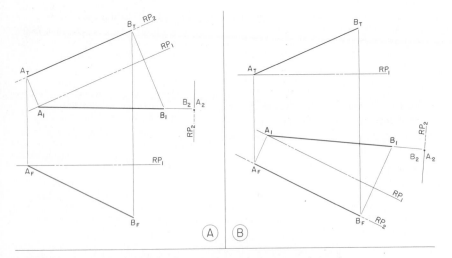

FIG. 8.55. End view of a line. (*Always* projected from a normal view.)

the position of a plane definitely, either *three points* or *two intersecting lines* in the plane must be specified. In Fig. 8.56*A*, three points, *A*, *B*, and *C*, specify a plane. Note also that any pair of intersecting lines, *AB* and *AC*, *AB* and *BC*, or *BC* and *CA*, would specify the same plane. A *pair of parallel lines* will also specify a plane.

8.18. EDGE VIEW OF A PLANE.

The edge view of a plane will be obtained when the direction of observation is aligned with some line of the plane. In other words, if an end view of a line of the plane is obtained, the plane will appear in its edge view. The plane of Fig. 8.56*A* is horizontal and therefore contains many horizontal-profile lines that would appear as points in the front view; the plane thus appears as an edge in the front view. The plane at Fig. 8.56*B* is positioned so that no lines in it will appear as points in the top view, but horizontal-profile lines will appear as points in the front view, giving the edge view shown. Similarly, a plane containing frontal-profile lines will appear as an edge in the top view, and a plane containing horizontal-frontal lines will appear as an edge in a side view. A plane positioned as just described is said to "recede" in the view in which the plane appears as an edge. Thus, in Fig. 8.56*B*, the plane is known as a frontal receding plane.

The plane of Fig. 8.56*C* is skew, and no lines in it, in either the front, top, or side view, will appear as points. If, however, a line is drawn on the plane in a position so that it appears in true length in one of the views, the end view of the line and the resulting edge view of the plane may be obtained. Line *CD* of

plane *ABC* in Fig. 8.56*C* is a frontal line, therefore appearing in true length at $C_F D_F$ in the front view of the plane. An auxiliary projected from the front view and taken in the direction of $C_F D_F$ will show the point view of *CD* and the edge of plane *ABC*. The frontal reference plane RP_1 is located for the auxiliary at a convenient distance from the front view and perpendicular to the projector from $C_F D_F$. This reference plane will appear again as an edge in the top view and will be perpendicular to the rays between front and top views;

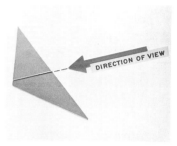

Edge view of a plane.

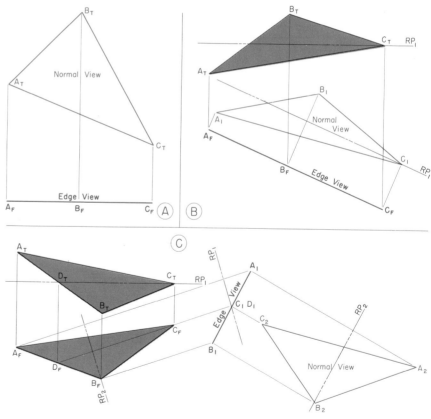

FIG. 8.56. Edge and normal views of a plane: (*A*) principal, (*B*) inclined, and (*C*) skew positions.

for convenience and simplicity of location, RP_1 is taken through $C_T D_T$. Measurements from RP_1, in the top view, transferred to the rays of projection for points A and B and laid off from RP_1, in the auxiliary view, will locate A_1 and B_1. The frontal line CD appears as a point at $C_1 D_1$. It should be noted that all frontal lines in plane ABC will appear as points in this edge view and that the edges AB, BC, and CA all align on one single line in the edge view.

If a horizontal line is drawn on a plane, an auxiliary projected from the top view and taken in the direction of the line will give the edge view; and if a profile line is placed on a plane, an auxiliary projected from the side view and aligned with the line will give the edge view of the plane. *Never* is more than *one* auxiliary required to obtain the edge view of a plane.

Summary

A plane in skew position is the general case (Fig. 8.56C).

1. Draw either a horizontal, frontal, or profile line on the plane. The end view of this line will give the edge view of the plane.

2. Draw the edge view of the plane by drawing projectors parallel to the normal view of the line on the plane; in Fig. 8.56, this is D_F, C_F.

3. Draw the reference plane line for the edge view perpendicular to the projectors to the edge view.

4. Draw a reference plane line perpendicular to the projectors between the view the edge view is projected from and the view adjacent in projection to this view, and draw the reference plane line in this latter view (Fig. 8.56C).

5. Measure distances from the reference plane described in (4), and lay

these distances off from the reference plane in the edge view. Remember that a distance from a reference plane, toward the view the edge view is projected from, should always be laid off in that same direction, i.e., from the reference plane, toward the view the edge view is projected from.

6. Connect points in the auxiliary view to form the edge view.

8.19.   NORMAL VIEW OF A PLANE. The normal view of a plane will be obtained when the viewing direction is perpendicular to the plane. In Fig. 8.56A, the plane ABC is horizontal; the direction of observation for the top view is perpendicular to the horizontal and therefore gives the normal view of plane ABC in the top view.

Plane ABC of Fig. 8.56B appears as an edge in the front view, as does the plane of Fig. 8.56A, but the plane is not horizontal, and therefore the top view does not give the normal view. An auxiliary, however, aligned perpendicular to the edge view will result in a normal view. The projectors in Fig. 8.56B are drawn perpendicular to the edge view (the front view), thus establishing the viewing direction perpendicular to the edge view. The reference plane RP_1 is perpendicular to these projectors and is located in the top view perpendicular to the projectors between top and front views. Measurements then made from RP_1 in the top view and transferred to RP_1 in the auxiliary complete the location of A_1, B_1, and C_1, the normal view of plane ABC.

Plane ABC of Fig. 8.56C is skew. Therefore the edge view will have to be made as described in paragraph 8.18 before the normal view can be constructed. In Fig. 8.56C, the rays of

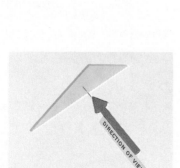

Normal view of a plane.

projection for the normal view are drawn perpendicular to the edge view. The reference plane RP_2 is then located perpendicular to these rays. This reference plane RP_2 will appear again as an edge in the front view and will be perpendicular to the rays of projection from the front view to the edge view. Measurements then made from RP_2 in the front view and transferred to RP_2 in the second auxiliary view will locate A_2, B_2, and C_2, the normal view of plane ABC.

Summary

The normal view of a plane is always projected *from* the edge view.

1. Draw projectors for the normal view perpendicular to the edge view.

2. Draw a reference plane line perpendicular to the projectors to the normal view (Fig. 8.56C).

3. Draw a reference plane line perpendicular to the projectors between the view the normal view is projected from and the view previously adjacent in projection to that view, and draw the reference plane line in this latter view (Fig. 8.56C).

4. Measure from the reference plane described in (3), and lay these distances off from the reference plane line in the normal view.

5. Connect points in the normal view.

8.20.   OTHER METHODS.   The foregoing methods of making normal, point, and edge views, by employing auxiliary views, are the standard and most-used methods. However, in some cases the following methods are used. Study these methods thoroughly, and refer to them again when necessary.

8.21.   NORMAL VIEW OF A LINE BY ROTA-TION.   As explained before in paragraph

8.13, a line in a horizontal plane appears in true length in the top view, a line in a frontal plane appears in true length in the front view, and a line in a profile plane appears in true length in either side view. Therefore, if a *skew* line is rotated so that it coincides with, or is parallel to, one of the planes of projection, the true length of the line will appear in one of the principal views.

Figure 8.57 shows an oblique line AB. In (A) the line has been rotated until it is frontal, thus giving the true length in the front view. The axis of rotation is perpendicular to the horizontal plane and therefore appears as a point in the top view. With center at A_T, an arc is drawn from B_T intersecting a frontal plane through A_T at B_{RT}, the rotated position of B (in the same frontal

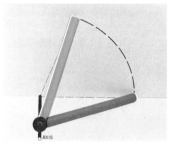

Rotation, normal view.

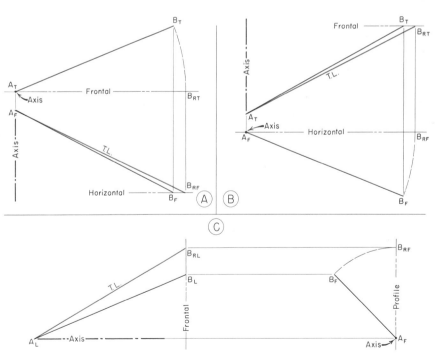

FIG. 8.57.   True length of a line by rotation, rotated (A) to a frontal plane, (B) to a horizontal plane, and (C) to a frontal plane.

plane as A). As B rotates, it must move in a plane perpendicular to the axis of rotation; and, in this case, because the axis is perpendicular to the horizontal, B must move in a horizontal plane. Therefore, a horizontal plane through B_F, intersected by projection from B_{RT}, locates the front view B_{RF}, the rotated position of point B. The true length of the line AB is then the distance from A_F (which remained stationary during the rotation) to B_{RF}.

Figure 8.57B shows the same line rotated until it is horizontal. The axis of rotation is perpendicular to frontal (horizontal-profile). With center at A_F, an arc from B_F brings B to coincidence with the horizontal plane through A_F at B_{RF}. Point B must move in a frontal plane (perpendicular to the horizontal-profile axis); the intersection of the projector from B_{RF} with the frontal plane through B_T locates B_{RT}; and the true length of the line is $A_T B_{RT}$.

Figure 8.57C shows a rotation similar to the others, but here the rotation is made by using the front and left-side views of a line. In the front view the arc $A_F B_F$ to B_{RF} with center at A_F brings point B to coincidence with a profile plane through A_F. Then, perpendicular to the horizontal-profile axis through A, point B must move in a frontal plane; the intersection of this plane from B_L at B_{RL} locates the rotated position of B at B_{RL}, and the true length is $A_L B_{RL}$. Note that when a line is rotated to a profile plane, only the side view (normal view of the profile plane) will show the true length of the line.

Study each illustration of Fig. 8.57, carefully visualizing the position of the axis in each case. Also, note and remember the important point that the *plane of rotation of a point will be perpendicular to the axis of rotation*.

Summary

The true length of a line (by rotation) is found by rotating the line into one of the *principal planes* of projection.

1. Decide on a plane (horizontal, frontal, or profile) into which the line will be rotated (Fig. 8.57A, B, or C).

2. One end (point) of the line will remain stationary. Decide on the end that is not to move.

3. With a compass, swing an arc to rotate the opposite end of the line into the same plane (frontal, horizontal, or profile) as the end of the line that remains stationary (Fig. 8.57A, B, or C).

4. During rotation, all points of the line must rotate in parallel planes perpendicular to the axis of rotation. (a) (Fig. 8.57A) horizontal planes. (b) (Fig. 8.57B) frontal planes. (c) (Fig. 8.57C) frontal planes.

5. Locate the plane through the point at the end of the line in which that point rotates. Again, this plane will be perpendicular to the axis of rotation.

6. Project the new (rotated) position of the line, and draw the line (Fig. 8.57A, B, and C).

8.22. TRUE LENGTH BY DIAGRAM. The true length of a line may also be found by a *true-length diagram*. This method is not employed in problems where the normal view of a line may be needed to locate some point or element, but where nothing more than the true length is required; for example, in the development of a surface, the use of a true-length diagram is a simple but accurate method. In Fig. 8.58, line AB is a skew line which may be considered as the hypotenuse of a right-angled triangle having AC as a horizontal leg and BC as a vertical leg. If the true length of these legs is found and the right angle

True length of a line by true-length diagram.

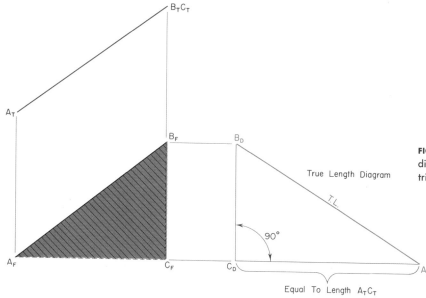

FIG. 8.58. True length of a line by true-length diagram. Horizontal and vertical legs of a right triangle are employed.

laid out, the hypotenuse will be determined. A diagram is prepared to one side of the front view (in this case, the right side). The projection of $B_F C_F$ to the diagram transfers the true length of the vertical leg to $B_D C_D$. The true length of the horizontal leg is the distance $A_T C_T$ (the top view of the horizontal leg). Therefore, if this distance is transferred by dividers or compass to the diagram at $C_D A_D$, the distance $B_D A_D$ on the diagram will be the true length of line AB. This method is very useful when a number of true lengths, for example, elements of a cone or cylinder, must be found.

Summary

1. Draw (or project to a true-length diagram) the vertical leg of a triangle having the given line as the hypotenuse (Fig. 8.58).

2. Measure the length of the horizontal leg of the triangle (with dividers or a compass), and lay this distance off on the diagram (Fig. 8.58).

3. Draw the hypotenuse of the triangle. This is the true length (Fig. 8.58).

8.23. SPECIFICATION OF A PLANE BY "STRIKE" AND "DIP." Instead of the usual specification by either three points or two intersecting lines, as described in paragraph 8.17, the position of a plane may be described by strike and dip. This method is used principally on mining, oil-prospecting, and other geologic maps. The *strike* of a plane is defined as the direction of a horizontal line on the plane. Thus in Fig. 8.59, the line *AB,* a horizontal line, may be designated as the strike of a plane by specification of its direction as shown in the top view. The direction may be given either as shown or by an azimuth from either magnetic or true north. *Dip* is defined as the true angle of the plane downward from the horizontal; a part of the specification is *on which side* of the strike line the plane passes below the horizontal. Therefore, in Fig. 8.59 the small arrow perpendicular to the strike

Strike and dip.

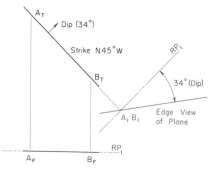

FIG. 8.59. Edge view of a plane specified by strike and dip. The edge view is shown by an auxiliary view.

line $A_T B_T$ shows that the plane dips on *that* side of the strike line, and the accompanying angle of 34° completes the specification. Thus on a map the location of the strike line, the elevation of a point on the line, and the dip specification will give complete information as to the location of the plane relative to other points on, over, or under the earth's surface.

Strike and dip specification of a plane is not restricted, however, to geologic maps. The *position* of the plane is much easier to visualize when strike and dip are given instead of either three points or two intersecting lines, and for this reason the method may be used advantageously in the solution of problems of a general nature.

8.24. EDGE VIEW OF A PLANE SPECIFIED BY STRIKE AND DIP. Specifying the edge view of a plane by the method of strike and dip is simple because the strike line is a horizontal line on the plane and the end view of this line is easily determined. In Fig. 8.59, the end view of strike line AB is $A_1 B_1$. The horizontal reference

plane RP_1 through AB appears as an edge in the auxiliary view, and the true angle of dip may therefore be laid out in the auxiliary view. Note that the angle of dip must be laid out below RP_1, because reversing it by mistake would make the plane dip on the wrong side of the strike line. Note that the edge view of the plane will be seen in the auxiliary view since the strike line (a line of the plane) appears as a point in this view. Also note that an auxiliary projected from the *top* view *must* be used.

Summary

The edge view of a plane, specified by strike and dip, is located by drawing the end view of the strike line.

1. Draw a projector aligned with the strike line.

2. Draw a reference plane line perpendicular to the projector. This line represents a horizontal plane.

3. Draw the other view of the reference plane through the front view of the strike line.

4. The end view of the strike line is on the projector and on the reference plane.

5. Lay out the dip angle from the end view of the strike line, measuring the angle from the horizontal reference plane. This line is the edge view of the plane (Fig. 8.59).

8.25. NORMAL VIEW OF A PLANE SPECIFIED BY STRIKE AND DIP. To find the normal view of a plane (specified by strike and dip), three points must be assumed on the plane because the strike and dip specification does not include located points that may be used for projection of a normal view. In Fig. 8.60, the strike line BC and the dip angle of 36° specify the plane. First the

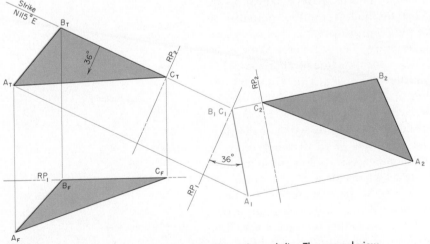

FIG. 8.60. Normal view of a plane specified by strike and dip. The normal view must be projected from the edge view.

edge view of the plane is made, as described in paragraph 8.24, by making the end view of *AB* and laying out the dip angle. Then the two points *B* and *C* (the ends of the strike line) and any third point *A* on the plane may be taken as three points on the plane. Point *A* is assumed at any convenient position in the top view A_T and may then be projected to this first auxiliary, where it will lie on the edge view at A_1. Projection is then made to the front view by projecting from A_T, measuring the height of *A* from RP_1 in the auxiliary, and transferring to the front view, to locate A_F. Finally a second auxiliary view, C_2, B_2, and A_2, is established by projecting in a direction perpendicular to the edge view. This is the normal view of triangle *ABC* on the strike and dip plane. Since other assumed triangles similar to *ABC* would, of course, serve the purpose as well, the three points used may be picked purely for purposes of convenience.

Summary

1. Draw the edge view of the plane, as explained in paragraph 8.24 and shown in Figs. 8.59 and 8.60.

2. Locate any point on the edge view of the plane (point *A*, Fig. 8.60).

3. Project the point to top and front views and draw the triangle representing the plane. The triangle is made up of two points on the strike line and the selected point (Fig. 8.60).

4. Draw the normal view of the plane by projecting a second auxiliary perpendicular to the edge view (Fig. 8.60). If necessary, refer back to Fig. 8.59.

8.26.   NORMAL VIEW OF A PLANE BY ROTATION.

The normal view of a plane may be made by rotating the plane until it comes into coincidence with one of the planes of projection. If the plane is rotated until it is horizontal, the normal view will be seen in the top view; if it is rotated to a frontal position, the front view will show the normal view; and if it is rotated to a profile position, either side view will show the normal view. The edge view of the plane is not needed as an intermediate step (as in the use of auxiliary views to obtain a normal view) because the plane can be rotated directly to either a horizontal, frontal, or profile position. However, the consideration of an edge view will help to explain the procedure. Therefore, in Fig. 8.61, a plane *ABC* is shown with an edge view as the front view. If a horizontal-profile axis is placed at point *A*, this axis will appear as a point in the front view and as a true-length line in the top view. The plane can then be rotated about this axis until it is horizontal. The path of rotation of any point in the plane (in this case) will lie in a frontal plane through the point because frontal planes

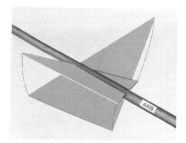

Normal view of a plane by rotation.

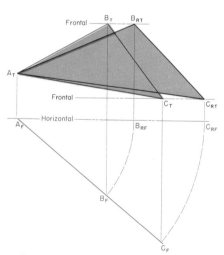

FIG. 8.61.   Normal view of a plane obtained by a rotated view. In this case, the plane is rotated to the horizontal.

are perpendicular to the horizontal-profile axis. Therefore the path of rotation of point B will be $B_F B_{RF}$ in the front view and $B_T B_{RT}$ in the top view, and for point C the path of rotation is $C_F C_{RF}$ in the front view and $C_T C_{RT}$ in the top view. Naturally, since the axis is at A, point A does not move. Thus the plane has been rotated to a horizontal position as shown at A_F, B_{RF}, and C_{RF}. The normal view of ABC is then seen in the new top view, A_T, B_{RT}, and C_{RT}.

If the plane is skew as in Fig. 8.62, a similar procedure may be followed. A horizontal axis BD is located on the plane. This axis will appear as a point in the auxiliary view at $B_1 D_1$ because the auxiliary has been made in a direction looking along the axis BD. Therefore the edge view, A_1, B_1, D_1, and C_1, is obtained. In this edge view, the plane can be rotated to a horizontal position at A_{R1}, B_1, D_1, and C_{R1}. During this rotation, the points B and D will remain

stationary because they are on the axis, and points A and C will rotate in planes perpendicular to the axis (in this case, the vertical planes marked on Fig. 8.62). Therefore, the new position (the rotated position and the new top view) becomes A_{RT}, B_T, and C_{RT}, the normal view of the plane. Study Fig. 8.62 carefully, noting the position of the axis of rotation and the path of each point as it rotates. Note also that the axis of rotation lies in the plane.

The foregoing will serve as a background for an explanation of the rotation of a skew plane to a normal position by a quick and accurate method without the use of an edge view. Figure 8.63*A* is practically a duplicate of Fig. 8.62 but with some additions for analysis. In the edge view at A_1, B_1, D_1, and C_1, the crosshatched area represents a right-angled triangle with a vertical leg V, a horizontal leg H, and hypotenuse HYP. The hypotenuse of this triangle is the

FIG. 8.62. Rotation of a plane to obtain a normal view by employing an auxiliary view.

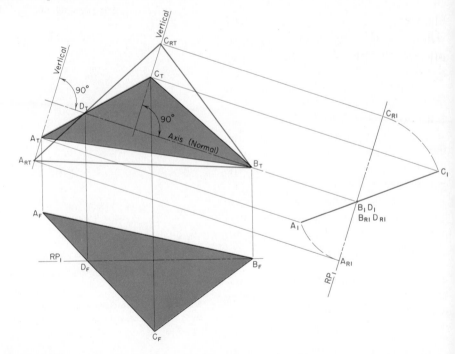

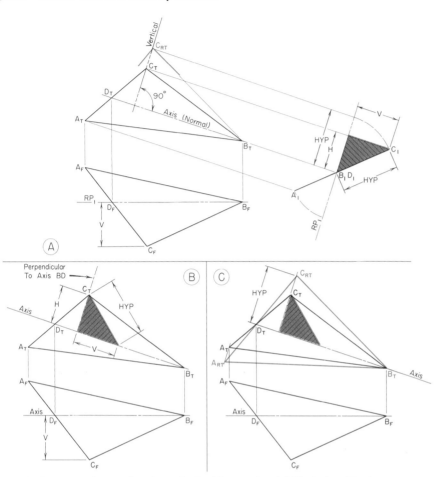

FIG. 8.63.   Normal view of a plane obtained by rotation. (*A*) Vertical and horizontal legs of right triangle shown by auxiliary view. (*B*) and (*C*) Vertical and horizontal legs shown on principal views.

true distance of point C from the axis BD. To prove this fact, note that axis BD appears as a point in the auxiliary view and that C_1 to B_1D_1 is then the shortest (true) distance from point to line. We know from plane geometry that, if the two legs of a right-angled triangle can be determined, the hypotenuse will also be determinable. Further, an examination of Fig. 8.63*B* will show that the vertical leg and the horizontal leg of Fig. 8.63*A* may be obtained without

the edge view of Fig. 8.63*A*. On Fig. 8.63*B*, the vertical leg V is the vertical distance of point C to the horizontal axis BD (measured in the front view). Also, the horizontal leg H is the horizontal perpendicular distance (in the top view) from axis BD to point C. Therefore, because point C must rotate in a plane perpendicular to axis BD, the vertical leg may be laid out along the axis as shown from the point where the horizontal leg intersects the axis. The hypotenuse may then be found as marked on Fig. 8.63*B*.

Finally all the above discussion is brought to completion at Fig. 8.63*C*, where the simplest and most practical method is shown. First, axis *BD* is located. Second, the path of rotation for point *C* is located, perpendicular to the true length of axis *BD* (in the top view). Third, the vertical leg for point *C* is taken with dividers or compass from the front view and laid off along axis *BD* in the top view. Fourth, the hypotenuse is spaced on the dividers or compass from the top view. Fifth, the hypotenuse is laid off from the axis, thus locating point C_{RT}, the revolved position of point *C*. A similar procedure is followed for point *A*, and the lines $A_{RT}C_{RT}$, $C_{RT}B_T$, and $B_T A_{RT}$ are drawn. This completes the normal view of plane *ABC*.

Note that, if desired, the plane may be rotated to a frontal position instead of horizontal. If this is done, the construction in the view where the axis appears in true length will be identical with the top view just discussed, as will be the construction in the accompanying view. To see the relationship, turn Fig. 8.63*C* upside down so that the former front view is now the top view and the former top view is the front view.

Summary

General case: Fig. 8.63*B* and *C*

1. Locate an axis of rotation on the plane. This may be either a horizontal, frontal, or profile line on the plane. In Fig. 8.63, the line is horizontal.

2. Points of the plane will rotate in planes *perpendicular* to the axis. Locate these planes for necessary points of the plane. In Fig. 8.63, these planes are vertical because the axis is horizontal.

3. Locate a triangle as shown in Fig. 8.63*B*, giving the vertical and horizontal legs and determining the hypotenuse, the true distance of a point *from* the axis. Do this for each point needed, as for (*A*) and (*C*) of Fig. 8.63.

4. Lay out each hypotenuse as shown in Fig. 8.63*C*.

5. Connect the points located. This is the normal view of the plane.

8.27.   METHODOLOGY.   The constructions given in this chapter will be used repeatedly for solving the problems in the chapters following. The student should, therefore, learn so thoroughly all the methods of determining point, edge, and normal views that the constructions may be made without the slightest hesitation. Remember that a firm foundation is the basis for understanding more complicated problems.

The explanations in the following chapters assume that the student knows the constructions in this chapter, that he understands the theory behind them, and that he can apply them with confidence.

8.28.   TERMS OF REFERENCE FOR AUXILIARY VIEWS.   In this text, emphasis is given to the *purpose* for which auxiliary views are made; namely, to show the *edge view* or *normal view* of a surface. This practice is basic to the representation of solid objects, and, fundamentally, an auxiliary view used to depict a surface needs no further identification than the designation *edge view* or *normal view*. However, auxiliaries are named in various ways in other texts on engineering drawing and graphics, and for this reason the following terms of reference are given:

Reference Group 1

Elevation auxiliary or *auxiliary elevation*. Any view made by looking in a horizontal direction but inclined to frontal and profile planes. These are the views illustrated in Fig. 8.7*B* to *E*.

Right auxiliary.   Any view made by looking from the right side in a frontal direction but inclined to horizontal and profile planes. See Fig. 8.7*F* and *G*.

Left auxiliary.   Any view made by looking from the left side in a frontal direction but inclined to horizontal and profile planes. See Fig. 8.7*H* and *J*.

Front auxiliary.   Any view made by looking from the front in a profile direction but inclined to horizontal and frontal planes. See Fig. 8.7*K* and *L*.

Rear auxiliary.   Any view made by looking from the rear in a profile direction but inclined to horizontal and frontal planes. See Fig. 8.7*M* and *N*.

Reference Group 2

Top-adjacent auxiliary.   Any auxiliary view projected from the top view. Such auxiliaries are the same as elevation auxiliaries (group 1). See Fig. 8.7*B* to *E*.

Front-adjacent auxiliary.   Any auxiliary view projected from a front view. Such auxiliaries are the same as right-and-left auxiliaries. See Fig. 8.7*F* to *J*.

Side-adjacent auxiliary.   Any auxiliary projected from a side view. Such auxiliaries are the same as front-and-rear auxiliaries. See Fig. 8.7*K* to *N*.

Reference Group 3

Oblique view.   This is the normal view of a skew (oblique) surface and is projected from an edge view. See Figs. 8.38 to 8.40.

Reference Group 4

Auxiliary-adjacent auxiliary view.   This is the normal view of a skew surface, projected from an edge view. See Figs. 8.38 to 8.40.

These terms of reference are used in books on descriptive geometry. However, since the book on descriptive geometry you are using with this text may give other terms, the space below is provided for listing them.

_____

_____

_____

_____

_____

_____

_____

_____

_____

_____

_____

_____

_____

_____

_____

PROBLEMS

GROUP 1. NORMAL VIEWS OF INCLINED SURFACES

8.1.1 to 8.1.7. Draw the given views and add the normal view of the inclined surface using the reference plane indicated.

8.1.8. Draw the front view, partial top view, and normal view of the inclined surface.

8.1.9. Draw the partial front view, right-side view, partial top view, and normal view of the inclined surface.

8.1.10. Draw the front view, partial top view, and normal view of the inclined surfaces.

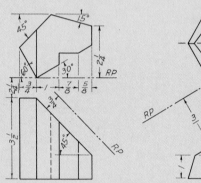

PROB. 8.1.1. Locking wedge.

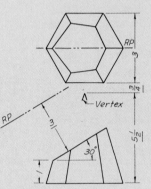

PROB. 8.1.2. Statue base.

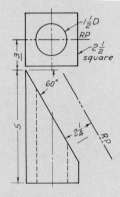

PROB. 8.1.3. Rod slide.

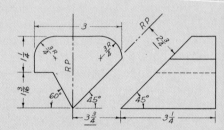

PROB. 8.1.4. Fulcrum.

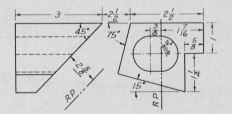

PROB. 8.1.5. Adjustable pawl.

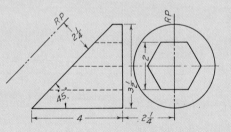

PROB. 8.1.6. Hexagonal-shaft lock.

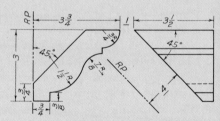

PROB. 8.1.7. Molding.

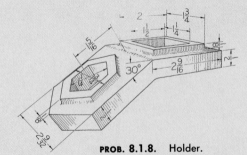

PROB. 8.1.8. Holder.

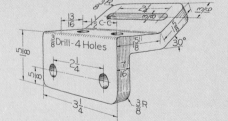

PROB. 8.1.9. Slotted anchor.

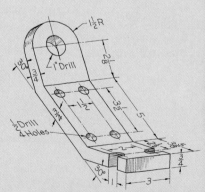

PROB. 8.1.10. Connector strip.

8.1.11. Draw the top view, partial front view, and normal view of the inclined surfaces.

8.1.12. Draw the front view, partial top view, and normal view of the inclined surface.

8.1.13. Draw the front view, partial right-side view, and normal view of the inclined surface. Draw the normal view before completing the front view.

8.1.14. Draw the front view, partial top view, and normal view of the inclined surface.

8.1.15. Draw the front view, partial top view, and normal view of the inclined surface.

8.1.16. Draw the front view, partial top and right-side views, and normal view of the inclined surface.

8.1.17. Draw the front view, partial top and left-side views, and normal view of the inclined surface.

8.1.18 and 8.1.19. Determine what views and partial views will best describe the part. Sketch the proposed views before making the drawing with instruments.

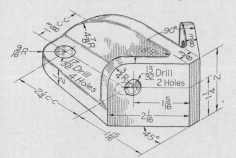

PROB. 8.1.11. Push plate.

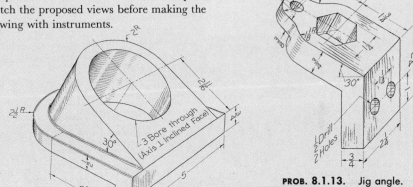

PROB. 8.1.12. Bevel washer.

PROB. 8.1.13. Jig angle.

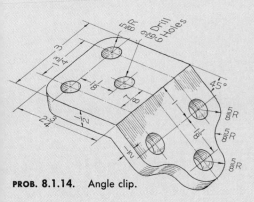

PROB. 8.1.14. Angle clip.

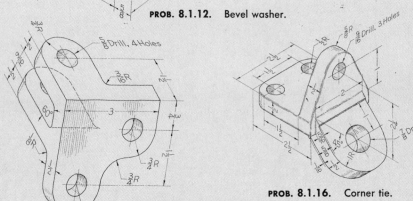

PROB. 8.1.15. Angle Swivel.

PROB. 8.1.16. Corner tie.

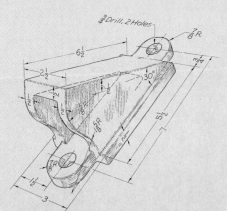

PROB. 8.1.17. Channel support.

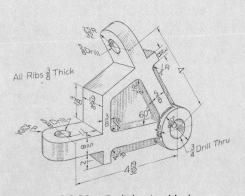

PROB. 8.1.18. Radial swing block.

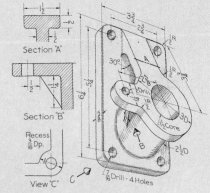

PROB. 8.1.19. Angle-shaft base.

8.1.20. Draw the front view, partial bottom view, and normal view of the inclined surface.

8.1.21. Draw the front view, partial left-side and bottom views, and normal view of the inclined surface.

8.1.22 and 8.1.23. Determine what views and partial views will best describe the part.

8.1.24. Draw the given front view and add the views necessary to describe the part.

8.1.25. Draw the front view, partial left-side view, and normal view of the inclined surface.

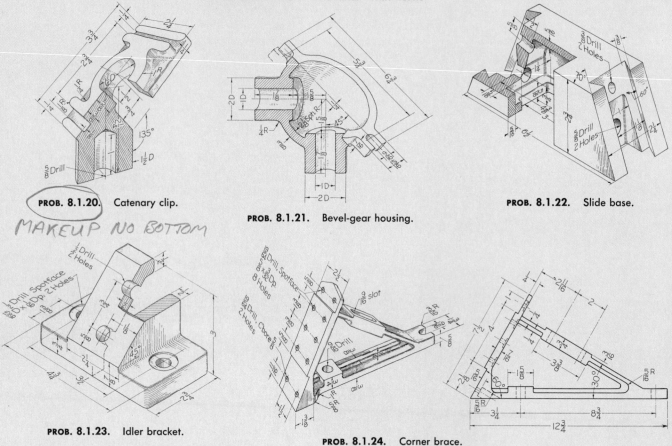

PROB. 8.1.20. Catenary clip.

MAKEUP NO BOTTOM

PROB. 8.1.21. Bevel-gear housing.

PROB. 8.1.22. Slide base.

PROB. 8.1.23. Idler bracket.

PROB. 8.1.24. Corner brace.

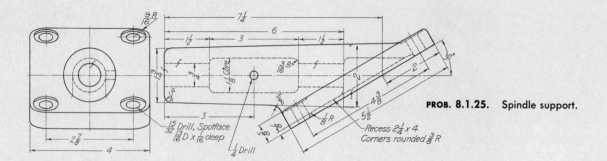

PROB. 8.1.25. Spindle support.

8.1.26 and 8.1.27. This pair of similar objects has the upper lug in two different positions. Layouts are for 11- × 17-in. paper. Draw the views and partial views as indicated on the layouts.

8.1.28. Draw the front view; partial top, right-side, and left-side views; and normal view of the inclined surface. Use decimal scale for layout.

8.1.29. Draw the views and partial views that will best describe the part.

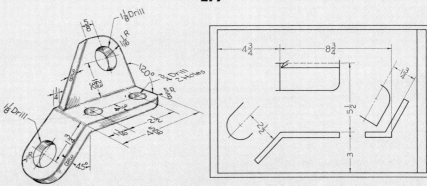

PROB. 8.1.26. Spar clip, 90°.

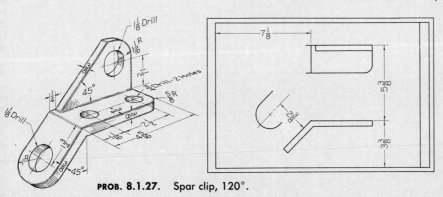

PROB. 8.1.27. Spar clip, 120°.

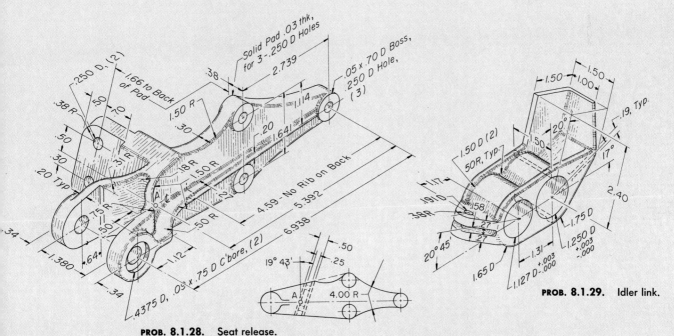

PROB. 8.1.28. Seat release.

PROB. 8.1.29. Idler link.

8.1.30. Draw top and front views and a normal view of the inclined face. Will the normal view of the inclined face show the true cross section of the square hole?

8.1.31. Draw front, top, and side views and normal views of the inclined surfaces.

8.1.32. Front and right-side views of the shaft-locator wedge are shown on a layout for 11- × 17-in. paper. Add normal view of the inclined faces at centerline position shown.

PROB. 8.1.30.   Actuator bracket.

PROB. 8.1.31.   Assembly-fixture base.

PROB. 8.1.32.   Shaft-locator wedge.

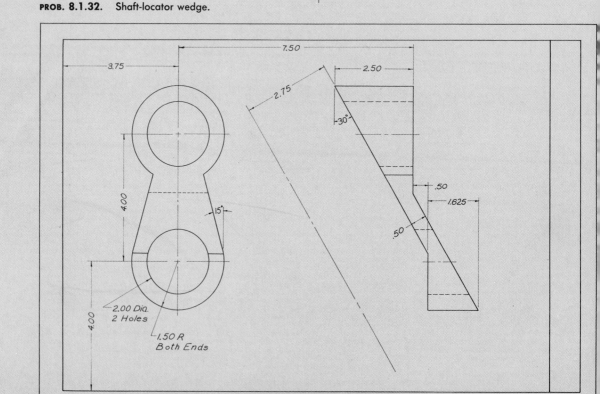

GROUP 2.   NORMAL VIEWS OF SKEW SURFACES

8.2.1.   Draw the partial front and top views, edge view showing the contour of the slot, and normal views of the skew surface.

8.2.2.   Draw the partial front and top views, and edge and normal views of the skew surface. Draw the normal view before completing the edge view.

8.2.3.   Draw the partial front and top views, and edge and normal views of the skew surface.

8.2.4.   Draw the views given, omitting the lugs in the top view. Add normal views to describe the lugs.

8.2.5.   Draw the views given, using edge and normal views to obtain the shape of the lugs.

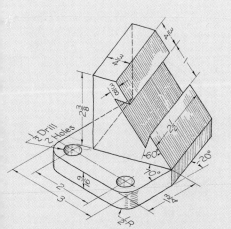

PROB. 8.2.1.   Dovetail clip.

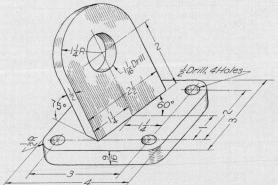

PROB. 8.2.2.   Anchor base.

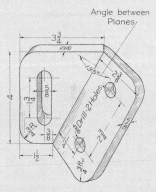

PROB. 8.2.3.   Adjusting clip.

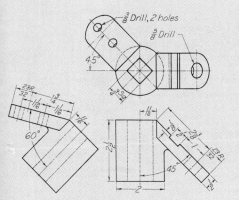

PROB. 8.2.4.   Bar-strut anchor.

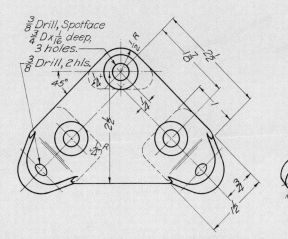

PROB. 8.2.5.   Cable anchor.

8.2.6. Draw the partial top, front, and side views. Add edge and normal views to describe the lugs.

8.2.7. Draw the top and front views and use edge and normal views to describe the slots

and skew surfaces. The part is symmetrical about the main axis.

8.2.8. Draw the spar clip, using the layout shown for 11- × 17-in. paper. Note that an edge and two normal views are required.

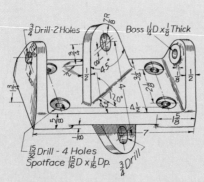

PROB. 8.2.6. Transverse connection.

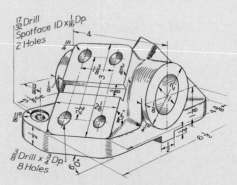

PROB. 8.2.7. Chamfer-tool base.

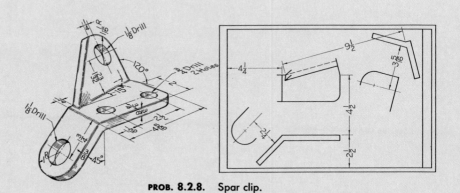

PROB. 8.2.8. Spar clip.

8.2.9. Draw the views given, using edge and normal views to describe the lugs.

8.2.10. Draw top and front views and auxiliary views that will describe the skew surface.

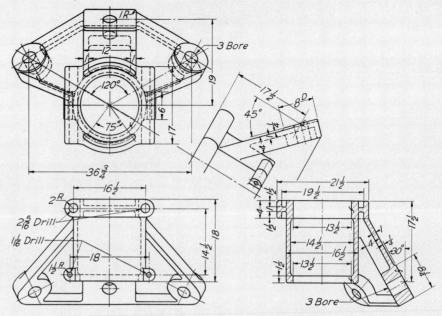

PROB. 8.2.9. Crane-masthead collar and cap.

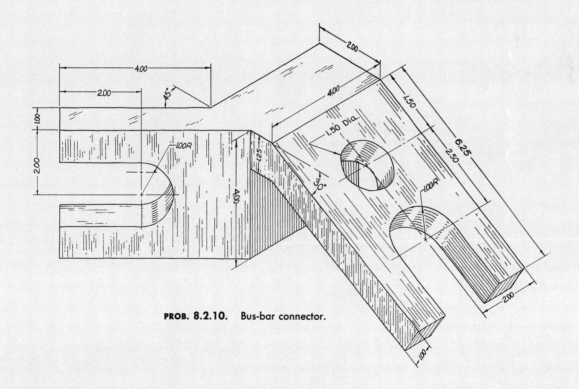

PROB. 8.2.10. Bus-bar connector.

8.2.11. Shown on layout for 11- × 17-in. paper are partial front and right-side views and partial auxiliary views that describe the position and shape of the skew surface. Complete front, right-side, and first auxiliary views.

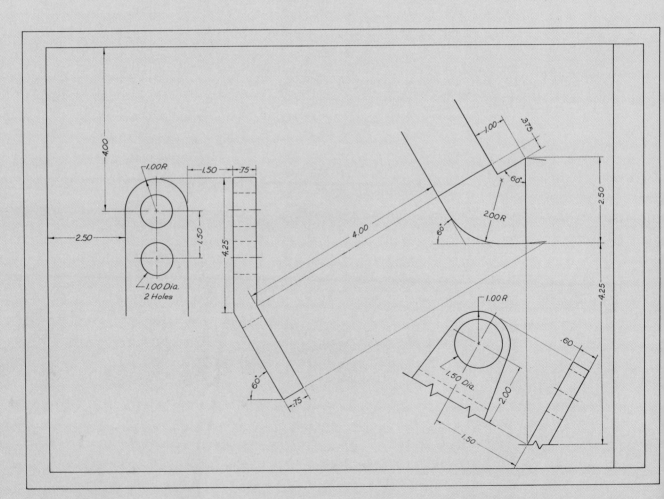

PROB. 8.2.11. Valve control-shaft bracket.

8.2.12. Shown on layout for 11- × 17-in. paper are partial top and front views and auxiliaries that describe the position and shape of the clamp portion of the part. Complete the top and front views.

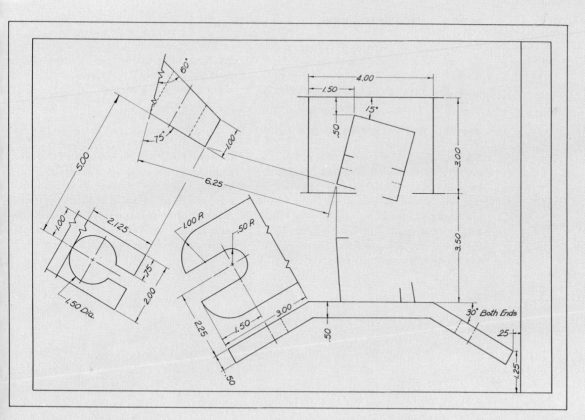

PROB. 8.2.12. Bipod shaft clamp.

GROUP 3. NORMAL VIEW OF A LINE

8.3.1. Find, by the use of an auxiliary projected from the top view, the true length of AB. Scale: $1'' = 1'\text{-}0''$.

8.3.2. Using the layout given for Prob. 8.3.1, determine, by projecting in a frontal direction, the true length of AB. Scale: ⅜ size.

8.3.3. Using the layout of Prob. 8.3.1, determine, in an auxiliary projected from the right-side view, the true length of AB. Scale: $¾'' = 1''$.

GROUP 4. NORMAL AND END VIEWS OF A LINE

8.4.1. Using the layout of Prob. 8.3.1, show the end view of AB by projecting from a first auxiliary view projected from the top view. Identify all reference planes, and label all points.

8.4.2. Using the layout of Prob. 8.3.1, show the end view of AB by projecting from a first auxiliary view projected from the front view. Identify all reference planes, and label all points.

8.4.3. Using the layout of Prob. 8.3.1, consider AB as the center line of a 3½-in. (nominal size) American Standard pipe. Show the end view of the pipe by projecting from a normal view of the center line AB projected from the side view. Scale ½ size.

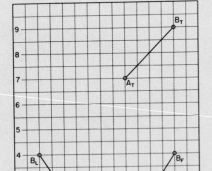

PROB. 8.3.1.

GROUP 5. EDGE VIEW OF A PLANE

8.5.1. Show the view of RSP by projecting parallel to a horizontal line of RSP.

8.5.2. Using the layout given for Prob. 8.5.1, determine the edge view of RSP by projecting parallel to a frontal line of RSP.

8.5.3. Using the layout of Prob. 8.5.1, draw the view of RSP when seen from the rear along a profile line of sight.

GROUP 6. EDGE AND NORMAL VIEWS OF A PLANE

8.6.1. Using the layout of Prob. 8.5.1, draw the normal view of RSP by projecting from an edge view of RSP projected from the top view. Label all points and identify the reference planes used.

8.6.2. Using the layout of Prob. 8.5.1, determine the true size and shape of RSP when projecting from an edge view of RSP projected from the front view. Label all points, and identify the reference planes used.

8.6.3. Using the layout of Prob. 8.5.1, first show the edge view of RSP in an edge view projected from the side view, then draw the normal view of RSP. Label all points, and identify all reference planes used.

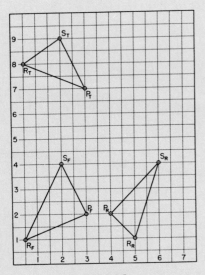

PROB. 8.5.1.

GROUP 7. EDGE VIEW OF A PLANE DEFINED BY SPECIFICATION OF STRIKE AND DIP

8.7.1. Show the edge view of the plane that strikes as shown through *A*. The plane dips 45° in a northwesterly direction. Consider north at the top of the plate.

8.7.2. Using the layout of Prob. 8.7.1, determine the edge view of the plane that strikes as shown through point *A*. The plane dips 60° in a southeasterly direction. Consider north at the top of the plate.

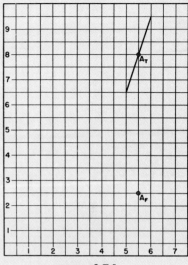

PROB. 8.7.1.

GROUP 8. NORMAL VIEW OF A PLANE DEFINED BY SPECIFICATION OF STRIKE AND DIP

8.8.1. *XYZ* is an equilateral triangle which strikes and dips through point *X* as indicated. *Y* is to the rear of *X*. Draw the top and front views of *XYZ*.

8.8.2. *EG* is 2½ in. long and makes an angle of 45° with *EF*. *EF* and *G* lie in the plane that strikes and dips through point *E* as shown. Draw the top and front views of *EF* and *EG*. Scale: full size.

GROUP 9. NORMAL VIEW OF A PLANE BY THE METHOD OF ROTATION

8.9.1. Draw the normal view of *LMO* by rotating the plane about a horizontal axis. Solve by using an edge view.

8.9.2. Using the layout of Prob. 8.9.1, draw the normal view of *LMO* by rotating the plane about a frontal axis. Solve by using an edge view.

8.9.3. Using the layout of Prob. 8.9.1, draw the normal view of *LMO* by rotating the plane about a horizontal axis. Solve by using only the views given.

8.9.4. Using the layout of Prob. 8.9.1, draw the normal view of *LMO* by rotating the plane about a frontal axis. Solve by using only the views given.

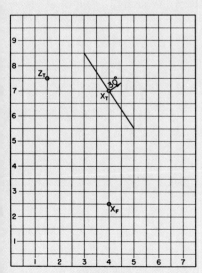

PROB. 8.8.1.

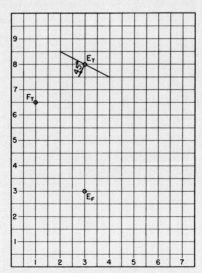

PROB. 8.8.2.

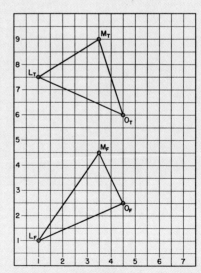

PROB. 8.9.1.

The study of points and straight lines continues the study of auxiliary views, extending their use to solve space problems. The determinations of space relationships, true distances, true lengths, parallelism, perpendicularity, angularity, and specified relationships are typical.

Points and Straight Lines in Space

9.1. Modern machines and structures are made up of many complicated elements and surfaces, but the predominating component will probably always be the straight line. This is so because forces act along straight lines, thus dictating the design in many respects; also, manufacturing economy and other practical considerations demand the use of straight-line elements. Many of the complicated surfaces of parts may be made up of straight-line elements. Thus the point and straight line become basic elements of study.

9.2. FUNDAMENTAL ITEMS. A point which moves in one unchanging direction generates a straight line. Any two points of a straight line determine the direction of the line, and the distance between the two points is the length of a segment of the line. The length of a line is indefinite since it may be extended through and beyond the two points which determine its direction. The student should have a thorough working knowledge of the various line positions as described in paragraph 8.13 and Figs. 8.42 and 8.43.

287

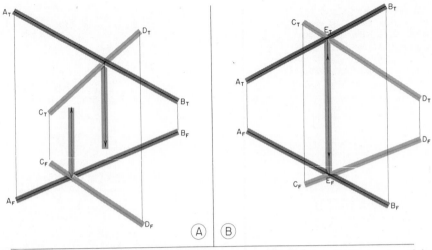

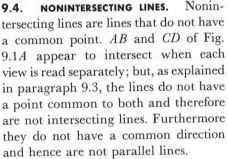

FIG. 9.1. Nonintersecting lines (*A*) and intersecting lines (*B*). To intersect, the crossing of the lines must be in projection in all views.

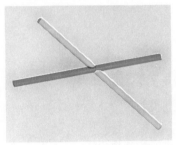

Intersecting lines

Skew lines

Parallel lines

9.3. INTERSECTING LINES. Lines which pass through the same point are intersecting lines. The common point is the point of intersection. A single orthographic view does not give sufficient information to determine whether existing lines do or do not intersect. Examination of the front view only of Fig. 9.1*A* does not justify the conclusion that *AB* and *CD* intersect, because the crossing of the lines is only the projection in the front view. The top view shows a crossing not in projection with the crossing in the front view; therefore there is no common point, and the lines do not intersect. On the other hand, if both the front and the top views of Fig. 9.1*B* are read by following along the projector from E_F, it can be seen that point *E* lies on both *AB* and *CD*, and the lines therefore intersect. Thus if two views (or more) show the lines to have a common point, the lines intersect. This intersecting-line principle is an important tool for solving many space problems. Points in various orthographic views may be located at the intersection of projectors as explained in many of the examples following.

Summary

Examine two or more orthographic views to see whether or not the apparent crossing of the lines is in projection.

1. If the crossing of the lines in two or more views is *not* in projection, the lines do *not* intersect.

2. If the crossing of the lines in two or more views *is* in projection, the lines *intersect.*

9.4. NONINTERSECTING LINES. Nonintersecting lines are lines that do not have a common point. *AB* and *CD* of Fig. 9.1*A* appear to intersect when each view is read separately; but, as explained in paragraph 9.3, the lines do not have a point common to both and therefore are not intersecting lines. Furthermore they do not have a common direction and hence are not parallel lines.

Lines are called skew if they are at an angle to each other or to the planes of projection (see Fig. 8.43 and paragraph 8.13). Specifically, the terminology is "skew to each other" or "skew to the planes of projection" (or both). Note specifically that skew lines *may* or *may not* intersect.

Summary

Examine two views (or more) to determine:

1. That a line is at an angle to the planes of projection and is therefore a skew line (to the planes of projection).

2. That a *pair* of lines are skew to each other (Fig. 9.1*A*).

9.5. **PARALLEL LINES.** Lines which have a common direction are parallel lines. Different views of parallel lines will not alter or change their direction; consequently parallel lines will remain parallel regardless of the number of views made. Figure 9.2 shows the top, front, and right-side views of two parallel lines *AB* and *CD*. Note that in each view the lines are parallel. This orthographic principle of parallel-line relationship is of great value to the designer. It can be used not only to solve space problems but also to check for projection errors on drawings where the geometric relationships are of a parallel nature, such as those in a parallelogram, opposite sides of a rectangle, etc.

Lines may appear to be parallel in one view and yet not be parallel. Two principal views are *usually* sufficient to determine whether lines are parallel, but, theoretically, it will require either three principal views or two principal views and an auxiliary view. For example, if the lines are both profile, the front and top views will show the lines parallel (actually they *are* in parallel planes) and a side or auxiliary view will clearly show that the lines are either parallel or not parallel.

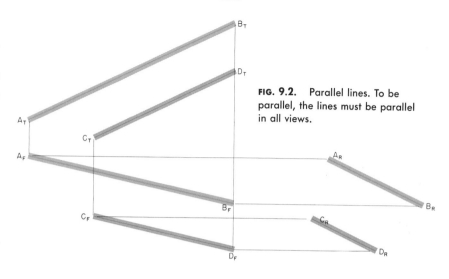

FIG. 9.2. Parallel lines. To be parallel, the lines must be parallel in all views.

9.6. **PERPENDICULAR LINES.** Lines are perpendicular if their directions are at an angle of 90° to each other. Perpendicular lines may be intersecting or nonintersecting. When perpendicular lines are represented on a drawing, they appear perpendicular in those views

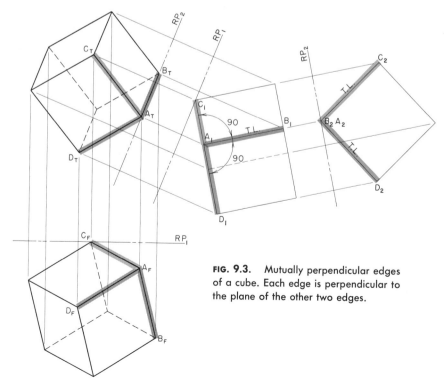

FIG. 9.3. Mutually perpendicular edges of a cube. Each edge is perpendicular to the plane of the other two edges.

Summary

1. Parallel lines will appear parallel in all orthographic views.

2. Always check three views to be certain of parallelism.

Perpendicular intersecting lines

Perpendicular nonintersecting lines

where *one* or *both* of the lines are shown in true length. Figure 9.3 shows the top, front, and first and second auxiliary views of a cube in space. The adjacent edges *AB*, *AC*, and *AD* are, by the geometry of a cube, mutually perpendicular. In the top and front views, none of the adjacent edges *AB*, *AC*, or *AD* appears at 90° to each other, as none of the edges is in true length in these views. In the first auxiliary view, *AB* is shown in true length and thereby will be seen perpendicular to the plane containing *AC* and *AD*. Note that edges *AC* and *AD* are not in true length in the first auxiliary view, yet they still appear perpendicular to edge *AB*. The second auxiliary view has been established by projecting in the direction of edge *AB*; *AB* therefore appears as a point in the second auxiliary view. Because *AB*, *AC*, and *AD* are the mutually perpendicular edges of a cube, the view showing *AB* as a point will also show *AC* and *AD* in true length. This may be understood by noting that the projectors for the second auxiliary view, being parallel to A_1B_1, are necessarily perpendicular to A_1C_1 and A_1D_1, thus giving the true length of *AC* and *AD* in the auxiliary view.

Summary

1. Perpendicular lines will appear perpendicular *only* when one of the lines is in true length (normal view).
2. Three mutually perpendicular lines will appear perpendicular when (*a*) one of the lines is in true length (normal view), (*b*) one of the lines appears as a point (end view).

Figure 9.4 shows the construction necessary to establish one line perpendicular to another. The front and top views of *AB* and the front view (only)

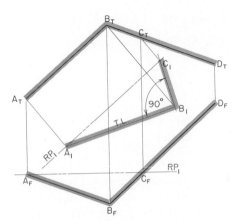

FIG. 9.4. A line perpendicular to and intersecting another line. True perpendicularity appears only in a view showing the true length of *one* of the lines.

of *BD* were given as initial information. Since neither line appears in true length in either the top or front view, a normal view of one of the lines must be made in order to establish the perpendicular relationship between the two lines. A normal view of *AB* (A_1B_1) is the required view. In this view, the direction of *BD* is drawn perpendicular to *AB* intersecting RP_1 at *C*. The top view of *C* is at the intersection of the projectors from C_F and C_1. The top view of *BD* is then drawn through point C_T, locating D_T by intersection of the projector from the front view.

Summary

1. Draw the normal view of the given line.
2. In the normal view of the given line, draw the second line perpendicular.
3. Locate a point on the second line by (*a*) projection or (*b*) measurement from a given view.
4. Complete the projection.

Frequently, after the direction of a line has been established, it is necessary to determine the true length of a segment of that line. In Fig. 9.5, BC is to be drawn perpendicular to AB, and the length of BC is to be determined. The top and front views of AB and the front view of BC are given initially. As in the problem of Fig. 9.4, a normal view of AB is first made; on this view the direction of BC is established perpendicular to AB. C_1 is located in the auxiliary view by measurement from RP_1 in the front view and by transferring this distance to the auxiliary view. Then C may be located in the top view by projection from C_1 and from C_F. The true length of BC can now be determined by a second auxiliary view made in a direction perpendicular to B_1C_1. Note again how the two perpendicular lines AB and BC appear in the second auxiliary view; AB appears as a point, and BC appears in true length.

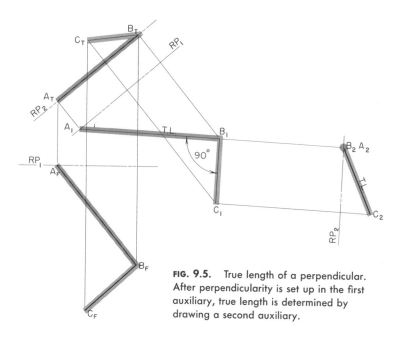

FIG. 9.5. True length of a perpendicular. After perpendicularity is set up in the first auxiliary, true length is determined by drawing a second auxiliary.

Summary

1. Draw the normal view of the given line.

2. In the normal view of the given line, draw the second line perpendicular.

3. Locate a point on the second line by (*a*) measurement or (*b*) projection from a given view.

4. Draw a second auxiliary giving the normal view of the second line, and measure the true length.

In Fig. 9.6, a line of specified length is drawn perpendicular to a given line. The top and front views of AB and the front view of AC are given. AD (to some specified length) is to be drawn perpendicular to AB. D is to be on AC. AC is drawn perpendicular to AB in the normal view (the auxiliary projected from the top view). C_T is located at the intersection of the projectors from C_1 and C_F.

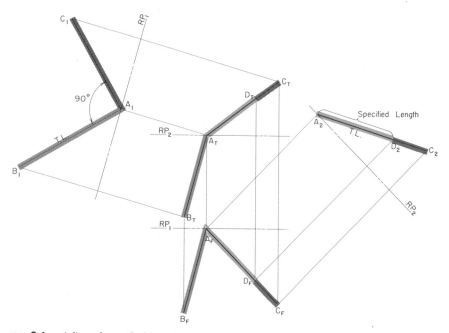

FIG. 9.6. A line of specified length perpendicular to and intersecting another line. The specified length must be set up in a true-length view of the perpendicular.

An auxiliary projected perpendicular to the front view of AC determines the true length of AC. AD is laid off to the specified length on A_2C_2 in this view. D is then projected on line AC to the front and top views.

Summary

1. Draw the normal view of the given line.

2. In the normal view of the given line, draw the second line perpendicular.

3. Locate a point on the second line by (*a*) measurement or (*b*) projection from a given view.

4. Complete the projection of the second line.

5. Draw another auxiliary, giving the normal view of the second line.

6. In the normal view of the second line, lay off the required length.

7. Complete the projection.

The example shown in Fig. 9.7 has the same requirements as that of Fig.

9.6 but differs in the method of solution. AD, of a specified length, is to be established perpendicular to AC. D is on AB. The top and front views of AC and the front view of AB are given.

AB is drawn perpendicular to the normal view of AC, as shown in the auxiliary view projected from the front view. The projection is now continued from this auxiliary view to the second auxiliary view in a direction parallel to AC, thus establishing the end view of AC and the normal view of AB. A_2D_2, of specified length, is laid off on A_2B_2. D on line AB is then projected back to the first auxiliary and then to front and top views.

Summary

1. Draw the normal view of the given line.

2. In the normal view of the given line, draw the second line perpendicular.

3. Locate a point on the second line

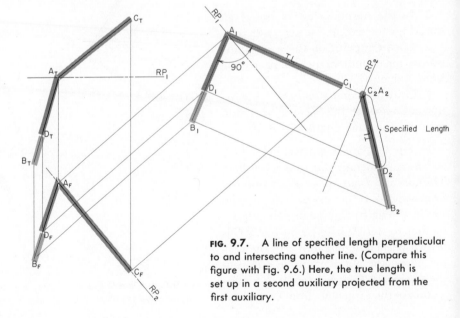

FIG. 9.7. A line of specified length perpendicular to and intersecting another line. (Compare this figure with Fig. 9.6.) Here, the true length is set up in a second auxiliary projected from the first auxiliary.

by (*a*) measurement or (*b*) projection from a given view.

4. Draw a second auxiliary, projected from the first auxiliary, giving the normal view of the second line.

5. In the normal view of the second line, lay out the required length.

6. Complete the projection.

9.7. DISTANCE FROM A POINT TO A LINE.

The distance from a point to a line is construed as the shortest distance between the point and the line; the shortest distance is measured along a perpendicular from the point to the line.

Figure 9.8 shows the construction necessary to determine the length of *CD*, the shortest distance from point *C* to line *AB*. Since *AB* is not in true length in either the top or front view, a normal

view of *AB* is established in the first auxiliary view. A perpendicular from point *C* to *AB* can be drawn in the auxiliary view. *CD* is the required distance, but it should be clearly understood that *CD* is not in true length in the auxiliary view. The true length of *CD* must be determined. A normal view of *CD* is obtained in the second auxiliary view (projected from the first auxiliary) by projecting *in the direction of AB*. This gives the true length of the shortest distance from point *C* to line *AB*.

Summary

1. Draw the normal view of the given line, and project the given point to this view.

2. In the normal view of the line, draw a perpendicular from the given point to the line. This represents the

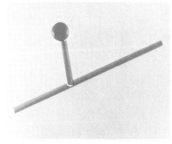

Shortest distance, point to line

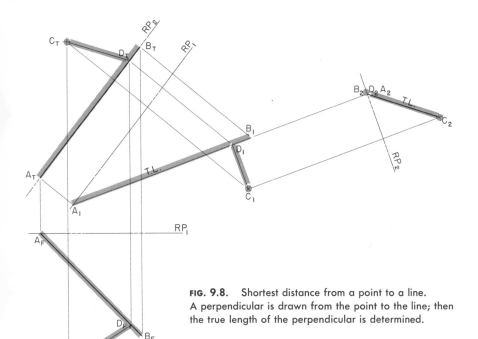

FIG. 9.8. Shortest distance from a point to a line. A perpendicular is drawn from the point to the line; then the true length of the perpendicular is determined.

plane of *all perpendiculars* through the point to the line.

3. Locate the intersection of the perpendicular and the given line, in the normal view of the given line. Project the intersection to the other views.

4. Draw a normal view of the perpendicular from point to line. This is the true length of the shortest distance from point to line.

9.8 THREE MUTUALLY PERPENDICULAR LINES.

The corner of any rectangular solid is a condition of three mutually perpendicular lines. The representation of three mutually perpendicular lines frequently occurs on engineering drawings. In Fig. 9.9, *AB*, *BD*, and *BC* have been drawn mutually perpendicular to each other, the top and front views of *AB* and the front view of point *C* having been given. *BD* is to be of some specified length, with *D* above point *B*.

A normal view of *AB* is first made.

In this view, the direction of *BD* and *BC* can be established as perpendicular to *AB*. C_1 can now be located on RP_1. The top view of *C* can now be located by projection. D_1 is somewhere above *B*, as stated in the problem. A second auxiliary view is projected in the direction of B_1A_1, showing *AB* as a point. *BC* and *BD* will appear in true length in this second auxiliary view. The direction B_2C_2 can be determined by projecting C_1 to the second auxiliary view and measuring from RP_2. A_2D_2 can now be drawn perpendicular to B_2C_2. *D* can now be located in the second auxiliary view at the specified distance from *B*. The first auxiliary, top, and front views of point *D* can then be located by projection and measurement from proper reference planes.

Summary

1. Draw the normal view of the completely specified line. In this view, draw

Three mutually perpendicular lines

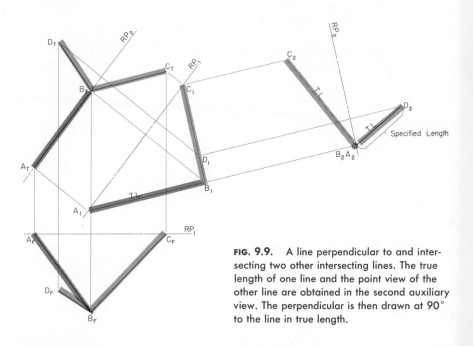

FIG. 9.9. A line perpendicular to and intersecting two other intersecting lines. The true length of one line and the point view of the other line are obtained in the second auxiliary view. The perpendicular is then drawn at 90° to the line in true length.

a perpendicular which represents the plane of the other two lines.

2. From specifications given, locate the end of one of the partially specified lines (for example, point C_A of Fig. 9.9). Project this point back to the other views.

3. Draw the end view of the completely specified line by making a second auxiliary. Carry the second line (determined in step 2) to this view.

4. Lay out the third perpendicular in the second auxiliary, and project it back to the other views.

9.9. COMMON PERPENDICULAR. The shortest distance between two nonintersecting lines is measured along the *one and only* perpendicular that intersects *both* lines. In Fig. 9.10, FE has been determined as the shortest distance between lines AB and CD. AB and CD are given. FE is to be determined. First, an auxiliary A_1B_1, showing the true length of AB, is made; then a second auxiliary view, showing the point view

of AB, is projected. In this view, the shortest distance F_2E_2 can be established perpendicular to D_2C_2 because AB appears as a point and FE will appear in true length and is therefore drawn perpendicular to CD. The shortest distance FE between lines AB and CD can then be measured in the second auxiliary view. To project FE back to the top and front views, FE is first projected to the first auxiliary view by projecting point E, which is on CD, from the second to the first auxiliary view. AB is normal in the first auxiliary view, and therefore F_1E_1 is drawn perpendicular to A_1B_1 from point E_1. FE can now be located in the top and front views by intersecting F on AB and E on CD. Problems of this type should be checked to ascertain that no mistake has been made in projecting points to the wrong line. In this problem, points F and E should be checked in the top and second auxiliary views for corresponding measurements from RP_2 and in the front and first auxiliary views for measurements from

Common perpendicular

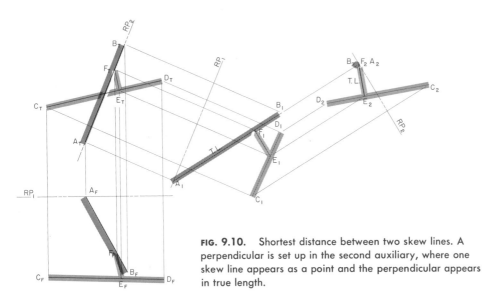

FIG. 9.10. Shortest distance between two skew lines. A perpendicular is set up in the second auxiliary, where one skew line appears as a point and the perpendicular appears in true length.

RP_1 in the front and first auxiliary views.

Summary

1. Draw the normal view of line A of the pair of lines. Carry line B into this auxiliary.

2. Draw the end view of line A, and carry line B into this second auxiliary.

3. Draw the common perpendicular in the second auxiliary by emanating it from the point view of line A and making it perpendicular to line B.

4. Draw the common perpendicular in the first auxiliary by projecting the intersection on line B from the second auxiliary and then drawing the common

perpendicular at right angles to line A.

5. Complete the projection in the other views.

9.10.   LINE THROUGH A POINT PERPEN-DICULAR TO TWO NONINTERSECTING LINES. In Fig. 9.11 the top and front views of AB and CD are given as two noninter-secting lines. Through point P a line OP is to be located perpendicular to AB and CD, with point O and P equi-distant from any particular point of AB. The two auxiliary views show the con-struction necessary to obtain the solu-tion. The true length of AB has been determined in the first auxiliary view. Point P and line CD are then projected

Line perpendicular to two skew lines

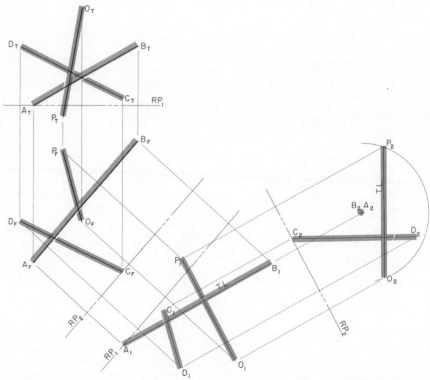

FIG. 9.11.   A line through a point perpendicular to two skew lines. The perpendicular is set up in the second auxiliary view, which shows the point of one skew line.

to this view. The direction of *OP* can be established in this view, but point *O* cannot be located to satisfy the solution. The direction for the second auxiliary view is taken to show the end view of *AB*; O_2P_2 will appear in true length and can be drawn perpendicular to C_2D_2. As *O* and *P* must be equidistant from any particular point of *AB*, point *O* can be located on the circle arc that passes through point *P* with *AB* as a center.

Because the direction of line *OP* has been established in the first auxiliary view as perpendicular to *AB*, point *O* can now be projected from the second auxiliary view to the first auxiliary view. The top and front views of point *O* can now be established by projection and measurement from the reference planes, and line *OP* can be drawn.

Summary

1. Draw the normal view of one of the given lines (line *A*), and project the other line (line *B*) and the given point into this view.

2. Draw the end view of line *A*, and project line *B* and the given point to this view.

3. Draw the required line perpendicular to line *B*, and fix the ends at equal distances from *AB*.

4. Project the required line back to the first auxiliary, where it will appear perpendicular to line *A*.

5. Complete the views.

9.11. THE ANGLE BETWEEN TWO INTERSECTING LINES. The angle between two intersecting lines will lie in the plane of the lines and therefore appears in true size in a view which shows both the true length and true relationship of the lines. The required view is thus a normal view of the plane of the lines, which may be obtained either by auxiliaries (edge and normal views) or by rotation, as explained in paragraphs 8.18, 8.19, and 8.26.

Angle between Lines by Edge and Normal Views. Figure 9.12 shows two intersecting lines, *AB* and *AC*. The angle between these two lines is to be determined. The two lines, *AB* and *AC*, may be considered as designating a plane *ABC*. A horizontal line *BD* of the plane *ABC* appears in true length in the top view, and a view (first auxiliary) made to obtain the point view of *BD* gives the edge view of the plane at $A_1B_1D_1C_1$. A view (second auxiliary) then made by projecting in a direction perpendicular to the edge view gives the normal view at $A_2B_2C_2$. In this normal view, the true length and relationship of both lines, *AB* and *AC*, is shown, and the true angle between the lines is angle *R*. Incidentally, the angle between *AB* and *BC*

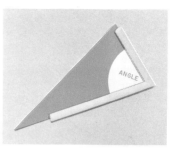

Angle between lines

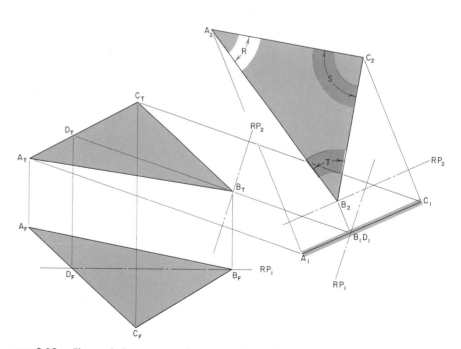

FIG. 9.12. The angle between two intersecting lines (edge-and-normal-view method). The two intersecting lines form a plane. The normal view of the plane shows the true angle.

(angle T) and the angle between BC and CA (angle S) are also shown on Fig. 9.12.

Summary

1. Draw the edge view of the plane of the two intersecting lines.

2. Draw the normal view of the plane of the two intersecting lines.

3. The true angle between the lines appears in the normal view.

Angle between Lines by Rotation. Figure 9.13 duplicates the given data of Fig. 9.12, but in Fig. 9.13 the normal view of lines AB and AC is obtained by rotation. A horizontal line BD of the plane ABC serves as an axis of rotation because it appears in true length in the top view at $B_T D_T$. The point view of the axis at $B_A D_A$ gives an axis about which the plane may be *rotated to the horizontal* at $A_{R1} B_{R1} C_{R1}$. The rotation of any point occurs in a plane perpendicular to the axis. Thus a perpendicular from C_T (to the axis) and a projection from C_{R1} to

the top view locates C_{RT}, the rotated position of C in the top view. Similarly, a perpendicular to the axis from A_T and a projection from A_{R1} to the top view locates A_{RT}, the rotated position of A. Lines then connecting A_{RT}, C_{RT}, B_T, and A_{RT} form the normal view of ABC, and the angle between AB and AC is angle R.

Summary

1. Draw the edge view of the plane of the two intersecting lines.

2. In the edge view, rotate the plane into coincidence with the reference plane for the auxiliary.

3. Project back from the auxiliary (to the view the auxiliary was projected from) where the rotated position of each point lies on a perpendicular through the point to the axis of rotation.

4. Complete the normal view (rotated view) by connecting points.

The auxiliary view of Fig. 9.13 and the rotation procedure in that view are not necessary constructions if advantage

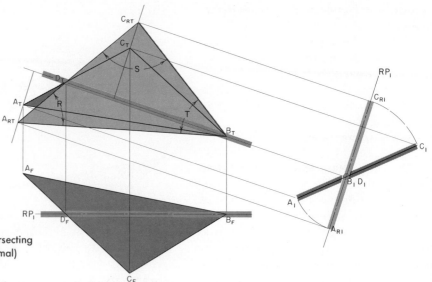

FIG. 9.13. The angle between two intersecting lines (rotation method). The rotated (normal) view shows the true angle.

is taken of the fact that the distance of any point from the axis is the hypotenuse of a triangle having vertical and horizontal legs, as explained previously in paragraph 8.26 and Fig. 8.63. Figure 9.14 shows the same given conditions as Fig. 9.13. A horizontal axis BD is drawn as before. Then, because any point, as it rotates, must move in a plane perpendicular to the axis, lines $O_T C_T$ and $K_T A_T$, extended, give the *path* of points C and A as they rotate. Points B and D, on the axis, of course do not move at all. The distance $M_F C_F$ is the vertical leg and $C_T O_T$ the horizontal leg of a triangle having $C_T N_T$ as the hypotenuse, which is the *actual distance* of point C from the axis. Thus $C_T N_T$ laid off at $O_T C_{RT}$, on the perpendicular previously drawn, gives C_{RT} as the rotated position of point C. Similarly, vertical distance $A_F J_F$ laid off at $K_T L_T$, where $A_T K_T$ is the mating horizontal leg, gives $L_T A_T$ as the hypotenuse and true distance of point A from the axis, which laid off at $K_T A_{RT}$ locates A_{RT}, the rotated position of point A. Now, connecting A_{RT}, C_{RT}, B_T, and A_{RT} determines the normal view of ABC, and the true angle between AC and AB is angle R. Note that line $A_{RT} C_{RT}$ must pass through point D_T because D is on the axis and is also a point on line AC.

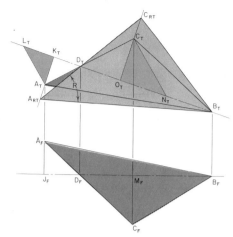

FIG. 9.14. The angle between two intersecting lines (rotation method). The rotated (normal) view shows the true angle.

Summary

1. Draw an axis of rotation.

2. In the view where the axis of rotation appears normal, draw paths of rotation for each point, perpendicular to the axis.

3. To determine the true distance of a point from the axis: (*a*) Measure one leg of the right-angled triangle in the view that is in direct projection with the view in which the axis appears normal (in Fig. 9.14, the front view). (*b*) The other leg of the right-angled triangle appears as the distance from the axis in the view in which the axis is normal. (*c*) Step off the two legs, and determine the hypotenuse (see Fig. 8.63 for illustration).

4. Determine the distance of each point from the axis as in (3), and lay this distance *from* the axis, and on the perpendicular to the axis, *through* the point.

5. Connect points to complete the rotated view.

9.12. SPECIFIED ANGLE BETWEEN TWO INTERSECTING LINES. If the angle between a pair of intersecting lines is specified, and not to be determined, the solutions are similar to those of paragraph 9.11, except that the angle will be laid out in a normal view, thus locating one of the lines.

Specified Angle by Edge and Normal Views. In Fig. 9.15, AB is a given line and C a point in the plane of line AE that is to make a specified angle with AB. The normal view of plane ABC is thus a view where both *AB* and *AE* appear in true length and therefore a view in which the specified angle may be laid out. In Fig. 9.15, edge and normal views are made as explained before for Fig. 9.12. Then, in the normal view the angle may be laid out and is shown at $B_2A_2E_2$ on Fig. 9.15. Point *E* has been conveniently located *on* line *BC* and can therefore be easily projected back to E_1 (the edge view) and thence to E_T and E_F.

Summary

1. Draw an edge view of the *plane* of the lines.

2. Draw a normal view of the plane of the lines.

3. In the normal view, lay out the required angle between the lines.

4. Project back to the other views to complete the solution.

Specified Angle by Rotation. The shortest method, from the standpoint of con-

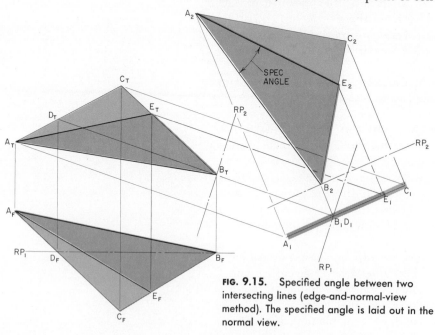

FIG. 9.15. Specified angle between two intersecting lines (edge-and-normal-view method). The specified angle is laid out in the normal view.

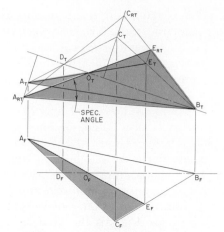

FIG. 9.16. Specified angle between two intersecting lines (rotation method). The specified angle is laid out in the rotated normal view.

struction and number of views required, is the rotation method shown in Fig. 9.16. The given information is the same as for Fig. 9.15, but in Fig. 9.16 the normal view of the plane has been determined by rotation. In the normal view, at $A_{RT}E_{RT}$ the line *AE* is drawn at the specified angle to *AB*. To counterrotate the line back to the given views, point *E* must move in a plane perpendicular to the axis and thus, in the top view, moves from E_{RT} to E_T on line *BC*. The front view of point E may then be found by projection from E_T to E_F. Note also that point *O*, where line *AE* crosses the axis of rotation, will remain fixed. With this fact, a line from A_T through point O_T, extended to C_TB_T, will determine E_T, *or* this construction will check on the accuracy of location of point E_T by the previously explained construction.

Summary

1. Draw the normal view of the plane of the lines by rotation.

2. Lay out the angle in the normal view.

3. Project back to the original views.

9.13. ANGULAR RELATIONSHIPS: NOR-MAL AND POINT VIEWS. The examples of paragraphs 9.11 and 9.12 present the general case where the two lines, for which an angular relationship is required, are both skew. This condition may not always prevail. One line may appear in true length in one of the views. In such a special case, an auxiliary view made to obtain the true length of both lines gives a simple and direct solution.

Angle between Lines. In Fig. 9.17, line AB is vertical and appears as a point in the top view. Line AC is a skew line (to the planes of projection). If an auxiliary is made to give the true length of AC, as shown in the figure, the true relationship and true length of both lines, AC and AB, will be obtained in this view. Note that the top view of ABC is the edge view of the plane of both lines. Therefore, in the auxiliary projected from the top view both lines are normal, and the true angle may be measured.

Summary

1. Draw an auxiliary view that will show the normal view of *both* lines. (This is the normal view of the *plane* of the lines.)

2. Measure the angle.

If one of the lines is in an inclined position—as the horizontal line AB of Fig. 9.18—but the other line skew to the planes of projection (line BC), then two views will be required. The first auxiliary $A_1B_1C_1$ gives the point view of AB. The second auxiliary view $A_2B_2C_2$, taken in a direction perpendicular to B_1C_1, gives the true length of BC *and* AB. The true angle may then be measured in the second auxiliary.

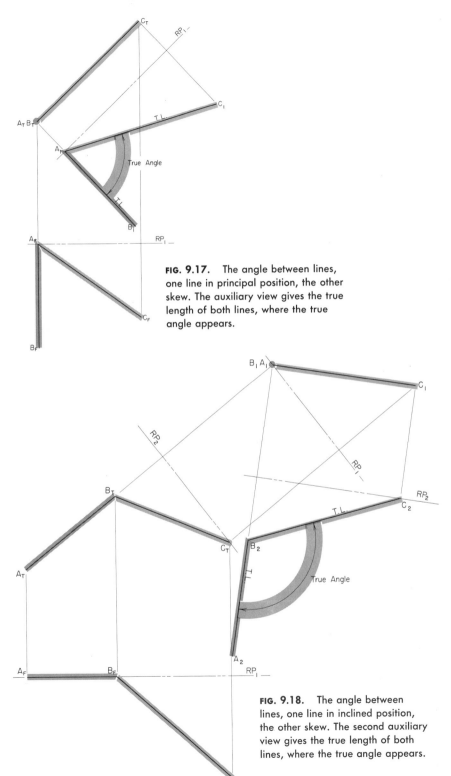

FIG. 9.17. The angle between lines, one line in principal position, the other skew. The auxiliary view gives the true length of both lines, where the true angle appears.

FIG. 9.18. The angle between lines, one line in inclined position, the other skew. The second auxiliary view gives the true length of both lines, where the true angle appears.

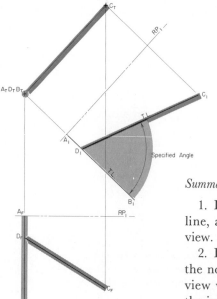

FIG. 9.19. A specified angle between two intersecting lines, one line in principal position, the other skew. The angle is laid out in the auxiliary view, where both lines appear normal.

Summary

1. Draw the point view of the inclined line, and carry the skew line into this view.

2. Draw a second auxiliary showing the normal view of the skew line. This view will also give the normal view of the inclined line.

3. Measure the angle in the second auxiliary.

Specified Angle between Lines. In Fig. 9.19, line AB and point C are given. A line CD is to be drawn making a specified angle with AB and of course intersecting AB. The auxiliary projected from the top view and taken in a direction perpendicular to the edge view of ABC will show the normal view of AB and, even though not yet drawn, the normal view of any line CD that intersects AB at D. Thus in this view, the line CD may be laid out at a specified angle with AB and the position of D determined. Measurement from RP_1 will then locate point D in the front view.

Summary

1. Draw the normal view of the plane of both lines.

2. Lay out the angle in the normal view.

3. Project back to the other views.

The solution when one line is skew and the other inclined (lying in a plane of projection) is given in Fig. 9.20. The first auxiliary $A_1B_1C_1$ gives the edge view of the plane of the lines, and the second auxiliary view $A_2B_2C_2$, taken perpendicular to $A_1B_1C_1$, gives the normal view of both lines, where the specified angle may be laid out. The intersection D on AB may then be carried back to the top and front views.

Summary

1. Draw the edge view of the *plane* of both lines.

2. Draw the normal view of the plane of both lines.

3. Lay out the angle in the normal view.

4. Project back to the other views.

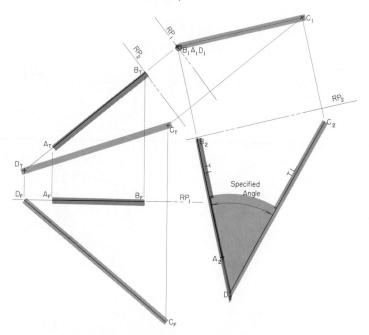

FIG. 9.20. A specified angle between two lines, one line in inclined position, the other skew. The true angle is laid out in the second auxiliary, where both lines appear normal.

PROBLEMS

The following problems are shown on a grid with coordinate lines ½ in. apart. The markings at the left and bottom indicate inches. Thus these problems may be plotted in a space 7½ by 10 in. on standard 8½- by 11-in. coordinate paper or on paper prepared for the purpose.

GROUP 1. TRUE LENGTHS

9.1.1. Find the true length of *AB*. Scale: ½ size.

9.1.2. Find the perimeter of the triangle *ABC*. Scale: full size.

9.1.3. The line *CL* slopes upward from *C* with a 60 per cent grade. Draw the front view of *CL*. Find the distance from *C* to *L*. Scale: $1'' = 50'$.

9.1.4. Line *AB* is to be established with a bearing of N60°E with a 60 per cent positive grade from *A*. The distance from *A* to *B* is 336 ft. Draw the top and front views of *AB*. Scale: $1'' = 100'$.

9.1.5. A power-line pole is supported by two guy wires. *E* and *D* are the points on the ground where the guy wires are to be attached.

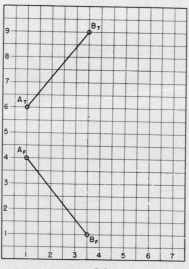

PROB. 9.1.1.

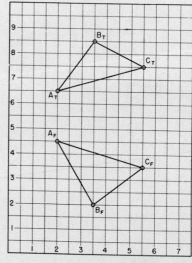

PROB. 9.1.2.

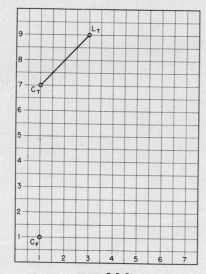

PROB. 9.1.3.

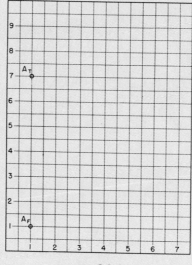

PROB. 9.1.4.

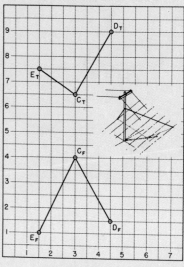

PROB. 9.1.5.

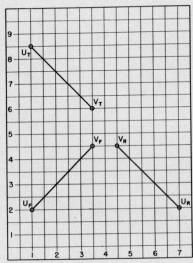

PROB. 9.1.6.

Find the length of the guy wires from point *C* in the pole. Disregard lengths for attaching. Scale: $1'' = 10'$.

9.1.6. Line *OP* is to be established with a grid azimuth of 213°45'. The line slopes down from *P* with a grade of 66⅔ per cent. The length of *OP* is 84 ft. Draw the top and front views of *OP*. Scale: $1'' = 20'$.

GROUP 2. POINTS ON LINES

9.2.1. Point *W* is on *UV* and is 6½ in. from *V* toward *U*. Locate the top, front, and right-side views of point *W*. Scale: ¼ size.

9.2.2. Point *D* is on line *AB*. Point *C* is ½ in. above point *A*. Draw the front view of *CD*. What is the true length of *CD*? Scale: full size.

9.2.3. *AB* is 14 in. long. *B* is to the rear of *A*. *C* is on *AB* and is 4¼ in. in front of *B*. Complete the top, front, and right-side views of *ABC*. Find the true distance from *B* to *C*. Scale: ¼ size.

9.2.4. A series of six points is to be located on line *AB*. Points 1 and 6 are to be ¾ in. from *A* and *B* respectively. The remaining points are to be equidistant from each other. What is the true distance between points 3 and 4?

Show on drawing where measurement is taken.

9.2.5. The line segment *AB* is to be divided into five equal spaces. Locate the top and front views of these divisions. Find the true length of the subdivisions. Scale: ½ size.

9.2.6. Line segment *AB* is three times as long as line segment *CD*. Point *A* is below point *B*. Draw the front view of point *A*. What is the length of line segment *CD*? Line segment *AB*? Scale: half size.

9.2.7. An electric power line is to be supported at eight points which lie in a straight line *CD*. Each of the supports is to be equally spaced along the cable. What is the true length of the cable between each support (neglecting the sag of the cable)? What is the grade of the cable? Scale: $1'' = 1,000'$.

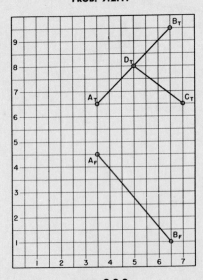

PROB. 9.2.1.

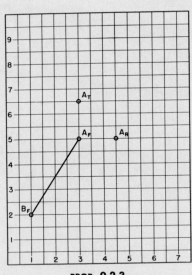

PROB. 9.2.3.

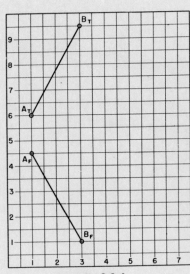

PROB. 9.2.4.

PROB. 9.2.2.

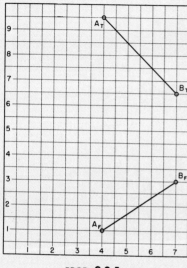

PROB. 9.2.5.

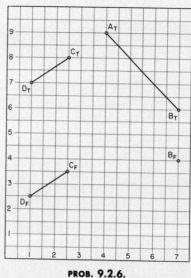

PROB. 9.2.6.

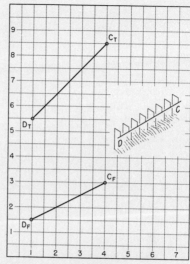

PROB. 9.2.7.

GROUP 3.   INTERSECTING LINES

9.3.1.   The horizontal line *CD* intersects the profile line *EF*. Draw the front view of *CD*. What is the true distance from *E* to *D*? Scale: 1″ = 1′-0″.

9.3.2.   *AB* has a bearing of N60°W and intersects the line *XY* at point *C*. *B* is 3¾ in.

below *X*. Complete the top and front views of *AB* and *C*. What is the true length of *BC*? Scale: ½ size.

9.3.3.   *AC* intersects the profile line *RS* at point *B*. Complete the top view of *ABC*.

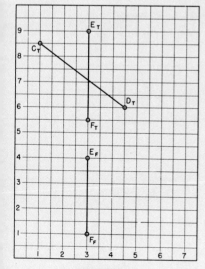

PROB. 9.3.1.

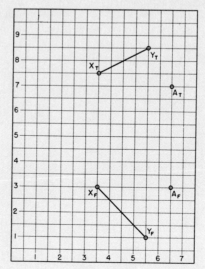

PROB. 9.3.2.

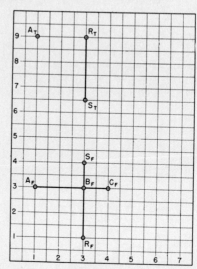

PROB. 9.3.3.

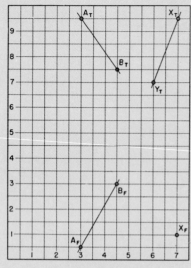

PROB. 9.3.4.

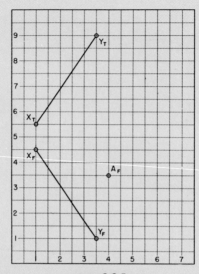

PROB. 9.3.5.

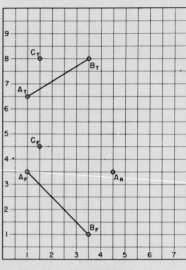

PROB. 9.4.1.

9.3.4. *AB* and *XY* represent the center lines of two air ducts. Center line *XY* is to intersect *AB* at point *Z*. Complete the top and front views of *XYZ*. Find the true length of *BZ*. Scale: ⅛″ = 1′-0″.

9.3.5. Point *B* is on line *XY*. *AB* is 3 in. long. Point *A* lies above point *B*. Complete the top and front views of *AB*. Scale: full size.

GROUP 4.   PARALLEL LINES

9.4.1. *CD* is parallel and equal in length to *AB*. Complete the top, front, and right-side views of *AB* and *CD*.

9.4.2. *AB* is one edge of a sheet-metal plate. This plate has the geometric shape of a rhom-

bus. One of the adjacent edges lies along *AC*. Complete the top and front views of the plate.

9.4.3. *XY* is one side and point *C* the geometric center of a parallelogram. Complete the top and front views of the parallelogram.

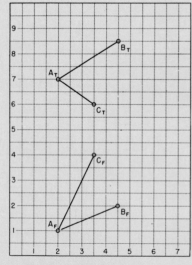

PROB. 9.4.2.

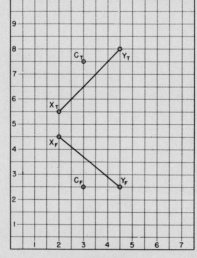

PROB. 9.4.3.

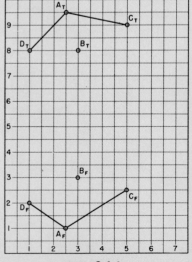

PROB. 9.4.4.

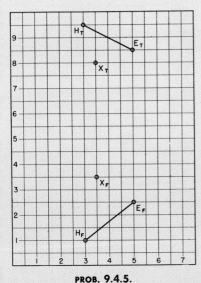

PROB. 9.4.5.

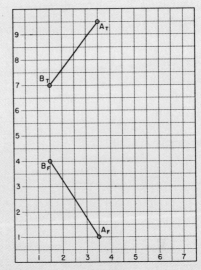

PROB. 9.5.1.

PROB. 9.5.2.

9.4.4.   *AB*, *AD*, and *AC* are three edges of a parallelepiped. Complete the top and front views, and show visibility.

9.4.5.   *HE* is an edge of a right section of a regular hexagonal shaft. Point *X* is the geometric center of this section. Complete the top and front views of this section.

GROUP 5.   PERPENDICULAR LINES

9.5.1.   Line *EF* is perpendicular to line *GH*. Locate *GH* in the top view.

9.5.2.   *AB* is a diagonal of a square. The other diagonal is horizontal. Draw the top and front views of the square.

9.5.3.   *OP* is the base side of an equilateral triangle. The altitude of this triangle is frontal.

Complete the top and front views of the triangle *OPQ*.

9.5.4.   *AB*, *BD*, and *BC* are three mutually perpendicular lines. *BD* and *BC* are equal in length. Point *D* is below *B*. Show the top and front views of the three lines.

9.5.5.   Shown in the sketch is a pictorial

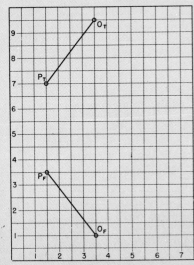

PROB. 9.5.3.

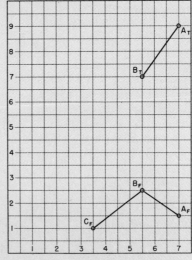

PROB. 9.5.4.

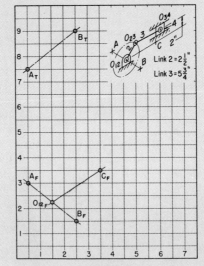

PROB. 9.5.5.

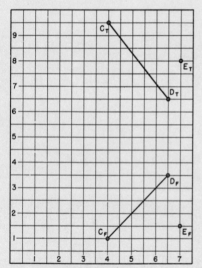

PROB. 9.5.6.

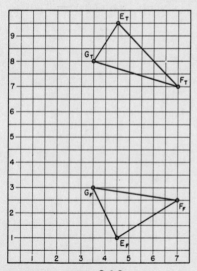

PROB. 9.6.1.

PROB. 9.6.2.

kinematic diagram of a slidecrank mechanism. Find the maximum stroke of link 4. Show in the top and front views the limiting positions of center 0,3,4. Scale: ⅜ size.

9.5.6. Shown in the sketch is a pictorial kinematic drawing of a four-bar mechanism.

Link 2 rotates about center line *A* with a constant velocity. When link 2 becomes perpendicular to link 3, link 4 has reached its maximum velocity. Locate in the top and front views all possible positions of centers 0,2,3 and 0,3,4 as link 4 obtains maximum velocity.

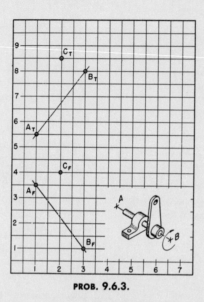

PROB. 9.6.3.

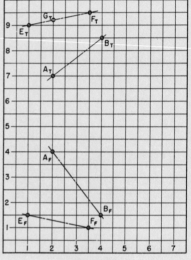

PROB. 9.6.4.

GROUP 6.   DISTANCE FROM A POINT TO A LINE

9.6.1. Determine the shortest distance from point *E* to the line *CD*.

9.6.2. *EF* is the base of a triangular steel plate. Find the area of the surface *EFG*. Scale: ¼ size.

9.6.3. Find the diameter of the circular path of point *C* as it revolves about the center line *AB*. Scale: ⅜ size.

9.6.4. *AB* and *EF* are the center lines of two pipes. They are to be connected from *G* on *EF* using a standard tee (90°) on *AB*. Draw the top and front views of the connecting-pipe center line. What is the center-line distance of the connecting pipe? Scale: ½″ = 1′-0″.

9.6.5. The spur gear *G* drives the pinion gear *H*. Gear *G* rotates at 200 rpm. *X* is a point on the pitch diameter of gear G. The speed of a spur gear is inversely proportional to its pitch diameter. What is the rpm of shaft *CD*? Scale: ¼ size.

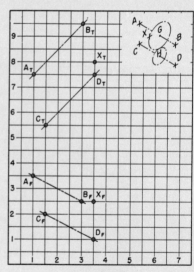

PROB. 9.6.5.

GROUP 7. COMMON PERPENDICULAR

9.7.1. Draw the top and front views of the common perpendicular between the lines AB and CD. What is the true length of this perpendicular? Scale: ½ size.

9.7.2. Find the minimum distance between lines AB and CD and AB and CE. Scale: ¼ size.

9.7.3. AB and CD are the center lines of two pipes which are to be connected with another pipe using standard tees (90°). Draw the top and front views of this center line.

9.7.4. AB is the axis of a 24-in.-diameter pipe. The pipe is to pass through a 6-in.-thick wall shown in the top view. What is the minimum size of a rectangular opening which must be cut in the wall to permit passage of the pipe? The opening is to have horizontal and vertical edges and is to be cut through the wall in a direction perpendicular to the wall. Scale: $1'' = 1'-0''$.

9.7.5. A cable attached at point R must be secured along line AB. The attachment along AB must be as close to point B as possible, and yet the cable should clear line EF by 12 in. Draw the top and front views of the cable. Scale: $1'' = 1'-0''$.

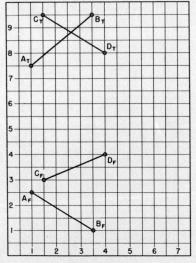

PROB. 9.7.1.

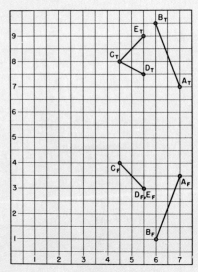

PROB. 9.7.2.

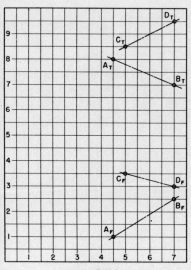

PROB. 9.7.3.

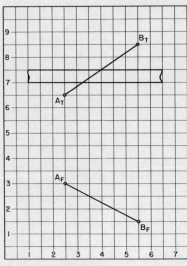

PROB. 9.7.4.

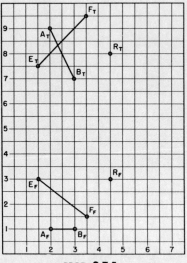

PROB. 9.7.5.

GROUP 8.   ANGLE BETWEEN LINES

9.8.1.   Show the true size of each of the interior angles of the triangle *ABC*.

9.8.2.   Show the true size of the angle between lines *AB* and *BC*.

9.8.3.   Show the true size of the angle between lines *AB* and *BC*.

9.8.4.   Show the true size of the angle that guy wires *LO*, *MO*, and *NO* make with the TV tower.

9.8.5.   Show the true size of the angle that *CL* makes with both *ED* and *XP*.

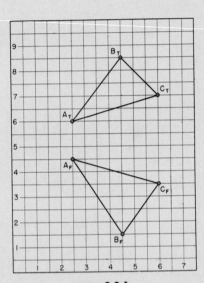

PROB. 9.8.1.

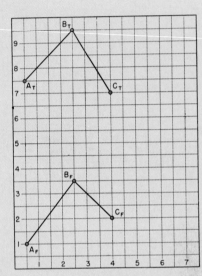

PROB. 9.8.2.

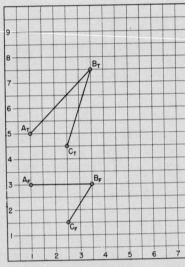

PROB. 9.8.3.

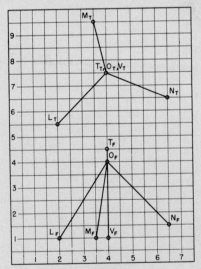

PROB. 9.8.4.

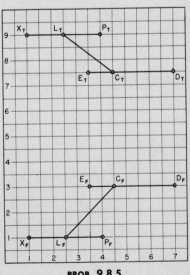

PROB. 9.8.5.

GROUP 9. LINES MAKING SPECIFIED ANGLES WITH EACH OTHER

9.9.1. *CD* makes an angle of 60° with *AB*. *D* is on the line segment *AB*. Draw the top and front views of *CD*.

9.9.2. Draw a line *BE* that makes an angle of 60° with *CD*. Point *E* is on *CD*. Also draw a line *AF* that makes an angle of 45° with *CD*. Point *F* lies on *CD*.

9.9.3. *RS* and *PQ* are the center lines of two members of a steel structure. Find the center line of a member from point *Q* that makes an angle of 60° with *RS*.

In addition, locate a member through point

P that makes an angle of 45° with *RS*.

9.9.4. Find the connector from the midpoint of line *AB* that will make an angle of 67½° with line *CD*.

9.9.5. *JK* is the center line of a pipe. Another pipe with a center line through point *P* is to connect to the pipeline *JK*, using a standard 45° lateral. The connection is to be as close to *J* as possible. Draw the top and front views of the center line of that portion of the lateral from *P* to *JK*.

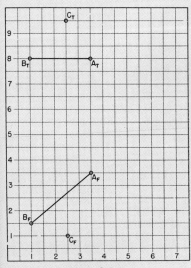

PROB. 9.9.1.

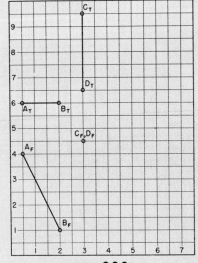

PROB. 9.9.2.

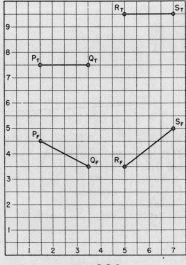

PROB. 9.9.3.

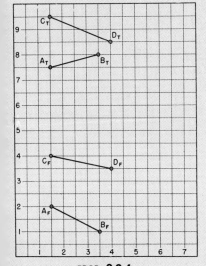

PROB. 9.9.4.

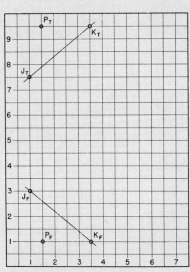

PROB. 9.9.5.

Curved Lines in Space

10

10.1. Chapters 9 and 11 deal with the problems of straight lines and also with the problems of straight lines and their relationships to planes. In addition to straight lines and planes, machines and structures will also contain various curves and combinations of straight and curved lines. The trained engineer must therefore be familiar with the mathematical and graphic theory of curves and the practical construction of them.

10.2. **DEFINITIONS.** A *curved line* is generated by a point moving in a constantly changing direction, according to some mathematical or graphic law. Curved lines may be classified as either single-curved or double-curved.

A *single-curved line* is a curved line having all points of the line in a plane. Single-curved lines are often called plane curves.

A *double-curved line* is a curved line having no four consecutive points in the same plane. Double-curved lines are also known as space curves.

A *tangent* to a curved line is a line, either straight or curved, that passes through two points on the curve that are infinitely close together. Note that this definition of tangency places the tangent in the plane of the curve for single-curved lines and in an instantaneous plane of the curve for double-curved lines.

Circle in skew position

A *normal* to a single-curved line will be a line in the plane of the curve and perpendicular to a straight line connecting two consecutive points of the curve. A normal to a double-curved line will be a line perpendicular to the instantaneous plane of the curve at the point of contact with the curve. A normal is perpendicular to the tangent at the same point of contact with the curve.

10.3. PLAN FOR STUDY. Because even the simplest plane curve, the circle, becomes an ellipse when in a skew position, it is necessary to study the plane curves in simple positions before attempting solutions in skew positions. (Plane curves—the circle, ellipse, parabola, hyperbola, cycloid, involute, and spiral—are discussed in Chap. 3.) Then the space problems of plane curves may be studied.

10.4. PLANE CURVES IN SPACE. A plane curve may, of course, lie in a horizontal, frontal, or profile plane, in which case the normal view of the curve will appear in one of the principal views. If the curve is in an inclined or skew plane, extra construction will be necessary before the principal views of the curve can be drawn. With the exception of a circle in a skew position, when the diameters of an ellipse may be located by special projective methods (explained in paragraph 10.5), a normal view of the curve is required.

10.5. A CIRCLE IN A SKEW POSITION. *By Plotting Points.* In designating the position of a circle in space, either the position of the central axis (axis of rotation) will have to be given or the plane of the circle defined. In Fig. 10.1, the axis *AB* of a circle with center at *O* has been located. The diameter of the circle is given. The axis *AB* is skew; therefore, an auxiliary view will be required to get the normal view. If now the end view of axis *AB* is made as at $B_2O_2A_2$, the plane of the circle will appear normal because the plane of the circle must be perpendicular to the axis of rotation. In this second auxiliary view, the circle may then be drawn. In the first auxiliary view, the axis appears in true length, and therefore the plane of the circle,

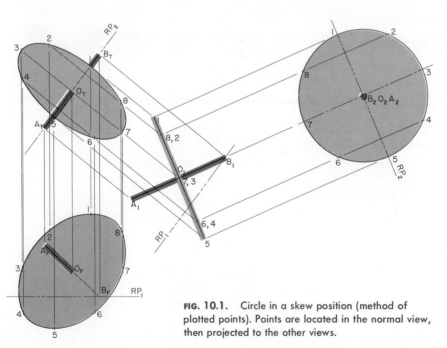

FIG. 10.1. Circle in a skew position (method of plotted points). Points are located in the normal view, then projected to the other views.

perpendicular to the axis, will appear as an edge. Thus points, for example, 1 to 8 in Fig. 10.1, located on the circle in the second auxiliary view (end view of axis) may be projected to the first auxiliary view, where they are located on the edge view of the circle. Next, these points may be projected to the top view and then to the front view, thus determining points on the elliptical curves through which smooth curves may be drawn.

Summary

1. Draw an auxiliary view showing the normal view of the circle axis and the edge view of the circle plane.

2. Draw a second auxiliary view, projected from the first auxiliary, showing the point view of the axis. Draw the normal view of the circle in this view.

3. Locate points on the circle in the normal view of it; project back to the edge view (first auxiliary) and then to the other views.

By Locating Major and Minor Diameters. The above problem can also be solved, without bringing points back from the normal view, by locating the major and minor diameters needed for each view. In any view of a circle in a skew position where the circle appears as an ellipse, the major diameter of the ellipse will be perpendicular to the axis of the circle, and the minor diameter of the ellipse will coincide (on the drawing) with the axis of the circle. This may be proved by examining the auxiliary views of Fig. 10.2. Axis AB and the diameter of the circle with center at O are given. The auxiliary view, projected from the right-side view, gives the true length of axis AB. From O, the plane of the circle and the diameter GH may then be laid out

at G_1H_1, perpendicular to A_1B_1. One diameter of the circle appears as a point at J_1K_1. Projection of this diameter back to the side view shows JK in true length in the side view. Because this diameter is in true length, it has not been foreshortened and is therefore the major diameter of the ellipse in this, the side view. Note that JK is perpendicular to the circle axis AB in the side view. Diameter GH is in true length at G_1H_1 in the auxiliary. Its position in the side view will therefore be perpendicular to the rays of projection between side view and auxiliary, and, as this diameter contains point O (the center), GH must appear in coincidence with the axis AB. Because GH is the perpendicular bisector of JK, the major diameter, it is the minor diameter. Also, GH is the

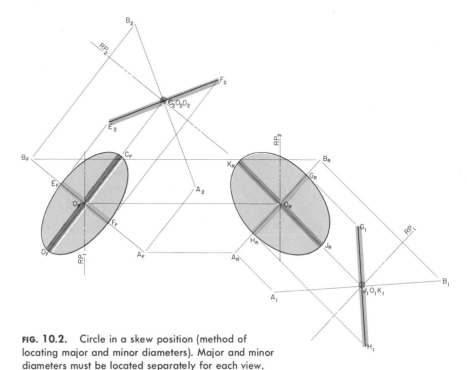

FIG. 10.2.   Circle in a skew position (method of locating major and minor diameters). Major and minor diameters must be located separately for each view.

diameter foreshortened to the greatest degree, proving again that it is the minor diameter. Thus, having established the major and minor diameters for the ellipse, we can draw the curve by either the concentric-circle or trammel method to complete the view. The front view of Fig. 10.2 may be established in a similar way by employing the auxiliary shown (projected from the front view) and determining the major diameter CD and the minor diameter EF.

Summary

1. From one of the views, project an auxiliary that shows the true length of the circle axis.

2. In the auxiliary view, at the circle center, lay out the edge view of the circle (perpendicular to the circle axis).

3. Project back to the view from the auxiliary: (*a*) The diameter which appears as a point at the circle center in the auxiliary projects to the view in true length perpendicular to the circle axis and is the major diameter of the ellipse. (*b*) The diameter of the circle which appears in true length perpendicular to the circle axis in the auxiliary projects to the view foreshortened and in coincidence with the circle axis and is the minor diameter.

4. Draw the ellipse by either trammel or concentric-circle method.

5. Repeat (1), (2), (3), and (4) for the other given view.

10.6. A CIRCLE IN A SKEW POSITION: SIMPLIFIED METHOD. *By Trammel.* If advantage is taken of the facts just presented in paragraph 10.5 and, in addition, a knowledge of the trammel method is applied, a circle in a skew position may be drawn without the necessity of extra views. In Fig. 10.3, the rotation

axis AB, the center, and the diameter of the circle are given. It has been shown in paragraph 10.5 that the major diameter in each view will be perpendicular to the axis of rotation and equal in length to the diameter of the circle. Therefore, the major diameters, $E_T F_T$ for the top view and $C_F D_F$ for the front view (of Fig. 10.3) can be drawn. The major diameter $E_T F_T$ is in true length in the top view and will therefore be a horizontal line $E_F F_F$ in the front view. This gives two points, E_F and F_F, in the front view that are on the elliptical curve. Then by employing a trammel (trammel 2 in Fig. 10.3) with point X as the plotting end, distance XZ is marked off equal to one-half the major diameter. Now with point X located at point F_F and point Z on the minor diameter (extended), a mark at point Y, where the

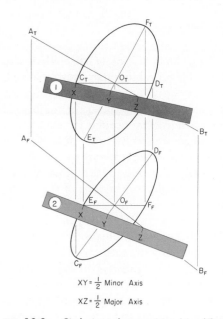

$$XY = \tfrac{1}{2} \text{ Minor Axis}$$

$$XZ = \tfrac{1}{2} \text{ Major Axis}$$

FIG. 10.3. Circle in a skew position (simplified trammel method). No auxiliary views are required.

trammel intersects the major diameter, will give distance XY equal to one-half the minor diameter. The trammel may then be moved as described in paragraph 3.50 to plot points on the curve. The top view is drawn similarly, employing major diameter $E_T F_T$, points C_T and D_T (either one) on the curve, and trammel 1, shown.

Summary

1. In the top view, draw the major diameter for the ellipse (equal to the circle diameter) through the circle center and perpendicular to the circle axis. This major diameter projects to the front view as a horizontal line. Make the projection to the front view.

2. In the front view, draw the major diameter for the ellipse (equal to the circle diameter) through the circle center and perpendicular to the circle axis. This major diameter projects to the top view as a frontal line. Make the projection to the top view.

3. On a piece of paper to be used as a trammel, mark off a distance equal to one-half the major diameter (points X and Y of Fig. 10.3).

In the top view, place the plotting end (point X) of the trammel at one end of the *projected* major diameter *from the front* view. Place point Z on the circle axis, the position of the minor diameter. Make a mark (point Y) at the point the trammel crosses the major diameter. Now, points Y and Z follow the major and minor diameters respectively, and point X locates points on the ellipse for the top view.

4. Repeat *all operations* listed in (3), but make another trammel (based on the different minor diameter in the front view) to plot the ellipse for the front view.

By Concentric-circle Method. An equivalent construction may be made by using the concentric-circle method shown in Fig. 10.4, in place of the trammel method of Fig. 10.3. In Fig. 10.4, as before in Fig. 10.3, the axis AB, the center O, and the diameter of the circle are given. The major diameters, $E_T F_T$ in the top view and $C_F D_F$ in the front view, and the projection of these diameters to the other view, $E_F F_F$ in the front view and $C_T D_T$ in the top view, are projected, giving points on the curve in each view, as described for the trammel method. Then, to draw the top view, the major-diameter circle for the ellipse is drawn and point C_T projected (perpendicular to the major diameter) to the circle at C_{MT}. This is the revolved position of point C on the ellipse to its original position on the major-diameter circle. If then the radial line $C_{MT} O_T$ is drawn and a projector perpendicular to

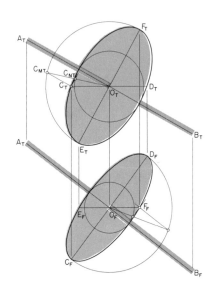

FIG. 10.4. Circle in a skew position (simplified concentric-circle method). No auxiliary views are required.

the minor diameter (also perpendicular to $A_T B_T$) drawn to intersect the radial line at C_{NT}, the distance $C_{NT} O_T$ is the length of one-half the minor diameter. The minor-diameter circle then drawn, as shown, completes the construction necessary to plot the curve by the concentric-circle method of paragraph 3.52. Construction for the front view is similar, as indicated on the figure.

Summary

1. In both views, draw the major diameters for the ellipses, through each circle center and perpendicular to each circle axis. Draw the major-diameter circle in each view.

2. Project each major diameter to the other view. The front-view major diameter is frontal in the top view. The top-view major diameter is horizontal in the front view. This locates two points *on the ellipse* in each view.

3. In each view, from one of the points on the ellipse, project a line to the major-diameter circle, parallel to the circle axis. From this point on the major-diameter circle, draw a radial line to the circle center. From the same point on the ellipse, draw a line perpendicular to the circle axis, and intersect the radial line. This intersection is a point on the minor-diameter circle. Draw the minor-diameter circle.

4. Draw each ellipse by the concentric-circle method (see paragraph 3.52).

10.7.   ANY PLANE CURVE IN A SKEW POSITION. If the position of the plane in which a plane curve lies is known and orientation of the plane curve on its plane is fixed, the curve may be laid out and drawn in any required view. The plane of the curve will probably occur as the surface of some object and is

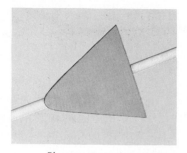

Plane curve in skew position

therefore fixed in space. The curve on the plane may occur as a geometrical shape, produced either by design requirements or by some necessary structural feature or, in some cases, by an intersection of some surface with the plane. Because of the numerous possibilities, the plane curve may be either a geometrical shape or some general curve not governed by mathematical laws.

In paragraphs 5.23 and 5.24, the circle on a skew plane, an ellipse on a skew plane (produced by intersection with a cylinder), and the projection of a general curve on a plane have been discussed. Also, in Chap. 14, the intersections of various surfaces with planes are shown. In paragraphs 10.5 and 10.6, the circle in skew position was given. Note in every case that, if the plane is known or can be determined, the curve can then be located on the plane. The normal view of the plane will be required in order to lay out the curve.

The principles just presented may be illustrated by Fig. 10.5, in which line AB is the central axis of a parabola. Point F on AB is the focus of the parabola and point P is a point on the curve. This information fixes the curve and the plane of the curve: First, by considering that ABP is the plane of the curved line, PX in plane ABP is drawn horizontal. Then an auxiliary projected from the top view in the direction of $X_T P_T$ will give the edge view of the plane at $B_1 F_1 X_1 P_1 A_1$. A second auxiliary view now made perpendicular to the edge view gives the normal view of the plane, and $A_2 B_2 F_2$ and P_2 are required points in this view. The directrix of the parabola will be perpendicular to axis AB and may be located by drawing an arc with center at P through F_2 as shown. The directrix is then tangent to

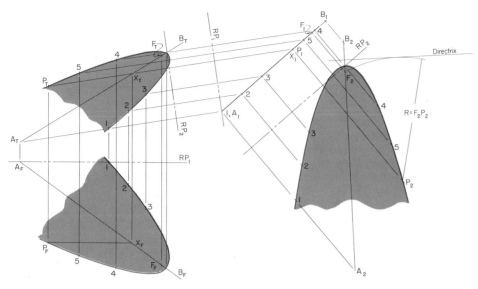

FIG. 10.5. A plane curve in a skew position. Points are plotted in the normal view, then projected back to the other views.

this arc. Now that the axis, the focus, and the directrix are located, the curve may be drawn in the second auxiliary view. Points now located on the curve (1 to 5, as shown) may be projected to the edge view and thence to the top and front views, completing the views required.

Any other geometrical curve may be drawn as described for the parabola of Fig. 10.5 if enough information is available to orient the plane and curve. For example, if the curve is an ellipse, the plane and either the position of the major diameter and minor diameter or the major diameter and a point on the curve must be known.

Nongeometrical curves may be laid out in the normal view if their true configuration is known.

Summary

1. The plane of the curve and its position on the plane must be established.

2. Draw the edge view of the curve plane.

3. Draw the normal view of the curve plane. Lay out the curve in this view.

4. Locate points on the curve and project back to all other views.

10.8. DOUBLE-CURVED LINES. The scarcity of geometrical double-curved lines, by comparison with the numerous single-curved lines, is surprising. There are only two double-curved lines, the cylindrical and the conical helix, much used in engineering work. These curves are defined and explained in Chap. 3, paragraphs 3.70 to 3.73

Double-curved lines will, however, often occur as the lines of intersection between two curved solids or surfaces. These lines are not geometrical lines but double-curved lines of general form. It will be interesting to note the double-curved lines of intersection that occur in the figures of Chap. 14.

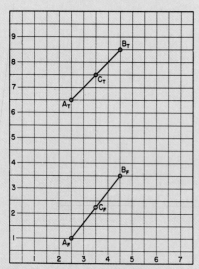

PROB. 10.1.1.

PROBLEMS

To be of value both as drawing exercises and as solutions, geometrical problems should be worked very accurately. The pencil must be kept extremely sharp, and comparatively light lines must be used. A point should be located by two intersecting lines, and the length of a line should be indicated by short dashes across the line.

GROUP 1. A CIRCLE (AXIS GIVEN) IN SKEW POSITION

10.1.1. *AB* is the axis and *C* the center of a circle of 2 in. diameter. Draw top, front, elevation auxiliary, and normal views by plotting points on the circle. Scale: full size.

10.1.2. *AB* is the axis and *C* the center of a circle of 3½ in. diameter. Draw the top and front views by locating major and minor diameters of the elliptical representation for each view. Scale: ½ size.

10.1.3. *AB* is the axis and *C* the center of a circle of 16 in. diameter. Draw top and front views by the trammel method. Scale: ¼ size.

10.1.4. *AB* is the axis and *C* the center of a circle of 15 in. diameter. Draw top and front views by the concentric-circle method. Scale: ¼ size.

10.1.5. *AB* is the axis, *C* the center, and *P* a point on the circumference of a circle. Draw top, front, and any other necessary views of the circle.

GROUP 2. A PLANE CURVE (AXIS GIVEN) IN SKEW POSITION

10.2.1. *ABC* is the plane and *C* the center of an ellipse whose major diameter is horizontal and 2½ in. long and whose minor diameter is 1¾ in. Draw top, front, and other necessary views of the ellipse. Scale: full size.

10.2.2. Using the layout for Prob. 10.1.1., *AB* is the axis of an elliptical cylinder with a right section at point *C*. The elliptical section has the major diameter frontal and 2¾ in. long. The minor diameter is 2 in. Draw top, front, and other necessary views of the right section and the limiting-element lines. Scale: full size.

10.2.3. *AB* is the axis of a parabola with focus at point *B*. Point *P* is a point on the parabola. Draw front, top, and other necessary views.

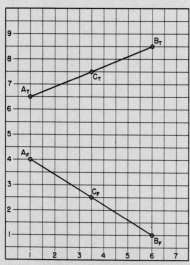

PROB. 10.1.2.

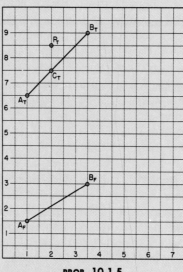

PROB. 10.1.5.

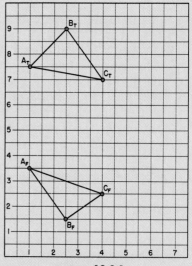

PROB. 10.2.1.

PROBS. 10.1.3. and 10.1.4.

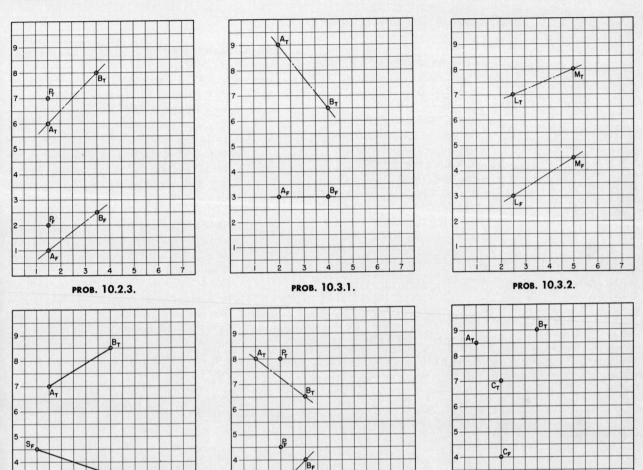

PROB. 10.2.3.   PROB. 10.3.1.   PROB. 10.3.2.

PROB. 10.3.3.   PROB. 10.3.4.   PROB. 10.3.5.

GROUP 3. THE CIRCLE (AXIS OR POSITION GIVEN)

10.3.1. *AB* is the axis and *B* is the center of a circle of 2½ in. diameter. Draw the top and front views of the circle. Scale: full size.

10.3.2. *LM* is the axis and *L* is the center of a 6-in.-diameter circle. Draw the top and front views of the circle. Scale: ⅜ size.

10.3.3. *AB* is the major diameter of the elliptical top view of a circle. The major diameter of the elliptical front view of the

circle lies along line *ST*. Draw the top and front views of the circle.

10.3.4. *P* is a point on the circumference of a circle whose axis is *AB*. Draw the top and front views of the circle.

10.3.5. *A, B,* and *C* are points on the circumference of a circle. Draw the top and front views of the circle and its axis.

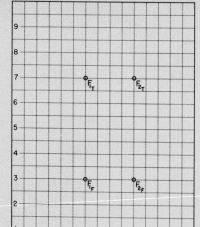

PROB. 10.4.1.

GROUP 4.   THE ELLIPSE (A VARIETY OF PROBLEMS)

10.4.1. F_1 and F_2 are the foci of an ellipse whose major diameter is 4 in. long. The plane of the ellipse makes a 30° angle with the frontal plane. Scale: ¾ size. Draw the top and front views of the ellipse.

10.4.2. Draw the top, front, and normal views of the conic section cut from the cone V by the plane whose edge view is CD.

10.4.3. RS is the center line of a 1½-in.-diameter drill which passes through the plane $ABCD$. Using conjugate diameters, draw the top and front views of the hole in the plane. Scale: ¾ size.

10.4.4. A concrete arch bridge is to span a river. The top and front views of the bridge piers are shown. The bridge arch is to be a semiellipse with a major diameter AB. A point on the arch 12 ft from the edge of the pier is to be 25 ft above the base of the pier. Draw the top and front views of the arch. What is the maximum distance vertically between the arch and the base of the pier? Scale: ⅛″ = 1′-0″.

10.4.5. Line PQ is tangent to an ellipse whose diameters are AB and CD. P is on the curve and directly above the right-hand focus. Draw the front view of line PQ.

10.4.6. V is the vertex of an oblique cone. Its circular base is 3½ in. in diameter, is centered at B, and lies in the plane ABC. Draw the top and front views of the cone, showing visibility. The base ends of the contour elements are to be located by a precise method. Scale: ½ size.

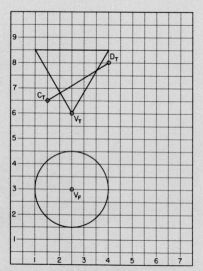

PROB. 10.4.2.

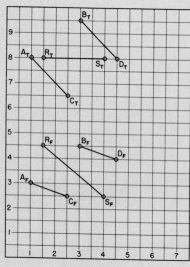

PROB. 10.4.3.

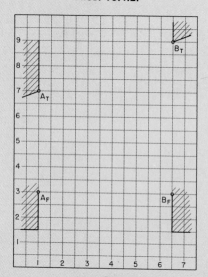

PROB. 10.4.4.

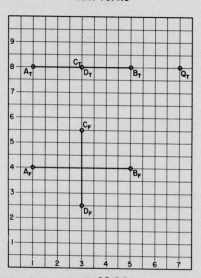

PROB. 10.4.5.

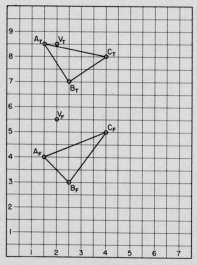

PROB. 10.4.6.

10.4.7. Points A, A', and C are points on a semiellipse. Point B is one end of the minor diameter which is 2½ in. long. Draw the top and front views of the ellipse. Scale: full size.

GROUP 5. THE PARABOLA (A VARIETY OF PROBLEMS)

10.5.1. XY is the directrix and F is the focus of a frontal parabola. Draw the front view of the parabola as far as the line CD.

10.5.2. Draw the top, front, and normal views of the parabola cut from the cone V by the plane that contains the line AB.

10.5.3. One of the cables of a suspension bridge is anchored to its towers at A and B. The loaded cable closely assumes the shape of a parabola with its focus at F. Determine the sag at the center measured with respect to the chord AB. Scale: $1'' = 50'$. Optional: Draw the curve.

10.5.4. GH is the tube of a 105-mm howitzer which is firing at a target on the mountain side represented by the plane TUV. The highest point on the parabolic trajectory of the shell is at X. Find the map and elevation views of the point of impact of the shell. Neglect air resistance.

10.5.5. The superstructure of the Rio Blanco bridge near Vera Cruz, Mexico, consists essentially of two arches leaning against each other in a manner similar to that shown in the pictorial sketch. In this problem, the arches are parabolic and are in contact at their vertices. The vertex and two other points on one of the arches are shown orthographically at V, A, and B. Draw the plan view of the arch.

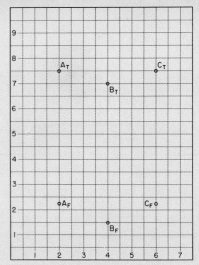

PROB. 10.4.7.

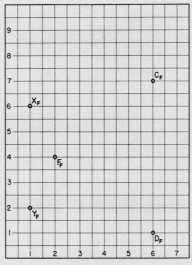

PROB. 10.5.1.

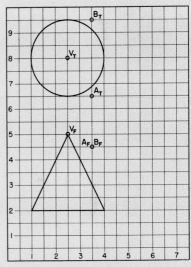

PROB. 10.5.2.

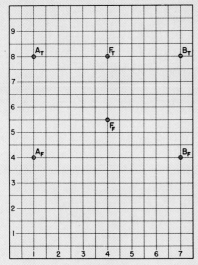

PROB. 10.5.3.

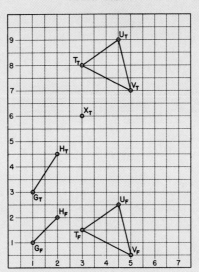

PROB. 10.5.4.

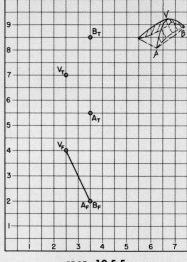

PROB. 10.5.5.

GROUP. 6. THE HYPERBOLA (A VARIETY OF PROBLEMS)

10.6.1. Given the foci F_1 and F_2 and the vertices V_1 and V_2 of a frontal hyperbola, draw the front view of both branches, extending them to the limiting lines L_1 and L_2.

10.6.2. F_1 and F_2 are the foci of the normal view of a hyperbola. P is a point on one of its branches. Draw the normal view of both branches of the hyperbola. Extend the view to the limits of the graph field.

10.6.3. Draw the top and normal views of both branches of the hyperbola which is cut from the cone V by the plane whose edge view appears as line ST.

10.6.4. M is the map location of a 4.2-in. mortar whose maximum range is approximately 2,500 yards. Friendly listening posts are located at A, B, and C. Reports from enemy mortars located generally to the north have been detected by the listening posts. There is a difference of 1.09 sec between the time when a given report is heard at A and the time when the same report is heard at B. The corresponding difference for posts B and C is 3.82 sec. The speed of sound under the conditions of this problem is 1,100 ft per sec. All points involved in this problem are at the same elevation. Scale: $1'' = 1,000$ yards. Locate all the enemy positions which are in range of the weapon at M. (*Hint.* The listening posts may be regarded as the foci of hyperbolas which pass through the enemy positions.)

GROUP 7. DOUBLE-CURVED LINES (refer to Chap. 3)

10.7.1. Draw one turn of a right-hand cylindrical helix having a cylinder diameter of 3 in. and a lead of 4 in. Scale: full size.

10.7.2. Draw one turn of a left-hand cylindrical helix having a cylinder diameter of 4 in. and a lead of 3 in. Locate a point on the helix 270° from point of beginning.

10.7.3. Draw one turn of a left-hand conical helix. The cone base is 3 in. in diameter, the altitude 4 in. The lead is 3 in., starting at the cone base.

10.7.4. Draw one turn of a right-hand conical helix starting at the apex of a cone whose elements make an angle of 40° with the axis. The lead is 3 in.

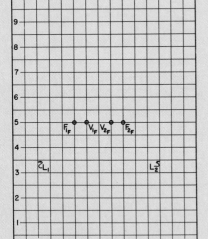

PROB. 10.6.1.

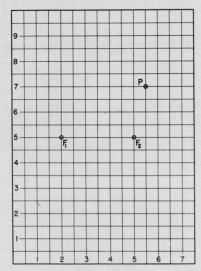

PROB. 10.6.2.

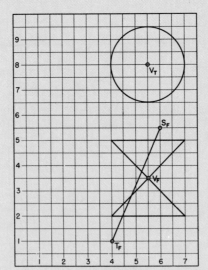

PROB. 10.6.3.

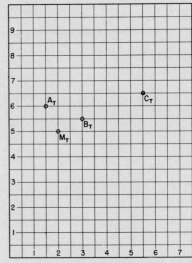

PROB. 10.6.4.

GROUP 8. THE INVOLUTE (refer to Chap. 3)

10.8.1. Draw one complete turn of the involute of the circle about *C*. Start at point *P* and proceed counterclockwise. Use at least 16 points.

10.8.2. *P* is a point on the involute of circle *A*. The involute unwinds clockwise. Draw the curve from its origin to the limit of the graph field.

10.8.3. *A* and *B* are the centers of two 20° involute spur gears. The direction of rotation of the driving gear *B* is indicated. Their pitch circles are tangent at the pitch point *P*. The profile of the gear teeth is an involute of the base circle. The base circles of both gears are tangent to the line of action. The tooth profile between the base and root circles is a radial line. Draw the contacting profiles of the two teeth which are touching (one profile on each gear). These profiles both pass through point *P*. Scale: full size.

GROUP 9. THE CYCLOID (refer to Chap. 3)

10.9.1. Draw one lobe of the cycloid generated by point *A* on circle *C* as the circle rolls along line *AB*. The origin of the curve is at *A*.

10.9.2. *ABCD* is a chute, of cycloidal profile, which is designed so as to permit objects to slide or roll from elevation *AB* to elevation *LM* in the shortest possible time. The chute terminates at its tangent line in the horizontal plane through *LM*. Complete the top and front views of the chute.

10.9.3. The arrangement and critical dimensions of the cycloidal impellers of a blower are shown in the design sketch. Draw the front view of the entire upper half of the left-hand impeller. Scale: ¼ size.

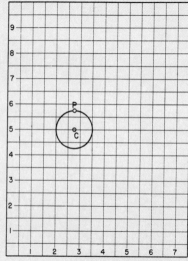

PROB. 10.8.1.

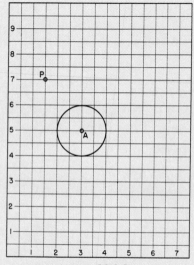

PROB. 10.8.2.

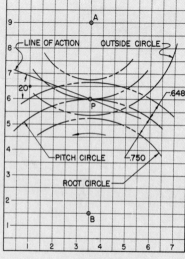

PROB. 10.8.3.

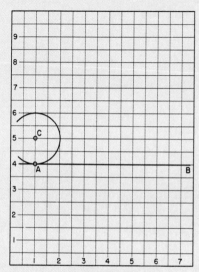

PROB. 10.9.1.

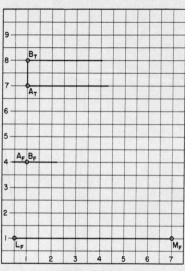

PROB. 10.9.2.

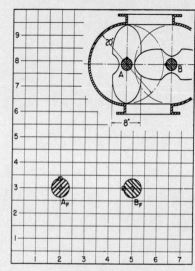

PROB. 10.9.3.

GROUP 10.   THE HELIX (refer to Chap. 3)

10.10.1. Draw the front view of the helix which lies on the cylinder about axis *AB*. The lead is 4 in. and the curve rises counterclockwise from point *P*. The upper end of the helix is at elevation *A*. Scale: full size.

10.10.2. The tangent of the helix angle of the helix on the cylinder about axis *CD* is 0.4. The helix starts at point *P* and rises clockwise. The upper end of the helix is at elevation *C*. Draw the front view of the helix.

10.10.3. *P*, *Q*, and *R* are points on the helix that rises counterclockwise around the cylinder whose axis is *LM*. Find the front view of point *R*.

10.10.4. *RT* is the axis of a right-hand double-flight helicoidal screw conveyer whose pitch is 12 in. *P* is a point on the outer edge of one of the flights. Draw the top view of the outer edge of each flight through the axial distance *RT*. Scale: ⅛ size.

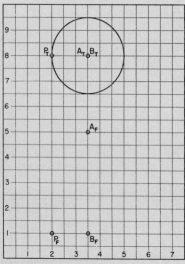

PROB. 10.10.1.

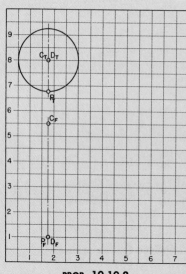

PROB. 10.10.2.

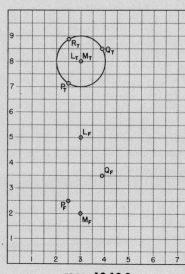

PROB. 10.10.3.

10.10.5. *AB* is the axis and the free height of a compression coil spring of five complete turns. The helix *angle,* when the spring is fully compressed, is two-thirds of the helix *angle* at free height. The bottom of the spring is fixed at elevation *B*. Find the elevation of the top of the spring when the spring is fully compressed.

10.10.6. *AB* is the axis of two concentric cylinders. On the smaller cylinder, there is a helix which rises clockwise from *P* and has a lead of 2 in. *PT* is a line which moves continually tangent to the helix on the smaller cylinder. Draw the front view of one turn of the helix traced on the larger cylinder by point *T*. Scale: full size.

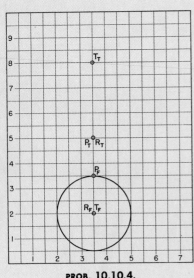

PROB. 10.10.4.

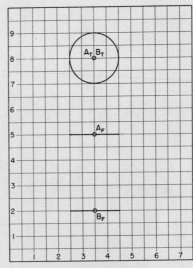

PROB. 10.10.5.

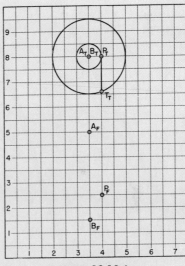

PROB. 10.10.6.

The study of straight lines and planes further extends the application of auxiliary views to the solution of space problems. Typical determinations: line and plane relationships, parallelism, perpendicularity, angularity, shortest distance, and specified relationships.

Lines and Planes in Space

11

11.1. In the previous chapter, the importance of straight lines as they occur in a variety of engineering problems has been discussed, and the diversity of their relationships has been explained. Straight lines occur often in machines, structures, etc., but probably they will more often be found *in combination with planes*. Consequently the study of straight lines and planes is a continuing investigation of line relationships as they occur with planes and with lines and points in planes. Also discussed here are the relationships of planes to other planes. It is interesting to note that, in the solution of *plane* problems, *lines* are used to establish one plane relative to another. Thus this chapter brings together the elements of engineering geometry, exclusive of curved lines and surfaces, which are treated in the chapters following.

Geometric plane figures and solids occur frequently in engineering work. Illustrations of various forms are given in Fig. 3.101. The most common are prisms and pyramids.

A *prism* is a polyhedron whose bases or ends are equal parallel polygons and whose lateral faces are parallelograms. A right prism is one whose lateral faces are rectangles; all others are called oblique prisms. The axis of a prism is a straight line connecting the centers of the bases. A truncated prism is that portion of a prism lying between one of its bases and a plane which cuts all its lateral edges.

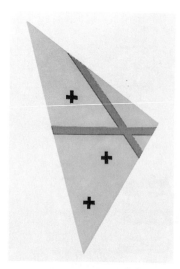

Points and lines in a plane

A *pyramid* is a polyhedron whose base is a polygonal plane and whose other surfaces are triangular planes meeting at a point called the vertex. The axis is a line passing through the vertex and the mid-point of the base. The altitude is a perpendicular from the vertex to the base. A pyramid is *right* if the altitude coincides with the axis; it is *oblique* if they do not coincide. A *truncated pyramid* is that portion of a pyramid lying be-tween the base and a cutting plane which cuts all the lateral edges. The *frustum* of a pyramid is that portion of a pyramid lying between the base and a cutting plane parallel to the base which cuts all the lateral edges.

11.2.   POINTS AND LINES IN A PLANE.   A point may be established in a plane by locating any convenient line in the plane which passes through the point.

In Fig. 11.1, the top view of P is initially given as a point in plane ABC. To locate the front and right-side views of point P, a line lying in the plane of ABC is drawn through the point. This line intersects AB at D and BC at point E. Both D and E are projected to the front view on AB and BC, respectively. This locates the front view of DE, a line of ABC. Point P is now projected to the front view of line DE. Point P is estab-lished in the right-side view by first pro-jecting DE to the right-side view and then projecting P from the front view to the right-side view of DE.

Summary

To locate a line in a plane, locate the points where the line intersects the boundaries of the plane. Project these points to all views.

To locate a point in a plane, draw a line of the plane through the point, project the line to all views, and project the point to all views of the line.

11.3.   HORIZONTAL, FRONTAL, AND PROFILE LINES OF A SKEW PLANE.   Any horizontal line in a skew plane either lies in, or is parallel to, some horizontal plane. To establish a horizontal line in a skew plane, the line is first drawn in a view where the horizontal plane appears as an edge,

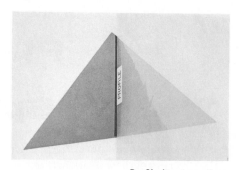

Profile line in a plane

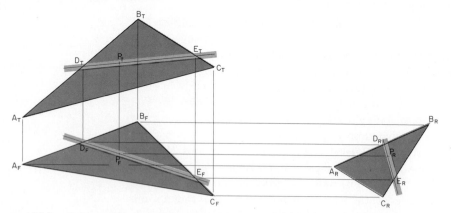

FIG. 11.1.   Points and lines in a plane. Any point in a plane lies on some line of the plane, and, conversely, any line of a plane contains many points in the plane.

such as the front, side, or any auxiliary view projected from the top view. Similarly, a frontal line is first established in a view where the frontal plane appears as an edge, such as the top, side, or auxiliary view projected from the front view. Likewise, a profile line must first be established in either the top, front, or auxiliary view projected from a side view, where a profile plane appears as an edge. All horizontal lines *in a given plane* (other than horizontal) are parallel. Similarly, all frontal lines (in a plane other than frontal) are parallel and all profile lines (in a plane other than profile) are parallel.

Figure 11.2*A* shows the top and front views of a skew plane *ABC*. To establish the horizontal line *BD* in *ABC*, the front view is drawn first. The top view of *BD* is located by projecting *D* to the top view on *AC*. Then *BD* is horizontal and is shown in true length in the top view.

Figure 11.2*B* shows the same plane *ABC*. To establish the frontal line *AE* in the plane *ABC*, the top view is drawn through *A*, intersecting *BC* at *E*. The front view of *AE* is established by projecting *E*, which is on *BC*, to the front view. The line *AE* is in true length in the front view.

In Fig. 11.2*C*, the top, front, and right-side views of the same plane *ABC* are shown. To establish the profile line *CF* in *ABC*, either the front or the top view is first drawn through point *C*, in-

Horizontal line in a plane

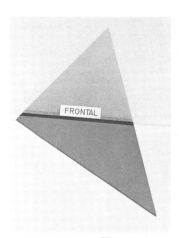

Frontal line in a plane

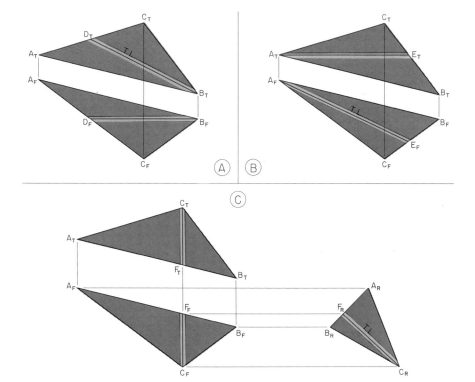

FIG. 11.2. (*A*) A horizontal line *BD* in a plane. (*B*) A frontal line *AE* in a plane. (*C*) A profile line *CF* in a plane.

tersecting *AB* at *F*. The right-side view of *CF* is drawn by projecting the front view of *F*, which is on *AB*, to the right-side view. The right-side view shows the profile line *CF* in true length.

Summary

To locate a horizontal line in a plane, draw the line in horizontal position in the front view and then project to the other views.

To locate a frontal line in a plane, draw the line in frontal position in the top view and then project to the other views.

To locate a profile line in a plane, draw the line in profile position in top and front views and then project to the side view.

Line parallel to a plane and plane parallel to a line

11.4. PARALLEL RELATIONSHIPS OF LINES AND PLANES. *A Line Parallel to a Plane.*

A line is parallel to a plane if it is parallel to *any line* of that plane. Parallelism between a line and a plane can be easily recognized in a view that shows the plane as an edge because, in this view, *all* lines in the plane appear coincident. However, only *one* line of the plane is needed. Figure 11.3*A* shows the necessary construction to draw *DE* parallel to *ABC*. The top and front views of *ABC*, the top view *DE*, and the front view of point *D* are initially given. The top view of *CF* is established in *ABC*, parallel to *DE*. The intersection *F* on *AB* is projected to the front view. *CF* is drawn in the front view. Through the front view of point *D*, *DE* is drawn parallel to *CF*, establishing *DE* parallel to *ABC*.

Summary

To locate a line parallel to a plane:

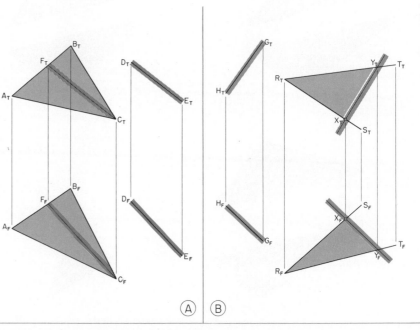

FIG. 11.3.   (*A*) A line parallel to a plane. (*B*) A plane parallel to a line.

1. Draw a line on the plane parallel to a given view of the line to be located parallel to the plane.

2. Draw the line (to be located) parallel to the line of the plane in all other views.

A Plane Parallel to a Line. Figure 11.3*B* shows the construction of a plane *RST* that is parallel to *HG*. The top and front views of *HG* and *RS* and the top view of *RT* are given. Through any point on *RS* (in this example, point *X*), the top and front views of a line are drawn parallel to *HG*. This construction constitutes a plane parallel to *HG*, formed by two intersecting lines: (1) *RS* and (2) the line through *X* parallel to *HG*. Point *Y* in the top view is at the intersection of *RT* and the line through *X*. Point *Y* is projected to the front view on the line through *X*. Then the front view of *RT* may be drawn through point *Y*. Note that plane *RST* now contains a line *XY*, which is parallel to *HG*.

Summary

1. Draw a line on the plane, parallel to the given views of the line to which the plane is to be parallel.

2. Use this line of the plane to project to the other views and determine the plane.

Similarly, a plane may be established parallel to any two skew lines. For example, having any two skew lines *AB* and *RS* given, two intersecting lines are drawn in the plane, one parallel to *AB* and the other parallel to *RS*. Actually, this is what has been done in Fig. 15.3*B*, but in this case the plane is coincident with one of the skew lines. If the plane is separated from both of the skew lines, Fig. 11.4 will illustrate the procedure. *AB* and *PQ* are the given skew lines,

and point *Y* is a point in a plane which is to be made parallel to *AB* and *PQ*. From point *Y*, a line *YX* is drawn parallel (in both views, top and front) to *PQ*; also, *YZ* is drawn parallel to *AB*, thus establishing a plane *YZX* parallel to *AB* and *PQ* because the plane contains a line parallel to each of the given lines.

Summary

1. Draw, through a given point of the plane, a line parallel to line *A*, to which the plane is to be parallel.

2. Draw, through the same given point of the plane, a line parallel to line *B*, to which the plane is to be parallel.

3. The two lines so drawn, parallel to lines *A* and *B*, determine a plane parallel to *A* and *B*.

The requirement of a plane parallel to two skew lines might also include a determination of the distance from the plane to the skew lines. When this re-

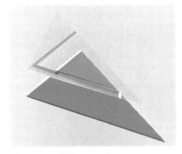

Plane parallel to a plane

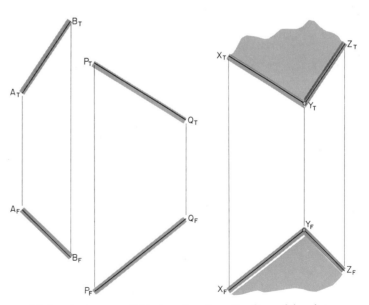

FIG. 11.4. A plane parallel to two skew lines. Two lines of the plane are drawn parallel repectively to the two skew lines.

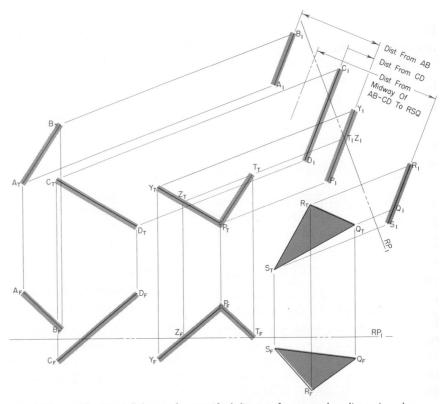

FIG. 11.5. A plane parallel to and a specified distance from two skew lines. An edge view of a parallel plane is used to determine the distance.

quirement exists, Fig. 11.5 illustrates the method employed. *AB* and *CD* are skew lines. A plane through *P* is to be drawn parallel to *AB* and *CD* and the distance from the plane to the lines determined. Drawing *PY* parallel to *CD* and *PT* parallel to *AB* determines a plane *PTY* parallel to *AB* and *CD* and through point *P*. The lines *PT* and *PY* may be made any convenient length. Then if an edge view of *PTY* is made (in this case, by making an auxiliary projected from the top view and in the direction of *TZ*, a line of *PTY*) and if *AB* and *CD* are projected to this auxiliary view, *AB*, *CD*, and *PTY* will be parallel to each other, and the distances from the lines to the plane are measured as shown on the figure.

Summary

1. Draw the plane parallel to the given skew lines as described in the previous paragraph.

2. Draw the edge view of one of the planes. Carry the second plane into this view. Being parallel, *both* planes appear as edges, and the distance between them can be measured.

It follows now that it is possible to locate a plane parallel to a pair of skew lines and at a certain distance *from* the skew lines. Again, Fig. 11.5 will illustrate. *AB* and *CD* are given skew lines. The *top* view of *RSQ* is given. The problem is to locate *RSQ* so that it is a specified distance from a position *midway* between lines *AB* and *CD* and *lower* than *AB* and *CD*. Any plane (in this case, *PTY*) is drawn, as before, parallel to the two skew lines; also, the edge view is made of *PTY* with accompanying lines *AB* and *CD* as before. The position midway between *AB* and *CD* can now be located in the auxiliary view and the required distance to *RSQ* measured. Projection from the top view of *RSQ* to the line established for the edge view now locates $R_1S_1Q_1$, making it possible then to measure $R_1S_1Q_1$ distances from the reference plane and to transfer these distances to the front view, completing the solution.

In the next paragraph, the construction of a plane *parallel to a* plane is discussed, but it is interesting to note in Figs. 11.4 and 11.5 that if the skew lines were *intersecting* lines, they would constitute a plane; then the problems of Figs. 11.4 and 11.5 would be changed to the problem of a plane parallel to a plane.

Summary

1. Draw *any* plane parallel to the given skew lines.
2. Draw the edge view of this plane, and carry the skew lines into the view. Any distance of a parallel plane *from* the skew lines can now be located. Draw the *edge view* of the required plane.
3. Project from a given view to the edge view of the required plane and complete the views.

Parallel Planes. Two intersecting lines that are parallel to any two lines of a given plane will define a plane parallel

to the given plane. In Fig. 11.6, the plane *XYZ* has been constructed parallel to *ABC* by drawing, through point *X*, lines *XY* and *XZ* parallel to, respectively, *AC* and *AB*. In this example, the top and front views of *X* were known, and so the distance between planes *ABC* and *XYZ* was fixed. However, if the problem requires that the parallel plane be located at a specified distance from *ABC* or, in this example, if the distance between the planes is required, the auxiliary view shown may be employed to obtain the solution. If the planes are parallel, the edge views will be parallel, and the true distance between the planes may be measured in the edge view of both.

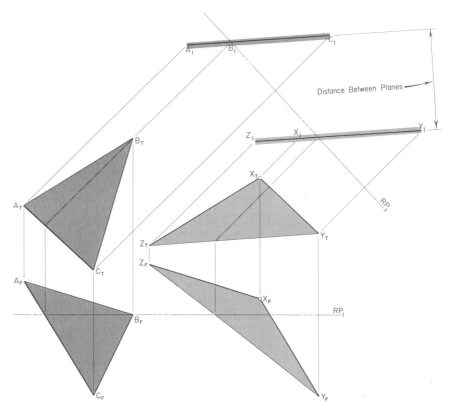

FIG. 11.6. Parallel planes. To set up one plane parallel to the other, in an edge view the required plane is made parallel to the given plane.

Line perpendicular to a plane and plane perpendicular to a line

Summary

1. To locate a plane parallel to another plane, draw any two intersecting lines that are parallel to any two lines of the given plane. These two lines determine a plane parallel to the given plane.

2. If the distance between the planes is required, draw the edge view of one plane, and carry the other plane into this view. *Both* planes must appear as edges because they are parallel, and the distance between the planes can now be measured.

Parallel Planes a Specified Distance Apart. If the requirement is that two planes be made parallel and a specified distance apart, Fig. 15.6 will also illustrate the solution. In this case, the top and front views of plane *ABC* and the top view of *XYZ* are given.

First, an auxiliary view $A_1B_1C_1$, giving the edge view of *ABC*, is drawn as in the figure. Second, the edge view of the second plane (in this case, *XYZ*) may now be drawn at the required distance from plane *ABC*. Third, projection from the given top view of *XYZ* will now establish $X_1Y_1Z_1$. Fourth, measurements from the reference plane in the auxiliary view for *X*, *Y*, and *Z* and projection from the top view of *X*, *Y*, and *Z* will determine the front view of *XYZ*. If the front view of *XYZ*—instead of the top view—had been given, measurements from the reference plane in the front view would establish $X_1Y_1Z_1$ on the edge view; then projection from the auxiliary and front views would finish the solution by locating the top view at the intersection of projectors from auxiliary and front views.

Summary

1. Draw the edge view of the given plane.

2. Establish the distance from the given plane, and draw the edge view of the required plane.

3. Project to the edge view of the required plane (from a given view) and complete the views.

11.5.   A LINE PERPENDICULAR TO A PLANE. A line perpendicular to a plane is perpendicular to every line in that plane.

A line drawn perpendicular to a single line of a given plane would not necessarily be perpendicular to that plane because the line could rotate about the single line of the plane; but if a line is drawn *perpendicular to two nonparallel lines* of a plane, then the perpendicular direction of that line with respect to the plane is established.

Figure 11.7 shows *MN* established through point *N* perpendicular to plane *ABC*, using the principles of perpendic-

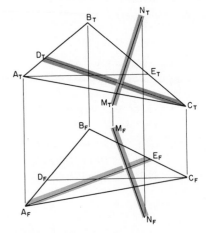

FIG. 11.7.   A line perpendicular to a plane, made perpendicular to true-length lines of the plane.

ular-line relationships discussed in paragraph 9.6. The horizontal line CD is established in plane ABC and is in true length in the top view. The top view of MN, through N, is drawn perpendicular to CD. The top view of M is arbitrarily located on the line for the purposes of this illustration. A frontal line AE is drawn in the top view, and its direction and true length are then shown in the front view. The front view of MN is drawn perpendicular to AE. The top view of M is projected to the front view. Thus line MN has been established perpendicular to ABC by drawing it perpendicular to lines CD and AE, two nonparallel lines of plane ABC.

Problems dealing with skew planes frequently involve true lengths of lines in the plane. Become observant, and notice any lines that may already exist in true length in any given view of a plane. Also, become competent in placing horizontal, frontal, or profile lines in a skew plane. This is a convenient way of establishing lines in true length

in any principal view of a plane to be used in establishing the relationship of other lines to the plane.

Summary

To establish a line perpendicular to a plane:

1. Draw the top view of the line perpendicular to a horizontal line of the plane.

2. Draw the front view of the line perpendicular to a frontal line of the plane.

3. (Sometimes required.) Draw the side view of the line perpendicular to a profile line of the plane.

11.6. DISTANCE FROM A POINT TO A PLANE. The distance from a point to a plane is construed as the shortest distance that can be measured between the point and the plane; this measurement will lie on a perpendicular dropped from the point to the plane.

In Fig. 11.8, the shortest distance from point N to the plane ABC has be-

Shortest distance, point to plane

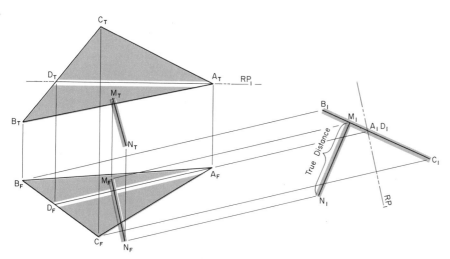

FIG. 11.8. Shortest distance from a point to a plane. This is the length of the line drawn from the point perpendicular to the plane.

termined. An edge view of the plane is first drawn as shown in the auxiliary view projected from the front view. Point N is located in this view. A line drawn from point N perpendicular to the plane, intersecting the plane at M, is now drawn. In this auxiliary view MN is in true length, and the true length of MN is the distance from N to the plane. As explained in paragraph 15.5, a line perpendicular to a plane is perpendicular to *all* lines of the plane and will appear at 90° to any true-length line of the plane.

Thus the direction of MN is established in the front view perpendicular to AD, a frontal line of the plane. The front view of M is located by projection. Similarly, the top view of MN may be drawn by establishing the direction perpendicular to a horizontal line of the plane. However, in this case MN in the top view has been located by projection from the front view and the measurement from the auxiliary. Note also that, because MN is in true length in the auxiliary view, the direction of MN in the front view must be perpendicular to the rays of projection connecting front and auxiliary views.

A further statement can be made with reference to the graphics shown in the auxiliary view: If *a line is perpendicular to a plane,* it will appear in true length in any view where the plane appears as an edge and will appear at 90° to the edge view.

Summary

1. Draw the edge view of the plane, and carry the specified point to this view.

2. Draw the perpendicular to the plane, and measure the distance from the point to the plane.

3. If the views are to be completed, project back from the edge view where

(a) the front view of the perpendicular will be perpendicular to a frontal line of the plane, and (b) the top view of the perpendicular will be perpendicular to a horizontal line of the plane.

11.7. A PLANE PERPENDICULAR TO A LINE. A plane perpendicular to a given line can be established by drawing two intersecting lines perpendicular to the given line. This can most readily be accomplished by using lines that appear in true length in one of the views. Therefore, if front and top views are to be drawn, a horizontal and a frontal line will be employed. The problem of Fig. 11.9 will illustrate the procedure. A plane, containing point A, perpendicular to the given line MN is to be drawn. AC, a horizontal line, is in true length in the top view and is therefore drawn perpendicular to MN. Frontal line AB is in true length in the front view and is

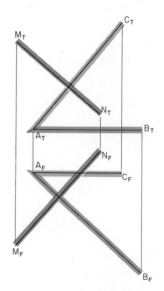

FIG. 11.9. A plane perpendicular to a line. The plane is determined by drawing two true-length lines perpendicular to the given line.

therefore drawn perpendicular to *MN*. Then *AC* and *AB* are two intersecting lines which form a plane perpendicular to *MN*. Since this construction conversely satisfies the conditions for perpendicularity given in paragraph 11.5, the plane *ABC* has been established perpendicular to line *MN*.

Summary

1. From the top view of a specified point of the plane, draw a horizontal line perpendicular to the given line. Complete, by drawing the front view of the horizontal line.

2. From the front view of the same specified point of the plane, draw a frontal line perpendicular to the given line. Complete, by drawing the top view of the frontal line.

3. The two intersecting lines thus drawn constitute a plane perpendicular to the given line.

11.8.   A PLANE PERPENDICULAR TO A PLANE.

A plane containing *one line perpendicular to a given plane* will be perpendicular to the given plane. In Fig. 11.10, *XYZ* is to be drawn perpendicular to the given plane *ABC*. The top and front views of *ABC*, the front view of *XYZ*, and the top view of *XY* are initially known. Through any point in plane *XYZ*, such as *P,* a *line* is drawn *perpendicular* to *ABC*, as outlined in paragraph 11.5 on drawing a line perpendicular to a plane. Thus $P_F Q_F$ is drawn perpendicular to the frontal line of *ABC,* and the top view of the line through *P* is drawn perpendicular to the horizontal line of *ABC*. At this stage of construction, the top and front views of a plane have been established, defined by two intersecting lines —*XY* and the line through *P*; this plane is perpendicular to *ABC* since the line through *P* is perpendicular to *ABC*. The top view of *Z* is located according to the

Plane perpendicular to a plane

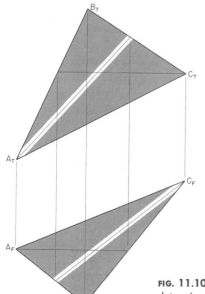
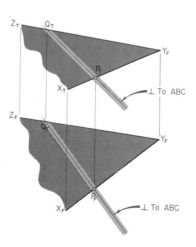

FIG. 11.10.   A plane perpendicular to a plane. The determined plane must contain one line that is perpendicular to the given plane.

principles of paragraph 11.2, by first projecting Q_F to Q_T on the line through point P_T.

Summary

For a line that is perpendicular to the given plane and lying in the required plane:

1. Draw the front view of the line perpendicular to a frontal line of the given plane.

2. Draw the top view of the line perpendicular to a horizontal line of the given plane.

3. Establish the line in the required plane by intersections on a given view. Then complete the second view by projection.

11.9.   THREE MUTUALLY PERPENDICULAR PLANES.   Two of three mutually perpendicular planes can be drawn perpendicular to each other by the construction given in paragraph 11.8. Then a third

perpendicular plane may be found by establishing two intersecting lines through any point of the third plane, each perpendicular to one of the other two planes. In Fig 11.11, a plane containing the given line DE and the front view of point F is drawn perpendicular to the given plane ABC. A line EZ perpendicular to ABC through point E establishes this plane perpendicular to ABC by the principles of paragraph 11.5. The front view of point Z is arbitrarily selected and located in the top view of this plane according to the principles of paragraph 11.2. The top view of point F is similarly located by projecting the front view of F to the top view of DZ. Point G is a known point of a third plane. Through G a line GK, perpendicular to ABC, and another line GH, perpendicular to DEF, establish a plane perpendicular to ABC and DEF. Thus ABC, DEF, and GHK are three mutually perpendicular planes.

Three mutually perpendicular planes

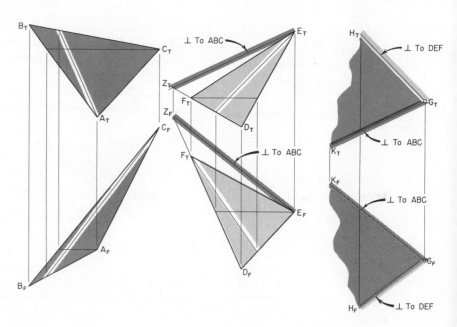

FIG. 11.11.   Three mutually perpendicular planes. Each plane must contain one line that is perpendicular to the other two planes.

Summary

1. Establish plane B perpendicular to plane A by the explanation of paragraph 15.8.

2. Establish plane C perpendicular to planes A and B. (a) Draw a line through a known point of plane C and perpendicular to plane A. The front view of this line is perpendicular to a frontal line of plane A, and the top view is perpendicular to a horizontal line of plane A. (b) Draw a line through the same known point of plane C and perpendicular to plane B. The top view of this line is perpendicular to a horizontal line of plane B and the front view is perpendicular to a frontal line of plane B.

11.10.   THE ANGLE BETWEEN A LINE AND A HORIZONTAL (H), FRONTAL (F), AND PROFILE (P) PLANE.   The true size of the angle between a line and a plane may be seen in any orthographic view which shows the line in true length and the plane as an edge.

The angle between a line and a plane is measured between the given line and the *plane trace* (intersection), on the given plane, formed by a plane passed through the given line and perpendicular to the given plane. The true size of the angle can be seen in an orthographic view which shows the normal view of the passed plane; the normal view of the passed plane will show the given line in true length and the given plane as an edge.

In Fig. 11.12, the true size of angle H—the angle that line AB makes with horizontal planes—is shown in the first auxiliary view projected from the top view. This view has been projected in a direction perpendicular to AB. Therefore, AB appears in true length, and the

horizontal reference plane shows as an edge. The second auxiliary view projected from the front view in a direction perpendicular to AB shows AB in true length and the frontal reference plane as an edge; therefore, the angle that AB makes with frontal planes (angle F) appears in true size. The third auxiliary view projected from the right-side view in a direction perpendicular to AB shows the true size of angle P, the angle that AB makes with the profile plane.

Summary

For the angle between a line and a horizontal plane, draw a normal view of the line, projected from the top view. The reference plane is horizontal. The true angle appears between the reference plane and line.

For the angle between a line and a frontal plane, draw a normal view of the line, projected from the front view.

Angle between a line and an H, F, or P plane and specified angle between an H, F, or P plane

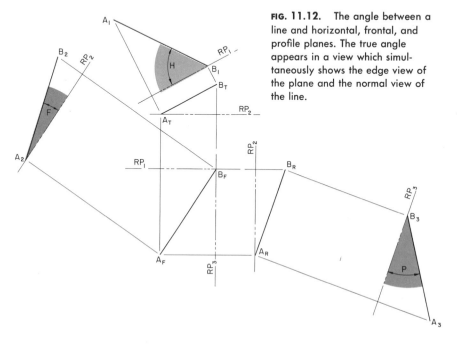

FIG. 11.12.   The angle between a line and horizontal, frontal, and profile planes. The true angle appears in a view which simultaneously shows the edge view of the plane and the normal view of the line.

The reference plane is frontal. The true angle appears between the reference plane and line.

For the angle between a line and a profile plane, draw a normal view of the line, projected from a side view. The reference plane is profile. The true angle appears between the reference plane and line.

11.11.   LINES MAKING GIVEN ANGLES WITH THE HORIZONTAL, FRONTAL, AND PROFILE PLANES.   *Cone Method.*   To draw a line through a given point at a specified angle with one of the principal planes of projection, the line may be established as an element of a right-circular cone (paragraphs 3.46 and 12.5) with the apex at the given point. The base of the

cone must be parallel to the principal plane, and the base angle of the cone equal to the specified angle. If the length of the line is specified, the element length (slant height) of the cone should be made equal to this length. If no other conditions of the problem are specified, then each element of the cone will satisfy the condition of the problem; the number of possible solutions will be infinite.

In Fig. 11.13*A*, *AB* is to be drawn making a specified angle *H* with the horizontal plane. The top-view direction of *AB*, the true length of *AB*, and the front view of *A* are known. A right-circular cone is established with the apex at *A*, a base angle equal to the specified angle *H*, and the element length equal to the true length of *AB*. Point *B* is then located on the base of the cone to satisfy

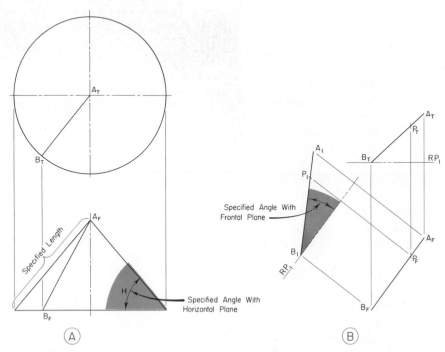

FIG. 11.13.   A line making a specified angle with one of the principal planes. (*A*) Cone method. (*B*) Auxiliary-view method.

the conditions of the problem and from there projected to the top view. In this example, *B* is below and to the left of *A*, but *B* might have been specified to be above *A*.

Summary

For a line making a specified angle with horizontal planes, draw a cone whose elements make the required angle with horizontal planes. Any specific element of this cone is the required line.

For a line making a specified angle with frontal planes, draw a cone whose elements make the required angle with frontal planes. Any specific element of this cone is the required line.

For a line making a specified angle with profile planes, draw a cone whose elements make the required angle with profile planes. Any specific element of this cone is the required line.

Auxiliary-view Method.   Figure 11.13*B* shows another solution of a similar problem, using an auxiliary view. The line direction in the front view is specified by $B_F P_F$, and B_T is given. An angle with frontal planes is also specified. An auxiliary view perpendicular to $A_F B_F$ will show the line in true length. Therefore, projectors from $B_F P_F$ are drawn, a reference plane assumed through *B* (in auxiliary and top views), and the specified angle with frontal planes laid out in the auxiliary view. Point P_1 then may be located on the true length of the required line in the auxiliary view. Point *P* may be located in the top view by projection from the front view and measurement from the auxiliary. Finally, the specified length of *AB* may be measured in the auxiliary view and projected to front and top views.

Note in both examples of Fig. 11.13 that a specified angle with a given plane must be laid out in a view showing the true length of the line and the edge view of the plane.

Summary

For a line making a specified angle with horizontal planes:

1. The top view and one point of the line must be specified.

2. Draw a view projected perpendicular to the top view of the line. In this view, the reference plane is horizontal. Draw the line at the required angle from the horizontal reference plane in this auxiliary view. Complete, by projection to other views.

For a line making a specified angle with frontal planes:

1. The front view and one point of the line must be specified.

2. Draw a view projected perpendicular to the front view of the line. In this view, the reference plane is frontal. Draw the line at the required angle from the reference plane in this auxiliary view. Complete, by projection to other views.

For a line making a specified angle with profile planes:

1. The side view and one point of the line must be specified.

2. Draw a view projected perpendicular to the side view of the line. In this view, the reference plane is profile. Draw the line at the required angle from the reference plane in this auxiliary view. Complete, by projection to other views.

A Line Making Specified Angles with Two Planes of Projection.   To draw a line through a given point, making specified angles with *two* of the principal planes, the line may be established as a common element (intersection) of two cones. The apexes of both cones are located at the given point, and their bases are constructed parallel to the respective principal planes. No intersection of the cones is possible unless the sum of the base angles ranges from 0 to 90° inclusive. To facilitate the determination of lines of intersection of the two cones, the element lengths (slant heights) must be made equal. In Fig. 11.14*A*, two right circular cones have been constructed with apexes at the center *C* of a sphere. The element lengths are equal to the radius of the sphere. The bases intersect because they are lines (curved) of a common surface. Lines drawn through the apexes and intersections of the bases are elements of both cones (the straight-line intersection of the cones).

Considering both nappes of each cone, we find the circular bases intersecting at eight different points. Drawing straight-line elements of the cones from the points of intersection on the bases through the apexes gives four straight lines of intersection. These four lines are all possible solutions of the problem. Further specifications must be added to limit the solution to one line.

In Fig. 11.14*B*, *OM* is to be established through the given point *O* making a specified angle *H* with the horizontal plane and an angle *F* with the frontal plane. *H* plus *F* is somewhere between 0 and 90°. The front view of a right circular cone with a horizontal base and apex at *O* is constructed with a base angle equal to *H*. *OV* is the true length (in the front view) of any element of this cone. The top view of another right circular cone with apex at *O* is constructed in the top view with the base angle equal to *F*. The element length of this cone is made equal in length to *OV*, the element length of the other cone, to ensure intersection of the bases. *M* is then located at one of the intersections of the two bases and is, in this case, in front and to the right of point *O*. The projection of point *M* to either view should pass through the intersection of the bases; this should be checked for each problem to verify that no mistakes have been made in construction of the cones.

Summary

1. Draw a cone (with apex at a given point) whose elements make the required angle with *one* of the planes of projection (horizontal, frontal, or profile).

2. Draw a cone (with apex at the same given point) whose elements are the same length as the elements of the

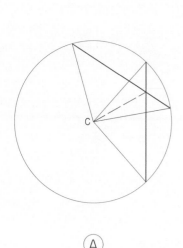

FIG. 11.14.   A line making specified angles with two of the principal planes. The line is determined by the intersection of two cones.

first cone and make the required angle with a second plane of projection.

3. The intersection of the bases of these cones and the apex determine the required line.

11.12.   ANGLE BETWEEN A LINE AND A SKEW PLANE: EDGE-VIEW METHOD.   As explained in paragraph 11.10, the true angle between a line and a plane will be observed when the edge view of the plane and the true length of the line are obtained in the same view. A convenient method of accomplishing this is to make an edge view of the plane and project the line along with the plane; then, by placing the line on the surface of a cone, the line may be rotated, *without changing*

the relationship of line and plane, until the line shows in true length. Then the true length of the line and the edge view of the plane will show the true angle between the two.

Figure 11.15 is an illustration using this edge-view and cone method for finding the angle between line *DE* and the plane *ABC*. An auxiliary view that shows the edge view of *ABC* is established, and *DE* is projected to this view. A right circular cone using *DE* as an element is constructed with the apex at *D*; then *E* is a point on the circular base. The base is drawn parallel to *ABC*. The limiting element of this cone is determined as the true length of *DE*, obtained by rotation as shown. The true size of

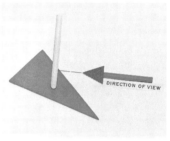

Angle between a line and a plane (edge-view method)

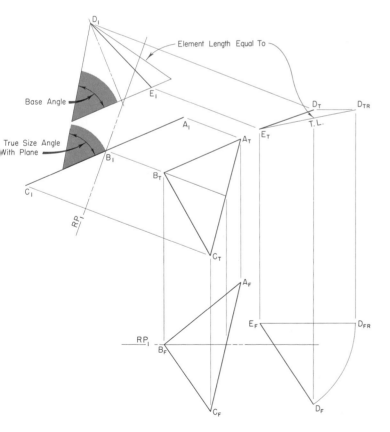

FIG. 11.15.   The angle between a line and a skew plane (edge-view method). The true angle appears in a view showing the edge view of the plane and the normal view (by rotation) of the line.

Angle between a line and a plane
(complementary-angle method)

the base angle is shown between the limiting element and the base. All elements of a right circular cone make the same angle with the base of the cone. Since the base of the cone is parallel to *ABC*, *DE* makes an angle with *ABC* equal in size to the base angle. The cone can be constructed using point *D* or point *E* as the apex and the other point as a point on the base. The base of the cone *must* be constructed parallel to the given skew plane.

Summary

1. Draw a view giving the edge view of the plane, and project the line to this view.

2. Determine the true length of the line.

3. Using one end of the line as apex, set up a cone with element length equal to the line length and base parallel to the edge view of the plane.

4. The angle between line and plane is the base angle of the cone.

11.13. ANGLE BETWEEN A LINE AND A SKEW PLANE: COMPLEMENTARY-ANGLE METHOD. Another method (as contrasted with the method of paragraph 11.12) of finding the angle between a line and a plane is to select some point on the line and draw from it a perpendicular to the plane; the angle between the line and the perpendicular will be the complement of the angle between the line and plane.

Figure 11.16 shows the above method for finding the true size of angle *Y* between line *NO* and the given skew plane. From point *O* a line is drawn perpendicular to the plane *ABC*, using the principles given in paragraph 11.5. The included angle formed by the perpendicular and *NO* is the complement of the required angle. A normal view of this angle is now required. A horizontal line drawn through the front view of *N* intersects the perpendicular at *M*, forming the plane *MNO*. An edge view of this plane is shown in the first auxiliary

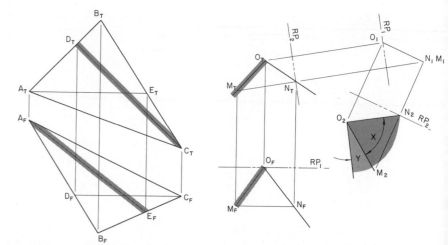

FIG. 11.16. The angle between a line and a skew plane (complementary-angle method). From a point on the line, a perpendicular is drawn to the plane. The angle between the given line and plane is the complement of the angle between the given line and the perpendicular.

view, projected from the top view. A normal view of *MNO* is established in the second auxiliary view by projecting perpendicular to the edge view of *MNO*. Angle *X*, the complement of the required angle, is shown in true size in the second auxiliary view. Angle *X* is subtracted graphically from 90°, leaving as the remainder angle *Y*, the angle that *ON* makes with the plane *ABC*.

Summary

1. From one end of the line, draw a line perpendicular to the plane.
2. Select a point on the perpendicular, and consider the given line and perpendicular as a plane. Draw the edge and normal views of this plane.
3. The angle between the given line and plane is the complement of the angle between the given line and the perpendicular.

11.14.   THE ANGLE BETWEEN PLANES.   *Intersection Given.*   The angle between two planes is measured in a plane perpendicular to both planes. Therefore, if the line of intersection between the two planes is given, a normal view of the angle between the two planes can be seen in that view where the line of intersection shows as a point. Figure 11.17 shows the construction necessary to determine the true size of the angle between planes *ABC* and *ABD*. A view of the two planes with the line of intersection *AB* showing in true length is drawn as shown in the first auxiliary view. A second auxiliary view which shows the end view of *AB* and each plane as an edge is established. The true size of the angle is measured in this view.

Summary

1. Draw the normal view of the line

Angle between planes (intersection given)

Angle between planes (complementary-angle method)

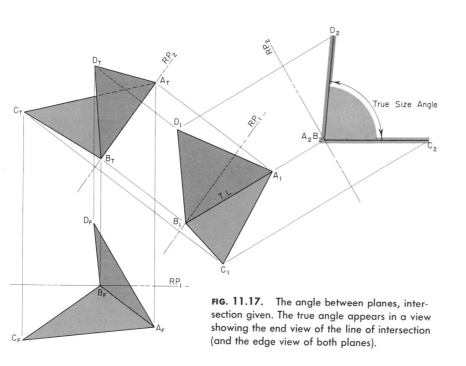

FIG. 11.17.   The angle between planes, intersection given. The true angle appears in a view showing the end view of the line of intersection (and the edge view of both planes).

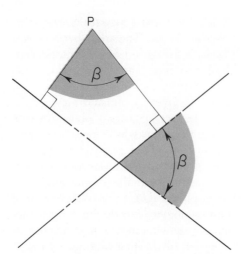

FIG. 11.18. The angle between planes. The true angle appears in a plane which is perpendicular to both given planes.

of intersection between the planes, and carry the planes into this view.

2. Draw the end view of the line of intersection, and carry the planes into this view. This view gives the edge view of both planes.

3. The angle between the planes is (according to standard practice) the acute angle.

Complementary-angle Method. In case the line of intersection is not given, further advantage may be taken of the opening statement of this section. From any convenient point drop a perpendicular to each plane. These two lines form a plane perpendicular to both given planes. The angle between the perpendiculars is equal to the angle between the two planes. There are *two* angles between a pair of intersecting lines, one the supplement of the other. The *acute* angle is generally accepted as the standard method of specification. This principle is illustrated in Fig. 11.18. In Fig. 11.19, the true size of the angle between planes XYZ and ABC is to be determined. The top and front views of P are established in any convenient position relative to the given planes. From P a line PR is drawn perpendicular to XYZ, and also from P a line PS is drawn perpendicular to ABC, using the principles outlined in paragraph 11.5 on drawing a line perpendicular to a plane. RS is conveniently established as a frontal line. The included angle RPS is equal to the angle between planes but does not show in true size in either the top or the front view. A normal view of RPS is shown, using the method of rotation as outlined in paragraph 8.26.

Summary

1. Select any convenient point in space.

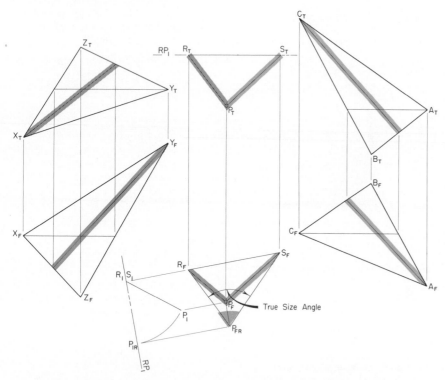

FIG. 11.19. The angle between planes (perpendicular-line method). From a point, a perpendicular is drawn to each plane. The angle between the perpendiculars is the angle between the planes.

2. From this point, draw a perpendicular to each plane.

3. Select points on each perpendicular, and considering the two intersecting perpendiculars as forming a plane, either by rotation or by an edge and normal view, determine the angle between the perpendiculars.

4. If the angle between the perpendiculars is acute (standard practice), this is the designated angle between the planes. If the angle is obtuse, find its supplement.

11.15. A PLANE MAKING SPECIFIED ANGLES WITH OTHER PLANES.

The previous paragraphs have stated that the true angle between planes is seen in a view where both planes appear as edges and that this view will be had when the line of intersection of the planes appears as a point. These facts may be applied to locate a plane at a specified angle with another plane.

Specified Angle between a Skew Plane and a Horizontal, Frontal, or Profile Plane. If the line of intersection of the planes is given, this problem is capable of a single solution; otherwise there will be an infinite number of answers. For example, in Fig. 11.20, the top view of plane ABC and the front view of AB are given, along with a specification of an angle that this plane is to make with frontal planes. Line AB is frontal and is, therefore, the intersection with a frontal plane through AB. Consequently, if the auxiliary view, giving the point view of AB, is made as shown, the edge view of a frontal plane through AB and the edge view of ABC will both appear with AB as their line of intersection. In this view, then, the specified angle may be laid out. Then point C, measured from the top view (distance X) and located on the auxiliary

view, completes the location of ABC at the specified angle with frontal planes. Point C in the front view then lies at the intersection of projectors from the top and auxiliary views.

To lay out a plane making a specified angle with horizontal planes, an auxiliary projected from the top view *must* be used. In this view the edge view of the plane and of *all* horizontal planes will be seen. For a plane making a specified angle with profile planes, an auxiliary projected from a side view must be used. In this view, the edge view of the plane and of *all* profile planes will be seen.

Summary

To draw a plane making a specified angle with horizontal planes:

1. Project an auxiliary from the top view, showing the line of intersection between the required plane and a horizontal plane.

2. The reference plane is horizontal. Set up the required angle between the

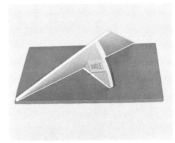

Angle between a plane and an H, F, or P plane

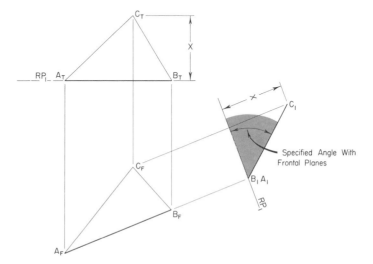

FIG. 11.20. A plane making a specified angle with a frontal plane. The angle is set up in a view showing the edge view of all frontal planes.

horizontal reference plane and the required plane.

3. Finish the projection by location of a point on the required plane from given information, and then project to the other views.

To draw a plane making a specified angle with frontal planes, proceed as in (1), but project the auxiliary from the front view. This view will show the edge view of the frontal reference plane.

To draw a plane making a specified angle with profile planes, proceed as in (1), but project the auxiliary from the side view. This view will show the edge view of the profile reference plane.

Specified Angle between Two Skew Planes. Again, if the line of intersection between the planes is given, the problem is capable of a single solution. In Fig. 11.21, plane *CJV* is a given skew plane. The

top view of *CJS*, in a *second* plane to be located at a specified angle with *CJV*, is given. The line of intersection is *CJ*. The first auxiliary view, perpendicular to *CJ*, gives the true length of *CJ*; the second auxiliary view gives the point view of *CJ* and the edge view of *CJV*. In this view, then, the specified angle may be laid out, thus locating the edge view of *CJS*. Point *S* may now be measured from RP_2 in the top view (distance *Z*) and transferred to the second auxiliary view, locating S_2. The first auxiliary view of *S* then lies at the intersection of projectors from the top and second auxiliary views at S_1. The front view of *S* is then found by projection from the top view and measurement from RP_1.

Summary

1. Draw the normal view of the line of intersection.

2. Draw the end view of the line of intersection. In this view, set up the required angle between planes.

3. Locate a point on the required plane (from given information) and complete the projection.

Specified Angle between a Plane and Two of the Three Planes of Projection. Any skew plane will make some angle, which can be determined (paragraph 11.14), with all three planes of projection. If two of the three angles are specified, the plane will be fixed in four possible positions which can then be restricted to give a single solution.

An excellent method of determining a plane at specified angles with two of the planes of projection is first to draw a line making complements of the angles (paragraph 11.11) which the plane is to make and then to draw a plane perpendicular to the line. The sum of the

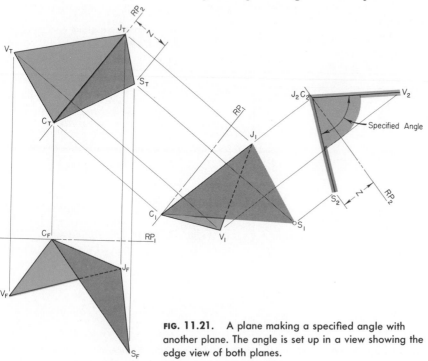

FIG. 11.21. A plane making a specified angle with another plane. The angle is set up in a view showing the edge view of both planes.

angles the plane makes with two of the planes of projection must be between 90 and 180°; otherwise the solution is impossible. In Fig. 11.22, a plane making a specified angle *H* with horizontal planes and a specified angle *F* with frontal planes is to be determined. The plane is to pass through point *P* and have a direction in space that dips forward and to the left of *P*. Therefore, a line perpendicular to this plane has a direction (from any point on the line) downward, rearward, and toward the right. First, determine by subtraction the complements of the angles the plane is to make; then, from any point such as *A* draw the required line as described in paragraph 11.11. Second, through point *P* draw a plane perpendicular to the line. In Fig. 11.22, the plane *PQR* is the re-quired plane designated by horizontal line *PQ* and frontal line *PR*, which are both perpendicular to *AB*.

Summary

1. Draw two cones, (*a*) one having elements that make the *complement* of the angle the plane is to make with projection plane *A* (horizontal, frontal, or profile), (*b*) the other with its apex coincident with the first cone, having elements of the same length, and having elements that make the complement of the angle the plane is to make with projection plane *B* (horizontal, frontal, or profile).

2. Determine the line of intersection of the two cones. (The bases intersect.)

3. Draw a plane perpendicular to the line of intersection of the cones. This

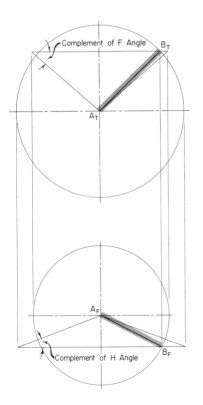

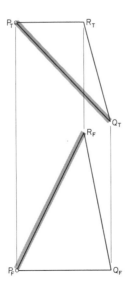

FIG. 11.22. A plane making specified angles with two of the principal planes. A line is drawn making complements of the required angles. Then the plane is drawn perpendicular to the line.

Common perpendicular

plane will make the required angles with the two planes of projection.

11.16. SHORTEST LINE INTERSECTING TWO SKEW LINES: PLANE METHOD.

The shortest distance between two skew lines is the perpendicular distance between the parallel planes that contain each of them. This distance is measured in that view which shows the edge view of the planes.

In Fig. 11.23, it is required to find the shortest distance between the two skew lines *AB* and *MN*. By using one of the given skew lines *AB*, a plane *ABC* is established parallel to *MN* by drawing a line through *B* parallel to *MN* in both top and front views. *C* is conveniently located by drawing *AC* horizontal. An edge view of *ABC* is established in the first auxiliary view by projection in the direction of *AC*. *MN* is projected to this auxiliary view. Note the appearance of *AB* and *MN* in this view. The lines, in space, actually are not parallel, but they appear parallel in this view, because the plane containing *MN* parallel to *ABC*, if drawn, would appear as an edge in

this view. In this view the true length of the shortest distance (common perpendicular) between the skew lines can be measured as the perpendicular distance between the planes.

In general, this would satisfy the requirements of many clearance problems of this type; but if the *location* of the perpendicular is required in addition, one more view will be necessary. A second auxiliary view is established by projecting in a direction perpendicular to *ABC*. This view shows a normal view of each of the skew lines, and the shortest distance between the two lines must therefore appear as a point in this view. The common perpendicular *XY* between the two skew lines appears as a point at the crossing of *MN* and *AB*. *XY* is located in the first auxiliary, top, and front views by projecting *X* and *Y* to intersect, respectively, *MN* and *AB*.

Summary

1. Draw a plane through one of the skew lines parallel to the second skew line.

2. Draw the edge, then the normal

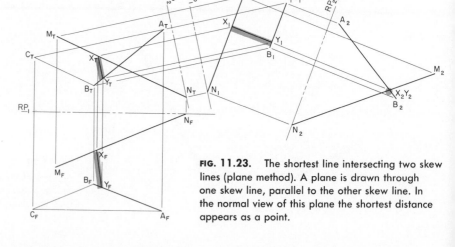

FIG. 11.23. The shortest line intersecting two skew lines (plane method). A plane is drawn through one skew line, parallel to the other skew line. In the normal view of this plane the shortest distance appears as a point.

view of this plane. The normal view shows the normal view of *both* skew lines.

3. In the normal view, the shortest line connecting the skew lines appears as a point at the crossing of the skew lines. Project this shortest line back to all other views.

11.17.   SHORTEST HORIZONTAL LINE INTERSECTING TWO SKEW LINES.   The true length of the shortest horizontal line intersecting two skew lines is the horizontal distance between the parallel planes that contain each of the skew lines.

In Fig. 11.24, it is required to find the line *XY*, the shortest horizontal line intersecting *AB* and *MN*. The plane *ABC* is established in both top and front views parallel to *MN*, similar to the procedure given in paragraph 11.16. *AC* is constructed as a horizontal line. The

auxiliary view, projected from the top view and in the direction of *AC*, establishes the edge view of *ABC*. *MN* is projected to this view. The plane parallel to *ABC* and containing *MN* will appear as an edge in this view. The true length of the shortest distance can be measured in this auxiliary view. Other auxiliary views which would show the planes as edges could be drawn, but only in an auxiliary view projected from the top view could the direction of a horizontal line (parallel to RP_1) between the two planes be determined. The *location* of the shortest horizontal line, however, cannot be determined in this view. Since the shortest horizontal line appears in true length in the first auxiliary view, a second auxiliary view is drawn, projected from the first auxiliary view in a direction parallel to the horizontal. This view

Shortest horizontal line connecting two skew lines

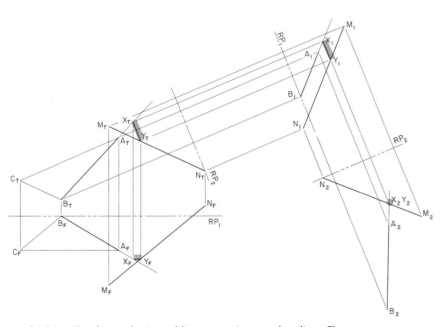

FIG. 11.24.   The shortest horizontal line connecting two skew lines. Three steps are required: (*A*) a plane through one skew line, parallel to the other skew line; (*B*) a view in a horizontal direction, showing the edge view of the planes of both lines; and (*C*) a view in a horizontal direction, showing the shortest line as a point.

is, in this case, *another* auxiliary with a horizontal viewing direction. Therefore, *XY* appears as a point in the second auxiliary view and is located at the crossing of the two skew lines *MN* and *AB*. *XY* is projected back to the first auxiliary, top, and front views by locating *X* and *Y*, respectively, on *AB* and *MN*.

Summary

1. Draw a plane through one line, parallel to the second line.

2. Draw an auxiliary view, projected from the top view, giving the edge view of the plane. Draw both skew lines in this view.

3. Draw a second auxiliary view taken in a direction parallel to the reference plane for the first auxiliary. Project both skew lines to this view, where the shortest horizontal appears as a point at the crossing of the skew lines.

4. Project the shortest horizontal back to the other views.

Simplified Method. Figure 11.25 shows another and shorter method of solving the problem just explained (Fig. 11.24) by employing the following theory: *The shortest horizontal line between two parallel planes is the line perpendicular to all horizontal lines of both planes.* It follows then that, in order to find the shortest horizontal line between two skew lines, a plane may be passed through one of the skew lines parallel to the other. A view now made looking in a horizontal direction and also perpendicular to a horizontal line of this plane will show the shortest horizontal (between the two skew lines) as a point at the crossing of the two skew lines.

In Fig. 11.25, *ABC* is constructed parallel to *MN* as in Fig. 11.24. From

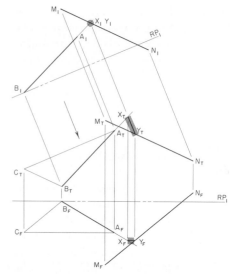

FIG. 11.25. The shortest horizontal line connecting two skew lines (simplified method). Two steps are required: (*A*) a plane through one skew line, parallel to the other skew line; (*B*) a view in a horizontal direction, perpendicular to a true-length line of the plane, showing the point view of the shortest horizontal.

the above principles, an auxiliary view has been projected from the top view in a direction perpendicular to *AC*, a horizontal line of plane *ABC*, thereby obtaining a view which will show the shortest horizontal line as a point. The auxiliary view of *XY* is located at the crossing of *AB* and *MN*. Then *XY* is located in the top and front views by projecting *X* and *Y* to *AB* and *MN*, respectively.

Note that the second auxiliary view of Fig. 11.24 and the auxiliary view of Fig. 11.25 are identical. The projectors for the second auxiliary view of Fig. 11.24 are perpendicular to the projectors between the top and first auxiliary view, therefore showing the space dimension of true height in this particular second auxiliary view; consequently, if a view is projected from the top view with projectors parallel (physical relationship on the sheet) to those of the second auxiliary view, the two views will be identical. This same relationship exists in a side view projected from the front view and in a side view in the alternate position.

Summary

1. Draw a plane through one of the lines, parallel to the second line.

2. Draw an auxiliary view, projected from the top view, and in a direction perpendicular to a horizontal line of the plane. In this view the shortest horizontal appears as a point at the crossing of the two skew lines.

3. Project back to the other views.

11.18.   SHORTEST FRONTAL LINE INTERSECTING TWO SKEW LINES.   The *true length* of the shortest frontal line intersecting two skew lines can be determined as the

frontal distance between the parallel planes that contain the two lines. The location of the shortest frontal line can be determined in that view where the frontal line will show as a point at the crossing of the two skew lines.

In Fig. 11.26, the determination of the shortest frontal line *XY* which intersects the skew lines *AB* and *MN* is illustrated. The solution is identical with that of paragraph 11.17 and Fig. 11.24, except that an auxiliary projected from the front view is used in order to determine the frontal-line direction and the direction of the second auxiliary view.

Summary

1. Draw a plane through one line, parallel to the second line.

2. Draw an auxiliary view, projected from the front view, giving the edge view of the plane. Carry both skew lines into this view.

Shortest frontal line connecting two skew lines

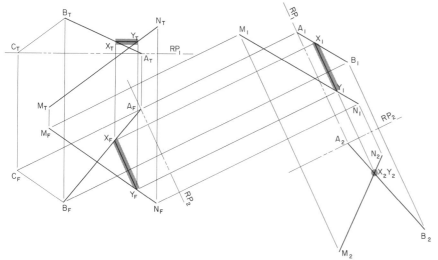

FIG. 11.26.   The shortest frontal line connecting two skew lines. Three steps are required: (*A*) a plane through one skew line, parallel to the other skew line; (*B*) a view in a frontal direction, showing the edge view of the planes of both lines; and (*C*) a view in a frontal direction, showing the shortest line as a point.

Shortest profile line connecting two skew lines

Shortest grade line between two skew lines

3. Draw a second auxiliary view, projected from the first auxiliary and taken in a direction parallel to the frontal reference plane of the first auxiliary. In this view, the shortest frontal line connecting the skew lines appears as a point at the crossing of the skew lines.

4. Project back to the other views.

Simplified Method. Figure 11.27 shows the shorter solution (similar to Fig. 11.25 for a horizontal line), using an auxiliary projected from the front view and made perpendicular to the frontal line *CA* of the plane *ABC*.

Summary

1. Draw a plane through one line, parallel to the second line.

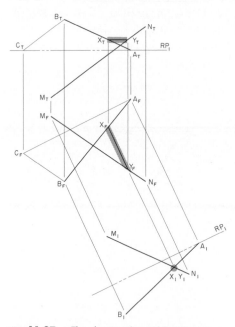

FIG. 11.27. The shortest frontal line intersecting two skew lines (simplified method). Two steps are required: (*A*) a plane through one skew line, parallel to the other skew line; (*B*) a view in a frontal direction, perpendicular to a true-length line of the plane showing the point view of the shortest frontal.

2. Draw an auxiliary view, projected from the front view and in a direction perpendicular to a frontal line of the plane. In this view, the shortest frontal line between the two skew lines appears as a point at the crossing of the two skew lines.

3. Project back to the other views.

The shortest profile line connecting two skew lines is found by using the principles given in this section and in paragraph 11.17, with the exception that an auxiliary projected from a side view must be used.

11.19. SHORTEST LINE OF SPECIFIED GRADE INTERSECTING TWO SKEW LINES. All shortest lines *intersecting two skew lines,* that are horizontal, vertical, at a specified grade, or perpendicular, will lie in *vertical* planes which are perpendicular to horizontal lines on parallel planes passed through the two skew lines. Furthermore, these shortest lines will intersect a horizontal axis parallel to the parallel planes of the skew lines. These facts may be used advantageously to find any of the shortest lines listed above. For example, assume that the shortest 25 per cent grade connector between two skew lines is required. In Fig. 11.28, a plane *DCE* is passed through one skew line *DC* parallel to *AB*, the other skew line. *DE* is made horizontal for convenience. The first auxiliary projected from the top view in the direction of *DE* then gives the edge view of *DCE*. The vertical line connecting the two skew lines appears as a point in the top view at the crossing of *AB* and *CD*. This line *RS* is readily located by projection to the auxiliary view. The shortest line (common perpendicular) will appear as a point at the crossing of *AB* and *CD* in the

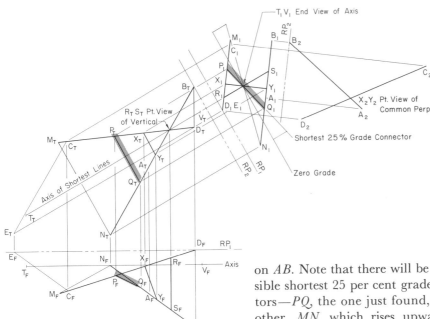

FIG. 11.28. The shortest line of specified grade intersecting two skew lines. Four steps are required: (*A*) a plane through one skew line, parallel to the other skew line; (*B*) a view made in a horizontal direction, showing the edge view of the planes of both skew lines; (*C*) a view in a horizontal direction, showing the shortest horizontal as a point; and (*D*) setting up the shortest grade line.

second auxiliary view which shows *AB* and *CD* in true length. This common perpendicular *XY* is readily located in the auxiliary view by projection back from the second auxiliary view. These two shortest lines, *RS* and *XY*, cross in the first auxiliary view and locate the point view of the axis of shortest lines. This axis *TV* may then be located in the top and front views. Since all shortest lines pass through *TV* in the first auxiliary view, other shortest lines may now be found. The shortest 25 per cent grade connector required in this problem may be laid out at the proper relationship with horizontal planes and passing through *TV* in the first auxiliary view. (*Grade* is defined as units of vertical rise over 100 units of horizontal run.) The 25 per cent grade line of this problem, *PQ*, located in the first auxiliary view, may then be projected back to top and front views, where *P* lies on *CD* and *Q*

on *AB*. Note that there will be two possible shortest 25 per cent grade connectors—*PQ*, the one just found, and another, *MN*, which rises upward from *TV*, while *PQ* descends from *TV* as both lines progress forward and to the right from *TV*.

Summary

1. Draw a plane through one line, parallel to the second line.

2. Draw an auxiliary view, projected from the top view, to give the edge view of the plane.

3. Draw a second auxiliary view, projected from the first auxiliary, and in a direction to give the normal view of the plane. In this view at the crossing of the two skew lines is located the point view of the common perpendicular. Project the common perpendicular back to the first auxiliary.

4. In the top view, the shortest vertical between the skew lines appears as a point at the crossing of the two skew lines. Project this line to the first auxiliary.

5. In the first auxiliary, the point of crossing of the shortest vertical and the

common perpendicular locates the *end view* of the *axis* of all shortest lines. Through this point in the first auxiliary, draw a line making the required grade.

6. Project the grade line back to the top view, where it will appear perpendicular to the axis of shortest lines; then project to the front view.

Simplified Method. Taking advantage of all the facts presented in paragraphs 11.16 and 11.17 and thus far in 11.18, a shorter solution of a problem similar to Fig. 11.28 is possible. In Fig. 11.29, *BN* and *DM* are two skew lines. Assume that the shortest line connector making 15° with the horizontal is wanted. A plane *DCE* parallel to *BN* is passed through *DM*, and *DE* of this plane is

made horizontal. Then the auxiliary projected from the top view in the direction of *DE* gives the edge view of *DCE*. Line *BN* is projected to this view. The vertical *RS* appears as a point in the top view and is projected to the auxiliary at R_1S_1. Any shortest line (as stated before) will lie in a vertical plane perpendicular to horizontal lines of the parallel planes containing the two skew lines and will therefore appear at right angles to *ED* (a horizontal line of *DCE*). One such line, *XY*, is selected at random, but in a convenient place in the top view at X_TY_T. This line projected to the auxiliary will cross *RS*, the vertical, at *TV*, thus locating the axis of shortest lines. In the auxiliary view, through *TV*, the line G_1H_1 making 15° with horizontal planes may then be drawn and projected back to top and front views. The other possible line making 15° with horizontal planes, *PQ*, is also drawn in the auxiliary at P_1Q_1. Both 15° lines *GH* and *PQ* are in true length in the auxiliary view. *PQ* is obviously the shorter of the two.

If a line at some angle to the frontal was required (instead of the line of Fig. 11.29 making an angle with horizontal planes), an auxiliary projected from the front view (giving the edge view of a plane through one line parallel to the other) would be employed in place of the auxiliary (projected from the top view) of Fig. 11.29.

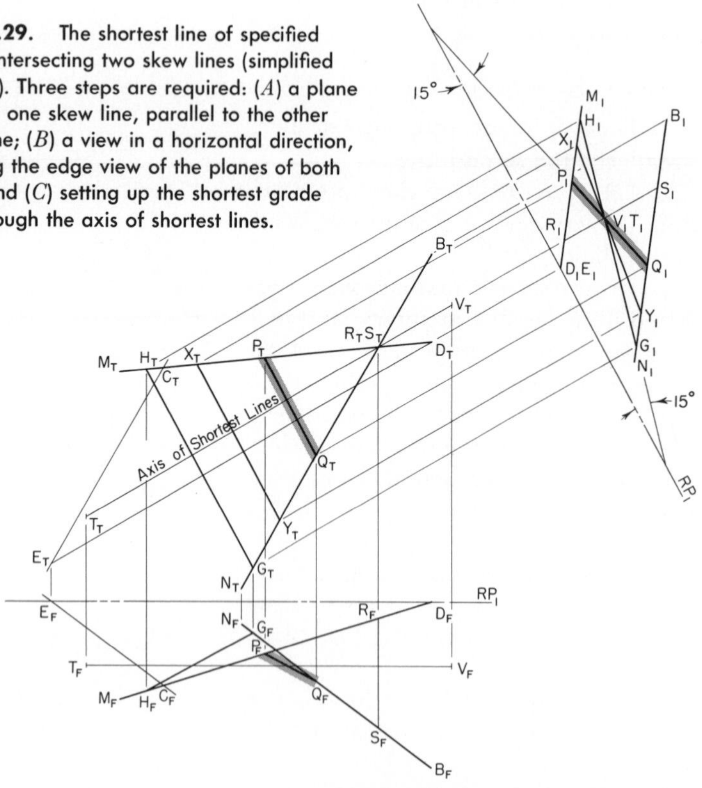

FIG. 11.29. The shortest line of specified grade intersecting two skew lines (simplified method). Three steps are required: (*A*) a plane through one skew line, parallel to the other skew line; (*B*) a view in a horizontal direction, showing the edge view of the planes of both lines; and (*C*) setting up the shortest grade line through the axis of shortest lines.

Summary

1. Draw a plane through one line, parallel to the second line.

2. Draw the edge view of the plane, by projecting an auxiliary from the top view.

3. The intersection of the two skew lines in the top view is the position (point view) of a vertical line connecting the two skew lines. Project this line to the

auxiliary. Any grade line will appear in the top view perpendicular to the rays of projection between the top view and the auxiliary. Draw any such grade line, and project it to the auxiliary.

The intersection of the vertical and any grade line in the auxiliary is the *point view* of the *axis* of shortest lines. Project this axis to the top view.

4. Draw the required grade line in the auxiliary view. This line will pass through the point view of the axis, and its grade is measured from the horizontal reference plane.

5. Project the required grade line to top and front views.

11.20.   SHORTEST LINE OF SPECIFIED BEARING INTERSECTING TWO SKEW LINES.   A *line of specified bearing* is a line having a particular map direction, or "heading." This means that the line will lie in, or be parallel to, a vertical plane whose direction is the specified bearing. There are an infinite number of lines of specified bearing that will intersect two skew lines, but only one shortest line.

The required line may be established parallel to the bearing plane in all views that show the plane as an edge. Also, the length of any shortest line between two skew lines will be seen in a view in which the lines *appear* parallel, that is, in a view giving the edge view of the parallel planes containing the lines. Therefore, in order to find the shortest line of specified bearing between two skew lines, we must draw a view which simultaneously shows the edge of the bearing plane and the edge views of parallel planes containing the skew lines.

In Fig. 11.30, *AB* and *CD* are given skew lines, and plane *BP* is a plane establishing the *direction* of bearing of a line which will later be determined as the shortest line of this bearing which

intersects *AB* and *CD*. The line *BX*, parallel to *CD*, establishes a plane *ABX* through *AB*, parallel to *CD*. Next, an auxiliary view made in a direction perpendicular to the bearing plane *BP* establishes a view in which the bearing plane appears normal. This is the first auxiliary view $A_1B_1C_1D_1$, projected from the top view. Any view now projected from this first auxiliary view will show the bearing plane as an edge. Furthermore, a view projected parallel to a normal line in plane *ABX* will also show *ABX* as an edge. Points *X* and *Y* in plane *ABX* have been located where the

Shortest line of specified bearing between two skew lines

FIG. 11.30.   The shortest line of specified bearing intersecting two skew lines. The simplest method requires four steps: (*A*) a plane parallel to the line of specified bearing; (*B*) a plane through one skew line, parallel to the other skew line; (*C*) a view showing the normal view of the bearing plane; and (*D*) a view in a direction perpendicular to the line of intersection between the parallel plane and the bearing plane, and also showing the edge view of the bearing plane.

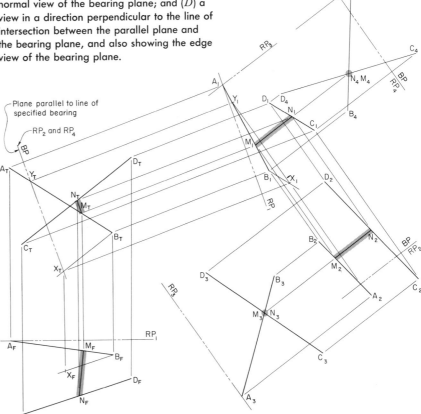

bearing plane intersects AB and BX; hence XY is in the bearing plane and will appear normal (where the bearing plane appears normal) in the first auxiliary view. A second auxiliary view now made looking in a direction parallel to X_1Y_1 will show the edge view of the bearing plane (marked BP in the view) and will show AB and CD parallel to each other (because they lie in parallel planes). In the second auxiliary view any line parallel to BP and intersecting AB and CD will have the proper bearing and meet all specifications of the problem except for the location of the *shortest* line. A third auxiliary view (D_3C_3, A_3B_3) now projected in the direction of the bearing plane BP in the second auxiliary view will again give the edge view of the bearing plane and will, at the crossing of A_3B_3 and C_3D_3, reveal the position of the shortest line of the specified bearing. This is line M_3N_3 in the new view, which, projected to the second auxiliary view at M_2N_2, shows the line to be parallel to the bearing plane. From M_2N_2 the line may then be projected back to all other views.

Summary

1. Draw a plane through one of the skew lines, parallel to the second skew line.

2. Draw the edge view of a "bearing plane," in the top view, parallel to the required bearing line.

3. Make an auxiliary view, projected from the top view, showing the normal view of the bearing plane. Carry all lines to this view.

4. Draw a second auxiliary view projected from the first auxiliary, showing the edge view of both the bearing plane and the plane parallel to one skew line. The direction of this view is determined by the direction of the line of intersection

of the two planes, which appears in true length in the first auxiliary. Carry both skew lines to this view.

5. Draw a third auxiliary view projected from the second auxiliary and in a direction to again get the *edge view* of the bearing plane. Carry both skew lines to this view. The crossing of the skew lines in this view is the point view of the shortest line of the specified bearing, connecting the two skew lines. Project this line back to all other views.

The shorter and simpler solutions of paragraphs 11.17 to 11.19 may also be applied to the above solution. Note in Fig. 11.30 that the view $A_4B_4C_4D_4 \ldots$, projected perpendicular to X_1Y_1, is a view made in exactly the same viewing direction in space as the view $A_3B_3 \ldots$. Thus the two extra views, (1) the first auxiliary and (2) the fourth view $A_4B_4 \ldots$, are the only views needed for a solution.

Summary

1. Draw a plane through one of the skew lines, parallel to the second skew line.

2. Draw the edge view of a "bearing plane" in the top view, parallel to the required bearing line.

3. Make an auxiliary view, projected from the top view, showing the normal view of the bearing plane. Carry all lines to this view.

4. Draw a second auxiliary, projected from the first auxiliary and made in a direction perpendicular to the line of intersection between the bearing plane and the plane parallel to one of the skew lines. Carry all lines to this view.

5. In the second auxiliary view, the point view of the required shortest line of specified bearing appears at the crossing of the skew lines. Project this line back to all other views.

PROBLEMS

GROUP 1.   POINTS IN PLANES

11.1.1.   Points X, Y, and Z lie in the plane ABC. Draw the top and front views of triangle XYZ.

11.1.2.   Find the top view of point S, which lies in the plane PQR.

11.1.3.   Lines AC and BD lie in the plane $KLMN$. AC is parallel to KL and is $1'$-$6''$ long. C is above A. BD is a horizontal line, and D is $1'$-$9''$ to the left of N. Scale: $\frac{3}{4}'' = 1'$-$0''$. Draw the top and front views of AC and BD.

11.1.4.   A plane roof structure is supported by three pipe supports at A, B, and C. Measured from the floor, the pipes are 9, 11, and 5 ft long, respectively. A hole for a ventilator is to have its center on the roof surface 8 ft above the floor and 6 ft from the roof end of support A. Scale: $\frac{1}{4}'' = 1'$-$0''$.

11.1.5.   A circle is to be drawn on the plane surface $ABCD$. The circle is to be centered at point A and have a 3-in. radius. Show top and front views of four points on the circle.

11.1.6. AB is a tunnel lying in the ore vein that strikes and dips as shown. Draw the top view of the tunnel.

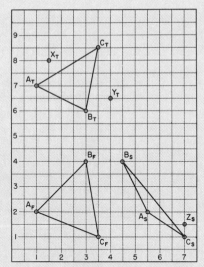

PROB. 11.1.1.

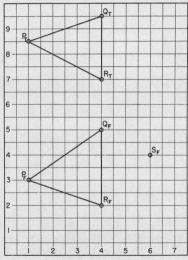

PROB. 11.1.2.

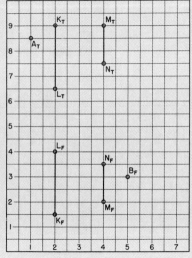

PROB. 11.1.3.

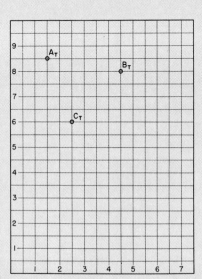

PROB. 11.1.4.

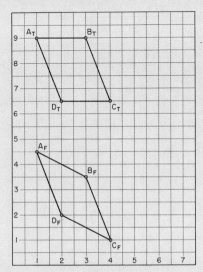

PROB. 11.1.5.

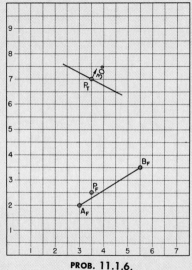

PROB. 11.1.6.

GROUP 2.   PLANE FIGURES

11.2.1.   *PQ* is the hypotenuse of a right triangle. The third corner, *R*, lies on line *PS*. Complete the top and front views of the triangle.

11.2.2.   *KL* and *KM* are the legs of an isosceles right triangle. *M* is above *K* and 18 in. behind *L*. Scale: ⅛ size. Complete the top and front views of the triangle *KLM*.

11.2.3.   *AB* is one diagonal of a rhombus. The third corner, *C*, lies on line *BG*. Draw the top and front views of the rhombus *ABCD*.

11.2.4.   *AB* is one side of a regular hexagon lying in the plane *ABM*. The hexagon lies in front of *AB*. Draw the top and front views of the hexagon.

11.2.5.   *AB* and *KL* are the bases of two similar isosceles triangles. The altitude of the triangle *KLM* is 2¼ in., and *M* is behind *K*. The vertex, *C*, of triangle *ABC* is above and 1¼ in. behind *A*. Scale: ¾ size. Draw the top and front views of the triangle *ABC*.

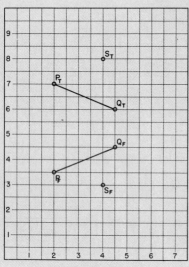

PROB. 11.2.1.

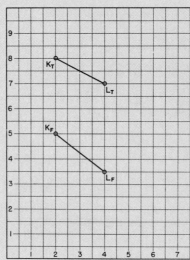

PROB. 11.2.2.

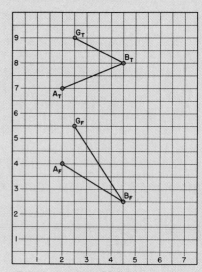

PROB. 11.2.3.

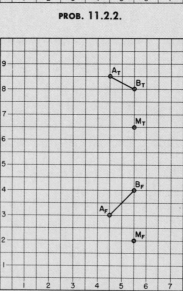

PROB. 11.2.4.

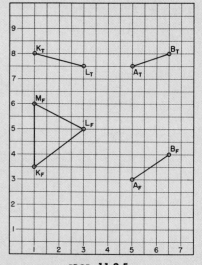

PROB. 11.2.5.

GROUP 3.   LINES PARALLEL TO PLANES, PLANES PARALLEL TO LINES, AND PLANES PARALLEL TO PLANES

11.3.1.   Line *WV* is parallel to plane *ABC*. Draw the front view of line *WV*.

11.3.2.   *DE* is the center line of a shaft supported by two identical bearings. *FGH* is the plane of the base of these bearings. Complete the front view of the plane.

11.3.3.   Plane *ABC* is parallel to lines *DE* and *FG*. Draw the top view of plane *ABC*.

11.3.4.   *AB* and *CD* represent two members in a bridge structure. The shortest possible horizontal catwalk is to be constructed between the two members. Draw the top and front views of the center line of the catwalk.

11.3.5.   *JK* and *LM* are the center lines of two conduits in an irrigation system. It has been decided to install a bypass connection between these conduits. Maximum hydraulic efficiency requires a 24-in. pipe on a 25 per cent grade. Draw the plan and elevation views of the center line of the bypass so as to use the least amount of pipe. How much pipe is required (center to center)? Scale: $1'' = 30'$.

11.3.6.   Planes *ABC* and *RST* are parallel. Complete the front view of *ABC*.

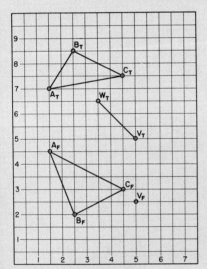

PROB. 11.3.1.

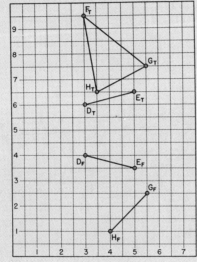

PROB. 11.3.2.

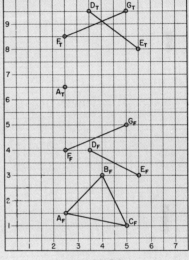

PROB. 11.3.3.

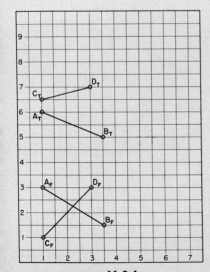

PROB. 11.3.4.

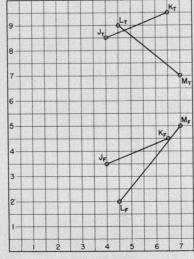

PROB. 11.3.5.

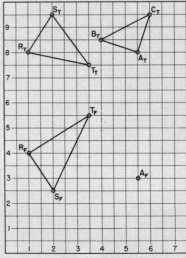

PROB. 11.3.6.

11.3.7. Planes *ABC* and *RST* are parallel. Complete the top and front views of *RST*.

11.3.8. Planes *ABC* and *KLM* are parallel. *KLM* is 1¼ in. away from, and generally below, *ABC*. Scale: ⅜ size. Draw the top view of *KLM*.

11.3.9. Line *AB* is parallel to line *CD*. Plane *ABCD* is parallel to plane *KLMN*. Draw the top and front views of lines *AB* and *CD*. What

is the distance between planes *ABCD* and *KLMN*? Scale: full size.

11.3.10. An ore vein strikes and dips as shown at *P*. Another vein, *R*, is parallel to, above, and 40 ft away from, vein *P*. Point *R* is 20 ft above and 60 ft east of *P*. Scale: 1″ = 50′. Draw the top and front views of vein *R* in terms of strike and dip.

GROUP 4. LINE PERPENDICULAR TO PLANE AND DISTANCE FROM POINT TO PLANE

11.4.1. Complete the front view of *PO*, a line which is perpendicular to plane *ABC*. Use auxiliary-view method.

11.4.2. Complete the top and front views of *PO*, a line perpendicular to plane *ABC*. Use normal-line relationships.

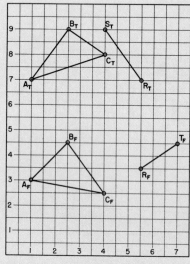

PROB. 11.3.7.

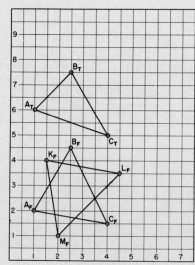

PROB. 11.3.8.

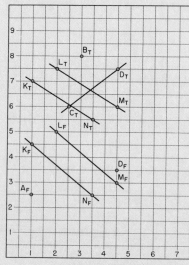

PROB. 11.3.9.

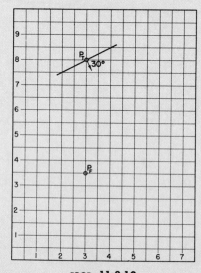

PROB. 11.3.10.

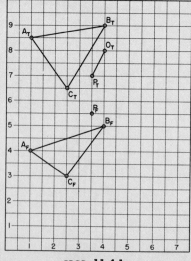

PROB. 11.4.1.

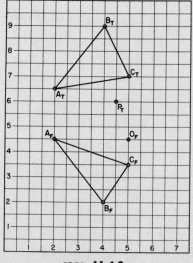

PROB. 11.4.2.

11.4.3. A point moves in a circular path passing through points A, B, and C. Draw the top and front views of the axis of rotation.

11.4.4. Draw the normal view of the distance from point P to the plane ABC.

11.4.5. Draw the top, front, and auxiliary views of line MN, which is perpendicular to plane KLM. MN is 72 in. long and N is above M. Scale: 3/16″ = 1′-0″.

11.4.6. A 7-in. diameter wheel rolls in a straight line across the plane surface RSTU from point P in a direction perpendicular to

RS. Locate, in the top and front views, the center C of the wheel when its line of contact with the plane intersects UT. Scale: 1/4 size.

11.4.7. AB and LM are tubing lines in a hydraulic system. An equalizing connection is to be made between line LM and the straight segment passing through B. The connecting line is to be perpendicular to the plane of AB. Draw the top and front views of the connection. How long is the connection? Scale: 3/4 size.

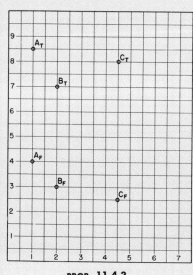

PROB. 11.4.3.

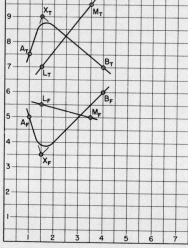

PROB. 11.4.4.

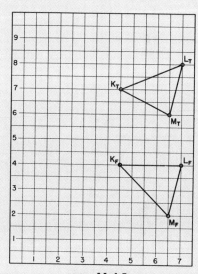

PROB. 11.4.5.

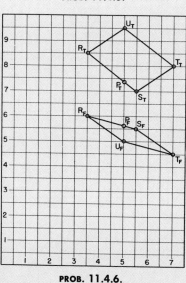

PROB. 11.4.6.

PROB. 11.4.7.

GROUP 5. PLANES PERPENDICULAR TO LINES

11.5.1. Draw the plane *ABC* perpendicular to the line *DA*. Use the auxiliary-view approach.

11.5.2. Draw the plane *JLM* perpendicular to the line *JK*. Use normal-line relationships.

11.5.3. *AB* is the shaft of a spur gear. Points *P*, *O*, and *T* are on the circumference and in the plane of a meshing gear. Scale: ⅜ size. What is the center-to-center distance between the gear shafts?

11.5.4. *AB* is the center line of a pipe of 10 in. diameter. The end of the pipe has been cut off through point *B* in a direction perpendicular to its center line. Draw the top and front views of 12 equally spaced points on the end of the pipe. Scale: 1½″ = 1′-0″. Optional: Draw the curve.

11.5.5. *AB* and *CD* are the center lines of the shafts of two belt pulleys. The pulleys are driven in opposite directions by a crossed belt. One straight run of the belt is horizontal and passes through *P*. Draw the top and front views of the straight portions of the belt.

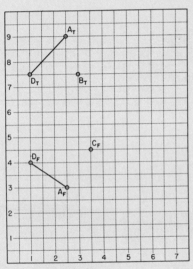

PROB. 11.5.1.

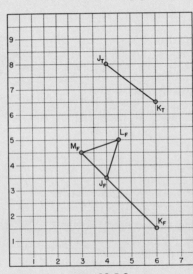

PROB. 11.5.2.

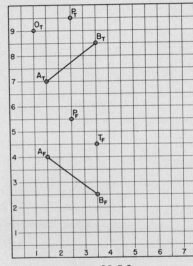

PROB. 11.5.3.

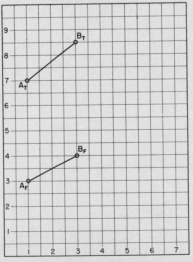

PROB. 11.5.4.

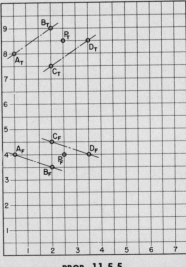

PROB. 11.5.5.

GROUP 6. PERPENDICULAR PLANES

11.6.1. Plane *XYZ* is perpendicular to plane *ABC*. Complete the front view of plane *XYZ*.

11.6.2. Plane *RST* is perpendicular to planes *ABC* and *JKL*. Complete the top and front views of plane *RST*.

11.6.3. Draw the top view of plane *PQR*, which is perpendicular to planes *ABC* and *ABD*.

11.6.4. Plane *ACD* is perpendicular to plane *ABC*. Plane *AFG* is perpendicular to both planes *ABC* and *ACD*. Draw the top and front views of planes *ACD* and *AFG*.

11.6.5. A concrete pier for a radar antenna is to be built on a hillside. *AB* is one of the edges of its square base, which lies in plane *ABK*. The pier, which is a right prism, has an altitude of 8 ft. The bulk of the pier lies above and in front of *AB*. Draw the top and front views of the pier. Scale: ¼″ = 1′-0″.

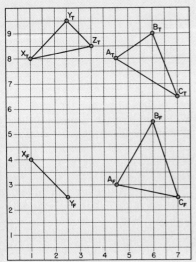

PROB. 11.6.1.

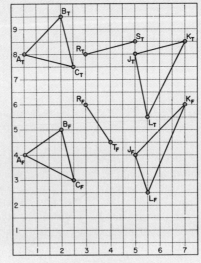

PROB. 11.6.2.

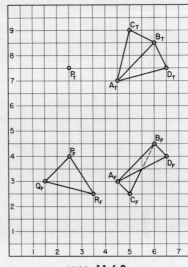

PROB. 11.6.3.

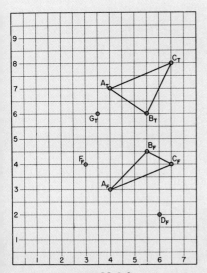

PROB. 11.6.4.

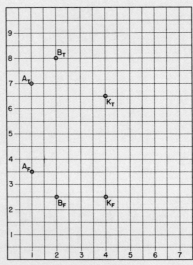

PROB. 11.6.5.

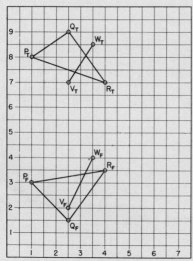

PROB. 11.7.1.

GROUP 7.   ANGLE BETWEEN A LINE AND A PLANE

11.7.1.   Determine the true size of the angles the line *AB* makes with the horizontal, frontal, and profile planes.

11.7.2.   Find the true size of the angle between the line *VW* and the plane *PQR*. Use auxiliary and oblique views only.

11.7.3.   Find the true size of the angle between the line *LM* and the plane *DEF*. Use only one auxiliary view.

11.7.4.   Find the true size of the angle between the line *PQ* and the plane *KLM*. Use the complementary-line method.

11.7.5.   A gin pole, *BT*, is supported and pivoted about its base *B* by four guy lines, which are anchored at ground level at points *W*, *X*, *Y*, and *Z*. The maximum permissible angle of lean of the pole is 45° from the vertical. Draw the plan view of the maximum area which can be served by the vertical load line. The hook can be raised and lowered independently.

11.7.6.   The design of the anchorages in Prob. 11.7.5 is affected by the maximum angle that can exist between the pole and the guy lines. Find the true size of this angle for line *WT*.

GROUP 8.   ANGLE BETWEEN PLANES

11.8.1.   Find the true size of angle between planes *RSTU* and *STVW*.

11.8.2.   Find the true size of angle between planes *ABC* and *DEF*.

11.8.3.   Find the true size of the angle between the lateral surfaces of the pyramidal column base.

11.8.4.   Plane *ABC* is one side of a trough whose right section is an equilateral triangle. The altitude of the right section is 1¾ in. Draw the top and front views of the right section *ADE* of the trough. Point *A* is a lower rear corner of the right section. Scale: full size.

11.8.5.   *RS* is the lower edge of a chute for conveying packages between the floors of a building. The surface of the chute is inclined at an angle of 40° above the horizontal and is rectangular in shape. The ceiling is 11 ft above the bottom of the chute. Draw the plan and elevation views of the chute from its bottom to the ceiling. How many square feet of material are required for the surface of the chute? Scale: ¼″ = 1′-0″.

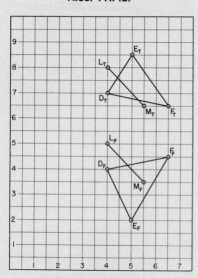

PROB. 11.7.2.

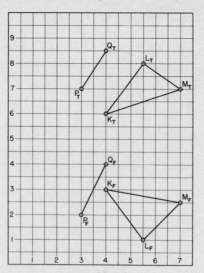

PROB. 11.7.4.

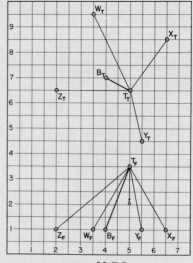

PROB. 11.7.5.

PROB. 11.7.3.

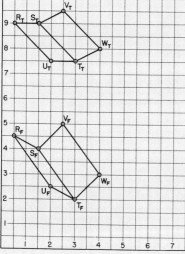

PROB. 11.8.1.

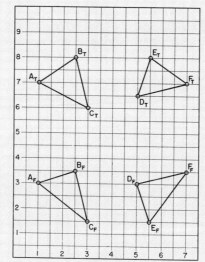

PROB. 11.8.2.

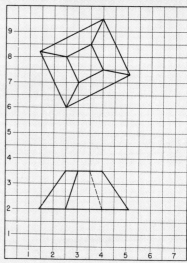

PROB. 11.8.3.

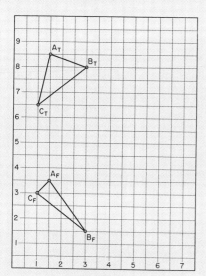

PROB. 11.8.4.

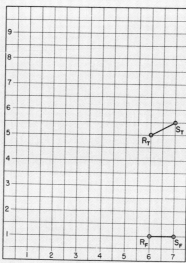

PROB. 11.8.5.

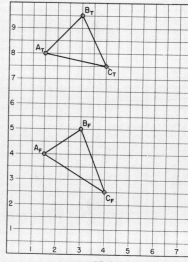

PROB. 11.9.1.

GROUP 9.   PLANES MAKING SPECIFIED ANGLES

11.9.1.   Draw the top and front views of line *CD*, which lies in the plane *ABC* and makes an angle of 45° with all profile planes. *CD* is 1½ in. long and *D* is above *C*. Scale: ¾ size.

11.9.2.   The Buckeye Vein strikes and dips as shown at *B*. A tunnel is to be dug in the vein, starting at point *A* and proceeding uphill in a westerly direction at a 20 per cent grade. The upper end of the tunnel is at the same elevation as *B*. Draw the map and elevation views of the tunnel.

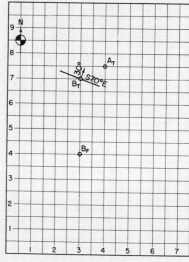

PROB. 11.9.2.

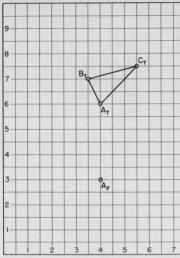

PROB. 11.9.3.

11.9.3. Draw the front view of *ABC*, a plane which makes angles of 40 and 75° respectively, with all horizontal and frontal planes. Plane *ABC* slopes downward toward the left front.

11.9.4. Complete the top and front views of plane *ABC*, which makes an angle of 60° with both the frontal and profile planes. Plane *ABC* slopes downward to the right rear.

11.9.5. The plane *XYZ* makes an angle of 45° with plane *ABC* and an angle of 60° with plane *BCD*. Draw the front view of plane *XYZ*. Use the plane which slopes downward to the left and whose strike line is most nearly profile.

11.9.6. Plane *RSTU* is a portion of a belt conveyer whose direction of travel is indicated. This conveyer is to be unloaded by a rectangular plow blade so as to discharge the material to the right. The blade makes an angle of 45° with the belt and an angle of 75° with a plane that is perpendicular to the belt and parallel to the direction of travel. The top of the blade is 1 ft above the belt. The length of the blade is limited by the edges of the belt. Point *A* is one corner of the blade. Scale: $\frac{1}{4}'' = 1'\text{-}0''$. Draw the top and front views of the blade.

11.9.7. A pencil of light is emitted from source *S* and reflected from an 8- by 12-in. rectangular mirror at point *R* so as to pass through a target at point *T*; the mirror is centered at *R* and has its longer edge parallel to the plane of the light rays. Scale: $\frac{3}{4}'' = 1'\text{-}0''$. Draw the top and front views of the mirror.

11.9.8. Complete the front view of the plane *PQR*, which makes angles of 60 and 30° with lines *AB* and *CD*, respectively. *PQR* dips northeasterly.

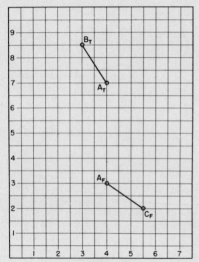

PROB. 11.9.4.

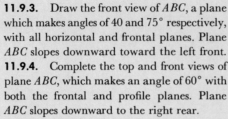

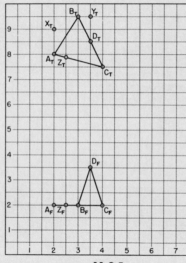

PROB. 11.9.5.

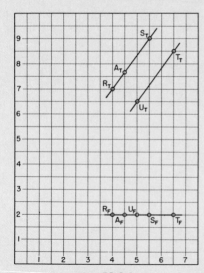

PROB. 11.9.6.

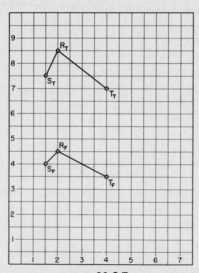

PROB. 11.9.7.

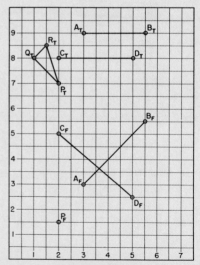

PROB. 11.9.8.

GROUP 10. SHORTEST LINE BETWEEN TWO SKEW LINES

11.10.1. Draw front, top, and any other necessary views of the shortest horizontal line between the lines *AB* and *CD*.

11.10.2. Using the layout for Prob. 11.10.1, determine the shortest distance between lines *AB* and *CD*. Scale: ¼ size.

11.10.3. Using the layout for Prob. 11.10.1, draw top, front, and any other necessary views of the shortest line connecting *AB* and *CD* that makes 15° with horizontal planes.

11.10.4. Draw front, top, and any other necessary views of the shortest frontal line between the lines *RS* and *TU*.

11.10.5. Using the layout for Prob. 11.10.4, determine the shortest distance between lines *RS* and *TU*.

11.10.6. Using the layout of Prob. 11.10.4, draw top, front, and any other necessary views of the shortest line connecting *RS* and *TU* that makes 10° with frontal planes.

11.10.7. *AB* and *CD* are skew lines. Locate the shortest line, parallel to bearing plane *BP*, that intersects *AB* and *CD*. Use the first method of paragraph 11.20.

11.10.8. *RS* and *TU* are skew lines to be intersected by the shortest line parallel to the bearing plane *BP* shown. Use the first method of paragraph 11.20.

11.10.9. *BP* is the bearing direction of the shortest line *PQ* intersecting *XY* and *MN*. Locate *PQ* by the simplified method of paragraph 11.20.

11.10.10. *PQ* and *RS* are skew lines and *BP* is the bearing *direction* of the shortest line *XY* (of this bearing) that intersects *PQ* and *RS*. Locate *XY* by the simplified method of paragraph 11.20.

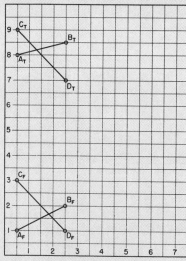

PROB. 11.10.1.

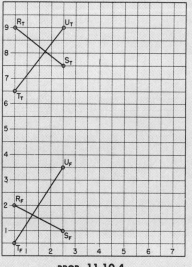

PROB. 11.10.4.

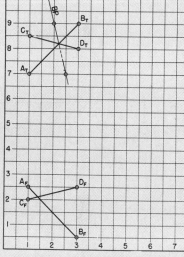

PROB. 11.10.7.

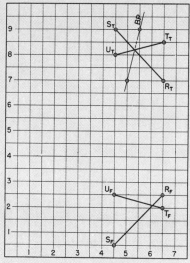

PROB. 11.10.8.

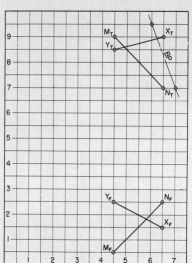

PROB. 11.10.9.

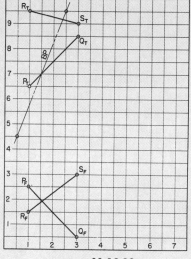

PROB. 11.10.10.

Curved and Warped Surfaces: Construction and Determination in Space

12

12.1. In all science and engineering, but particularly in the mechanical phases of engineering, curved surfaces will frequently occur. Geometrically, shafts, bolts, rivets, and pipes are cylinders; hoppers, tanks, ducts, and discharge devices frequently occur as cones or portions of cones; transitions and blends often are oblique cones or convolutes; and we all observe in everyday life the double-curved and warped surfaces of automobile bodies, ship hulls, and aircraft fuselages and wings. Nevertheless, a knowledge of curved surfaces is important in the nonmechanical fields. In physics and other sciences, the theories of light, heat, sound, electronics, etc., will involve the cylinder, cone, paraboloid, and other surfaces. As a class, curved surfaces probably have a greater and more varied application than any other single portion of engineering geometry.

12.2. CLASSIFICATION OF SURFACES. A surface may be considered to be generated by a line, called the *generatrix,* which moves according to some law. Surfaces may thus be divided into two general classes: (1) those which can be generated by a moving *straight* line and (2) those which can be generated only by a moving *curved* line. The first are called *ruled surfaces;* the second, *double-curved surfaces.* Any position of the generatrix is called an *element* of the surface.

Ruled surfaces may be divided into (1) planes, (2) single-curved surfaces, and (3) warped surfaces.

373

The plane may be generated by a straight line moving so as to touch two other intersecting or parallel straight lines or a plane curve or a point and a straight line.

Single-curved surfaces have their elements either parallel or intersecting. In this class are the cylinder, the cone, and a third surface, the convolute, in which only consecutive elements intersect.

Warped surfaces have no two consecutive elements either parallel or intersecting. There is a great variety of warped surfaces. The surface of a screw thread and that of an airplane wing are two examples.

Double-curved surfaces are generated by a curved line moving according to some law. The commonest forms are surfaces of revolution, made by revolving a curve about an axis in the same plane, as the sphere, torus or ring, ellipsoid, paraboloid, hyperboloid, etc.

12.3. SINGLE-CURVED SURFACES.

A single-curved surface, as the name implies, is a surface having curvature in one direction only. A single-curved surface may be generated by a straight-line generatrix moving (1) parallel to itself and intersecting a curved directrix not coplanar with the line (cylinder) or (2) so that consecutive elements intersect each other and intersect two curved-line directrices (convolute) or (3) in contact with a point directrix and a curved directrix not coplanar with the point (cone).

12.4. CYLINDERS.

A cylinder, Fig. 12.1, is a single-curved surface generated by the motion of a straight-line generatrix remaining parallel to itself and constantly intersecting a curved directrix. The various positions of the generatrix are elements of the surface. It is a *right cylinder* when the elements are perpendicular to the bases, an *oblique cylinder* when they are not. A *truncated cylinder* is that portion which lies between one of its bases and a cutting plane that cuts all the elements. The axis is the line joining the centers of the bases. Cylinders and cones do not necessarily have closed base surfaces.

A cylinder may be represented by drawing two views, usually (1) a view showing the end view of the axis and (2) a view showing the normal view of the axis (Fig. 12.2*A*). This is the simplest

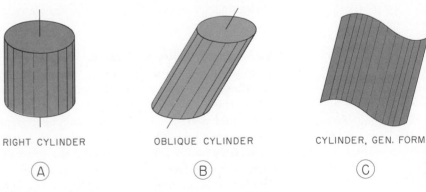

RIGHT CYLINDER　　　　OBLIQUE CYLINDER　　　　CYLINDER, GEN. FORM

(A)　　　　　　　(B)　　　　　　　(C)

FIG. 12.1. Forms of cylinders. All forms have parallel elements.

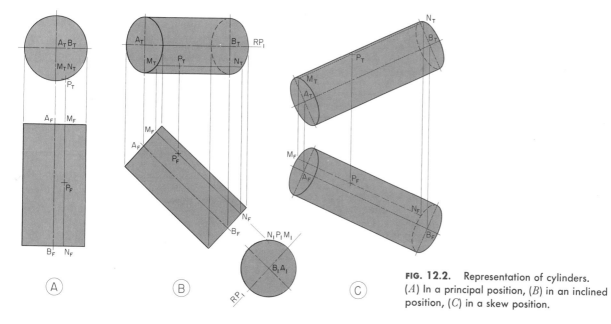

FIG. 12.2. Representation of cylinders. (*A*) In a principal position, (*B*) in an inclined position, (*C*) in a skew position.

possible position. The cylinder might be located in space as at (*B*), where the axis is frontal. In this case, right sections for bases at (*A*) and (*B*) will appear as edges in the front view, and either (1) projection to the top view will determine major and minor diameters—as explained in paragraph 10.5—to plot the elliptical curves, or (2) the end view shown may be employed to plot points on the curves. If the axis is in a skew position as at (*C*), either a normal view or a normal view and an end view of the axis may be made and the cylinder then laid out in these views, as described for case (*B*). Another way is to lay out the base curves by treating them as circles in skew position, using one of the methods of paragraph 10.6.

A point on the surface of a cylinder is located by realizing the fact that a point must lie on an element of the cylinder. Thus, in Fig. 12.2, if point *P* is known in either the top or front view,

the adjacent view (top or front view) may be determined by projecting point *P* to the element of the cylinder on which it lies.

Summary

Representation

Draw two views, a view showing the normal view of the axis and a view showing the end view of the axis.

Location of an element

Through any given point, draw a line parallel to the axis and connecting the bases, or, depending upon problem requirements, locate the element in the view showing either the normal view or the end view of the axis; then project to the other views.

Location of a point

Draw an element through the point, and project the element to the other views. Then project the point to the element in all views.

RIGHT CONE   OBLIQUE CONE   CONE, GEN. FORM

Ⓐ   Ⓑ   Ⓒ

FIG. 12.3. Forms of cones. All have elements intersecting a common point (apex).

12.5.   CONES.   A cone (Fig. 12.3) is a single-curved surface generated by the movement, along a curved directrix, of a straight-line generatrix, one point of which is fixed and not coplanar with the directrix. The directrix is the base, and the fixed point (point directrix) is the vertex of the cone. Each position of the generatrix is an element of the surface. The axis is a line connecting the vertex and the center of the base. The altitude is a perpendicular dropped from the vertex to the base. A cone is *right* if the axis and altitude coincide; it is *oblique* if they do not coincide. A *truncated cone* is that portion lying between the base and a cutting plane which cuts all the elements. The *frustum of a cone* is that portion lying between the base and a cutting plane parallel to the base which cuts all the elements.

A cone may be determined by the position and shape of a base curve and the position of the apex. Figure 12.4*A* is the simplest position, with the end (top view) and the true length (front

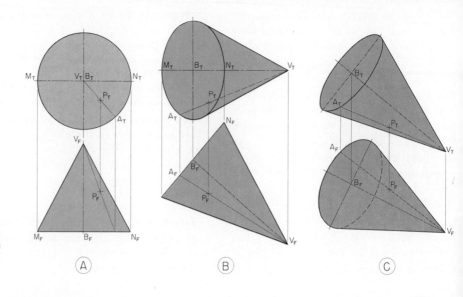

FIG. 12.4. Representation of cones. (*A*) In a principal position, (*B*) in an inclined position, (*C*) in a skew position.

Ⓐ   Ⓑ   Ⓒ

view) of the axis. In Fig. 12.4*B*, the front view shows the base as an edge. The right-circular base in this view may be drawn perpendicular to the axis and then projection made to the top view to locate the diameters of the ellipse, as explained in paragraph 10.5. At *C*, the axis is in a skew position, the base may be determined by the simplified methods of paragraph 10.6, or, if preferred, a true-length and end view of the axis will make possible the location of points in the end view to project back to the top and front views and locate the base curves.

Any point on a cone lies on some element of the cone. Figure 12.4 shows a point *P* assumed to have been located in one of the views and then projected to the other view by locating the point on an element of the cone through the point.

Summary

Representation

Draw two views, a view showing the normal view of the axis and a view showing the end view of the axis.

Location of an element

Through any given point, draw a line from the apex to the base, or, depending on problem requirements, locate the element in a view showing either the normal view or the end view of the axis; then project to the other views.

Location of a point

Draw an element from the apex, through the point and to the base. Draw the element in the other views; then project the point to the element.

12.6. CONVOLUTES. The term "convolute" is derived from the Latin *volvere*, "to roll." This mathematically and graphically means "to form by a rolling element." Specifically, the rolling element is either a tangent plane or a line. Thus any surface formed by the location of elements produced by tangency of a line or plane may be termed a convolute. There are two forms, conical and helical, in general use (Fig. 12.5).

12.7. THE CONICAL CONVOLUTE. The conical convolute, commonly known as the "convolute transition," Fig. 12.5*A*, is generated by a straight-line generatrix in contact with two curved-line directrices, the generatrix moving so as to lie always in a plane tangent to the curved-line directrices. Adjacent elements, infinitely close together, will be planar and will intersect. The surface will revert to a right circular cone when both

CONVOLUTE

(A)

HELICAL CONVOLUTE

(B)

CONVOLUTE, GEN. FORM

(C)

FIG. 12.5. Forms of convolutes. All have elements formed by a tangent to a curve.

directrices are circular right sections and are coaxial. Note in Fig. 12.4A that a series of planes, tangent to the cone, would produce elements at the lines of tangency.

Figure 12.6 illustrates the construction of a conical convolute. The pictorial view at (A) shows how an element of the surface is located. Any plane placed against both base curves will, of course, contact both curves and form a line connecting the points of contact. This line will be an element of the surface. In the plane contacting the base curves, there will be tangents to the base curves, lines PQ and OQ on the figure. Thus if an element, say, through point P on the lower base is wanted, a tangent is drawn emanating from point P. Then Q is located on this tangent *at the intersection of base planes*. Finally, a tangent from point Q to the upper base and the tangent point O when located will determine the element OP.

Figure 12.6B shows the orthographic construction when the base planes are parallel. Assume that an element through point Y is wanted. From Y_T a tangent YR is drawn. The base planes,

being parallel, intersect at infinity; therefore, a tangent XS parallel to YR will locate X, the other end of element YX. Note the construction shown for accurate location of the tangent points. A number of elements similar to YX, evenly spaced around either base, will complete the representation.

Figure 12.6C illustrates the construction when the base planes intersect at a finite distance. Any tangents to the base curves will, of course, lie in the plane of the curves. The intersection of the base planes at C_F is projected to the top view, where the line of intersection appears as a true-length line. Any pair of tangents to both base curves will intersect on this line. It follows then that a tangent constructed to the ellipse at point B and extended to C_T locates the intersection of a tangent to the upper base curve. From C_T, then, a line drawn to the upper base curve is the tangent line, and the tangent point A, then determined by the method of paragraph 3.55, completes the location of element AB. Other elements, similar to AB, are then located to complete the representation.

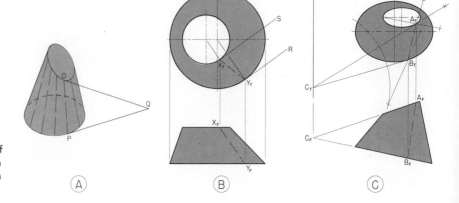

FIG. 12.6. Representation of conical convolutes. (A) Pictorial representation of tangent plane, (B) conical convolute with parallel bases, (C) conical convolute with nonparallel bases.

Summary

1. Locate and draw the two base curves.

2. Determine the planes of the bases and the line of intersection of these planes. (If the bases are parallel, the line of intersection is at infinity.)

3. Draw a tangent from a point on one base, and extend this tangent to the intersection of the base planes.

4. Draw a tangent *from* the point now located on the intersection of the base planes *to* the second base. Determine the point of tangency of this line with the base.

5. Connect the two points of tangency thus located on the bases. This is one element of the convolute formed by a plane tangent to the bases.

6. Repeat the process (1) through (5) to locate all necessary elements and to adequately determine the surface.

12.8.   THE HELICAL CONVOLUTE.   The helical convolute is a surface generated by a straight-line generatrix moving so as to be tangent always to a helix. From a given diameter of the generating cylinder and the lead, the helix is plotted; then tangents to the helix will locate elements of the helical convolute. In Fig. 12.7, the axis of the surface is centered at O. The top view is the end, and the front view the true length of the axis. In the top view, the smaller circle is the diameter of the generating cylinder for the helix. In this case, the circumference has been divided into six parts; therefore, the lead divided into six parts will locate positions, along the axis, of the generating point, and projection from the top view will then locate points on the helical curve in the front view, as described in paragraph 3.72. Or if

the helix angle is drawn as shown on Fig. 12.7, by projecting the lead from the front view and laying out the circumference, sixth points of the circumference may be projected to the developed helix at A_D, B_D, C_D, etc., and then to the front view.

Tangents to the helical curve may now be determined by first drawing them in the top view, tangent to the circle representing the generating cylinder at A_T-1_T, B_T-2_T, C_T-3_T, etc. The outer circle through 1, 2, 3, etc., is the given outer limit for the convolute. Tangent A-1 is frontal and will appear in true length in the front view. Also, the tangent at point A will appear parallel to the helix angle. Thus, A_F-1_F drawn parallel to $A_D B_D \ldots A_D$ establishes one element of the convolute surface. Any tangent (element) of the convolute will have the same directional relationship to the axis. In other words, if tangent B-2 were rotated around the axis O until B-2 is frontal, then B-2 would be parallel, in the front view, to the developed helix $A_D B_D \ldots A_D$. Further, the difference be-

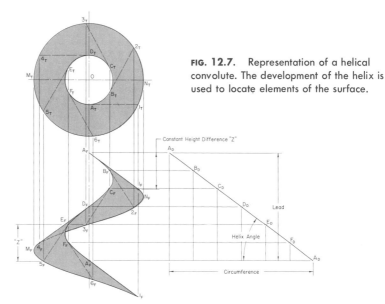

FIG. 12.7.   Representation of a helical convolute. The development of the helix is used to locate elements of the surface.

tween the inner point *B* and the outer point 2, *measured parallel to the axis,* will be identical for any of the tangents. To locate any tangent then, say *E*-5, this constant distance (in this case, constant height difference *Z*) is measured for frontal tangent *A*-1; next, the projector for point 5 on tangent *E*-5 is drawn to the front view; third, constant distance *Z* is measured as shown, locating point 5. All the other tangent elements, *B*-2, *C*-3, etc., are of course located in the same way. Smooth curves through the points for both helices complete the representation.

Summary

1. Determine and draw two views of the generating cylinder. Also draw a concentric cylinder to limit the surface.
2. Draw the helix (on the generating cylinder) on which the convolute is to be generated.
3. Determine the helix angle by drawing a development of the helix. This is a rectangular plot of lead versus circumference.
4. Draw a tangent to the generating helix that appears normal in the view showing the normal view of the generating cylinder's axis.
5. Determine the distance, *parallel to the axis* between the two ends of the normal tangent drawn in (4). This is the distance *Z* of Fig. 12.7.
6. Project all points of tangency of tangents to the generating helix (drawn in the end view) to the view showing the normal view of the axis.
7. Draw projection lines to the view showing the normal view of the axis, from all points of intersection of the tangents to the generating cylinder with the limiting cylinder.
8. Use the constant distance *Z* by measuring parallel to the axis in the

normal view of the axis from the tangent point of a tangent line on the generating cylinder to locate the point of intersection of the tangent line with the limiting cylinder. Draw all tangents in this view.
9. Draw the two helices formed on the generating cylinder and the limiting cylinder.

12.9. TANGENTS TO SINGLE-CURVED SURFACES.   The convolutes are constructed of tangents, and the necessity of constructing any tangent line or plane (other than the ones used in generating the surface) is rare. On the other hand, some problems involving a cylinder or cone may require a tangent line or plane to be located. A tangent has been defined as a line that passes through two consecutive points of a curve that are infinitely close together. When this conception is applied to a surface, it follows then that a line passing through two consecutive points of the surface will be tangent to the surface. Cylinders and cones contain an unlimited number of possible base curves or sections. For the cylinder: the circle, ellipse, and straight line, and for the cone: the straight line, circle, ellipse, parabola, and hyperbola. A line tangent to any one of these possible base curves or sections will be tangent to the surface. Also, any line tangent to a surface will lie in a plane that is tangent to the surface. Note particularly that an element of a cylinder or a cone is also a tangent of the surface.

Tangents to a Cylinder.   Figure 12.8 illustrates lines and planes tangent to a cylinder. The cylinder is right circular. Therefore, the end view will show the edge view of any plane tangent to the cylinder. For a tangent plane containing point *O*, the point is located in the end view at O_1 and the tangent O_1R_1 drawn. *R* lies on an element of the cylinder.

Thus any other point on the same element, such as Q, will now determine a plane ORQ tangent to the cylinder.

The problem can also be solved without the end view. Assume a tangent plane containing point P, on the cylinder, is wanted. Through point P in the front view, a section parallel to the bases is drawn. This section will be a circle, as shown in the top view. Then a *tangent* from point P and the *element* through P will determine the tangent plane. Point O in this case may be assumed in any convenient place on the tangent through P.

Any line tangent to the cylinder will lie in the tangent plane. Thus OR, OP, OS, and OQ are lines tangent to the cylinder through point O.

Summary

1. Draw the two required views of the cylinder axis. This is the space location of the cylinder.

2. Draw an end view of the axis. In this view, lay out the cylinder's end view. Now complete the other views of the cylinder by projection back from the end view.

3. In the end view, locate the plane of any required tangent to the cylinder. This plane appears as an edge tangent to the cylinder through any point *on* the cylinder or as an edge through any point *not on* the cylinder, tangent to the cylinder.

4. Project any specified tangent line, lying in the tangent plane, back to the other views. The tangent line *must* contact the cylinder on an element of the cylinder which is the line of intersection between the tangent plane and cylinder.

Tangents to a Cone. In Fig. 12.9, a plane containing point O, tangent to the cone, is required. Through point O, a plane is passed parallel to the base

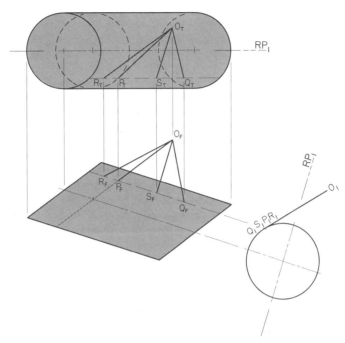

FIG. 12.8. Tangents to a cylinder. Any tangent line lies in a plane tangent to the cylinder.

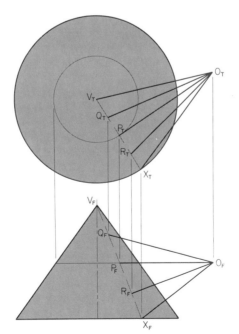

FIG. 12.9. Tangents to a cone. Any tangent line lies in a plane tangent to the cone.

plane (horizontal). This plane cuts from the cone the circle shown; a tangent *OP* to this circle then establishes a line tangent to the cone. The element of the cone through *P* is then drawn at *VX*. The plane tangent to the cone is then *PXO* or *VPO*, established by an element and a tangent to a base curve of the cone. Any line in this tangent plane will be a line tangent to the cone. Thus *QO*, *PO*, *RO*, and *XO* are line tangents.

Summary

1. Draw two required views of the cone axis. If these views are not an end view and a normal view of the axis, draw them.

2. Through any point on the required tangent line, either on the cone or outside the cone surface, draw a tangent to the cone that is parallel to the base. Draw the element of the cone through the tangent point on the cone. A plane is now formed consisting of the element of the cone and any point on the tangent line to the cone.

3. Locate any required tangent line in the tangent plane, according to problem requirements.

12.10.   DOUBLE-CURVED SURFACES.   Engineering structures and mechanical parts often are made up of, or employ, surfaces that are completely curved. Examples of surfaces of this type are the streamlined surfaces of aircraft and automobile bodies, boat and ship hulls, parabolic and ellipsoid reflectors, and many others. Because no straight-line element can be drawn on a completely curved surface, it is said to be double-curved.

The generating curve may be either a geometrical curve or a curve of general form, and the generating curve may be controlled in various ways; moreover, the generating curve may be either constant or variable. The variety of forms is therefore unlimited.

12.11.   CLASSIFICATION.   Double-curved surfaces may be classified as follows:

Surfaces of revolution are surfaces generated by revolving a curved-line generatrix about a straight line as an axis. If the generatrix lies in the same plane as the axis, the surface generated will conform to the curve of the generatrix.

Surfaces of general form are surfaces generated by moving a constant or variable curved-line generatrix along a noncircular curved path.

12.12.   SURFACES OF REVOLUTION.   A surface of revolution may be formed by employing any curve as a generating line. Geometrical curves, however, usually one of the conics, are most common, as illustrated pictorially in Fig. 12.10. At (*A*) is shown a sphere, generated by revolving a circle around one of its diameters. Figure 12.10*B* illustrates a prolate ellipsoid generated by revolving an ellipse about its major diameter. (*C*) is an oblate ellipsoid formed by revolving an ellipse about its minor diameter. The paraboloid at (*D*) is generated by revolving a parabola about its central axis. This is the surface of parabolic reflectors. The hyperboloid (*E*) is formed by revolving a hyperbola about its central axis. The hyperboloid of revolution may also be formed by revolving a straight line around an axis, as described in paragraph 12.30, and in this form is a warped surface. It is interesting to note that the circular hyperboloid is the only warped surface that is also a surface of revolution. (*F*) is a torus, formed by revolving a circle around an axis which

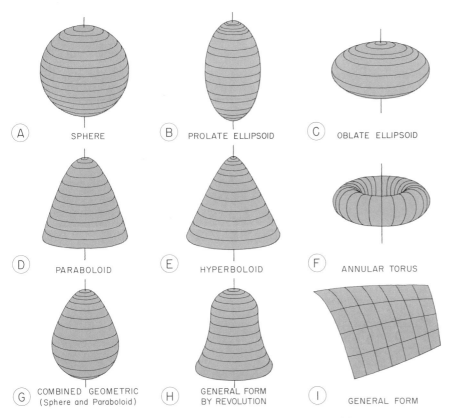

A. SPHERE
B. PROLATE ELLIPSOID
C. OBLATE ELLIPSOID
D. PARABOLOID
E. HYPERBOLOID
F. ANNULAR TORUS
G. COMBINED GEOMETRIC (Sphere and Paraboloid)
H. GENERAL FORM BY REVOLUTION
I. GENERAL FORM

FIG. 12.10. Forms of double-curved surfaces. All forms are generated by a curve.

is not a diameter of the circle. If the axis lies within the circle, a closed torus will be formed; if the axis is outside the circle, an annular torus is formed. Any curve, either open or closed, may be employed to form a torus. Odd curves are often used in architecture to form a decorative torus on columns or on circular moldings.

Geometric curves may, of course, be combined to form a surface of revolution. An example is shown at (*G*). Furthermore, any nongeometric curve may be rotated about an axis, producing a surface of revolution as, for example, the bell-shaped surface at (*H*). The completely general form of a double-curved

surface is indicated at (*I*). This might be a portion of an automobile body, airplane fuselage, or ship hull.

12.13. REPRESENTATION. Because a surface of revolution is generated by the revolution of a line around an axis, it is necessary to have one view showing the axis as a point and another view showing the axis in true length. In most cases, the surface will be drawn in a simple position, where top and front or front and side views will be the point and true length of axis views. However, when the surface is in some inclined or skew position, one or more extra views must be made. Figure 12.11 shows a paraboloid

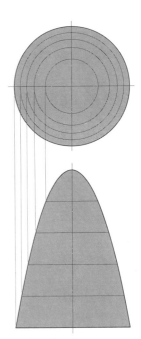

FIG. 12.11. Representation of a double-curved surface. (A paraboloid in a principal position.)

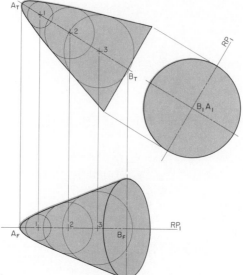

FIG. 12.12. Representation of a double-curved surface by the tangent-sphere method. (Inclined position.)

in a simple position. The front view shows the normal view, and the top view shows the end view of the axis. The outline of the front view will be the true shape of the parabola and the top view will be a circle showing the base diameter. Sections of the surface perpendicular to the axis are circular. Therefore, if planes of circular sections are located in the front view and then projected to, and drawn as circles in, the top view (as shown on Fig. 12.11), these circular sections will be circular elements of the surface.

When the surface of revolution is in an inclined position as in Fig. 12.12 or in a skew position as in Fig. 12.13, the method of tangent spheres is a most convenient method of drawing the outline. Circles representing spheres are drawn tangent to the surface outline in a view where the normal view of the axis shows the true-surface outline. Then

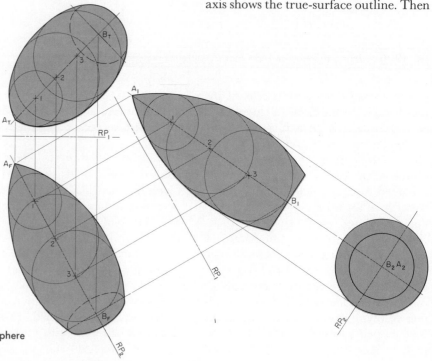

FIG. 12.13. Representation of a double-curved surface by the tangent-sphere method. (Skew position.)

if these sphere centers are projected to the axis in any other view and the circles representing the spheres drawn in that view, the outline of the view will be a curve tangent to the circles. In Fig. 12.12, the axis is horizontal. Circles are drawn in the top view tangent to the true-surface outline, using any convenient series of centers such as 1, 2, 3, as shown. The circle centers are then projected to the front view of the axis, and the circles (diameters identical to the top view) are then drawn in the front view. A curve drawn tangent to these circles gives the front-view outline. The ellipse representing the base may be drawn as described in paragraph 10.6. The end view of the axis and accompanying base circle may be drawn if desired.

For a skew position such as Fig. 12.13, an auxiliary view showing the normal view of the axis must be made and the true-surface outline laid out. Then tangent spheres in the auxiliary view may be projected to the other views, as shown, to complete the representation. The second auxiliary view showing the axis as a point may be drawn, if desired, although it is not necessary to the representation. The outline of the base will be elliptical and may be drawn as described in paragraph 10.6.

Summary

1. Draw two views of the axis of the surface of revolution. If one of these views (because of space position) is not a normal view of the axis, draw it.

2. In the normal view of the axis, from specifications, lay out the surface.

3. In the normal view, select a number of centers on the axis, and draw circles, representing spheres, that are tangent to the surface.

4. Project all of the sphere centers to the other views, and draw all circles representing the spheres in all views.

5. Draw curves tangent to the spheres, to complete the views.

12.14. LOCATION OF A POINT ON A SURFACE OF REVOLUTION. The specification for the location of a point on a surface of revolution must in some way be referred to the axis of the surface, for if it is not, the problem becomes one of finding where a line intersects the surface. In Fig. 12.14, the point P has been specified as somewhere on a plane at distance D below A (one end of the axis) and at a distance Q from the base of the surface containing point B, the other end of the axis. First, in the auxiliary view showing the true length of the axis

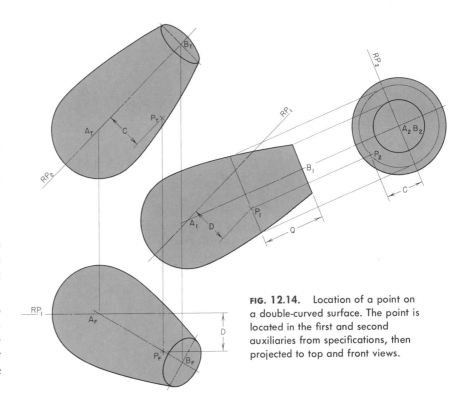

FIG. 12.14. Location of a point on a double-curved surface. The point is located in the first and second auxiliaries from specifications, then projected to top and front views.

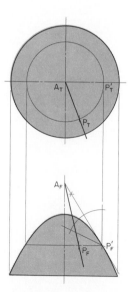

FIG. 12.15. A line tangent to a double-curved surface. The line lies in a plane tangent to the surface. This line tangent intersects the surface axis.

AB, the distances D and Q may be laid out and the point P located, as shown at P_1. Second, the circle of the surface upon which P_1 lies is drawn in the second auxiliary view showing the end view of axis AB. Third, point P may be located in the second auxiliary view because it must lie on the circle and be in projection with P_1. Finally, the top view may then be located by projection from P_1 and by measurement of distance C from RP_2.

The front view of P may then be found by projection from the top view to the horizontal plane on which point P was originally specified.

Many variations of the specification for the location of point P are possible. As an example, point P may be specified on some vertical, horizontal, or profile plane and at some distance from either end of the axis. Another possible specification is to locate the point on a particular circle of the surface and at some distance from one end of the axis with, in addition, a plane specification on which the point must lie.

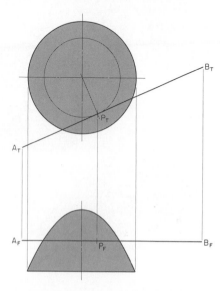

FIG. 12.16. A line tangent to a double-curved surface. The line lies in a plane tangent to the surface. This line is parallel to the surface base.

Summary

1. Draw two views of the axis of the surface. If these two views are not a normal and end view, draw auxiliaries showing these.

2. From specifications, locate the point in one of the views.

3. Project or measure (as may be necessary) to locate the point in the normal view, where it will lie on a circle of the surface, the location of which must be given in the specifications for the point.

4. Draw, in the end view, the circle the point lies on, and project the point to it. This now establishes the point on the surface of revolution.

5. Project the point location to the other views.

12.15.   A LINE OR PLANE TANGENT TO A SURFACE OF REVOLUTION.   A line tangent to a surface of revolution must lie in a plane tangent to the surface at the same point. Thus a line tangent, unless special conditions prevail, is best found by first finding or locating a plane tangent. Special conditions of line tangency are illustrated by Figs. 12.15 and 12.16. In Fig. 12.15, a tangent is drawn through point P so that the tangent intersects the axis. If the point P is revolved about the axis until it falls on a limiting element of the surface at P', a tangent to the true generating curve of the surface will pass through the axis, as shown. The intersection with the axis will not move under counterrevolution, and thus the tangent through point P will be a line drawn through points A and P.

Figure 12.16 illustrates a tangent to a circular section of a surface of revolution. The tangent must lie in a plane perpendicular to the axis, as shown by the front view, and be tangent to the circular section, as shown on the top view.

Summary

A line tangent intersecting the axis of the surface (Fig. 12.15)

1. In the normal view of the surface axis, rotate the point to the surface limit (normal view of the surface curve). Draw the tangent to the curve at the point, and extend the tangent to intersect the surface axis.

2. Now, counterrevolve the tangent by simply drawing a line from the intersection of tangent and axis through the actual point location.

3. Project the tangent to the end view, and to any other views.

A line tangent in a plane perpendicular to the surface axis (Fig. 12.16)

1. In the end view of the surface axis, draw the circle that the point lies on, and draw the tangent to the circle at the point.

2. Project the tangent to the normal view of the surface axis, where the tangent will be located through the point and perpendicular to the surface axis.

3. Project to any other views.

Lines tangent in any position other than those described and illustrated by Figs. 12.15 and 12.16 are not easily found because a section of the surface cut by a plane through the line and normal to the surface must be made. However, a *line tangent* drawn in a *plane tangent* is a direct and straightforward solution. Figure 12.17 illustrates a surface of revolution with its axis in a skew position to which a plane and line tangent are to be drawn at point *P*. Two tangent lines through point *P* will determine a plane tangent. On the true-

length view of the axis, a tangent *VT* through point *P* and intersecting the axis is laid out by the method of Fig. 12.15. On the end view of the axis, a tangent *RS* through point *P* (tangent to a circular section) is laid out by the method of Fig. 12.16. The plane *RST* made from these two tangent lines is then the required tangent plane at point *P*.

Any line through point *P* in plane *RST* will be a line tangent to the surface of revolution. Line *PW* is shown in Fig. 12.17 as an example of a horizontal line through point *P* and tangent to the ellipsoidal surface.

Summary

1. In the normal view of the surface axis, lay out a tangent line through the point and intersecting the surface axis by the method of Fig. 12.15.

2. In the end view and normal view of the surface axis, lay out a tangent

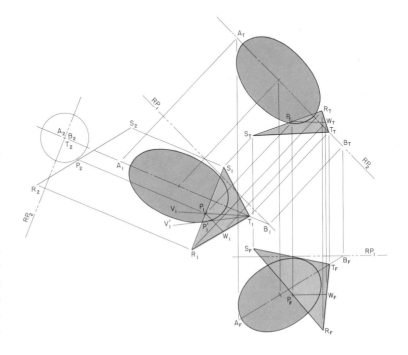

FIG. 12.17. Line and plane tangents to a double-curved surface. The plane tangent is formed of two intersecting line tangents.

through the point and perpendicular to the surface axis by the method of Fig. 12.16. Locate any two convenient points on this tangent.

3. The two points on the tangent just located and the point of intersection with the axis on the tangent first located constitute a plane through the point on the surface, tangent to the surface. Any line in this plane, through the point, is a tangent line to the surface at the point.

4. Locate whatever is required by problem specifications in the tangent plane and project to the other views.

12.16. WARPED SURFACES.   The major portion of all surfaces used in making up machines and structures will be found to consist of the simpler forms such as planes, prisms, pyramids, cylinders, and cones. Occasionally, however, a surface is required to form a smooth connection, or "blend," between two planes or similar simple surfaces. The surface required to make such a transition must usually be formed by a generating line with a constantly changing direction, and the surface is then said to be warped.

12.17. DEFINITIONS AND CLASSIFICATION. A *warped surface* is a surface generated by a straight line moving so that no two consecutive positions are parallel or lie in the same plane. The line and plane elements used in generating warped surfaces are given in the definitions following:

The *generatrix* is a straight line moving so as to form the required surface.

The *directrices* are the straight or curved lines that the generatrix continuously contacts.

The *director* is that plane to which the generatrix is constantly parallel.

An *axis* is a center line around which a generatrix may revolve; or an axis is a line around which a surface is symmetrical.

The *elements* are straight lines shown on the surface, indicating different plotted positions of the generatrix.

Warped surfaces may be classified as ruled surfaces because they are generated by the motion of a straight line. The hyperboloids may be double-ruled as it is possible to draw two elements through any point on the surface. All the other warped surfaces are single-ruled.

By definition, no two consecutive elements on a warped surface may be parallel or intersect. Therefore, the relationships between the director and directrices or between the directrices (if there is no director) are restricted. The directrices may not intersect or be parallel, and no directrix may lie in the plane director; for if such conditions exist, either an impossible surface or a plane or single-curved surface will result. If two line directrices intersect or are parallel, a plane surface will result. If a line directrix is placed so as to form the axis of curved line directrices, a single-curved surface will be formed.

Warped surfaces may be generated in several different ways:

1. By moving the generating line so as to contact two nonparallel, nonintersecting line directrices and also remain parallel to a plane director.

2. By moving the generating line so as to follow a space-curve directrix and also remain at a constant angle to a line directrix.

3. By moving the generating line so as to contact three nonparallel, nonintersecting line directrices.

Warped surfaces may be classified according to their family grouping; the following outline also gives the method of generation in each case:

I. Single-ruled Surfaces

A. Cylindrical forms
  1. *Cylindroid,* generated by two curved directrices and a plane director
  2. *Cow's horn,* generated by two curved directrices and one straight directrix

B. Conical forms
  1. *Right conoid and oblique conoid,* generated by a curved directrix, a straight directrix, and a plane director
  2. *Warped cone,* generated by two curved directrices and a straight directrix

C. Helicoidal forms
  1. *Cylindrical helicoid (right or oblique),* generated by a cylindrical helix and a generatrix having a constant angle with a straight directrix
  2. *Conical helicoid (right or oblique),* generated by a conical helix and a generatrix having a constant angle with a straight directrix

D. General forms: *Ruled surfaces of airfoils and streamlined shapes*

II. Double-ruled Surfaces

A. Circular form: *Hyperboloid of revolution,* generated by a straight generatrix revolving about a straight nonparallel, nonperpendicular directrix

B. Elliptical form: *Elliptical hyperboloid,* generated by a straight generatrix moving in contact with three straight directrices

C. Parabolic form: *Parabolic hyperboloid,* generated by a straight generatrix moving in contact with two straight directrices and parallel to a plane director

12.18. SINGLE-RULED SURFACES: CYLINDRICAL FORMS. The cylindrical forms of warped surfaces make a transition between two cylindrical surfaces, either right or oblique. These warped surfaces are often used in vaulted ceilings or arched passageways and where cylindrical flumes or ducts change in size and direction.

12.19. THE CYLINDROID. A cylindroid is a warped surface formed by a generatrix moving parallel to a plane director and in contact with two curved directrices. Figure 12.18*A* shows the surface pictorially.

The cylindroid shown in Fig. 12.18*B* has a plane director appearing as an edge in the top view. The front-curved directrix *AB* is circular. The rear-curved directrix *CD* is elliptical. The projected size of the curved directrices perpendicular to the plane director must be

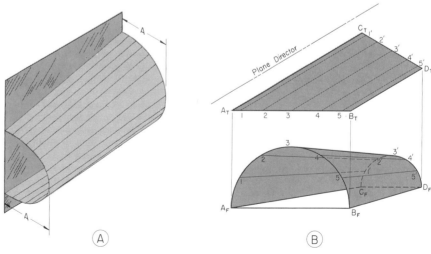

FIG. 12.18. The cylindroid. (*A*) Pictorial representation, (*B*) orthographic representation.

identical; for if they are not the same, some position of the generatrix (parallel to the plane director) will not intersect both directrices. This is shown by dimension A on the pictorial illustration. Successive positions of the generatrix, 1-1', 2-2', etc., are drawn parallel to the edge view of the plane director and then projected to the front view.

If a cylindroid is to be drawn in a skew position or if the plane director is a skew plane, an auxiliary view showing the edge of the plane director will have to be drawn, in which view the generatrix positions may be shown and then projected back to the principal views.

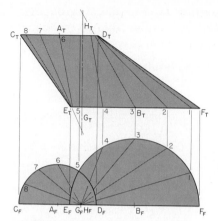

FIG. 12.20.   Construction of the cow's horn. Elements are located in the front view, then projected to the top view.

Summary

1. Draw two views of the cylindroid. (*a*) A view showing the edge view of the plane director. (*b*) Any other view in direct projection with the first view in which the curved directrices can be conveniently drawn. (Remember that the maximum and minimum projected distances of the curved directrices, perpendicular to the plane director, must be identical.)

2. In the view showing the edge view,

draw elements parallel to the plane director that intersect the two curved directrices.

3. Project the elements to the second view.

12.20.   THE COW'S HORN.   The *cow's horn* is a warped surface generated by a line moving in contact with two curved directrices and intersecting a third straight directrix employed as an axis. Figure 12.19 shows the surface pictorially and identifies the directrices and generatrix.

The cow's horn is usually designed with circular directrices although it may be made with ellipses. The cow's horn should not be confused with the sometimes similar warped cone, because the cow's horn has its axis placed in a position so that one central element of the surface intersects the axis at infinity; whereas the warped cone has its axis through the center of each base.

Figure 12.20 shows the construction of a typical cow's horn. The two curved directrices (in this case, circles) are *CD*

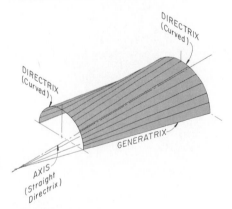

FIG. 12.19.   The cow's horn. All elements intersect the curved directrices and the axis.

with center A and EF with center B. The axis is GH, located on the line of centers. The elements (positions of the generatrix) are first drawn in the front view so as to intersect both directrices and the axis. The elements, 1, 2, etc., are then projected to the top view. Element 5 will intersect the axis at infinity.

Note that some of the elements will intersect the axis on one end of the surface, and others will intersect on the opposite end. The elements *do not* intersect the axis at a common point.

Summary

1. Draw a view showing the normal view of the two curved directrices and the point view of the axis.

2. Draw a view in direct projection with the first view, showing the normal view of the axis and the edge view of the planes of the curved directrices.

3. In the point view of the axis, draw elements that intersect the axis and both curved directrices.

4. Project these elements to the view showing the normal view of the axis.

12.21.   SINGLE-RULED SURFACES: CONICAL FORMS.   Conical-form warped surfaces are used to make a transition between two curved surfaces or from a curved surface (usually a cylinder) to a plane. They are, in a practical way, found approximated in the surfaces of some jets and nozzles and on some bits and forming tools. One common use is for the transition between a curved and flat ceiling. As the surfaces are not easily developable, they are not so common as similar transitions that are formed by plane surfaces and portions of oblique cones.

12.22.   THE CONOID.   A *conoid* is a warped surface formed by a generatrix moving parallel to a plane director and in contact with a curved directrix and a straight directrix. If the straight directrix is perpendicular to the plane director, the surface is a right conoid; if not perpendicular, the surface is an oblique conoid. Figure 12.21A illustrates a right conoid, and Fig. 12.21B illustrates an oblique conoid.

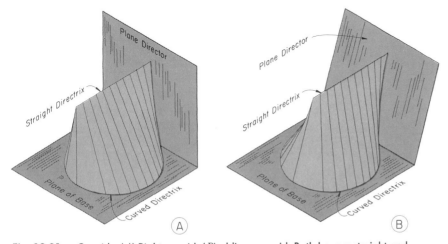

Fig. 12.21.   Conoids. (A) Right conoid, (B) oblique conoid. Both have a straight and a curved directrix. Elements are parallel to a plane director.

12.23.   THE RIGHT CONOID.   In the typical right conoid in Fig. 12.22*A*, the line *AB* is the straight-line directrix and the circular base is the curved directrix. The plane director is, in this case, a vertical plane and perpendicular to the horizontal-line directrix *AB*, thus satisfying the conditions necessary to obtain a right conoid. Positions of the generatrix will be parallel to the edge view of the plane director. The intersections of the generatrix thus are easily obtained in the top view and are then projected to the front view.

Note that the length of the straight directrix must be the same as the distance across the base, perpendicular to the plane director. If those distances were not identical, the generatrix could not remain parallel to the plane director and intersect both line directrices.

A right conoid may, of course, be in a skew position in space instead of the regular position shown in Fig. 12.22*A*. The problem, however, may be solved by making an auxiliary view to get the edge view of the plane director and, in this view, setting up positions of the generatrix and then projecting the intersections back to the principal views.

Summary

1. Draw two views of the specified right conoid, one showing the edge view and the other the normal view of the base (curved directrix). Draw the

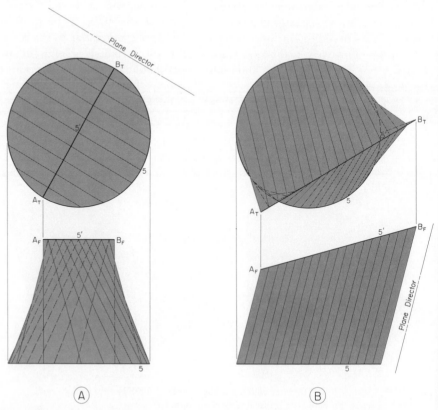

FIG. 12.22.   Construction of the conoid. (*A*) Right conoid, (*B*) oblique conoid.

straight-line directrix (normal in the view showing the normal view of the base and perpendicular to the plane director) in both of these views.

2. In the view showing the normal view of the base, draw the edge view of the plane director.

3. In the view now showing the normal view of the curved-line directrix, the normal view of the straight-line directrix, and the edge view of the plane director, draw elements parallel to the plane director that intersect both the curved and straight directrices.

4. Project the elements to the other view.

12.24. THE OBLIQUE CONOID. Figure 12.22*B* illustrates a typical oblique conoid. The plane director in this case shows as an edge in the front view. The straight directrix *AB* is a line inclined to the base, therefore satisfying the conditions for an oblique conoid. Successive positions of the generatrix are drawn parallel to the edge view of the plane director and then projected to the top view.

Note that the projected length of the straight directrix must be the same as the projected size of the curved directrix in a direction perpendicular to the plane director.

An oblique conoid in a skew position in space may be drawn as described in paragraph 12.23.

Summary

1. Draw two views of the base (curved-line directrix), one a normal view and the other an edge view. Draw the *position* (not necessarily the correct length) of the straight-line directrix in these views.

2. If one of the views drawn will not show the edge view of the plane director, draw a view that does. In this view, draw elements parallel to the plane director that intersect both the straight and curved directrices. The limiting elements intersecting the curved-line directrix will determine the length of the straight directrix.

3. Project to the other view or views.

12.25. THE WARPED CONE. The warped cone is a warped surface formed by a generatrix moving in contact with two curved directrices and intersecting a third directrix located as a central axis.

The definitions of the warped cone and the cow's horn are similar. This similarity is, however, only superficial. The axis of a warped cone is central, whereas that of the cow's horn is not; the elements of a warped cone all intersect the axis on one end, whereas the elements of a cow's horn intersect half on one end and half on the other; also, the form of a warped cone is conical, and the cow's horn is cylindrical. Figure 12.23 pictorially represents a typical warped cone.

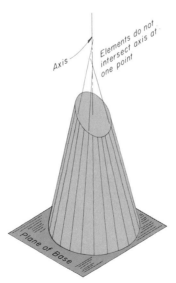

FIG. 12.23. The warped cone. All elements intersect two curved directrices and a straight directrix (axis).

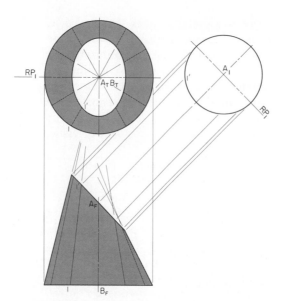

FIG. 12.24. Construction of the warped cone. Elements are located in the top view, then projected to the front view.

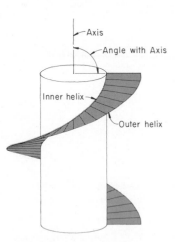

FIG. 12.25. The cylindrical helicoid. The elements emanate from a cylindrical helix.

Figure 12.24 is an orthographic drawing of a warped cone. In this case, the lower base is circular, with center at *B*. The upper base is also circular, but inclined to the base, and with center at *A*. The axis *AB* is located so as to pass through the center of both bases. The surface will be a warped cone instead of a right cone because the upper base is not a section of a right cone.

Elements of the surface are located by dividing the base into a convenient number of parts and drawing elements to intersect the upper base and the axis. In this case the elements must first be drawn in the top view where the axis appears as a point and then projected from the top view to the front view to complete the representation of the surface. In any case where the axis does not appear as a point in one of the regular views, a point view must be made before the elements can be drawn. The ele-

ments may be extended to the axis in the front view if desired; and if they are so extended, the intersections will be at different points, proving that the surface is warped instead of the surface of a right or oblique cone.

Summary

1. Draw two views, one an end view and the other a normal view of the axis. Use auxiliary views for construction of the base curves, as needed.

2. Divide the larger base into a convenient number of parts.

3. In the end view of the axis, draw elements that intersect both bases and the axis.

4. Project the elements to the view showing the normal view of the axis.

12.26.   **SINGLE-RULED SURFACES: HELICOIDAL FORMS.** Helicoidal surfaces are warped surfaces in which one of the directrices is a helix. These surfaces are very common: they are present on screw threads, coil springs, twist drills, spiral chutes, and other similar elements or structures.

12.27.   **CYLINDRICAL HELICOIDS.** A cylindrical helicoid is a warped surface formed by a generatrix having a constant angle with a straight directrix and moving in contact with a cylindrical helix (curved directrix). If the angle with the axis is 90° (generatrix perpendicular to the axis), the surface will be a right helicoid. If the angle is other than 90°, the surface will be an oblique helicoid. Figure 12.25 is a pictorial drawing of a cylindrical helicoid.

Figure 12.26 shows the construction of a cylindrical right helicoid. The straight directrix is *AB*. The generatrix *CD* is perpendicular to the axis *AB*. The space curve DD' is a cylindrical helix. Positions of the generatrix are first located in the top view by dividing the enclosing cylinder into a convenient number of equal parts. These points are then connected to the axis AB, thus intersecting the inner cylinder and producing successive positions of the generatrix, 1, 2, 3, etc. The helix and positions of the generatrix may then be drawn. The lead of the helix, laid out as shown, is divided into the same number of equal parts used in dividing the enclosing cylinder. This procedure is necessary since a helix is defined as a point moving at a constant rate around an axis and at the same time moving at a constant rate parallel to the axis. Dividing the lead (distance traveled parallel to the axis in one revolution) into equal parts locates a series of planes upon which successive positions of the generatrix will lie. Positions of the generatrix may then be plotted in the front view by projecting the top-view position to the proper plane in the front view.

Summary

1. Draw two views, one the end view and the other the normal view of the axis.

2. From specifications, draw inner and outer limiting cylinders of the required surface.

3. Divide the larger cylinder (for accuracy) in the end view into a convenient number of equal parts, and draw radial lines to the axis. This represents successive positions of the generatrix in the end view.

4. Lay out the lead along the normal view of the axis, and divide it into the same number of equal parts used in dividing the end view. This represents

successive positions of the generatrix as it moves along the axis.

5. Plot positions of the generatrix by projection from the end view to the normal view of the axis, remembering that as the generatrix moves one unit around the axis it also moves one unit along the axis.

An oblique cylindrical helicoid is identical to a right cylindrical helicoid except that the acute angle of the generatrix with the axis is less than 90°. The inner end of the generatrix therefore starts at a different level than the outer end, as shown by the front view of Fig. 12.27. The lead for each helix is laid out and divided individually into the same number of equal parts as the top view. The front view may then be completed by projecting successive posi-

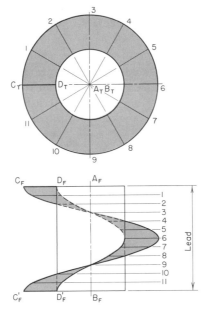

FIG. 12.26. Construction of a cylindrical right helicoid. The elements are perpendicular to (and intersect) the axis.

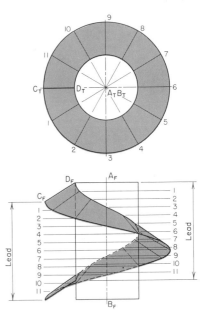

FIG. 12.27. Construction of a cylindrical oblique helicoid. The elements are at an angle to the axis but (in this case) intersect the axis.

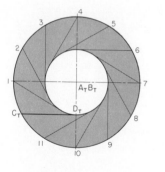

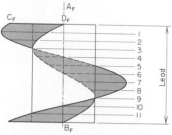

FIG. 12.28. Construction of a cylindrical oblique helicoid. The elements (in this case) do not intersect the axis but are in planes perpendicular to the axis.

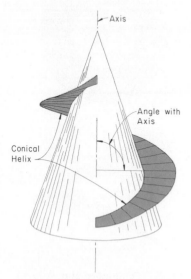

FIG. 12.29. The conical helicoid. The elements emanate from a conical helix.

tions of the inner and outer ends of the generatrix to the proper plane position, as indicated in Fig. 12.27.

Any oblique helicoidal surface must have the generatrix at some angle to the axis, but the generatrix need not intersect the axis. Figure 12.28 shows an oblique cylindrical helicoid in which the generatrix *DC* does not intersect the axis. Note that the method of layout is identical to Fig. 12.27 except for the difference in relative position of the generatrix. Also note that the elements, in this case, are horizontal.

Summary

1. Draw two views of the axis, one an end view and the other a normal view.

2. Draw inner and outer cylinders to limit the required surface.

3. Divide the larger cylinder (for accuracy) in the end view into a convenient number of equal parts, and draw successive positions of the generatrix in the end view.

4. Draw one position of the generatrix in the end view that will appear normal in the normal view of the axis. In this normal view, lay out the angle that the generatrix is to make with the axis. This determines the "space distance," parallel to the axis, between the inner and outer limiting ends of the generatrix.

5. Using the space distance just determined, lay out two identical leads, one for the helix on the inner cylinder, the other for the helix on the outer cylinder, and offset along the axis by the space distance.

6. Plot successive positions of the generatrix in the normal view of the axis by projection from the end view, remembering that as the generatrix moves one unit around it moves one unit along the axis.

12.28. CONICAL HELICOIDS. A conical helix is a space curve defined as a point moving at a uniform rate around an axis and at the same time moving at a uniform rate along the axis and on the surface of a cone. Figure 12.29 illustrates the surface pictorially. Figure 12.30 illustrates the construction of a conical right helicoid. The axis is *AB*, and generatrix *CD* is perpendicular to it. The generatrix positions are to be plotted for each one-twelfth of one complete rotation. Thus the top view is divided into 12 parts by drawing lines through the axis at increments of 30°. The lead is also divided into 12 equal parts. The helix (which represents movement on the cone surface of the point *C*) is plotted by first locating circular sections of the

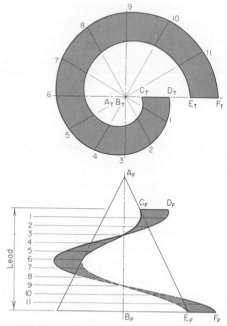

FIG. 12.30. Construction of a conical right helicoid. The elements intersect the conical helix and the axis and are perpendicular to the axis.

cone on which plotted positions of point C will lie. In Fig. 12.30, these circular sections are cut by planes 1, 2, 3, etc. On these circles, at successive positions of the lead, are found the several points representing the helical movement of point C. For example, on plane 1 of the lead and position 1 of the top view is found the first point, and at plane 2 and position 2 of the top view is found the second point. Note that the points in the top view lie on the circle cut by planes 1, 2, 3, etc. After the top view has been drawn, the points may be projected to the front view. The generatrix CD will appear the same length in the top view for all positions and may now be drawn, locating the outer helix from the inner helix. Then, to complete the front view, positions of point D are projected to the proper lead plane. The visibility is then determined and the curves drawn in.

A conical oblique helicoid is drawn in a similar manner with, of course, the exception that the generatrix will be drawn at an angle to the axis.

Summary

1. Draw two views of the axis, one an end view and the other a normal view.

2. In these views, draw the cone upon which the conical helix is to be generated.

3. In the end view, divide the base of the cone into a convenient number of equal parts, and using these points, draw successive positions of the generatrix.

4. Lay out the lead along the axis in the normal view, and divide the lead into the same number of equal parts used in dividing the end view.

5. Plot positions of the generatrix in the normal view of the axis by projection from the end view, remembering that as the generatrix moves one unit around

the axis it also moves one unit along the lead.

12.29. DOUBLE-RULED SURFACES: THE HYPERBOLOIDS. All double-ruled warped surfaces may be classed as hyperboloids because the principal contour of the surface is hyperbolic. However, in most cases other conic sections, circles, ellipses, and parabolas, may also be cut from the surface by properly selected planes. The hyperboloids may be designed in either circular, elliptical, or parabolic form. The elliptical form is rather limited in practical uses, but the circular form is common and important because of its application in hypoid gearing. The parabolic form is often used as the transition surface for ducts, dams, retaining walls, bridges, and other concrete structures.

All the hyperboloids—circular, elliptical, or parabolic—are basically generated by a straight line moving so as to be in contact with three nonparallel, nonintersecting directrices. However, the circular form, called the "hyperboloid of revolution," must have the directrices located so that their relationship to a central axis is the same for all three directrices, and the parabolic form must have all three directrices in parallel planes. Thus it is evident that the elliptical form is the general case and that the circular and parabolic forms are special arrangements. Conversely, the directrices for an elliptical hyperboloid must be carefully chosen, or the circular or parabolic form may be generated.

The directrices for any hyperboloid will be elements of the surface for the second generation. Therefore, any three elements of one generation may be taken as directrices for the second generation. Every element of the first generation will

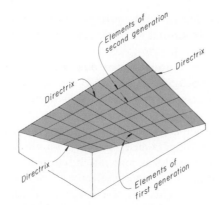

FIG. 12.31. The hyperboloid. The elements intersect three nonparallel, nonintersecting directrices.

intersect every element of the second generation, proving that both generations form the same surface.

Figure 12.31 shows pictorially the three nonparallel, nonintersecting directrices for a hyperboloid. The elements are positions of the generatrix intersecting all three directrices. Note that elements of the second generation must have as their directrices three elements of the first generation.

Figure 12.32 is an orthographic drawing of a hyperboloid, illustrating the method of location for elements that intersect all three directrices. The directrices are lines AB, CD, and EF. If the end view of one of the directrices is obtained, all elements in that view must, in order to intersect that directrix, pass through the directrix where it appears as a point. In Fig. 12.32, directrix CD is horizontal, and therefore an auxiliary projected from the top view and taken in the direction of $C_T D_T$ will show CD as a point. Directrices AB and EF are projected to this view. Then any straight line through $C_A D_A$ intersecting AB and CD (line 2-6, etc.) will be an element of

the surface. The elements may then be projected back to the top view and to the front view. If the second generation is desired, elements F-1, 3-5, and B-4 may be taken as directrices and an end view of one of these directrices employed, as described for the first generation, to give elements for the second generation. Although the surface just described is an elliptical hyperboloid, this example gives the basic theory necessary to a complete understanding of the generation of all the hyperboloids.

The explanations following for the circular, elliptical, and parabolic hyperboloids are the useful and practical methods.

12.30. THE CIRCULAR HYPERBOLOID. This hyperboloid is often called the hyperboloid of revolution because, as the cross section perpendicular to the axis must be circular, it may be generated

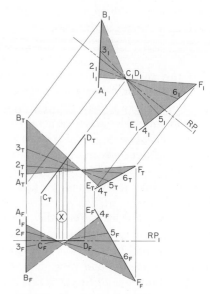

FIG. 12.32. Construction of the hyperboloid. The three nonparallel, nonintersecting directrices are AB, CD, and EF.

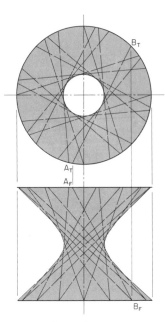

FIG. 12.33. Orthographic representation of a circular hyperboloid. The elements intersect a gore circle and two circular directrices.

by a single generatrix revolving about an axis.

Figure 12.33 is the representation of a circular hyperboloid. The generatrix AB, having a fixed relationship (nonparallel and nonintersecting) to the axis, will describe circles on any plane perpendicular to the axis. The smallest circle described is known as the *gore circle*. The simplest and most direct construction is first to locate and draw two circles representing the circular path of points on the generatrix at the extremities of the surface parallel to the axis. Next, draw the gore circle in the top view. All positions of the generatrix must contact the gore circle and the two extremity circles and thus are drawn tangent to the gore circle in the top view, crossing the two extremity circles. For convenience, one extremity circle may be

divided into a number of equal parts, thus producing evenly spaced elements of the representation.

The elements located in the top view are then projected down to the front view from their intersection with the two extremity circles.

Following the basic theory of the hyperboloids as described in paragraph 12.27, it is interesting to note that elements of one generation will be directrices for the second generation. Figure 12.34 shows three elements of one generation taken as directrices and marked Dir. 1, Dir. 2, and Dir. 3. Three elements of the second generation, A_1B_1, A_2B_2, and A_3B_3, intersect all three directrices. As an example in reading the drawing

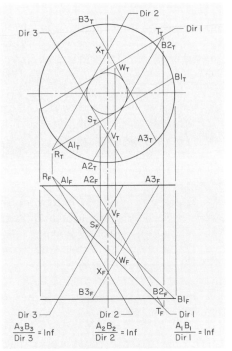

FIG. 12.34. Elements and directrices of a circular hyperboloid. Any three elements of one generation are three nonparallel, nonintersecting directrices of the second generation.

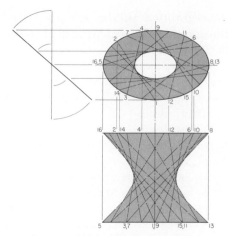

FIG. 12.35. The elliptical hyperboloid. The elements intersect a gore ellipse and two elliptical directices.

of Fig. 12.34, Dir. 1 intersects A_1B_1 at infinity, A_2B_2 at T, and A_3B_3 at W. Similarly, A_1B_1 intersects Dir. 1 at infinity, Dir. 2 at R, and Dir. 3 at S.

Summary

To draw a circular hyperboloid:

1. Draw two views of the axis, an end view and a normal view.

2. Draw two circles concentric with the axis, representing maximum limits of the surface.

3. In the end view of the axis, draw a gore circle, representing the minimum limit of the surface from the axis.

4. Draw elements in the end view that are tangent to the gore circle and intersect the two extremity circles.

5. Project the elements to the view showing the normal view of the axis.

12.31. THE ELLIPTICAL HYPERBOLOID. The general hyperboloid form is the elliptical hyperboloid, as described in paragraph 12.29. However, in order to control the elliptical shape wanted, the layout

should be made by locating two ellipses representing the path of points on the generatrix in planes perpendicular to the axis. In Fig. 12.35, two ellipses representing the extremities of the surface have been drawn by revolving circles, as shown, to obtain the required minor diameters. Positions of the generatrix are found by drawing the gore ellipse and drawing the generatrix positions tangent to the gore ellipse. Thus, in Fig. 12.35, elements 1-2, 3-4, 5-6, etc., are positions of the generatrix of the required surface. The second generation may be made by reversing the direction of the generatrix relative to the axis.

Figure 12.36 shows that the elliptical hyperboloid may be formed by a generatrix in contact with three straight-line directrices. A_1B_1, A_2B_2, and A_3B_3 are elements of one generation. Three

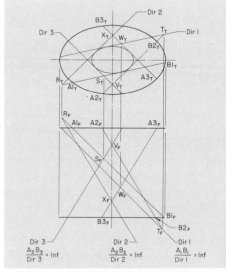

FIG. 12.36. Elements and directrices of an elliptical hyperboloid. Any three elements of the first generation are three nonparallel, nonintersecting directrices of the second generation.

elements of the opposite generation are taken as directrices and are marked Dir. 1, Dir. 2, and Dir. 3. Note that Dir. 1 intersects A_1B_1 at infinity, A_2B_2 at T, and A_3B_3 at W. Similarly, A_1B_1 intersects Dir. 1 at infinity, Dir. 2 at R, and Dir. 3 at S.

Summary

To draw an elliptical hyperboloid:

1. Draw two views of the axis, an end view and a normal view.

2. Draw an auxiliary view, projected from the end view, and in this auxiliary view lay out the edge view of two circular maximum limits for the surface and a minimum limit or gore circle. Rotate the edge views in the auxiliary view so that when projection back to the end view is made, ellipses of the required proportion (major diameter versus minor diameter) are obtained.

3. Draw the elliptical limits (maximum and minimum) in the end view, and project to the view showing the normal view of the axis.

4. Draw elements in the end view that are tangent to the gore ellipse, and intersect the limiting ellipses.

5. Project the elements to the view showing the normal view of the axis.

12.32. THE PARABOLIC HYPERBOLOID.
The parabolic hyperboloid is one of the most common and useful of all hyperboloids, used for the warped surfaces of ducts, dams, and retaining walls and in bridges and culverts. It is also often found in the external surfaces of castings and forgings of mechanical parts. The name "hyperbolic parabolic" has been generally accepted for this warped surface. However, it is apparent from the classification in paragraph 12.27 that the term parabolic hyperboloid is more

accurate and logical. Figure 12.37 illustrates the surface pictorially.

Definition. The *parabolic hyperboloid* is the surface formed by a generating line moving parallel to a plane director and in contact with two straight noninter-secting, nonparallel directrices.

Figure 12.38 illustrates the general case: The lines AB and CD are the two directrices and form the two limiting ends of the surface. The generatrix will constantly contact lines AB and CD and be parallel to a plane director. Because lines AB and CD are nonintersecting and nonparallel and are also of different length, the plane director will be a skew plane that must be parallel to the two limiting positions AD and BC of the generatrix. To locate the plane director, a point view of one position of the generatrix may be obtained, and a second position of the generatrix carried into

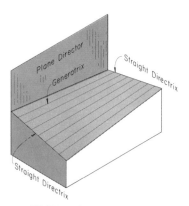

FIG. 12.37. The parabolic hyperboloid. The elements are parallel to a plane director and intersect two straight-line directrices.

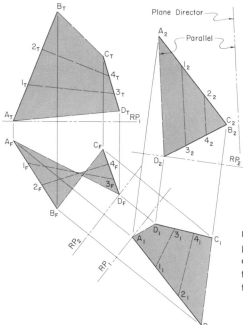

FIG. 12.38. Construction of a parabolic hyperboloid. In the second auxiliary, the elements are parallel to the plane director and intersect the directrices.

this point view will then indicate the direction for the edge view of the plane director. In Fig. 12.38, the generatrix position BC has been selected for the point view. The auxiliary view of BC is B_1C_1 and shows the true length of BC. AD is carried into this view. The point view of BC is B_2C_2, and the generatrix position AD is carried from the first auxiliary to the view showing the point view of BC. AD is shown in this view at A_2D_2. The line AD is not in true length in this view, but a receding plane passed parallel to AD will also be parallel to BC. This plane will be the necessary plane director and is marked on the figure. All positions of the generatrix will be parallel to the plane director and may now be drawn. They are indicated in the point view of BC by 1-3 and 2-4. The generatrix positions may now be carried back to the first auxiliary view and then to the principal views. Note that 1-3 and 2-4 divide the directrix lines AB and CD into equal parts but that successive positions of the generatrix are nonparallel and nonintersecting. The plotted positions of the

generatrix form elements of the parabolic hyperboloid.

The surface just discussed may be said to be in a skew position because the positions of the directrix and plane director are skew. Often, however, the directrices may be in a skew position, but the plane director may be either horizontal, frontal, or profile, thus simplifying the solution and position of the surface in space. Figure 12.39 shows at (A) a parabolic hyperboloid with a vertical plane director, at (B) one with a horizontal plane director. Note in each case that the projected lengths of the directrices perpendicular to the plane director must be the same.

Summary

1. The surface is formed by a generatrix moving in contact with two nonparallel, nonintersecting lines and parallel to a plane director.

2. Elements of the surface divide the plane directrices into proportional parts.

3. A point view of one element of the surface and another element in that view will determine the edge view of the plane director.

4. Elements of the surface are nonintersecting, nonparallel lines.

5. Only a portion of a complete parabolic hyperboloid is ever used practically, the portion which is bounded by the two directrices and two limiting elements. The complete surface extends to infinity.

If it is not necessary in a practical case to locate the plane director, any parabolic hyperboloid may be drawn in the principal views by dividing the directrices into equal parts and then connecting these points with lines to show successive positions of the generatrix. Note that in Fig. 12.38 the positions of

FIG. 12.39.   Parabolic hyperboloids.
(A) Plane director vertical,
(B) plane director horizontal.

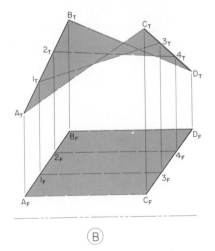

the generatrix, 1-3 and 2-4, divide both directrices *AB* and *CD* into equal parts. Figure 12.40 shows a method (based on the above fact) for drawing the principal views. Here the top view is selected for dividing the lines. Note that here is employed the familiar scale method of drawing a perpendicular from one end of the line and orienting a scale with convenient divisions so that points located may be projected back as perpendiculars to the line. Thus *AB* and *CD* have been equally divided and the generatrix positions drawn in the top view and then projected to the front view. If, after this method has been used to draw the principal views, the position of the plane director is required, it may be found by proceeding as in Fig. 12.38.

Summary

To draw a parabolic hyperboloid:

1. Draw two views of the two line directrices.

2. Divide each directrix into the same number of equal parts.

3. Draw elements connecting proportionate points of division of the directrices.

Figure 12.41 illustrates the fact that a parabolic hyperboloid may be formed by a generatrix in contact with three straight-line directrices. As stated before, the three directrices must lie in parallel planes. In Fig. 12.41, *AB* and *CD* are taken as two of the directrices. A point view is made of directrix *CD*, and directrix *AB* is carried to the point view. Then if a third directrix, for example, *EF*, is drawn parallel to *AB*, all three directrices will lie in parallel planes. The third directrix *EF* is carried back to the principal views, and it is evident from these views that all the elements intersect all three directrices.

Summary

Elements of one generation can be taken as directrices of the second generation. All elements of one generation intersect all elements of the second generation; thus any three elements of one generation can determine the surface and may be taken as three straight-line directrices which elements of the second generation must intersect.

The parabolic hyperboloid may also be constructed by drawing the two limiting parabolas for the surface as shown in Fig. 12.42. As explained before, all the elements must lie in parallel planes so that it is necessary (in this case) to lcoate and draw the plane director. In Fig. 12.43, the plane director appears as an edge in the front view, and all the elements are drawn parallel to it. The plane director and elements for the second generation must be reversed but have the same relationship to the vertical axis of the surface.

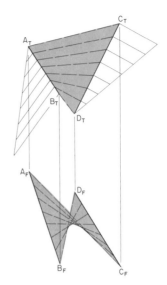

FIG. 12.40. Construction of a parabolic hyperboloid. In this example, the directrices are divided into equal parts to locate elements.

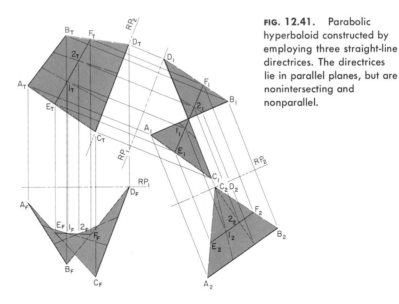

FIG. 12.41. Parabolic hyperboloid constructed by employing three straight-line directrices. The directrices lie in parallel planes, but are nonintersecting and nonparallel.

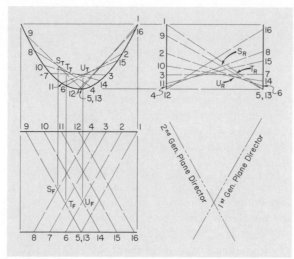

FIG. 12.42. A parabolic hyperboloid constructed by limiting parabolas. The elements intersect a gore parabola and two limiting parabolas.

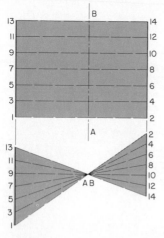

FIG. 12.43. A parabolic hyperboloid with frontal plane director. The elements are parallel to a frontal plane.

Summary

1. Draw two limiting parabolas of the surface.

2. Locate the plane director.

3. Draw elements parallel to the plane director.

12.33.   ELEMENT RELATIONSHIPS OF A PARABOLIC HYPERBOLOID. Any element of a parabolic hyperboloid is not only a line about which the generatrix of the second generation rotates but also a line which the generatrix will constantly touch. In Fig. 12.43, a parabolic hyperboloid is drawn in a simple position with the plane director frontal. Every position of the generatrix, 1-2, 3-4, etc., contacts line *AB*, one element (second generation) of the surface. Note, incidentally, that the element *AB* becomes the third straight-line directrix of Fig. 12.41. If the parabolic hyperboloid is in a skew position, a special element may be located by setting up a plane through one line directrix parallel to the other line directrix, as shown by plane *DEF* of

Fig. 12.44. An edge view of the plane *DEF* then results in a view in which the two line directrices appear as seen at A_1B_1 and C_1D_1 of Fig. 12.44. In this view, all positions of the generatrix will pass through a common point X_1Y_1, the point view of the special element. The point view of the element at X_1Y_1 may be found by drawing, in the top view, the vertical position of the generatrix 5-6 and projecting it to the auxiliary view and then setting up any element such as 1-2 in the auxiliary view. All elements of the surface are perpendicular to *XY*. Therefore, 1-2 may be located at any convenient place in the top view, perpendicular to *XY*, and then projected to the auxiliary view. These two positions, 5-6 and 1-2, of the generatrix determine the point view X_1Y_1, from which X_TY_T and X_FY_F may be located. Note that the plane director in this case will be a vertical plane and will appear as an edge in the top view, parallel to 1-2, 3-4, etc., and that the auxiliary view will be the normal view of the plane director. The element just described is the basis for locating all shortest lines intersecting two skew lines as discussed in paragraphs 11.16 to 11.20. Note that this is a special case of the parabolic hyperboloid in which the plane director is parallel to a group of shortest lines of the surface. Elements of the surface *do not* divide the directrices equally, as in Figs. 12.40, 12.43, and 12.45, because the elements have not been located in equal increments parallel to the plane director.

As indicated above, there are an infinite number of elements, and any element of one generation may be taken as the third line directrix for the second generation. Therefore, a point view of any element will locate a third line directrix for the other generation. Also, by obtaining the point view of an element, the position of the plane director will be determined. Both of these facts are illustrated by Fig. 12.45. The top and front views of a parabolic hyperboloid have been drawn by dividing AB and CD equally for one generation and BC and AD for the second generation. Then an element 7-8 is selected at random for the true-length and point view at the left side of the figure. Note in the point view of 7-8 that AB, CD, 7-8, 9-10, and 11-12 all appear parallel to each other and that the plane director will therefore appear as an edge in this view. Element 5-6 of the second generation has been selected for a point view at the right side of the figure. Here BC, 5-6, 3-4, 1-2, and AD all appear parallel, and the plane director for the second generation can be established. Thus we conclude that any element will be the third line directrix of the opposite generation and that the point view of any element will give a view in which the edge view of the plane director of that generation (of which the element is a member) will appear.

Summary

1. All elements of one generation intersect all elements of the second generation.

2. Any three elements of one generation may be taken as three straight-line directrices of the surface.

3. The space position of the plane director can be found by drawing a plane through any one element, parallel to any other element of the same generation. Then determine the edge view of the plane.

4. Because the line directrices are elements of the opposite generation, the

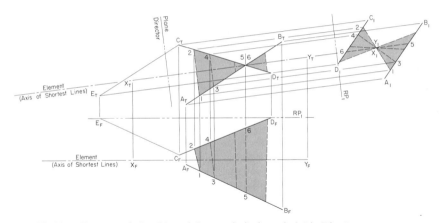

FIG. 12.44. Element relationships of the parabolic hyperboloid. Of prime significance is the fact that one element is an axis of shortest lines.

plane director for this generation can be found by drawing a plane through one line directrix, parallel to the other line directrix.

5. The shortest element length of a generation is the perpendicular distance

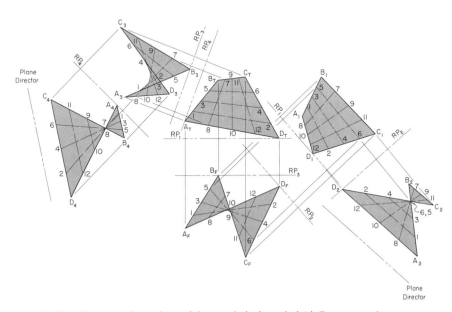

FIG. 12.45. Element relationships of the parabolic hyperboloid. Two generations are shown on this figure. Elements of one are directrices of the other.

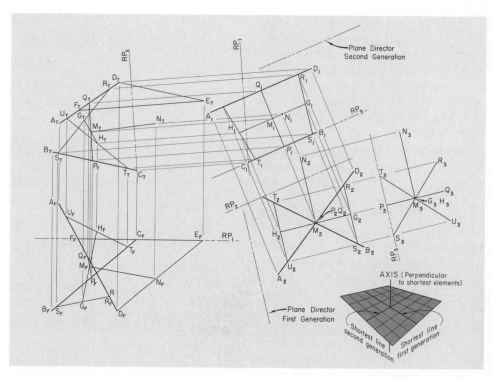

FIG. 12.46. Axis of symmetry of a parabolic hyperboloid. The axis is perpendicular to the shortest lines of each generation.

between the parallel planes containing the directrices.

6. The shortest element of a generation intersects an "axis of shortest lines," as does the shortest vertical, horizontal, or specified grade element. This axis is a specific third straight-line directrix.

7. The plane directors for each generation are not the same plane. Each is parallel to all elements of its own generation and is found by locating a plane through one *element* parallel to another *element* of the *same generation*.

12.34. THE AXIS OF SYMMETRY OF A PARABOLIC HYPERBOLOID. The *axis of symmetry,* or "central axis," of a parabolic hyperboloid is a line about which the surface is coextensive and proportional; the surface "balances" about its central axis. The axis of symmetry may be found by locating the shortest line of

each generation and then erecting a perpendicular at the intersection of the shortest lines. However, before this is possible, *the surface itself must be symmetrical.* No central axis can exist for *any* surface that is *asymmetrical.* A symmetrical parabolic hyperboloid is one in which the surface progresses in a uniform manner on opposite sides of the axis. Therefore, the axis must intersect *an element of the surface that is symmetrical to the directrices.* Furthermore, the only possible line symmetrical to two skew-line directrices is the *common perpendicular* of the directrices. Therefore, if the surface is made so that it is symmetrical about the common perpendicular between each pair of directrices for the two generations, the surface will be symmetrical and an axis can be located.

Figure 12.46 will illustrate the determination of a symmetrical parabolic hyperboloid and the location of its central axis. Lines AD and BC are taken as directrices of the first generation. The surface will be symmetrical about the common perpendicular PQ, which has been located by the method of paragraph 11.16. In the second auxiliary view, PQ appears as a point at P_2Q_2, and both directrices AD and BC appear in true length. An axis symmetrical to AD and BC will show in true length and will be the bisector of the angle between A_2D_2 and B_2C_2. This axis MN must also be symmetrical to directrices for the second generation. Therefore, two directrices, R_2S_2 and T_2U_2, are drawn equidistant from the point view of PQ at P_2Q_2 and parallel to M_2N_2. The directrices RS and TU will have a common perpendicular GH, which intersects PQ at M. The axis must, of course, also be symmetrical to the directrices RS and TU. This symmetry is shown by the view at $R_3S_3T_3U_3$, which is a third auxiliary projected from the second auxiliary and made in a direction to give the true length of RS and TU. All lines may now be projected back to the top and front views. Note, in the second and third auxiliary views, that axis MN is perpendicular to the common perpendicular for each pair of directrices. The plane director for each generation is shown on the figure. Also note that, in each case, the plane director is parallel to the directrices of the opposite generation and also parallel to the central axis.

Summary

To draw a parabolic hyperboloid symmetrical about an axis:

1. Locate and draw two views of the *position* (only) of the directrices of the first generation. The length of the directrices must not be a determining factor.

2. Draw a plane through one directrix parallel to the other directrix.

3. Draw the edge view (first auxiliary) of the plane, then the normal view (second auxiliary).

4. The shortest element of the first generation will appear as a point at the crossing of the directrices.

5. To be symmetrical, the second generation must have its shortest element intersect the shortest element of the first generation at the mid-point of both elements. Therefore, in the second auxiliary, draw two elements of the first generation that are symmetrical with the shortest element of the first generation.

6. Now, draw a third auxiliary projected from the second, showing the normal view of all three elements of the first generation. These three elements constitute straight-line directrices for the second generation, and in the third auxiliary all three appear in true length (normal). Moreover, in the third auxiliary, the shortest element of the second generation will appear as a point at the crossing of the two selected symmetrical elements of the first generation (directrices for the second generation). Draw the axis of the surface perpendicular to both shortest elements (in the third auxiliary). The axis appears normal in this view.

7. Project the axis back to the second auxiliary, where it will again appear normal because it is perpendicular to the shortest elements of both generations. (In the second auxiliary one shortest element appears normal; the other shortest element appears as a point.)

8. Project all lines back to the original views.

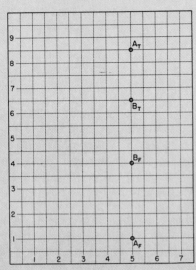

PROB. 12.1.1.

PROBLEMS

GROUP 1.   THE CYLINDER

12.1.1.   *AB* is the axis of a cylinder whose circular right section is 2 in. in diameter. The base at *B* is frontal; the base at *A* is horizontal. Draw the top and front views of the cylinder, showing visibility. Scale: ¾ size.

12.1.2.   *AB* is the axis of a cylinder whose circular right section is 4 in. in diameter. The bases are frontal and contain points *A* and *B*. Draw the top and front views of the cylinder, showing visibility. Scale: ⅜ size.

12.1.3.   *CD* is the axis of a cylinder of circular right section. Its circular base about point *D* is shown. Draw the conjugate diameters of the elliptical front view of the base about *D*. One of these diameters is frontal. *Optional:* Complete the views.

12.1.4.   Draw a view which shows the true shape of the right section of the cylinder *LM*.

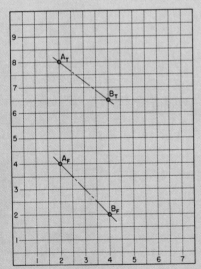

PROB. 12.1.2.

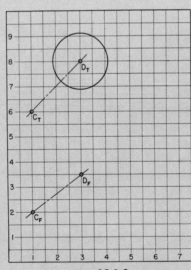

PROB. 12.1.3.

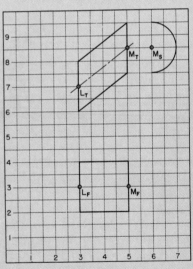

PROB. 12.1.4.

12.1.5. The axis, *AB*, and contour elements of a cylindrical surface are shown. Find the top view of *P*, a point on the rearward portion of the surface.

12.1.6. Planes *POT* and *LMN* are tangent to cylinder *AB*. Complete the top view of plane *POT* and the front and right-side views of plane *LMN*.

12.1.7. Draw the top view of plane *PLM*, which is tangent to the upper surface of the

cylinder *CD*. Draw the front view of plane *PQR*, which is tangent to the lower surface of cylinder *CD*.

12.1.8. *UV* is the axis of a circular cylinder. Point *T* is on a right section of the cylinder. Draw the top and front views of a point *X*, which is the intersection between the tangent to the cylinder right section at *T* and the plane whose edge view is shown at line *EV*.

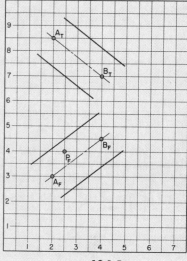

PROB. 12.1.5.

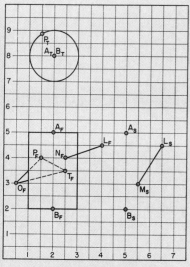

PROB. 12.1.6.

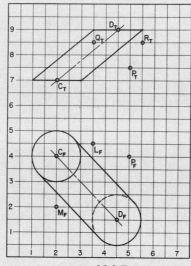

PROB. 12.1.7.

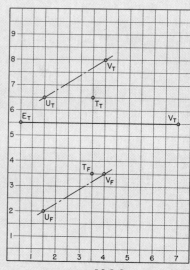

PROB. 12.1.8.

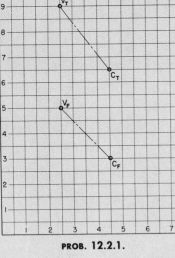

PROB. 12.2.1.

GROUP 2. THE CONE

12.2.1. *VC* is the axis of a right-circular cone. The base is 3 in. in diameter and is centered about *C*. Draw the top and front views of the cone, showing visibility. Scale: full size.

12.2.2. *A* is the vertex and *AB* is the axis of a cone. The right section about *B* is a circle of 6 in. diameter. The base is frontal and contains *B*. Draw the top and front views of the major and minor diameters of the elliptical base. Scale: ⅜ size. *Optional:* Draw the curve and complete the views.

12.2.3. Centered at *A* and *B* are two circular bases cut from an oblique cone. Find the top and front views of the vertex of the cone. Find the true length of the longest element on the surface of the cone between the bases *A* and *B*.

12.2.4. *VA* is the axis of a right-circular cone. Its base is 6 in. in diameter and contains point *A*. Another right-circular cone, whose axis is *VD*, is tangent to cone *VA* along the upper frontal element of cone *VA*. The vertex angle of cone *VD* is 50°, and its base contains point

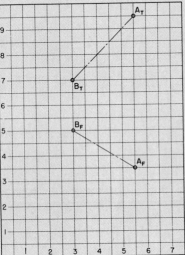

PROB. 12.2.2.

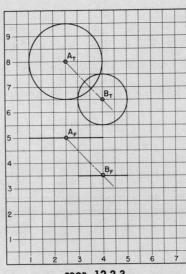

PROB. 12.2.3.

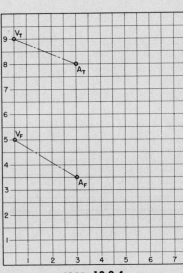

PROB. 12.2.4.

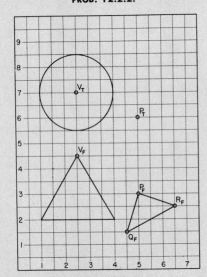

PROB. 12.2.5.

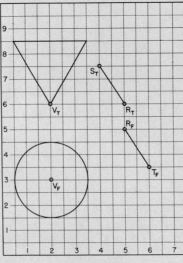

PROB. 12.2.6.

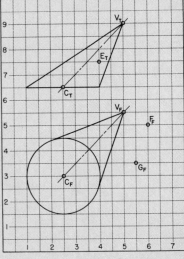

PROB. 12.2.7.

D. The cones have equal slant heights. Draw the top and front views of the axis of cone *VD*. Scale: half size. *Optional:* Complete the views of the cones.

12.2.5. Draw the top view of *PQR*, a plane which is tangent to the rearward surface of cone *V*.

12.2.6. Complete the top and front views of *RST*, a plane which is tangent to the lower surface of cone *V*.

12.2.7. Draw the top and front views of *EFG*, a plane which is tangent to the upper surface of the cone *VC*. Point *E* is on the surface of the cone.

GROUP 3.   THE CONVOLUTE

12.3.1. *XY* is the axis of a helical convolute. The directing helix begins at point *P* and rises clockwise. Its lead is the distance *XY*. The surface is limited by the outer cylinder. Its elements slope downward. Draw the top and front views of the convolute, between elevations *X* and *Y*, using 12 equally spaced elements. Draw the involute intersection which the surface makes with the horizontal plane through *X*. Show visibility.

12.3.2. The two pipe openings at *A* and *B* are to be connected by a conical-convolute transition piece. Draw the top and front views of the five elements whose ends are shown in the front view.

12.3.3. The two duct openings at *A* and *B* are to be connected by a conical-convolute transition piece. Draw the top and front views of the contour elements and four additional well-spaced elements of the convolute surface.

12.3.4. *AB* and *CD* are the minor and major diameters, respectively, of the elliptical end of a conical-convolute transition piece. Point *E* is the center of the circular end of the piece. Draw the top and front views of the contour elements and the four additional elements whose ends are indicated at 1, 2, 3, and 4. Points 1 and 2 are on the upper surface of the transition piece.

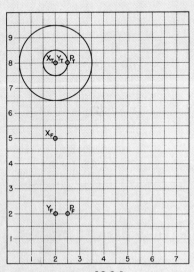

PROB. 12.3.1.

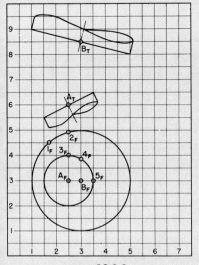

PROB. 12.3.2.

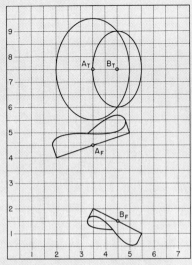

PROB. 12.3.3.

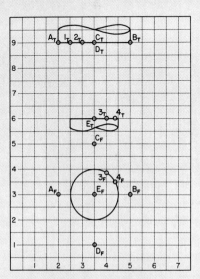

PROB. 12.3.4.

GROUP 4.   THE SPHERE

12.4.1.   Two plane sections through a sphere are shown at C and D. Draw the top and front views of the sphere.

12.4.2. A and B are two plane sections through a sphere. Draw the top and front views of the sphere and the front view of the section through B.

12.4.3.   Top and front views of a spherical ball joint and its cuplike sockets are shown. What is the total angular movement of the ball permitted in a vertical plane? In a plane shown in edge view as line TV? (The limiting condition of travel is determined by interference of the ball stud with the sockets.)

12.4.4.   Find the top and front views of X, the center of a sphere which rests in the pocket formed by the spheres A, B, and C. Sphere X is the same size as the given spheres.

12.4.5.   Complete the top and front views of PQR, a plane that is tangent to the sphere about S. P is on the upper surface of the sphere. Show the visibility of the plane.

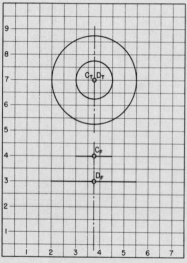

PROB. 12.4.1.

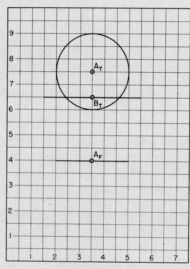

PROB. 12.4.2.

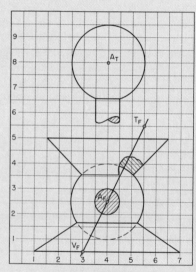

PROB. 12.4.3.

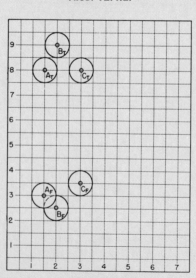

PROB. 12.4.4.

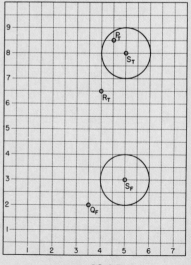

PROB. 12.4.5.

GROUP 5.   THE ELLIPSOID

12.5.1.   *AB* is the major diameter of a prolate ellipsoid. Its minor diameter is one-third the length of the major diameter. Draw the top and front views of the ellipsoid. Draw the view of the ellipsoid in which its major diameter will appear as a point.

12.5.2.   The lower portion of a cylindrical water tank is shown in the front view. The bottom of the tank is half of an ellipsoid which fits smoothly onto the rest of the tank. The

lowest point on the bottom is 4 ft below *T*. Draw the top, front, and right-side views of the tank bottom. Scale: ¼″ = 1′-0″. Is the tank bottom oblate or prolate?

12.5.3.   Point *P* represents a pulley through which a taut rope passes. The rope is attached to swivels which are anchored at *A* and *B*. Draw the top and front views of the locus of point *P*.

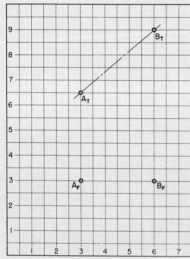

PROB. 12.5.1.

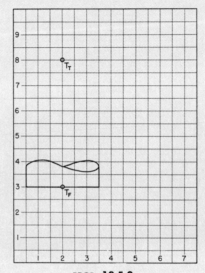

PROB. 12.5.2.

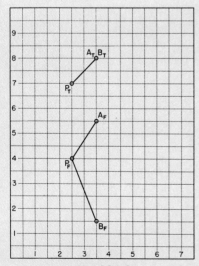

PROB. 12.5.3.

GROUP 6.   THE PARABOLOID

12.6.1.   *XY* is the directrix and *F* is the focus of the generatrix of a parabolic mirror. The axial length of the mirror is 4 in. Draw the top, front, and half right-side views of the mirror. Scale: half size.

12.6.2.   *XY* is the directrix and *F* is the focus of a generating parabola. Draw the top, front, and half right-side views of the surface created by the parabola as it revolves about its directrix. The height of the surface is *XY*.

12.6.3.   Point *F* is the focus of a parabola whose directrix lies along line *AB*. Draw the top and front views of the paraboloid generated by this parabola. The axial length of the surface is 1½ in. Scale: full size.

12.6.4.   *XY* is the directrix and *F* is the focus of the generatrix of a paraboloid. Plane *RST* is tangent to the paraboloid at *T*, which is on the upper portion of the surface. Draw the top and front views of plane *RST*.

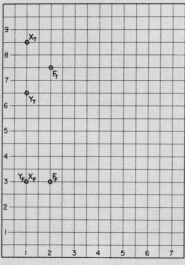

PROB. 12.6.1.

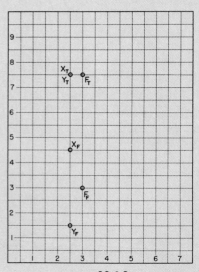

PROB. 12.6.2.

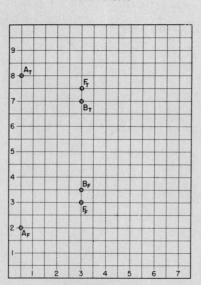

PROB. 12.6.3.

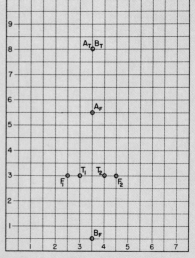

PROB. 12.6.4.

GROUP 7.   THE HYPERBOLOID

12.7.1. *AB* is the conjugate axis, F_1 and F_2 are the focuses, and T_1 and T_2 are the ends of the transverse axis of a frontal hyperbola. This hyperbola is the generatrix of a hyperboloid of revolution of one sheet. The altitude of the hyperboloid is *AB*. Draw the top and front views of 12 equally spaced elements of each generation of the hyperboloid.

12.7.2. The ellipses whose diameters are *AB* and *CD* with centers at *O* and *T* are the bases of an elliptical hyperboloid. The gore ellipse has diameters *EF* and *GH*. Draw the top and front views of six equally spaced elements of each generation.

12.7.3. *ABCD* is one wing of the projection-screen structure for an outdoor automobile theater. It is desired to cover this surface with sheet metal, thus forming a parabolic hyperboloid. Draw the plan, front-elevation, and side-elevation views of nine horizontal and seven profile elements, equally spaced, which represent the locations of the supporting members. These elements are in addition to the boundary elements shown.

12.7.4. *AB* and *CD* are the boundaries of a parabolic hyperboloid. (*a*) Draw the top and front views of eight elements of each generation. (*b*) Using *AB* and *CD* as directrices, draw the view of the surface which shows the edge view of the plane director and the elements parallel thereto.

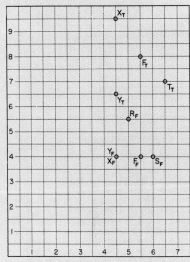

PROB. 12.7.1.

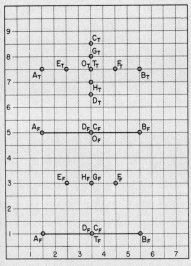

PROB. 12.7.2.

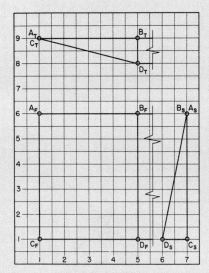

PROB. 12.7.3.

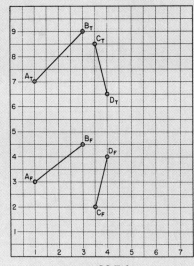

PROB. 12.7.4.

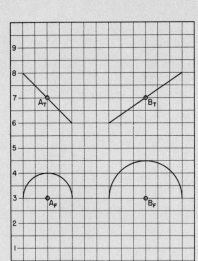

PROB. 12.8.1.

GROUP 8.   THE CYLINDROID

12.8.1.   The semiellipses centered at A and B are the directrices of a cylindroid whose plane director is frontal. Draw the top and front views of 10 elements, the ends of which are equally spaced around the front view of ellipse B.

12.8.2.   The semiellipses centered at C and D are the directrices of a cylindroid whose plane director is horizontal. Draw the top and front views of 10 elements, the ends of which are equally spaced around the front view of the ellipses.

12.8.3.   Curves AB and CD are the directrices of a cylindroid. The plane director appears as an edge in the front view and is parallel to the line of tangency between the two curves. Draw the top and front views of 10 elements, the ends of which are equally spaced around the front view of curve AB.

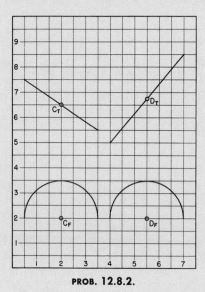

PROB. 12.8.2.

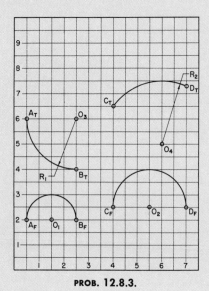

PROB. 12.8.3.

GROUP 9.   THE CONOID

12.9.1.   Circle C and line AB are the directrices of a right conoid. Draw the top, front, and right-side views of the conoid, employing 10 elements whose intersections with AB are equally spaced.

12.9.2. BC is a bowstring truss which supports the end of the arched roof of a warehouse. The roof of the office wing of the building terminates in the straight line AD. Draw the plan and elevation views of the positions of nine equally spaced joists which support the conoidal surface connecting AD and BC.

12.9.3.   Line AB and circle C are the directrices of an oblique conoid. Draw the top and front views of the conoid, employing 12 equally spaced elements.

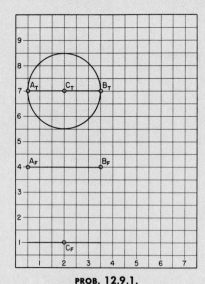

PROB. 12.9.1.

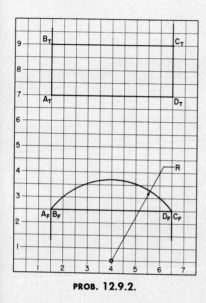

PROB. 12.9.2.

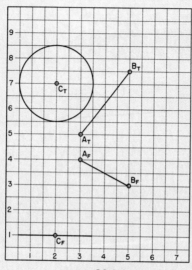

PROB. 12.9.3.

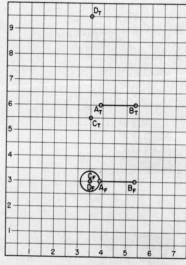

PROB. 12.10.1.

GROUP 10. THE HELICOID

12.10.1. *CD* is the center line of the 2-in.-diameter shaft of a right-hand right-helicoidal screw conveyer. The outside diameter of the screw is 10 in. The lead is 8 in. The first element of the surface is *AB*. Draw the top and front views of one turn of the conveyer, employing 16 equally spaced elements. Show visibility. Scale: ⅜ size.

12.10.2. *CD* is the axis of a right-hand oblique helicoidal chute. The chute is attached to a column of 1 ft diameter. The outside diameter of the chute is 2 ft, and its lead is 6 ft. The elements slope upward from the center and make an angle of 60° with the axis. Starting with element *AB*, draw the top and front views of one-half turn of the chute, using eight equally spaced elements. Show visibility. Scale: 1″ = 1′-0″.

12.10.3. *CD* is the axis of an earth auger bit. The blade of the bit is a right-hand right-conical helicoid. The design cone is given. The lead is one-half the altitude of the cone. Starting with element *AB*, draw the top and front views of one turn of the auger-bit blade. Show visibility.

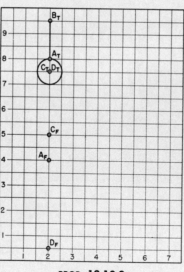

PROB. 12.10.2.

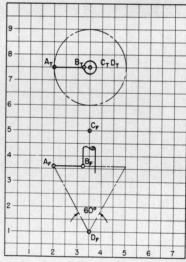

PROB. 12.10.3.

In the design of structures and machines, the external forces acting *upon the structure or the forces to be* produced *by the machine are original information. From this information the forces in individual members or components may be calculated graphically and mathematically. For proper design to achieve needed strength of the typical structures pictured, the individual member forces must first be known. Shown at the left, beams and trusses; in the center, a support structure of a large suspension bridge; at the right, the main boom and cable system of a large crane.*

Vector Quantities: Determination and Resolution in Space

13

13.1. Many engineering problems involve only simple measurable quantities such as volume, mass, and temperature, which may have their *magnitude* represented either by a single real number or by a linear distance and are therefore called "scalar" quantities. Often, however, there will be quantities such as velocity, acceleration, force, or displacement which have *magnitude, direction,* and a point of application or *position.* Because of these additional properties, such quantities cannot be represented by a single numerical value and are called "vector" quantities.

Figure 13.1 will assist in showing the difference between scalar and vector quantities. Any mass, such as the weight shown in the figure, will have its magnitude represented by a single number (ounces, pounds, etc.) and is therefore a scalar quantity. But if this mass is now placed on a beam supported as shown, the weight becomes a *force* (directed downward by gravity), which bears on the beam at the point of application or position of the weight. Thus we now have a vector quantity, a force, having magnitude, direction, and position.

FIG. 13.1. Illustration of scalar and vector quantities. The weight is a scalar quantity. The *force* of the weight on the beam is a vector quantity.

The typical analysis of vector problems can also be illustrated by Fig. 19.1. The weight, placed as shown, will produce a force directed to the beam, which in turn produces forces downward at each end of the beam where the supports are placed. In order for the beam to remain in equilibrium, the supports must resist the downward pressure by equal and opposite forces. If the weight is centrally located, the force on each support will be equal; if the weight is off center as shown, one support receives more force than the other. To find the force on each support is a typical problem of vector analysis.

Vector problems may be solved equationally, but these methods are sometimes more complicated and laborious than graphical methods, which are simple and direct and, furthermore, aid greatly in visualization and analysis of any problem.

13.2.   DEFINITIONS.   Other necessary items, such as resultants and components, will be defined later, but at the outset it is necessary to define the fundamentals.

A *scalar quantity* is a quantity having magnitude only and has its measure described by a single number or by a linear distance. Examples are volume (cubic feet), temperature (degrees), mass (pounds), and pressure (pounds per square inch).

A *vector quantity* is a quantity having magnitude, direction, and position and is described by a specification of all three details. The position, in some cases, may be either general or so obvious that description may not be vital to the solution; in other cases, position is very important. In all cases, magnitude and direction must be given. Force, velocity,

acceleration, and displacement are examples of vector quantities.

A *force* is the action of one body on another body. A force, therefore, never exists alone. Forces always occur in pairs, one acting on a body and the body then resisting the action—every action has an equal and opposite reaction.

A *vector* is the graphical representation of a vector quantity. It consists of a straight line whose length, to scale, represents the magnitude and whose direction and position are fixed by orthographic views.

A *line of action* is a direction along which a vector quantity acts.

An *origin* is either the point of application of a vector quantity or the intersection of the lines of action of two or more vector quantities.

A *free vector* is a vector representing magnitude and direction only and may be drawn anywhere in the plane of the vector quantity.

A *localized vector* is a vector showing magnitude, direction, and position and must be laid out along the line of action of the vector quantity.

A *space diagram* is a drawing which represents the body and the action lines of all the vector quantities (Fig. 13.7).

A *vector diagram* is a drawing containing free vectors (magnitude and direction only) which represent the forces on a body (Fig. 13.7).

As this discussion goes forward, and these terms occur, the student is urged to reread the definitions carefully.

13.3.   CLASSIFICATION OF FORCE SYSTEMS. Any number of forces, considered as a group, constitute a force system.

A *coplanar system* is one in which all the forces lie in the same plane, Fig. 13.2*A* and *C*.

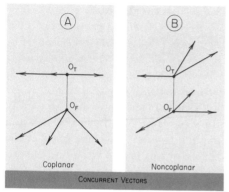
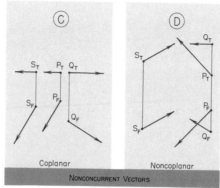

FIG. 13.2. Classification of vector quantities.

A *noncoplanar system* is one in which the forces do not lie in a common plane, Fig. 13.2*B* and *D*.

A *concurrent system* is one in which two or more forces have their line of action through a common point, Fig. 13.2*A* and *B*.

A *nonconcurrent system* is one in which the lines of action do not intersect as a common point, Fig. 13.2*C* and *D*.

Thus systems may be: coplanar and concurrent, coplanar and nonconcurrent, noncoplanar and concurrent, noncoplanar and nonconcurrent.

A *parallel system* is one in which all the forces are parallel. This system is not necessarily coplanar.

A *nonparallel system* is one in which the forces are not parallel and may be either coplanar or noncoplanar.

A *collinear system* is one in which all forces have the same line of action.

13.4. THE GRAPHIC VECTOR. To lay out a vector, as stated in the definition, the position, direction, and magnitude must be known. The position is located on an orthographic drawing of the structure or machine involved. Assume that a simple beam of a structure is to be loaded at its center with a weight of

1,750 lb. Figure 13.3 shows the beam laid out to scale. The vector is then drawn at the beam's center, the point of application or *position* of the force. The direction of the force is downward (force of gravity) so that the arrowhead may be placed on the direction line, as shown. The length of the vector is proportional to the magnitude and the vector scale used in Fig. 13.3 is 1 in. = 100 lb. Naturally, the vector scale will have no relationship whatever to the space scale for the orthographic drawing because one scale is in terms of weight (pounds) and the other in distance (feet).

In this case, the space diagram and vector are superimposed. This is to show that position, direction, and magnitude of the force are represented by the vector. Later, the vector diagram will be separated from the space diagram.

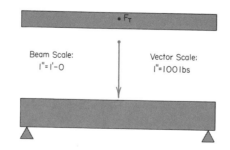

FIG. 13.3. Space diagram and vector. Note that the space scale and vector scale are independent because they represent different magnitudes.

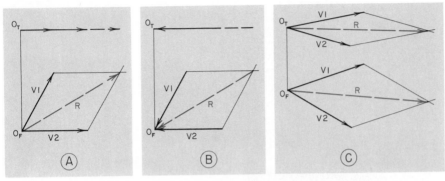

FIG. 13.4. The parallelogram law applied. The resultant is the diagonal of the parallelogram constructed with two vectors as sides.

13.5.   RESULTANTS. A resultant is a vector quantity which will replace two or more vector quantities and have the same action. Any system of *concurrent* vectors and also any system of *coplanar nonconcurrent* vectors can be added geometrically to give a single vector that will have the same effect as the original system. The process of finding a resultant is called *composition*. Resultants are determined by applying either the parallelogram or triangle laws, the principles of which may be employed to form a vector polygon.

13.6.   THE PARALLELOGRAM LAW. *Two concurrent nonparallel vectors, acting either away from (Fig. 13.4A) or toward (Fig. 13.4B) their origin will have a resultant which is the diagonal of a parallelogram constructed on the two vectors.* Note that in Fig. 13.4A the resultant acts in a direction away from the origin and in Fig. 13.4B in a direction toward the origin. Proof of the validity of this law may be had experimentally.

In Fig. 13.4A and B, the original vectors $V1$ and $V2$ and the resultants R are all in true length in the front view. In Fig. 13.4C, however, vectors $V1$ and $V2$ are in skew positions and, therefore, not in true length in either view. Nevertheless, the parallelogram law can be applied to find the resultant of Fig. 13.4C. The parallelogram is drawn as before by making the sides parallel, in both views, to $V1$ and $V2$. The resultant, R, is the diagonal as before but is a skew line. A true length view of R will then give the magnitude of the resultant.

13.7.   THE TRIANGLE LAW. *Two concurrent nonparallel vectors acting either toward or away from their origin may be drawn as two sides of a triangle, and the third side will be the resultant.* Figure 13.5A is a copy of the vector parallelogram of Fig. 13.4A. Note that $V1$ could be moved to an alternate position on the opposite side, and the resultant would be the same as indicated in Fig. 13.5B. Also, note that $V2$ could be moved to the top of the parallelogram, with $V1$ remaining in the original position, and a different triangle obtained, but with the same resultant. Thus the triangle construction is a simplification of the parallelogram.

Figure 13.5C shows how the vector triangle can be used to find the resultant when the two concurrent vectors do not

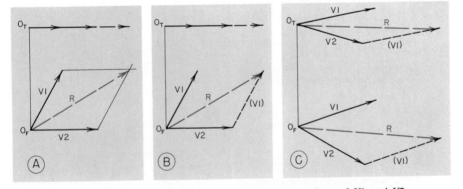

FIG. 13.5. The triangle law applied. In each case, R is the resultant of $V1$ and $V2$.

appear in true length in the given views. A line parallel to and of the same length as $V1$ is drawn from the end of $V2$, giving the resultant R from O to the end of $V1$ in the new position. The true length of R will give the magnitude of the resultant. Compare Figs. 13.5C and 13.4C.

In the above constructions, $V1$ becomes a free vector because it can be (and is) moved away from its line of action.

Note in Fig. 13.5A and B that, if R is replaced by a vector in the opposite direction, the resultant of $V1$, $V2$, and R will be zero. This is evidence of the validity of the construction.

If vectors are collinear, both the vector polygon and vector triangle will degenerate into a straight line, and the vectors are directly additive or subtractive, whichever the case may be.

13.8. THE VECTOR POLYGON.

When three or more coplanar vectors exist, the vector triangle is expanded into a vector polygon. To prove this statement, in Fig. 13.6 three vectors $V1$, $V2$, and $V3$ have been laid out in successive order with the origin of $V2$ at the end of $V1$ and the origin of $V3$ at the end of $V2$. Then $R2$ is the resultant of $V1$, $V2$, and $V3$. To prove the construction, $V1$ and $V2$ form a vector triangle with $R1$ as the resultant; then $R1$ and $V3$ form a second vector triangle with $R2$ as the resultant; and because $R1$ is the resultant of $V1$ and $V2$, the resultant of $V1$, $V2$, and $V3$ is $R2$. Any number of vectors may be composed in this way to find the resultant of the system. The paragraphs following will illustrate the use of a vector polygon for concurrent coplanar and noncoplanar forces.

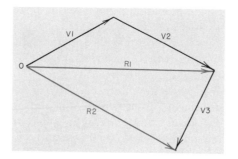

FIG. 13.6. A vector polygon. $R1$ is the resultant of $V1$ and $V2$; and $R2$ is the resultant of $R1$ and $V3$.

13.9. CONCURRENT COPLANAR FORCES.

Figure 13.7A is the space diagram for three coplanar forces, $F1$, $F2$, and $F3$, concurrent at point O. These forces are to be composed into a resultant. The vector diagram at (B) is made by selecting an origin O at any convenient place on the paper and then drawing the vectors parallel to the directions established by the space diagram, making the length of the vectors to scale, representing the magnitude of each. Any successive order may be chosen, but care must

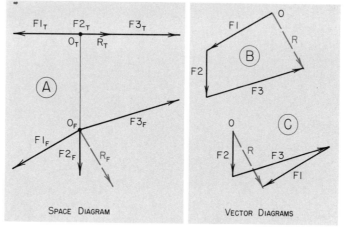

FIG. 13.7. The resultant of concurrent coplanar forces. Vectors at (B) and (C) are drawn parallel to the directions on the space diagram (A). Note the differing order of layout in (B) and (C) but the same resultant.

be taken to maintain the given direction of each vector. Thus at (B), $F1$, $F2$, and $F3$ are laid out in that order and R, the resultant, is the line necessary to close the diagram. The magnitude of R is found by scaling the line. At (C), the order starting from O is $F2$, $F3$, and $F1$. Note that R, the resultant, has the same direction and length as in diagram (B). The resultant can then be transferred to the space diagram, where it will be concurrent at O with the original forces, which it replaces, and will be parallel to R on the vector diagram.

Vectors $F1$, $F2$, and $F3$ on the vector diagram are free vectors because they have been moved away from a definite line of action in order to determine the resultant. Note, however, that when the resultant is placed back on the space diagram it becomes the representation of a vector quantity which has magnitude, direction, and position and is now a localized vector.

Summary

See general summary, paragraph 13.22.

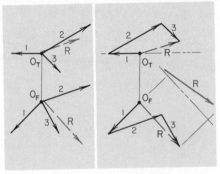

SPACE DIAGRAM   VECTOR DIAGRAM

FIG. 13.8. The resultant of concurrent noncoplanar forces. Two views are required for the vector diagram, and the vector diagram and the magnitude of the resultant are determined by an auxiliary view.

13.10.   CONCURRENT   NONCOPLANAR FORCES. Any two concurrent forces will be coplanar, but three or more *may or may not* be coplanar. The space diagram of Fig. 13.8 shows three forces, 1, 2, and 3, that are not coplanar but are concurrent at O. The vector diagram for these forces will be similar to Fig. 13.7, but because the forces are noncoplanar and therefore cannot all appear in true length in one view, the polygon becomes a *space* polygon requiring two views. To make the diagram, a point O is selected. Next, vector 1 is drawn parallel to force direction 1 on the space diagram. The length of vector 1 is made (to some convenient scale) equal in length to the magnitude of force 1. Then vectors 2 and 3 are drawn by laying out their direction, drawing a true-length view and on it measuring the magnitude, and then projecting to top and front views R, the resultant, is the line necessary to close the diagram. The magnitude of R is found by determining its true length as shown by the auxiliary view. R may be transferred back to the space diagram by drawing it parallel in both views to R on the vector diagram. This locates the line of action of the resultant.

Summary

See general summary, paragraph 13.22.

13.11.   THEORY OF TRANSMISSIBILITY. Before going on to a study of nonconcurrent forces, it will be necessary to understand the theory of transmissibility, which states that *the external effect of a force on a rigid body is unchanged for all points of application along the line of action.* To explain this theory, in Fig. 13.9A, a force is directed *away from* a point of application, O. At (B), the same force is directed

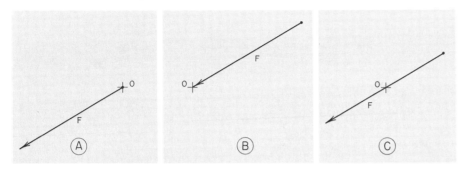

FIG. 13.9. Transmissibility. Any force may act on a body by (*A*) pulling, (*B*) pushing, (*C*) pulling and pushing. The *external* effect is identical.

toward point *O*. In other words, the point *O* in the first case is being pulled upon and in the second it is being pushed. The external effect on the body is the same. At Fig. 13.9*C*, the point of application has been moved away from point *O*, but the effect on *O* is still identical. Thus we conclude that a vector, representing a force, may be moved along the line of action without changing the external effect.

For future reference, however, it should be noted that the *internal* effect on a body may not be the same. Stress and deformation may be greatly influenced by the point of application.

Summary

See general summary, paragraph 13.22.

13.12. NONCONCURRENT COPLANAR FORCES. *Line-of-action Method.* The theory of transmissibility may be employed to find the resultant of nonconcurrent coplanar forces. As shown in Fig. 13.10*A*, if two vectors are coplanar and nonparallel, their lines of action will intersect, and by the theory of transmissibility, this intersection may then be considered as the origin of the forces. Therefore, if the vectors of Fig. 13.10*A* are moved along the lines of action to the origin, as shown at Fig. 13.10*B*, the resultant can be found by the parallelogram method. As illustrated at (*C*), the resultant may also be found by using a vector triangle.

The foregoing principles may be applied to find the resultant of three or

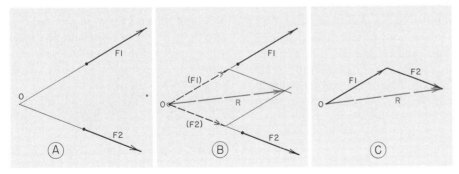

FIG. 13.10. Transmissibility applied. Vectors are moved along their line of action to an origin.

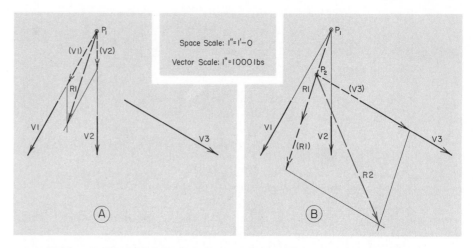

FIG. 13.11. Resultant of coplanar nonconcurrent forces (line-of-action method). At (*A*), *V*1 and *V*2 are composed into resultant *R*1; then at (*B*), *R*1 and *V*3 are composed into *R*2. Note the theory of transmissibility applied here.

more nonconcurrent coplanar vectors. In Fig. 13.11, three forces are represented by vectors *V*1, *V*2, and *V*3. At (*A*), the lines of action of *V*1 and *V*2 have been extended to their intersection at P_1, the point through which *V*1 and *V*2 both act. *V*1 and *V*2 are then moved with their bases at P_1 and the resultant *R*1 found by the parallelogram method. As shown at (*B*), the resultant *R*1 and vector *V*3 act through point P_2, the intersection of the lines of action of *R*1 and *V*3. If now *R*1 and *V*3 are moved with their bases at P_2, the resultant *R*2 may be found. This is the resultant of all three forces, and its magnitude, direction, and position are now determined. In this solution, the space and vector diagrams are superimposed. An identical solution could have been accomplished by first finding the resultant of *V*2 and *V*3 and then finding the final resultant with *V*1.

Summary

See general summary, paragraph 13.22.

13.13. COMPONENTS. Before proceeding to other solutions, it will be necessary to define and study components. *A component is one of the two or more forces into which a single force may be converted.* Collectively, the components will have the same action as the original force. The process of determining components of a force is called *resolution.* Figure 13.12 will illustrate the fundamentals. *V*1 is an original force represented by a vector. *C*1 and *C*2 are components of *V*1. The conception of components is actually the reverse of the triangle law for a resultant because if *C*1 and *C*2 were original vectors, then *V*1 is the resultant. It should also be noted that *C*3 and *C*4 are com-

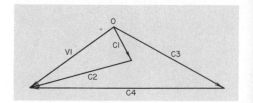

FIG. 13.12. Components. *C*1 and *C*2 are components of *V*1, as also are *C*3 and *C*4.

ponents of $V1$. The number of components into which a single force may be resolved is infinite.

If the directions of the lines of action of two components are known, a vector diagram may be made to find the magnitude of both components. In Fig. 13.13, the space diagram shows a force V. The directions of two components $C1$ and $C2$ are also known. Therefore, in the vector diagram, $C1$ and $C2$ are drawn parallel (to $C1$ and $C2$ on the space diagram) from the two ends of $V1$. These lines will intersect at O, now giving the magnitude of $C1$ and $C2$.

Summary

See general summary, paragraph 13.22.

13.14. NONCONCURRENT COPLANAR FORCES. *Component-polygon Method.* The space diagram of Fig. 13.14 shows two nonconcurrent coplanar forces, $F1$ and $F2$, for which the magnitude, direction, and position of the resultant are to be found. First, a vector diagram is made by drawing $F1$ and $F2$ parallel to the space directions and making their length equal to their magnitude, according to the vector scale. This now gives the magnitude and direction of the resultant R. The *position* of the resultant must now be found. Any point O may be selected (convenience is the criterion) and lines drawn from O to points 1, 2, and 3, the intersection of the vectors. These lines O-1, O-2, and O-3 may now be considered as components $C1$ and $C2$ of $F1$, $C2$ and $C3$ of $F2$, and $C1$ and $C3$ of R. The component $C2$ is a common component of $F1$ and $F2$, and for $F1$ acts in a direction from O to 2; for $F2$ it acts in a direction from 2 to O. Therefore, the action of $C2$ is zero because of equal and opposite forces. The position of the re-

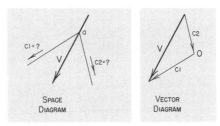

FIG. 13.13. Component magnitudes determined by known directions. The components on the vector diagram are drawn parallel to the directions predetermined on the space diagram.

sultant can now be located by drawing the components $C1$, $C2$, and $C3$ on the space diagram. The component $C2$ cancels out between forces $F1$ and $F2$ and has no action on the resultant. Therefore $C'2$ is drawn parallel to $C2$ giving the line ab on the space diagram. $C1$ is a component of both $F1$ and R. A line $C'1$ is therefore drawn from a on $F1$, parallel to $C1$. Also, $C3$ is a component of $F2$ and R. A line $C'3$ is therefore drawn from b parallel to $C3$. These lines, $C'1$ and $C'3$, then intersect at c which is a point through which the resultant R acts. It will make no difference where, on $F1$ and $F2$, the line $C'2$ varies in position, a different point c will be obtained, but it will be on the line of action of R. Thus the magnitude, direction,

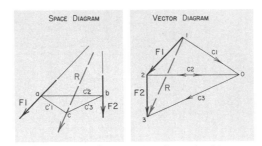

FIG. 13.14. Resultant position determined by component polygon. Component directions determined on the vector diagram are transferred (parallel) to the space diagram to locate the resultant position.

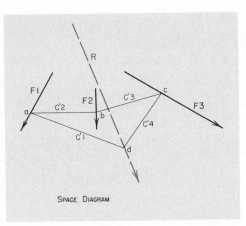
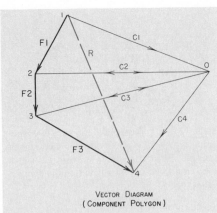

FIG. 13.15. Resultant position determined by component polygon. Component directions determined on the vector diagram are transferred (parallel) to the space diagram to locate the resultant position.

and position of R have now been determined.

Figure 13.15 illustrates a similar case but for three forces. The vector diagram of the forces and a group of components concurrent at some point O are arranged as in the previous example. This time, however, there will be two common (equal and opposite) components, $C2$ and $C3$. These are drawn on the space

diagram first, making $C'2$ parallel to $C2$, locating ab connecting $F1$ and $F2$. Then, from b on $F2$, $C'3$ is drawn parallel to $C3$, locating c on $F3$. Now $C'1$ from a parallel to $C1$ and $C'4$ from c parallel to $C4$ locate d, a point through which R acts. On the theory of transmissibility, any point d through which R acts will have the same external effect on the body of the material.

The component method just described is especially useful when the forces are almost parallel, causing the intersection of their lines of action to be beyond the limits of the drawing. If the forces are parallel, it is the only practical method.

Summary

See general summary, paragraph 13.22.

13.15. PARALLEL NONCONCURRENT CO-PLANAR FORCES. As explained in paragraph 13.3, when concurrent forces are parallel, they will be collinear (act along the same line) and are, therefore, directly additive or subtractive. For nonconcurrent parallel forces, the lines of action will not be the same so that extra construction is necessary to find the position of the resultant. The component-polygon method is best because the line-of-action method involves the use of components and, for several forces, becomes somewhat laborious and confusing.

In Fig. 13.16, the space diagram shows three parallel forces of different magnitude. Since the forces are parallel, the vector triangle degenerates into a straight line, as shown. The resultant will be the summation of the three vectors $F1$, $F2$, and $F3$ and will lie along the straight line of the three vectors. To find the position of the resultant, a point O is selected at random and components $C1$, $C2$, $C3$, and $C4$ drawn (as in Fig.

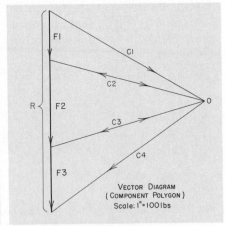

FIG. 13.16. Resultant position of parallel coplanar forces. Component directions determined on the vector diagram are transferred (parallel) to the space diagram to locate the resultant position.

13.15). The rest of the construction is the same as described in paragraph 13.14. Note again that components $C2$ and $C3$ are each common components of two forces and $C'2$ and $C'3$ are thus the connecting lines between forces $F1$ and $F2$ and $F2$ and $F3$ on the space diagram.

Summary

See general summary, paragraph 13.22.

13.16. COPLANAR FORCES IN INCLINED AND SKEW POSITIONS. It is evident from the foregoing chapters of this book that the various points, lines, and planes of modern machines and structures do not always occur in simple positions or rela-

tionships. Consequently, the stresses introduced on machine parts and elements of structures will often be in inclined or skew planes. This apparent complication, however, is not serious since the normal view of such planes may be easily obtained, where the forces will appear in their true relationship. This normal view then becomes the space diagram for forces, and from it a component polygon may be made to determine a resultant. The resultant may then be located on the space diagram.

In Fig. 13.17, forces $F1$, $F2$, and $F3$ lie in plane $ABCD$, a plane in an inclined position. The auxiliary shown is

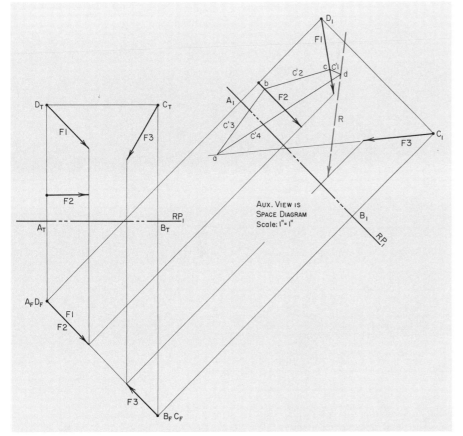

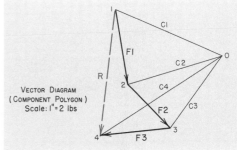

FIG. 13.17. Resultant of coplanar forces in an inclined position. The normal view of the plane of the forces becomes the space diagram.

a normal view of all the force directions, gives their true relationship, and becomes the space diagram. The vector diagram and determination of the resultant's position, magnitude, and direction are identical to the description given in paragraph 13.14.

Figure 13.18 is a similar case except that the forces lie in a skew plane. After the normal view of the plane of the forces has been found, the solution is

again the same as that given in paragraph 13.14.

Summary

See general summary, paragraph 13.22.

13.17.   RESOLUTION OF COPLANAR CONCURRENT FORCES.   In paragraph 13.13, it was shown how a vector could be resolved into two components concurrent with the vector by constructing a vector

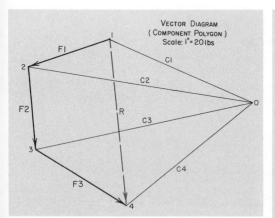

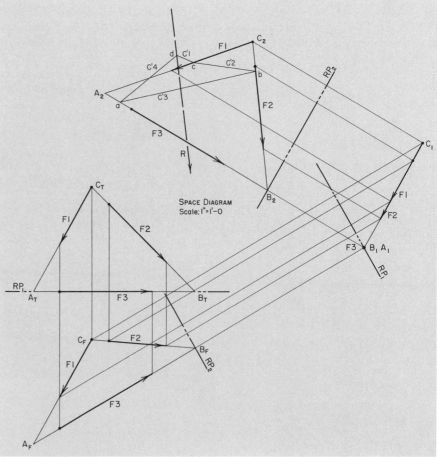

FIG. 13.18.   Resultant of coplanar forces in a skew position. The second auxiliary view is the space diagram.

triangle with sides parallel to the components desired. Nevertheless, certain conditions must be met before the problem has only *one* answer. If the direction and magnitude of a vector are considered as *two* conditions, then $N - 2$ conditions must be known before the problem has a single solution. For example, in Fig. 13.19A, the directions of two desired components are known. *Six* conditions are involved, the magnitude and direction of the vector F and the magnitudes and directions of both components. *Four* conditions are known, the magnitude and direction of F and the directions of the components. Therefore, the limit of $N - 2$ is satisfied, and the problem can be solved on the vector diagram by laying out the directions of both components. In Fig. 13.19B, again six conditions are involved, but this time the direction of one component and the magnitude of the other give a total of four known conditions. The problem is then solved as shown by laying out the direction of one component and the

magnitude of the other. In Fig. 13.19C, the directions of three desired components are known; thus eight conditions are involved (two conditions for four vectors), but only five (four directions and one magnitude) are known. The problem will have an infinite number of answers, as shown at (D), by *assuming* three components, or at (E), where two other possible solutions are shown; but if the magnitude of one component had been known, as indicated at (F), the problem has only one solution: Component $C3$ can be laid out, and then the known directions of $C1$ and $C2$ will determine their magnitude.

Even though the conditions stated above are met, a single vector cannot be resolved into *nonconcurrent* components unless the components are parallel (concurrent at infinity). The resolution of a vector into parallel components will be discussed in paragraph 13.22.

Summary

See general summary, paragraph 13.22.

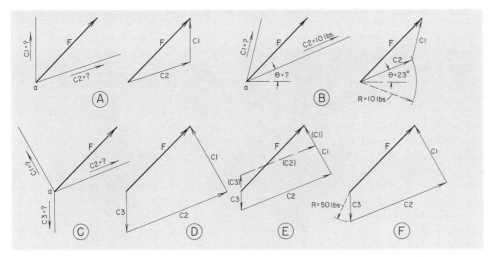

FIG. 13.19.   Conditions for determination of components. Directions and magnitudes of $N - 2$ must be known before the problem has a single solution.

13.18. RESOLUTION OF COPLANAR CONCURRENT FORCES IN EQUILIBRIUM. When concurrent coplanar forces are placed in equilibrium, the resultant of all forces must be zero; also, there will be only two possible components for a given force, for if there are more, equilibrium will be upset and the components become indeterminate. For example, in the space diagram of Fig. 13.20, a weight is supported by two members AO and BO. If a third support *in the plane* of AO and BO is added, one support will share more load than it should and the determination of stress in the supports is impossible. Thus the $N - 2$ conditions mentioned previously must be maintained.

To find the forces in members AO and BO, in the vector diagram, V_D is laid off vertically to scale and equal to the magnitude of the force (1,000 lb). Then V_B parallel to OB and V_A parallel to OA will intersect, determining the two com-

ponents of V_D. These are the forces in OA and OB. For the system to remain in equilibrium, the direction of V_B must be upward and to the right and that of V_A must be upward and to the left. Note that these directions of force make V_A and V_B in *opposition* to V_D, thus placing the whole system in balance. In the vector diagram, the front view shows all forces in true length.

Summary

See general summary, paragraph 13.22.

13.19. RESOLUTION OF NONCOPLANAR CONCURRENT FORCES. When noncoplanar concurrent forces are placed in equilibrium, three component forces will be *required* to maintain equilibrium, and thus $N - 3$ conditions will be necessary. One might be asked why $N - 2$ conditions are the limit for coplanar and $N - 3$ the limit for noncoplanar forces. This is because more than *two* compo-

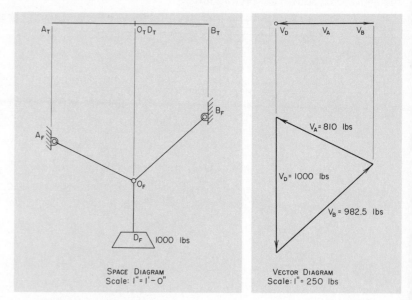

FIG. 13.20. Resolution of forces in equilibrium. In this case, one magnitude and two directions are known.

nents for coplanar and more than *three* for noncoplanar forces are indeterminate. Also, if there is only one component, the forces will be collinear—*two* are required to make the forces coplanar, and *three* are required for a noncoplanar system. Note in the space diagram of Fig. 13.21 that, if a fourth supporting member is added, one member will take more (or less) load and throw the system out of balance. Remember that a rigid four-legged table often requires a wedge under one leg to prevent tilting.

The resolution of components for noncoplanar concurrent systems may be accomplished by either obtaining a point view of any one of the vectors or making an edge view of two unknown vectors.

Summary

See general summary, paragraph 13.22.

13.20. RESOLUTION BY A POINT VIEW. To resolve a force into three noncoplanar concurrent forces (components), at least *one* view should be made in which one force appears as a point and the other three appear either in true length or foreshortened. If *both* views of the vector diagram show all four vectors foreshortened or in true length, the determination can only be made by trial-and-error methods, which are tedious and time-consuming. The point view of *any* one of the vectors will give a straightforward solution.

Resolution by the Point View of a Known Quantity. Figure 13.21 shows by the space diagram that a weight is supported by three members, *OA, OB,* and *OC.* The weight gives vector V_D, which appears as a point in the top view and in true length in the front view of the vector diagram. The directions of all the

vectors can now be established in both views. Any order may be selected, and in this case V_B is laid off from the base of V_D and, of course, must be parallel in both views to *OB.* Then V_A is drawn from the tip of V_D, parallel in both views to *OA.* The vector V_C may now be laid off in both views, parallel to *OC,* but its actual location cannot be found before some extra construction. Therefore, V_C is drawn first as line 2-3 in the top view, which is then projected to the front view. This trial line would place V_A as line 2-1 in the front view, and V_A *must* emanate from the tip of V_D. Thus it is necessary now to *move* the V_C line until the polygon of vectors can be closed.

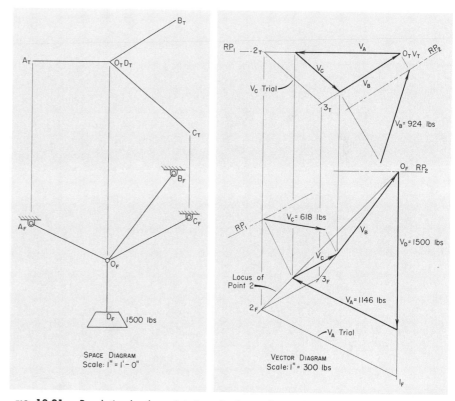

FIG. 13.21. Resolution by the point view of a known force. The vector directions are established; then the vector polygon is closed by employing an intermediate trial line.

Point 3 of the trial line will move along the directional line for V_B, and point 2 will have a locus that is a line connecting point 2 and O (the base of V_D). To prove this relationship, draw several trial lines for V_C. Finally, then, where the directional line for V_A crosses the "locus of points 2" in the front view determines the end of V_A and one end of

V_C, and V_C then drawn parallel to OC closes the polygon. The true length of vectors will now give the magnitudes needed. V_A is in true length in the front view and may be scaled there. The auxiliary projected from the front view gives the true length of V_C. The auxiliary projected from the top view gives the true length of V_B.

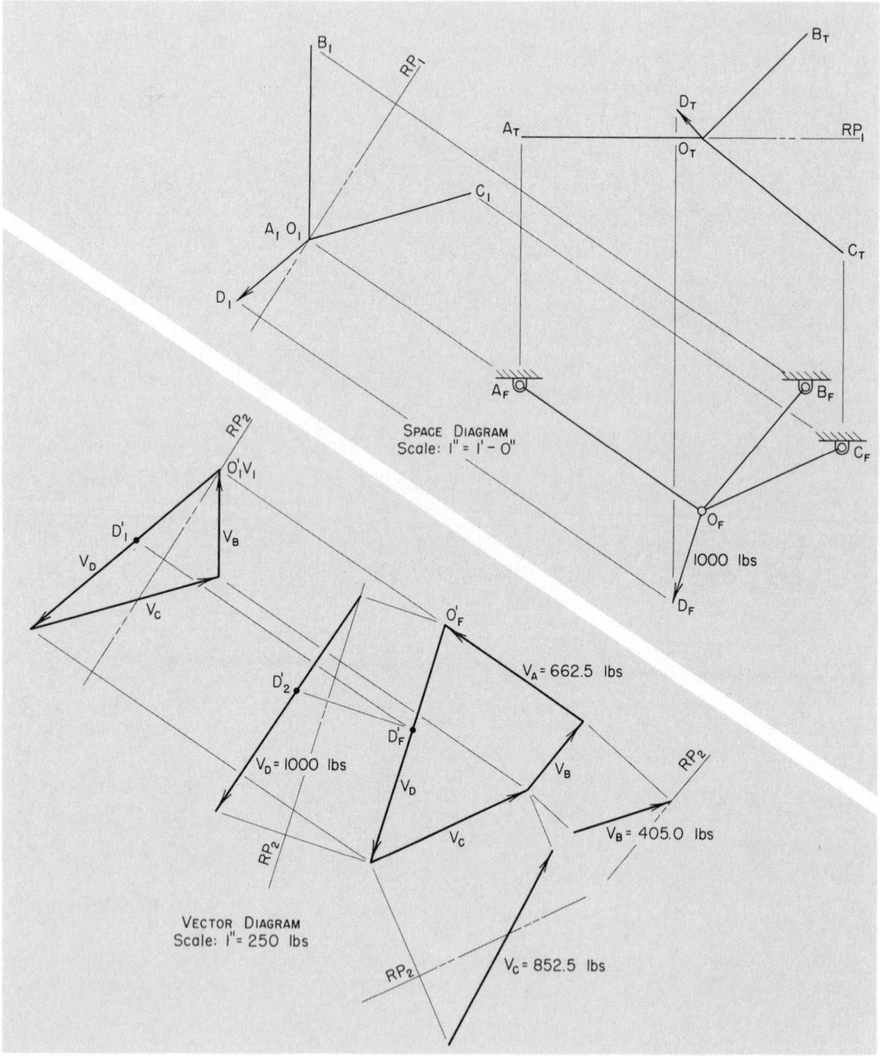

Resolution by the Point View of an Unknown Quantity. In any particular problem, one of the forces, known or unknown, may appear as a point. There is also the possibility that *none* of the forces will appear as a point in the views given, and therefore the point view of one force will have to be made before laying out the vector diagram. A system of this type is shown in Fig. 13.22. The direction of OA, however, is frontal, and the auxiliary projected from the front view will give the point view of OA. The diagram will employ views *projectively matching* the front and auxiliary views of the space diagram. To start the vector diagram, the known force in the direction of OD must first be located. Therefore, some point O' for the diagram is selected and $O'D'$ laid out parallel to front and auxiliary views. Then a true length view of $O'D'$ (shown here projected from the front view of $O'D'$) gives a view in which the magnitude of the force in OD may be laid out. Next, in the auxiliary view, where V_A (the vector representation of the force in OA) appears as a point, the directions of V_B, parallel to OB, and V_C, parallel to OC, will make a closed vector polygon. Now, projection of the intersection of V_C and V_B (in the auxiliary view) to the front view and the *directions* of V_A, V_B, and V_C in the front view make possible the completion of the polygon in the front view. Finally,

FIG. 13.22.   Resolution by a point view of an unknown force. The vector polygon is determinate in the point and normal views of the unknown force.

the separate auxiliaries for V_B and V_C give the magnitude of these forces, and because V_A is frontal, it can be scaled in the front view. Note that the directional arrows on the vectors place the system in equilibrium because V_C, V_B, and V_A *oppose* (act in reverse direction to) V_D.

Summary

See general summary, paragraph 13.22.

13.21. RESOLUTION BY THE EDGE VIEW OF THE PLANE OF TWO UNKNOWN QUANTITIES.

Whether or not some force directions are in true length or appear as points in the given views, resolution can always be had by making the edge view of the plane of two of the unknowns. In Fig. 13.23, the plane of OC and OA has been selected for the edge view. Thus the view made looking in the direction of CX, a horizontal line of plane OAC, gives the edge view in the auxiliary projected from the top view. The vector diagram may now be started by selecting a point O and locating the known force vector V_D parallel to OD in top and auxiliary views. In the true length view for V_D, the magnitude of V_D is measured and then projected back to top and auxiliary views. Next, the vectors can be partially located in the auxiliary view by drawing V_B parallel to O_1B_1 and a line for V_A and V_C parallel to $O_1C_1A_1$. Going now to the top view, V_B can be established in direction by drawing it parallel to O_TB_T. Projection of the intersection of V_B and V_AC_A in the auxiliary, to the top view, locates the end of V_B. Having V_B established in both views, V_A parallel to O_TA_T and V_C parallel to O_TC_T complete the top view of the vector polygon. Finally, projection of the intersection of V_C and V_A in the top view, to the auxiliary view,

determines V_C and V_A in the auxiliary view. True lengths of V_A, V_B, and V_C, as shown, then give the needed magnitudes.

Summary

See general summary, paragraph 13.22.

13.22. SUMMARY.

A vector quantity has the characteristics of magnitude, direction, and location. Forces, velocity, and displacement are examples of vec-

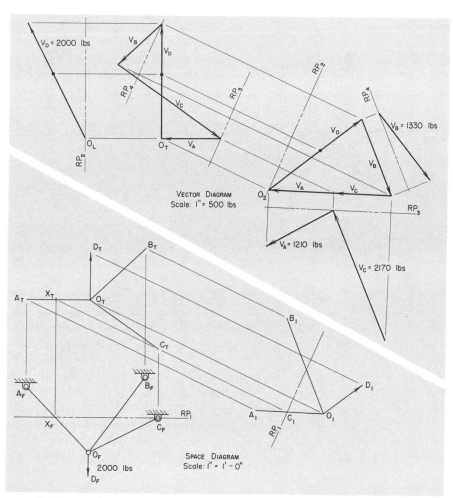

FIG. 13.23. Resolution by the edge view of the plane of two unknown forces. Determination is possible because *in the edge view* two vectors coincide in direction.

tor quantities. These quantities are represented graphically by a vector which is an arrow drawn so that its length is proportional to the magnitude of the quantity, while the point of action and the direction of action are correctly shown with respect to some reference. Vectors can be broadly classified as *coplanar* or *noncoplanar,* with each of these classifications being further subdivided into *concurrent* and *nonconcurrent* vectors. Two or more vectors acting together can be replaced by a single vector known as the *resultant,* which creates the same action as the multiple vectors. The usual vector problem consists of a number of vectors of varying magnitudes and directions whose resultant must be known before further solution of the problem can be attempted. Vectors are combined graphically by simple geometric methods applied through orthographic projection drawings. Coplanar vectors require one orthographic view, while noncoplanar vectors require more than one view.

The methods appropriate for resolution of various vector systems are related to the vector classifications. Before cataloging the methods, it should be noted that vectors are often considered to be the resultant of several arbitrary and often imaginary vectors. These vectors are called *components* and are often used to simplify problems involving vectors. Thus, a vector acting in a diagonal direction can be considered to be the resultant of two imaginary vectors, one vertical and the other horizontal. Suggested methods for determining the resultant of the action of various vectors acting together are given in the following outline.

Concurrent-coplanar

1. Parallelogram method
2. Triangle law method
3. Vector polygon method

Nonconcurrent-coplanar

1. Line-of-action method
2. Component-polygon method

Concurrent-noncoplanar

Line-of-action method using auxiliary views (also called the space polygon method)

Nonconcurrent-noncoplanar

No simple graphical method listed

The principles of earlier chapters in the text dealing with the relationships of points, lines, and planes are often helpful in determining the resultant of several vectors. Methods for solving noncoplanar concurrent vector problems utilize point views of one vector, edge views of the plane of two unknown vectors, and a normal view of the plane of two vectors. None of these methods give a final answer in one step but rather provide a method of combining several vectors at a time to form a resultant which in turn may be combined with other vectors or resultants to further the problem into a final resultant.

Any vector problem may be solved by the method of combining two vectors to form a resultant, combining this resultant with a new vector to obtain a second resultant, combining this resultant with a fourth vector to form a new resultant, and by this process eliminating the vectors one at a time until only one resultant remains. Although lengthy and cumbersome, this method will give results if any of the other methods are forgotten.

PROBLEMS

Selections from the following problems may be made and the figures constructed to any desired scale on 8½- by 11-in. or 11- by 17-in. drawing sheets. The direction and position of all given vectors are indicated in the problem illustrations; the magnitudes of the vectors are stated in the problems listed below.

RESULTANTS AND COMPONENTS

Determine the magnitude, position, and direction of the resultant of the given force system.

13.1.1. $F1 = 250$ lb, $F2 = 300$ lb.
13.1.2. $F1 = 250$ lb, $F2 = 200$ lb.
13.1.3. $F1 = 190$ lb, $F2 = 170$ lb.
13.1.4. $F1 = 300$ lb, $F2 = 350$ lb.
13.1.5. $F1 = 200$ lb, $F2 = 250$ lb, $F3 = 170$ lb.
13.1.6. $F1 = 200$ lb, $F2 = 200$ lb, $F3 = 250$ lb.
13.1.7. $F1 = 160$ lb, $F2 = 100$ lb, $F3 = 150$ lb.
13.1.8. $F1 = 160$ lb, $F2 = 220$ lb, $F3 = 200$ lb.
13.1.9. $F1 = 170$ lb, $F2 = 160$ lb, $F3 = 170$ lb.
Resolve the given force into the components indicated.
13.1.10. $F = 220$ lb.
13.1.11. $F = 210$ lb, $C1 = 240$ lb.

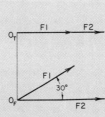

PROB. 13.1.1.

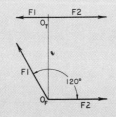

PROB. 13.1.2.

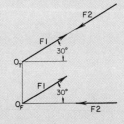

PROB. 13.1.3.

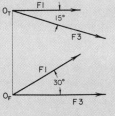

PROB. 13.1.4.

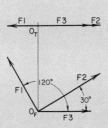

PROB. 13.1.5.

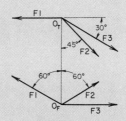

PROB. 13.1.6.

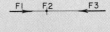
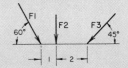

PROB. 13.1.7.

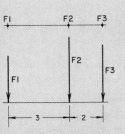

PROB. 13.1.8.

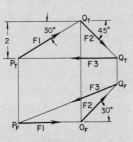

PROB. 13.1.9.

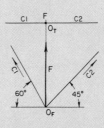

PROB. 13.1.10.

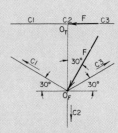

PROB. 13.1.11.

Geometric surfaces are combined in many ways to form useful objects of scientific value, practical shapes for machines and structures, and also significant forms used in architecture and many decorative arts. The meeting of geometric shapes (intersections) and the translation of shapes to a flat plane (developments) are important aspects of engineering design and construction.

Surface Intersections and Developments

14.1. In making orthographic drawings, it is necessary to represent the *lines of intersection* between the various surfaces of a wide variety of objects. Nearly every line on a drawing is a line of intersection, generally the intersection of two planes, giving a straight line, or of a cylinder and a plane, giving a circle or an ellipse. The term "intersection of surfaces" refers, however, to the more complicated lines that occur when geometric surfaces such as planes, cylinders, and cones intersect one another. These lines of intersection are shown by one of two basic methods: (1) *conventional intersections,* ordinarily used to represent a fillet, round, or runout, as explained in paragraph 7.23 and shown in Fig. 7.43, or (2) *plotted intersections,* used when an intersection must be located accurately for purposes of dimensioning or for development of the surfaces. In sheet-metal combinations the intersection *must* be found before the piece can be developed. In this chapter we are concerned solely with the methods of projecting plotted intersections and with the procedures employed for the development of surfaces. *Development* is defined as the unfoldment of a surface to a plane.

Because intersections and developments both are detailed treatments of plane, curved, and warped surfaces, the student should become familiar with all forms. Various figures, solids, and surfaces are illustrated in Fig. 3.101. Definitions and detailed

14

descriptions of prisms and pyramids are given in paragraph 11.1. Definitions and classifications of curved and warped surfaces are given in Chap. 12.

14.2. INTERSECTIONS OF PLANE SURFACES.

The intersection of a line and a plane is a *point* common to both. The intersection of two planes is a *line* common to both. After mastering the graphic methods of locating intersections (paragraphs 14.3 to 14.10), apply the principles you have learned to finding the line of intersection between objects made up of plane surfaces (prisms and pyramids, paragraphs 14.11 to 14.13). The method of solution for the intersection of other polyhedrons should follow logically from the examples given.

14.3. INTERSECTION OF A LINE AND A PLANE, BOTH IN PRINCIPAL POSITIONS.

Principal positions of planes are horizontal, frontal, or profile. Principal positions of lines occur when the lines are *not* inclined to any principal plane; thus a line is (1) horizontal-frontal, (2) horizontal-profile, or (3) frontal-profile. Therefore, if the line is parallel to, or lies in, the principal plane, no single point of intersection is possible, but in positions when the line is perpendicular to the plane, a single point exists. To illustrate, Fig. 14.1 shows a rectangular object made up of horizontal, frontal, and profile planes with an accompanying horizontal-profile line *AB*. Because the line is parallel to horizontal and profile planes, the line and these planes do not intersect except at infinity. However, the line is perpendicular to the frontal plane, and there is a single point of intersection, observed in the top view at P_T and in the side view at P_R, where the front of the object appears as an edge.

The front view of the intersection is coincident with $A_F B_F$ at P_F because this is the end view of line *AB*.

Thus it is established that *the intersection of a line and plane is a point on the line coincident with the edge view of the plane.* The point of intersection of a line and plane is often called a "piercing point."

Summary

1. Locate the intersection by inspection in any view which shows the line and the edge view of the plane; then project the point to any other views.

2. On a practical object, the point of intersection must lie within the confines of the plane.

14.4. INTERSECTION OF AN INCLINED LINE WITH PLANES IN PRINCIPAL POSITIONS.

Two points of intersection are possible, one with each plane to which the line is not parallel. For example, Fig. 14.2 shows a frontal line *AB* and an object made up of horizontal, frontal, and profile planes. The line will not intersect any frontal plane (except at infinity). The intersection with the profile plane (right

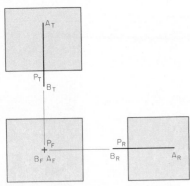

FIG. 14.1. Intersection of a line and a plane. In this case, the line is perpendicular to the plane.

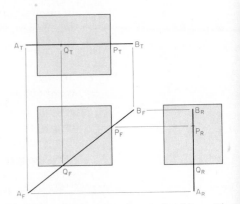

FIG. 14.2. Intersection of an inclined line with planes. In this case, the line intersects the horizontal and profile sides of an object.

side) is seen at P_T and P_F, where the plane appears as an edge, and is then easily projected to P_R. The intersection with the horizontal (bottom) is observed at Q_F and Q_R, where the plane appears as an edge, and is projected from Q_F to Q_T.

Observe that line AB does not intersect the top or left side of the object, but if the top and side planes were extended, a point of intersection would exist.

Summary

1. Locate the intersection by inspection in any view which shows the line and the edge view of the plane.

2. Project the point of intersection to the other views.

3. On a practical object, the point of intersection must lie within the confines of the plane.

14.5.   INTERSECTION OF A SKEW LINE WITH PLANES IN PRINCIPAL POSITIONS.   Theoretically, a skew line (a line inclined to

all principal planes) will intersect all three principal planes. However, on a rectangular object, depending upon the length and position of the line, only one or two intersections exist. Figure 14.3 illustrates all possibilities. At (A), the skew line from point A inside the object emanates upward, backward, and to the right, and obviously intersects the top (horizontal) surface of the object at P, observed first at P_F and P_R, where the top surface appears as an edge, and then projected to P_T. But line AB does not intersect any other surface of the object.

At (B) line AB is seen to intersect two surfaces of the object, the right side at Q and the front at P. Note that in each case the points are found first where the surface appears as an edge, Q_T and Q_F for point Q and P_T and P_R for point P.

At (C) the top surface of the object is extended so that three intersections are possible. Physically this occurs on an object when two rectangular shapes are offset or when a base or lug extends. The line AB intersects the right side at

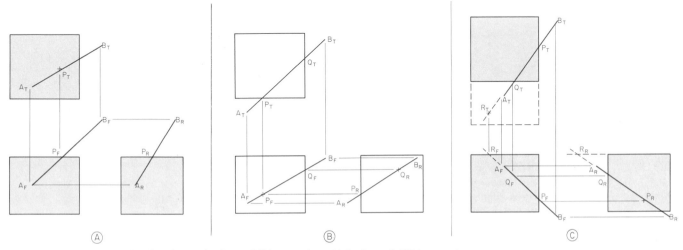

FIG. 14.3.   Intersection of a skew line with planes. (A) Intersection with horizontal; (B) intersection with frontal and profile; (C) intersection with horizontal, frontal, and profile.

P and the front at Q. The top surface and the line give an intersection at R, shown on the figure with dashed lines for the extensions.

Note in every case of Fig. 14.3 that the intersection is found by observing where the line intersects the surface *in the edge view* of the surface. For horizontal, frontal, and profile surfaces, two views always show the surface as an edge.

Thus it is easily seen that, for example, at (B), the line crosses the edge view of the right side of the object in the top view at Q_T and in the front view at Q_F, and because point Q falls *within the confines* of the surface, a real point of intersection has been found. Also observe at (A) that line AB *apparently* crosses the edge view of the right side of the object *in the top view*. Nevertheless, reading the front view, line AB is seen to miss the right side, and there is therefore no intersection of AB with the right side. To illustrate further, line AB of Fig.

14.4A apparently intersects the edge view of the top surface, as observed in the front view. But projecting Q_F to the top view at Q_T on AB, we see that Q_T falls within the confines of the top surface of the object and is therefore an intersection. However, at (B), when Q_F is projected to the top view, Q_T is outside the confines of the top surface, and there is no intersection. From this it is clear that to determine a real point of intersection, (1) *two views must be consulted,* and (2) *the apparent point of intersection in one view must project within the confines of the surface in another view.*

Summary

1. Locate the intersection by inspection in any view which shows the line and the edge view of the plane.

2. Project the point of intersection to the other views.

3. On a practical object, the point of intersection must lie within the confines of the plane.

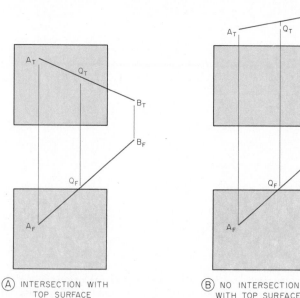

FIG. 14.4. To determine an intersection. The intersection (piercing point) must fall within the surface area in two (or more) views.

(A) INTERSECTION WITH TOP SURFACE

(B) NO INTERSECTION WITH TOP SURFACE

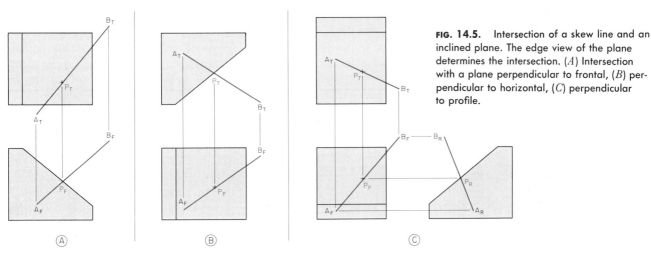

FIG. 14.5. Intersection of a skew line and an inclined plane. The edge view of the plane determines the intersection. (*A*) Intersection with a plane perpendicular to frontal, (*B*) perpendicular to horizontal, (*C*) perpendicular to profile.

14.6. INTERSECTION OF A SKEW LINE WITH INCLINED PLANES. An inclined plane appears as an edge in one view, and because of this, its intersection with any line is easily found. In Fig. 14.5*A* the inclined surface appears as an edge in the front view. The apparent intersection P_F is projected to P_T on A_TB_T, where it is seen that P_T falls within the confines of the inclined surface and therefore is a real point of intersection. Figure 18.5 shows the principle applied at (*B*) to a surface inclined to front and side and at (*C*) to a surface inclined to top and front. Note that at (*B*) the intersection will be located first in the top view, and at (*C*) it will be found first in the side view.

Summary

1. Locate the intersection by inspection in the view which shows the line and the edge view of the plane.

2. Project the point of intersection to the other views.

3. On a practical object, the point of intersection must lie within the confines of the plane.

14.7. INTERSECTION OF A SKEW LINE WITH A SKEW SURFACE. *General Case.* A skew surface does not appear as an edge in any principal view, so if the methods of paragraphs 14.3 to 14.6 are used, an edge view will have to be made. This is illustrated in Fig. 14.6, where the edge

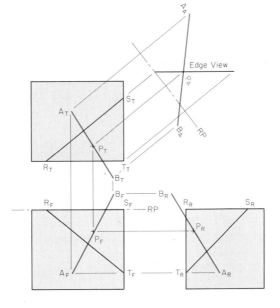

FIG. 14.6. Intersection of a skew line and a skew plane. An auxiliary (edge view) determines the intersection.

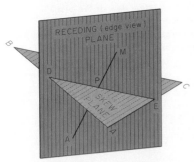

FIG. 14.7. Intersection of a line and a plane. The point of intersection is common to the line, the plane, and a receding plane used for determination of the intersection.

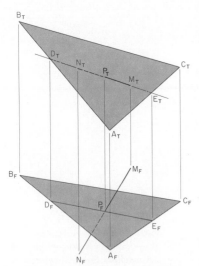

FIG. 14.8. Construction for finding the intersection of a line and a plane. (Figure 14.7 helps to visualize this construction.)

view has been made by looking in the direction of *SR*, a horizontal line of the skew surface. Line *AB* is now projected into the edge view, and the intersection *P* is located and then projected back to top, front, and side views.

It is not necessary, however, to employ an extra view (edge). The intersection of a line and a plane is a point common to both. A given line will intersect all lines of the plane which pass through the point of intersection. The intersection therefore can readily be determined by locating a *line of the plane* which intersects the given line.

The pictorial example of Fig. 14.7 illustrates the theory of finding the intersection *P* of line *MN* with a skew plane *ABC*. To find a line of *ABC* which intersects *MN*, a vertical plane containing *MN* is passed through *ABC*, thereby establishing *DE* as the straight-line intersection between the vertical plane and *ABC*. *DE* and *MN* are nonparallel lines of a common plane (vertical plane) and therefore must intersect; their common point is point *P*. Since point *P* is on line *DE*, it is a point in plane *ABC*. Therefore, *P* is a point common to plane *ABC* and the given line *MN*.

Figure 14.8 illustrates the orthographic procedure of finding the point of intersection of a line *MN* and a skew plane *ABC*. A vertical plane, which appears as an edge in the top view, is passed through *MN*, cutting the top view of *AB* at *D* and the top view of *AC* at *E*. Then, *DE* is the line of intersection of the vertical plane and *ABC*. *DE* is located in the front view by projecting points *D* and *E* to the front view on *AB* and *AC*, respectively. The intersection of *MN* and *DE*, point *P*, is located in the front view where *MN* intersects *DE*. (*DE* and *MN* both lie in the same verti-

cal plane.) Point *P* is projected to the top view on *MN*, completing the top and front views of point *P*, the intersection of line *MN*, and the skew plane *ABC*. An identical solution may be had by using a receding plane through the front view of line *MN*. The intersection of the receding plane and the given plane is then projected to the top view, where the intersection with line *MN* locates point *P*. A practical example is shown in Fig. 14.9, where *AB* is a line and *RST* a skew plane. A plane *appearing as an edge in the top view,* passed through *AB*, will intersect *RS* at Z_T and *RT* at X_T, and these points, projected to the front view at Z_F and X_F, establish *ZX* as the line of intersection between the edge-view plane and *RST*, the skew plane. The front view shows the intersection of *AB* with *ZX* at P_F, the point common to line, skew plane, and edge-view plane. To complete, *P* is projected to the top view at P_T.

Often, it happens that one edge of a skew surface is profile, as is *ST* in Figs.

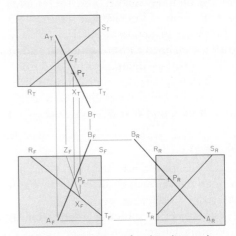

FIG. 14.9. Intersection of a skew line and a skew plane. The intersection is determined by a receding plane (edge-view plane in the top view) passed through line *AB*.

14.9 and 14.10, and when the line, in this case *AB*, is in a position like that of Fig. 14.10, the intersection (with the skew plane) of an edge-view plane through the line is not easily projected. An accepted method in such cases is to *extend* the skew plane to eliminate the profile edge. In Fig. 14.10, *RS* has been extended to *U*, making the skew surface *RUT* still the *same* surface but larger. An edge-view plane (in the top view), passed as before, gives *XZ* as its line of intersection with *RUT*. Point *P*, the point common to edge-view plane, skew plane, and line, is then located first in the front view at P_F and then projected to top and side views.

Summary

1. Pass a receding plane through the line (a plane appearing as an edge coincident with the line in either the top, front, or side view).

2. Determine the line of intersection between the receding plane and the given plane, and project this line to an adjacent view.

3. The point of intersection lies at the intersection of the *given line* with the *line of intersection* between the given plane and the receding plane.

4. On a practical object, the point of intersection must lie within the confines of the plane.

5. An alternate method is to draw an auxiliary showing the edge view of the plane, locate the intersection by inspection in the auxiliary, and then project to the other views.

14.8. **INTERSECTION OF SEVERAL LINES WITH A PLANE.** Frequently problems occur which require the intersection of many lines with a plane. Figure 14.11 is an example of such a problem, re-

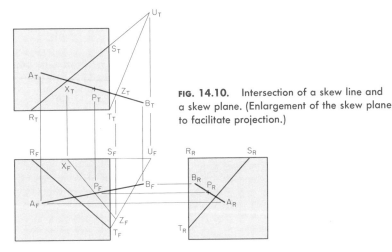

FIG. 14.10. Intersection of a skew line and a skew plane. (Enlargement of the skew plane to facilitate projection.)

quiring the determination of the intersection of the skew plane *ABC* and the parallelepiped *MNOPQR*. The problem is solved by determining the intersection of the edges of the parallelepiped with the given plane and drawing the consecutive lines of intersection on the parallelepiped between the points deter-

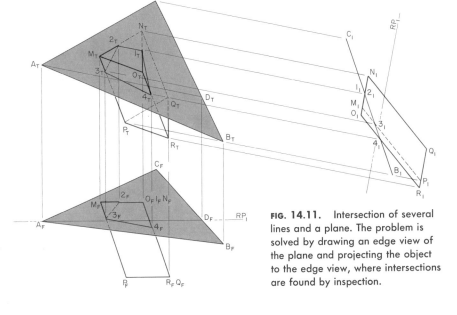

FIG. 14.11. Intersection of several lines and a plane. The problem is solved by drawing an edge view of the plane and projecting the object to the edge view, where intersections are found by inspection.

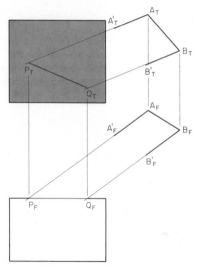

FIG. 14.12. Intersection of a skew plane with a plane in principal position. The edge view of the principal plane determines the intersection.

mined. The solution illustrated in Fig. 14.11 first requires that an edge view of the plane be established as shown in the auxiliary view projected from the top view. The parallelepiped is projected to the auxiliary view. The auxiliary view clearly shows where the plane *ABC* cuts through the parallelepiped, as at points 1 to 4 on lines *NO*, *MN*, *MP*, and *OR*, respectively. The numbered points are projected back to the top and front views and the consecutive lines of intersection drawn in both views.

The points of intersection 1 to 4 could have been determined by the procedure outlined in paragraph 14.7, but the time required for the necessary construction would be excessive compared to the edge-view method just described.

Summary

1. Draw an auxiliary showing the edge view of the given plane.

2. Project the several lines (usually a plane figure or solid) to the auxiliary view.

3. Locate the several points of intersection by inspection in the auxiliary view and project these points to the other views.

14.9. INTERSECTION OF A SKEW PLANE WITH A PLANE IN A PRINCIPAL POSITION. Any line of a given plane will intersect a second plane *on the line of intersection* between the two planes. Therefore, to establish the line of intersection between two planes, the intersection either of two lines of one plane with the other plane, or one line of each plane with the opposite plane, will establish two points on the line of intersection of the planes. The simplest case is when one of the planes is in a principal position such as the top surface of the object in Fig.

14.12. Lines *A-A'* and *B-B'* are edges of a skew plane, which, extended, are seen to intersect the top surface of the rectangular object at *P* and *Q*, as explained in paragraph 14.5.

Summary

1. In the edge view of the principal plane, locate the points of intersection of any two lines of the skew plane.

2. Project the points of intersection to the other views.

3. Connect the points of intersection with a straight line in all views.

14.10. INTERSECTION OF A SKEW PLANE WITH AN INCLINED PLANE. Figure 14.13 is similar to Fig. 14.12, but the intersection this time is with the inclined surface of the object. The intersection is again found by extending *A-A'* and *B-B'* to the edge view of the inclined surface. Refer to paragraph 14.6.

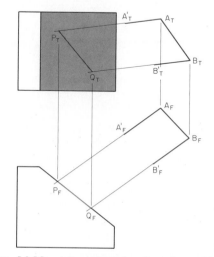

FIG. 14.13. Intersection of a skew plane with an inclined plane. The edge view of the inclined plane determines the intersection.

Summary

1. In the edge view of the inclined plane, locate the points of intersection of any two lines of the skew plane.

2. Project the points of intersection to the other views.

3. Connect the points of intersection with a straight line in all views.

14.11. INTERSECTION OF TWO SKEW PLANES.

General Case. The intersection of two planes is a straight line. To determine the location and direction of the line of intersection, it is necessary to determine two points on this line. The points are necessarily common to both planes. In Fig. 14.14, the line of intersection between planes ABC and DEF is to be established by locating points O and P, two points common to both planes, by the procedure outlined in paragraph 14.7. O is the intersection of

DE and plane ABD. A front receding plane is passed through the front view of DE, cutting AC at M and BC at N. MN is the line of intersection between the front receding plane and ABC. MN is then located in the top view, intersecting DE at point O, which is the intersection of DE and ABC. O is located in the front view by projecting O from the top view onto the front view of DE. Similarly, a vertical plane is passed through AC, cutting DF at R and EF at Q. RQ is the line of intersection between the vertical plane and DEF. RQ is then projected to the front view, intersecting AC at point P, the intersection of AC with plane DEF. Point P is then projected to the top view. Points O and P are common to both planes and must therefore be on the line of intersection between planes ABC and DEF. The top and front views of OP are extended to any desired length, as

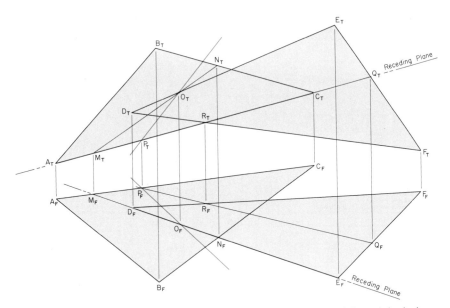

FIG. 14.14. Intersection of two skew planes. Receding planes passed through both skew planes determine the intersection.

the given planes are indefinite in extent. As a check on correctness and accuracy of the solution, a third point may be located. A receding plane in either view may be employed to do this; of course, for the solution to be correct, all three points must align on the same straight line—the line of intersection.

Another conception may be used to find the intersection of two planes: Any plane intersecting a second plane will intersect that plane in a straight line all points of which are common to both planes. It follows then that the two given planes may be cut by a receding plane, giving a line of intersection of the receding plane and each of the given planes. These two lines of intersection will intersect at a point which is common to both given planes, thus giving one point on the line of intersection of the given planes. This operation repeated with a second receding plane will

give a second point, thus determining the line of intersection of given planes. Therefore, in Fig. 14.15, the receding plane in the top view will cut RS from plane PTY and WU from CJV. The intersection of RS and WU in the front view at O_F is then projected to the top view, where O_T lies on the receding plane used.

Similarly, the receding plane in the front view will cut PF from plane PTY and CE from plane CJV. The intersection of PF and CE in the top view at N_T is then projected to the front view, where N_F lies on the receding plane used. Thus O and N are common to planes PTY and CJV and determine the line of intersection.

This method would be employed whenever the triangles representing the planes do not conveniently cross as they do in Fig. 14.14. Also, later, in the solution of problems involving curved sur-

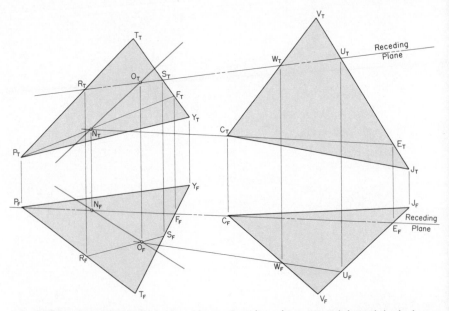

FIG. 14.15. Intersection of two skew planes. Receding planes passed through both skew planes determine the intersection.

faces, cutting planes will be chosen to pass through two surfaces but will not necessarily be placed at any particular edge or element of either surface. A practical case is shown in Fig. 14.16. As before, the points of intersection of two lines determine the intersection of the planes. In Fig. 14.16 two edge-view (in the front view) planes have been passed through A-A' and B-B' extended. The edge-view planes then intersect the skew plane $RSTU$ in lines WX and YZ. Then P_T and Q_T, the intersections of A-A' and B-B' extended in the top view, determine the top view of the line of intersection, which, projected to the front view at P_F and Q_F, completes the solution. Compare Fig. 14.16 (edge-view plane in front view is used) with Fig. 14.9 (edge-view plane in top view is used). An edge-view plane can also be passed in a side view whenever it is convenient to do so.

Summary

1. Pass receding (edge-view) planes through two lines of one of the given planes.

2. Locate the lines of intersection between the receding planes and the second given plane.

3. Locate the points of intersection between the two lines (through which receding planes were passed) and the lines of intersection between receding planes and second given plane. Project these two points to the other views.

4. Draw straight lines connecting the two points in all views.

Alternative method:

1. Pass a receding plane through both given planes.

2. Determine the lines of intersection with the receding plane and both given

planes. These lines of intersection intersect at a point common to both given planes.

3. Repeat (1) and (2) to find a second point common to both given planes.

4. The two common points thus found determine the line of intersection of the given planes.

14.12. INTERSECTION OF PLANES WHEN STRIKE AND DIP SPECIFICATIONS ARE GIVEN.

A point common to two planes can be located at the intersection of two strike lines, one in each plane, provided the lines are at the same elevation. Two such points will determine the direction and location of the straight-line intersection between the two planes.

In Fig. 14.17, the plane on the left is defined in both the top and front views by the strike AB and the 45° angle of dip. Note the elevation of AB at 1,620 ft. The plane on the right is defined by

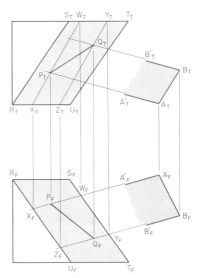

FIG. 14.16.   Intersection of two skew planes. For convenient projection, receding planes are passed through two lines of the skew plane to determine the intersection.

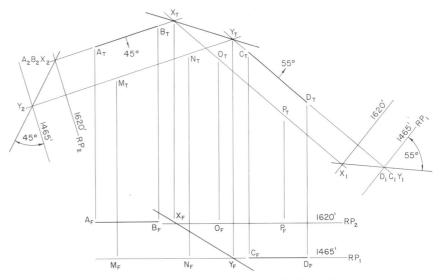

FIG. 14.17.   Intersection of two skew planes (planes specified by strike and dip). Two auxiliaries (edge views of the planes), projected from the top view, determine the intersection.

the strike *CD* and the 55° angle of dip. Note the elevation of *CD* at 1,465 ft.

In the first auxiliary view (projected from the top view in the direction of *CD*) *CD* appears as a point; and the plane will necessarily appear as an edge, drawn 55° below the horizontal as prescribed by the angle of dip. At an elevation of 1,620 ft (the same elevation as *AB*) a horizontal line *OP* is drawn in the auxiliary view. The top view of *OP* is drawn parallel to *CD*, extended to intersect the top view of *AB* at *X. AB* and *OP* are two horizontal lines at the same level or elevation. The front view of *X* is located at the 1,620-ft level. Point *X* is common to both planes and is a point on the line of intersection of the two planes.

In the second auxiliary view projected from the top view in the direction of *AB*, the edge view of the plane is determined and drawn 45° below the horizontal as presented. At an elevation of 1,465 ft (same elevation as *CD*), a horizontal line *MN* is located in the plane. *MN* is projected to the top view and drawn parallel to *AB*, extended to intersect the top view of *CD* at *Y. CD* and *MN* are two horizontal lines at the same level or elevation. *X* and *Y* are two points common to both planes and are on the line of intersection between the two planes. The top and front views of the line of intersection are now drawn through points *X* and *Y*.

Summary

1. Draw auxiliary views showing the point view of both strike lines.
2. In the auxiliary views, draw the edge views of the planes, through the point views of the strike lines and dipping on the side of the strike line indicated by specifications.

3. A point on the line of intersection between the planes lies at the intersection of strike lines which are *at the same level* on each plane, therefore: (*a*) If the two given strike lines are at the same level, their intersection in the top view is one point on the line of intersection. Find a second point by measuring a distance below the original strike lines in the front view and both auxiliaries and projecting the two new strike lines to the top view, where they intersect. Project the two points thus determined on the line of intersection to the front view, and connect the points in both views with straight lines. (*b*) If the given strike lines are at different levels, draw a strike line on each plane at the level of the other plane. Then, proceed as in (*a*).

14.13. **TO FIND THE INTERSECTION OF TWO PRISMS (FIG. 14.18).** In general, find the line of intersection of a surface on one prism with all surfaces on the other.

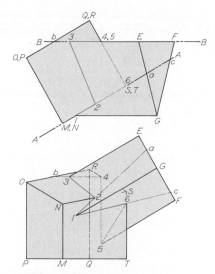

FIG. 14.18. Intersection of two prisms. Receding planes as described in paragraphs 14.9 to 14.12 are used to determine the intersection.

Then take a surface adjacent to the first, and find its intersection with the other prism. Continue in this manner until the complete line of intersection of the prisms is determined.

The method of locating end points on the line of intersection of two surfaces depends upon the position of the surfaces as follows:

Both Surfaces Receding. Their intersection appears as a point in the view in which they recede. Project the intersection to an adjacent view, locating the two ends of the intersection on the edges of one or both intersecting surfaces so that they will lie within the boundaries of the other surface. The intersection 4-5 of surfaces *QRST* and *EF*-3 was obtained in this manner.

One Surface Receding, the Other Skew. An edge of the skew surface may appear to pierce the receding surface in a view in which these conditions exist. If, in an adjacent view, the piercing point lies on the edge of the skew surface and within the boundaries of the other surface, then it is an end point on the intersection of the surfaces. Point 5, lying on edge *F*-5 of the skew surface *FG*-1-5 and the surface *QRST,* is located in the top view in this manner. Point 1 was similarly established. Point 6, lying on edge *ST,* is found by passing a vertical plane *AA* through edge *ST.* Plane *AA* cuts line *c*-1 from plane *GF*-5-1, giving point 6 where line *c*-1 crosses *ST.*

Both Surfaces Skew.   Find the piercing point of an edge on one surface with the other surface, as follows: Pass a receding plane through an edge of one surface. Find the line of intersection of the receding plane and the other surface as explained above. The piercing point of the edge and surface is located where the line of intersection, just found, and the

edge intersect. Repeat this operation to establish the other end of the line of intersection of the surfaces. Point 3, on the line of intersection 2-3 of the oblique surfaces *NORS* and *EG*-1-3, was found in this manner by passing the receding plane *BB* through edge *E*-3, finding the intersection *b*-4 of the surfaces, and then locating point 3 at the intersection of *b*-4 and *E*-3.

Summary

Both surfaces receding

The intersection appears as a point in this view. Project the intersection to other views.

One surface receding, the other skew

An edge of the skew surface observed to intersect the receding surface locates an intersection. If, when projected to an adjacent view, it lies within the boundaries of the receding surface, an end point on the line of intersection is located.

Both surfaces skew

Pass a receding plane through an edge of one surface. Find the line of intersection between the receding plane and the second surface. In an adjacent view, the intersection is the intersection of the edge of the first surface with the line of intersection between receding plane and second surface. To be an end point on the line of intersection, the point must fall within the boundaries of the second surface.

14.14.   TO FIND THE INTERSECTION OF TWO PYRAMIDS.   In general, find where one edge on one pyramid pierces a surface of the other pyramid. Then find where a second edge pierces, and so on. To complete the line of intersection the piercing points of the edges of the second pyramid with surfaces of the first will

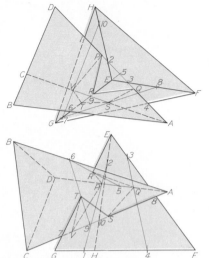

FIG. 14.19. Intersection of two pyramids. Receding planes as described in paragraphs 14.9 to 14.12 are used to determine the intersection.

probably also have to be found. Figure 14.19 illustrates the method. Find where edge *AD* pierces plane *EHG* by assuming a vertical cutting plane through edge *AD*. This plane cuts line 1-2 from plane *EHG*, and the piercing point is point *P,* located first on the front view and then projected to the top view. Next, find where *AD* pierces plane *EFG* by using a vertical cutting plane through *AD*. This plane cuts line 3-4 from plane *EFG*, and the piercing point is point *Q.*

Having a point *P* on plane *EHG* and point *Q* on plane *EFG*, the piercing point of edge *EG* with plane *ABD* will have to be found in order to draw lines of intersection. A vertical plane through *EG* cuts line 5-6 from plane *ABD*, and the intersection is point *R* on edge *EG*. Thus edges of the "first" pyramid pierce surfaces of the "second," and edges of the second pierce surfaces of the first. Continue in this manner until the complete line of intersection *PRQSTV* has been found.

The use of a vertical cutting plane to obtain the piercing points is perhaps the simplest method and the easiest to visualize. Nevertheless, it should be noted that a plane receding either from the frontal or profile planes could also be used. As an example of the use of a plane receding from the frontal, consider that such a plane has been passed through line *CA* in the front view. This plane cuts line 7-8 from plane *EFG*, and the point of intersection is *S* on line *CA*. The use of a plane receding from the profile would be basically the same but would, of course, require a side view.

Summary

Find where edges of pyramid *A* intersect surfaces of pyramid *B*. To complete the line of intersection find where (as necessary) edges of pyramid *B* intersect surfaces of pyramid *A*. (Reference: paragraph 14.7.)

14.15.   TO FIND THE LINE OF INTERSECTION BETWEEN A PRISM AND A PYRAMID (FIG. 14.20). The method, basically, is the same as for two pyramids. Thus, a vertical plane through edge *G* cuts line 1-2 from surface *AED*, and a vertical plane through edge *K* cuts line 3-4 from surface *AED*, giving the two piercing points *P* and *Q* on surface *AED*. A vertical plane through edge *AE* cuts elements 7 and 8 from the prism and gives piercing points *R* and *T*. Continue in this manner until the complete line of intersection *PQS-TVR* is found.

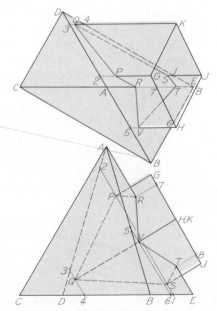

FIG. 14.20. Intersection of a pyramid and a prism. Receding planes as described in paragraphs 14.9 to 14.12 are used to determine the intersection.

Summary

Find where edges of the pyramid intersect surfaces of the prism and complete by finding where any necessary edges of the prism intersect surfaces of the pyramid. (Reference: paragraph 14.7.)

14.16.   INTERSECTIONS OF CURVED SURFACES.

The line of intersection of two curved surfaces, as was the case for plane surfaces, is a line all points of which are common to both surfaces. There may be more than one line of intersection between two curved surfaces. For example, a small pipe which passes completely through a larger pipe will intersect the larger pipe in two lines, one line as it *enters* and another as it *leaves*.

The line of intersection of any two surfaces may be found by either one of the following methods:

Selected-line Method.   Select a sufficient number of lines of one surface. Find the point where each one of these lines pierces the other surface. A line joining these piercing points will be the line of intersection of the two surfaces. This method was used in paragraph 14.11 to find the line of intersection of two plane surfaces.

Cutting-plane Method.   Pass a sufficient number of cutting planes through each of the given surfaces simultaneously. Each plane will "cut" a line (straight or curved) from each of the given surfaces. These lines will intersect either in a point or points common to the two given surfaces. A line connecting these points will be the line of intersection of the given surfaces. This method was also used in paragraph 14.11 to find the line of intersection of two plane surfaces.

Cutting-sphere Method.   In finding the line of intersection between two double-curved surfaces, sometimes a plane will cut circles from one of the surfaces but parabolas, hyperbolas, etc., from the other surface. In such cases, it may be possible to use a cutting sphere, thus obtaining *circles* from both surfaces and simplifying the solution.

In attacking any problem of surface intersection, always examine the problem carefully to discover the *simplest* lines possible to cut from each surface.

In applying any of the general methods outlined above, exercise care, or the solution of the problem may become more complicated than necessary. In applying the selected-line method, for example, lines from one surface should be selected by giving primary consideration to the method that will be used to find where these lines pierce the other surface. In applying the cutting-plane method, planes should be selected that will cut *simple* lines (either straight lines or circles) from each of the given surfaces.

For purposes of analyzing the problems of geometric curved-surface intersection, curved surfaces may be divided into two classes: (1) single-curved surfaces of revolution and (2) double-curved surfaces of revolution.

Summary

Selected-line method

1. Select a number of lines (elements) of one surface.

2. Determine where these lines intersect the second surface.

3. Draw a smooth curve through the intersections.

Cutting-plane method

1. Pass a number of planes through each of the surfaces simultaneously. Use planes that will cut simple lines (straight lines or circles) from each surface.

2. Draw a smooth curve through the intersections.

Cutting-sphere method (for intersections of double-curved surfaces whose axes intersect)

1. Centered at the intersection of the axes, draw spheres of varying size. The spheres will cut circles from both surfaces.

2. Determine the intersections of circles cut from the surfaces.

3. Draw a smooth curve through the intersections.

14.17. INTERSECTION OF A SINGLE-CURVED SURFACE AND A LINE.

In paragraph 14.7, directions were given for finding the point of intersection between a line and plane. Basically, the same method is used to find the intersection of a line and a single-curved surface. If a cutting plane is passed through the line and the intersection of the cutting plane with the single-curved surface found, this intersection will cross the line in points common to the line, the cutting plane, and the single-curved surface. The cutting plane is preferably passed through the single-curved surface so that it will cut a straight line. This means that for a cone the plane will be passed through the apex, or for a cylinder it will be parallel to the axis.

14.18. INTERSECTION OF A CYLINDER AND A LINE.

The problem of finding the intersection of a cylinder and a line is illustrated pictorially in Fig. 14.21A. A plane passed parallel to the axis of a cylinder will cut straight-line elements from the cylinder. Therefore, in Fig. 14.21A, lines from A and B parallel to the cylinder axis will determine a plane that contains AB and is also parallel to the cylinder axis. These lines intersect the base plane of the cylinder at R and S. Points 1 and 2, where RS cuts the base

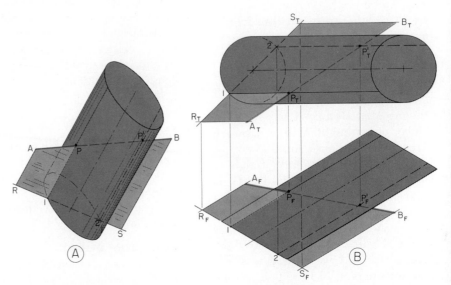

FIG. 14.21. Intersection of a line and a cylinder. (A) Pictorial aid to theory explanation, (B) orthographic construction. A receding plane passed through the line parallel to the cylinder axis cuts straight-line elements from the cylinder and provides determination of the intersection.

curve, determine the ends of two elements of the cylinder in plane *ABRS*. The intersections of *AB* and the elements at *P* and *P'* are then points which are common to the line *AB*, the cutting plane, and the cylinder.

Figure 14.21*B* illustrates the orthographic solution. From *A* and *B*, lines are drawn parallel to the cylinder axis to intersect the base plane at *R* and *S*. The lines *AB*, *BS*, *SR*, and *RA* now form a plane passed through *AB*, parallel to the cylinder axis. The line *RS* then cuts the base curve at 1 and 2, thus locating elements of the cylinder. The elements intersect *AB* at *P* and *P'*, the piercing points.

Summary

1. Pass a plane through the line, parallel to the cylinder axis.

2. Determine the intersection of the plane with the base curve of the cylinder, and draw the two elements of the cylinder cut by the plane.

3. The two points of intersection of the line and cylinder are the intersections of the line and the two cylinder elements.

14.19. INTERSECTION OF A CONE AND A LINE. Figure 14.22*A* illustrates pictorially the problem of finding the points where a line pierces a cone. A cutting plane *VXY*, containing the given line *AB* and passing through the apex *V* of the cone, is selected. A plane passing through the apex of a cone will intersect the cone in straight lines. The lines of intersection of the cutting plane and the cone are lines *V*-1 and *V*-2. These lines are determined by finding the line of intersection *RS* between the cutting plane and the *base plane* of the cone and then finding the points 1 and 2 where this line crosses the *base curve*. Line *AB* intersects both lines *V*-1 and *V*-2, establishing the points *P* and *P'* where line *AB* pierces the cone.

The orthographic solution is illustrated in Fig. 14.22*B*. Convenient points *X* and *Y* on line *AB* are selected so that plane *VXY* (a plane containing the apex of the cone and line *AB*), extended, will intersect the base plane of the cone in the line *RS*. In the top view, *RS* cuts the base curve at 1 and 2, thus locating elements *V*-1 and *V*-2, which then intersect *BA* at *P* and *P'*, the piercing points of line *AB* and the cone.

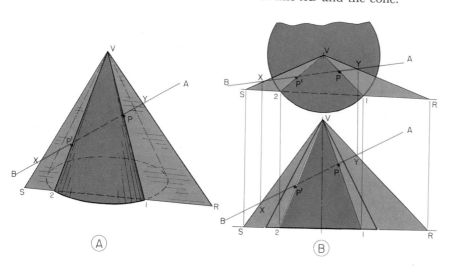

FIG. 14.22. Intersection of a line and a cone. (*A*) Pictorial aid to theory explanation, (*B*) orthographic construction. A plane passed through the line and the cone apex cuts two elements from the cone and provides determination of the intersection.

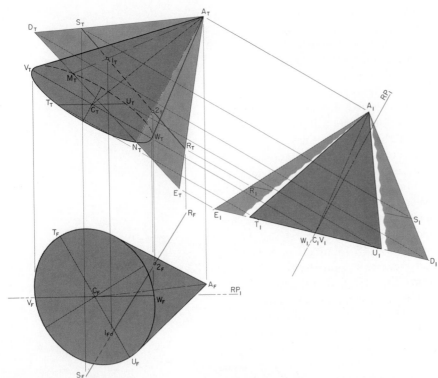

FIG. 14.23. Intersection of a line and cone, both in skew position. An auxiliary view showing the edge view of the cone base is employed to simplify the determination.

give the edge view of the base, and having the point view at V_1A_1, any other point in the plane of the base allows completion of the edge view of the base in the auxiliary view. TU, the front-view major diameter, may be employed for this purpose. TU is frontal and may therefore be located in the top view. Then projection from T and U to the auxiliary and measurement from the front view locates points in the auxiliary through which the edge view of the base may be drawn. Now, through RS in the auxiliary a plane ARS will pass through the apex of the cone and contain line RS. Then, AR and AS, extended to the base plane, locate a line of plane ARS in the base plane of the cone at E_1D_1. This line ED, projected back to AR and AS (extended) in the top view, will reveal the points M and N where plane ARS intersects the base curve. Thus, two elements, MA and $NA,$ are cut from the cone. These elements intersect RS at points 1 and 2, the piercing points of RS with the cone. The front view of points 1 and 2 may be found by projecting 1 and 2 to RS in the front view. The location of elements MA and NA in the front view allows checking for accuracy. Note in Fig. 14.23 that the top view and auxiliary have the same relationship to the solution as do the top and front views of Fig. 14.22.

Summary

1. Pass a plane through the line and through the apex of the cone.

2. Determine the intersection of the plane and the base plane and base curve of the cone; then determine the two elements cut from the cone by the plane.

3. The two points of intersection of the line and cone are the intersections of the line and the elements cut from the cone.

If the line and cone are both in a skew position as in Fig. 14.23, an extra view will assist in getting an accurate solution. If either the major and minor or the conjugate diameters of the cone's base are given, these diameters may be employed to get the edge view of the base. In Fig. 14.23, the major and minor diameters are given for each elliptical representation in top and front views of the base. The base is circular but not a right section of the cone, and the cone is therefore an oblique cone. The top-view major diameter VW is a horizontal line and is in true length. An auxiliary view then made as a point view of VW (by projecting from the top view) will

14.20. INTERSECTION OF ANY SINGLE-CURVED (RULED) SURFACE AND A LINE.

The problem of finding the piercing point of a line and any ruled surface is illustrated pictorially in Fig. 14.24*A*. A plane passed through the line will cut a line (often curved) from the surface. This line of intersection between cutting plane and surface may be located by finding where the cutting plane intersects elements of the surface. Then where the given line intersects the *surface intersection* of the cutting plane, there is a point common to the given line and surface. Figure 14.24*B* shows the orthographic construction. A receding plane in the top view through *AB* cuts elements of the surface. These points of intersection on the elements may then be projected to the front view, locating the front view of the line of intersection between cutting plane and ruled surface. The intersection at *P* is then a point common to the given line and ruled surface. The above method is useful in finding the piercing point of a line and either a geometrical ruled surface, such as one of the hyperboloids, or a ruled (or single-curved) surface of general form.

Summary

1. Pass a receding plane through the line.

2. Determine the intersection of the receding plane and the ruled surface by finding intersections of elements of the ruled surface with the plane.

3. The intersection of the line and ruled surface is the intersection of the line with the line of intersection between the ruled surface and the receding plane.

14.21. INTERSECTION OF A SINGLE-CURVED SURFACE AND A PLANE.

In the solution of these problems, either the selected-line

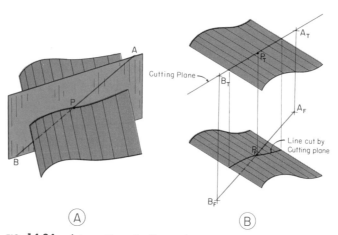

FIG. 14.24. Intersection of a line and a ruled surface. (*A*) Pictorial aid to theory explanation, (*B*) orthographic construction. A plane passed through the line cuts a curve from the ruled surface.

or the cutting-plane method may be used. However, the selected-line method is usually used when the edge view of the plane is given or a rearrangement of views can easily be made in which the plane will show as an edge. The cutting plane is usually used in all other cases. A straight line or circle can always be cut from a single-curved surface by a cutting plane.

14.22. INTERSECTION OF A CYLINDER AND A PLANE.

Figure 14.25 illustrates both the selected-line and the cutting-plane method of finding the intersection of a cylinder and plane. At *A*, a selected line of the plane, such as *AX*, is seen to intersect the cylinder in the top view where the cylindrical surface appears as an edge. Therefore, element *P* of the cylinder will contain point *Z*, one point on the line of intersection. A number of selected lines of the plane will give points to plot the complete curve of intersection. Note that line *AX* also intersects the cylinder at point *Y*, on element *Q*.

At Fig. 14.25*B*, a vertical cutting plane is shown. This plane, parallel to the cylinder axis, will cut elements of the cylinder at *T* and *U* and will also cut a line *RS* from the plane *ABC*. Points *Z* and *X* are then points common to cutting plane, given plane, and cylinder and are two points on the line of intersection sought. A series of planes similar to the one shown will give other points to complete the line of intersection.

Summary

Selected-line method

1. Draw a number of lines on the plane and determine where these lines intersect the cylinder. Draw an end view of the cylinder if necessary.

2. Draw a smooth curve through the points of intersection.

Cutting-plane method

1. Pass a number of planes through the given plane and parallel to the cylinder axis. These planes cut elements from the cylinder and lines from the plane. Points on the line of intersection occur at the intersection of cylinder elements and plane line, cut by the same plane.

2. Draw a smooth curve through the points of intersection.

14.23. INTERSECTION OF A CONE AND A PLANE.

Figure 14.26*A* illustrates pictorially the determination of the line of intersection between a cone and a plane by the selected-line method. Lines (elements) of the cone, such as *V*-1, *V*-2, etc., will respectively intersect the plane at *a, b,* etc. If the edge view of the plane appears in one of the views, as in 14.26*B*, the solution is quite simple. Selected elements of the cone, *V*-1, *V*-2, etc., are drawn in both views. These elements are seen to intersect the plane in the front view at *a,b,* etc. Projection of these points to the top view then gives points through which a smooth curve is drawn to complete the solution. The edge view of the plane (within the confines of the cone) is, of course, the intersection in the front view.

If the plane intersecting the cone is in a skew position, as in Fig. 14.27, the cutting-plane method would probably be preferred because of the simplicity of the solution. Any plane passed through the apex of the cone will cut straight lines from the cone. Therefore, in Fig. 14.27*A*, if vertical cutting planes are employed, all passing through the apex *V*, these planes will cut lines such as *V*-2 and *V*-8 from the cone. At the same time, such a cutting plane will cut *XZ* from the plane. *XZ* then intersects *V*-2 at *b* and *V*-8 at *h*, giving two points on

FIG. 14.25. Intersection of a plane and a cylinder. Receding planes passed parallel to the cylinder axis and (*A*) through selected lines of the plane or (*B*) parallel to each other cut straight-line elements from both surfaces.

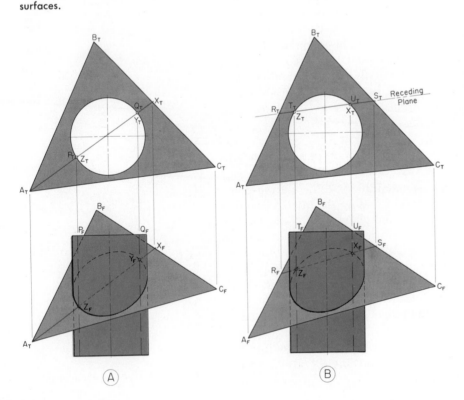

the line of intersection. A series of planes thus passed and points found will complete the solution.

Even though the above plane method is simple and requires only the given views for solution, one might prefer to draw an extra view (auxiliary), as at Fig. 14.27*B*, where, by projecting parallel to a horizontal line of the plane, *the plane appears as an edge.* In this event, selected lines of the cone are seen to intersect the plane in the auxiliary view (where the plane appears as an edge), and the solution becomes basically the same as in Fig. 14.26*B*. In addition, of course, points located first in the auxiliary view and then in the top view will have to be found in the front view by projection from the top view and measurement from the auxiliary, indicated typically by distance *X* on the figure.

Summary

Two views given, one view showing the edge view of the plane

1. Draw elements of the cone in both views.

2. Observe where elements of the cone intersect the edge view of the plane.

3. Project the points of intersection to the adjacent view, and draw a smooth curve through the points.

Two views given, the plane in skew position

1. Draw elements of the cone in both views.

2. Pass receding planes through the cone elements, and determine the lines of intersection between receding planes and given plane.

3. Points of intersection of given cone and plane lie at the intersection of elements and plane line cut by a receding plane. Draw smooth curves through the points in both views.

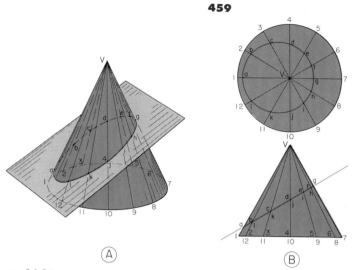

FIG. 14.26.   Intersection of a plane and a cone (cone in principal position, plane in inclined position). (*A*) Pictorial aid to explanation, (*B*) orthographic construction. Points are determined in the edge view of the plane, then projected to the top view.

Two views given, the plane in skew position (alternate method)

Draw a view showing the edge view of the plane, then proceed as in (1).

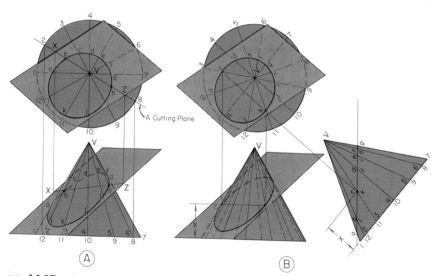

FIG. 14.27.   Intersection of a plane and a cone. (*A*) By employing cutting planes to cut straight-line elements from the cone, (*B*) by employing an edge view of the plane.

14.24.   INTERSECTION OF TWO RULED SURFACES.   In determining the line of intersection of two ruled surfaces either the selected-line or the cutting-plane method may be used. However, when the selected-line method is used, cutting planes will have to be employed to find the points where the selected lines pierce the other surface. Therefore, no matter which analysis is applied, the construction involved will be the same as if the cutting-plane analysis had been applied. As a result, problems involving the intersection of ruled surfaces should be solved using the cutting-plane analysis. Planes are selected, when possible, to cut *straight lines* from each of the given ruled surfaces simultaneously.

14.25.   INTERSECTION OF TWO CYLINDERS (FIG. 14.28).   Cutting planes parallel to the axis of a cylinder will cut straight-line elements from the cylinder. The frontal cutting planes *A, B, C,* and *D, parallel to the axis of each cylinder,* cut elements from each cylinder, the intersections of which are points on the curve. The pictorial sketch shows a slice cut by a plane from the object, which has been treated as a solid in order to illustrate the method more easily.

When the axes of the cylinders do not intersect, as in Fig. 14.29, the same method is used. Certain "critical planes" give the limits and turning points of the curve. Such planes should always be taken through the contour elements. For the position shown, planes *A* and *D* give the depth of the curve, the plane *B* the extreme height, and the plane *C* the tangent or turning points on the contour element of the vertical cylinder. After the critical points have been determined, a sufficient number of other cutting planes are used to give an accurate curve.

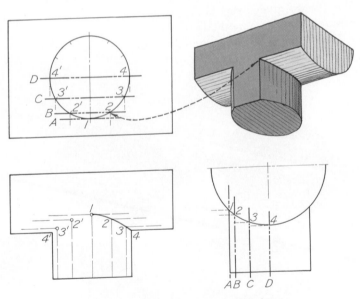

FIG. 14.28.   Intersection of two cylinders. Planes cut straight-line elements from both.

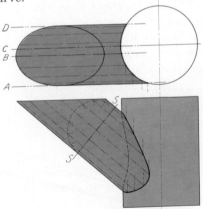

FIG. 14.29.   Intersection of two cylinders, axes not intersecting. Planes, parallel to each of the axes, cut straight-line elements from both surfaces.

14.26. INTERSECTION OF TWO CYLINDERS:

GENERAL CASE. Figure 14.30 illustrates pictorially at *A* and orthographically at *B* the determination of the line of intersection of two cylinders. As explained before, a plane passed *parallel to the axis* of a cylinder will cut straight-line elements from the cylinder. Logic then dictates that a plane parallel to the axes of *two* cylinders will cut straight-line elements from both.

Following the theory of paragraph 11.4 (drawing a plane parallel to two skew lines) in Fig. 14.30*A*, line *XS* is made parallel to one cylinder axis and line *XR* parallel to the other cylinder axis. *RS* is located so that it will be *in the plane of the bases of both cylinders.* Thus a line parallel to *RS* will cut the base curves of both cylinders and locate points, such as 1 through 7 (shown), which will fix the location of elements of each cylinder which lie in the same plane and will therefore determine points on the line of intersection. The details of projection are shown in Fig. 14.30*B*. First, for the method to be applied, *both cylinder bases must lie in the same plane,* preferably horizontal, frontal, or profile. If the original views do not include bases in one plane, they can be made so by finding the cylinder intersections with a common plane, as explained in paragraph 14.22. In this case (Fig. 14.30*B*), the bases are in a horizontal plane. Second, a plane must be established parallel to both cylinder axes. This construction is shown at *XRS*, where point *X* has been assumed at any convenient place, and then *XR* is drawn parallel to the left cylinder axis and *XS* parallel to the right cylinder axis. *RS* is made horizontal *because the bases are horizontal,* thus producing a line of intersection *RS* of plane *XRS* with a horizontal plane. The direction of $R_T S_T$

will fix the direction of the intersection with horizontal planes of *any* plane parallel to both cylinders. Lines *Z, Z', Z",* and *Z"'*, drawn parallel to *RS*, are therefore the intersections of planes parallel to both cylinders with the horizontal base plane of the cylinders. Third, the horizontal intersection of any plane passed as described will cut the base curves of the cylinders. For example, plane *Z'* cuts the base of the left cylinder at points 2 and 8 and the base of the right cylinder at 6 and 12. The elements of the cylinders then emanate from these points and intersect in four points, 2, 6, 8, and 12, which are points on the line of intersection. The top view is drawn first, and then the elements and points are projected down to the front view. The numbering system of Fig. 14.30 is

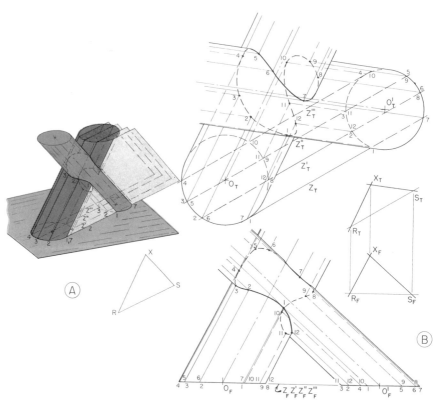

FIG. 14.30. Intersection of two cylinders, edge view of bases given. Cutting planes passed parallel to the axes of both cylinders and the cutting plane intersections with the bases make for an easy solution.

similar to the one described for Fig.
14.34. Notice in this case that 2 and 12,
cut by plane Z', are on the bottom side
of the cylinders and that points 6 and 8
are on the upper side. Note also that
plane Z is the foremost plane that will
cut both cylinders and that Z''' is the
rearmost. Except for a plane tangent to
one of the cylinders, four points on the
line of intersection are obtained by each
cutting plane. The visibility is determined by inspection after the line of
intersection is plotted.

Summary

1. At a convenient place on the sheet,
draw a plane consisting of (*a*) a line
parallel to one cylinder axis, (*b*) a line
parallel to the other cylinder axis, and
(*c*) a line parallel to the base planes of
both cylinders.

2. Draw a line, parallel to the line of
the plane that is parallel to the base
planes of the cylinders, that cuts the
base curve of both cylinders. This represents the intersection, with the base
planes, of a plane parallel to both cylinder axes. This plane cuts elements from
both cylinders that emanate from the
points where the line crosses (and intersects) the base curves.

3. Draw the elements of the cylinders
which will intersect in four points common to both cylinders.

4. Continue the process described in
(2) and (3) to determine a sufficient
number of points on the line of intersection to draw smooth curves.

**14.27. INTERSECTION OF A CYLINDER AND
A CONE (FIG. 14.31).** Cutting planes
may be taken, as at (*A*), so as to pass
through the vertex of the cone and parallel to the axis of the cylinder, thus

cutting the straight-line elements from
both cylinder and cone; or, as at (*B*),
with a right-circular cone, when the
cylinder's axis is parallel or perpendicular to the cone's axis, cutting planes
may be taken parallel to the base so as
to cut circles from the cone. Both systems of planes are illustrated in the figure. The pictorial sketches show slices
taken by each plane through the objects,
which have been treated as solids in
order to illustrate the method more
easily. Some judgment is necessary in
the selection of both the direction and
the number of cutting planes. More
points need to be found at the places of
sudden curvature or change of direction
of the projections of the line of
intersections.

In Fig. 14.31*A* the cutting planes appear as edges in the right-side view,
where the cylinder surface also appears
as an edge. The observed intersections
in the side view are then projected to
the cone elements formed by the cutting planes, in the top and front views,
to complete the solution.

At (*B*), horizontal cutting planes cut
circles from the cone and straight-line
elements from the cylinder. The top
view then reveals intersections of cone
circles and cylinder elements. Projection
to the front view will complete the
solution.

Figure 14.32*A* illustrates the determination of the line of intersection of a
cone and a cylinder by the cutting-plane
method. The axes of both surfaces of
Fig. 14.32*A* are vertical. Therefore, any
vertical plane that passes through the
apex of the cone will cut straight-line
elements from the cone, and these vertical planes will also cut elements from
the cylinder. One such cutting plane is
shown on the figure. This plane cuts

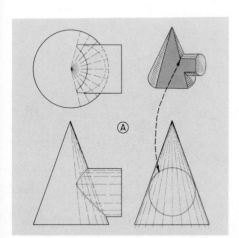

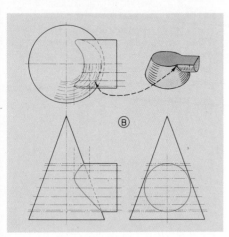

FIG. 14.31. Intersection of a cylinder and
cone. (*A*) elements of the cone are observed
to intersect the cylinder in the side view
(edge view of cylinder); or (*B*) horizontal
planes cut circles from both surfaces and
locate points common to both.

elements *V*-1 and *V*-2 from the cone and at the same time cuts elements 1′ and 2′ from the cylinder. Element *V*-1 of the cone intersects element 1′ of the cylinder, and element *V*-2 of the cone intersects element 2′ of the cylinder, thus locating two points on the line of intersection. A number of vertical planes thus employed will give points to locate the curve in the front view. The line of intersection in the top view is, of course, the circle shown, the end view of the cylinder.

It should be noted that the problem of Fig. 14.32*A* may also be solved by cutting both surfaces with horizontal planes, thus obtaining a circle from each surface. The intersections of circles may be found in the top view and then be projected to the front view.

Figure 14.32*B* illustrates the determination of the line of intersection for another cone-and-cylinder combination. In the views given (top and front), it can be seen that no suitable cutting plane can be employed to determine the line of intersection if simple lines are to be cut from each surface. Planes parallel to plane *A* will cut straight lines from the cylinder but a hyperbola from the cone. Planes parallel to plane *B* will cut circles from the cone but ellipses from the cylinder. Planes parallel to plane *C* will cut straight lines from the cylinder but ellipses from the cone. It is now evident that some other method may give an easier solution. The auxiliary view shown, giving the end view of the cylinder, offers the advantage that planes may be passed through the apex of the cone and also parallel to the cylinder axis without burdensome extra construction. One such plane is shown, which cuts a line *V*-1 from the cone and which also cuts elements 1′ and 1″ from the

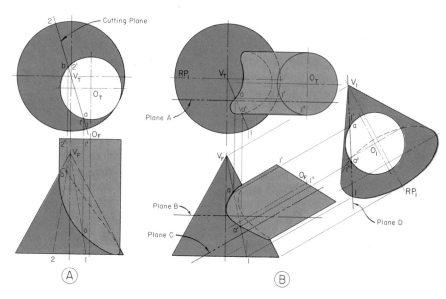

FIG. 14.32. Intersection of a cylinder and a cone. Cutting planes are used to cut straight-line elements from both surfaces (through the cone apex, parallel to the cylinder axis).

cylinder. These elements intersect at *a* and *a*′ (first located in the front view), giving two points on the line of intersection. Additional planes similar to the one illustrated will determine other points to complete the intersection.

Summary

1. Pass planes simultaneously through both the cylinder and the cone. Remember that a plane perpendicular to the cylinder axis will cut a circle; a plane parallel to the axis will cut elements. Also, a plane perpendicular to the cone axis will cut a circle; a plane through the apex will cut elements.

2. Determine intersections of elements and/or circles cut from cone and cylinder by each cutting plane.

3. Draw smooth curves through the points of intersection.

14.28. INTERSECTION OF TWO CONES. Figure 14.33 illustrates another variation of the intersection of single-curved surfaces, this time for two cones. Employing only top and front views (given), no series of planes either horizontal, frontal, profile, or receding in any view will cut simple lines from the surfaces. Yet, as shown in Fig. 14.32 and explained in paragraph 14.27, if a plane is passed through the apex of a cone, it will cut straight-line elements from the cone. It follows then that if a plane is passed through the apexes of *both* cones, straight-line elements will be cut from both cones. Therefore, *a plane passed through a line connecting the apex points of both cones* should give a relatively simple position.

A point view of the line connecting the apex points of the cones of Fig. 14.33 is had in the auxiliary view shown at $V'V$, and this view, having the *point view of a line through which a plane is passed*, gives the edge view of the plane. One such plane (2) is shown, which cuts an element V-2 from one cone and an element V'-2′ from the other. These two elements intersect at 2″, giving one point on the line of intersection of the cones. A series of planes passed as described will give other points to plot the complete line of intersection.

Summary

1. Draw a line connecting the apex points of both cones.

2. Draw a point view of the line connecting the cone apexes. Carry the projection of the cones to this view.

3. Planes passed through the point view of the line connecting the apex points will cut elements from both cones.

4. Elements cut from both cones (by a cutting plane) intersect. Project the points of intersection to the given views and draw smooth curves.

Intersection of Two Cones, Edge Views of Bases Given. In Fig. 14.33, the edge views of the bases of both cones appear in the front view, but when the point view of the line connecting the apexes is made in this new view, the base curves must be plotted. Depending, to some extent, on the position of the cones, a better solution might be to pass planes through the apexes of both cones, determining where the planes intersect the base planes of the cones. Figure 14.34*A* illustrates the principle pictorially. Line V-V' connecting the apex points is extended to P and P', where the line intersects the base planes. Then a point such as X, chosen on the line of intersection of the base planes, will make a plane $PP'X$ which contains a line $P'X$ cutting the base curve of one cone and a line PX cutting the base curve of the other. Elements of each cone thus located (by cutting the base curves) will intersect in four points on the line of intersection.

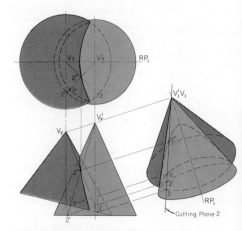

FIG. 14.33. Intersection of two cones. Cutting planes are passed through the apexes of both cones, thus cutting straight-line elements from both surfaces.

The orthographic drawing at Fig. 14.34*B* will illustrate the details of construction. Apex line *V-V′* is extended to intersect the base planes at *P* and *P′*. The line of intersection of the base plane appears as a point in the front view and as a line in the top view. A point *X* selected on the base-plane intersection in the top view produces *P′X*, points 2 and 8 on the base of the left cone, and *PX* and points 6 and 12 on the right cone. These elements 2-*V′*, 8-*V′*, 6-*V*, and 12-*V*, intersect at 2, 6, 8, and 12 in the cutting plane and on both cones. Elements 2-*V′*, 8-*V′*, 6-*V*, and 12-*V* then located in the front view allow projection of 2, 6, 8, and 12 to the front view. Other points are located by shifting the plane to another position, such as *PP′X′* and *PP′X″*. In the illustration, elements cut from each cone by each cutting plane are numbered alike so that identically numbered elements intersect at a point designated by the number. This method of determining the line of intersection of two cones is sometimes called "the swinging-plane method."

Summary

1. Draw a line connecting the apex points of both cones.

2. Extend the base planes (edge view) to determine the intersection of the base planes and also the intersections of the line connecting the apex points and the base planes.

3. Line now drawn in the base planes, from the intersection of one base plane and cone apex line, to the intersection of base planes, then to the opposite intersection of base plane and cone apex line, cutting the base curves of both cones, will determine elements of both cones,

cut by the same plane. These cone elements intersect in four points common to both cones.

4. Continue the process as in (3) with other lines in the base planes (representing different planes through the apex of both cones) until a sufficient number of points common to both cones have been determined. Draw smooth curves through the points.

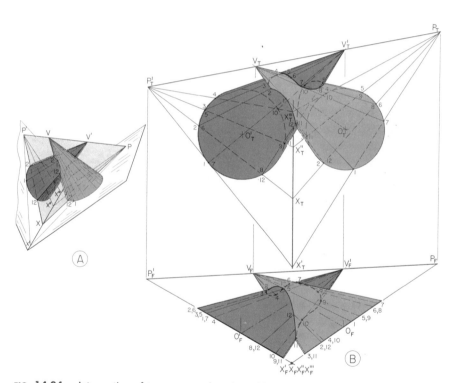

FIG. 14.34. Intersection of two cones, edge view of bases given. Cutting planes passed through the apexes of both cones and the cutting plane intersections with the bases make for an easy solution.

14.29. INTERSECTION OF DOUBLE-CURVED SURFACES OF REVOLUTION.

Double-curved surfaces of revolution present problems somewhat more complicated than do single-curved surfaces because straight lines cannot be cut from a double-curved surface. However, the geometric double-curved surfaces, the ellipsoid, paraboloid, etc., are surfaces of revolution and circles may therefore be cut by planes perpendicular to the axis of revolution.

14.30. INTERSECTION OF A SURFACE OF REVOLUTION AND A LINE.

Because no straight line can be drawn on a surface of revolution, any plane passed through the surface will be a curve. In finding the points of intersection of a line and a surface of revolution, it is necessary to pass a plane through the line. The curve resulting from the intersection of the cutting plane and the surface of revolution will then intersect the line to locate the points of intersection of line and surface.

Figure 14.35 illustrates the intersection of a skew line AB and a surface of revolution (hyperboloid). A vertical cutting plane is passed through the line AB. To find the intersection of the cutting plane and the surface of revolution a number of horizontal planes are passed through both. Plane Z, for example, cuts a circle from the surface of revolution. This circle in the top view is seen to intersect the edge view of the cutting plane at point X_T. Point X_F, then projected from the top view, locates one point on one curve of intersection between the vertical plane through AB and the hyperboloid. Other points so located will plot the curves, shown in the front view, which intersect the line AB at P_F and Q_F, the points of intersection of AB and the hyperboloid.

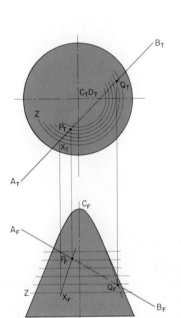

FIG. 14.35. Intersection of a double-curved surface (hyperboloid) and a line. The solution is accomplished by passing a plane through the line and then plotting the plane intersection with the double-curved surface.

Summary

1. Pass a receding plane through the line, parallel to the axis of the surface of revolution.

2. Determine the intersection of the receding plane and surface of revolution by passing planes perpendicular to the axis of the surface of revolution. Points of intersection lie on the receding plane and on circles cut by the planes perpendicular to the axis. Draw the line of intersection between the surface of revolution and the receding plane. The points of intersection of the given line and the surface of revolution lie at the intersection of the line and the line of intersection between the receding plane and the surface of revolution.

14.31. INTERSECTION OF A DOUBLE-CURVED SURFACE AND A PLANE.

Figure 14.36 shows a double-curved surface of revolution (a paraboloid) to be intersected by the plane ABC. The axis of the paraboloid is vertical. Horizontal planes are perpendicular to the vertical axis and will therefore cut circles from the double-curved surface. Horizontal planes will cut straight lines from the plane. For example, a horizontal plane through point c on line BC will cut a horizontal line from plane ABC. The top view of the horizontal line through c is found by projection as shown. The horizontal plane c also cuts a circle from the paraboloid. This circle appears as an edge in the front view and also appears in its true diameter. The circle is then drawn in the top view. The line in plane ABC and the circle then intersect at two points, 3 and 3′, located first in the top view and then projected to the front view. A series of planes through a, b, c, d, etc., will give points to plot the intersection.

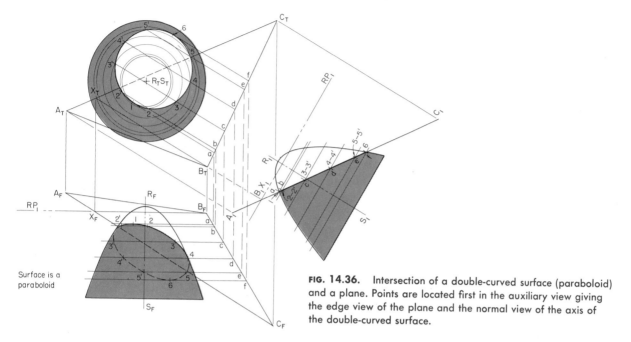

Surface is a
paraboloid

FIG. 14.36. Intersection of a double-curved surface (paraboloid) and a plane. Points are located first in the auxiliary view giving the edge view of the plane and the normal view of the axis of the double-curved surface.

The problem could also have been solved by employing the auxiliary view shown, where the axis of the double-curved surface appears in true length and the plane appears as an edge. Horizontal planes located in the auxiliary view will cut circles from the double-curved surface and will show the intersections of the passed plane and *ABC* as points. These intersections are projected to the top view (on the circle cut from the double-curved surface) and then located in the front view by projection from the top view and measurement from the auxiliary.

If the axis of the double-curved surface is in a skew position instead of vertical, two extra views will be required: (1) an auxiliary view giving the true length and (2) a second auxiliary view, projected from the first auxiliary, giving the point view of the axis of the paraboloid. The plane *ABC* is projected

into these views. Thus the first and second auxiliary views will have the same relationship as the top and front views of Fig. 14.36. The problem is then solved in the auxiliary views, and the line of intersection is projected back to top and front views.

Summary

1. Pass planes perpendicular to the axis of the surface of revolution. These planes cut circles from the surface of revolution and straight lines from the given plane.

2. Project the circles and straight lines to an adjacent view where their intersection is first located; then project to the first view. Draw smooth curves through the points of intersection.

3. If the given views do not contain a normal view of the axis of the surface of revolution, draw an auxiliary view to show it. Then proceed as in (1) and (2).

14.32. INTERSECTION OF TWO DOUBLE-CURVED SURFACES OF REVOLUTION.

As explained before, the simplest line that can be cut from a double-curved surface of revolution is a circle. Also, if the axes of two double-curved surfaces are at an angle to each other, a circle could be obtained from one surface but a curve would be cut from the other, producing a difficult solution. An alternate, and better, method may be applied if the axes of the surfaces intersect. A sphere with its center at the intersection of the axes will cut circles from both surfaces.

Figure 14.37 illustrates the sphere method of finding the line of intersection between a paraboloid and hyperboloid. The axes of the two surfaces intersect at point E. In the front view (where both axes appear in true length), a circle, with center at E_F, is drawn representing a sphere, such as, for example, the circle marked "sphere 2" on the figure. This sphere will intersect the surface having axis AB and produce a circle which appears as an edge perpendicular to axis AB. Also, the same sphere will intersect the surface having axis CD and produce a circle which appears as an edge perpendicular to axis CD. These two edge views intersect at 2 and 2 in the front view. These points 2 are common to the sphere and both double-curved surfaces. To get the top view, points 2 lie on the circle cut from the surface having axis AB. The size of the sphere is altered to get more points. In Fig. 14.37, sphere 1 is the smallest sphere used because a smaller one will not cut one of the surfaces. Sphere 3 is the largest that will give points on the line of intersection.

It is possible of course, and even probable, that the axes of two double-curved surfaces of revolution may not intersect. In this event, the sphere method in pure

form cannot be applied; but with alterations, the principle can be employed. Figure 14.38 shows two double-curved surfaces of revolution whose axes do not intersect. The intersection is to be found. A sphere with center arbitrarily located at O will cut two circles from the surface having axis AB, as indicated on the figure. This sphere will also cut a curve from the surface with axis CD, which may be found by passing planes through the sphere and perpendicular to CD. The end view of the axis of surface CD will show the circles cut from both the sphere and surface CD as true circles and will also show the intersections 1, 2, 3, 4, 3', and 2', where the sphere and surface CD have common points. These points, 1, 2, 3, 4, 3', and 2', projected back to the front view, locate the curve shown, which intersects the circles cut from surface AB at points X, Z, Z', and X', which are then common to both double-curved surfaces. The top views of points X and X' lie on the upper circle cut by the sphere from surface AB, and points Z and Z' lie on the lower circle. A sufficient number of points to complete the line of intersection may be found by repeating the process, starting each time with a different size of sphere.

The above method may seem to be somewhat complicated, but compared with other methods it is not. For instance, if both surfaces were simply cut by horizontal planes, circles would be cut from surface AB, but the curve cut from CD would have to be plotted in the top view by finding intersections of right sections of CD with the original cutting plane, a tedious process. Note in Fig. 14.38 that the cutting planes passed perpendicular to CD and the resulting circles (right sections of CD) in the end view will remain constant throughout the completion of the solution.

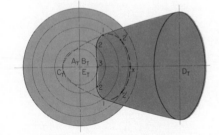

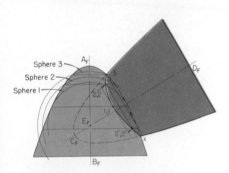

FIG. 14.37. Intersection of two double-curved surfaces (axes intersecting, sphere method). Selected spheres with centers at the intersection of the axes of the surfaces cut circles from both.

Summary

Axes intersecting

1. Centered at the intersection of the axes, draw a series of spheres, varying in size.

2. Each sphere cuts a circle from each surface of revolution, and these circles intersect in points on the line of intersection. Connect the determined points in a smooth curve.

Axes not intersecting

1. Draw a sphere centered at an arbitrary point on the axis of surface *A*. This sphere cuts two circles from the surface. The sphere will also cut a curve from surface *B*. Draw an end view of the axis of surface *B,* and in this view, determine the curve cut from surface *B* by passing planes perpendicular to the axis of surface *B*, thereby cutting circles from both the surface and the sphere. Project the determined points (actually a curve) back to the view from which the end view was projected, where the curve of surface *B* and the circle of surface *A* intersect to give points on the line of intersection of both surfaces of revolution.

2. Project points found to the adjacent view.

3. Continue the process, using a different size sphere each time.

4. Draw a smooth curve through located points to show the line of intersection.

14.33.   DEVELOPMENTS. In many different kinds of construction full-size patterns of some or all of the faces of an object are required; for example, in stonecutting, a template or pattern giving the shape of an irregular face, or in sheet-metal work, a pattern to which a sheet may be cut so that when rolled, folded, or formed it will make the object.

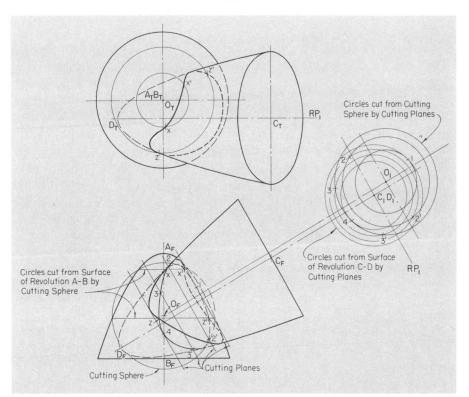

The complete surface laid out in a plane is called the "development" of the surface.

Surfaces about which a thin sheet of flexible material (such as paper or tin) can be wrapped smoothly are said to be developable; these include objects made up of planes and single-curved surfaces only. Warped and double-curved surfaces are nondevelopable; and when patterns are required for their construction, they can be made only by methods that are approximate, but, assisted by the ductility or pliability of the material, they give the required form. Thus while a ball cannot be wrapped smoothly, a two-piece pattern developed approximately and cut from leather can be stretched and sewed on in a smooth cover, or a flat disk of metal can be die-stamped, formed, or spun to a hemispherical or other shape.

FIG. 14.38. Intersection of two double-curved surfaces (axes not intersecting). A modified sphere method is used. Selected sphere cuts circles from one surface and a curve from the other.

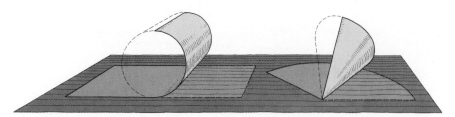

FIG. 14.39. Theory of development. The surface is composed into a plane by unfoldment.

14.34. BASIC CONSIDERATIONS. We have learned the method of finding the true size of a plane surface by projecting its normal view. If the true size of all the plane faces of an object are found and joined in order at their common edges so that all faces lie in a common plane, the result will be the developed surface. Usually this may be done to the best advantage by finding the true length of the edges.

The development of a right cylinder is evidently a rectangle whose width is the altitude and length the rectified circumference (Fig. 14.39); and the development of a right-circular cone is a circular sector with a radius equal to the slant height of the cone and an arc equal in length to the circumference of its base (Fig. 14.39).

As illustrated in Fig. 14.39, developments are drawn with the inside face

up. This is primarily the result of working to inside rather than outside dimensions of ducts. This procedure also facilitates the use of fold lines, identified by punch marks at each end, along which the metal is folded in forming the object.

In laying out real sheet-metal designs, an allowance must be made for seams and lap and, in heavy sheets, for the thickness and crowding of the metal; there is also the consideration of the commercial sizes of material as well as the question of economy in cutting. In all of this some practical shop knowledge is necessary. Figure 14.55 and paragraph 14.46 indicate the usage of some of the more common joints, although the developments given in this chapter will be confined to the principles.

14.35. TO DEVELOP A TRUNCATED HEXAGONAL PRISM (FIG. 14.40). First draw two projections of the prism: (1) a normal view of a right section (a section or cut obtained by a plane perpendicular to the axis) and (2) a normal view of the lateral edges. The base *ABCDEF* is a right section shown in true size in the bottom view. Lay off on line *AA* of the development the perimeter of the base. This line is called by sheet-metal workers the "stretchout" or "girth" line. At points *A, B, C,* etc., erect perpendiculars called "measuring lines" or "bend lines," representing the lateral edges along which the pattern is folded to form the prism. Lay off on each of these its length *A*-1, *B*-2, *C*-3, etc., as given on the front view. Connect the points 1, 2, 3, etc., in succession, to complete the development of the lateral surfaces. Note on the pattern that the inside of the lateral faces is toward the observer. For the development of the entire surface in one piece, attach the true sizes

FIG. 14.40. Development of a prism. The true size of each side is laid out in successive order.

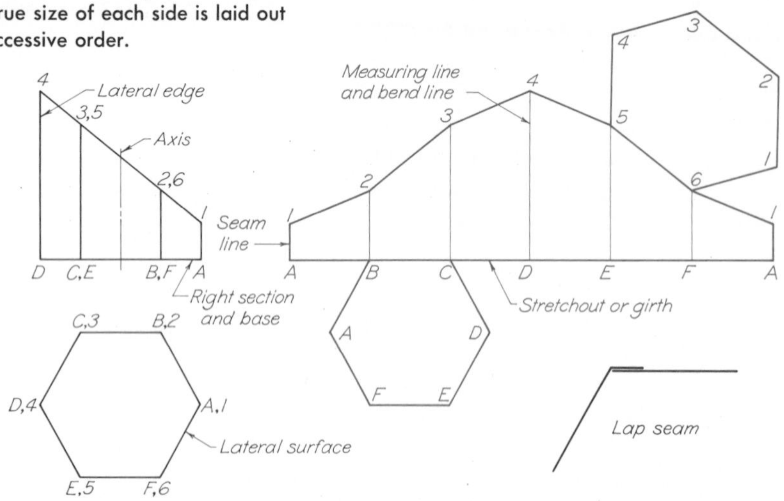

14.37. To Develop an Oblique Pyramid

of the upper end and the base as shown, finding the true size of the upper end by an auxiliary (normal) view as described in paragraph 8.4. For economy of solder or rivets and time, it is customary to make the seam on the shortest edge or surface. In seaming along the intersection of surfaces whose dihedral angle is other than 90°, as is the case here, the lap seam lends itself to convenient assembling. The flat lock could be used if the seam were made on one of the lateral faces.

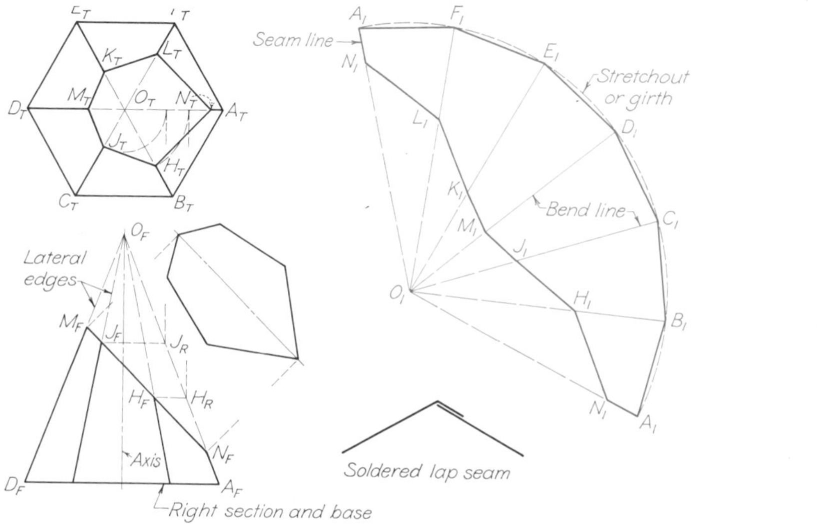

14.36. TO DEVELOP A TRUNCATED RIGHT PYRAMID (FIG. 14.41).

Draw the projections of the pyramid which show (1) a normal view of the base or right section and (2) a normal view of the axis. Lay out the pattern for the pyramid, and then superimpose the pattern of the truncation.

Since this is a portion of a right regular pyramid, the lateral edges are all of equal length. The lateral edges OA and OD are parallel to the frontal plane and consequently show in their true length on the front view. With center O_1, taken at any convenient place, and a radius $O_F A_F$, draw an arc that is the stretchout of the pattern. On it step off the six equal sides of the hexagonal base, obtained from the top view, and connect these points successively with each other and with the vertex O_1, thus forming the pattern for the pyramid.

The intersection of the cutting plane and lateral surfaces is developed by laying off the true length of the intercept of each lateral edge on the corresponding line of the development. The true length of each of these intercepts, such as OH and OJ, is found by rotating it about the axis of the pyramid until they

coincide with $O_F A_F$. The path of any point, as H, will be projected on the front view as a horizontal line. To obtain the development of the entire surface of the truncated pyramid, attach the base; also find the true size of the cut face and attach it on a common line.

The lap seam is suggested for use here also for convenient assembling.

The right-rectangular pyramid, Fig. 14.42, is developed in a similar way, but as the edge OA is not parallel to the plane of projection, it must be rotated to $O_F A_R$ to obtain its true length.

14.37. TO DEVELOP AN OBLIQUE PYRAMID (FIG. 14.43).

Since the lateral edges are unequal in length, the true length of each

FIG. 14.41. Development of a pyramid. This is a right pyramid. The true lengths of all edges (from the vertex to the base) are equal.

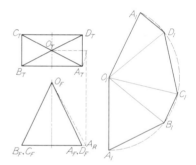

FIG. 14.42. Development of a pyramid. The true length from vertex to base is found by rotating one edge until frontal.

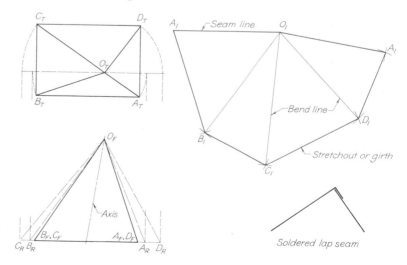

FIG. 14.43. Development of an oblique pyramid. Each lateral edge is of different length. The true length for each must be determined.

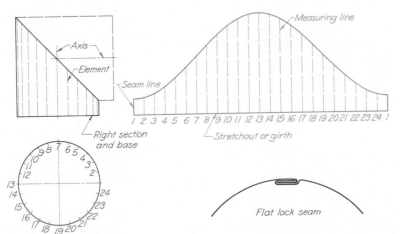

FIG. 14.44. Development of a cylinder. The cylinder is treated as a many-sided prism.

of a cylinder is similar to the development of a prism. Draw two projections of the cylinder: (1) a normal view of a right section and (2) a normal view of the elements. In rolling the cylinder out on a tangent plane, the base or right section, being perpendicular to the axis, will develop into a straight line. For convenience in drawing, divide the normal view of the base, here shown in the bottom view, into a number of equal parts by points that represent elements. These divisions should be spaced so that the chordal distances closely enough approximate the arc to make the stretchout practically equal to the periphery of the base or right section. Project these elements to the front view. Draw the stretchout and measuring lines as in Fig. 14.40, the cylinder now being treated as a many-sided prism. Transfer the lengths of the elements in order, by projection or with dividers, and join the points thus found by a smooth curve, sketching it in freehand very lightly before fitting the french curve to it. This development might be the pattern of one-half of a two-piece elbow. Three-piece, four-piece, or five-piece elbows can be drawn similarly, as illustrated in Fig. 14.45. As the base is symmetrical, only one-half of it need be drawn. In these cases, the intermediate pieces, as B, C, and D, are developed on a stretch-out line formed by laying off the perimeter of a right section. If the right section is taken through the middle of the piece, the stretchout line becomes the center line of the development.

Evidently any elbow could be cut from a single sheet without waste if the seams were made alternately on the long and short sides. The flat lock seam is recommended for Figs. 14.44 and 14.45, although other types could be used.

must be found separately by rotating it parallel to the frontal plane. With O_1 taken at any convenient place, lay off the seam line O_1A_1 equal to O_FA_R. With A_1 as center and radius A_1B_1 equal to the true length of AB, describe an arc. With O_1 as center and radius O_1B_1 equal to O_FB_R, describe a second arc intersecting the first in vertex B_1. Connect the vertices O_1, A_1, and B_1, thus forming the pattern for the lateral surface OAB. Similarly, lay out the patterns for the remaining three lateral surfaces, joining them on their common edges. The stretchout is equal to the summation of the base edges. If the complete development is required, attach the base on a common line. The lap seam is suggested as the most suitable for the given conditions.

14.38.   TO DEVELOP A TRUNCATED RIGHT CYLINDER (FIG. 14.44). The development

FIG. 14.45. Development of an elbow (cylinders). Note the identity of A and E and of B and D.

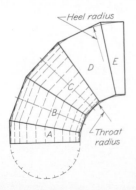

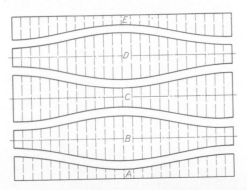

The octagonal dome (Fig. 14.46) illustrates an application of the development of cylinders. Each piece is a portion of a cylinder. The elements are parallel to the base of the dome and show in their true lengths in the top view. The true length of the stretchout line for sections A and A' shows in the front view at $O_F H_F$. By considering $O_T H_T$ as the edge of a plane cutting a right section, the problem is identical with the preceding problem.

Similarly, the stretchout line for sections B, B', D, and D' shows in true length at $O_F K_R$ in the front view, and for section C and C' at $O_S M_S$, in the side view.

The true shape of hip rafter ON is found by rotating it until it is parallel to the frontal plane, as at $O_F N_R$, in the same manner as in finding the true length of any line. A sufficient number of points should be taken to give a smooth curve.

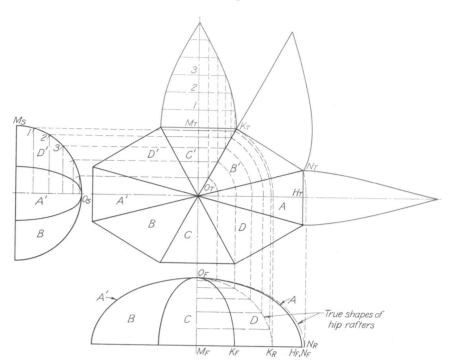

FIG. 14.46. Development of a dome (cylinders). Each cylindrical portion is unrolled separately.

14.39. TO DEVELOP A TRUNCATED RIGHT-CIRCULAR CONE (FIG. 14.47).

Draw the projections of the cone which will show (1) a normal view of the base or right section and (2) a normal view of the axis. First develop the surface of the complete cone and then superimpose the pattern for the truncation.

Divide the top view of the base into a sufficient number of equal parts so that the sum of the resulting chordal distances will closely approximate the periphery of the base. Project these points to the front view, and draw front views of the elements through them. With center A_1 and a radius equal to the slant height A_F-1_F, which is the true length of all the elements, draw an arc, which is the stretchout, and lay off on it the chordal divisions of the base, ob-

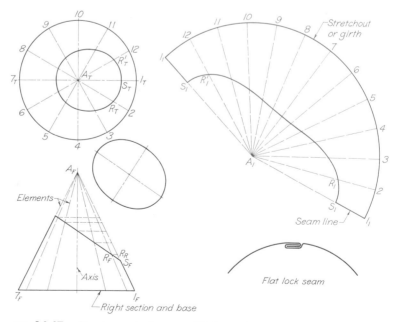

FIG. 14.47. Development of a cone. This is a right cone. All elements from vertex to base are the same length.

tained from the top view. Connect these points 1_1, 2, 3, etc., with A-1, thus forming the pattern for the cone. Find the true length of each element from vertex to cutting plane by rotating it to coincide with the contour element A-1, and lay off this distance on the corresponding line of the development. Draw a smooth curve through these points. The flat lock seam along element S-1 is recommended, although other types could be employed. The pattern for the inclined surface is obtained from the auxiliary (normal) view.

14.40. TRIANGULATION. Nondevelopable surfaces are developed approximately by assuming them to be made of narrow sections of developable surfaces. The commonest and best method for approximate development is that of triangulation, that is, the surface is assumed to be made up of a large number of triangular strips, or plane triangles with very short bases. This method is used for all warped surfaces and also for oblique cones. Oblique cones are single-curved surfaces and thus are theoretically capable of true development, but they can be developed much more easily and accurately by triangulation, a simple method which consists merely of dividing the surface

into triangles, finding the true lengths of the sides of each, and constructing them one at a time, joining these triangles on their common sides.

14.41. TO DEVELOP AN OBLIQUE CONE (FIG. 14.48). An oblique cone differs from a cone of revolution in that the elements have different lengths. The development of the right-circular cone is, practically, made up of a number of equal triangles which meet at the vertex and whose sides are elements and whose bases are the chords of short arcs of the base of the cone. In the oblique cone each triangle must be found separately.

Draw two views of the cone showing (1) a normal view of the base and (2) a normal view of the altitude. Divide the true size of the base, here shown in the top view, into a sufficient number of equal parts so that the sum of the chordal distances will closely approximate the length of the base curve. Project these points to the front view of the base. Through these points and the vertex, draw the elements in each view. Since this cone is symmetrical about a frontal plane through the vertex, the elements are shown only on the front half of it. Also, only one-half of the development is drawn. With the seam on the shortest element, the element OC will be the center line of the development and can be drawn directly at O_1C_1, as its true length is given at O_FC_F. Find the true length of the elements by rotating them until parallel to the frontal plane or by constructing a "true-length diagram." The true length of any element would be the hypotenuse of a triangle, one leg being the length of the projected element as seen in the top view and the other leg being equal to the altitude of the cone. Thus to make the diagram, draw the leg OD coincid-

FIG. 14.48. Development of an oblique cone. A true-length diagram is used to obtain the lengths of the elements.

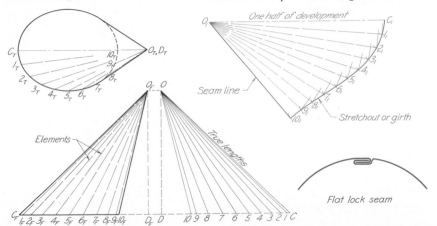

14.43. Transition Pieces

ing with or parallel to $O_F D_F$. At D and perpendicular to OD, draw the other leg, on which lay off the lengths D-1, D-2, etc., equal to D_T-1_T, D_T-2_T, etc., respectively. Distances from O to points on the base of the diagram are the true lengths of the elements.

Construct the pattern for the front half of the cone as follows: With O_1 as center and radius O-1, draw an arc. With C_1 as center and radius C_T-1_T, draw a second arc intersecting the first at 1_1; then O_1-1_1 will be the developed position of the element O-1. With 1_1 as center and radius 1_T-2_T, draw an arc intersecting a second arc with O_1 as center and radius O-2, thus locating 2_1. Continue this procedure until all the elements have been transferred to the development. Connect the points C_1, 1_1, 2_1, etc., with a smooth curve, the stretch-out line, to complete the development. The flat lock seam is recommended for joining the ends to form the cone.

14.42. A CONIC CONNECTION BETWEEN TWO PARALLEL CYLINDRICAL PIPES OF DIFFERENT DIAMETERS.

This is shown in Fig. 14.49. The method used in drawing the pattern is an application of the development of an oblique cone. One-half of the elliptical base is shown in true size in an auxiliary view, here attached to the front view. Find the true size of the base from its major and minor diameters, divide it into a number of equal parts so that the sum of these chordal distances closely approximates the periphery of the curve, and project these points to the front and top views. Draw the elements in each view through these points, and find the vertex O by extending the contour elements until they intersect. The true length of each element is found by using the vertical distance between its ends as the vertical

leg of the diagram and its horizontal projection as the other leg. As each true length from vertex to base is found, project the upper end of the intercept horizontally across from the front view to the true length of the corresponding element to find the true length of the intercept. The development is drawn by laying out each triangle in turn, from vertex to base, as in paragraph 14.41, starting on the center line $O_1 C_1$ and then measuring on each element its intercept length. Draw smooth curves through these points to complete the pattern. Join the ends with a flat lock seam.

14.43. TRANSITION PIECES.

These are used to connect pipes or openings of different shapes of cross section. Figure 14.50, showing a transition piece for con-

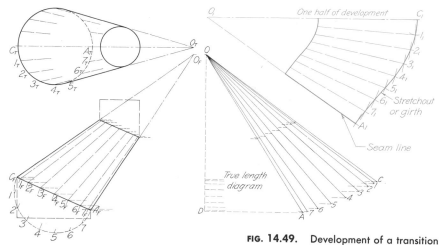

FIG. 14.49. Development of a transition (oblique cone). This transition connects two cylindrical pipes of different diameters and offset in position.

FIG. 14.50. Development of transition. This transition connects a cylindrical with a rectangular pipe. The surface is made up of planes and portions of oblique cones.

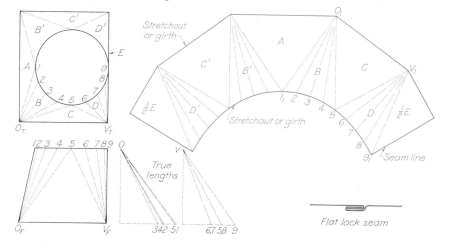

necting a round pipe and a rectangular pipe, is typical. Transition pieces are always developed by triangulation. The piece shown in Fig. 14.50 is made up of four triangular planes, whose bases are the sides of the rectangle, and four parts of oblique cones, whose common bases are arcs of the circle and whose vertices are at the corners of the rectangle. To develop it, make a true-length diagram as in Fig. 14.48. When the true length of *O*-1 is found, all the sides of triangle *A* will be known. Attach the development of cones *B* and *B'*, then those of triangles *C* and *C'*, and so on.

Figure 14.51 is another transition piece joining a rectangular to a circular pipe whose axes are nonparallel. By using a partial right-side view of the round opening, the divisions of the bases of the oblique cones can be found (as the object is symmetrical, one-half only of the opening need be divided). The true lengths of the elements are obtained as in Fig. 14.49.

With the seam line the center line of the plane *E* in Figs. 14.50 and 14.51, the flat lock is recommended for joining the ends of the development.

FIG. 14.51. Development of a transition. This transition connects cylindrical and rectangular pipes with nonparallel axes. The surface is made up of planes and portions of oblique cones.

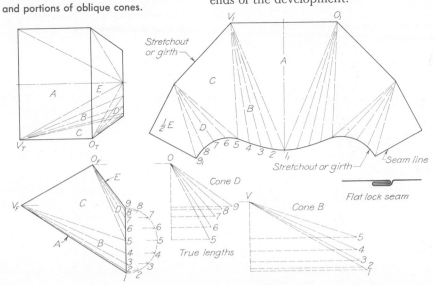

14.44. TRIANGULATION OF WARPED SURFACES.

The approximate development of a warped surface is made by dividing it into a number of narrow quadrilaterals and then splitting each of these quadrilaterals into two triangles by a diagonal, which is assumed to be a straight line, although really a curve. Figure 14.52 shows a warped transition piece to connect an ovular (upper) pipe with a right-circular cylindrical pipe (lower). Find the true size of one-half the elliptical base by rotating it until horizontal about an axis through 1, when its true shape appears on the top view. The major diameter is $1\text{-}7_R$, and the minor diameter through 4_R will equal the diameter of the lower pipe. Divide the semiellipse into a sufficient number of equal parts, and project these to the top and front views. Divide the top semicircle into the same number of equal parts, and connect similar points on each end, thus dividing the surface into approximate quadrilaterals. Cut each into two triangles by a diagonal. On true-length diagrams find the lengths of the elements and the diagonals, and draw the development by constructing the true sizes of the triangles in regular order. The flat-lock seam is recommended for joining the ends of the development.

14.45. TO DEVELOP A SPHERE.

The sphere may be taken as typical of double-curved surfaces, which can be developed only approximately. It may be cut into a number of equal meridian sections, or lunes, as in Fig. 14.53, and these may be considered to be sections of cylinders. One of these sections, developed as the cylinder in Fig. 14.53, will give a pattern for the others.

Another method is to cut the sphere

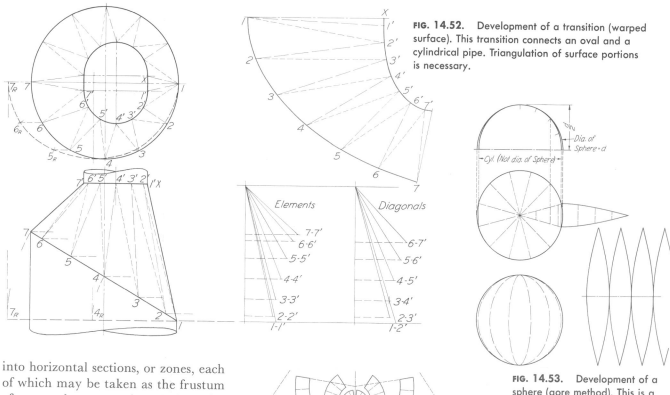

FIG. 14.52. Development of a transition (warped surface). This transition connects an oval and a cylindrical pipe. Triangulation of surface portions is necessary.

Elements

7-7'
6-6'
5-5'
4-4'
3-3'
2-2'
1-1'

Diagonals

6-7'
5-6'
4-5'
3-4'
2-3'
1-2'

FIG. 14.53. Development of a sphere (gore method). This is a double-curved surface and development is only approximate.

into horizontal sections, or zones, each of which may be taken as the frustum of a cone whose vertex is at the intersection of the extended chords (Fig. 14.54).

14.46. JOINTS, CONNECTORS, AND HEMS.

There are numerous joints used in seaming sheet-metal ducts and in connecting one duct to another. Figure 14.55 illustrates some of the more common types, which may be formed by hand on a break or by special seaming machines. No attempt to dimension the various seams and connections has been made here because of the variation in sizes for different gages of metal and in the forming machines of manufacturers.

Hemming is used in finishing the raw edges of the end of the duct. In wire hemming, an extra allowance of about 2½ times the diameter of the wire is made for wrapping around the wire. In flat hemming, the end of the duct is bent over once or twice to relieve the sharp edge of the metal.

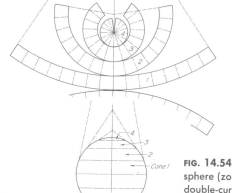

FIG. 14.54. Development of a sphere (zone method). This is a double-curved surface and development is only approximate.

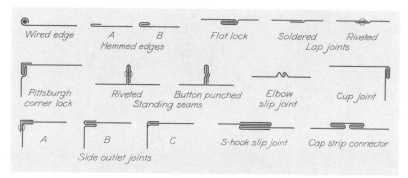

FIG. 14.55. Joints and finished edges. These are used in constructing sheet-metal parts.

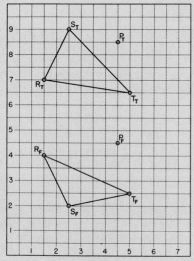

PROB. 14.1.1.

PROBLEMS

INTERSECTIONS

In the study of intersections, a purely theoretical approach may be used without any reference whatever to practical utility where the lines, planes, and surfaces form pipes, ducts, or other real objects. On the other hand, some may prefer to teach the subject by applying the theory on useful objects. For these reasons, the problems on intersections are given first from the standpoint of pure theory and then from a more practical standpoint. Note that, even though the surfaces are geometrical, they are the ducts, hoppers, transitions, etc., that will often be found in practical work.

GROUP 1. INTERSECTION OF LINES AND PLANES

14.1.1. Locate the top and front views of P, the point where the line JK pierces the plane EFG.

14.1.2. Determine the shortest distance from point P to the plane RST.

14.1.3. Determine the intersection of line AB with planes KLM, LMN, and LNO. Draw the top and front views of all points of intersection.

14.1.4. The entrances to three vertical mine shafts on a mountainside are shown at R, S, and T. These shafts give access to the ore vein that strikes and dips as shown at P. Scale: $1'' = 100'$. Find the depths of the shafts.

14.1.5. Lines AB and CD are to be connected by a single straight line passing through point P. Draw top and front views of the line.

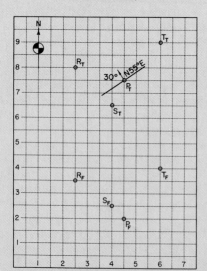

PROB. 14.1.2.

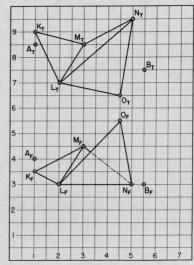

PROB. 14.1.3.

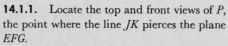

PROB. 14.1.4.

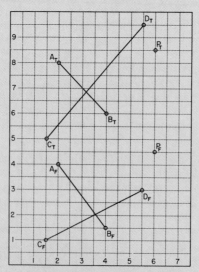

PROB. 14.1.5.

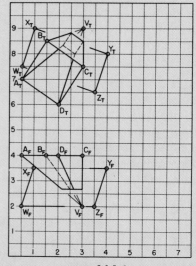

PROB. 14.1.6.

14.1.6. An outside storage bin discharges through the pyramidal hopper *VABCD* which passes through a roof, a portion of which is shown by points *WXYZ*. Draw the plan and elevation views of the roof opening which fits snugly around the hopper.

14.1.7. *AB* is the axis of a duct of irregular cross section. The duct is to be cut off in the direction determined by plane *KLM*. Show the top and front views of the cut. Determine the true shape of the cap which will fit this cut. (Neglect bend-overs, etc.)

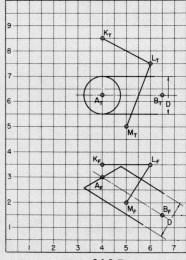

PROB. 14.1.7.

GROUP 2. INTERSECTION OF PLANES

14.2.1. Find the line of intersection between the planes *ABC* and *DEF*. Show visibility.

14.2.2. Find the line of intersection between the planes *MNO* and *RST*.

14.2.3. Find the intersection of the three planes *ABC*, *JKL*, and *RST*.

14.2.4. Find the line of intersection and complete the views of the two hollow sheet-metal shapes shown. The top of the right-hand shape is enclosed.

14.2.5. Draw the top and front views of the line of intersection between ore veins *V* and *W*. What is the grade of this line?

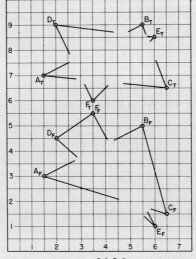

PROB. 14.2.1.

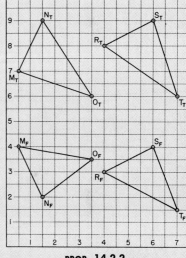

PROB. 14.2.2.

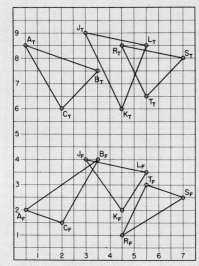

PROB. 14.2.3.

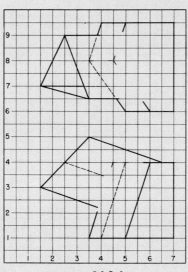

PROB. 14.2.4.

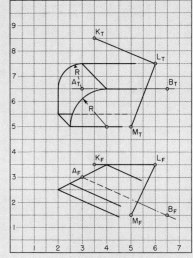

PROB. 14.2.5.

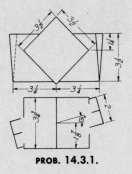

PROB. 14.3.1.

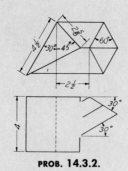

PROB. 14.3.2.

Selections may be made from the following problems. Construct the figures accurately in pencil without inking. Any practical problem can be resolved into some combination of the "type solids," and the exercises given illustrate the principles involved in the various combinations.

GROUP 3.   INTERSECTIONS OF PRISMATIC DUCTS

14.3.1. to 14.3.3.   Find the line of intersection, considering the prisms as pipes opening into each other. Use care in indicating visible and invisible parts of the line of intersection. **14.3.4. to 14.3.6.**   Find the line of intersection, indicating visible and invisible parts and considering prisms as pipes opening into each other.

14.3.7.   Find the intersection between the two prismatic ducts.

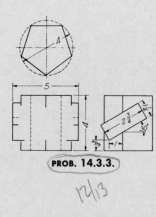

PROB. 14.3.3.

12/13

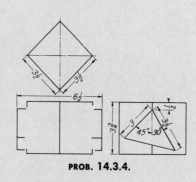

PROB. 14.3.4.

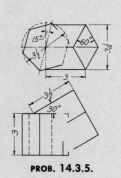

PROB. 14.3.5.

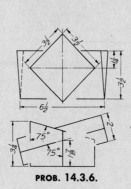

PROB. 14.3.6.

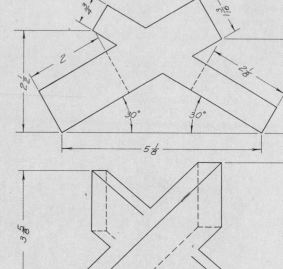

PROB. 14.3.7.   Prismatic ducts.

14.3.8. The layout as illustrated shows a tower and proposed conveyor-belt galleys. Find the intersection between the tower and the main supply galley.

14.3.8*A.* Same layout as Prob. 14.3.8. After solving Prob. 14.3.8, find the intersection between the two galleys.

GROUP 4.   INTERSECTIONS OF PYRAMIDAL OBJECTS

14.4.1. to 14.4.5.   Find the lines of intersection.

14.4.6.   Find the line of intersection between the prismatic duct and hopper.

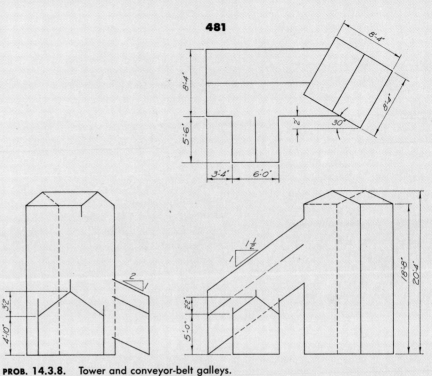

PROB. 14.3.8.   Tower and conveyor-belt galleys.

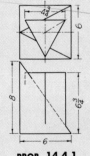

PROB. 14.4.1.

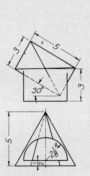

PROB. 14.4.2.

PROB. 14.4.3.

PROB. 14.4.4.

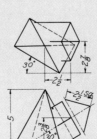

PROB. 14.4.5.

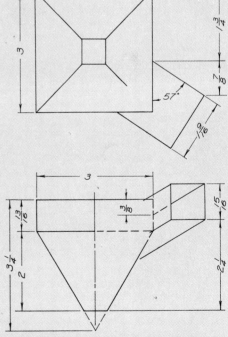

PROB. 14.4.6.   Prismatic duct and hopper.

GROUP 5.   INTERSECTIONS OF SINGLE-CURVED SURFACES

14.5.1.   Find the points X and Z where line AB pierces the 2-in.-diameter right-circular cylinder OP. Find the points R and S where line CD pierces this cylinder.

14.5.2.   Find the points X and Z where line AB pierces the 2-in.-diameter right-circular cylinder OP.

14.5.3.   Draw the top view of the line of intersection between plane A and the 2-in.-diameter right-circular cylinder OP. Draw the front view of the line of intersection between plane B and this cylinder.

14.5.4.   Draw the top and front views of the line of intersection between plane ABC and the 2-in.-diameter right-circular cylinder OP. Complete the cylinder and show visibility.

14.5.5.   Find the point P where line AB pierces the surface of the cylindroid $XZX'Z'$. XZ and $X'Z'$ are the curved-line directrices of the cylindroid. Its plane director is the vertical plane director shown.

14.5.6 and 14.5.7.   Find the points X and Z where line AB pierces the cone VO. Show visibility of line AB.

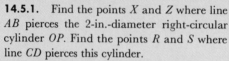

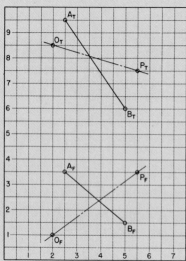

PROB. 14.5.1.

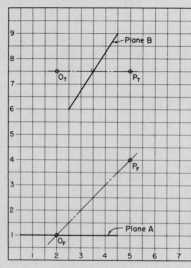

PROB. 14.5.2.

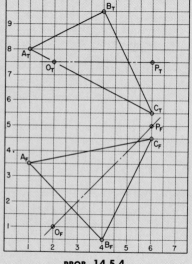

PROB. 14.5.3.

PROB. 14.5.4.

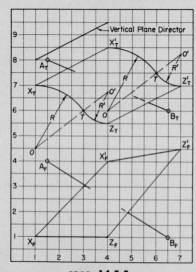

PROB. 14.5.5.

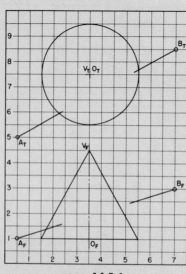

PROB. 14.5.6.

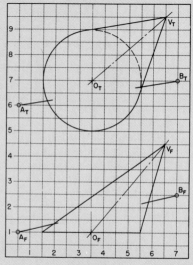

PROB. 14.5.7.

14.5.8. (a) Draw the front view of the line of intersection between plane *A* and cone *VO*. (b) Draw the top view of the line of intersection between plane *B* and cone *VO*. (c) Draw the top view of the line of intersection between plane *C* and cone *VO*. (d) What is the name of the conic section cut by each of the planes?

14.5.9. Draw the front view of the line of intersection between plane *A* and cone *VO*.

Draw the top view of the line of intersection between plane *B* and cone *VO*.

14.5.10. Draw the top view of the line of intersection between plane *ABC* and cone *VO*. Complete the cone and show visibility.

14.5.11 to 14.5.13. Complete the views of cylinders *AB* and *CD*, showing their line of intersection.

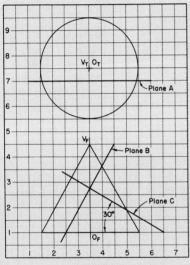

PROB. 14.5.8.

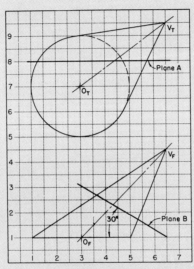

PROB. 14.5.9.

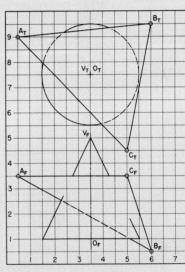

PROB. 14.5.10.

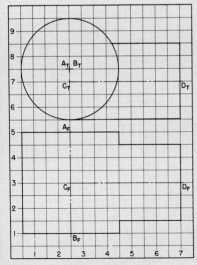

PROB. 14.5.11.

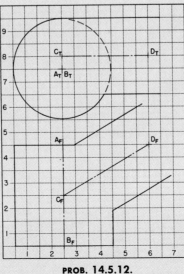

PROB. 14.5.12.

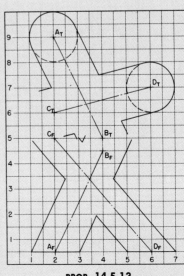

PROB. 14.5.13.

14.5.14 to 14.5.16. Complete the views of cones *VO* and *XP*, showing their line of intersection.

14.5.17. Draw the top view of the line of intersection between the cone *VO* and the cylinder *AB*.

14.5.18. Draw the top and front views of the line of intersection between the cone *VO* and the cylinder *AB*. Cylinder *AB* is a 3-in.-diameter right-circular cylinder.

14.5.19. Complete the views of the cone *VO* and the cylinder *AB*, showing their line of intersection.

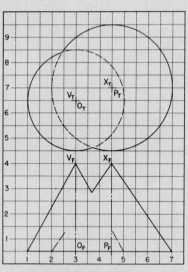

PROB. 14.5.14.

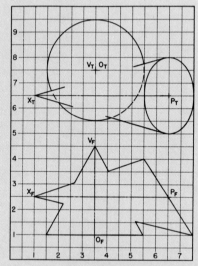

PROB. 14.5.15.

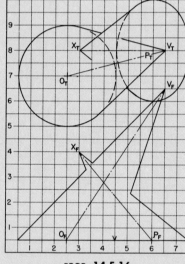

PROB. 14.5.16.

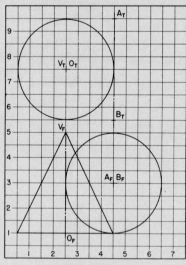

PROB. 14.5.17.

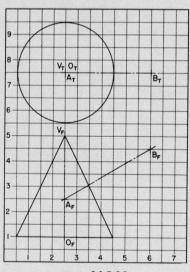

PROB. 14.5.18.

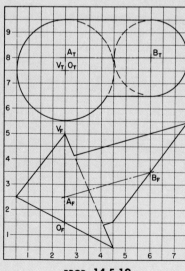

PROB. 14.5.19.

GROUP 6.   INTERSECTIONS OF CYLINDRICAL DUCTS

14.6.1 to 14.6.3.   Find the line of intersection, indicating visible and invisible portions and considering cylinders as pipes opening into each other.

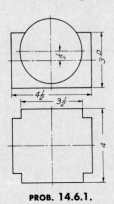

PROB. 14.6.1.

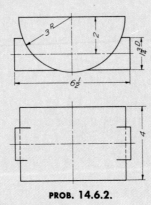

PROB. 14.6.2.

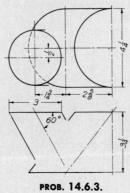

PROB. 14.6.3.

14.6.4.   The layout shows a pump casing composed of a cylinder and elbow. Find the intersection between the cylinder and elbow.

14.6.5.   The layout shows a portion of a liquid oxygen pumping system consisting of pipes A, B, C, and D. Find the intersection of the pipes.

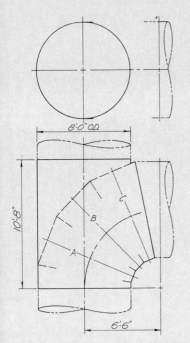

PROB. 14.6.4.   Pump casing.

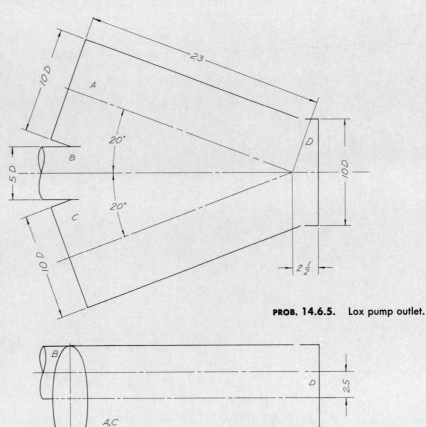

PROB. 14.6.5.   Lox pump outlet.

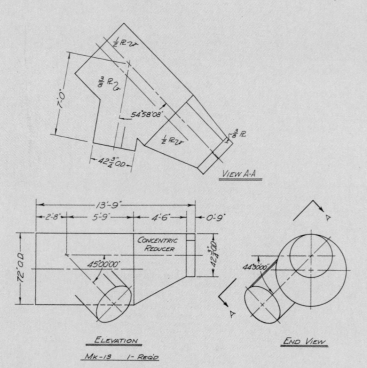

14.6.6. The layout shows an oblique pipe meeting a cylindrical inlet in a power-station piping system. Find the intersection between the inlet and pipe.

PROB. 14.6.6.   Power-station piping.

GROUP 7.   INTERSECTIONS OF CONIC OBJECTS AND DUCTS

14.7.1 to 14.7.11.   Find the line of intersection.

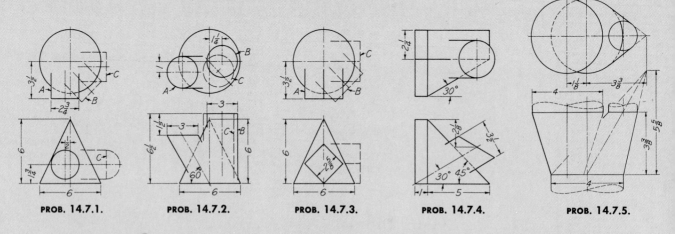

PROB. 14.7.1.   PROB. 14.7.2.   PROB. 14.7.3.   PROB. 14.7.4.   PROB. 14.7.5.

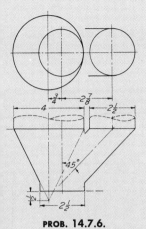

PROB. 14.7.6.

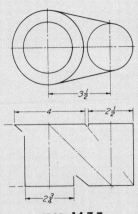

PROB. 14.7.7.

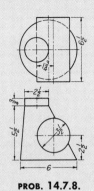

PROB. 14.7.8.

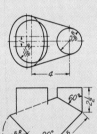

PROB. 14.7.9.

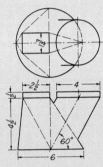

PROB. 14.7.10.

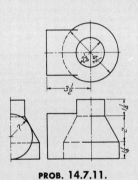

PROB. 14.7.11.

14.7.12. The layout shows the plan view of an intake manifold consisting of a conical connector intersected by two cylindrical pipes. Find the intersection of the pipe that enters the side of the conical connector. The axes of the two shapes intersect. Solve this problem using only the plan view.

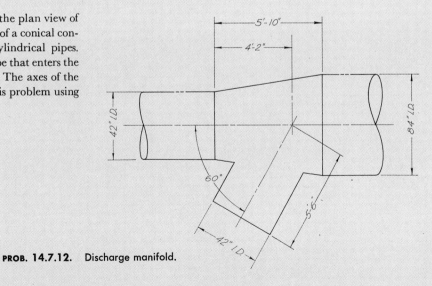

PROB. 14.7.12.   Discharge manifold.

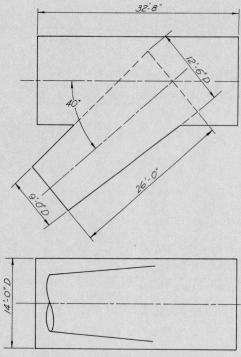

PROB. 14.7.13.   "Kaplan-system" outlet.

14.7.13. The layout shows the cylindrical outlet pipe and conical inlet pipe of a "Kaplan-system" outlet. Find the intersection of the two shapes, using the cutting-sphere method.

14.7.14. The layout shows a right circular cylinder and an elliptical-base cone. Find the intersection of the two surfaces.

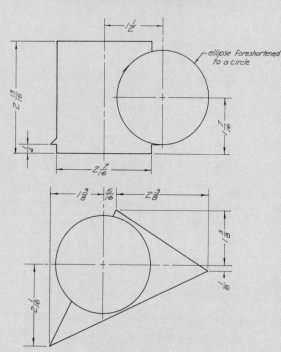

PROB. 14.7.14.   Cylinder and cone.

GROUP 8.   INTERSECTIONS OF DOUBLE-CURVED SURFACES

14.8.1.   (*a*) Find the points *X* and *Z* where line *AB* pierces the sphere *O*. (*b*) Draw the front view of the line of intersection between sphere *O* and a vertical plane containing line *AB*.

14.8.2.   Draw the front view of the line of intersection between sphere *O* and cylinder *AB*.

14.8.3.   Draw the top and front views of the line of intersection between sphere *O* and the lower portion of cone *VO*.

14.8.4.   Draw the top and front views of the line of intersection between sphere *O* and the surface of revolution generated by revolving the parabola about axis *AB*. Point *A* is the focus of the parabola; the line shown is its directrix.

Not only may the foregoing problems be used for exercises in finding the lines of intersection between various surfaces but, after the lines of intersection have been found, the individual surfaces may be developed.

Problems intended for later development should be drawn very accurately because the accuracy of the development will depend upon the drawing from which it was made. Expecially, the line of intersection should be accurately found.

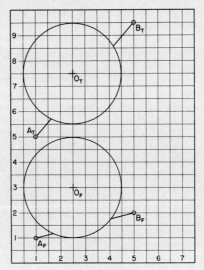

PROB. 14.8.1.

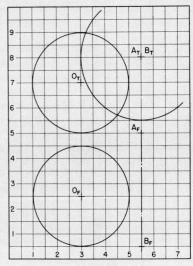

PROB. 14.8.2.

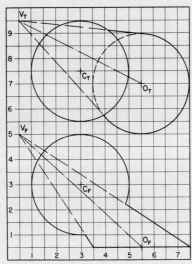

PROB. 14.8.3.

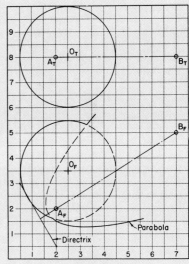

PROB. 14.8.4.

DEVELOPMENTS

GROUP 9.   DEVELOPMENTS OF PRISMS

14.9.1 to 14.9.6.   Develop lateral surfaces of
the prisms.

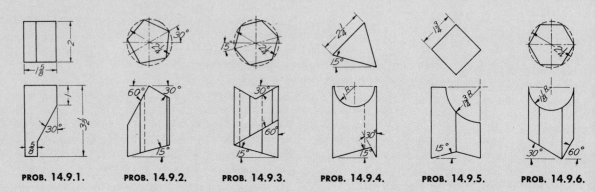

PROB. 14.9.1.   PROB. 14.9.2.   PROB. 14.9.3.   PROB. 14.9.4.   PROB. 14.9.5.   PROB. 14.9.6.

GROUP 10.   DEVELOPMENTS OF PYRAMIDS

14.10.1 to 14.10.3.   Develop lateral surfaces
of the hoppers.

14.10.4 and 14.10.5.   Develop lateral surfaces of the pyramids.

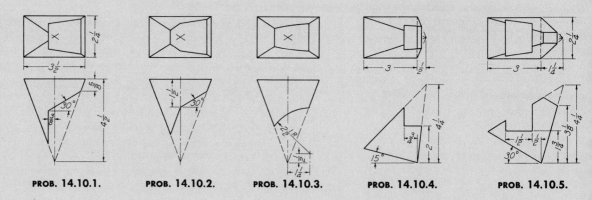

PROB. 14.10.1.   PROB. 14.10.2.   PROB. 14.10.3.   PROB. 14.10.4.   PROB. 14.10.5.

GROUP 11. DEVELOPMENTS OF CYLINDERS

14.11.1 to 14.11.7. Develop lateral surfaces
of the cylinders.

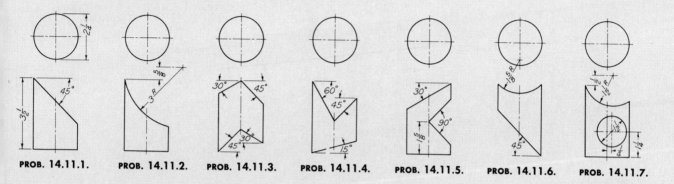

PROB. 14.11.1.   PROB. 14.11.2.   PROB. 14.11.3.   PROB. 14.11.4.   PROB. 14.11.5.   PROB. 14.11.6.   PROB. 14.11.7.

14.11.8. Develop the oblique pipe section of
the power-station piping of Prob. 14.6.6. Also
develop the cylindrical inlet, showing the
opening to be made for the oblique pipe.

GROUP 12. DEVELOPMENTS OF COMBINATIONS OF PRISMS AND CYLINDERS

14.12.1 to 14.12.3. Develop lateral surfaces.

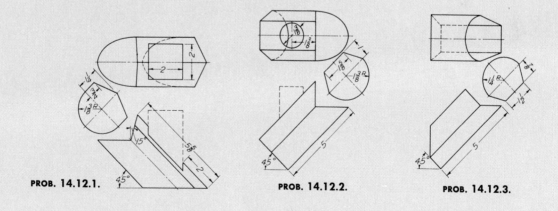

PROB. 14.12.1.   PROB. 14.12.2.   PROB. 14.12.3.

GROUP 13.   DEVELOPMENTS OF CONES

14.13.1 to 14.13.5.   Develop lateral surfaces.

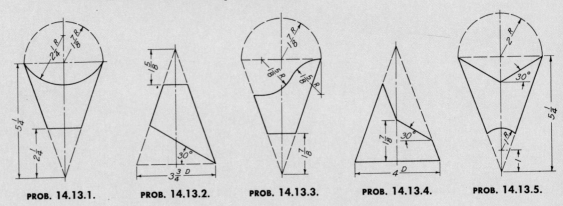

PROB. 14.13.1.   PROB. 14.13.2.   PROB. 14.13.3.   PROB. 14.13.4.   PROB. 14.13.5.

14.13.6.   Develop the concentric reducer for the power-station piping of Prob. 14.6.6.

GROUP 14.   DEVELOPMENTS OF COMBINATIONS OF SURFACES

14.14.1 to 14.14.4.   Develop lateral surfaces of the objects.

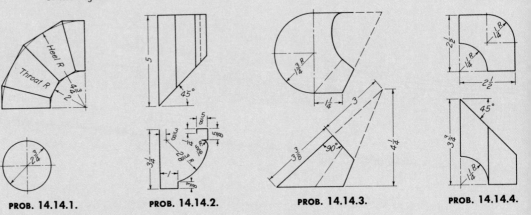

PROB. 14.14.1.   PROB. 14.14.2.   PROB. 14.14.3.   PROB. 14.14.4.

14.14.5.   Develop the cylindrical pipe for the pump casing of Prob. 14.6.4.

14.14.6.   Develop the elbow sections, A, B, and C, of the pump casing, Prob. 14.6.4.

GROUP 15.   DEVELOPMENTS OF CONES AND TRANSITION PIECES

14.15.1 to 14.15.8.   Develop lateral surfaces of the objects.

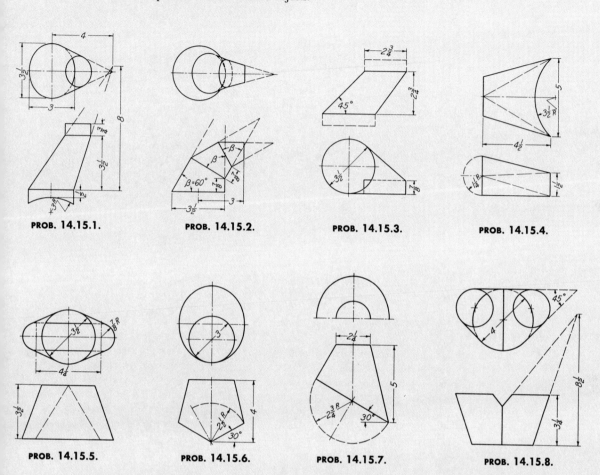

PROB. 14.15.1.   PROB. 14.15.2.   PROB. 14.15.3.   PROB. 14.15.4.

PROB. 14.15.5.   PROB. 14.15.6.   PROB. 14.15.7.   PROB. 14.15.8.

GROUP 16. DEVELOPMENTS OF FURNACE-PIPE FITTINGS

14.16.1 to 14.16.8. Develop surfaces and make paper models.

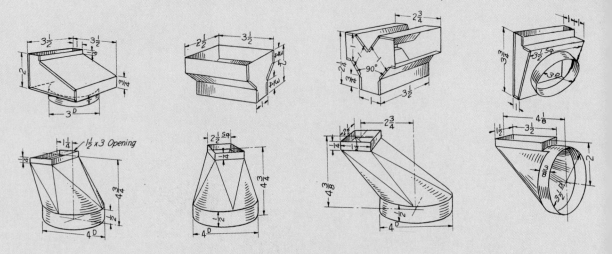

PROBS. 14.16.1 to 14.16.8.

GROUP 17. SPECIALITIES

There are innumerable combinations of geometric shapes and, sometimes, nongeometric forms used in modern engineering work that, fundamentally, are problems of layout and intersection and then either development or representation. The following three problems are typical examples.

14.17.1. The diverter-duct system for a VTOL jet consists essentially of a formed elbow and a cylinder. A typical layout is shown in Prob. 14.17.1. Find the intersection between the cylinder and elbow. Develop the cylinder and make an accurate representational drawing of the elbow.

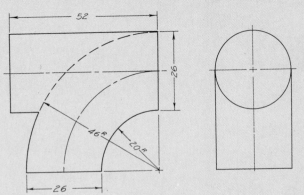

PROB. 14.17.1. Diverter-duct system.

14.17.2. The evaporator shown in the layout consists of a combustion sphere and cone. Connected to this combination is a steam outlet *A* and an exhaust pipe *B*. Find all intersections and then develop the parts that can be developed.

14.17.3. The microwave horn reflector antenna consists essentially of three surfaces: a cone, a cylinder, and a paraboloid of revolu- tion, which, if chosen correctly, should intersect one another on the same curve. To verify this construction, lay out the complete horn according to the dimensions shown in the illustration. Then, find the intersection between the cone and cylinder and between the cylinder and paraboloid. Develop all parts that can be developed.

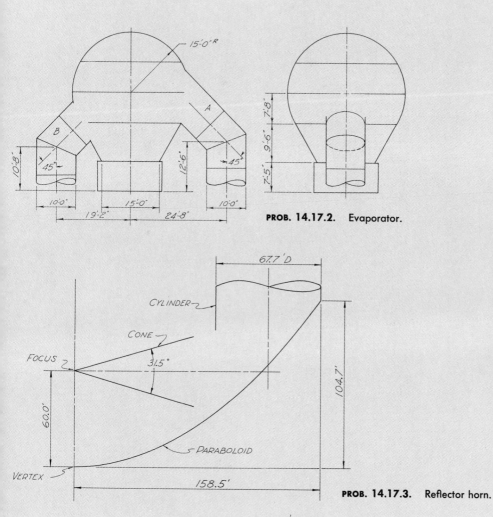

PROB. 14.17.2.   Evaporator.

PROB. 14.17.3.   Reflector horn.

Dimensions and notes on a drawing give both the necessary factual information for the detailed size of every part of an object and the information necessary for processing and manufacturing. Thus, with the shape description, the dimensions and notes complete the drawing so that manufacture and assembly can be carried out exactly as originally conceived by the designer.

Size Description: Dimensions, Notes, Limits, and Precision

15

15.1. After the shape of an object has been described by orthographic (or pictorial) views, the value of the drawing for the construction of the object depends upon dimensions and notes that describe the *size*. In general, the description of shape and size together gives complete information for producing the object represented.

The dimensions put on the drawing are *not necessarily* those used in making the drawing but are those required for the proper functioning of the part after assembly, selected so as to be readily usable by the workers who are to make the piece. Before dimensioning the drawing, study the machine and understand its functional requirments; then put yourself in the place of the patternmaker, diemaker, machinist, etc., and mentally construct the object to discover which dimensions would best give the information.

15.2. **METHOD.** The basic factors in dimensioning practice are:

1. *Lines and Symbols.* The first requisite is a thorough knowledge of the elements used for dimensions and notes and of the weight and spacing of the lines on the drawing. These lines, symbols, and techniques are the "tools" for clear, concise representation of size.

2. *Selection of Distances.* The most important consideration for the ultimate operation of a machine and the proper working of

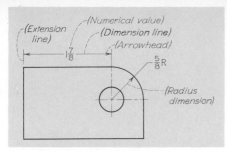

FIG. 15.1. Dimensions.

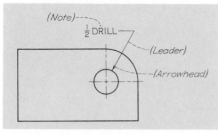

FIG. 15.2. A note.

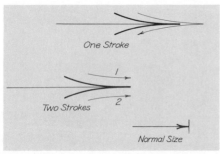

FIG. 15.3. Open-style arrowhead strokes.

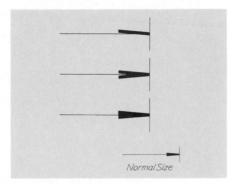

FIG. 15.4. Solid-style arrowhead strokes.

the individual parts is the selection of distances to be given. This selection is based upon the functional requirements, the "breakdown" of the part into its geometric elements, and the requirements of the shop for production.

3. *Placement of Dimensions.* After the distances to be given have been selected, the next step is the actual placement of the dimensions showing these distances on the drawing. The dimensions should be placed in an orderly arrangement that is easy to read and in positions where they can be readily found.

4. *Dimensioning Standard Features.* These include angles, chamfers, standard notes, specifications of holes, spherical shapes, round-end shapes, tapers, and others for which, through long usage and study, dimensioning practice has been standardized.

5. *Precision and Tolerance.* The ultimate operation of any device depends upon the proper interrelationship of the various parts so that they operate as planned. In quantity production, each part must meet standards of size and position to assure assembly and proper functioning. Through the dimensioning of the individual parts, the limits of size are controlled.

6. *Production Methods.* The method of manufacturing (casting, forging, etc.) affects the detailed information given on the drawing proper, and in notes and specifications. The operations of various shops must be known, in order to give concise information.

LINES AND SYMBOLS

15.3. **DIMENSION FORMS.** Two basic methods are used to give a distance on

a drawing: a *dimension* (Fig. 15.1) or a *note* (Fig. 15.2).

A dimension is used to give the distance between two points, lines, or planes, or between some combination of points, lines, and planes. The numerical value gives the actual distance, the dimension line indicates the direction in which the value applies, and the arrowheads indicate the points between which the value applies. Extension lines refer the dimension to the view when the dimension is placed outside the view.

A note provides a means of giving explanatory information along with a size. The leader and arrowhead refer the word statement of the note to the proper place on the drawing. Notes applying to the object as a whole are given without a leader in some convenient place on the drawing.

The lines and symbols used in dimensioning are dimension lines, arrowheads, extension lines, leaders, numerical values, notes, finish marks, etc.

15.4. **LINE WEIGHTS.** Dimension lines, extension lines, and leaders are made with fine full lines the same width as center lines so as to contrast with the heavier outlines of the views. Note the line widths given in the alphabet of lines, Figs. 2.56 and 2.57.

15.5. **ARROWHEADS.** These are carefully drawn freehand. The sides of the arrowhead are made either in one stroke, toward the point and then away from it, or in two strokes toward the point, as shown in enlarged form in Fig. 15.3. The general preference is for the solid head, as in Fig. 15.4. The solid head is usually made narrower and slightly longer than the open head and has practically no curvature to the sides. It

FIG. 15.5. Incorrect arrowheads. The first two examples show mistakes in placement. The last three illustrate shapes that are extremely poor.

is made in one stroke and then filled, if necessary, without lifting the pen or pencil; a rather blunt pencil or pen is required for this style of head. The bases of arrowheads should not be made wider than one-third the length. All arrowheads on the same drawing should be the same type, open or solid, and the same size, except in restricted spaces. Arrowhead lengths vary somewhat depending upon the size of the drawing. A good general length for small drawings is ⅛ in. and for larger drawings 3⁄16 in.

Poor arrowheads ruin the appearance of an otherwise carefully made drawing. Avoid the incorrect shapes and placements shown in Fig. 15.5.

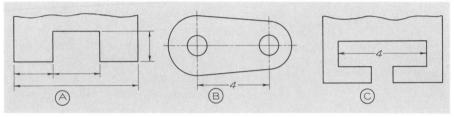

FIG. 15.6. Dimension terminals.

15.6. EXTENSION LINES.

These extend from the view to a dimension placed outside the view. They should not touch the outline of the view but should start about 1⁄16 in. from it and extend about ⅛ in. beyond the last dimension line (Fig. 15.6A). This example is printed approximately one-half size.

Dimensions may also terminate at *center lines* or *visible outlines of the view*. Where a measurement between centers is to be shown, as at (B), the center lines are continued to serve as extension lines, extending about ⅛ in. beyond the last dimension line. Usually the outline of the view becomes the terminal for arrowheads, as at (C), when a dimension must be placed inside the view. This might occur because of limited space, when extension lines crossing parts of the view would cause confusion, or when long extension lines would make the dimension difficult to read.

Extension lines for an angular dimension are shown in Fig. 15.7A, with one of the extension lines used for a linear dimension, a common occurrence.

Extension lines should not be broken where they cross each other or an outline of a view, as shown in Fig. 15.6A and 15.7A. However, when space is restricted and the extension lines come close to arrowheads, the extension lines may be broken for clarity, as in Fig. 15.7B.

Where a point is located by extension lines alone, the extension lines should pass through the point, as at (C).

15.7. LEADERS.

These are *straight* (not curved) lines leading from a dimension value or an explanatory note to the feature on the drawing to which the note applies (Fig. 15.8). An arrowhead is used at the pointing end of the leader but never at the note end. The note end of the leader should terminate with a short horizontal bar at the mid-height of the lettering and should run to the beginning or the end of the note, never to the middle.

Leaders should be drawn at an angle to contrast with the principal lines of the drawing, which are mainly horizontal and vertical. Thus leaders are usually drawn at 30°, 45°, or 60° to the horizontal; 60° looks best. When

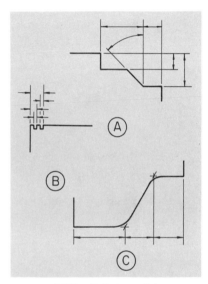

FIG. 15.7. Technique of drawing extension lines.

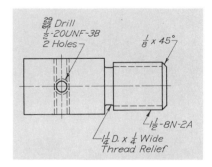

FIG. 15.8. Leaders for notes. Observe that the leader emanates from the *beginning* or the *end* of the lettered information.

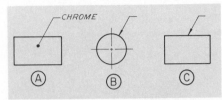

FIG. 15.9. Leaders. (*A*) special terminal; (*B*) and (*C*) proper angle.

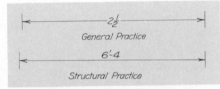

FIG. 15.10. Placement of dimension values.

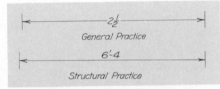

FIG. 15.11. Technique for lettering values with common fractions.

several leaders are used, the appearance of the drawing is improved if the leaders can be kept parallel.

The ANSI allows the use of a "dot" for termination of a leader, as in Fig. 15.9*A*, when the dot is considered to be a clearer representation than an arrowhead. The dot should fall within the outline of the object.

When dimensioning a circular feature with a note, the leader should be *radial* as shown at (*B*). A leader directed to a flat surface should meet the surface at an angle of *at least* 30°; an angle of 45° or 60° as at (*C*) is best.

If possible *avoid* crossing leaders; *avoid* long leaders; *avoid* leaders in a horizontal or vertical direction; *avoid* leaders parallel to adjacent dimension lines, extension lines, or crosshatching; and *avoid* small angles between leaders and the lines they terminate on.

15.8. FIGURES. For dimension values, figures must be carefully lettered in vertical or inclined style. In an effort to achieve neatness, the beginner often gets them too small. One-eighth inch for small drawings and $\frac{5}{32}$ in. for larger drawings are good general heights.

The general practice is to leave a space in the dimension line for the dimension value (Fig. 15.10). It is universal in structural practice and common in architectural practice to place the value above a continuous dimension line (Fig. 15.10).

15.9. COMMON FRACTIONS. These should be made with the fraction bar parallel to the guide lines for making the figure and with the numerator and denominator each somewhat smaller than the height of the whole number so that the *total* fraction height is twice that of the integer (Fig. 15.11). Avoid

the incorrect forms shown. The figures should not touch the fraction bar.

15.10. FEET AND INCHES. Indicate these thus: 9'-6". When there are no inches, it should be so indicated, as 9'-0", 9'-0½". When dimensions are all in inches, the inch mark is preferably omitted from all the dimensions and notes unless there is some possibility of misunderstanding; if that is the case, "1 bore," for example, should be given for clarity as "1" bore."

In some machine industries, all dimensions are given in inches. In others where feet and inches are used, ANSI recommends that dimensions up to and including 72 in. be given in inches and greater lengths in feet and inches.

In structural drawing, length dimensions should be given in feet and inches. Plate widths, beam sizes, etc., are given in inches. Inch marks are omitted, even though the dimension is in feet and inches (Fig. 15.10).

In the United States, if no foot or inch marks appear on a drawing, the dimension values indicate inches unless a different unit of measurement is indicated by a general note. Drawings made in foreign countries employing the metric system are commonly dimensioned in millimeters.

15.11. READING DIRECTION OF FIGURES. This is arranged according to the aligned system or the unidirectional system.

The *aligned system* is the older of the two methods. The figures are oriented to be read from a position *perpendicular* to the dimension line; thus the guide lines for the figures will be parallel to the dimension line, and the fraction bar in line with the dimension line (Fig. 15.12). The figures should be arranged so as to be read from the *bottom* or *right*

15.12. Systems of Writing Dimension Values

side of the drawing. Avoid running dimensions in the directions included in the shaded area of Fig. 15.12; if this is unavoidable, they should read downward with the line.

The *unidirectional system* originated in the automotive and aircraft industries, and is sometimes called the "horizontal system." All figures are oriented to read from the bottom of the drawing. Thus the guide lines and fraction bars are horizontal regardless of the direction of the dimension (Fig. 15.13). The "avoid" zone of Fig. 15.12 has no significance with this system.

Notes must be lettered horizontally and read from the bottom of the drawing in either system.

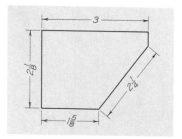
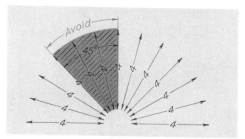

FIG. 15.12. Reading direction of values (aligned system). The drawing is read from the bottom and right side.

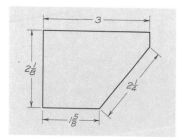
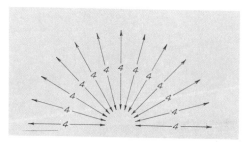

FIG. 15.13. Reading direction of values (unidirectional system). The drawing is read from the bottom.

15.12. SYSTEMS OF WRITING DIMENSION VALUES.

Dimension values may be given as common fractions, ¼, ⅜, etc., or as decimal fractions, 0.25, 0.375, etc.; and from these, three systems are evolved.

The *common-fraction system,* used in general drawing practice, including architectural and structural work, has all dimension values written as units and common fractions, as 3½, 1¼, ⅜, ¹⁄₁₆, ³⁄₃₂, ¹⁄₆₄. Values thus written can be laid out with a steel tape or scale graduated in sixty-fourths of an inch.

The *common-fraction, decimal-fraction system* is used principally in machine drawing whenever the degree of precision required calls for fractions of an inch smaller than those on the ordinary steel scale. To continue the use of common fractions below ¹⁄₆₄, such as ¹⁄₁₂₈ or ¹⁄₂₅₆, is considered impractical. The method followed is to give values: (1) in units and common fractions for distances not requiring an accuracy closer than ¹⁄₆₄ in.; and (2) in units and decimal fractions, as 2.375, 1.250, 0.1875, etc.,

for distances requiring greater precision. The decimal fractions are given to as many decimal places as needed for the degree of precision required.

The *complete decimal system* uses decimal fractions exclusively for all dimension values. This system has the advantages of the metric system but uses the inch as its basis, thus making it possible to use present measuring equipment.

The ANSI complete decimal system[1] uses a two-place decimal for all values where common fractions would ordinarily be used. The digits after the decimal point are preferably written to even fiftieths, .02, .10, .36, etc., so that when halved, as for radii, etc., two-place decimals will result. Writing the values in even fiftieths allows the use of scales divided in fiftieths (Fig. 15.14), which are much easier to read than scales divided in hundredths.

Dimension values for distances requiring greater precision than that expressed by the two-place decimal are written to three, four, or more decimal places as needed for precision.

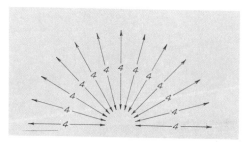

FIG. 15.14. Decimal scale. Graduations are in fiftieths.

[1] Y14.5—1966.

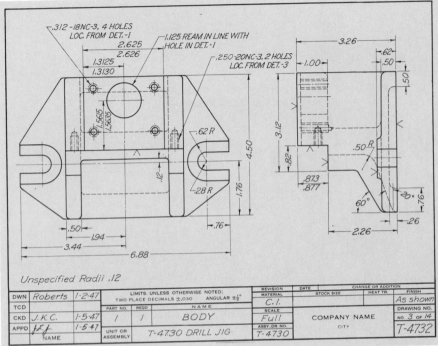

Unspecified Radii .12

DWN	Roberts	1-2-47	LIMITS, UNLESS OTHERWISE NOTED: TWO PLACE DECIMALS ±.030 ANGULAR ±½°		REVISION	DATE	CHANGE OR ADDITION			
TCD					C. I.	STOCK SIZE	HEAT TR.	FINISH As shown		
CKD	J.K.C.	1-5-47	PART NO.	REQD	NAME	MATERIAL		SCALE	COMPANY NAME	DRAWING NO.
APPD	J.E.J.	1-5-47	1	1	BODY	Full			CITY	NO. 3 of 14
	NAME		UNIT OR ASSEMBLY		T-4730 DRILL JIG	ASSY. DR. NO. T-4730				T-4732

FIG. 15.15. A drawing dimensioned in the decimal system.

Figure 15.15 is a detail drawing dimensioned according to the ANSI decimal system. The advantage of this system in calculating, adding, and checking and in doing away with all conversion tables, as well as in lessening chances for error, is apparent.

Designers and draftsmen working in the complete decimal system find it necessary to think in terms of tenths and hundredths of inches instead of common fractions. New designs must be made in decimal sizes without reference to common fractional sizes. However, until standard-stock materials, tools, and commercial parts are available in decimal sizes, some dimensions will have to be given as the decimal equivalent of a common fraction. Thus, for example, a standard ⅜-16UNC-2A thread would be given as 0.375-16UNC-2A.

Decimal equivalents of some common fractions come out to a greater number of decimal places (significant digits)

than is necessary or desirable for use as a dimension value, and in such cases the decimal should be adjusted, or "rounded off," to a smaller number of decimal places. The following procedure from the SAE Aerospace–Automotive Drafting Standard[2] is recommended:

When the figure beyond the last figure to be retained is less than 5, the last figure retained should not be changed. Example: 3.46325, if cut off to three places, should be 3.463.

When the figure beyond the last figure to be retained is more than 5, the last figure retained should be increased by 1. Example: 8.37652, if cut off to three places, should be 8.377.

When the figure beyond the last place to be retained is exactly 5 with only zeros following, the preceding number, if even, should be unchanged; if odd, should be increased by 1. Example: 4.365 becomes 4.36 when cut off to two places. Also, 4.355 becomes 4.36 when cut off to two places.

15.13. FINISH MARKS. These are used to indicate that certain surfaces of metal parts are to be machined and that allowance must therefore be provided for finish. Finish marks need not be used for parts made by machining from rolled stock, as the surfaces are necessarily machined. Neither are they necessary on drilled, reamed, or counterbored holes or on similar machined features when the machining operation is specified by note. Also, when limit dimensions are given, the accuracy required is thereby stated, and a finish mark on the surface is unnecessary.

The standard finish mark recommended by the ANSI is a 60° V with its point touching the line representing the

[2] Section A.6 (1963).

edge view of the surface to be machined. The V is placed on the "air side" of the surface. Figure 15.16 shows the normal size of the V and its position for lines in various directions as given on a drawing.

Finish marks should be placed on all views in which the surface to be machined appears as a line, including dashed lines. If the part is to be machined on all surfaces, the note "Finish all over," or "FAO," is used, and the marks on the views are omitted.

In addition to using the finish mark to indicate a machined surface, it may be necessary in some cases to indicate the degree of smoothness of the surface. The ANSI gives a set of symbols to indicate the degree of smoothness of a surface, the various conditions of *surface quality*. These symbols are explained and illustrated in paragraph 15.79.

15.14. SCALE OF THE DRAWING.
Even though a workman is never expected to scale a distance on a drawing to obtain a dimension value, the scale to which the drawing is made should be stated in the title block. Standard scales are listed in Fig. 2.34.

15.15. REVISION OF DIMENSIONS.
As a project is being developed, changes in design, in engineering methods, etc., may make it necessary to change some drawings either before or after they have been released to the shop. If the change is a major one, the drawing may have to be remade. But in many cases it is merely a question of altering the dimension values and leaving the shape description unchanged. For changes in dimensions, the out-of-scale dimensions should be indicated by one of the methods in Fig. 15.17. Drawing changes should be listed in tabular form, in con-

nection with the title block or in the upper right corner, with reference letters and the date, as explained in paragraph 19.19.

15.16. ABBREVIATIONS.
Many abbreviations are used on drawings to save time and space. The common ones such as DIA, THD, MAX, MIN, ID, and OD are universally understood. Uncommon abbreviations such as PH BRZ (Phosphor bronze) should be used cautiously because of the possibility of misinterpretation. Abbreviations should conform to the SAE Aerospace–Automotive Drafting Standard, Sec. Z.1.

15.17. DECIMAL POINTS.
These should be made distinctly, in a full letter space, and should be aligned with the bottom edges of digits and letters.

15.18. DASHES.
These are used in many standard expressions such as ½—20 and should be made clearly, one letter space in length, at the mid-height of letters or digits and parallel to the direction of the expression.

SELECTION OF DISTANCES

15.19. THEORY OF DIMENSIONING.
Any object can be broken down into a combination of basic geometric shapes, principally prisms and cylinders. Occasionally, however, there will be parts of pyramids and cones, now and then a double-curved surface, and rarely, except for surfaces of screw threads, a warped surface. Any of the basic shapes may be positive or negative, in the sense that a hole is a negative cylinder. Figure 5.98 illustrates a machine part broken down into its fundamental shapes.

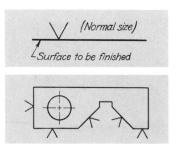

FIG. 15.16. The ANSI finish mark. It indicates removal of material to produce the desired surface.

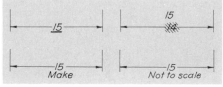

FIG. 15.17. Out-of-scale dimensions.

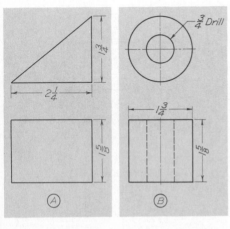

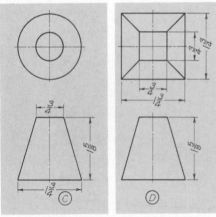

FIG. 15.18. Size dimensions. (*A*) prism; (*B*) cylinder; (*C*) cone; (*D*) pyramid.

If the *size* of each of these elementary shapes is dimensioned and the relative position of each is given, measuring from center to center, from base lines, or from surfaces, the dimensioning of any piece can be done systematically. Dimensions can thus be classified as dimensions of *size* and dimensions of *position*.

15.20. DIMENSIONS OF SIZE. Since every solid has three dimensions, each of the geometric shapes making up the object must have its height, width, and depth indicated in the dimensioning.

The *prism,* often in plinth or flat form, is the most common shape and requires three dimensions for square, rectangular, or triangular (Fig. 15.18*A*). For regular hexagonal or octagonal types, usually only two dimensions are given, either the distance "across corners" and the length or the distance "across flats" and the length.

The *cylinder,* found on nearly all mechanical pieces as a shaft, boss, or hole, is the second most common shape. A cylinder obviously requires only two dimensions, diameter and length (*B*). Partial cylinders, such as fillets and rounds, are dimensioned by radius instead of diameter. A good general rule is to dimension complete circles with the diameter and circle arcs (partial circles) with the radius.

Right cones can be dimensioned by giving the altitude and the diameter of the base. They usually occur as frustums, however, and require the diameters of the ends and the length (*C*). Sometimes it is desirable to dimension cone frustums as *tapers* or with an angular dimension, as described in paragraph 15.41.

Right pyramids are dimensioned by

giving the dimensions of the base and the altitude. Right pyramids are often frustums, requiring dimensions of both bases (*D*).

Oblique cones and *pyramids* are dimensioned in the same way as right cones and pyramids but with an additional dimension parallel to the base to give the offset of the vertex.

Spheres are dimensioned by giving the diameter and other surfaces of revolution by dimensioning the generating curve.

Warped surfaces are dimensioned according to their method of generation; and as their representation requires numerous sections, each of these must be fully dimensioned by ordinate and abscissa dimensions.

15.21. DIMENSIONS OF POSITION. After the basic geometric shapes have been dimensioned for size, the position of each relative to the others must be given. *Position must be established in height, width, and depth directions.* Rectangular shapes are positioned with reference to their faces, cylindrical and conic shapes with reference to their center lines and their ends.

One basic shape will often coincide or align with another on one or more of its faces. In such cases the alignment serves partially to locate the parts and eliminates the need of a dimension of position in a direction perpendicular to the line of coincidence. Thus in Fig. 15.19, prism *A* requires only one dimension for complete positioning with respect to prism *B*, as two surfaces are in alignment and two in contact.

Coincident center lines often eliminate the need for position dimensions. In the cylinder in Fig. 15.18*B* the center lines of the hole and of the cylinder

15.23. Correlation of Dimensions

coincide, and no dimensions of position are needed. The two holes of Fig. 15.19 are on the same center line, and the dimension perpendicular to the common center line positions both holes in that direction.

15.22. SELECTION OF DIMENSIONS. The dimensions arrived at by reducing the part to its basic geometric shapes will, in general, fulfill the requirements of practical dimensioning. However, sometimes other dimensions are required to ensure satisfactory functioning of the part and to give the information in the best way from the standpoint of production.

The draftsman must therefore correlate the dimensions on drawings of mating parts to ensure satisfactory functioning and, at the same time, select dimensions convenient for the workmen to use.

Here our study of drawing as a language must be supplemented by a knowledge of shop methods. To be successful, the machine draftsman must have an intimate knowledge of pattern-making, foundry practice, forging, and machine-shop practice, as well as, in some cases, sheet-metal working, metal and plastic die casting, welding, and structural-steel fabrication.

The beginning student who is without this knowledge should not depend upon his instructor alone but should learn by observing work going through the shops and reading books and periodicals on methods used in modern production work.

The *selection of dimensions of size* arrived at by shape breakdown will usually meet the requirements of the shop since the basic shapes result from the fundamental shop operations. However, a shop often prefers to receive dimensions of

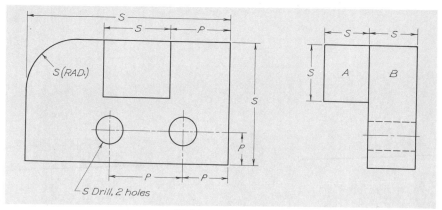

FIG. 15.19. Dimensions of size and position. S indicates size, P position.

size in note form rather than as regular dimensions when a shop process is involved, such as drilling, reaming, counterboring, and punching.

Selecting dimensions of position ordinarily requires more consideration than selecting dimensions of size because there are usually several ways in which a position might be given. In general, positional dimensions are given between finished surfaces, center lines, or a combination thereof (Fig. 15.22). Remember that rough castings or forgings vary in size; so do not position machined surfaces from unfinished surfaces—except in one situation: A machined surface may be positioned from an unmachined surface only when the *initial*, or *starting*, dimension gives the position for the first surface to be machined—a position from which the other machined surfaces will in turn be positioned. *Coinciding center lines of unfinished and finished surfaces often take the place of a starting dimension.*

The position of a point or center by offset dimensions from two center lines or surfaces (Fig. 15.20) is preferable to angular dimensions (Fig. 15.21) unless the angular dimension is more practical from the standpoint of construction.

15.23. CORRELATION OF DIMENSIONS. Mating parts must have their dimensions correlated so that the two parts will

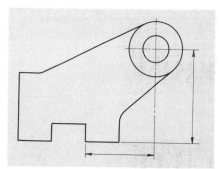

FIG. 15.20. Position by offsets.

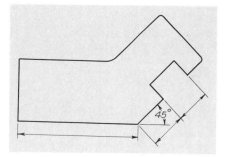

FIG. 15.21. Position by angle.

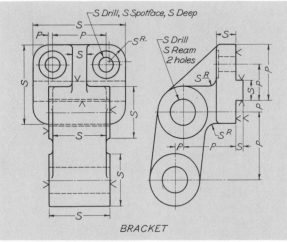

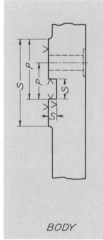

FIG. 15.22. Correlation of dimensions. Dimensions must be given so that parts will assemble properly.

FIG. 15.23. An example of dimensioning. See text for detailed explanation.

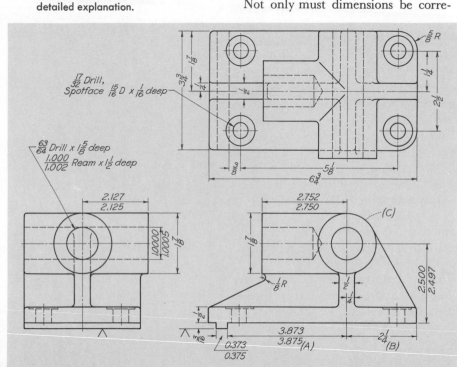

lated with the dimensions of the mating part, but the accuracy to which these distances are produced must meet certain requirements, or the parts still may not fit and function properly. Distances between the surfaces or center lines of finished features of an object must usually be more accurately made than distances between unfinished features. In Fig. 15.23, note that the position dimensions between center lines or surfaces of finished features are given as three-place decimals, as dimension A. Dimensions of position for unfinished features are given as common fractions, as dimension B. The decimal dimensions call for greater precision in manufacture than do the common fractions. Dimension B is in this case used by the patternmaker to position cylinder C from the right end of the piece. The machinist will first locate the finished hole in this cylinder, making it concentric with the cylinder; then all other machined surfaces will be positioned from this hole, as, for example, the spline position by dimension A. The four spot-faced holes are positioned with reference to each other with fractional dimensions since the holes are oversize for the fastenings used, allowing enough shifting of the fastenings in the holes so that great accuracy in location is not necessary. The mating part, with its holes to receive the screws, would be similarly dimensioned.

Study Fig. 15.23 and note the classification, size, and position of each dimension.

fit and function as intended. Figure 15.22 illustrates this principle. Note that the tongue of the bracket is to fit the groove in the body, and that the drilled holes in both pieces must align. Study the dimensioning of both pieces and observe that the dimensions of position (P) are correlated so that the intended alignment and fitting of the parts will be accomplished.

Not only must dimensions be corre-

15.24. SUPERFLUOUS DIMENSIONS. *Duplicate* or *unnecessary* dimensions are to be avoided because they may cause confusion and delay. When a drawing is changed or revised, a duplicate dimension may not be noticed and changed along with its counterpart; hence a distance will have two different values, one incorrect. An unnecessary dimension is any dimension, other than a duplicate, that is not essential in making the piece. Because of the allowable variation permitted the manufacturer on each dimension (see paragraph 15.54), difficulties will be encountered if unnecessary dimensions occur when parts are to be interchangeable. Actually, if the proper dimensions have been selected, it will be possible to establish a point on the object in any given direction with only one dimension. Unnecessary dimensions always occur when all the individual dimensions are given, in addition to the overall dimension (Fig. 15.24). One dimension of the series must be omitted if the overall dimension is used, thus allowing only one possible positioning from each dimension (Fig. 15.25).

In architectural and structural work, where the interchangeability of parts is usually irrelevant, unnecessary dimensions cause no difficulty and all dimensions are given.

Although it is important not to "over-dimension" a part, it is equally important to give all the dimensions that are needed to locate every point, line, or surface of the object. Every dimension that the workman will require in making the part must be given.

Dimensions for similar features, such as the thickness of several ribs obviously of the same size, need not be repeated (Fig. 15.26). Also, such details as the size of fillets and rounds can be provided for with a general note. Any superfluous or omitted dimensions can be easily discovered by mentally going through the manufacture, or even the drawing, of the part, checking each dimension as it is needed.

15.25. REFERENCE DIMENSIONS. Occasionally, for reference and checking, all dimensions in a series are given as well as the overall dimension. In such cases one dimension is marked with the abbreviation "REF" as shown in Fig. 15.26. According to ANSI definition, a reference dimension is "a dimension without tolerance, used for informational purposes only, and does not govern machining or inspection operations."

15.26. DIMENSIONS FROM DATUM. Datum points, lines, and edges of surfaces of a part are features that are assumed to be exact for purposes of computation or reference, and *from* which the position of other features is established. In Fig. 15.27*A* the left side and bottom surfaces of the part are the datum surfaces, and at (*B*) the center lines of the central hole in the part are datum lines. Where positions are specified by dimensions from a datum, different features are always positioned from this datum and *not* with respect to one another.

15.27. SELECTION OF A DATUM. A feature selected to serve as a datum must be clearly identified and readily recognizable. Note in Fig. 15.27 that the datum lines and edges are obvious. On an actual part, the datum features must be accessible during manufacture so that there will be no difficulty in making measurements. In addition, *corresponding*

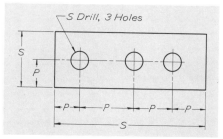

FIG. 15.24. One unnecessary dimension.

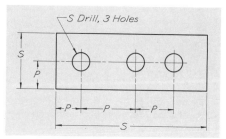

FIG. 15.25. Unnecessary dimension omitted.

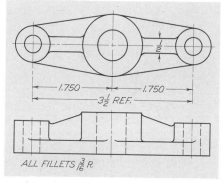

FIG. 15.26. One reference dimension.

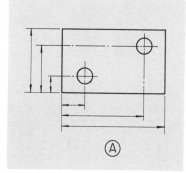

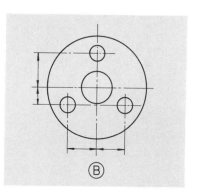

FIG. 15.27. Dimensions from datum. (*A*) Datum surfaces; (*B*) datum center.

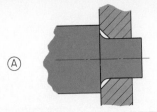

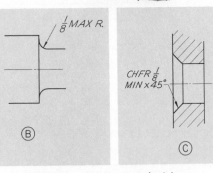

FIG. 15.28. Maximum and minimum sizes. Mating edges at (A) are dimensioned as at (B) and (C) so that there will be no assembly interference.

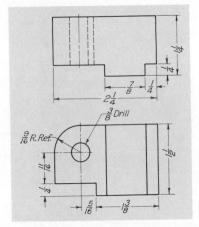

FIG. 15.29. The contour principle. Dimensions are placed where the feature dimensioned is most easily recognized.

FIG. 15.30. Dimensions for cylinders. (A) shows usual practice for cylindrical parts; (B), (C), and (D), for holes.

features on mating parts must be employed as datum features to assure assembly and proper functioning.

A datum surface (on a physical part) must be more accurate than the allowable variation on any dimension of position which is referred to the datum. Thus, it may be necessary to specify the perfection of datum surfaces for flatness, straightness, roundness, etc. See paragraphs 15.77 and 15.78.

15.28.   BASIC DIMENSIONS.   Any dimension on a drawing specified as BASIC is a *theoretical* value used to describe the exact size, shape, or position of a feature. It is used as a reference from which permissible variations are established.

15.29.   MAXIMUM AND MINIMUM SIZES. In some cases a maximum or a minimum size represents a limit beyond which any variation in size cannot be permitted, but in the *opposite* direction there is no difficulty. To illustrate, Fig. 15.28A shows a shaft and hub assembly. If the change in diameter of the shaft (rounded) is too large or the hub edge (chamfer) too small, the hub will not seat against the shaft shoulder, but if the shaft radius is somewhat smaller or the hub edge somewhat larger, no difficulty exists. Therefore in the dimensioning of both, at (B) and (C), MAX and MIN are applied to the dimensions. This method is often used in connection with depths of holes, lengths of threads, chamfers, and radii.

PLACEMENT OF DIMENSIONS

15.30.   PLACEMENT   OF   DIMENSIONS. After the distances have been selected, it is possible to decide (1) the *view* on which the distance will be indicated, (2) the particular *place* on that view, and (3) the *form* of the dimension itself. Numerous principles, some with the force of a rule, can be given, but in all cases the important consideration is *clarity*.

15.31.   VIEWS: *The Contour Principle.* One of the views of an object will usually describe the shape of some detailed feature better than will the other view or views, and the feature is then said to be "characteristic" in that particular view. In reading a drawing, it is natural to look for the dimensions of a given feature wherever that feature appears most characteristic, and an advantage in clarity and in ease of reading will certainly result if the dimension is placed there. In Fig. 15.29 the rounded corner, the drilled hole, and the lower notched corner are all characteristic in, and dimensioned on, the front view. The projecting shape on the front of the object is more characteristic in the top view and is dimensioned there.

Dimensions for prisms should be placed so that two of the three dimensions are on the view showing the contour shape and the third on one of the other views (Figs. 15.18 and 15.29).

Dimensions for cylinders, the diameter

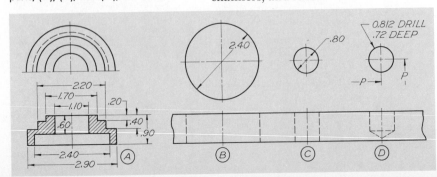

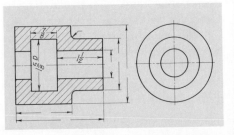

FIG. 15.31.   Dimensions inside the view.

15.31. Views

and length, are usually best placed on the noncircular view (Fig. 15.30A). This practice keeps the dimensions on one view, a convenience for the workman. Occasionally a cylindrical hole is dimensioned with the diameter at an angle on the circular view, as indicated at (B). This practice should never be used unless there is a clear space for the dimension value. In some cases, however, the value can be carried outside the view, as at (C). When a round hole is specified by a note, as at (D), the leader should point to the circular view if possible. The note has an advantage in that the diameter, operation, and depth can all be given together. Giving the diameter on the circular view as at (B), (C), and (D) may make for ease of reading, as the dimensions of position will probably be given there also, as indicated at (D). When it is not obvious from the drawing, a dimension may be indicated as a diameter by following the value with the letter D, as shown in Fig. 15.31.

PRINCIPLES FOR THE PLACEMENT OF DIMENSIONS

1. Dimensions outside the view are preferred, unless added clearness, simplicity, and ease of reading will result from placing some of them inside. For good appearance, dimensions should be kept off the cut surfaces of sections. When it is not possible to do this, the section lining is omitted around the numbers, as shown in Fig. 15.31 (see paragraph 15.35).

2. Dimensions between the views are preferred unless there is some reason for placing them elsewhere, as in Fig. 15.29 where the dimensions for the lower notched corner and the position of the hole must come at the bottom of the front view.

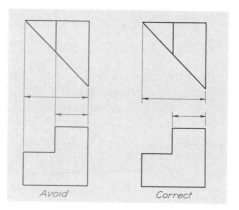

FIG. 15.32. Dimensions applied to one view only.

3. Dimensions should be applied to one view only; that is, with dimensions between views, the extension lines should be drawn from one view, not from both views (Fig. 15.32).

4. Dimensions should be placed on the view that shows the distance in its true length (Fig. 15.33).

5. Dimension lines should be spaced, in general, ½ in. away from the outlines of the view. This applies to a single dimension or to the first dimension of several in a series.

6. Parallel dimension lines should be spaced uniformly with at least ⅜ in. between lines.

7. Values should be midway between the arrowheads, except when a center line interferes (Fig. 15.34) or when the values of several parallel dimensions are staggered (Fig. 15.35).

8. Continuous or staggered dimension lines may be used, depending upon convenience and readability. Continuous dimension lines are preferred where possible (Figs. 15.36 and 15.37).

9. Always place a longer dimension line outside a shorter one to avoid crossing dimension lines with the extension lines of other dimensions. Thus an overall dimension (maximum size of piece in a given direction) will be outside all other dimensions.

FIG. 15.37. Dimensions staggered.

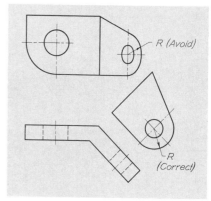

FIG. 15.33. Dimensioned distance given in normal view.

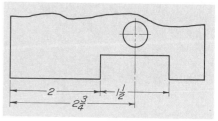

FIG. 15.34. Values midway between arrowheads.

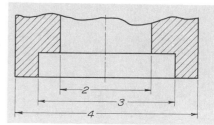

FIG. 15.35. Values staggered for clarity.

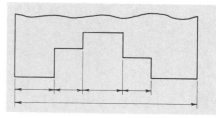

FIG. 15.36. Dimensions arranged in continuous form.

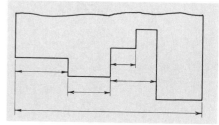

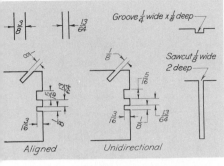

FIG. 15.38. Dimensions in limited space.

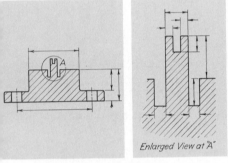

FIG. 15.39. Use of enlarged view to clarify dimensions.

10. Dimensions should never be crowded. If the space is small, follow one of the methods given in paragraph 15.32.

11. Center lines are used to indicate the symmetry of shapes, and frequently eliminate the need for a positioning dimension. They should be considered as part of the dimensioning and drawn in finished form at the time of dimensioning. They should extend about ⅛ in. beyond the shape for which they indicate symmetry unless they are carried further to serve as extension lines. Center lines should not be continued between views.

12. All notes must read horizontally (from the bottom of the drawing).

CAUTIONS

1. Never use a center line, a line of a view, or an extension line as a dimension line.

2. Never place a dimension line on a center line or place a dimension line where a center line should properly be.

3. Never allow a line of any kind to pass through a dimension figure.

4. Never allow the crossing of two dimension lines or an extension line and a dimension line.

5. Avoid dimensioning to dashed lines if possible.

15.32. DIMENSIONING IN LIMITED SPACE. Dimensions should never be crowded into space too small to contain them. One of the methods in Fig. 15.38 can be used where space is limited. Sometimes a note is appropriate. If the space is small and crowded, an enlarged removed section or part view can be used (Fig. 15.39).

15.33. ORDER OF DIMENSIONING. A systematic order of working is a great help in placing dimensions. Figure 15.40 illustrates the procedure. First complete the shape description (*A*). Then place the extension lines and extend the center lines where necessary (*B*), thus planning for the location of both size and position dimensions; study the placement of each dimension and make alterations if desirable or necessary. Add the dimension lines (*C*). Draw arrowheads and leaders for notes (*D*). Then add values and letter notes (*E* and *F*).

It is desirable to add the notes *after* the dimensions have been placed. If the notes are placed first, they may occupy a space needed for a dimension. Because of the freedom allowed in the use of leaders, notes may be given in almost any available space.

15.34. DIMENSIONING OF AUXILIARY VIEWS. In placing dimensions on an auxiliary view, the same principles of dimensioning apply as for any other drawing, but special attention is paid to the contour principle given in paragraph 15.31. An auxiliary view is made for the purpose of showing the normal view (size)

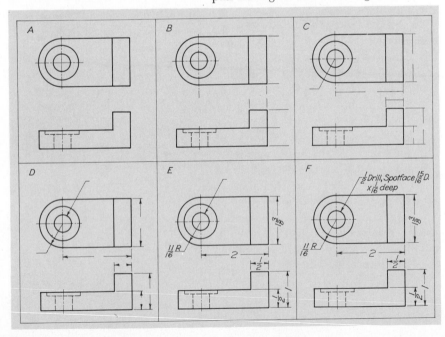

FIG. 15.40. Order of dimensioning. See text for details.

15.37. Dimensioning Pictorial Drawings

of some inclined or skew face, and for this reason the dimensioning of the face should be placed where it is easiest to read, *which will be on the normal view.* Note in Fig. 15.41 that the spacing and size of holes as well as the size of the inclined face are dimensioned on the auxiliary view. Note also the angle and dimension of position tying the inclined face to the rest of the object could not be placed on the auxiliary view.

15.35. DIMENSIONING OF SECTIONAL VIEWS.

Dimensions that must be placed on sectional views are usually placed outside the view so as not to be crowded within crosshatched areas. However, sometimes a dimension *must* be placed across a crosshatched area. When this is the case, the crosshatching is left out around the dimension figures, as illustrated in Fig. 15.31. Examples showing dimensioning practice on sectional views are given in Probs. 19.2.3, 19.2.4, and 19.3.11.

15.36. DIMENSIONING A HALF SECTION.

In general, the half section is difficult to dimension clearly without some possibility of crowding and giving misleading or ambiguous information. Generous use of notes and careful placement of dimension lines, leaders, and figures will in most cases make the dimensioning clear; but if a half section cannot be clearly dimensioned, an extra view or part view should be added on which to describe the size.

Inside diameters should be followed by the letter *D* and the dimension line carried over the center line, as in Fig. 15.42, to prevent the possibility of reading the dimension as a radius. Sometimes the view and the dimensioning can both be clarified by showing the

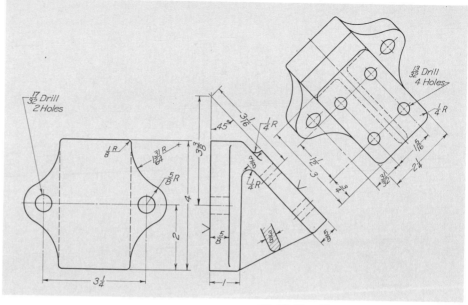

FIG. 15.41. Dimensioning on an auxiliary (normal) view.

dashed lines on the unsectioned side. Dimensions of internal parts, if placed inside the view, will prevent confusion between extension lines and the outline of external portions.

15.37. DIMENSIONING PICTORIAL DRAWINGS.

Pictorial drawings are often more difficult to dimension than orthographic drawings because there is one view instead of several, and the dimensioning may become crowded unless the placement is carefully planned. In general, the principles of dimensioning for orthographic drawings should be followed whenever it is possible.

FIG. 15.42. Dimensioning a half section.

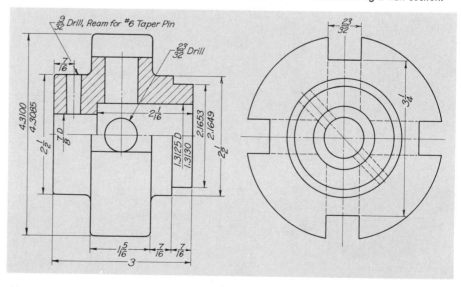

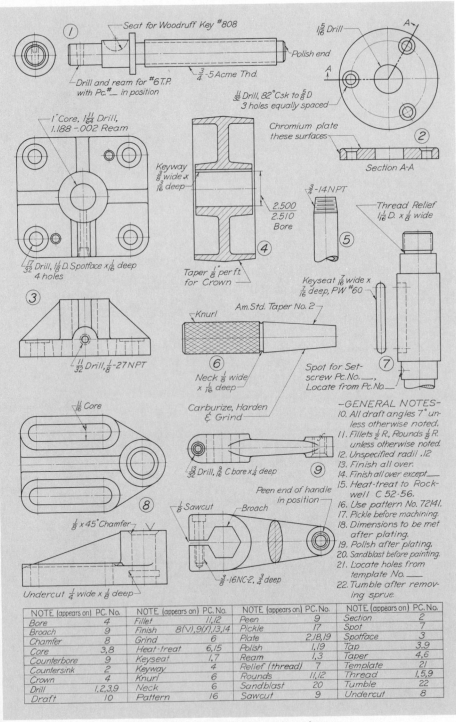

Seat for Woodruff Key #808

Polish end

Drill and ream for #6T.P. with Pc.#___ in position

$\frac{3}{4}$-5 Acme Thd.

$1\frac{5}{16}$ Drill

$\frac{11}{16}$ Drill, 82°Csk to $\frac{5}{8}$ D 3 holes equally spaced

Chromium plate these surfaces

Section A-A

1"Core, $1\frac{11}{64}$ Drill, 1.188 -.002 Ream

Keyway $\frac{3}{8}$ wide x $\frac{3}{16}$ deep

2.500 2.510 Bore

$\frac{3}{4}$-14NPT

Thread Relief $1\frac{1}{16}$ D. x $\frac{1}{8}$ wide

$\frac{17}{32}$ Drill, $1\frac{1}{8}$ D.Spotface x $\frac{1}{16}$ deep 4 holes

Taper $\frac{1}{8}$" per ft. for Crown

Keyseat $\frac{7}{16}$ wide x $\frac{7}{16}$ deep, PW #60

Am.Std. Taper No. 2

Knurl

$\frac{11}{32}$ Drill, $\frac{1}{8}$-27NPT

Neck $\frac{1}{8}$ wide x $\frac{1}{16}$ deep

Spot for Set-screw Pc.No.___, Locate from Pc.No.___

Carburize, Harden & Grind

$\frac{11}{16}$ Core

$\frac{13}{32}$ Drill, $\frac{9}{16}$ C bore x $\frac{1}{4}$ deep

Peen end of handle in position

$\frac{1}{8}$ Sawcut

Broach

$\frac{1}{8}$ x 45° Chamfer

$\frac{3}{8}$-16NC-2, $\frac{3}{4}$ deep

Undercut $\frac{1}{4}$ wide x $\frac{1}{8}$ deep

-GENERAL NOTES-

10. All draft angles 7° un-less otherwise noted.
11. Fillets $\frac{1}{8}$ R, Rounds $\frac{1}{8}$ R. unless otherwise noted.
12. Unspecified radii .12
13. Finish all over.
14. Finish all over except___
15. Heat-treat to Rock-well C 52-56.
16. Use pattern No. 72141.
17. Pickle before machining.
18. Dimensions to be met after plating.
19. Polish after plating.
20. Sandblast before painting.
21. Locate holes from template No.___
22. Tumble after remov-ing sprue.

NOTE (appears on)	PC. No.	NOTE (appears on)	PC. No.	NOTE (appears on)	PC. No.	NOTE (appears on)	PC. No.
Bore	4	Fillet	11,12	Peen	9	Section	2
Broach	9	Finish	8(V),9(V),13,14	Pickle	17	Spot	7
Chamfer	8	Grind	6	Plate	2,18,19	Spotface	3
Core	3,8	Heat-treat	6,15	Polish	1,19	Tap	3,9
Counterbore	9	Keyseat	1,7	Ream	1,3	Taper	4,6
Countersink	2	Keyway	4	Relief (thread)	7	Template	21
Crown	4	Knurl	6	Rounds	11,12	Thread	1,5,9
Drill	1,2,3,9	Neck	6	Sandblast	20	Tumble	22
Draft	10	Pattern	16	Sawcut	9	Undercut	8

FIG. 15.43. Recommended wording of notes.

The following rules should be observed:

1. Dimension and extension lines should be placed so as to lie *in* or *per-pendicular* to the face on which the dimension applies. See Probs. 19.1.4 and 19.1.5.

2. Dimension numerals should be placed so as to lie in the plane in which the dimension and extension lines lie. See Probs. 19.1.8 and 19.1.14.

3. Leaders for notes and the lettered note should be placed so as to lie in a plane parallel or perpendicular to the face on which the note applies. See Probs. 19.1.18 and 19.4.7.

4. Finish may be indicated by the standard finish symbol (**V**). The symbol is applied *perpendicular to* the face with its point touching a short line lying in the surface. The symbol and line should be parallel to one of the principal axes. If the symbol cannot be applied in the above manner, the finish symbol may be attached to a leader pointing to the face. See Probs. 19.1.5 and 19.1.18.

5. Lettering of dimension values and of notes should be made so that the lettering appears to lie in or parallel to one of the principal faces of the pictor-ial drawing. To do this, the lettering must be the *pictorial representation of ver-tical figures*. Note the placement and lettering of the dimension values and the notes in Probs. 19.4.2 and 19.4.4.

The ANSI Standard permits lettering of pictorial drawings according to the unidirectional system, with either verti-cal or slant lettering, to allow use of mechanical lettering devices. If the uni-directional system is employed,

1. Dimension values are lettered to read from the bottom of the sheet.

2. Notes are lettered so that they lie *in the picture plane*, to read from the bottom of the sheet. Notes should be kept off the view, if possible.

DIMENSIONING STANDARD FEATURES

15.38.   NOTES.   These are word statements giving information that cannot be given by the views and dimensions. They almost always specify some standard shape, operation, or material, and are classified as *general* or *specific*. A general note applies to the entire part, and a specific note applies to an individual feature. Occasionally a note will save making an additional view; or even an entire drawing, for example by indicating right- and left-hand parts.

Do not be afraid to put notes on drawings. Supplement the graphic language with the English language whenever added information can be conveyed by so doing, but be careful to word the note so clearly that the meaning cannot possibly be misunderstood.

General notes do not require the use of a leader and should be grouped together above the title block. Examples are "Finish all over," "Fillets ¼R, rounds ⅛R, unless otherwise specified," "All draft angles 7°," "Remove burs," etc.

Much of the information provided in the title strip of a machine drawing is a grouping of general notes. Stock size, material, heat-treatment, etc., are general notes in the title of the drawing of Fig. 15.106.

Specific notes almost always require a leader and should therefore be placed fairly close to the feature to which they apply. Most common are notes giving an operation with a size, as "½ Drill, 4 holes."

Recommended wordings for notes occurring more or less frequently are given in Fig. 15.43.

When lower-case lettering is used, capitalization of words in notes depends largely on company policy. One common practice is to capitalize all important words. However, for long notes, as on civil engineering or architectural drawings, the grammatical rules for capitalization usually prevail.

15.39.   ANGLES.   The dimension line for an angle is a circle arc with its center at the intersection of the sides of the angle (Fig. 15.44). The value is placed to read horizontally, with the exception that in the aligned system large arcs have the value aligned with the dimension arc. Angular values should be written in the form 35°7′ with no dash between the degrees and the minutes.

15.40.   CHAMFERS.   Chamfers may be dimensioned by note, as in Fig. 15.45*A*, if the angle is 45°. The linear size is understood to be a short side of the chamfer triangle; the dimensioning without a note shown at (*B*) is in conformity with this. If the chamfer angle is other than 45°, it is dimensioned as at (*C*).

15.41.   TAPERS.   The term "taper" as used in machine work usually means the surface of a cone frustum. The dimensioning will depend on the method of manufacture and the accuracy required. If a standardized taper (see Appendix) is used, the specification should be accompanied by one diameter and the length as shown at (*A*) in Fig. 15.46. The general method of giving the diameters of both ends and the taper per foot is illustrated at (*B*). An

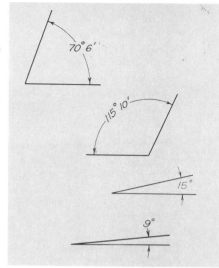

FIG. 15.44.   Dimensioning of angles.

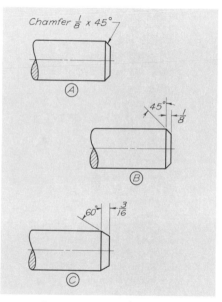

FIG. 15.45.   Dimensioning of chamfers.

FIG. 15.46.   Dimensioning of tapers.

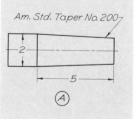

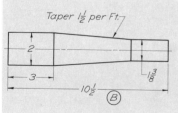

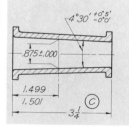

FIG. 15.47. Dimensioning of batters and slopes.

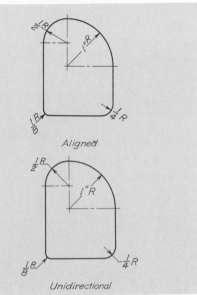

Aligned

Unidirectional

FIG. 15.48. Dimensioning of radii.

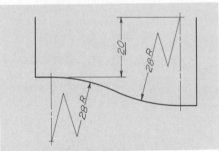

FIG. 15.49. Dimensioning of radii having inaccessible centers. Note that the positioning dimension is marked out of scale.

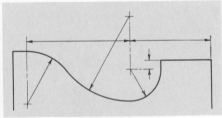

FIG. 15.50. Dimensioning a curve made up of radii. The position of centers must be given.

alternate method is to give one diameter, the length, and the taper per foot. Taper per foot is defined as the difference in diameter in inches for 1 ft of length. The method of dimensioning for precision work, where a close fit between the parts as well as a control of entry distance is required, is shown at (C). Because inaccuracy results from measuring at one end, a gage line is established where diameter is to be measured. The entry distance is controlled through the allowable variation in locating the gage line, and the fit of the taper is controlled by the accuracy called for in the specification of the angle.

15.42. BATTERS, SLOPES, AND GRADE. *Batter* is a deviation from the vertical, such as is found on the sides of retaining walls, piers, etc., and *slope* is a deviation from the horizontal. Both are expressed as a ratio with one factor equal to unity, as illustrated in Fig. 15.47. *Grade* is identical with slope but is expressed in percentage, the inclination in feet per hundred feet. In structural work angular measurements are shown by giving the ratio of run to rise with the larger side 12 in.

15.43. ARCS. Arcs should be dimensioned by giving the radius on the view that shows the true shape of the curve. The dimension line for a radius should always be drawn as a radial line at an angle (Fig. 15.48), never horizontal or vertical; and only one arrowhead is used. There is no arrowhead at the arc

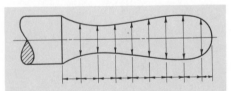

FIG. 15.51. A curve dimensioned by offsets.

center. The numerical value should be followed by the letter *R*. Depending upon the size of the radius and the available space for the value, the dimension line and value are both inside the arc, or the line is inside and the value outside, or, for small arcs, both are outside, as shown in the illustration.

When the center of an arc lies outside the limits of the drawing, the center is moved closer along a center line of the arc and the dimension line is jogged to meet the new center (Fig. 15.49). The portion of the dimension line adjacent to the arc is a radial line of the true center. A curved line made up of circle arcs is dimensioned by radii with the centers located, as in Fig. 15.50.

15.44. CURVES. Curves for which great accuracy is not required are dimensioned by offsets, as in Fig. 15.51. For greater accuracy, dimensions from datum features, as in Fig. 15.52, are recommended. Note in Fig. 15.52 that *any* pair of dimensions (indicated at *x*) could be given to greater accuracy than the others, in order to position a point for which greater accuracy is required.

15.45. SHAPES WITH ROUNDED ENDS. These should be dimensioned according to their method of manufacture. Figure 15.53 shows several similar contours and the typical dimensioning for each. The link (*A*), to be cut from thin material, has the radius of the ends and the center distance given as it would be laid out. At (*B*) is shown a cast pad di-

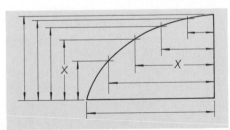

FIG. 15.52. A curve dimensioned from datum edges.

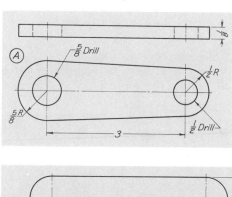

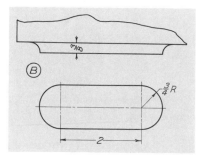

FIG. 15.53. Dimensioning of round-end shapes.

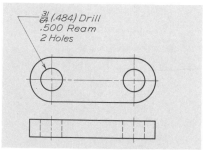

FIG. 15.54. Dimensioning of drilled and reamed holes.

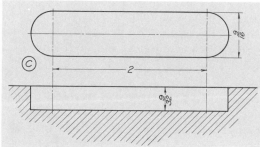

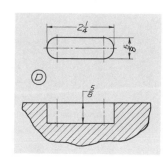

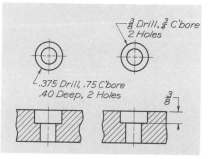

FIG. 15.55. Dimensioning of counterbored holes.

mensioned as at (*A*), with the dimensions most usable for the patternmaker. The drawing at (*C*) shows a slot machined from solid stock with an end-milling cutter. The dimensions give the diameter of the cutter and the travel of the milling-machine table. The slot at (*D*) is similar to that at (*C*) but it is dimensioned for quantity production, where overall length, not table travel, is wanted for gaging purposes. Pratt and Whitney keys and key seats are dimensioned by the method shown at (*D*).

15.46. DIMENSIONS AND SPECIFICATIONS FOR HOLES.

Drilled, reamed, bored, punched, or cored holes are usually specified by note giving the diameter, operation, and depth if required. If there is more than one hole of the same kind, the leader needs to point to but one hole, and the number of holes is stated in the note (Fig. 15.54). Several operations involving one hole may be grouped in a common note. Figures

15.54 to 15.57 show typical dimensioning practice for drilled and reamed, counterbored, countersunk, and spot-faced holes.

The ANSI specifies that standard drill sizes be given as decimal fractions, such as 0.250, 0.375, 0.750, and 1.500. If the size is given as a common fraction, the decimal equivalent should be added.

The leader to a hole should point to the *circular* view if possible. The pointing direction is toward the center (Fig. 15.9*B*). With concentric circles, the arrowhead should touch the inner circle (usually the first operation) unless an outer circle would pass through the arrowhead. Then, the arrow should be drawn to touch the outer circle.

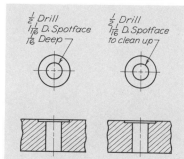

FIG. 15.57. Dimensioning of spot-faced holes.

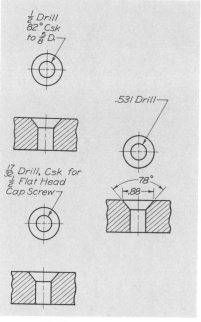

FIG. 15.56. Dimensioning of countersunk holes.

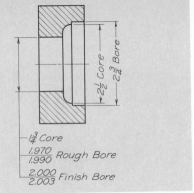

FIG. 15.58. Method of specifying several operations on a hole.

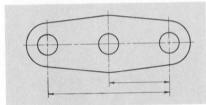

FIG. 15.59. Dimensions of position for holes.

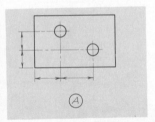

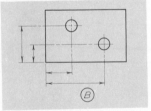

FIG. 15.60. Dimensions of position for holes.

Holes made up of several diameters and involving several stages of manufacture may be dimensioned as shown in Fig. 15.58. This method combines notes with the regular dimensions.

Threaded holes are dimensioned and specified as described in Chap. 16.

15.47. POSITIONING OF HOLES. Mating parts held together by bolts, screws, rivets, etc., must have holes for fastenings positioned from common datum surfaces or lines in order to assure matching of the holes. When two or more holes are on an established center line, the holes will require a dimension of position in one direction only (Fig. 15.59). If the holes are not on a common center line, they will require positioning in two directions, as in Fig. 15.60. The method at (B) is preferred when it is important to have the positions of both holes established from datum features (left and lower sides of the part).

The coordinate method for the positioning of holes (Fig. 15.61A) is preferred in precision work. The hole circle is often drawn and its diameter given for reference purposes, as in the figure. The diameter of a hole circle is invariably given on the circular view. The datum lines in this case are the center lines of the part.

Hole circles are circular center lines, often called "bolt circles," on which the centers of a number of holes are located.

One practice is to give the diameter of the hole circle and a note specifying the size of the holes, the number required, and the spacing, as in Fig. 15.61B. If one or more holes are not in the regular equally spaced position, their location may be given by an offset dimension, as shown at (C).

Figure 15.62 shows holes located by polar coordinates. This method should be used only when modern, accurate shop equipment is available for locating holes by angle.

15.48. CYLINDRICAL SURFACES. Cylindrical surfaces on a drawing having an end view may be dimensioned as in Fig. 15.63A; if there is no end view, "DIA" should be placed after each value as in Fig. 15.63B.

15.49. SPHERICAL SURFACES. Spherical surfaces should be dimensioned as in Fig. 15.64, by placing "SPHER" after the dimension value.

15.50. CURVED SURFACES. A position on a curved part may be misconstrued unless there is a specification showing the *surface* of the part to which the dimension applies, as in Fig. 15.65.

15.51. THREADS, FASTENERS, KEYWAYS, AND KEYSEATS. The dimensioning of these is given in Chap. 16.

FIG. 15.61. Positioning of holes on "hole circles." (A) from datum lines; (B) equally spaced; (C) one hole offset.

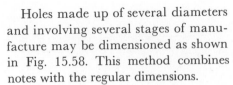

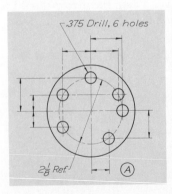

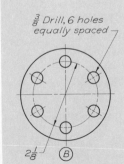

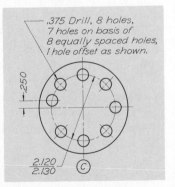

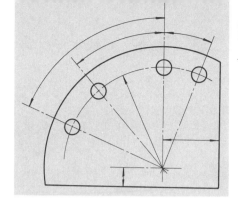

FIG. 15.62. Holes positioned by angle from datum line.

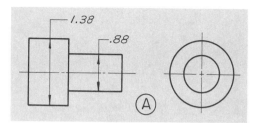

FIG. 15.63. Dimensioning of cylinders. (A) end view shown; (B) no end view.

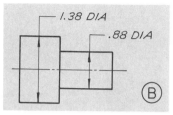

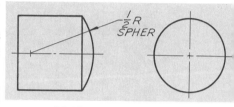

FIG. 15.64. Dimensioning a spherical surface.

15.52. THE METRIC SYSTEM.

A knowledge of the metric system is advantageous, as it is used on all drawings from countries where this system is standard and with increasing frequency on drawings made in the United States. The first instance of international standardization of a mechanical device is that of ball bearings, which have been standardized in the metric system.

Scale drawings in the metric system are not made to English or American scales, but are based on divisions of 10 as full size and then 1 to 2, 1 to 2½, 1 to 5, 1 to 10, 1 to 20, 1 to 50, and 1 to 100. The unit of measurement is the millimeter (mm), and the figures are all understood to be millimeters, without any indicating marks. Figure 15.66 is an example of metric dimensioning. A table of metric equivalents is given in the Appendix.

15.53. STANDARD SIZES, PARTS, AND TOOLS.

In dimensioning any machine part, it is often necessary to specify some standard thickness or diameter or the size produced by some standard tool. The ANSI Standard, prevailing company standard, or manufacturer's standard should be consulted in order to assure giving correct information.

Wire and sheet-metal gages are given by number and are followed by the equivalent thickness or diameter in decimal form.

Bolts and screws are supplied in fractional and numbered sizes.

Keys are available in manufacturer's numbered sizes or, for square and flat keys, in fractional sizes.

Rivets, depending upon the variety, are supplied in fractional or numbered sizes.

Drills are available in numbered, lettered, fractional, and metric sizes.

Reamers, milling cutters, and other standard tools are available in a variety of standard sizes.

The Appendix gives tables of standard wire and metal gages, bolt and screw sizes, key sizes, etc. ANSI or manufacturer's standards will give further information required.

PRECISION AND TOLERANCE

15.54. PRECISION AND TOLERANCE.

In the manufacture of any machine or structure, quality is a primary consideration. The manufacturing care put into the product determines its quality in

FIG. 15.65. Dimensioning a position on a curved surface.

FIG. 15.66. A metric drawing. Dimensions are in millimeters.

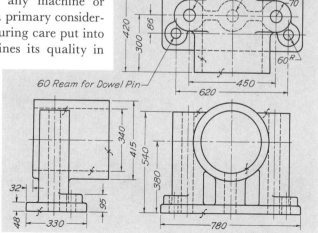

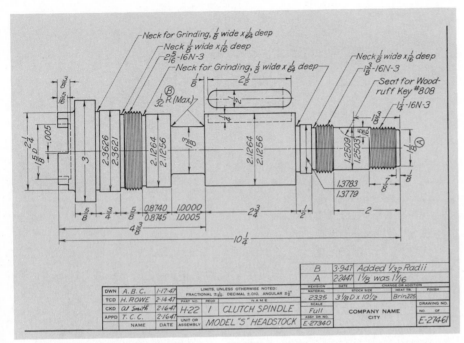

FIG. 15.67. Toleranced dimensions. The title strip gives tolerances on fractional, decimal, and angular dimensions. All other tolerances are specified directly as limits.

Tolerance is the allowable variation for any given size and provides a practical means of achieving the precision required. The tolerance on any given dimension varies according to the degree of precision necessary for the particular surface. For nonmating surfaces, the tolerance may vary from 0.01 in. for small parts to as much as 1 in. on very large parts. For mating surfaces, tolerances as small as a few millionths of an inch are sometimes necessary (for extremely close-fitting surfaces), but usually surfaces are finished to an accuracy of 0.001 to 0.010, depending upon the function of the part. Figure 15.67 shows variously toleranced dimensions on a machine drawing. Methods of expressing tolerances are given in paragraph 15.61.

In some cases, particularly in structural and architectural work, tolerances are not stated on the drawing but are given in a set of specifications or are understood to be of an order standard for the industry.

relation to competitive products on the market and, in part, its accompanying relative cost and selling price.

Precision is the degree of accuracy necessary to ensure the functioning of a part as intended. As an example, a cast part usually has two types of surfaces: mating surfaces and nonmating surfaces. The mating surfaces are machined to the proper smoothness and to be at the correct distance from each other. The nonmating surfaces, exposed to the air and with no important relationship to other parts or surfaces, are left in their original rough-cast form. Thus mating surfaces ordinarily require much greater manufacturing precision than nonmating surfaces. The dimensions on a drawing must indicate which surfaces are to be finished and the degree of precision required in finishing. However, because it is impossible to produce any distance to an absolute size, some variation must be allowed in manufacture.

15.55. FITS OF MATING PARTS. The working parts of any machine have some definite relationship to their mating parts in order to achieve a particular function, such as free rotation, free longitudinal movement, clamping action, permanent fixed position, etc. To ensure the proper relationship, the old practice was to mark the drawings of both parts with the same fractional dimension and add a note such as "running fit" or "drive fit," leaving the difference in size required (the allowance) to the experience and judgment of the machinist.

The tongue of Fig. 15.68 is to slide longitudinally in the slot. Thus, if the slot is machined first and measures 1.499 in. and the machinist, from his experience, assumes an allowance of

0.004 in., he will carefully machine the tongue to 1.495 in.; the parts will fit and function as desired. In making up a second machine, if the slot measured, say, 1.504 in. after machining, the tongue would be made 1.500 in. and an identical fit obtained; but the tongue of the first machine would be much too loose in the slot of the second machine, and the tongue of the second would not enter the slot of the first. The parts would, therefore, not be interchangeable.

Since it is not possible to work to absolute sizes, it is necessary where interchangeable assembly is required to give the dimensions of mating parts with "limits," that is, the maximum and minimum sizes within which the actual measurements must fall in order for the part to be accepted. The dimensions for each piece are given by three- or four-place decimals, the engineering department taking all the responsibility for the correctness of fit required.

Figure 15.69 shows the same tongue and slot as in Fig. 15.68 but dimensioned for interchangeability of parts. In this case, for satisfactory functioning, it has been decided that the tongue must be at least 0.002 in. smaller than the slot but not more than 0.006 in. smaller. This would provide an average fit similar to that used in the previous example. The maximum and minimum sizes acceptable for each part are then figured.

The value 1.500 in. has been assigned as the size of the minimum acceptable slot. This value minus the minimum clearance, 0.002 in., gives a size for the maximum tongue of 1.498. The maximum allowable clearance, 0.006, minus the minimum allowable clearance, 0.002, gives the amount, 0.004, available as the total manufacturing tolerance for both parts. This has been evenly divided and applied as 0.002 to the slot and 0.002 to the tongue. Thus the size of the maximum slot will be the size of the minimum slot *plus* the slot tolerance, or 1.500 + 0.002 = 1.502. The size of the minimum tongue will be the size of the maximum tongue *minus* the tongue tolerance, or 1.498 − 0.002 = 1.496.

A study of Fig. 15.69 will show that, made in any quantity, the two parts will allow interchangeable assembly and that any pair will fit approximately as any other pair, as planned. This system is essential in modern quantity-production manufacture. Quantity-production and unit-production methods are discussed in paragraph 15.80.

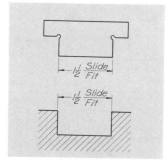

FIG. 15.68. Dimensioning a fit. According to this practice the machinist fits one part to the other.

15.56. NOMENCLATURE. The terms used in limit dimensioning are so interconnected that their meaning should be clearly understood before a detailed study of the method is attempted.

The following are adapted from ANSI definitions:

Nominal Size. The nominal size is the designation that is used for the purpose of general identification.

Dimension. A dimension is a geometric characteristic such as diameter, length, angle, or center distance.

Size. Size is a designation of magnitude. When a value is assigned to a dimension, it is referred to as the size of that dimension.

Allowance. An allowance is an intentional difference between the maximum material limits of mating parts. (See definition of "Fit.") It is a minimum clearance (positive allowance) or maximum interference (negative allowance) between mating parts.

Tolerance. A tolerance is the total permissible variation of a size. The tolerance is the difference between the limits of size.

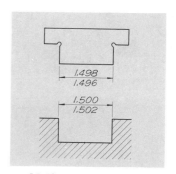

FIG. 15.69. Dimensioning a fit with limits. Tolerance on tongue, 0.002 in.; tolerance on groove, 0.002 in.; allowance, 0.002 in.

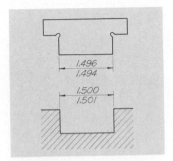

FIG. 15.70. An example of limit dimensioning. Tolerance on tongue, 0.002 in.; tolerance on groove, 0.001 in.; allowance, 0.004 in.

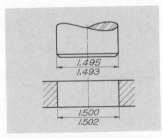

FIG. 15.71. A clearance fit. The tightest fit is 0.005 in. clearance; the loosest, 0.009 in. clearance.

Basic Size. The basic size is that size from which the limits of size are derived by the application of allowances and tolerances.

Design Size. The design size is that size from which the limits of size are derived by the application of tolerances. When there is no allowance, the design size is the same as the basic size.

Actual Size. An actual size is a measured size.

Limits of Size. The limits of size are the applicable maximum and minimum sizes.

Maximum Material Limit. A maximum material limit is the maximum limit of size of an external dimension or the minimum limit of size of an internal dimension.

Minimum Material Limit. A minimum material limit is the minimum limit of size of an external dimension or the maximum limit of size of an internal dimension.

Tolerance Limit. A tolerance limit is the variation, positive or negative, by which a size is permitted to depart from the design size.

Unilateral Tolerance. A unilateral tolerance is a tolerance in which variation is permitted only in one direction from the design size.

Bilateral Tolerance. A bilateral tolerance is a tolerance in which variation is permitted in both directions from the design size.

Unilateral Tolerance System. A design plan that uses only unilateral tolerance is known as a Unilateral Tolerance System.

Bilateral Tolerance System. A design plan that uses only bilateral tolerances is known as a Bilateral Tolerance System.

Fit. Fit is the general term used to signify the range of tightness which may result from the application of a specific combination of allowances and tolerances in the design of mating parts.

Actual Fit. The actual fit between two mating parts is the relation existing between them with respect to the amount of clearance or interference that is present when they are assembled.

Clearance Fit. A clearance fit is one having limits of size so prescribed that a clearance always results when mating parts are assembled.

Interference Fit. An interference fit is one having limits of size so prescribed that an interference always results when mating parts are assembled.

Transition Fit. A transition fit is one having limits of size so prescribed that either a clearance or an interference may result when mating parts are assembled.

Basic-Hole System. A basic-hole system is a system of fits in which the design size of the hole is the basic size and the allowance is applied to the shaft.

Basic-Shaft System. A basic-shaft system is a system of fits in which the design size of the shaft is the basic size and the allowance is applied to the hole.

In illustration of some of these terms, a pair of mating parts is dimensioned in Fig. 15.70. In this example the *nominal size* is 1½ in. The *basic size* is 1.500. The *allowance* is 0.004. The *tolerance* on the tongue is 0.002, and on the slot it is 0.001. The *limits* are, for the tongue, 1.496 (maximum) and 1.494 (minimum) and, for the slot, 1.501 (maximum) and 1.500 (minimum).

15.57. GENERAL FIT CLASSES. The fits established on machine parts are classified as follows:

A *clearance fit* is the condition in which the internal part is smaller than the external part, as illustrated by the dimensioning in Fig. 15.71. In this case the largest shaft is 1.495 in. and the smallest hole 1.500 in., leaving a clearance of 0.005 for the tightest possible fit.

An *interference fit* is the opposite of a clearance fit, having a definite interference of metal for all possible conditions. The parts must be assembled by pressure or by heat expansion of the external member. Figure 15.72 is an illustration. The shaft is 0.001 in. larger than the hole for the loosest possible fit. The allowance in this case is 0.003 in. interference.

A *transition fit* is the condition in which either a clearance fit or an interference fit may be had. Figure 15.73 illustrates a transition fit; the smallest shaft in the largest hole results in 0.0003 in. clearance and the largest shaft in the smallest hole results in 0.0007 in. interference.

15.58. SELECTIVE ASSEMBLY.

Sometimes the fit desired may be so close and the tolerances so small that the cost of producing interchangeable parts is prohibitive. In such cases tolerances as small as practical are established; then the parts are gaged and graded as, say, *small, medium,* and *large.* A small shaft in a small hole, medium in medium, or large in large will produce approximately the same fit allowance. Transition and interference fits often require a selection of parts in order to get the amount of clearance or interference desired. Antifriction bearings are usually assembled selectively.

15.59. BASIC-HOLE AND BASIC-SHAFT SYSTEMS.

Production economy depends to some extent upon which mating part is taken as a standard size. In the *basic-hole system,* the minimum size of the hole is taken as a base from which all

variations are made; the hole can often be made with a standard tool.

Where a number of different fits of the same nominal size are required on one shaft, as, for example, when bearings are fitted to line shafting, the *basic-shaft system* is employed, in which the maximum shaft size is taken as the basic size.

15.60. UNILATERAL AND BILATERAL TOLERANCES.

A unilateral tolerance is one in which the total allowable variation is in *one* direction, plus or minus (not both) from the basic value. A bilateral tolerance is one in which the tolerance is divided, with part plus and the remainder minus from the basic value.

15.61. METHODS OF EXPRESSING TOLERANCES.

Tolerances may be *specific,* given with the dimension value; or *general,* given as a note in the title block. The general tolerances apply to all dimensions not carrying a specific tolerance. The general tolerance should be allowed to apply whenever possible, using specific tolerances only when necessary. If no tolerances are specified, the value usually assumed for fractional dimensions is $\pm\frac{1}{64}$ in.; for angular dimensions $\pm\frac{1}{2}°$; and for decimal dimensions plus or minus the nearest significant figure, as, for example, ± 0.01 in. for a two-place decimal and ± 0.001 in. for a three-place decimal.

There are several methods of expressing tolerances. The method preferred in quantity-production work, where gages are employed extensively, is to write the two limits representing the maximum and minimum acceptable sizes as in Fig. 15.74. An internal dimension has the *minimum* size above the line, and an external dimension has the *maximum* size above the line. This ar-

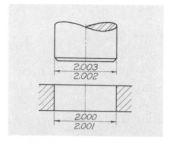

FIG. 15.72. An interference fit. The loosest fit is 0.001 in. interference; the tightest, 0.003 in. interference.

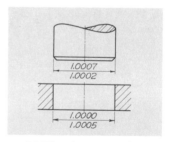

FIG. 15.73. A transition fit. The loosest fit is 0.0003 in. clearance; the tightest, 0.0007 in. interference.

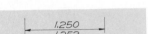

FIG. 15.74. A tolerance expressed as limits.

FIG. 15.75. Tolerances plus and minus.

rangement is for convenience in machining.

Another method is to give the basic size followed by the tolerance, plus and minus (with the plus above the minus), as in Fig. 15.75. If only one tolerance value is given, as at (*B*), the other value is assumed to be zero.

Unilateral tolerances are expressed by giving the two limits, as in Fig. 15.74, or by giving one limiting size and the tolerance,

$$\text{as } 2.750 + 0.005$$
$$\text{or } 2.750 \begin{array}{c} +0.005 \\ -0.000 \end{array};$$

for fractional dimensions,

$$\frac{1}{2} - \frac{1}{32} \text{ or } \frac{1}{2} \begin{array}{c} +0 \\ -\frac{1}{32} \end{array};$$

for angular dimensions,

$$64°15'30'' + 0°45'0''$$
$$\text{or } 64°15'30'' \begin{array}{c} +0°45'0'' \\ -0°0'0'' \end{array}.$$

Bilateral tolerances are expressed by giving the basic value followed by the divided tolerances, both plus and minus (commonly equal in amount),

$$\text{as } 1.500 \begin{array}{c} +0.002 \\ -0.002 \end{array} \text{ or } 1.500 \pm 0.002;$$

for fractional dimensions,

$$1\frac{1}{2} \begin{array}{c} +\frac{1}{64} \\ -\frac{1}{64} \end{array} \text{ or } 1\frac{1}{2} \pm \frac{1}{64};$$

for angular dimensions,

$$30°0' \begin{array}{c} +0°10' \\ -0°10' \end{array} \text{ or } 30°0' \pm 0°10'.$$

Millimeter Tolerance Equivalents. Because of expanding world-wide use, drawings are, when necessary, dimensioned in a dual system giving both *inch* and *metric* tolerances. Therefore, it is necessary to know the tolerance equivalents and the standards for "rounding off" the values. This information is given in the Appendix.

15.62.   DECIMAL PLACES.   A dimension value should be carried to the same number of decimal places as the tolerance. For example, with a tolerance of 0.0005 on a nominal dimension of 1½ in., the basic value should be written 1.5000. Tolerances for common fractional values should be given as common fractions, as ⅞ ± ¹⁄₆₄. Tolerances for decimal values should be given as decimal fractions, as 0.750 ± 0.010.

15.63.   FUNDAMENTALS FOR TOLERANCE SELECTION.   Before the engineer can decide on the precision necessary for a particular part and specify the proper fits and tolerances, he must have experience in the manufacturing process used and understand the particular mechanism involved. The following quotation from the ANSI Standard is pertinent: "Many factors, such as length of engagement, bearing load, speed, lubrication, temperature, humidity, and materials, must be taken into consideration in the selection of fits for a particular application."

A table of fits, such as the ANSI table of cylindrical fits (Appendix) explained in paragraph 15.67, may be taken as a guide for ordinary work.

In many cases practical experience is necessary in determining the fit conditions guaranteeing proper performance. Often it is difficult to determine the definite size at which performance fails, and critical tolerances are sometimes determined through exhaustive testing of experimental models.

It is essential to know the precision attainable with various machine tools and machining methods. As an example, holes to be produced by drilling must not be specified to a smaller tolerance than can be attained by drilling. Attainable manufacturing precision is discussed in paragraph 15.64. A knowledge of kinds and types of equipment is needed to assure that the tolerances specified can be attained.

15.64. MANUFACTURING PRECISION.

The different manufacturing processes all have inherent minimum possible accuracies, depending upon the size of the work, the condition of the equipment, and, to some extent, the skill of the workmen. The following *minimum* tolerances are given as a guide and are based on the assumption that the work is to be done on a quantity-production basis with equipment in good condition. Greater precision can be attained by highly skilled workmen on a unit-production basis.

In general, the following are recommended as tolerances for dimensions having *no effect on the function of the part;* for sizes of 0 to 6 in., $\pm\frac{1}{64}$; 6 to 18 in., $\pm\frac{1}{32}$; 18 in. and larger, $\pm\frac{1}{16}$ (or more).

Sand Castings. For unmachined surfaces, a tolerance of $\pm\frac{1}{32}$ is recommended for small castings and a tolerance of $\pm\frac{1}{16}$ for medium-sized castings. On larger castings the tolerance should be increased to suit the size. Small and medium-sized castings are rarely below the nominal size since the pattern is "rapped" for easy removal from the sand, and this tends to increase the size.

Die Castings and Plastic Molding. A tolerance of $\pm\frac{1}{64}$ or less can easily be held with small and medium-sized parts; for large parts, the tolerance should be increased slightly. Hole-center distances can be maintained within 0.005 to 0.010, depending on the distance of separation. Certain alloys can be die-cast to tolerances of 0.001 or less.

Forgings. The rough surfaces of drop forgings weighing 1 lb or less can be held to $\pm\frac{1}{32}$; for weights up to 10 lb,

$\pm\frac{1}{16}$; for weights up to 60 lb, $\pm\frac{1}{8}$. Because of die wear, drop forgings tend to increase in size as production from the die increases.

Drilling. For drills from no. 60 to no. 30, allow a tolerance of $+0.002 - 0.000$; from no. 29 to no. 1, $+0.004 - 0.000$; from $\frac{1}{4}$ to $\frac{1}{2}$ in., $+0.005 - 0.000$; from $\frac{1}{2}$ to $\frac{3}{4}$ in., $+0.008 - 0.000$; from $\frac{3}{4}$ to 1 in., $+0.010 - 0.000$; from 1 to 2 in., a tolerance of $+0.015 - 0.000$.

Reaming. In general, a tolerance of $+0.0005 - 0.0000$ can be held with diameters up to $\frac{1}{2}$ in. For diameters from $\frac{1}{2}$ to 1 in., $+0.001 - 0.000$; from 1 in. and larger, $+0.0015 - 0.0000$.

Lathe Turning: Rough Work. For diameters of $\frac{1}{4}$ to $\frac{1}{2}$ in., allow a total tolerance of 0.005; for diameters of $\frac{1}{2}$ to 1 in., 0.007; for diameters of 1 to 2 in., 0.010; for diameters of 2 in. and larger, 0.015.

Finish Turning. For diameters of $\frac{1}{4}$ to $\frac{1}{2}$ in., allow a total tolerance of 0.002; for diameters of $\frac{1}{2}$ to 1 in., 0.003; for diameters of 1 to 2 in., 0.005; for diameters of 2 in. and larger, 0.007.

Milling. When single surfaces are to be milled, tolerances of 0.002 to 0.003 can be maintained. When two or more surfaces are to be milled, the most important can be toleranced to 0.002 and the remainder to 0.005. In general, 0.005 is a good value to use with most milling work.

Planing and Shaping. These operations are not commonly used with small parts in quantity-production work. For larger parts, tolerances of 0.005 to 0.010 can be maintained.

Broaching. Diameters up to 1 in. can be held within 0.001; diameters of 1 to 2 in., 0.002; diameters of 2 to 4 in., 0.003. Surfaces up to 1 in. apart can be held within 0.002; 1 to 4 in. apart, 0.003; 4 in. apart and over, 0.004.

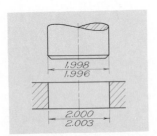

FIG. 15.76. Limits calculated from maximum and minimum clearances. See text for details.

Threads. Tolerances for ANSI threads are provided on the pitch diameter through the thread class given with the specification. For a given class, the tolerances increase as the size of the thread increases.

Grinding. For both cylindrical and surface grinding, a tolerance of 0.0005 can be maintained.

15.65. SELECTION OF TOLERANCES. A common method of determining and applying tolerances is to determine at the outset how much clearance or interference there can be between the mating parts *without impeding their proper functioning.* The difference between the tightest and loosest conditions will be the *sum* of the tolerances of both parts. To obtain tolerances for the individual parts, take half of this value; or if it seems desirable because of easier machining on one part, use slightly less tolerance for that part, with a proportionately larger tolerance for the part more difficult to machine. The following example will illustrate the procedure:

Assume that a running fit is to be arranged between a 2-in. shaft and bearing. It has been determined that in order to provide clearance for a film of oil, the parts cannot fit closer than 0.002 in., and in order to prevent excessive looseness and radial movement of the shaft, the parts cannot be looser than 0.007 in. The calculations follow:

Fit		Clearance
Loosest	= 0.007 max	
Tightest	= 0.002 min (allowance)	
Difference	= 0.005 (sum of tolerances)	
½ diff.	= 0.0025 (possible individual tolerance)	

Assuming that the shaft will be ground and the bearing reamed, 0.002 can be used for the shaft tolerance and 0.003 for the bearing tolerance since these values conform better to the precision attainable by these methods of production.

Figure 15.76 illustrates the completed dimensions. Note that the minimum hole is taken as the basic size of 2.000 and the tolerance of 0.003 applied. Then the largest shaft size will be the basic size minus the value for the tightest fit (the allowance); the shaft tolerance then subtracted from the maximum shaft size gives the minimum shaft size. From the figure, the 2.003 bearing minus the 1.996 shaft gives 0.007, the loosest fit; the 2.000 bearing minus the 1.998 shaft gives 0.002, the tightest fit.

15.66. ANSI PREFERRED LIMITS AND FITS FOR CYLINDRICAL PARTS.[3] This standard conforms with the recommendations of American-British-Canadian conferences. Agreement has been reached for diameters up to 20 in., and larger diameters are under study.

15.67. DESIGNATION OF ANSI FITS. The standard ANSI fits are designated by symbols that facilitate reference for educational purposes. These symbols are not to be shown on manufacturing drawings; instead, sizes should be specified. The letter symbols used are as follows:

> RC, running or sliding fit
> LC, locational clearance fit
> LT, transition fit
> LN, locational interference fit
> FN, force or shrink fit

[3] Excerpted from ANSI Preferred Limits and Fits for Cylindrical Parts (B4.1—1967) with the permission of the publisher, the American Society of Mechanical Engineers, 345 East 47th Street, New York, N.Y. 10017.

These letter symbols are used in conjunction with numbers for the class of fit; thus FN4 represents a class 4 force fit. Each symbol (two letters and a number) represents a complete fit, for which the minimum and maximum clearance or interference and the limits of size for the mating parts are given in the Appendix.

15.68. DESCRIPTION OF FITS.

The following is a description of each class of fit, with a reference in each case to the tables in the Appendix.

Running and Sliding Fits (Table 1). These fits provide a similar running performance, with suitable lubrication allowance, throughout the range of sizes. The clearances for the first two classes, used chiefly as slide fits, increase more slowly than for the other classes, so that accurate location is maintained, even when this is at the expense of free relative motion.

RC 1, *close sliding fits* accurately locate parts that must assemble without perceptible play.

RC 2, *sliding fits* are for accurate location, but with greater maximum clearance than RC 1. Parts move and turn easily but do not run freely, and in the larger sizes may seize with small temperature changes.

RC 3, *precision running fits* are about the closest fits expected to run freely, and are for precision work at slow speeds and light journal pressures. They are not suitable under appreciable temperature differences.

RC 4, *close running fits* are chiefly for running fits on accurate machinery with moderate surface speeds and journal pressures, where accurate location and minimum play are desired.

RC 5 and RC 6, *medium running fits*

are for higher running speeds, heavy journal pressures, or both.

RC 7, *free running fits* are for use where accuracy is not essential, where large temperature variations are likely, or under both these conditions.

RC 8 and RC 9, *loose running fits* are for materials such as cold-rolled shafting and tubing, made to commercial tolerances.

Locational Fits (Tables 2, 3, and 4). These fits determine only the location of mating parts and may provide rigid or accurate location—as in interference fits—or some freedom of location—as in clearance fits. They fall into three groups:

LC, *locational clearance fits* are for normally stationary parts that can be freely assembled or disassembled. They run from snug fits for parts requiring accuracy of location, through the medium clearance fits for parts such as spigots, to the looser fastener fits where freedom of assembly is important.

LT, *transition locational fits* fall between clearance and interference fits for application where accuracy of location is important, but small amount of clearance or interference is permissible.

LN, *locational interference fits* are used where accuracy of location is of prime importance, and for parts needing rigidity and alignment with no special requirements for bore pressure. Such fits are not for parts that transmit frictional loads from one part to another by virtue of the tightness of fit; these conditions are met by force fits.

Force Fits (Table 5). A force fit is a special type of interference fit, normally characterized by maintenance of constant bore pressures throughout the range of sizes. Thus the interference varies almost directly with diameter, and to maintain the resulting pressures

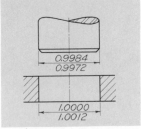

FIG. 15.77. An ANSI clearance fit. This one is class RC 6. Tolerance on shaft, 0.0012 in.; tolerance on hole, 0.0012 in.; allowance, 0.0016 in. clearance.

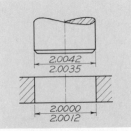

FIG. 15.78. An ANSI interference fit. This one is class FN 4. Tolerance on shaft, 0.0007 in.; tolerance on hole, 0.0012 in.; allowance, 0.0042 in. interference.

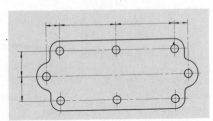

FIG. 15.79. Successive dimensioning. Tolerances accumulate.

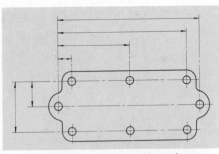

FIG. 15.80. Dimensions from datum. Position from datum is subject to only one tolerance, but the center distance between two holes positioned from datum is subject to variation of two tolerances.

within reasonable limits, the difference between its minimum and maximum value is small.

FN 1, *light drive fits* require light assembly pressures and produce more or less permanent assemblies. They are suitable for thin sections, long fits, or cast-iron external members.

FN 2, *medium drive fits* are for ordinary steel parts or for shrink fits on light sections. They are about the tightest fits that can be used with high-grade cast-iron external members.

FN 3, *heavy drive fits* are suitable for heavier steel parts or for shrink fits in medium sections.

FN 4 and FN 5, *force fits* are for parts that can be highly stressed, or for shrink fits where heavy pressing forces are impractical.

15.69. EXAMPLES OF DIMENSIONING STANDARD ANSI FITS. Assume that a 1-in. shaft is to run with moderate speed but with a fairly heavy journal pressure. The fit class chosen is RC 6. From Table 1 (Appendix) the limits given are:

Hole: $\begin{array}{l} +1.2 \\ -0 \end{array}$

Shaft: $\begin{array}{l} -1.6 \\ -2.8 \end{array}$

These values are thousandths of an inch. The basic size is 1.0000. Therefore, for the hole, 1.0000 + 0.0012 gives 1.0012 as the maximum limit, and 1.0000 + 0.0000 gives 1.0000 for the minimum limit. For the shaft, 1.0000 − 0.0016 gives 0.9984 for the maximum limit, and 1.0000 − 0.0028 gives 0.9972 for the minimum limit. The dimensioning is shown in Fig. 15.77. To analyze the fit, the tightest condition (largest shaft in smallest hole) is 1.0000 − 0.9984, or 0.0016, clearance. This is the

allowance. The loosest condition (smallest shaft in largest hole) is 1.0012 − 0.9972, or 0.0040, clearance. The values of these two limits are given in the table under "limits of clearance."

To illustrate further, suppose a 2-in. shaft and hub are to be fastened permanently with a drive fit. The hub is high-grade steel. Fit FN 4 has been chosen. Table 5 gives:

Hole: $\begin{array}{l} +1.2 \\ -0 \end{array}$

Shaft: $\begin{array}{l} +4.2 \\ +3.5 \end{array}$

These values are in thousandths of an inch. The basic size is 2.0000. Thus, for the hole 2.0000 + 0.0012 gives 2.0012 for the maximum limit, and 2.0000 − 0.0000 gives 2.0000 as the minimum limit. For the shaft, 2.0000 + 0.0042 gives 2.0042 for the maximum limit, and 2.0000 + 0.0035 gives 2.0035 for the minimum limit. The limits of fit are 0.0023 minimum interference and 0.0042 maximum interference. The allowance is 0.0042. The dimensioning of this fit is shown in Fig. 15.78.

Note in both the above cases that, in dimensioning, the maximum limit of the hole and the minimum limit of the shaft are placed below the dimension line. This is for convenience in reading the drawing and to help prevent mistakes by the machinist.

The ANSI fits are based on standard hole practice. Note in the tables (1 to 5) that the minimum hole size is always the basic size.

15.70. CUMULATIVE TOLERANCES. Tolerances are said to be cumulative when a position in a given direction is controlled by more than one tolerance. In Fig. 15.79 the holes are positioned one from another. Thus, the distance between two holes separated by two, three, or four dimensions will vary in position by the sum of the tolerances on all the dimensions. This difficulty can be eliminated by dimensioning from *one* position, which is used as a datum for all dimensions, as shown in Fig. 15.80. This system is commonly called baseline dimensioning.

Figure 15.81 is a further example of the effect of cumulative tolerances. The position of surface *Y* with respect to surface *W* is controlled by the additive tolerances on dimensions *A* and *B*. If it is important, functionally, to hold surface *Y* with respect to surface *X*, the dimensioning used is good. If, however, it is more important to hold surface *Y* with respect to surface *W*, the harmful effect of cumulative tolerances can be avoided by dimensioning as in Fig. 15.82. Cumulative tolerance, however, is always present; in Fig. 15.82 the position of surface *Y* with respect to surface *X* is now subject to the cumulative tolerances of dimensions *A* and *C*.

In machine drawing, overdimensioning a drawing may cause confusion in the shop due to cumulative tolerances. This is illustrated in Fig. 15.83, where one of the surfaces will be positioned by two dimensions, both of which are subject to a tolerance. Thus surface *Z* may be positioned with respect to surface *W* by means of dimensions *A*, *B*, and *D* and be within ±0.003 in. of the basic position; this variation is inconsistent with the tolerance on dimension *E*. The situation can be clarified by assigning smaller tolerances to dimensions *A*, *B*, and *D* so that, cumulatively, they will be equal to ±0.001 or less. This is poor practice, however, since it will probably increase the production cost. Another

solution is to increase the tolerance on dimension *E* to ±0.003 if the function of the part will permit. The best solution, however, is to eliminate one of the four dimensions, since one dimension is superfluous. If all four dimensions are given, one should be marked "REF," and its tolerance thus eliminated.

15.71. TOLERANCE BETWEEN CENTERS. In all cases where centers are arranged for interchangeable assembly, the tolerance on shafts, pins, etc., and the tolerance on bearings or holes in the mating pieces will affect the possible tolerance between centers. In Fig. 15.84, observe that smaller tolerances on the holes would necessitate a smaller tolerance on the center distances. A smaller allowance for the fit of the pins would make a tighter fit and reduce the possible tolerances for the center-to-center dimensions. Study carefully the dimensions of both pieces.

15.72. TOLERANCE OF CONCENTRICITY. Tolerance of concentricity is a special case of tolerance in which there is a coincidence of centers. In most cases, concentric cylinders, cones, etc., generated about common axes in manufacture, will be concentric to a degree of precision more than adequate for functional requirements, and no statement is required on the drawing concerning the allowable variation. However, mating pairs of two (or more) precise, close-fitting, machined cylindrical surfaces must have the axes of adjoined cylinders closely coinciding in order to permit assembly of the parts; thus it is sometimes necessary to give the permissible deviation from concentricity. Since the center lines of adjoining cylinders coincide on a drawing, the tolerance

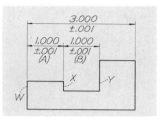

FIG. 15.81. Control of surface position through different toleranced dimensions. Here one dimension is successive.

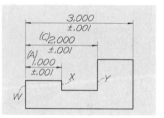

FIG. 15.82. Control of surface position through different toleranced dimensions. All dimensions are from datum.

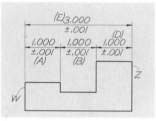

FIG. 15.83. Control of surface position through different toleranced dimensions. This drawing is overdimensioned.

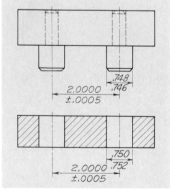

FIG. 15.84. Tolerance on centers. The parts will not assemble unless all features are held within the limits shown.

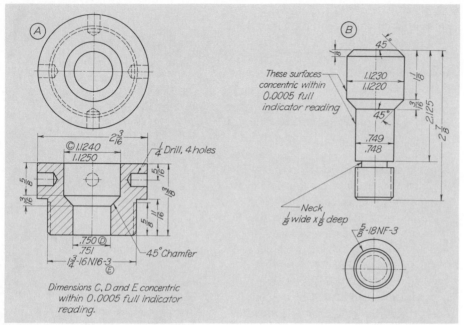

FIG. 15.85. Tolerance of concentricity. (*A*) shown by general note; (*B*) shown by note with leaders to surfaces.

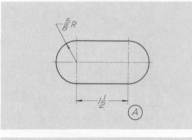

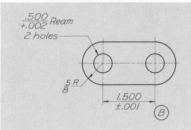

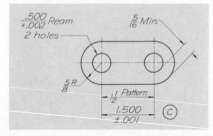

0.035 in. for a length of 1 in. and can be used as a basis for computing the tolerance in any given problem.

As an example, assume an allowable variation of 0.007 in.; then $(0.007/0.035) \times 1° = \frac{1}{5}°$ is the angular tolerance at 1 in. If the length is assumed as 2 in., the tolerance would be one-half the tolerance computed for 1 in., or $\frac{1}{5}° \times \frac{1}{2} = \frac{1}{10}°$, or $0°6'$.

15.74. COINCIDING CENTER LINES AND DIMENSIONS. In many cases the center lines for two different features of a part will coincide. Often one center line is for an unfinished feature and the other (and coincident) center line for a finished feature. Figure 15.86*A* shows the drawing of a link dimensioned for the patternmaker. If holes are to be machined in this link, the drawing would be as at (*B*); the patternmaker would not use the dimension between centers, as shown, but would assume the nominal dimension of 1½ in. with the usual pattern tolerance of $\pm\frac{1}{32}$ in. The clearest dimensioning in this case would be as at (*C*).

In any instance where there is a coincidence of centers, it may be difficult to indicate the limits within which the coincidence must be maintained. At (*C*) there are actually two horizontal center lines, one for the cast link and another for the hole centers. One method of controlling the deviation from coincidence is to give the wall thickness as a minimum, which is understood to apply in all radial directions.

In cases where the coincident center lines are both for finished features with differing tolerances, there may be a serious ambiguity on the drawing unless the dimensioning is specially arranged. Figure 15.87*A* shows a milled slot with

cannot be given as a dimension. One method of indicating it is to mark the diameters with reference letters and give the tolerance in note form as in Fig. 15.85*A*. The reference letters can be dispensed with if the note is applied directly to the surfaces, as at (*B*).

15.73. TOLERANCE FOR ANGULAR DIMENSIONS. When it is necessary to give the limits of an angular dimension, the tolerance is generally bilateral, as $32 \pm \frac{1}{2}°$. When the tolerance is given in minutes, it is written $\pm 0°10'$; and when given in seconds, it is written $\pm0'30''$. Where the location of a hole or other feature depends upon an angular dimension, the length along the leg of the angle governs the angular tolerance permitted. A tolerance of $\pm1°$ gives a variation of

FIG. 15.86. Coinciding center lines and dimensions. Clarification is obtained by giving dimensions for separate operations.

nominal dimensions and, on the coincident center lines, two accurate holes with a closely toleranced center distance. Unless the dimensioning is cleared by two separate dimensions, as shown, the machinist would not know the difference in tolerance. A somewhat more difficult case is shown at (*B*) where pairing holes are diagonally opposite. Unless all the holes are to be tolerated the same on their center distance, the dimensioning must be made clear with notes, as shown.

15.75. POSITIONAL TOLERANCES.

Figures 15.61 and 15.62 show holes positioned by rectangular or polar coordinates. This method of positioning by tolerances on two dimensions produces a square tolerance zone for the common case where the positioning dimensions are at right angles to each other. The engineering intent can often be specified more accurately by giving information that states the *true position,* with tolerances to indicate how far actual position on the part can vary from true position. True position denotes the basic or theoretically exact position of a feature. This method results in a circular tolerance zone when the tolerance applies in all directions from true position.

Features such as holes may be allowed to vary in any direction from the specified true position. Features such as slots may be allowed to vary from the specified true position on either side of the true-position plane. Thus there are two methods of applying true-position tolerances. Both methods are shown in Fig. 15.88.

When a feature is allowed to vary in any direction, a note in one of the following forms should be used:

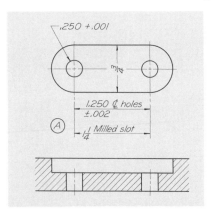

(*a*) 6 holes located at true position within 0.010 dia.

(*b*) 6 holes located within 0.005*R* of true position.

When features are allowed to vary from a true-position plane, a note in one of the following forms should be used:

(*a*) 6 slots located at true position within 0.010 wide zone.

(*b*) 6 slots located within 0.005 either side of true position.

When a feature is allowed to vary in any direction from true position, the position of the feature is given by untoleranced dimensions, as shown in Figs. 15.88 and 15.89. The fact that there is no allowable variation on the positioning dimensions should be indicated either on the drawing, in the title block, or in a separate specification, by a note —"Dimensions locating true position are basic." If this is not done, the word "basic" should be shown on each dimension subject to true-position tolerance.

15.76. MAXIMUM MATERIAL CONDITION.

Since all features of a part have allowable variations in size, for *mating* parts the least favorable assembly condition exists when the mating parts are both at their maximum material condition. This means that a hole is at its minimum size and a shaft at its maximum.

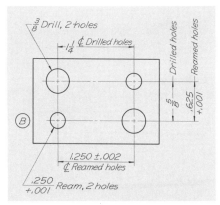

FIG. 15.87. Coinciding center lines and dimensions. Clarification is obtained by giving dimensions for separate features.

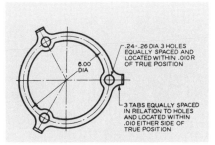

FIG. 15.88. True position dimensioning (ANSI).

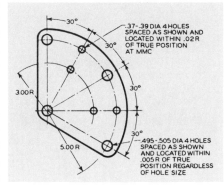

FIG. 15.89. True position dimensioning (ANSI).

FIG. 15.90. Zone tolerances (ANSI).

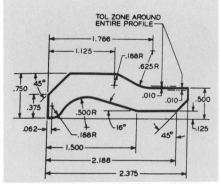

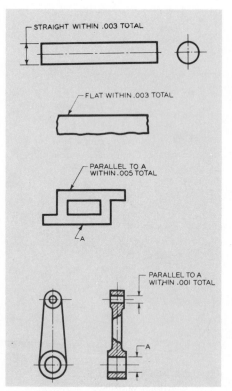

FIG. 15.91. Form tolerances. Straightness, flatness, and parallelism (ANSI).

FIG. 15.92. Form tolerances. Squareness (ANSI).

In terms of the cylindrical surface of a hole, it means that no point on the surface will be inside a cylinder having a diameter equal to the *actual* diameter of the hole, minus the true-position tolerance (diameter or twice the radius of the tolerance circle), the axis of the cylinder being at true position.

Where the maximum material condition applies, it is stated by the addition of "maximum material condition" to the true-position note, or by using the abbreviation "MMC," as shown in Fig. 15.89. Also, MMC may be stated in a general note or a specification.

In some cases it may be necessary to state a positional tolerance without reference to MMC. This is done by the reference "regardless of feature size" (abbreviated RFS), as shown on Fig. 15.89, or by a general note or specification.

In most cases the datum for true position is obvious from the dimension-ing itself, but where there may be any doubt, the positional tolerance note should read "XX holes located within .xxxR of true position in relation to datum *A*." Of course, datum *A* must be clearly marked on the drawing.

For a complete discussion of true-position tolerancing and related details, see ANS Y14.5—1966.

15.77. ZONE TOLERANCES. A zone tolerance may be specified where a uniform variation can be permitted along a contour, as in Fig. 15.90. For complete coverage, see ANS Y14.5—1966.

15.78. FORM TOLERANCES. Tolerances of form state how far actual surfaces may vary from the perfect geometry implied by the drawing. The methods of indicating straightness, flatness, and parallelism are shown in Fig. 15.91; squareness in Fig. 15.92; angularity, symmetry, concentricity, and roundness in Fig. 15.93; and parallelism with a surface and another hole in Fig. 15.94. For complete details on form tolerances, see ANS Y14.5—1966.

15.79. SURFACE QUALITY. The proper functioning and wear life of a part frequently depend upon the smoothness quality of its surfaces. ANSI Standard B46.1—1962 defines the factors of surface quality and describes the meaning

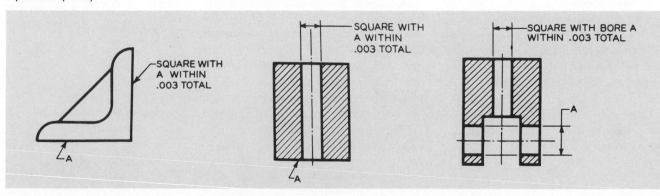

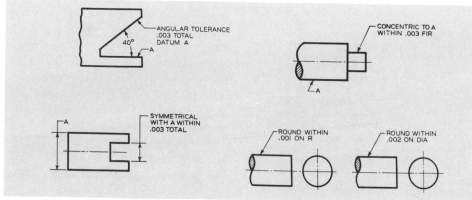

FIG. 15.93.   Form tolerances. Angularity, symmetry, concentricity, and roundness (ANSI).

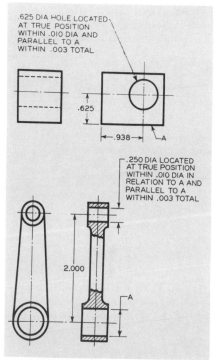

FIG. 15.94.   Form tolerances. Parallel to surface and parallel to hole (ANSI).

and use of symbols on drawings. Any surface, despite its apparent smoothness, has minute peaks and valleys, the height of which is termed "surface roughness" and which may or may not be superimposed on a more general "*waviness.*" The most prominent direction of tool marks and minute scratches is called "lay."

Roughness, produced principally by cutting edges and tool feed, is expressed as the arithmetical average from the mean in microinches (Fig. 15.95).

Roughness width is rated in inches as the maximum permissible spacing between repetitive units of the surface pattern (Fig. 15.95).

Roughness-width cutoff is the maximum width in inches of surface irregularities to be included in the measurement of roughness height (Fig. 15.95).

Waviness designates irregularities of greater spacing than the roughness, resulting from factors such as deflection and vibration (Fig. 15.95). The height is rated in inches as peak-to-valley height. The width is rated in inches as the spacing of adjacent waves.

Lay is the direction of the predominant surface pattern, produced by tool marks or grains of the surface ordinarily determined by the production method used (Fig. 15.95).

Although other instruments are used, the common method of measuring surface roughness employs electrical amplification of the motion of a stylus over the surface.

The symbol for indicating surface irregularities is a "check mark" with the

FIG. 15.95.   Surface roughness (ANSI).

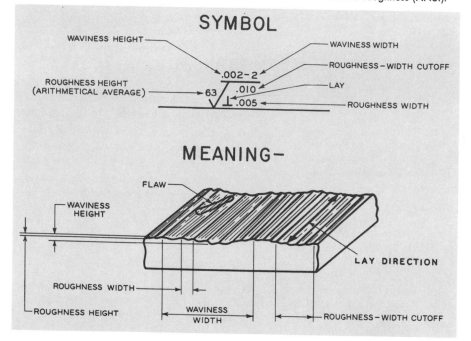

FIG. 15.96. Symbol. The roughness-height rating is placed at the left of the long leg.

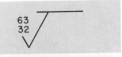

FIG. 15.97. Symbol. The specification of maximum and minimum roughness height indicates the allowable range.

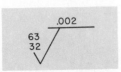

FIG. 15.98. Symbol. The maximum waviness-height rating is placed above the horizontal extension.

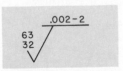

FIG. 15.99. Symbol. The maximum waviness-width rating is placed to the right of the waviness-height rating.

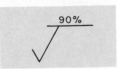

FIG. 15.100. Symbol. To specify the contact area, when required, the percentage value is placed above the extension line.

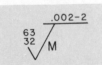

FIG. 15.101. Symbol. Lay designation is given by the lay symbol placed to the right of the long leg.

TABLE 15.1

Recommended roughness-height values (microinches)				
0.25	5	20	80	320
0.5	6	25	100	400
1.0	8	32	125	500
2.0	10	40	160	600
3.0	13	50	200	800
4.0	16	63	250	1000

Recommended waviness-height values (inches)					
0.00002	0.00008	0.0003	0.001	0.005	0.015
0.00003	0.0001	0.0005	0.002	0.008	0.020
0.00005	0.0002	0.0008	0.003	0.010	

Recommended roughness-width-cutoff values (inches)					
0.003	0.010	0.030	0.100	0.300	1.0000

horizontal extension as shown in Figs. 15.96 to 15.103. Symbols for lay and the application of the symbols on a drawing are shown in Fig. 15.104. The caption explains each case.

Values for roughness height, waviness height, and roughness-width cutoff are shown in Table 15.1.

Figure 15.105 is a chart adapted from several sources, giving the range of surface roughness for various methods.

PRODUCTION METHODS

15.80. PRODUCTION METHODS AND DIMENSIONING PRACTICE. Production methods can be classified as (1) *unit production,* when one or only a few devices or structures are to be built, and (2) *quantity* or *mass production,* when a large number of practically identical ma-

chines or devices are to be made with the parts interchangeable from one machine to another.

Unit-production methods almost always apply to large machines and structures, especially if they are custom-made. The large size to some extent eliminates the need for great accuracy. Each individual part is produced to fit or is fitted to the adjacent parts, frequently on the job, by experienced workmen in accordance with common fractional dimensions and directions given on the drawings. Since interchangeability of parts is no object, tolerances are not ordinarily used.

Similar methods are employed for unit production of smaller machines and mechanical devices. The drawings may have common fractional dimensions exclusively, on the assumption that the parts will be individually fitted in the shop. If this practice is followed, the manufacturing group accepts the responsibility for the proper functioning of the machine, and in some cases even for designing some of the parts. Skilled workmen are employed for this work. Usually one machine is completed before another is started, and the parts are not interchangeable.

Quantity-production methods are used whenever a great many identical products are made. After a part has been detailed, the operations-planning group of the engineering department plans the shop operations step by step. Then special tools are designed by the tool-design group so that, in production, semiskilled workmen can perform operations that would otherwise require skilled work-

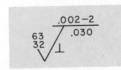

FIG. 15.102. Symbol. The roughness-width-cutoff rating is placed below the horizontal extension.

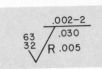

FIG. 15.103. Symbol. When it is required, the maximum roughness-width rating is placed at the right of the lay symbol.

men. These tools, built by a highly skilled toolmaker, simplify and greatly increase the rate of production.

One workman performs a single operation on a part; then it is passed to a second workman, who performs another operation; and so on until the part has been completed. Specially designed tools and equipment make it possible to produce economical parts that have dimensional exactness consistent with the requirements for interchangeability. The assembly may also be made by semiskilled workers using special assembly fixtures and tools.

With this system nothing can be left to the judgment of the workman. In preparing drawings intended for quantity production, the engineering department must assume full responsibility for the success of the machine by making the drawings so exact and complete that, if followed to the letter, the resulting parts cannot fail to be satisfactory. The engineering department alone is in a position to correlate corresponding dimensions of mating parts, establish dimensional tolerances, and give complete directions for the entire manufacturing job.

It is sometimes expedient for concerns doing unit or small-production work to follow the methods of the quantity-production system. The advantage they gain is interchangeability of parts, which can be produced without reference or fitting to mating parts.

15.81. PRINCIPLES FOR THE SELECTION OF DIMENSIONS.
Systematic selection of dimensions demands consideration of the *use* or *function* of the part and the *manufacturing process* to be used in producing it.

The *functional principle* recognizes that it is essential to dimension between points or surfaces associated through their functional relationship with points or surfaces of mating parts. This is accomplished by correlating the dimensions on a drawing of one part with the mating dimensions on the drawing of a mating part and arranging the tolerances of these dimensions to ensure interchangeability and proper functioning.

The *process principle,* or "workman's rule," as it is sometimes called, recognizes that the work of manufacture can be made easier by giving directly the dimensions the shop will find most convenient to "work to" in producing the part. Here a knowledge of manufacturing processes and procedure is necessary, as explained in Chap. 17.

In some cases there may be a conflict between these two principles. Whenever

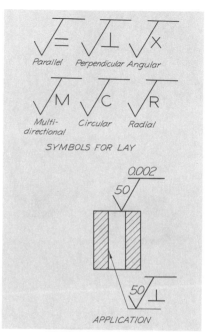

FIG. 15.104. Lay symbols and application of surface-quality symbols on the drawing.

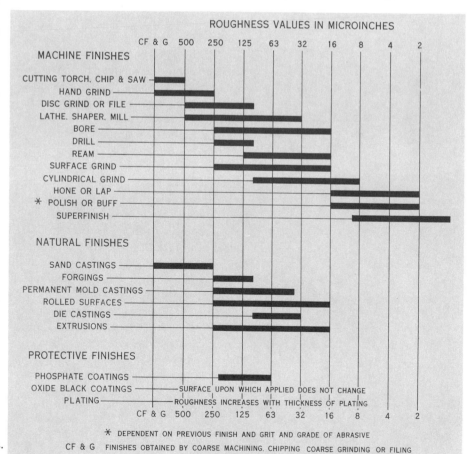

FIG. 15.105. Surface-roughness values.

there is, the functional principle must take precedence, as any attempt to satisfy both principles would result in overdimensioning, as described in paragraph 15.24, causing confusion for the workmen and possible malfunctioning of the part. With few exceptions, however, dimensions can be chosen to satisfy both principles.

15.82.   PROCEDURE FOR THE SELECTION OF DIMENSIONS.   A systematic procedure for selecting dimensions is of course desirable. The following steps can serve as a guide:

1. Carefully study the part along with its mating part or parts. Pay particular attention to the mating and controlling surfaces. Plan dimensions meeting functional requirements before placing any dimensions on the drawing so that you can correlate dimensions of mating parts.

2. Study the part to determine whether or not the manufacturing processes can be simplified by an alteration of any of the functional dimensions. Do not make changes if the functioning of the part would be impaired in any way.

3. Select the nonfunctional dimensions, being guided by the process principle, so that the dimensions will be readily usable by the workmen. Avoid overdimensioning and duplication.

In general, dimensions for mating surfaces are governed by the functional and process principles, and the dimensions for nonmating surfaces are governed by the process principle only.

Occasionally the manufacturing process will not be known at the time of dimensioning. This may happen when there are optional methods of manufacture, all equally good, or when the details of the manufacturing equipment

of a contracting firm are not known. When this is the case, the dimensions should be selected and toleranced in a logical manner so that the part, regardless of the method by which it is produced, cannot fail to be satisfactory. The size and location dimensions arrived at by the shape-breakdown system described in paragraph 15.22 apply here to a great extent since these dimensions fulfill most production requirements. Contracting firms often redraw incoming part drawings, dimensioning them for the most economical production with their own shop equipment.

15.83.   METHODS OF PART PRODUCTION. In following the process principle, the basic methods of part production—casting, forging, etc.—as described in Chap. 17, must be known. The manufacturing procedures followed with the particular type of part involved are then considered in selecting the dimensions. The only workman to be considered in dimensioning a part cut from solid stock is the machinist. For parts produced by casting, the workmen to be considered are the patternmaker (for sand castings) or the diemaker (for die castings) and, for finishing, the machinist. Forged parts subject to quantity production are dimensioned for the diemaker and machinist. For parts produced from sheet stock, the template maker, the diemaker, and the machinist must be considered; information for making the template and for forming the blank is obtained from a detail drawing showing the part as it should be when completed. In every case one drawing, appropriately dimensioned, must show the finished part.

The paragraphs that follow give examples of the dimensioning of machine parts for quantity production.

15.84. DIMENSIONING A PART MACHINED FROM STOCK.

Figure 15.106 is a detail drawing of the stud from the rail-transport hanger in Prob. 19.3.13. Study this assembly drawing to determine the function of the stud. The stud is produced by machining on a lathe. Cold-rolled steel stock, 1¼ in. in diameter, is used. The stock diameter is the same as the large end of the stud, thus eliminating one machining operation.

Shape breakdown of the part results in a series of cylinders each requiring two dimensions—diameter and length. The important functional dimensions have been marked (on Fig. 15.106) with the letters *A*, *B*, *C*, and *D*. Diameter *A* is given to correlate with the bore of the bearings; a four-place decimal limit provides for the desired fit. Dimension *B* is a three-place decimal limit to correlate with a similar dimension for the hole in the hanger. Dimension *C* is made 0.03 in. larger than the combined width of the two bearings in order to allow the inner races of the bearings to "creep." Dimension *C*, a two-place decimal, can vary ±0.030 in., but clearance for the bearings is assured under all conditions. Dimension *D* is made approximately 0.05 in. less than the length of the hanger hub to ensure that the nut will bear against the hanger rather than on the shoulder of the stud.

Functional dimensions need not always be extremely accurate. Note that dimensions *C* and *D*, with the relatively broad tolerance of two-place decimals, will allow the part to function as intended.

The thread specification can be con-

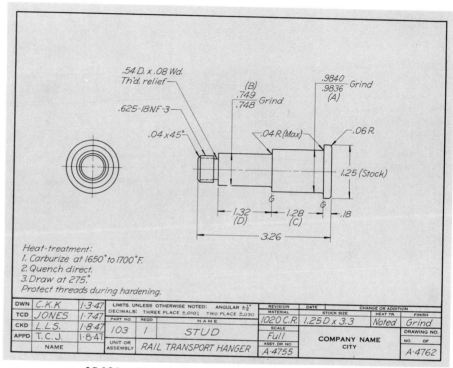

FIG. 15.106. Dimensioning a part machined from stock.

sidered as a functional dimension with the tolerance provided through the thread class.

The remainder of the dimensions selected are those that best suit shop requirements. Note that the thread length and over-all dimension cannot both be given, or the part would be overdimensioned.

15.85. DIMENSIONING A CASTING.

The dimensions required for sand castings can be classified as those used by the patternmaker and those used by the machinist. Since a cast part has two distinct phases in its manufacture, we will discuss a particular case first with the drawings made according to the multiple system explained in Chap. 17,

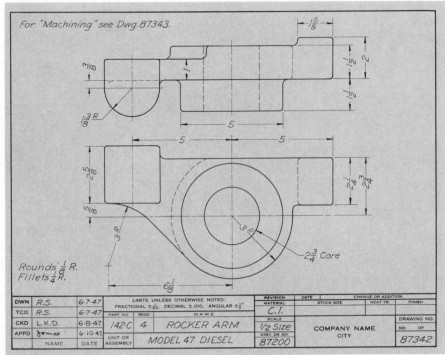

FIG. 15.107. Dimensioning an unmachined casting.

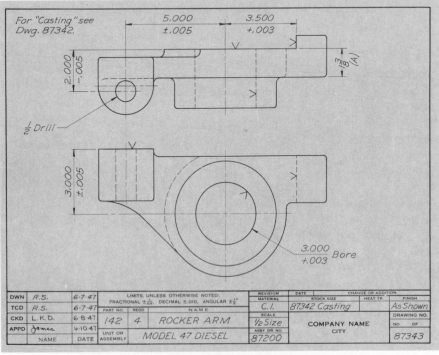

FIG. 15.108. Dimensions for machining a casting.

one for the patternmaker (Fig. 15.107) and one for the machinist (Fig. 15.108).

The *casting drawing* gives the shape of the unmachined casting and carries dimensions for the patternmaker only. Shape breakdown will show that each geometric shape has been dimensioned for size and then positioned, thus providing dimensions easily usable by the workman. Some of the dimensions might be altered, depending upon how the pattern is made; the most logical and easily usable combination should be given. Note that the main central shape is dimensioned as it would be laid out on a board. Note also that several of the dimensions have been selected to agree with required functional dimensions of the machined part although the dimensions employed have been selected so as to be directly usable by the patternmaker; they also achieve the *main objective,* which is to state *the sizes that the unmachined casting must fulfill when produced.*

The *machining drawing* shows only the dimensions required by the machinist. These are almost all functional dimensions and have been selected to correlate with mating parts. It is important to note that a starting point must be established in each of the three principal directions for machining the casting. In this case a starting point is provided by (1) the coincidence of the center lines of the large hole and cylinder (positioning in two directions) and (2) dimension *A* to position the machined surface on the back, from which is positioned the drilled hole. Dimension *A* is a common fraction carrying the broad tolerance of ±1/64 in., as there is no functional reason for working to greater precision.

Figure 15.109 is a drawing of the same part used in Figs. 15.107 and 15.108 but with the casting drawing dispensed with and the patternmaker's dimensions incorporated in the drawing of the finished part. In combining the two drawings, some dimensions have been eliminated, as the inclusion of all the dimensions of both drawings would result in over-dimensioning; thus the patternmaker must make use of certain machining dimensions in his work. In working from the drawing in Fig. 15.109, the patternmaker provides for machining allowance, being guided by the finish marks. In the drawing in Fig. 15.107 the engineering department provides for the machining allowance by showing and dimensioning the rough casting oversize where necessary for machining, and no finish marks are used.

15.86. DIMENSIONING A DROP FORGING.
Figure 15.110 is a drawing of a drop forging showing, at the left, the unmachined forging and, at the right, the machined forging. The drawing of the unmachined forging carries the dimensions it must fulfill when produced; these dimensions have been selected so as to be most useful to the diemaker for producing the forging dies. As the draft on drop forgings is considerable, it is shown on the drawing and dimensioned (usually) by a note. If the draft varies for different portions of the part, the angles may be given on the views. The dimensions parallel to the horizontal surfaces of the die are usually given so as to specify the size at the *bottom of the die cavity*. Thus, in dimensioning, visualize the draft as stripped off; then its apparent complication will no longer be a difficulty.

The machining drawing shows the dimensions for finishing. These are all functional, selected from the standpoint of the required function of the part. Study the illustration carefully.

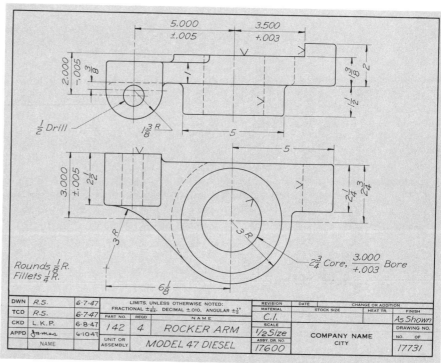

FIG. 15.109. All dimensions for a casting.

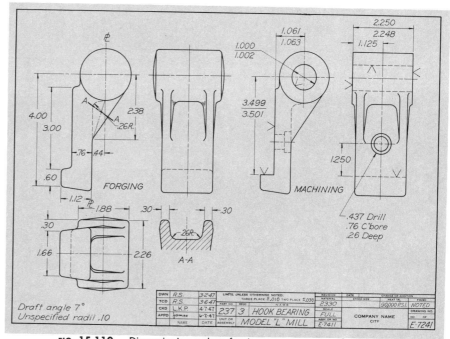

FIG. 15.110. Dimensioning a drop forging.

15.87. DIMENSIONING A SHEET-METAL PART. Parts to be made of thin materials are usually drawn showing the part in its finished form, as in Fig. 15.111. The template maker first uses the drawing to lay out a flat pattern of the part. If only a few parts are to be made, this template will serve as a pattern for cutting the blanks. Then the part will be formed and completed by hand. If a large number of parts are to be made, the diemaker will use the template and drawing in making up the necessary dies for blanking, punching, and forming. The work of both template maker and diemaker is simplified by giving the dimensions to the same side of the material inside or outside, whichever is more important from the functional standpoint, as shown in Fig. 15.111. Dimensions to rounded edges (bends) are given to the theoretical sharp edges, which are called *mold lines*. The thickness of the material is given in the "stock" block of the title strip. Note in the figure that the holes are positioned in groups (because of functional requirements) and that important functional dimensions are three-place decimals.

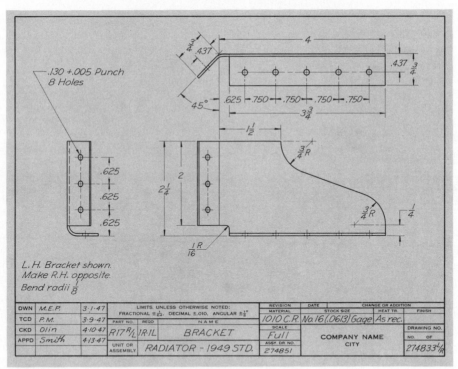

FIG. 15.111. Dimensioning a sheet-metal part.

PROBLEMS

The following problems are given as studies in dimensioning in which the principles presented in this chapter are to be applied. Attention should be given to the methods of manufacture, as described in Chap. 17. Assume a function for the part in order to fix the position of finished surfaces and limit possibilities in the selection of dimensions.

GROUP 1.   DIMENSIONED DRAWINGS FROM PICTORIAL VIEWS

The problems that are presented in pictorial form in Chaps. 5 to 8 can be used as dimensioning problems. Either dimension a drawing you have already made as an exercise in shape description or, for variety, select another. Because of the difference in method of representation, the dimensions on a pictorial drawing and those on an orthographic drawing of the same object will not necessarily correspond; therefore, pay no attention to the placement of dimensions on the pictorial drawings except for obtaining the sizes needed. A selection of 12 problems, graded in order of difficulty, is given below.

15.1.1.   Make a dimensioned orthographic drawing of Prob. 5.2.1, beam support. No finished surfaces.

15.1.2.   Make a dimensioned orthographic drawing of Prob. 5.2.5, slotted wedge. Slot and base are finished.

15.1.3.   Make a dimensioned orthographic drawing of Prob. 5.2.8, corner stop. Slot at top, cut corner, and base are finished.

15.1.4.   Make a dimensioned orthographic drawing of Prob. 5.2.11, guide base. Vertical slot, boss on front, and base are finished.

15.1.5.   Make a dimensioned orthographic drawing of Prob. 5.2.19, shifter fork. All contact surfaces are finished.

15.1.6.   Make a dimensioned orthographic drawing of Prob. 5.2.29, shaft guide. L-shaped pad and end of hub are finished.

15.1.7.   Make a dimensioned orthographic drawing of Prob. 8.1.13, jig angle. Finished all over.

15.1.8.   Make a dimensioned orthographic drawing of Prob. 8.1.19, angle-shaft base. Base and slanting surface are finished.

15.1.9.   Make a dimensioned orthographic drawing of Prob. 8.1.18, radial swing block. All contact surfaces are finished.

15.1.10.   Make a dimensioned orthographic drawing of Prob. 8.2.6, transverse connection. Base pads are finished.

15.1.11.   Make a dimensioned orthographic drawing of Prob. 8.2.7, chamfer-tool base. Contact surfaces are finished.

15.1.12.   Make a dimensioned orthographic drawing of the desurger case.

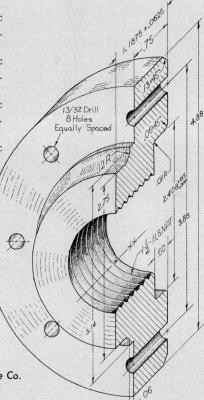

PROB. 15.1.12.   Desurger case. Courtesy of Westinghouse Air Brake Co.

GROUP 2. DIMENSIONED DRAWINGS FROM MODELS

Excellent practice in dimensioning is afforded by making a detail drawing from a pattern, casting, or forging or from a model made for the purpose. Old or obsolete patterns can often be obtained from companies manufacturing a variety of small parts, and "throw-out" castings or forgings are occasionally available. In taking measurements from a pattern, a shrink rule should be used; allowance must be made for finished surfaces.

GROUP 3. PIECES TO BE DRAWN AND DIMENSIONED

The problem illustrations are printed to scale, as indicated in each problem. Transfer distances with dividers or by scaling, and draw the objects to a convenient scale on paper of the size to suit. For proper placement of dimensions, more space should be provided between the views than is shown in the illustrations.

Use the aligned or horizontal dimensioning system, as desired. It is suggested that some problems be dimensioned in the complete decimal system.

15.3.1. Stud shaft, shown half size. Machined from steel-bar stock.

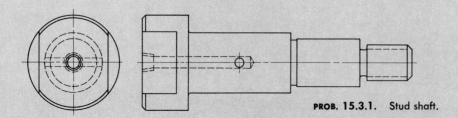

PROB. 15.3.1. Stud shaft.

15.3.2. Shaft bracket, shown half size. Malleable iron. Hole in base is drilled and counterbored for a socket-head cap screw. Base slot and front surface of hub are finished. Hole in hub is bored and reamed. The function of this part is to support a shaft at a fixed distance from a machine bed, as indicated by the small pictorial view.

15.3.3. Idler bracket, shown half size. Cast iron. Hole is bored and reamed. Slot is milled.

15.3.3*A.* See Prob. 15.3.3. Draw and dimension the right-hand part.

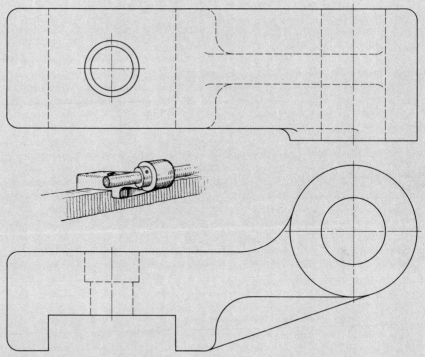

PROB. 15.3.2. Shaft bracket.

PROB. 15.3.3. Idler bracket, left hand.

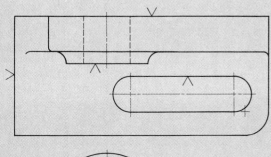

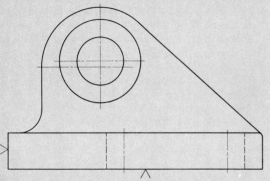

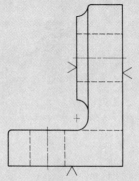

15.3.4. Filter flange, shown half size. Cast aluminum. The small holes are drilled. Add spot faces.

15.3.5. Boom-pin rest. Steel drop forging. shown half size; draw half size or full size. Add top view if desired. Show machining allowance with alternate position lines, and di-mension as in Fig. 17.8. All draft angles 7°. Holes are drilled, corner notches milled.

15.3.5*A.* Same as Prob. 15.3.5., but make two drawings; (*a*) the unmachined forging dimensioned for the diemaker and (*b*) the machined forging dimensioned for the machinist. Reference: Fig. 15.110.

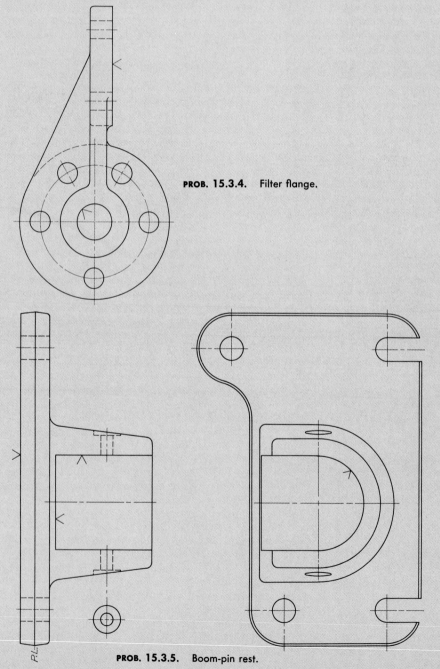

PROB. 15.3.4. Filter flange.

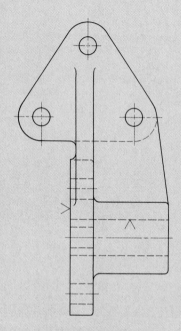

PROB. 15.3.5. Boom-pin rest.

15.3.6. Clutch lever. Aluminum drop forging. Shown half size, draw full size or twice size. Add top view if desired. Holes are drilled and reamed; ends of hub are finished; left-end lug is straddle milled; slot in lower lug is milled. Show machining allowance with alternate position lines, and dimension as in Fig. 17.8. All draft angles 7°.

15.3.6*A***.** Same as Prob. 15.3.6, but make two drawings: (*a*) the unmachined forging dimensioned for the diemaker and (*b*) the machined forging dimensioned for the machinist. Reference: Fig. 15.110.

15.3.7. Radiator mounting clip, LH, no. 16 (0.0625) steel sheet. Shown half size. Holes and slot are punched. Reference: Fig. 15.111.

15.3.8. Pulley bracket. Shown half size. Aluminum sheet, 24-ST, 0.032 in. thick. Reference: Fig. 15.111.

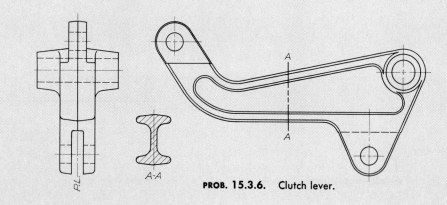

PROB. 15.3.6. Clutch lever.

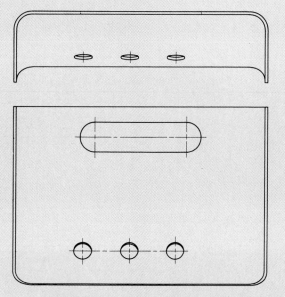
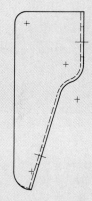

PROB. 15.3.7. Radiator mounting clip, left hand.

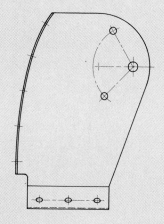
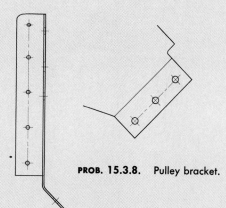

PROB. 15.3.8. Pulley bracket.

15.3.9. Using the scale shown, draw and dimension the check-valve body.

15.3.10. Using the scale shown, draw and dimension the hydrostatic pressure housing.

Draw to convenient scale on paper of a size adequate for clear representation. Use either the fractional or decimal system.

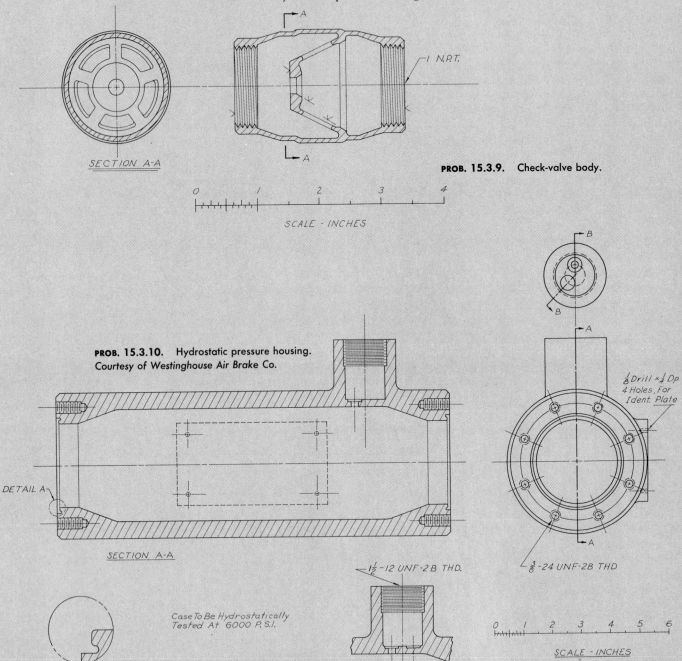

SECTION A-A

PROB. 15.3.9. Check-valve body.

SCALE - INCHES

PROB. 15.3.10. Hydrostatic pressure housing.
Courtesy of Westinghouse Air Brake Co.

DETAIL A

SECTION A-A

DETAIL A
View Enlarged Four Times

Case To Be Hydrostatically
Tested At 6000 P.S.I.

$1\frac{1}{2}$-12 UNF-2B THD.

SECTION B-B

$\frac{1}{8}$ Drill x $\frac{1}{2}$ Dp
4 Holes, for
Ident. Plate

$\frac{3}{8}$-24 UNF-2B THD.

SCALE - INCHES

15.3.11. Using the scale shown, draw and dimension the universal-joint housing. Use a scale and paper size adequate for clear representation. Either the fractional or decimal system may be used.

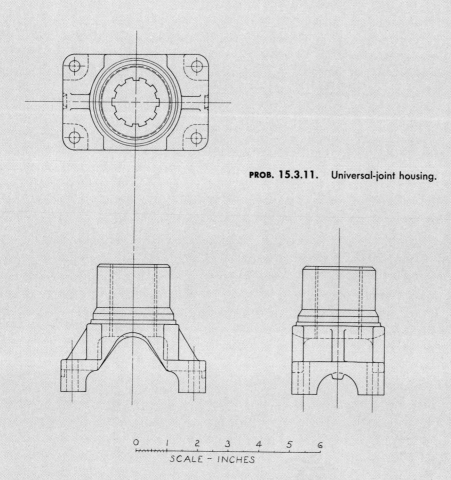

PROB. 15.3.11. Universal-joint housing.

SCALE – INCHES

15.3.12. Using dividers on the scale shown, draw and dimension the universal joint. Note that the flexing-rod portions are helical. Use either the fractional or decimal system.

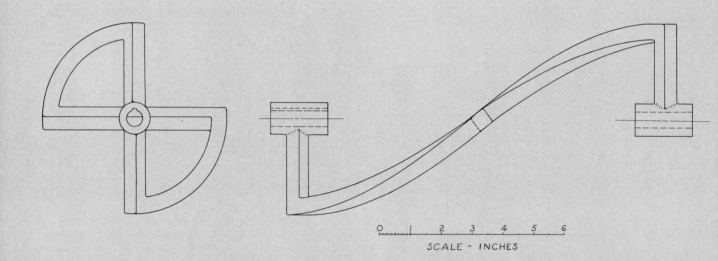

SCALE - INCHES

PROB. 15.3.12. Universal joint.

GROUP 4. DIMENSIONED DRAWINGS FROM AN ASSEMBLY OR DESIGN DRAWING

The assembly drawings given in the problem section of Chap. 19 are well suited for exercises in dimensioning detail working drawings. The assembly shows the position of each part, and the function can be understood by a study of the motion, relationship, etc., of the different parts. Note particularly the mating and controlling surfaces and the logical reference surfaces for dimensions of position. Inasmuch as the dimensioning of an assembly drawing is crowded, and it will probably not even have the same views as the detail drawing of one of the parts, disregard the position and selection of the assembly dimensions, and use them only to obtain sizes. The following are suggested:

15.4.1. Detail drawing of shaft, Prob. 19.3.3.

15.4.2. Detail drawing of bushing, Prob. 19.3.3.

15.4.3. Detail drawing of bracket, Prob. 19.3.3.

15.4.4. Detail drawing of body, Prob. 19.3.7.

15.4.5. Detail drawing of hanger, Prob. 19.3.13.

15.4.6. Detail drawing of rack, Prob. 19.3.9.

15.4.7. Detail drawing of rack housing, Prob. 19.3.9.

15.4.8. Detail drawing of cover, Prob. 19.3.9.

15.4.9. Detail drawing of base, Prob. 19.3.1.

15.4.10. Detail drawing of base, Prob. 19.7.3.

15.4.11. Detail drawing of jaw, Prob. 19.7.3.

15.4.12. Detail drawing of screw, Prob. 19.7.3.

15.4.13. Detail drawing of screw bushing, Prob. 19.7.3.

15.4.14. Detail drawing of body (drop forging), Prob. 19.4.7.

15.4.15. Detail drawing of base, Prob. 19.7.1.

15.4.16. Detail drawing of frame, Prob. 19.7.1.

15.4.17. Detail drawing of frame, Prob. 19.7.2.

15.4.18. Detail drawing of ram, Prob. 19.7.2.

15.4.19. Detail drawing of pinion shaft, Prob. 19.7.2.

15.4.20. Detail drawing of base, Prob. 19.7.2.

15.4.21. Detail drawing of cover, Prob. 19.7.2.

15.4.22. Detail drawing of sleeve ball, Prob. 19.7.2.

15.4.23. Detail drawing of stud ball, Prob. 19.7.2.

15.4.24. Detail drawing of body, Prob. 19.4.5.

15.4.25. Detail drawing of spring, Prob. 19.4.5.

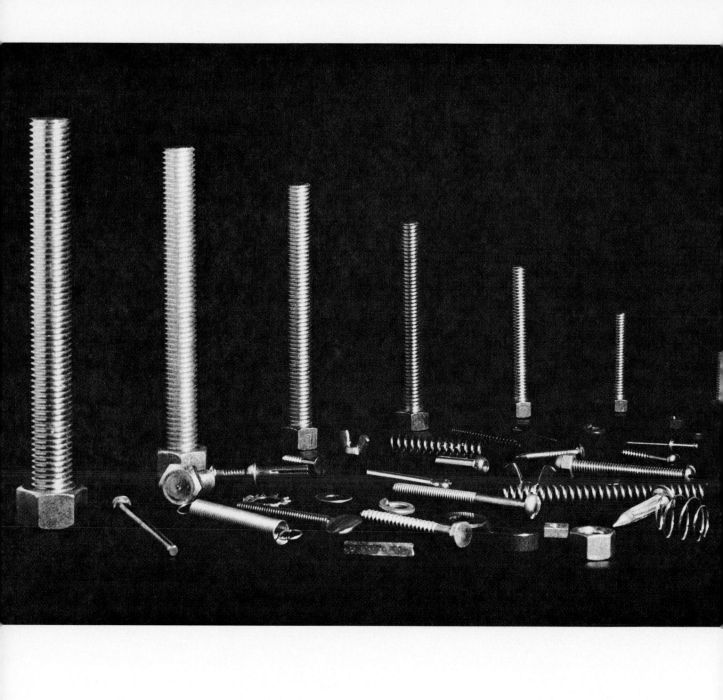

Practically every machine or structure made of more than one single piece must have a fastener or fasteners to hold the pieces together or, often, to allow for disassembly. Many forms are needed in order to fasten similar and dissimilar materials temporarily or permanently. The picture displays a diversity of screw threads and fasteners.

Machine Elements: Threads, Fasteners, Keys, Rivets, and Springs

16

16.1. A screw thread is the functional element used on bolts, nuts, cap screws, wood screws, and the like and on shafts or similar parts employed for transmitting power or for adjustment. Screw threads occur in one form or another on practically all engineering products. Consequently, in making working drawings, there is the repeated necessity to *represent* and *specify* screw threads.

16.2. **HISTORY.** The earliest records of the screw are found in the writings of Archimedes (278 to 212 B.C.). Although specimens of ancient Greek and Roman screws are so rare as to indicate that they were seldom used, there are many from the later Middle Ages; and it is known that crude lathes and dies were used to cut threads in the latter period. Most early screws were made by hand, by forging the head, cutting the slot with a saw, and fashioning the screw with a file. In America in colonial times wood screws were blunt on the ends; the gimlet point did not appear until 1846. Iron screws were made for each threaded hole. There was no interchanging of parts, and nuts had to be tied to their own bolts. In England, Sir Joseph Whitworth made the first attempt to set up a uniform standard in 1841. His system was generally adopted there but not in the United States.

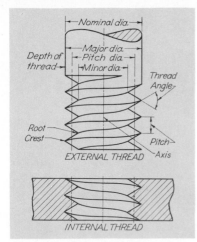

FIG. 16.1. Screw-thread terminology. See paragraph 16.4 for details.

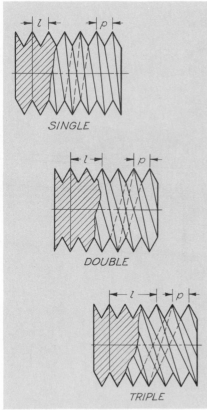

FIG. 16.2. Multiple threads. Note that, for a single thread, lead and pitch are identical values; for a double thread, lead is twice the pitch; and for a triple thread, lead is three times the pitch.

16.3. STANDARDIZATION. The initial attempt to standardize screw threads in the United States came in 1864 with the adoption of a report prepared by a committee appointed by the Franklin Institute. The system, designed by William Sellers, came into general use and was known as the "Franklin Institute thread," the "Sellers thread," or the "United States thread." It fulfilled the need for a general-purpose thread at that period; but with the coming of the automobile, the airplane, and other modern equipment, it became inadequate. Through the efforts of the various engineering societies, the Bureau of Standards, and others, the National Screw Thread Commission was authorized by act of Congress in 1918 and inaugurated the present standards. The work has been carried on by the ANSI and by the Interdepartmental Screw Thread Committee of the U.S. Departments of Defense, Army, Navy, Air Force, and Commerce. Later, these organizations, working in cooperation with representatives of the British and Canadian governments and standards associations, developed an agreement covering a general-purpose thread that fulfills the basic requirements for interchangeability of threaded products produced in the three countries. The "Declaration of Accord" establishing the Unified Screw Thread was signed in Washington, D.C., on November 18, 1948.

Essential features of the Unified and other threads are given in this chapter, while standards covering them are listed in the Appendix.

16.4. SCREW-THREAD TERMINOLOGY

Screw Thread (Thread). A ridge of uniform section in the form of a helix on the external or internal surface of a cylinder or cone.

Straight Thread. A thread formed on a cylinder (Fig. 16.1).

Taper Thread. A thread formed on a cone.

External Thread (Screw). A thread on the external surface of a cylinder or cone (Fig. 16.1).

Internal Thread (Nut). A thread on the internal surface of a cylinder or cone (Fig. 16.1).

Right-hand Thread. A thread which, when viewed axially, winds in a clockwise and receding direction. Threads are always right-hand unless otherwise specified.

Left-hand Thread. A thread which, when viewed axially, winds in a counterclockwise and receding direction. All left-hand threads are designated "LH."

Form. The profile (cross section) of the thread. Figure 16.3 shows various forms.

Crest. The edge or surface that joins the sides of a thread and is farthest from the cylinder or cone from which the thread projects (Fig. 16.1).

Root. The edge or surface that joins the sides of adjacent thread forms and coincides with the cylinder or cone from which the thread projects (Fig. 16.1).

Pitch. The distance between corresponding points on adjacent thread forms measured parallel to the axis (Fig. 16.1). This distance is a measure of the size of the thread form used.

Lead. The distance a threaded part moves axially, with respect to a fixed mating part, in one complete revolution. See multiple thread (below) and Fig. 16.2.

Threads per Inch. The reciprocal of the pitch and the value specified to govern the size of the thread form.

Major Diameter. The largest diameter of a screw thread (Fig. 16.1).

Minor Diameter. The smallest diameter of a screw thread (Fig. 16.1).

Pitch Diameter. On a straight thread, the diameter of an imaginary cylinder, the surface of which cuts the thread forms where the width of the thread and groove are equal (Fig. 16.1). The clearance between two mating threads is controlled largely by closely toleranced pitch diameters.

Depth of Thread. The distance between crest and root measured normal to the axis (Fig. 16.1).

Single Thread. A thread having the thread form produced on but one helix of the cylinder (Fig. 16.2). See multiple thread (below). On a single thread, the lead and pitch are equivalent. Threads are always single unless otherwise specified.

Multiple Thread. A thread combination having the same form produced on two or more helices of the cylinder (Fig. 16.2). For a multiple thread, the lead is an integral multiple of the pitch, that is, on a *double thread* the lead is twice the pitch, on a *triple thread,* three times the pitch, etc. A multiple thread permits a more rapid advance without a coarser (larger) thread form. Note that the helices of a double thread start 180° apart; those of a triple thread, 120° apart; and those of a quadruple thread, 90° apart.

16.5. THREAD FORMS.

Screw threads are used on fasteners, on devices for making adjustments, and for the transmission of power and motion. For these different purposes, a number of thread forms are in use (Fig. 16.3). The dimensions given in the figure are those of the basic thread forms. In practical usage,

clearance must be provided between the external and internal threads.

The *sharp V,* formerly used to a limited extent, is rarely employed now; it is difficult to maintain sharp roots in quantity production. The form is of interest, however, as the basis of more practical V-type threads; also, because of its simplicity, it is used on drawings as a conventional representation for other (V-type) threads.

V-type threads are employed primarily on fasteners and for making adjustments. For these purposes, the standard thread form in the United States is the *American National.* This form is also the basis for the Unified Screw Thread standard of the United States, Canada, and Great Britain and as such is known as the *Unified* thread. As illustrated in Fig. 16.3, the form is that of the maximum external thread. Observe that while the crest may be flat or rounded, the root is rounded by design or as a result of tool wear. The American National thread is by far the most commonly used thread in this country.

The 60° *stub* form is sometimes preferred when, instead of multiple threads, a single National-form thread would be too deep.

FIG. 16.3. Thread profiles. See paragraph 16.5 for the explanation of each type.

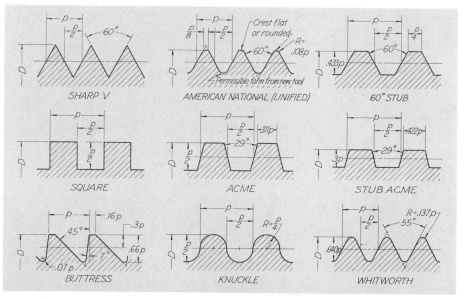

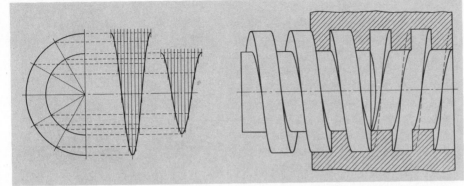

FIG. 16.4. True representation of a square thread, external and internal. Each thread (crest and root) line is a plotted helix.

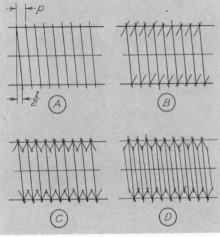

FIG. 16.5. Stages in construction for drawing a single V thread. Lay out pitch and half-lead and draw crest lines (*A*), start thread contour (*B*), complete thread contour (*C*), and draw root lines (*D*).

The former British standard was the *Whitworth*, at 55°, with crests and roots rounded. The *British Association Standard*, at 47½°, measured in the metric system, is used for small threads. The *French* and the *International Metric Standards* have a form similar to the American National but are dimensioned in the metric system.

The V shapes are not desirable for transmitting power since part of the thrust tends to burst the nut. This does not happen when a *square thread* is used as it transmits all the forces nearly parallel to the axis of the screw. The square thread can have, evidently, only half the number of threads in the same axial space as a V thread of the same pitch, and thus in shear it is only half as strong. Because of manufacturing difficulties, the square-thread form is sometimes modified by providing a slight (5°) taper to the sides.

The *Acme* has generally replaced the square thread because it is stronger, more easily produced, and permits the use of a disengaging or split nut.

The *Stub Acme* is a strong thread suited to power applications where space limitation makes it desirable.

The *buttress*, for transmitting power in only one direction, has the efficiency of the square and the strength of the V thread. It was formerly produced with a perpendicular pressure flank (face); the newer 7° slope is more easily manufactured. Sometimes called the "breechblock" thread, it is used to withstand the pressure on breech blocks of large guns.

The *knuckle* thread is especially suitable when threads are to be molded or rolled in sheet metal. It can be observed on glass jars and in a shallow form on bases of ordinary incandescent lamps.

Internal screw threads are produced by cutting, while external threads are made by cutting or rolling. Tests show that rolled threads are considerably stronger than cut threads. Through cold forging, rolling adds toughness and strength to the threaded portion.

16.6. THREAD REPRESENTATION. The true representation of a screw thread is almost never used in making working drawings. In true representation, the crest and root lines (Fig. 16.4) appear as the projections of helices (see Helix, paragraph 3.71), which are extremely laborious to draw. Where true representation is desirable, on advertising, elaborate display drawings, etc., templates can be made of cardboard or celluloid to assist in drawing the helices.

On practical working drawings, threads are given a semiconventional or symbolic representation, which provides thread pictures adequate for manufacturing purposes.

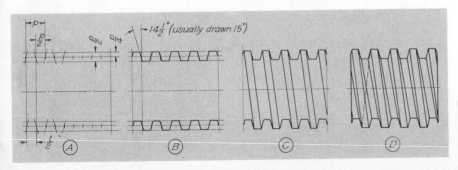

FIG. 16.6 Stages in drawing a single Acme thread. Because of the shape of the thread, the pitch diameter must first be located (*A*); then the thread form is drawn (*B*), and completed (*C*) and (*D*).

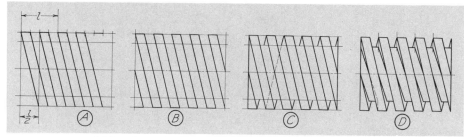

FIG. 16.7. Stages in drawing a double square thread. The lead is twice the pitch. Note that after spacing the lead and pitch (A), crest and root lines are drawn (B) and (C); then the base line of the thread is added (D).

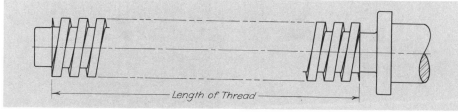

16.7. SEMICONVENTIONAL REPRESENTATION.

This simplifies the drawing of the thread principally by conventionalizing the projection of the helix into a straight line. Where applicable with certain thread forms, further simplifications are made. For example, the 29° angle of the Acme and 29° stub forms are drawn at 30°, and the American National form is represented by the sharp V. In general, true pitch should be shown, although a small increase or decrease in pitch is permissible so as to have even units of measure in making the drawing. Thus seven threads per inch may be increased to eight, or four and one-half may be decreased to four. Remember this is only to simplify the drawing—the actual threads per inch must be specified in the dimensioning.

To draw a thread semiconventionally, you must know whether it is external or internal, the form, the major diameter, the pitch, its multiplicity, and whether it is right- or left-hand. Figure 16.5 illustrates the stages in drawing an American National, or sharp V; Fig. 16.6, an Acme; and Fig. 16.7, a square thread. Figure 16.5, showing the V thread, illustrates the method of drawing a thread semiconventionally. At (A) the diameter is laid out, and on it the pitch is measured on the upper line. This thread is a single thread; therefore, the pitch is equal to the lead, and the helix will advance $p/2 = l/2$ in 180°. This distance is laid off on the bottom diameter line, and the crest lines are drawn in. One side of the V form is drawn at (B), and it is completed at (C). At (D), the root lines are added. As can be seen from Figs. 16.5 to 16.7, the stages in drawing any thread semiconventionally are similar; the principal difference is in the thread form.

The square thread in Fig. 16.7 is double, while that in Fig. 16.8 is single and left-hand. Observe in Fig. 16.8 that it is unnecessary to draw the threads the whole length of a long screw. If the thread is left-hand, the crest and root lines are slanted in the opposite direction from those shown in Figs. 16.5 to 16.7, as illustrated by the left-hand square thread in Fig. 16.8. Figure 16.9

FIG. 16.8. Thread representation on a long screw. The "repeat" lines save much drawing time.

FIG. 16.9. Semiconventional thread representation. This method is used for threads drawn 1 in. or larger on both assembly and detail drawings.

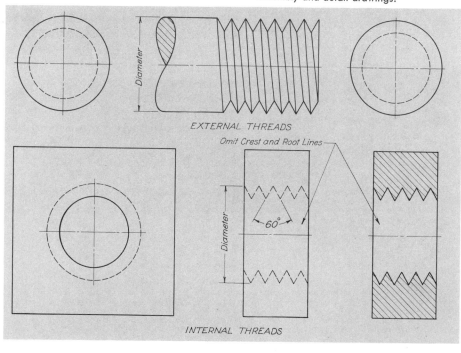

EXTERNAL THREADS

INTERNAL THREADS

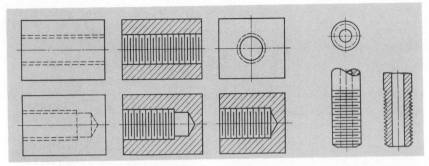

FIG. 16.10. ANSI regular thread symbols. These are used for threads drawn under 1 in. on assembly drawings.

illustrates semiconventional treatment for both external and internal V threads. Note that the crest and root lines are omitted on internal threads.

In general, threads should be represented semiconventionally except for the smaller sizes, which are ordinarily pictured by means of the ANSI thread symbols. It is suggested that threads of 1 in. and larger in actual measurement on the drawing be represented semiconventionally.

16.8. THREAD SYMBOLS. The ANSI provides two types of thread symbols: "regular" and "simplified." It is recommended that the ANSI symbols be used for indicating the smaller threads, those drawn under 1 in., and that the regular symbols be used on assembly drawings and the simplified symbols on detail drawings. The following paragraphs describe these symbols in detail.

FIG. 16.11. ANSI simplified thread symbols. These are used for threads drawn under 1 in. on detail drawings.

16.9. ANSI REGULAR THREAD SYMBOLS (FIG. 16.10). The regular symbols omit the profile on longitudinal views and indicate the crests and roots by

lines perpendicular to the axis. However, exceptions are made for internal threads not drawn in section and external threads drawn in section as shown in the figure.

16.10. ANSI SIMPLIFIED SYMBOLS (FIG. 16.11). The simplified symbols omit both form and crest lines and indicate the threaded portion by dashed lines parallel to the axis at the approximate depth of thread. The simplified symbols are less descriptive than the regular symbols, but they are quicker to draw and for this reason are preferred on detail drawings.

16.11. TO DRAW THE ANSI SYMBOLS. The two sets of symbols should be carefully studied and compared. Note that the regular and simplified symbols are identical for hidden threads. Note also that the end view of an external thread differs from the end view of an internal thread but that regular and simplified end-view symbols are identical.

No attempt need be made to show the actual pitch of the threads or their depth by the spacing of lines in the symbol. Identical symbols may be used for several threads of the same diameter but of different pitch. Only in the larger sizes for which the symbols are used could the actual pitch and the true depth of thread be shown without a confusion of lines that would defeat the purpose of the symbol. The symbols should therefore be made so as to read clearly and look well on the drawing, without other considerations.

To draw a symbol for any given thread, only the major diameter and length of thread must be known, and for a blind tapped hole, the depth of the tap drill is also needed.

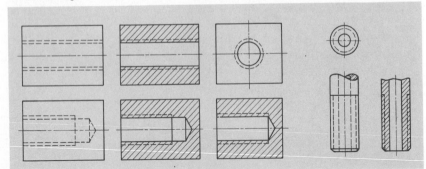

16.11. To Draw the ANSI Symbols

A *regular or simplified symbol for a tapped hole* is drawn in the stages shown in Fig. 16.12. The lines representing depth of thread are not drawn to actual scale but are spaced so as to look well on the drawing and to avoid crowding.

A *regular symbol for a tapped hole in section* is drawn in the stages shown in Fig. 16.13. The lines representing the crests are spaced by eye or scale to look well and need not conform to the actual thread pitch. The lines representing the roots of the thread are equally spaced by eye between the crest lines and are usually drawn heavier. Their length need not indicate the actual depth of thread but should be kept uniform by using light guide lines.

A *simplified symbol for an external thread* is drawn in the stages shown in Fig. 16.14. The 45° chamfer extends to the root line of the thread. Note that in the end view the chamfer line is shown.

A *regular symbol for external threads* is drawn in the stages shown in Fig. 16.15. The chamfer is 45° and to the depth of thread. Crest lines are spaced by eye or scale. Root lines are spaced by eye, are usually drawn heavier, and need not conform to actual thread depth.

Line Spacings. Table 16.1 gives suggested values of "pitch" and "depth of thread" for purposes of drawing the

TABLE 16.1. Suggested Values for Drawing Thread Symbols

Major diam. of thread D	Pitch p for dwg. purposes	Depth of thread $p/2$ for dwg. purposes
⅛ and ³⁄₁₆	¹⁄₁₆ scant	¹⁄₃₂ scant
¼ and ⅜	¹⁄₁₆	¹⁄₃₂
½ and ⅝	⅛	¹⁄₁₆
¾ and ⅞	³⁄₁₆	³⁄₃₂

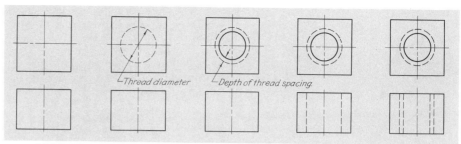

FIG. 16.12. Stages in drawing internal-thread symbols in external views. Regular and simplified symbols are identical here. See Table 16.1 for suggested depth of thread spacing.

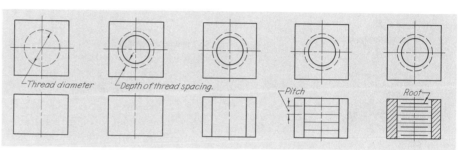

FIG. 16.13. Stages in drawing regular internal-thread symbols in sectional views. See Table 16.1 for suggested depth of thread and pitch spacing.

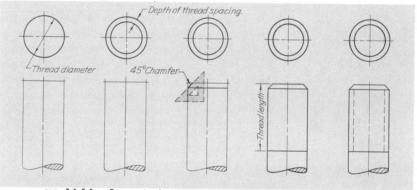

FIG. 16.14. Stages in drawing simplified external-thread symbols. See Table 16.1 for suggested depth of thread spacing.

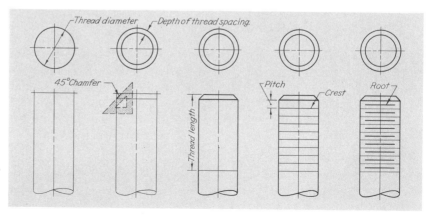

FIG. 16.15. Stages in drawing regular external-thread symbols. See Table 16.1 for suggested depth of thread and pitch spacing.

ANSI symbols. Figure 16.16 shows both regular and simplified symbols, full size, drawn according to the values given in Table 16.1. No distinction is made in the symbol between coarse and fine threads.

16.12. THREADS IN SECTION. Figure 16.4 shows the true form of an internal square thread in section. Observe that the far side of the thread is visible, causing the root and crest lines to slope in the opposite direction from those on the external thread. Figure 16.9 shows the semiconventional treatment for V threads 1 in. or longer in diameter. Note that the crest and root lines are omitted. The regular and simplified symbols for threads in section are shown in Figs. 16.10 and 16.11. When two pieces screwed together are shown in section, the thread form should be drawn to aid in reading (Fig. 16.17). With small diameters, it is desirable to decrease the number of threads per inch, thus eliminating monotonous detail and greatly improving the readability of the drawing.

16.13. UNIFIED AND AMERICAN (NATIONAL) SCREW THREADS. The Unified thread standards adopted by the United States, Canada, and Great Britain for the bulk of threaded products basically constitutes the ANSI Standard "Unified Screw Threads" (B1.1—1960). The form of thread employed has been described in paragraph 16.5 and is essentially that of the former (1935) American Standard. Threads produced according to the former and present standards will interchange. Important differences between the two standards are in the liberalization of manufacturing tolerances, the provision of allowances for most classes of threads, and the changes in thread

designations. The new ANSI Standard contains, in addition to the Unified diameter-pitch combinations and thread classes (adopted in common by the three countries), additional diameter-pitch combinations and two thread classes retained from the 1935 standard.

16.14. THREAD SERIES. Threads are classified in "series" according to the number of threads per inch used with a specific diameter. For example, an American (Unified) thread having 20 threads per inch applied to a ¼-in. diameter results in a thread belonging to the coarse-thread series, while one with 28 threads per inch on the same diameter gives a thread belonging to the fine-thread series.

In the United States the thread forms that have been subjected to series standardization by the ANSI include the Unified or American National, the Acme, Stub Acme, pipe threads, buttress, and the knuckle thread as used on electric sockets and lamp bases. Except for the Unified, or American National, only one series is provided for each of the thread forms so standardized (see Appendix for Acme and Stub Acme threads and for pipe threads).

The ANSI Standard "Unified Screw Threads" covers six series of screw threads and, in addition, certain other preferred special diameter-pitch combinations. In the descriptions of the series which follow, the letters "U" and "N" used in the series designations stand for the words "Unified" and "National (form)," respectively.

The *coarse-thread series*, designated "UNC" or "NC," is recommended for general use where conditions do not require a fine thread.

The *fine-thread series*, designated

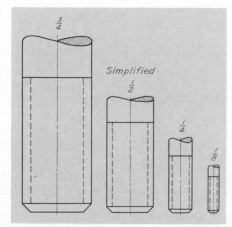

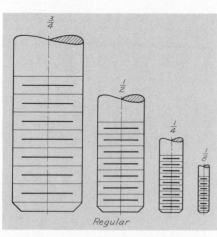

FIG. 16.16. Thread symbols, actual drawing size.

"UNF" or "NF," is recommended for general use in automotive and aircraft work and where special conditions require a fine thread.

The *extrafine-thread series,* designated "UNEF" or "NEF," is used particularly in aircraft work, which requires an extremely shallow thread or a maximum number of threads within a given length.

The *8-thread series,* designated "8N," is a uniform-pitch series using eight threads per inch for all diameters concerned. Bolts for high-pressure pipe flanges, cylinder-head studs, and similar fasteners against pressure require that an initial tension be set up by elastic deformation of the fastener and that the components be held together so that the joint will not open when steam or other pressure is applied. To secure a proper initial tension, it is not practicable that the pitch should increase with the diameter of the thread, as the torque required to assemble would be excessive. Accordingly, for such purposes, the 8-thread series has come into general use in many classes of engineering work and as a substitute for the coarse-thread series.

The *12-thread series,* designated "12UN" or "12N," is a uniform-pitch series using 12 threads per inch for all diameters concerned. Sizes of 12-pitch threads from ½ to 1¾ in. in diameter are used in boiler practice, which requires that worn stud holes be retapped with the next larger size. The 12-thread series is also widely used in machine construction for thin nuts on shafts and sleeves and provides continuation of the fine-thread series for diameters larger than 1½ in.

The *16-thread series,* designated "16UN" or "16N," is a uniform-pitch series using 16 threads per inch for all diameters concerned. This series is in-

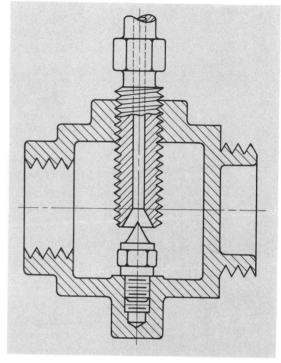

FIG. 16.17. Threads in section, actual drawing size.

tended for applications requiring a very fine thread, such as threaded adjusting collars and bearing retaining nuts. It also provides continuation of the extrafine-thread series for diameters larger than 2 in.

Special threads, designated "UN," "UNS," or "NS," as covered in the standards include nonstandard or special combinations of diameter, pitch, and length of engagement.

The diameter-pitch combinations of the above series will be found in the Appendix, where the Unified combinations (combinations common to the standards of the United States, Canada, and Great Britain) are printed in bold type.

16.15. UNIFIED AND AMERICAN SCREW-THREAD CLASSES. A class of thread is distinguished by the tolerance and allowance specified for the member threads and is therefore a control of the looseness or tightness of the fit between mating screws and nuts. The Unified and American (National) and Acme are at present the only threads in this country standardized to the extent of providing several thread classes to control the fit.

The classes provided by the ANSI Standard "Unified Screw Threads" are classes 1A, 2A, and 3A, applied to *external threads only;* classes 1B, 2B, and 3B, applied to *internal threads only;* and classes 2 and 3, applied to *both external and internal threads.* These classes are achieved through toleranced thread dimensions given in the standards.

Classes 1A and 1B are intended for ordnance and other special uses where free assembly and easy production are important. Tolerances and allowance are largest with this class.

Classes 2A and 2B are the recognized standards for the bulk of screws, bolts, and nuts produced and are suitable for a wide variety of applications. A moderate allowance provides a minimum clearance between mating threads to minimize galling and seizure.

Classes 3A and 3B provide a class where accuracy and closeness of fit are important. No allowance is provided.

Classes 2 and 3, each applying to both external and internal threads, have been retained from the former (1935)

American Standard. No allowance is provided with either class, and tolerances are in general closer than with the corresponding new classes.

16.16. UNIFIED THREADS. Not all the diameter-pitch combinations listed in the American Standard "Unified and American Standard Screw Threads" appear in the British and Canadian standards. Combinations used in common by the three countries are called Unified threads and are identified by the letter U in the series designation; they are printed in bold type in the Appendix table. Unified threads may employ classes 1A and 1B, 2A and 2B, and 3A and 3B only. When one of these classes is used and the U does not appear in the designation, the thread conforms to the principles on which Unified threads are based.

The Unified and American National screw-thread table (Appendix) indicates the classes for which each series has data tabulated in the standards. Threads of standard diameter-pitch combinations but of a class for which data are not tabulated in the standard are designated UNS if a Unified combination and NS if not.

16.17. ACME AND STUB ACME THREADS. Acme and Stub Acme threads have been standardized by the ANSI in one series of diameter-pitch combinations (see Appendix). In addition, the standard provides for two general applications of Acme threads: general purpose and centralizing. The three thread classes 2G, 3G, and 4G, standardized for general-purpose applications, have clearances on all diameters for free movement. Centralizing Acme threads have a close fit on the major diameter

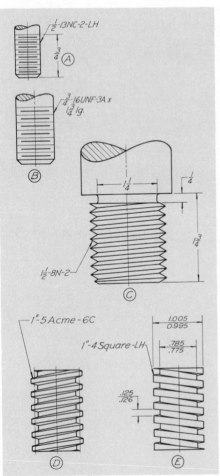

FIG. 16.18. Specifications of external threads. (*A*) is American National, (*B*) Unified, (*C*) American National, (D) Acme, (E) square.

to maintain alignment of the screw and nut and are standardized in five thread classes, 2C, 3C, 4C, 5C, and 6C. The Stub Acme has only one thread class for general usage.

16.18. BUTTRESS THREADS. Buttress threads have been standardized in a different fashion from the other types. Thread form and class of fit is completely defined. Thread series is not defined, but a table of recommended thread diameters and associated thread pitches is provided. Since the number of associated thread pitches varies from three to eleven (depending upon the thread diameter), the designation of a thread series would merely add complication. Three classes of fit are standard: class 1 (free), class 2 (medium), and class 3 (close).

16.19. THREAD SPECIFICATION. The orthographic views of a thread are necessary in order to locate the position of the thread dimensionally on the part. In addition, the views describe whether the thread is external or internal. All other information, called the "specification," is normally conveyed by means of a note or dimensions and a note. In addition to appearing on drawings, the specification may be needed in correspondence, on stock and parts lists, etc.

Features of a thread on which information is essential for manufacture are form, nominal (major) diameter, threads per inch, and thread class or toleranced dimensions. In addition, if the thread is left-hand, the letters LH must be included in the specification; also, if the thread is other than single, its multiplicity must be indicated.

In general, threads other than the Unified and American National, Acme, Stub Acme, and buttress require toler-

anced dimensions to control the fit (Fig. 16.18*E*).

Unified and American National threads are specified completely by note. The form of the specification always follows the same order: The nominal size is given first, then the number of threads per inch and the series designation (UNC, NC, etc.), and then the thread class (Fig. 16.18*A* to *C*). If the thread is left-hand, the letters LH follow the class (Fig. 16.18*A*). Examples:

¼-20UNC-3A	¼-20NC-2
1-12UNF-2B-LH	1-20NEF-3
2-8N-2	2-12UN-2A
2-16UN-2B	2-6NS-2A

Note that, when the Unified-thread classes are employed, the letters A and B indicate whether the thread is external or internal.

Acme and Stub Acme threads are also specified by note. The form of the specification follows that of the Unified (Fig. 16.18*D*). Examples:

1¾-4Acme-2G (general-purpose class 2 Acme; 1¾ in. major diameter, 0.25 in. pitch; single, right-hand)

1-5Acme-4C-LH (centralizing class 4 Acme; 1 in. major diameter, 0.2 in. pitch; single, left-hand)

2½-0.333p-0.666L-Acme-3G (general-purpose class 3 Acme; 2½ in. major diameter, 0.333 in. pitch, 0.666 in. lead; double, right-hand)

¾-6Stub Acme (Stub Acme; ¾ in. major diameter, 0.1667 in. pitch; right-hand)

Buttress threads can be completely specified by note but require one additional item of information in addition to diameter, threads per inch, type of thread, and class of fit: the direction of pressure as exerted by the internal

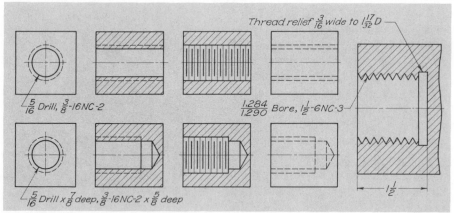

FIG. 16.19. Specifications of internal threads. All shown here are American National.

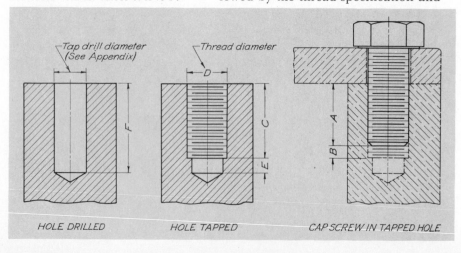

FIG. 16.20. Proportions for tapped holes. See Table 16.2 for values of *A* to *F*.

HOLE DRILLED   HOLE TAPPED   CAP SCREW IN TAPPED HOLE

member (screw). The following symbols are recommended for this purpose:

(← screw *pushing* to left (screw pressure flank facing left)

←(screw *pulling* to right (screw pressure flank facing right)

Note that the arrow points left but that the parenthesis mark indicates the direction of pressure flank. Where the buttress thread is multiple, the pitch and lead distances should be given instead of threads per inch. Examples:

⅝-20(←N. Butt.-1
4-8←(N. Butt.-2LH
10-0.1p-0.2L(←N. Butt.-1

16.20.   TAPPED-HOLE   SPECIFICATIONS. Always specify by note, giving the tap-drill diameter and depth of hole followed by the thread specification and

length of thread (Fig. 16.19). For tap-drill sizes, see the Appendix. It is general commercial practice to use 75 per cent of the theoretical depth of thread for tapped holes. This gives about 95 per cent of the strength of a full thread and is much easier to cut.

16.21.   DEPTH OF TAPPED HOLES AND ENTRANCE LENGTH.   For threaded rods, studs, cap screws, machine screws, and similar fasteners, the depth of tapped holes and entrance length may be found by using an empirical formula based on the diameter of the fastener and the material tapped. See Fig. 16.20 and Table 16.2.

16.22.   THREADED FASTENERS.   All engineering products, structures, etc., are composed of separate parts that must be held together by some means of fastening. Compared with permanent methods of fastening, such as welding and riveting, threaded fasteners provide an advantage in that they can be removed, thus allowing disassembly of the parts. As distinguished from other fastening devices such as pins, rivets, and keys, a *threaded* fastener is a cylinder of metal with a screw thread on one end and, usually, a head on the other.

The quantity of threaded fasteners used each year is tremendous. Many varieties are obtainable, some standardized and others special. The standardization of such widely used products results in uniform and interchangeable parts obtainable without complicated and detailed specification and at low cost. Standardized fasteners should be employed wherever possible.

Most fasteners have descriptive names, as the "setscrew," which holds a part in a set, or fixed, position. The bolt derives its name from an early-English use; it

TABLE 16.2. Detailed Depths for Drilling and Tapping Holes in Common Materials

Material	Entrance length for cap screws, etc., A	Thread clearance at bottom of hole B	Thread depth C	Unthreaded portion at bottom of hole E	Depth of drilled hole F
Aluminum	$2D$	$4/n$	$2D + 4/n$	$4/n$	$C + E$
Cast iron	$1\frac{1}{2}D$	$4/n$	$1\frac{1}{2}D + 4/n$	$4/n$	$C + E$
Brass	$1\frac{1}{2}D$	$4/n$	$1\frac{1}{2}D + 4/n$	$4/n$	$C + E$
Bronze	$1\frac{1}{2}D$	$4/n$	$1\frac{1}{2}D + 4/n$	$4/n$	$C + E$
Steel	D	$4/n$	$D + 4/n$	$4/n$	$C + E$

A = entrance length for fastener.
B = thread clearance at bottom of hole.
C = total thread depth.
D = diameter of fastener.

E = unthreaded portion at bottom of hole.
F = depth of tap-drill hole.
n = threads per inch.

was employed as a fastener or pin for bolting a door. Five types—the bolt, stud, cap screw, machine screw, and setscrew—represent the bulk of threaded fasteners.

16.23. AMERICAN STANDARD BOLTS AND NUTS.

A *bolt* (Fig. 16.21A), having an integral head on one end and a thread on the other end, is passed through clearance holes in two parts and draws them together by means of a nut screwed on the threaded end.

Two major groups of bolts have been standardized: round-head bolts and wrench-head bolts (sometimes called "machine bolts").

Round-head bolts are used as through fasteners with a nut, usually square. Eleven head types have standard proportions and include carriage bolts, step bolts, elevator bolts, and spline bolts. Several head types are intended for wood construction and have square sections, ribs, or fins under the head to prevent the bolts from turning. These bolts are hot or cold formed, with no machining except threading; hence they present a somewhat coarse and irregular appearance. A table in the Appendix shows the various head forms and gives nominal dimensions suitable for drawing purposes.

Wrench-head (machine) bolts have two standard head forms: square and hexagonal. Although intended for use as a through fastener with a nut, machine bolts are sometimes used as cap screws. Nuts to match the bolthead form and grade are available, but any nut of correct thread will fit a bolt. Machine bolts vary in grade from coarsely finished products resembling round-head bolts to a well-finished product matching a hexagon cap screw in appearance. Dimensions for drawing purposes are given in the Appendix.

16.24. STUDS.

A *stud* (Fig. 16.21B) is a rod threaded on each end. As used normally, the fastener passes through a clearance hole in one piece and screws permanently into a tapped hole in the

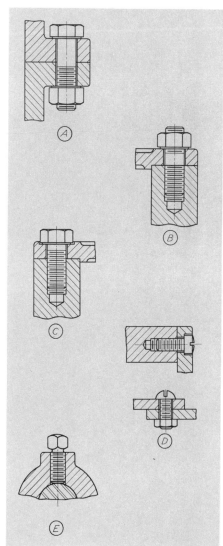

FIG. 16.21. Common types of fasteners. (A) bolt; (B) stud; (C) cap screw; (D) machine screws; (E) setscrew.

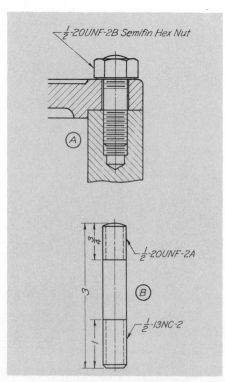

FIG. 16.22. Stud and nut. (*A*) is the assembly drawing and (*B*) is the detail drawing of the stud.

other. A nut then draws the parts together. The stud (Fig. 16.22) is used when through bolts are not suitable for parts that must be removed frequently, such as cylinder heads and chest covers. One end is screwed tightly into a tapped hole, and the projecting stud guides the removable piece to position. The end to be screwed permanently into position is called the "stud end"; and the opposite end, the "nut end." The nut end is sometimes identified by rounding instead of chamfering. Studs have not been standardized by the ANSI. The length of thread on the stud end is governed by the material tapped, as indicated in paragraph 16.20. The threads should jam at the top of the hole to prevent the stud from turning out when the nut is removed. The fit of the thread between the stud and tapped hole should be tight.

The length of thread on the nut end should be such that there is no danger of the nut binding before the parts are drawn together. The name "stud bolt" is often applied to a stud used as a through fastener with a nut on each end. The stud, a nonstandard part, is usually described on a detail drawing

(Fig. 16.22*B*). The nut, being a standard part, is described by note on the assembly drawing (Fig. 16.22*A*) or on the parts list.

16.25.   CAP SCREWS. A *cap screw* (Fig. 16.21*C*) passes through a clearance hole in one piece and screws into a tapped hole in the other. The head, an integral part of the screw, draws the parts together as the screw enters the tapped hole. Cap screws are used on machine tools and other products requiring close dimensions and finished appearances. They are well-finished products; for example, the heads of the slotted- and socket-head screws are machined, and all have chamfered points. The five types of heads shown in Fig. 16.23 are standard. Detail dimensions and length increments are given in the Appendix.

16.26.   MACHINE SCREWS. A *machine screw* (Fig. 16.21*D*) is a small fastener used with a nut to function in the same manner as a bolt; or without a nut, to function as a cap screw. Machine screws are small fasteners used principally in numbered diameter sizes. The finish is regularly bright, and the material used

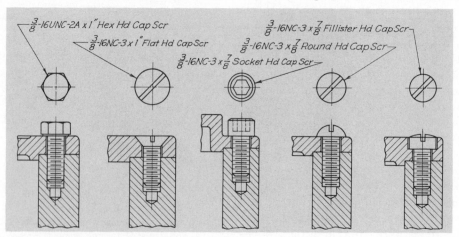

FIG. 16.23.   American Standard cap screws.
Note that the head type is given in the specification.

is commonly steel or brass. The nine standardized head shapes (Fig. 16.24), except for the hexagon, are available in slotted form as shown or with cross recesses (Fig. 16.25). The size of the recess varies with the size of the screw. Two recess types occur: intersecting slots with parallel sides converging to a sharp apex at the bottom of the recess (the same driver is used for all size recesses) and large center opening, tapered wings, and a blunt bottom (five sizes of drivers needed).

The hexagon machine screw is not made with a cross recess but may be optionally slotted. Dimensions for drawing machine screw heads will be found in the Appendix.

16.27.   SETSCREWS.

A *setscrew* (Fig. 16.21*E*) screws into a tapped hole in an outer part, often a hub, and bears with its point against an inner part, usually a shaft. Setscrews are made of hardened steel and hold two parts in relative position by having the point set against the inner part. The American Standard square-head and headless screws are shown in Fig. 16.26. Types of points are shown in Fig. 16.27. Headless setscrews are made to comply with the safety code of factory-inspection laws, which are strict regarding the use of projecting screws on moving parts. Square-head setscrews have head proportions following the formulas in Fig. 16.26 and can be drawn by using the radii suggested there. A neck or a radius may be used under the head, and the points have the same dimensions as headless screws. Dimensions for headless setscrews are given in the Appendix.

16.28.   AMERICAN STANDARD NUTS.

These are available in two wrench-type styles: square and hexagonal. In addition to the plain form usually associated with bolts, several special-purpose styles are available. Jam, hexagonal slotted, and hexagonal castle nuts are shown in Fig. 16.28. Machine screw and stovebolt nuts are made in small sizes only.

16.29.   STANDARD FASTENERS.

The ANSI Standards provide uniform dimensions and proportions for all fasteners (except studs) listed in the preceding paragraphs. With the exception of machine bolts, the only options for any of the preceding fasteners are the head style and thread series. Wrench head bolts are available in two head styles, two head weights, three finishes, and three thread series. Table 16.3 lists the available standard options, and paragraph 16.30 describes the differences:

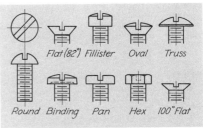

FIG. 16.24.   American Standard machine-screw heads.

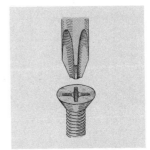

FIG. 16.25.   Recessed head and driver.

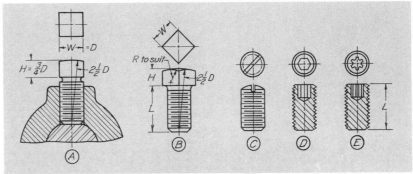

FIG. 16.26.   American Standard setscrews. (*A*) and (*B*) square head; (*C*), (D), and (E) headless.

FIG. 16.27.   American Standard setscrew points.

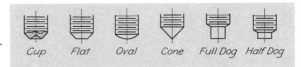

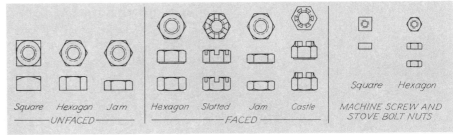

FIG. 16.28.   American Standard nuts.

TABLE 16.3.   Available Types and Thread Details of Standard Fasteners

Fastener group	Head styles	Thread series	Thread class
Round-head bolts	All	UNC	2A
Cap screws	Hexagonal	UNC, UNF, 8UN	2A
	Slotted		2A
	Socket		3A
Machine screws	All	NC, NF	2
Setscrews	Socket	UNC, UNF, 8UN, UNC, UNF	3A
	Square		2A
	Slotted		2A

Wrench-head (Machine) Bolts

Finish class	Square		Hexagonal		Thread	
	Regular	Heavy	Regular	Heavy	Series	Class
Unfaced	X	...	X	X	UNC	2A
Semifinished	...	...	X	X	UNC	2A
Finished	...	...	X	X	UNC, UNF, 8UN	2A

American Standard Nuts

Finish class	Square		Hexagonal			Hexagonal slotted		
	Regular	Heavy	Regular	Heavy	Thick	Regular	Heavy	Thick
Unfaced	X	X	X	X				
Semifinished	...	...	X	X	...	X	X	
Finished	...	...	X	...	X	X	...	X

16.30.   FASTENER TERMS.   *Nominal Diameter*.   The basic major diameter of the thread.

Width across Flats—W.   The distance separating parallel sides of the square or hexagonal head or nut, corresponding with the nominal size of the wrench. See table in Appendix for dimension *W*.

Tops of Boltheads and Nuts.   The tops of heads and nuts are flat with a chamfer to remove the sharp corners. The angle of chamfer with the top surface is 25° for the square form and 30° for the hex-agonal form; both are drawn at 30°. The diameter of the top circle is equal to the width across flats.

Washer Face.   The washer face is a circular boss turned or otherwise formed on the bearing surface of a bolthead or nut to make a smooth surface. The diameter is equal to the width across flats. The thickness is 1/64 in. for all fasteners. A circular bearing surface can be obtained on a nut by chamfering the corners. The angle of chamfer with the bearing face is 30°; the diameter of the circle is equal to the width across flats.

Fastener Length. The nominal length is the distance from the bearing surface to the point. For flat-head fasteners and for headless setscrews it is the over-all length.

Regular Series. Regular boltheads and nuts are for general use. The dimensions and the resulting strengths are based on the theoretical analysis of the stresses and on results of numerous tests.

Heavy Series. Boltheads and nuts in this series are for use where greater bearing surface is necessary. Therefore, for the same nominal size, they are larger in over-all dimensions than regular heads and nuts. They are used where a large clearance between the bolt and hole or a greater wrench-bearing surface is considered essential.

Thick Nuts. These have the same dimensions as regular nuts, except that they are higher.

Class of Finish. Unfaced bolts and nuts are not machined on any surface except the threads. The bearing surface is plain. Dimensional tolerances are as large as practicable.

Semifinished Boltheads and Nuts. These have a smooth bearing surface machined or formed at right angles to the axis (see Fig. 16.29). For boltheads, this is a washer face; and for nuts, a washer face or a circular bearing surface produced by chamfering the corners. Dimensional tolerances of the fastener are otherwise the same as for the unfaced group.

Finished Bolts and Nuts. These differ from the semifinished in two ways: The bearing surface may be washer-faced or produced by double chamfering (see Fig. 16.29). Dimensional tolerances are smaller than for the semifinished form. Finished hexagonal bolts have dimensional tolerances and workmanship similar to hexagonal cap screws.

16.31. **STANDARD FASTENER SPECIFICATIONS.** All standard fasteners may be specified on drawings or parts lists by notes. The following items may be included in a fastener specification in the order listed. Obviously, many of the items will not apply to some fastener types.

1. Thread specification (without length)
2. Fastener length
3. Fastener series (bolts only)
4. Class of finish (bolts only)
5. Material (if other than steel)
6. Head style or form
7. Point type (setscrews only)
8. Fastener group name

Sample specifications follow. Note carefully the machine-bolt notes.

½-13UNC-2A × 3
   Reg Sq Bolt

¼-20UNC-2A × 4
   Reg Semifin Hex Bolt

⅜-16UNC-2A × 3½
   Hvy Semifin Hex Bolt

¾-16UNF-2A × 2½
   Finished Hex Bolt (omit Reg)

⅝-11UNC-2A × 4¼
   Hvy Finished Hex Bolt

#10-24NC-2 × 2
   Brass Slotted Flat Hd Mach Scr

#6-32NC-2 × ½
   Recess Fil Hd Mach Scr

¼-20UNC-2A × ¾
   Sq Hd Cone Pt Setscrew

½-13UNC-3A × 2
   Soc, Flt Pt Setscrew

See Fig. 16.23 for cap-screw notes.

16.32. **THE DRAWING OF FASTENERS.** Before drawing a fastener, its *type, nominal diameter,* and *length,* if a bolt or screw, must be known. Knowing the type and diameter, other dimensions can be found in the tables (see Appendix).

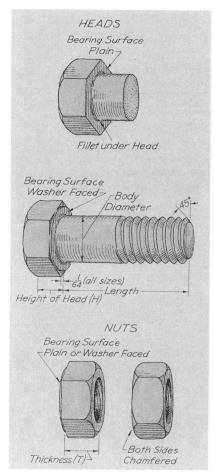

FIG. 16.29. Details of form for hexagonal bolts and nuts.

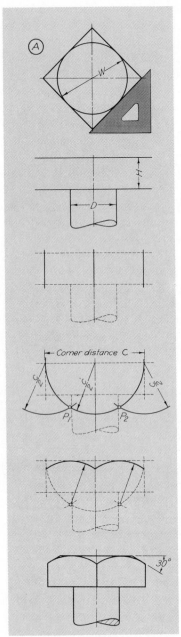

END VIEW OF SQUARE BOLTHEAD

Draw a circle of diameter W, and then draw the square with T square and 45° triangle.

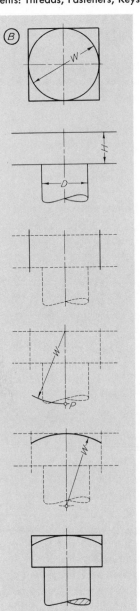

FACE VIEW OF SQUARE BOLTHEAD

1. Establish the diameter and the height of head.

2. Draw, lightly, the vertical edges of the faces, projecting from the end view.

3. Set compass to radius of $C/2$, and draw the circle arcs locating centers P_1 and P_2.	3. Set compass to radius of W, and draw the circle arc locating the center P.

4. Draw chamfer arcs, using radii and centers shown.

5. Complete the views. Show 30° chamfer on across-corners view.

FIG. 16.30. (A) Stages in drawing a square head across corners. (B) Stages in drawing a square head across flats.

16.33.   TO DRAW SQUARE AND HEXAGON-FORM FASTENERS.

Square and hexagonal heads and nuts are drawn "across corners" in all views showing the faces unless a special reason exists for drawing them "across flats." Figure 16.30 shows stages in drawing square heads both across corners and across flats, and Fig. 16.31 shows the same for hexagonal heads. The principles apply equally to the drawing of nuts. The following information must be known: (1) type of head or nut, (2) whether regular or heavy, (3) whether unfinished or semifinished,

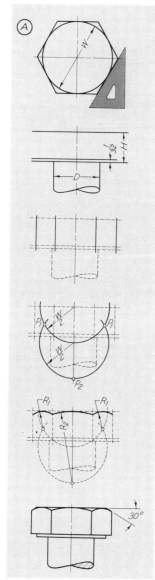

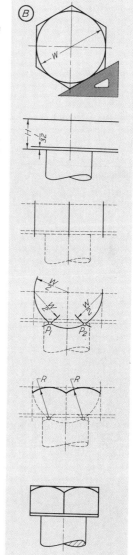

• END VIEW OF HEXAGONAL BOLTHEAD

Draw a circle of diameter W, and then draw the hexagon with T square and 30-60° triangle.

FACE VIEW OF HEXAGONAL BOLTHEAD

1. Establish the diameter, height of head, and washer-face thickness. The actual thickness of the washer face for all fasteners is 1/64 in. but may be increased up to 1/32 in. for the drawing.

2. Draw, lightly, the vertical edges of the faces, projecting from the end view.

3. With radius of $W/2$ draw the circle arcs locating centers P_1 and P_2.

4. Draw chamfer arcs, using radii and centers shown.

5. Complete the views. Washer-face diameter is equal to W. For across-corners view, show 30° chamfer.

FIG. 16.31 (A) Stages in drawing a hexagonal head across corners. (B) Stages in drawing a hexagonal head across flats.

and (4) the nominal diameter. Using this information, additional data W (width across flats), H (height of head), and T (thickness of nut) are obtained from the tables (see Appendix).

Figure 16.32 shows a regular semifinished hexagonal bolt and nut, drawn by the method of Fig. 16.31, showing the head across flats and the nut across corners. The length is selected from the bolt-

FIG. 16.32.   American Standard regular hexagonal semifinished bolt and nut. See Appendix for detailed sizes.

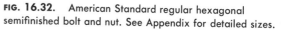

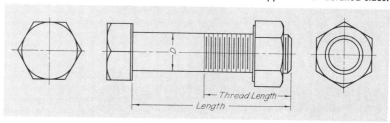

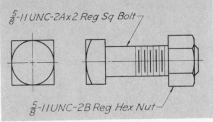

FIG. 16.33. ANSI regular square bolt and regular unfaced hexagonal nut. See Appendix for detailed sizes.

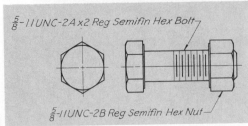

FIG. 16.34. ANSI regular semifinished hexagonal bolt and regular semifinished hexagonal nut. See Appendix for detailed sizes.

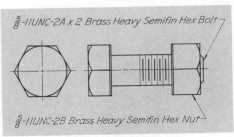

FIG. 16.35. ANSI heavy semifinished hexagonal bolt and heavy semifinished hexagonal nut. See Appendix for detailed sizes.

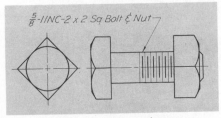

FIG. 16.36. ANSI regular unfaced square bolt and nut. See Appendix for detailed sizes.

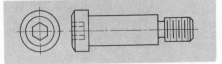

FIG. 16.37. American Standard shoulder screw. The body is accurately finished. See Appendix.

FIG. 16.38. American Standard plow bolts.

length tables and the length of thread determined from the footnote to the bolt table (see Appendix). Observe that the washer face shown in Fig. 16.31 will occur only with semifinished hexagonal fasteners and is sometimes omitted from the drawings of these. Other views of bolts and nuts are shown in Figs. 16.33 to 16.36.

The drawing may require considerable time when, for example, clearance conditions necessitate an accurately drawn fastener, using exact dimensions from tables. Often, however, the representation of fasteners may be approximate or even symbolic because the note specifications invariably accompany and exactly specify them. If an accurate drawing of the fastener is not essential, the W, H, and T dimensions of hexagonal and square heads and nuts may be obtained from the nominal diameter and the following formulas; the resulting values will be quite close to the actual

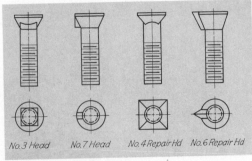

No.3 Head   No.7 Head   No.4 Repair Hd   No.6 Repair Hd

dimensions. For the regular series, $W = 1\frac{1}{2}D$, $H = \frac{2}{3}D$, and $T = \frac{7}{8}D$; for the heavy series, $W = 1\frac{1}{2}D + \frac{1}{8}$ in., $H = \frac{3}{4}D$, and $T = D$.

A wide variety of *templates* to facilitate the drawing of fasteners is available.

16.34. SPECIALIZED FASTENERS. There are a great many special fasteners, a number of which are the developments of the companies that supply a variety of forms. The common types are discussed in the following paragraphs.

16.35. SHOULDER SCREWS (FIG. 16.37). These are widely used for holding machine parts together and providing pivots, such as with cams, linkages, etc. They are also used with punch and die sets for attaching stripper plates and are then commonly called "stripper bolts." Threads are coarse series, class 3. Detail dimensions are given in the Appendix.

16.36. PLOW BOLTS (FIG. 16.38). These are used principally in agricultural equipment. The No. 3 and No. 7 heads are recommended for most new work. Threads are coarse series, class 2A. For particulars and proportions, see ANS B18.9—1958.

16.37. AMERICAN STANDARD TAPPING SCREWS. Tapping screws are hardened fasteners that form their own mating internal threads when driven into a hole of the proper size. For certain conditions and materials, these screws give a combination of speed and low production cost, which makes them preferred. Many special types are available. The ANSI has standardized head types conforming with all machine-screw heads except the binding and 100° flat heads. For drawing purposes, dimensions of machine-screw heads may be used. Sizes conform, in general, with machine-screw sizes. The ANSI provides three types of thread and point combinations (Fig. 16.39). The threads are 60° with flattened crest and root; types (*A*) and (*B*) are interrupted threads, and all fasteners are threaded to the head. Full details are given in ANS B18.6.1—1961.

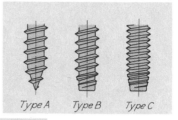

FIG. 16.39. American Standard tapping screw points. These are hardened and made to form their own thread in a drilled or punched hole.

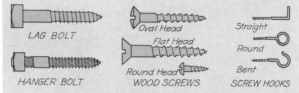

FIG. 16.40. Fasteners used in wood.

16.38. FASTENERS FOR WOOD.

Many forms of threaded fasteners for use in wood are available. Some are illustrated in Fig. 16.40. Threads are interrupted, 60° form, with a gimlet point. The ANSI has standardized lag bolts with square heads and also wood screws with flat, round, and oval heads. Lag bolt-heads follow the same dimensions and, in general, the same nominal sizes as regular square bolts. For specific information see ANS B18.10—1963. Wood screws follow the same head dimensions and, in general, the same nominal sizes as the corresponding flat-, round-, and oval-head machine screws. The nominal sizes, however, are carried to higher numbers. See table in the Appendix. Like machine screws, wood-screw heads may be plain slotted or have either style of cross recess. Several kinds of finish are available, for example, bright steel, blued, or nickel-plated. Material is usually steel or brass.

16.39. OTHER FORMS OF THREADED FASTENERS.

Many other forms of threaded fasteners, most of which have not been standardized, are in common use. Figure 16.41 illustrates some of these.

16.40. LOCK NUTS AND LOCKING DEVICES (FIG. 16.42).

Many different locking devices are used to prevent nuts from working loose. A screw thread holds se-

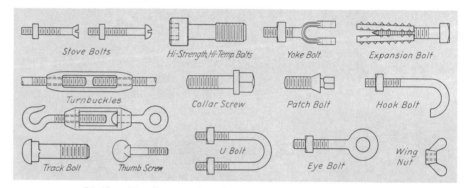

FIG. 16.41. Miscellaneous threaded fasteners. Many special fasteners are available.

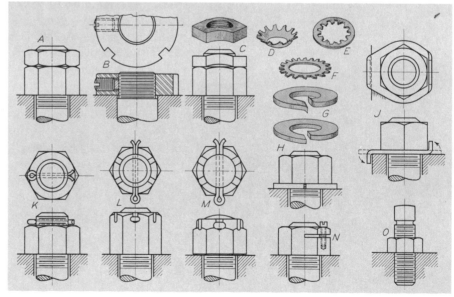

FIG. 16.42. Various locking devices. See paragraph 16.40.

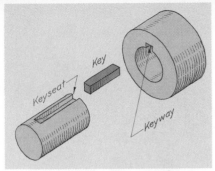

FIG. 16.43. Key nomenclature.

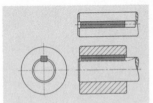

FIG. 16.44. Square (or flat) key. One-half of the key is in the keyway, one-half in the key seat.

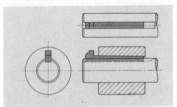

FIG. 16.45. Gib-head key. The head shape provides removal.

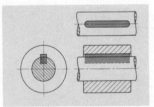

FIG. 16.46. Pratt and Whitney key. The ends of the key are rounded.

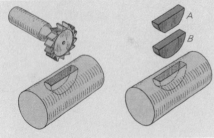

FIG. 16.47. Woodruff keys, cutter, and key seat. This is most widely used.

curely unless the parts are subject to impact and vibration, as in a railroad-track joint or an automobile engine. A common device is the *jam nut* shown at (*A*). *Slotted nuts* (*L*) and *castle nuts* (*M*), to be held with a cotter or wire, are commonly used in automotive and allied work. For additional information on jam, slotted, and castle nuts, see paragraph 16.28.

At (*B*) is shown a *round nut* locked by means of a setscrew. A brass plug is placed under the setscrew to prevent damage to the thread. This is a common type of adjusting nut used in machine-tool practice. (*C*) is a *lock nut*, in which the threads are deformed after cutting. Patented *spring washers,* such as are shown at (*D*), (*E*), and (*F*), are common devices. Special patented nuts with plastic or fiber inserts or with distorted threads are in common use as locking devices. The locking action of (*J*), (*K*), (*N*), and (*O*) should be evident from the figure.

16.41. ANSI STANDARD PLAIN AND LOCK WASHERS. There are four standard ANSI spring lock washers: light, medium, heavy, and extra heavy. These are shown in Fig. 16.42*G* and *H* and are specified by giving nominal diameter and series, for example,

½ Heavy Lock Washer

ANSI plain washers are also standardized in four series—light, medium, heavy, and extra heavy—and are specified by giving nominal diameter and series, for example,

⁷⁄₁₆ Light Plain Washer

FIG. 16.48. Keys for light duty. (*A*) saddle, (*B*) flat, (*C*) Nordberg.

Dimensions of ANSI plain and lock washers are given in the Appendix.

16.42. KEYS. In making machine drawings there is frequent occasion for representing key fasteners, used to prevent the rotation of wheels, gears, etc., on their shafts. A key is a piece of metal (Fig. 16.43) placed so that part of it lies in a groove, called the "key seat," cut in a shaft. The key then extends somewhat above the shaft and fits into a "keyway" cut in a hub. Thus, after assembly, the key is partly in the shaft and partly in the hub, locking the two together so that one cannot rotate without the other.

16.43. KEY TYPES. The simplest key, geometrically, is the square key, placed *half* in the shaft and *half* in the hub (Fig. 16.44). A flat key is rectangular in cross section and is used in the same manner as the square key. The gib-head key (Fig. 16.45) is tapered on its upper surface and is driven in to form a very secure fastening. Both square and flat (parallel and tapered stock) keys have been standardized by the ANSI. Tables of standard sizes are given in the Appendix.

The Pratt and Whitney key (Fig. 16.46) is a variation on the square key. It is rectangular in cross section and has rounded ends. It is placed two-thirds in the shaft and one-third in the hub. The key is proportioned so that the key seat is square and the keyway is half as deep as it is wide. Sizes are given in the Appendix.

Perhaps the most common key is the Woodruff (Fig. 16.47). This key is a flat segmental disk with a flat (*A*) or round (*B*) bottom. The key seat is semicylindrical and cut to a depth so that *half* the *width* of the key extends above the shaft and into the hub. Tables of dimensions are given in the Appendix. A good basic rule for proportioning a Woodruff key to a given shaft is to have the width of the key one-fourth the diameter of the shaft and its radius equal to the radius of the shaft, selecting the standard key that comes nearest to these proportions. In drawing Woodruff keys, take care to place the center for the arc above the top of the key to a distance equal to one-half the thickness of the saw used in splitting the blank. This amount is given in column E of the table in the Appendix.

Figure 16.48 shows three keys for light duty: the saddle key (A), the flat key (B), and the pin, or Nordberg, key (C), which is used at the end of a shaft, as, for example, in fastening a handwheel.

Figure 16.49 shows some forms of heavy-duty keys. (A) is the Barth key, (B) the Kennedy key, and (C) the Lewis key for driving in one direction. In the latter two, the line of shear is on the diagonal.

For very heavy duty, keys are not sufficiently strong and splines (grooves) are cut in both shaft and hub, arranged so that they fit one within the other (Fig. 16.50). (A) and (B) are two forms of splines widely used instead of keys. (B) is the newer ANSI involute spline (B5.15—1960).

16.44.   SPECIFICATION OF KEYS.   Keys are specified by note or number, depending upon the type.

Square and flat keys are specified by a note giving the width, height, and length, for example,

½ Square Key 2½ Lg
½ × ⅜ Flat Key 2½ Lg

Plain taper stock keys are specified by giving the width, the height at the large end, and the length. The height at the large end is measured at the distance W (width) from the large end. The taper is 1 to 96 (see Appendix). For example,

⅜ × ⅜ × 1½ Square Plain Taper Key
½ × ⅜ × 1¼ Flat Plain Taper Key

Gib-head taper stock keys are specified by giving, except for name, the same information as for square or flat taper keys (see Appendix), for example,

¾ × ¾ × 2¼ Square Gib-head Taper Key
⅞ × ⅝ × 2½ Flat Gib-head Taper Key

Pratt and Whitney keys are specified by number or letter (see Appendix), for example,

Pratt and Whitney Key No. 6

Woodruff keys are specified by number (see Appendix).

Dimensions and specifications of other key types may be found in handbooks or manufacturers' catalogues.

16.45.   DIMENSIONING KEY SEATS AND KEYWAYS.   The dimensioning of the *seat* and *way* for keys depends upon the purpose for which the drawing is intended. For unit production, when the keys are expected to be fitted by the machinist, nominal dimensions may be given, as in Fig. 16.51. For quantity production, the limits of width (and depth, if necessary) should be given as in Fig. 16.52. Pratt and Whitney key seats and keyways are dimensioned as in Fig. 16.53. Note that

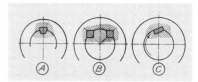

FIG. 16.49.   Keys for heavy duty. (A) Barth, (B) Kennedy, (C) Lewis.

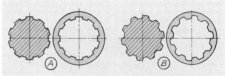

FIG. 16.50.   Splined shafts and hubs. (A) straight-radial, (B) involute. Both provide strong resistance to torque forces.

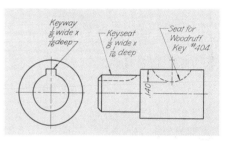

FIG. 16.51.   Nominal dimensions of key seats and keyways (square and Woodruff). See paragraph 16.45.

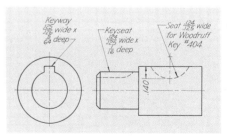

FIG. 16.52.   Limit dimensions of key seats and keyways (square and Woodruff). See paragraph 16.45.

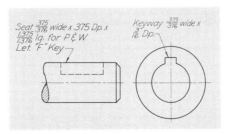

FIG. 16.53.   Dimensioning for a Pratt and Whitney key seat and keyway.

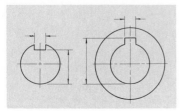

FIG. 16.54. Dimensions of keyway and key seat for interchangeable assembly. These correspond to sizes on gages used.

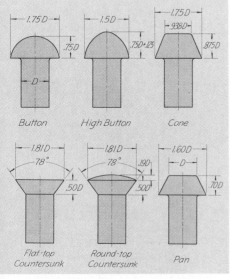

Button   High Button   Cone

Flat-top Countersunk   Round-top Countersunk   Pan

FIG. 16.55. Large rivet heads. These are used for structural steel.

FIG. 16.56. Lap and butt joints. See paragraph 16.46.

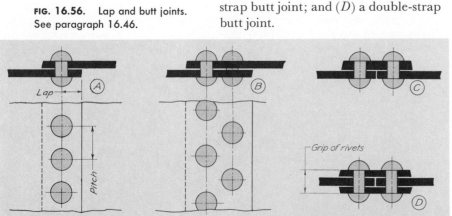

the *length* of the key seat is given to correspond with the specification of the key. If interchangeability is important and when careful gaging is necessary, the dimensions should be given as in Fig. 16.54 and the values expressed with limits.

16.46. **RIVETS.** Rivets are used for making permanent fastenings, generally between pieces of sheet or rolled metal. They are round bars of steel or wrought iron with a head formed on one end and are often put in place red hot so that a head can be formed on the other end by pressing or hammering. Rivet holes are punched, punched and reamed, or drilled larger than the diameter of the rivet, and the shank of the rivet is made just long enough to give sufficient metal to fill the hole completely and make the head.

Large rivets are used in structural-steel construction and in boiler and tank work. In structural work, only a few kinds of heads are normally needed: the button, high button, and flat-top countersunk heads (Fig. 16.55).

For boiler and tank work, the button, cone, round-top countersunk, and pan heads are used. Plates are connected by either lap or butt joints. Figure 16.56*A* is a single-riveted lap joint; (*B*) is a double-riveted lap joint; (*C*) is a single-strap butt joint; and (*D*) a double-strap butt joint.

Large rivets are available in diameters of ½ to 1¾ in., by increments of even ⅛ in. The length needed is governed by the "grip," as shown at Fig. 16.56*D*, plus the length needed to form the head. Length of rivets for various grip distances may be found in the handbook "Steel Construction" published by the American Institute of Steel Construction.

Small rivets are used for fabricating light structural shapes and sheet metal. ANSI small-rivet heads are shown in Fig. 16.57. Small rivets are available in diameters of 3/32 to 7/16 in., by increments of even 1/32 in. to ⅜ in. diameter.

Tinners', coopers', and belt rivets are used for fastening thin sheet metal, wood, leather, rubber, etc. Standard heads and proportions are given in the Appendix.

16.47. **SPRINGS.** A spring can be defined as an elastic body designed to store energy when deflected. Springs are classified according to their geometric form: helical or flat.

16.48. **HELICAL SPRINGS.** These are further classified as (1) compression, (2) extension, or (3) torsion, according to the intended action. On working drawings, helical springs are drawn as a single-line convention, as in Fig. 16.58; or semiconventionally, as in Figs. 16.59 to 16.61, by laying out the diameter (*D*) and pitch (*P*) of coils and then drawing a construction circle for the wire size at the limiting positions and conventionalizing the helix with straight lines. Helical springs may be wound of round-, square-, or special-section wire.

Compression springs are wound with the coils separated so that the unit can be compressed, and the ends may be open or closed and may be left plain or ground,

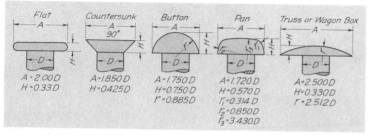

FIG. 16.57. ANSI Standard small-rivet heads. These are used principally for thin material.

FIG. 16.58. Conventional representation of springs. The single-line treatment saves drawing time.

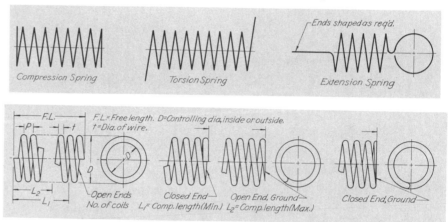

FIG. 16.59. Representation and dimensioning of compression springs.

as shown in Fig. 16.59. The information that must be given for a compression spring is as follows:

1. Controlling diameter: (*a*) outside, (*b*) inside, (*c*) operates inside a tube, or (*d*) operates over a rod

2. Wire or bar size

3. Material (kind and grade)

4. Coils: (*a*) total number and (*b*) right- or left-hand

5. Style of ends

6. Load at deflected length of __

7. Load rate between __ inches and __ inches

8. Maximum solid height

9. Minimum compressed height in use

Extension springs are wound with the loops in contact so that the unit can be extended, and the ends are usually made as a loop, as shown in Fig. 16.60. Special ends are sometimes required and are described by the ANSI. The information that must be given for an extension spring is as follows:

1. Free length: (*a*) over-all, (*b*) over coil, or (*c*) inside of hooks

2. Controlling diameter: (*a*) outside diameter, (*b*) inside diameter, or (*c*) operates inside a tube

3. Wire size

4. Material (kind and grade)

5. Coils: (*a*) total number and (*b*) right- or left-hand

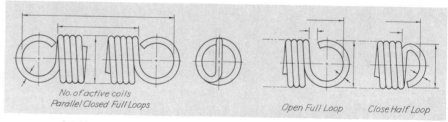

FIG. 16.60. Representation and dimensioning of extension springs.

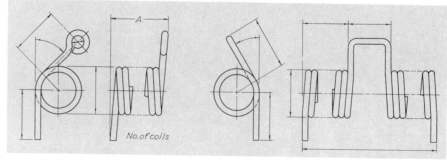

FIG. 16.61. Representation and dimensioning of torsion springs.

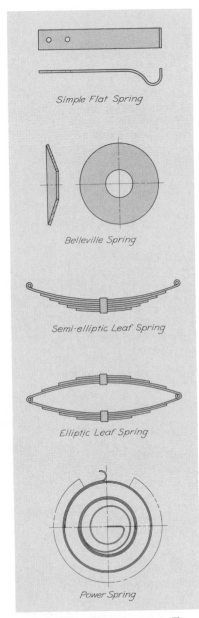

Simple Flat Spring

Belleville Spring

Semi-elliptic Leaf Spring

Elliptic Leaf Spring

Power Spring

FIG. 16.62. Flat spring types. The variety is such that these require individual representation and specification.

6. Style of ends

7. Load at inside hooks

8. Load rate, pounds per 1-in. deflection

9. Maximum extended length

Torsion springs are wound with closed or open coils, and the load is applied torsionally (at right angles to the spring axis). The ends may be shaped as hooks or as straight torsion arms, as indicated in Fig. 16.61. The information that must be given for a torsion spring is as follows:

1. Free length (dimension A, Fig. 16.61)

2. Controlling diameter: (a) outside diameter, (b) inside diameter, (c) operates inside a hole, or (d) operates over a rod

3. Wire size

4. Material (kind and grade)

5. Coils: (a) total number and (b) right- or left-hand

6. Torque, pounds at ___ degrees of deflection

7. Maximum deflection (degrees from free position)

8. Style of ends

16.49.   FLAT SPRINGS. A flat spring can be defined as any spring made of flat or strip material. Flat springs (Fig. 16.62) are classified as (1) simple flat springs, formed so that the desired force will be applied when the spring is deflected in a direction opposite to the force; (2) power springs, made as a straight piece and then coiled inside an enclosing case; (3) Belleville springs, stamped of thin material and shaped so as to store energy when deflected; and (4) leaf springs, in elliptic or semielliptic form, made of several pieces of varying length, shaped so as to straighten when a load is applied. The information that must be given for a flat spring is as follows:

1. Detailed shape and dimensions of the spring shown in a drawing

2. Material and heat-treatment

3. Finish

16.50.   MANUFACTURERS' SPECIALTIES. A common problem in all commercial drafting rooms is the design and representation of parts to accommodate manufacturers' specialties such as fasteners, keys, rivets, springs, and ball bearings. Also necessary is the specification of the specialty, including the trade name or other pertinent information such as the size and company number. These are the principal reasons why the following descriptions and accompanying problems are given. There are many industrial companies that manufacture fastening specialities. Many of these are made specifically for the purpose of supplying a low-cost product. Others are designed for speed of assembly. Still others are devised for special uses or to replace standard fasteners, keys, or springs. Most of these designs are not standardized and possibly never will be, either because the manufacturing companies are continually improving the component characteristics and forms or because they are patented devices.

It is impossible to give complete coverage here to all obtainable products or even to list all varieties made by a particular manufacturer. However, the following paragraphs describe some well-known and widely used parts. National organizations such as the ASME supply comprehensive lists of manufacturers' products, and the advertising in current periodicals is a good source of information. Descriptive literature is obtainable from the manufacturers.

Self-threading nuts are inexpensive heat-treated spring-steel parts that are easily assembled on an unthreaded stud, shaft, rod, wire, pin, or tube of suitable dimensions and material. Details of *PALNUTS,* made by The Palnut Company, Mountainside, N.J., are given in the Appendix.

Push-on fasteners are spring-steel washerlike parts that are pushed onto an unthreaded stud, shaft, rod, wire, pin, or tube and make a permanent, quick, and inexpensive fastening by means of the gripping action of the specially designed hole in the part. *PUSHNUTS,* made by The Palnut Company, Mountainside, N.J., are given in the Appendix.

Rivet-nuts are, as the name implies, a combination of a rivet and nut. They are tubular rivets with internal threads and have a body so designed that a hand or power assembly tool, which engages the thread, causes the shank to expand and fill the prepared hole in the part to be attached. *RIVNUTS,* made by the B. F. Goodrich Company, Akron, Ohio, are given in the Appendix.

ROLLPINS are parts similar to standard straight or tapered pins but are tubular in form with a slotted and chamfered longitudinal opening. They are made of heat-treated spring steel and can be used to replace a grooved pin, key, rivet shaft, cotter pin, setscrew, clevis pin, hinge pin, dowel pin, bolt and nut, rivet, or taper pin. *ROLLPINS,* made by the Elastic Stop Nut Corporation of America, Union, N.J., are given in the Appendix.

Retaining rings are tempered spring-steel rings designed as either an external ring to fit into a groove on a shaft or as an internal ring to be fitted into a groove in a hub. Their principal use is to locate or prevent axial movement of a shaft in a hub. They are made in a great variety of forms and sizes. *WALDES TRUARC* retaining rings, made by Waldes Kohinoor, Inc., Long Island City, New York, N.Y., are given in the Appendix.

Drive rivets are "blind"-type rivets consisting of a slotted and cored body and a steel grooved pin. In the installation the body is inserted in prepared holes in the parts to be fastened and then the pin is driven into the body. There are many sizes and lengths. *SOUTHCO* aluminum drive rivets and steel drive rivets are given in the Appendix. These rivets are made by the Southco Division of the South Chester Corporation, Lester, Penna.

PROBLEMS

GROUP 1. HELICES

16.1.1. Draw three complete turns of a helix; diameter, 3 in.; pitch, 1¼ in. See Chap. 3.
16.1.2. Draw three complete turns of a conic

helix, end and front views, with 1½-in. pitch, whose large diameter is 4 in. and small diameter is 1½ in. See Chap. 3.

GROUP 2. SCREW THREADS

16.2.1. Draw in section the following screw-thread forms, 1-in. pitch: American National, Acme, stub Acme, square.
16.2.2. Draw two views of a square-thread screw and a section of the nut separated; diameter, 2½ in.; pitch, ¾ in.; length of screw, 3 in.
16.2.3. Same as Prob: 16.2.2 but for V thread with ½-in. pitch.
16.2.4. Draw screws 2 in. in diameter and 3½ in. long: single square thread, pitch ½ in.; single V thread, pitch ¼ in.; double V thread, pitch ½ in.; left-hand double square thread, pitch ½ in.

16.2.5. Working space, 7 by 10½ in. Divide space as shown and in left space draw and label thread profiles, as follows: at A, sharp V, ½-in. pitch; at B, American National (Unified), ½-in. pitch; at C, square, 1-in. pitch; at D, Acme, 1-in. pitch. Show five threads each at A and B and three at C and D.

In right space, complete the views of the object by showing at E a 3½-4UNC-2B threaded hole in section. The thread runs out at a 3¹⁷⁄₃₂-in.-diameter by ¼-in.-wide thread relief. The lower line for the thread relief is shown. At F, show a 1¾-5UNC-3A thread. The thread is 1 in. long and runs out at a neck that is 1⅜ in. in diameter by ¼ in. wide. The free end of the thread should be chamfered at 45°. At G, show the shank threaded ⅝-18UNF-3A by 1 in. long; at H, show ⅜-16UNC-2B through tapped holes in section, four required. Completely specify all threads.
16.2.6. Working space, 7 by 10½ in. Complete the views and show threaded features as follows: at A, a ½-20UNF-3B through tapped hole; at B, a ⅝-11UNC-2B by ¾-in.-deep tapped hole with tap drill 1⅛ in. deep; at C, a ⅜-16UNC-2B by ¼-in.-deep tapped hole with the tap drill through to the 1-in. hole; at D, a 1½-8N-2 threaded hole running out at the large cored hole. Completely specify all threads.
16.2.7. Complete the offset support, showing threaded holes as follows: at A, 1⅜-6UNC-2B; at B, ½-13NC-2; at C, ⅝-18UNF-3B. A and C are through holes. B is a blind hole to receive a stud. Material is cast iron. Specify the threaded holes.
16.2.8. Complete the views of the cast-steel rocker, showing threads as follows: on center line A-A, 2-8N-2; on center line B-B, a

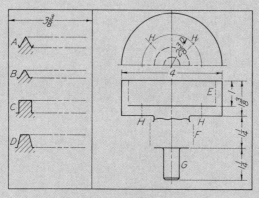

PROB. 16.2.5. Screw threads.

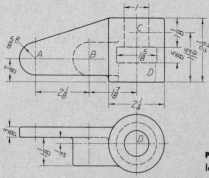

PROB. 16.2.6. Intermediate lever.

½-20UNF-2B tapped hole, ⅝ in. deep, with tap drill ⅞ in. deep; on center line *C-C*, a 2¾-12UN-2A external thread; on center line *D-D*, a ⅞-14UNF-3A external thread.

16.2.9. Minimum working space, 10½ by 15 in. Complete the views of the objects, and show threads and other details as follows: *upper left*, on center line *A-A*, show in section a ¾-10UNC-2B tapped hole, 1½ in. deep, with tap-drill hole 2½ in. deep. At *B*, show a 1¾-8N-2 external thread in section. At *C*, show a ¾-10UNC-2A thread in section. From *D* on center line *A-A*, show a ¼-in. drilled

hole extending to the tap-drill hole. At *E*, show six ¼-in. drilled holes, ¼ in. deep, equally spaced for spanner wrench. *Upper right*, at *F*, show a 1½-6UNC-2A thread. *Lower left*, at *G*, show (three) ⅜-16UNC-2B through holes. At *H*, show a ⅞-9UNC-2B tapped hole, 1⅛ in. deep, with the tap-drill hole going through the piece. On center line *K-K*, show a ⅞-14UNF-3B through tapped hole. *Lower center*, at *M*, show a ⅝-18UNF-3A thread 1¾ in. long. *Lower right*, on center line *P*, show a 2-4½UNC-2B hole in section.

Completely specify all threads.

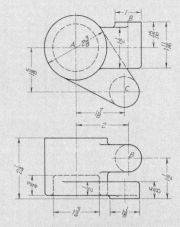

PROB. 16.2.7. Offset support.

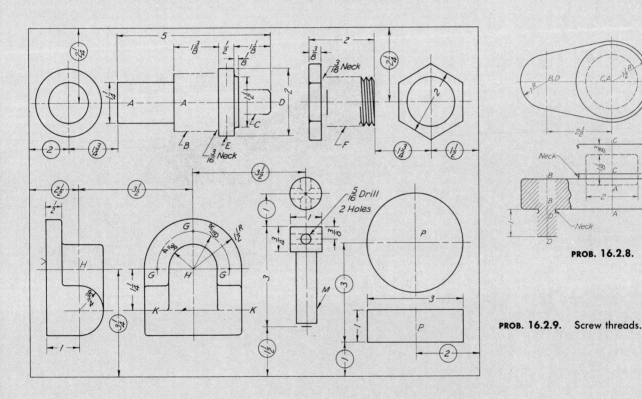

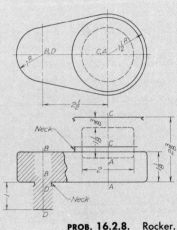

PROB. 16.2.8. Rocker.

PROB. 16.2.9. Screw threads.

GROUP 3. **THREADED FASTENERS**

16.3.1. Draw one view of regular semi-finished hexagonal bolt and nut, across corners; diameter, 1 in.; length, 5 in.

16.3.2. Same as Prob. 16.3.1 for a heavy unfinished bolt and nut.

16.3.3. Same as Prob. 16.3.1 for a square bolt and nut.

16.3.4. Draw four ½- by 1½-in. cap screws, each with a different kind of head. Specify each.

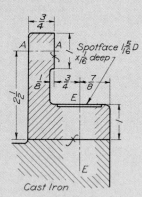

PROB. 16.3.5. L lug.

16.3.5. Show the pieces fastened together on center line *E-E* with a ¾-in. hexagonal-head cap screw and light lock washer. On center line *A-A* show a ⅜- by 1½-in. shoulder screw.

16.3.6. Show pieces fastened together with a ¾-in. square bolt and heavy square nut. Place nut at bottom.

16.3.7. Fasten pieces together with a ¾-in. stud and regular semifinished hexagonal nut.

16.3.8. Fasten pieces together with a ¾-in. fillister-head cap screw.

16.3.9. Draw one view of a round-head square-neck (carriage) bolt; diameter, 1 in.; length, 5 in.; with regular square nut.

16.3.10. Draw one view of a round-head rib-neck (carriage) bolt; diameter, ¾ in.; length, 4 in.; with regular square nut.

16.3.11. Draw two views of a shoulder screw; diameter, ¾ in.; shoulder length, 5 in.

16.3.12. Draw two views of a socket-head cap screw; diameter, 1¼ in.; length, 6 in.

16.3.13. Draw the stuffing box and gland, showing the required fasteners. At *A*, show ½-in. hexagonal-head cap screws (six required). At *B*, show ½-in. studs and regular semi-finished hexagonal nuts. Specify fasteners.

16.3.14. Draw the bearing plate, showing the required fasteners. At *C*, show ½-in. regular semifinished hexagonal bolts and nuts (four required). At *D*, show ½-in. socket setscrew. At *E*, show ½-in. square-hand setscrew. Setscrews are to have cone points. Specify fasteners.

Problems 16.3.13 and 16.3.14 may be drawn together on an 11- by 17-in. sheet or on separate sheets, showing full diameter of flanges.

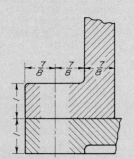

PROB. 16.3.6. Double cover.

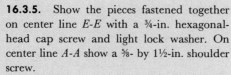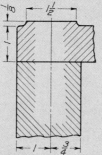

PROB. 16.3.7. Bracket and support.

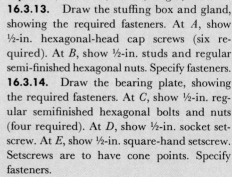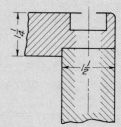

PROB. 16.3.8. Centered closure.

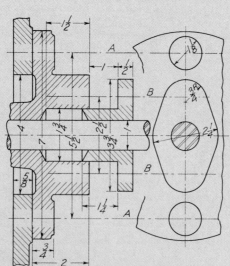

PROB. 16.3.13. Stuffing box and gland.

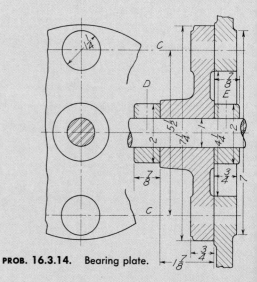

PROB. 16.3.14. Bearing plate.

16.3.15. Draw the ball-bearing head, showing the required fasteners. At *A*, show ½- by 1¾-in. regular semifinished hexagonal bolts and nuts (six required), with heads to left and across flats. Note that this design prevents the heads from turning. At *B*, show 5/16- by ¾-in. fillister-head cap screws (four required). At *C*, show a ⅜- by ½-in. slotted flat-point setscrew with fiber disk to protect threads of spindle. Specify fasteners.

16.3.16. Draw the plain bearing head, showing the required fasteners. At *D*, show ½- by 2-in. studs and regular semifinished hexagonal nuts (six required); spot-face 1 in. diameter by 1/16 in. deep. At *E*, show ⅜- by 1-in. hexagonal-head cap screws (four required). At *F*, show a 7/16- by ⅞-in. square-head cup-point setscrew. At *G*, show a ⅛-27NPT hole with a pipe plug. Show the 11/32-in. tap drill through for gun packing the gland. Specify fasteners.

Problems 16.3.15 and 16.3.16 may be drawn together on an 11- by 17-in. sheet or on separate sheets, showing full diameter of flanges.

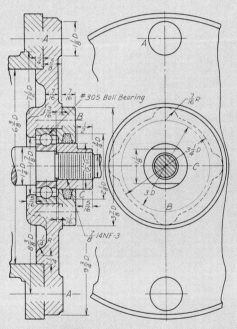

PROB. 16.3.15. Ball-bearing head.

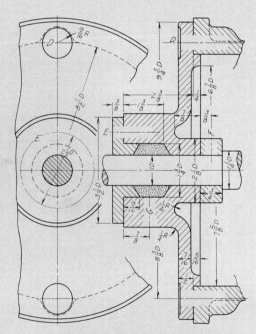

PROB. 16.3.16. Plain bearing head.

GROUP 4.   KEYS

Key sizes are given in the Appendix.

16.4.1. Draw hub and shaft as shown, with a Woodruff key in position.
16.4.2. Draw hub and shaft as shown, with a square key 2 in. long in position.

16.4.3. Draw hub and shaft as shown, with a gib-head key in position.
16.4.4. Draw hub and shaft as shown, with a Pratt and Whitney key in position.

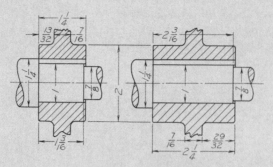

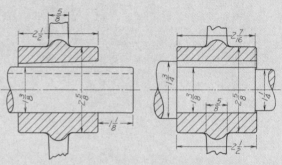

PROB. 16.4.1. Hub and shaft.   **PROB. 16.4.2.** Hub and shaft.   **PROB. 16.4.3.** Hub and shaft.   **PROB. 16.4.4.** Hub and shaft.

GROUP 5.   RIVETS

16.5.1. Draw top view and section of a single-riveted butt joint 10⅝ in. long. Pitch of rivets is 1¾ in. Use cone-head rivets.

16.5.2. Draw a column section made of 15-in. by 33.9-lb channels with cover plates as shown, using ⅞-in. rivets (dimensions from the handbook of the American Institute of Steel Construction). Use button-head rivets on left side and flat-top countersunk-head rivets on right side so that the outside surface is flush.

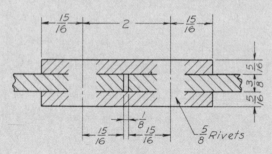

PROB. 16.5.1. Butt joint.

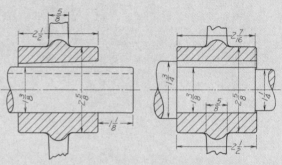

PROB. 16.5.2. Column.

GROUP 6.   SPRINGS

16.6.1. Draw a compression spring as follows: inside diameter, ¾ in.; wire size, ⅛ in. diameter; coils 14, right-hand; squared and ground ends; free length, 3½ in.

16.6.2. Draw a compression spring as follows: outside diameter, 1 in.; wire size, ³⁄₃₂ in. diameter; coils 12, left-hand; open ends, not ground; free length, 4 in.

16.6.3. Draw an extension spring as follows: free length over coils, 2 in.; outside diameter, 1⅛ in.; wire size, ⅛ in. diameter; coils 11, right-hand; the ends parallel, closed loops.

16.6.4. Draw an extension spring as follows: free length inside hooks, 2¾ in.; inside diameter, ¾ in.; wire size, ⅛ in. diameter; coils 11, left-hand; the ends parallel, closed half loops.

16.6.5. Draw a torsion spring as follows: free length over coils ¾ in.; inside diameter, 1⅛ in.; wire size, ⅛ in. diameter; coils 5, right-hand; ends straight and turned to follow radial lines to center of spring and extend ½ in. from outside diameter of spring.

16.6.6. A compression spring made of 26-gage steel wire with an outside diameter of 2 in. has 8 active coils wounld to a pitch of ½ in. Determine the free length if:

(a) The spring has open ends.

(b) The spring has closed ends.

(c) The spring has open ends ground.

(d) The spring has closed ends ground.

16.6.7A. If the above spring is compressed solid, determine its outside diameter.

16.6.7B. If the above spring has a pitch tolerance of ±0.015 in. and an outside-diameter tolerance of ±0.015-in. dia., determine the maximum outside diameter. (*Note:* The wire manufacturers' tolerance on the wire diameter is ±0.001 in.)

16.6.8. Redesign the ball-bearing heads of Prob. 16.3.15 using a lubricated and sealed-for-life type of bearing held in place with a retainer ring.

GROUP 7.   MANUFACTURERS' SPECIALTIES

16.7.1. Two sheets of 16-gage steel are to be fastened together with a Rivnut. This Rivnut is to be ¼-in. dia., flathead, open end, keyless, aluminum. Specify Rivnut and draw inserted on center line, but not upset. Draw nine times actual size.

16.7.2. Same as Prob. 16.7.1. Two sheets of 16-gage steel are to be fastened together with a Rivnut. This Rivnut is to be 0.221-in. dia., flathead, closed end, keyed, steel. Specify Rivnut and draw inserted on center line, but not upset. Draw nine times actual size.

16.7.3. A ¼-in. steel plate is to be fastened to a sheet of 16-gage steel by a Rivnut. This is to be a countersunk head, ¼-in. dia., closed end, keyless, steel Rivnut.

(a) Draw and specify Rivnut with fastener inserted on center line, but not upset. Draw three times size.

(b) Completely specify the flathead machine screw of maximum length that will fasten a ⅛-in. plate to the above after upsetting.

16.7.4. Same as Prob. 16.7.3. A ¼-in. steel plate is to be fastened to a sheet of 16-gage sheet metal by a Rivnut. This is to be a countersunk head, 0.490-in. dia., open end, keyless, corrosion-resistant steel Rivnut. Specify Rivnut and draw on center line with Rivnut inserted, but not upset. Draw three times size.

16.7.5. Two sheets of 16-gage sheet metal are to be fastened together with a ⅛-in. dia. aluminum drive rivet made by the Southco Division of the South Chester Corporation. Show a universal head drive rivet in position on center line but not upset. Specify the rivet and draw nine times actual size.

16.7.6. Same as Prob. 16.7.5, but full brazier head instead of universal head.

16.7.7. Two ¼-in. plates are to be fastened together with a Southco ³⁄₁₆-in. dia. aluminum drive rivet. Show an all-purpose liner head drive rivet in position on center line, but not upset. Specify the rivet and draw three times actual size.

16.7.8. Same as Prob. 16.7.7, but for 100° countersunk head.

16.7.9. Same as Prob. 16.7.7, but for full brazier head.

16.7.10. Same as Prob. 16.7.7, but for universal head.

16.7.11. Same as Prob. 16.7.7, but for round ply-head.

16.7.12. Same as Prob. 16.7.7, but for flat ply-head.

16.7.13. A ¼-in. plate is to be fastened to a 1-in. thick plywood member. The fastening device is to be a Southco ¼-in. dia. aluminum drive rivet. The plywood is to have a ¾-in. deep hole. Show a 100° countersunk head drive rivet in place on center line, but not upset. Specify the rivet and draw three times actual size.

16.7.14. Same as Prob. 16.7.13, but for universal head.

16.7.15. Same as Prob. 16.7.13, but for full brazier head.

PROB. 16.7.1.   Layout.

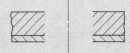

PROB. 16.7.3.   Layout.

PROB. 16.7.5.   Layout.

PROB. 16.7.7.   Layout.

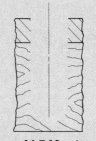

PROB. 16.7.13.   Layout.

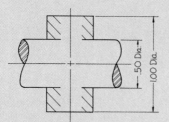

PROB. 16.7.16. Layout.

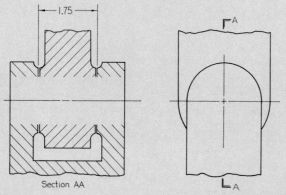

Section AA

PROB. 16.7.17. Layout.

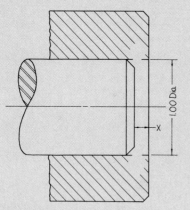

PROB. 16.7.18. Layout.

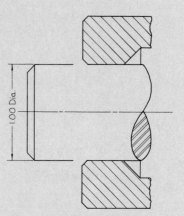

PROB. 16.7.19. Layout.

16.7.16. Draw and dimension the limits of the drilled hole in the external collar necessary to hold a Rollpin in place. Show and specify the Rollpin in position on center line and draw three times actual size.

16.7.17. Draw and dimension the limits of the drilled hole in the outer member necessary to hold a ⅜-in. dia. Rollpin. The inner member is to have a minimum clearance of 0.003 in. Dimension the maximum and minimum diameter of the drilled hole in the inner member. Show and specify the Rollpin in position on the center line. Draw three times actual size.

16.7.18. Show and specify a Waldes Truarc 5000 series retaining ring in position to limit the axial travel of the shaft, until it reaches a minimum distance X, as shown in the Appendix on retaining rings. Determine and show the dimension X and the complete groove dimensions as well as the maximum 45° chamfer dimension. Draw three times actual size.

16.7.19. Show and specify a Waldes Truarc 5100 series retaining ring in position to limit axial travel of the shaft. Determine and show the groove dimensions and the maximum 45° chamfer allowable on the external member. Draw three times actual size.

16.7.20. Same as Prob. 16.7.19, but use series 5133 E ring.

GROUP 8.   DESIGN PROBLEMS

16.8.1. The shaft and bar shown are to be joined so that a light torque can be transmitted from one member to the other. The parts must be readily disassembled. Show at least three ways of solving this problem. In each case give the instructions and dimensions required to complete the design.

16.8.2. A shaft passing through a fixed panel is to have a plastic knob fastened to it. Its angular motion is to be limited to 45° of travel. Select appropriate standard fasteners, and make a drawing showing them installed. Give whatever instructions and dimensions are required to complete the design. (*Note:* This is a large production design and time and cost are important factors.)

16.8.3. The ½-in. dia. shaft shown must be able to move axially ¾ in. in the frame without rotating. The block must be rigidly attached to this shaft. The two ⅜-in. dia. shafts must be free to rotate in the block with no appreciable axial movement. Select appropriate standard fasteners to complete this design. Make necessary drawings showing any additional machining operations, and an assembly drawing. Give complete instructions and all necessary dimensions to complete this design.

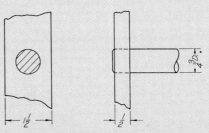

PROB. 16.8.1.   Layout.

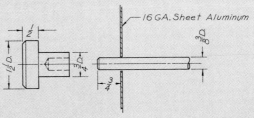

PROB. 16.8.2.   Layout.

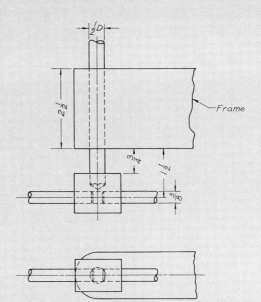

PROB. 16.8.3.   Layout.

From the very beginning of an original design through to the procedure of preparing drawings for construction and assembly, careful thought must be given to machining and processing methods. Ignorance in this area will certainly lead to inefficient and costly production. Therefore all designers, draftsmen, detailers, and others involved in development and construction must have a good knowledge of shop methods.

Drawings: Specification for Manufacture

17

17.1. The test of any working drawing for legibility, completeness, and accuracy is the production of the object or assembly by the shop without further information than that given on the drawing. A knowledge of shop methods will, to a great extent, govern the effectiveness and completeness of the drawing. Study the glossary of shop terms to become familiar with the terms and the form of designation in notes. This chapter is given as an introduction to those on design and working drawings.

The relation of drawings and the prints made from them to the operations of production is illustrated in the accompanying chart (Fig. 17.1). This chart shows in diagrammatic form the different steps in the development of drawings and their distribution and use in connection with shop operations from the time the order is received in the plant until the finished machine is delivered to the shipping room.

17.2. EFFECT OF THE BASIC MANUFACTURING METHOD ON THE DRAWING. In drawing any machine part, consider first the manufacturing process to be used, as on this depends the representation of the detailed features of the part and, to some extent, the choice of dimensions. Special or unusual methods may occasionally be used, but most machine parts are produced by (1) casting, (2) forging, (3) machining from standard stock, (4) welding, or (5) forming from sheet stock.

585

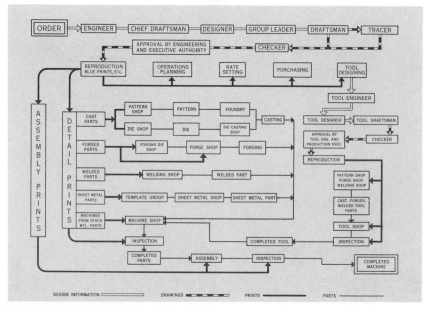

FIG. 17.1. Development and distribution of drawings. This shows the routing of drawings, prints, and parts through all design and manufacturing units.

Each of the different methods produces a characteristic detailed shape and appearance of the parts, and these features must be shown on the drawing.

Figure 17.2 shows and lists typical features of each method and indicates the differences in drawing practice.

17.3. THE DRAWINGS. For the production of any part, a detail working drawing is necessary, complete with shape and size description and giving, where needed, the operations that are to be performed by the shop. Machined surfaces must be clearly indicated, with dimensions chosen and placed so as to be useful to the various shops without the necessity of adding or subtracting dimensions or scaling the drawing.

Two general practices are followed: (1) the "single-drawing" system, in which only one drawing, showing the finished part, is made to be used by all the shops involved in producing the part; and (2) the "multiple-drawing" system, in which different drawings are prepared, one for each shop, giving only the information required by the shop for which the drawing is made.

The second practice is recommended, as the drawings are easier to dimension without ambiguity, somewhat simpler and more direct, and therefore easier for the shop to use. Figure 17.3 is a single drawing, to be used by the pattern shop and the machine shop. Figures 15.107 and 15.108 are multiple drawings, Fig. 15.107 for the patternmaker and Fig. 15.108 for the machine shop.

17.4. SAND CASTINGS. Figure 17.3 shows (in the title strip) that the material to be used is cast iron (*C.I.*), indicating that the part will be formed by pouring molten iron into a mold (in this case a "sand mold"), resulting in a sand casting.

After casting, subsequent operations produce the finished part. Figure 17.4

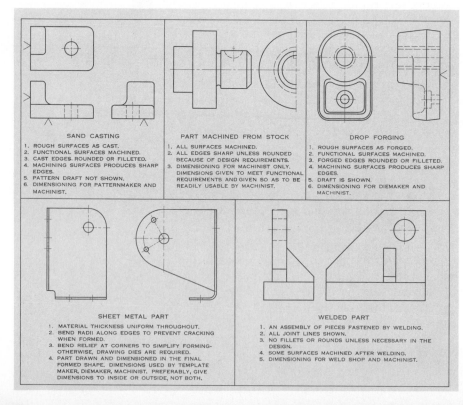

FIG. 17.2. Drawing requirements for different manufacturing methods.

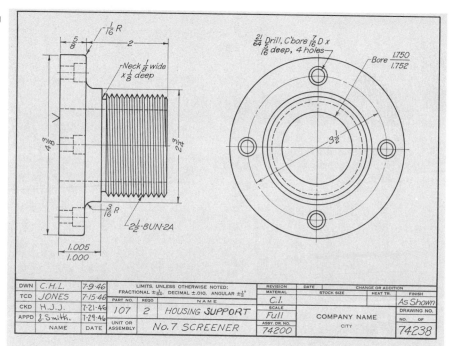

illustrates the shop interpretation of the casting drawing in Fig. 17.3 and indicates the order of operations to be performed.

17.5. THE PATTERN SHOP.

The drawing is first used by the patternmaker, who makes a pattern, or "model," of the part in wood. From this, if a large quantity of castings is required, a metal pattern, often of aluminum, is made. The patternmaker provides for the shrinkage of the casting by making the pattern oversize, using a "shrink rule" for his measurements. He also provides additional metal (machining allowance) for the machined surfaces, indicated on the drawing by (1) finish marks, (2) dimensions indicating a degree of precision attainable only by machining, or (3) notes giving machining operations. The patternmaker also provides the "draft," or slight taper, not shown on the drawing, so that the pattern can be withdrawn easily from the sand. A "core box," for making sand cores for the hollow parts of the casting, is also made in the pattern shop. A knowledge of patternmaking is a great aid in dimensioning, as almost all the dimensions are used by the patternmaker, while only the dimensions for finished features are used by the machine shop.

17.6. DRAWINGS OF CASTINGS.

A casting drawing is usually made as a single drawing of the machined casting, with dimensions for both the patternmaker and the machinist (Fig. 17.3). If the multiple-drawing system is followed, a drawing of the unmachined casting, with allowances for machining accounted for and with no finish marks or finish dimensions, is made for the patternmaker; then a second drawing for the

FIG. 17.5. A pattern drawing. This is a drawing of the pattern for the casting in Fig. 17.3.

machinist shows the finished shape and gives machining dimensions.

For complicated or difficult castings, a special "pattern drawing" may be made (Fig. 17.5), showing every detail of the pattern, including the amount of draft, the parting line, "core prints" for supporting the cores in the mold, and the pattern material. Similar detail drawings may also be made for the core boxes.

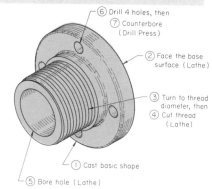

FIG. 17.4. Interpretation of the casting drawing in Fig. 17.3. These are the operations that must be performed to produce the part.

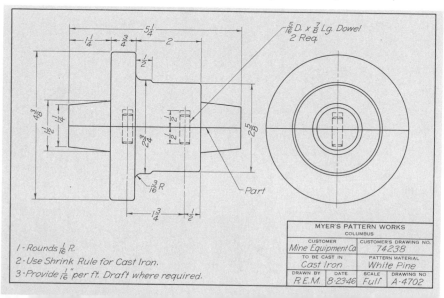

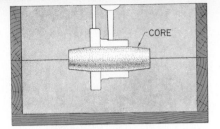

FIG. 17.6. Cross section of a two-part mold. This shows the cavity produced by the pattern in Fig. 17.5.

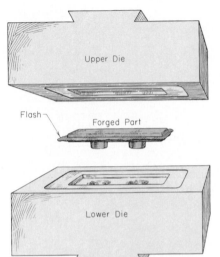

FIG. 17.7. Drop-forging dies and the forged part. These are the dies for the part shown in Fig. 17.8.

17.7. THE FOUNDRY. The pattern and core box or boxes are sent to the foundry, and sand molds are made so that molten metal can be poured into the molds and allowed to cool, forming the completed rough casting. Figure 17.6 is a cross section of a two-part mold, showing the space left by the pattern and the core in place. Only in occasional instances does the foundryman call for assistance from the drawing, as his job is simply to reproduce the pattern in metal.

Permanent molds, made of cast iron coated on the molding surfaces with a refractory material, are sometimes an advantage in that the mold can be used over and over again, thus saving the time to make an individual sand mold for each casting. This method is usually limited to small castings.

Die castings are made by forcing molten metal under pressure into a steel die mounted in a special die-casting machine. Alloys with a low melting point are used in order to avoid damaging the die. Because of the accuracy possible in mak-

ing a die, a fine finish and accurate dimensions of the part can be obtained; thus machining may be unnecessary.

17.8. FORGINGS. Forgings are made by heating metal to make it plastic and then forming it to shape on a power hammer with or without the aid of special steel dies. Large parts are often hammered with dies of generalized all-purpose shape. Smaller parts in quantity may warrant the expense of making special dies. Some small forgings are made with the metal cold.

Drop forgings are the most common and are made in dies of the kind shown in Fig. 17.7. The lower die is held on the bed of the drop hammer, and the upper die is raised by the hammer mechanism. The hot metal is placed between the dies, and the upper die is dropped several times, causing the metal to flow into the cavity of the dies. The slight excess of material will form a thin fin, or "flash," surrounding the forging at the parting plane of the dies (Fig. 17.7). This flash is then removed in a "trimming" die made for the purpose. Considerable draft must be provided for release of the forging from the dies.

17.9. DRAWINGS OF FORGINGS. Forging drawings are prepared according to the multiple-drawing system, one drawing for the diemaker and one for the machinist (Fig. 17.110); or the single-drawing system, one drawing for both (Fig. 17.8). In either case the parting line and draft should be shown and the amount of draft specified. On the single drawing (Fig. 17.8), the shape of the finished forging is shown in full outline, and the machining allowance is indicated by "alternate-position" lines, thus completing the shape of the rough forging. This single

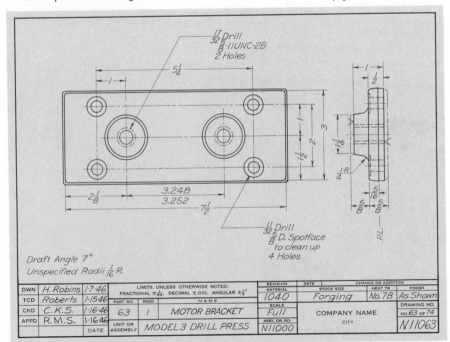

FIG. 17.8. A working drawing of a forged part. Note the indication of parting line and extra material for machining.

drawing combines two drawings in one, with complete dimensions for both die-maker and machinist.

Figure 17.9 illustrates the shop interpretation of the forging drawing in Fig. 17.8 and indicates the order of operations to be performed.

17.10. THE MACHINE SHOP. The machine shop produces parts machined from stock material and finishes castings, forgings, etc., requiring machined surfaces. Cylindrical and conic surfaces are machined on a lathe. Flat or plane surfaces are machined on a planer, shaper, milling machine, broaching machine, or in some cases (facing) a lathe. Holes are drilled, reamed, counterbored, and countersunk on a drill press or lathe; holes are bored on a boring mill or lathe. For exact work, grinding machines with wheels of abrasive material are used. Grinders are also coming into greatly increased use for operations formerly made with cutting tools. In quantity production many special machine tools and automatic machines are in use. The special tools, jigs, and fixtures made for the machine parts are held in the toolroom ready for the machine shop.

17.11. FUNDAMENTALS OF MACHINING. All machining operations remove metal, either to make a smoother and more accurate surface, as by planing, facing, milling, etc., or to produce a surface not previously existing, as by drilling, punching, etc. The metal is removed by a hardened steel, carbide, or diamond cutting tool (machining) or an abrasive wheel (grinding); the product, or "work piece," as well as the tool or wheel, being held and guided by the machine. When steel cutting tools are used, the

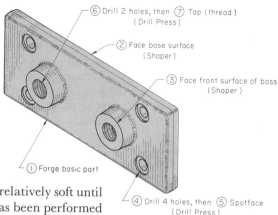

⑥ Drill 2 holes, then ⑦ Tap (thread) (Drill Press)
② Face base surface (Shaper)
③ Face front surface of boss (Shaper)
① Forge basic part
④ Drill 4 holes, then ⑤ Spotface (Drill Press)

FIG. 17.9. Interpretation of the forging drawing in Fig. 17.8. These are the separate manufacturing steps.

product must remain relatively soft until after all machining has been performed upon it, but if diamond-tipped tools are used or if grinding wheels are employed, the product may be hardened by heat-treatment before finishing.

All machining methods are classified according to the operating principle of the machine performing the work:

1. The surface may be *generated* by moving the work with respect to a cutting tool or the tool with respect to the work, following the geometric laws for producing the surface.

2. The surface may be *formed* with a specially shaped cutting tool, moving either work or tool while the other is stationary.

The forming method is, in general, less accurate than the generating method, as any irregularities in the cutter are reproduced on the work. In some cases a combination of the two methods is used.

17.12. THE LATHE. Called the "king of machine tools," the lathe is said to be capable of producing all other machine tools. Its primary function is machining cylindrical, conic, and other surfaces of revolution, but with special attachments it can perform a great variety of operations. Figure 17.10 shows the casting made from the drawing of Fig. 17.3

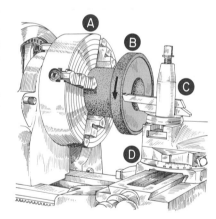

FIG. 17.10. Facing. The chuck (*A*) holds the part (*B*) and revolves it in the direction shown. The tool in the holder (*C*) is brought against the work surface by the lathe carriage, and the motion of the tool across the face is controlled by the cross slide (*D*).

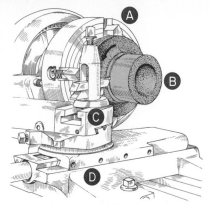

FIG. 17.11. Turning. The chuck (*A*) holds the part (*B*) and revolves it in the direction shown. The tool in the holder (*C*) is brought against the work surface by the cross slide, and the motion of the tool is controlled by the lathe carriage (*D*).

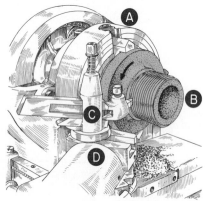

FIG. 17.12. Threading. The chuck (*A*) holds the part (*B*) and revolves it in the direction shown. The tool, ground to the profile of the thread space, in the holder (*C*) is brought into the work surface by the angled cross slide (*D*), and the rate of travel is controlled by gears and a lead screw that moves the lathe carriage.

FIG. 17.13. Boring. The chuck (*A*) holds the part (*B*) and revolves it in the direction shown. The boring bar with the tool in the holder (*C*) is brought against the work surface by the cross slide, and advance is controlled by the lathe carriage (*D*).

held in the lathe chuck. As the work revolves, the cutting tool is moved across perpendicular to the axis of revolution, removing metal from the base and producing a plane surface by generation. This operation is called *facing*. After being faced, the casting is turned around, and the finished base is aligned against the face of the chuck, bringing the cylindrical surface into position for *turning* to the diameter indicated in the thread note on the drawing. The neck shown at the intersection of the base with the body is turned first, running the tool into the casting to a depth slightly greater than the depth of the thread. The cylindrical surface is then turned (generated) by moving the tool parallel to the axis of revolution (Fig. 17.11). Figure 17.12 shows the thread being cut on the finished cylinder. The tool is ground to the profile of the thread space, carefully lined up to the work, and moved parallel to the axis of revolution by the lead screw of the lathe. This operation is a combination of the fundamental processes, the thread profile being formed while the helix is generated.

The hole through the center of the casting, originally cored, is now finished by *boring*, as the cutting of an interior surface is called (Fig. 17.13). The tool

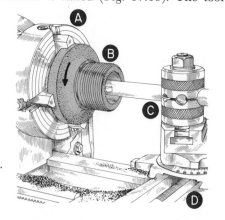

is held in a boring bar and moved parallel to the axis of revolution, thus generating an internal cylinder.

Note that in these operations the dimensions used by the machinist have been (1) the finish mark on the base and thickness of the base, (2) the thread note and outside diameter of the thread, (3) the dimensions of the neck, (4) the distance from the base to the shoulder, and (5) the diameter of the bored hole.

Long cylindrical pieces to be turned in the lathe are supported by conic centers, one at each end. Figure 17.22 illustrates the principle.

17.13.   THE DRILL PRESS. The partially finished piece of Fig. 17.3 is now taken to the drill press for drilling and counterboring the holes in the base according to the dimensions on the drawing. These dimensions give the diameter of the drill, the diameter and depth of the counterbore, and the location of the holes. The casting is clamped to the drill-press table (Fig. 17.14) and the rotating drill brought into the work by a lever operating a rack and pinion in the head of the machine. The cutting is done by two ground lips on the end of the drill (Fig. 17.24). Drilling can also be done in a lathe, the work revolving while the drill is held in and moved by the tailstock. In Fig. 17.15 the drill has been replaced by a counterboring tool (Fig. 17.24) of which the diameter is the size specified on the drawing and which has a cylindrical pilot on the end to fit into the drilled hole, thus ensuring concentricity. This tool is fed in to the depth shown on the drawing.

Study the drawing of Fig. 17.3 with the illustrations of the operations, and check, first, the dimensions that would

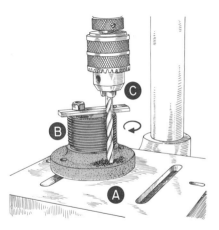

FIG. 17.14. Drilling. The table (*A*) supports the part (*B*), sometimes clamped as shown. The drill in the chuck (*C*) revolves in the direction shown, and is forced downward by a gear and rack in the drill-press head, to make the hole.

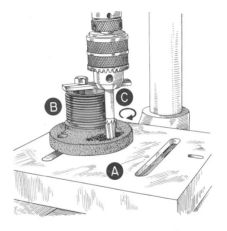

FIG. 17.15. Counterboring. The table (*A*) supports the part (*B*), sometimes clamped as shown. The counterboring tool with piloted end to fit the previously drilled hole is held in the chuck (*C*) and revolves in the direction shown. The gear and rack in the drill-press head bring the tool into the work.

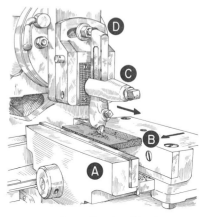

FIG. 17.16. Shaping. The vise (*A*) holds the part (*B*). The tool in the holder (*C*) is forced across the work surface by the ram (*D*) in the forward-stroke direction shown. The tool lifts on the return stroke by the pivot head on the ram. To make successive cuts, the table holding (*A*) and (*B*) moves in the direction shown.

be used by the patternmaker and, second, those required by the machinist.

17.14. THE SHAPER AND THE PLANER.

The drop forging of Fig. 17.8 requires machining on the base and boss surfaces.

Flat surfaces of this type are machined on a shaper or a planer. In this case the shaper (Fig. 17.16) is used because of the relatively small size of the part. The tool is held in a ram that moves back and forth across the work, taking a cut at each pass forward. Between the cuts, the table moves laterally so that closely spaced parallel cuts are made until the surface is completely machined.

The planer differs from the shaper in that its bed, carrying the work, moves back and forth under a stationary tool. It is generally used for a larger and heavier type of work than that done on a shaper.

17.15. PARTS MACHINED FROM STANDARD

STOCK. The shape of a part will often lend itself to machining directly from standard stock, such as bars, rods, tubing, plates, and blocks, or from extrusions and rolled shapes, such as angles and channels. Hot-rolled (HR) and cold-rolled (CR) steel are common materials.

Parts produced from stock are usually finished on all surfaces, and the general note "Finish all over" on the drawing eliminates the use of finish marks. Figure 17.17 is the drawing of a part to be made from bar stock. Note the specification of material, stock size, etc., in the title.

FIG. 17.17. Working drawing of a part machined from stock. Note the specification of material and stock size in the title block.

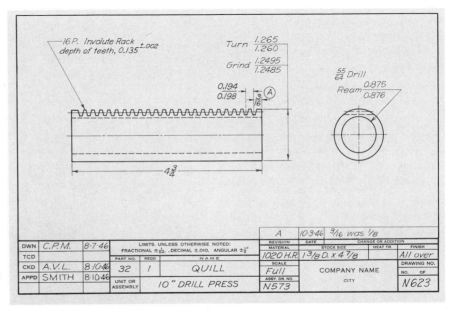

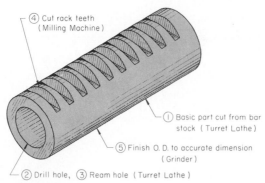

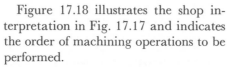

FIG. 17.18. Interpretation of the drawing in Fig. 17.17. This lists machining operations.

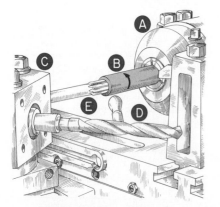

FIG. 17.19. Turret-lathe operations (drilling and reaming). The chuck (*A*) holds, indexes (for length), and rotates the stock (*B*) in the direction shown. The turret (*C*) swings the drill (*D*) and reamer (*E*) successively into position.

Figure 17.18 illustrates the shop interpretation in Fig. 17.17 and indicates the order of machining operations to be performed.

17.16.   THE TURRET LATHE.   The *quill* of Fig. 17.17, produced in quantity, may be made on a turret lathe, except for the rack teeth and the outside-diameter grinding. The stock is held in the collet chuck of the lathe. First the end surface is faced, and then the cylindrical surface (OD) is turned. The work piece is then ready for drilling and reaming. The turret holds the various tools and swings them around into position as needed. A center drill starts a small hole to align the larger drill, and then the drill and reamer are brought successively into position. The drill provides a hole slightly undersize, and then the reamer, cutting with its fluted sides, cleans out the hole and gives a smooth surface finished to a

size within the dimensional limits on the drawing. Figure 17.19 shows the turret indexed so that the drill is out of the way and the reamer in position. At the right is seen the cutoff tool ready to cut the piece to the length shown on the drawing.

17.17.   THE MILLING MACHINE.   The dimensions of the rack teeth (Fig. 17.17) give the depth and spacing of the cuts and the specifications for the cutter to be used. This type of work may be done on a milling machine. The work piece is held in a vise and moved horizontally into the rotating milling cutter, which, in profile, is the shape of the space between the teeth (Fig. 17.20). The cuts are spaced by moving the table of the machine to correspond with the distance shown on the drawing. Note that this operation is a forming process, as the shape depends upon the contour of the cutter. With several cutters mounted together (gang milling), a number of teeth can be cut at the same time.

There are many types of milling cutters made to cut on their peripheries, their sides, or their ends, for forming flat, curved, or special surfaces. Three milling cutters are shown in Fig. 17.21.

17.18.   THE GRINDER.   The general purpose of grinding is to make a smoother and more accurate surface than can be

FIG. 17.20. Milling. The vise (*A*) holds the part (*B*) to the table (*C*), which moves laterally to index cuts and longitudinally, in the direction shown, for individual cuts. The milling cutter (*D*) revolves in the direction shown.

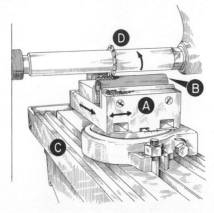

FIG. 17.21. Milling cutters.

obtained by turning, planing, milling, etc. In many cases pieces hardened by heat-treatment will warp slightly; and as ordinary machining methods are impractical with hardened materials, such parts are finish-ground after hardening.

The limit dimensions for the outside diameter of the quill (Fig. 17.17) indicate a grinding operation on a cylindrical grinder (Fig. 17.22). The abrasive wheel rotates at high speed, while the work piece, mounted on a mandrel between conic centers, rotates slowly in the opposite direction. The wheel usually moves laterally to cover the surface of the work piece. The work piece is gaged carefully during the operation to bring the size within the dimensional limits shown on the drawing and to check for a cylindrical surface without taper. The machine for flat surfaces, called a "surface grinder," holds the work piece on a flat table moving back and forth under the abrasive wheel. The table "indexes" laterally after each pass under the work.

17.19. LAPPING, HONING, AND SUPERFINISHING.

These are methods of producing smooth, accurate, mirrorlike surfaces after grinding. All three methods use fine abrasives (1) powdered and carried in oil on a piece of formed soft metal (lapping) or (2) in the form of fine-grained compact stones (honing and superfinishing) to rub against the surface to be finished and reduce scratches and waviness.

17.20. THE BROACHING MACHINE.

A broach is a long, tapered bar with a series of cutting edges (teeth), each successively removing a small amount of material until the last edge forms the shape desired. For flat or irregular external surfaces, the broach and work

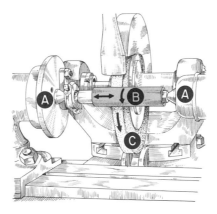

FIG. 17.22. Grinding. The cone centers (A) hold the mandrel, which mounts and rotates the part (B) in the direction shown. The wheel (C) moves laterally to traverse the entire surface of (B).

piece are held by the broaching machine, and the broach is passed across the surface of the work piece. For internal surfaces, the broach is pulled or pushed through a hole to give the finished size and shape.

Some machined shapes can be more economically produced by broaching than by any other method. Figure 17.23 shows several forms of broaches and the shapes they produce.

17.21. SMALL TOOLS.

The shop uses a variety of small tools, both in powered machines and as hand tools. Figure

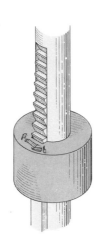

Broaching a Keyway

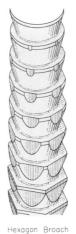

Hexagon Broach

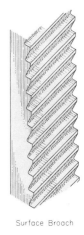

Surface Broach

FIG. 17.23. Broaches. Each tooth takes its small cut as the broach is forced across or through the work piece.

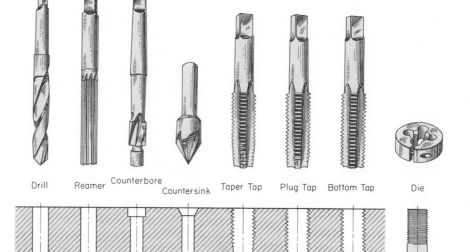

Drill   Reamer   Counterbore   Countersink   Taper Tap   Plug Tap   Bottom Tap   Die

FIG. 17.24.   Small tools.

17.24 shows a *twist drill*, available in a variety of sizes (numbered, lettered, fractional, and metric) for producing holes in almost any material; a *reamer,* used to enlarge and smooth a previously existing hole and to give greater accuracy than is possible by drilling alone; a *counterbore* and a *countersink,* both used to enlarge and alter the end of a hole (usually for screwheads). A *spot-facing tool* is similar to a counterbore. *Taper, plug,* and *bottoming taps* for cutting the thread of a tapped hole and a die for threading a rod or shaft are also shown.

17.22.   WELDED PARTS.   Simple shapes cut from standard rod, bar, or plate stock can be combined by welding to form a finished part. Some machining after the welding process is frequently necessary.

17.23.   PARTS FROM STANDARD SHEET.   A relatively thin sheet or strip of standard thickness may first be cut to size "in the flat" and then bent, formed, punched,

etc., to form the final required part. The drawing should be made so as to give information for the "template maker" and the information required for bending and forming the sheet. Sometimes separate developments (Chap. 14) are made. The thickness of sheet stock is specified by giving (1) the gage (see table, Appendix) and the equivalent thickness in decimals of an inch or (2) only the decimal thickness (the practice followed in specifying aluminum sheet). Figure 15.111 shows a working drawing of a sheet-metal part.

17.24.   PLASTICS.   Plastics are available either in standard bar, rod, tubing, sheet, etc., from which parts can be made by machining, or in granular form to be used in "molding," a process similar to die-casting, in which the material is heated to a plastic state and compressed by a die (compression molding) or injected under pressure into a die (injection molding). Metal inserts for threads, wear bushings, etc., are sometimes cast into the part. Consideration should be given the diemaker when dimensioning the drawing.

17.25. HEAT-TREATMENT. This is a general term applied to the processing of metals by heat and chemicals to change the physical properties of the material.

The glossary of shop terms gives definitions of such heat-treatment processes as annealing, carburizing, casehardening, hardening, normalizing, and tempering.

The specification of heat-treatment may be given on the drawing in several ways: (1) by a general note listing the steps, temperatures, and baths to be used, (2) by a standard heat-treatment number (SAE or company standard) in the space provided in the title block, (3) by giving the Brinell or Rockwell hardness number to be attained, or (4) by giving the tensile strength, in pounds per square inch, to be attained through heat-treatment.

Figures 17.8, 15.67, 15.106, and 15.110 illustrate these methods.

17.26. TOOLS FOR MASS PRODUCTION. Many special machine tools, both semi-automatic and fully automatic, are used in modern factories. These machines are basically the same as ordinary lathes, grinders, etc., but contain mechanisms to control the movements of cutting tools and produce identical parts with little attention from the operator once the machine has been "tooled up." Automatic screw machines and centerless grinders are examples of these special tools.

17.27. JIGS AND FIXTURES. Jigs for holding the work and guiding the tool and fixtures for holding the work greatly extend the production rate for general-purpose machine tools.

17.28. INSPECTION. Careful inspection is an important feature of modern production. Good practice requires inspection after each operation. For production in quantity, special gages are usually employed, but in small-quantity production, the usual measuring instruments, calipers and scale, micrometers, dial gages, etc., are used. For greater precision in gaging, electrical, air, or optical gages are often employed.

17.29. ASSEMBLY. The finished separate pieces come to the assembly department to be put together according to the assembly drawings. Sometimes it is desirable or necessary to perform some small machining operation during assembly, often drilling, reaming, or hand finishing. In such cases the assembly drawing should carry a note explaining the required operation and give dimensions for the alignment or location of the pieces. If some parts are to be combined before final assembly, a subassembly drawing or the detail drawings of each piece will give the required information; "⅛ drill in assembly with piece No. 107" is a typical note form for an assembly machining operation.

Design is one of the most important studies in engineering because upon good design rests the ultimate success of a machine or structure. Design as such encompasses many areas of endeavor from the world of art to that of applied science. In this chapter we are concerned principally with the fundamentals of greatest interest to the engineer.

Fundamentals of Design

18.1. INTRODUCTORY. The word "design" has many meanings. A digest of various dictionary definitions is: to plan, conceive, invent, and to designate so as to transmit the plan to others. *Design* has many purely artistic connotations. For example, the design of fabrics, clothing, furniture, etc. In engineering, design has come to mean that broad category of invention leading to the production of useful devices.

Design, from the latin "designare" (to mark out), is the process of developing plans, schemes, directions, and specifications for something new. Thus it is within context to speak of Hitler's designs for world conquest; the design (conception) of a book, play, or motion picture; or the design of fabric, clothing, furniture, appliances, or other completely physical objects. Design is distinguished from production and craftsmanship: design is the creative original plan, and the production and craftsmanship are a part of the execution of the plan.

Design means creation in the purest sense. Specifically, design does not go beyond creation, and it logically follows that the execution of a design, that is, the carrying out of the plan by presentation, action, production, manufacture, craftsmanship, and use are not design at all but are simply and positively the products of the design. Also, when examining a finished product,

597

it is proper to speak of the *design* of it, and by this term of reference we mean the original plan or scheme and not the product itself.

A design may be presented by means of drawings, models, patterns, specifications, or other similar methods of communication. By whatever means the design is made known, every detail important to consummation must be given. This will include such items as materials and their capabilities, the methods of adapting the materials to their purpose or work, the relationship of parts within the whole, and the effect of the finished product upon those who may see it, use it, or become involved with it.

Design is a word used more or less loosely in all the arts in referring to composition, style, decoration, or any relationship of the parts of a complete entity. In some areas, notably in architecture and in product design, art and engineering affect each other, so that complete freedom is often somewhat restricted. Usually, painters, poets, musicians, and some others can design with great freedom.

Logically, one who designs is called a designer. All designers must be experi-

FIG. 18.1. Aesthetic design. The design has no function other than to decorate.

enced and educationally organized and oriented. In other words a designer must know a great deal about what he is attempting to design or he will fail miserably. As an example, suppose that a person who has never fished and knows nothing about the sport, attempts to design a fishing reel. Because of his ignorance of such aspects as weight, balance, line capacity, drag characteristics, and over-all performance such a person is completely incapable of producing a good design. Nevertheless, most good engineering designers are capable of designing a wide variety of devices because of their knowledge of materials, processes, production methods, and other related aspects. Designers may be likened to executives in large companies, especially such people as editors and directors. The executive will decide policies and business methods and then transmit his ideas to colleagues who carry out the executive orders. A designer conceives his design and then transmits his plans to others who produce the product. This does not mean, however, that a designer never is involved in production. Especially in the fine arts, a designer may actually produce the product himself.

Design in a broad sense can be, and often is, classified according to its relationship to practicality. Thus, *abstract design* has no relationship whatever to useful or physical objects and is intended only to create a visual interest or impact. The frontispiece of this chapter is an example of abstract design. Much of so-called "modern" art is abstract design. *Aesthetic design* is a design applied to some useful object. The design is intended for decorative purposes alone, and has nothing whatever to do with the usefulness of the object. Figure 18.1 shows the design of a lace mantilla, a traditional head

covering for women. The design is aesthetic only and performs no practical purpose in effectively covering the head. Other examples of aesthetic design are found in furniture, architecture, motorcars, appliances, floor coverings, and other useful objects where the design per se has no function but to decorate and create an aesthetic impact. *Aesthetic functional* design is that category of design where aesthetic and functional aspects are closely allied. An example is shown in Fig. 18.2. This is the new Baldwin theatre organ, a fine musical instrument as well as an outstanding aesthetic and traditional design. To see how function affects aesthetics note that the seat must be wide enough at the base to cover the width of the 32-note pedal board. Thus, the aesthetic design of the seat must be accommodated to functional requirements. The curved console is not only

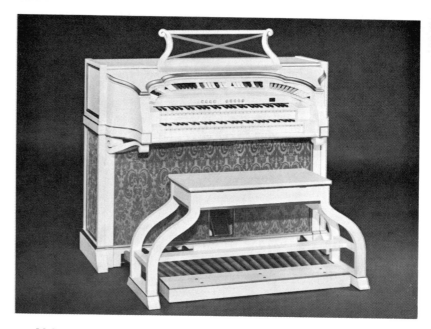

FIG. 18.2. Aesthetic-functional design. Aesthetics and functionalism are affected by each other.

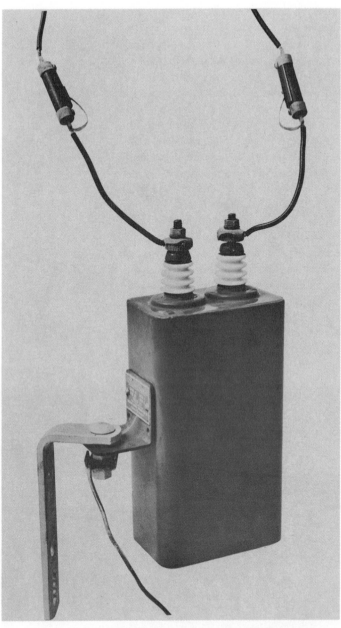

FIG. 18.3. Purely functional design. Aesthetics plays no part, and is not considered important in any way.

traditional and aesthetically interesting but also has a function in that the tabs controlling the voices on the two manuals are more convenient to the organist. It is interesting to note here that the Baldwin theatre organ contains completely transistorized tone generators and amplifiers and the most modern of speaker systems, and the cabinet proper must be sized and designed for acoustics and to accommodate the fundamental parts of the instrument. *Purely functional design* is any design where function is completely dominant with aesthetics not considered at all. An example is shown in Fig. 18.3, a picture of a 3KVAR, 250-volt single-phase 60-cycle capacitor used on electric transmission lines. This piece of equipment is completely functional and aesthetics plays no part in the design. Other examples are machines such as lathes, boring machines, motors, power tools, conveyors, material-handling equipment, and the great bulk of manufacturing and production equipment.

Even though aesthetic considerations may be present in engineering design, the emphasis in this discussion must necessarily be restricted to good functional engineering design. However, never entertain the thought that pure function always prevails as the governing factor. As an example, in early automotive design the machine proper was designed, and then the body was designed to cover the machine. Recent automotive design shows that because of body shape, many components have been redesigned and moved from former positions in order to accommodate to body design.

Some of the best examples of design in all aspects are to be found in automotive and commercial aircraft design. Purely aesthetic features are evidenced in colors used; elegance of fabric, plastic, or leather in upholstery; finish and appearance of appointments, body lines, and artistic configuration. Functional-aesthetic features are obvious in such aspects as artful and functional controls, dials, instruments, glass areas, seat comfort, and safety features. Purely functional design is clearly manifested by examination of the power supply and all of its auxiliaries and components.

There are many categories of engineering design, such as machine design and structural design. Paralleling this, the designer working in a particular field is designated by his field or subclassification in it: for example, machine designer, appliance designer, structural designer, automotive parts designer, etc.

Even though the field of design is broad, all designers think and produce in much the same manner. Simply put, the designer draws upon his background of knowledge and experience in producing a new entity. Thus, every designer must have (1) knowledge in his field, (2) experience, (3) inventive ability, (4) a knowledge of materials and processes, and (5) the ability to represent (draw) so as to transmit his designs to others.

All this is not quite as difficult as one might think. The real key lies mostly in the ability to *draw*, both freehand and with instruments; it is then the creation develops. At this time all the designer's knowledge, experience, and skill are brought to fruition. As he thinks of ways to solve the problem—considering methods, materials, combinations, and arrangement of components—he records his thoughts and develops his design. Because of the creative aspect, designing is personally very interesting and satisfying.

It is our purpose in this chapter to describe the processes of creation and development and to give advice on what authorities consider to be good design.

18.2.   THE NECESSARY BACKGROUND OF KNOWLEDGE AND EXPERIENCE.   No designing is possible for people unfamiliar with the problem at hand and with the possible methods of solution. Thus, first of all, a designer must have a thorough knowledge of all the elements involved. This means also that for every particular "field of endeavor," the background will be dictated by that field. Nevertheless, no field today is quite "pure." As an example, in mechanical engineering there will most certainly be many cases where an electrical application is an important part of the mechanical device, and vice versa. Therefore, a diversified background is a distinct advantage. Furthermore, the necessary background will vary considerably, depending upon the extent of scientific education and training required. For example, a designer working in one of the aerospace fields must have extensive study in physics, chemistry, mathematics, etc., while a designer working for a company which manufactures small home appliances would probably not need anything beyond basic courses. Further, it should be noted that in conference with many top executives and designers in the aerospace as well as in highly technical electronics fields, it has been learned that a number of men having a terminal technical training of only two years have, nevertheless, through experience of a few years, become valuable to the company as designers of fairly complex machines. It is the judgement of this author, however, that the extent of technical training dictates the extent to which a designer can expect to work on highly technical equipment. But it may also be said that experience in the field will make up to some extent for a lack of formal education.

Every designer, no matter what the field or the product, *must* have a thorough training in graphics. Without it, a designer would fail completely because as the design conception proceeds, the designer's own thinking must be recorded in the form of sketches and drawings. Furthermore, as the design is developed it must be discussed with and approved by such people as the chief designer, chief engineer, and management executives. This means that clear and concise communication is necessary, which is accomplished through the sketches and drawings made by the designer. The design drawings will often be augmented and supported by mathematical data and diagrams, sometimes including computer data, but the designer's sketches and drawings and his discussion and explanation are the most significant aspect of communication. As has often been said, although it is quite impossible to describe even a simple component in words, communication is very simply and directly accomplished with a drawing.

Figure 18.4 is an example of a very early design drawing by Leonardo da Vinci (dating from about A.D. 1500). Because of his great ability to represent graphically, da Vinci was able to convey a design with great clarity in a single drawing.

In addition to the ability to express himself graphically, a designer must have a complete knowledge of processes, materials, methods of fastening and of assembly, types of finishes, and economical methods of production, as well as a knowledge of aesthetic values.

The paragraphs following give information on how a designer carries his work forward to produce the good design of a complete entity made with good components, and the thought he must give to drawings, materials, processes, fastening, assembly, finishes, economics, and aesthetics.

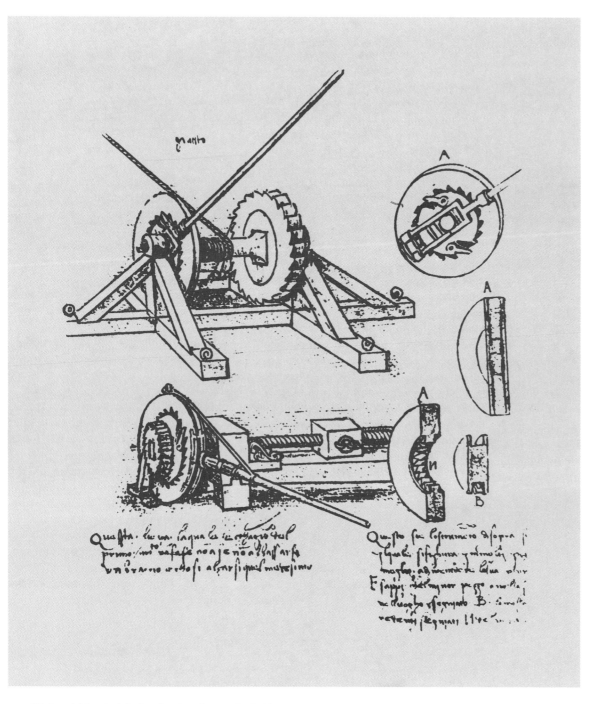

FIG. 18.4. A historical design drawing. Leonardo da Vinci (about A.D. 1500).

18.3. PROCEDURE—HOW A DESIGNER THINKS. *First,* in approaching a new project, the designer must recognize and thoroughly understand every phase of the problem. This will include all information necessary to state what the device is expected to accomplish and the pertinent data such as speeds, pressures, temperatures, and operating conditions. Also, statements of relative size and appearance are often included.

Second, the search for solutions is started, and here the real ability to create shows itself. In the beginning, conventional solutions will come to mind, and there may be several of them. Then, as the investigation continues, newer, more modern, and previously unheard-of answers may appear. At this stage the designer should let his imagination really "run rampant." Every unusual physical, chemical, and electrical application, use of material, combination of elements, and their relationships, should be carefully studied. A number of possible solutions will probably emerge. Sensitivity to the problem, the ability and desire to create, coupled with originality and the worker's ability to analyze and synthesize, characterizes this stage of the work. Perseverance and persistence offer the key to success here.

While the solutions are being composed, the designer must make sketches for his own use. To be sure, these may be very "rough" and may lack detailed information, but they will probably include many written notes giving information for later use. This is where real ability and facility in the use of the graphic language play a very important role. An active mind and fluency at recording the mind's products of originality on paper combine to produce at successful solutions.

Third, all of the solutions should be evaluated. This analysis must include feasibility of the design from every standpoint—from every engineering detail to economics and aesthetics. This must be done carefully and honestly because it is principally self-evaluation. Personal idiosyncrasies and preferences should be subservient to a completely "open mind."

Fourth, either decide on the best solution or continue the search for a better solution.

Fifth, obtain approval of the design. The practice here, varies with the size of the organization. Company practice prevails.

Sixth, refine and correct the original design and make more complete sketches as a guide before starting a formal design drawing. Some alterations may be a result of the approval conference on the design.

Seventh, make a formal design drawing. This drawing must show all information that will be needed by detailers who will make the individual part drawings, subassemblies, and assemblies.

Eighth, obtain final approval of the design.

A comparison of this thought procedure with the formal design procedure illustrated on the opposite page will help the student to understand how one informs the other.

DESIGN PROCEDURE

PHASE ONE—THE PROJECT

A. Discussion with management, engineering, client.
B. Statements and specification of the design problem.
C. Collection of all pertinent information.

PHASE TWO—FORMULATION

A. Recognition of requirements.
B. Definition of requirements.
C. Consideration of previous designs.
D. Assembly of all original data needed—mathematical, graphical, mechanical, electrical, etc.

PHASE THREE—CONCEPTS

A. Preliminary design sketches.
B. Preliminary design data giving materials, methods, construction details, and projected characteristics.

PHASE FOUR—ANALYSIS

A. Critical analysis of all design concepts.
B. Selection of most promising design or designs.

PHASE FIVE—DESIGN CONFERENCE

A. Discussion of preliminary designs with engineering, management, client.
B. Approval of design or designs.

PHASE SIX—REFINEMENT

A. More complete drawings and specifications of selected design or designs.
B. More complete data supporting projected design.

PHASE SEVEN—DESIGN CONFERENCE

A. Discussion of refined design or designs.
B. Approval of most promising design.

PHASE EIGHT—SYNTHESIS

A. Projected design supported by mathematical, graphical, and computer-aided and combined systems data.
B. Investigation of all physical aspects and proof of soundness of the design.

PHASE NINE—MODELS

A. Components.
B. Mock-ups.
C. Models of critical features.

PHASE TEN—TESTING

A. Proof of operating characteristics of components.
B. Proof of soundness of complete entity.

PHASE ELEVEN—CONFERENCE

A. Final discussion with originating authority.
B. Approval of final design.

PHASE TWELVE—FINAL PREPARATION

A. Final design drawings.
B. Final specifications.

PHASE THIRTEEN—TRANSMITTAL

A. Transmittal of final design drawings and specifications to originating authority.

NOTE: In the outline above three conferences (Phases 5, 7, and 11) are scheduled with the originating authority, engineering, and management. This is usual, but it does *not* mean that these are the only conferences during the development of the project. The designer confers frequently with colleagues, and with engineers, components suppliers, materials experts, and others, to obtain information and confirm design features.

18.4. DRAWINGS. Design drawings are not like other drawings (assembly and detail drawings) previously discussed in this text. The difference is that design drawings supply the information *from which* assembly and detail drawings will be made. Design drawings may be divided into two classes, *preliminary* and *final.*

Preliminary design drawings, for the most part, are sketches, although some (usually in the later stages of design) may be instrument drawings. Figures 18.5 to 18.8 illustrate preliminary design drawings. These are made freehand. While working up the sketches, the designer is keenly attentive to the solution of the problem, as described in paragraph 18.3. As the creative process goes forward every aspect of the final design must be considered and recorded.

As an example of how the design thinking and the preliminary drawings are brought forward together, Figs. 18.5 to 18.8 illustrate a series of design drawings made for a nutcracker. The first drawing, Fig. 18.5, shows that the designer conceived a lever and base with fixed and pivoted pads between which the nut would be placed. It is immediately obvious that when the shell breaks, the release of counter force will allow the lever to descend at once and crush the nut meat. The second design, Fig. 18.6, is a refinement over the first design with the linkage arranged so that when the actuating lever descends to its maximum, the holding pads will come to a minimum separation, but no closer together.

FIG. 18.5. Design sketch of nutcracker. This is the first of a series.

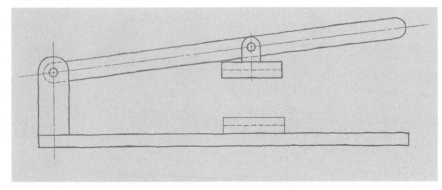

FIG. 18.6. Design sketch of nutcracker. This is a refinement of the first sketch (Fig. 18.5).

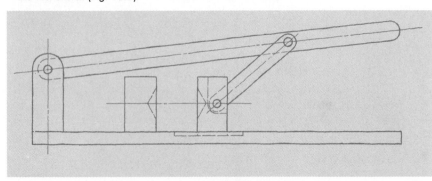

A further refinement is seen in Fig. 18.7, where the linkage is reversed to place it away from the hand position on the operating lever. Finally, in Fig. 18.8, the basic arrangement of Fig. 18.7 is refined to include an adjustable distance between the holding pads. Also at this time a more accurate and complete drawing is made, and some basic dimensions and details, including material types, are added.

A much more sophisticated and complex example of design thinking is described below. The accompanying drawings are shown in Figs. 18.9 to 18.14. The final design drawing prepared for presentation at an engineering and management conference, is shown in Fig. 18.15. For purposes of authenticity the following is an excerpt from the designer's file of notes and comments on the design through all stages of development.

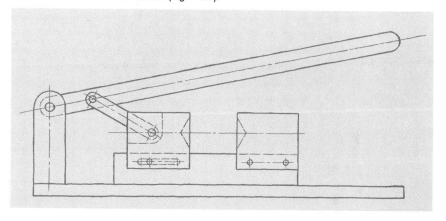

FIG. 18.7. Design sketch of nutcracker. This is the third in a series, a refinement of the second (Fig. 18.6).

FIG. 18.8. Design drawing of nutcracker. This represents the final design which is the culmination of progressive thinking and refinement in solving the problem.

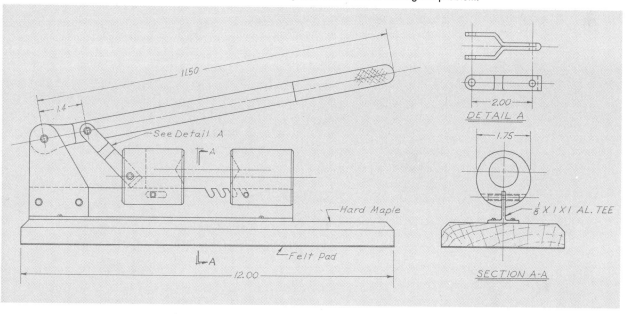

DESIGN PROBLEM 2016

Problem

Design a device to collect seawater samples at any desired depth. This device, on one trip to sea bottom and back, must collect at least six samples and preferably two or three times that number.

Operating Conditions

Salt water, depth nearly seven miles, maximum pressure about six tons per square inch, water significantly compressible at this pressure.

Preliminary Solutions and Comments (see sketches, Figs. 18.9 to 18.14)

Design 1 (Fig. 18.9). A pull on the actuator cable will swing arm in and up, tripping lever and opening port. Slacking off on cable permits return spring to move arm out again. The next pull will open the next chamber above, etc. A spring to close each port after its chamber fills will be required.

Disadvantages: Too complicated. Cables will twist together and tangle. Leverage is good, but may not be sufficient to open ports at high pressures. Operation will always be uncertain.

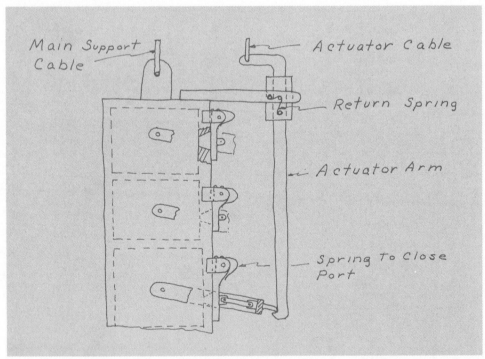

FIG. 18.9. Preliminary design sketch 1 of water sampler.

Design 2 (Fig. 18.10). A pull on the actuator cable will index the external cylinder relative to the internal cylinder containing the collecting chambers. Each index will line up a pair of holes between the two cylinders permitting each chamber to fill in turn.

Disadvantages: Sealing off chambers will be difficult. Cable stretch and tangling will make indexing inaccurate and uncertain. Cylinders may stick together, making indexing uncertain.

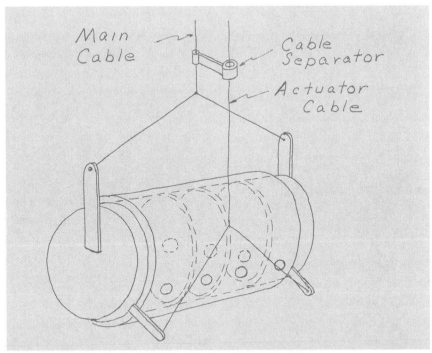

FIG. 18.10. Preliminary design sketch 2 of water sampler.

Design 3 (Fig. 18.11). Each chamber contains a preloaded spring pressing a ground valve into its seat. Each spring is carefully loaded to permit the valve to open at a definite pressure.

Disadvantages: Spring calibration will change with corrosion and use. Temperature and salinity variations will prevent pressure from varying as a straight-line function of depth, i.e., depth at which each chamber opens will be uncertain.

Note: Electrical contacts could be designed to send signal to surface indicating when chamber opened. A premeasured suspension cable will then indicate depth.

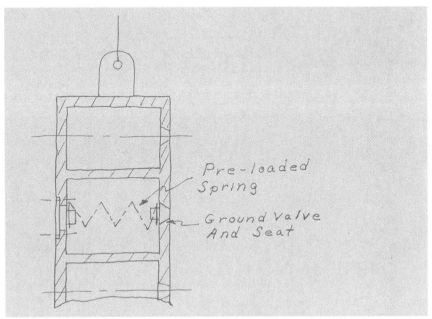

FIG. 18.11. Preliminary design sketch 3 of water sampler.

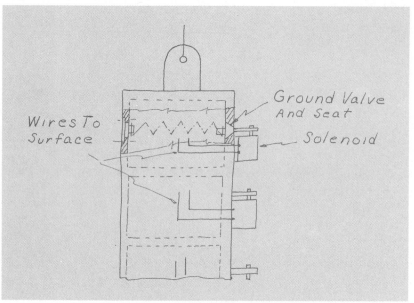

FIG. 18.12. Preliminary design sketch 4 of water sampler.

Design 4 *(Fig. 18.12)*. This design is basically the same as design 3. A solenoid plunger engages an extension on the valve so that it will stay closed until an electrical impulse from the surface retracts the plunger. Spring for each depth will exert less force than comparable spring from design 3.

Disadvantages: Too many wires to run to surface. Trapped air may not allow cylinders to fill completely. Trapped air and slight expansion of water brought up from great depth will build high internal cylinder pressure at surface. Both high external and internal pressures (at different times) makes cylinder design difficult. Removing water samples will be a problem.

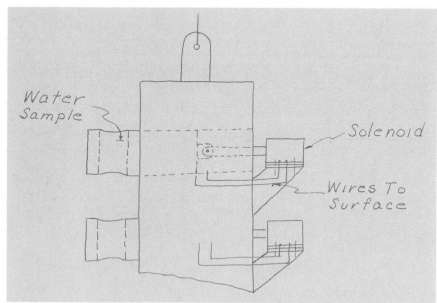

FIG. 18.13. Preliminary design sketch 5 of water sampler.

Design 5 *(Fig. 18.13)*. The chambers used to collect samples are cut into close-fitting Teflon-coated pistons. Water flows continually through chambers until solenoids retract them into housing. Samples are collected from bottom, coming up. As internal pressure builds up, it will tend to bleed off around piston. External water will not contaminate sample as long as some positive pressure remains in chamber.

Disadvantages: Too many solenoids and too many wires. All electrical systems will have to be specially designed to withstand the pressure. Solenoid will have to stay energized to hold sample in place. It may be impossible to get a reasonable-sized solenoid to give a stroke that is long enough.

Design 6 (Fig. 18.14). Each chamber remains in open water as in design 5 until it is pushed into the housing. A single solenoid operated repeatedly indexes the tripper vertically up the housing. After the solenoid indexes the proper number of times, the tripper engages the trip pin holding one of the cylinders in place. As the trip pin is lifted, the compression spring pushes the cylinder into the housing, collecting a sample. The solenoid continues indexing the tripper vertically, with each current impulse from surface tripping each of the cylinders in turn.

Disadvantages: Complicated. Electrical components must be specially designed.

Notes: This looks good enough to make a design layout and to contact manufacturers of solenoids about the electrical design.

The electrical current can be monitored at the surface with an oscilloscope to tell if solenoid has indexed properly with each current impulse sent to it.

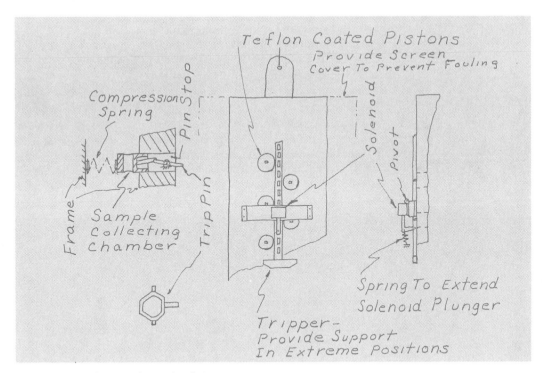

FIG. 18.14. Preliminary design sketch 6 of water sampler.

**PRESENTATION TO ENGINEERING-
MANAGEMENT CONFERENCE**

This explanation accompanies the design drawing, Fig. 18.15:

The solenoid (1) is energized, thus moving the trip arm (2) with trip lugs (3) up the housing (4). When the solenoid is deenergized, the return spring (5) pulls the solenoid arm out and over the trip arm and positions the solenoid arm in the next slot on the trip arm. This action is possible because of the hinging of the solenoid mount plate (6). The trip arm is not pushed down by this action due to the spring-loaded antireversing pawl (7), which locks into a slot in the trip arm. As the trip arm moves up, the trip lugs trip the trigger mechanism (8) built within the cylinder.

The piston (9) is then forced into the housing by the spring force of the load spring (10). This operation is continued, triggering cylinders at required depths. The cylinders are machined into the lower portion of the housing, with the upper portion of the housing not bored, but used to serve as additional weight and support for the trip arm during its upward motion.

When this device is brought to the surface, water samples are obtained from each cylinder by opening the individual petcock (11) for each cylinder in turn.

To reload this device a threaded tee wrench is passed through the hole in the housing support for the load spring and screwed into the piston. The piston is then retracted, and the trigger mechanism is reset manually.

This entire device should be surrounded by a wire cage to prevent fouling.

Final design drawings. Figure 18.15 is an example of a typical final design drawing. It represents the culmination of previous design sketches into a final, complete and accurate drawing, accompanied by all necessary data and specifications. From this drawing, detail and assembly drawings will be made. See also Fig. 19.1.

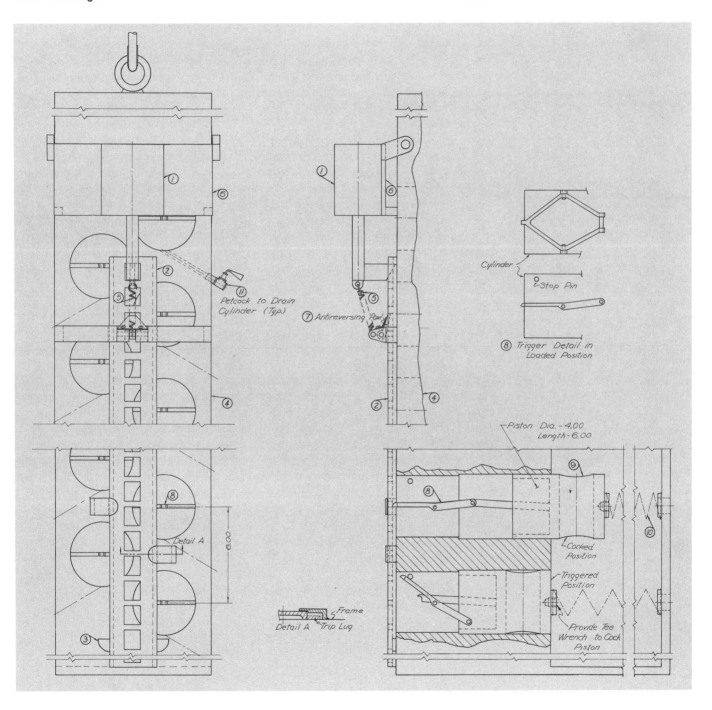

FIG. 18.15.   Design drawing of water sampler.

18.5. MANDATORY RELATIONSHIPS OF DESIGN, MATERIALS AND CONSTRUCTION. In any design, a prime factor is consideration of materials to be used. This is because, to some extent, the fastening of parts, their relationship, and often their detailed shape and the aesthetic appearance of the complete entity are affected by the materials used. More important reasons, however, are the conditions under which the machine is expected to operate. For example, a machine to be used in both tropical and extremely cold climates will have to be made of materials not adversely affected by either climate. In the hot and humid climate, parts deteriorate because of heat, corrosion due to humidity, and damage by fungous growths. On the other hand, in an extremely cold climate, contraction causes reduction of clearances and parts may "freeze" in position. Also, in extreme cold some materials become brittle and crack or break, operational difficulties are caused by cold "gummy" lubricants, and hazards are created by frost and ice. The same conditions prevail for many aircraft parts. From summertime ground temperatures of plus 90°F or so, in a very short time, an airplane may be flying at 30,000 ft where the temperature may be of the order of minus 40°F. Even if a device will still operate at two temperature extremes, the operational characteristics, especially in delicate instruments, may change radically, making either insulation or maintenance at a constant temperature (or both) a necessary part of the design.

The actual details of construction also have much to do with the successful operation of a machine. Inadequate bearing surfaces or insufficient lubrication will cause the machine to have a short operating life before repair or replacement. Protective seals against contaminants, abrasive materials, or corrosive liquids and gases, are frequently necessary. Even "foolproof" design and construction against mishandling is important. The designer himself, or another engineer familiar with the equipment might operate a particular machine with a sensitive regard for its lacks or inadequacy, but, especially when home appliances or other devices operated by laymen are designed, precautions against mishandling must be provided. Control knobs that come off and get lost; levers that break; screws and nuts that readily loosen and drop off; multiple ("stacked") controls so made that the careless person can inadvertently move two or more while adjusting one; finishes that rust, corrode, pit, and wear off; parts that are difficult to keep clean, and many other similar factors are all abominations that will cause the purchaser and user to take a very dim view of the relative quality of the device. The cardinal rule is to design and dictate construction details to provide as many guards against damage to the device as is consistent with the price range of the product.

To summarize the foregoing discussion, it may be said that the design, the materials used, and the details of construction are all so closely interrelated for ultimate success of the device that they must be considered simultaneously.

Through consultations and discussions with designers in many different fields, the author has formed the opinion that all designers do not think in exactly the same way. Indeed, the same designer may not approach any particular problem according to a fixed pattern. Nevertheless, most designers consider the material first and then, closely following, will think of the design of the part and how it is attached to mating parts. This is because the material used more or less determines the detailed shape of a part. For example a cast part will have a somewhat different configuration than that of a sheet-metal part or a part machined from solid material. If the part is designed before the material and method of production is determined, some adjustments in the design will probably have to be made. Following this philosophy, the next four paragraphs give (18.6) characteristics of materials, (18.7) methods of parts production, (18.8) good design and proportioning of parts, and (18.9) assembly—fastening and joining of parts.

18.6. CHARACTERISTICS OF MATERIALS. It is impossible, in the space available in this text, to give all available information on materials. Complete listings would include all detailed characteristics of strength, heat-treatment, resistance to corrosion, hardness, toughness, wear resistance, machinability, ductility, and so many others that the descriptions would fill a large book. The summarized material following, however, will serve as a guide to the principal characteristics and uses of most common materials. Detailed information will be found as needed in the standards of the ANSI, ASME, ASTM, ASM, AISE, and SAE, and in such publications as *Machinery's Handbook and Materials in Design Engineering,* a periodical published by the Reinhold Publishing Corp., 430 Park Avenue, New York, N.Y. Also see Glossary. It is not considered to be within our premise to engage here in a discussion of the strengths of materials.

FERROUS METALS

CAST IRON—GRAY. Widely used because of the ease with which a great variety of parts can be made. Good machining properties; can be joined by welding; can be brazed; fairly resistant to corrosion.

CAST IRON—NODULAR AND DUCTILE FORMS. Similar to ordinary gray irons, but with controlled alloy composition for ductility and strength. Good machinability; can be welded by most fusion processes; fairly resistant to corrosion.

CAST IRON—MALLEABLE. The malleableizing process produces a structure similar to steel. Good machining qualities; can be joined by welding, brazing, and soldering. Resistant to corrosion in rural, industrial, and marine atmospheres, both fresh and salt water.

CAST IRON—WHITE AND ALLOY. These irons are compounded to obtain special properties. Nickel, chromium, and molybdenum are added for wear and abrasion resistance. Large amounts of silicon, nickel, and aluminum produce irons resistant to heat and corrosion.

IRON—INGOT. Available as sheets, strips, wire, and rail sections. Readily joined by resistance, arc, and gas welding. Corrosion resistance is poor—all types are rusted by oxygen and water at room temperature.

IRON—WROUGHT. Available as tubular products, plates, sheets, bars, structural shapes, wire, chain; fair corrosion resistance (better than carbon steels).

STEEL, CARBON—HARDENING GRADES. Available as hot- and cold-rolled strips, bars, rods, and mill shapes, these steels are almost always heat-treated to give hardness, strength, and resistance to wear. Depending upon composition, machining qualities are fair to excellent. Forging qualities are good; welding requires special practices. Corrosion resistance is poor—all types are rusted by oxygen and water at room temperature.

STEEL, CARBON—CARBURIZING GRADES. Available in all mill forms, these steels are for case-hardening by carburizing, giving a strong, tough core and a very hard "skin." They can be welded, but some grades require special practice. Machining qualities vary from poor to excellent; forging qualities are generally good. Corrosion resistance is poor —all types are rusted by oxygen and water at room temperature.

STEEL, NITRIDING—WROUGHT. These steels are treated by nitriding to give an extremely hard outer surface and are heat-treated for toughness and strength. Can be welded by the atomic hydrogen process. Most uses of these steels are based on resistance to wear. If the nitrided outer layer is not removed, the case is quite corrosion-resistant to alkalis, oils, combustion products, and to fresh and salt water.

STEEL, ALLOY—WROUGHT. This class of steels in both carburizing and hardening grades (AISI 1340 to 9255) offers a variety for various purposes where different degrees of hardness and strength are required. In general, corrosion resistance is fair (better than that of plain, or non-alloy, carbon steels).

STEEL, HIGH-STRENGTH—WROUGHT. Available in most standard mill forms and structural shapes, these niobium- (columbium-) and vanadium-bearing carbon steels are used principally for structural purposes.

STEEL, ULTRA-HIGH-STRENGTH—WROUGHT. Available in most standard wrought forms, these steels are used primarily where a high strength-to-weight ratio is required. Readily welded.

STEEL, FREE-CUTTING—WROUGHT. Available in cold-drawn shapes, these steels are used for a variety of parts such as studs, nuts, fasteners, collars, dowels.

STEEL, HIGH-TEMPERATURE—WROUGHT. Available in sheets, strips, plates, bars, forgings, tubing, these steels are used for such parts as turbine buckets, jet-engine compressor blades, etc., where high strength at high temperature is required. Good resistance to atmospheric corrosion.

STEEL, STAINLESS AUSTENITIC—WROUGHT. Obtainable in sheets, strips, plates, bars, wire, and tubing, these steels, as the name implies, are for corrosion-resistant applications. These stainless steels have a fair index of machinability and are readily welded. Depending upon composition, grades vary from general purpose to types which resist both corrosion and heat.

STEELS, STAINLESS FERRITIC—WROUGHT. These stainless steels are general-purpose grades having fair to excellent machinability and fair weldability, which are used in such applications as automobile trim, kitchen equipment, and chemical equipment. Some grades also resist corrosion at high temperature.

STEELS, MARTENSITIC STAINLESS—WROUGHT. These stainless steels have good corrosive resistance to weather and water and to some chemicals; used for instruments, cutlery, springs, and applications requiring good mechanical properties at high temperatures.

STEELS, STAINLESS AGE-HARDENABLE—WROUGHT, CAST. These stainless steels are used for structural parts where a high strength-weight ratio is required or for parts requiring high strength, good resistance to corrosion, and ease of fabrication.

IRON-BASE SUPERALLOYS (Cr-Ni)—WROUGHT. These alloys are used for highly stressed parts at elevated temperatures; corrosion resistance excellent; machinability and weldability only fair.

IRON-BASE SUPERALLOYS (Cr-Ni-Co)—CAST, WROUGHT. These alloys have good resistance to corrosion at elevated temperatures; used for such parts as gas-turbine blades, vanes, and nozzles.

STEEL, CARBON—CAST. These steels have good machinability and weldability; poor corrosion resistance; used for applications requiring good to high strength, good machinability, toughness, wear, and fatigue resistance.

STEELS, ALLOY—CAST. Properties are similar to those of cast carbon steels except that high-temperature properties are better. Some of these steels are intended for applications requiring high strength, wear resistance, high hardness, and high fatigue resistance.

STEELS, STAINLESS—CAST. These stainless steels, in a variety of compositions, are easily welded by metal arc. Corrosion resistance is excellent, including strong reducing and oxidizing media. Tensile strengths from about 70,000 to 140,000 psi.

ALLOYS, HEAT-RESISTANT—CAST. These metals have good machinability, can be welded by all common methods, and maintain good mechanical properties at high temperatures.

STEELS, TOOL—WROUGHT. These steels, in a variety of compositions, are used principally for machine tools and dies where strength, toughness, and resistance to wear are required.

NONFERROUS METALS

ALUMINUM AND ITS ALLOYS—WROUGHT AND CAST. Most of the alloys for wrought forms are available in sheets, plates, rods, bars, tubes, extrusions, and structural shapes. This class of metals offers a wide variety of compositions all having high resistance to rural atmospheres. Some have good resistance to fresh and sea water and also to organic acids, anhydrides, aldehydes, esters, ketones, petroleum derivatives, ammonium compounds, and other commercial chemicals. Machinability and weldability are good. The uses are many and varied—electrical conductors, chemical equipment, cooking utensils, architectural applications, pressure tubes, bus and truck bodies, transportation equipment, auto and appliance trim, screw machine products, pipe and hardware, structural parts for aircraft, transmission cases, among others.

COBALT-BASE ALLOYS—CAST, WROUGHT. Wrought forms are sheets, bars, billets, forgings, and wire. These metals are used for high-temperature applications requiring strength and corrosion resistance.

TUNGSTEN, TANTALUM, MOLYBDENUM. These metals are used for a variety of electrical applications such as filaments, contacts, capacitors and for such aerospace applications as rocket nozzles, heat shields, radiation shields, and structural parts.

NIOBIUM (COLUMBIUM) AND ITS ALLOYS. These metals are used principally for parts requiring good strength at elevated temperatures, especially in missile and space-vehicle structures and components.

COPPER AND ITS ALLOYS—WROUGHT, CAST. Available in pure form and in combination with many other metals. Alloys include phosphorus, tellurium, sulfur, zirconium, beryllium, chromium. Commercial bronze is 90% copper, 10% zinc. Red brass is 85% copper, 15% zinc. Other brasses have more zinc and less copper down to yellow brass, which is 65% copper and 35% zinc. Muntz metal is 60% copper and 40% zinc. When the copper-zinc combination is altered by the addition of lead, so-called leaded bronzes and brasses are produced. All alloys have good resistance to rural, marine, and industrial atmospheres. With some exceptions, joining by soldering and welding is excellent. Wrought forms are sheets, rods, strips, plates, bars, wire, foil, tubes, and pipe. Uses include a wide variety of electrical, architectural, and mechanical applications; copper is outstanding for thermal and electrical conductivity; copper, bronze, and brass are also used extensively for artistic and decorative purposes.

LEAD AND ITS ALLOYS.   Lead is used in pure form (chemical lead) and combined with tellurium for chemical apparatus. Common soft lead (Pb 99.73 +) is used commercially for such applications as storage batteries, cable sheathing, alloying, and coatings. The wrought forms (1% to 9% Sb) are commonly used for roofing and flashing, extruded pipe, and corrosion-resistant applications requiring more strength than soft lead. All forms are resistant to sulfuric, sulfurous, phosphoric, and chromic acids, but are attacked by acetic, formic, and nitric acids. Very resistant to all atmospheres and to fresh and salt water.

MAGNESIUM ALLOYS.   Magnesium alloys are available in wrought sheets, rods, bars, and extrusions and also for sand and die castings. Because of their lightness and strength, these alloys are particularly useful in aircraft, missile, and aerospace applications, and for the same reasons are also used extensively in such applications as electronic housings, office machines, appliances, luggage, cameras and optical equipment, and sporting goods, among others. Magnesium has good resistance to atmospheres, but it is attacked by salt water unless its surface is finished.

NICKEL AND ITS ALLOYS.   Many different alloys are available. Nickel 200 and 201, Duranickel, and Monel 400 and K-500 are commonly used for parts requiring a combination of strength, ductility, and corrosion resistance. Inconel is used extensively for applications where oxidizing and carburizing atmospheres at elevated temperatures are present. Monel 411 and 505 are used extensively for food-handling equipment, tanks, boilers, valve seats, liners, bushings. Low-expansion nickel alloys are valuable for length-standard bars, bimetal thermostats and similar low-expansion applications. Nickel-base superalloys are much used in jet-engine, missile, and furnace applications where high-temperature strength and resistance to corrosion are important factors.

PRECIOUS METALS.   The precious metals are, of course, much used for jewelry and other art applications, but are also valuable for engineering purposes. The following entries indicate typical uses.

Gold.   Lining of chemical equipment, high-melting solder alloys, dentistry. Gold does not oxidize when heated in air.

Silver.   Electrical contacts, corrosion-resistant equipment, photographic equipment, brazing alloys. Does not oxidize when heated in air. Resists most dilute mineral acids and alkalis.

Platinum.   Chemical equipment, electrical contacts, catalysts, laboratory equipment, thermocouples. Very good oxidation resistance, but is dissolved by aqua regia.

Palladium.   Electrical contacts, catalysts, hydrogen production, dental alloys. Resists hydrofluoric, acetic, and phosphoric acids.

Rhodium.   Electrodeposits for nontarnishing finishes, mirrors, thermocouples, catalysts. Resistant to most acids.

Ruthenium.   Hardener for platinum and palladium. Resistant to most acids.

Osmium.   Pen tips, small wear-resistant parts, electrical contacts, instrument pivots. Resistant to common acids.

Iridium.   Alloys with platinum for electrical contacts, hypodermic needles, thermocouples. Resistant to common acids.

TIN AND ITS ALLOYS.   Many alloys are available. Soft tin is used for food-can linings, beverage-can linings, pipe for handling beverages, liners for food-handling equipment. Resists atmospheres and waters, but is attacked by strong acids and alkalis. Hard tin is used for collapsible tubes and foil. White metal and pewter are used for jewelry and ornamental holloware for table service. Other alloys (Sn, Sb, Cu, Pb) are used for bearings and die-cast parts. Tin-lead-antimony alloys are used for bearing liners under light, medium, and heavy loads and speeds.

TITANIUM AND ITS ALLOYS.   Titanium is characterized by its superior resistance to corrosive attacks by sea water and most chloride salt solutions. Titanium is mostly used for parts requiring a high-strength formability and weldability. Also for parts requiring a high strength-to-weight ratio.

ZINC AND ITS ALLOYS.   Zinc and zinc alloys are available in rolled plates, strips, and sheets; also in extruded rods and shapes and drawn rods and wire. Zinc is an important metal in the alloying of copper-base metals and is much used for coating of steel (galvanizing), but is also used in pure form and as a base metal for alloys. Zinc may be fabricated by drawing, bending, roll-forming, stamping, swaging, coining, and extruding and is easily soldered and welded. Common uses are for dry-battery cases, flashing, weatherstrip, lithoplates, automotive parts, household items, office equipment, hardware. Zinc is very resistant to atmospheres and to moisture- and acid-free hydrocarbons, but it is attacked by strong acids and bases.

ZIRCONIUM AND ITS ALLOYS.   Available as ingots, billets, sheets, strips, bars, rods, tubes, and wire, zirconium is very ductile and workable and is very easily fabricated. It may be welded under inert atmosphere and can be brazed and soldered. Principal uses are for chemical equipment, flash-bulb filler, fuel-cladding in water, steam-, or gas-cooled nuclear reactors. Resistant to hydrochloric, nitric, and sulfuric acid and to alkalis at all concentrations and temperatures, zirconium is attacked by hydrofluoric acid and aqua regia.

PLASTICS AND RUBBER

ABS RESINS—MOLDED, EXTRUDED. These plastics in grades designed for medium to very high impact, low-temperature impact, and heat-resistant service are all highly resistant to aqueous acids, alkalis, salts, and are also resistant to phosphoric and hydrochloric acids and alcohols. Disintegrated by sulfuric and nitric acids; soluble in esters and ketones. Typical uses are for piping, appliance housings and wheels, housewares, garden equipment, office equipment, cases, luggage.

ACRYLICS—CAST, MOLDED, EXTRUDED. These plastics in general-purpose and high-impact grades are all resistant to weak acids, alkalis, and some hydrocarbons, but are attacked by esters, ketones, aromatic and chlorinated hydrocarbons, and concentrated acids. Typical uses are for transparent enclosures, electronic parts; drafting equipment; decorative parts; household, office, and automotive parts; knobs and keys for office, musical, and electronic equipment.

ALKYDS—MOLDED. These plastics in granular, putty, and glass-reinforced grades, are all resistant to weak acids but are attacked by alkalis. They are almost unattacked by organic alcohols, hydrocarbons, and fatty acids. Typical uses are for ignition, switch, and circuit-breaker parts; resistors; capacitors; and other electronic parts.

CELLULOSE ACETATE—MOLDED, EXTRUDED. These plastics are all resistant to salt and fresh water and to dilute acetic and sulfuric acid, but are decomposed by strong acids, and dissolved by acetone and ethyl acetate. Typical uses are for photographic film base, tape, appliance housings, optical parts, handles and knobs, toys, buttons.

CELLULOSE ACETATE, BUTYRATE, AND PROPIONATE—MOLDED; EXTRUDED. These plastics are all unaffected by fresh and salt water, 3% hydrogen peroxide, weak acids, and white gasoline, but are softened or dissolved by ethyl alcohol, acetone, ethyl acetate, ethylene dichloride, carbon tetrachloride, and toluene. Typical uses are for decorative parts, knobs and handles, pipe, pens, telephones, steering and control wheels, tooth brushes, optical parts.

CELLULOSE NITRATE AND ETHYL CELLULOSE—MOLDED, EXTRUDED. These plastics are resistant to weak sulfuric, acetic, and hydrochloric acids and to weak sodium hydroxide and sodium carbonate. Attacked by strong acids, ethyl alcohol, acetone, toluene, and gasoline. Typical uses are for fountain pens, spectacle frames, drawing instruments, radio housings, handles, and knobs.

CHLORINATED POLYETHER, PHENOXY, AND POLYALLOMER. Chlorinated polyether is unaffected by both organic and inorganic chemicals except fuming nitric and sulfuric. Phenoxy is very resistant to waters, acids, alkalis, aliphatic hydrocarbons, oils, and greases, but is attacked by many organic solvents. Polyallomer is unaffected by strong acids and bases and only slightly affected by chlorinated compounds and aliphatic hydrocarbons. Typical uses are for valves, pipes, lining, coatings, housings, electrical conduits, film.

DIALLYL PHTHALATES—MOLDED. These plastics are all unaffected by weak acids, alkalis, and organic solvents, and only slightly affected by strong acids and alkalis. Typical uses are for connectors, plugboards, housings, appliance parts, insulators, resistors, aircraft leading edges, nose cones, ducts, decorative sheets for laminating wood and fabric.

EPOXIES—CAST, MOLDED. These plastics are highly resistant to water and strong alkalis, and are somewhat less resistant to sulfuric and acetic acid and oxidizing agents. Typical uses are for coatings for electrical components, patching and repair compounds, glues, electrical moldings, coatings for marine hulls and parts, paints, and protective finishes.

MELAMINES—MOLDED. There are many forms. All are resistant to weak acids and alkalis, organic solvents, greases, and oils, but they are attacked by strong acids and alkalis. Unfilled melamine is used for decorative buttons, moldings, and general ornamental applications. Cellulose-electrical is used for general mechanical and electrical applications at elevated temperatures. Glass fiber is used for applications requiring high shock resistance, good electrical properties, and resistance to burning. Alpha-cellulose–mineral forms are used for applications requiring low shrinkage, good dimensional stability, and good molding characteristics. The alpha-cellulose form is a general-purpose class for electrical and mechanical applications such as tableware, kitchenware, and lighting fixtures. Mineral-electrical is for elevated temperature and electrical applications such as ignition parts and terminal blocks. Fabric forms are for applications requiring improved impact strength.

PHENOLICS—MOLDED. These plastics are resistant to waters and atmospheres, but are severely attacked by strong acids and alkalis. Resistance to weak acids, alkalis, and organic solvents varies with the reagent and with the material formulation. Several types are available: mechanical and chemical, general-purpose, transparent, arc-resistant (mineral), and rubber phenolic (wood flour, flock, fabric, asbestos). Typical uses are for instrument panels, knobs, coil forms, cases, fuse blocks, handles, connector plugs, photographic tanks and related equipment, furniture hardware, instrument casings, molds, and dies.

POLYAMIDES (NYLONS)—MOLDED, EXTRUDED. Many forms are available. In general, polyamides are inert to organic chemicals, esters, ketones, alcohols, hydrocarbons, weak acids, common solvents, and petroleum products. They also resist alkalis and salt solutions, but are attacked by phenols, strong acids, and strong oxidizing agents. Typical uses are for bearings, bushings, coil forms, abrasion-resistant sheathing and coating, electrical insulation, lines, cords, and ropes, seals, tubing, rods, sheets, laminations.

POLYESTERS—CAST. These plastics are attacked by strong acids, alkalis, ketones, and chlorinated solvents. Typical uses are for castings for electrical components and high-temperature applications.

POLYSTYRENES—MOLDED, EXTRUDED. These plastics are resistant to alkalis, salts, lower alcohols, glycols, and waters, and are somewhat resistant to mineral and vegetable oils. They are attacked by higher alcohols, gasoline, and strong oxidizing agents; soluble in aromatic and chlorinated hydrocarbons. Typical uses are for electrical parts, insulators, coil forms, rigid containers, instrument panels, housewares, storage-battery cases, drafting instruments, instrument housings, knobs, panels for electric parts and refrigerators.

POLYETHYLENES—MOLDED, EXTRUDED. These plastics are resistant to atmospheres and waters, and to acids and alkalis at normal temperature. They are attacked by oxidizing acids such as nitric and fuming sulfuric. Typical uses are for containers for drugs, squeeze bottles for drugs and toiletries, kitchen utility ware, tank liners, sealing rings, battery parts, wrapping films for food and clothing, high-frequency insulation, pipe, tubing.

POLYPROPYLENES—MOLDED, EXTRUDED. These plastics are resistant to most acids, alkalis, and saline solutions and to organic solvents. Typical uses are for appliances, television and radio housings, housewares, wire coatings, luggage, automotive parts, containers, packaging.

POLYCARBONATES—MOLDED, EXTRUDED. These plastics are resistant to most organic solvents. They are attacked by strong acids and alkalis. Typical uses are for appliance parts, gears, bearings, bushings, electrical parts, housings, electronic components, aircraft and automotive parts, portable tool housings.

POLYVINYL CHLORIDE—MOLDED, EXTRUDED. Polyvinyl chloride and polyvinyl chloride acetate in nonrigid and rigid forms are resistant to alkalis and weak acids, but are not resistant to strong acids, ketones, and esters. Vinylidene chloride is resistant to all common acids and alkalis. Typical uses are for nonrigid general-purpose garden hose, protective garments, small solid tires, flexible grips, tubes; nonrigid electrical low-tension power cable and wiring insulation, appliance cords; rigid hoods, ducts, tanks, chemical piping, panels, phonograph records.

POLYVINYL ALCOHOL—MOLDED, EXTRUDED. This plastic resists organic solvents and petroleum products, but is attacked by strong acids. Typical uses are for adhesives, sizing and coatings for fabric and paper, chemical tubing, gaskets, diaphragms, packages for chemicals.

POLYVINYL BUTYRAL—MOLDED, EXTRUDED. This plastic is resistant to alkalis, aliphatics, and hydrocarbons, but is attacked by strong acids. Typical uses are as laminating sheet for safety glass, textile waterproofing, structural adhesive, coatings, and primers.

POLYVINYL FORMAL—MOLDED, EXTRUDED. This plastic is resistant to alcohols, esters, and ketones, except those having a high acetate content. It is attacked by strong acids. The principal use is for wire and cable coatings requiring toughness and adhesion.

FLUOROCARBONS—MOLDED, EXTRUDED. These plastics are resistant to most chemicals and solvents with (in some forms) the exception of alkali metals. Typical uses are for chemical piping, gaskets, diaphragms, electrical insulation, connectors, coil forms, anti-adhesive coatings, bearings, bushings, wear surfaces, molded components, laminates.

SILICONES—MOLDED. These plastics are resistant to gasoline and petroleum oils, and to sulfuric and hydrochloric acids. Typical uses are for connector plugs, switch parts, insulators, jet-engine parts, ignition systems, guided-missile parts.

UREAS—MOLDED. These plastics have high resistance to organic solvents, oils, and greases; not resistant to acids and alkalis. Typical uses are for housings for radios, business machines, and food equipment; toilet seats; electric switches and plugs; cosmetic containers.

PLASTIC FILMS. Plastic films are available in the following materials: cellophane, fluorocarbon, polypropylene, nylon, polycarbonate, polyester, polystyrene, polyethylene, polyvinyl chloride, and rubber hydrochloride.

PLASTIC LAMINATES, GLASS REINFORCED—MOLDED. These are available in the following: phenolic, polyester (rigid) silicone, and epoxy. Typical uses are: air ducts, airframe components, missile nose cones, fuel tanks, printed circuits, roto blades, luggage, boats, car bodies, machine housings, chemical tanks, high-frequency equipment, high-strength components, pressure tanks, high-strength tubing and pipe.

PLASTIC AND RUBBER FOAMS—FLEXIBLE. Polyethylene, silicone, urethane, vinyl, natural rubber, neoprene, butadiene-acrylonitrile, and butadiene-styrene are typical flexible foams. Uses include a variety of applications for thermal insulation, cushioning, vibration isolation, flotation, packaging, shock absorption, filtering.

PLASTIC FOAMS—RIGID. Cellulose acetate, epoxy, urethane, silicone, phenolic, and polystyrene are typical rigid foams. Uses include vibration insulation, cushioning, thermal insulation, packaging, void filling, buoyancy components and pipe coverings.

RUBBER, HARD—MOLDED, EXTRUDED. Hard rubber is used for molded parts and is obtainable in sheets, rods, and tubes. Typical uses are for chemical tanks and apparatus and for electrical and electronic components.

RUBBER, NATURAL AND SYNTHETIC—MOLDED, EXTRUDED. The following lists typical materials and uses:

Natural rubber and butadiene-styrene.   Used for pneumatic tires and tubes, power transmission belts, gaskets, hose, tank linings, sound and shock absorption, seals.

Butyl.   Used for pneumatic tires and tubes, steam hose, diaphragms, flexible electrical insulation.

Butadiene-acrylonitrile.   Used for diaphragms, self-sealing tank applications, aircraft hose, gaskets, shock mountings, gasoline and oil hose.

Chloroprene.   Used for petroleum tubes, hoses, tank linings, electric insulation, special tires.

Polysulfide.   Used for gaskets, diaphragms, seals, shock mountings, hose, chemical applications for solvents.

Silicone.   Used for high- and low-temperature electric insulation, gaskets, seals, O-rings, diaphragms.

Urethane.   Used for special aircraft tires, commercial tires, shoe heels, and allied products.

Polyacrylate.   Used for petroleum hose, gaskets, seals, and O-rings for resistance to high pressures in lubricating systems, especially where sulfur is present.

Polybutadiene.   Used for seals, gaskets, belting, and pneumatic tires, and in combination with other rubbers to increase resistance to abrasion and to produce greater resilience.

Vinylidene-fluoride-hexafluoropropylene.   Used for seals, gaskets, diaphragms, flexible mounts, coated fabrics.

Fluorosilicone.   Used for seals, gaskets, O-rings, etc., where resistance to high-temperature solvents or oils is necessary.

Ethylene propylene.   Used for weather stripping, hose, tubing, belts, automotive and appliance parts, electric insulation, footwear.

Chlorosulfonated polyethylene.   Used for chemical and petroleum hose and tubing, tank linings, wire and cable sheathing, footwear, flooring, building products.

Polytrifluorochloroethylene.   Used for seals, gaskets, O-rings, tubing and diaphragms.

CERAMICS, GLASS, CARBON, AND MICA

CERAMICS—FIRED PARTS. The following lists materials and typical uses:

Polycrystalline glass.   Used for heatproof cookware and parts requiring stability under temperature changes, also for high-temperature, high-frequency applications in electronics.

Cordierite.   Used for insulators, terminal blocks, heater-coil supports, foundry parts, fuel-burner tips, and similar high-temperature applications.

Forsterite.   Used principally for low-loss insulators.

Standard electrical ceramic.   Used for low- and high-voltage insulators, high-temperature wire supports, lightning-arrester parts, suspension (strain) insulators, x-ray equipment (rods and tubes).

Refractory mullite.   Used for high-temperature insulators, spark-plug cores, high-temperature laboratory ware.

Steatite.   Used for electronic tube sockets, electric line insulators, electrical component spacers and bushings, thermostat components.

Zircon.   Used for electronic tube sockets, coil forms, component spacers, printed circuit plates.

REFRACTORY CERAMICS AND CERMETS—FIRED OR SINTERED PARTS.
Refractory ceramics and cermets (composite materials consisting of an intimate mixture of ceramic and metallic components) are used for a wide variety of mechanical and electrical applications. Cermets are usually sintered, that is, powdered elements are combined, pressed to form the part, and then heated to about half the melting temperature (on the absolute scale) so that the elements fuse together with increased contact area to form a homogeneous crystalline structure. Refractory ceramics are used for pots, dishes, bowls, tableware, insulators, switch parts, connector blocks, spacers, and for magnetic, piezoelectric, and high-dielectric-constant parts. Sintered cermets are important because of their qualities of high strength, high thermal-shock resistance, high corrosion resistance, high wear resistance, high-temperature resistance, and hardness. Depending upon composition, sintered cermets are used successfully for bearings, bushings, seal parts, gears, friction parts, cutting and drilling tools, etc., and in such electric applications as insulators, capacitors, dielectrics, microwave parts, nuclear-reactor elements, filaments.

INDUSTRIAL GLASS. Many forms are commercially available: soda-lime glass is used for general plate applications and lamp bulbs; alumina-silicate for blown ware; soda-zinc for pressed ware; high-lead for radiation shielding; potash-lead for capacitors; borosilicate for electric insulation, industrial glassware, ultraviolet-light transmission; high-silica for high-temperature applications.

CARBON AND GRAPHITE—MOLDED, EXTRUDED. Carbon, graphite, and carbon-graphite combinations are used for a variety of mechanical and electrical applications. Typical uses are for bearings, seals, pistons, wear surfaces, pump and valve parts, battery carbons, electric contacts, welding carbons, brushes for electric motors. Chemical uses include pumps, valves, fittings, pipe, and filtering media.

MICA-MOLDED SHEET. Natural muscovite is used for furnace peepholes, gage glass, capacitors, tube spacers, high-temperature insulators, and spacers. Glass-bonded and ceramoplastic mica are used for high-temperature insulators, computer parts, and electromechanical devices requiring high stability.

FIBERS—NATURAL, SYNTHETIC, AND INORGANIC; FELTS, WOODS, PAPERS

FIBERS—NATURAL. Vegetable fibers, specifically, cotton, flax, jute, hemp, rami, manila, sisal, and hennaquin, and zoological fibers of wool, horsehair, and silk are used extensively for thread, cord, and rope which are combined to form mats and fabric. Loose or cut fibers are formed into mats, pads, and felts.

FIBERS—SYNTHETIC. Regenerated cellulose, cellulose esters, fluorocarbon, acrylics, polyamides, polyesters, vinyl, and polyethylene are used for monofilament and multifilament fibers. These are used principally in thread, cord, pad, and rope applications and for the making of fabric.

FIBERS—INORGANIC. Glass, asbestos, and aluminum silicate in crude fiber or chopped, are used for insulation, pads, additives to plastics, reinforcement. Asbestos is made into rolls, sheets, and plates for thermal insulation. Glass fibers are made into threads and woven into cloth both for decorative purposes and for engineering applications such as thermal insulation, filtering, wicks, air filters.

FELTS—NATURAL. Natural fibers, principally cotton and wool, are made into felts, usually supplied in sheets and rolls. These are used in many ways by cutting, laminating, coating, impregnating, cementing, molding and shaping to form a variety of components. Commonly used for bearing seals, vibration mounts, lubricators and wicks, grease retainers, weatherstrips, dust shields, noise and vibration dampers.

FELTS—SYNTHETIC. Synthetic fibers of polyester, polypropylene, rayon, nylon, and acrylics are made into felts. Uses are similar to those of natural-fiber felts, but particularly for cases where the chemical resistive qualities of the synthetics are needed.

WOODS. Natural wood (cut boarding) is a structural material familiar to almost everyone. Its use should not be overlooked in selecting materials. Hardboard (fibrous), particle board, softboard, and plywood panels are widely used for structural, insulation, and decorative purposes.

PAPERS. Papers of wood, cotton, and linen are used extensively for electric insulation, spacers, gaskets, washers, and seals. Papers are treated with oils, plastics, and resins to extend useful applications.

COATINGS AND FINISHES

COATINGS—SPRAYED METAL. Sprayed metal coatings are used for several purposes, for example, to increase corrosion resistance, to increase hardness and wear resistance, or to provide better bearing surfaces. Aluminum is used for corrosion and heat resistance; babbitt for bearing properties; brass and bronze for appearance and resistance to corrosion and wear; copper for electrical conductivity; lead, tin, zinc, Monel, nickel, and stainless steel for corrosion resistance; steel for hardness.

COATINGS—ELECTRODEPOSITED. Coatings deposited electrically are used to improve appearance, to increase electrical qualities, and to increase resistance to wear, to corrosion, or to specific environments. Not all metals can be satisfactorily deposited on all base metals.*

COATINGS—CERAMIC, CERMET, AND REFRACTORY. Fired porcelain enamel frits and refractory materials are used as corrosion-resistant coatings and also for color appeal and decorative effect. Examples are refrigerators, ranges, food-handling equipment, photographic trays and chemical laboratory equipment, and parts subjected to oxidation and high temperatures. These coatings are especially valuable for use on ferrous metals. Flame-applied ceramics and cermets, depending upon the material used, give coatings that are resistant to wear, abrasion, heat, oxidation, and to thermal and mechanical shock.

COATINGS—HOT-DIP. These coatings, used principally on steel, cast iron, and copper, provide corrosion resistance at low cost. The materials used are aluminum, zinc, lead, tin, and lead-tin. Examples of use are for roofing, nails, wire, outdoor and indoor hardware, barrels, cans, food cans, kitchen utensils, electronic parts, printed circuits.

COATINGS—IMMERSION. These coatings can be applied to most ferrous and nonferrous metals, with a few exceptions. Materials used are nickel, tin, copper, gold, silver, and platinum. Examples of use are for decorative finishes, corrosion protection, increased conductivity (electronic parts and printed circuits), facilitation of soldering and brazing.

* Consult detailed listings given by suppliers, standards, or such sources as the supplements of *Materials in Design Engineering* magazine.

COATINGS—DIFFUSION. Diffusion coatings are produced by the application of heat while the base material is in contact with a powder or solution. Common diffusion coatings on steel are carburizing, chromizing, cyaniding, nitriding, sherardizing, calorizing. Most diffusion coatings are intended to obtain hard and wear-resistant surfaces and to increase resistance to corrosion.

COATINGS—VAPOR-DEPOSITED. Vapor-deposited metalizing consists of vaporization or evaporation of a metal in a vacuum chamber, where it then condenses on all cool surfaces. Most metals and nonmetals can be used as base materials to be coated. Examples are mirrors and optical reflectors, metalized plastics, lens coatings, costume jewelry, instrument parts.

COATINGS—ORGANIC. These consist of alkyds, celluloses, epoxies, phenolics, silicones, vinyls, rubbers, and others. They are used for color, decoration, and resistance to corrosion.

COATINGS—CHEMICAL CONVERSION. These are chemical coatings which react with the base metal to produce a surface structure that will improve paint bonding, corrosion resistance, decorative properties, and wear resistance. Phosphate, chromate, anodic, and oxide coatings are common.

COATINGS—RUST-PREVENTION. These are oils, petroleum derivatives, and waxes that form a film which will resist attack, principally from industrial and rural atmospheres.

FINISHES—MECHANICAL. Sandblasting, peening, hammering, wire brushing, wheel or belt polishing, burnishing, and buffing are used to produce a decorative finish. Surfaces obtained vary from dull (sandblasting) to very bright (buffing).

FACINGS. Facings are overlays applied by welding operations. The purpose is to produce a hard surface designed for special service conditions, usually resistance to wear and abrasion. Typical materials used for facing are carbon steels, chromium and chromium-nickel steels, and cobalt, nickel, and tungsten alloys.

COMPOSITES

LAMINATES—PLASTIC-METAL. These consist of a metal (steel, aluminum, or magnesium) precoated with a plastic film. At the present time, vinyl and polyester predominate. They are available in a wide variety of textures and colors.

LAMINATES—METAL-WOOD. The most common are wood cores with steel or aluminum faces. These are used extensively in automotive, appliance, and architectural applications.

LAMINATES—BONDED COMBINATIONS. Practically any material can be combined with plastics by adhesive bonding. Common varieties are plastic laminates faced with copper, silver, gold, aluminum, vulcanized fiber, asbestos.

LAMINATES—BIMETALLIC. These are composite material wherein aluminum or magnesium alloys are molecularly bonded to a ferrous metal. The advantages are that the strength and other characteristics of ferrous metals are retained along with the high heat conductivity and other characteristics of light metals.

LAMINATES—HONEYCOMB. These include a wide variety of materials and structures. Their greatest advantage lies in a structural core separating two facings of high-strength material, thus combining light weight and strength because the high-strength material is some distance from the neutral axis. Common facing materials are steel, aluminum, stainless steel, superalloys, plastics, and plywood. Core materials include paper (impregnated), aluminum, steel, stainless steel, superalloys, and plastics.

LAMINATES, GENERAL-PURPOSE—SHEET, ROD, TUBE. These laminates include phenolics with canvas, asbestos, paper, asbestos cloth, glass cloth; also, melamine, epoxy, and polyester with glass cloth. Typical uses are for switch panels, electronic insulation, printed circuits, terminal blocks, motor parts, electric appliance insulation.

LAMINATES, MECHANICAL—SHEET, ROD, TUBE. These laminates of phenolic with cotton canvas or cotton-linen canvas and melamine with cotton canvas are for mechanical purposes. Typical uses are for gears, pinions, pulleys, knobs, bushings, cams, threaded and tapped parts.

LAMINATES, ELECTRICAL—SHEET, ROD, TUBE. These laminates of phenolic with paper, cotton, linen, glass cloth, or nylon and silicone with glass cloth are used for a variety of electrical applications. Typical uses are for panels for electrical and electronic purposes, terminal blocks, coil forms, switch rotors and stators, wave-change switch parts and electronic applications where low-loss insulation is needed.

METALS—PRECLAD AND PRECOATED. Base metals, principally steel, aluminum, copper, bronze, and brass, precoated with such metals as aluminum, copper, lead, silver, gold, nickel, platinum, and stainless steel are available as sheets, rods, strips, tubing, and wire. Also available are base metals with coatings of alkyd, polyvinyl chloride, vinyl lacquer, or enamel. Preplated or precoated metals often have an economic advantage because they can be fabricated without further finishing.

18.7. METHODS OF PARTS PRODUCTION. As in the case of the listing of materials in paragraph 18.6, it is impossible to give here all details of parts production. The following descriptions are only a guide; detailed information may be found in textbooks on parts production and processing. See Glossary.

CASTING

SAND CASTINGS. Moist sand is packed around a pattern and the pattern is then removed. Molten metal is poured into the cavity left by the pattern. When the metal solidifies, the sand mold is broken away and the casting removed.

SHELL-MOLD CASTINGS. Sand mixed with a thermosetting plastic is placed in a heated metal pattern in which the sand mixture solidifies, forming a mold or "shell." Molten metal poured into the shell solidifies, and the shell is then broken away.

PERMANENT-MOLD CASTINGS. Mold cavities are machined into two or more metal blocks which are hinged or clamped together. After molten metal is poured into the mold cavity and allowed to solidify, the mold is removed.

PLASTER-MOLD CASTINGS. A slurry of gypsum and other ingredients is poured over a pattern and allowed to set. The pattern is then removed and the mold is baked. Next, molten metal is poured into the mold and allowed to solidify, and the mold is then broken away.

INVESTMENT CASTINGS. A refractory slurry is formed around a pattern of wax, meltable plastic, or frozen mercury. After the slurry sets up, the pattern is melted out, and the mold is baked. Molten metal is then poured into the mold and allowed to solidify, after which the mold is broken away.

DIE CASTINGS. Molten metal is forced under pressure into a closed steel die. When the metal solidifies, the die is opened and the casting ejected.

CENTRIFUGAL CASTINGS. A mold of sand, graphite, or metal is rotated; molten metal introduced into the mold is thrown to the mold wall, where it remains by centrifugal force until solidified.

CONTINUOUS CASTING. Molten metal (usually a copper alloy such as bronze) is fed into a mold, rapidly cooled and withdrawn, and then cut to the desired length.

FORGING

OPEN-DIE FORGINGS. Mechanical hammering is applied to metal heated to the plastic state. The desired shape is achieved by turning and manipulating the workpiece between hammer blows.

CLOSED-DIE FORGINGS. Compressive forces produced by a mechanical or hydraulic hammer are applied to metal heated to the plastic state and placed between dies having cavities which will form the desired shape. In some cases several successive dies are required.

UPSET FORGINGS. Metal heated to the plastic state is gripped by dies which also compress to form the desired shape.

OTHER FORMING OPERATIONS

COLD HEADING. This is similar to upset forging, except that the metal is worked cold. Common practice is to feed wire (up to 1-in. diameter) to a gripping die with a portion protruding. The force of a punch against the protruding end forms a "head" on the part. Head shape is determined by the shape of the punch die.

IMPACT EXTRUSIONS. *Forward* extrusions are produced by placing a preformed thick metal blank in a die and striking the blank with a high-velocity punch. The metal flows forward through an opening in the die. *Rearward* extrusions are made by placing a thick metal blank in the bottom of a die cavity. The blank is struck by a high-velocity punch and the metal flows upward around the punch.

DIE EXTRUSIONS. Metal heated to the plastic state is forced through a die having an opening of the desired cross-sectional shape. The metal emerges from the die in a continuous piece, which is then cut to the desired length.

STAMPINGS. Parts made of plate, strip, and sheet stock are produced by one or more of these operations: cutting, forming, drawing. *Cutting* operations include blanking, punching, shearing, piercing, notching, etc.; the metal is parted by stressing beyond the ultimate strength. *Forming* includes bending, stretch forming, coining, embossing; the metal is stressed beyond the yield point and permanently deformed. *Drawing* is an operation in which a flat blank is pressed into the desired shape.

SPUN PARTS. A preformed or flat metal blank is drawn over a male spinning (rotating) form by the application of pressure from either a round-ended or roller-ended tool. The method is restricted to surfaces of revolution.

SCREW-MACHINE PARTS. Bar or tube stock is fed through the hollow spindles of an automatic lathe. The stock is indexed and clamped in a collet chuck, and is then cut by various tools carried on a turret and/or tool slides. Operations performed include turning, facing, threading, tapping, drilling, boring, reaming, and other similar cutting operations.

POWDERED METAL AND CERMET PARTS. Powdered metal combinations are compressed in a die to the desired finished form. The part is then sintered (heated) in a furnace at a temperature of one-half to two-thirds of the melting point of the base constituent, which produces a homogeneous structure.

ELECTROFORMING. This is a process in which a mandrel, having a shape which is the reverse mating form of the part wanted, is placed in an electroplating bath and plated until the desired thickness is obtained. The electrodeposited part is then separated from the mandrel.

TUBING AND FORMED TUBE PARTS. Tubing is produced by extruding, by piercing or drawing of rod, or by bending and welding of sheet, strip, or plate. Tube parts are produced by forming a tube by methods such as bending, swaging, upsetting, flaring, spinning, and machining.

PLASTICS. Plastics, basically, are molded. There are many ways in which the molding can be accomplished, but fundamentally the process consists of placing or forcing the material in a plastic, powdered, or liquid state into a mold where the material solidifies and then is ejected or removed. The details of all the processes are too extensive to be given here, but injection moldings, extrusions, sheet moldings, blow moldings, slush and dip moldings, compression moldings, transfer moldings, and reinforced moldings are common methods. Plastics can also be cast. Sheets, tubes, etc., can be cut and machined. Inserts for fastening and for wear surfaces can be molded in place.

RUBBER. Rubber is molded in a manner similar to the molding of plastic. Uncured rubber is forced or placed in a mold where under heat and pressure the rubber vulcanizes. Extrusions and die-cut parts from sheets and other shapes are also common.

CERAMICS, GLASS, CARBON, GRAPHITE. Ceramics are formed by extruding, injection molding, pressing and casting. Glass is formed by blowing, pressing, drawing, and sintering. Carbon and graphite are formed by molding and extruding.

18.8. GOOD DESIGN AND PROPORTIONING OF PARTS. There are principles of design that govern the shape and proportion of machine parts. These principles have been determined by geometry, by experience in part-production methods, by calculations of strength, and by testing procedures. Study the descriptions and accompanying illustrations carefully, remember all the details you can, and refer back to the discussion when necessary.

Corners. Sharp corners are dangerous. In cast parts cracks may occur at a sharp corner, due to cooling strains. In other parts (forged, molded, etc.) breaks caused by overstressing will always start at a sharp corner. A corner like that shown in Fig. 18.16 is very poor design. Design with a rounded corner as shown in Fig. 18.17 if at all possible. The minimum inside radius is usually about one-half the metal thickness, making the minimum outer radius about one and one-half times the metal thickness.

Tee sections. For the same reasons given for outside corners, sharp corners should never be used on tee sections. Figure 18.18 represents a dangerous condition and is poor design. The rounded inside corners in Fig. 18.19 show good design. The radius is usually a minimum of about one-half the metal thickness.

Differences in Metal Thickness. When joined sections vary greatly in metal thickness, especially in castings and forgings, cooling strains may produce cracks and warping. Figure 18.20 is very poor design because of the wide difference in metal thickness and also because of the sharp corners. Keep joined sections as uniform as possible and avoid sharp corners, as in Fig. 18.21.

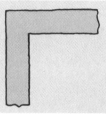

FIG. 18.16. Sharp corner. Poor design.

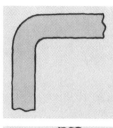

FIG. 18.17. Rounded corner. Good design.

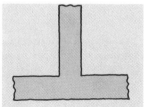

FIG. 18.18. Sharp inside corner. Poor design.

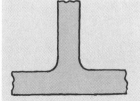

FIG. 18.19. Rounded inside corner. Good design.

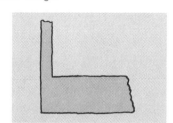

FIG. 18.20. Wide difference in metal thickness. Poor design.

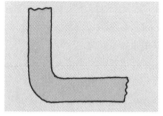

FIG. 18.21. Uniform section. Good design.

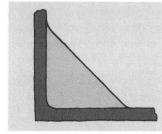

FIG. 18.22. Design for small ribs.

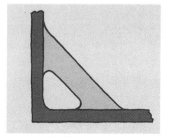

FIG. 18.23. Design for large ribs.

Ribs. Small ribs can be designed as solid ribs, as in Fig. 18.22. However, for large ribs it is best to open the inside of the rib, as in Fig. 18.23. The opened inside design is especially good for lightweight parts because the inside portion of the rib, structurally, adds very little strength.

FIG. 18.24. Stiffening ribs. Poor design because of an unstable geometry.

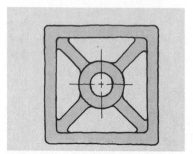

FIG. 18.26. Stiffening ribs. Good design because of stable geometric shapes.

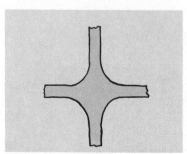

FIG. 18.27. Corner radius too large. Poor design.

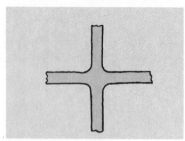

FIG. 18.28. Proper corner radius. Good design.

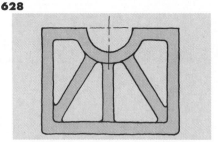

FIG. 18.25. Stiffening ribs. Good design because of stable geometric shapes.

Bracing Ribs or Supports. Internal bracing should be designed according to geometrical principles. The ribs of Fig. 18.24 lend very little stiffness to the part because the geometry of the part is based on the square, which is an unstable shape. Stiffening ribs based on the triangle, a stable shape, should be employed if possible, as shown in Figs. 18.25 and 18.26. These designs are for torsioned stiffening only and are not applied to beam stiffening.

Size of Corner Radii. We have seen before that corners should be rounded for several reasons. However, if the corner radius is too large for intersecting members, as in Fig. 18.27, too much material is left at the intersection and the design becomes poor because of wide differences in metal thickness. Keep the radius to a reasonable (minimum) value of about half the metal thickness, as in Fig. 18.28.

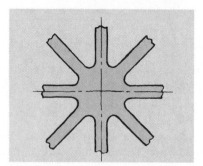

FIG. 18.29. Several intersecting members produce a great difference in metal thickness. Poor design.

When several (five or more) members intersect, as in Fig. 18.29, even a small corner radius will not solve the problem and the difference in metal thickness becomes critical. The solution of the problem is to relieve the center of the part with a hole, as in Fig. 18.30, regardless of whether the hole has any function for the part or not.

Good Proportions. Many combinations of hubs, ribs, holes, corner sections, flanges, and other elements occur in machine parts. It is impossible to describe all combinations, but the following examples will cover the bulk of the elements usually combined. Please note that the values given for corner radii are *maximum* values. Also note that the proportioning is based on the theory that differences in metal thickness should be "blended" into each other. This produces the best insurance against distortion and cracking during cooling and develops the maximum strength capability of the part.

Figure 18.31 shows good proportioning for a corner rib.

Figure 18.32 shows good proportioning for a centralized hub.

Figure 18.33 shows good proportions for a flared section (hub) on one side only of the section.

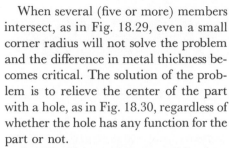

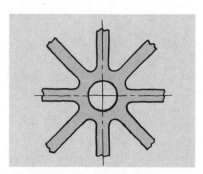

FIG. 18.30. Great difference in metal thickness relieved with a hole. Good design. Compare with Fig. 18.29.

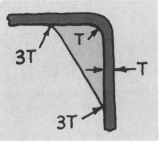

FIG. 18.31. Good proportioning for a corner rib. Radius values are maximum.

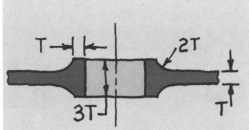

FIG. 18.32. Good proportioning for a centralized hub. Radius value is maximum.

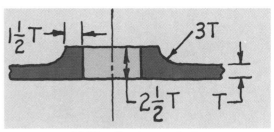

FIG. 18.33. Good proportioning for a flared hub. Radius value is maximum.

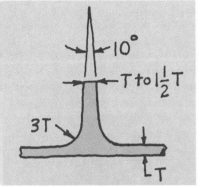

FIG. 18.34. Good proportioning for a support rib. Radius value is maximum.

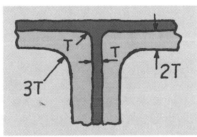

FIG. 18.35. Good proportioning for a ribbed tee section. Radius values are maximum.

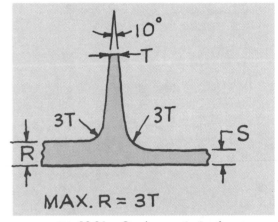

MAX. R = 3T

FIG. 18.36. Good proportioning for a support rib for unequal body sections. Radius values are maximum.

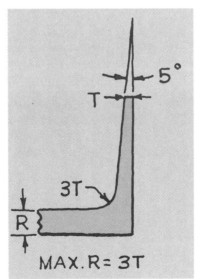

MAX. R = 3T

FIG. 18.37. Good proportioning for an end rib. The radius value is maximum.

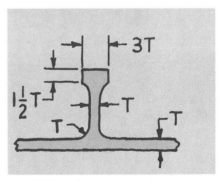

FIG. 18.38. Good proportioning for a flanged rib. Radius value is maximum.

Figure 18.34 shows good proportions for a support rib. Note that the tapered section of the rib provides a good blend of metal thickness from the body section.

Figure 18.35 shows good proportions for a ribbed tee section.

Figure 18.36 shows good proportions for a support rib on a section having two different thicknesses. Note that the thinner section (S) is any thickness less than $R = 3T$ and that the radius values of $3T$ are maximum values. The tapered rib gives a good blend between the rib and body section.

Figure 18.37 shows good proportions for an end rib. The tapered form provides a good blend between the rib and body.

Figure 18.38 shows good proportions for a flanged rib. The flanged section provides extra strength.

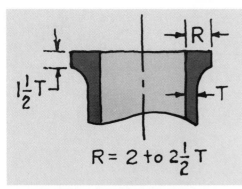

FIG. 18.39. Good proportioning for a flange at the end of a tube.

$$R = 2 \text{ to } 2\frac{1}{2}T$$

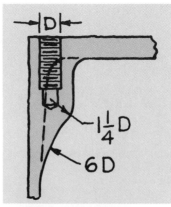

FIG. 18.40. Good proportioning for extra material needed for a tapped hole in a thin wall.

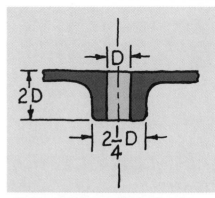

FIG. 18.41. Good proportioning based on the diameter of hole needed.

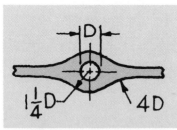

FIG. 18.42. Good proportioning for an enlarged portion.

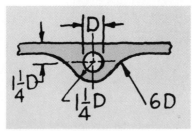

FIG. 18.43. Good proportioning for an enlarged section.

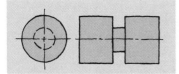

FIG. 18.44. A machined part with sharp edges. Poor design.

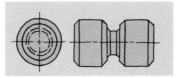

FIG. 18.45. A machined part with chamfered edges. Good design.

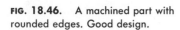

FIG. 18.46. A machined part with rounded edges. Good design.

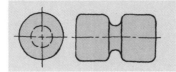

FIG. 18.47. Keyseat bottom and shaft correspond. Poor design.

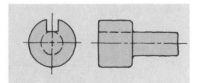

Figure 18.39 shows good proportions for a flange at the end of a tube.

Figure 18.40 shows good proportions for extra material needed for a tapped hole in a thin wall section.

Figure 18.41 shows good proportions for a hub. The sizes given are based on the diameter of the hole needed.

Figure 18.42 shows good proportions for a symmetrical enlarged section necessary to provide a hole equal to, or larger than, a wall section.

Figure 18.43 shows an enlarged section similar to Fig. 18.42, but for a nonsymmetrical section.

Figure 18.44 shows a simple cylindrical part machined from solid bar stock. The sharp edges weaken the part and even though it may not be highly stressed, they may cause difficulties in assembly and malfunctioning later. A better design is shown in Fig. 18.45, where the edges are chamfered. An even better design is shown in Fig. 18.46, where the edges are rounded.

Figure 18.47 shows a keyseat designed so that its bottom surface corresponds with the smaller shaft diameter. This is poor design because the machining of the keyseat will probably cut into (or score) the shaft. The part should be designed for clearance between the bottom of the seat and the shaft, as in Fig. 18.48.

It is not impossible to cut a completely sharp corner at the change in diameter of a headed shaft, bolt, nut, or similar part, but it is difficult and expensive, and the part may be unreliable. When such a part must seat on a mating part, the certain interference because of an imperfect sharp corner can be relieved by necking the shaft as in Fig. 18.49. However, the neck requires an extra machining operation and also weakens the shaft. A better method, especially for highly stressed parts and for threaded parts, is to round the intersection of head and body and chamfer the mating part as in Fig. 18.50. The round radius must be less than the right-angle legs of the chamfer.

Parts can be severely weakened by poorly chosen placement of keyseats, grooves, and other similar elements. Notice in Fig. 18.51 that the keyway severely weakens the rounded end portion of the part. The difficulty is easily eliminated by placing the keyway as shown in Fig. 18.52.

In round parts such as hubs and collars there is no position for a keyway that will not weaken the part. An example is shown in Fig. 18.53. One solution of the problem is to add extra material by flaring the hub, as in Fig. 18.54. The flared portion is usually designed with a radius and straight tangent portions connecting to the hub outer diameter.

In good machinery, finished-surface seats are always provided for fasteners. A simple unfinished surface, like that shown in Fig. 18.55, is poor design. Surfaces are finished either by adding a boss with machined surface as in Fig. 18.56 or by spot-facing the surface as in Fig. 18.57.

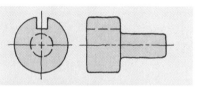

FIG. 18.48. Clearance between keyseat bottom and shaft. Good design.

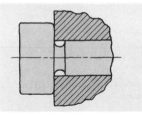

FIG. 18.49. Necking of a shaft to eliminate interference. Allowable design for lightly stressed parts.

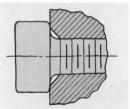

FIG. 18.50. Round on shaft and chamfer on mating part eliminate interference. Good design.

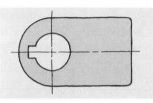

FIG. 18.51. Keyway in a position that severely weakens the part. Poor design.

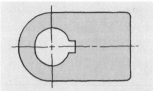

FIG. 18.52. Keyway position does not weaken the part. Good design.

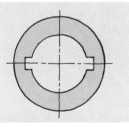

FIG. 18.53. Hub is weakened by keyways. Poor design.

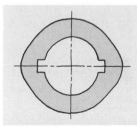

FIG. 18.54. Extra material added to hub so that keyways will not weaken the part. Good design.

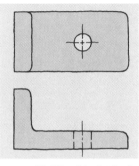

FIG. 18.55. No finished surface for bolt or screw seat. Poor design.

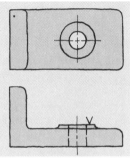

FIG. 18.56. Seat for bolt or screw provided by a finished boss. Good design.

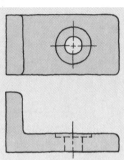

FIG. 18.57. Seat for bolt or screw provided by spotface. Good design.

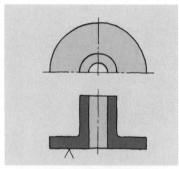

FIG. 18.58. Full finished surface on base of hub. Good design when a complete flat surface is needed.

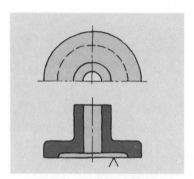

FIG. 18.59. Center portion of hub base relieved to save machining. Good design.

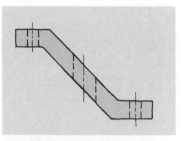

FIG. 18.60. Drilled hole at an angle to the part surface. Poor design.

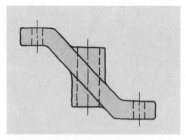

FIG. 18.61. Normal surface provided for drilled hole. Good design.

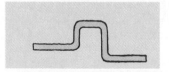

FIG. 18.62. Formed sheet-metal part with 90° bends and small bend radii. Poor design.

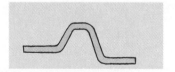

FIG. 18.63. Formed sheet-metal part with bends less that 90° and bend radii (internal) greater than the metal thickness. Good design.

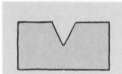

FIG. 18.64. Sharp-pointed notch. Poor design.

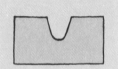

FIG. 18.65. Round-bottomed notch. Good design.

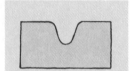

FIG. 18.66. All corners of notch rounded. Good design.

It is not necessary to finish the complete base surface of a hub or similar part unless for some functional reason a completely flat surface is needed. Figure 18.58 shows a part with the complete base surface machined. When the complete flat surface is not necessary, the center portion can be relieved, as in Fig. 18.59. This saves machining time and produces a good seating surface.

Parts should never be designed so that a hole must be drilled at an angle to a surface, as in Fig. 18.60. Even though a drill jig is used, the design will cause drill breakage, inaccuracy, and severe wear on the drill bushing. Provide a normal surface for the hole by building up the piece as in Fig. 18.61.

In parts formed from sheet metal two practices should be avoided if possible. First, full 90-degree bends will cause undue stretching of the material by the die and the part may be difficult to strip from the die. Second, small radii less than the metal thickness (internal) may cause cracking of the material at the bend. Such a poorly designed part is shown in Fig. 18.62. Unless full 90-degree bends are needed for some functional reason, a far better design is to use bends of less than 90 degrees and radii equal to the metal thickness (internal) or larger, as shown in Fig. 18.63.

Sharp pointed notches in sheet metal parts should be avoided because stress breaks will start at the sharp point. For this reason Fig. 18.64 is poor design. It costs no more and is much safer to provide a round bottom on the notch as in Fig. 18.65, or, better still, to provide also rounds at the upper ends of the notch as in Fig. 18.66.

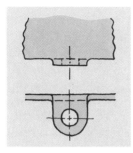

FIG. 18.67. No corner notches for bend relief. Poor design.

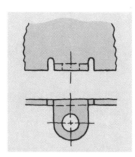

FIG. 18.68. Corner notches provided for bend relief. Good design.

When bent lugs are needed on a sheet-metal part for fastening or a similar purpose, notches should be provided at the sides of the lug. In Fig. 18.67 notches are not provided and because of the bend radius required, undue stretching and distortion will occur at the sides of the lug. Side notches, such as shown in Fig. 18.68, will eliminate the difficulty. Note also in Fig. 18.68 that the outer surface can be brought flush with the side surface of the part proper.

Bent stiffening flanges on round corners of sheet-metal parts must be specially designed or crowding and crinkling of the metal will occur, as shown in Fig. 18.69. A design with notches to relieve the crowding of the material will solve the problem, as indicated in Fig. 18.70.

Formed flanges on the outside rounded corners of sheet-metal parts are almost impossible to make without undue stretching, weakening, and cracking of the material, as indicated in Fig. 18.71. The solution of the problem is to provide notches, as in Fig. 18.72.

Formed parts of spherical or similar shape should not be made as in Fig. 18.73, without a flange for stiffening. A flange, such as shown in Fig. 18.74, makes for a much more stable part and also provides a seating surface, often needed.

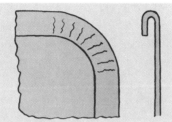

FIG. 18.69. Bent flange on round corner causes crowding of the metal. Poor design.

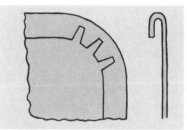

FIG. 18.70. Notches are used to relieve the crowding of metal on a bent corner flange. Good design.

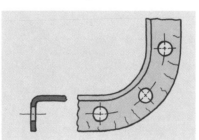

FIG. 18.71. Formed outside flange on rounded corner produces breaks in the material. Poor design.

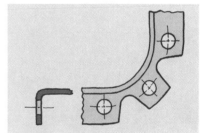

FIG. 18.72. Notches on the outside formed flange on a rounded corner prevent material stretching and breakage. Good design.

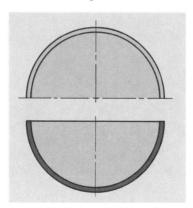

FIG. 18.73. Spherical part without flange. Poor design.

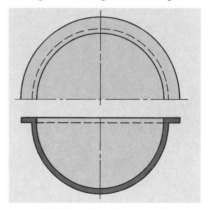

FIG. 18.74. Spherical part with flange. Good design.

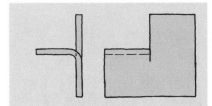

FIG. 18.75. Bent portion of part formed by shearing and bending. Poor design.

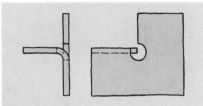

FIG. 18.76. Bent portion of part formed by shearing to a terminal hole and bending. Good design.

When a portion of a sheet-metal part must be made by shearing or cutting and bending over as in Fig. 18.75, breakage because of overstressing or fatigue will start from the end of the sheared or cut surface. The sheared or cut line should be terminated by a hole (drilled or punched), as in Fig. 18.76. The hole contour will distribute stresses and prevent breakage.

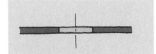

FIG. 18.77. Drilled hole in sheet metal.

FIG. 18.78. Punched (or drilled) and formed hole in sheet metal.

Holes in sheet metal made by punching or drilling are satisfactory when a completely flat surface is needed, as in Fig. 18.77. However, a stronger hole can be made by punching or drilling and forming, as in Fig. 18.78. Another advantage of a hole so made is that it may be tapped to receive a screw.

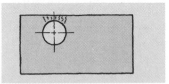

FIG. 18.79. Hole too close to the edge causes distortion and possible breakage. Poor design.

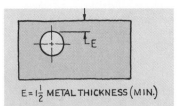

$E = 1\frac{1}{2}$ METAL THICKNESS (MIN.)

FIG. 18.80. Proper setback for a punched hole in sheet metal. Good design.

Punched holes too close to the edge of a sheet-metal part may cause distortion and possible breakage of the material, as indicated in Fig. 18.79. The hole should be set back with the minimum edge distance shown in Fig. 18.80.

If the corner of a sheet-metal pan does not have to be closed for functional purposes, an economical part can be made by relieving the corner as shown in Fig. 18.81.

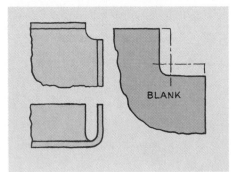

BLANK

FIG. 18.81. Corner relief for a formed sheet-metal pan. Economical design.

If possible, sheet metal parts should be designed so that maximum use can be made of the stock without excessive scrap, as indicated in Fig. 18.82.

Sheet-metal parts should be designed so as to simplify the shape of the blank unless there is some functional reason for not doing so. The design of the part shown in Fig. 18.83 produces an irregular blank and excessive scrap from the blanking operation.

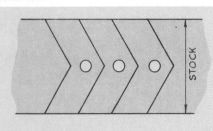

STOCK

FIG. 18.82. Maximum use of stock. Good design.

A more economical design is shown in Fig. 18.84, where the blank has straight sides. By reversal in the blanking operation excessive scrap is eliminated and maximum use of the stock is attained.

18.9. ASSEMBLY—FASTENING AND JOINING OF PARTS. There are many methods of joining parts. The designer should be familiar with all possible methods and should select the method (in any particular case) that will satisfactorily hold the parts together and also be economical from the standpoints of cost, repair and replacement, and general maintenance. In any particular machine several different methods may be used depending somewhat on whether the fastening is to be permanent or removable. The following lists describe the most common methods.

Mechanical Fasteners. These include bolts and screws, rivets, special springs, snap rings, O-rings, rollpins, and keys. For details, see Chap. 16.

Adhesives. Adhesives are classified by *bonding type* (heat, pressure, time, catalyst, vulcanizing); *form* (liquid, paste, powder, mastic); *flow* (flowable or nonflowable); *vehicle* (solvent dispersion, water emulsion, or complete solids); or chemical composition, which is the most significant.

Natural adhesives of casein, blood albumin, hide, bone, fish, starch, rosin, shellac, asphalt, sodium silicate, or glycerin-litharge are used for wood, paper, cork, packaging, textiles, some metals, and plastics.

Thermoplastic adhesives of polyvinyl acetate, polyvinyl alcohol, acrylic, cellulose, nitrate, and asphalt are used for practically all materials, but principally for nonmetallics such as wood, leather, cork, and paper.

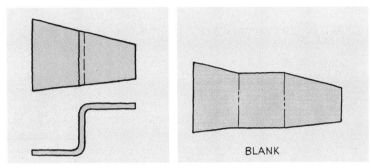

FIG. 18.83. Irregular blank. Poor design.

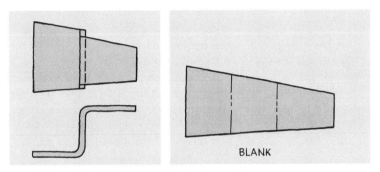

FIG. 18.84. Simplified shape of blank. Good design.

Thermosetting adhesives of phenolic, resorcinol, phenolresorcinol, epoxy, urea, melamine, and alkyd are used for many metals and nonmetals. Specifically, epoxies are used to join dissimilar materials, metals and plastics; phenolics for metal, glass, and wood; ureas and melamines for wood; alkyds for metal laminations.

Elastomeric adhesives of natural rubber, butadiene-styrene, neoprene, and silicone are used for wood, rubber, fabric, foil, paper, leather, plastic film, and for tape.

Almost all adhesives are strongest in shear, somewhat weaker in tension, and weakest in peel strength. Therefore, in the design of the joint strength is an important consideration.

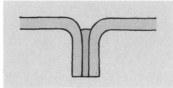

FIG. 18.35. Adhesive-bonded joint. Weak in tension because of peel.

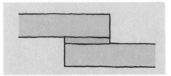

FIG. 18.86. Adhesive-bonded butt joint. Weak in tension because of bond strength and lack of bond area.

FIG. 18.87. Adhesive lap joint. Better in tension than the joints of Figs. 18.85 and 18.86.

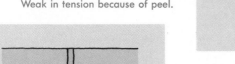

FIG. 18.88. Adhesive-bonded joint. Better in tension than the joints of Figs. 18.85, 18.86, or 18.87.

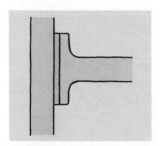

FIG. 18.89. Right-angle member flared for greater area of bonded joint.

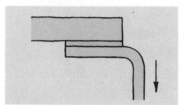

FIG. 18.90. Adhesive-bonded joint for right angle. Poor design.

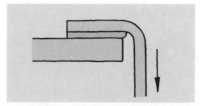

FIG. 18.91. Adhesive-bonded joint for right angle. Good design.

A joint like that shown in Fig. 18.85 is weak in tension because, as the parts joined are stressed, the metal will distort and will be peeled away from the adhesive bond.

A simple butt joint like that shown in Fig. 18.86 is not strong in tension because of the weakness of the bond itself, and also because in most joints of this type the actual bond area is limited.

A better joint may be made by lapping the parts as in Fig. 18.87. This puts the bond in shear, but as the parts are stressed, some distortion due to the offset will occur and the adhesive may peel.

Probably the best joint in tension is that shown in Fig. 18.88, where tension on the joint will not distort the members and the adhesive remains in shear.

When an adhesive bond is used for a right-angle member as in Fig. 18.89, the member should be flared as shown to get a greater bonding area.

When a joint is designed as in Fig. 18.90 for a right-angle corner, the adhesive bond will be in peel and will be weak. The joint should be designed as in Fig. 18.91, where the adhesive bond is in shear.

Adhesive-bonded joints are not used for highly stressed parts because of the relatively low strength of adhesives. However, adhesive joints and connections may be very satisfactory and economical for lightly stressed parts and for attaching coverings, medallions, name plates and similar parts which are not stressed at all.

Solders. Many combinations of solder metals are commercially available. *Tin-lead* solders are used for general-purpose applications on ferrous and nonferrous metals for joining and coating. *Tin-lead-antimony* solders are used for machine and torch soldering and coating of metals, except galvanized iron. *Tin-antimony* solders are used for joints on copper in electrical, plumbing, and heating applications. *Tin-silver* solders are used principally for work on fine instruments. *Tin-zinc* solders are used to join aluminum. *Lead-silver* solders are used on copper, brass, and similar metals (with torch heating). *Cadmium-zinc* solders are used for soldering aluminum. *Cadmium-silver* solders are used for joining aluminum to aluminum and to dissimilar metals. *Zinc-aluminum* solders are used for high-strength aluminum joints.

Brazing. Brazing is the operation of joining two similar or dissimilar metals by partial fusion with a metal or alloy applied under very high temperature. Brazing alloys include aluminum-silicon, copper-phosphorus, silver, gold, copper, copper-zinc, magnesium, and nickel.

Welding. Welding is the operation of joining two similar metals with a fused joint of the same or very similar metal. Steel, cast iron, copper and copper alloys, nickel alloys, and aluminum can be welded.

The accompanying table lists joinability of common materials by various procedures.

Joinability of Materials*

	Arc welding	Oxyacet-ylene welding	Resistance welding	Brazing	Soldering	Adhesive bonding	Threaded fasteners	Riveting and stitching
Cast iron	X	X				X	X	X
Carbon and low-alloy steels	X	X	X	X		X	X	X
Stainless steels	X	X	X	X		X	X	X
Aluminum magnesium	X	X	X	X		X	X	X
Copper and its alloys	X	X	X	X	X	X	X	X
Nickel and its alloys	X	X	X	X	X	X	X	X
Titanium	X		X			X	X	
Lead, zinc	X	X			X	X	X	X
Thermoplastics	X	X	X			X	X	X
Thermosets						X	X	X
Elastomers						X		X
Ceramics						X	X	
Glass		X				X	X	
Wood						X	X	X
Leather						X		X
Fabric						X		X
Dissimilar metals				X	X	X	X	X
Metals to nonmetals						X	X	X
Dissimilar nonmetals						X		X

* The crossmark ($\times$) in the table indicates common practice. Difficult and unreliable methods are not given.

18.10. AESTHETICS. The aesthetics of any completely new and original creation can usually be designed with freedom because there is no other similar entity to compare or compete with. The choice of configuration, colors, contrasts, materials, and other similar factors offers extensive opportunity for experiment. The designer may try a number of combinations, build mock-ups, and then choose the most appealing.

The aesthetics or "styling" of products built previously, but redesigned for a new model, are affected somewhat by the former model and also by what most industries call styling trends. As examples, note the trends in each year's models of automobiles, refrigerators, radios, television receivers, and other well-known products. Each year, new ways are found to combine colored finishes, chrome or other metal trim, plastics, leather, wood, and many other materials. Configurations are improved and "cleaned up." Operative elements such as knobs and levers are altered to give interesting and pleasing appearances.

The aesthetics of any product, new or redesigned, presents no simple problem. The project requires artistic ability, a keen color sense, good judgment of configurations and combinations, and an instinct for supplying the factors that appeal strongly to most buyers and users. This may sound difficult to a person who thinks that he has no artistic ability. A measure of success can be attained, however, by diligent and purposeful study, observation, and work.

Consider the following list of factors.

Configuration. The "overall shape" of any product gives the first and most important impact. As an example, automobiles are made in many colors and color combinations, but the particular model is at once recognized by its distinctive shape. In designing the configuration of a product, try to find a combined shape that is recognizable, distinctive, and functionally reasonable. Attempts to cover function with a shape that has no relationship to function usually fail. Experiment with every possible combination of shapes, blended curves, and surfaces. If the product is redesigned (new model), attempt to find distinctive forms that follow styling trends.

Colors. After configuration, color probably has the most important impact. Choose colors or combinations that are traditionally accepted, but also try new shades, tints, and combinations.

Contrasts. Contrasts can be obtained in many ways. Examples are combining a dark color with a light color; combining a rough texture with a smooth texture; combining definitely different materials (leather and gold, wood and metal, fabric and wood or metal, etc.); combining materials with differences in reflectance (bright finish and dull finish); combinations of color, material, texture, brightness.

Details. Small details should not be overlooked. Quite often the success of a design lies in attention to the apparently insignificant parts. The color, material, texture, or relative brightness of a small part may add a definite distinction to the product. Small details to be considered are such items as knobs, handles, lights and lighting accessories, indicators, meters, dials, and other similar appurtenances.

Accents. Accents are the smaller but very important features of aesthetic design exemplified by a decorative line of contrasting color, texture, or material on an otherwise plain surface; a decorative medallion or name plate so placed as to add to the overall composition; any small detail that adds distinction to an otherwise plain, uninteresting configuration.

Models. The best way to study the aesthetics of a product is to make several models of the design and then use a number of different combinations of colors, textures, and materials for later appraisal of the overall impact.

Appraisal. In a company of any significant size the appraisal of styling is usually made by a group. This is a very sound method, because the appraisal will represent the combined thinking of several people. If, however, the judgment must be made by one or two persons only, the cardinal rule is to make every attempt to be as objective as possible.

18.11. SUMMARY OF DESIGN PROCEDURE. The accompanying diagrammatic outline has been assembled from recorded standard practices in a number of large engineering companies and from discussion with a number of designers who are personal friends. Thus this outline represents an authentic cross section of usual procedure in this country.

DESIGN PROCEDURE

PHASE ONE—THE PROJECT

A. Discussion with management, engineering, client.
B. Statements and specification of the design problem.
C. Collection of all pertinent information.

PHASE TWO—FORMULATION

A. Recognition of requirements.
B. Definition of requirements.
C. Consideration of previous designs.
D. Assembly of all original data needed—mathematical, graphical, mechanical, electrical, etc.

PHASE THREE—CONCEPTS

A. Preliminary design sketches.
B. Preliminary design data giving materials, methods, construction details, and projected characteristics.

PHASE FOUR—ANALYSIS

A. Critical analysis of all design concepts.
B. Selection of most promising design or designs.

PHASE FIVE—DESIGN CONFERENCE

A. Discussion of preliminary designs with engineering, management, client.
B. Approval of design or designs.

PHASE SIX—REFINEMENT

A. More complete drawings and specifications of selected design or designs.
B. More complete data supporting projected design.

PHASE SEVEN—DESIGN CONFERENCE

A. Discussion of refined design or designs.
B. Approval of most promising design.

PHASE EIGHT—SYNTHESIS

A. Projected design supported by mathematical, graphical, and computer-aided and combined systems data.
B. Investigation of all physical aspects and proof of soundness of the design.

PHASE NINE—MODELS

A. Components.
B. Mock-ups.
C. Models of critical features.

PHASE TEN—TESTING

A. Proof of operating characteristics of components.
B. Proof of soundness of complete entity.

PHASE ELEVEN—CONFERENCE

A. Final discussion with originating authority.
B. Approval of final design.

PHASE TWELVE—FINAL PREPARATION

A. Final design drawings.
B. Final specifications.

PHASE THIRTEEN—TRANSMITTAL

A. Transmittal of final design drawings and specifications to originating authority.

NOTE: In the outline above three conferences (Phases 5, 7, and 11) are scheduled with the originating authority, engineering, and management. This is usual, but it does *not* mean that these are the only conferences during the development of the project. The designer confers frequently with colleagues, and with engineers, components suppliers, materials experts, and others, to obtain information and confirm design features.

DESIGN PROJECTS

A series of design projects is presented on the following pages. The projects are designed to tax the ingenuity of the student without requiring any special knowledge of engineering mechanics or higher mathematics.

Each project has an accompanying suggested solution. These solutions are deliberately left undimensioned and incomplete so that the minimum requirement for the student is to complete the design and make a set of working drawings. They do not necessarily represent the best possible design for the project. The student is urged to consider as many other ideas as possible, weighing all such factors as cost and reliability before making a final selection.

Use of standard purchased parts such as roll-pins, retainer rings, screws, etc., is encouraged.

DESIGN PROJECT 18.1.

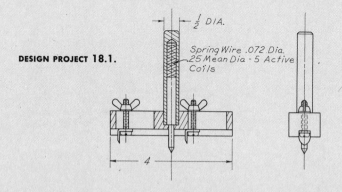

18.1. Design a device to be used in a drill press to cut circular gaskets from sheet cork, rubber, etc. It must cut gaskets to varying sizes, as large as 4-in. outside diameter, with the interior hole adjusting down as small as practicable.

The design indicated makes use of a spring-loaded centering pin to keep the material from slipping during the cutting. Torque must be transmitted from the spring tube to the cutter bar by some fastening device not shown. If this design is used, the means incorporated to make this connection must permit the parts to be disassembled for spring replacement and sharpening of the center pin.

DESIGN PROJECT 18.2.

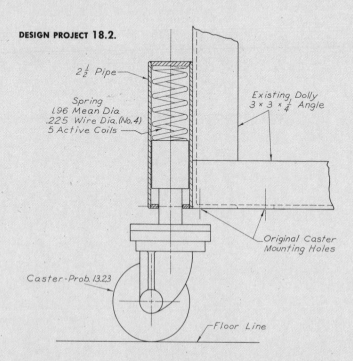

18.2. An industrial dolly made from steel angle is to be rebuilt to carry delicate electronics instruments. The dolly is equipped with four casters similar to that shown in Prob. 19.2.3.

Design a new caster mount to absorb shock incurred when the dolly is used on rough floors. A design load of about 100 lb per caster (including dolly) is to be carried.

The suggested design makes use of a compression spring having a spring constant of 100 psi, with a total deflection of 2 in.

18.3. Design a rust-resistant portable stand suitable for holding serving trays, campers' cookstoves, laundry baskets, etc. This stand is to be folded into as small and neat a package as possible.

The suggested solution makes use of aluminum angles and flat aluminum bar stock. The fasteners are threadless pins held in place by pushnuts (see Appendix).

DESIGN PROJECT 18.3.

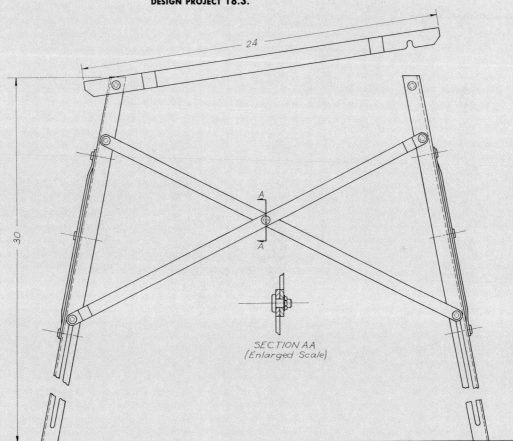

SECTION AA
(Enlarged Scale)

18.4.   Design a portable solar stove suitable for survey parties and campers, for use in relatively sunny climates. It must be lightweight and disassemble to pack into a small box. A parabolic reflector at least 3 ft in diameter must be used, and its focal point must not be too precise or it will tend to burn a hole in a small container. The reflector must be on an adjustable mounting so that it can be focused on the sun at different times of the day and year, and at different latitudes.

The suggested solution consists of a reflector made of eight properly developed segments of polished sheetmetal. These segments lie flat when not in use, and are bent to the proper shape by fasteners holding the segment edges together.

DESIGN PROJECT 18.4.

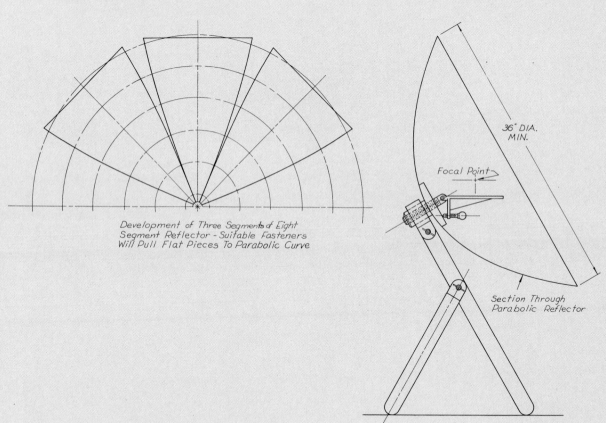

Development of Three Segments of Eight Segment Reflector - Suitable Fasteners Will Pull Flat Pieces To Parabolic Curve

36" DIA. MIN.

Focal Point

Section Through Parabolic Reflector

18.5. A small brass shell is fed from a hopper into the existing supply tube shown, that in turn supplies a press which further processes the part. All parts must have the closed end down.

Design a device to turn those pieces which have the open end down. The hopper feeds the pieces at such a rate that they do not touch each other.

One possible solution is shown; it utilizes an adjustable pin which enters the open end of those pieces that need turning. Gravity will then flip the pieces as indicated. The closed ends of the other pieces will hit the pin, the pieces will bounce up and fall without turning.

The design must be mounted on the existing 6-in. I-section column shown.

18.6. An industrial drying process is supplied with warm air through an 8-in.-diameter round duct. A variable-diameter orifice is to be installed in the duct to control the airflow. To aid in maintaining laminar flow the opening is to be kept approximately round and concentric in the duct. The diameter must reduce down to approximately one-half of the original diameter.

Design a suitable device for this service.

The solution indicated is based on the idea of six curved blades pivoted outside the periphery of the duct and moved in and out of the airstream by a control ring which is concentric with the duct.

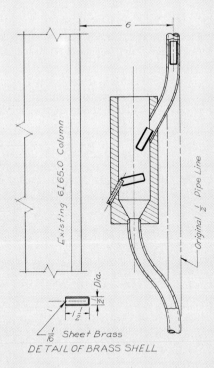

DESIGN PROJECT 18.5.

DETAIL OF BRASS SHELL

DESIGN PROJECT 18.6.

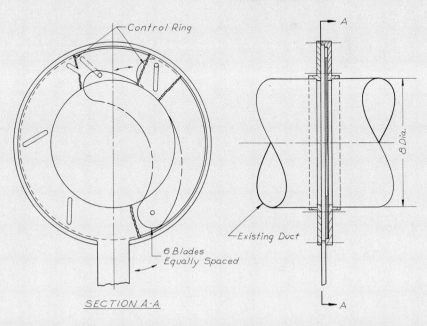

SECTION A-A

18.7. Many mechanical devices are lubricated for life at the time of assembly. This requires that a metered amount of oil be placed in the machine.

Design a device that will meter out 2 fluid ounces of oil with a single "push-pull" motion of the operator (1 U.S. fluid ounce = 1.805 cubic inches).

Some adjustment is desirable so that precise control is possible. Oil must not flow when the device is not in use.

The partial solution indicated uses two pistons, mounted on a single rod, sliding back and forth in a carefully finished cylinder.

Air trapped in the cylinder may impede movement of either the oil or the piston. The plastic float valve indicated will permit air to enter and leave the cylinder, but will trap the oil.

DESIGN PROJECT 18.7.

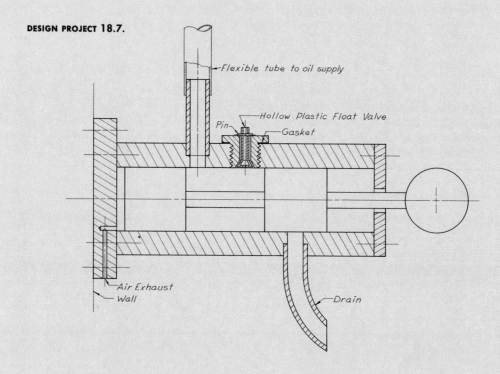

18.8. A "tin"-can food-container manufacturing plant is supplying cans directly to a food processer. The flow of cans must be equally divided and supplied to the two conveyor belts which will be installed as shown. Design a device and make the necessary assembly, working, and installation drawings for this.

The solution indicated consists of a "tee" member pivoted as shown. Each can will rotate the member in one direction or the other, evenly dividing the flow.

The cans are 4 in. in diameter and 4¾ in. high. They are supplied spaced out so that they do not touch each other.

DESIGN PROJECT 18.8.

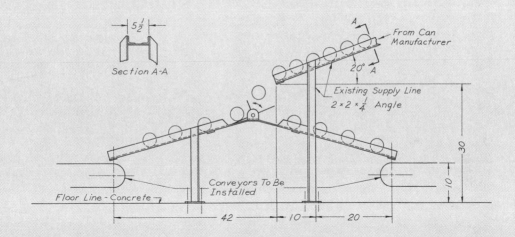

DESIGN PROJECT 18.9.

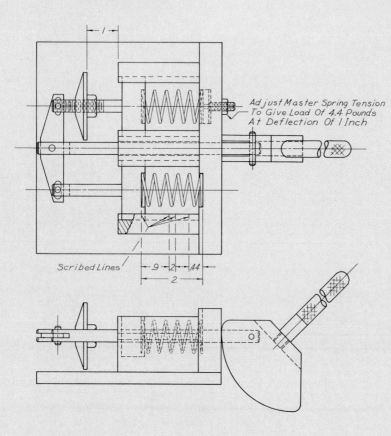

Adjust Master Spring Tension
To Give Load Of 4.4 Pounds
At Deflection Of 1 Inch

Scribed Lines

18.9. Design a device to check the compression-type coil spring specified below for the following:

Spring rate (pounds to deflect spring 1 inch)
Maximum free length
Maximum length when compressed solid

Specification of spring: 1-in. mean diameter, .0625-in.-diameter wire, five active coils, ends squared and ground, 2-in. maximum free length, 0.44-in. maximum solid length, and 4.4 psi spring rate. A load of 4.4 lb must deflect spring from 0.9 to 1.1 in.

The device indicated is one possible solution. A cam turned by hand deflects the master spring 1 in. (It is carefully set to give a force of 4.4 lb at 1-in. deflection.) If the two shoes are equidistant from the center pivot, the spring under test will carry a 4.4-lb load. Lines scribed on the base then will show, if the spring is within tolerance. The other lines scribed on the base will show, if spring meets length-tolerance specifications.

18.10. An electrical manufacturer makes transformer cores by welding or riveting stacks of thin steel laminations together. Because of the variation in thickness of the laminations due to the rolling tolerance (both total thickness variation and variation from side to side on the same sheet) neither the number of laminations per stack, nor the height of the stack are good measures of the ideal stack. As the electrical properties are primarily a function of the mass of steel in the core, the cores are best gaged by weight.

The lamination shown is stamped from a 22-gage sheet steel and is to be used in a core weighing 1.4 lb with as little variation as possible.

The ultimate goal is an automatic machine to receive the laminations directly from the punch press, select the stock, and feed it to an automatic welder. However, because of the complexity of the problem, a hand-powered, hand-loaded, hand-unloaded experimental machine is to be designed and tried first.

A partial solution is shown. Complete this design or prepare an alternate design to handle this problem.

DESIGN PROJECT 18.10.

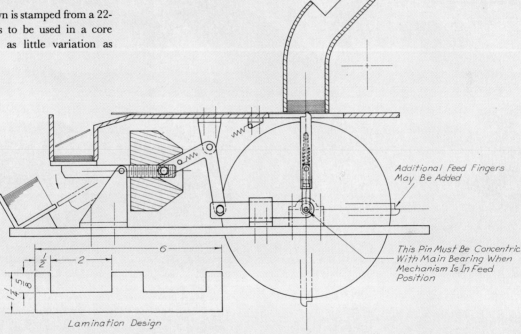

Additional Feed Fingers
May Be Added

This Pin Must Be Concentric
With Main Bearing When
Mechanism Is In Feed
Position

Lamination Design

After a single component, unit or subassembly, complete machine, mechanism or structure has been designed, developed and tested, a series of drawings is made giving all information necessary for manufacture. Known as working drawings, they include such items as detail drawings of individual parts, drawings of a subassembly or complete entity, parts lists, material specifications, manufacturing program, tooling, special tools, dies, fixtures, and many others.

Working Drawings

19.1. DEFINITION. A working drawing is any drawing used to give information for the manufacture or construction of a machine or the erection of a structure. Complete knowledge for the production of a machine or structure is given by a *set* of working drawings conveying all the facts fully and explicitly so that further instructions are not required.

The description given by the set of drawings will include:

1. The full graphic representation of the shape of each part (shape description).

2. The figured dimensions of each part (size description).

3. Explanatory notes, general and specific, on the individual drawings, giving the specifications of material, heat-treatment, finish, etc. Often, particularly in architectural and structural work, the notes of explanation and information concerning details of materials and workmanship are too extensive to be included on the drawings and so are made up separately in typed or printed form and called the "specifications"—thus the term "drawings and specifications."

4. A descriptive title on each drawing.

5. A description of the relationship of each part to the others (assembly).

6. A parts list or bill of material.

A set of drawings will include, in general, two classes of drawings: *detail drawings,* giving the information included in items

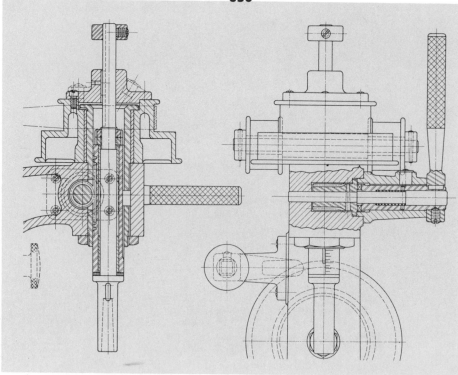

FIG. 19.1. A portion of a design drawing. Notes and specifications accompany the drawing.

1 to 4; and an *assembly drawing,* giving the location and relationship of the parts, item 5.

19.2. ENGINEERING PROCEDURE. When a new machine or structure is designed, the first drawings are usually in the form of freehand sketches on which the original ideas, scheming, and inventing are worked out. These drawings are accompanied or followed by calculations to prove the suitability of the design. Working from the sketches and calculations, the design department produces a *design assembly* (also called a "design layout" or "design drawing") (Fig. 19.1). This is a preliminary pencil drawing on which more details of the design are worked out. It is accurately made with instruments, full size if possible, and shows the shape and position of the various parts. Little attempt is made to show all the intricate detail; only the

essential dimensions, such as basic calculated sizes, are given. On the drawing, or separately as a set of written notes, will be the designer's general specifications for materials, heat-treatments, finishes, clearances or interferences, etc., and any other information needed by the draftsman in making up the individual drawings of the separate parts.

Working from the design drawing and notes, draftsmen (detailers) then make up the individual detail drawings. Figure 19.2 shows a detail drawing taken from the design drawing of Fig. 19.1. On a detail drawing, all the views necessary for complete shape description of a part are provided, and all the necessary dimensions and manufacturing directions are given. Dimension values for nonmating surfaces are obtained by scaling the design drawing, and the more critical values are determined from the design notes and from drafting-room standards. The detailer correlates the dimensions of mating parts and gives all necessary manufacturing information.

The set of drawings is completed with the addition of an assembly drawing and a parts list or bill of material.

If a machine is to be quantity produced, "operation" or "job" sheets will be prepared describing the separate manufacturing steps required and indicating the use and kind of special tools, jigs, fixtures, etc. The tool-design group, working from the detail drawings and the operation sheets, designs and makes the drawings for the special tools needed.

19.3. ASSEMBLY DRAWINGS. An *assembly drawing* is, as its name implies, a drawing of the machine or structure put together, showing the relative positions of the different parts.

The term "assembly drawings" includes preliminary design drawings and layouts, piping plans, unit assembly drawings, installation diagrams, and final complete drawings used for assembling or erecting the project.

The design drawing is the preliminary layout on which the scheming, inventing, and designing are accurately worked out. The assembly drawing is in some cases made by tracing from the design drawing. More often it is drawn from the dimensions of the detail drawings; this provides a valuable check on the correctness of the detail drawings.

The assembly drawing sometimes gives the over-all dimensions and the distances between centers or from part to part of the different pieces, thus fixing the relation of the parts to each other and aiding in erecting the machine. However, many assembly drawings need no dimensions. An assembly drawing should not be overloaded with detail, particularly hidden detail. Unnecessary dashed lines should not be used on any drawing, least of all on an assembly drawing.

Assembly drawings usually have reference letters or numbers designating the different parts. These "piece numbers," sometimes enclosed in circles (called "balloons" by draftsmen) with a leader pointing to the piece (Fig. 19.3), are used in connection with the details and bill of material.

A *unit assembly drawing* or subassembly (Fig. 19.3) is a drawing of a related group of parts used to show the assembly of complicated machinery where it would be practically impossible to show all the features on one drawing. Thus, in the drawing of a lathe, there would be included unit assemblies of groups of

FIG. 19.3. A unit assembly drawing. For complex machines, a number of units may be used in place of one complete assembly drawing.

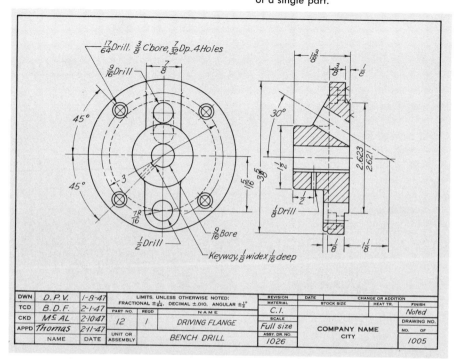

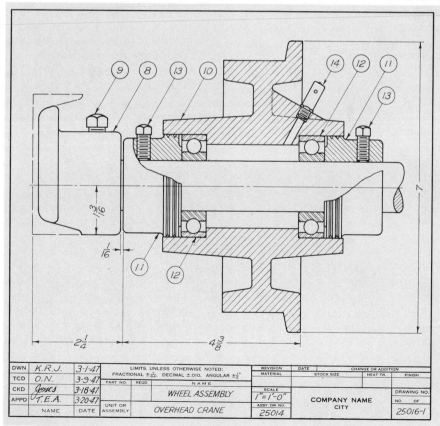

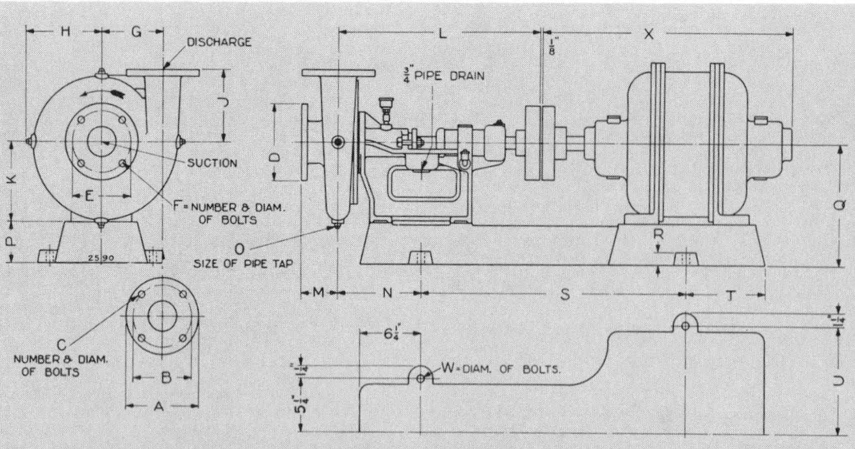

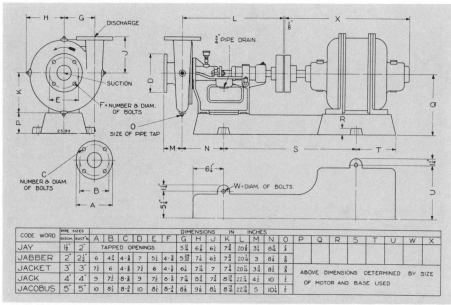

CODE WORD	PIPE SIZES DISCH.	PIPE SIZES SUCT'N	A	B	C	D	E	F	G	H	J	K	L	M	N	O	P	Q	R	S	T	U	W	X
JAY	1 1/2"	2"	TAPPED OPENINGS						5 13/16	6 7/8	6 1/2	7 3/4	20 3/8	3 1/4	8 3/16	3/8								
JABBER	2"	2 1/2"	6	4 3/4	4-5/8	7	5 1/2	4-5/8	5 29/32	7 1/4	6 1/2	7 3/4	20 7/16	3	8 1/4	3/8								
JACKET	3"	3"	7 1/2	6	4-5/8	7 1/2	6	4-5/8	6 1/4	7 11/16	7	7 3/4	20 11/16	3 3/4	8 1/2	3/8	ABOVE DIMENSIONS DETERMINED BY SIZE OF MOTOR AND BASE USED							
JACK	4"	4"	9	7 1/2	8-5/8	9	7 1/2	8-5/8	7 11/16	8 3/4	7 3/4	8 13/16	22 11/16	4 1/2	10	1/2								
JACOBUS	5"	5"	10	8 1/2	8-3/4	10	8 1/2	8-3/4	8 1/8	9 1/8	8 1/4	8 13/16	22 15/16	5	10 1/4	1/2								

FIG. 19.4. An outline assembly drawing (tabular). Tabulation gives the dimensions for different-sized units.

FIG. 19.5. A detail drawing. Note the completeness of manufacturing information given on the drawing.

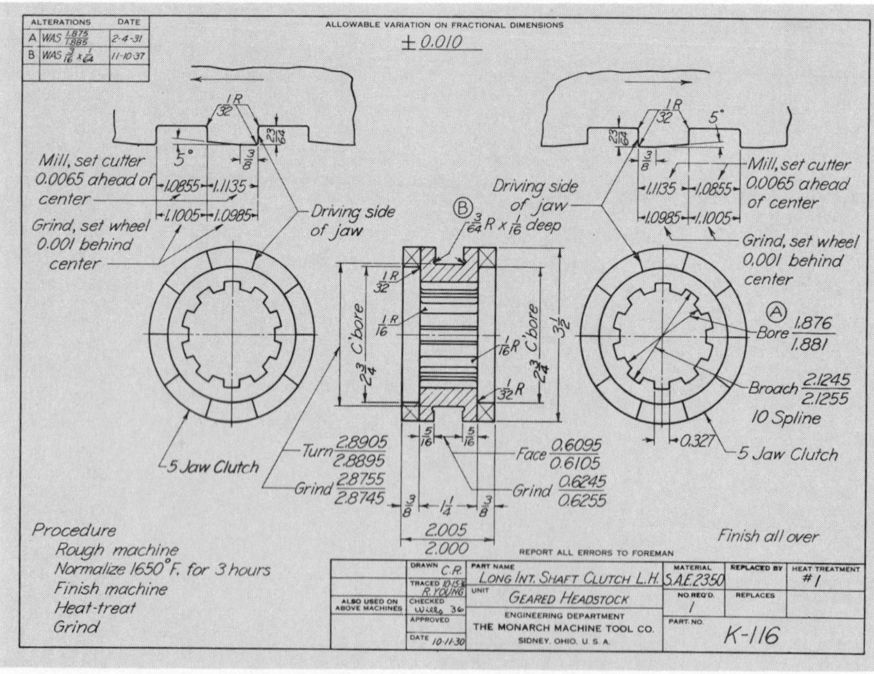

parts such as the headstock, tailstock, gearbox, etc.

An *outline assembly drawing* is used to give a general idea of the exterior shape of a machine or structure, and contains only the principal dimensions (Fig. 19.4). When it is made for catalogues or other illustrative purposes, dimensions are often omitted. Outline assembly drawings are frequently used to give the information required for the installation or erection of equipment and are then called *installation drawings.*

An *assembly working drawing* gives complete information for producing a machine or structure on one drawing. This is done by providing adequate orthographic views together with dimensions, notes, and a descriptive title. The figure for Prob. 19.3.7 is an example.

A *diagram drawing* is an assembly showing, symbolically, the erection or installation of equipment. Erection and piping and wiring diagrams are examples. Diagram drawings are often made in pictorial form.

19.4. DETAIL DRAWINGS. A *detail* drawing is the drawing of a single piece, giving a complete and exact description of its form, dimensions, and construction. A successful detail drawing will tell the workman *simply* and *directly* the shape, size, material, and finish of a part; what shop operations are necessary; what limits of accuracy must be observed; the number of parts wanted; etc. It should be so exact in description that, if followed, a satisfactory part will result. Figure 19.5 illustrates a commercial detail drawing.

Detailing practice varies somewhat according to the industry and the requirements of the shop system. For example, in structural work, details are often grouped together on one sheet, while in modern mechanical practice a separate sheet is used for each part.

If the parts are grouped on one sheet, the detailed pieces should be set, if possible, in the same relative position as on the assembly and, to facilitate reading, placed as nearly as possible in natural relationship. Parts of the same material or character are usually grouped together, as, for example, forgings on one sheet, castings on another, and parts machined from stock on another. A subtitle must be provided for each part, giving the part number, material, number required for each assembly, etc.

The accepted and best system in mechanical work is to have each piece, no matter how small, on a separate sheet. As described in paragraph 17.3, if the single-drawing system is followed, one drawing will be used by all shops. If the multiple system is used, a separate drawing must be made for each shop; thus there may be a *pattern drawing,* a *casting drawing,* and a *machining drawing,* all for a single cast part. A detail drawing should be a complete unit for the purpose intended and should not be dependent in any way upon any other detail drawing.

19.5.   TABULAR DRAWINGS.

A tabular drawing, either assembly or detail, is one on which the dimension values are replaced by reference letters, an accompanying table on the drawing listing the corresponding dimensions for a series of sizes of the machine or part, thus making one drawing serve for the range covered. Some companies manufacturing parts in a variety of sizes use this tabular system of size description, but a serious danger with it is the possibility of misreading the table. Figure 19.4 shows a tabular assembly drawing.

19.6.   STANDARD DRAWINGS.

To avoid the difficulties experienced with tabular drawings, some companies make a "standard drawing," complete except for the actual figured dimensions. This drawing is reproduced by offset printing or black-and-white reproduction on vellum paper, and the reproductions are dimensioned separately for the various sizes of parts. This method gives a separate complete drawing for each size of part; and when a new size is needed, the drawing is easily and quickly made. Figure 19.6 shows a standard drawing, and Fig. 19.7 the drawing filled in, making a completed working drawing.

19.7.   STANDARD PARTS.

Purchased or company standard parts are specified by name and size or by number and, consequently, do not need to be detailed. All standard parts, such as bolts, screws, antifriction bearings, etc., are shown on the assembly drawing and are given a part number. The complete specifications for their purchase are given in the parts list.

Sometimes, however, a part is made by *altering* a standard or previously produced part. In this case a detail drawing is made, showing and specifying the original part with changes and dimensions for the alteration.

19.8.   THE BILL OF MATERIAL, OR PARTS LIST.

This is a tabulated statement, usually placed on a separate sheet in the case of quantity production (as in Prob. 19.2.4) or on the assembly drawing in other cases (as in Prob. 19.3.12). This table gives the piece number, name, quantity, material, sometimes the stock size of raw material, detail drawing numbers, weight of each piece, etc. A final column is usually left for remarks.

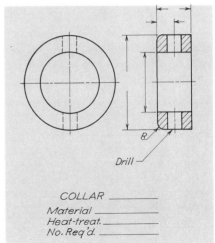

FIG. 19.6.   A standard drawing. This is reproduced on tracing paper to provide the shape description needed for the drawing.

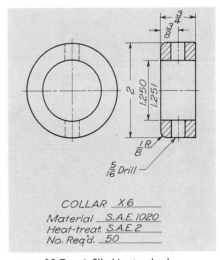

FIG. 19.7.   A filled-in standard drawing. With the addition of dimensions a standard drawing becomes a completed drawing to be used for manufacturing purposes.

The term "bill of material" is ordinarily used in structural and architectural drawing. The term "parts list" applies more accurately in machine-drawing practice. In general, the parts are listed in the order of their importance, with the larger parts first and the standard parts such as screws, pins, etc., at the end.

The blank ruling for a bill of material should not be crowded. Lines should never be spaced closer than ¼ in.; 5⁄16 or ⅜ in. spacing is better, with the height of the lettering not more than half the space and centered between the lines. Instead of being lettered, bills of material are frequently typed on forms printed on thin paper. Intensifying the impression by typing with carbon paper on the back increases the opacity of the letters, and a clearer blueprint will result.

19.9. SET OF DRAWINGS. A *complete set* of working drawings consists of detail sheets and assembly sheets, the former giving all necessary information for the manufacture of each of the individual parts which cannot be purchased and the latter showing the parts assembled as a finished unit or machine. The set includes the bill of material or parts list and may also contain special drawings for the purchaser, such as foundation plans or oiling diagrams.

19.10. MAKING A WORKING DRAWING: BASIC CONCEPTS. Although pictorial drawings are used to some extent in special cases, the basis of all working drawings is orthographic projection. Thus, to represent an object completely, at least two views are ordinarily needed, often more. The only general rule is: *make as many views as are necessary to describe the object clearly—and no more.* In-

stances may occur in which the third dimension is so evident as to make one view sufficient, as, for example, in the drawing of a shaft or bolt. In other cases, perhaps a half-dozen views will be required to describe a piece completely. Sometimes half, partial, or broken views can be used to advantage.

Select for the front view the face showing the largest dimension, preferably the obvious front of the object when in its functioning position, and then decide what other views are necessary. A vertical cylindrical piece, for example, would require only a front and a top view; a horizontal cylindrical piece, only a front and a side view. Determine which side view to use or whether both are needed. The one with the fewest dashed lines should be preferred. In some cases the best representation will be obtained by using *both* side views with all unnecessary dashed lines omitted. See whether an auxiliary view or a note will eliminate one or more other views and whether a section is better than an exterior view. One statement can be made with the force of a rule: *If anything in clearness can be gained by violating a principle of projection, violate it.*

Paragraphs 7.12 to 7.26 give a number of examples of conventions that are in violation of theoretical representation but are in the interest of clearness. The draftsman must remember that his responsibility is to the reader of the drawing and that he is not justified in saving himself any time or trouble at the expense of the drawing, by making it less plain or easy to read. The time so saved by the draftsman may be lost to the company a hundredfold in the shop, where the drawing is used not once but repeatedly.

There is a *style* in drawing, just as

there is in literature, which indicates itself in one way by ease of reading. Some drawings stand out, while others, which may contain all the information, are difficult to decipher. Although dealing with mechanical thought, there is a place for some artistic sense in mechanical drawing. The number, selection, and disposition of views; the omission of anything unnecessary, ambiguous, or misleading; the size and placement of dimensions and lettering; and the contrast of lines are all elements in the style.

In commercial drafting, *accuracy* and *speed* are the two requirements. The drafting room is an expensive department, and time is an important element. The draftsman must therefore have a ready knowledge not only of the principles of drawing but of the conventional methods and abbreviations and of any device or system that will save time without sacrificing clearness.

The usual criticism of the beginner by the employer is the result of the former's lack of appreciation of the necessity for speed.

19.11. MATERIALS USED FOR WORKING DRAWINGS.

Working drawings go to the shop in the form of blueprints, black-line prints, or other similar forms of reproduction, and the drawings must therefore be made on translucent material, either directly or as tracings. Pencil drawings may be made on tracing paper or on pencil cloth; inked drawings, on tracing paper or on tracing cloth.

Tracing paper is a thin translucent material, commonly called "vellum." Considerable time and expense may be saved by making the original pencil drawing on this material. Excellent prints can be obtained if the lines are of sufficient blackness and intensity.

Pencil cloth is a transparentized fabric with one or both sides of its surface prepared to take pencil so that the original drawing can be made on it and prints made either from the pencil drawing directly or after it has been inked. Some of the newer cloths are moisture resistant, others are really waterproof. Pencil cloth is made for pencil drawings, and perfect blueprints can be made from drawings made on it with sharp, hard pencils. Ink lines, however, do not adhere well and have a tendency to chip or rub off in cleaning.

Tracing cloth is a fine-thread fabric sized and transparentized with a starch preparation. The smooth side is considered by the makers as the working side, but most draftsmen prefer to work on the dull side, which will take pencil marks. The cloth should be fastened down smoothly over the pencil drawing and its selvage torn off. To remove the traces of grease that sometimes prevent the flow of ink, dust the tracing cloth with chalk or prepared pounce (a blackboard eraser may be used) and then rub it off with a cloth. Carbon tetrachloride is an effective cleaning agent. Rub a moistened cloth over the surface—any excess will evaporate in a moment.

A *plastic material,* known as "Mylar,"[1] is now available for both pencil and ink drawings. It is evenly translucent, has a fine matte surface, good lasting qualities, and requires no special storage precautions.

19.12. DRAWING SIZES.

Drawing paper and cloth are available in rolls of various widths and in standard trimmed sizes. Most drafting rooms use standard sheets, printed with border and title block. The recommended sizes shown in Table 19.1, based on multiples of 8½ by 11 in. and 9

[1] DuPont Manufacturing Co.

TABLE 19.1. Finished Flat-sheet Sizes

Designation	Width	Length	Designation	Width	Length
A	8½	11	A	9	12
B	11	17	B	12	18
C	17	22	C	18	24
D	22	34	D	24	36
E	34	44	E	36	48
F*	28	40	F*	28	40

* Not a multiple of the basic size. To be used when width of E size is not adaptable.

by 12 in., permit the filing of prints in a standard letter file.

Figure 19.8 shows the most common trimmed sizes. Larger drawings can be made on rolled stock of standard width, with the length as a multiple of 11 or 12 in., not to exceed 144 in.

19.13. ORDER OF PENCILING. After the scheming, inventing, and calculating have been done and the design drawing has been completed, the order of procedure for making the detail drawings is:

1. Select a suitable standard sheet or lay off a sheet to standard size, with the excess paper to the right, as a convenient space for making sketches and calculations, and block out the space for the title.

2. Decide what scale to use, choosing one large enough to show all dimensions without crowding, and plan the arrangement of the sheet by making a little preliminary freehand sketch, estimating the space each view will occupy and placing the views to the best advantage for preserving, if possible, a balance in the appearance of the sheet. Be sure to leave sufficient space *between* views for the dimensions.

3. Draw the center lines for each view, and on these "block in" the views by laying off the principal dimensions and outlines, using *light, sharp, accurate* pencil lines. Center lines are drawn for the axes of symmetry of all symmetrical views or parts of views. Thus every cylindrical part should have a center line—the projection of the axis of the piece. Every circle should have two center lines intersecting at its center.

4. Draw the views, beginning with the most dominant features and progressing to the subordinate. Carry the different views on together, projecting a characteristic shape as shown on one view to the other views and *not* finishing one view before starting another. Draw the lines to the final finished weight (wherever possible), using a minimum of construction. *Never* make a drawing lightly and "heavy" it later.

5. Finish the projections, putting in last the minor details. Check the projec-

FIG. 19.8. ANSI trimmed sizes of paper and cloth. ANSI sizes are based on multiples of 8½ by 11 in. and 9 by 12 in. (see Table 19.1).

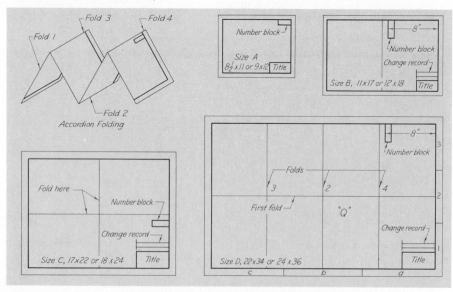

tions and make sure that all views are complete and correct.

6. Draw all necessary dimension lines; then put in the dimension values.

7. Draw guide lines for the notes, and then letter them.

8. Lay out the title.

9. Check the drawing carefully.

The overrunning lines of the constructive stage should not be erased before tracing or inking. These extensions are often convenient in showing the stopping points. Avoid unnecessary erasing as it abrades the surface of the paper so that it catches dirt more readily.

As an aid in stopping tangent arcs in inking, it is desirable to mark the tangent point on the pencil drawing with a short piece of the normal to the curve at the point of tangency.

Figure 19.9 illustrates the stages of penciling.

19.14. ORDER OF INKING. To ensure good printing, the ink should be perfectly black and the ruling pens in good condition. Red ink should not be used unless it is desired to have some lines inconspicuous on the print. Blue ink will not print well. Sometimes, on maps, diagrams, etc., it is desirable to use colored inks on the tracing to avoid confusion of lines; in such cases, add a little Chinese white to the colored inks and it will render them sufficiently opaque to print.

Ink lines can be removed from tracing cloth by rubbing with a hard pencil eraser, slipping a triangle under the tracing to give a harder surface. The rubbed surface should afterward be burnished with a burnisher or fingernail. In tracing a part that has been section-lined, a piece of white paper can be slipped under the cloth and the section lining

done without reference to the section lines underneath.

Tracing cloth is sensitive to atmospheric variations, often changing overnight so as to require restretching. If a large tracing cannot be finished in one day, some views should be finished and no figure left only partly traced.

In making a large tracing, it is well to cut the required piece from the roll and lay it exposed, flat, for a short time before fastening it down.

Water will ruin a tracing on starch-coated cloth, and moist hands or arms should not come in contact with it. Form the habit of keeping the hands off drawings. In both drawing and tracing on

FIG. 19.9. Order of penciling. (1) Layout; (2) details progress to (3); completion at (4). See paragraph 19.13.

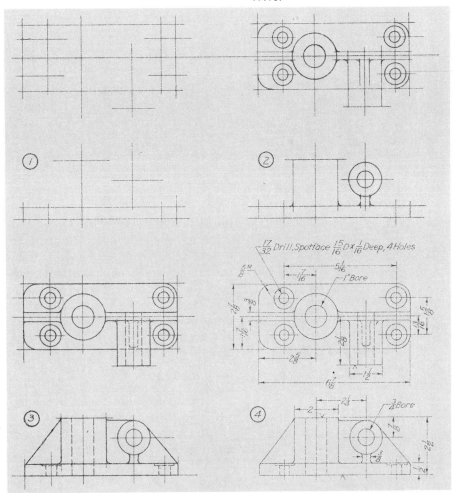

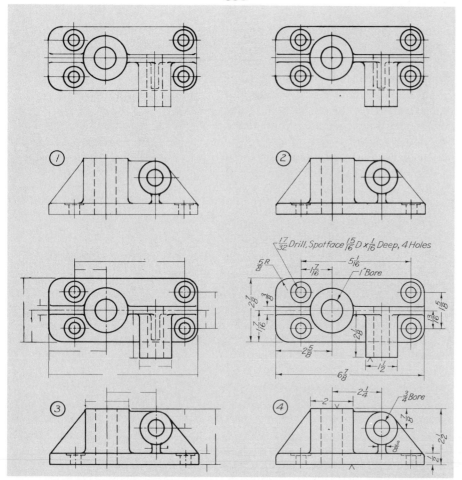

FIG. 19.10. Order of inking. (1) Layout; (2) details progress to (3); completion at (4). See paragraph 19.14.

3. Ink any irregular curved lines.

4. Ink straight full lines in this order: horizontal, vertical, and inclined.

5. Ink straight dashed lines in the same order.

6. Ink center lines.

7. Ink extension and dimension lines.

8. Ink arrowheads and dimensions.

9. Section-line all areas representing cut surfaces.

10. Letter notes and titles. (On tracings, draw pencil guide lines first.)

11. Ink the border.

12. Check the inked drawing.

Figure 19.10 shows the stages of inking.

19.15. TITLE BLOCKS. The title of a working drawing is usually placed in the lower right-hand corner of the sheet, the size of the space varying with the amount of information to be given. The spacing and arrangement are designed to provide the information most helpful in a particular line of work.

In general, the title of a machine drawing should contain the following information:

1. Name of company and its location

2. Name of machine or unit

3. Name of part (if a detail drawing)

4. Drawing number

5. Part number (if a detail drawing)

6. Number of parts required (for each assembly)

7. Scale

8. Assembly-drawing number (given on a detail drawing to identify the part in assembly)

9. Drafting-room record: names or initials of draftsman, tracer, checker, approving authority; each with date

10. Material

To these, depending upon the need for the information, may be added:

large sheets, it is a good plan to cut a mask of drawing paper to cover all but the view being worked on. Unfinished drawings should be covered overnight.

Tracings can be cleaned of pencil marks and dirt by wiping with a cloth moistened with benzine or carbon tetrachloride. To prevent smearing when using this method of cleaning, borders and titles should be printed in an ink not affected by benzine.

Order of Inking

1. Ink all full-line circles, beginning with the smallest, and then circle arcs.

2. Ink dashed circles and arcs in the same order as full-line circles.

11. Stock size
12. Heat-treatment
13. Finish
14. Name of purchaser, if special machine
15. Drawing "supersedes" and "superseded by"

Form of Title. Every drafting room has its own standard form for titles. In large offices the blank form is often printed in type on the tracing paper or cloth. Figures 19.11 and 19.12 are characteristic examples.

A form of title that is used to some extent is the *record strip,* a strip marked off across the lower part or right end of the sheet, containing the information required in the title and space for the recording of orders, revisions, changes, etc., that should be noted, with the date, as they occur. Figure 19.13 illustrates one form.

It is sometimes desired to keep the records of orders and other private information on the tracing but not to have them appear on the print. In such cases a record strip is put outside the border and trimmed off the print before sending it out.

To Letter a Title. The title should be lettered freehand in single-stroke capitals, vertical or inclined—not both styles in the same title. Write out the contents on a separate piece of paper; then refer to paragraph 4.15, where full instructions have been given.

19.16. **ZONING.** As an aid in locating some item on a large drawing, the lower and right borders may be ruled and marked as shown on the *D*-size drawing in Fig. 19.8. Item *Q* would be located in zone *b*2. A separate column in the change-record block is often used to indicate the position of each drawing change.

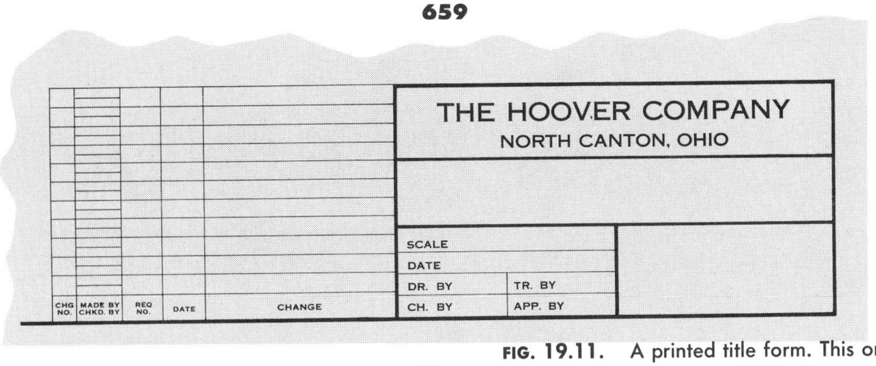

FIG. 19.11. A printed title form. This one contains a "change-record" block.

19.17. **CHECKING.** When a working drawing is finished, it must be checked by an experienced person, who, in signing his name to it, becomes responsible for any errors. This is the final "proof-reading" and cannot be done by the one who has made the drawing nearly so well as by another person. In small offices all the work is checked by the chief draftsman, or sometimes draftsmen check one another's work; in large drafting rooms one or more checkers are employed who devote all their time to this kind of work. All notes, computations, and checking layouts should be preserved for future reference.

Students can gain experience in this work by checking one another's drawings. To be effective, checking must be done in an absolutely systematic way and with thorough concentration.

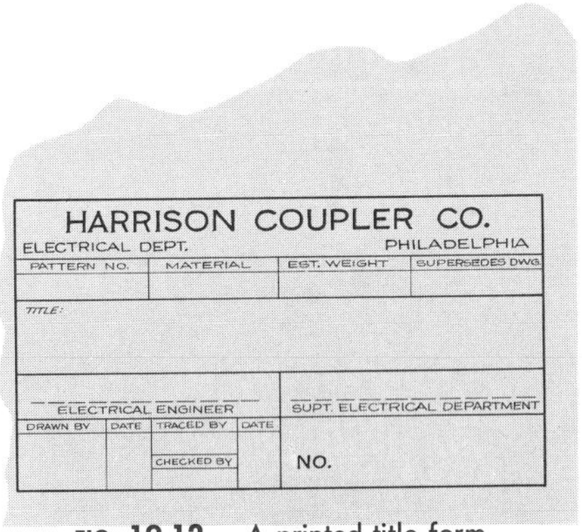

19.18. **ORDER OF CHECKING.** Each of the following items should be gone through separately. As each dimension or feature is verified, a check mark in colored pencil should be placed on or above it and corrections indicated with a different-colored pencil.

1. Put yourself in the position of those who are to read the drawing, and find out whether it is easy to read and

FIG. 19.12. A printed title form. This one is for an electrical department.

FIG. 19.13. A strip title. This type extends across one side of the drawing.

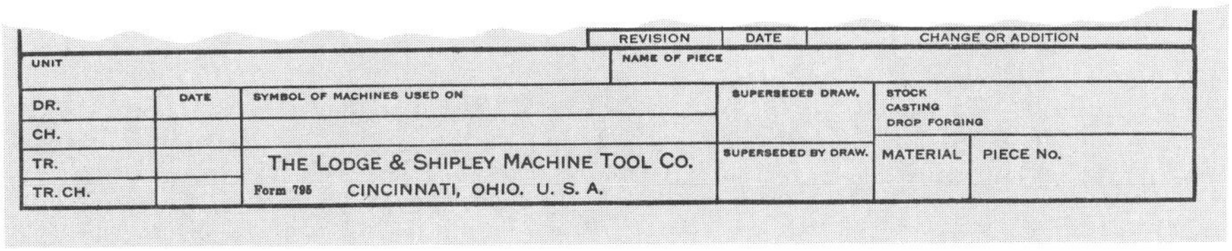

tells a straight story. Always do this before checking any individual features, in other words, before you have had time to become accustomed to the contents.

2. See that each piece is correctly designed and illustrated and that all necessary views are shown but none that is not necessary.

3. Check all the dimensions by scaling and, where advisable, also by calculation. Preserve the calculations.

4. See that dimensions for the shop are given as required by the shop and that the shop is not left to do any adding or subtracting in order to get a needed dimension.

5. Check for tolerances. See that they are neither too "fine" nor too "coarse" for the particular conditions of the machine, so that they will not, on the one hand, increase unnecessarily the cost of production or, on the other, impair accuracy of operation or duplication.

6. Go over each piece and see that finishes are properly specified.

7. See that every specification of material is correct and that all necessary ones are given.

8. Look out for "interferences." This means that each detail must be checked with the parts that will be adjacent to it in the assembled machine to see that proper clearances have been allowed.

9. When checking for clearances in connection with a mechanical movement, lay out the movement to scale, figure the principal angles of motion, and see that proper clearances are maintained in all positions, drawing small mechanisms to double size or larger.

10. Check to see that all the small details such as screws, bolts, pins, and rivets are standard and that, where it is possible, stock sizes have been employed.

11. Check every feature of the title or record strip and bill of material.

12. Review the drawing in its entirety, adding such explanatory notes as will increase its efficiency.

19.19. ALTERATIONS. Once a drawing has been printed and the prints have been released to the shop, any alterations or changes should be recorded on the drawing and new prints issued. If the changes are extensive, the drawing may be *obsoleted* and a new drawing made which *supersedes* the old drawing. Many drawing rooms have "change-record" blocks printed in conjunction with the title, where minor changes are recorded (Fig. 19.11). The change is identified in the record and on the face of the drawing by a letter.

New designs may be changed so often that the alterations cannot be made fast enough to reach the shop when needed. In this case sketches showing the changes are rapidly made, reproduced, and sent to the shop, where they are fastened to each print of the drawing. These sketches, commonly known as "engineering orders," are later incorporated on the drawing.

Portions of a drawing can be canceled by drawing closely spaced parallel lines, usually at 45°, over the area to be voided.

19.20. WORKING SKETCHES. Facility in making freehand orthographic drawings is an essential part of the equipment of every engineer. Routine men such as tracers and detailers may get along with skill and speed in mechanical execution, but the designer must be able to record his ideas freehand. In all inventive mechanical thinking, in all preliminary designing, in all explanations and instructions to draftsmen, freehand sketching is the mode of expression. Its mastery means mastery of the language, and it is gained only after full proficiency in drawing with instruments has been acquired. It is mastery which the engineer, inventor, designer, chief draftsman, and contractor, with all of whom time is too valuable to spend in mechanical execution, must have.

Working sketches may be made in orthographic or pictorial form. Chapter 5 gives the fundamentals for orthographic freehand drawings, and Chap. 6 discusses pictorial sketching.

19.21. KINDS OF WORKING SKETCHES.

Working sketches can be divided into two general classes: (1) those made before the structure is built and (2) those made after the structure is built.

In the first class are included the sketches made in connection with the designing of the structure. These can be classified as (*a*) *scheme* or *idea* sketches, used in studying and developing the arrangement and proportion of parts; (*b*) *computation sketches,* made in connection with the figured calculations for motion and strength; (*c*) *executive sketches,* made by the chief engineer, inventor, or consulting engineer to give instructions for special arrangements or ideas that must be embodied in the design; (*d*) *design sketches,* used in working up the schemes and ideas into suitable form so that the design drawing can be started; and (*e*) *detail sketches,* made as substitutes for detail drawings.

The second class includes (*a*) *detail sketches,* drawn from existing models or parts, with complete notes and dimensions, from which duplicate parts can be constructed directly or from which work-

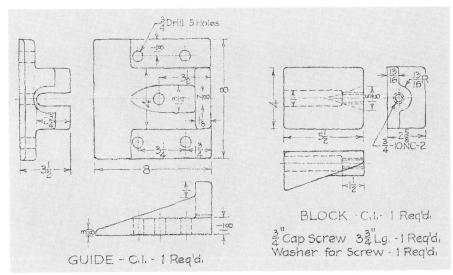

GUIDE - C.I. - 1 Req'd.

BLOCK - C.I. - 1 Req'd.
¾" Cap Screw 3¾" Lg. - 1 Req'd.
Washer for Screw - 1 Req'd.

FIG. 19.14. A detail sketch. This is a sketch of two parts, the guide and block, parts for a leveling device.

ing drawings can be made (Fig. 19.14); (*b*) *assembly sketches,* made from an assembled machine to show the relative positions of the various parts, with center and location dimensions, or sometimes for a simple machine, with complete dimensions and specifications; and (*c*) *outline* or *diagrammatic sketches,* generally made for the purpose of location: sometimes, for example, to give the size and location of pulleys and shafting, piping, or wiring, that is, information for use in connection with the setting up of machinery; sometimes to locate a single machine, giving the over-all dimensions, sizes, and center distances for foundation bolts and other necessary information.

19.22. MAKING A WORKING SKETCH.

In making a working sketch, the principles of projection and the rules of practice for working drawings are to be remembered and applied. A systematic order should be followed for both idea sketches and sketches from objects, as listed below:

1. Visualize the object.

2. Decide on the treatment, orthographic or pictorial.

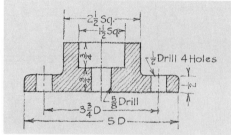

FIG. 19.15. A one-view sketch. Notes and the dimensioning details make another view unnecessary.

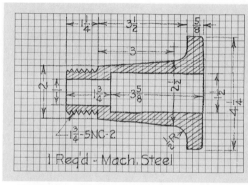

FIG. 19.16. A sketch on coordinate paper.

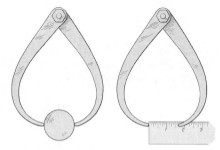

FIG. 19.17. Outside caliper. It is used for measuring diameters or thicknesses.

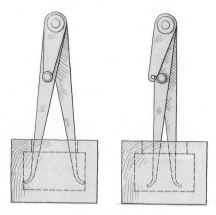

FIG. 19.18. Inside transfer caliper. It is used for measuring internal distances when a shoulder prevents direct removal.

3. Determine the view or views.
4. Determine the size of the sketch.
5. Locate the center lines.
6. Block in the main outlines.
7. Complete the detail.
8. Add dimension lines and arrowheads.
9. Put on the dimension values.
10. Letter notes and title, with date.
11. Check the drawing.

Before a good graphic description of an object or idea can be developed, it is essential that the mental image of it be definite and clear. The clearness of the sketch is a direct function of this mental picture. Hence the first step is to concentrate on visualization, which leads directly to the second step: determination of the best method of representation.

The method of representation will probably not be just the same as would be used in a scale drawing. For example, a note in regard to thickness or shape of section will often be used in a working drawing to save a view (Fig. 19.15); thus one view of a piece that is circular in cross section would be sufficient. In other cases additional part views and extra sections may be sketched rather than complicate the regular views with added lines that might confuse the sketch, although the same lines might be perfectly clear in a measured drawing.

The third step is to determine the view (pictorial) or views (orthographic). Draw the object in its functioning position, if possible, but if another position will show the features to better advantage, use it. A machine should, of course, be represented right-side up, in its natural working position. If symmetrical about an axis, often only one-half need be sketched. If a whole view cannot be made on one sheet, it may be put on two, each part being drawn up to a break line used as a datum line.

The fourth step is to proportion the size of the sketch to the sheet. Have it large enough to show all detail clearly, but allow plenty of room for dimensions, notes, and memorandums. Small parts can be sketched larger than full size. Do not try to crowd all the views on one sheet of paper. Use as many sheets as may be required, but name each view, indicating the direction in which it is taken. Sometimes one view alone will require a whole sheet.

In drawing on plain paper, the location of the principal points, centers, etc., should be so judged that the sketches will fit on the sheet, and the whole sketch, with as many views, sections, and auxiliary views as are necessary to describe the piece, will be drawn in as nearly correct proportion as the eye can determine, *without making any measurements.*

Cross-section Paper. Sketches are often made on coordinate paper ruled faintly in ¹⁄₁₆, ⅛, or ¼ in., used simply as an aid in drawing straight lines and judging proportions, or for drawing to approximate scale by assigning suitable values to the unit spaces. The latter use is more applicable to design sketches than to sketches from the object (Fig. 19.16).

In order to gain skill through practice, sketches should be made entirely freehand. However, in commercial work the engineer often saves time by making a hybrid sketch, drawing circles with the compass or even with a coin from his pocket, ruling some lines with a pocket scale or a triangle and making some freehand but always keeping a workmanlike quality and good proportion.

19.23. DIMENSIONING AND FINISHING.

After completing the views of a piece, go over it and add *dimension lines* for all the dimensions needed for its construction, drawing extension lines and arrowheads carefully and checking to see that none is omitted.

The dimension values are now added. If the sketch is made from reference drawings and specifications, these sources give the dimension values. If the sketch is of an existing part or model, measurements must be made to determine the dimension values, as explained in paragraph 19.24.

Add all remarks and notes that seem to be of possible value. The title should be written or lettered on the sketch.

Always Date a Sketch. Valuable inventions have been lost through inability to prove priority because the first sketches had not been dated. In commercial work the draftsman's notebook with sketches and calculations is preserved as a permanent record, and its sketches should be made so as to stand the test of time and be legible after the details of their making have been forgotten.

19.24. MEASURING AND DIMENSIONING.

Before adding values, *if the sketch is of an existing model or part,* the object has not been handled, and so the drawing has been kept clean. The measurements for the dimensions indicated on the drawing are now needed. A flexible rule or steel scale will serve for getting most of the dimensions. Never use a draftsman's scale for measuring castings, as it would become soiled and its edges marred. The diameter of cylindrical shapes or the distance between outside surfaces can be measured by using outside calipers and scale (Fig. 19.17); and the sizes of holes or internal surfaces, by using inside calipers. Figure 19.18 illustrates the inside transfer caliper, used when a projecting portion prevents removing the ordinary caliper. The outside transfer caliper is used for a similar condition occurring with an outside measurement. The depth of a hole is easily measured with the depth gage (Fig. 19.19*A*). Screw threads are measured by calipering the body diameter and either counting the number of threads per inch or gaging with a screw-pitch gage (Fig. 19.19*B*). A fillet-and-round gage measures radii, the gage fitting to the circular contour (Fig. 19.19*C*). It is often necessary to lay a straightedge across a surface, as in Fig. 19.20. This type of measurement could be made

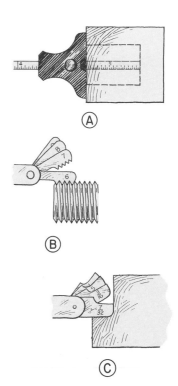

FIG. 19.19. Gages. (*A*) depth gage; (*B*) screw-pitch gage; (*C*) fillet-and-round gage.

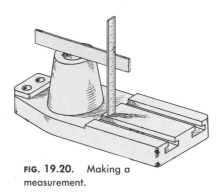

FIG. 19.20. Making a measurement.

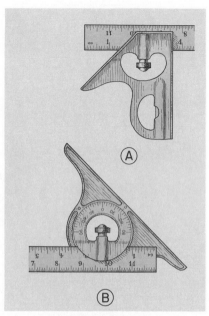

FIG. 19.21. Combination square. (*A*) standard head; (*B*) adjustable head.

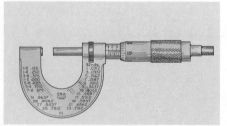

FIG. 19.22. Outside micrometer caliper.

conveniently with a combination square or with a surface gage. The combination square has two different heads, the regular 90-45° head (Fig. 19.21*A*) for a variety of measurements, and the protractor head (Fig. 19.21*B*) for measuring or laying out angles. For accurate measurements, outside or inside micrometer calipers are necessary. The outside type is illustrated in Fig. 19.22. Readings to 0.001 in. are easily obtained. Accurate measurements of holes can be made with a telescopic gage in conjunction with an outside micrometer.

A variety of gages made for special purposes, such as a wire gage, gage for sheet metal, can be used as occasion demands. With some ingenuity, measurements can often be made with the simpler instruments when special ones are not available.

Always measure from finished surfaces, if possible. Judgment must be exercised in measuring rough castings so as not to record inequalities.

In finding the distance between centers of two holes of the same size, measure from the edge of one to the corresponding edge of the other. Curves are measured by coordinates or offsets, as shown in Figs. 19.51 and 19.52. A curved outline can be recorded by laying a sheet of paper on it and making a rubbing.

19.25.   CHECKING THE SKETCH.   The final step is to check the sketch. It is a curious fact that when a beginner omits a dimension, it is usually a basic, vital one, such as that of the center height of a machine or an over-all length.

Sketches are not always made on paper with a printed title, but essentially the same information as for an instru-

ment drawing should be recorded in some convenient place on the sheet. All notes and special directions should be checked for accuracy along with the drawing proper. In general, follow the order of checking given in paragraph 19.17.

19.26.   REPRODUCTION OF DRAWINGS. Working drawings go to the shop in the form of prints made from the original drawings. Several different printing processes are in use, all of which give the best results from tracings inked on tracing cloth or paper. However, quite satisfactory prints can be obtained from pencil drawings on translucent paper when the penciling is done skillfully, with uniform, opaque lines. In fact, most of the drawings of industry are not inked; only those of a permanent nature, such as maps, charts, etc., and tracings that must be printed a great many times, are inked.

Blueprints.   The simplest and most generally used copying process is the blueprinting process, in which the prints are made by exposing a piece of sensitized paper and a tracing in close surface contact with each other to sunlight or electric light in a printing frame or machine made for the purpose. On exposure to the light, a chemical action takes place, which, when fixed by washing in water, gives a strong blue color. The parts protected from the light by the black lines of the tracing wash out, leaving the white paper.

Vandyke Paper.   This is a thin sensitized paper that turns dark brown when exposed to light and properly "fixed." A reversed negative of a tracing can be made on it by exposing it to light with the inked side of the drawing next to the sensitized side of the paper; then this negative can be printed on blueprint paper, giving a positive print with blue lines on white.

BW Prints and Directo Prints. These have black lines on a white ground and are made directly from the original tracing, in a blueprinting machine (and developed by hand) or in a special machine made for the purpose. They are used extensively when positive prints are desired.

Ozalid Prints. This process is based on the chemical action of light-sensitive diazo compounds. It is a contact method of reproduction in which the exposure is made in a regular blueprinting machine or an ozalid "whiteprint" machine, and the exposed print is developed dry with ammonia vapors in a developing machine. Standard papers giving black, blue, and maroon lines on a white ground are available. Dry developing has the distinct advantage of giving prints without distortion, and it also makes possible the use of transparent papers, cloth, and foils, which effects savings in drawing time, as these transparent replicas can be changed by additions or erasures and prints made from them without altering the original tracing.

Photostat Prints. These are extensively used by large corporations. By this method, a print with white lines on a dark background is made directly from any drawing or tracing, to any desired reduction or enlargement, through the use of a large, specially designed camera. This print can be again photostated, giving a brown-black line on a white ground. This method is extremely useful to engineers for drawings to be included in reports and for matching drawings of different scales which may have to be combined into one.

Duplicating Tracings. Tracings with all the qualities of ordinary inked ones are made photographically from pencil drawings by using a sensitized tracing cloth.

Lithoprinting. When a number of copies of a drawing (50 or more) are needed, they may be reproduced by lithoprinting, a simplified form of photolithography, at comparatively small cost.

Copying Methods. Copying methods such as the mimeograph, ditto machine, and other forms of the hectograph or gelatin pad are often used for small drawings.

Photo-copying Methods. Negative copies on high-contrast film are reproduced on paper or cloth either to the same size as the original or to a reduced or increased size. Micromaster copies (Keuffel & Esser Co.) are well known. The reproductions are very good, and when the process is used for reproduction of an old drawing, wrinkles and other blemishes can be eliminated by using opaque on the film negative.

19.27. FILING AND STORING DRAWINGS. Drawings are filed in steel or wooden cabinets made for the purpose. Many engineering offices store their drawings in fireproof vaults and remove them only for making alterations or for printing. Photographic copies are sometimes made as a separate permanent record. Drawings are always filed flat or rolled. Prints, however, are folded for filing or mailing. The usual method is the "accordion" fold illustrated in Fig. 19.8. To aid in the filing of accordion-folded prints, a supplementary number block may be added, as shown.

PROBLEMS

GROUP 1.   DETAIL DRAWINGS

This group of problems gives practice in making drawings with sectional views, auxiliaries, and conventional representation.

Several methods of part production are included: casting, forging, forming of sheet metal, and plastic molding.

19.1.1. Make complete working drawing with necessary sectional views. Cast iron.

19.1.2. Working drawing of friction-shaft bearing. Cast iron.

19.1.3. Working drawing of mixing-valve body. Cast brass.

19.1.4. Working drawing of conveyor hanger. Determine what views and part views will best describe the piece. Cast steel.

19.1.5. Working drawing of strut base. Determine what views and part views will best describe the piece. Cast aluminum.

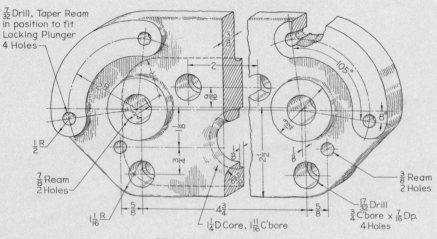

PROB. 19.1.1.   Gear-shifter bracket.

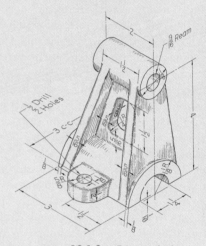

PROB. 19.1.2.   Friction-shaft bearing.

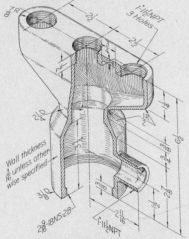

PROB. 19.1.3.   Mixing-valve body.

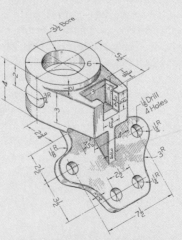

PROB. 19.1.4.   Conveyor hanger.

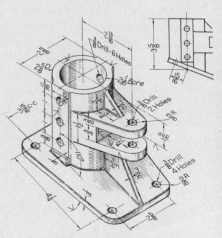

PROB. 19.1.5.   Strut base.

19.1.6. Draw given front view. Add part views and auxiliaries to describe the piece best. Cast aluminum.

19.1.7. Working drawing of valve cage. Cast bronze.

19.1.8. Determine what views and part views will most adequately describe the piece. Malleable iron.

19.1.9. Working drawing of water-pump cover. Aluminum alloy die casting.

19.1.10. Working drawing of slotted spider. Malleable iron.

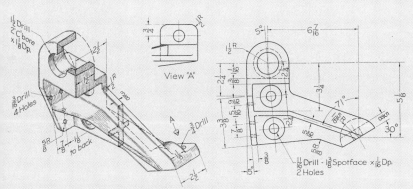

PROB. **19.1.6.** Hinge bracket.

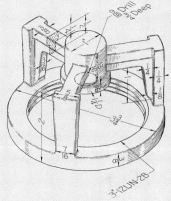

PROB. **19.1.7.** Valve cage.

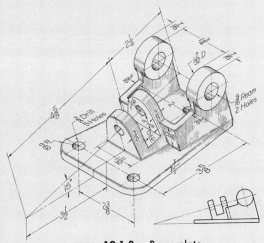

PROB. **19.1.8.** Brace plate.

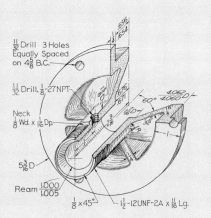

PROB. **19.1.9.** Water-pump cover.

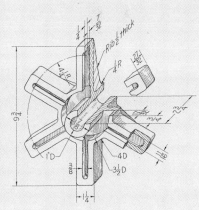

PROB. **19.1.10.** Slotted spider.

19.1.11. Make working drawing of relief-valve body. Cast brass.

19.1.12. Working drawing of breaker. Steel.

19.1.13. Working drawing of meter case. Molded bakelite.

19.1.14. (*a*) Make detail working drawings on same sheet, one for *rough* forging and one for *machining;* or (*b*) make one detail drawing for forging and machining. Alloy steel.

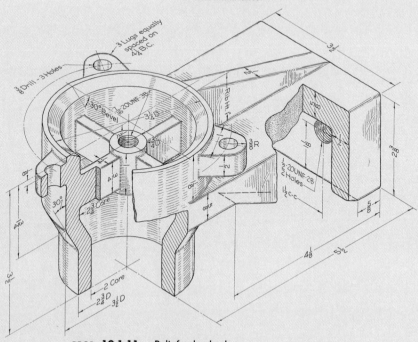

PROB. 19.1.11. Relief-valve body.

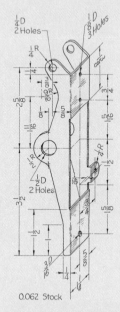

0.062 Stock

PROB. 19.1.12. Breaker.

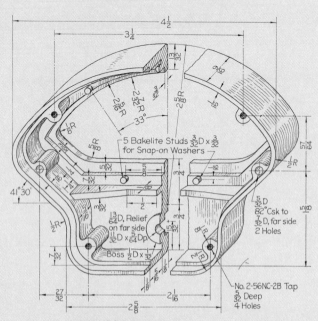

PROB. 19.1.13. Meter case.

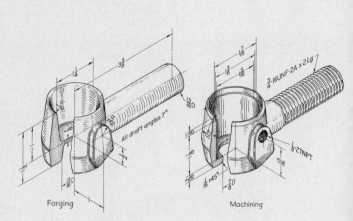

Forging

Machining

PROB. 19.1.14. Steering knuckle.

Problems

19.1.15. Working drawing of automotive connecting rod. Drop forging, alloy steel. Drawings same as Prob. 19.1.14.

19.1.16. Working drawing of puller body. Press forging, steel. Drawings same as Prob. 19.1.14.

19.1.17. Make working drawing of buffer stand. Steel drop forging. Drawings same as Prob. 19.1.14.

19.1.18. Working drawing of torque-tube support. Drop forging, aluminum alloy. Drawings same as Prob. 19.1.14.

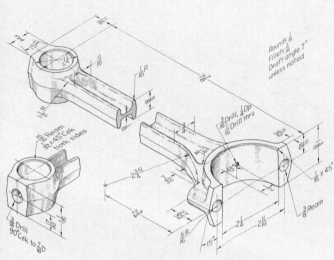

PROB. 19.1.15. Automotive connecting rod.

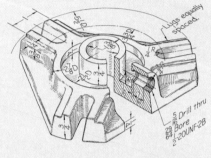

PROB. 19.1.16. Puller body.

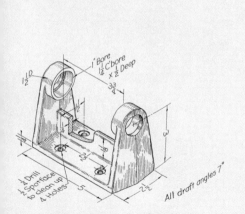

PROB. 19.1.17. Buffer stand.

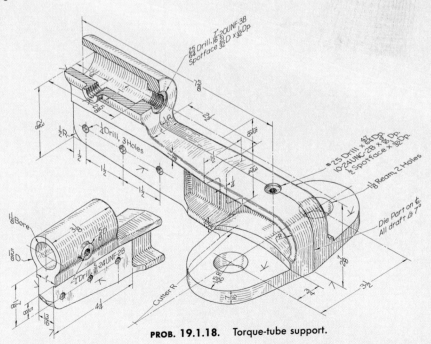

PROB. 19.1.18. Torque-tube support.

19.1.19. Working drawing of supply head. Cast iron.

19.1.20. Working drawing of bearing block, cast iron.

19.1.21. Working drawing of elevator control bracket. Aluminum alloy, welded.

19.1.22. Working drawing of flap link. High-strength aluminum alloy.

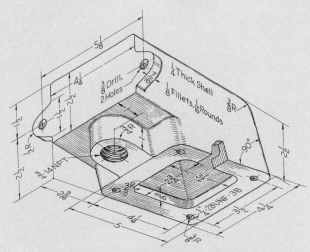

PROB. 19.1.19. Supply head.

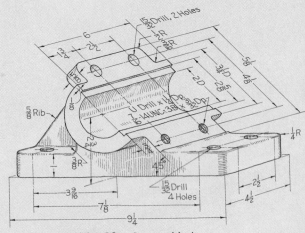

PROB. 19.1.20. Bearing block.

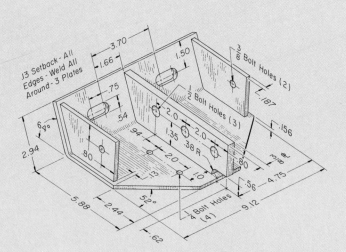

PROB. 19.1.21. Elevator control bracket.

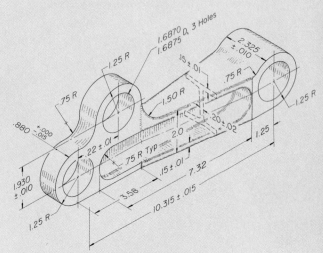

PROB. 19.1.22. Flap link.

19.1.23. Working drawing of wing fitting. High-strength aluminum alloy.

19.1.24. Working drawing of micro-switch bracket. Aluminum sheet, 0.15 thick.

19.1.25. Working drawing of tab link. High-strength aluminum alloy.

19.1.26. Working drawing of drag strut. High-strength aluminum alloy.

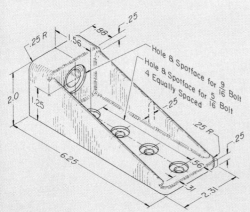

PROB. 19.1.23. Wing fitting.

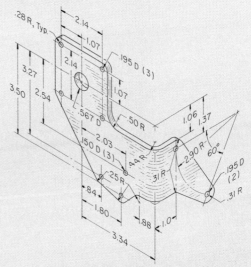

PROB. 19.1.24. Micro-switch bracket.

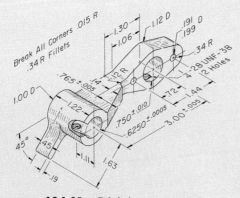

PROB. 19.1.25. Tab link.

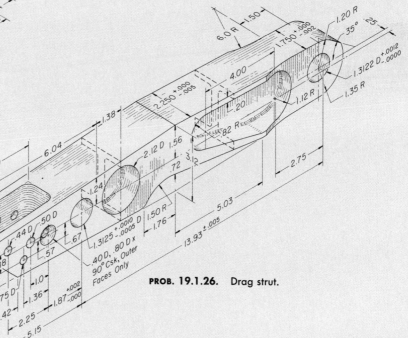

PROB. 19.1.26. Drag strut.

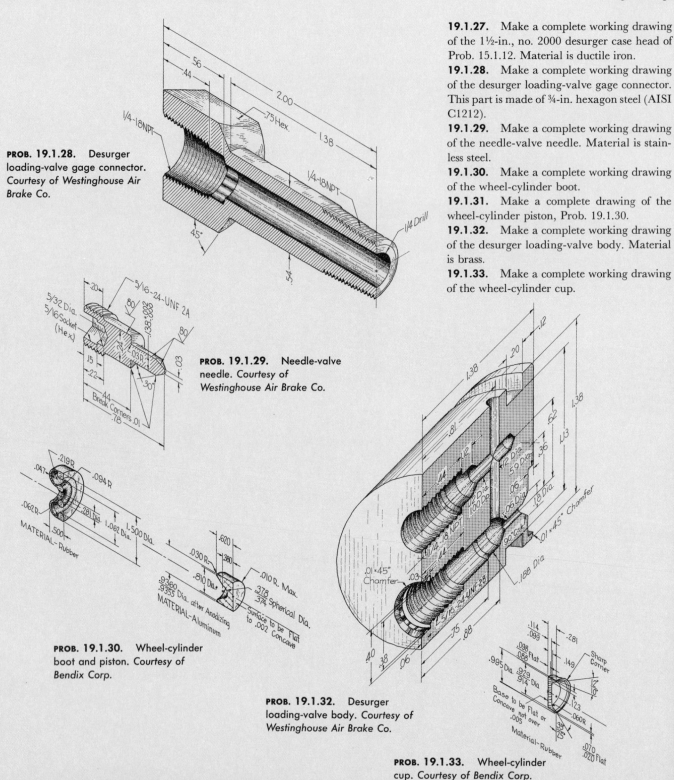

PROB. 19.1.28. Desurger loading-valve gage connector. *Courtesy of Westinghouse Air Brake Co.*

PROB. 19.1.29. Needle-valve needle. *Courtesy of Westinghouse Air Brake Co.*

PROB. 19.1.30. Wheel-cylinder boot and piston. *Courtesy of Bendix Corp.*

PROB. 19.1.32. Desurger loading-valve body. *Courtesy of Westinghouse Air Brake Co.*

PROB. 19.1.33. Wheel-cylinder cup. *Courtesy of Bendix Corp.*

19.1.27. Make a complete working drawing of the 1½-in., no. 2000 desurger case head of Prob. 15.1.12. Material is ductile iron.

19.1.28. Make a complete working drawing of the desurger loading-valve gage connector. This part is made of ¾-in. hexagon steel (AISI C1212).

19.1.29. Make a complete working drawing of the needle-valve needle. Material is stainless steel.

19.1.30. Make a complete working drawing of the wheel-cylinder boot.

19.1.31. Make a complete drawing of the wheel-cylinder piston, Prob. 19.1.30.

19.1.32. Make a complete working drawing of the desurger loading-valve body. Material is brass.

19.1.33. Make a complete working drawing of the wheel-cylinder cup.

GROUP 2.   AN ASSEMBLY DRAWING FROM THE DETAILS

19.2.1.   Assembly drawing of sealed shaft unit. Bracket and gland are cast iron. Shaft, collar, and studs are steel. Bushing is bronze. Drill bushing in assembly with bracket.

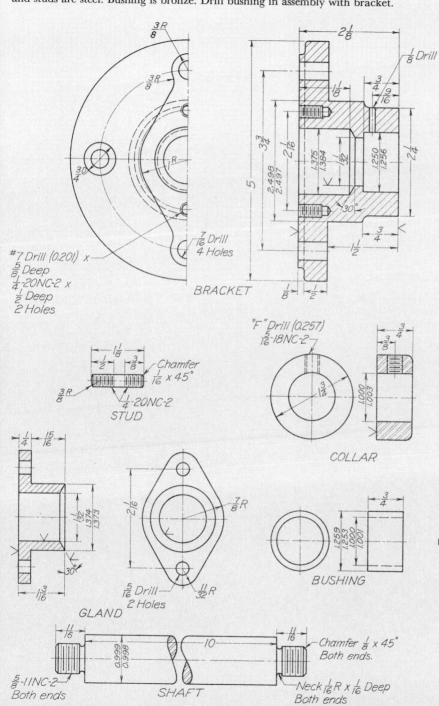

PROB. 19.2.1.   Sealed shaft unit.

19.2.2. Make an assembly drawing of the crane hook from details given. Standard parts 7 to 10 are not detailed; see Appendix or handbook for sizes.

19.2.3. Make an assembly drawing, front view in section, of caster.

19.2.3*A.* Redesign caster for ball-bearing installation.

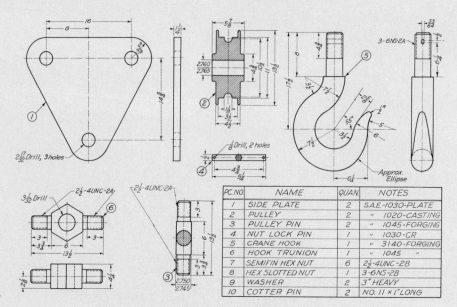

PC. NO.	NAME	QUAN.	NOTES
1	SIDE PLATE	2	S.A.E.-1030-PLATE
2	PULLEY	2	" 1020-CASTING
3	PULLEY PIN	2	" 1045-FORGING
4	NUT LOCK PIN	1	" 1030-CR
5	CRANE HOOK	1	" 3140-FORGING
6	HOOK TRUNION	1	" 1045
7	SEMIFIN HEX NUT	6	2½-4UNC-2B
8	HEX SLOTTED NUT	1	3-6NS-2B
9	WASHER	2	3" HEAVY
10	COTTER PIN	2	NO. 11 × 1" LONG

PROB. 19.2.2. Crane hook.

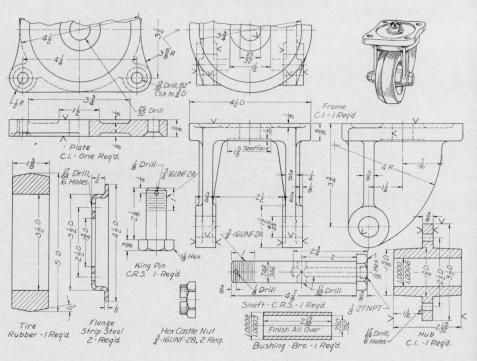

PROB. 19.2.3. Caster.

19.2.4. Make an assembly drawing of the Brown and Sharpe rotary geared pump, with top view, longitudinal section, and side view. Show direction of rotation of shafts and flow of liquid with arrows. Give dimensions for base holes to be used in setting; also give distance from base to center of driving shaft and size of shaft and key.

For the parts that are not detailed, see the parts list.

PARTS LIST									
BROWN AND SHARPE No. 1 ROTARY GEARED PUMP									
PC. NO.	DRAW SIZE	NAME	QUAN.	MAT.	STOCK		USED ON		REMARKS
					DIA.	LGTH.	NAME	PC. NO.	
101		Base	1	C.I.					
102		Body	1	C.I.					
103		Cover	1	C.I.					
104		Pulley	1	C.I.					
105		Gland	1	C.I.					
106		Gland Bushing	1	Bro.					
107		Gear Bushing	4	Bro.					
108		Driving Gear	1	S.A.E. #1045	1 9/16	5 7/8			
109		Driven Gear	1	S.A.E. #1045	1 9/16	2 9/16			
110		Gasket	2	Sheet Copper			Body	102	#26 B&S Gage (0.0159)
111		#10-32 x 1 5/8 Slotted Hex. Hd. Mach. Scr. & Nut	4				Cover	103	
112		#10-32 x 1 5/8 Slotted Hex. Hd. Cap Scr.	2				Cover	103	
113		#10-32 x 7/8 Slotted Hex. Hd. Cap Scr.	2				Gland	105	
114		Woodruff Key #405	1				Driving Gear	108	
115		3/8 x 3/8 Headless Set Scr., 3/8-16NC-2	1				Pulley	104	
116		3/16 x 1 7/16 Dowel Pin	2	C.R.S.			Cover	103	
		Packing	To Suit						Garlock Rotopac #239

PROB. 19.2.4. Rotary geared pump and parts list.

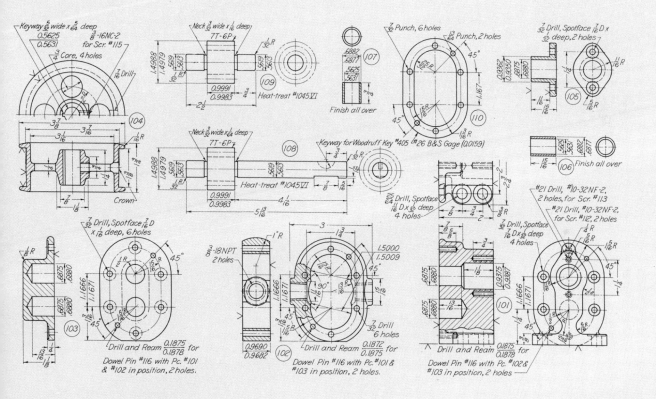

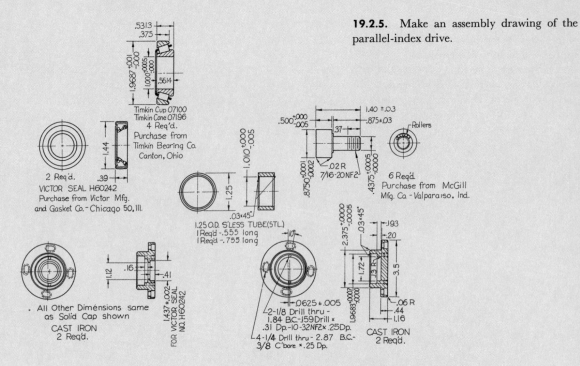

19.2.5. Make an assembly drawing of the parallel-index drive.

PROB. 19.2.5. Parallel-index drive. *Courtesy of Commercial Cam and Machine Co.*

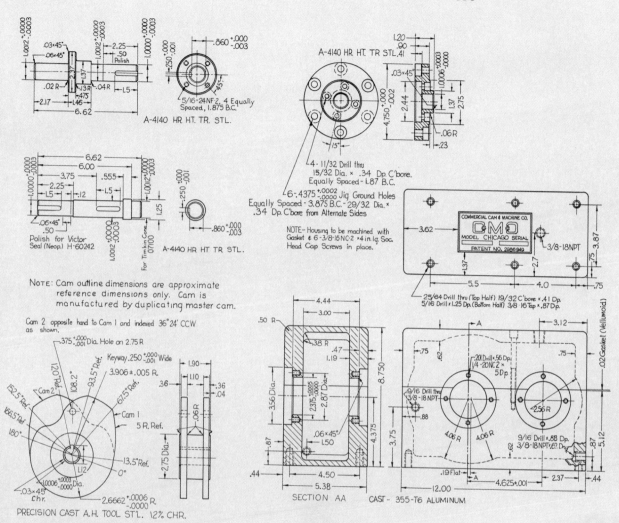

PROB. 19.2.5. Parallel-index drive. Courtesy of Commercial Cam and Machine Co.

Problems

GROUP 3. DETAIL DRAWINGS FROM THE ASSEMBLY

19.3.1. Make detail drawings of the jig table.
Parts, cast iron.

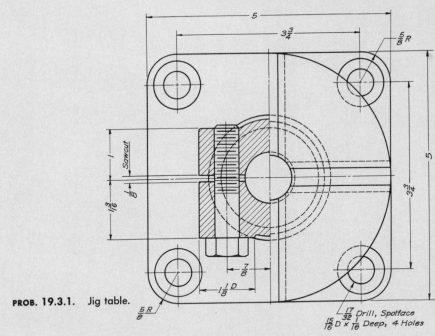

PROB. 19.3.1. Jig table.

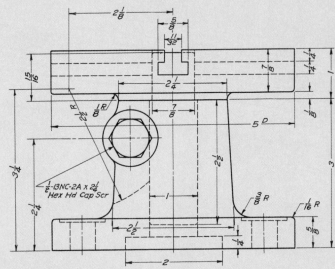

19.3.2. Make detail drawings of the door catch.

19.3.3. Make detail drawings of belt drive. The pulley and bracket are cast iron; the gear and shaft, steel. The bushing is bronze.

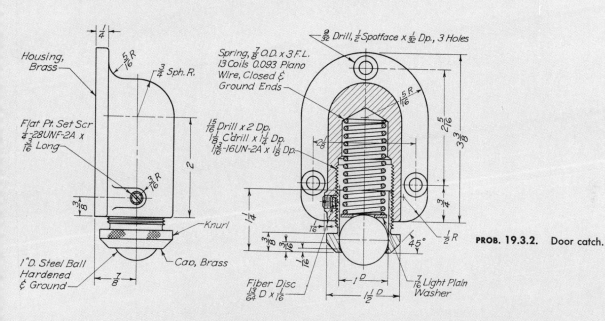

PROB. 19.3.2. Door catch.

PROB. 19.3.3. Belt drive.

19.3.4. Make detail drawings of swing table.

19.3.5. Make detail drawings of sealed ball joint.

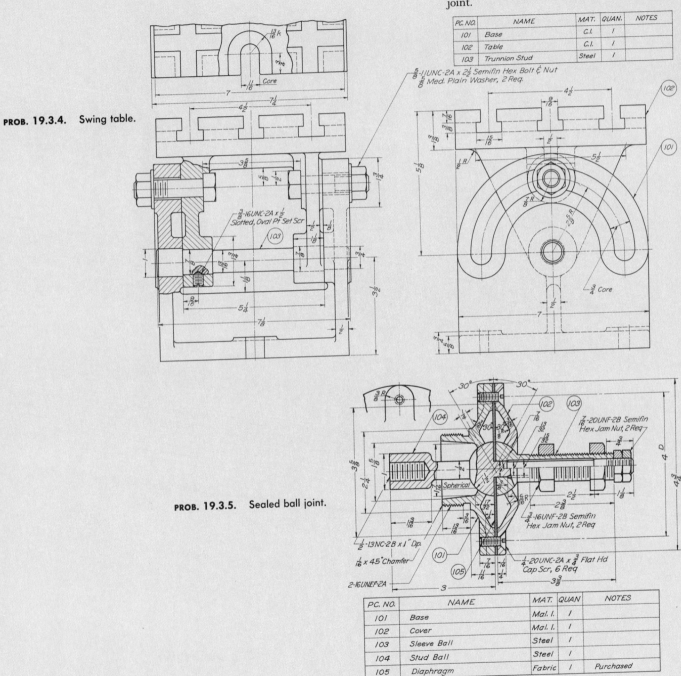

PROB. 19.3.4. Swing table.

PC. NO.	NAME	MAT.	QUAN.	NOTES
101	Base	C.I.	1	
102	Table	C.I.	1	
103	Trunnion Stud	Steel	1	

PROB. 19.3.5. Sealed ball joint.

PC. NO.	NAME	MAT.	QUAN	NOTES
101	Base	Mal. I.	1	
102	Cover	Mal. I.	1	
103	Sleeve Ball	Steel	1	
104	Stud Ball	Steel	1	
105	Diaphragm	Fabric	1	Purchased

19.3.6. Make detail drawings of belt tightener. The bracket, pulley, and collar are cast iron. The bushing is bronze; the shaft, steel.

19.3.7. Make detail drawings of rotary pressure joint.

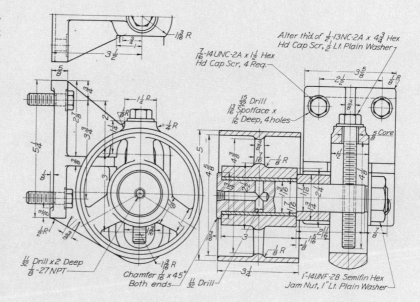

PROB. 19.3.6. Belt tightener.

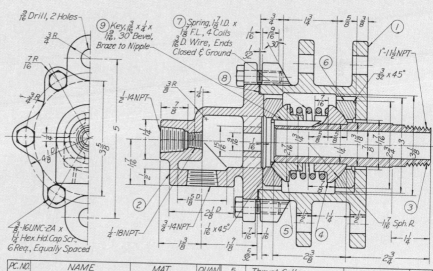

PROB. 19.3.7. Rotary pressure joint.

PC. NO.	NAME	MAT.	QUAN.				
1	Body	C.I.	1	5	Thrust Collar	C.I.	1
2	Head	C.I.	1	6	Seal Ring	No. 61 Graphitar	2
3	Nipple Tube	Steel	1	7	Spring	Stainless Steel	1
4	Nipple Body	C.I.	1	8	Gasket	Durabla	1
				9	Key	Steel	1

19.3.8. Make detail drawings of ball-bearing idler pulley.

19.3.9. Make detail drawings of butterfly valve.

19.3.10. Make detail drawings for V-belt drive.

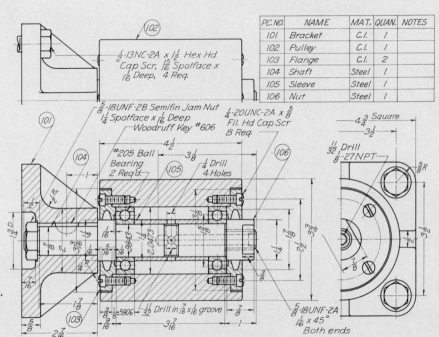

PC. NO.	NAME	MAT.	QUAN.	NOTES
101	Bracket	C.I.	1	
102	Pulley	C.I.	1	
103	Flange	C.I.	2	
104	Shaft	Steel	1	
105	Sleeve	Steel	1	
106	Nut	Steel	1	

PROB. 19.3.8. Ball-bearing idler pulley.

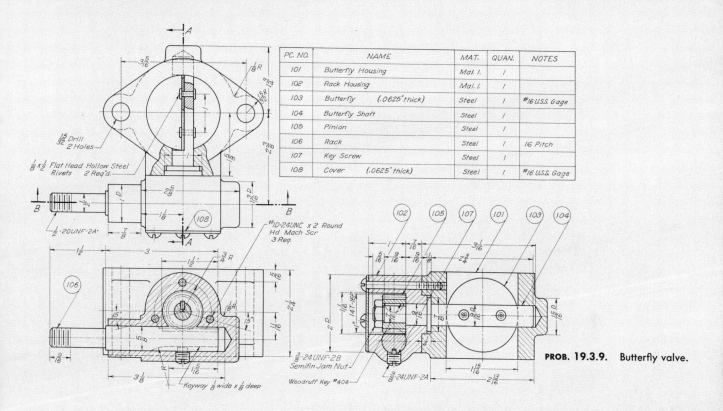

PC. NO.	NAME		MAT.	QUAN.	NOTES
101	Butterfly Housing		Mal. I.	1	
102	Rack Housing		Mal. I.	1	
103	Butterfly	(.0625" thick)	Steel	1	#16 U.S.S. Gage
104	Butterfly Shaft		Steel	1	
105	Pinion		Steel	1	
106	Rack		Steel	1	16 Pitch
107	Key Screw		Steel	1	
108	Cover	(.0625" thick)	Steel	1	#16 U.S.S. Gage

PROB. 19.3.9. Butterfly valve.

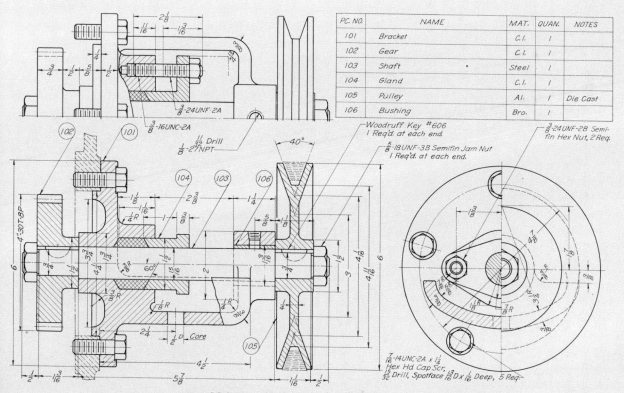

PC. NO.	NAME	MAT.	QUAN.	NOTES
101	Bracket	C.I.	1	
102	Gear	C.I.	1	
103	Shaft	Steel	1	
104	Gland	C.I.	1	
105	Pulley	Al.	1	Die Cast
106	Bushing	Bro.	1	

PROB. 19.3.10. V-belt drive.

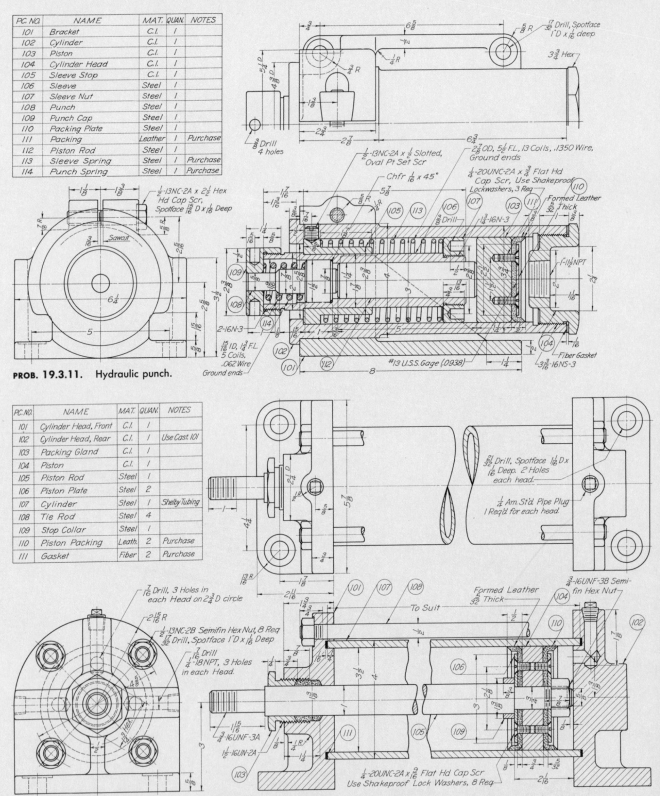

PC. NO.	NAME	MAT.	QUAN.	NOTES
101	Bracket	C.I.	1	
102	Cylinder	C.I.	1	
103	Piston	C.I.	1	
104	Cylinder Head	C.I.	1	
105	Sleeve Stop	C.I.	1	
106	Sleeve	Steel	1	
107	Sleeve Nut	Steel	1	
108	Punch	Steel	1	
109	Punch Cap	Steel	1	
110	Packing Plate	Steel	1	
111	Packing	Leather	1	Purchase
112	Piston Rod	Steel	1	
113	Sleeve Spring	Steel	1	Purchase
114	Punch Spring	Steel	1	Purchase

PROB. 19.3.11. Hydraulic punch.

PC. NO.	NAME	MAT.	QUAN.	NOTES
101	Cylinder Head, Front	C.I.	1	
102	Cylinder Head, Rear	C.I.	1	Use Cast. 101
103	Packing Gland	C.I.	1	
104	Piston	C.I.	1	
105	Piston Rod	Steel	1	
106	Piston Plate	Steel	2	
107	Cylinder	Steel	1	Shelby Tubing
108	Tie Rod	Steel	4	
109	Stop Collar	Steel	1	
110	Piston Packing	Leath.	2	Purchase
111	Gasket	Fiber	2	Purchase

PROB. 19.3.12. Double-acting air cylinder.

19.3.11. Make detail drawings of hydraulic punch. In action, the punch assembly proper advances until the cap, piece 109, comes against the work. The assembly (piece 106 and attached parts) is then stationary, and the tension of the punch spring (piece 114) holds the work as the punch advances through the work and returns.

19.3.12. Make detail drawings of double-acting air cylinder. Length of stroke to be assigned. Fix length of cylinder to allow for clearance of 1 in. at ends of stroke. Note that pieces 101 and 102 are identical except for the extra machining of the central hole in piece 101 for the shaft, packing, and gland. Make separate drawings for this piece, one for the pattern shop and two for the machine shop.

19.3.13. Make detail drawings of rail-transport hanger. Rail is 10-lb ASCE.

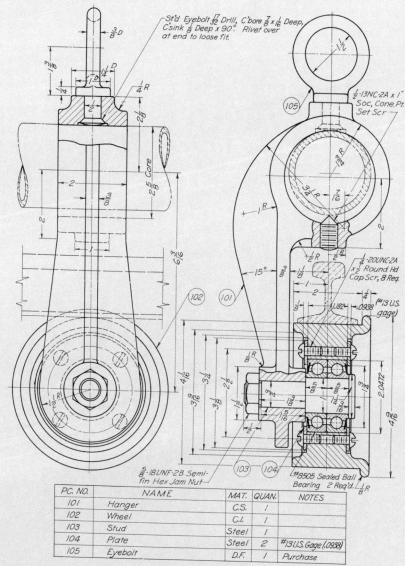

PROB. 19.3.13. Rail-transport hanger.

PC. NO.	NAME	MAT.	QUAN.	NOTES
101	Hanger	C.S.	1	
102	Wheel	C.I.	1	
103	Stud	Steel	1	
104	Plate	Steel	2	#13 U.S. Gage (.0938)
105	Eyebolt	D.F.	1	Purchase

19.3.14. Make detail drawings of the laboratory pump. Materials are shown on the assembly drawing.

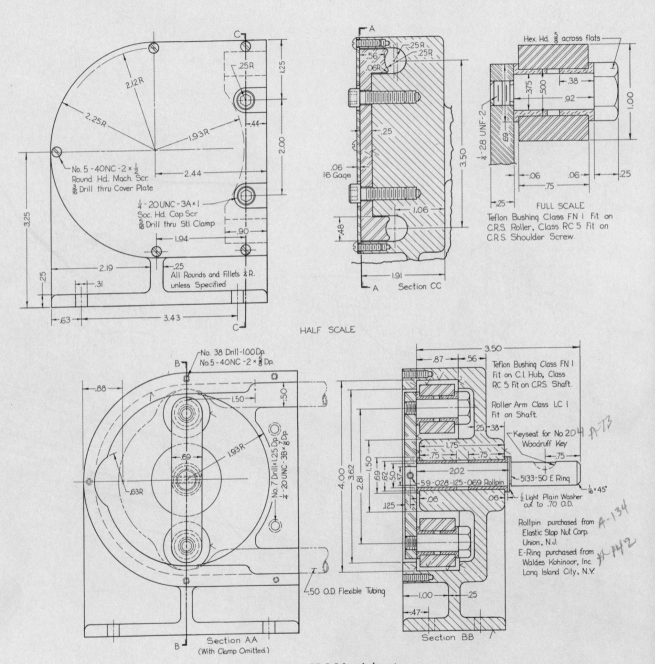

PROB. 19.3.14. Laboratory pump.

GROUP 4. A SET OF DRAWINGS FROM AN EXPLODED PICTORIAL

The problems that are given in this group have been arranged as complete exercises in making a set of working drawings. Remember that the dimensions given on the pictorial views are to be used only to obtain distances or information needed. In some cases the data needed for a particular part may have to be obtained from the mating part.

The detail drawings should be made with each part on a separate sheet. Drawings of cast or forged parts may be made in the single-drawing or the multiple-drawing system described in Chap. 15.

The assembly drawing should include any necessary dimensions, such as number, size, and spacing of mounting holes, that might be required by a purchaser or needed for checking with the machine on which a subassembly is used.

For the style and items to be included in the parts list, see Prob. 19.2.4.

19.4.1. Make a complete set of working drawings for the antivibration mount.

19.4.2. Make a complete set of drawings for pivot hanger, including detail drawings, assembly drawing, and parts list. All parts are steel. This assembly consists of a yoke, base, collar, and standard parts.

PROB. 19.4.1. Antivibration mount.

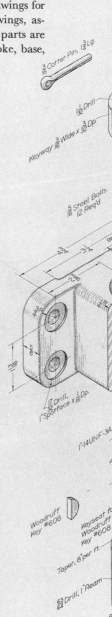

PROB. 19.4.2. Pivot hanger.

19.4.3. Make a complete set of drawings for pump valve. The valve seat, stem, and spring are brass; the disk is hard-rubber composition. In operation, pressure of a fluid upward against the disk raises it and allows flow. Pressure downward forces the disk tighter against the seat and prevents flow.

19.4.4. Make a complete set of working drawings for the cartridge-case trimmer. Note that some of the dimensions will have to be obtained from the mating part. A tabular drawing may be made of the case holder, covering holders for various cartridge cases. The dimensions to be tabulated are (a) holder length, (b) diameter, and (c) taper of hole.

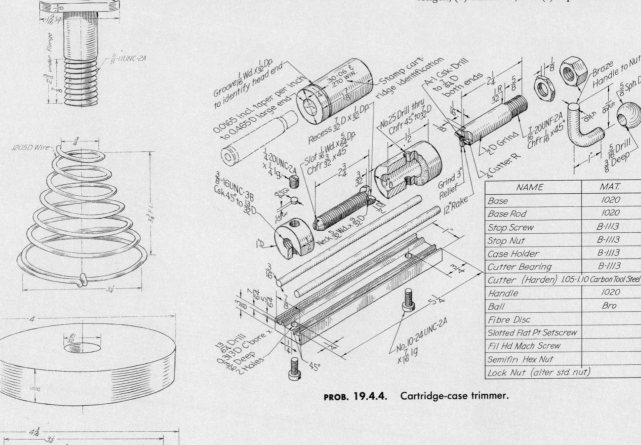

NAME	MAT.
Base	1020
Base Rod	1020
Stop Screw	B-1113
Stop Nut	B-1113
Case Holder	B-1113
Cutter Bearing	B-1113
Cutter (Harden)	1.05-1.10 Carbon Tool Steel
Handle	1020
Ball	Bro
Fibre Disc	
Slotted Flat Pt Setscrew	
Fil Hd Mach Screw	
Semifin Hex Nut	
Lock Nut (alter std. nut)	

PROB. 19.4.4. Cartridge-case trimmer.

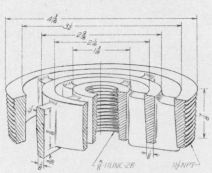

PROB. 19.4.3. Pump valve.

19.4.5. Make a complete set of working drawings of the hydraulic check valve. Spring is stainless steel; gasket is soft aluminum; all other parts are steel.

19.4.6. Make a complete set of working drawings of the boring-bar holder. All parts are steel. Note that the *body* is made in one piece, then split with a ⅛-in.-wide cut (exaggerated in the picture). The holder can be seen in use in Fig. 17.13.

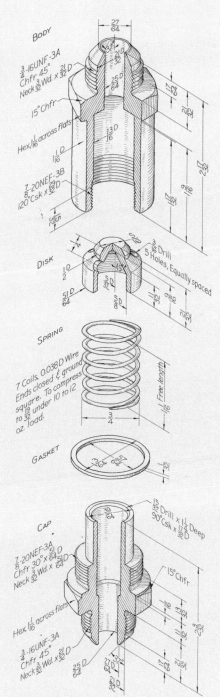

PROB. 19.4.5. Hydraulic check valve.

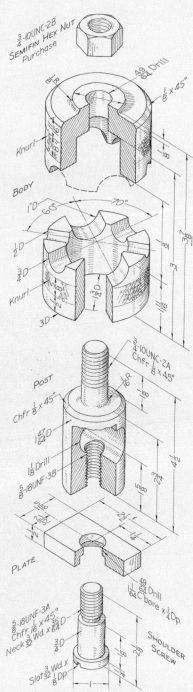

PROB. 19.4.6. Boring-bar holder.

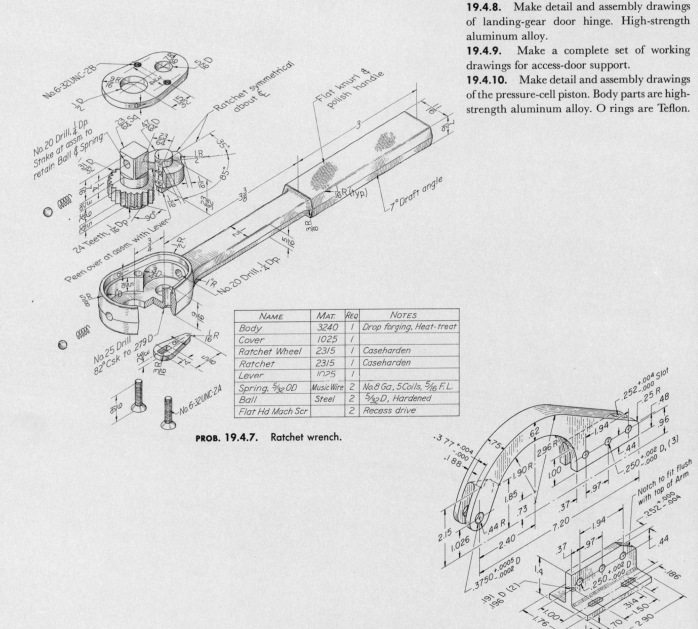

19.4.6*A.* Design three boring bars (see Fig. 17.13) to fit the boring-bar holder, and make a tabular drawing.

19.4.7. Make a complete set of working drawings of the ratchet wrench.

19.4.8. Make detail and assembly drawings of landing-gear door hinge. High-strength aluminum alloy.

19.4.9. Make a complete set of working drawings for access-door support.

19.4.10. Make detail and assembly drawings of the pressure-cell piston. Body parts are high-strength aluminum alloy. O rings are Teflon.

Name	Mat.	Req	Notes
Body	3240	1	Drop forging, Heat-treat
Cover	1025	1	
Ratchet Wheel	2315	1	Caseharden
Ratchet	2315	1	Caseharden
Lever	1025	1	
Spring, 5/32 OD	Music Wire	2	No.8 Ga, 5 Coils, 5/16 F.L.
Ball	Steel	2	5/32 D, Hardened
Flat Hd Mach Scr		2	Recess drive

PROB. 19.4.7.   Ratchet wrench.

PROB. 19.4.8.   Landing-gear door hinge.

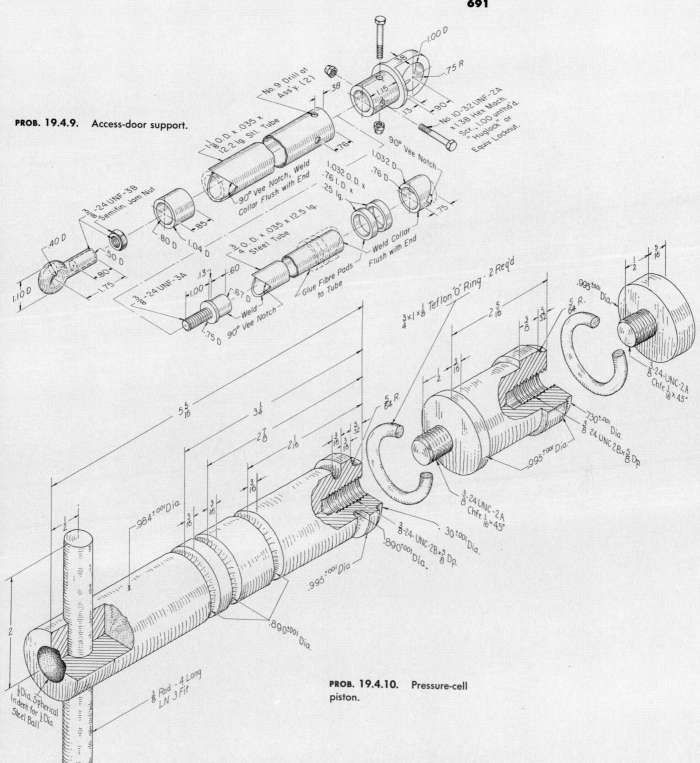

PROB. 19.4.9. Access-door support.

No.9 Drill at Ass'y. (2)

1.00 D

.38

.75 R

.90

.13

1.15

.38

No. 10-32 UNF-2A x 1.38 Hex Mach. Scr., 1.00 unthd'd. "Huglock" or Equiv. Locknut.

90° Vee Notch

1 O.D. x .035 x 8 12.2 lg. Stl. Tube

.76

90° Vee Notch, Weld Collar Flush with End

1.032 D

.76 D

.75

3/8-24 UNF-3B Semifin. Jam Nut

.85

.80 D

1.04 D

1.032 O.D. x .76 I.D. x .25 lg.

3/4 O.D. x .035 x 12.5 lg. Steel Tube

Weld Collar Flush with End

.40 D

.50 D

.80

1.75

1.10 D

3/8-24 UNF-3A

.13

.60

1.00

.67 D

Weld

90° Vee Notch

.75 D

Glue Fibre Pads to Tube

3/4 x 1 x 1/8 Teflon "O" Ring · 2 Req'd

2 5/16

3/8

5/32

5/64 R.

1/2

5/16

.995 ±.001 Dia.

1/2

3/16

5/64 R.

3/8-24-UNC-2A Chfr. 1/16 x 45°

.730 ±.001 Dia.

3/8-24 UNC-2B x 5/8 Dp.

.995 ±.001 Dia.

5 5/16

3 1/4

2 7/8

2 1/16

3/16

3/16

5/32

.984 ±.001 Dia.

3/16

3/16

3/8-24-UNC-2A Chfr. 1/16 x 45°

.30 ±.001 Dia.

3/8-24-UNC-2B x 5/8 Dp.

.890 ±.001 Dia.

.995 ±.001 Dia.

.890 ±.001 Dia.

1/2 Dia. Spherical Indent for 1/2 Dia. Steel Ball

2

3/8 Rod - 4 Long LN 3 Fit

PROB. 19.4.10. Pressure-cell piston.

19.4.11. Make a complete set of working drawings of the pivot nut and adjusting screw.

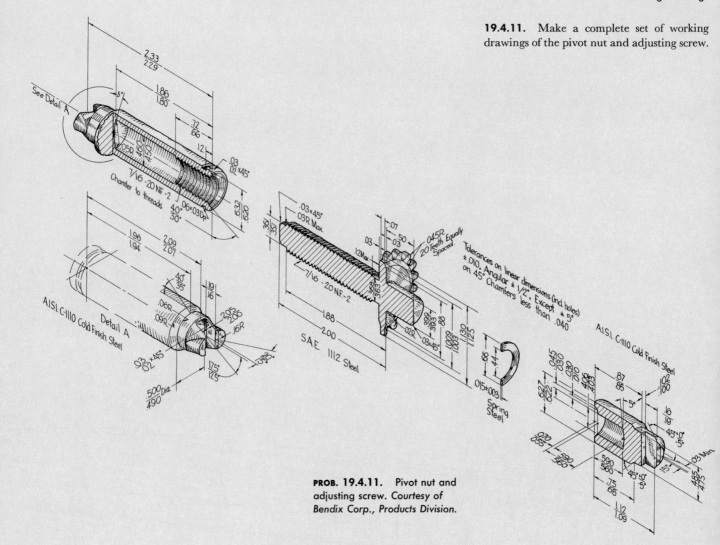

PROB. 19.4.11. Pivot nut and adjusting screw. *Courtesy of Bendix Corp., Products Division.*

GROUP 5. A SET OF DRAWINGS FROM A PICTORIAL ASSEMBLY

19.5.1. Make a complete set of working drawings of the high-tension coil mount.
19.5.2. Make a complete set of working drawings of the pipe clamp. The flange is cast steel.
19.5.3. Make a complete set of working

drawings of the stay-rod pivot. Parts are malleable iron.
19.5.4. Make a complete set of working drawings of the tool post. All parts are steel.
19.5.5. Make a unit-assembly working drawing of the wing-nose rib.

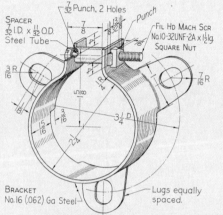

PROB. 19.5.1. High-tension coil mount.

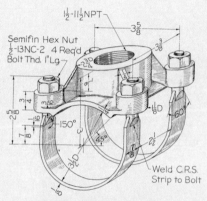

PROB. 19.5.2. Pipe clamp.

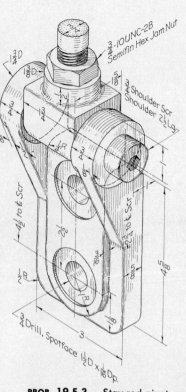

PROB. 19.5.3. Stay-rod pivot.

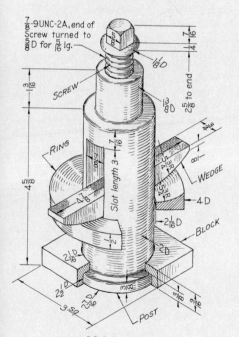

PROB. 19.5.4. Tool post.

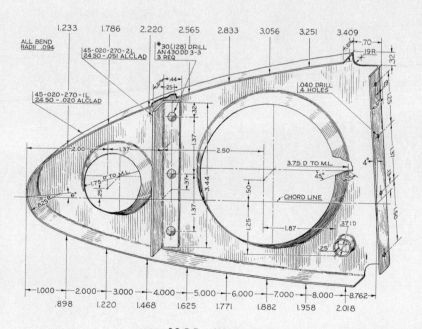

PROB. 19.5.5. Wing-nose rib.

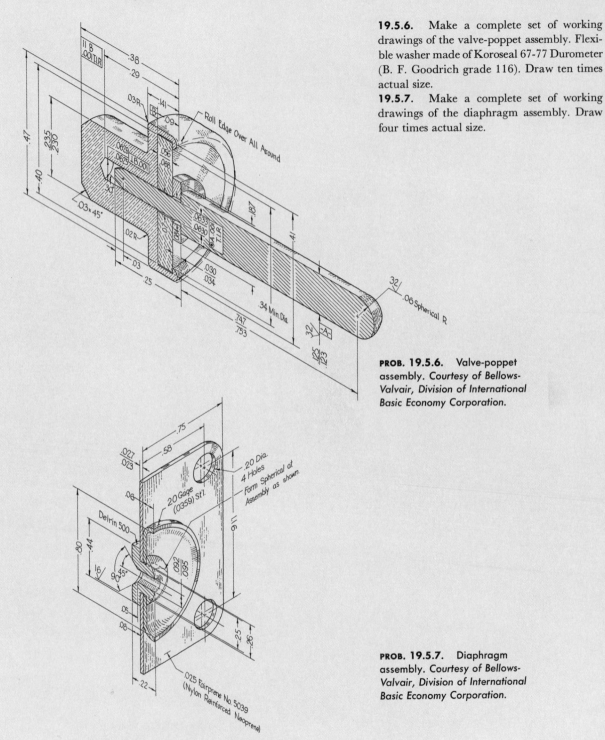

19.5.6. Make a complete set of working drawings of the valve-poppet assembly. Flexible washer made of Koroseal 67-77 Durometer (B. F. Goodrich grade 116). Draw ten times actual size.

19.5.7. Make a complete set of working drawings of the diaphragm assembly. Draw four times actual size.

PROB. 19.5.6. Valve-poppet assembly. *Courtesy of Bellows-Valvair, Division of International Basic Economy Corporation.*

PROB. 19.5.7. Diaphragm assembly. *Courtesy of Bellows-Valvair, Division of International Basic Economy Corporation.*

GROUP 6. WORKING DRAWINGS FROM PHOTO-DRAWINGS

Photo-drawings are coming into use commercially, especially in the processing industries. These problems give practice in making detail and assembly drawings, and illustrate the possibilities of drawings produced from photographs of models or test parts.

19.6.1. Detail drawing of conveyor link. SAE 1040 steel.

19.6.2. Detail drawing of hydro-cylinder support. Aluminum sheet.

19.6.3. Detail drawing of lift-strut pivot. Forged aluminum.

19.6.4. Detail drawing of length adjuster-tube. SAE 1220 steel.

19.6.5. Detail and unit assembly of pivot shaft. Shaft is bronze; nuts are steel.

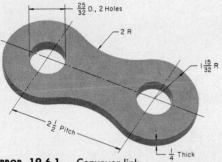

PROB. 19.6.1. Conveyor link.

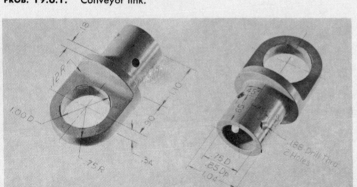

PROB. 19.6.3. Lift-strut pivot.

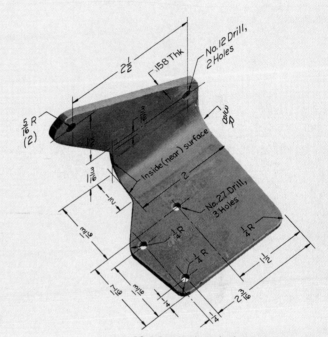

PROB. 19.6.2. Hydro-cylinder support.

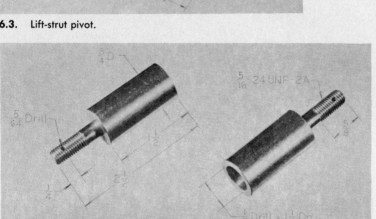

PROB. 19.6.4. Length adjuster-tube.

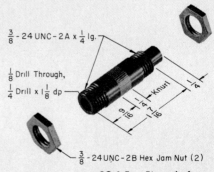

PROB. 19.6.5. Pivot shaft.

19.6.6. Detail drawing of third terminal (temperature control). Material is red brass (85% CU).

19.6.7. Set of working drawings of conveyor link unit. All parts are steel.

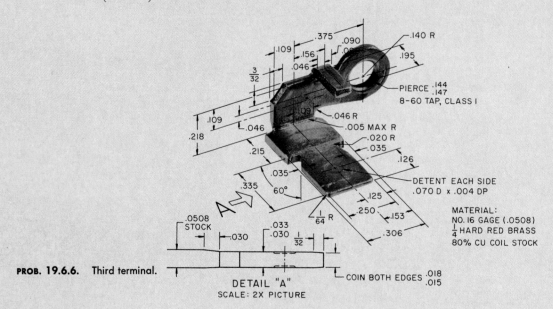

PROB. 19.6.6. Third terminal.

DETAIL "A"
SCALE: 2X PICTURE

PROB. 19.6.7. Conveyor link unit.

GROUP 7. A SET OF DRAWINGS FROM THE DESIGN DRAWING

19.7.1. Marking machine. From design drawing, shown half size, make complete set of drawings. Base, piece 1, is malleable-iron casting. Frame, piece 2, is cast iron. Ram, piece 3, is 1020 HR; bushing, piece 4, is 1020 cold-drawn tubing; heat-treatment for both is carburize at 1650 to 1700°F, quench direct, temper at 250 to 325°F. Spring, piece 5, is piano wire, No. 20 (0.045) gage, six coils, free length 2 in., heat-treatment is "as received." Marking dies and holders are made up to suit objects to be stamped.

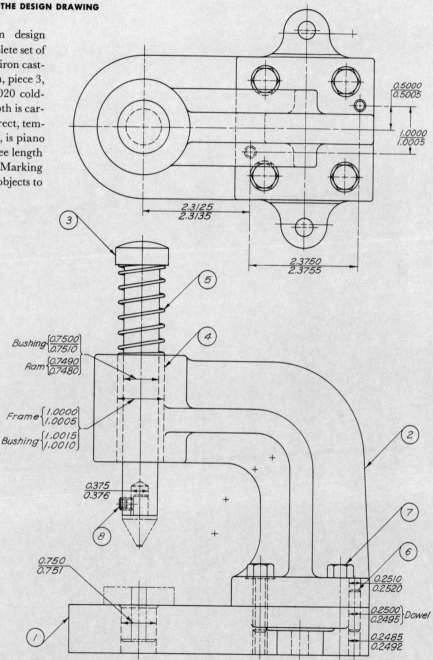

PROB. 19.7.1. Marking machine (one-half size).

19.7.2. Arbor press. From design drawing, shown one-quarter size, make complete set of drawings. All necessary information is given on the design drawing.

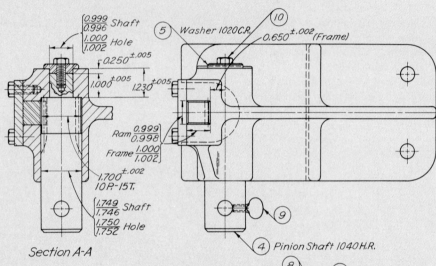

Section A-A

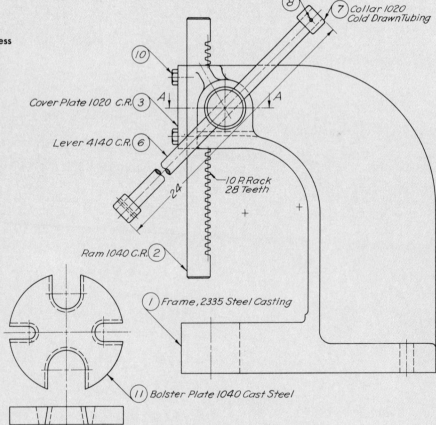

PROB. 19.7.2. One-ton arbor press (one-quarter size).

19.7.3. Number 2 flanged vise. From design drawing, make complete set of drawings, including details, parts list, and assembly. Design drawing is shown one-third size. All necessary information will be found on the design drawing.

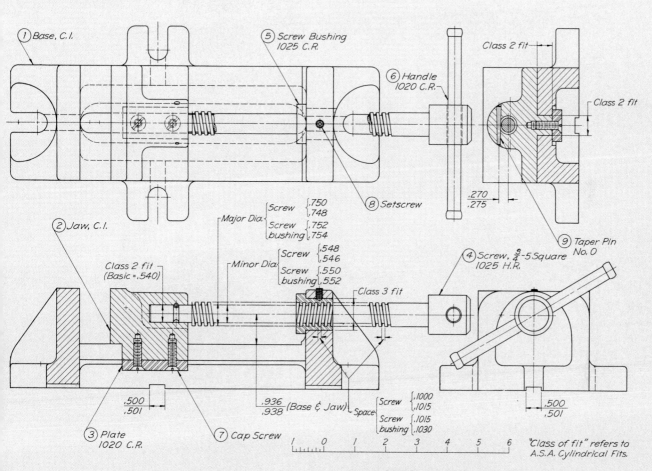

PROB. 19.7.3. No. 2 flanged vise (one-third size).

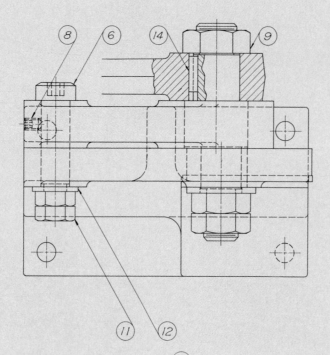

PC. NO.	NAME	MAT.	REQ	NOTES
1	Base	2335	1	Steel Casting
2	Jaw	2335	1	Steel Casting
3	Eccentric	2340 HR	1	
4	Blade	1095 HR	2	
5	Handle	1040	1	Drop Forging
6	Shoulder Screw		1	.
7	Flat Head Cap Screw		4	
8	Socket Set Screw		1	Flat Point
9	Semifin Hex Jam Nut		1	
10	Semifin Hex Jam Nut		2	
11	Semifin Hex Jam Nut		2	
12	Cut Washer	1112 CR	1	
13	Cut Washer	1112 CR	1	
14	Key	Key Stock	1	

PROB. 19.7.4.   Bench shears, 2¾-in. (one-half size).

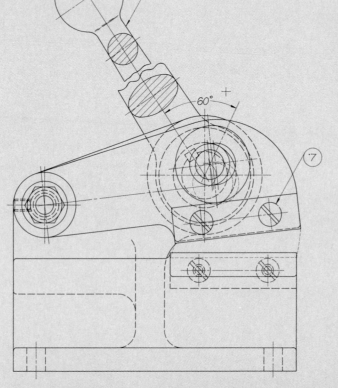

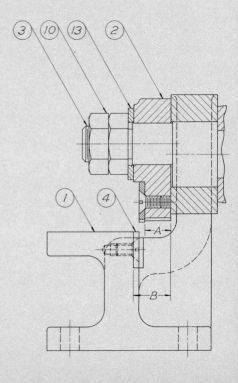

19.7.4. Bench shears. Design drawing is half size. Make a complete set of drawings. For dimensions where close fits are involved, either the decimal limits or the tolerance to be applied to the scaled basic size are given on the design drawing. Heat-treatments should be specified as follows: for base and jaw, "normalize at 1550°F"; for eccentric, "as received"; for blade, "to Rockwell C57-60"; for handle, none. Finish for blades, "grind." Washers are special but may be specified on the parts list by giving inside diameter, outside diameter, and thickness. The key may be specified on the parts list by giving width, thickness, and length.

Following are some specifications for limits and tolerances:

Diameter of shoulder screw and hole in both base and jaw:

Screws (as manufactured): $\dfrac{0.623}{0.621}$

Hole: $\dfrac{0.624}{0.626}$

Diameter of eccentric and hole in handle:

Eccentric: $\dfrac{0.999}{0.997}$

Handle: $\dfrac{0.999}{1.001}$

Diameter of eccentric and hole in base:

Eccentric: $\dfrac{1.3745}{1.3740}$

Base: $\dfrac{1.3750}{1.3755}$

Diameter of eccentric and width of slot in jaw:

Eccentric: $\dfrac{0.874}{0.872}$

Jaw: $\dfrac{0.875}{0.877}$

Width of keyway in both handle and eccentric:

Key (as purchased): $\dfrac{0.250}{0.249}$

Key seat and keyway: $\dfrac{0.250}{0.251}$

Depth of keyway and key seat in both handle and eccentric:

$\frac{3}{32}'' + \frac{1}{64} - 0$

Control of clearance between blades:

Thickness of blade: $\dfrac{0.1250}{0.1245}$

Dimension A: $\dfrac{0.562}{0.561}$

Dimension B: $\dfrac{0.812}{0.813}$

Tolerance on shoulder screw and eccentric hole locations: For base and jaw (two dimensions on each part)

± 0.002

Limits for eccentric offset:

Center to center: $\dfrac{0.248}{0.252}$

Length of handle:

Center of hub to center of ball: 12 in.

19.7.5.   The overriding clutch is shown half size. From this design drawing make a complete set of working drawings. The frame is made of cast iron and the shaft is cold-rolled steel. Other parts are as indicated.

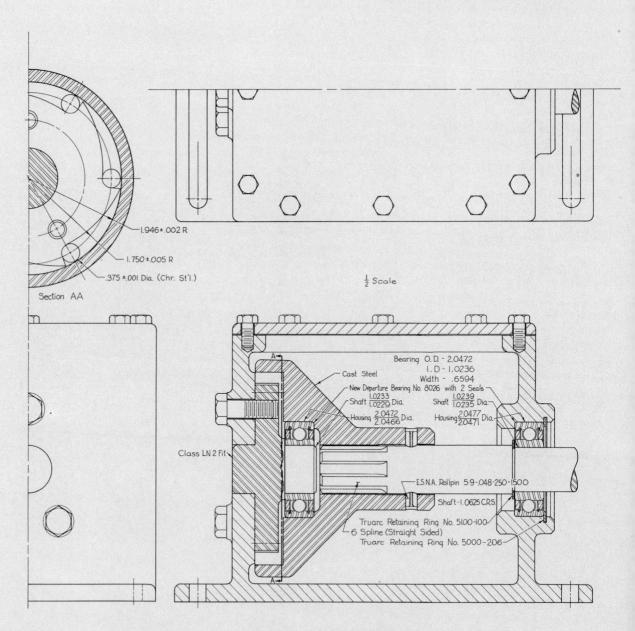

1.946 ± .002 R

1.750 ± .005 R

.375 ± .001 Dia. (Chr. St'l.)

Section AA

½ Scale

A

Cast Steel

Bearing O.D. - 2.0472
I. D - 1.0236
Width - .6594

New Departure Bearing No. 8026 with 2 Seals

Shaft $\frac{1.0233}{1.0229}$ Dia.   Shaft $\frac{1.0239}{1.0235}$ Dia.

Housing $\frac{2.0472}{2.0466}$ Dia.   Housing $\frac{2.0477}{2.0471}$ Dia.

Class LN 2 Fit

E.S.N.A. Rollpin 5 9 -.048-.250 -1500

Shaft - 1.0625 C.R.S.

Truarc Retaining Ring No. 5100-100
6 Spline (Straight Sided)
Truarc Retaining Ring No. 5000-206

A

PROB. 19.7.5.   Overriding clutch.

No.	No. Reqd	Description	Size	Material
1	1	Shaft	1 Dia. × 13	Stn. Stl.
2	1	Base	.375 × 1 × 16.5	Stn. Stl.
3	3	Lug	.375 × 1 × 1	Stn. Stl.
4	2	Clamp Ring	1.375 Dia × 2	Stn. Stl.
5	4	Lug	.188 × .375 × 2	Stn. Stl.
6	1	Frame	.188 × 2 × 9	Stn. Stl.
7	2	Clamp Bolt	.375 Dia. × 3.5	Stn. Stl.
8	1	Spur Gear	20 Teeth - 20°Press. Angle 10 Pitch - .75 Face Width	Stn. Stl.
9	2	Taper Pin	No. 1	Stn. Stl.
10	2	Bushing	1 Dia. × .312	Nylon
11	1	Shaft	.50 Dia. × 2.125	Stn. Stl.
12	1	Bearing Block	.75 × 1 × 2	Nylon
13	1	Rack	.75 × 1 × 7.5	Stn. Stl.
14	1	Handle	.50 Dia. × 8	Stn. Stl.
15	1	Hub	1 Dia. × .75	Stn. Stl.
16	4	Self Tapping Rd. Hd. Screw	No. 8 × .50 Long	Stn. Stl.
17	1	Press Plate	.75 × 3 × 4	Stn. Stl.
18	1	Bone Juice Drain	.875 Dia × 3	Stn. Stl.
19	1	Bone Juice Plate	.75 × 5 × 6	Stn. Stl.
20	1	Web	.50 × 1.50 × 5	Stn. Stl.

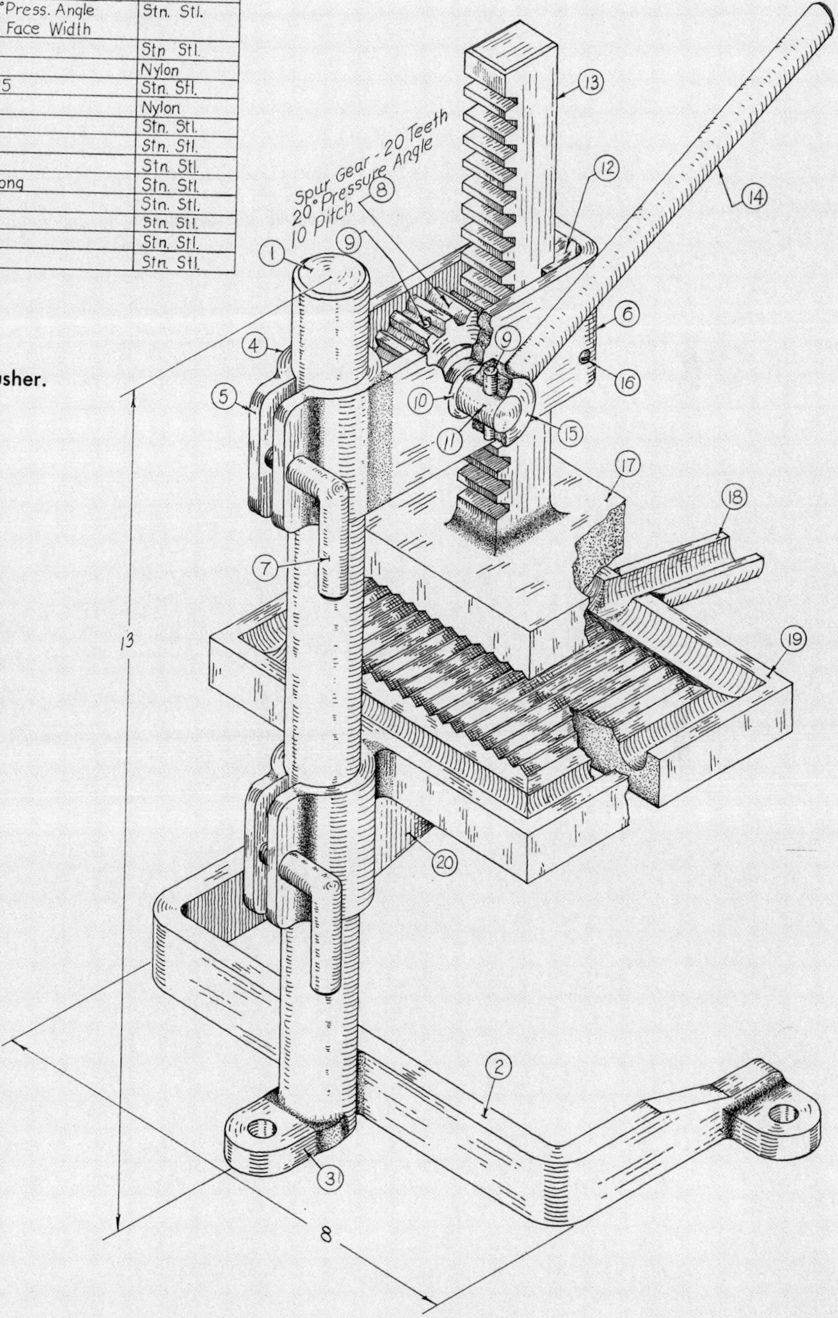

PROB. 19.7.6. Bone crusher.

19.7.6. The illustration for this problem is a pictorial design drawing, made for presentation to a medical research group. The device, a bone crusher, is proposed for use by doctors of veterinary medicine in the laboratory analysis of bone disease. Fundamentally, the machine consists of parts welded together as shown by the drawing and indicated on the bill of materials. Make a complete set of drawings, including details, working drawings, subassembly drawings if necessary, and the assembly drawing.

Spur Gear - 20 Teeth
20° Pressure Angle
10 Pitch

19.7.7. A common problem in all manufacturing projects is the planning and execution of methods to promote speed, consistent quality of parts, and economy in production. Quite often, parts can be made as a portion or segment of a basic shape. For example, rings can be cut into segments and extruded shapes can be cut to length quickly and economically to produce brackets, clips, etc. Bars, tubes, and rolled shapes also can be cut to length to produce parts of required shape.

A fine example of intelligent production planning is given in the following problem.

The M-14 rifle has a curved aperture in its sighting mechanism offering a challenge to produce the simple and economical part

shown in the illustration. Essentially the part is a serrated sector of a circle having a tapered hole. The aperture is made of SAE 1041 steel heat-treated to Rockwell C40-45 after machining, then phosphate-coated for corrosion protection. A unique process of external and internal broaching is an important phase of the processing to achieve the necessary economy.

Since the body is a portion of a true circle, it was decided to produce the part from steel tubing, broaching where possible. Engineers of National Broach & Machine Co. assisted in making a study to recommend processing sequences with tooling that would produce the part to desired tolerances. Special Red Ring broaches were chosen for three operations.

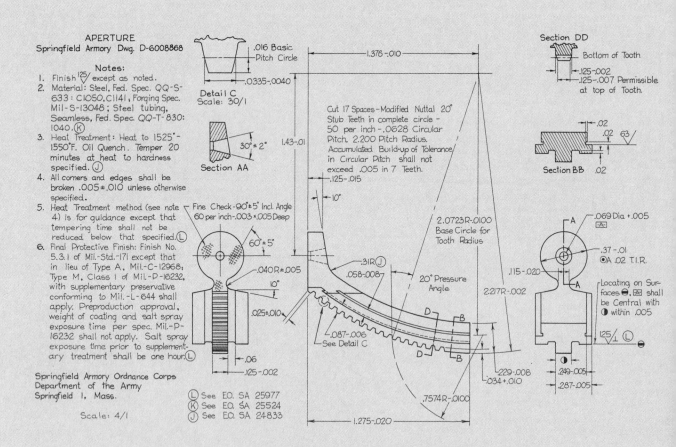

PROB. 19.7.7. M-14 rifle aperture.

Operation 1:
Machine and cut off.

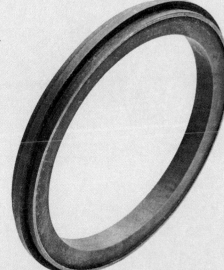

Operation 2:
Face and undercut.

Operation 1. First a ring is turned, bored, cut off and faced on a four-spindle, 4¾-in. Conomatic bar machine. The ⅛-in. width of the serrated tooth section is held to 0.001 in.

Operation 2. Next the ring is faced and undercut on both sides in an Ex-Cell-O two-spindle boring machine.

Operation 3. The ring is then broached on a 40-ton Colonial horizontal broaching machine. The internal broach shapes the ID of the ring which will later be cut to form eight peephole gun parts. Broaching operation takes 30 sec.

Operation 3:
Broach inside diameter.

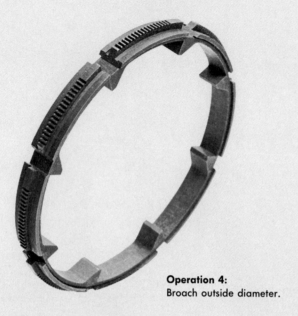

Operation 4:
Broach outside diameter.

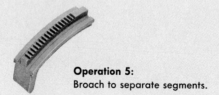

Operation 5:
Broach to separate segments.

Operation 6:
Broach radius.

Operation 7:
Drill peep hole.

Operation 4. The next operation uses two broaches on a 20-ton Oilgear vertical machine that notches and serrates the OD and forms eight segments.

The tool for this sequence is an internal pot-type broach that traverses over the ring mounted on a long fixture. First the rings are finished on the notched OD and serrated with one set of tools. The 2.217-in. OD is held to 0.002 in. while sixteen 0.0628-in. circular pitch 20° P.A., involute serrations are broached on each of the eight sections. Time: 30 sec.

Operation 5. After a number of rings have been finished, broach inserts are removed and replaced with another set of inserts that cut the ring into eight aperture parts and finish broach each part to length. Time: another 30 sec.

Operation 6. Next Red Ring external surface broaches form the ⅜-in.-dia. circular portion around the peephole on a 5-ton Cincinnati vertical broaching machine. This takes 20 sec.

Operation 7. Final machining is the 0.069-in. peephole, which has a 30° included-angle conical section. It is drilled on a Hamilton drill press equipped with a four-station index fixture and special drilling tool. The hole must be accurately positioned within 0.002 in. of the center line of the gear section.

This part is an excellent example of how four broaching operations equipped with properly conceived broaching tools can cut production costs and make a precise component with a total production time of only 110 sec/part.

From the final part drawing of Prob. 19.7.7, make separate drawings to show the part at the completion of each stage of manufacture, as shown by the pictures accompanying Prob. 19.7.7 and designated as Operations 1 through 7.

This problem and the explanation accompanying it is given through the courtesy of the National Broach & Machine Co. and by Dale O. Miller, Jr., of Rochester Gear, Inc., a personal friend of the author of this text.

GROUP 8. WORKING SKETCHES

19.8.1. Select one of the problems in Group 1, and make a detail working sketch.

19.8.2. Select one of the problems in Group 2, and make an assembly sketch.

19.8.3. Select a single part from one of the assemblies of Groups 3 to 5, and make a working sketch.

19.8.4. Select a single part from one of the Probs. 19.1.1 to 19.4.7, and make a pictorial working sketch.

19.8.5. Select one of the problems that are given in Group 3, and make detail working sketches.

19.8.6. Select one of the problems in Group 4 or 5, and make a complete set of working sketches.

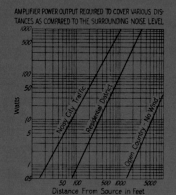

AMPLIFIER POWER OUTPUT REQUIRED TO COVER VARIOUS DIS-
TANCES AS COMPARED TO THE SURROUNDING NOISE LEVEL

Watts / Distance From Source in Feet

Noisy City Traffic / Residential District / Open Country - No Wind

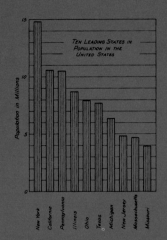

TEN LEADING STATES IN
POPULATION IN THE
UNITED STATES

Population in Millions

New York / California / Pennsylvania / Illinois / Ohio / Texas / Michigan / New Jersey / Massachusetts / Missouri

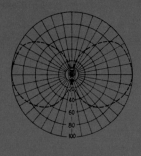

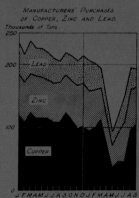

MANUFACTURERS' PURCHASES
OF COPPER, ZINC AND LEAD

Thousands of Tons

LEAD
ZINC
COPPER

J F M A M J J A S O N D J F M A M J J A S
1948   1949

WEIGHT PERCENTAGE ANALYSIS FOR AN
INTERNALLY BRACED CABIN MONOPLANE

26.4% / 22.4% / 33.1% / 15.6%
Wing Group / Body Group / Power Plant / Fixed
Tail Group 2.5% / Equip.

Miscellaneous
17.8%

Blasting Powder
14.0%

Dynamite
52.3%

Permissibles
14.3%

Nitroglycerine
1.6%

11.75

3.70   4.30   4.55   5.40

HR Carbon   HR Alloy   CF Carbon   CF Alloy   Wrought
Steel   Steel   Steel   Steel   Iron

MILL PRICE OF BAR STOCK
Cents per Pound

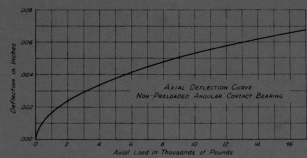

Deflection in Inches

.008

.006

.004

.002

.000

AXIAL DEFLECTION CURVE
NON-PRELOADED ANGULAR CONTACT BEARING

0   2   4   6   8   10   12   14   16

Axial Load in Thousands of Pounds

Charts, graphs, and diagrams are used to display graphically data of technical tests, observations, and determinations in all scientific fields. Some typical applications: chemical composition; strength of materials; hydraulic flow, pressure, and device performance; electrical and electronic measurements; heat, light, and sound determinations; physical properties of solids, liquids, and gases; representation of mathematical calculations. There are many other applications—too numerous to record here. Charts, graphs, and diagrams are not only valuable tools for the engineer's purposes in his technical work, but they are also significant and useful in explanations and presentations to lay personnel.

Charts, Graphs, and Diagrams: Introduction to Graphic Solutions

20

20.1. This chapter is given as an introduction to the use of graphic methods in tabulating data for analysis, solving problems, and presenting facts. We will discuss the value of this application of graphics in engineering and suggest ways of studying the subject further.

The graphic chart is an excellent method for presenting a series of quantitative facts quickly. When properly constructed, charts, graphs, and diagrams constitute a powerful tool for computation, analysis of engineering data, and the presentation of statistics for comparison or prediction.

20.2. CLASSIFICATION. Charts, graphs, and diagrams fall roughly into two classes: (1) those used for purely technical purposes and (2) those used in advertising or in presenting information in a way that will have popular appeal. The engineer is concerned mainly with those of the first class, but he should be acquainted also with the preparation of those of the second and understand their potential influence. The aim here is to give a short study of the types of charts, graphs, and diagrams with which engineers and those in allied professions should be familiar.

It is assumed that the student is familiar with the use of rectangular coordinates and that such terms as "axes," "ordinates," "abscissas," "coordinates," and "variables" are understood.

20.3.　REPRESENTATION OF DATA: RECTI-LINEAR CHARTS. Because the preliminary chart work in experimental engineering is done on rectilinear graph paper, the student should become familiar with this form of chart early in his course. The rectilinear chart is made on a sheet ruled with equispaced horizontal lines crossing equispaced vertical lines. The spacing is optional. One commercial graph paper is divided into squares of ¹⁄₂₀ in., with every fifth line heavier, to aid in plotting and reading. Sheets are available with various other rulings, such as 4, 6, 8, 10, 12, and 16 divisions per inch.

It is universal practice to use the upper right-hand quadrant for plotting experimental-data curves, making the lower left-hand corner the origin. In case both positive and negative values of a function are to be plotted, as occurs with many mathematical curves, the origin must be placed so as to include all desired values.

Figure 20.1 shows a usual form of rectilinear chart, such as might be made for inclusion in a written report.

20.4.　DRAWING THE CURVE. In drawing graphs from experimental data, it is often a question whether the curve should pass through all the points plotted or strike a mean between them. In general, observed data not backed up by definite theory or mathematical law are shown by connecting the points plotted with straight lines, as in Fig. 20.2A. An empirical relationship between curve and plotted points may be used, as at (B), when, in the opinion of the engineer, the curve should exactly follow some points and go to one side of others. Consistency of observation is indicated at (C), in which case the curve should closely follow a true theoretical curve.

20.5.　TITLES AND NOTATION. The title is an important part of a chart, and its wording should be clear and concise. In every case, it should contain sufficient description to tell what the chart is, the source or authority, the name of the observer, and the date. Approved practice places the title at the top of the sheet, arranged in phrases symmetrically about a center line. If it is placed within the ruled space, a border line or box should set it apart from the sheet. Each sheet of curves should have a title; and when more than one curve is shown on a sheet, the different curves should be drawn so as to be easily distinguishable. This can be done by varying the character of the lines, using full, dashed, and dot-and-dash lines, with a tabular key for identification, or by lettering the names of the curves directly along them. When the charts are not intended for reproduction, inks of different colors can be used.

20.6.　TO DRAW A CHART. In drawing a coordinate chart, the general order is: (1) compute and assemble all data; (2) determine the size and kind of chart best adapted and whether to use printed or plain paper; (3) determine, from the

FIG. 20.1. A rectilinear chart. This type of chart shows how one variable changes with respect to another. Corresponding values can be determined.

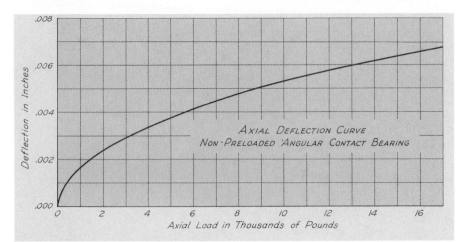

limits of the data, the scales for abscissas and ordinates to give the best effect to the resulting curve; (4) lay off the independent variable (often *time*) on the horizontal, or *X,* axis and the dependent variable on the vertical, or *Y,* axis; (5) plot points from the data and pencil the curves; (6) ink the curve; (7) compose and letter the title and coordinates.

The construction of a graphic chart requires good draftsmanship, especially for the lettering, but in engineering and scientific work the primary considerations are judgment in the proper selection of coordinates, accuracy in plotting points and drawing the graph, and an understanding of the functions and limitations of the resulting chart.

When the chart is drawn on a printed form, to be blueprinted, the curve can be drawn on the reverse side of the paper, enabling erasures to be made without injuring the ruled surface.

Green is becoming the standard color for printed forms. Blue will not print or photograph; red is trying on the eyes.

If the curve is for purposes of computation, it should be drawn with a fine, accurate line; if for demonstration, it should be fairly heavy, for contrast and effect.

The following rules are adapted from ANS Y15 (formerly ASA Z15):

Standards for Graphic Presentations

1. A graph should be free of all lines and lettering that are not essential to the reader's clear understanding of its message.

2. All lettering and numbers on a graph should be placed so as to be easily read from the bottom and from the right-hand side of the graph, not the left-hand side.

3. Standard abbreviations should be used where space is limited as, for example, in denoting the unit of measurement in scale captions.

4. The range of scales should be chosen so as to ensure effective and efficient use of the coordinate area in attaining the objective of the chart.

5. The zero line should be included if visual comparison of plotted magnitudes is desired.

6. When it is desired to show whether the rate of change of the dependent variable is increasing, constant, or decreasing, a logarithmic vertical scale should be used in conjunction with an arithmetical horizontal scale.

7. The horizontal (independent variable) scale values should usually increase from left to right and the vertical (dependent variable) scale values from bottom to top.

8. Scale values and scale captions should be placed outside the grid area, normally at the bottom for the horizontal scale and at the left side for the vertical scale. On wide graphs the vertical scale may be repeated at the right.

9. For arithmetical scales, the scale numbers shown on the graph and the space between coordinate rulings should preferably correspond to 1, 2, or 5 units of measurement, multiplied or divided by 1, 10, 100, etc.

10. The use of many digits in scale numbers should be avoided.

11. The scale caption should indicate both the variable measured and the unit of measurement. For example: EXPOSURE TIME IN DAYS.

12. Coordinate rulings should be limited in number to those necessary to guide the eye in making a reading to the desired degree of approximation. Closely spaced coordinate rulings are appropriate for computation charts but not for graphs intended primarily to show relationship.

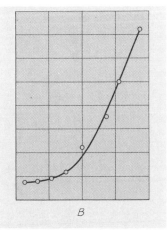

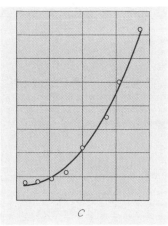

FIG. 20.2. Methods of drawing curves. (*A*) "curve" for data not supported by theory and therefore not necessarily producing a smooth curve; (*B*) and (*C*) curves for data known to produce smooth curves.

13. Curves should preferably be represented by solid lines.

14. When more than one curve is presented on a graph, relative emphasis or differentiation of the curves may be secured by using different types of line, that is, solid, dashed, dotted, etc., or by different widths of line. A solid line is recommended for the most important curve.

15. The observed points should preferably be designated by circles.

16. Circles, squares, and triangles should be used rather than crosses or filled-in symbols to differentiate observed points of several curves on a graph.

17. Curves should, if practicable, be designated by brief labels placed close to the curves (horizontally or along the curves) rather than by letters, numbers, or other devices requiring a key.

18. If a key is used, it should preferably be placed within the grid in an isolated position, and enclosed by a light line border—grid lines, if convenient.

19. The title should be as clear and concise as possible. Explanatory material, if necessary to ensure clearness, should be added as a subtitle.

20. Scale captions, designations, curves, and blank spaces should, so far as practicable, be arranged to give a sense of balance around vertical and horizontal axes.

21. The appearance and the effectiveness of a graph depend in large measure on the relative widths of line used for its component parts. The widest line should be used for the principal curve. If several curves are presented on the same graph, the line width used for the curves should be less than that used when a single curve is presented.

22. A simple style of lettering, such as Gothic with its uniform line width and no serifs, should in general be used.

20.7. LOGARITHMIC SCALES. An important type of chart is that in which the divisions are made proportional to the logarithms of the numbers instead of to the numbers themselves, and accordingly are not equally spaced. When ruled logarithmically in one direction with equal spacing at right angles, the spacing is called "semilogarithmic."

FIG. 20.3. A semilogarithmic chart. The ordinate axis (in this case) is logarithmic, the abscissa uniform.

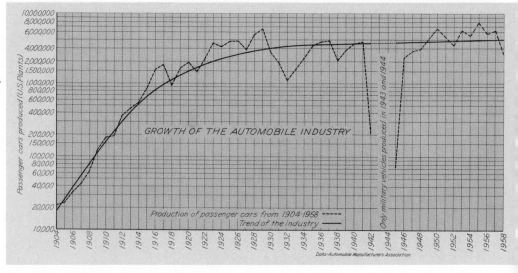

Logarithmic spacing may be directly from the graduations on one of the scales of a slide rule. Logarithmic paper is sold in various combinations of ruling. It is available in one, two, three, or more cycles; in multiples of 10; and also in part-cycle and split-cycle form. In using logarithmic paper, interpolations should be made logarithmically; arithmetical interpolation with coarse divisions might lead to considerable error.

20.8. SEMILOGARITHMIC CHARTS.

These charts have equal spacing on one axis, usually the X axis, and logarithmic spacing on the other axis. Owing to a property by virtue of which the slope of the curve at any point is an exact measure of the rate of increase or decrease in the data plotted, the semilogarithmic chart is frequently called a "ratio chart." Often called the "rate-of-change" chart as distinguished from the rectilinear, or "amount-of-change," chart, it is extremely useful in statistical work as it shows at a glance the rate at which a variable changes. By the use of this chart it is possible to predict a trend, such as the future increase of a business, growth of population, etc.

In choosing between rectilinear ruling and semilogarithmic ruling, the important point to consider is whether the chart is to represent *numerical* increases and decreases or *percentage* increases and decreases. In many cases it is desirable to emphasize the percentage, or rate, change, not the numerical change; for these a semilogarithmic chart should be used.

An example of a semilogarithmic chart is given in Fig. 20.3. This curve was drawn from data compiled for the *World Almanac*. The dashed line shows the actual production by years, and the full line is the trend curve, the extension of which predicts future production.

Exponential equations of the form $y = ae^{bx}$ plot on semilogarithmic coordinates as a straight line. This represents the type of relationship in which a quantity increases or decreases at a rate proportional to the amount present at any time. For example, the passage of light through a translucent substance varies (in intensity) exponentially with the thickness of material.

20.9. LOGARITHMIC CHARTS.

These are charts in which both abscissas and ordinates are spaced logarithmically. Any equation of the form $y = ax^b$, in which one quantity varies directly as some power of another, will plot as a straight line on logarithmic coordinates. Thus, multiplication, division, powers, and roots are examples. Figure 20.4 shows a logarithmic plot of sound intensity (and the power required to produce it) which varies as a power of the distance from the source. Other examples are the distance-time relationship of a falling body and the period of a simple pendulum.

20.10. POLAR CHARTS.

The use of polar coordinate paper for representing intensity of illumination, intensity of heat, polar forms of curves, etc., is common. Figure 20.5 shows a candle-power distribution curve for an ordinary Mazda B lamp, and Fig. 20.6 the curve for a certain type of reflector. The candle power in any given direction is determined by reading off the distance from the origin to the curve. Use of polar forms of curves enables the determination of the foot-candle intensity at any point.

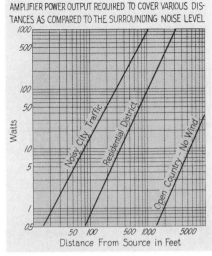

FIG. 20.4. A logarithmic chart. Both ordinate and abscissa are divided logarithmically.

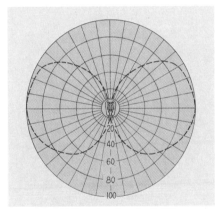

FIG. 20.5. A polar chart. This type is used when direction from a point (pole) must be shown.

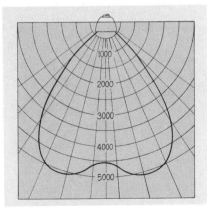

FIG. 20.6. A polar chart. This one shows the area of illumination from a reflector.

20.11.   TRILINEAR CHARTS.   The trilinear chart, or "triaxial diagram," as it is sometimes called, affords a valuable means of studying the properties of chemical compounds consisting of three elements, alloys of three metals or compounds, and mixtures containing three variables. The chart has the form of an equilateral triangle, the altitude of which represents 100 per cent of each of the three constituents. Figure 20.7, showing the ultimate tensile strength of copper-tin-zinc alloys, is a typical example of its application. The usefulness of such diagrams depends upon the geometric principle that the sum of the perpendiculars to the sides from any point within an equilateral triangle is a constant and is equal to the altitude.

20.12.   CHOICE OF TYPE AND PRESENTATION.   The function of a chart is to reveal facts. It may be entirely misleading if wrong paper or coordinates are chosen. The growth of an operation plotted on a rectilinear chart might, for example, entirely mislead an owner analyzing the trend of his business, while if plotted on a semilogarithmic chart, it would give a true picture of conditions. Intentionally misleading charts have been used many times in advertising; the commonest form is the chart with a greatly exaggerated vertical scale. In engineering work it is essential to present the facts honestly and with scientific accuracy.

20.13.   ANALYSIS OF EXPERIMENTAL DATA. So far we have discussed only the representation of data. In many cases representation alone, on suitable coordinates gives an accurate description—for, from the plot, the *value* of one variable relative to a second variable can be ascertained. Nevertheless, the equation of a relationship can often be obtained from the data. To do this, the data must be plotted on coordinates that will "justify" the curve to a straight line. The equation of a straight line on any system of coordinates is easily determined. Equations thus resolved are known as *empirical* equations.

The standard procedure is first to plot the data on rectangular coordinates. If a straight line results, it is known that the equation is of the first degree (linear). If a curve results from the plot, the equation is of a higher form, and semilogarithmic coordinates or logarithmic coordinates should be tried; if the data justifies to a straight line on either system, the equation can be determined.

20.14.   RECTANGULAR PLOTS: LINEAR EQUATIONS.   If a plot of data results in a straight line on rectilinear coordinates, the equation is of the first degree. Figure 20.8 shows a plot that justifies to a straight line on rectilinear coordinates. To determine the equation of the line, select two points, such as y_1x_1 and y_2x_2 shown in Fig. 20.8. Then by simple proportion

FIG. 20.7.   A trilinear chart. This type is used to represent properties of three combined elements.

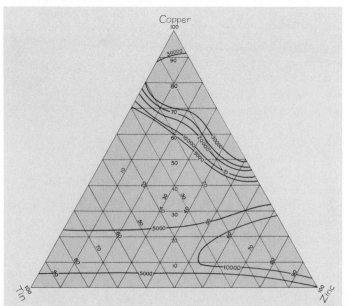

$$\frac{y - y_1}{x - x_1} = \frac{y_2 - y_1}{x_2 - x_1}$$

and from Fig. 14.8

$y_1 = 13.8, y_2 = 43.5; x_1 = 8, x_2 = 35.0$

substituting,

$$\frac{y - 13.8}{x - 8.0} = \frac{43.5 - 13.8}{35.0 - 8.0}$$

whence,

$$\frac{y - 13.8}{x - 8.0} = 1.1$$

and $y = 5.0 + 1.1x$

Thus, this equation is of a straight line, $y = a + bx$, where $a = 5.0$ and $b = 1.1$.

The coefficient 1.1 is the slope of the line and the constant 5.0 is the ordinate-axis intercept.

20.15. LOGARITHMIC PLOTS: POWER EQUATIONS.

If the data justifies to a straight line on logarithmic coordinates, the equation is a power relationship of the form $y = ax^b$. Figure 20.9 shows a plot that justifies to a straight line on logarithmic coordinates. Two selected points give

$x_1 = 2.5 \qquad y_1 = 3.8$
$x_2 = 55.0 \qquad y_2 = 26.5$

Because the plot is logarithmic,

$$\frac{\log y - \log 3.8}{\log x - \log 2.5} = \frac{\log 26.5 - \log 3.8}{\log 55.0 - \log 2.5}$$

whence,

$$\log y = 0.330 + 0.628 \log x$$

and

$$y = 2.14 x^{0.628}$$

20.16. SEMILOGARITHMIC PLOTS: EXPONENTIAL EQUATIONS.

If plotted data justifies to a straight line on semilogarithmic coordinates, the equation is

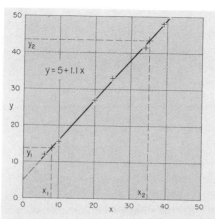

FIG. 20.8. A straight-line plot on rectilinear coordinates. The equation of the line is linear, $y = a + bx$.

an exponential form, $y = ae^{bx}$ or $y = a10^{bx}$ (for base 10 logarithms). Figure 20.10 shows a typical plot. Two selected points give

$x_1 = 0.8 \qquad y_1 = 3.8$
$x_2 = 4.5 \qquad y_2 = 50.0$

Writing the equation of the straight line,

$$\frac{\ln y - \ln 3.8}{x - 0.8} = \frac{\ln 50.0 - \ln 3.8}{4.5 - 0.8}$$

whence,

$$\ln y = 0.777 + 0.697x$$

and

$$y = 2.18 e^{0.697x}$$

20.17. NOMOGRAPHY.

After the equation of a relationship has been determined, specific values of the variables can be found by substitution in the equation. To facilitate such calculations, a chart called a nomogram can be made in which the variables are represented by plotted scales arranged so that a straightedge placed across the scales will give corresponding values of the variables. A simple example of a nomogram (conversion chart) is shown in Fig. 20.11.

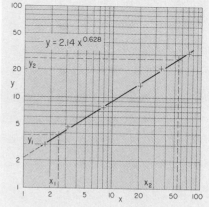

FIG. 20.9. A straight-line plot on logarithmic coordinates. The equation of the line is a power form, $y = ax^b$.

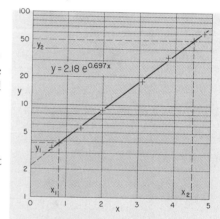

FIG. 20.10. A straight-line plot on semilogarithmic coordinates. The equation of the line is an exponential form, $y = ae^{bx}$.

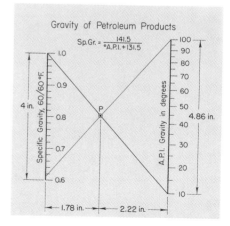

FIG. 20.11. A nomogram. This one is a conversion chart for specific gravity to degrees API.

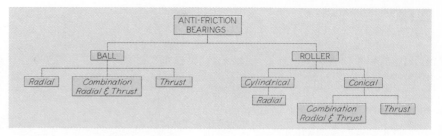

FIG. 20.12.　A classification chart. This type of chart shows the relationship of parts of a whole.

The construction of a nomogram requires a knowledge of functional scales, chart forms, and the necessary mathematics. Thus, nomography is a special graphic field. For a discussion of it, see Chap. 21.

20.18.　GRAPHIC CALCULUS.　Considered in the same light as nomography, this is a specialized field of chart construction in which the rates of change of variables are determined graphically. For a discussion of graphic calculus, see Chap. 23.

FIG. 20.13.　A flow sheet. This is an effective way to show the fundamentals of a process or method.

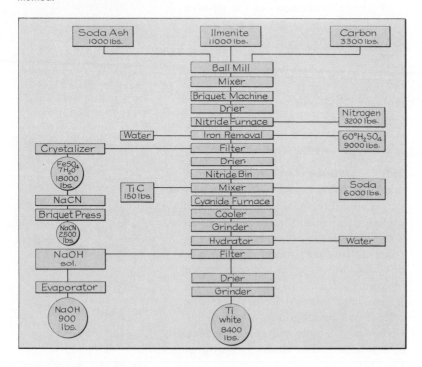

20.19.　CLASSIFICATION CHARTS, ROUTE CHARTS, AND FLOW SHEETS.　The uses to which these three classes of charts can be put are widely different; but their underlying principles are similar, and so they have been grouped together for convenience.

A *classification chart,* illustrated in Fig. 20.12, is intended to show the subdivisions of a whole and the interrelation of its parts with one another. Such a chart often takes the place of a written outline as it gives a better visualization of the facts than can be achieved with words alone. A common application is an organization chart of a corporation or business. It is customary to enclose the names of the divisions in rectangles, although circles or other shapes may be used. The rectangle has the advantage of being convenient for lettering, while the circle can be drawn more quickly and possesses greater popular appeal. Often a combination of both is used.

The *route chart* is used mainly for the purpose of showing the various steps in a process, either of manufacturing or other business. The *flow sheet,* illustrated in Fig. 20.13, is an example of a route chart applied to a chemical process. Charts of this type show in a dynamic way facts that might require considerable study to be understood from a written description. Figure 17.1, showing the course of a drawing through the shops, illustrates a different form of route chart.

20.20. POPULAR CHARTS.

Engineers and draftsmen are frequently called upon to prepare charts and diagrams that will be understood by nontechnical readers. For such charts it is often advisable to present the facts, not by means of curves on coordinate paper, but in a way that is more easily read, even though the representation may be somewhat less accurate. Charts for popular use must be made so that the impression they produce is both quick and accurate. They are seldom studied critically but are taken in at a glance; hence the method of presentation requires the exercise of careful judgment and the application of a certain amount of psychology.

20.21. BAR CHARTS.

The bar chart is a type of chart easily understood by nontechnical readers. One of its simplest forms is the *100 per cent bar* for showing the relations of the constituents to a given total. Figure 20.14 is an example. The different segments should be crosshatched, shaded, or distinguished in some other effective manner, the percentage represented should be placed on the related portion of the diagram or directly opposite, and the meaning of each segment should be clearly stated. Bars may be placed vertically or horizontally, the vertical position giving an advantage for lettering and the horizontal an advantage in readability, as the eye judges horizontal distances readily.

Figure 20.15 is an example of a *multiple-bar chart,* in which the length of each bar is proportional to the magnitude of the quantity represented. Means should be provided for reading numerical values represented by the bars. If it is necessary to give the exact value rep-

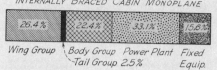

WEIGHT PERCENTAGE ANALYSIS FOR AN INTERNALLY BRACED CABIN MONOPLANE

26.4% | 22.4% | 33.1% | 15.6%

Wing Group | Body Group | Power Plant | Fixed Equip.
Tail Group 2.5%

FIG. 20.14. A 100 per cent bar chart. This is a simple and impressive method of showing percentages of a whole.

FIG. 20.15. A multiple-bar chart. Each bar gives (graphically) the magnitude of the item represented.

resented by the individual bars, the values should not be lettered at the ends of the bars as this would increase their apparent length. This type of chart is made horizontally, with the description at the base, and vertically. The vertical form is sometimes called the "pipe-organ chart." When vertical bars are drawn close together, touching along the sides, the diagram is called a "staircase chart." This chart is more often made as the "staircase curve," a line plotted on coordinate paper representing the profile of the tops of the bars.

A *compound-bar chart* is made when it is desirable to show two or more components in each bar. It is really a set of 100 per cent bars of different lengths set together in pipe-organ or horizontal form.

20.22. PIE CHARTS.

The "pie diagram," or 100 per cent circle (Fig. 20.16) is much inferior to the bar chart but is used constantly because of its popular appeal. It is a simple form of chart and, except for the lettering, is easily constructed. It can be regarded as a 100 per cent bar bent into circular

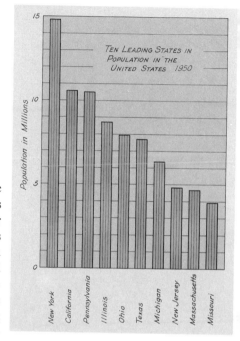

TEN LEADING STATES IN POPULATION IN THE UNITED STATES 1950

Population in Millions

New York | California | Pennsylvania | Illinois | Ohio | Texas | Michigan | New Jersey | Massachusetts | Missouri

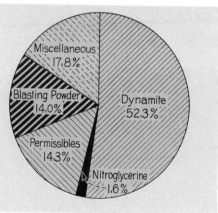

Miscellaneous 17.8%

Blasting Powder 14.0%

Permissibles 14.3%

Dynamite 52.3%

Nitroglycerine 1.6%

FIG. 20.16. A pie chart. This chart shows percentages of a whole. Compare it with a 100 per cent bar chart.

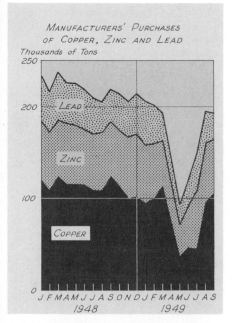

FIG. 20.17. A strata chart. The individual charts are superimposed.

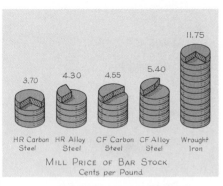

FIG. 20.18. A pictorial chart. Pictorialism adds to popular interest but detracts from accuracy of representation.

form. The circumference of the circle is divided into 100 parts, and sectors are used to represent percentages of the total.

To be effective, this diagram must be carefully lettered and the percentages marked on the sectors or at the circumference opposite the sectors. For contrast, it is best to crosshatch or shade the individual sectors. If the original drawing is to be displayed, the sectors may be colored and the diagram supplied with a key showing the meaning of each color. The percentage notation should always be placed where it can be read without removing the eyes from the diagram.

20.23.   STRATA AND VOLUME DIAGRAMS. The use of strata and volume diagrams has been common although they are usually the most deceptive of the graphic methods of representation. Figure 20.17 is a strata chart showing a change in amounts over a period of time. The area between the curves is shaded to emphasize each variable represented. However, in reading it should be remembered that the areas *between* curves have no significance.

20.24.   PICTORIAL CHARTS. Pictorial charts were formerly much used for comparisons, for example of costs, populations, standing armies, livestock, and various products. It was customary to represent the data by human or other figures whose heights were proportional to numerical values or by silhouettes of the animals or products concerned whose heights or sometimes areas were proportional. Since volumes vary as the cubes of the linear dimensions, such charts are grossly misleading. Bar charts or charts such as the one shown in Fig.

20.18, where the diameter of the column is constant, should be used for the type of comparisons that are shown in pictorial charts.

20.25.   CHARTS FOR REPRODUCTION. Charts for reproduction by the zinc-etching process should be carefully penciled to about twice the size of the required cut. Observe the following order in inking: First, ink the circles around plotted points; second, ink the curves with strong lines. A border pen is useful for heavy lines, and a Leroy pen (in socket holder) may be used to advantage, particularly for dashed lines. Third, ink the title box and all lettering; fourth, ink the coordinates with fine black lines, putting in only as many as are necessary for easy reading and breaking them wherever they interfere with title or lettering or where they cross plotted points.

20.26.   CHARTS FOR DISPLAY. Large charts for demonstration purposes are sometimes required. These can be drawn on sheets 22 by 28 in. or 28 by 44 in. known as "printer's blanks." The quickest way to make them is with show-card colors and single-stroke signwriter's brushes. Large bar charts can be made with strips of black adhesive tape. Lettering can be done with the brush or with gummed letters.

20.27.   STANDARDS. Many standards are available for graphic presentations of data. Of particular interest are the ANSI Standards for graphical symbols (Y32), letter symbols (Y10), and time-series charts (Y15.2—1960), and ANS Y15.1 "Guide for Preparing Technical Illustrations for Publications and Projection."

20.28. THE ADVANTAGE OF COLOR.

Even though "black-and-white" charts, graphs, and diagrams are satisfactory for statistical and scientific purposes, the use of color will add greatly to readability, separation, and emphasis. In black and white, line codes (dashes, etc.) must be used and areas can be emphasized only by crosshatching. In color, lines stand out prominently and areas are easily distinguished. Especially for popular charts, color is almost mandatory. Today, many of the charts in good periodicals, corporate reports, promotional charts, and many others are being done in color. The use of color is increasing rapidly. Note the use of color techniques in all of the illustrations in this chapter, especially Figs. 20.12, 20.13, 20.15, and Figs. 20.19 to 20.23.[1] Also, compare Fig. 20.19 with Fig. 20.20.

20.29. PRINCIPLES FOR THE USE OF COLOR.

The use of color always requires some artistic judgment and consequently it is difficult to give definitive rules. Nevertheless, the following principles will serve as a guide.

Backgrounds. A pure white background for a chart is not nearly so effective as a background made of a light tint of color. This is because a white background, even if it is outlined, is the same value as the page itself. A background made as a light tint adds cohesiveness and vigor to the charts. Notice the use of tinted backgrounds in all the charts in this chapter.

[1] Figures 20.19 to 20.23 are supplied through the courtesy of Mr. W. Anthony Dowell of the Palm Beach office of Merrill Lynch, Pierce, Fenner and Smith and are adapted from the U.S. Industrial Outlook, 1965, by the U.S. Department of Commerce.

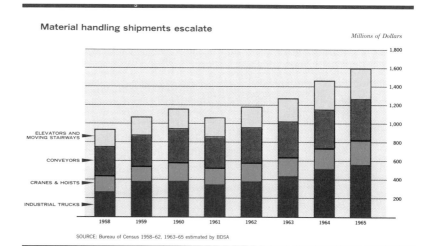

Material handling shipments escalate

Millions of Dollars

SOURCE: Bureau of Census 1958–62, 1963–65 estimated by BDSA

FIG. 20.19. A multiple-bar chart in color. Basic colors and tints are used. Compare with Fig. 20.20.

White lines and areas. White lines and areas can be produced only if a tinted background is employed. This adds one more color to any series used and is quite effective. Notice the white area in Fig. 20.23 and the white line in Fig. 20.22.

Values of tints. Tints of a color are made either by diluting the color with white or, in printing, by the use of screens which reduce the color intensity. In printing, the screens are rated in per-

FIG. 20.20. The chart of Fig. 20.19 in "black and white" and tints. Compare with Fig. 20.19.

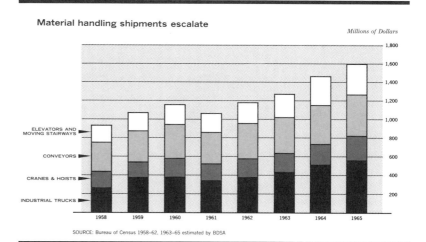

Material handling shipments escalate

Millions of Dollars

SOURCE: Bureau of Census 1958–62, 1963–65 estimated by BDSA

centage, which means that a 75% screen will print (in actual minute areas) 75% of the color and 25% white (blank area). Thus a 30% screen would print 30% of the color and 70% as blank area. For the dilution of a color with white when applying color by hand, it is advantageous to think of the color *value* also in percentage because it is easy to judge color intensity, for example, as approximately ¾ the intensity of the pure color. The actual dilution *will not* be the same as the value of the intensity; the dilution must be made by carefully adding white, and then judging the intensity. Note the various intensities of colors used in the illustrations of this chapter.

Contrast. Contrast may be defined as the degree of dissimilarity. Thus, high contrast is had when a color of strong intensity is placed adjacent to a color of very weak intensity. Low contrast is had when two colors of about the same intensity are placed together. High contrast will accentuate the areas and low contrast will diminish the impact of the areas. Notice the gradual (low-contrast) changes in both color and value of the areas in Fig. 20.19 and also the high con-

trast and accentuation of the darkest and white areas of Fig. 20.29. If emphasis is needed, use high contrast. If a subtle change is desirable, use low contrast.

Adjacent areas. Adjacent areas are well defined and easily read if they are made of different colors. Notice in Fig. 20.21 that adjacent areas are different colors and also that different values of the colors have been used. Maximum separation of areas occurs when a strong color and value is placed next to a weak color and value. In some cases maximum separation is needed, in others a more gradual change is desirable. For example, in Fig. 20.20 the stronger colors are used at the bottom of the bars and the weaker colors at the top. This is done not only for the sake of stability of the bars, but because, if adjacent areas of the bars are made as high-contrast areas, the bars become "spotty" in appearance and the value of a continuous bar is lost.

Adjacent lines. The best separation of lines occurs when adjacent lines are contrasty, either in color or value, or both. Note the use of alternate brown and red lines in Fig. 20.22 and the contrasting white line at the top.

Choice of Colors. The actual choice of colors is almost entirely one of artistic judgment, but this is often tempered by other factors. Colors at the high (wavelength) end of the spectrum are known as "cold" colors. Colors at the low end of the spectrum are known as "warm" colors. The colors of nature are the blue of the sky; the greens of trees, grass, and shrubbery; and the browns of tree trunks, soil, and rock. Note that these colors comprise a cold color, a medium color, and a warm color. However, even though we view the colors of nature daily and are not disturbed by them, such colors are not commonly put together in

FIG. 20.21. A series of pie charts in color. Readability and appeal is superior to single-color rendition.

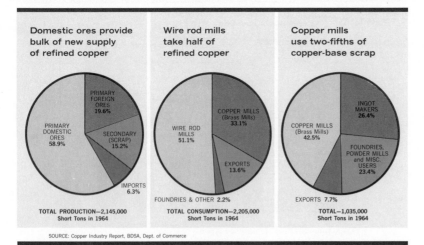

Domestic ores provide bulk of new supply of refined copper

PRIMARY FOREIGN ORES 19.6%
PRIMARY DOMESTIC ORES 58.9%
SECONDARY (SCRAP) 15.2%
IMPORTS 6.3%
TOTAL PRODUCTION—2,145,000 Short Tons in 1964

Wire rod mills take half of refined copper

COPPER MILLS (Brass Mills) 33.1%
WIRE ROD MILLS 51.1%
EXPORTS 13.6%
FOUNDRIES & OTHER 2.2%
TOTAL CONSUMPTION—2,205,000 Short Tons in 1964

Copper mills use two-fifths of copper-base scrap

INGOT MAKERS 26.4%
COPPER MILLS (Brass Mills) 42.5%
FOUNDRIES, POWDER MILLS and MISC. USERS 23.4%
EXPORTS 7.7%
TOTAL—1,035,000 Short Tons in 1964

SOURCE: Copper Industry Report, BDSA, Dept. of Commerce

a chart. Also, strange as it may seem to the layman, a study of the colors of the spectrum and other scientific aspects of color transmission and reflectance will be of little help in the choice of colors to be used for a chart, graph, or diagram. This is because the *only* important considerations are those of pleasing and visually effective combinations, contrasts, and color values. Colors that are not pleasingly compatible should not be used together unless a startling or garish effect is wanted. For example, violet, purple, and yellow are almost never used for charts. The colors used most are blues, greens, reds, browns, white, and black. The symbolic colors of a company or organization may also play a part in the choice, as for example, the blue and white of the Pure Oil Company or the red, white, and blue of The Standard Oil Company. Of interest is the fact that blue has predominated recently in the annual reports of many large companies. In addition, many of the charts and graphs in such magazines as *Scientific American* have been printed in black, shades of black (gray), red, blue, and green with occasionally some yellow, but black, gray, and red are predominant.

The best practice is to lay out the chart and then try several colors by holding colored sheets or strips over the chart to judge finally the most pleasing and effective combination.

20.30.   COLOR FOR PRIMARY CHARTS.   By the term "primary charts" is meant the chart that is made by hand for use directly. This excludes reproduction. Color may be applied in the form of colored inks, water color, or tempera. All of these may be used in a ruling pen for making lines or applied with a brush for

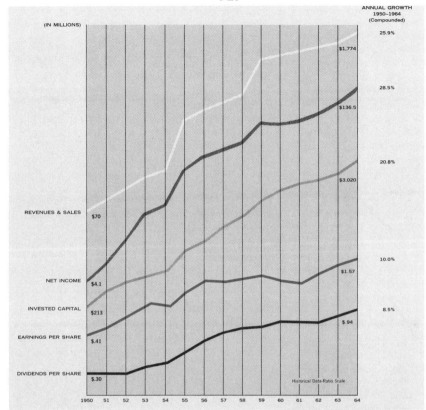

areas. Chart-Pak (Chart-Pak Inc., River Road, Leeds, Mass.) colored acetate fiber strip, available in many colors and widths, is a convenient method of coloring for line graphs and bar charts. Colored paper can be used for backgrounds, with the chart drawn *on* the colored paper.

20.31.   COLOR FOR REPRODUCED CHARTS. When the chart is made exclusively for reproduction, the basic chart is outlined and drawn in india ink as would be done for a black-and-white chart, with the exception that areas are not blacked-in. Then, an overlay sheet of tracing paper or drafting film such as Mylar is placed over the chart and fastened with drafting (or transparent) tape. On this overlay sheet directions are lettered or writ-

FIG. 20.22.   A graph in color. Note that one more colored line is produced by employing a tinted background with the white line on it.

ten, designating the colors to be used for lines and areas. The engraver, following these directions, will then make plates for the printing of each color. In giving the directions for color and color value, either an approximate value must be given, such as *light blue,* or an exact value must be designated, such as 30% blue.

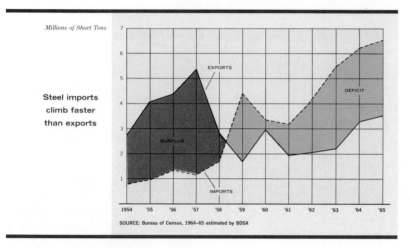

Steel imports climb faster than exports

FIG. 20.23. A strata chart in color. Note that the overlap of colored strata produces readability for the *surplus* area and the separation of strata emphasizes the *deficit* area.

PROBLEMS

These problems are given for practice in preparing various types of charts, graphs, and diagrams for technical or popular presentation.

20.1.1. The data given below were obtained in a tension test of a machine-steel bar. Plot the data on rectangular coordinates, using the elongation as the independent variable, the applied load as the dependent variable.

Applied load, lb per sq in.	Elongation per in. of length
0	0
3,000	0.00011
5,000	0.00018
10,000	0.00033
15,000	0.00051
20,000	0.00067
25,000	0.00083
30,000	0.00099
35,000	0.00115
40,000	0.00134
42,000	0.00142

20.1.2. A test of the corrosive effect of 5 per cent sulfuric acid, both air-free and air-saturated, on 70 per cent nickel, 30 per cent copper alloy (Monel) over a temperature range from 20 to 120°C resulted in the data tabulated below. Plot this data on rectangular coordinates with corrosion rate as ordinate versus temperature as abscissa.

Temp., °C	Corrosion rate, MDD (mg per sq dm per day)	
	Acid sat. with air	Acid air-free, sat. with N_2
20	195	35
30	240	45
40	315	50
50	425	63
60	565	70
70	670	74
80	725	72
83	715	70
85	700	68
92	580	57
95	470	42
101	60	12

20.1.3. In testing a small 1-kw transformer for efficiency at various loads, the following data were obtained: Watts delivered: 948, 728, 458, 252, 000. Losses: 73, 62, 53, 49, 47.

Plot curves on rectangular coordinate paper showing the relation between percentage of load and efficiency, using watts delivered as the independent variable and remembering that efficiency = output ÷ (output + losses).

20.1.4. The following data were obtained from a test of an automobile engine:

Rpm	Length of run, min	Fuel per run, lb	Bhp
1,006	11.08	1.0	5.5
1,001	4.25	0.5	8.5
997	7.53	1.0	13.0
1,000	5.77	1.0	16.3
1,002	2.38	0.5	21.1

Plot curves on rectangular coordinate paper, showing the relation between fuel used per brake horsepower-hour and brake horsepower developed. Show also the relation between thermal efficiency and brake horsepower developed, assuming the heat value of the gasoline to be 19,000 Btu per lb.

20.1.5. During a given year the consumption of wood pulp by various grades in the United States was as shown in the table.

Grade of pulp	Consumption in paper and board manufacture, tons
Sulfate	8,380,864
Sulfite	3,331,668
Groundwood	2,483,980
Defibrated, exploded, etc.	971,912
Soda	564,355
All other	754,331
Total (all grades)	16,487,110

Show these facts by means of a 100 per cent bar, a pie diagram, and a multiple-bar chart.

20.1.6. Put the data of Fig. 20.16 into 100 per cent bar form.

20.1.7. Put the data of Fig. 20.14 into pie-chart form.

20.1.8.   A test of the resistance of alloy steels to high-temperature steam resulted in the data tabulated below. Represent the results of the test graphically by means of a multiple-bar chart.

Corrosion of Steel Bars in Contact with Steam at 1100°F for 2,000 Hr

Steel	Average penetration, in.
SAE 1010	0.001700
1.25 Cr-Mo	0.001169
4.6 Cr-Mo	0.000956
9 Cr 1.22 Mo	0.000694
12 Cr	0.000045
18-8-Cb	0.000012

20.1.9.   From the data below, plot curves showing the "thinking distance" and "braking distance." From these curves, plot the sum curve "total distance." Title "Automobile Minimum Travel Distances When Stopping—Average Driver."

Mph	Ft per sec	Thinking distance, ft	Braking distance, ft
20	29	22	18
30	44	33	40
40	59	44	71
50	74	55	111
60	88	66	160
70	103	77	218

20.1.10.   Make a semilogarithmic chart showing the comparative rate of growth of the five largest American cities from 1880 to 1950. Data for this chart are given below:

Population

City	1880	1890	1900	1910
New York, N.Y.	1,911,698	2,507,414	3,437,202	4,766,883
Chicago, Ill.	503,185	1,099,850	1,698,757	2,185,283
Philadelphia, Pa.	847,170	1,046,964	1,293,697	1,549,008
Los Angeles, Calif.	11,181	50,395	102,479	319,198
Detroit, Mich.	116,340	205,876	285,704	465,766

City	1920	1930	1940	1950
New York, N.Y.	5,620,048	6,930,446	7,454,995	7,835,099
Chicago, Ill.	2,701,705	3,376,438	3,396,808	3,606,436
Philadelphia, Pa.	1,823,779	1,950,961	1,931,334	2,064,794
Los Angeles, Calif.	576,673	1,238,048	1,504,277	1,957,692
Detroit, Mich.	993,678	1,568,662	1,623,452	1,838,517

20.1.11.   On polar coordinate paper, plot a curve for the first set of data given below as a solid line (Fig. 20.6) and a curve for the second set as a broken line (Fig. 20.5). The lower end of the vertical center line is to be taken as the zero-degree line. The curves will be symmetrical about this line, two points being plotted for each angle, one to the left and one to the right. Mark the candle power along this center line also.

Angle, °	(1) **Mazda lamp and porcelain enameled reflector,** candle power	(2) **Type S-1 sun lamp,** candle power
0	600	1,000
5	655	925
10	695	790
15	725	640
20	760	460
25	800	350
30	815	260
35	825	205
40	830	170
45	815	150
50	785	130
55	740	120
60	640	0
65	485	—
70	330	—
75	200	—
80	90	—
85	25	—
90	0	—

20.1.12.   On trilinear coordinate paper plot the data given below. Complete the chart, identifying the curves and lettering the title below the coordinate lines (Fig. 20.7).

Freezing Points of Solutions of Glycerol and Methanol in Water

Weight, per cent			Freezing points, °F
Water	Methanol	Glycerol	
86	14	0	+14
82	8	10	+14
78	6	16	+14
76	24		− 4
74	2	24	+14

Freezing Points of Solutions of Glycerol and Methanol in Water (Cont.)

Weight, per cent			Freezing points, °F
Water	Methanol	Glycerol	
71	17	12	− 4
70	0	30	+14
68	32	0	−22
65	10	25	− 4
62	23	15	−22
60	40	0	−40
58	5	37	− 4
57	17	26	−22
55	0	45	− 4
54	28	18	−40
53	47	0	−58
52	10	38	−22
50	20	30	−40
47	31	22	−58
45	0	55	−22
42	7	51	−40
39	12	49	−58
37	0	63	−40
36	8	56	−58
33	0	67	−58

20.1.13. Thermal conductivities of a bonded-asbestos-fiber insulating material at various mean temperatures are tabulated below:

Mean temperature (hot to cold surface) T, °F	Thermal conductivity K, Btu per hr-sq ft-°F temp diff-in. thickness
100	0.365
200	0.415
320	0.470
400	0.520
460	0.563
600	0.628
730	0.688
900	0.780

Plotting the data on uniform rectangular coordinates with thermal conductivity as ordinate and mean temperature as abscissa, evaluate the constants a and b in the linear equation $K = a + bT$ relating the variables.

20.1.14. Corrosion tests on specimens of pure magnesium resulted in values for weight increase in pure oxygen at 525°C tabulated in the next column:

Elapsed time T, hr	Weight increase W, mg per sq cm	Elapsed time T, hr	Weight increase W, mg per sq cm
0	0	11.5	1.00
2.0	0.17	20.0	1.68
4.0	0.36	24.1	2.09
8.2	0.65	30.0	2.57

Plotting the data on uniform rectangular coordinates with weight increase as ordinate and elapsed time as abscissa, evaluate the constant a in the linear equation $W = aT$ relating the variables.

20.1.15. Approximate rates of discharge of water under various heads of fall through a 1,000-ft length of 4-in. pipe having an average number of bends and fittings are tabulated below:

Head of fall H, ft	Discharge Q, gal per min	Head of fall H, ft	Discharge Q, gal per min
1	35.8	20	159.7
2	50.6	25	178.9
4	71.6	30	195.8
6	87.7	40	225.8
9	107.5	50	252.2
12	123.7	75	309.8
16	142.9	100	357.9

Plotting the data on logarithmic coordinates with discharge as ordinate and head as abscissa, evaluate the constants a and b in the power equation $Q = aH^b$ relating the variables.

20.1.16. Creep-strength tests of a high-chromium (23 to 27 per cent) ferritic steel used in high-temperature service resulted in the stress values, to produce a 1 per cent deformation in 10,000 hr at various temperatures, tabulated in the right margin:

Plotting the data on semilogarithmic coordinates with stress as ordinate on a logarithmic scale and temperature as abscissa on a uniform scale, evaluate the constants a and b in the exponential equation $S = a10^{bT}$ relating the variables.

Temperature T, °F	Stress S, lb per sq in.
1,000	6,450
1,100	2,700
1,200	1,250
1,300	570
1,400	270

20.1.17. COLORED CHARTS. Select any of Probs. 20.1.1 to 20.1.16, and draw in color, following the suggestions given in paragraph 20.30.

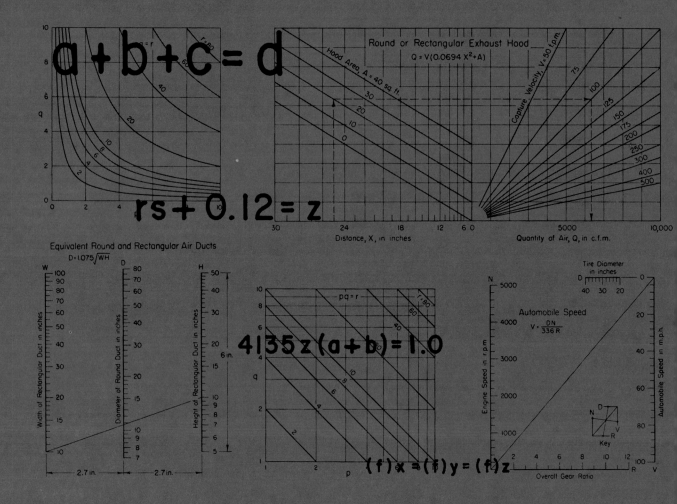

$a+b+c=d$

$rs+0.12=z$

$4|35z(a+b)=1.0$

$(f)x=(f)y=(f)z$

Round or Rectangular Exhaust Hood
$Q = V(0.0694 X^2 + A)$

Distance, X, in inches

Quantity of Air, Q, in c.f.m.

Equivalent Round and Rectangular Air Ducts
$D = 1.075\sqrt{WH}$

Width of Rectangular Duct in inches

Diameter of Round Duct in inches

Height of Rectangular Duct in inches

2.7 in.

2.7 in.

$pq = r$

Tire Diameter in inches

Automobile Speed
$V = \dfrac{DN}{336R}$

Engine Speed in r.p.m.

Automobile Speed in m.p.h.

Key

Overall Gear Ratio

Graphic
Solutions
of
Equations

21

21.1. In engineering, calculations are constantly being made for research, design, and production. Most of these calculations involve an algebraic equation; a smaller number concern empirical data for which an equation may not exist. The majority of these calculations are made by mathematical methods, but if they involve (*a*) repetitive solutions of an algebraic equation, (*b*) usage by nontechnical personnel, or (*c*) solutions by trial and error, graphic methods will often reduce calculation time, minimize errors, and provide a visual conception of the relationship of the factors involved. Even if the actual calculations are performed by a computing device, a graphic solution will provide a rapid and reasonably accurate method of checking the resulting data, and empirical data can often be processed by graphic methods in a fraction of the time required to obtain a mathematical solution.

First, the graphic methods appropriate to the solution of various types of problems will be discussed. Then, the actual construction of the graphic solutions will be given. Since several forms of a graphic solution usually may be used to solve any given problem, the problems will be catalogued by their mathematical components and suitable solution methods. Problems can be broadly classed as those having an algebraic equation or those utilizing empirical data and can be further subdivided according

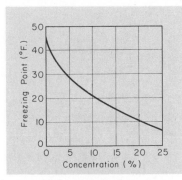

FIG. 21.1. A typical *x-y* plot on cartesian coordinates.

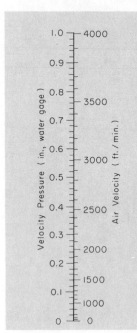

FIG. 21.2. A conversion chart.

to the number of variables involved. The graphic solutions suggested are not the only ones possible for each problem but are considered to be the simplest and most commonly used.

21.2. TWO-VARIABLE EQUATION GIVEN.

A common equation for this problem is represented as $f(y) = f(x)$. Its simplest graphic solution is the familiar *x-y* plot (Fig. 21.1), and should not be underestimated. A carefully drawn plot provides all the values of x and y which solve the equation, and also the slope of the curve gives an estimate of the rate of change of the variables. Often this qualitative information can be as valuable as the actual values of the variables. The *x-y* plot can be made on various coordinate systems, and the principles of Chaps. 20 and 22 are helpful in choosing the correct system to use. The x-y plot is recommended for transmitting information among persons of technical training because not even the equation reveals as much information, except after careful study.

If the sole purpose of the graphic solution is to provide values of x and y which satisfy the equation or if non-technical personnel are likely to be involved, a conversion chart provides a better method of presentation. This chart (Fig. 21.2) consists of two parallel scales so graduated that matching values of x and y are adjacent to each other. (For this discussion, *matching values* are those values of the variables which provide a distinct solution of the equation.) The conversion chart inherently contains little chance for error since no lines are drawn to connect matching values of x and y, as is necessary with the *x-y* plot. However, because all matching values of x and y are *adjacent*, the conversion

chart is ideally suited to problem solutions by trial and error. Conversion charts can be constructed from the equation or directly from an *x-y* plot, but the direct method is recommended only if an accurate *x-y* plot is available or will be needed for other purposes.

21.3. THREE-VARIABLE EQUATION GIVEN.

Two basic forms of such an equation are $f(p) + f(q) = f(r)$ and $f(p) f(q) = f(r)$. An *x-y* plot (Fig. 21.3) for this type of equation will reveal that a separate curve exists for each value of the variable chosen as the parameter.[1] Unless the curves can be rectified to straight lines, the labor of drawing enough curves to provide an accurate representation of the problem becomes too great for practical purposes. If the equation is $p + q = r$ or $pq = r$, the *x-y* plot becomes quite simple as these curves rectify easily to straight lines on rectangular coordinates. This kind of *x-y* plot is often called a *network chart* (see Figs. 21.4 to 21.7). The accuracy of a network chart is primarily determined by the degree of subdivision of the original coordinate system. With

---

[1] The term "parameter" is here used in the graphic sense that a parameter is a *line* of constant value representing the locus of a mathematical constant.

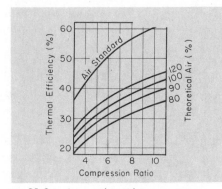

FIG. 21.3. An *x-y* plot with parameters.

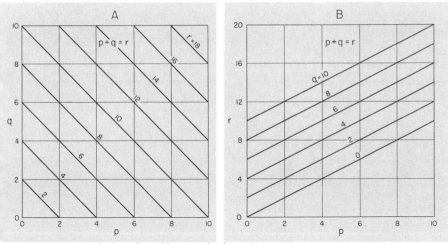

FIG. 21.4.   Network chart for addition and subtraction.

the straight-line curves it is a simple matter to draw additional parameter lines as they are needed. Thus interpolation is not a serious difficulty.

An equation stating the relationship of three variables can be represented on rectangular coordinates as a *family* of straight or curved lines. Two of the variables plot as coordinates along the axes, and the third as parameters. When the function is either addition or subtraction, the family of lines (parameters) are straight and parallel to each other, which is demonstrated by plotting an equation such as $p + q = r$, as shown in Fig. 21.4A. If one of the variables (p) is plotted on the x axis and the other (q) on the y axis, the sum of the two is represented by a series of parameters (r). To make the plot, take arbitrary values of p and q and plot the parameter r for these values. Thus $p = 4$ and $q = 6$ locate $r = 10$ at the intersection of coordinates. Also, $p = 8$ and $q = 2$ give $r = 10$, another point on the parameter $r = 10$. A third point for $r = 10$ shows that the parameter is a straight line. Now the parameter $r = 10$ connects $p = 10$ on the x axis with $q = 10$ on the

y axis. Therefore, all parameters pass through their own value on x and y axes and can be drawn in without further plotting of points. To prove this fact, note that the intercepts on the x axis of the parameters are all for $q = 0$ and on the y axis for $p = 0$.

The same chart can be used for subtraction by simply rewriting the equation $p + q = r$ in the form $p = r - q$ or $q = r - p$. For subtraction, then, one coordinate and the parameters are used as the two variables for which the sum is wanted. For $r - q = p$, the sum is read on the x axis.

A chart such as Fig. 21.4B employs the parameters for one of the variables for which the sum, with another variable, is wanted. In this case, for $p + q = r$, values of p are plotted on the x axis, values of q are the parameters, and the sum r is plotted on the y axis. Again, as in Fig. 21.4A, two or three random values of p and q (or p and r, solving for q) can be selected and points on the parameter plotted. Then since the parameter passes through its own value on the y axis, all parameters can be drawn in and their values marked.

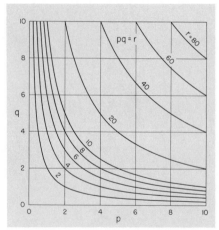

FIG. 21.5. Network chart for multiplication on rectilinear coordinates.

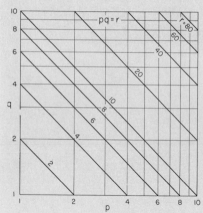

FIG. 21.6. Network chart for multiplication on logarithmic coordinates.

To use Fig. 21.4B for subtraction, the equation is rewritten to $r - q = p$. Then the coordinate line for a value of r, intersecting the parameter line for a value of q, locates the coordinate line on which the sum p is read.

The multiplication of two variables to obtain a third, $pq = r$, when plotted on uniform rectangular coordinates with the product r as parameter, results in a series of hyperbolic curves, as shown in Fig. 21.5. The asymptotes of the hyperbolas are the x and y axes. This is, of course, a usable chart for $pq = r$, but the plotting of the hyperbolas is laborious —and not nearly so accurate as the plotting of straight-line parameters. If, however, the equation is written in logarithmic form, $\log p + \log q = \log r$, the equation becomes one of addition, and straight-line parameters are obtained. Values of p and q can be plotted either as values of $\log p$ and $\log q$ on rectilinear coordinates or as values of p and q on logarithmic coordinates, as in Fig. 21.6. Note that the spacing of the parameters in Fig. 21.6 is also logarithmic.

Another method of multiplying two variables is shown in Fig. 21.7A. If one of the variables, in this case, q, is plotted as a series of parameters on uniform rectangular coordinates, the product is then one of the coordinate values and the parameters are straight lines. The construction of the chart is indicated by a study of Fig. 21.7A.

The concurrent straight lines of Fig. 21.7A, representing the equation $pq = r$, can be plotted on oblique coordinates as shown in Fig. 21.7B. In this case, the coordinates of p are the oblique lines, q is represented as parameters, and the coordinates of r are rectangular. It is also possible to make both coordinates of p and r oblique, although there is little reason for doing so.

Division of variables can be accomplished by rewriting the equation and employing the chart accordingly. In Fig. 21.7A, if the equation $pq = r$ is rewritten to $q = r/p$, then values of r and p on the chart intersect to locate the quotient q.

A better general method for the solution of three-variable equations is by

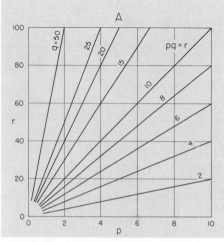

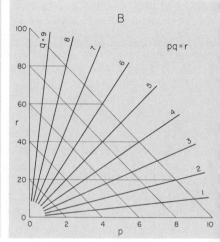

FIG. 21.7. Network charts for multiplication using parameters on (*A*) cartesian coordinates and (*B*) oblique coordinates.

means of an alignment chart or nomograph. The *nomograph* consists of three functional scales, each graduated in terms of one of the variables, which are arranged so that matching values of p, q, and r lie on a straight line connecting the scales (Fig. 21.8). Although the scales may be curved or straight and can be arranged in various patterns, the simplest nomograph consists of three parallel straight scales. If this nomograph has scales graduated with equal distances between divisions, it will solve the equation $f(p) \pm f(q) = f(r)$. The graduations and positions of the scales are controlled by formulas related to the equation being solved. If this same form of nomograph has the scales graduated to conform to a logarithmic pattern like a standard slide-rule scale, the chart will solve the equation $f(p) f(q) = f(r)$. To avoid the difficulty of graduating all scales to logarithmic form, a nomograph shaped like a capital letter N or Z (Fig. 21.9) and having one or two of its scales uniformly divided is often used. The N or Z chart (Fig. 21.9) is preferable when the calculations normally occur for large values of the variables, the three-parallel logarithmic-scale form better when the calculations most often made are for small values of the variables.

The nomograph offers several distinct advantages over other methods of problem solution. Most important is the ability to visually check the solution to a problem. Obviously, the only chance for error is to misread the values where the "matching-point line" or tie line intersects the scales. For trial and error solutions or repetitive solutions, the nomograph is rapid and easy to use.

Nomographs can be developed from mathematical formulas related to the equation to be solved or can be obtained by graphic manipulation of an $x - y$ plot of the equation. If the equation is given (or can be obtained), it is usually simpler to develop a nomograph by formula. Use of the x-y plot is best limited to empirical data for which no equation can be easily obtained.

If only a few selected values of a third variable are to be used in calculations, a form of nomograph known as a *pivot-point* nomograph (Fig. 21.10) is sometimes used. The general rules for three-scale nomographs are followed, but instead of the complete scale, only the needed values of the third variable are shown by small crosses.

21.4. FOUR-OR-MORE-VARIABLE EQUATION GIVEN.

A basic rule of most graphic solutions is that variables may be combined only in groups of three. Four-or-more-variable equations must be rewritten so that no more than three variables are used at any one time. In most cases arbitrary variables which are common to two parts of the rewritten equation must be used. It is necessary to rewrite the equation $f(p) + f(q) + f(r) = f(s)$ as two simultaneous equations each containing three variables. Thus $f(p) + f(q) = K$ could be one equation, and the second equation would

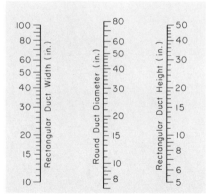
FIG. 21.8. A parallel-scale nomograph.

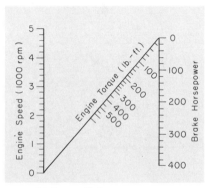
FIG. 21.9. A Z chart.

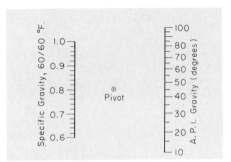
FIG. 21.10. A pivot-point nomograph or conversion chart.

then be $K + f(r) = f(s)$. The nomograph to solve the original equation consists then of two standard three-scale nomographs, each to solve one of the derived equations. Since one scale is common to both nomographs, a total of five scales is used. Normally the arbitrary scale (Fig. 21.11) is not graduated but is used as a pivot scale for tie lines connecting the first two variables and the second pair of variables. The diagram below will assist in clarifying the method and indicating how additional variables may be handled. The diagram is actually for a five-variable equation as answer 3 is variable 5.

```
Variable 1 . . .
                  :  . . Answer  1  . . .
Variable 2 . . :                       :  . . Answer  2  . . .
Variable 3 . . . . . . . . . . . . :                       :  . . Answer  3
Variable 4 . . . . . . . . . . . . :                                    :
```

Network charts may be used to solve equations of four or more variables if the variables have simple functions. As with the nomograph, a common pivot scale is used to join two parts of the problem. This common scale may or may not be graduated, but if it is, the graduations are identical for both problem parts which it joins.

21.5. SPECIAL SLIDE RULES. Most problems which can be solved by means of a nomograph can also be solved by a slide rule (Fig. 21.12) using scales especially developed for the purpose. Problems having more than four variables will require two or more sliding members in the slide rule. Problems involving addition and multiplication require "slip gauge" scales as the common scale between the addition and multiplication parts of the slide rule. The slide rule is the easiest to use and read of all graphic solutions for equations of three or more variables, but the problem of constructing the physical components precludes its use unless ease of reading is the major consideration. Thorough knowledge of the principles of slide rule design will assist in determining the problems for which a slide rule is justified.

21.6. SPECIAL GRAPHIC SOLUTIONS. The discussion to this point has indicated methods of representing algebraic equations of various forms, but in each case only one equation was involved. Two specialized, but extremely simple, graphic solutions are available for manipulation of two equations. Although limited to two-variable equations, any number of equations could be combined two at a time by these methods.

21.7. SIMULTANEOUS EQUATIONS. Any single equation relating two variables will be satisfied by an indefinite number of pairs of the variables. If two equations relating the same two variables are known, there will be a definite number of pairs of the variables that will satisfy

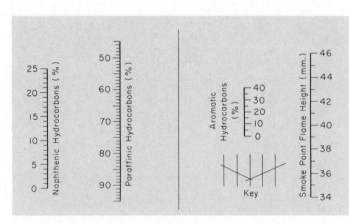

FIG. 21.11. A four-variable parallel-scale nomograph.

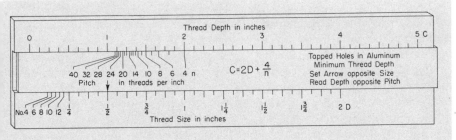

FIG. 21.12.   A special slide rule.

both equations. The number of solutions will depend upon the form of the equations and whether or not negative values are considered.

The solution of simultaneous equations can be, and often is, done algebraically, but in cases where the data are empirical (and no mathematical equation can be written), the algebra fails completely. Also, in many cases where the equations are complicated—especially when they are in cubical, logarithmic, or power form—the algebraic solution may be very complicated and time-consuming. For these reasons and because of the advantage of having a graphic record of the relationship, it may be desirable to solve the problem graphically. Figure 21.13 shows the solution of a pair of simultaneous equations by graphic means. Each equation is plotted separately as shown. The point (or points) where the curves intersect is a point(s) common to the locus of both equations and has coordinates of x and y values that satisfy both equations. The values of x and y obtained by this method may not perfectly satisfy the equations but are usually accurate enough for practical purposes.

21.8.   ADDITION AND SUBTRACTION OF FUNCTIONS.   It is often necessary to add (or subtract) two or more functions of a variable quantity. For example, in deter-

mining the total cost of a product, the costs of raw materials, labor, tooling, factory overhead, etc., all combine to make up the total. Some of the costs may be constant for the number of pieces produced; others may be variable. The total-cost curve or equation will be the sum of all the other curves or functions. Figure 21.14 shows the plots of two individual functions, $y_1 = 20 - 0.24x$ and $y_2 = 10 + 0.01x^2$. The addition of these two functions algebraically produces a third function, $y_3 = 30 - 0.24x + 0.01x^2$. The curve of this function may be obtained graphically by adding the ordinate height of the lower curve to the ordinate height of the upper curve at a number of selected x values. This method is limited to rectilinear coordinates. If the functions are plotted on logarithmic coordinates, addition of the ordinate heights will produce multiplication of the functions. Further study of the principles governing special slide rules (paragraph 21.15) will aid in providing an explanation of this.

For purposes of analysis, graphic addition of functions (on uniform rectilinear coordinates, as described) has a distinct advantage over mathematical calculations: the true representation of all the relationships is shown.

21.9.   FUNCTIONAL SCALES.   The scale is a fundamental element of the graphic

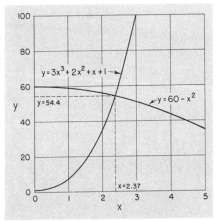

FIG. 21.13.   Solution of simultaneous equations.

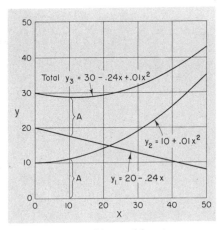

FIG. 21.14.   Addition of functions.

language. In previous chapters, the types and uses of standard drafting scales have been given, and their employment in problems of orthographic projection drawing, pictorial drawing, dimensioning and working drawings, engineering geometry, vector geometry, and for charts, graphs, and diagrams has been discussed. In fact, engineers, architects, and others use graphic scales repeatedly and extensively in the layout of drawings and in the measurement of the distances resulting from graphic constructions. But the full importance of functional graphic scales is realized only when their many other uses are known.

The scale is one of the most common objects of modern civilization. Any normal home has scales on its furnace thermostat, air conditioner thermostat, water heater, radio, television, and oven. The list seems endless; yet the number of devices bearing scales in a home is as nothing compared to the number of machines and instruments utilizing scales to be found in any modern factory. With the exception of scales used for direct measurement of length, such as the yardstick, carpenter's rule, and draftsman's scale, all scales have certain common characteristics. They do not measure temperature, speed, or radio frequency *directly* but, instead, measure linear and angular displacement. The thermometer scale indicates the expansion of a liquid, change of electrical resistance of a thermocouple, or differing rates of expansion of a bimetal strip subjected to temperature changes.

Careful analysis will show that all scales measure displacement, but *indicate the value of the variable causing that displacement.* The liquid-column thermometer indicates by the length of its liquid column the temperature causing that amount of expansion of the liquid reservoir. All functional scales will be found to follow the same principle. The scale measures the displacement of an indicating device; the numerical value of the occurrence which caused the displacement is marked on the scale at that point; the displacement of the scale is related to the measured occurrence by an equation or function. Mastery of this principle is absolutely essential in the construction of functional scales used in graphic solutions.

21.10.   DEFINITION.   A *scale* is a line or stem along which small marks or *graduations* appear at intervals. Numbers or *calibrations* appear at certain of the graduations, and the stem may be curved or straight. A *functional scale* is a scale on which the distance between calibrations is proportional to the difference of *values of the scale function* at each of the calibrations. In mathematical terms, a number or calibration x will appear at a distance $f(x)$ along the scale stem. An equation $L_x = f(x)$ is said to be the equation of the scale calibrations. The distance L is in arbitrary units. Since $L = 0$ when $f(x) = 0$, this point is defined as the *origin* of the scale, and all measurements and calculations start at this point. Distances measured along the scale in a certain direction from the origin are positive in direction; distances measured along the scale in the opposite direction are negative. The positive and negative directions are determined by the sign of the function, and normally, positive scale directions are measured to the right or upward.

21.11.   CLASSIFICATION.   Scales are classified as uniform or nonuniform, according to the characteristics of the function of the scale. Classification of the scales is often necessary to make an intelligent choice of the constants to be used in computation of the scale graduations.

A *uniform scale* (Fig. 21.15A and B) represents a linear function and therefore has evenly spaced graduations. The distances between calibrations, having equal increments, are also equal. The distance from the origin to any calibration is proportional to both the numerical value of the calibration and the value of the function at that point. Uniform scales will result from equations such as $L = 4.5x$ and $L = 7x + 5.7$.

A *nonuniform* scale (Fig. 21.16 A, B, C, and D) represents a nonlinear function and therefore has graduations which are unevenly spaced. The distances between calibrations, having *equal* increments, are also *unequal*. Because of the uneven distances between calibrations, the increments of the calibrations will often have to be changed. A standard slide rule will give evidence of this fact. The distance from the origin to any calibration is proportional to the value of the function of the variable at that point and is *not* proportional to the numerical value of the calibration. Nonuniform scales result from equations such as $L = x^2$, $L = 1/x$, $L = \log x$.

21.12.   THE SCALE EQUATION.   The definition of a functional scale includes a simple equation relating the calibrations to the distances along the scale stem. This equation, $L = f(x)$, is inconvenient to use since L is in arbitrary units and is always equal to $f(x)$. To permit the use of definite length units and to permit flexibility in determining total scale lengths, a proportionality factor m is introduced. The scale equation to be

used for all calculations and locations of graduations on the scale stem is therefore written

$$d = m\,f(x)$$

where d is the distance from the origin to the calibration having the numerical value of x.

The distance d is commonly measured in either inches or centimeters, from the origin of the scale where $f(x) = 0$ and along the stem of the scale. All graduations of the scale can be located by this equation, but, usually, only selected *major* graduations are located by calculation.

The proportionality factor m is termed the "modulus" of the scale. The *modulus* is a simple numerical constant introduced into the scale equation to provide suitable distances for the desired total scale length.

The term "range" is commonly used to indicate the difference of function values at the maximum and minimum

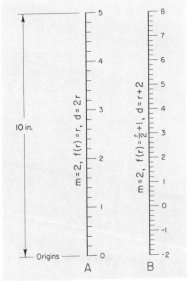

FIG. 21.15.   Uniform functional scales.

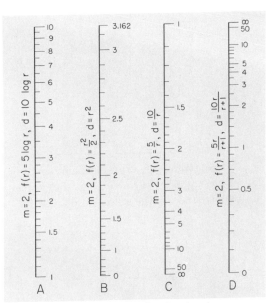

FIG. 21.16.   Nonuniform functional scales.

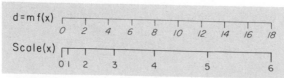

FIG. 21.17. A scale for $f(x) = x^2$.

scale values. Since many scales will not start at the origin, it is necessary to determine the scale length by means of the relationship

$$d_2 - d_1 = m[f(x_2) - f(x_1)]$$

This equation is often abbreviated as $L = mR$, where L is the length of the scale, m is the modulus, and R is the range of the function.

An example (Fig. 21.17) will aid in clarifying these relationships. The calculations necessary to develop a graphic scale will prove most useful if a definite format is used. If a scale is to be developed for the function x^2, a simple table is used with columns for the three major items to be evaluated—x, $f(x)$, and $d = m f(x)$. For example, if $f(x) = x^2$,

x	$f(x)$	$d = m f(x)$
		Let $m = 0.5$
0	0	0
1	1	0.5
2	4	2.0
3	9	4.5
4	16	8.0
5	25	12.5
6	36	18.0

The values of x are known as the values of the variable (or the scale values) and are the values to be used for calibrations. The values of $f(x)$ represent the distance (in arbitrary units) along the scale, at which the calibrations or scale values (x) will appear. The origin is the point on the scale where $f(x) = 0$ and is the reference point for all measurements. For this example the origin occurs at $x = 0$. The distances (d) are the *measurements in inches* along the scale to each of the calibrations or scale values. The proportionality factor or modulus m was completely arbitrary in this case. For later calculations it will be chosen with some thought to the end result. The function range for the scale values chosen is $36 - 0$ or 36 units. The length of the scale is 18 in. If the requirement had been that x was to have a minimum value of 4 and a maximum value of 10 (Fig. 21.18), the table of calculations could have included one additional column to calculate the position of the scale calibrations from the first scale number.

x	$f(x)$	$d = m f(x)$	$d' = d - 8$
4	16	8.0	0
6	36	18.0	10.0
8	64	32.0	24.0
10	100	50.0	42.0

The fourth column provides a convenient measuring point when the origin does not lie within the limits of the scale as chosen. The function range of this scale is $100 - 16 = 84$ units, and its length is 42 in. The simple equation $L = mR$ would have given the same results since $42 = 0.5 \times 84$.

Obviously some compromise is desirable here since a scale 42 in. long is too large for most purposes. Since the function range will remain 84 units for the scale values chosen, the modulus is chosen to provide a suitable scale length. A modulus of 0.2 would give a scale

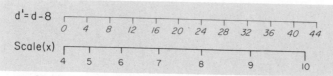

FIG. 21.18. A scale for $f(x) = x^2$.

length of 16.8 in., and 0.1 would give 8.4 in. The function range should always be determined *before* choosing a modulus so that a suitable scale length can be obtained.

A simple uniform scale (Fig. 21.19) for the equation $f(x) = x - 6$ can be used to illustrate positive and negative directions of scale measurements. The calculation form for the scale range of 0 to 10 is

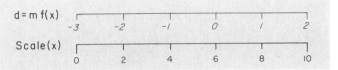

FIG. 21.19. A scale for $f(x) = x - 6$.

x	$f(x)$	$d = mf(x)$ Let $m = 0.5$
0	−6	−3
2	−4	−2
4	−2	−1
6	0	0
8	2	1
10	4	2

The origin of this scale is at $x = 6$. Measurements for the values of x are made from this point in both directions along the scale. If the numbers greater than 6 are measured to the right of the origin, the numbers less than 6 are measured to the left. The negative direction is due to the function values' becoming negative and has no direct relationship to the values of the variable x. If the equation had been $f(x) = x + 6$, the function values would have remained positive until x was less than −6. The origin of this scale is at $x = -6$ (where $f(x) = 0$).

The location of the origin of a scale and the concept of the positive and negative directions are most important for the proper orientation of the scales of conversion charts and nomographs.

21.13. TO GRADUATE AND CALIBRATE A SCALE. The steps in construction of a scale are the same whether the scale is

single or is to be combined with other scales.

1. Determine the scale equation.
2. Determine the scale range.
3. Determine either the scale length or the modulus.
4. Calculate the desired calibrations or graduations.
5. Construct the skeleton scale with stem and graduations.
6. Label the scale calibrations and legends.

The steps for construction of a scale are the same whether the scale is uniform or nonuniform, but the amount of calculation is usually considerably less for the uniform scale. Experience will teach shortcuts for many of the construction steps.

Assume that a scale (Fig. 21.20) is to be constructed to represent the equation $f(x) = 2/x + 1$. This equation is non-linear and therefore will produce a nonuniform scale. All major calibrations must be calculated for this scale. The scale range must next be chosen. Assume x to vary from 0.2 to 20.

$f(x) = 2/x + 1$	x	$f(x)$
	0.2	11
	20	1.1

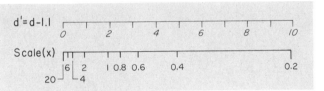

FIG. 21.20. A scale for $f(x) = 2/x + 1$.

The function range can be easily determined as $11 - 1.1 = 9.9$ units, and the modulus of the scale length must then be chosen. Although any value can be chosen for either of these items, a little thought given to a good compromise value will often simplify calculations. If we assume that the scale is to be 8 in. in length, the simple equation for scale length ($L = mR$) reveals that the modulus will be 80/99 or 0.888. . . . Since this modulus must be used for all calculations concerning the scale, it is a poor choice mathematically. Choosing m as 0.9 will not change the scale length significantly and will simplify the calculations considerably. But choice of m as 1.0 will further simplify the calculations. This choice will produce a scale length of 9.9 in. No rules can be given since each scale must meet different requirements, but careful choice of the modulus is emphasized for proper problem solution. For simplicity assume m to be 1 in this case.

Theoretically, the position of all graduations must be calculated. For practical purposes, however, it is usually adequate to calculate major calibrations and obtain all other graduations by proportion. A scale the size of the example should have 10 to 15 calculated graduations. The calculations for the equation $f(x) = 2/x + 1$ are:

x	$f(x)$	$d = m f(x)$ $m = 1$	$d' = d - 1.1$
0.2	11	11	9.9
0.4	6	6	4.9
0.6	4.3	4.3	3.2
0.8	3.5	3.5	2.4
1.0	3	3	1.9
2	2	2	0.9
4	1.5	1.5	0.4
6	1.3	1.3	0.2
8	1.25	1.25	0.15
10	1.2	1.2	0.1
20	1.1	1.1	0

The calculation table reveals a fact that is often ignored. The scale values from 0.2 to 0.4 cover only about 2 per cent of the scale range but represent more than half the scale length. If this region of the scale is to be even reasonably accurate, it must have calculated calibrations or graduations appearing at distance increments of not greater than one-tenth the scale length. Unless the number of readings involving this portion of the scale is substantially greater than 2 per cent of the total, it is advisable to delete the scale range from 0.2 to 0.4 or 0.5. The values most often read should occupy a major part of the scale length. Values which are only occasionally encountered must be omitted from the scale so that the majority of values will be covered more accurately.

The scale (Fig. 21.20) can now be constructed with each calculated graduation accurately located. The examples of Fig. 21.15 and 21.16 give the relative sizes of the calibrations and graduations. If the correct letter height is taken as $\frac{1}{8}$ in., the longest graduation is approximately $\frac{3}{16}$ in. long. The stem of the scale is drawn first; then the origin or first scale graduation is located. All calculated graduations are located from this point. Additional graduations are uniformly spaced between the calculated graduations. Graphic methods are available to graduate the intervening distances more accurately than by the uniform-space method, but the results are seldom worth the effort for short scales. Greater scale accuracy is obtained by calculating the position of more graduations. Calibrations and legends are added to the scale to complete it. Care should be exercised to ensure that the calibration intervals permit easy interpolation. Calibration intervals of 1, 2, 5, or 10 cause the least difficulty.

To illustrate uniform-scale construction, assume the scale to represent the equation $f(x) = 4x - 2$. This is a linear function and is represented by a uniform scale. Usually a uniform scale will require calculations only to determine the function range and the resulting scale length. Assume the scale values to vary from 0 to 10.

$f(x) = 4x - 2$	x	$f(x)$
	0	−2
	10	38

From the calculations the function range is seen to be 40 units. Although the modulus is not needed for this scale, it will be needed if the scale is to be combined with other scales. The construction of this scale requires the balancing of two conditions—length and modulus. The scale is to be divided into 10 equal parts and these parts into similar equal subdivisions. The scale length should be chosen to permit easy graduation into the required number of parts. Thus a 5-in. scale length is ideally suited for this purpose. Each integral value of x is spaced ½ in. from the previous one. The modulus will be used in calculations when the scales are combined in conversion charts and nomographs, so the modulus should not be a value that is difficult to use in calculations. For a scale length of 5 in., the modulus would be ⁵⁄₄₀ or ⅛. Five inches, then, is an easily divided scale length and produces a convenient value of the modulus.

If the scale length had been chosen as 8 in., the modulus would now be ⁸⁄₄₀ or ⅕, a simpler fraction to use. But the scale would now require 10 equal divisions in a length of 8 in., not quite so simple a task as for a length of 5 in. The actual construction of the physical

scale is the same as for a nonuniform scale, and the discussion will not be repeated.

21.14.   GRAPHIC METHODS OF GRADUATING A SCALE. The preceding paragraphs have indicated general methods for graduating a scale, regardless of its equation. Uniform scales representing linear functions are usually graduated by placing the correct number of scale divisions within the required scale length. This can be accomplished directly with the draftsman's scale, using one of the proportional methods of Chap. 2. Figure 21.21*A* illustrates graduation of a scale where the length has been chosen to provide ½-in. lengths for unit intervals of x. Figure 21.21*B* illustrates the familiar proportional method of dividing a distance (in this case, 4.8 in. into six equal parts). A third method of graduating the scale is by means of a scale chart (Fig. 21.21*C*), which is also called a *modulus chart*. A single scale of any convenient length and containing 10 major graduations is first constructed. All graduations of this scale are projected to a single point. Any line drawn parallel to the original scale will intersect these projectors or rays to produce

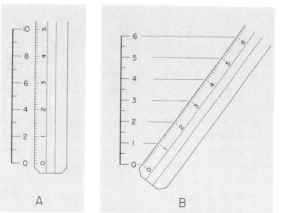

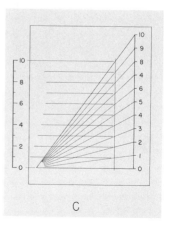

FIG. 21.21.   Graphic graduation of scales.

a scale having the same number of divisions as the original but in a different length. If the original scale in the illustration is 10 in. long, the figure illustrates construction of a scale with a scale range of 0 to 10 and a scale length of 8 in. Scales having ranges greater than 10 can be obtained by "stacking" the necessary scale segments end to end.

Nonuniform scales can also be graduated by this method, but only the logarithmic scale is used often enough to warrant construction of a permanent scale chart. The master scale (Fig. 21.22) is graduated in terms of log x for $x = 1$ to $x = 10$. The resulting graduations

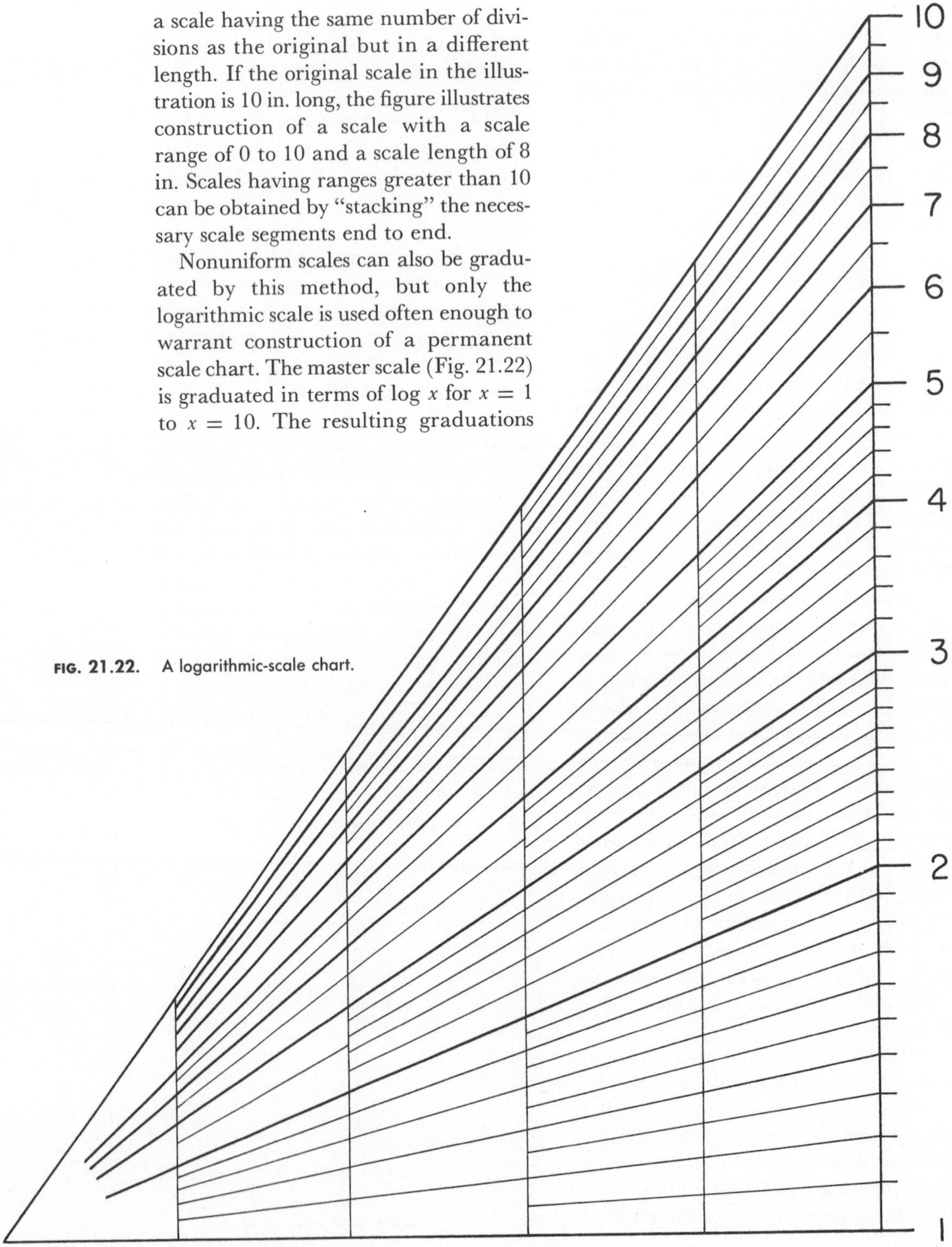

FIG. 21.22. A logarithmic-scale chart.

are projected to the concurrent point to form proportionality rays. Lines drawn parallel to the original scale may be graduated as logarithmic scales of the desired length by the method of Fig. 21.21C. Additional logarithmic cycles may be stacked to produce a scale of the desired range. The use of a scale chart for graduating logarithmic scales reduces the number of calculations for construction to just three items—(a) the length of a log cycle, (b) the number of cycles in the complete scale (or the total scale length), and (c) the modulus.

21.15. CONVERSION CHARTS FOR THE SOLUTION OF EQUALITIES. A *mathematical equality* is an expression in which the function of one variable is equal to the function of another variable. Mathematically, $f(x) = f(y)$. If the equation can be solved for one variable in terms of the other, with all terms containing x on one side of the equation and all terms containing y on the opposite side, the relationship can be represented graphically by scales representing $f(x)$ and $f(y)$ placed on opposite sides of a common scale stem. To illustrate this, take two standard drafting scales, one fractional (sixteenths) and the other decimal (tenths), and place them side by side as in Fig. 21.23. This is the graphic counterpart of the familiar decimal-equivalent table as the two scales provide a convenient method of converting fractional parts of an inch to decimal parts. Although it is possible to write a scale equation for such a conversion chart, the only real difference between the two scales is the number of graduations placed in a given length. Obviously, the major graduations of the scales are in inches.

The basic reason for making a conversion scale can again be illustrated by

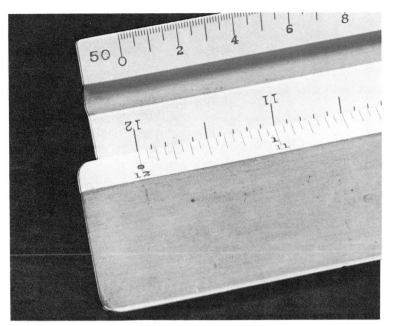

FIG. 21.23. Illustration of equality (conversion scales).

two drafting scales as in the previous example. One scale (Fig. 21.24) can be a standard inch scale and the other a metric scale graduated in centimeters. The scale equation for each scale will be of the form $d_x = m_x f(x)$ and $d_y = m_y f(y)$. Since the basic premise of conversion scales is that they represent $f(x) = f(y)$, certain deductions may be made concerning the scale equations. If matching values of x and y are to be opposite each other on the scales, the distances locating these values must also be equal. If $d_x = d_y$ for all values and $f(x) = f(y)$, it is evident that $m_x = m_y$. Also the distance measurements (d) must be made from a common point or origin. The following two principles

FIG. 21.24. Conversion scales for relating inches and centimeters.

prevail for all conversion charts and should be carefully noted.

1. Conversion chart scales have a common origin.

2. Conversion chart scales have a common modulus.

To apply this information to the construction of a conversion chart such as the one illustrated in Fig. 21.24, the following steps are used.

If a conversion chart is to be made to convert inches to centimeters, the equation of equality is

$$\text{Inches} = \frac{\text{centimeters}}{2.54}$$

Care should be exercised in determining the equality as it is often confused with the statement of conversion. For the example given, the *conversion* statement is that 1 in. equals 2.54 cm. The *equality* is that inches equal the number of centimeters divided by 2.54. Most conversion chart difficulties can be traced to confusion about the equality.

The calculation and construction of the scales proceeds as with any graphic scale:

$$I = \frac{C}{2.54}$$

Let I vary from 0 to 15, and let the scale length be 15 in.

I scale	I	$f(I)$	$d = m f(I)$ Let $m = 1$
$f(I) = I$ Uniform scale	0	0	0
	15	15	15
C scale	C	$f(C)$	$d = m f(C)$ From above $m = 1$
$f(C) = C/2.54$ Uniform scale	0	0	0
	38.1	15	15
	40	15.75	15.75

The calculations for the C scale indicate two items which require careful attention. If the basic equality is correct, then $f(I)_{max} = f(C)_{max}$. The maximum value of $f(I)$ is 15, and the maximum value of $f(C)$ must also be 15. The value of C corresponding to this is 38.1. This is a poor value (because it is a fractional value) to use as the terminal value for the scale. Wherever possible, the scales should be terminated on *whole-number* values to assist in interpolation. Therefore the range of the C scale should be reduced to 38 or increased to 39 or 40. The calculation and resulting scale length for the terminal value of 40 is shown. Only rarely is it possible to have an equal scale length for both sides of a conversion chart, but the initial calculations always assume equal scale functions and lengths.

The steps necessary to the construction of a conversion chart are outlined as follows:

1. Determine the mathematical equality of the chart.

2. Select the scale range for one of the scales.

3. Calculate the function range of this scale. (The simplest method is to partially complete the table of calculations so that the function calculations need not be repeated.)

4. Select the scale length or the modulus. (In either case, the modulus must be obtained.)

5. Prepare a table of calculations for the second scale. Initially use the same function range as for the first scale. Adjust the function range of this second scale to provide a suitable terminal value.

To illustrate the necessary steps, consider the making of a conversion chart for the equation $p = 2q + 4$, as shown in Fig. 21.25. Both sides of this equality are linear and will be represented by uniform scales. Therefore the only calculations will be of scale length and the number of equal divisions within this length.

The scale range of the p scale is to be from 0 to 10, and the scale length is to be 4.5 in.

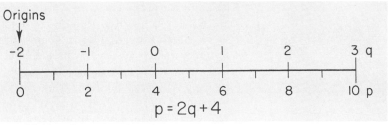

FIG. 21.25.   Conversion chart for $p = 2q + 4$.

p scale	p	$f(p)$	$d = mf(p)$
			$m = 4.5$
$) = p$ iform	0	0	0
	10	10	4.5

q scale	q	$f(q)$	$d = mf(q)$
			From above
			$m = 4.5$
$) = 2q + 4$ iform	-2	0	0
	3	10	4.5

In calculating the q scale, the values of $f(q) = 0$ and 10 are used to obtain the minimum and maximum values for q of -2 and $+3$. If these terminal values are not whole numbers, the scale should be lengthened or shortened to provide whole numbers. Although the origin[2] is not needed for this problem, it is identified on Fig. 21.25 as a pair of matching values which are the common origins of the two scales.

Actual construction of the two scales consists in placing 10 equal divisions in a length of 4.5 in. for the p scale. The q scale is divided into five equal parts in a length of 4.5 in. The two scales are so oriented that the scale values of $q = -2$ and $p = 0$ are adjacent to each other on the common stem. These are matching values, and the point they represent is a matching point. Although the match-

ing values chosen are for the scale origins, any pair of matching values may be used, as the origin is not always included within the scale range. A matching point must align the scales if they are to represent the equality.

Another example of a uniform-scale chart (Fig. 21.26) will help clarify the use of matching points. The chart is to provide a conversion from degrees centigrade to degrees Fahrenheit. The centigrade scale is to have a range of 0 to 100 degrees, and the scale length is to be 4.75 in. The equality is $°C = \frac{5}{9}(°F - 32)$.

C scale	C	$f(C)$	$d = mf(C)$
			From $L = mR$
			$m = 0.0475$
$f(C) = C$ Uniform	0	0	0
	100	100	4.75

F scale	F	$f(F)$	$d = mf(F)$
			From above
			$m = 0.0475$
$f(F) = 5/9(F - 32)$ Uniform	32	0	0
	212	100	4.75

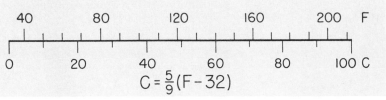

$$C = \frac{5}{9}(F - 32)$$

FIG. 21.26.   Conversion chart relating degrees centigrade to degrees Fahrenheit.

[2] An *origin* is defined as the point at which the function of the variable is zero.

The terminal values for the F scale are not the most desirable and should be changed. Figure 21.26 indicates the results if the terminal values are 40 and 210. The scale can be graduated by placing 180 equal divisions in the scale length of 4.75 in. or by placing 170 (or 17) equal divisions in 4.48 in. In either case, the two scales must be aligned at a matching point. If the F scale is graduated to 32°, the origin is a convenient matching point ($F = 32$, $C = 0$). If the F scale is only graduated to 40, matching points might be chosen as $F = 50$ and $C = 10$ or $F = 140$ and $C = 60$. Any point can be used for the matching point, but the two points chosen have whole-number values and are easy to use.

Conversion charts for nonlinear equations producing nonuniform scales are often needed. The basic processes of chart construction remain the same for them as for uniform-scale charts, but the amount of calculation is usually greater. Where it is possible, the use of a scale chart to graduate the scales will greatly relieve the monotony encountered otherwise.

An example of a nonuniform-scale conversion chart (Fig. 21.27) is one representing the equality $p = 4q^2$. This equation may be used directly to construct a conversion chart which will have one uniform scale and one nonuniform scale. If we assume values of p to vary from 1 to 10, we can let the length of the scale be 5 in. The table of calculations will require complete calculations for all graduations of the q scale, but only the scale length calculations are needed for the p scale.

p scale	p	$f(p)$	$d = m f(p)$ Let $m = 0.5$	d'
$f(p) = p$ Uniform	1	1	0.5	0
	10	10	5.0	4.5

q scale	q	$f(q)$	$d = m f(q)$ From above $m = 0.5$	d'
$f(q) = 4q^2$ Nonuniform	0.5	1	0.5	0
	0.6	1.44	0.72	0.22
	0.7	1.96	0.98	0.48
	0.8	2.56	1.28	0.78
	0.9	3.24	1.62	1.12
	1.0	4.00	2.00	1.50
	1.1	4.84	2.42	1.92
	1.2	5.76	2.88	2.38
	1.3	6.76	3.38	2.88
	1.4	7.84	3.92	3.42
	1.5	9.00	4.50	4.00
	1.58	10.00	5.00	4.50

The terminal value of the q scale should be increased or decreased, and in the figure it has been reduced to 1.50 for the maximum. Suitable matching points for these scales are $p = 1$ and $q = 0.5$, $p = 4$ and $q = 1$, and $p = 9$ and $q = 1.5$.

Scale charts are not commonly obtainable for squared scales and, in addition, require more labor to construct than the actual scale itself. Since logarithmic-scale charts are easily obtainable and can also be constructed from log cycle graph paper, an equation of the type given above is often rewritten in logarithmic form. The equation then becomes $\log p = 2 \log q + \log 4$, as shown in Fig. 21.28. Let the scale range be the same as before and the scale be approximately the same length. While all calculations can be made for a scale

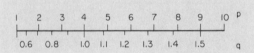

FIG. 21.27. A conversion chart for $p = 4q^2$.

of this type, the quickest method is to calculate only the length of each log cycle and the values of one matching point.

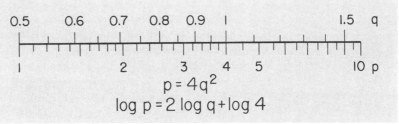

FIG. 21.28.   A conversion chart for $p = 4q^2$ using logarithmic scales.

	p	$f(p)$	$d = mf(p)$	d'
p scale			Let $m = 5$	
$f(p) = \log p$	1	0	0	0
Log scale	10	1	5	5
	q	$f(q)$	$d = mf(q)$	d'
q scale			From above $m = 5$	
$f(q) = 2 \log q$	1	0	0	0
Log scale	10	2	10	10

Solution of the original equation indicates that matching points can easily be used where $q = 1$ and $p = 4$ or where $q = 0.5$ and $p = 1$. Other matching points can be obtained, but these two offer convenient values to work with. Construction of the conversion chart (of Fig. 21.28) consists in first determining the log scale which has a cycle length of 5 in. and the scale which has a cycle length of 10 in. The 5-in. cycle is transferred directly to the paper and labeled for values of p from 1 to 10. The 10-in. cycle will not be used in its entirety but will have only portions of the upper and lower ends used. The 10-in. cycle is aligned with the existing 5-in. cycle scale at either of the matching points. The scale divisions from 0.5 to 1.0 are then marked along the p scale. The remaining segment of the scale is marked off by moving the 10-in. log cycle so that the opposite end is aligned at $p = 4$ and $q = 1$. The portion of the scale from 1 to 1.5 is divided, calibrations are labeled, and the scale legends placed along the scales to complete the chart. The accuracy of the completed chart depends upon the use of an ac-curate scale chart. If a commercial scale chart is not available, the labor spent in constructing an accurate chart is usually considerably less than that used in calculating and graduating all the scales for a conversion chart or a nomograph.

Figure 21.29 illustrates another conversion chart employing logarithmic scales. It should be noted that the H scale for this chart uses portions of three log cycles, but each cycle is the same length, and only the scale numbers are different for each portion of the various cycles.

The logarithmic-scale chart should be used with discretion because the format of the scales makes accurate reading of scale values increasingly difficult as the scale values become larger. Uniform scales obviously have the *same* ease (or difficulty) of reading anywhere within the scale range.

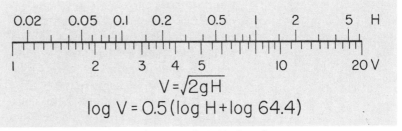

FIG. 21.29.   A conversion chart using logarithmic scales.

21.16. NOMOGRAPHY. Mathematical equations containing three or more variables are found in every phase of engineering work. Many of these equations must be solved repeatedly. The nomograph offers one method of relieving the drudgery of repetitive calculations. Although some equations do not lend themselves to nomographs, the great majority of equations of three or more variables can be made into a nomograph.

A nomograph consists of three or more scales arranged and graduated so that any straight line, called a *tie line,* drawn to intersect the three scales will intersect them at scale values which are distinct solutions of the equation. For most nomographs, the tie line will be limited to intersecting three scales at a time. For this reason, only three-variable nomographs will have construction methods given in this text. Additional variables may be added two at a time to the result from a preceding group of three. The construction of four-or-more-variable nomographs consists in repeating the three-variable construction a sufficient number of times to give a final answer.

21.17. NOMOGRAPH CONSTRUCTION METHODS. The construction of a nomograph to represent a specific equation may follow any one of three different procedures, depending upon the equation form and the extent to which it is desired to become involved with theoretical considerations. In the case of certain equations involving simple addition or multiplication of terms, the nomograph can be constructed by laying out two scales of suitable form along parallel straight stems. Each scale is graduated in terms of one of the variables from the equation. The equation is solved mathematically to obtain sets of corresponding values of the variables. Then, points on the third scale, which may be straight or curved, are located graphically by the intersection of pairs of tie lines. An adaptation of this method, known as "graphic anamorphosis," is described in Chap. 22, for construction of a nomograph from empirical data. Both of these methods are to be used when the methods listed below fail to produce a result.

The standard procedure differentiates the form of the chart according to the geometrical combination of the scales and associates each form with a particular form of equation. Each chart form is analyzed geometrically to establish rules for locating and graduating the scales.

Another procedure involves writing the chart equation as a vanishing third-order determinant of special form. The elements of the determinant provide functions of each variable which permit the scales to be plotted in a coordinate system. This method is valuable for equations which either do not fit or are difficult to fit to one of the standard geometric forms.

The design and construction of a nomograph require time and effort. The limitations on accuracy inherent in all graphic methods must be considered. Care must be employed in locating and graduating the scales to obtain the best possible accuracy.

21.18. PARALLEL-SCALE NOMOGRAPHS—GEOMETRIC METHOD. Relationships between three variable quantities are often of such a nature that they can be expressed by equations of the form

$$f(p) + f(q) = f(r)$$

where $f(p)$, $f(q)$, and $f(r)$ are each an

algebraic function of a single variable. This type of relationship may be represented by a nomograph of three parallel straight scales. Each scale is calibrated with values of one of the variables, and the scales are so located and graduated that a straight line cuts them at values of p, q, and r which satisfy the equation. The unknown values of any one of the variables may be determined by drawing a tie line to connect known values of the other two.

The construction of a parallel-scale chart is shown diagrammatically in Fig. 21.30. Two vertical scales, the p scale with a modulus m_p and the q scale with a modulus m_q, are located a suitable distance apart. The scales are graduated according to the scale equations

$$d_p = m_p f(p) \qquad \text{and} \qquad d_q = m_q f(q)$$

A vertical scale for r is next located between the p and q scales at a distance a from the p scale and a distance b from the q scale. The origin of the r scale is located on a straight line joining the origins of the p and q scales. The three points of origin satisfy the chart equation, since, by definition, the origin of a scale is the point representing the zero value of the scale function and $0 + 0 = 0$.

Any straight line connects three values, p^*, q^*, and r^*, on the three scales. The distance c on the p scale is equal to the product of the scale modulus and the scale function:

$$c = m_p f(p^*)$$

and, similarly, on the q and r scales:

$$e = m_q f(q^*) \qquad g = m_r f(r^*)$$

Lines parallel to the base line form two similar triangles in which corresponding sides and altitudes are in the same ratio:

$$\frac{g - c}{e - g} = \frac{a}{b}$$

Substituting equivalent values for c, e, and g, we get

$$\frac{m_r f(r^*) - m_p f(p^*)}{m_q f(q^*) - m_r f(r^*)} = \frac{a}{b}$$

Collecting terms, we have

$$m_p f(p^*) + \frac{a}{b} m_q f(q^*)$$

$$= \left(1 + \frac{a}{b}\right) m_r f(r^*)$$

To reduce this equation to the original chart equation, the coefficients of the three terms must be equal:

$$m_p = \frac{a}{b} m_q = \left(1 + \frac{a}{b}\right) m_r$$

If the first two coefficients are equal, then

$$\frac{a}{b} = \frac{m_p}{m_q}$$

Thus, the location of the center scale must be such that the distances a and b are in the same ratio as the moduli of the two outside scales. *This is the first rule for the construction of the parallel-scale nomograph.*

If the first and third coefficients are equal, then

$$m_p = \left(1 + \frac{a}{b}\right) m_r = \left(1 + \frac{m_p}{m_q}\right) m_r$$

and

$$m_r = \frac{m_p m_q}{m_p + m_q}$$

The center-scale modulus must equal the product of the two outside-scale moduli divided by their sum. *This is the second rule for the construction of the parallel-scale nomograph.*

It is not necessary to use the straight

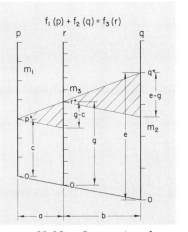

$f_1(p) + f_2(q) = f_3(r)$

FIG. 21.30. Construction of a parallel-scale chart.

line connecting the scale origins as a base line for the vertical location of the r scale on its stem. In many cases, the scale origins should not be included in the ranges of scale values. Any straight tie line joining values of p, q, and r that satisfy the chart equation may serve as a base line.

Assume that a nomograph is to be made to represent the equation

$$E = 1.85 + 0.917\,(G - G_w)$$

where E = terminal voltage in volts of a lead-cell storage battery. (E varies from 2.04 to 2.14.)

G = specific gravity of the electrolyte. (G varies in relationship to the other variables.)

G_w = specific gravity of water at the cell temperatures. (G_w varies from 0.98 to 1.00.)

This equation fits the form of a three-parallel-straight-scale nomograph, and all of the scales will be uniform. (All the scale equations will be linear.)

Although the equation may be used in its present form, inspection reveals that dividing both sides by 0.917 will simplify the equation so that only one variable will have a modifying constant. Thus, the equation which will be used to construct the nomograph is

$$G_w + 1.09E = G + 2.02$$

The construction of the nomograph (Fig. 21.31) is as follows.

First, a table is made to give the values needed for each scale:

Assume length = 4 in.
therefore m = 200

G_w scale	G_w	$f(G_w)$	$d = m\,f(G_w)$	d'
$f(G_w) = G_w$	0.98	0.98	196	0
uniform	1.00	1.00	200	4

Assume length = 6 in.
therefore m = 55

E scale	E	$f(E)$	$d = m\,f(E)$	d'
$f(E) = 1.09E$	2.04	2.2236	122.3	0
uniform	2.14	2.3326	128.3	6

$$m = \frac{200 \times 55}{200 + 55} = 43.1$$

G scale	G	$f(G)$	$d = m\,f(G)$	d'
$f(G) = G + 2.02$	1.18	3.16	136.20	0
uniform	1.1836	3.1636	136.35	0.15
	1.3126	3.3326		
	1.32	3.30	142.23	6.03

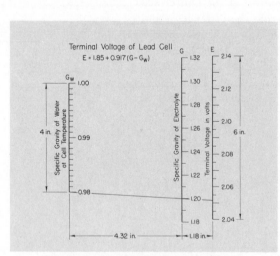

FIG. 21.31. A parallel-scale chart for the terminal voltage of a lead cell.

The calculations for the G_w and E scales are self-explanatory. The scale lengths are assumed, and the resulting modulus is calculated. The simplest method of determining the modulus in this case is to use the formula $L = mR$. Thus for the G_w scale, $L = 4$ and $R = (1.00 - 0.98)$. From this, $m = 200$. For the E scale,

$$m = \frac{L}{R} = \frac{6}{2.3326 - 2.2236} = 55$$

The G scale is calculated from values of $f(G)$. The maximum value of $f(G)$ for G would be the sum of the maximum values of the functions for the other two scales since $f(G) = f(G_w) + f(E)$. The maximum value of $f(G)$ for G is 3.3326, which corresponds to a scale value of 1.3126 for G. The minimum value of G is similarly found to be 1.1836. Both of these values are undesirable terminal values for a scale, so arbitrary terminal values of 1.18 and 1.32 are assigned. The modulus is calculated from the equation for the center-scale modulus. The length of the scale is calculated, as is the distance from the terminal value of the scale to the minimum scale value resulting from addition of functions. The values of $G_w = 0.98$, $E = 2.04$, and $G = 1.1836$ lie on a base tie line. The value of $G = 1.1836$ will be difficult to locate on the scale since the scale is unlikely to be graduated to smaller increments than 0.001. Therefore the distance from the scale terminal value to the intersection of the base line is calculated.

The spacing of the scales is obtained from the equation

$$\frac{a}{b} = \frac{m_A}{m_B} = \frac{200}{50}$$

If $a + b = 5.5$ in., $a = 4.32$ in. and $b = 1.18$ in.

An experienced nomographer would not need to make a complete table, but would follow steps of calculation somewhat as outlined below.

1. *Equation*

   $$G_w + 1.09E = G + 2.02$$

2. *Scale Ranges*

   $G_w = 0.98$ to 1.00
   $E = 2.04$ to 2.14

3. *G_w Scale*

   $f(G_w) = G_w$
   Range: $1.00 - 0.98 = 0.02$
   Scale length: Assume 4 in.
   Modulus: $\dfrac{4}{.02} = 200$

   Divide scale into 20 major units in 4 in. of length. Label every 0.1 increment.

4. *E Scale*

   $f(E) = 1.09\,E$
   Range: $1.09\,(2.14 - 2.04) = 0.109$
   Scale length: Assume 6 in.
   Modulus: $\dfrac{6}{0.109} = 55$

   Divide scale into 20 units in 6 in. of length. Label every 0.02 increment.

5. *G Scale*

   $f(G) = G + 2.02$
   Max. value G: 1.3126   Use 1.32
   Min. value G: 1.1836   Use 1.18
   Range: $1.32 - 1.18 = 0.14$
   Modulus: $\dfrac{200 \times 55}{200 + 55} = 43.1$
   Scale length: $43.2 \times 0.14 = 6.3$ in.

Divide scale into 14 equal units in 6.3 in. of length. Label every 0.02 increment.

6. *Scale Spacing*

Chart width: Assume 5.5 in.

$$\frac{a}{b} = \frac{m_A}{m_B} = \frac{200}{55}$$

$$a = 4.32,\ b = 1.18$$

7. *Base Tie Line*

$G_w = 0.98,\ E = 2.04,\ G = 1.1836$
or $G_w = 0.98,\ G = 1.20,\ E = 2.052$

Equations involving three variables are often of the form

$$f(p)\ f(q) = f(r)$$

A nomograph of the Z form will represent this equation (multiplication of functions), but the Z chart has certain disadvantages. Rewriting the basic equation in logarithmic form will place it in the standard three-parallel-scale format:

$$\log f(p) + \log f(q) = \log f(r)$$

This equation can be used to construct a nomograph following the steps of the previous example with one exception. If a scale chart is used to obtain the logarithmic scales, the length of the log cycle (for each scale) must be known in order to make the chart.

An illustration of the calculations for and construction of a parallel logarithmic-scale nomograph follows.

Both round and rectangular air ducts are used in heating and air conditioning systems, and their sizes for equal air-handling capacity are related by

$$D = 1.075\ \sqrt{WH}$$

where D = diameter of round duct, in.
W = width of rectangular duct, in.
H = height of rectangular duct, in.

Construction of a nomograph (Fig. 21.32) to represent this equation requires either full calculations for each scale (log functions are nonlinear) or the use of a logarithmic-scale chart. If a scale chart is used, the necessary calculations are as follows.

1. *Equation*

$$0.5 \log W + 0.5 \log H = D - \log 1.075$$

2. *Scale Ranges*

$W = 10$ to 100
$H = 5$ to 50

3. *W Scale*

$f(W) = 0.5 \log W$

Range: $0.5\ (\log 100 - \log 10) = 0.5$

Scale length: Assume 6 in.

Modulus: $\dfrac{6}{0.5} = 12$

Cycle length:
$12[0.5\ (\log 10 - \log 1)] = 6.0$ in.

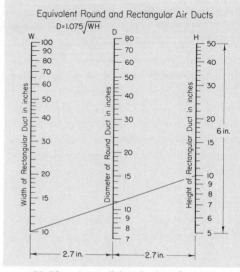

Equivalent Round and Rectangular Air Ducts
$D = 1.075\sqrt{WH}$

FIG. 21.32. A parallel-scale chart for equivalent air ducts.

4. *H Scale*

$f(H) = 0.5 \log H$

Range: $0.5 (\log 50 - \log 5) = 0.5$

Scale length: Assume 6 in.

Modulus: $\dfrac{6}{0.5} = 12$

Cycle length:
$12[0.5 (\log 10 - \log 1)] = 6$ in.
(Note that the scale uses parts of two log cycles, 5 to 10 from one cycle and 10 to 50 from the other.)

5. *D Scale*

$f(D) = \log D + \log 1.075$

Max. value D:
$1.075 \sqrt{100 \times 50} = 70.7$ Use 80

Min. value D:
$1.075 \sqrt{10 \times 5} = 7.07$ Use 7

Modulus: $\dfrac{12 \times 12}{12 + 12} = 6$

Cycle length:
$6 (\log 10 - \log 1) = 6$ in.

6. *Chart Width* $= 5.4$ in.

Scale spacing:

$\dfrac{a}{b} = \dfrac{12}{12}$ For $a + b = 5.4$, $a = 2.7$,
         and $b = 2.7$

7. *Tie Line*

Connects $W = 10$, $H = 10$, and $D = 10.75$

21.19. *Z* **CHARTS—TWO PARALLEL AND ONE TRANSVERSE SCALE.** It has been shown that the relationship in which one term is equal to the product of two others,

$$f(p)\, f(q) = f(r)$$

may be represented by a nomograph of three parallel straight logarithmic scales. This equation may also be represented

by a nomograph of two parallel scales and a third transverse scale. The parallel scales run in opposite directions from a base line joining their origins. The diagonal scale extending along the base line may represent values of either p or q. Its origin coincides with the origin of the r scale.

The construction of the Z or N chart, as it is often called, is shown diagrammatically in Fig. 21.33. Two vertical scales, the p scale with a modulus m_p and the r scale with a modulus m_r, are located a convenient distance apart. The scales are graduated according to the scale equations

$$d_p = m_p\, f(p) \qquad \text{and} \qquad d_r = m_r\, f(r)$$

so as to run in opposite directions from a base line. The q scale lies along the base line with its origin at the origin of the r scale. Thus, by the separation of the p and r scales, the base line is inclined at an angle, provides a chart of rectangular proportions, and makes for sharp intersections between the scales and the tie lines drawn across them.

Any straight line connects three values of p^*, q^*, and r^* on the three scales. The distance a on the p scale is equal

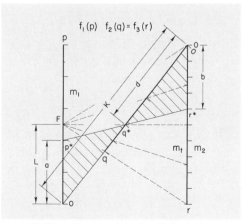

FIG. 21.33.   Construction of a *Z* chart.

to the product of the scale modulus and the value of the scale function:

$$a = m_p \, f(p^*)$$

And, similarly, on the r scale,

$$b = m_r \, f(r^*)$$

Corresponding sides of the similar triangles formed by the base line and tie line are in the same ratio:

$$\frac{a}{b} = \frac{K - d}{d}$$

where K = length of transverse scale intermediate to p and r scales

d = distance from its origin to graduation q^*

Substituting equivalent values for a and b, we get

$$\frac{m_p \, f(p^*)}{m_r \, f(r^*)} = \frac{K - d}{d}$$

$$f(p^*) \, \frac{m_p d}{m_r \, (K - d)} = f(r^*)$$

In order for this equation to be equivalent to the original chart equation,

$$\frac{m_p d}{m_r \, (K - d)} = f(q^*)$$

Solving for d, we have

$$d = \frac{K \, f(q^*)}{m_p/m_r + f(q^*)}$$

The scale equation giving the distance from the origin to any point on the q scale is

$$d_q = \frac{K \, f(q)}{m_p/m_r + f(q)}$$

Scale distances for graduating the scale may be obtained by substituting specific values of q in the equation. This process is complicated because the scale does not have a constant modulus. Since the ratio m_p/m_r is always positive, the length

K represents all positive values of the function $f(q)$ from zero to infinity. There is a rapid convergence of values at the seldom-used upper end of the scale.

A more convenient method for graduating the transverse scale involves projection from a temporary scale on the stem of the r scale to a focus F located on the stem of the p scale. The equation of the temporary scale is

$$d_t = m_t \, f(q)$$

and the distance L, locating the focus, is related to the temporary scale modulus m_t by the equation

$$\frac{L}{m_t} = \frac{m_p}{m_r}$$

In some cases, a more precise location of the graduations of the transverse scale may be effected through the use of a different focus and temporary scale for different portions of the transverse scale. The temporary scale and projectors are a construction only and do not form a part of the completed chart.

The location of the transverse scale depends upon the position of the origins of the parallel scales. These origins are not always included within the ranges of the scale values. When they are not, the transverse scale is located by similar triangle geometry or by the intersection of a pair of tie lines for each scale graduation.

As an example of Z-chart construction, engine brake horsepower is given by the formula

$$BHP = \frac{2\pi \, NT}{33,000}$$

where BHP = brake horsepower

N = engine speed, rpm

T = braking torque, lb-ft

A nomograph for the above relationship is shown in Fig. 21.34.

Construction of the chart may be summarized as follows.

1. *Chart Equation*

   $NT = 5,250\ BHP$

2. *N Scale* (speed)

   $f(N) = N$

   Range: $5,000 - 0 = 5,000$

   Scale length: Assume 6.25 in.

   Modulus: $\dfrac{6.25}{5,000} = 0.00125$

   Divide scale into 25 equal units in 6.25 in. of length. Label every fifth unit.

3. *BHP Scale* (brake horsepower)

   $f(BHP) = 5,250\ BHP$

   Range: $5,250\ (400 - 0) = 2,100,000$

   Scale length: Assume 6 in.

   Modulus: $\dfrac{6}{2,100,000} = 0.00000286$

   Divide the scale into 20 equal units in 6 in. of length. Label every fifth graduation.

4. *T Scale* (torque)

   $f(T) = T$

   Range: $500 - 0 = 500$

   Location of focus: Assume $L = 5$ in.

   Temporary-scale modulus:

   $\dfrac{5}{m_t} \times \dfrac{0.00125}{0.00000286}$ and $m_t = 0.0114$

   Temporary-scale length:
   $0.0114 \times 500 = 5.70$ in.

   Temporary-scale equation:
   $d_t = 0.0114T$

   (Divide the temporary scale into 25 equal units in 5.7 in. of length.) The

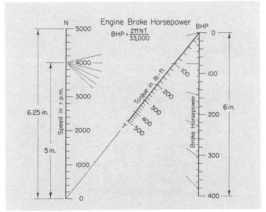

FIG. 21.34. A Z chart for engine brake horsepower.

temporary scale is laid out on the stem of the *BHP* scale and is transferred to the *T* scale by projectors converging at the focus.

21.20. CHART LAYOUT. The preceding discussion dealt with the preparation of the basic types of nomographs, and in each case, chart layout is based on rules which result from a geometric analysis of the chart form. Chart construction can be simplified once a chart form is identified as representing a particular type of equation. Two scales of suitable type and modulus are laid out along properly located stems. Next, corresponding values of the variables are obtained by repeated substitutions in the chart equation. Then, pivot points or points on a third scale are obtained from intersections of appropriate tie lines.

This method is useful for the construction of nomographs whose form has been found by determinant methods. Since simple determinant methods described in this text do not include a variable-scale modulus, the determinant is often used to find the form of the chart, and the layout is then made by locating intersecting tie lines.

The use of tie lines to locate a pivot point on a conversion chart or a third scale on a nomograph is illustrated in Fig. 21.35A. In constructing the conversion chart at (A) for the equation $2p = r$, the two scales are first located parallel to one another and at a suitable distance apart. The scales are graduated to any convenient length but not necessarily the same. Since the equation contains only linear functions of p and r, the scales are uniform. They may be subdivided by any of the graphic methods for dividing a line into equal parts. A value of p is substituted into the equation, the corresponding value of r determined, and a tie line drawn to connect these values on the scales. The process is repeated to obtain a second tie line, and the intersection of the tie lines is the locus of point P, the pivot. A third tie line may be used to check the accuracy of the location of point P.

The p and r scales of the nomographs in Fig. 21.35B and C may be located and subdivided in the same manner as in Fig. 21.35A. The q scale is then plotted a point at a time by assigning a specific numerical value to q and then using the same procedure used to locate the pivot on the conversion chart at (A). In the figure, the value $q = 0$ was located by means of a tie line connecting $p = 0$ and $r = 0$ and another tie line connecting $p = 5$ and $r = 10$. The scale is completed by drawing a line or stem through the series of plotted q values. Since the equation in example (B) involves only addition of terms, the q scale is uniform and parallel to the p and r scales. In example (C), where multiplication is involved, the q scale is nonuniform and is not parallel to the other two.

The graphic method for locating pivot points or scales produces an accurate and usable chart and, in many cases, reduces the time and effort involved in preparation. Nevertheless, a fundamental understanding of chart form is necessary, else the third scale may evolve as a curve that cannot be used or as a scale too short for practical use. The parallel scales first drawn must be properly designed. Plotting one of these as a uniform scale when it should be nonuniform to satisfy the chart equation would result in tie-line intersections that could not be checked by a third tie line. The procedure should not be used unless the general arrangement and type of graduations are known for the outer two scales.

21.21. DETERMINANTS. A valuable tool for the construction of three-scale nomo-

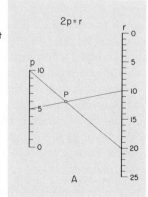
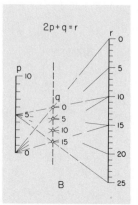
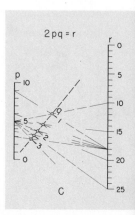

FIG. 21.35. Graphic method of chart construction.

graphs is obtained by relating their geometry to a vanishing third-order determinant. Construction of a nomograph from a determinant requires some information about determinants and the mathematical manipulations which may be performed on them. The following paragraphs provide sufficient background and mathematical information for the successful construction of a nomograph.

A third-order determinant is a square array of nine elements arranged in three rows and three columns and designated by

$$\begin{vmatrix} x_1 & y_1 & z_1 \\ x_2 & y_2 & z_2 \\ x_3 & y_3 & z_3 \end{vmatrix} = D$$

The value of a determinant is the sum of all possible products $x_i y_j z_k$ ($i \neq j \neq k$) with proper regard for sign:

$$\begin{aligned} & 1,2,3 \\ D = x_i y_j z_k &= x_1 y_2 z_3 + x_2 y_3 z_1 + x_3 y_1 z_2 \\ & (i \neq j \neq k) \\ & \quad - x_1 y_3 z_2 - x_3 y_2 z_1 - x_2 y_1 z_3 \end{aligned}$$

We can imagine the value of the third-order determinant to be obtained as follows: Rewrite the first two horizontal rows below the determinant, and draw six diagonals through the three middle values, y_2, y_3, and y_1, as shown:

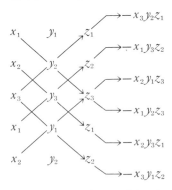

Compute the products of the three ele-

ments in each diagonal, and find the algebraic sum of these products. Consider the products of diagonals sloping downward to the right as positive and those of diagonals sloping upward to the right as negative.

Only determinants of algebraic functions whose value is zero are used to construct nomographs. Mathematically,

$$D = f(p, q, r) = 0$$

Certain properties of vanishing or zero-valued determinants are stated below. These properties will be used repeatedly in the construction of nomographs from determinants.

1. Any two rows or columns of a zero-valued determinant may be interchanged.

$$D = \begin{vmatrix} x_1 & y_1 & z_1 \\ x_2 & y_2 & z_2 \\ x_3 & y_3 & z_3 \end{vmatrix} = \begin{vmatrix} x_1 & z_1 & y_1 \\ x_2 & z_2 & y_2 \\ x_3 & z_3 & y_3 \end{vmatrix}$$

$$= \begin{vmatrix} x_2 & y_2 & z_2 \\ x_1 & y_1 & z_1 \\ x_3 & y_3 & z_3 \end{vmatrix} = 0$$

2. Any constant multiple of the elements in one row (or column) may be added to the elements of another row (or column).

$$D = \begin{vmatrix} x_1 & y_1 & z_1 \\ x_2 & y_2 & z_2 \\ x_3 & y_3 & z_3 \end{vmatrix} = \begin{vmatrix} (x_1 + az_1) & y_1 & z_1 \\ (x_2 + az_2) & y_2 & z_2 \\ (x_3 + az_3) & y_3 & z_3 \end{vmatrix}$$

$$= \begin{vmatrix} x_1 & y_1 & (z_1 - by_1) \\ x_2 & y_2 & (z_2 - by_2) \\ x_3 & y_3 & (z_3 - by_3) \end{vmatrix} = 0$$

3. All elements in any row (or column) may be multiplied by the same constant.

$$D = \begin{vmatrix} x_1 & y_1 & z_1 \\ x_2 & y_2 & z_2 \\ x_3 & y_3 & z_3 \end{vmatrix} = \begin{vmatrix} ax_1 & by_1 & z_1 \\ ax_2 & by_2 & z_2 \\ ax_3 & by_3 & z_3 \end{vmatrix} = 0$$

21.22. DETERMINANT THEORY OF NOMOGRAPHIC CHARTS.

The use of determinants for the construction of nomographs will be limited[3] in this text to determining the form that the nomograph will take, although the scales will be graduated by the methods of paragraph 21.10.

The basic assumption concerning nomographs is that they consist of three or more scales graduated and arranged so that matching values of the original equation would lie on a straight line connecting the scales. If three scales of curved form are considered to be the general form of the nomograph scale, they can be placed in an x-y coordinate system as shown in Fig. 21.36. If we assume that points which satisfy the equation of the nomograph will lie on a straight line connecting the three scales, the relationships involving these three points can be developed by plane geometry. The three points on the scales intersected by the tie line will have the coordinates of x_a, y_a; x_b, y_b; x_c, y_c. From similar triangles,

$$\frac{x_c - x_a}{y_c - y_a} = \frac{x_c - x_b}{y_c - y_b}$$

Clearing fractions, we have

$$x_a y_b + x_b y_c + x_c y_a$$
$$- x_a y_c - x_b y_a - x_c y_b = 0$$

This equation is also the expansion of a third-order determinant

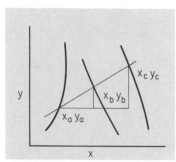

FIG. 21.36. General form of a nomograph in cartesian coordinates.

[3] Methods of determinant manipulation exist in which the determinant will provide the equation for each of the nomograph scales complete with variable modulus, but this discussion limits itself to more elementary material. If further information is required on this subject, several comprehensive texts on nomography have complete information on the use of determinants for the construction of nomographs.

$$\begin{vmatrix} y_a & x_a & 1 \\ y_b & x_b & 1 \\ y_c & x_c & 1 \end{vmatrix} = 0$$

The preceding statement is the basis for all nomographic construction from determinants, but the actual use of the determinant involves two separate concepts. The *first concept* is purely mathematical and simply states that the expansion of the determinant produces the complete original equation of the nomograph. To illustrate this concept, assume that a nomograph is to be constructed to solve the equation $A - 2B = C$. Without regard to the method of obtaining the determinant, expansion of the following determinant will produce the original equation.

$$\begin{vmatrix} A & 1 & 1 \\ 2B & 1 & 0 \\ C & 0 & 1 \end{vmatrix} = A - 2B - C$$

The reader should verify this fact by using the rules for determinant expansion given in paragraph 21.11.

This concept is fundamental to the entire process, and it is mandatory that the original determinant can be expanded to obtain the original equation. *Regardless of any further manipulations performed upon a determinant, this mathematical concept must be satisfied first.* For this reason, no rules are given for the development of a determinant from the equation since more than one combination is usually possible. Thus, trial and retrial is the keynote in arranging the terms of the equation in the best position in a determinant.

The *second concept* is the relationship of the determinant to the location of points (or lines) in a coordinate system. Although this phase of the determinant is only a by-product of the mathematical process, the coordinate concept will ultimately produce the information for construction of a nomograph.

To illustrate this concept, determinants as a mathematical entity can be ignored. Assume that points and lines are to be located in the principal orthographic projection planes by means of height, width, and depth measurements. If a point A has the coordinates of 4 units height, 3 units width, and ½ unit depth, it lies in a horizontal plane 4 units above an arbitrary horizontal reference plane, in a profile plane 3 units to the right of a profile reference plane, and in a frontal plane ½ unit behind a frontal reference plane. The coordinates for point A are given as 4, 3, ½ since the order was arbitrarily predetermined as height, width, and depth. Points B and C are similarly located with respect to the original reference planes. Thus the three points and their coordinates are tabulated

$$A: \quad 4, \quad 3, \quad ½$$
$$B: \quad 2, \quad 1, \quad 0$$
$$C: \quad 3, \quad ½, \quad 2$$

The nine coordinates are now in exactly the positions of the nine elements of a third-order determinant. In general form the coordinates of the three points can be given by the coordinate array

$$\begin{matrix} H_A & W_A & D_A \\ H_B & W_B & D_B \\ H_C & W_C & D_C \end{matrix}$$

where H, W, and D are abbreviations for height, width, and depth, respectively.

Simple nomographs are usually constructed in one plane only, which means that all three points must have a common height, width, or depth coordinate. The depth measurement is usually selected as common and is *assigned a*

value of unity to avoid arithmetic problems when the coordinate array is used as a determinant for expansion. The coordinate array for points A, B, and C is

$$\begin{matrix} H_A & W_A & 1 \\ H_B & W_B & 1 \\ H_C & W_C & 1 \end{matrix}$$

The mathematical determinant seldom provides a full column of ones, so manipulation of the determinant is required to accomplish this end. As in the preceding instance concerning formation of the determinant, experience and patience will provide the knowledge needed to obtain the proper coordinate-array determinant from the mathematical determinant. The rules governing manipulation of determinants are listed in paragraph 21.11 and must be adhered to strictly. However, the choice of operation and the number of operations are completely at the option of the person constructing the nomograph.

Straight lines can also be indicated by this coordinate notation simply by replacing one numerical coordinate with a variable. A vertical straight line will have a fixed width and depth measurement, but its height measurement can be as long as needed. Coordinate notation for such a line is

$$A, \quad 2, \quad 1$$

A horizontal-frontal line B has coordinates

$$1½, \quad B, \quad 1$$

Another vertical line C has the coordinates

$$C, \quad 5, \quad 1$$

The nine-element array resulting is

$$\begin{matrix} A & 2 & 1 \\ 1½ & B & 1 \\ C & 5 & 1 \end{matrix}$$

This is not a zero-valued determinant and would not produce a nomograph, but three straight lines could be located on orthographic projection planes by such a coordinate array.

In nomographic work, the height coordinate is usually represented by the symbol y and the width coordinate by the symbol x, to correspond to the cartesian coordinate system normally used for mathematical plotting. These symbols represent distances in x and y directions for any specified point on the nomograph scales. Construction of graphic scales has shown that the distance along a scale to a specified point is equal to $mf(x)$. If $m = 1$, then x_A (or d) $= f(A)$. The general form of the coordinate array from which a nomograph will be constructed is

$$\begin{vmatrix} f(A) & g(A) & 1 \\ f(B) & g(B) & 1 \\ f(C) & g(C) & 1 \end{vmatrix} = 0$$

Adding the vertical side marks and setting the array equal to zero is unnecessary for practical purposes but should be done as a reminder of the mathematical-determinant origin of this construction coordinate array.

Any set of three points which lie on a straight line and which satisfy an equation involving $f(A)$, $g(A)$, $f(B)$, $g(B)$, $f(C)$, and $g(C)$ will have y and x coordinates which can be substituted into the determinant and cause it to equal zero. The use of $f(A)$ and $g(A)$, etc., should not be confused with the actual function of the variable A which the nomograph is attempting to represent. The term $f(A)$ in the determinant structure simply represents the manner in which the points on scale A vary in a vertical direction while $g(A)$ indicates the horizontal relationships of these

same points. Thus to represent the function A^2 on a scale it is expedient to separate A^2 into $A \times A$ in the mathematical determinant. Later manipulation might then rearrange the determinant, for example, so that the vertical coordinate, $f(A) = A$ and the horizontal coordinate, $g(A) = 1/A$.

Each row (horizontal) of the construction form of the nomograph is the scale equation of the variable indicated, expressed in terms of the vertical and horizontal coordinates of the scale. The majority of simple nomographs do not have scales having both the vertical and horizontal coordinates as variables so that the process is not as complicated as it might first appear.

To illustrate how each row of the construction determinant is used, assume that the following construction determinant has been obtained from the desired mathematical determinant.

$$\begin{vmatrix} 2A & 1 & 1 \\ 0 & B & 1 \\ C^2 & 0 & 1 \end{vmatrix} = 0$$

To construct this nomograph on paper, first assign some convenient point the value of $y = 0$ and $x = 0$. The second element of each row is the horizontal or x coordinate, and the third row contains an $x = 0$ coordinate. The first element of this row is the y coordinate and indicates that the points are to follow a pattern of C^2. The sign is positive so the scale extends upward from the $y = 0$ point. If we assume a scale range of $C = 0$ to 5, 25 y-coordinate divisions will be needed to cover this scale which lies along the y axis (since $x = 0$ for all points). The length of each y-coordinate division is arbitrary, but it must be the same for all three scales. The second row of the determinant indicates that a scale is to be graduated along the x axis ($y = 0$) in a linear pattern [$g(B) = B$]. Although almost any range of B could be assumed, the first row of the determinant indicates a scale to range upwards parallel to the y axis and at one x unit to the right of the y axis. Thus the range of the B scale must be adjusted so that $x = 1$ or $B = 1$ is suitable for proper separation of the two vertical scales. Figure 21.42 illustrates a nomograph of this type. The A scale must be graduated using the same y-coordinate divisions as were assigned the C scale so that A is to range from 0 to 12.5 if the scales are to be the same length.

Careful study of each row of the construction determinant will assist the nomographer in determining the scale forms for the nomograph and suggest shortcuts for scale graduation. Straight-line scales which lie either horizontal or vertical are characterized by determinant rows such as $2F$, ½, 1; 0.2, R, 1; 1, D, 1. The first scale is vertical, and the second two are horizontal. Straight-line scales which are neither vertical nor horizontal have determinant rows such as W, W, 1; T, $2T$, 1; $2K$, K, 1. Each of these scales must be graduated by measuring first vertically and then horizontally. Thus to find the point $T = 2$ of the second scale, a vertical measurement of 2 y units is made, and then horizontally from this point a measurement of 4 x units is made. Scales which are curved will have determinant rows such as H, H^2, 1; S, $2S^{1/2}$, 1; P^2, P^3, 1. These scales are graduated by the same combination of vertical and horizontal measurements used for the preceding slant straight lines. Notice especially that in the actual construction of a nomograph the best procedure is usually to employ the determinant as a guide to the format

and then apply the methods of paragraph 21.10 to actually graduate the scales.

It must be emphasized that the x and y units are purely arbitrary in size and thus need not be equal. But once the length has been established for one scale, it must be used for all three scales. This will not create a major problem for the nomographer if he studies the requirements of all three scales before starting construction.

The steps leading to the construction of a nomograph by the determinant method may be outlined as follows:

1. Construct a third-order determinant using zeros, ones, and terms of the original equation so that the determinant may be mathematically expanded to obtain the original equation.
2. Using permissible manipulations, rearrange the determinant so that the following conditions are met:
   a. Elements of one column are all ones.
   b. Elements of any row do not contain a variable found in any other row. This means that variables relating to scale A must appear in the same row, as must variables relating to scale B and scale C.
   c. Each row must contain either (la) a scale-related variable and a numerical constant, or (lb) two scale-related variables, and (2) a one.
3. Assign lengths to the x- and y-coordinate divisions to match the requirements of the scale ranges.
4. Using the first element of each row as the y coordinate and the second element of each row as the x coordinate, plot the three scales.

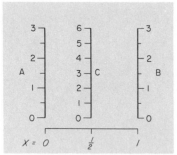

FIG. 21.37. Nomograph for $A + B = C$ by determinants.

To illustrate the process, a nomograph is to be constructed which will represent the equation $A + B = C$ or $A + B - C = 0$. First, the mathematical determinant is needed. This is usually constructed crossword-puzzle fashion by using zeros, ones, and the terms A, B, and C in the nine positions found in the determinant. The determinant which can be found by this method is

$$\begin{vmatrix} A & 0 & 1 \\ B & 1 & 0 \\ C & 1 & 1 \end{vmatrix} = 0$$

Expansion of this determinant produces $A + B - C = 0$, the original equation. Thus the first condition of nomograph construction is fulfilled. The second condition, that all elements of one column (vertical) be ones, is not met by either column 2 or column 3. Since any column of a determinant may be interchanged with another column without changing the value of the determinant, it is not necessary to attempt to change column 3 into ones but merely to obtain one column of all ones. Interchanging will permit column 1 to be the vertical coordinates, column 2 the horizontal coordinates, and column 3 the ones.

If column 2 is *added* to column 3, the zero is eliminated in column 3.

$$\begin{vmatrix} A & 0 & 1 \\ B & 1 & 1 \\ C & 1 & 2 \end{vmatrix} = 0$$

Dividing row 3 by the divisor 2 places the determinant in the final construction form.

$$\begin{vmatrix} A & 0 & 1 \\ B & 1 & 1 \\ \dfrac{C}{2} & \dfrac{1}{2} & 1 \end{vmatrix} = 0$$

This determinant meets all three conditions imposed on the proper construc-

tion determinant so that it now may be used to construct a nomograph. This determinant indicates a vertical scale (x = constant) at $x = 0$ extending upward with a scale equation of $d_A = A$. At $x = 1$ another vertical scale extending upward and having a scale equation of $d_B = B$ is constructed. Midway between these scales, at $x = \frac{1}{2}$, a third vertical scale extending upward with a scale equation of $d_C = C/2$ is constructed. All measurements made in the y direction use the same units of length —any arbitrary units. The x units are also arbitrary but need not be the same as for the y direction. Because the modulus of all scales is unity, the ranges for the A and B scales must be approximately equal if the scales are to be of approximately equal lengths. The completed nomograph is shown in Fig. 21.37.

A nomograph to represent the equation $AB = C$ can be constructed from a determinant by the following steps:

1. By trial and error the determinant is set up.

$$\begin{vmatrix} A & 1 & 0 \\ 0 & B & 1 \\ -C & 0 & 1 \end{vmatrix} = 0$$

2. Column 2 is added to column 3.

$$\begin{vmatrix} A & 1 & 1 \\ 0 & B & 1 + B \\ -C & 0 & 1 \end{vmatrix} = 0$$

3. Row 2 is divided by $(1 + B)$.

$$\begin{vmatrix} A & 1 & 1 \\ 0 & \dfrac{B}{1 + B} & 1 \\ -C & 0 & 1 \end{vmatrix} = 0$$

This determinant indicates a scale extending upward at $x = 1$ and graduated in terms of A. At $x = 0$ a scale is to extend downward and is to be graduated in terms of C. A third scale is to be placed on the $y = 0$ level (horizontal) and is to be graduated in terms of $B/(1 + B)$, using x units for measurement. The location of the scale graduations can be seen in Fig. 21.38. For $B = 0$, $x = 0$. For $B = 2$, $x = \frac{2}{3}$. For $B = \infty$, $x = 1$.

The nomograph indicated is based on an x-y coordinate system, but no restriction is made as to the angle between the coordinate axes. The usual 90° system provides the nomograph shown in Fig. 21.38, but a superior version of the nomograph will result if the coordinate axes are at an angle of 45°, as shown in Fig. 21.39. The nomograph will now resemble the conventional Z or N chart and will be easier to use because of the improved tie-line intersections between scales. Skewing of the coordinate axes is often helpful for curved-scale or concurrent-scale nomographs.

Obtaining the determinant which represents the given equation can be accomplished by several methods, but only one method can be said to work for all equations. It relies more on the experience of the operator than on method, and is somewhat like working a crossword puzzle. The operator places the various elements of the equation by trial and error into the determinant framework which can be expanded to provide the original equation. Several further examples of equations will be given to aid in understanding the mechanism of determinant methods.

Consider the construction of a nomograph to represent the equation

$$\frac{1}{A} + \frac{1}{B} = \frac{1}{C}$$

This equation is obviously in the form of a three-parallel-straight-scale nomo-

graph with nonuniform scales. The scale equation without a modulus is $d_x = 1/x$ for all the scales. This is not a desirable scale equation as the large values of x will all be crowded into a very short scale length. Placing the equation in the determinant form may provide a clue to a better format. Since the expansion of a determinant is the summation of products, the equation is expanded so that its terms are also products.

$$BC + AC = AB$$

By trial and error,

$$\begin{vmatrix} C & C & 1 \\ 0 & A & 1 \\ B & 0 & 1 \end{vmatrix} = 0$$

This determinant represents a nomograph which will be much easier to construct and use. It is already in the final construction form, and no further manipulation will be needed. As shown in Fig. 21.40, a scale graduated uniformly in terms of B is to extend upward along the y axis at $x = 0$. A scale graduated uniformly in terms of A is to extend to the right along the x axis at $y = 0$. The third scale is also uniformly graduated and extends upward to the right at 45° (or half the angle between axes) from the origin of the other two scales at $x = 0$ and $y = 0$. The C scale must be divided by plotting the points using the coordinate system. Thus the location of the point $C = 2$ is found by the intersection of the coordinate lines, $x = 2$ and $y = 2$. The third scale can also be divided by the method of paragraph 21.10.

An equation where the determinant method greatly simplifies the problem is

$$\frac{B}{C} + \frac{1}{A} = \frac{1}{B}$$

Although the apparent form of this equa-

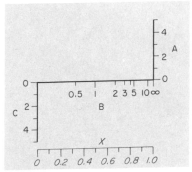

FIG. 21.38. Nomograph for $AB = C$ using cartesian coordinates.

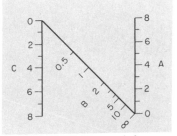

FIG. 21.39. Nomograph for $AB = C$ using skewed or oblique coordinates.

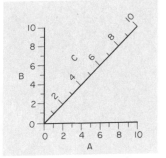

FIG. 21.40. Nomograph for $\frac{1}{A} + \frac{1}{B} = \frac{1}{C}$.

tion is that of the three-parallel-straight-scale nomograph, the term containing two variables prevents use of the standard geometry. Expanding the equation to obtain the summation of products gives

$$AB^2 + BC - AC = 0$$

By trial and error,

$$\begin{vmatrix} A & 0 & 1 \\ B & B^2 & 1 \\ 0 & C & 1 \end{vmatrix} = 0$$

Again this determinant is in the final construction form and needs no further manipulation. The nomograph (Fig. 21.41) represented by this determinant has the same general arrangement as the previous example. The A scale is along the y axis at $x = 0$ and is graduated in terms of A. The C scale is along the x axis at $y = 0$ and is graduated in terms of C. The third scale is still upward to the right but no longer at $45°$. The coordinates indicate that the scale is curved. A table of coordinates can be developed to graduate this scale.

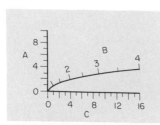

FIG 21.41. Nomograph for $\dfrac{B}{C} + \dfrac{1}{A} = \dfrac{1}{B}$.

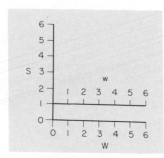

FIG. 21.42. Nomograph for $W = S(W - w)$.

B	x_B	y_B
0	0	0
1	1	1
2	4	2
3	9	3
4	16	4

The third scale can also be graduated by the method of paragraph 21.10. The determinant proves that the third scale is curved and therefore is a legitimate answer. A major advantage of determinant methods is to prove the format of the nomograph. Often the determinant cannot be used directly to graduate the scales because of the problem of unvarying moduli, but merely knowing

the form of the scales permits construction of a nomograph which might otherwise be impossible.

To illustrate how a determinant aids in determining the form that a nomograph will take for a given equation, suppose a nomograph is required to represent the equation

$$W = S\,(W - w)$$

where $W =$ weight of an object in air, gm

$w =$ weight of the object in water, gm

$S =$ specific gravity of the object

By trial and error,

$$\begin{vmatrix} S & 0 & 1 \\ 1 & w & 1 \\ 0 & W & 1 \end{vmatrix} = 0$$

This determinant is in final construction form and may be used directly. The determinant indicates a scale uniformly graduated in terms of S and extending upward from $x = 0$. A second scale is graduated uniformly in terms of w and extends to the right from $y = 1$. The third scale is graduated uniformly in terms of W and extends to the right from $y = 0$. This nomograph (Fig. 21.42) is extremely easy to use and construct but offers some chance for inaccuracy if the specific gravity is being determined from the weights of the object in the two media. Another difficulty with this nomograph is that specific gravities considerably larger than unity require a very long S scale if the distance from $S = 0$ to $S = 1$ is to be sufficiently large to give accurate intersections. Skewing the axes of the coordinate system will improve the usefulness of this nomograph.

A second determinant can be found which also is a solution to the equation.

$$\begin{vmatrix} W & -W & 1 \\ 1 & -S & 0 \\ w & 0 & 1 \end{vmatrix} = 0$$

This determinant is not in the final construction form and must be manipulated to produce that form. Adding column 1 to column 3 and dividing each row by the resulting term in column 3 produces

$$\begin{vmatrix} \dfrac{W}{1+W} & \dfrac{-W}{1+W} & 1 \\ 1 & -S & 1 \\ \dfrac{w}{1+w} & 0 & 1 \end{vmatrix} = 0$$

The nomograph which results from this determinant is shown in Fig. 21.43. Either nomograph offers advantages and disadvantages which must be compromised by the constructor. This example shows that determinant methods may provide more than one form of nomograph for any equation and that the construction of a successful nomograph relies on experience and patience, combined with good fortune in finding the best solution. If all the formal methods described in this chapter fail, the graphical-anamorphosis method of Chap. 22 will sometimes provide a nomograph. The nomographer seeking the best answer to a problem is advised to outline all solutions which can be found and then select the best method.

21.23. NOMOGRAPHS FOR EQUATIONS OF MORE THAN THREE VARIABLES—GEOMETRIC METHOD. A relationship involving four variable quantities may be such that it . can be represented by a nomographic chart composed of two 3-variable nomographs. The nomographs are combined by arranging them so that a scale of one is superimposed upon an identically constructed scale of the other. The coin-

ciding common scales are ungraduated since the stem serves only as a pivot scale or line at which the tie lines for each of the component nomographs will intersect.

An equation of the form

$$f(p) + f(q) + f(r) = f(s)$$
or $\qquad f(p) + f(q) = -f(r) + f(s)$

can be represented by a nomograph composed of two parallel-scale nomographs. The equation is rewritten as two 3-variable equations by equating each side of the second form of the above to an arbitrary quantity K. Thus

$$f(p) + f(q) = K$$
and $\qquad K = f(s) - f(r)$

The equations could also be written by rearrangement of the terms so that

$$f(p) + K = f(s)$$
and $\qquad K - f(q) = f(r)$

Each of these pairs of three-variable equations may be represented by a standard three-parallel-straight-scale nomograph. As shown in Fig. 21.44, the major difference between the two pairs of nomographs is the position that the K or pivot scale occupies. For the first pair of equations, the K scale is the center scale, and the tie lines connecting the outer scales of each pair will intersect at the pivot scale, forming a large X. The K scale for the second pair of equations is one of the outer scales so that both scales of one pair will lie on one side of the pivot scale and the two scales of the other pair will lie on the other side of the pivot scale. If more than four variables are to be combined to form a nomograph, the second method permits easier addition of further three-variable nomographs at the end of the "string" of existing nomographs.

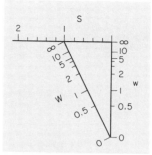

FIG. 21.43. Nomograph for $W = S(W - w)$ in second form.

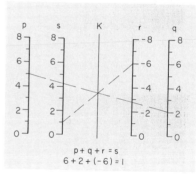

FIG. 21.44. A four-variable parallel-scale chart.

The major consideration in the construction of any nomograph of more than three variables must be the *common* characteristics of the K or pivot scale. Whatever modulus is chosen or calculated for the K scale for one group of variables *must* be used for the K scale with the second group. This often means that some thought must be given to the interlocking nature of this modulus before the problem is started.

As a practical example of a four-variable-equation nomograph (Fig. 21.45) the smoke point of a kerosene or diesel fuel is measured as the height in millimeters of a flame that can be maintained without smoking when the fuel is burned in a standard lamp. The smoke point may be evaluated from the hydrocarbon content of the fuel through the use of the formula

$$S = 0.48P + 0.32N + 0.20A$$

where S = smoke-point flame height, mm

P = paraffinic-hydrocarbon content, per cent

N = naphthenic-hydrocarbon content, per cent

A = aromatic-hydrocarbon content, per cent

The formula may be replaced by two 3-variable equations:

$$0.32N - K = -0.48P$$
and $$S - K = 0.20A$$

Each of these equations can be represented by a standard three-scale nomograph, each related to the other through the common (K) scale. Construction of such a chart may be outlined as follows.

1. *N Scale*

$f(N) = 0.32N$

Range: $0.32 (25 - 0) = 8.0$

Scale length: Assume 5 in.

Modulus: $\dfrac{5}{8} = 0.625$

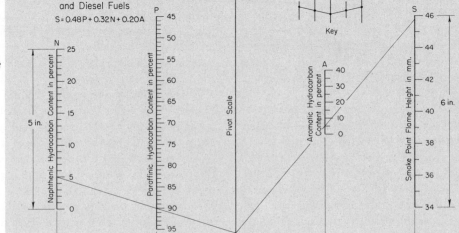

FIG. 21.45. A parallel-scale chart for the smoke point of kerosene.

Divide scale into 25 equal graduations in a length of 5 in. Label every fifth graduation.

2. *K Scale* (Common or pivot scale)

$$f(K) = -K$$

Modulus: Assume 0.5

This scale requires no graduations, and consequently no scale range or length can be given.

3. *P Scale*

$$f(P) = -0.48P$$

Range: $-0.48 (95 - 45) = -24$

Modulus: $\dfrac{0.625 \times 0.5}{0.625 + 0.5} = 0.278$

Scale length: $0.278 \times (-24) = 6.67$ in.

Divide the scale into 50 equal parts in 6.67 in. of length. Label every fifth graduation. The scale values range from 45 at the top to 95 at the bottom since the negative function value reverses the scale direction.

4. *Scale Spacing*

Chart width: Assume 5.75 in.

$$\frac{a}{b} = \frac{m_N}{m_K} = \frac{0.625}{0.5}$$

$$a = 3.19, b = 2.56$$

5. *Base Tie Line*

Arrange the scales so that a line connecting the middle values of the N and P scales is approximately horizontal. A tie line connecting $N = 5$, $P = 90$ is drawn for future connection with the tie line from the other side of the nomograph. The value of K intersected by the tie line is 44.8.

6. *S Scale*

$$f(S) = S$$

Range: $46 - 34 = 12$

Scale length: Assume 6 in.

Modulus: $\dfrac{6}{12} = 0.5$

Divide the scale into 12 equal parts in 6 in. of length. Label every second graduation.

7. *K Scale*

$$f(K) = -K$$

$m = 0.5$ from assumption of step 2

8. *A Scale*

$$f(A) = 0.20A$$

Range: $0.2 (40 - 0) = 8$

Modulus: $\dfrac{0.5 \times 0.5}{0.5 + 0.5} = 0.25$

Scale length: $0.25 \times 8 = 2$ in.

Divide the scale into 8 equal graduations, labeling every second division. Each division is ¼ in. from the next.

9. *Scale Spacing*

Chart width: Assume 5.75 in.

$$\frac{a}{b} = \frac{m_S}{m_K} = \frac{0.5}{0.5}$$

$$a = 2.88, b = 2.88$$

10. *Base Tie Lines*

$$N = 5, P = 90, K = 44.8, A = 5,$$
$$S = 45.8$$

A key is provided to indicate the correct manner for locating the tie lines on the chart. The tie lines must intersect at the pivot scale. The value of any one of the variables can be determined by locating the tie lines connecting the given values of the other three. The completed chart is shown in Fig. 21.45.

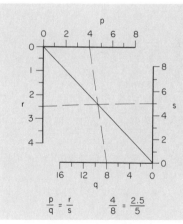

FIG. 21.46. A proportionality or double-Z chart.

21.24. PROPORTIONALITY CHARTS. An equation of four variables expressed in the form

$$\frac{f(p)}{f(q)} = \frac{f(r)}{f(s)}$$

can be represented by a nomographic chart which combines two 3-variable Z charts about a common transverse scale. The chart (Fig. 21.46) so formed consists of one graduated scale for each of the four variables plus an ungraduated transverse pivot scale. If a set of four values of the variables is to satisfy the equation, the straight tie line joining the values of p and q must intersect the tie line joining the values of r and s at a point on the pivot scale.

The construction of the double-Z or proportionality chart can be shown by plane geometry to require that the moduli of the various scales retain the ratio

$$\frac{m_p}{m_q} = \frac{m_r}{m_s}$$

As an example of an equation for which a proportionality chart can be made, automobile speed is related to engine speed, overall gear ratio, and tire diameter by the formula

$$V = \frac{DN}{336R}$$

where V = automobile speed, mph
D = tire diameter, in.
N = engine speed, rpm
R = overall gear ratio

This relationship may be represented by a proportionality chart (Fig. 21.47) if the equation is rearranged to the form

$$\frac{N}{336V} = \frac{R}{D}$$

Chart construction follows the usual outline.

1. *N Scale*

$f(N) = N$

Range: $5,000 - 0 = 5,000$

Scale length: Assume 6.25 in.

Modulus: $\frac{6.25}{5,000} = 0.00125$

Divide the scale into 25 equal divisions in 6.25 in. of length. Label every fifth division.

2. *V Scale*

$f(V) = 336V$

Range: $336 (100 - 0) = 33,600$

Modulus: $\frac{6.25}{33,600} = 0.000186$

Divide the scale into 25 equal divisions in 6.25 in. of length. Label every fifth graduation.

3. *D Scale*

$f(D) = D$

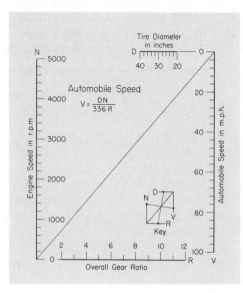

FIG. 21.47. A double-Z chart for automobile speed.

Range: $40 - 20 = 20$

Scale length: Assume 1.2 in.

Modulus: $\dfrac{1.2}{20} = 0.06$

Scale starting point $= 0.06 \times 20 = 1.2$ in. from origin. Divide the scale into 10 equal divisions in 1.2 in. of length beginning at 1.2 in. from origin. Label every fifth division.

4. *R Scale*

$f(R) = R$

Range: $12 - 2 = 10$

Modulus: $\dfrac{0.00125}{0.000186} = \dfrac{m_R}{0.06}$

$$m_R = 0.403$$

Scale length: $0.403 \times 10 = 4.03$ in.

Scale starting point: $0.403 \times 2 = 0.806$ in. from origin

Divide the scale into 10 equal divisions in 4.03 in. of length starting at 0.806 in. from the origin. Label every second graduation.

A key is provided to indicate the correct manner for locating the tie lines on the chart. The tie lines must intersect at the transverse pivot scale. Figure 21.47 is the completed chart.

Other combinations of three-scale nomographs to represent equations of four variables are possible. A common type has an equation of the form

$$f(p) + f(q) = f(r)f(s)$$

This equation can be represented by a combination of a three-parallel-scale nomograph and a Z chart. One scale of the parallel-scale nomograph is common to one of the "legs" of the Z chart as in Fig. 21.48. The principles of each chart type are followed, using a fixed modulus for the common scale.

The process of combining basic nomographs may be expanded to cover the representation of equations in five or more variables. As the form of the chart becomes more complex, however, it becomes more cumbersome to use and its value as a means of solving an equation diminishes.

Nomographs representing four-or-more-variable equations can be constructed by the straightforward graphic chart-layout methods (paragraph 21.10), but the amount of labor involved will be great. Unless no standard geometric method for nomograph construction seems to fit, the use of graphic chart-layout methods should be avoided. Although other geometric methods are possible, the following example of a nomograph for a four-variable equation, which combines a Z chart and a determinant chart, presents a good solution for some difficult equations.

Assume that a nomograph is to be constructed to represent the equation

$$\frac{I}{W} = \left(\frac{T}{2\pi}\right)^2 r + r$$

The best method of determining the format for such an equation is to write the equation as simple letters for each term. Thus the equation shown could be written

$$\frac{A}{B} = C^2D + D^2$$

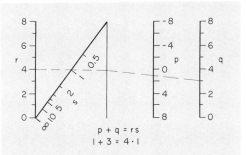

FIG. 21.48. A four-variable combination-type chart.

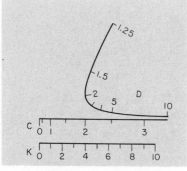

FIG. 21.49. A nomograph for $K = C^2D + D^2$.

If $A/B = K$ is considered as the first half of the combination nomograph, then $K = C^2D + D^2$ is the second half. The first equation is the form for a Z chart and creates no problems. The resulting Z chart is shown on the right side of Fig. 21.50. The second equation is in a form that is not recognizable as any of the simple forms. The use of a determinant will assist in formulating a nomograph for this equation. The equation

$$C^2D + D^2 - K = 0$$

can be represented by the determinant

$$\begin{vmatrix} 0 & K & 1 \\ 1 & C^2 & 0 \\ -D & -D^2 & 1 \end{vmatrix} = 0$$

Adding column 1 to column 3, multiplying row 3 by -1, and finally dividing row 3 by $D - 1$ produces the determinant

$$\begin{vmatrix} 0 & K & 1 \\ 1 & C^2 & 1 \\ \dfrac{D}{D-1} & \dfrac{D^2}{D-1} & 1 \end{vmatrix} = 0$$

A schematic layout of the resulting nomograph is shown in Fig. 21.49. This determinant chart, combined with the

FIG. 21.50. A nomograph for $\dfrac{I}{W} = \left(\dfrac{T}{2\pi}\right)^2 r + r^2$.

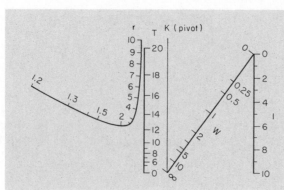

Z chart for the first equation, produces the completed nomograph (Fig. 21.50). The very simplicity of the method recommends it as a solution whenever some portion of an equation is not recognizable as representing one of the standard geometrical forms.

21.25. SPECIAL SLIDE RULES. Any slide rule consists of two or more scales which can be moved laterally with respect to each other. Any pair of scales having such lateral movement can provide the graphic equivalent of addition, subtraction, multiplication, division, and combinations of these processes. All slide rules are based upon this simple principle. Although this discussion deals only with straight scales for slide rules, the scales can be curved and in some cases must be curved. Any equation which can be represented by a nomograph can also be represented by a special slide rule, although the slide rule may be cumbersome and impractical. Special slide rules are usually intended to solve only one equation and are designed to provide the least possible slide settings necessary to obtain the answer. Special slide rules are also usually intended to have each pair of factors set opposite each other on the various scales so that the use of indexes and indicators is kept at a minimum. The standard engineer's slide rule is a general-purpose instrument and often requires reading a partial answer and resetting this value on another scale.

To demonstrate the use of sliding scales, take a pair of standard drafting scales, as indicated in Fig. 21.51, and place them as shown with the origin (zero) of one scale (B) indexed (matched) with any desired division of the other scale (A). Pairs of values will occur along

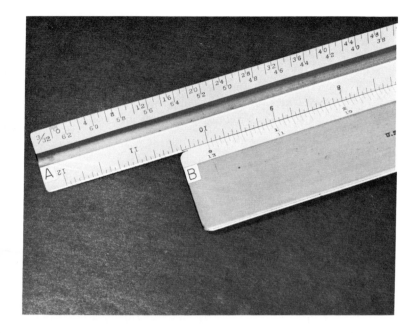

FIG. 21.51. Illustration of sliding scales.

the A and B scales, and these values will conform to the equation

$$A = 10 - B$$

If the direction of either the A or B scale had been reversed, the scales would have been arranged so that addition was performed. If the answer to the addition operation is to appear at the index (origin) of one of the scales, it can be seen that the illustration is correctly arranged to solve the problem $8 + 2 = 10$. Throughout the discussion, it will be assumed that the most logical type of slide rule will have the two factors of the problem set together on opposite scales and the answer found opposite an indicator or index. Since the same scale arrangement will provide both addition and subtraction, the need for an easy-to-use format becomes more evident.

The examples of Fig. 21.52 illustrate the principles of sliding scales. At A, a standard conversion chart consisting of

two fixed adjacent scales is shown; distance a obviously equals distance b. At B, a center scale is made movable with respect to two outer fixed scales; the distances a and b total the distance c. If the slide rule is to follow the assumption that the answer is to be *opposite an index,* the slide rule will solve the equation $c - b = a$. Moving the index or zero point of the a and c scales to the *opposite* (right) end of the scale, the slide rule will solve $c' + b' = a'$ when values of c' and b' are set opposite each other. Thus, the operations of addition and subtraction are dependent upon three items, (1) scale form, (2) scale direction, and (3) alignment of indexes or matching points.

At C, an additional d scale has been added to the slide rule. If *all* zero points are at the *left,* the slide rule obviously solves the equation distance d minus distance b is equal to distance a minus distance c. If $a - c = d - b$, then by re-

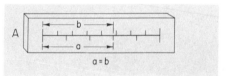

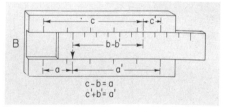

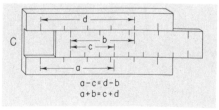

FIG. 21.52. Sliding scales for addition and subtraction.

arrangement, $a + b = c + d$. Although they are not arranged in the best order, all values will be found opposite each other on the paired scales. A more convenient arrangement for the equation $a + b = c + d$ would be to have the a and b scales paired and the c and d scales paired.

To provide a simple rule for arranging slide rule scales, consider example (B) of Fig. 21.52. The equation solved is $c - b = a$. Rewriting the equation as $c - b - a = 0$ and setting the values in a vertical line, the order in which the scales will be placed on the slide rule is

$$\begin{bmatrix} \text{Scale order 1} \\ c - b - a = 0 \end{bmatrix} \quad \begin{array}{l} c \rightarrow \\ -b \rightarrow \\ \text{index} \\ -a \rightarrow \end{array}$$

The direction of each scale for increasing values is shown by the arrows. If the equation is to be $c' + b' = a'$ as in the second part of example (B) of Fig. 21.52, the scale arrangement is

$$\begin{bmatrix} \text{Scale order 2} \\ c' + b' - a' = 0 \end{bmatrix} \quad \begin{array}{l} \leftarrow c' \\ b' \rightarrow \\ \text{index} \\ \leftarrow -a' \end{array}$$

From this information a very simple method can be developed, which will give the correct *direction* of any scale on a slide rule so that it will perform the operation desired. The equation of the slide rule is written with all the terms on one side of the equation and the other side equal to zero. The letters representing the terms are then placed in a vertical column in the order in which the scales will be arranged on the slide rule. If a scale contains only an index, that scale must be included in the column in the correct position. A column of *alternating* plus and minus signs is placed in front of the letters, and another column of *alternating* signs is placed following the letters but with the signs arranged so that each letter in the column has only one plus and one minus sign attached. For example,

$$\begin{bmatrix} \text{Scale order 1} \\ c - b - a = 0 \end{bmatrix} \quad \begin{array}{l} - c + \rightarrow \\ + b - \rightarrow \\ - \text{index} + \\ + d - \rightarrow \end{array}$$

For the equation

$$c - b = a \quad \text{or} \quad c - b - a = 0$$

the direction of scales (for increasing values) is to the right for all letter scales. Thus the direction of increasing values on the scales is shown to be *in the direction of the sign in the column which matches the sign of the term in the equation*. The second equation $c' + b' = a'$ or $c' + b' - a' = 0$ will be found to have the scale directions of c' and a' reversed from scale order 1, but the direction of the b scale remains the same as before. This is important. Starting the first column of signs with a plus instead of a minus will provide the *same* scale arrangement of increasing values as shown in the example. For

$$c' + b' - a' = 0,$$

$$\begin{bmatrix} \text{Scale order 2} \\ c' + b' - a' = 0 \end{bmatrix} \quad \begin{array}{l} \leftarrow + c - \\ - b + \rightarrow \\ + \text{index} - \\ \leftarrow - a + \end{array}$$

Example (C) of Fig. 21.52 can also be obtained by this method, and the scales can be rearranged to provide a different pairing of variables. The present arrangement of scales as shown in the figure is shown to solve the equation $a + b = c + d$ or $a + b - c - d = 0$.

The scale direction form is

$$\begin{bmatrix} \text{Scale order 3} \\ a + b - c - d = 0 \end{bmatrix} \quad \begin{array}{l} + d - \rightarrow \\ - b + \rightarrow \\ + c - \rightarrow \\ - a + \rightarrow \end{array}$$

Matching signs of the equation with the form would cause each of the scales to increase in value to the right. Still using the same equation with a new scale arrangement on the slide rule, in which the a and b scales are paired as are the c and d scales, would change the scale-direction form to

$$\begin{bmatrix} \text{Scale order 4} \\ a + b - c - d = 0 \end{bmatrix} \quad \begin{array}{l} - a + \rightarrow \\ \leftarrow + b - \\ \leftarrow - c + \\ + d - \rightarrow \end{array}$$

Matching signs for this new slide rule form would cause the a and d scales to increase to the right while the b and c scales would increase to the left. If it is desirable the a and d scales can increase to the left while the b and c scales increase to the right. This method is for slide rule operation in which the values of the variables are paired on adjacent scales and the *index of the scale* is not used as an indicator of values. That this mode of operation is different from the standard used with the usual engineer's slide rule should be noted.

21.26. CONSTRUCTION OF SLIDE RULES. Slide rules to solve equations of the form $f(a) + f(b) = f(c)$ or $f(a) + f(b) + f(c) = f(d)$ are normally constructed like a standard engineer's slide rule with a body having two outer fixed scales and a sliding center part having two more scales, each of which is adjacent to a scale on the body. For equations of three variables, one of the scales on the

slide is only an index or indicating arrow, but its relationship to the other scales of the rule is governed by the same restrictions that the scale representing a fourth variable would have. Since slide rules are related to conversion charts by being adjacent scales, the same rules govern their construction: The moduli of all scales must be the same, and all scales must have a common origin. Just as with conversion charts, the scales often do not include the origin within the scale range, and the usual method of aligning scales is by means of matching points. The scales of a slide rule are calculated without respect to alignment or direction on the rule. Position and direction of the scales are determined as the scales are actually being placed on the rule. Assume that a slide rule is to be constructed to solve the equation $p + 2q = r - 4$. The p scale is to vary from 0 to 10. The scales of this rule will be calculated exactly as the scales for a nomograph would be. (The completed slide rule and a typical problem solution are shown in Fig. 21.53.)

1. *p Scale*

   $f(p) = p$

   Range: $10 - 0 = 10$

   Length: Assume 10 in.

   Modulus: $\dfrac{10}{10} = 1$

   Divide the scale into 10 equal divisions in 10 in. of length.

2. *q Scale*

   $f(q) = 2q$

   Length: 10 in. from above

   Modulus: 1 from above

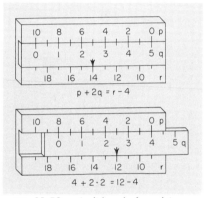

FIG. 21.53. A slide rule for solving $p + 2q = r - 4$.

Range: $1 \times 10 = 10$. Therefore q must vary from 0 to 5.

Divide the scale into 5 equal parts in 10 in. of length.

3. *r Scale*

$$f(r) = r - 4$$

Max. r: $10 + 2(5) + 4 = 24$

Min. r: $0 + 2(0) + 4 = 4$

Modulus: 1 from above

Length: $1 \times (24 - 4) = 20$ in. Obviously this scale will not fit on a rule intended to have 10-in. scales. Some change will have to be made in the range of values to be placed on the r scale. If we assume that the usual values encountered in problems will lie midway between the maximum and minimum, the r scale can vary from 9 to 19 which provides a range of 10 and a length of 10 in. Divide the scale into 10 equal parts in 10 in. of length.

4. *Scale Arrangement*

The scales are to be placed on the rule so that the p scale is on the upper body, the q scale adjacent on the slide, an *index* arrow on the lower half of the slide, and the r scale on the lower body.

5. *Scale Direction*

To determine the direction of increasing scale values for each scale, rewrite the equation, and use the scale-direction form. For

$$p + 2q - (r - 4) = 0$$

$$\leftarrow + p -$$
$$- q + \rightarrow$$
$$+ \text{ index } -$$
$$\leftarrow - r +$$

The p scale is to increase to the left, the q scale to the right, and the r scale to the left.

6. *Matching Points*

For $p = 10$, $q = 0$, place the index arrow at $r = 14$.

The previous slide rule for three variables is actually the same as a slide rule for four variables since the index is at a point which corresponds to a value of zero for some fourth variable. If the equation for the slide rule had been $p + 2q = s + (r - 4)$, all calculations could have been made just as in the previous example, with one exception. Wherever the index arrow or the index scale is mentioned, the terms $s = 0$ or the s scale must be substituted. The scale direction of the p, q, and r scales would remain the same while the s scale is seen to increase to the right from the rewritten equation $p + 2q - s - (r - 4) = 0$. The matching points would be at $p = 10$, $q = 0$, $s = 0$, and $r = 14$. The completed slide rule is shown in Fig. 21.54. Slide rules involving four variables usually involve considerable balancing of the scale ranges to obtain optimum results. If the p and q scales are required to have the ranges given, the only choice of range would be for the s and r scales. Regardless of the range chosen for the r scale, the matching points must remain the same so that any change of the r scale will cause a corresponding change in the s scale. Experience should be obtained in "juggling" the scale ranges of simple slide rules as shown in the illustration, before complicated slide rules are attempted.

A typical slide rule or slide chart to solve a practical problem is shown in

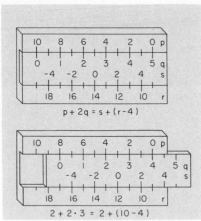

FIG. 21.54. A slide rule for solving $p + 2q = s + (r - 4)$.

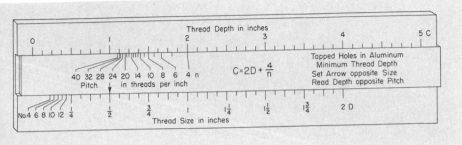

FIG. 21.55. A slide rule for minimum thread depth.

Fig. 21.55. The minimum thread depth of a hole tapped in aluminum is given by the equation $C = 2D + 4/n$, where C is the thread depth in inches, D is the thread diameter, and n is the number of threads per inch. This equation is designed to provide approximately equal strengths of the tapped hole and the threaded fastener to be used in the hole. A major difference in this slide rule from the previous examples can be seen in the method of labeling the calibrations. The slide rule is calibrated in exactly the same terms that would be used by either a machinist or a designer concerned with this problem. The calculations leading to the construction of this slide rule follow the same pattern as for the first slide rule discussed. It should be noted concerning the direction of scales that if the equation is rewritten as $2D + 4/n - C = 0$ and the scale-direction form used to determine the scale direction, the n scale seemingly does not obey the rule. The scale-direction form is intended to determine the direction of increasing function values of the scale, and the function $4/n$ increases in a direction opposite that of increasing values of n. This distinction between scale values and function values normally must be made only for scales whose function is a reciprocal.

The construction of nomographs has already indicated that problems involv-

ing multiplication and division can be solved as addition or subtraction of the logarithms of the factors. The slide rule is limited to the addition of distances but can be constructed to provide multiplication of numbers by using logarithmic scales in place of the uniform scales of addition problems. The construction of logarithmic scales follows the methods used in nomographs while the location and direction of scales follow the methods illustrated for an addition-type slide rule.

Assume that a slide rule is to be constructed to solve the equation $pq^2 = 0.2r$. This expression can be rewritten in logarithmic form suitable for the construction and direction of scales.

$$\log p + 2 \log q = \log r + \log \tfrac{1}{5}$$

The values of p are to vary from 1 to 10, and the scale is to be 10 in. long. (The resulting slide rule is shown in Fig. 21.56.)

1. *p Scale*

$f(p) = \log p$

Range: $\log 10 - \log 1 = 1$

Length: Assume 10 in.

Modulus: $\dfrac{10}{1} = 10$

Cycle length: $10 (\log 10 - \log 1) = 10$ in.

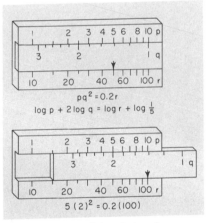

FIG. 21.56. A slide rule to solve $pq^2 = 0.2r$.

2. *q Scale*

$f(q) = 2 \log q$

Length: 10 in. from above

Modulus: 10 from above

Range: $\dfrac{10}{10} = 1$. Therefore q must vary from 1 to $\sqrt{10}$ or 1 to 3.1623.

Cycle length: $10 \, (2 \log 10 - 2 \log 1) = 20$ in.

3. *r Scale*

$f(r) = \log r$

Max. r: 500

Min. r: 5

This range of values will require three log cycles, which in turn will make the scale 30 in. long. Values of r varying from 10 to 100 will be chosen so that the scale will be 10 in. long. Cycle length: 10 in.

4. *Scale Arrangement*

Scale p on upper body, scale q on upper slide, *index* on lower slide, and r scale on lower body.

5. *Scale Direction*

$\log p + 2 \log q - \log r + \log \tfrac{1}{5} = 0$

$$- p + \rightarrow$$
$$\leftarrow + q -$$
$$- \text{index} +$$
$$+ r - \rightarrow$$

The p scale is to increase to the right, the q scale to the left, and the r scale to the right.

6. *Matching Points*

$p = 10$, $q = 1$, index at $r = 50$

The addition of a fourth variable to the equation $pq^2 = 0.2 \, rs$ would create a slide rule as shown in Fig. 21.57. The

s scale replaces the index scale in all calculations and would require knowledge of the cycle length of the s scale, the direction of the scale, and the matching points including the s scale.

The equation $\log p + 2 \log q - \log r - \log s + \log \tfrac{1}{5} = 0$ indicates that the cycle length of the s scale would be $10(\log 10 - \log 1) = 10$ in. The direction of the s scale would increase to the left. Matching points would be $p = 10$, $q = 1$, $r = 50$ at $s = 1$.

A practical slide rule involving four factors is one for calculating the displacement of an internal combustion engine from the formula

$$V = \frac{\pi D^2 S N}{4}$$

where V = displacement, cu. in.
S = stroke, in.
N = number of cylinders
D = bore of cylinders, in.

Combining constants, we get

$$V = 0.7854 D^2 S N$$

In logarithmic form

$$- \log V + 2 \log D + \log S + \log N + \log 0.7854 = 0$$

The log cycles for the V, S, and N scales will be equal in length while the cycle for the D scale will be twice as long.

The scale direction form

$$+ V - \rightarrow$$
$$- S + \rightarrow$$
$$\leftarrow + N -$$
$$- D + \rightarrow$$

indicates that the V scale increases to the right, the S scale to the right, the N scale to the left, and the D scale to the right. The completed slide rule is shown in Fig. 21.58. Matching points are

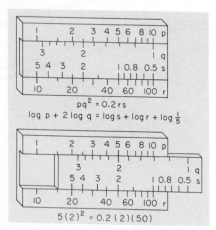

FIG. 21.57. A slide rule to solve $pq^2 = 0.2 \, rs$.

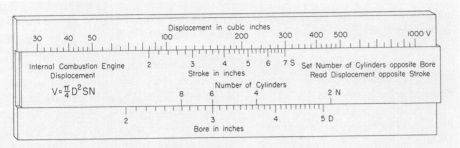

FIG. 21.58. A slide rule for the displacement of an internal combustion engine.

$N = 6$, $D = 3$, $S = 4$, and $V = 169.6$.

Slide rules can be designed for more-than-four-variable equations, and the process is identical with that for slide rules of three and four variables. Equations of five and six variables require the use of two slides in place of one, with considerable complication in the mechanical construction. Methods of constructing slide rules for more than four variables or for those involving combined addition and multiplication operations are beyond the scope of this text.

21.27. SUMMARY. The majority of equations of two or three variables may be represented by a conversion chart, nomograph, or special slide rule. Any equation may also be represented by a standard x-y plot, and the principles outlined in Chap. 22 should be used to determine the proper coordinate system. An equation of two variables may be represented by two adjacent functional graphic scales. Equations of three variables may often be represented by a three-scale nomograph, using geometric methods, scale-layout methods, or determinant methods. Generally, any equation which can be represented by a nomograph can also be represented by a special slide rule. Equations which do not fit any of the methods indicated should be considered in the same

category as empirical data and the methods of Chap. 22 used to represent the equation. Equations of four or more variables should be considered as two or more three-variable equations with a common arbitrary variable linking the three-variable equations. Nomographs to represent a four-variable equation consist of 2 three-variable nomographs having a common pivot scale. Thus a total of five scales is needed to represent a four-variable equation.

Nomographs, conversion charts, and slide rules are all dependent upon functional graphic scales to represent the function of the variable appearing in the equation. A functional scale has the scale calibrations appearing at distances proportional to the value of the function of the variable at the scale graduation having the value of x. A proportionality factor called the *modulus* is used to convert the function values into inches. The scale equation $d = mf(x)$ states this fact mathematically. The *origin* of the scale is defined as the point on the scale where $f(x) = 0$.

Conversion charts relate equations of two variables to graphic scales. Conversion charts have two adjacent graphic scales, each graduated in terms of one of the two variables. Both scales use the same modulus and have a common origin.

Nomographs represent equations of three variables by three graphic scales arranged and graduated so that values which are solutions of the equation lie on a straight line connecting the scales. Geometric methods may be found for many forms of nomographs, but the most common forms are (*a*) the three-parallel-straight-scale chart and (*b*) the *Z* chart.

The three-parallel-straight-scale nomograph represents the equation of the form $A + B = C$. The A and B scales are the outer scales while C scale is between the A and B scales. The modulus of the center scale is equal to the product of the outer-scale moduli, divided by the sum of the outer-scale moduli. The distance from the A scale to the C scale bears the same ratio to the distance from the B scale to the C scale as the A- and B-scale moduli. This form of nomograph may also be used to represent an equation of the form $AB = C$ if the equation is rewritten in the logarithmic form. Thus $AB = C$ becomes $\log A + \log B = \log C$.

The *Z* chart may be used to represent the equation form $AB = C$. The chart consists of two parallel straight scales representing the A and C variables, arranged at a convenient distance apart and with their origins at opposite ends. A transverse scale connecting the outer-scale origins represents the B variable. The A and C scales are graduated according to the function of the variable they represent, while the transverse scale must be graduated by a series of tie lines connecting appropriate values on the outer scales. A formula for determining a temporary scale along one of the outer scales may also be used to assist in graduating the transverse scale.

Determinants may also be used to analyze the form of nomograph which will represent an equation of three variables. A vanishing third-order determinant consisting of nine terms arranged in three columns and three rows is used, and expansion of the determinant must produce the original equation. In construction form, the determinant must have one column of all ones and no row containing a variable found in another row. The elements in each row (excluding the ones) are the x and y coordinates of the graduations on scales for a nomograph. Often the determinant is used to select the nomograph form, and simple scale-layout methods are used to construct the nomograph.

A slide rule to represent an equation of no more than four variables consists of a body and a slide. A functional scale may be placed on each side of the joint separating the body from the slide; thus a total of two scales on the body and two on the slide is possible. An index replaces one scale for equations of three variables. All scales of the slide rule have the same modulus. A scale-direction form relating the sign of the scale variable to the direction of increasing scale values facilitates construction.

PROBLEMS

The problems listed below are arranged according to the number of variables involved in the equation. Appropriate solution methods are listed for each of the problem groups. The teacher is to specify the method used to represent each problem assigned. Where the range of a variable is not given, limiting values of the variable should either be assigned or be determined by substitution in the problem equation. Scales should be carefully graduated and calibrated, and each is to have a legend indicating the quantity represented and the unit of measurement. Each chart is to have a descriptive title with its equation.

GROUP 1. ONE-VARIABLE PROBLEMS

These problems are to be used as exercises in the construction of functional scales. The completed scales should be accompanied by all calculations used in their construction.

21.1.1. $f(r) = 6.5r, r = 0$ to 10

21.1.2. $f(s) = 0.4r^3 - 20, s = 0$ to 5

21.1.3. $f(t) = 8/t, t = 1$ to 50

21.1.4. $f(u) = 1 - \log u, u = 1$ to 10

21.1.5. $f(v) = v/(v - 1), v = 2$ to 20

21.1.6. $f(w) = w(w - 1), w = 1$ to 4

GROUP 2. TWO-VARIABLE PROBLEMS

These problems can be represented by x-y plots, conversion charts, pivot-point nomographs, and if desired, two-scale slide rules.

21.2.1. Pressure conversion

$$P = 0.434H$$

where P = pressure, lb per sq in.
H = head, 0 to 50 ft water

21.2.2. Flow conversion

$$W = 500Q$$

where W = weight of water, lb per hr
Q = volume of water, 0 to 50 gal per min

21.2.3. Fuel oil

$$H = 18,300 + 40G$$

where H = heating value, Btu per lb
G = API gravity, 10 to 34°

21.2.4. Low-pressure steam

$$H = 1,050 + 0.473T$$

where H = heat content above water at 32°F, Btu per lb
T = temperature, 200 to 500°F

21.2.5. Concrete

$$S_{28} = S_7 = 30 \sqrt{S_7}$$

where S_{28} = probable 28-day strength, lb per sq in.
S_7 = 7-day test strength, 1,000 to 3,000 lb per sq in.

21.2.6. Heavy liquids, liquors, and acids

$$B = 145 - \frac{145}{S}$$

where B = Baumé gravity, °
S = specific gravity, 60/60°F, 1.0 to 1.6

21.2.7. Round brass bar stock

$$W = 2.92D^2$$

where W = weight, lb per ft
D = diameter, 0 to 6 in.

21.2.8. Simple pendulum

$$T = 2\pi \sqrt{\frac{L}{g}}$$

where T = period of oscillation, sec
L = centroidal distance, 0 to 10 ft
g = acceleration due to gravity, 32.2 ft per sec²

21.2.9. Sharp-crested 90° V-notch weir

$$Q = 2.5H^{2.5}$$

where Q = discharge (water), cu ft per sec
  H = head above sill, 0.5 to 2.0 ft

21.2.10. Standard annealed copper wire

$$L = \frac{3,000}{(10)S/10}$$

where L = breaking load, lb
  S = wire size, 0 to 16 AWG

21.2.11. Power conversion

$$HP = 0.746KW$$

where HP = horsepower
  KW = electric power, 0 to 100 kw

21.2.12. Wrought-aluminum alloys

$$T = 575B$$

where T = approximate tensile strength, lb per sq in.
  B = Brinell hardness, 20 to 120

21.2.13. Moist air

$$S = 0.238 + 0.48H$$

where S = humid heat, Btu per lb per °F
  H = humidity, 0 to 0.15 lb water vapor per lb dry air

21.2.14. Viscosity conversion

$$K = 0.22S - \frac{180}{S}$$

where K = kinematic viscosity, centistokes
  S = Saybolt Universal viscosity, 30 to 60 sec

21.2.15. Round steel bar stock

$$W = 2.67D^2$$

where W = weight, lb per ft of length
  D = diameter, 0 to 6 in.

21.2.16. Uniformly loaded shaft

$$f = 211.4\sqrt{\frac{1}{d}}$$

where f = fundamental frequency of transverse vibration, cycles per min
  d = static deflection, 0.01 to 1 in.

GROUP 3. THREE-VARIABLE PROBLEMS

These problems can be represented by x-y plots, network charts, nomographs, and special slide rules.

21.3.1. Equation

$$2p + q = r$$

p = 0 to 10
q = 0 to 25
r = 0 to 40

21.3.2. Equation

$$3p = q = 50 - r$$

p = 0 to 10
q = 0 to 20
r = 0 to 45

21.3.3. Equation

$$2pq = r$$

p = 0 to 10
q = 0 to 10
r = 0 to 50

21.3.4. Equation

$$\frac{pq}{2} = r - 10$$

p = 0 to 10
q = 0 to 20
r = 0 to 50

21.3.5. Ohm's law

$$I = \frac{E}{R}$$

where I = current, 0 to 10 amp
E = voltage, 0 to 120 volts
R = resistance, 1 to 20 ohms

21.3.6. Air flow

$$TP = SP + VP$$

where TP = total pressure, in. water
SP = static pressure, 0 to 10 in. water
VP = velocity pressure, 0 to 2.5 in. water

21.3.7. Pressure conversion

$$P_A = P_G + 0.49B$$

where P_A = absolute pressure, lb per sq in.
P_G = gauge pressure, 0 to 25 lb per sq in.
B = barometric pressure, 28 to 32 in. mercury

21.3.8. Insulation

$$T_M = \frac{T_H - T_C}{2}$$

where T_M = arithmetic mean of temperature, °F
T_H = temperature, hot side, 200 to 1200°F
T_C = temperature, cold side, 80 to 200°F

21.3.9. Tube swaging

$$L = 4.08(D_1 - D_2) + 0.13$$

where L = length of runout, 0 to 5 in.
D_1 = outside diameter of tube before swaging, ¼ to 4 in.
D_2 = outside diameter of tube after swaging, ³⁄₁₆ to 3 in.

21.3.10. Sharp-crested submerged rectangular weir

$$Q = 3.33BH^{1.5}$$

where Q = discharge, cu ft water per sec
B = width, 1 to 10 ft
H = head above sill, 0.5 to 2 ft

21.3.11. Dry air

$$D = \frac{P}{0.754(T + 460)}$$

where D = density, lb per cu ft
P = absolute pressure, 16 to 30 in. mercury
T = temperature, -40 to 180°F

21.3.12. Air ducts

$$D = 1.075 \sqrt{WH}$$

where D = diameter of equivalent round duct, in.
W = width of rectangular duct, 10 to 100 in.
H = height of rectangular duct, 5 to 50 in.

21.3.13. Roll crusher

$$F = 0.04D + X$$

where F = maximum feed particle size, in.
D = diameter of rolls, 18 to 72 in.
X = distance between roll faces, 0.25 to 2.5 in.

21.3.14. Gear drive

$$C = \frac{D_w + D_G}{2}$$

where C = center distance, in.
D_w = worm-pitch diameter, 1 to 6 in.
D_G = gear-pitch diameter, 5 to 30 in.

21.3.15. Tapped holes in cast iron

$$T = 1.5D + \frac{4}{P}$$

where T = thread depth, in.
D = nominal thread diameter, ¼ to 3 in.
P = pitch, 4 to 32 threads per in.

21.3.16. Falling body

$$h = h_0 - \frac{gt^2}{2}$$

where h = height, ft
h_0 = initial height, 0 to 500 ft
t = elapsed time, 0 to 5 sec
g = acceleration due to gravity, 32.2 ft per sec^2

21.3.17. Lead storage cell

$$E = 1.850 + 0.917(G - G_w)$$

where E = terminal voltage, 2.04 to 2.14 volts
G = specific gravity of electrolyte, 1.18 to 1.32
G_w = specific gravity of water at cell temperature, 0.98 to 1.00

21.3.18. Gear drive

$$C = \frac{D_G + D_P}{2}$$

where C = center distance, 2 to 15 in.
D_G = gear-pitch diameter, 2 to 20 in.
D_P = pinion-pitch diameter, 2 to 10 in.

21.3.19. Bronze bearing stock

$$W = 3.72 \frac{\pi}{4}(D_o{}^2 - D_i{}^2)$$

where W = weight, 0 to 120 lb per ft of length
D_o = outside diameter, 1 to 8 in.
D_i = inside diameter, ½ to 6 in.

21.3.20. Ohm's law

$$E = IR$$

where E = electromotive force, volts
I = current, 1 to 15 amp
R = resistance, 1 to 10 ohms

21.3.21. Roller bearing

$$L = \frac{60SH}{10^6}$$

where L = minimum life, millions of revolutions
S = speed, 100 to 10,000 rpm
H = minimum life, 1,000 to 20,000 hr

21.3.22. Cylindrical storage tank

$$C = 7.48 \frac{\pi}{4} D^2 H$$

where C = capacity, gal
D = diameter, 1 to 10 ft
H = height, 1 to 30 ft

21.3.23. Resistances in parallel

$$\frac{I}{R} = \frac{1}{R_1} + \frac{1}{R_2}$$

where R = equivalent resistance, ohms
R_1 = resistance, 0 to 25 ohms
R_2 = resistance, 0 to 25 ohms

21.3.24. Capacitors in series

$$\frac{1}{C} = \frac{1}{C_1} + \frac{1}{C_2}$$

where C = equivalent capacitance, μf
C_1 = capacitance, 0 to 500 μf
C_2 = capacitance, 0 to 1,000 μf

21.3.25. Spur gear

$$N = PD$$

where N = number of teeth, 0 to 250
P = pitch diameter, 0 to 25 in.
D = diametral pitch, 3 to 30 teeth per in.

21.3.26. Roller chain sprocket

$$N = \frac{4D}{P} + 5$$

where N = minimum number of teeth, 5 to 55
D = bore diameter, 0.25 to 3 in.
P = chain pitch, 0.25 to 1 in.

21.3.27. Rectangular beam

$$I = \frac{BH^3}{12}$$

where I = moment of inertia, in.^{4}
B = beam-section breadth, 0 to 12 in.
H = beam-section height, 0 to 20 in.

21.3.28. Roller bearing

$$L = \frac{C}{P} 3.33$$

where L = minimum life, millions of revolutions
C = dynamic capacity, 0 to 100,000 lb
P = applied load, 0 to 25,000 lb

GROUP 4. PROBLEMS OF FOUR OR MORE VARIABLES

Problems of this type can be represented by network charts, combined nomographs, and special slide rules.

21.4.1. Equation

$$2p + q = r + s$$

$p = 0$ to 10
$q = 0$ to 40
$r = 0$ to 30
$s = 0$ to 20

21.4.2. Equation

$$pq = r + 4s$$

$p = 0$ to 10
$q = 0$ to 10
$r = 0$ to 40
$s = 0$ to 5

21.4.3. Equation

$$pq = rs^2$$

$p = 1$ to 10
$q = 1$ to 15
$r = 1$ to 10
$s = 1$ to 4

21.4.4. Joggle in sheet-metal flange

$$A = 0.27(4.3D + R + T)$$

where A = joggle-relief encroachment, in.
D = joggle depth, 0 to 0.5 in.
R = flange-bend radius, 0 to 1.0 in.
T = sheet-metal thickness, 0 to 0.20 in.

21.4.5. Spherical pressure vessel

$$S = \frac{PD}{4T}$$

where S = circumferential stress, lb per sq in.
P = internal pressure, 0 to 250 lb per sq in.
D = internal diameter, 5 to 25 in.
T = shell thickness, 0.2 to 1.0 in.

21.4.6. Pipe insulation

$$B = \frac{0.38L}{DT}$$

where B = applied cost, dollars per board ft
L = applied cost, 0.50 to 10.00 dollars per lin ft
D = outside diameter of insulation, 3 to 20 in.
T = thickness of insulation, 1 to 5 in.

21.4.7. Moist air

$$D = 1.326 \left(\frac{B - 0.38W}{T + 460} \right)$$

where D = density, lb per cu ft
B = barometric pressure, 28 to 32 in. mercury
W = water-vapor pressure, 0 to 3 in. mercury
T = temperature, 40 to 140°F

21.4.8. Sheet-metal bend

$$B = A(0.0175R + 0.0078T)$$

where B = bend allowance, in.
A = angle through which sheet metal is bent, 0 to 120°
R = bend radius, 0 to 2.0 in.
T = sheet-metal thickness, 0 to 0.25 in.

21.4.9. Fuel combustion

$$W = 11.5C + 4.3(8H - O)$$

where W = theoretical combustion (air), 5 to 15 lb per lb fuel
C = weight of carbon, 0.40 to 0.95 lb per lb fuel
H = weight of hydrogen, 0 to 0.15 lb per lb fuel
O = weight of oxygen, 0 to 0.40 lb per lb fuel

21.4.10. Belt drive

$$L = 1.57(D_1 + D_2) + 2C$$

where L = approximate length of belt, 25 to 200 in.
D_1 = pitch diameter, large sheave, 2 to 48 in.
D_2 = pitch diameter, small sheave, 2 to 24 in.
C = center distance, 10 to 60 in.

21.4.11. Cylindrical tank

$$S = \frac{PD}{2T}$$

where S = circumferential stress, 200 to 20,000 lb per sq in.
P = internal pressure, 10 to 250 lb per sq in.
D = internal diameter, 6 to 36 in.
T = wall thickness, 0.2 to 1.0 in.

21.4.12. Water pump

$$B = \frac{QH}{39.6E}$$

where B = brake horsepower, 0.1 to 10
Q = discharge, 10 to 200 gal per min
H = head, 20 to 100 ft water
E = efficiency, 40 to 80 per cent

21.4.13. Coil spring

$$S = 2.55\frac{PD}{d^3}$$

where S = torsional stress, 0 to 120,000 lb per sq in.
P = applied load, 0 to 350 lb
D = mean coil diameter, 0.5 to 3 in.
d = wire diameter, 0.1 to 0.3 in.

21.4.14. Physical pendulum

$$I = \frac{g}{4\pi^2}WLT^2$$

where I = moment of inertia, 0 to 40,000 lb-ft^2
W = weight, 100 to 2,000 lb
L = centroidal distance, 0 to 15 ft
T = period of oscillation, 0 to 5 sec
g = acceleration due to gravity, 32.2 ft per sec^2

GROUP 5.   ROOTS OF EQUATIONS

21.5.1. Solve graphically for the roots of the quadratic equation

$$x^2 - 4.2x + 2.5 = 0$$

21.5.2. Solve graphically for the roots of the equation

$$0.25x^2 - 1.85x^{0.7} + 1 = 0$$

21.5.3. Solve graphically for the square root of 7.55. (*Hint.* Solve for the roots of the equation $x^2 - 7.55 = 0$.)

GROUP 6.   SIMULTANEOUS EQUATIONS

21.6.1. Solve simultaneously, by graphic means, the two equations

$$y = 0.5x^2 \qquad y = x + 1.7$$

21.6.2. Solve simultaneously, by graphic means, the two equations

$$y = e^x \qquad y = 10 - 0.4x$$

GROUP 7. ADDITION OF FUNCTIONS

21.7.1. Plot graphically the equation $y = e^x + x^{2.5}$ for values of x from 0 to 5. Values of e^x and $x^{2.5}$ are given in the table for various values of x.

x	e^x	x	$x^{2.5}$
0	1.00	0	0
0.8	2.23	1.0	1.00
1.6	4.95	2.0	5.65
2.6	13.5	2.5	9.86
3.2	24.5	3.0	15.6
3.9	49.4	3.5	22.9
4.4	81.5	4.0	32.0
4.8	121.5	4.5	43.0
5.0	148.4	5.0	53.0

21.7.2. The annual fixed costs for insulating a certain steam-pipe installation can be expressed as $C_F = 35S + 40$ in dollars per year, where S is the thickness of insulation in inches. The annual cost of heat lost from the installation can be expressed as $C_H = 105/S$ in dollars per year. Plot the total annual cost $C_F + C_H$ for values of S from 0 to 6 in., and determine the optimum thickness of insulation.

21.7.3. A quantity A is equal to the sum of two components, B and C, which vary with time T. Values of B and C, measured experimentally at various time values, are given in the table. Determine graphically the maximum value of A and the time at which it occurs.

T	B	T	C
0	3.0	0	4.4
1.5	1.6	2.0	5.8
2.8	1.1	3.8	6.8
3.5	1.2	5.0	7.0
4.6	1.6	6.0	6.8
6.5	2.4	7.2	6.5
8.0	3.1	8.6	5.4
10.0	4.0	10.0	4.2

I	M	Er.	% Er.	Ex	I	M
00005	.0013	+.0000118	+2.36	.00127	.090	2.3
0001	.0025	-.0000157	-1.57	.00254	.100	2.5
0002	.0051	+.0000079		00508	.200	5.1
0003	.0076	-.000			.300	7.
0004	.0102	+.			.400	10
0005	.013				500	
0006	.015				00	
0007	.018				0C	
0008	.0?				0	
0009						
0010						
0015						
0020						
002						
002						

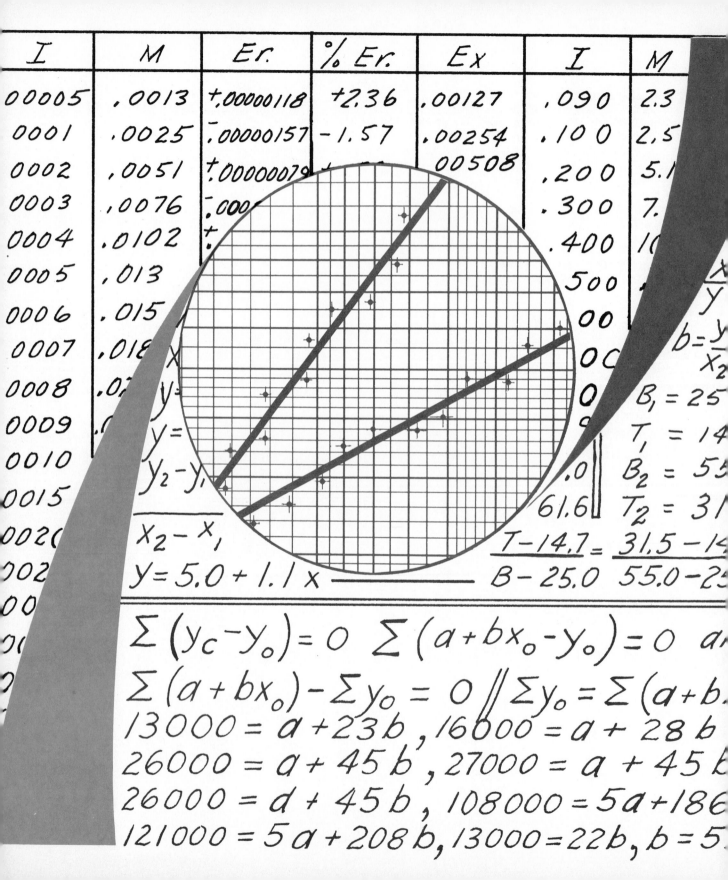

$$\frac{y_2 - y_1}{x_2 - x_1}$$

$$y = 5.0 + 1.1x$$

$$b = \frac{y}{x_2}$$

$B_1 = 25$

$T_1 = 14$

$B_2 = 55$

$T_2 = 31$

61.6

$$\frac{T - 14.7}{B - 25.0} = \frac{31.5 - 14}{55.0 - 25}$$

$$\Sigma(y_c - y_0) = 0 \quad \Sigma(a + bx_0 - y_0) = 0$$

$$\Sigma(a + bx_0) - \Sigma y_0 = 0 \quad \| \quad \Sigma y_0 = \Sigma(a + b}$$

$$13000 = a + 23b, \quad 16000 = a + 28b$$

$$26000 = a + 45b, \quad 27000 = a + 45b$$

$$26000 = d + 45b, \quad 108000 = 5a + 186$$

$$121000 = 5a + 208b, \quad 13000 = 22b, \quad b = 5$$

The determination of an empirical
equation requires three steps: (1) the
collection and recording of data
(green background area), (2) a
graphic plot of the data (red center
circle), and (3) the calculation of
an equation from the plot (brown
background area).

Graphic Solutions of Empirical Data

22.1. The engineer's work most often deals with physical quantities and the manner in which they vary with respect to one another. In research and development as well as in the design of machinery and equipment, in the functioning of processes, and in the operation of plants, it is necessary to determine the relationships between variable quantities through tests and observations. Controlled changes are brought about in one variable and corresponding changes measured in another. As a continuous operation proceeds, simultaneous readings of the variables are often made by automatic recording devices. Then results of a test are recorded as a set of tabulated values of the variables. This experimental procedure is used extensively in research, both basic and practical.

These experimental data seldom remain in tabular form but are processed to provide a more convenient format for future

Automatic recording instruments

experiments. When the data represent a relationship in which the quantities vary according to some mathematical law, the algebraic equation relating the variables is found. Both graphic and mathematical methods can be used to determine the equation representing empirical data. And even when the experimental data do not represent a known mathematical relationship or when the relationship is obscure, the data can often be processed directly from an x-y plot into a graphic chart of the type described in Chap. 21.

FIG. 22.1.   Plotting empirical data.

22.2.   GRAPHIC REPRESENTATION OF DATA.

After data have been obtained from an experiment, the relationship between variables can be studied. In some very simple cases, examination of the numerical values alone may suffice to reveal the desired information concerning the changes taking place. However, in most cases it is necessary to examine the data graphically.

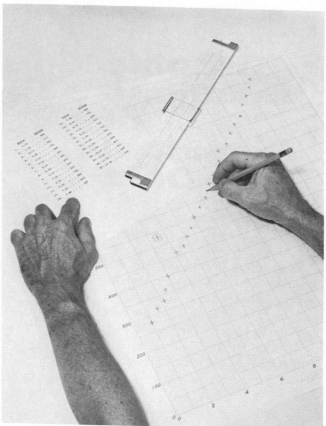

A relationship given in graphic form by plotting the data on uniform rectangular coordinates (Fig. 22.1) indicates that a definite relationship exists if a smooth line can be drawn passing through the points or very close to them. If a smooth curve cannot be drawn through the data points, no definite relationship exists and no further graphic manipulation can be performed.

Any x-y plot of experimental data which has a smooth curve passing either through or near the data points should be examined for characteristics that indicate a mathematical relationship. Any smooth curve which does not seem to obey one of the simple mathematical relationships should be left as an x-y plot or processed into a conversion chart or nomograph by one of the methods of graphic scale distortion explained later in the chapter.

22.3. PLOTTING EMPIRICAL DATA.

Accurate determination of the mathematical relationship of empirical data or production of a nomograph by scale-distortion methods requires the most accurate obtainable *x-y* plot of the data. Therefore initial plotting of the data points must be done with care if the plot is to have any value.

The equation of the data relationship is determined from the plot in many cases. Accuracy of the location of data points and of the line drawn through the points is essential. A prime requisite is that the plot be large enough that accuracy as near that of the data as possible can be obtained. Printed cross-sectional paper is available in rolls 20 in. wide and in cut sheets up to 16 by 20 in.

Coordinate Divisions and Scales. It is much easier to use cross-sectional paper divided in tenths. The divided units may be inches or centimeters, chosen according to the necessary size of the plot and the decimal places of the values of observed data. The scale used can then be easily adjusted to suit, using 1, 2, 5, 10, or 20 (or more) smallest divisions per unit. (The paper employed in Fig. 22.1 is divided into tenths of an inch.)

Coordinate Axes. It is common practice to plot the independent variable as abscissa (*x* axis) and the dependent variable as ordinate (*y* axis).

Plotted Points. The plotted point is best recorded as a pair of light, sharp, intersecting lines at right angles to each other, a method more accurate than either dots or circles. (See Fig. 22.1 and other illustrations in this chapter.)

22.4. REPRESENTATIVE LINES.

The purpose of drawing a line through a series of plotted points is to obtain a single line representation that will account for and minimize experimental error. Later, an equation of the line will be derived, or a nomograph or conversion chart can be constructed from the line (or lines, if there are parameters). Therefore, the line drawn through a series of plotted points must be representative of the data.

Although there may be errors in reading the instruments used in conducting the experiment, these errors tend to "balance out" by being over in one case and under in another, so the representative line should strike an average between the plotted points.

In many cases, the observed data will so closely fit a single line that the line can be drawn purely "by eye." However, in cases where the errors of observation are greater, it may be difficult to judge the position of a representative line and be reasonably sure that the line is the best that can be obtained. The graphic aids illustrated in Fig. 22.2 may then be employed to advantage.

Making a reading

Checking automatic recorder

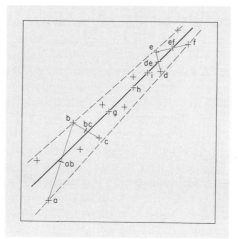

FIG. 22.2. Obtaining the representative line by means of the envelope of the data.

First, it is a help to draw an envelope of the data (the two dotted lines of Fig. 22.2), which encloses all the plotted points. Certainly the representative line must fall somewhere near the middle of the envelope if there are both plus and minus errors in the data. Also, points may have an average struck between them to aid in fixing the position of the best line. In Fig. 22.2, the mid-point *ab* between points *a* and *b* is an average between *a* and *b,* and the final line should come close to this point. Other average points, *bc* between *b* and *c* and *de* between *d* and *e,* give a series of "average points" which the representative line should pass through, or miss only by a small distance. Note that the averages between points such as *g, h,* and *i* will fall on the line. This method is really a method of selected averages because the average of two points such as *a* and *c,* both of which apparently contain minus errors, or points such as *b* and *e,* which contain plus errors, is not considered. A very accurate representative line may be obtained in this way, especially if the plot is large enough to easily distinguish variations between the plotted points.

Errors in observed data that are all plus or minus, caused by an instrument out of adjustment and therefore reading consistently high or low, will not show up in the plot but must be corrected before the experiment is performed. Occasionally there will be a "wild" point in a plot (the encircled point of Fig. 22.1) which falls some distance from the line indicated by all other points. Obviously, such a point is in error because of a misread instrument, a reading made at the wrong time, or a mistake in recording the reading, and therefore should be eliminated. Note again that, to get the best representative line, the plot of the data should be large.

The ultimate purpose of the representative line is to provide the basis for obtaining the equation of the experimental data or for constructing a conversion chart or nomograph. The equation of the data can only be obtained if the representative line is a straight or curved line when plotted on the proper coordinate system. Since a conversion chart or nomograph can be made from either a straight or curved representative line, it is desirable to make preliminary plots on various coordinate systems to determine whether or not a straight line or curve can be plotted on any one of the systems. Preliminary plots should be accurate enough to indicate curvature or straightness of the data line but need not be made with the care used for the final plot.

There are numerical methods of evaluation that fit a straight line to plotted points. These methods involve consideration of the residuals (deviations) of plotted points from the calculated line. If the ordinate of a point is y_o and the calculated ordinate of the straight line at the same value of x is y_c, then the residual is $R = y_o - y_c$. The method of averages provides the equation of a straight line for which the algebraic sum of the residuals approaches zero. The method of least squares provides the equation of a straight line for which the sum of the squares—and therefore the sum of the absolute values of the residuals—is a minimum.

The numerical methods offer one advantage and a corresponding disadvantage over the graphic methods of determining the equation of a straight line. The advantage is that the plot of the data need only be accurate enough to determine the type of coordinate system on which the data would rectify to, or plot as, a straight line. Thus, no large, accurate plot is needed. The disadvantage is that the amount of computation required is large, extreme care being required to prevent calculation errors. For most engineering work the numerical methods do not offer any tangible advantages over carefully drawn graphic methods, although each method has a time and a place when it should be used.

Remember that no method will produce accurate results from inaccurate data; and if the data are accurate, the graphic methods will do an accurate job.

22.5. EMPIRICAL EQUATIONS.

Since errors may be present in the original observations and drafting inaccuracies may be involved in plotting points and drawing a representative line, a derived equation will represent the relationship only approximately and only within the range of the test data. The derived equation is called an "empirical" equation to distinguish it from theoretically derived formulas expressing physical, chemical, or other laws.

If the points as plotted on rectilinear coordinates appear to lie on, or very nearly on, a straight line, a linear (first-degree) equation of the form $y = a + bx$ will represent the plotted data. If the points as plotted on rectilinear coordinates deviate systematically from a straight line, the equation representing the data is usually of the power, exponential, or periodic-term form, or even a combination of any or all of the types.

The procedure for determining which, if any, of the three types of equation discussed in the examples to follow will fit the particular set of data under examination consists of determining the coordinate system on which the data rectifies to, or lies in, a straight line. The data values may be plotted directly on the correct coordinate system, or the proper functions of the values may be plotted on rectilinear coordinates to produce rectification. Thus the data values might be plotted on logarithmic coordinates, or the logarithms of the data might be plotted on rectilinear coordinates. Normally, less work is involved if the data values are plotted directly on the proper coordinates. Once rectification is obtained, the constants of the equation type related to the particular coordinate system are obtained by either graphic or analytical methods.

22.6. LINEAR EQUATIONS.

Empirical data which plot as a virtually straight line on rectilinear (uniform) coordinates are known to have an equation of the general form $y = a + bx$, where a and b are constants. This equation is in the slope-intercept form, with a as the y intercept and b as the slope of the line. The various methods by which the constants of the equation can be evaluated are illustrated below. The first two methods rely upon an accurate and carefully drawn plot of the data and the resulting representative line and are the methods commonly listed as graphic. The second two methods are essentially numerical and require only a sufficiently accurate plot to prove that the data will rectify on the coordinate system chosen.

Slope-intercept Method. Figure 22.3 illustrates the graphic procedure for determination of the equation from observed data recorded in an experiment. These data are plotted as shown in the figure, using light, sharp, intersecting

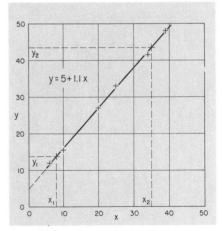

FIG. 22.3. Data and curve for a linear equation.

lines for the location of points. Then the best straight-line representative of the data is drawn through as many of the points as possible, striking an average between points not on the line.

The y intercept of this representative line will be the value of a in the equation and may be measured directly from the y scale (at $x = 0$). In this case, the value is seen to be 5.0. To complete the equation, the slope b is measured. If the scales used for x and y are identical, the slope can be measured directly from the line by drawing a horizontal line and a vertical line from two selected points on the line to represent a tangent and then measuring and calculating the value of the tangent. This method is not desirable since there is always the possibility of mistakenly using it to obtain the slope when the x and y scales are not identical. The general method of calculating the slope from two selected points on the representative line is preferred since no confusion can result from deciding whether or not the method can be used. In Fig. 22.3, two selected points on the line (shown by the dashed line extending to the axes) will have the coordinates of x_1, y_1 and x_2, y_2. The tangent is found from the equation

$$\frac{y_2 - y_1}{x_2 - x_1} = b$$

$$\frac{43.5 - 13.8}{35.0 - 8.0} = \frac{29.7}{27} = 1.1$$

The equation of the line is

$$y = 5 + 1.1x$$

Note especially that this method as well as the following one requires the slope and the intercept to be calculated from the representative line rather than from the experimental data. This point

is often neglected, and the equation obtained by use of the data can be extremely inaccurate. The purpose of the representative line is to average graphically all the data values and thereby eliminate the effects of various inaccuracies.

Method of Selected Points. The equation of a straight line plotted on rectilinear coordinates may be evaluated by reading coordinates of two selected points on the line, x_1, y_1 and x_2, y_2, and substituting in the equation

$$\frac{y - y_1}{x - x_1} = \frac{y_2 - y_1}{x_2 - x_1}$$

This equation simply states the fact that the slope of a straight line is everywhere constant and sets up a proportion between corresponding changes in x and y values.

From the graph of Fig. 22.3, coordinates of two selected points are

$$x_1 = 8 \qquad x_2 = 35.0$$
$$y_1 = 13.8 \qquad y_2 = 43.5$$

Substituting in the equation, we get

$$\frac{y - 13.8}{x - 8.0} = \frac{43.5 - 13.8}{35.0 - 8.0}$$

$$\frac{y - 13.8}{x - 8.0} = 1.1$$

$$y = 5.0 + 1.1x$$

It should be noted that the coefficient 1.1 is the slope of the line

$$b = \frac{y_2 - y_1}{x_2 - x_1}$$

and that the constant term 5.0 is the ordinate-axis intercept a.

Figure 22.4 shows a practical example of the determination of an equation by the method of selected points. Brinell hardness and tensile strength of a num-

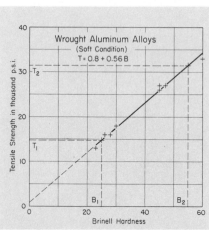

FIG. 22.4. Data and curve for a linear equation.

ber of wrought-aluminum alloys in the soft or annealed condition are tabulated. These data are plotted on uniform rectangular coordinates in Fig. 22.4, and a representative straight line is drawn through the points. Coordinates of two selected points on the line are

$$B_1 = 25 \qquad B_2 = 55$$
$$T_1 = 14.7 \qquad T_2 = 31.5$$

Writing the equation of the straight line, we get

$$\frac{T - 14.7}{B - 25} = \frac{31.5 - 14.7}{55 - 25}$$
$$T = 0.8 + 0.56B$$

It seems reasonable to make a comparison between the slope-intercept method and the method of selected points. In the slope-intercept method, the y-intercept value may be read from the graph, but the slope must be obtained by a pair of selected points; in the method of selected points, the equation is determined solely from the selected points. Also, in many cases, the y intercept will not appear on the graph. For these reasons and because the method of selected points works equally well for power and exponential equations, it will be the only graphic method used for the remaining equation types.

Method of Averages. As stated earlier, the numerical methods of obtaining the equation representing empirical data require only a sufficiently accurate plot of the data to determine the coordinate system on which the data plots as a straight line. The actual equation is determined from the data only.

If empirical data having the coordinates x_o, y_o are plotted on a rectilinear coordinate system, the data will lie on or near a straight line, if they obey a linear relationship. For each data

point having an observed x value of x_o, there will be a y value of y_o for the observed value and y_c for the calculated value which lies exactly on the straight line representing the data. Thus every point on the line having coordinates x_o, y_c deviates from the observed data having coordinates x_o, y_o by a vertical distance $y_c - y_o$.

The vertical deviations are used instead of the horizontal solely because the independent variable x is likely to be more accurate than the dependent variable y. For a straight line to represent exactly the average of all data points, the sum of the deviations of the calculated and observed values must be equal to zero (the plus and minus deviations must cancel). Mathematically,

$$\Sigma(y_c - y_o) = 0$$

Since $y_c = a + bx_o$,

$$\Sigma(a + bx_o - y_o) = 0$$
$$\Sigma(a + bx_o) - \Sigma y_o = 0$$
or $\qquad \Sigma y_o = \Sigma(a + bx_o)$

Since there are two constants to be determined, the simplest procedure is to divide the data into two groups and obtain summations of each of the groups. Thus two simultaneous equations in a and b will be obtained. For the data of Fig. 22.4, the first five readings could be the first summation, and the second five readings could be the second summation. Since a typical equation would be

$$13,000 = a + 23b$$

the summation can be tabulated:

13,000	= a	+	23b
16,000	= a	+	28b
26,000	= a	+	45b
27,000	= a	+	45b
26,000	= a	+	45b
108,000	= 5a	+	186b

Equation (1) of the summations is

$$108,000 = 5a + 186b$$

Equation (2) of the summations is obtained by summing the second group of five data points, and the equation is

$$121,000 = 5a + 208b$$

Subtracting Eq. (1) from Eq. (2), we have

$$13,000 = 22b$$
$$b = 591$$

Substituting the value of b in Eq. (1), we get

$$108,000 = 5a + 109,920$$
$$a = -384$$

The equation of the line by this method is

$$T = -384 + 591B$$

Dividing by 1,000 places it in the values of the equation found by the method of selected points:

$$T = -0.384 + 0.591B$$

To illustrate that no method can be more accurate than the data, the equation obtained by summing the first, third, fifth, seventh, and ninth data points and the second, fourth, sixth, eighth, and tenth data points is

$$T = 3.2 + 0.5B$$

Wide variations in equations obtained by various summations indicate that the data do not accurately fit a straight line, and therefore the equation can only be used to obtain values requiring no greater accuracy than that afforded by the extreme values of equations which can be found.

The data of Fig. 22.3 indicate a much higher degree of correlation. Summation of the first and second halves of the data gives an equation

$$y = 4.97 + 1.1x$$

Summation of the first, third, and fifth points and the second, fourth, and sixth points gives an equation

$$y = 6.6 + 1.18x$$

Although the method of averages is one of the most widely used in obtaining equations from empirical data, its use does not guarantee more accurate results than those afforded by graphic methods.

Method of Least Squares. This method is similar to the method of averages except for the premise that the best line to represent data has the sum of the squares of the y deviations as a minimum.

$$\Sigma(y_c - y_o)^2 = \text{minimum}$$

or

$$\Sigma(a + bx_o - y_o)^2 = \text{minimum}$$

Partial differentiation of this equation with respect to the quantities a and b gives the following equations.

For a $\quad\quad \Sigma(a + bx_o - y_o) = 0$
For b $\quad\quad \Sigma(ax_o + bx_o^2 - x_o y_o) = 0$

Since two separate equations are involved in this method, the data do not need to be divided into two groups for summation.

Easier handling of the equations will result if they are rewritten.

$$\Sigma y_o = na + b\Sigma x_o \quad\quad (1)$$
$$\Sigma x_o y_o = a\Sigma x_o + b\Sigma x_o^2 \quad\quad (2)$$

where n is the number of data points.

The necessary terms for these equations can be tabulated using the data of Fig. 22.4.

x_0	y_0	$x_0 y_0$	x_0^2
23	13	299	529
28	16	448	784
45	26	1,170	2,025
45	27	1,215	2,025
45	26	1,170	2,025
47	27	1,269	2,209
45	27	1,215	2,025
26	16	416	676
30	18	540	900
60	33	1,980	3,600
394	229	9,722	16,798

Substituting in Eqs. (1) and (2), we get

$$229 = 10a + 394b$$
$$9,722 = 394a + 16,798b$$

From these equations $a = 6.47$ and $b = 0.544$. Thus the equation for the data is

$$T = 6.47 + 0.544B$$

This method is considered to give the most accurate results for fitting an equation to empirical data but is obviously the most complicated method to use.

By this method the data of Fig. 22.3 have an equation of

$$y = 8.2 + 0.953x$$

Each method gives different results then, but the correlation between results is in direct proportion to the closeness with which the data fit a straight line. The data of Fig. 22.3 lie very close to a straight line, and the equations found by the various methods correlate closely. The data of Fig. 22.4 only approximate a straight line, and the resulting equations vary considerably.

The method of selected points is accurate enough for data closely fitting a straight line that it precludes the use of either of the numerical methods unless extreme accuracy is needed. The method of least squares gives the equation most closely fitting the data mathematically but offers no great advantage in accuracy unless the data points do not lie close to a straight line. For most purposes the method of selected points or the method of averages should be used for data closely fitting a straight line, while the method of selected points or the least-squares method should be used for data only approximating a straight line.

22.7. EQUATIONS OF POWER RELATIONSHIPS. Power relationships occur frequently in nature. The distance-time relationship of a falling body, the period of a simple pendulum, and the velocity of free discharge of water from an orifice are power relationships.

The power equation $y = ax^b$, in which one quantity varies directly as some power of another, plots on the uniform rectangular coordinates of Fig. 22.5A as a family of parabolic and hyperbolic

FIG. 22.5. Plots of power equations.

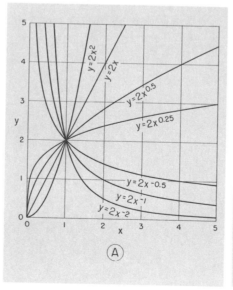

(A)

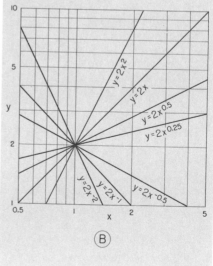

(B)

curves passing through the point (1,*a*). When the exponent *b* is equal to unity, the curve is a straight line through the origin. For other positive values of *b*, the curves are parabolic, symmetrical with respect to the *y* axis for values of *b* greater than 1 and symmetrical with respect to the *x* axis for values of *b* less than 1. Negative values of *b* result in hyperbolic curves having their coordinate axes as asymptotes, one variable decreasing as the other increases. When placed in logarithmic form, the equation becomes $\log y = \log a + b \log x$, in which $\log y$ and $\log x$ are variable and $\log a$ and *b* are constant terms. Hence, curves of this type may be rectified either by plotting the logarithms of *x* and *y* on rectilinear coordinates or by plotting *y* versus *x* directly on logarithmic coordinates as in Fig. 22.5*B*.

An example of data giving a power equation is shown in Fig. 22.6, where a test resulted in tabulated values of two variables, as shown.

These data plot on uniform coordinates as a curved line but when plotted on logarithmic coordinates as in Fig. 22.6, rectify to a straight line.

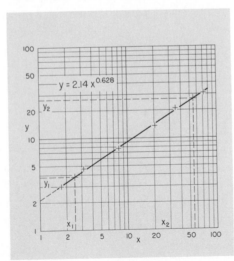

FIG. 22.6. Data and representative line for a power equation.

The representative straight line is drawn through the points. Coordinates of two selected points on the line are

$$x_1 = 2.5 \qquad y_1 = 55.0$$
$$x_2 = 3.8 \qquad y_2 = 26.5$$

The equation of a straight line by the method of selected points is

$$\frac{\log y - \log 3.8}{\log x - \log 2.5} = \frac{\log 26.5 - \log 3.8}{\log 55.0 - \log 2.5}$$

Evaluating logarithms, we have

$$\log y = 0.330 + 0.628 \log x$$

or $\qquad y = 2.14x^{0.628}$

Note that the coefficient 2.14 is the ordinate-axis intercept obtained by extending the line to $x = 1$ and that the exponent 0.628 is the slope of the rectified curve. The *y* intercept occurs at the coordinate line $x = 1$ since $\log 1 = 0$. The value 1 is therefore the origin of the logarithmic scale.

The method of averages can also be used to obtain the equation of this line, and the same method is used as for the linear equation of paragraph 22.6. The summation equations must be written in the logarithmic form

$$\Sigma \log y = \Sigma \log a + b \Sigma \log x$$

Summing the first three data points of Fig. 22.6 gives

$$2.03571 = 3 \log a + 1.65128b$$

Summing the second three data points of Fig. 22.6 gives

$$3.94391 = 3 \log a + 4.71315b$$

Subtracting the first equation from the second gives

$$1.90820 = 3.06187b$$

Hence $\qquad\qquad b = 0.624$

Substituting this value of *b* in the first equation, we have

$$2.03571 = 3 \log a + 1.03040$$
$$3 \log a = 1.00531$$
Hence $a = 2.163$

The equation of the data by the method of averages is

$$y = 2.163x^{0.624}$$

The method of least squares may also be used to determine the equation of the data. The two summation equations to be used are

$$\Sigma \log y_o = n \log a + b \Sigma \log x_o$$

and

$$\Sigma(\log x_o \cdot \log y_o) = $$
$$\log a \Sigma \log x_o + b \Sigma(\log x_o)^2$$

Substituting the data in Eq. (1) gives

$$5.97962 = 6 \log a + 6.36443b$$

Substituting the data in Eq. (2) gives

$$7.55553 = 6.36443 \log a + 8.68434b$$

Solving for b, we get

$$7.27631 = 11.60007b$$
$$b = 0.627$$

Substituting the value of b in Eq. (1) and solving for a gives

$$5.98 = 6 \log a + 3.99$$
$$\log a = 0.331$$
$$a = 2.143$$

The equation of the data as determined by the method of least squares is

$$y = 2.143x^{0.627}$$

A practical example of data giving a power equation is shown in Fig. 22.7, where maximum sizes of particles passing United States Standard sieves of different mesh are tabulated as shown.

These data are plotted on logarithmic coordinates in Fig. 22.7 and a representative straight line drawn through the points. Coordinates of two selected points on the line are

$$N_1 = 25 \qquad N_2 = 250$$
$$D_1 = 660 \qquad D_2 = 57$$

Writing the equation of the straight line gives

$$\frac{\log D - \log 660}{\log N - \log 25} = \frac{\log 57 - \log 660}{\log 250 - \log 25}$$
$$\log D = 4.307 - 1.064 \log N$$

Hence

$$D = \frac{20{,}300}{N^{1.064}} \qquad \text{or} \qquad D = 20{,}300N^{-1.064}$$

Note that the reciprocal form of the equation or the negative exponent is produced by the negative slope of the line of Fig. 22.7. The solutions for the equations of this line by the methods of averages and least squares will not be repeated since they exactly parallel the procedures shown for the data of Fig. 22.6. The reader should use these methods to obtain equations of the line of Fig. 22.7 so that the equations may be compared with an equation of known correctness.

22.8.   EQUATIONS OF EXPONENTIAL RELA- TIONSHIPS.   In nature many physical

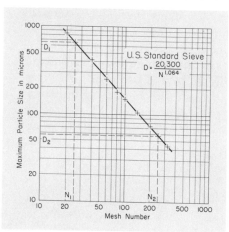

FIG. 22.7.   Data and representative line for a power equation.

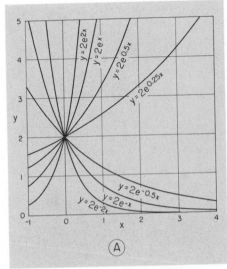

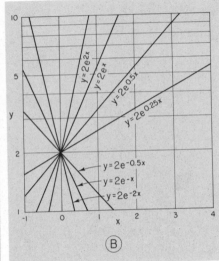

FIG. 22.8. Plots of exponential equations.

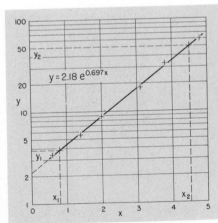

FIG. 22.9. Data and representative line for an exponential equation.

quantities increase or decrease at a rate proportional to the amount present at any time. As time varies arithmetically by a constant difference, the quantity changes geometrically by a constant factor. Exponential relationships involving time change are found in formulas for transient currents in an inductive electric circuit, for the decay of natural radioactivity, and for the increase in a sum of money at compound interest. Variables other than time may also be involved. The intensity of light passing through a transparent or translucent substance varies exponentially with the thickness of the material.

The exponential equation $y = ae^{bx}$ or $y = a10^{bx}$ plots on rectilinear coordinates of Fig. 22.8A as a family of curves passing through the point $(0,a)$ and having the x axis as asymptote. When placed in logarithmic form, the equation $y = ae^{bx}$ becomes

$$\ln y = \ln a + bx \ln e$$

Since $\ln e = 1$,

$$\ln y = \ln a + bx$$

Similarly the equation $y = a10^{bx}$ becomes

$$\log y = \log a + bx$$

Curves of this type may be rectified by plotting either $\ln y$ versus x or $\log y$ versus x on rectilinear coordinates or by plotting y versus x directly on semilogarithmic coordinates in which the y scale is logarithmic and the x scale uniform, as shown in Fig. 22.8B.

An example of data giving an exponential equation is shown in Fig. 22.9, where a test resulted in tabulated values of the two variables. These data plot on uniform coordinates as a curved line. However, when the data are plotted on semilogarithmic coordinates, as in Fig. 22.9, with a logarithmic y scale and a uniform x scale, a representative straight line may be drawn through the points. Coordinates of two selected points on the line are

$$x_1 = 0.8 \qquad x_2 = 4.5$$
$$y_1 = 3.8 \qquad y_2 = 50$$

Writing the equation of the straight line gives

$$\frac{\ln y - \ln 3.8}{x - 0.8} = \frac{\ln 50 - \ln 3.8}{4.5 - 0.8}$$
$$\ln y = 0.777 + 0.697x$$

Hence $\qquad y = 2.18e^{0.697x}$

If the use of logarithms to the base 10 is preferred, the equation of the straight line is written

$$\frac{\log y - \log 3.8}{x - 0.8} = \frac{\log 50 - \log 3.8}{4.5 - 0.8}$$
$$\log y = 0.338 + 0.302x$$

Hence $\qquad y = 2.18 (10)^{0.302x}$

The method of averages may be used to find the equation of the straight line for the exponential equation, and the summation equation becomes

$\Sigma \log y = \Sigma \log a + b \Sigma x$

Summing the first three data points produces Eq. (1):

$$2.22415 = 3 \log a + 4.0b$$

Summing the second three data points produces Eq. (2):

$$4.55193 = 3 \log a + 11.7b$$

Subtracting Eq. (1) from Eq. (2) gives

$$7.7b = 2.32778$$
$$b = 0.3025$$

Substituting the value of b in Eq. (1) and solving for a give

$$2.22415 = 3 \log a + 1.21$$
$$\log a = 0.33805$$
$$a = 2.178$$

The equation of the data by this method is

$$y = 2.178 \,(10)^{0.3025x}$$

The method of least squares may also be used to find the equation of the straight line, but extreme care is required to prevent errors caused by mixing logarithmic and linear values. The equations of summation are

$$\Sigma \log y_o = n \log a + b \Sigma x_o$$

and

$$\Sigma(x_o \log y_o) = \log a \, \Sigma x_o + b \, \Sigma x_o^2$$

Substituting the values of data points into Eq. (1), we get

$$6.7762 = 6 \log a + 15.7b$$

Substituting the values of the data into Eq. (2), we get

$$21.4525 = 15.7 \log a + 53.41b$$

Subtracting Eq. (1) from Eq. (2) gives

$$22.329 = 73.97b$$
$$b = 0.3018$$

Substituting this value in Eq. (1) gives

$$6.7762 = 6 \log a + 4.738$$
$$\log a = 0.3397$$
$$a = 2.186$$

The equation of the data by this method is

$$y = 2.186(10)^{0.3018x}$$

The value of 2.186 is the ordinate-axis intercept obtained by extending the representative line to $x = 0$, and the value 0.3018 is the slope of the rectified curve or representative line. The closeness with which values obtained by the various methods match indicates how closely the data approach a straight line. If the data lie on a straight line with little deviation, the method of selected points will give an equation of sufficient accuracy to satisfy the requirements of most problems. But if the data only approximate a straight line, either the method of selected points or the method of averages might give inaccurate results. Then the method of least squares will give the most reliable equation.

The various methods can be summarized as follows:

1. Accurate straight-line data points
   a. Use the method of selected points if an accurate x-y plot is available or desirable.
   b. Use the method of averages if an accurate x-y plot is not available or is not desired.
2. Approximate straight-line data
   a. Use the method of selected points for an approximate equation.
   b. Use the method of least squares for the most reliable equation.

A practical example of data yielding

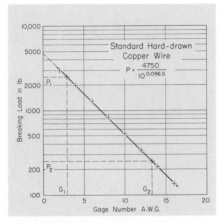

FIG. 22.10. Data and representative line for an exponential equation.

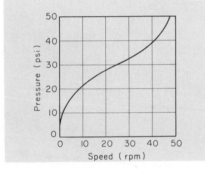

FIG. 22.11. Plot of empirical data.

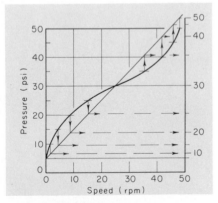

FIG. 22.12. Rectifying the curve of a plot of empirical data by single-scale distortion.

an exponential equation is shown in Fig. 22.10 with tabulated data from breaking loads of standard hard-drawn copper wire. The data are plotted on semilogarithmic coordinates and a representative line is drawn through the points. Coordinates of two selected points on the line are

$$G_1 = 2.9 \qquad G_2 = 13.3$$
$$P_1 = 2,500 \qquad P_2 = 250$$

Writing the equation of the straight line gives

$$\frac{\log P - \log 2,500}{G - 2.9} = \frac{\log 250 - \log 2,500}{13.3 - 2.9}$$
$$\log P = 3.677 - 0.96G$$
$$P = 4,750 \, (10)^{-0.096G}$$

The negative value of the exponent indicates the negative value of the slope of the representative line of Fig. 22.10.

22.9.   GRAPHIC SCALE DISTORTION.   Data which fail to conform to one of the simple mathematical relationships illustrated thus far in this chapter can be plotted on "special" coordinates which permit a straight line to be drawn for the representative line. The method of obtaining the special coordinates is solely graphic although a mathematical process could probably be developed. The resulting straight-line plot can be left in that form, made into a conversion chart, or if the data contains three variables, made into a nomograph. Both two- and three-variable data use the same principle of distorting the coordinates to permit drawing a straight line. No proofs will be offered for either data method as the two-variable method has an intuitive proof and the three-variable method has proofs offered in several texts restricted solely to graphic solutions.

22.10.   SINGLE-SCALE DISTORTION FOR TWO-VARIABLE DATA.   Any group of data which has two variables will conform to some equation of the general form $f(y) = f(x)$, the form used to construct a conversion chart in Chap. 21. Since the data are available but not the equation, it will be necessary to work directly from the data plot, using only the assumption that a conversion chart will represent the data. Two graphic methods will be shown, both of which actually produce the same results, with the exception that one method produces a straight-line plot as an intermediate answer. This method is included solely to illustrate how a data curve can be rectified by distorting coordinates.

The plot of empirical data having no particular relationship is shown in Fig. 22.11. A conversion chart will be found to result from a straight-line plot having a slope of unity. The x- and y-axis scales may be used directly as the opposite scales of the chart. The computation of the slope of a line is complicated by the lack of an equation so this method will be illustrated only to the point at which a rectified plot of the data is obtained. If the x and y coordinates are both equal, a straight line having a slope of 1 will make an angle of 45° with the axes. A 45° line drawn through the ordinate-axis intercept represents the desired straight line while the curve represents the actual data plot on rectilinear coordinates. For any value of x, the corresponding values of y are double, y for the curve and y for the straight line. These values must be numerically equal, which means that the ordinate scale must be distorted so that all values of y for the curve lie directly on the corresponding values of y for the straight line. Figure 22.12 illustrates the procedure.

All graduations of the *y* (ordinate) axis are projected horizontally to the original curve. The points of intersection are then projected vertically to the straight line. The straight-line intersections are then projected horizontally to the *y* axis (in this case the projection is to the right-hand *y* axis) and labeled with the same value as was at the opposite end of the various projections. The distorted *y* scale is now the correct scale for the rectified plot of the data. Because the coordinate system follows no particular mathematical relationship, the equation for the resulting rectified plot cannot be found from the coordinate system. Although a conversion chart can be made from the *x* and *y* scales that have been constructed, a simpler and more foolproof method eliminates the straight line as an intermediate.

This method is based on the fact that any point on the plot of the data has coordinates of y_1, x_1 and that these points satisfy the equation of the line so that $f(y_1) = f(x_1)$. To create this condition graphically, all graduations of the *y* axis are projected horizontally to the data curve. These intersections are then projected vertically to the *x* axis to produce a pair of adjacent scales in which corresponding values of *x* and *y* are opposite each other. Because this is the only condition required of a conversion chart, the two scales are now a conversion chart. The two scales can be removed from the plot and are shown separately in Fig. 22.14.

This method is limited to data for which the plotted curve has a slope that remains negative or positive. Curves having both negative and positive slopes must be divided into separate distorted plots for each differing curve portion.

The accuracy of this method is de-pendent upon the reliability of the original data and the care used in the graphic constructions. Inaccurate data and sloppy drafting will produce a conversion chart having even less usefulness than the original tabulated data. The conversion chart resulting from this method is theoretically correct; therefore, this method should be considered whenever an accurate *x-y* plot of the data is available. Although the original data plot was on rectilinear coordinates, the method is completely independent of the coordinate system, so the original plot can be made on any type of coordinates desired. And the size of various portions of the conversion chart can be controlled by correct choice of the coordinates of the original plot.

22.11. DOUBLE-SCALE DISTORTION FOR THREE-VARIABLE DATA.

The following methods are also called graphic ana-morphosis. For these methods a plot of data of three variables is normally made as a standard *x-y* plot with the third variable acting as a parameter. Figure 22.15 illustrates a plot of *y* versus *x* for each particular value of *z*. The plot is made on rectilinear coordinates for simplicity, but the method is not dependent upon any coordinate system. Each curve can have a separate conversion made for it, using the methods of paragraph 22.10, but the results will still have a separate chart for each value of *z*. A more usable chart will result if the data can be made into a nomograph. Producing a nomograph from the data requires first that the coordinates of the plot be so distorted that all of the curves are rectified and become straight lines. To consider the principle involved, two curves will be drawn and the procedure illustrated for them.

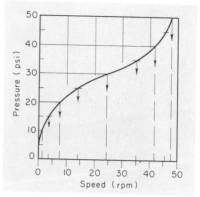

FIG. 22.13. Obtaining a conversion chart from a plot of empirical data.

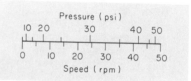

FIG. 22.14. A conversion chart obtained by single-scale distortion.

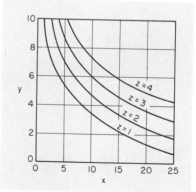

FIG. 22.15. A plot of empirical data having parameters.

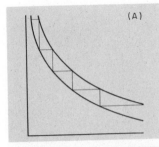

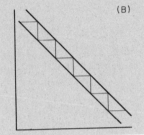

FIG. 22.16. Drawing "stair steps" preliminary to rectifying curves from empirical data.

Figure 22.16*A* shows a plot of *y* versus *x* for two values of *z*. If a series of "stair steps" are drawn within the curve as shown, the "treads" and "risers" will not be equal or uniform. Figure 22.16*B* illustrates another plot of *y* versus *x* for two values of *z* in which the two lines are straight and parallel, which is desirable in a rectified plot. The stair steps drawn between these two lines will be characterized by having all the risers of equal length and all the treads of equal length. The treads and risers may or may not be equal to each other. Both the *x* and *y* axes must have their scales distorted if this latter condition is to result from the first one. The process consists of determining the scale-distortion curve for each scale by plotting riser length for the curves versus riser length for the straight lines. The *y* scale then has a conversion chart made for *y* undistorted and *y* distorted. Similarly, the treads and the *x* axis are compared. Figure 22.17 shows the complete process.

The original *y*-versus-*x* plot is shown in the upper left-hand corner complete with stair steps. The desired straight-line *x-y* plot is shown in the lower right-hand corner with the *x* and *y* axes rotated so that the *y* axis is horizontal and the *x* axis is vertical. The two straight lines with their stair steps are completely arbitrary as to slope and distance apart of the curves. The best slope is usually about 45°, and the distance apart can be roughly estimated as matching the original curve spacing if no other spacing is desired. Projecting the riser heights horizontally to the right from the curves and vertically upward from the straight lines produces a series of points which will determine a curve of distortion. The curve is drawn as carefully as possible. Care should be exercised in projecting the various heights to be sure that corresponding risers are used. Projecting the tread widths vertically downward from the curves and horizontally to the left from the straight lines again gives a curve of distortion which is drawn through the intersection of the appropriate projection lines. Extreme care should be taken that the tread and riser projections are correctly matched.

The *y*-axis scale of the curves is projected horizontally to the riser-distortion curve, and the resulting intersections are projected vertically downward to the *y* axis of the straight lines. Similarly the graduations of the *x* axis are projected vertically downward to the tread-distortion scale and the resulting intersections projected horizontally to the *x* axis of the straight-line plot. Only the values of the scale graduations lying within the limits of the distortion curves may be used, and as a result the origin of the scales is often not available for distortion. Because the distortion curve is limited by the stair

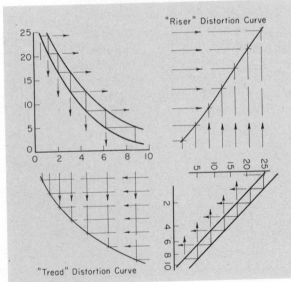

FIG. 22.17. Double-scale distortion to obtain rectification of curves of empirical data.

steps, several sets may have to be drawn before the treads and risers extend to the limits of the curves being rectified. For practical purposes the straight-line plot is seldom drawn with the stair steps, but an appropriate length is chosen for the risers and treads, and this distance is plotted in place of the projected distances from the straight-line plot. The method will be shown in detail in explanation of the rectification of more than two curves which follows.

Rectification of more than two curves at a time utilizes the same principles as for two curves except that the family of curves must belong to a group for which rectification can occur with only one distortion for each axis. If the axes must be separately distorted for each curve, no single set of axes can provide rectification for all the curves and the curves cannot be made into a nomograph. It is necessary to prove that the curves belong to the correct family by testing them three at a time for linearity. Figure 22.18 shows the test as a series of vertical and horizontal lines. If the test lines intersect at each of the curves as shown, the distortion of the coordinate scales will provide rectification of all the curves. The curves should be tested three at a time, with each test using two lines from a previous test and one untested line. Because of the complexity of this method, usually only two or three groups of three lines each, picked at random, are tested. If these lines pass the test, it is assumed that all lines will pass with sufficient accuracy for most problems.

In Fig. 22.19 a plot is shown of moisture content of air versus air temperature with parameters of relative humidity. These curves pass the test for linearity, and further scale distortion can begin. The stair steps of Fig. 22.17

may be drawn between any two curves of the group. In this particular case, the stair steps have been drawn between the 50 per cent and 80 per cent curves. The riser heights of the distorted plot shall equal the distance a. There are seven risers in the stair steps so seven lengths of a are laid out horizontally to the right of the curve-line plot. Vertical lines are drawn for each of the a distances. The risers are projected from the curves to the a distances. The resulting intersections are points which represent the curve of distortion drawn in Fig. 22.19. Similarly the tread widths of the distorted plot are picked as a distance b. There are seven treads in the curve plot so seven distances b are laid out vertically below the curve plot. Horizontal lines are drawn for each of the b distances. The curve-

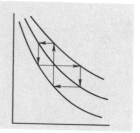

FIG. 22.18.   Test for linearity.

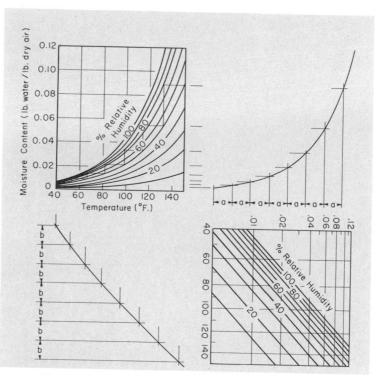

FIG. 22.19.   Double-scale distortion to obtain rectification of empirical curves.

plot treads are projected to the *b* lines, and the resulting intersections form the curve of distortion shown. The graduations of the *y* axis are projected to the riser-distortion scale and at right angles from these points to a new distorted *y* scale. Similarly the graduations of the *x* axis are projected to the tread-distortion scale and from this point at right angles to determine the new distorted *x* scale. Two selected points from each curve are used to determine the plot of the straight lines, using the distorted scales of *y* and *x*. Figure 22.19 shows the finished plot of the rectified lines.

It could be shown mathematically that the scales of the rectified plot can be used directly to form the outer two scales of a three-scale nomograph. Each recti-

fied line forms one pivot point of the third, which need not be straight or parallel to the other two scales. Normally the outer two scales are made parallel to each other although experience will show whether some slight deviation from parallelism might improve the resulting nomograph. Figure 22.20*A* illustrates the *y* and *x* scales of the rectified plot transferred to positions parallel to each other and at some convenient distance apart. Intersecting tie lines form the 100 per cent humidity point on the third scale. The coordinates or values to be used for these tie lines are taken from two selected points on either of the plots of the 100 per cent humidity line. Figure 22.20*B* illustrates the completed nomograph.

Double-scale distortion (graphic anamorphosis) requires extreme care in maintaining drafting accuracy for reliable results, but it will provide a nomograph when no equation is available or when the equation cannot be placed in any nomographic form. Producing a nomograph from an equation by this method will require plotting a series of parametric curves from which the rectified plot can be made. The amount of labor involved is considerable, and this method can therefore be recommended only for cases in which other methods cannot be applied.

22.12. SUMMARY. Empirical data are data from observations for which no equation for the data was known before the data was obtained. The data should first be plotted on rectilinear coordinates to determine whether rectification or a suggestion of the equation form occurs. Data which plot as a straight line on rectilinear coordinates have an equation of the form $y = a + bx$, where $a = y$ at

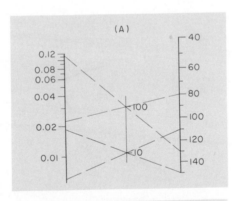

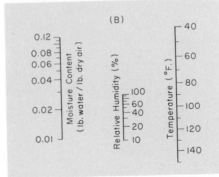

FIG. 22.20. A nomograph constructed from the scales of the rectified plot of empirical data.

$x = 0$ and b is the slope of the straight line. Data which plot as a straight line on logarithmic coordinates have an equation of the power form $y = ax^b$, where $a = y$ at $x = 1$ and b is the slope of the straight line. Data which plot as a straight line on semilogarithmic coordinates have an equation of the exponential type $y = a\,(10)^{bx}$, where $a = y$ at $x = 0$ and b is the slope of the straight line.

Three general and relatively accurate methods for the determination of the constants of the equations are (1) the method of selected points, (2) the method of averages, and (3) the method of least squares. The first two methods, which are graphic and numerical respectively, are recommended for data which plot in essentially a straight line. The last method, which is purely numerical, is recommended for data which plot with noticeable deviations from a straight line.

Data for which no simple equation form can be found (which do not plot as a straight line on any of the three coordinate systems mentioned) can be made into a conversion chart for two-variable data and a nomograph for three-variable data by the process of graphic scale distortion. Single-scale distortion produces a conversion chart from an accurate x-y plot on any coordinates by projecting the y-axis graduations to the curve and projecting the resulting intersections to the x axis. An x-y plot with parameters produces a nomograph using the scales from an x-y plot in which the curves rectified. The distorted scales of the rectified plot are obtained by drawing a stair step between two curves of the first plot and determining the scales which would cause this stair step to have risers of equal length and treads of equal length. Plots of more than two curves must meet the test for linearity for the method to be appropriate.

PROBLEMS

GROUP 1.   EMPIRICAL DATA OF KNOWN EQUATION FORM

The following problems are identified as to the form of equation which fits the given data. Preliminary plots of the data should be made on rectilinear coordinates in order to illustrate the characteristics of each type of equation.

22.1.1. Measurement of the electrical resistance of a 1-ft length of No. 0 AWG standard annealed copper wire at various temperatures resulted in the data shown in the accompanying table.

Temperature T, °C	Resistance R, μohms
14.0	96.00
19.2	97.76
25.0	100.50
30.0	102.14
36.5	105.00
40.1	105.75
45.0	108.20
52.0	110.60

After plotting the data on uniform rectangular coordinates with resistance as ordinate and temperature as abscissa, evaluate the constants a and b in the linear equation $R = a + bT$ relating the variables.

22.1.2. Approximate rates of discharge of water under various heads of fall through a 1,000-ft length of 4-in. pipe having an average number of bends and fittings are tabulated below:

Head of fall H, ft	Discharge Q, gal/min
1	35.8
2	50.6
4	71.6
6	87.7
9	107.5
12	123.7
16	142.9

Completed plots of the rectified data should include careful calibration of the scales, properly labeled scale captions, and the equation of the data with the constants evaluated.

Head of fall H, ft	Discharge Q, gal/min
20	159.7
25	178.9
30	195.8
40	225.8
50	252.2
75	309.8
100	357.9

After plotting the data on logarithmic coordinates with discharge as ordinate and head as abscissa, evaluate the constants a and b in the power equation $Q = aH^b$ relating the variables.

22.1.3. Creep-strength tests of a high-chromium (23 to 27 per cent) ferritic steel used in high-temperature service resulted in the stress values, to produce a 1 per cent deformation in 10,000 hr at various temperatures, tabulated below:

Temperature T, °F	Stress S, lb/sq in.
1,000	6,450
1,100	2,700
1,200	1,250
1,300	570
1,400	270

After plotting the data on semilogarithmic coordinates with stress as ordinate on a logarithmic scale and temperature as abscissa on a uniform scale, evaluate the constants a and b in the exponential equation $S = a10^{bT}$ relating the variables.

GROUP 2. EMPIRICAL DATA OF UNKNOWN EQUATION FORM

Preliminary plots should be made on recti-linear coordinates for data in all the following problems so that the equation form may be determined. Further preliminary plots of the data should be made on the correct coordinate system required for rectification. This will avoid loss of time and waste of large coordinate paper if an improper choice of coordinate has been made. Constants of the equations may be obtained graphically from an accurate recti-fied plot of the data or numerically by the method of averages or least squares. The completed plot of the data should include scales with proper graduations, calibrations, legends, and the equation with constants evaluated for the data as part of a descriptive title.

22.2.1. Spark-gap break-down voltages for smooth spherical electrodes 25 cm in diameter and in clean dry air at 25°C and 760 mm are tabulated below for various gap lengths:

Gap length L, cm	Peak voltage V, kv
5	0.16
10	0.32
15	0.48
20	0.64
25	0.81
30	0.98
35	1.15
40	1.32
45	1.49
50	1.66
60	2.01
70	2.37
80	2.74
90	3.11
100	3.49

22.2.2. Capacities of horizontal conveyer belts, carrying materials with a density of 50 lb per cu ft at a speed of 200 ft per min and running on standard 20° troughing idlers, are tabulated below:

Belt width W, in.	Capacity C, short tons (2,000 lb)/hr
12	29
18	68
24	125
30	200
36	290
42	406
48	550
54	716
60	900

22.2.3. Corrosion tests on specimens of pure magnesium resulted in values for weight increase in pure oxygen at 525°C tabulated below:

Elapsed time T, hr	Weight increase W, mg/sq cm
0	0
2.0	0.17
4.0	0.36
8.2	0.65
11.5	1.00
20.0	1.68
24.1	2.09
30.0	2.57

22.2.4. Solubility tables give the data tabulated below for the solubility of anhydrous potassium alum in water:

Temperature T, °C	Solubility S, g K_2SO_4 $Al_2(SO_4)_3$/100 g H_2O for saturated solution
0	3.0
10	4.0
20	5.9
30	8.39
40	11.70
50	17.00
60	24.75

22.2.5. Breaking loads for standard annealed copper wire are given in the table that follows:

Wire size G, AWG	Breaking load L, lb
0	2,980
1	2,430
2	1,930
3	1,530
4	1,210
5	962
6	762
7	605
8	480
9	380
10	314
11	249
12	197
13	156
14	124

22.2.6. Steam tables give the specific volume of saturated steam at various absolute pressures as tabulated below:

Absolute pressure P, lb/sq in.	Specific volume V, cu ft/lb
1	333.6
2	173.73
3	118.71
5	73.52
10	38.42
14.7	26.80
20	20.089
25	16.303
30	13.746
40	10.498

22.2.7. Thermal conductivities of a bonded-asbestos-fiber insulating material at various mean temperatures are tabulated below:

Mean temperature (hot to cold surface) T, °F	Thermal conductivity K, Btu/hr-sq ft-°F temp diff-in. thickness
100	0.365
200	0.415
320	0.470
400	0.520
460	0.563
600	0.628
730	0.688
900	0.780

22.2.8. Heat losses from horizontal bare-iron hot-water pipes at 180°F to still ambient air at 75°F are tabulated below:

Pipe size D, in.	Heat loss H, Btu/lin ft-24 hr
1	1,896
1¼	2,398
1½	2,746
2	3,430
2½	4,140
3	5,054
3½	5,771
4	6,493
4½	7,211
5	8,020
6	9,530
8	12,442
10	15,528
12	18,418
14	20,140
16	23,088
18	25,998

GROUP 3.   GRAPHIC SCALE-DISTORTION PROBLEMS

Since all forms of graphic scale distortion rely upon an x-y plot of the data, no problems will be presented labeled strictly for scale-distortion purposes. All the problems in groups 1 and 2 of this chapter may be used for single-scale-distortion problems. All the two-variable equations of the problems of Chap. 21 may be used to produce an x-y plot for single-scale-distortion problems. Any arbitrary curve may be drawn on x-y coordinates and rectified by single-scale distortion, and technical magazines are a further source of x-y plots which can be used for single-scale distortion.

Double-scale distortion requires an x-y plot with parameters to produce a "family" of curves. Plots of data of three variables can be found in technical publications, and scale distortion should be performed directly upon these plots. Any of the three-variable problems of Chap. 21 may be used to produce the required x-y plot, using one of the three variables as the parameter. The following data can be rectified by one of the methods used to find an equation from empirical data but also provide an excellent problem for double-scale distortion.

Plot the data carefully, and draw the curves as accurately as possible to minimize errors in drafting. The finished nomograph produced from this data should be drawn and labeled in accordance with the principles of Chap. 21.

22.3.1. The maximum free air delivered to a pressure vessel at any given pressure is related to the size of the safety valve as shown in the following table:

Gage pressure, psi	Valve diameter, in.								
	¼	½	¾	1	1¼	1½	2	2½	3
50		20	37	58	84	114	189	282	393
100		32	59	94	135	186	306	457	638
150		42	78	124	180	248	410	613	856
200		51	96	152	221	302	501	750	1,050
250		59	112	178	259	354	592	880	1,230
300		67	127	202	293	400	668	998	1,398
350		74	141	224	325	444	741	1,114	1,557
400	53	111	176	248					
500	61	129	224	286	374	472			
600	70	147	232	324					
800	84	177	242	390	509	634			
1,000	97	205	346	450					
1,200	109	230	386	500					

Graphic Calculus

23.1. In the previous chapter, the engineer's concern with the relationships of variable quantities was demonstrated, and it was pointed out that a relationship may be of any order, from a linear, or first-degree, equation to power and exponential types. There are, of course, more complicated forms. The determination of a *relationship,* however, may not furnish all the information required for engineering purposes. In any case, it may be necessary to know the *rate of change* of the variables, that is, how fast or how much a change is caused in one variable as the result of a change in the other variable. For a first-degree equation, the rate of change of the variables is constant. For other equations, the rate of change may be uniform or may vary according to a mathematical relationship. The rate of change for other situations may follow some mathematical law or, on the other hand, may not.

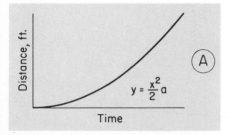

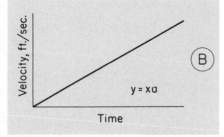

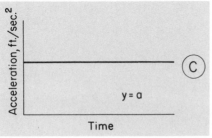

FIG. 23.1.   Derived curves.

Figure 23.1 illustrates an equational relationship in which a body is moving under constant acceleration. The time-distance curve *A* has an equation of $y = (x^2/2)a$, where y is distance, x is time, and a is the constant acceleration. By calculus, the first derivative will be $y = xa$, which is velocity, shown by curve *B* to change at a uniform rate. This is the *rate* of change of the distance-time relationship. The second derivative of $y = (x^2/2)a$ is $y = a$ (or the first derivative of $y = xa$ is $y = a$), the rate of change of the velocity (curve *B*), which is shown in curve *C* to be a constant, the acceleration, equal to a. The third derivative (the derivative of $y = a$, the acceleration) will be zero ($y = 0$). Thus we see that a derivative gives the rate of change of a relationship of *next higher order*. Conversely, if the series is started with the acceleration $y = a$, the curve of next higher order, the velocity $y = xa$, is the integral of $y = a$. Also, the distance-time curve $y = (x^2/2)a$ is the second integral of $y = a$ (or the first integral of $y = xa$). Therefore, an integral gives the *summation* for a relationship of lower order.

In many cases, the rate of change of a relationship will not be constant, nor will it vary according to any known mathematical law. In Fig. 23.2, a body is shown to be moving according to some changing velocity and acceleration. The first derivative, curve *B,* which has been produced by graphic methods, shows that the velocity does not change at any easily determinable mathematical rate. Also, the second derivative, the acceleration, curve *C,* follows a similar pattern for rate of change. Even though the possibility is remote that mathematical equations can be written in this case, the curves show how the rates vary and provide a means

of finding the value of the rate of change at any particular point on the curves. Thus the graphic counterpart of mathematical integration and differentiation becomes a *family* of curves on which all necessary relationships and rates of change may be determined. The engineer is often faced with problems similar to the foregoing example, where tabulated data representing a relationship are so complex that either no mathematical equation can be found or the computations become extremely difficult. In such cases, the operations of integration and differentiation, that is, of determining a related curve of next higher or lower degree, can be performed quickly and accurately by graphic methods.

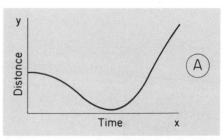

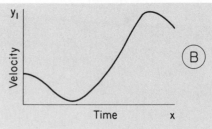

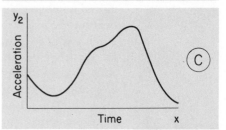

FIG. 23.2.   Derived curves.

23.2. **RATE OF CHANGE.** *The value of the derivative at any point of a curve is equal to the slope of the line drawn tangent to the curve at that point.* The solution of this mathematical problem led Leibnitz and Newton, independently of each other, to the discovery of the differential calculus.

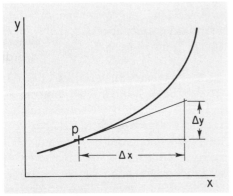

FIG. 23.3. Rate of change.

Graphically, the statement means that, if *at any point on a curve* (as, for example, point *p* of Fig. 23.3) *a tangent is drawn, the value of the tangent, $\Delta y/\Delta x$, is the rate of change at point p.* The application of this theorem to a series of points on a curve is fundamental to both graphic and symbolic calculus.

23.3. **LAWS OF GRAPHIC CALCULUS.** The methods of graphic calculus are based upon two laws of derived curves.

First Law. The slope at any point of a given curve relating two variables is numerically equal to the ordinate at the corresponding point of the derived curve of next lower degree (derivative curve). This law is illustrated in Fig. 23.4, where the slope at $x = 1$ of the curve of higher degree (y_1 versus x) is the tangent of the angle θ, or $\Delta y_1/\Delta x$. This slope is numerically equal to the ordinate *a* of the derivative curve (y_2 versus x) at the same point, $x = 1$. The slope reaches a maximum value *b* at $x = 2.6$, becomes zero at $x = 5.3$, and

then takes on negative values, reaching the value $-c$ at $x = 6$. Notice that the derivative curve (y_2 versus x) is plotted to *twice* the scale of the given curve (y_1 versus x), and on the given curve the y_1 scale is *half* that of the x scale.

Second Law. The area bounded by a given curve, any two ordinates, and the x axis is numerically equal to the difference between the two corresponding ordinates of the curve of next higher degree (integral curve). This law is illustrated in Fig. 23.5. The area under the curve of lower degree (y_2 versus x) over the interval from $x = 1$ to $x = 1.8$ is numerically equal to *a*, the *increase* in the value of y_1 *over the same interval*. Similarly, the area of the interval from $x = 1.8$ to $x = 2.6$ is numerically equal to *b*. The total ordinate of the curve of higher degree represents, at any given value of x, the *cumulative* area under the curve of lower degree up to that point. Thus y_1 reaches a maximum value at $x = 5.3$; then from $x = 5.3$ to $x = 6$, it decreases in value by the incre-

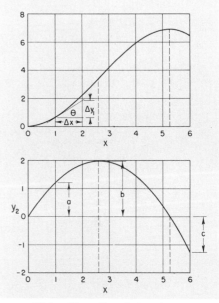

FIG. 23.4. Illustration of slope law.

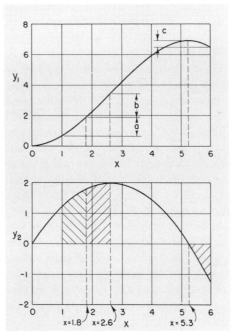

FIG. 23.5. Illustration of area law.

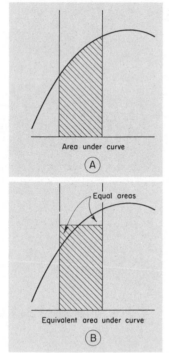

FIG. 23.6. Equivalent area of a strip.

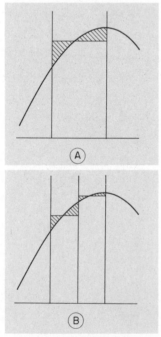

FIG. 23.7. Width of strip adjusted to obtain greater accuracy.

ment c as the area under the curve y_2 versus x becomes negative in sign.

Because slopes (tangents) are generally more difficult to measure or compare than are areas, the latter are preferred as the basis for graphic methods of calculus.

23.4. EQUIVALENT AREAS. In applying the *second law,* the area under the curve, for a number of vertical strips, is required. The area under the curve is found and used as an equivalent area, explained by Fig. 23.6, where at (A) the real area under a curve is shown and at (B) an equivalent rectangular area. If the two small almost triangular areas indicated at (B) are made *equal,* one area is additive and the other subtractive to make the rectangular area *identical in value* to the area under the curve. This is easily accomplished by locating a horizontal line which cuts the curve between the two ordinates so as to form a pair of equal "triangular" areas. The horizontal line is located graphically by using a triangle or transparent-blade T square so that both areas under consideration can be seen. When the triangular areas under consideration are small, the eye is quite sensitive to differences and a very good approximation of the position of the mean ordinate is obtained. Also, when the two triangular areas are of approximately the same *shape,* judgment of the two areas is simplified. For example, the two areas of Fig. 23.7A are not of the same shape because the curve changes more rapidly on one end than at the other; but if, as at (B), the vertical strip is made narrower (in this case, half of the previous strip), the difference in curvature is not so pronounced, the areas are smaller, and very good approximations can be

made. Thus we may say with the force of a rule that, *where the curvature is noticeably unequal, narrower strips should be used.*

The charts for graphic calculus should be made *large.* It is difficult to obtain accuracy in *any* graphic construction when the data plot is not of sufficient size to get results within the range of accuracy of the experimental data. Standard graph paper is available in cut sheets up to 16 by 20 in.

23.5. GRAPHIC INTEGRATION. *Chordal Method.* Of all the known methods for graphic integration, the chordal method is outstanding since it is as accurate as any, it does not require extra equipment, such as a mirror for locating tangents, and the construction is simple and direct.

The given curve of lower order, representing a relationship between y_2 and $x,$ is plotted on rectangular coordinates as shown in Fig. 23.8. Ordinates are then drawn to divide the chart area into a series of vertical strips. The number and spacing of the ordinates are determined by the shape of the curve: If the curvature either is sharp or reverses itself, the ordinates should be close together; conversely, where the curve is relatively flat, they may be spaced farther apart. On Fig. 23.8, the attempt has been made to locate the vertical strips so that mean ordinate distances can be accurately located.

Next, *mean ordinate heights* for the several strips are determined as described in paragraph 23.4. Thus, as illustrated by Fig. 23.9, the area under the curve in each strip has now been equated to the product of the mean ordinate times the width of the strip. For example, the area under curve pq is equal to the area of the rectangle whose upper boundary is $rw,$ and in similar fashion, all mean ordinate

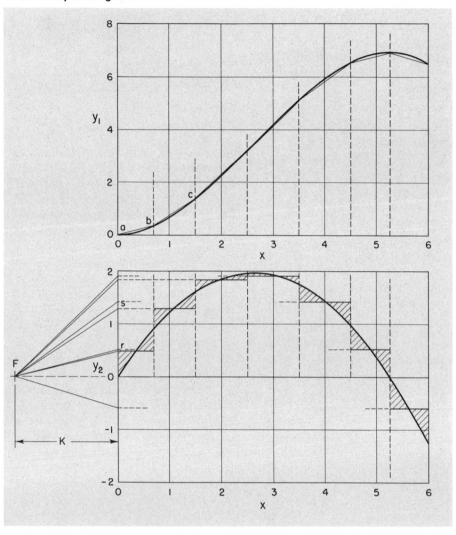

FIG. 23.8.   Graphic integration: chordal method.

FIG. 23.9.   Theory of chordal method.

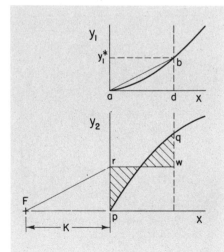

heights have been determined on Fig. 23.8.

Now the height of the mean ordinate of each strip is projected to a vertical line, which, in this case, is the y axis. A focus F (described in detail in paragraph 23.6) is located on the x axis (extended), and rays are drawn from the focus to the projected heights of the mean ordinates for each strip (illustrated in both Figs. 23.8 and 23.9).

The integral curve can now be started.

It is best to draw the integral curve above the given curve as in Fig. 23.8— even a separate piece of paper may be used if desired. The chart is started by laying out the axes y_1 and x in projection with the lower chart so that the same vertical strips on the given curve may be drawn for the integral curve.

Points on the integral curve (y_1 versus x) are located by starting at the origin and drawing a straight line across each strip *parallel* to the corresponding ray below, for example, *ab* parallel to *Fr* and then *bc* parallel to *Fs,* and so on until all points, *a, b, c,* etc., have been found. A smooth curve through the points is the integral curve.

23.6. FOCAL DISTANCE AND SCALES FOR THE CHORDAL METHOD.

The focal distance K (on Fig. 23.8) is related to the scales for $x, y_1,$ and y_2 by the formula

$$K = m_x \frac{m_{y2}}{m_{y1}}$$

where m_x = modulus for the x scale
m_{y1} = modulus for the y scale of integral curve
m_{y2} = modulus of the y scale of the given curve

In Fig. 23.9, the area under curve *pq* of the plot y_2 versus x is the product of the numerical value of the mean ordinate and the numerical value of strip width:

$$\text{Area} = \frac{pr}{m_{y2}} \frac{rw}{m_x}$$

In the plot y_1 versus x, the numerical value of the y_1 ordinate at point *b* is

$$y_1{}^* = \frac{bd}{m_{y1}}$$

If $y_1{}^*$ = area, then

$$\frac{bd}{m_{y1}} = \frac{pr}{m_{y2}} \frac{rw}{m_x}$$

whence
$$\frac{m_x m_{y2}}{m_{y1}} = \frac{pr}{bd} \frac{rw}{} \qquad (1)$$

From similar triangles *Frp* and *abd,*

$$\frac{K}{pr} = \frac{ad}{bd} = \frac{rw}{bd} \qquad (2)$$

From (2), we get

$$K = \frac{pr}{bd} \frac{rw}{} \qquad (3)$$

whence, from (1) and (3),

$$K = \frac{m_x m_{y2}}{m_{y1}}$$

In Fig. 23.8, the scale of y_2 is twice that of y_1. Therefore,

$$K = m_x {}^2\!/\!_1 \qquad \text{or} \qquad K = 2m_x$$

In other words, distance K is equal to two units of the x scale. Thus if both scales y_2 and y_1 are decided upon, the distance K may be determined. On the other hand, if a distance K is assumed, the y_1 scale may then be calculated.

The y_1-scale modulus m_{y1} of the integral curve must normally be smaller than the modulus m_{y2} of the given curve in order to keep the integral curve within reasonable proportions. The maximum value of y_1 may be estimated by remembering that the maximum value will be equal, *numerically,* to the *total* area under the curve. This total is the summation of all the individual areas in the strips and can be had by actually making the summation, but an easier way is indicated in Fig. 23.10, where a rectangular equivalent area is arranged so that areas $A + B$ balance area C. The product of the *y-mean ordinate* y_m and the total x value x_t then gives the maximum y_1-ordinate value. On Fig. 23.10, y_m = 1.25 (approximately), and x_t = 5.3; the product is 6.6 (approximately). The scale for y_1 can then be selected for good proportions of the integral curve and the K distance calculated to conform.

23.7. GRAPHIC DIFFERENTIATION.

Chordal Method. The integral curve y_1 versus x of Fig. 23.8 may be taken as a given curve, and y_2 versus x, the lower curve, then becomes the derivative curve of y_1 versus x. The chordal method just described is *reversible* and can be employed

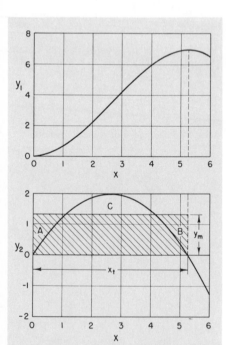

FIG. 23.10. Total (equivalent) area under curve.

as readily as before to plot the derivative curve. The steps are performed one by one in opposite order. First, chords of the given curve are drawn across each vertical strip. Then, a focus and the axes for the derivative curve are located, using a larger scale for the derivative curve. Next, rays from the focus, *parallel* to the chords, determine mean ordinates on the lower curve. A smooth line drawn across the horizontal mean-ordinate lines so as to balance out the triangular areas added on and cut off in each vertical strip then gives the derivative curve.

The above method of drawing a derivative curve is quite satisfactory for most cases, but sometimes it is somewhat difficult to draw a smooth curve to balance the areas on the lower curve. Also, for the best results and easiest solution, the chords of the given curve should be chosen carefully. Fortunately, however, for critical problems, some extra constructions may be made to aid in balancing the areas on the derivative chart. The first law states that the slope at any given point of the given curve will be numerically equal to the ordinate at the corresponding point of the derived curve. Also, from Fig. 23.9, it is readily seen that points p and q on the lower curve and a and b on the upper curve are points *on* the curves. By employing the above facts, graphic derivation may be accomplished simply and with accurate results. In Fig. 23.11A, a given curve with chord ab is shown, along with the derived curve prq. From the chordal method of paragraphs 23.5 and 23.6, it is known that a and b are points on the given curve for which p and q are corresponding points on the derived curve. There is also a y-mean height y_m for the area under the derived curve,

and at the point r where the y-mean height crosses the curve, a tangent t may be drawn on the given curve. From the first law, the slope at point t is equal to the ordinate value at r, and from the figure, it is seen that the ordinate value of r will be equal to y_m. Therefore, if a tangent *point* can be accurately located on the given curve to meet the above conditions, a definite point r can be found on the derived curve. From elementary geometry, it is known that for a circle arc, as shown at Fig. 23.11B, a tangent and a series of parallel chords will all have a radial line that is the perpendicular bisector of the chords. Thus if the given curve is divided into portions which closely approach *arcs*, the perpendicular bisectors of the chords will locate tangent points and, by projection to the derived curve, locate points on the curve. This is illustrated at Fig. 23.11C, where the given curve has been divided into segments and vertical strips have been determined by chords, $ab, bc,$ and cd. These chords have been chosen so that each portion of the curve is closely symmetrical about the perpendicular bisector of its chord. Note that where the curve is relatively flat the chord may be longer than where the curvature changes rapidly. The perpendicular bisectors of the chords then locate tangent points t_1 for ab, t_2 for bc, and t_3 for cd. These tangent points then projected down to the derived-curve chart will locate points r_1, r_2, and r_3 *on the mean-ordinate height lines.*

It is obvious that no curve, unless it is actually a circle arc, can have perfect symmetry about a chord. Nevertheless, if the chords are carefully chosen and made reasonably short, the conditions for a circle arc are approached so closely that the error is negligible. As a matter

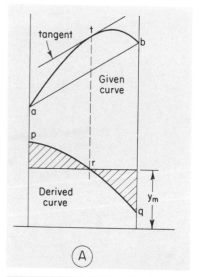

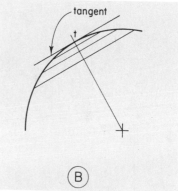

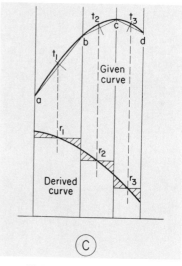

FIG. 23.11. Chords of given curve located to obtain derived curve.

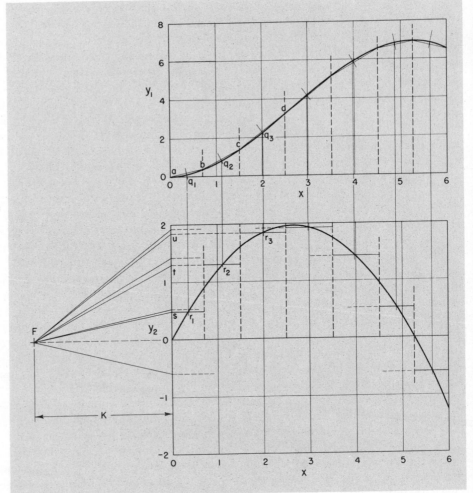

FIG. 23.12. Graphic differentiation: chordal method.

of fact, the whole system of calculus is based on methods of *limits* where a series of values of a variable approach a definite constant value. Thus the graphic procedure here described follows the fundamental theory of calculus.

Figure 23.12 illustrates the determination of a derivative curve, based on the foregoing methods. The given curve, y_1 versus x, is plotted on uniform rectangular coordinates as shown. A series of chords, *ab, bc, cd,* etc., is drawn as described for Fig. 23.11C so that the chords cut the curve to produce close symmetry of the curve

about the chord. The derivative chart is then started by determining a scale and focal distance K. Reversing the process described for integration, the maximum ordinate of y_1 versus x is 6.7 (approximately). From the second law, this value represents the total value of the area under the derivative curve, up to the corresponding value of x for $y_{1, max}$, in this case, $x = 5.3$. Therefore, $6.7/5.3 = 1.26$ (approximately), the y mean value of the area up to $x = 5.3$. If the same scale of y_1 versus x is used for the derived curve, the total height will be only about one-third that of the given curve. Thus an increase in scale is desirable. If the y_2-versus-x scale is to be three times that of y_1 versus x, then

$$K = \frac{m_x m_{y2}}{m_{y1}} = m_x \frac{3}{1}$$

or $\qquad K = 3m_x$

The K distance is then laid off equal to three times one unit of x, locating the focus F. Lines now drawn from the focus parallel to the chords on y_1 versus x, for example, Fs parallel to ab, Ft parallel to bc, and Fu parallel to cd, determine points s, t, u, etc., on the ordinate of y_2 versus x for projection to the strips, giving y-mean heights for the strips. The strips on both curves are formed by the intersections of the chords on y_1 versus x. Perpendicular bisectors of the chords on y_1 versus x will locate tangent points q_1, q_2, q_3, etc., which, projected down to y_2 versus x, locate points r_1, r_2, r_3, etc., on the y-mean height lines of the strips. A smooth curve through r_1, r_2, r_3, etc., is the derivative curve. As a check, it should be noticed that the derivative curve should balance the additive and subtractive areas from the y-mean area in each strip.

23.8. OTHER METHODS OF GRAPHIC INTEGRATION AND DIFFERENTIATION.

There are a number of other graphic methods for integration and differentiation based either on the use of tangents or on a combination of graphic and mathematical procedures. However, these methods all have one or more serious faults and will, therefore, not be described. Any method depending upon the drawing of a tangent to a curve is inaccurate because of the difficulty of drawing an accurate tangent. Any combination of graphics and mathematics

can be used only when the curve is parabolic or of a geometrical shape that allows the application of mathematical formulas.

23.9. CONSTANT OF INTEGRATION.

The graphic methods will integrate a given curve, and the algebraic methods will integrate an expression, but neither method will orient numerical values of an integral with a corresponding value of the given curve or expression. In all the graphic examples shown thus far, the curves have started at the origin of uniform rectangular coordinates where the constant of integration relating the curves is zero. This condition, however, may not always be the case. To explain, assume that an integral curve is to be determined that passes through $x = 1$ and $y = 4$ from a given curve having a slope of $2x$. Mathematically, this means that the curve to be determined will be the integral of $y = 2x$.

Since the slope at any point is dy/dx, by hypothesis,

$$\frac{dy}{dx} = 2x \qquad \text{and} \qquad dy = 2x\,dx$$

Integrating, we get

$$y = 2\int x\,dx$$

or $\qquad y = x^2 + C \qquad (1)$

where C is the constant of integration. The curve must pass through the point $x = 1$ and $y = 4$. Therefore, to satisfy Eq. (1),

$$4 = 1 + C \qquad \text{and} \qquad C = 3$$

Graphically, as shown in Fig. 23.13, the curve (straight line) of $y = 2x$ is plotted at y_2 versus x as shown. This is the given curve for which the integral curve is needed. In this case, a K distance of three units of x has been selected,

FIG. 23.13. Constant of integration.

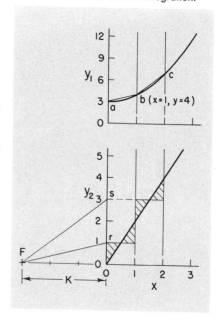

thus making the scale of y_1, the integral chart, one-third of the scale for y_2. Then y-mean areas are drawn for the strips on y_2 versus x, between $x = 0$, $x = 1$, and $x = 2$. Now focal lines Fr and Fs can be used to get chords on the integral curve. Remembering that the curve must pass through $x = 1$ and $y = 4$, point b (at these values) is located on the integral curve. Then chord ba parallel to Fr and chord bc parallel to Fs give points through which the integral curve may be drawn. It is seen now that the y intercept occurs at $y = 3$, the value of the constant of integration when $x = 0$, satisfying the equation $y = x^2 + C$. Thus the constant of integration simply moves the curve up or down on the y axis. If some other values of x and y had been given, the constant of integration would be changed but the integration would be identical.

In any practical case, the constant of integration is usually determinable by knowing either the relationship of given and integral values of a variable or by knowing *one point* on the integral curve.

It is also valuable to note that a constant does not affect the process of differentiation. Remember that, according to the first law, the *slope* of a given curve gives the ordinate height on the derivative curve and that the second law concurs by stating that the *difference* in ordinate value of a given curve gives the area under the derived curve.

23.10. EXAMPLE OF GRAPHIC INTEGRATION. Sometimes in a practical problem an instantaneous rate of change can be determined accurately through the use of measuring instruments or by calculation, but because of the nature of the problem, the *rate-of-change* curve will not follow known or readily determined

mathematical law. Therefore, the graphic method of integration is either the *only* or the *easiest* solution. For example, a small conservation dam is known, from a survey of the pool contour and bed, to contain 8,000,000 gal of water when full. Head, in feet of water behind the dam, is easily determined by direct measurement. Flow (gallons per hour) out of a drain pipe may be determined by calculation from head of water and pipe size. Nevertheless, because of the uneven contour of both the pool outline and bed, as the pool is drained, there is no simple relationship for rate of flow versus time. However, by graphic integration of the rate-of-flow curve (determined by a test), the number of gallons drained out may be determined, thus giving information to show (1) remaining capacity of the pool at any particular head, (2) flow rate for any particular head, and (3) time required to drain a given quantity of water from the pool. The data on the opposite page have been obtained from a test.

These data plotted on uniform rectangular coordinates on the lower chart of Fig. 23.14 give the rate-of-flow curve of H and GPH versus T. (Head and flow rate are directly related.) The integral of this rate curve will give the summation of the rate or, in this case, gallons capacity versus time. The head H corresponding to quantity at full stage and at lower stages has also been shown on the integral chart. Note that capacity at full stage is the constant of integration in this case and must be plotted first in making the integral curve. The integral curve is plotted as shown on Fig. 23.14 and described in paragraph 23.5.

To use the chart, assume that at head a it is desired to drain y_1 gal from the pool. The time required is then T_1. The

DRAIN RATES

Time T, hr	Head H, ft	GPH, gal/hr
0	30	205,000
4	29.4	203,000
8	28.6	200,000
12	27.4	198,600
16	25.8	190,000
20	23.4	180,000
24	20	167,000

Capacity at full stage: 8,000,000 gal
Head at full stage: 30.0 ft

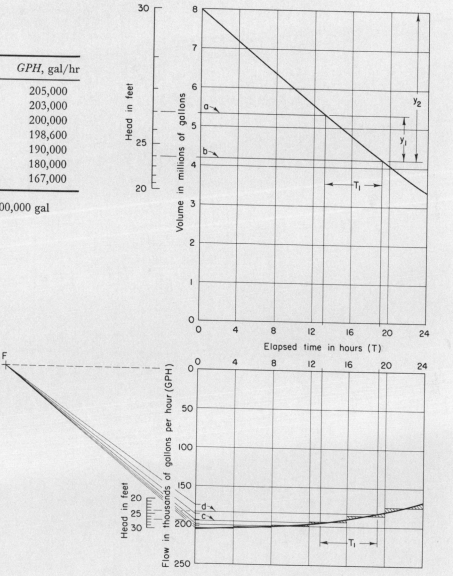

FIG. 23.14.   Example of graphic integration.

rate of flow at the beginning and end of the drain period can be read from c and d on the lower chart. The capacity to hold additional water coming down from the supply stream after this drain period is then y_2 on the integral chart. As

another example, assume at head a that the pool is drained for a time of T_1. Then y_1 gal have been taken out. Thus this chart of given and integral curves becomes the operating guide for the conservation and flood-prevention dam.

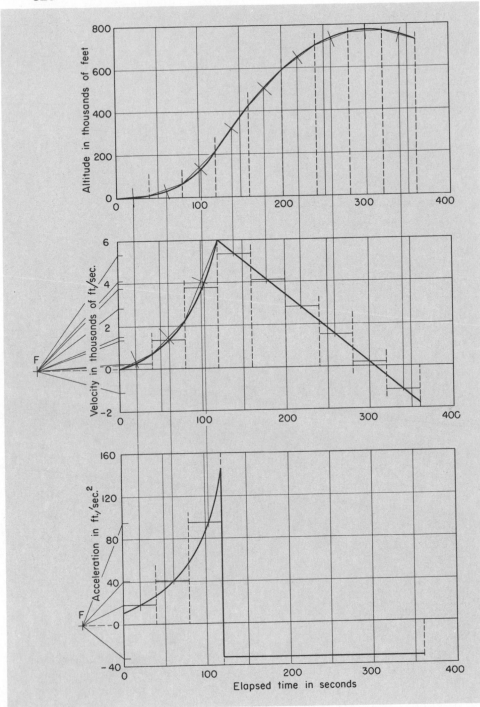

FIG. 23.15. Example of graphic differentiation.

23.11. EXAMPLE OF GRAPHIC DIFFERENTIA-TION. Many devices of science and engineering move with some varying rate of velocity and acceleration. Sometimes these varying rates are known to follow mathematical laws, but in other cases, it may be necessary to verify an assumed law, determine a law, or represent the rates of change (if no known mathematical relationship fits the data). In any case, the graphic method of differentiation will apply. For example, the movement of missiles and rockets may be closely estimated by mathematical means if the fundamentals such as gross weight, fuel capacity, burning rate of fuel, and engine thrust are known; but the actual *performance* may not follow the calculations exactly because of unforeseen variations caused either by unknown design characteristics or other imperfect aspects. Through the use of tracking devices, both optical and radar, and also by including instruments in the rocket itself, such as a recording altimeter, flight data may be obtained.

Figure 23.15 illustrates a case where a rocket, having a gross weight of 15,000 lb and engine thrust of 20,000 lb at sea level and a fuel-burning period of 120-sec duration, has been fired vertically from ground level. The data for altitude are plotted against time in the upper curve of Fig. 23.14. The rocket will accelerate until burnout of the fuel, then coast to its zenith, and finally fall as a free body. For guidance in future designing, not only should the rates of velocity and acceleration be determined but the important *maximum* acceleration is needed. All necessary information can be found by drawing the velocity and acceleration curves.

The velocity curve is the first derivative and is constructed as described in paragraph 23.7. Note that the focal distance (K of Fig. 23.15) has been chosen

to keep the velocity curve at a height consistent with the height of a given (original-data) curve. Maximum velocity occurs at burnout.

The acceleration curve will be the derivative of the velocity curve (the second derivative of the given-data curve). This is again plotted as described in paragraph 23.7. This curve shows that the acceleration is at a maximum at burnout, reduces *very* sharply from 146 ft per sec^2 to -32.2 ft per sec^2, and then is constant. Thus all needed information has been obtained by graphic methods, regardless of whether equations are possible to determine.

23.12. SUMMARY. The mathematical operations of differentiation and integration of calculus are dependent upon an equation of the function under investigation. The same operations can be performed on curves resulting from plots of empirical data by graphic methods. The graphic counterpart of differentiation is performed by plotting the numerical value of the slope of a curve at selected points x_0, x_1, x_2, etc. This operation and relationship is stated in the first law of graphic calculus: *The slope at any point of a given curve relating two variables is numerically equal to the ordinate at the corresponding point of the derived curve of next lower degree* (derivative curve). The definition of curves of lower and higher degree is based on the mathematical operations. Each successive differentiation produces a curve (or equation) of lower degree than the original. Integration produces a curve (or equation) of higher degree than the original. Graphic convention places integration curves above the original and differentiation curves below the original.

The graphic counterpart of integration is performed by plotting the total area under the curve bounded by the abscissa axis and the abscissa values of x_0 and x_1. Thus the area under the curve between x_0 and x_1 is plotted as a numerical value of the ordinate at x_1. Similarly the area under the curve between x_0 and x_2 is plotted as a numerical value of the ordinate at x_2. The second law of graphic calculus states this relationship: *The area bounded by a given curve, any two ordinates, and the x axis is numerically equal to the difference between the two corresponding ordinates of the curve of next higher degree* (integral curve).

Various graphic methods of accomplishing the operations of integration and differentiation are available. Graphic integration is best accomplished by either the method of equivalent areas or the chordal method. The method of equivalent areas is often modified slightly by using an overlay of fine squares which can be counted to provide a measurement of area sufficiently accurate for the purposes of the problem. The chordal method will normally be the more accurate method if careful drafting practices are followed. Graphic differentiation is accomplished by revers-

ing the chordal method of graphic integration. This relationship points out an interesting fact: If curve A is the derivative curve of curve B, then curve B is also the integral curve for curve A. If this relationship is understood, the graphic processes will be seen to be the same, only operated either forward or in reverse.

Graphic methods will not provide the constant of integration which is inherent in mathematical integration. If values of the integral curve are to be used in problem solution, the constant of integration must be obtained by mathematical methods. If the constant of integration cannot be found, the integral curve will be found to be correct, except that all values will be either too large or too small by some constant amount, C.

As in all graphic methods, the accuracy and usefulness of the results are directly determined by the accuracy of the original data and the care used in drafting. Graphic calculus theoretically provides perfect answers. Large, carefully drawn plots will accomplish this theoretical aim with adequate practical accuracy.

PROBLEMS

GROUP 1. GRAPHIC DIFFERENTIATION

23.1.1. Plot the following points, and draw a smooth curve through them. Construct the derivative curve.

x	y	x	y
0	1.0	5	5.6
1	2.2	6	6.1
2	3.3	7	6.5
3	4.2	8	6.8
4	5.0	9	7.0

23.1.2. Plot the following points, and draw a smooth curve through them. Construct the curve giving the rate of change of y with respect to x. Determine the value of x at which the value of y is a maximum.

x	y	x	y
0	0	270	75
40	19	332	80
90	38	410	81
173	60	450	80
220	69	500	76

23.1.3. The position of a body sliding down an inclined surface is measured at half-second intervals. Distance traveled S, in feet, is tabulated below against elapsed time T, in seconds. Plot the distance-versus-time curve, and construct the curve giving the velocity of the body at any instant.

T, sec	S, ft	T, sec	S, ft
0	0	3.0	2.17
0.5	0.06	3.5	2.92
1.0	0.25	4.0	3.88
1.5	0.54	4.5	4.83
2.0	0.98	5.0	6.00
2.5	1.49		

23.1.4. Measurements of the temperature θ, in degrees Fahrenheit, of a cooling body are tabulated below for values of elapsed time T, in minutes. Draw the derivative curve giving the rate of cooling at any time.

T, min	θ, °F	T, min	θ, °F
0	184	7	121
1	171	10	107
2	159	15	90
3	149	20	79
5	134		

23.1.5. An automobile accelerates from a standstill to a speed of 75 ft per sec in 30 sec. Values of the speed V, in feet per second, are given at right at 5-sec intervals of elapsed time T, in seconds. Plot the acceleration-versus-time curve.

T, sec	V, ft/sec	T, sec	V, ft/sec
0	0	20	58.8
5	23.1	25	67.3
10	37.5	30	75.0
15	49.0		

23.1.6. The population of the state of Ohio (United States Census) over the period from 1800 to 1950 is given below. Construct the curve showing the rate of population increase.

Year	Population	Year	Population
1800	45,365	1880	3,198,062
1810	230,760	1890	3,672,329
1820	581,434	1900	4,157,545
1830	937,903	1910	4,767,121
1840	1,519,467	1920	5,759,394
1850	1,980,329	1930	6,646,697
1860	2,339,511	1940	6,907,612
1870	2,665,260	1950	7,946,627

23.1.7. The work done by the explosion of a mixture of 1 cu ft of a fuel gas and X cu ft of air is given by the empirical formula $W = 85X - 3.1X^2$. For what value of X is the maximum work obtained? Solve graphically.

23.1.8. Annual costs C, in dollars (return on investment plus cost of heat lost), for various thicknesses T, in inches, of insulation for a piping system are tabulated at right. Plot the given data, construct the derivative curve, and determine the thickness of insulation for which the cost is a minimum.

T, in.	C, \$
1	275
2	174
3	165
4	190
5	225
6	260

x	y	x	y
0	0	5	4.20
1	1.50	6	4.65
2	2.41	7	5.10
3	3.10	8	5.55
4	3.69	9	6.00

GROUP 2.   GRAPHIC INTEGRATION

23.2.1. Plot the points listed at left, and draw a smooth curve through them. Construct the integral curve.

23.2.2. Determine graphically the value of π. (*Hint.* Construct a semicircle of 6-in. radius upon the x axis as diameter. Draw the integral curve. Divide the total area under the semicircle by 18.)

23.2.3. Determine graphically the value of ln 10. (*Hint.* Plot the curve representing the equation $y = 1/x$, and integrate graphically from $x = 1$ to $x = 10$.)

23.2.4. One pound of superheated steam is allowed to expand against a piston, isothermally at 400°F, from a pressure of 200 to a pressure of 40 lb per sq in. gage. Volumes V, in cubic inches, occupied by the steam at various pressures P, in pounds per square inch gage, are tabulated at left. Plot the pressure-versus-volume curve, and integrate it graphically to determine the work done on the piston. (*Hint.* Work $= \int P\, dV$.)

V, cu in.	P, lb/sq in. gage
3,770	200
4,200	180
4,730	160
5,390	140
6,240	120
7,400	100
9,030	80
11,530	60
15,870	40

23.2.5. The specific heat of water at atmospheric pressure C, in British thermal units per pound per degree Fahrenheit, is tabulated below against temperature T, in degrees Fahrenheit. Plot the tabulated points, and draw a smooth curve through them. Integrate graphically to obtain the amount of heat that is required to raise the temperature of 1 lb of water from freezing to boiling.

$$\left[\text{\textit{Hint.} Heat} = \int C\, dT = 180 + \int (C - 1)\, dT.\right]$$

T, °F	C, Btu/lb-°F	T, °F	C, Btu/lb-°F
32	1.0080	140	1.0001
50	1.0019	158	1.0013
68	0.9995	176	1.0029
86	0.9987	194	1.0050
104	0.9987	212	1.0076
122	0.9992		

23.2.6. A plate cam, sliding with uniform motion, is to elevate a follower during a 3-sec time interval. The cam length is 6 in. Velocities V, in inches per second, to be imparted to the follower are tabulated below against

T, sec	V, in./sec	T, sec	V, in./sec
0	0	1.70	0.665
0.30	0.21	2.00	0.59
0.50	0.34	2.30	0.455
0.75	0.48	2.50	0.34
1.10	0.62	2.75	0.175
1.25	0.655	3.00	0
1.50	0.68		

values of elapsed time T, in seconds. Plot the velocity-versus-time curve for the follower. Integrate graphically to obtain the distance-versus-time curve, and tabulate offsets at ½-in. intervals for machining the cam.

23.2.7. Soundings D, in feet, taken at points located at distances S, in feet, from one bank of a stream are tabulated below. Draw the integral curve to determine the cross-sectional area of the stream.

S, ft	D, ft	S, ft	D, ft
0	0	30	6.3
6	2.2	36	4.4
12	3.0	42	2.0
18	4.0	47.2	0
24	5.6		

23.2.8. An object starting from rest accelerates uniformly to a velocity of 24 ft per sec in 6 sec time, travels at constant velocity for 7.2 sec time, and then decelerates to a standstill in 4.8 sec time. Plot the acceleration-versus-time, the velocity-versus-time, and the distance-versus-time curves to describe the motion.

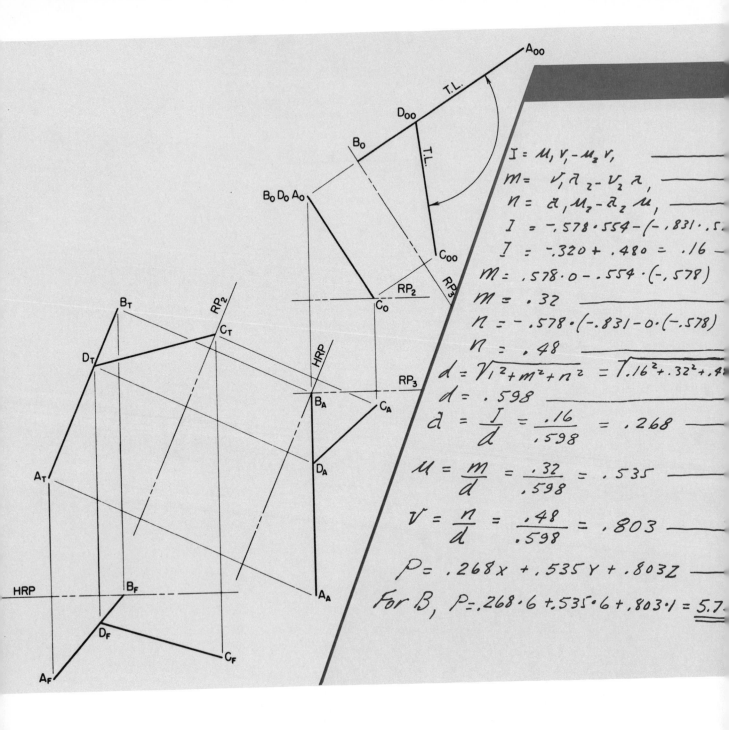

$$I = u_1 v_1 - u_2 v_1$$

$$m = v_1 a_2 - v_2 a_1$$

$$n = a_1 u_2 - a_2 u_1$$

$$I = -.578 \cdot .554 - (-.831 \cdot .5\ldots$$

$$\underline{I = -.320 + .480 = .16}$$

$$M = .578 \cdot 0 - .554 \cdot (-.578)$$

$$\underline{M = .32}$$

$$n = -.578 \cdot (-.831 - 0 \cdot (-.578)$$

$$\underline{n = .48}$$

$$d = \sqrt{I^2 + m^2 + n^2} = \sqrt{.16^2 + .32^2 + .4\ldots}$$

$$\underline{d = .598}$$

$$d = \frac{I}{d} = \frac{.16}{.598} = .268$$

$$u = \frac{m}{d} = \frac{.32}{.598} = .535$$

$$v = \frac{n}{d} = \frac{.48}{.598} = .803$$

$$P = .268 x + .535 Y + .803 Z$$

$$\text{For } B, \; P = .268 \cdot 6 + .535 \cdot 6 + .803 \cdot 1 = \underline{\underline{5.7\ldots}}$$

For practically all graphical representations and solutions there is a mathematical counterpart. Depending upon the type of solution needed and its accuracy, either graphical or mathematical (or both) routes may be taken. The illustration shows a typical graphical solution in the left portion and another typical mathematical determination at the right.

Graphical and Mathematical Counterparts

24

24.1. First of all, in the design and development stages of producing a product, especially when the physical entity is completely new, drawings are made representing initial conditions. Then, as alterations in design are made and development and testing are initiated, it may be either expedient or necessary to support some or all of the basic design by mathematical calculations. This is usually needed because of critical conditions requiring accuracy beyond that which can be attained by purely graphic methods. Thus it follows that the engineer must be familiar with the graphical-mathematical counterparts for the location of points, lines, planes, and surfaces in space.

The mathematics described in this chapter is the counterpart of the spatial geometry described earlier and is also compatible with standard texts on solid and analytical geometry. The operations involving point, line, and plane relationships are readily described either graphically or mathematically. For obvious reasons, original descriptions are given graphically, representing original conceptions. Then, the mathematical solution is given. The nomenclature used here corresponds with that used in mathematics texts.

This chapter provides the link between original (graphic) conceptions and mathematical support either by the usual methods or by computer.

Since the emphasis in this chapter is on the mathematical concepts, the illustrations are freehand sketches—common practice for the visualization of a mathematical problem.

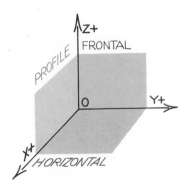

FIG. 24.1. The origin and axes for X, Y, and Z measurements from an origin O. The octant enclosed by horizontal, frontal, and profile planes extending forward, to the right of, and above the origin contain all positive values of X, Y, and Z.

24.2. THE COORDINATE SYSTEM. The standard coordinate system of analytic geometry places the *origin* for calculation at the intersection of three principal planes, horizontal, frontal, and profile, as shown in Fig. 24.1. The X axis lies at the intersection of the horizontal and profile planes and measured distances forward and rearward. Positive values of x are measured *forward* from the origin and negative values are measured *rearward* from the origin. The Y axis lies at the intersection of the frontal and horizontal planes and measures distances to the right and left. Positive values of y are measured to the *right* of the origin. The Z axis lies at the intersection of the profile planes and measures distances upward and downward. Positive values of z are measured *upward* from the origin and negative values of z are measured downward from the origin.

Notice in Fig. 24.1, that the space octant shown will contain all positive values of x, y, and z. The adjacent octant to the rear will contain negative values of x. The adjacent octant to the left will contain negative values of y. The adjacent octant below will contain negative values of z. In any given problem the origin may be located in any convenient position in space. However it is convenient to locate the origin below, behind, and to the left of major features in order to avoid the nuisance of dealing with negative values.

In plotting points in this three-dimensional system, each point will have three coordinates which will always be given in the order, x, y, z. Some typical plotting situations are illustrated in Figs. 24.2 and 24.3.

In some cases it may be desirable to locate the origin at certain given (or determined) distances from an existing point as illustrated in Fig. 24.4 and explained in the caption. Naturally, it also may be desirable to place the origin at some previously established point, as shown in Fig. 24.5 and described in the caption.

The student is cautioned to understand this coordinate system thoroughly before proceeding. The positive and negative designations can lead to trouble if one is not diligently accurate.

24.3. A LINE IN SPACE. The simple equation of a line in two-dimensional space ($Y = a + bX$) cannot be extra-

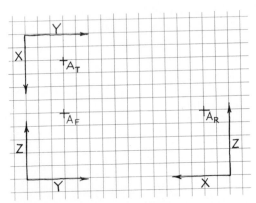

FIG. 24.2. Plotting of point $A(2,3,5)$.

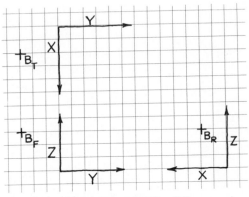

FIG. 24.3. Plotting of point $B(2,-3,3)$.

polated into three-dimensional space because, in two-dimensional space, a line has only two points or a slope and an intercept for a description. To describe a line in X,Y,Z space adequately, *three* conditions must be met. Hence the description of a line in X,Y,Z space must utilize some other method. The standard method, basically, is to measure the angle that the line makes with each of the three coordinate axes. To simplify the analysis consider a line AB through the origin as shown in Fig. 24.6. AB makes an angle α with the X axis, β with the Y axis and γ with the Z axis. These direction angles are unique to the line and no other line will have the same direction angles unless it is parallel to AB. The observant student should now note that only two direction angles are needed to describe a line adequately. This, of course, could be the basis of a system of line description since only two direction angles need be described. However, a more satisfactory method (a slight adaptation of this direction-angle method) is used because it is much more compatible with standard orthographic projection practice.

The measurement of direction angles is quite a problem mathematically although graphically it is a simple exercise in obtaining a normal view of a plane formed by two intersecting lines. Unfortunately, the limitations of graphic accuracy preclude using direction angles in place of an extremely precise mathematical solution. However, the relative size of the direction angle between 0° and 90° or between 90° and 180° will determine the algebraic signs to be used with the actual measurement. A knowledge of direction angles is absolutely essential to understanding the mathematical description of a line.

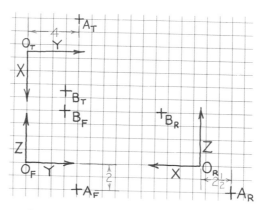

FIG. 24.4. Location of an origin 2 units above, 4 units to the left of, and 2½ units in front of a given point A. *Relative to the origin,* point A then becomes $A(-2\frac{1}{2}, 4, -2)$. Point B also shown is 3, 3, 4 *relative to the origin.*

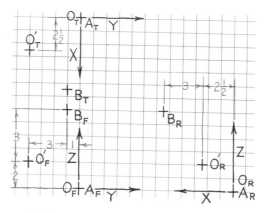

FIG. 24.5. Location of the origin at a given point A. The same *identical* point B of Fig. 24.4, relative to the origin at A then becomes $B(5\frac{1}{2}, -1, 5)$.

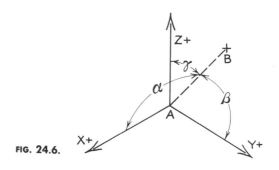

FIG. 24.6.

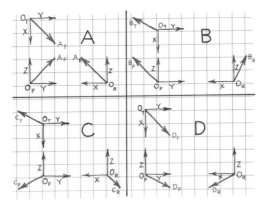

FIG. 24.7. Illustration of algebraic signs of lines in space.

24.4. METHOD OF DESCRIBING A LINE.
Line OA in Fig. 24.8 has projected dimensions on each of the coordinate axes which correspond to depth, width, and height of standard orthographic projection. We might call these values (l, m, n) *direction numbers*. Any line has a unique set of direction numbers, but it is the ratio between the numbers rather than the numbers themselves that is important. If the length of the line OA is made equal to one, the direction numbers l, m, and n become numerically equal to the cosine of the direction angle. Since any angle has only one cosine, the cosines of a set of direction angles are unique. Graphically the direction-angle cosines are merely the height, width, and depth measurements of a line of unit length. Direction cosines are easy to measure or to calculate and are the basis for the equations of a line in space. All future references to direction cosines will use λ as the direction cosine of angle α, μ for angle β, and ν for angle γ. Remember, α is the angle between the line and the X axis, β the angle to the Y axis, and γ the angle to the Z axis.

In order to assign the correct algebraic sign to the direction cosine, the size of the direction angle must be known. If the direction angle is 90° or less, the cosine is positive; if greater than 90°, the cosine is negative. From Fig. 24.7A–D it is seen that two parallel lines pointing in opposite directions would have identical direction cosines but of opposite sign. It is for this reason that a line must have a direction in space. In this context, all lines must "point" somewhere.

It was stated earlier that the orthographic height, width, and depth measurements of a line *one unit long* are numerically equal to the cosine of the direction angle. Since any angle can

Consider the lines described in Fig. 24.7 in standard views.

In Fig. 24.7A all direction angles are less than 90°. In Fig. 24.7B direction angle α between OB and the X axis is greater than 90°. Similarly direction angle β between OB and the Y axis is greater than 90°. Direction angle α between OB and Z axis is less than 90°. In Fig. 24.7C all direction angles are greater than 90°. In Fig. 24.7D direction angles α and β are less than 90° while direction angle α is greater than 90°. This information will be used in the discussion following.

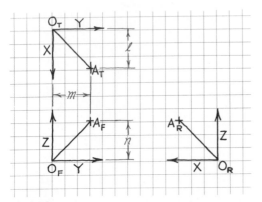

FIG. 24.8.

have only one cosine, this relationship is specific. Hence the depth of a unit line is numerically equal to λ, the direction cosine of α the angle between the line and the X axis. Depth is simply the difference of the x coordinates of the line. By similar deduction, width and height are related to the cosines μ and ν. From this knowledge, three equalities can be written about any line in space. Note that these equalities do not require that the line go through the origin although this is the basis for direction angles. The three equalities are:

$$\frac{\text{Depth}}{\lambda} = \frac{X_2 - X_1}{\lambda} = 1$$

$$\frac{\text{Width}}{\mu} = \frac{Y_2 - Y_1}{\mu} = 1$$

$$\frac{\text{Height}}{\nu} = \frac{Z_2 - Z_1}{\nu} = 1$$

By combining any two of the three equations a basic equation of a line is obtained

$$\frac{X_2 - X_1}{\lambda} = \frac{Y_2 - Y_1}{\mu}$$

$$\frac{X_2 - X_1}{\lambda} = \frac{Z_2 - Z_1}{\nu}$$

$$\frac{Y_2 - Y_1}{\mu} = \frac{Z_2 - Z_1}{\nu}$$

One of the theorems of analytical geometry is a help in calculating the direction cosines. The relationship is:

$$\lambda^2 + \mu^2 + \nu^2 = 1$$

24.5. CALCULATION OF DIRECTION COSINES. To calculate the direction cosines of a line, given the coordinates of two points on it, requires one bit of information not discussed as yet. The true length of a line segment whose ends have coordinates X_1, Y_1, Z_1, and X_2, Y_2, Z_2 is:

$$d = \sqrt{(X_2 - X_1)^2 + (Y_2 - Y_1)^2 + (Z_2 - Z_1)^2}$$

Previously it was mentioned that orthographic height, width, and depth are numerically equal to the direction cosines if the length of the line is equal to 1. For a line of length d the depth, height, and width are d times as long as for a line of length 1.

Therefore, each of the direction cosines is:

$$\lambda = \frac{\text{Depth}}{d} = \frac{X_2 - X_1}{d}$$

$$\mu = \frac{\text{Width}}{d} = \frac{Y_2 - Y_1}{d}$$

$$\nu = \frac{\text{Height}}{d} = \frac{Z_2 - Z_1}{d}$$

It can be seen that the above equations do not require that the line go through the coordinate origin. While all of the original assumptions were made on a line through the origin, any line in space has a parallel counterpart which goes through the origin. To illustrate the principle, consider the line $A(2,3,6)$-$B(5,6,10)$ and the line $C(0,0,0)D(3,3,4)$. A sketch of these lines, as in Fig. 24.9, will show that they are parallel although

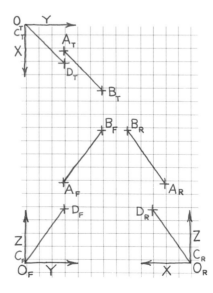

FIG. 24.9. Line $A(2,3,6)B(5,6,10)$ is parallel to line $C(0,0,0,)D(3,3,4)$. Therefore the direction cosines are identical.

only CD goes through the origin. Therefore, the direction cosines must be identical.

For line AB:

$$d = \sqrt{(5-2)^2 + (6-3)^2 + (10-6)^2}$$
$$d = \sqrt{3^2 + 3^2 + 4^2}$$
$$d = 5.83$$

$$\lambda = \frac{X_2 - X_1}{d} = \frac{5-2}{5.83} = \frac{3}{5.83} = .514$$

$$\mu = \frac{Y_2 - Y_1}{d} = \frac{6-3}{5.83} = \frac{3}{5.83} = .514$$

$$\nu = \frac{Z_2 - Z_1}{d} = \frac{10-6}{5.83} = \frac{4}{5.83} = .686$$

For line CD:

$$d = \sqrt{(3-0)^2 + (3-0)^2 + (4-0)^2}$$
$$d = 5.83$$

$$\lambda = \frac{X_2 - X_1}{d} = \frac{3}{5.83} = .514$$

$$\mu = \frac{Y_2 - Y_1}{d} = \frac{3}{5.83} = .514$$

$$\nu = \frac{Z_2 - Z_1}{d} = \frac{4}{5.83} = .686$$

Both lines have identical direction cosines and are, therefore, parallel. To double check, the sum of the squares of the direction cosines of each line equals 1.

The general equation of the line AB might be written as:

$$\frac{X-2}{.514} = \frac{Y-3}{.514} = \frac{Z-6}{.686}$$

For line CD:

$$\frac{X-0}{.514} = \frac{Y-0}{.514} = \frac{Z-0}{.686}$$

or

$$\frac{X}{.514} = \frac{Y}{.514} = \frac{Z}{.686}$$

Any two of the three parts of the equality is sufficient to describe the line.

The interaction between lines in space is essentially one of either intersection of lines or the angle between lines. Both of these conditions will be used in dealing with planes and are, therefore, essential to later work.

24.6. INTERSECTION OF LINES. Two lines in space intersect if they have a common coordinate point. Two lines which are known to intersect graphically might appear as in Fig. 24.10.

Line AB has the equation:

$$\frac{X-0}{.5} = \frac{Z-1}{.707}$$

Line CD has the equation:

$$\frac{X-0}{.5} = \frac{Z-3}{-.707}$$

The two equations become:

$$.707X = .5Z - .5$$
$$-.707X = .5Z - 1.5$$

Adding the two equations:

$$0 = Z - 2.$$
$$Z = 2.$$

FIG. 24.10.

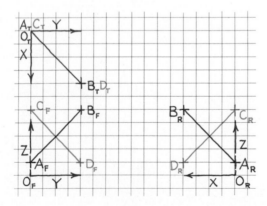

Substituting $Z = 2$ in the equation for line AB:

$$X = .707$$

Substituting $Z = 2$ in the equation for line CD:

$$X = .707$$

Therefore, the two lines have a common point at .707.

24.7. ANGLE BETWEEN LINES.

Angular relationships between lines require first that some method be derived that permits measuring the angle between two lines without regard to line magnitudes. If lines OA and OB are not parallel and intersect at the origin, a normal view of the plane formed by these two lines would reveal the angle between them in true size as shown by the normal view of Fig. 24.11. However, the law of cosines also states that the distance between the ends of the line segments, the segment AB, is related to segments OA and OB as follows:

$$\overline{AB}^2 = \overline{OA}^2 + \overline{OB}^2 - 2 \cdot \overline{OA} \cdot \overline{OB} \cos \theta$$

where θ is the angle between the two lines. If the segments OB and OA are each 1 unit long, the equation simplifies to $\overline{AB}^2 = 1 + 1 - 2 \cos \theta$.

$$\cos \theta = \frac{2 - \overline{AB}^2}{2} \quad (1)$$

The equations of lines OA and OB are

$$\frac{X}{\lambda_1} = \frac{Y}{\mu_1} = \frac{Z}{\nu_1}$$

and

$$\frac{X}{\lambda_2} = \frac{Y}{\mu_2} = \frac{Z}{\nu_2}$$

Since OA and OB are each 1 unit long, the point A has coordinates $X = \lambda_1$, $Y = \mu_1$, $Z = \nu_1$ and point B has coordinates $X = \lambda_2$, $Y = \mu_2$, $Z = \nu_2$.

This knowledge follows from the fact that the depth of a line of unit length is numerically equal to the direction cosine of the related angle. Similarly width and height are related to the other direction cosines.

Therefore

$$AB^2 = (\sqrt{(X_2 - X_1)^2 + (Y_2 - Y_1)^2 + (Z_2 - Z_1)^2})^2$$

$$\overline{AB}^2 = (\lambda_2 - \lambda_1)^2 + (\mu_2 - \mu_1)^2 + (\nu_2 - \nu_1)^2$$

$$\overline{AB}^2 = \lambda_1^2 + \mu_1^2 + \nu_1^2 + \lambda_2^2 + \mu_2^2 + \nu_2^2 - 2(\lambda_1\lambda_2 + \mu_1\mu_2 + \nu_1\nu_2)$$

since $\quad \lambda_1^2 + \mu_1^2 + \nu_1^2 = 1$

and $\quad \lambda_2^2 + \mu_2^2 + \nu_2^2 = 1,$

this simplifies to:

$$\overline{AB}^2 = 2 - 2(\lambda_1\lambda_2 + \mu_1\mu_2 + \nu_1\nu_2)$$

By substitution in Eq. (1), the cosine of the angle between two lines is:

$$\cos \theta = \lambda_1\lambda_2 + \mu_1\mu_2 + \nu_1\nu_2$$

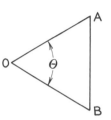

FIG. 24.11.

24.8. PARALLEL AND PERPENDICULAR LINES.

From the above equation we can define both parallel and perpendicular lines where the direction cosines of each line are given as

$$\lambda_1, \mu_1, \nu_1$$

and

$$\lambda_2, \mu_2, \nu_2$$

For parallel lines :

$$\lambda_1 = \lambda_2$$
$$\mu_1 = \mu_2$$
$$\nu_1 = \nu_2$$
$$\lambda_1\lambda_2 + \mu_1\mu_2 + \nu_1\nu_2 = 1 \text{ (cosine } 0° = 1)$$

For perpendicular lines:

$$\lambda_1\lambda_2 + \mu_1\mu_2 + \nu_1\nu_2 = 0$$
$$\text{(cosine } 90° = 0)$$

It will be noted that perpendicular lines are somewhat ambiguously de-

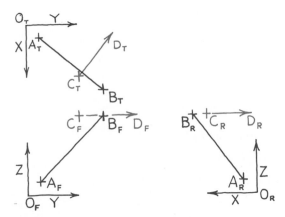

FIG. 24.12.

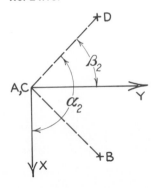

FIG. 24.13.

fined by this equation, but the student of graphics will recall that an infinite number of lines may be constructed perpendicular to another line. Hence additional information needs to be known about the line to be constructed perpendicular to a given line.

Example: Construct a horizontal line CD through point $C(4,4,6)$ perpendicular to line $A(1,1,1)B(5,6,6)$. See Fig. 24.12.

For line AB:

$$d = \sqrt{(5-1)^2 + (6-1)^2 + (6-1)^2}$$
$$d = \sqrt{16 + 25 + 25}$$
$$d = 8.13$$
$$\lambda_1 = \frac{5-1}{8.13} = .492$$
$$\mu_1 = \frac{6-1}{8.13} = .615$$
$$\nu_1 = \frac{6-1}{8.13} = .615$$

For line CD:

If the line is horizontal, the direction angle between this line and the Z axis is $90°$. The direction cosine is, therefore, 0. The direction cosines for line CD have the following relationships:

$$\nu_2 = 0$$
$$\lambda_2{}^2 + \mu_2{}^2 = 1$$
$$(\lambda^2 + \mu^2 + \nu^2 = 1, \text{ but } \nu = 0)$$
$$\lambda_2 = \sqrt{1 - \mu_2{}^2}$$

For the two lines to be perpendicular:

$$\lambda_1\lambda_2 + \mu_1\mu_2 + \nu_1\nu_2 = 0 \qquad (2)$$

Substituting the values for λ_1, μ_1, ν_1 and λ_2, μ_2, ν_2 in Eq. (2):

$$.492\sqrt{1 - \mu_2{}^2} + .615\mu_2 + .615 \cdot 0 = 0$$
$$.492\sqrt{1 - \mu_2{}^2} = -.615\mu_2$$

Squaring:

$$.242(1 - \mu_2{}^2) = .375\mu_2{}^2$$
$$.617\mu_2{}^2 = .242$$
$$\mu_2{}^2 = .392$$
$$\mu_2 = \pm.626$$

Therefore

$$\lambda_2 = \sqrt{1 - .392}$$
$$\lambda_2 = \pm.780$$

The simplest method of determining the correct values of the direction cosines is to draw a top view of lines AB and CD as though they went through the origin. From the sketch of Fig. 24.13 it can be seen that μ_2 should be $+(\beta_2$ less than $90°)$ and λ_2 should be $-(\alpha_2$ greater than $90°)$.

24.9. A LINE PERPENDICULAR TO TWO LINES. The particular situation of a line perpendicular to two other lines is the basis for several future references and hence is quite important. Line EF has direction cosines λ, μ, ν and is perpendicular to line $AB(\lambda_1,\mu_1,\nu_1)$ and to line $CD(\lambda_2,\mu_2,\nu_2)$. From paragraph 24.8 it is known that:

$$\lambda\lambda_1 + \mu\mu_1 + \nu\nu_1 = 0$$
$$\lambda\lambda_2 + \mu\mu_2 + \nu\nu_2 = 0$$

Solution of these two equations for λ, μ, and ν leads to this relationship

$$\frac{\lambda}{\begin{vmatrix} \mu_1 & \nu_1 \\ \mu_2 & \nu_2 \end{vmatrix}} = \frac{\mu}{\begin{vmatrix} \nu_1 & \lambda_1 \\ \nu_2 & \lambda_2 \end{vmatrix}} = \frac{\nu}{\begin{vmatrix} \lambda_1 & \mu_1 \\ \lambda_2 & \mu_2 \end{vmatrix}}$$

This indicates that the direction cosines of the line perpendicular to two other lines are proportional to determinants involving the direction cosines of the two given lines. Hence we can say that the direction numbers of the desired perpendicular line are:

$$l = \begin{vmatrix} \mu_1 & \nu_1 \\ \mu_2 & \nu_2 \end{vmatrix}$$

$$m = \begin{vmatrix} \nu_1 & \lambda_1 \\ \nu_2 & \lambda_2 \end{vmatrix}$$

$$n = \begin{vmatrix} \lambda_1 & \mu_1 \\ \lambda_2 & \mu_2 \end{vmatrix}$$

Direction numbers represent the height, width, and depth of a line of length d and can be converted to direction cosines by dividing by d where:

$$d = \sqrt{l^2 + m^2 + n^2}$$

Expanding the determinants:

$$l = \mu_1\nu_2 - \mu_2\nu_1$$
$$m = \nu_1\lambda_2 - \nu_2\lambda_1$$
$$n = \lambda_1\mu_2 - \lambda_2\mu_1$$
$$d = \sqrt{l^2 + m^2 + n^2}$$

$$\lambda = \frac{l}{d} \qquad \mu = \frac{m}{d} \qquad \nu = \frac{n}{d}$$

Applying these relationships to the preceding example of a horizontal line CD perpendicular to a line AB, construct a line EF perpendicular to both lines AB and CD. See Fig. 24.14.

From the example:

$$\lambda_1 = .492 \qquad \lambda_2 = -.78$$
$$\mu_1 = .615 \qquad \mu_2 = .626$$
$$\nu_1 = .615 \qquad \nu_2 = 0$$

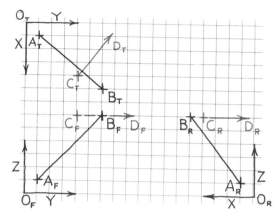

FIG. 24.14.

Direction numbers of the line EF are:

$$l = .615 \cdot 0 - .626 \cdot .615$$
$$l = -.385$$
$$m = .615 \cdot (-.78) - 0 \cdot .492$$
$$m = -.48$$
$$n = .492 \cdot .626 - (-.78) \cdot .615$$
$$n = .788$$

Converting to direction cosines,

$$d = \sqrt{-.385^2 + (-.48)^2 + .788^2}$$
$$d = 1.$$

The alert student will recognize this condition as a line of unit length. This cannot be predicted and *must* not be assumed to be true.

Therefore

$$\lambda = -.385$$
$$\mu = -.48$$
$$\nu = .788$$

If the line EF is to pass through the point $(2,3,1)$, the equation of the line EF is:

$$\frac{X - 2}{-.385} = \frac{Y - 3}{-.48} = \frac{Z - 1}{.788}$$

Plot this line on Fig. 24.14 to show proof of the relationship.

24.10. **A PLANE IN SPACE.** A study of graphics has already indicated that a plane may be represented by three non-collinear points or two intersecting lines. Either of these definitions is satisfactory from a mathematical standpoint but the concept of a plane defined by two intersecting lines leads to a more useful equation for certain purposes. Since any plane having initial conditions of three non-collinear points can also be expressed as formed by two lines which intersect at one of the three given points, this creates no real hardship.

A plane defined by three points A, B, and C can be said to be defined by two intersecting lines AB and BC. This plane has an "axis" which may be likened to the axis of a circle in the oblique position which is *a line perpendicular to the plane* or (specifically) to the lines AB and BC. We already have seen that such a line has direction cosines λ, μ, and which can be calculated from the direction cosines of the lines AB and BC. The equation of a plane having such a plane axis can be expressed as:

$$\lambda X + \mu Y + \nu Z = p$$

The magnitude of p will be found to be the distance along the plane axis between the coordinate origin and the plane: p is positive for planes which pass on the positive or first octant side of the origin.

To illustrate, find the equation of a plane $A(6,6,1)$, $B(1,1,6)$, $C(1,4,4)$. See Fig. 24.15.

For the line segment AB:

$$d = \sqrt{(1-6)^2 + (1-6)^2 + (6-1)^2}$$
$$d = \sqrt{25 + 25 + 25}$$
$$d = 8.67$$
$$\lambda_1 = \frac{\text{Depth}}{d} = \frac{1-6}{8.67} = -.578$$
$$\mu_1 = \frac{\text{Width}}{d} = \frac{1-6}{8.67} = -.578$$
$$\nu_1 = \frac{\text{Height}}{d} = \frac{6-1}{8.67} = .578$$

For the line segment BC:

$$d = \sqrt{(1-1)^2 + (1-4)^2 + (6-4)^2}$$
$$d = \sqrt{0 + 9 + 4}$$
$$d = 3.61$$
$$\lambda_2 = \frac{\text{Depth}}{d} = \frac{1-1}{3.61} = 0$$
$$\mu_2 = \frac{\text{Width}}{d} = \frac{1-4}{3.61} = -.831$$
$$\nu_2 = \frac{\text{Height}}{d} = \frac{6-4}{3.61} = .554$$

The plane axis is a line perpendicular to AB and BC. This line has direction numbers:

$$l = \mu_1\nu_2 - \mu_2\nu_1$$
$$m = \nu_1\lambda_2 - \nu_2\lambda_1$$
$$n = \lambda_1\mu_2 - \lambda_2\mu_1$$
$$l = -.578 \cdot .554 - (-.831) \cdot .578$$
$$l = -.320 + .480$$
$$l = .16$$
$$m = .578 \cdot 0 - .554 \cdot (-.578)$$
$$m = .32$$
$$n = -.578 \cdot (-.831) - 0 \cdot (-.578)$$
$$n = .48$$

FIG. 24.15.

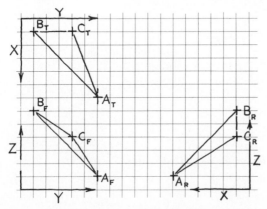

$$d = \sqrt{l^2 + m^2 + n^2}$$

$$d = \sqrt{.16^2 + .32^2 + 48^2}$$

$$d = .598$$

$$\lambda = \frac{l}{d}$$

$$\lambda = \frac{.16}{.598}$$

$$\lambda = .268$$

$$\mu = \frac{m}{d}$$

$$\mu = \frac{.32}{.598}$$

$$\mu = .535$$

$$\nu = \frac{n}{d}$$

$$\nu = \frac{.48}{.598}$$

$$\nu = .803$$

The basic equation of the plane is:

$$.268X + .535Y + .803Z = p$$

Substituting the values of any point on the plane into this equation gives the value of p. For point B:

$$.268 \cdot 1 + .535 \cdot 1 + .803 \cdot 6 = p$$

$$p = 5.621$$

For point A:

$$.268 \cdot 6 + .535 \cdot 6 + 803 \cdot 1 = 5.621$$

For point C:

$$.268 \cdot 1 + .535 \cdot 4 + .803 \cdot 4 = 5.620$$

which are identical if carried out to a sufficient number of decimal places.

Since this value is positive, the plane axis is in the positive coordinate area. Had the value of p been negative, it would have indicated that the distance from the origin to the plane was "pointed" in a negative direction and the

direction cosines had reversed signs. As with a line perpendicular to another line, some knowledge of the position of the plane with respect to the origin is needed. The axis of a plane can be pointed in either a negative or positive direction and the only indication of this is through the value of p. If the value of p is correct for the problem, then the direction cosines λ, μ, and ν have both correct magnitude and signs. If p is reversed in sign from what is expected, then the direction cosines have correct magnitude, but all signs must be reversed. (Note that parallel lines pointing in opposite directions have direction cosines of the same magnitude but opposite signs.)

Thus the correct equation for the plane ABC is:

$$.268X + .535Y + .803Z - 5.621 = 0$$

Relationships involving lines and planes require only manipulation of the basic operations already discussed.

24.11. LINE PERPENDICULAR TO A PLANE.

The form of the equation of a plane is such that the direction cosines of a line perpendicular to a plane are the coefficients of the planar equation.

Example: Construct a line $D(5,2,3)E$ perpendicular to the plane ABC of the preceding example. See Fig. 24.16.

FIG. 24.16.

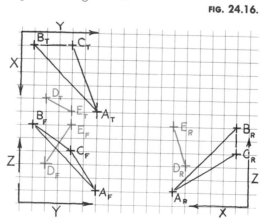

The equation of the plane ABC has been found to be

$$.268X + .535Y + .803Z - 5.621 = 0$$

Therefore, the direction cosines of a line perpendicular to this plane are:

$$\lambda = .268$$
$$\mu = .535$$
$$\nu = .803$$

Therefore, the equations used for line DE are:

$$\frac{X - 5}{.268} = \frac{Y - 2}{.535}$$

$$\frac{X - 5}{.268} = \frac{Z - 3}{.803}$$

$$\frac{Y - 2}{.535} = \frac{Z - 3}{.803}$$

24.12.   LINE PARALLEL TO A PLANE. A line parallel to a plane is perpendicular to the "axis" of the plane. This plane axis is a line perpendicular to the plane and has direction cosines equal to the coefficients of the planar equation. The problem becomes one of constructing a line perpendicular to another line.

Example: Construct a horizontal line $G(2,2,2)H$ parallel to the plane ABC of the preceding example. See Fig. 24.17.

Basically this problem is one of constructing GH perpendicular to line DE of the preceding example. This problem has been solved as part of paragraph 24.8. The three line equations for GH are:

$$\frac{X - 2}{-.894} = \frac{Y - 2}{.446}$$

$$\frac{X - 2}{-.894} = \frac{Z - 2}{0}$$

$$\frac{Y - 2}{.446} = \frac{Z - 2}{0}$$

24.13.   PLANE PERPENDICULAR TO A LINE. The direction cosines of the line are the coefficients of the planar equation. Substitution of the coordinates of a known point on the plane into the equation permits evaluation of p.

Example: Construct a plane $A(2,1,3)$,-B,C perpendicular to the line DE which has the equation

$$\frac{X - 1}{.4} = \frac{Y - 3}{.6}$$

See Fig. 24.18.

The line direction cosines are:

$$\lambda_1 = .4$$
$$\mu_1 = .6$$
$$\nu_1 = \sqrt{1. - .4^2 - .6^2} \text{ (from knowl-}$$
$$\text{edge that } \lambda_1{}^2 + \mu_1{}^2 + \nu_1{}^2 = 1)$$
$$\nu_1 = .694$$

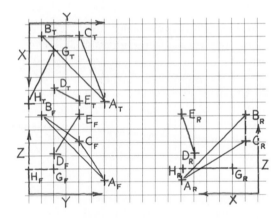

FIG. 24.17.

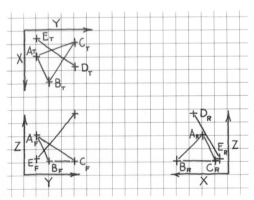

FIG. 24.18.

Therefore, the basic equation of the plane is:

$$.4X + .6Y + .694Z = p$$

Solving for p by substituting the co-ordinates of A in this basic equation

$$p = .4 \cdot 2 + .6 \cdot 1 + .694 \cdot 3$$
$$p = 3.48$$

The equation of the plane is:

$$.4X + .6Y + .694Z - 3.48 = 0$$

To plot the plane on Fig. 24.18:
 For $B = (4,2,Z)$

$$.4X + .6Y + .694Z - 3.48 = 0$$
$$.4 \cdot 4 + .6 \cdot 2 + .694Z = 3.48$$
$$.694Z = 3.48 - 1.6 - 1.2$$
$$Z = \frac{.68}{.694} = .980$$
$$B = (4,2,.98)$$

For $C = (X,4,1)$

$$.4X + .6 \cdot 4 + .694 \cdot 1 = 3.48$$
$$.4X = 3.48 - 2.4 - .694$$
$$X = \frac{.386}{.4} = .966$$
$$C = (.966,4,1)$$

24.14. A PLANE PARALLEL TO A LINE. A plane parallel to a line contains two lines of known direction, one parallel to the given line, the other perpendicular to the given line. Discussion of these two-line relationships has indicated that parallel lines have identical direction cosines. Perpendicular lines obey the relationship that

$$\lambda_1\lambda_2 + \mu_1\mu_2 + \nu_1\nu_2 = 0.$$

As the student of graphics knows, an infinite number of lines can be constructed perpendicular to a given line. It is therefore necessary to give some limit-

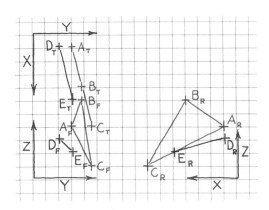

FIG. 24.19.

ing condition for any problem involving a line perpendicular to a line.

 Example: Construct a vertical plane $A(1,3,4),B,C$ parallel to line $D(1,2,3)$-$E(5,3,2)$. See Fig. 24.19.

 The direction numbers of DE (see paragraph 24.5) are:
 Depth

$$\frac{X_2 - X_1}{l} = 1, \quad \frac{5 - 1}{l} = 1, \quad l = 4$$

 Width

$$\frac{Y_2 - Y_1}{m} = 1, \quad \frac{3 - 2}{m} = 1, \quad m = 1$$

 Height

$$\frac{Z_2 - Z_1}{n} = 1, \quad \frac{2 - 1}{n} = 1, \quad n = 1$$

 To reduce to direction cosines, divide each direction number by d where:

$$d = \sqrt{1^2 + m^2 + n^2}$$
$$d = \sqrt{4^2 + 1^2 + (-1)^2}$$
$$d = \sqrt{18}$$
$$d = 4.24$$
$$\lambda_1 = \frac{4}{4.24} = .943$$
$$\mu_1 = \frac{1}{4.24} = .236$$
$$\nu_1 = \frac{-1}{4.24} = -.236$$

A vertical plane contains a line parallel to the Z axis and perpendicular to the X and Y axes. Direction cosines of such a line (of unit length) are:

$$\lambda_2 = 0.$$
$$\mu_2 = 0.$$
$$\nu_2 = 1.$$

At this point the problem is identical to the plane in space. The plane must be constructed parallel to the two given lines although the lines in themselves do not form a plane. Since parallel lines have identical direction cosines and the equation of a plane is developed solely from the direction cosines of the given lines, the problem is identical to the plane in space.

The line numbers of the plane (actually of a line perpendicular to the given lines) are :

$$l = \mu_1 \nu_2 - \mu_2 \nu_1$$
$$l = .236 \cdot 1 - 0 \cdot (-.236)$$
$$l = .236$$
$$m = \nu_1 \lambda_2 - \nu_2 \lambda_1$$
$$m = -.236 \cdot 0 - 1 \cdot .943$$
$$m = -.943$$
$$n = \lambda_1 \mu_2 - \lambda_2 \mu_1$$
$$n = .943 \cdot 0 - 0 \cdot .236$$
$$n = 0$$

Converting direction numbers to direction cosines:

$$d = \sqrt{l^2 + m^2 + n^2}$$
$$d = \sqrt{(.236)^2 + (-.943)^2 + 0^2}$$
$$d = \sqrt{.056 + .889}$$
$$d = .971$$
$$\lambda = \frac{l}{d}$$
$$\lambda = \frac{.236}{.971} = .243$$

$$\mu = \frac{m}{d}$$
$$\mu = \frac{-.943}{.971} = -.971$$
$$\nu = \frac{n}{d}$$
$$\nu = \frac{0}{.971} = 0$$

The basic equation of the plane is:

$$.243X - .971Y + 0 \cdot Z = p$$

Substituting the coordinates of point A into the basic equation:

$$.243(1) - .971(3) + 0(4) = p$$
$$p = -2.67$$

The complete equation of the plane is:

$$.243X - .971Y = 2.67$$

To prove the relationship:
For $B = (4, Y, 6)$

$$.243 \cdot 4 - .971Y = -2.67$$
$$-.971Y = 3.64$$
$$Y = 3.75$$

For $C = (7, Y, 1)$

$$Y = \frac{4.349}{.971} = 4.50$$

Thus, the plane obtained, as illustrated in Fig. 24.19, is observed to appear as an edge in the top view, is therefore a vertical plane, and is parallel to line DE. Mathematically, this is equationally true because the coefficient of Z is zero. If the problem had specified a plane receding from frontal, the line numbers which are also direction cosines of a unit line of a line of the plane would be:

$$l = \lambda = 1$$
$$m = \mu = 0$$
$$n = \nu = 0$$

The coefficient of X in the resulting equation will be zero and the plane will appear as an edge in the front view.

If the problem had specified a plane receding from profile, the line numbers of a line of the plane would be:

$$l = \lambda = 0$$
$$m = \mu = 1$$
$$n = \nu = 0$$

The coefficient of Y in the resulting equation will be zero and the plane will appear as an edge in a side view.

24.15. SHORTEST DISTANCE BETWEEN SKEW LINES. This problem is readily solved by methods already given. The shortest distance between two skew lines is a line perpendicular to each line. A line perpendicular to two lines is also the "axis" of a plane. We already know that the value of p in the planar equation is the distance between the plane and the origin as measured along the plane axis. Therefore, if a plane is passed through each of the skew lines (having as its plane axis the line perpendicular to each of the skew lines), the difference of p values is the distance between the parallel planes and hence the distance between lines.

Example: Determine the shortest distance between line $A(1,2,3)B(4,2,2)$, and line $C(5,6,3)D(3,4,2)$. See Fig. 24.20. The direction cosines of AB:

$$\lambda_1 = -.95$$
$$\mu_1 = 0.$$
$$\nu_1 = .316$$

The direction cosines of CD:

$$\lambda_2 = .667$$
$$\mu_2 = .667$$
$$\nu_2 = .333$$

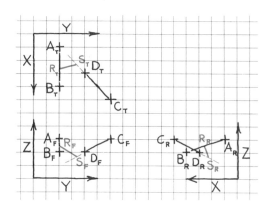

FIG. 24.20.

Direction numbers of a line perpendicular to these two lines:

$$l = -.211$$
$$m = .528$$
$$n = -.634$$

Converting to direction cosines:

$$\lambda = -.248$$
$$\mu = .621$$
$$\nu = -.745$$

The basic equation of each plane is:

$$-.248X + .621Y - .745Z = p$$

Substituting coordinates of A into the equation:

$$p = -.248(1) + .621(2) - .745(3)$$
$$p = -1.24$$

Substituting coordinates of C into the equation :

$$p = -.248(5) + .621(6) - .745(3)$$
$$p = .25$$

The distance between the parallel planes containing lines AB and CD and hence the distance between AB and CD is:

$$d = .25 - (-1.24)$$
$$= 1.49$$

24.16 SUMMARY: LINE AND PLANE RELATIONSHIPS. The basic relationships governing lines and planes are relatively few in number. Much of the problem of using these relationships is determining just where and how to use them. The graphics student has a counterpart in the auxiliary view. Frequently, the only difficulty in solving a problem is to find a suitable starting place. So it is with the mathematics of graphic problems. The basic tools are few, but the determination of a starting place is the real problem. The basic equations are:

1. Line relationships
   a. True length of a line:

$$d = \sqrt{(X_1 - X_2)^2 + (Y_1 - Y_2)^2 + (Z_1 - Z_2)^2}$$

   b. Direction cosines of a line:

$$\lambda = \frac{\text{depth}}{d}$$

$$\mu = \frac{\text{width}}{d}$$

$$\nu = \frac{\text{height}}{d}$$

   c. Basic equation of a line:

$$\frac{X - X_0}{\lambda} = \frac{Y - Y_0}{\mu} = \frac{Z - Z_0}{\nu}$$

   where x_0, y_0, z_0 are coordinates of a point on the line

   d. Angle between lines:

$$\cos \theta = \lambda_1 \lambda_2 + \mu_1 \mu_2 + \nu_1 \nu_2$$

   where $\cos 90° = 0$ and $\cos 0° = 1$

   e. A line perpendicular to two skew lines has direction numbers:

$$l = \mu_1 \nu_2 - \mu_2 \nu_1$$
$$m = \nu_1 \lambda_2 - \nu_2 \lambda_1$$
$$n = \lambda_1 \mu_2 - \lambda_2 \mu_1$$

   f. Direction numbers (l, m, n) of a line are defined as the depth, width, and height of a line of length d. To convert direction number to direction cosines see 1b.

2. Plane relationships
   A plane has an axis which is a line through the origin perpendicular to the plane. The direction cosines of this axis are the coefficients of the planar equation:

$$\lambda X + \mu Y + \nu Z = p$$

   where p is the distance between the plane and the origin measured along the axis.

Using this set of basic relationships, the student may apply his ingenuity to solving problems that involve other relationships.

3. Angular relationships
   a. *A line making specified angles* with principal projection planes. Any line making angles of a, b, and c with horizontal, frontal, and profile planes also makes angles of $90 - a$ with a line perpendicular to the horizontal, $90 - b$ with a line perpendicular to the frontal, and $90 - c$ with a line perpendicular to the profile. Since each of these perpendicular lines is also a coordinate axis, it can be seen that a line at angle a with the horizontal is also at $90 - a$ with the Z axis, angle b with the frontal is $90 - b$ with the X axis and angle c with the profile is $90 - c$ with the Y axis. Since only two direction angles are needed to describe a line, it

can be seen that the usual problem of a line making specified angles with H and F is easily solved.

b. *The angle between planes* has a graphical counterpart which is sometimes used to measure such an angle. Since each plane has an axis which is perpendicular to the plane, it is possible to measure the angle between the axes and relate this to the angle between planes. Since any pair of planes has two values, α and $180 - \alpha$ for the angle between planes, the axes also have values of α and $180 - \alpha$ as the angle between lines. The problem will dictate which value of the angle between axes is the desired angle between planes.

c. *The intersection of two planes* is a straight line containing two points common to both planes. The procedure for obtaining the equation of this line of intersection is to solve the two-plane equations simultaneously for a linear equation.

Example: Find the line of intersection between the plane

$$.3X + .7Y + .648Z - 4. = 0$$

and the plane

$$.5X + .707Y + .5Z - 3. = 0.$$

If the first equation is multiplied by $\dfrac{.707}{.700}$, the Y term will have the coefficient .707 and the equation becomes

$$.303X + .707Y + .654Z - 4.04 = 0$$

Subtracting the second equation from the first gives

$$-.197X + .154Z - 1.04 = 0$$

as the result.

Rearranging this equation:

$$.154Z = .197X + 1.04$$

Dividing both sides by .154:

$$Z = 1.28X + 6.75 = 1.28(X + 5.27)$$

$$Z = \frac{X + 5.27}{.782}$$

This can be put in more recognizable form by writing it as:

$$\frac{Z - 0.}{1.} = \frac{X + 5.27}{.782} \qquad (1)$$

This is the common form of the equation of a line. Unfortunately the denominators of this equation are direction numbers and not direction cosines. To convert direction numbers to direction cosines requires that we know all three direction numbers. Therefore, we must resolve the original two planar equations for a solution relating either X and Y or Y and Z. We shall pick Y and Z. The result of this operation is the equation:

$$.138Y + .174Z - 1.1 = 0$$

Dividing by .174 and rearranging gives:

$$Z = -.788Y + 6.32$$

$$= -.788(Y - 8.0)$$

$$= -\frac{1}{1.27}(Y - 8.)$$

This equation and Eq. (1) above have a common Z term. Thus we can write for the equation of the line:

$$\frac{X + 5.27}{.782} = \frac{Z}{1.} = \frac{Y - 8.}{1.27} \qquad (2)$$

From this we can obtain the direction numbers:

$$l = .782$$

$$m = -1.27$$

$$n = 1$$

The direction cosines which result from this set of direction numbers:

$$\lambda = .436$$

$$\mu = -.707$$

$$\nu = .558$$

To check these values, we can use the concept that the line of intersection of two planes is also a line perpendicular to the axes. Using the formulas of paragraph 24.8, we obtain direction cosines for a line perpendicular to the axes:

$$\lambda = -.436$$

$$\mu = .707$$

$$\nu = -.558$$

Thus the line determined in each case is the correct one but is (or may be) pointed in opposite directions depending upon which method we use.

To check the coordinates of the point which the line goes through we use the values found in Eq. (2). Point P has the coordinates -5.27, $0.$, and $+8$. The standard equation of a line through a point P having coordinates x, y, z is

$$\frac{X - x}{\lambda} = \frac{Y - y}{\mu} = \frac{Z - z}{\nu}$$

Substituting these values in the planar equations proves that the point is common to both, i.e., the equations equal zero.

24.17. SINGLE CURVED SURFACES. The student of graphics is familiar with the cylinder and the cone. The equations of these surfaces are most easily represented if we consider the axis of either the cone or cylinder to be one of the coordinate axes. For either the cone or cylinder this means that there are three equations which will fit depending on which coordinate axis is the axis of the surface. We shall limit ourselves to cylinders and cones having circular and elliptical right sections but other shapes can be used if the equation of the cross section is known.

24.18. CIRCULAR AND ELLIPTICAL CYLINDERS. Considering the circle as a special form of the ellipse in which the diameters are all equal, the equation of the right section of any cylinder takes the form

$$\frac{X^2}{a^2} + \frac{Y^2}{b^2} = 1$$

where a and b are the major and minor radii. Since the third coordinate of a cylinder is completely independent of the cross section, three cylinder equations evolve.

Cylinder having the Z axis and its axis coincident:

for any Z

$$\frac{X^2}{a^2} + \frac{Y^2}{b^2} = 1$$

Cylinder having the X axis and its axis coincident:

for any X

$$\frac{Z^2}{a^2} + \frac{Y^2}{b^2} = 1$$

Cylinder having the Y axis and its axis coincident:

for any Y

$$\frac{X^2}{a^2} + \frac{Z^2}{b^2} = 1$$

To illustrate, write the equation of a circular cylinder having a radius of 5 and a center located at $X = 3$, $Y = 2$, $Z = 1$. The axis of the cylinder is to be parallel to the Z axis.

A Z-axis cylinder of radius $= 5$ has the basic equation:

$$\frac{X^2}{5^2} + \frac{Y^2}{5^2} = 1$$

However, the X and Y of this equation are based on a center of $X = 0$, $Y = 0$. But for our problem the center is at $X = 3$, $Y = 2$. Thus all values of X are $+3$ too large and all values of Y are $+2$ too large. We can say that the true equation of this cylinder is:

$$\frac{(X - 3)^2}{25} + \frac{(Y - 2)^2}{25} = 1$$

24.19. CIRCULAR AND ELLIPTICAL CONES. Unlike the cylinder, the cross section of a cone is related to its position along the axis of the cone. If we consider a cone with a right section having major and minor radii a and b and this section is at a distance c from the vertex, we can see that the radii must be different for any other right section not at distance c from the vertex. This is accomplished by equating the ellipse not to 1 as in the cylinder but to a variable relationship involving c and specified distance along the axis for the desired point. A Z-axis cone has the equation:

$$\frac{X^2}{a^2} + \frac{Y^2}{b^2} = \frac{Z^2}{c^2}$$

As with the cylinder, there are three versions of this basic equation. The right side of the equation indicates that the axis of the cone is coincident with the coordinate axis named.

Example: Determine the equation of a right-circular Y-axis cone having the vertex at $X = 0$, $Y = 0$, $Z = 0$ and a point on the surface at $X = 3$, $Y = 4$, $Z = 2.5$. The general equation is:

$$\frac{X^2}{a^2} + \frac{Z^2}{b^2} = \frac{Y^2}{c^2}$$

For this cone $a = b = \sqrt{3^2 + 2.5^2}$
$$= \pm 3.91$$
and $\qquad c = 4$

Thus the equation of the cone becomes

$$\frac{X^2}{15.25} + \frac{Z^2}{15.25} = \frac{Y^2}{16}$$

24.20. COORDINATIONS USING AUXILIARY VIEWS. The mathematical counterpart of an auxiliary view is a realignment of the coordinate system used for the original problem. A normal view of an oblique surface is simply a rotation of coordinate axes until two of the coordinate axes are parallel to the surface and the third is perpendicular to the surface. In addition, the coordinate system may be moved to a new origin although all axes remain parallel in old and new positions. Thus a cone with a vertex at the origin has a simpler equation than one having the vertex not at the origin. Both of these processes of reorienting the direction of axes and relocating the origin are very powerful tools in using space geometry for problem solution.

24.21. TRANSLATIONS OF COORDINATE ORIGINS. Assuming a coordinate system x, y, z, it is desired to produce a new coordinate system x', y', z' having an origin x_0, y_0, and z_0 distant from the original. Any point in space that had original coordinates x, y, z has coordinates x', y', z' in the new system which are related by

$$x' = x - x_0$$
$$y' = y - y_0$$
$$z' = z - z_0$$

To illustrate, consider a point $A(3,4,2)$ in a coordinate system. A new coordinate system is to be set up parallel to the old one but with the new origin coinciding with point $X(1,3,4)$ of the old system. In the new system point A has the coordinates

$$x' = x - x_0 = 3 - 1 = 2$$
$$y' = y - y_0 = 4 - 3 = 1$$
$$z' = z - z_0 = 2 - 4 = -2$$

The student is urged to plot this example for visualization of the relationship.

By rearranging the basic equations, coordinates in a new system can be related to an old system.

$$x = x' + x_0$$
$$y = y' + y_0$$
$$z = z' + z_0$$

Translation of coordinates is a valuable tool for simplifying equations and is especially valuable for comparing geometrics that originally are not *equally* related to an origin.

24.22.   ROTATION OF AXES.   Any serious student of mathematical graphics will find invaluable the process of rotating a coordinate system while retaining the origin.

Any coordinate system which is rotated through some angle with respect to an original coordinate system has three axes or lines which make direction angles with the original axes. Since we must establish some frame of reference, we will state that the new x axis has direction cosines of λ_1 with the old x axis, λ_2 with the old y axis and λ_3 with the old z axis as measured in the old coordinate system. Similarly, the new y axis has direction cosines of μ_1, μ_2, μ_3 with the old axes and the new z axis has direction cosines

of ν_1, ν_2, ν_3 with the old axes. These nine direction cosines have certain known relationships.

$$\lambda_i^2 + \mu_i^2 + \nu_i^2 = 1 \quad \text{(for } i = 1, 2, 3)$$
$$\lambda_1^2 + \lambda_2^2 + \lambda_3^2 = 1$$
$$\mu_1^2 + \mu_2^2 + \mu_3^2 = 1$$
$$\nu_1^2 + \nu_2^2 + \nu_3^2 = 1$$

Coordinates of a point A in a new coordinate system using the coordinates of the point in the old coordinate system would be:

$$x' = \lambda_1 x + \lambda_2 y + \lambda_3 z$$
$$y' = \mu_1 x + \mu_2 y + \mu_3 z$$
$$z' = \nu_1 x + \nu_2 y + \nu_3 z$$

To illustrate the principle consider a new coordinate system with the new y axis rotated midway between the old x and y axes and at an angle of $54°44'$ with the old z axis.

We start by cataloging the angles or direction cosines that are known.

Angle between y and $z = 54°44'$
Angle between y' and x equals angle between y' and y

Therefore

$$\mu_3 = .577$$
$$\mu_2 = \mu_1$$

Since

$$\mu_1^2 + \mu_2^2 + \mu_3^2 = 1$$
$$2\mu_1^2 + .577^2 = 1$$
$$2\mu_1^2 = 1 - .333$$
$$\mu_1^2 = .333$$
$$\mu_1 = \pm.577$$

Since all angles are less than $90°$

$$\mu_1 = \mu_2 = .577$$

Since the new z axis is perpendicular to the new y axis, we recognize that the angle between z' and z is $35°16'$. Also the angles between z' and y and between z' and x are equal.

Therefore $\nu_3 = \cos 35°16' = .816$

Since

$$\nu_1 = \nu_2$$

and

$$\nu_1{}^2 + \nu_2{}^2 + \nu_3{}^2 = 1$$
$$2\nu_1{}^2 + .816^2 = 1$$
$$2\nu_1{}^2 = .666$$
$$\nu_1 = \pm.577$$

The angles between z' and x and between z' and y are greater than $90°$ so

$$\nu_1 = \nu_2 = -.577$$

Cataloging known direction cosines at this point:

$$\mu_1 = .577 \qquad \nu_1 = -.577$$
$$\mu_2 = .577 \qquad \nu_2 = -.577$$
$$\mu_3 = .577 \qquad \nu_3 = .816$$

From the relationship

$$\lambda_i{}^2 + \mu_i{}^2 + \nu_i{}^2 = 1 \qquad (i = 1, 3)$$

we obtain the values for $\lambda_1, \lambda_2, \lambda_3$

$$\lambda_1{}^2 + .577^2 + (-.577)^2 = 1$$
$$\lambda_1{}^2 = .333$$
$$\lambda_1 = \pm.577$$
$$\lambda_2{}^2 + .577^2 + (-.577)^2 = 1$$
$$\lambda_2{}^2 = .333$$
$$\lambda_2 = \pm.577$$
$$\lambda_3{}^2 + .577^2 + .816^2 = 1$$
$$\lambda_3{}^2 = 0$$
$$\lambda_3 = 0$$

The angle between x' and x is less than $90°$ so $\lambda_1 = .577$

The angle between x' and y is greater than $90°$ so $\lambda_2 = -.577$

If a point A is located at $(1,1,1)$ in the old coordinate system, it has coordinates x', y' and z' in the new system calculated by the following equations:

$$x' = \lambda_1 x + \lambda_2 y + \lambda_3 z$$
$$= .577 \cdot 1 - .577 \cdot 1 + 0 \cdot 1$$
$$= 0$$
$$y' = \mu_1 x + \mu_2 y + \mu_3 z$$
$$= .577 \cdot 1 + .577 \cdot 1 + .577 \cdot 1$$
$$= 1.731$$
$$z' = \nu_1 x + \nu_2 y + \nu_3 z$$
$$= -.577 \cdot 1 - .577 \cdot 1 + .816 \cdot 1$$
$$= -.338$$

The alert graphics student may note that this rotation is one which would have produced isometric drawings in conventional graphics. Continuing this rotation for a complete object and plotting the resulting rotated object will produce orthographic views, one of which will be a conventional isometric.

Rotation of axes is a valuable tool for simplifying problems which, otherwise, would be very difficult to solve. The equation of a cone whose axis is not parallel to coordinate axes is relatively simple to solve if the equation is first written for a coordinate-axis cone and then the axis system rotated to produce a new equation. To illustrate how rotation can simplify obtaining an equation, consider finding the equation of the cylinder

$$\frac{X^2}{9} + \frac{Y^2}{16} = 1$$

in the coordinate system illustrated above. We will expect the new equation to appear completely unlike the original equation which should serve to illustrate why reverse rotation can help simplify things. At this point we need some additional information, the equations for expressing x in terms of x', y', and z'.

$$x = \lambda_1 x' + \mu_1 y' + \nu_1 z'$$
$$y = \lambda_2 x' + \mu_2 y' + \nu_2 z'$$
$$z = \lambda_3 x' + \mu_3 y' + \nu_3 z'$$

For our problem we find

$$x = .577x' + .577y' - .577z'$$
$$y = -.577x' + .577y' - .577z'$$
$$z \text{ is not needed}$$

Therefore the equation of the cylinder becomes

$$\frac{(.577x' + .577y' - .577z')^2}{9}$$
$$+ \frac{(-.577x' + .577y' - .577z')^2}{16} = 1$$

where all values are primed.

This simplifies to:

$$8.33x^2 + 8.33y^2 + 8.33z^2 + 2.33xy$$
$$- 2.33xz - 8.33yz = 144$$

It can be seen that this equation would be difficult to develop without rotation. Note that this is the equation of an elliptical cylinder whose axis is tilted $35°16'$ from vertical. Thus, it is possible to rotate the above equation by the appropriate amount and return it to its original version. It can also be seen that if enough information is known about the equation of an object, it may be possible to vastly simplify the equation by rotation of axes.

Further, if the original equation had been the cumbersome version just produced (but information was known as to the position of the axis), rotation of the axis system to coincide with the axis of the cylinder would produce the simple cylinder equation originally used. Simplification of equations is a laborious process, but there are cases where this is the only reasonable solution.

PROBLEMS

The comprehensive study of graphical-mathematical counterparts demands that each phase, graphical and mathematical, be identified, solved, and compared. Thus, in the study of these counterparts, the most valuable training will be attained by accomplishing the solution of problems by both methods. Also, graphics and mathematics each provides a check on the other which, incidentally, is a very valuable procedure in engineering practice. To check the graphic solution, plot the mathematical determination of points, lines, points on planes, etc., on the graphic solution. To check the mathematical solution, compare measurements and the location of points, lines, etc., with the mathematical determination. Following this conception, the problem material listed below is ideally suited to comparative study.

Solve the following problems both graphically and mathematically, and compare the determinations.

24.1. A selection of problems from Chap. 9, Points and Straight Lines in Space.

24.2. A selection of problems from Chap. 10, Curved Lines in Space.

24.3. A selection of problems from Chap. 11, Lines and Planes in Space.

Professional Problems

25

25.1. As the preface states, the broad professional aspects of graphic knowledge and practice are continually expanding because, as the profession of engineering has really "come of age," with the attendant complexity, complication, and sophistication of adulthood, all aspects of the profession are brought to a similar high level. In other words, graphics is no longer the principal concern of designers and groups charged only with the production of drawings and specifications for manufacture, but now becomes a vital concern for the directing engineer in coordinating the total effort of engineering projects.

It also follows that the designers, chief draftsmen, group leaders, and draftsmen must embrace a new conception of professionalism in the areas of engineering training necessary for a complete understanding of problems transmitted by the specialized technical and engineering divisions.

Thus it becomes appropriate to include a series of professional problems in this textbook. The problems have been selected from a wide variety of engineering fields and interfield categories. For example, quite often mechanical, and/or electrical, electronics, or other physical or chemical determinations are necessary to the solution of a single problem. Solving a number of the problems following will help materially in giving the student of graphics some experience and, eventually, a command of the uses of graphics in the solution of problems typical of those faced continually by professional engineers.

The difficulty of classifying professional problems into categories or groups should be evident. However, since problems must be selected on the basis of needed experience, those of group 1 deal principally with projections, those of group 2 with structures, mechanics, and components, and those of group 3 with graphic solutions.

851

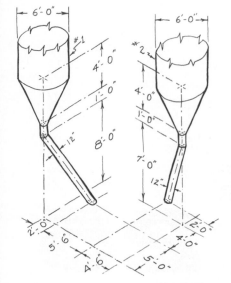

PROB. 25.1.1.

PROBLEMS

GROUP 1.   PROJECTIONS

25.1.1. A chemical processing plant has pipes leading through the floor from overhead vats, as illustrated. The chief draftsman has sketched the pertinent information, requesting that the following be determined:

(a) The size and shape of the hole the workmen must cut in the floor for the pipes to pass through.

(b) The true angle of the elbow leading from the bottom of vat 1.

(c) The true angle of the elbow leading from the bottom of vat 2.

(d) The development of the frustrum of the cone that forms the bottom of the vats.

25.1.2. An operations engineer has made a rough sketch showing the center lines of pipes *AB* and *CD* as they cut across the corner of a boiler complex. It is desired to connect these two pipes by means of a pipe *EF* (the shortest connecting line possible) to provide a bypass.

(a) Locate the center line of pipe *EF*, showing the distances from its terminal points to *A* and *C*, respectively. (Point *E* lies between *A* and *B*; and point *F* lies between *C* and *D*.)

(b) What is the true length of the center line of pipe *EF*?

(c) Since this is a specialized piece of work, individual joints must be designed and fabricated for this connection. As a first step in accomplishing this, determine the angles *CFE* and *AEF*.

25.1.3. Rigid electrical transmission elements are to be inserted in the miniaturized electrical connector box shown in the sketch which an engineer has made for the drafting group. The sketch shows that these elements must go from points *A*, *B*, and *C* to points *F*, *G*, and *H*, respectively. Voltage requirements are such that there must be at least 0.1-in. clearance between the center lines of these elements.

(a) Does the arrangement shown in the figure meet these specifications?

(b) What are the true lengths of each of these elements?

25.1.4. A project engineer requires a miniature electrical connector box in which rigid electrical transmission elements will be inserted. He has shown his requirements in sketch form and states that he desires to run an element from point *P* to some unestablished point *Q*. It is necessary for *PQ* to be perpendicular to the directions of both *AB* and *CD*. Also, point *Q* must lie in one of the faces of the connector box.

(a) Where must the hole *Q* be drilled? (*Hint:* Establish direction of line *PQ*, then determine where it pierces plane of the face.)

PROB. 25.1.2.

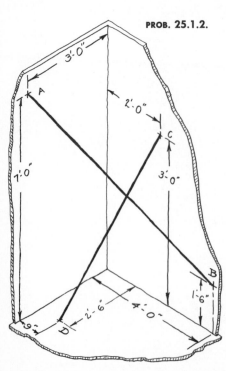

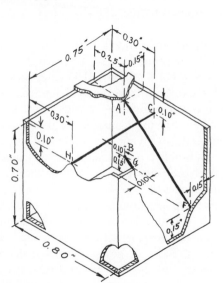

PROB. 25.1.3.

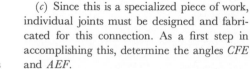

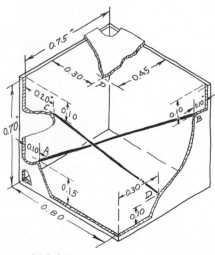

PROB. 25.1.4.

(b) Determine if the element PQ, established as described above, intersects either AB or CD.

(c) If PQ does not intersect either AB or CD, determine how much it misses each of these elements.

(d) What is the true length of element PQ?

25.1.5 In a certain electrical connector box a rigid electrical transmission element runs from A to B. Holes have been drilled at C and E for proposed elements CD, CF, and EK to enter. The supervising engineer has made a sketch of this situation. He desires that the following questions be answered and the requirements met.

(a) CD must be parallel to AB. Where must hole D be drilled?

(b) EF must be perpendicular to CD (part a, above), and also to AB; and it must intersect AB. Where must hole F be drilled?

(c) How far does EF (part b, above) miss CD?

(d) EK must be perpendicular to AB and CD, and 1 in. above AB. Where must hole K be drilled?

(e) What are the true lengths of: AB, CD, CF, and EK?

25.1.6. A resident engineer has made a sketch showing the broad requirements for a proposed cofferdam. The sheeting is to be a double row of 2×12's, tongue and groove; the horizontal and cross bracing is to be 6×8's. Cross bracing runs from A to F, A to H, D to G, D to E, etc.

Design this bracing, making pertinent orthographic drawings. Show details of the lap joints at the center where the braces cross each other; and details of the end cuts of the braces. Clearly specify all depths of cuts, and angles, and/or other information needed so that the shop can make these braces, exactly as designed, without further consultation with the engineer.

25.1.7. An architect has made a rough sketch of a steeple he is studying in an effort to decide the best type of lightning rod to install. He also wants to determine some pertinent information which the steel fabricators need. Here are the things he wants to know:

(a) The lightning rod CE has a rigid conductor acting as a ground wire designated as GHJ on the figure. It runs from point G (which is on the lightning rod 6″ above point C) parallel to the plane of the roof ACD, to point H. This point H lies in a plane perpendicular to AD, and a fourth of the distance from A to D. From said point H the conductor runs down the face of the steeple $ADFK$, parallel to it, and at the same distance from plane $ADFK$ as it is from plane ACD. What is the distance from the conductor to plane $ADFK$?

(b) What is the true length of the conductor GH?

(c) Determine the true angle GHJ.

(d) Determine the true length of the support at H.

(e) Determine the angle the support at H makes with the plane $ADFK$.

(f) Determine the angle between plane $ADFK$ and GH.

(g) Determine the angle between plane ADC and HJ.

(h) Determine the angle between the lightning rod and plane ACD.

(i) Determine the angle between planes ABC and ADC.

(j) Determine the angle between planes ADC and $ADFK$.

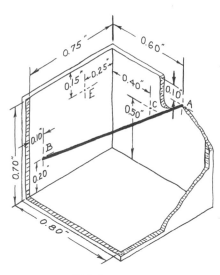

PROB. 25.1.5.

PROB. 25.1.6.

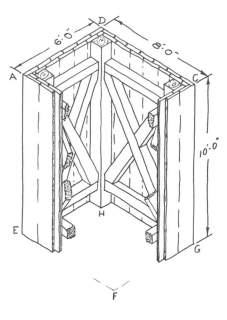

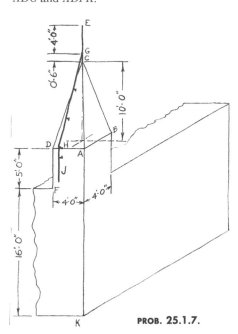

PROB. 25.1.7.

25.1.8. A helicoidal catwalk 2 ft wide must be placed around a spherical tank 30 ft in diameter so as to enable workmen to check gages and to gain access to the top of the tank. The helicoid will start at the maximum diameter of the sphere and continue at a 30° slope until it reaches the top.

(*a*) Make an orthographic drawing showing the top and front views of this catwalk.

(*b*) Determine the true length of the center line of this catwalk.

(*c*) Design an acceptable platform for the top of this spherical tank.

25.1.9. Due to the heavy loads on the stainless steel tank of Prob. 25.1.9 engineers have determined that a supporting member *EF* will be required to brace member *AB* against *CD*. The engineer in charge has made a sketch of the situation and would like to consider also several alternative situations:

(*a*) What would be the shortest possible supporting member *EF*?

(*b*) If *E* is on *AB* and *F* is on *CD*, how far would *E* be located from point *C* if the above shortest member were used?

(*c*) If it is required to use a member *EF* which is 8 ft in length, where will point *E* be

located on *AB*, and where will point *F* be located on *CD*?

(*d*) What length strut *EF* would be required to reach from point *G* (which lies on *CD* 2 ft from *C*) to point *B* (on *AB*), and makes an angle of 30° with *CD*?

25.1.10. A safety engineer for a power company has sketched a set of proposed guy wires that are to be installed on a mast near a transformer outlet, as shown. The transformer outlet is at point *E*.

(*a*) The safety engineer wants to know how far it is from *E* to the nearest guy wire.

(*b*) The advertising manager is considering designing an attractive sign that will lie in the plane *BAC*. He wants to know the true angle *BAC*.

(*c*) The advertising manager has an alternative sign in mind that would lie in the plane *CAO* and, therefore, he would like to know the true shape of this plane.

(*d*) The advertising manager has decided that the best design of a sign could be made if the angle *BAC* were 30°. The project engineer wants to know where the point *C* would be located on the circumference of the circle *BCD* if they were to make this angle 30°.

25.1.11. One of the uses of a laser beam is to help in the surveying work necessary in constructing tunnels. At the beginning of the tunnel the beam is set at a specified angle and bearing and aimed at a target. As excavation progresses, the target is moved forward into the tunnel and a minimum of error accrues.

The sketch shows contours of a hill through which it is proposed to construct a tunnel. Transfer this contour map to a blank sheet of paper and, working from this, furnish the following information:

(*a*) Specify the vertical angle and the bearing for the laser beam if the tunnel is to enter at *A* and emerge at *B*.

(*b*) Using the cross section shown and a ditch bottom slope of 0.2%, estimate the amount of earth required to be moved to drain the pond shown at *C*. (Show ditch location on plan, then draw original and finish profiles, and, finally, cross sections from which the yardage will be computed.)

(*c*) Estimate the amount of earth fill needed

PROB. 25.1.9.

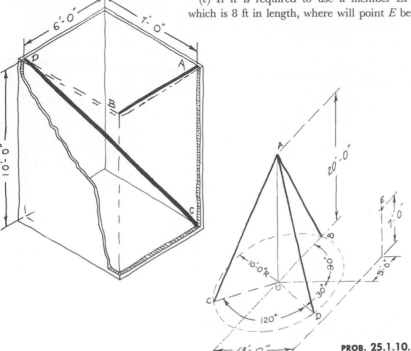

PROB. 25.1.10.

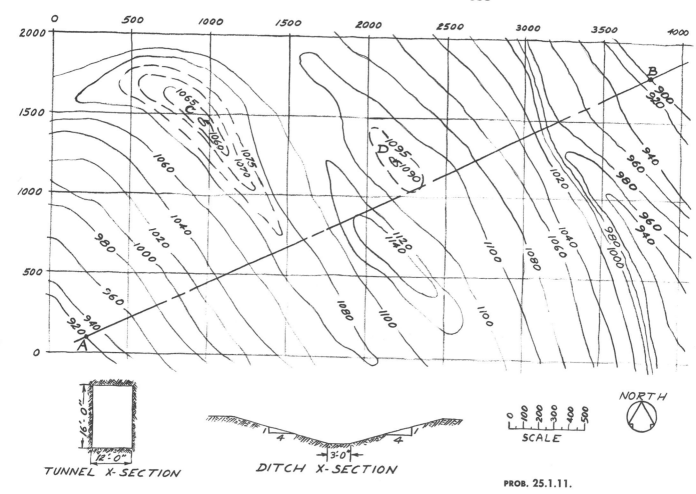

TUNNEL X-SECTION

DITCH X-SECTION

SCALE

NORTH

PROB. 25.1.11.

to fill pond D to elevation 1095. (Draw cross sections and derive the estimate from them.)

(*d*) Estimate the amount of earth that will have to be moved to build the tunnel.

Note: When the vertical distance is small compared with the horizontal distance, it is usually convenient to choose different scales. For example, the vertical scale could be 1 in. = 1 ft, while the horizontal scale could be 1 in. = 1000 ft (or any other set of values). They are not dependent upon each other so long as all views are kept in the horizontal plane and in planes that fold directly from this horizontal plane, i.e., in the first auxiliary off of the horizontal plane.

Percent grade would be shown by projecting an auxiliary view from a top view in a direction parallel to the bearing line, which would be shown in the top view. Horizontal distances would be measured using the horizontal scale (and they would be measured parallel to the above bearing line). Vertical distances would be perpendicular to said bearing line, and they would be measured using the vertical scale. Percent grade would be the ratio of this vertical distance (measured using the vertical scale) to the horizontal distance (measured using the horizontal scale); it must be this ratio and not an angle expressed in degrees.

Usually this view would produce a true-length line, but since the scales are different, the true length would be the square root of the sum of the squares of the vertical and horizontal distances.

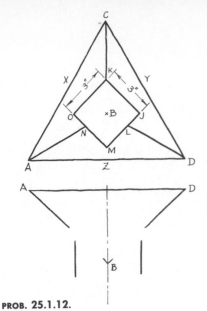

PROB. 25.1.12.

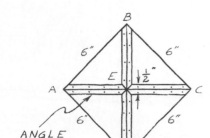

ANGLE
STRIPS
(4-⅝" HOLES)
(Each Strip)

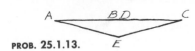

PROB. 25.1.13.

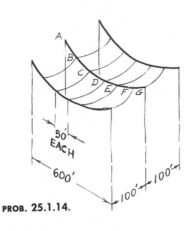

PROB. 25.1.14.

25.1.12. One of the parts of a machine which is being mass produced consists of a hopper welded to a hollow square outlet. The engineer has made a rough sketch of it as shown.

The hopper is formed by three mutually perpendicular planes, *ABC*, *CBD*, and *ABD*. All seams are fabricated by welding.

The industrial engineer in charge of the operation wants to know how many inches of weld are required to manufacture this part.

Two different options are being considered for this design, option A and option B. Determine the inches of weld needed for each option.

Option A		Option B	
Side	Length, in.	Side	Length, in.
X	10	X	19
Y	10	Y	23
Z	10	Z	17

25.1.13. An operations engineer has made a rough sketch showing the general design for a reflector, the angle between planes *ABE* and *DCE*. They will be manufactured by cutting triangular plates and fastening them together with strips cut to the proper shape and bent to the proper angle. The engineer wants to know:

(*a*) What is the angle between *ABE* and *ADE*, so that these strips can be formed to the proper angle?

(*b*) What is the true shape of the triangular planes?

(*c*) What is the true shape of the fastening strips, which are first stamped out of a flat piece of metal, and then bent to the proper angle?

(*d*) Show location of holes drilled in the fasteners, and also in the triangular plates so that they will fit when the strip is laid over the triangular plate.

(*e*) Make a satisfactory orthographic drawing of this strip, so that the shop can fabricate it.

25.1.14. The suspended roof system, for buildings that need large floor areas free of columns, is becoming more and more popular. The system follows the general principle of the suspension bridge.

The system of primary cables for such a structure, proposed for covering a football stadium, has been sketched by the resident engineer and is shown in Prob. 25.1.14. Secondary cables (not shown) will be strung from these primary cables and the roof, in turn, will be suspended from the secondary cables.

The engineer in charge has instructed the draftsman to assume that the primary cables hang as parabolas with a maximum sag of 26 ft at the center; *A* and *G* are the same elevation. Furthermore, it is assumed that this parabola approximates a series of cords (*AB*, *BC*, *CD*, *DE*, *EF*, *FG*) whose horizontal projections are equal.

Determine the angle that each of these cords makes with the horizontal plane, so that the engineer can proceed further with the design.

25.1.15. A solar stove is being designed for use in field research. It consists of a circular paraboloid, 6 ft in diameter, which will focus the sun's rays approximately at a point. The distance from the plane of the circular front to the parabolic surface at the center line is 18 in.

Determine the focal point of the parabolic surface.

25.1.16. It is required to brace certain pipes against each other in order to reduce vibrations in a crowded and complex layout of piping. Space requirements demand that the braces lie as shown in the rough sketch. The engineering group has tabulated control distances for four separate situations as listed below, part *A* through *D*, inclusive. All distances are shown in inches proceeding from *R* to *S* and from *P* to *Q*. Up, to the right, and forward are positive directions. *P* is directly above *R* in every case.

	Pipe *RS*			Pipe *PQ*			
	A	B	C	D	E	F	V
(*a*)	−4	4	4	4	−4	4	4
(*b*)	−6	5	4	1	−2	3	3
(*c*)	−2	4	3	2	−4	6	2

(*d*) In part *d*, shafts lie in horizontal planes at 30° angle with each other; *A*, *B*, *C*, *D*, *E*, and *F* are all zero; and *V* is 6 in.

PROB. 25.1.16.

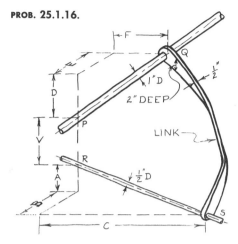

It is required that you design the link to be used for the brace, in each case. Make complete orthographic drawings for the link so that it can be fabricated. Provide a method of clamping the link to the pipe.

25.1.17. A shipment consisting of long lengths of shafting is being loaded into an industrial complex where clearances are very tight. At four distinct points (A through D, inclusive, listed below) clearance may be critical. One of the project engineers has made a rough sketch of the situation and asked a

PROB. 25.1.17.

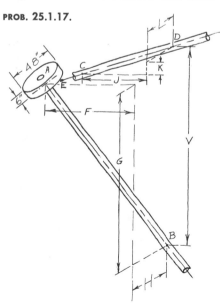

draftsman to tell him the true distance from a specified point C to the 48-in. pulley, 6 in. wide, at A. Consider the diameter of CD to be negligible. Briefly, it is the true length of CE that is desired.

All distances shown proceed from A to B and from C to D. Point B lies either directly below, or directly above, point D. Distance V is measured from B to D, upward being the positive direction for all measurements. To the right and forward are also positive directions.

		AB			CD		
	F	G	H	J	K	L	V
(a)	14′3″	−5′3″	−6′0″	10′6″	2′3″	−5′0″	8′0″
(b)	14′3″	4′0″	−6′0″	10′6″	1′6″	−5′9″	−1′6″
(c)	14′3″	−5′3″	−6′0″	10′6″	−2′3″	−4′6″	2′3″
(d)	14′3″	−5′3″	−6′0″	10′6″	−2′3″	−4′6″	8′0″

25.1.18. A project engineer has sketched some general ideas concerning a scaffold, and has asked for a design meeting the following requirements:

1. It is to be made entirely of some tubing which they have on hand. Two sizes are available, such that the smaller fits snugly into the larger.
2. Welds may be made where desirable.
3. It must be possible to dismantle the scaffold with a minimum of effort.
4. When dismantled it must lie as flat as possible for ease in moving and loading into trucks.
5. Sufficient cross braces must be provided to prevent lateral sway in all directions.
6. All units must be interchangeable and easily assembled.
7. Sufficient head room must be provided so that workers may stand and work on any level.

Assume you are the draftsman, and carry out the project engineer's assignment. Make orthographic drawings sufficiently complete so that the scaffold units may be fabricated.

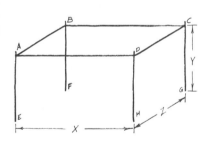

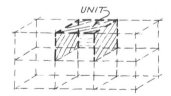

PROB 25.1.18.

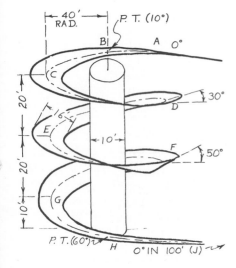

25.1.19. An amusement park is considering a new roller coaster. The design engineer has made a sketch of the plane of the tracks in an effort to study the varying elevation required as the car picks up speed as it descends. He has not worked on the design of the supporting structure and, therefore, it is not shown on the sketch.

Make an orthographic top, front, and end view of this track as it circles the vertical tower.

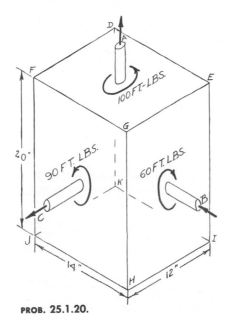

PROB. 25.1.20.

25.1.20. Moment vectors are shown as arrows of a specified length, which represent moments in a *plane perpendicular to the arrow*. The sense is determined by the "right-hand rule," i.e., if the arrow is considered to be grasped with the right hand so that the extended thumb is pointing in the direction of the arrow, the curled fingers of the right hand indicate the direction of the moment lying in a plane perpendicular to the arrow.

For example, the 100-ft-lb moment shown in plane *DEFG* in the illustration is represented by arrow *A*, 100 units in length, in the direction shown. In like manner arrows *B* and *C*, 60 and 90 units in length, respectively, rep-

resent the moments shown in planes *EGHI* and *FGHJ*.

These moment vectors may be added vectorially, like any other vectors.

In this problem it is assumed that an engineer in charge of a laboratory experiment has made a sketch of a gear box on which some predetermined torques will be placed. Requirements of the experiment are such that the resultant of torques *A*, *B*, and *C* must lie in a specified direction.

The head of the drafting group suggests the following: Draw a view of the gear box such that the resultant torque lies in the plane of the paper on which you are drawing (i.e., the vector representing the torque will be perpendicular to the plane of the paper).

This will be a view of the box as though seen along the line of the resultant torque, i.e., the view as seen when the resultant torque appears as a point. (Lugs inserted perpendicular to the plane of this view would have to carry only a tensile or compressive load; they would not be required to carry a transverse load.)

25.1.21. Read all explanatory notes concerning Prob. 25.1.20 and then draw a view of the gear box shown in the engineer's sketch of Prob. 25.1.21, so that the resultant torque lies in the plane of the paper, as was done in Prob. 25.1.20.

The vector representing the 90-ft-lb couple is perpendicular to plane *CDF*; and the vectors representing the 30-, 40-, and 60-ft-lb couples are perpendicular to planes *ABCDE*, *AGEJ*, and *EDFIJ*, respectively.

The chief draftsman has suggested the following approach: Show plane *CDF* as an edge, then the 90-ft-lb vector will appear as true length. It does not matter where this vector pierces plane *CDF*, since a couple is a "free" vector and therefore may be applied at any point. The next step is to project the 90-ft-lb vector back into the frontal and horizontal planes. The vector addition is now made in each of these planes; and the resultant in each of these planes is thereby determined. The point view of this resultant now determines the required view.

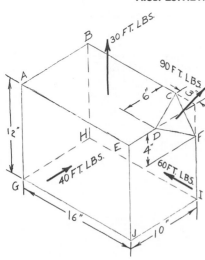

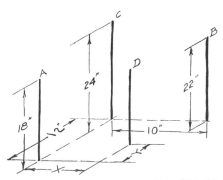

PROB 25.1.22.

25.1.22.   Various shapes are being tested in a wind tunnel, and the engineer has made a sketch illustrating the general layout. He requires the following information:

(*a*) The heights of the supports *A*, *B*, and *C* are shown in the sketch. Determine the height above a horizontal reference plane of support *D* if *ABCD* is to be a plane. For this, distance *X* is 12″ and distance *Y* is 8″.

(*b*) Determine the position and height above a horizontal reference plane that support *D* should be if *ABCD* is a circle. For this problem distance *X* is 6″, and piling *D* lies between *A* and *B* (rather than between *A* and *C*).

(*c*) *AB* is one conjugate diameter and *CD* is another conjugate diameter of an ellipse lying in plane *ABCD*. Determine the *X* and *Y* distances for point *D*, and the height of *D* above the horizontal plane.

(*d*) It has been decided to place four additional supports under the shape being tested in part *c*, above. One set, supports *E* and *F*, are to be placed at the extremities of the major diameter and another set, *G* and *H*, are to be placed at the extremities of the minor diameter. Determine the *X* and *Y* coordinates, and the heights above the horizontal reference plane for the supports *E*, *F*, *G*, and *H*.

25.1.23.   The "Electrotape" (a commercial product manufactured by Cubic Corporation, Electrotape Division, San Diego, California) is a precise electronic instrument for measuring distances across inaccessible terrain. It has a

wide range, extending from a few feet to about thirty miles. It is light in weight and easy to operate.

A resident engineer has roughly sketched the layout of some distances that are being measured with an Electrotape. Point *A* is 1620 ft lower than point *B* and the distance (measured along the slope, *not* the horizontal distance) is 2140 ft. Point *B*, which is essentially the same elevation as point *C*, is visible from point *C*; but point *A* is not. The Electrotape has determined that the distance from *C* to *B* is 3076 ft. The bearing from *C* to *B* is N27°E, and from *A* to *B* is N72°E.

Determine the horizontal distance from *C* to *A*.

25.1.24.   An architectural engineer has sketched the general layout of the supporting columns in an ultramodern building.

(*a*) Draw views that show the true shape of the faces, so that forms can be cut to the proper size.

(*b*) Design these forms and make orthographic drawings sufficiently complete so that the contractor can build them from your drawings. Make the faces of tempered masonite backed up by 2 × 6 tongue and groove sheathing. This is to be supported on 2 × 12's one foot center to center. In this design, keep in mind the ease of stripping the forms, after the concrete has set.

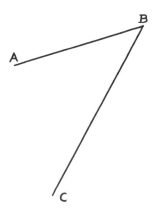

PROB. 25.1.23.

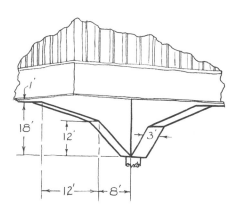

PROB. 25.1.24.

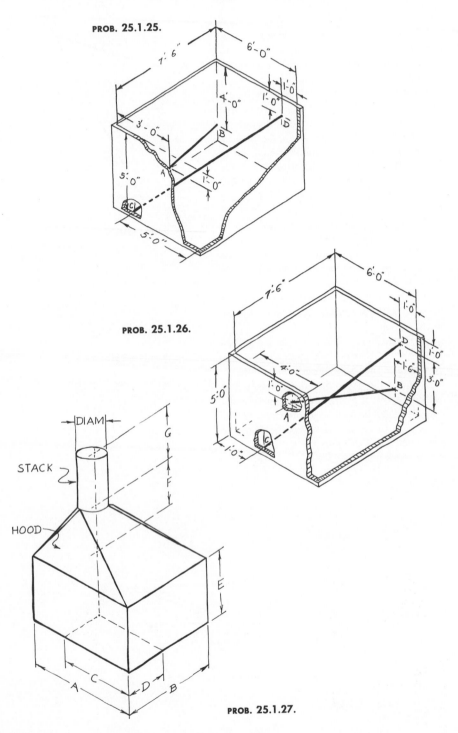

PROB. 25.1.25.

PROB. 25.1.26.

PROB. 25.1.27.

25.1.25. An engineer has made a sketch showing the center lines of pipes *AB* and *CD* as they pass through a steel chamber. For structural reasons it is desired to connect these two pipes together with a brace.

(*a*) If it is desired to brace these two pipes by means of the shortest horizontal member possible, show the location of the center line of the brace.

(*b*) If it is desired to brace these two pipes by means of the shortest member which is parallel to the face of *B* and *D*, show the location of the center line of this connecting brace.

(*c*) Design braces for both conditions. Both pipes are standard 2-in. steel.

25.1.26. The engineer in charge of air conditioning for a certain project has made a sketch showing the center line of a 36″ circular sheet metal duct running from *A* to *B* as it intersects a similar 24″ duct running from *C* to *D*. The center lines do not intersect, but the ducts themselves do.

(*a*) Draw orthographic views of this intersection.

(*b*) Develop a section of the pipe *AB* at this intersection sufficient in length to show how a flat piece of metal would have to be cut to fit properly.

(*c*) Same as part *b* for pipe *CD*.

25.1.27. A manufacturer of a line of gas burners desires to add a series of hoods to his product offerings. Dimensions for each specific case are as shown in the table below:

Case	A	B	C	D	E	F	G	Stack Diameter
(1)	4′	4′	2′	2′	4′	4′	3′	1′
(2)	6′	4′	6′	2′	4′	6′	3′	1′
(3)	6′	4′	6′	0′	4′	8′	3′	1′

(*a*) Develop the surfaces of one of the hoods.

(*b*) Make a model of one of the hoods.

25.1.28.   A part to be supplied to a manufac-turer of art objects is composed of an elliptical base capped by a top made of two half cones joined by planes, as illustrated in the sketch.

(a) Show the line of intersection of the elliptical base with the cap, in the front view.

(b) Develop the elliptical base.

(c) Develop the cap.

25.1.29.   Early steam engines usually incor-porated a governor which consisted of three balls that moved out due to centrifugal force when speed increased. This actuated a linkage (not shown in the figure) which connected to the throttle and regulated the speed.

An engineer in charge of renovating some antiques has made a sketch of this as shown. He desires to install a rod running from A to B in such a manner that it does not interfere with the action of this governor. He has speci-fied that the nearest position of the edge of the balls to the center line of the rod be 2 in.

He directs a draftsman to determine the missing distance, C or D, for the cases listed below:

Case	D	C
(a)	8″	?
(b)	4″	?
(c)	2″	?
(d)	?	1″
(e)	?	4″
(f)	?	5″
(g)	?	0″
(h)	0″	?

25.1.30.   Highway AB runs near highway CD at a certain location in mountainous ter-rain. The resident engineer has made a sketch showing pertinent data concerning these highways.

It is desired to join these two highways by a connecting road. Since highway standards in this vicinity do not allow a grade to exceed 6%, the engineer must know the location of the shortest possible straight road that will connect AB to CD lying on a 6% grade.

PROB. 25.1.28.

PROB. 25.1.29.

PROB. 25.1.30.

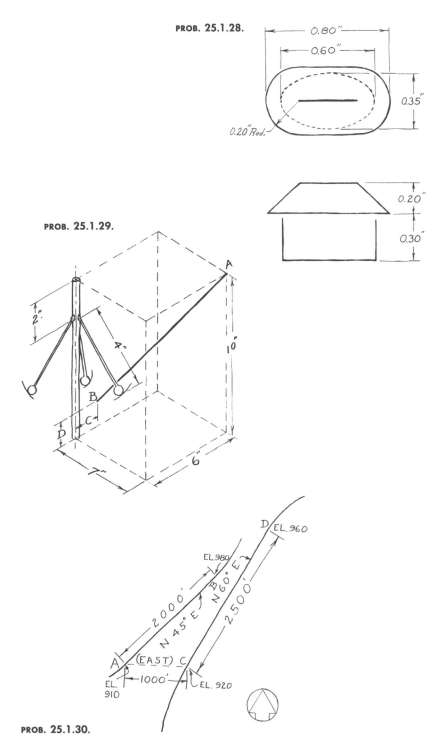

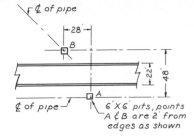

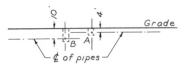

PROB 25.2.1.

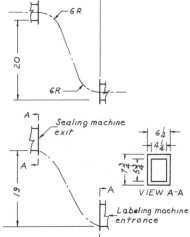

PROB. 25.2.2.

GROUP 2.   STRUCTURES, MECHANICS, AND COMPONENTS

25.2.1. A pneumatic tool called a Pneuma-gopher[1] pierces holes through the soil under roads, etc., for the installation of pipelines. Forward motion is produced by blows of an internal hammer. The tool is 45″ long and 3¾″ in diameter.

A pipe connection is to be made under a road using this tool from a "tee" at point *A* to the end of a pipe at *B*.

(*a*) Determine the location of the start of the hole in the pit and the direction of the hole.

(*b*) Where should the hole enter the second pit?

(*c*) Find the length of pipe needed.

25.2.2. Oil cans that exit from a sealing machine are to slide down a chute to a labeling machine. Each machine is located in the figure. Design the chute using helicoids and flat planes. *Note:* As a helicoid is a warped surface not readily fabricated from sheet metal, the design might take the form of several round rods bent to shape and connected with cross pieces. Can size is 4″ in diameter and 5″ high.

[1] Manufactured by Schramm Inc., West Chester, Pa.

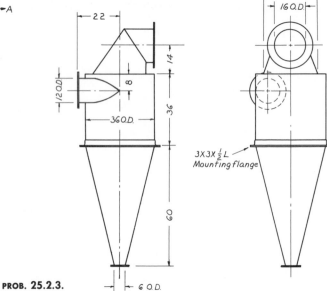

PROB. 25.2.3.

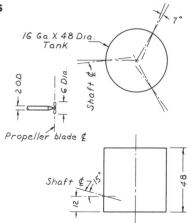

PROB. 25.2.4.

25.2.3. A dust collector (for removing dust, etc., from piped air or other gases) is shown. Make developments for each of the pieces shown.

25.2.4. A quenching tank for heat-treating steel is to be equipped with three propeller agitators installed on the center lines shown. The propeller is to clear the tank bottom by 6″.

(*a*) Determine the location and shape of the hole to be cut in the tank wall.

(*b*) Design a mounting bracket and locate it on the shaft housing from the propeller blade center line.

25.2.5. A commercially available butterfly valve contains a casting similar to the one shown. ⅜″ diameter holes will be drilled through the lugs followed by a 1″ diameter spotfacing operation to finish the washer seat. Draw the piece in its finished form.

25.2.6. A ventilating fan manufacturer is re-designing a fan to support the motor base from the shroud. Two pieces of 12-gage sheet steel are to be cut, bent, and spot welded to the shroud and base as shown. Develop these pieces showing dimensions, bend lines, angle of bend, etc.

25.2.7. A modernistic office building is to be built supported by columns with open parking underneath. To protect the columns from the

PROB. 25.2.5.

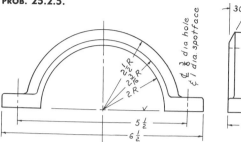

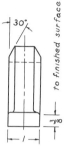

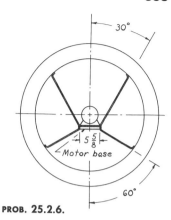

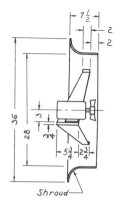

PROB. 25.2.6.

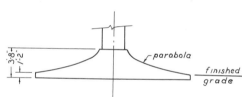

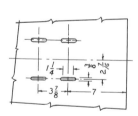

PROB. 25.2.7.

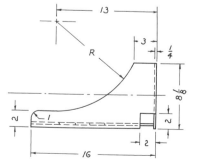

traffic, concrete bases are to be poured around the columns as shown. Develop the sheet metal shapes to be used in building the concrete forms.

25.2.8. An electric motor manufacturer is developing a line of motor mounts to be bolted directly to the driven equipment so that the motors can be direct-coupled to the load. Complete the top view of the prototype shown and develop the 16-gage sheet metal piece.

25.2.9. A new school building is to have a small auditorium built in the form of a pentagon. Five 4×6 timbers ($3\frac{5}{8}'' \times 5\frac{1}{2}''$) are to be joined together at the center as shown to support the roof. The roof surfaces are to have a slope of 4 ft in 12. Show how each timber is to be cut at the end so that they will fit together. Design some system to fasten the ends together. A clear plastic skylight running 4 ft down each slope, made from $\frac{1}{4}''$ thick acrylic, will cover this area. Determine the shape and size of the plastic pieces. (They will be joined by a special adhesive.) The skylight must clear the top of the timbers by $3''$ so that it can overlap the roof deck.

PROB. 25.2.9.

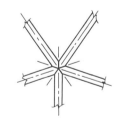

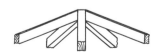

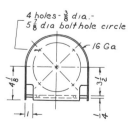

PROB. 25.2.8.

Hyperbolic cooling towers. Courtesy of the
Marley Company, Kansas City, Mo.

25.2.10. Many power plants are installing large hyperbolic natural-draft cooling towers similar to that shown. They are thin, light-weight concrete, often no more than 4″ thick. An open grid of beams at the bottom supports the shell and permits entry of air. In studying possible support designs for the water-diffusion grid in the tower, it is necessary to know the length of the support cables and the angle they make with the grid. Find this information. Determine the grid diameter.

25.2.11. An industrial building has a roof supported by split-ring connector timber trusses as shown. (The 4″ × 6″ struts all lie centered on the truss center lines.) An existing exhaust system is to be connected to the roof ventilator shown. Design the connecting duct-work showing bends, straight runs, etc. Keep the total length of duct as short as possible. (Minimum radius for turns is 45″ to the center line.)

25.2.12. A cylindrical storage bin with a conical hopper bottom is shown. Design the 6″ channel strut so that it will just touch the conical hopper. Design a pad to be attached to the strut to give support to the hopper.

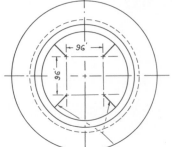

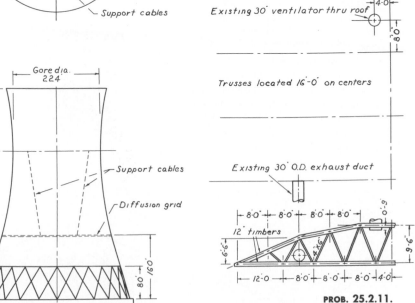

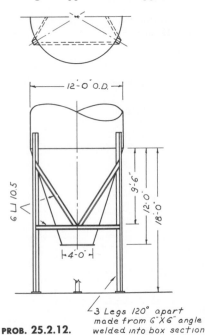

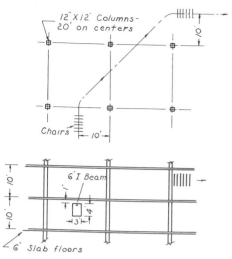

PROB. 25.2.13.

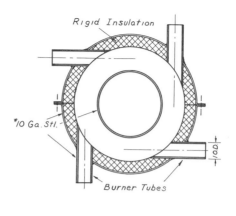

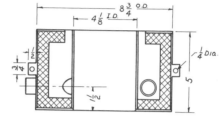

PROB. 25.2.14.

25.2.13. A manufacturer of steel folding card table chairs is setting up a production line in a reinforced concrete building. The chairs are moved on hangers on a trolley conveyor. This conveyor is to go from one floor to the next as shown. Standard turns for the 6″ I beam used are available for 30° and 45° bends (both hor. and ver.); the radius of curvature to the center line is 4′. Determine which bends to use, the length of straight track between them, and the location and size of the hole to be cut in the floor. A vertical clearance of 4′ and horizontal clearance of 3′ (as shown) must be maintained.

25.2.14. A power plant boiler manufacturer is building a series of muffle furnaces to be used in the field to stress relieve welds in boiler tubes. Portable torches are inserted through the burner tubes. Make a development of the outer shell.

25.2.15. A manufacturer storing and using large quantities of dry sand has a storage bin with a hopper bottom as shown. The corners are to be reinforced as shown. Develop the reinforcing pieces and determine the angle to which each is to be bent.

25.2.16. A cover for a traffic control light is shown. Draw a top view and complete the right side view. Make a development of the sheet metal piece.

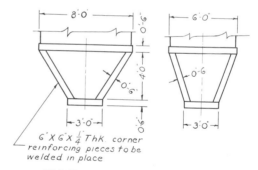

PROB. 25.2.15.

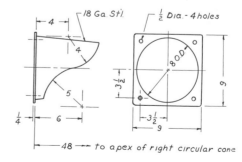

PROB. 25.2.16.

PROB. 25.2.18.

PROB. 25.2.17.

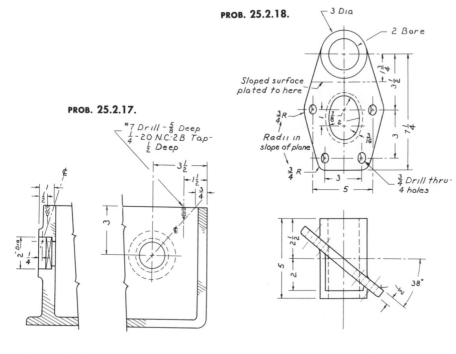

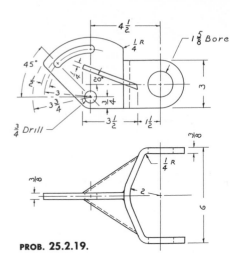

PROB. 25.2.19.

25.2.17. A manufacturer of speed reducers is producing a casting, part of which is shown. In an effort to increase the oil supply to the bearing indicated, a ⅛″-diameter hole is to be drilled along the center line shown. It will connect to a splash-supplied reservoir in the cover.

(*a*) Determine the length of the hole for cost-estimating purposes.

(*b*) How deep may the standard drill go and leave ¹⁄₁₆″ metal between the two holes?

25.2.18. The piece shown is to be mass-produced with the finished sloped surface (indicated) chromium plated. In figuring costs the area of this surface must be determined so that the amount of chromium used can be estimated. Determine the true shape of this surface and its area.

25.2.19. A manufacturer uses large quantities of a casting similar to the weldment shown. A study is under way to determine the relative cost of both pieces. Determine the true shape of the gusset and the number of inches of weld required to weld it in place. It is welded both sides.

25.2.20. Coal is to be gravity fed from a crusher directly to a rotating grate stoker in a power plant.

(*a*) Design a piece similar to that shown (made of ⅜″ plate) to give an even distribution of coal across the grate.

(*b*) Develop the various pieces to be welded together.

PROB. 25.2.20.

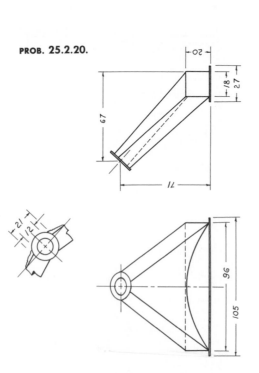

25.2.21.   An extension to a 3″ welded steel pipeline is to be installed as shown.

(*a*) Determine the number of degrees to be cut from standard elbows for each end of the connection and the length of straight pipe needed.

(*b*) Design a hanger to support the pipe from the I beam.

25.2.22.   A manufacturer of home tractors is having trouble with breakage of the adjustment pin on the plow attachment shown. The maximum drawbar pull is 1000 lb. Determine the maximum load this pin must carry.

25.2.23.   The bucket for a backhoe and its operating mechanism is shown. The hydraulic cylinder puts out a maximum thrust of 43,000 lb. Management wants to increase the thrust to 50,000 lb. Determine the maximum load at each pin in preparation for studying the effect on bearings and stress in the parts. The bucket can rotate 45° clockwise and 110° counterclockwise from the position shown.

25.2.24.   A commercially available tank filler cap is shown. Each spring exerts a 10-lb pull at the closed position. The spring rate is 15 lb/in. Determine how much tank pressure the cap will hold, the maximum load in each pin, and the maximum force needed to open the cap with atmospheric pressure in the tank.

25.2.25.   An appliance manufacturer is designing a cam to be die cast. A tapered roller follower (moving parallel to the axis) is to run in the groove indicated. The development of the path of the centroid of the cross section of the groove is shown. Make a complete drawing of the cam. It is an established fact that the product of the length of the centroidal path times the cross-sectional area will yield the volume of the solid generated. Use this to determine the volume of metal in the cam.

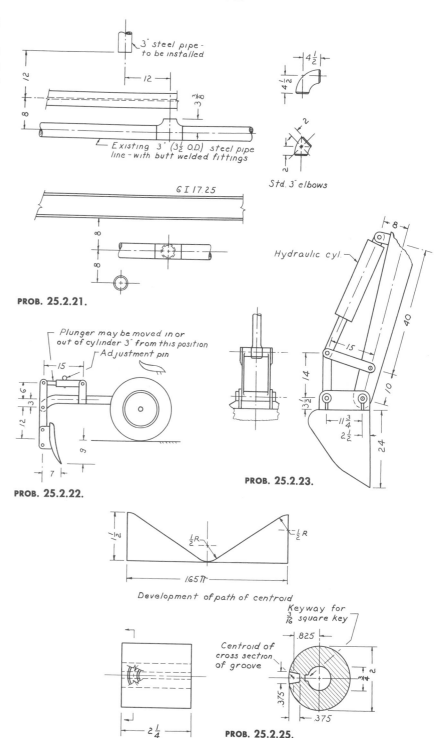

PROB. 25.2.21.

PROB. 25.2.22.

PROB. 25.2.23.

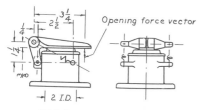

PROB. 25.2.24.

PROB. 25.2.25.

GROUP 3. GRAPHIC SOLUTIONS

25.3.1. Provide a graphic solution for the following: The tensile impact stress induced in a member by a weight w falling through a distance h onto the member can be calculated by means of the formula:

$$S_1 = S + S \sqrt{1 + \frac{2h}{e}}$$

where S_1 = the stress due to impact, psi

    S = the stress if the weight w were a static load, psi

    h = the distance through which the weight falls, in.

    e = the total deformation of the member due to the weight w acting as a static load, in.

25.3.2. The maximum pressure at a distance R from an underwater explosion was measured and the results are tabulated below. Determine the mathematical expression which best fits these data.

Explosive Charge 1 Pressure, psi	Explosive Charge 2 Pressure, psi	R, in.
640	390	0.8
210	130	2.0
130	75	3.0
85	52	4.0

PROB. 25.3.3.

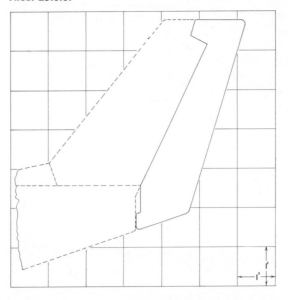

25.3.3. The rudder assembly of a modern single-engine light plane is shown in the figure. Determine the centroid of the movable (solid lines) part.

Assuming that the rudder is of uniform thickness, find the moment of inertia of the piece about the hinge line.

25.3.4. Provide a graphic solution for the following: The Rankine formula is used to determine the safe loading on a column. A column is a structural member subjected to an axial compressive load. The formula is:

$$\frac{P}{A} = \frac{18,000}{1 + \frac{(l/r)^2}{18,000}}$$

where $\dfrac{P}{A}$ = the allowable stress, psi

    $\dfrac{l}{r}$ = the slenderness ratio,

$$120 \le \frac{l}{r} \le 200.$$

(Members with ratios that are less than 120 are called posts and are analyzed by a different method. Members with ratios greater than 200 are rarely used.)

25.3.5. A series of U-shaped channels were fabricated and tested under a uniaxial compressive load.[2] The purpose of the tests was to determine the relationship between the total width of the base of the channel and the effective width. The effective width is defined as that portion of the base width that can be assumed to carry an equivalent uniform stress equal to the actual stress at the edges of the section. Because of local buckling of the compression element, the stress distribution across the section is nonlinear. Theoretical considerations indicate that the relationship will be of the form

$$\frac{b}{t}\beta = A + B\frac{t}{w\beta}$$

[2] A. L. Johnson and G. Winter, "Behavior of Stainless Steel Columns and Beams," *Journal of the Structural Division, ASCE,* vol. 92, no. ST5, Oct., 1966, pp. 97–118.

where w is the actual width, b is the effective width, t is the thickness, and β is a measure of the strain at the edges of the section. From the data tabulated below determine suitable values for A and B:

$\dfrac{b}{t}\beta$	$\dfrac{t}{w\beta}$	$\dfrac{b}{t}\beta$	$\dfrac{t}{w\beta}$
1.8433	0.5538	0.9551	0.7588
1.7182	0.2917	1.0410	0.7113
1.7512	0.2364	1.3676	0.6217
1.6393	0.2063	1.4553	0.5538
1.5885	0.1955	0.3869	1.9492
0.9715	0.9648	0.7577	1.0467
1.4541	0.5410	1.1126	0.8601
1.7126	0.4064	1.2096	0.7597
1.4573	0.3513	0.7210	1.3694
0.6569	1.4195		

25.3.6.   It can be shown that the total force acting on a submerged surface is equal to the area of the surface times the water pressure at the centroid of the surface. Thus

$$F_H = A \cdot \bar{c} \cdot \gamma$$

where A is the area of the surface, c is the depth of water to the centroid and γ is the unit weight of water. Determine the total force acting on the sluice gate shown.

25.3.7.   Provide a graphic solution for the following: The probable error is defined as the maximum error that will occur 50% of the time. That is, the actual error will be less than the probable error at least 50% of the time. The probable error can be calculated using the expression

$$E = 0.6745 \sqrt{\frac{v^2}{n-1}}$$

where v^2 = sum of the squares of the deviations from the mean
n = number of observations

25.3.8.   Subsidence is the term used to describe the deformation of the ground surface due to motion of a granular material beneath the surface. This motion can be caused when a cavity is filled in by surrounding material. Experiments[3] were performed to determine the shape of the deformation at the surface. From the data tabulated below determine an expression relating relative subsidence Sr to the horizontal distance from the point of greatest depression. Relative subsidence is defined as $Sr = Sez/Seo$, where Seo is the subsidence at $z = 0$. Try an equation of the form

$$Sr = Ae^{Bz\gamma},$$

for different integer values of γ.

Sr	z	Sr	z
1.00	0.0	.50	0.60
.94	0.15	.33	0.75
.82	0.30	.16	0.90
.66	0.45	.08	1.05

25.3.9.   Provide a graphic solution for the following: The relationship between horsepower (hp) and torque is given by the relationship

$$T_m = \frac{63{,}024 \text{ hp}}{N}$$

where T_m = torque, in.-lb
N = revolutions of shaft per minute

25.3.10.   Physical constraints on the form of the mathematical relationship between variables should be recognized and used to simplify the process of curve fitting. The following data were found from a uniaxial tension test on a steel bar. State the physical constraints on the relationship and indicate the limits of applicability of the equation.

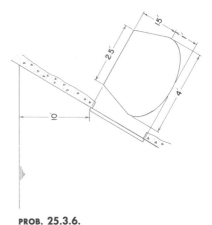

PROB. 25.3.6.

Load, lb P	Elongation, in. e	Load, lb P	Elongation, in. e
580	0.001	6850	0.010
1300	0.002	7700	0.011
1980	0.003	8200	0.012
2680	0.004	9050	0.013
3400	0.005	9550	0.014
4100	0.006	10250	0.188
4950	0.007	11150	0.250
5650	0.008	11770	0.313
6300	0.009		

[3] Arnold L. Sweet, "Validity of a Stochastic Model for Predicting Subsidence," *Journal of the Engineering Mechanics Division, ASCE*, vol. 91, no. EM2, Dec., 1965, pp. 111–128.

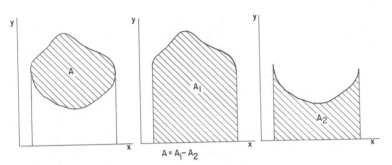

PROB. 25.3.11A.

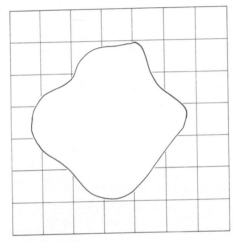

PROB. 25.3.11B.

25.3.11. Graphical integration can be used to determine the area of an irregular plane figure. Since the process of graphical integration is set up to determine the area between a curve and an axis, direct application of this method to the problem of the area of a plane figure is difficult. This difficulty can be overcome, however, if the boundary of the figure is broken into two curves at the limits of the figure. The area between each of these curves and the axis can be determined by the usual method of graphical integration. The desired area of the irregular figure will be the difference between these two areas. Problem 25.3.11A illustrates the procedure. Determine the area of the closed curve shown in Prob. 25.3.11B.

25.3.12. The centroid of a plane figure is defined as the center of the area. Since a point can be located by the intersection of two lines, the problem of finding the centroid of a plane figure reduces to finding the position of at least two lines passing through the centroid. The position of a line passing through the centroid is defined mathematically as

$$\bar{C} = \frac{\int_{c_1}^{c_2} C \cdot dA}{\int_{c_1}^{c_2} dA}$$

where C indicates the distance from an infinitesimal area dA to the reference axis and $\bar{C}$ is the distance from the reference axis to the centroid. To evaluate the first moment of the area about the axis ($\int C\,dA$) a curve must be plotted with ordinates equal to $C \cdot \Delta A$. See the figure for Prob. 25.3.12. Determine the centroid of the bulb channel shown in Prob. 25.3.13B.

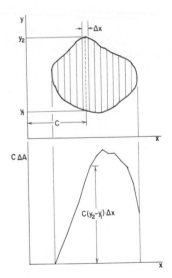

PROB. 25.3.12.

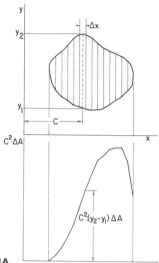

PROB. 25.3.13A.

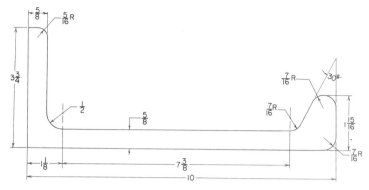

PROB. 25.3.13B.

25.3.13.   The first moment of an area is used to determine the position of the centroid of the area. The second moment of inertia has applications in engineering mechanics. It is defined mathematically as

$$I = \int_{C_1}^{C_2} C^2 \, dA$$

The graphical evaluation of this integral is similar to the evaluation of the first moment with the exception that a curve is plotted with ordinates equal to $C^2 \cdot \Delta A$. The illustration for Prob. 25.3.13A gives the details.

Determine the moment of inertia about a vertical axis through the centroid of the bulb channel shown in the illustration for Prob. 25.3.13B.

25.3.14.   Provide a graphic solution for the following: It is necessary for railway engineers to know both the distance and time required for a train to accelerate (decelerate) from one speed to another. The equations used in this determination are listed below. It should be recognized that these equations are only satisfactory for increments of speed less than 5 mph.

$$S = 70.2 \frac{(V_2^2 - V_1^2)}{a}$$

$$t = 95.7 \frac{(V_2 - V_1)}{a}$$

where S = distance required to accelerate from one speed to another, ft

t = time required to accelerate from one speed to another, sec

V_2 and V_1 = speeds, mph

a = accelerating force, lb/ton of total train weight

25.3.15.   Some physical relationships can be rectified over only a limited portion of their range. Experiments were performed to determine the relationship between the coefficient of contraction C_d, a measure of fluid discharge through an orifice, and the Reynolds number R, a parameter which characterizes the relative importance of viscous action. From a rectified plot of the data given below determine a suitable relationship and state its limits of applicability.

R	C_d	R	C_d
0.6	0.12	20.	0.64
0.8	0.14	40.	0.81
1.0	0.16	60.	0.90
1.9	0.20	80.	0.96
4.	0.3	100.	1.0
6.	0.37	200.	1.11
8.	0.43	400.	1.2
10.	0.49		

25.3.16. Provide a graphic solution for the following: In measuring distances with a steel tape an error is introduced in the measurement due to the sag of the tape. The correction to compensate for this error can be calculated using the formula:

$$C_s = \frac{w^2 l^3}{24 P^2}$$

where C_s = the correction for sag of tape between supports, ft
w = the weight of the tape per foot, lb/ft
l = the distance between supports, ft
P = the tension applied to the tape, lb
Range of w from 0.01 to 0.02 lb/ft. Range of P from 5 to 30 lb. Range of 1 from 20 to 100 ft.

25.3.17. Measurements of the capillary rise of water in manometer tubes were taken and recorded in table. Compare your fitted equation to the theoretical relationship for an air-water system. The theoretical relationship is

$$y = \frac{0.046}{D}$$

for water at 20°C.

Rise, in.	Tube diameter, in.
y	D
0.0840	0.22
0.0410	0.39
0.0180	0.53
0.0088	0.78
0.0010	1.11

25.3.18. The profile of a river bed was found by taking elevations of the bed with respect to a fixed datum at intervals of 10 ft. If the elevation of the water surface is 30 ft above the datum, determine the cross-sectional area of the river. What is the change in area if the water elevation increases to 45 ft?

Station	Elevation, ft	Station	Elevation, ft
0	59.5	11	12.5
1	58.0	12	13.5
2	53.5	13	17.5
3	48.0	14	33.5
4	43.0	15	37.5
5	37.0	16	41.0
6	31.5	17	44.5
7	23.0	18	47.5
8	20.0	19	52.0
9	17.5	20	57.5
10	15.0	21	60.5

25.3.19. Provide a graphic solution for the following: To produce the centripetal force necessary for nonlinear motion, railway engineers superelevate the outer rail of the track an amount dependent on the speed of the train and the radius of the curve. The equation used to evaluate this distance is:

$$E = 3.95 \frac{V^2}{R}$$

where E = the elevation of the outer rail, in.
V = the speed of the train, mph
R = the radius of the curve, ft

25.3.20. It is quite important to know the peak flows of a river basin because of an increasing concern with flooding and flood-control projects. The flow is a function of many factors among which are rainfall, the evaporation rate of the standing water, and the percentage of water absorbed into underground springs. Since this problem has so many variables, a statistical approach is often used in which the peak flow expected becomes a function of the area which drains into this particular river and the probability of rainfall for the period under study. The following data have been collected. From these data derive the empirical equations for 5-, 10- and 25-year peak flows.

Area, mi²	Flow, ft³/sec × 10³		
	5-year	10-year	25-year
20	2.1	2.6	3.0
50	3.7	4.5	5.5
100	6.0	7.0	8.7
500	17.0	20.0	25.0
1000	26.0	32.0	39.0
2000	40.0	50.0	60.0

25.3.21. A highway is to be built across irregular terrain. Elevations have been taken at 100-ft intervals along the center line of the proposed route and are tabulated below. The highway will start at station 1 + 0 at an elevation of 212 ft and proceed upward at a slope of 5% to station 11 + 0. From station 11 + 0 to station 15 + 0 there will be a vertical curve. Parabolas are used for vertical curves because they are easier to lay out in the field than circular arcs. From station $15 + 0$ the road descends at a slope of 2.5% to station $20 + 0$ where this section ends at an elevation of 253 ft. Determine the quantities of earth which must be removed or filled to construct the road. Assume cuts and fills are 100 ft wide and have vertical sides.

Station	Elevation	Station	Elevation
$1 + 0$	203	$11 + 0$	273
$2 + 0$	204	$12 + 0$	278
$3 + 0$	207	$13 + 0$	279
$4 + 0$	212	$14 + 0$	279
$5 + 0$	218	$15 + 0$	275
$6 + 0$	232	$16 + 0$	269
$7 + 0$	245	$17 + 0$	264
$8 + 0$	255	$18 + 0$	258
$9 + 0$	262	$19 + 0$	253
$10 + 0$	269	$20 + 0$	250

25.3.22. Provide a graphic solution for the following: The Manning formula is used to determine the velocity of flow in open channels. The formula applies only to steady uniform flow. The equation is

$$V = \frac{1.486}{n} R^{2/3} S^{1/2}$$

where V = the velocity of flow, ft/sec
R = the hydraulic radius, which is the ratio of the flow cross section to the wetted perimeter of the channel
S = the slope of the channel, ft/1000 ft
n = Manning's coefficient, a parameter which describes the relative roughness of the channel; n assumes values from 0.009 (very smooth) to 0.10 (very rough)

25.3.23. Highway engineers are interested in four properties of asphaltic materials in pavement design: (1) consistency, (2) variation in consistency with temperature, (3) durability, and (4) adhesiveness. The variation in consistency with temperature is very important since it affects not only the quality of the pavement over wide temperature ranges but affects mixing procedures as well. Viscosity is a measure of this consistency and has been found to vary with temperature. In the data tabulated below, notice that several readings of the dependent variable were taken so that the range of probable values could be identified. Find the limiting equations that define the region described by the given data.

Temperature, °F	Viscosity, stokes
80	2000000
80	1000000
80	900000
140	3000
140	2000
140	1500
210	50
210	40
210	25
350	1
350	0.7
350	0.5

25.3.24. The average value of a function $f(x)$ between the ordinates x_1 and x_2 is defined mathematically by

$$f(x)_{av} = \frac{1}{x_2 - x_1} \int_{x_1}^{x_2} f(x) \, dx$$

where $f(x)_{av}$ represents the average ordinate. Determine the average value of the function defined as follows.

$$f(x) = 2 \sin x, \qquad (0 \leq x \leq 0.5)$$
$$f(x) = 2x, \qquad (0.5 \leq x \leq 2.5)$$
$$f(x) = 3 - 0.6x, \qquad (2.5 \leq x \leq 5)$$

25.3.25. Provide a graphic solution for the following: The shear stress on an oblique plane of a bar subjected to an axial force can be found from the equation:

$$S_s = \frac{P}{2A} \sin 2\theta$$

where S_s = the shear stress, psi
P = the axial force, lb
A = the cross-sectional area of the bar, in.^{2}
θ = the angle which the plane makes with the axis of the bar

25.3.26. Industrial engineering studies have shown that labor-time relationships can be utilized in the optimization of production systems. One such study was concerned with the reduction in production time as the worker became more familiar with the operation. The performance of several operators was studied and the average production values for the group are presented below. What is the relationship between units produced and the average man-hours required to produce the unit?

Units produced	Average man-hours/unit
10	12.5
30	8.8
50	7.6
80	6.6
100	6.2
200	5.0
300	4.4
400	4.0
500	3.8
600	3.6
700	3.4
800	3.3
900	3.2
1000	3.1

25.3.27. Evaluate graphically the value of the integral

$$Q = \int_{-1}^{+1} \frac{dx}{(1 + 2x^2)^2}$$

Check your answer mathematically.

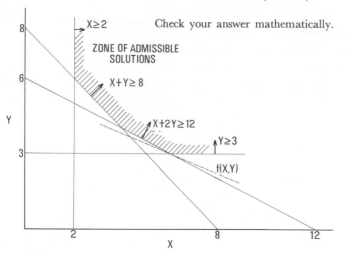

25.3.28. Problems in linear programming involve minimizing a function of several variables subject to a number of constraints on the variables. Problems involving two variables can be solved graphically. The following example will illustrate the procedure:

Minimize the function

$$f(x, y) = 2x + 5y = q,$$

for
$$x \geq 2$$
$$y \geq 3$$
$$x + y \geq 8$$
$$x + 2y \geq 12$$

The problem is to find acceptable values of x and y which will minimize the function $f(x, y)$. From the constraints it is immediately apparent that values of $x < 2$ and $y < 3$ are unacceptable. This fact is shown graphically in the figure. By plotting the two other equations of constraint the zone of acceptable solutions can be seen. Any point in this zone satisfies the four constraints. There is, however, only one point that will both satisfy the constraints and minimize the function. The function is a straight line with a slope of $-2/5$. If a line with this slope is plotted on the figure so that it just touches the acceptable zone, values of x and y which minimize the function will be found at the point of contact. From the illustration we get $x = 6$ and $y = 3$, to give $q = 27$. This is the smallest value for q which can be calculated using acceptable values of x and y.

A company has two warehouses which can supply a vendor. The vendor requires at least 50 units per month. Warehouse A has 40 units on hand and warehouse B has 25. If it costs $10 per unit to ship from warehouse A and $7.50 per unit from B what number should be shipped from each warehouse to minimize shipping costs?

What will be the effect on costs of a new union ruling that not more than 40% of the total can come from warehouse B?

PROB. 25.3.28.

25.3.29. Due to the high degree of competition in the construction industry, cost analyses must be made regularly so that bidding can be as accurate as possible. For construction machinery this requires that records be kept of both original and operating costs. The data below represent the cumulative costs for a tractor. These values are the totals spent up to a specific date for the initial cost and maintenance expenses. Graphically determine the original outlay for the machine and the expression for the maintenance costs. What is the equation that defines the total cumulative costs as shown?

End of year	Costs to date	End of year	Costs to date
1	$13,460	6	20,760
2	14,920	7	22,220
3	16,380	8	23,680
4	17,840	9	25,140
5	19,300	10	26,600

25.3.30. The illustration gives a velocity-versus-time diagram for an automobile. Construct acceleration-versus-time and displacement-versus-time diagrams.

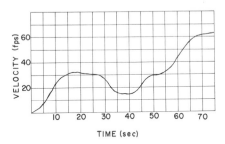

PROB. **25.3.30.**

25.3.31. It can be shown (see any text on strength of materials) that the deflection, curvature, bending moment, shear, and load on a beam are related mathematically by the expressions:

Curvature

$$\theta = \frac{dy}{dx}$$

Bending moment

$$\frac{M}{EI} = \frac{d\theta}{dx} = \frac{d^2y}{dx^2}$$

Shear

$$V = \frac{dM}{dx} = EI\frac{d^2\theta}{dx^2} = EI\frac{d^3y}{dx^3}$$

Load

$$Q = \frac{dV}{dx} = \frac{d^2M}{dx^2} = EI\frac{d^3\theta}{dx^3} = EI\frac{d^4y}{dx^4}$$

where EI is a constant depending upon the material properties and the cross section of the beam.

By successive integration determine the deflected shape of the beam shown in the illustration for Prob. 25.3.31. Note the boundary conditions (constants of integration) $M = 0$ at $x = 0, 1$; $y = 0$ at $x = 0, 1$.

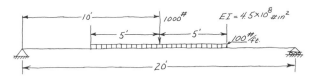

PROB. **25.3.31.**

APPENDIXES

Glossary

PART A. SHOP TERMS

anneal (*v.*)   To soften a metal piece and remove internal stresses by heating to its critical temperature and allowing to cool very slowly.

arc-weld (*v.*)   To weld by electric-arc process.

bore (*v.*)   To enlarge a hole with a boring tool, as in a lathe or boring mill. Distinguished from *drill*.

boss (*n.*)   A projection of circular cross section, as on a casting or forging.

braze (*v.*)   To join by the use of hard solder.

broach (*v.*)   To finish the inside of a hole to a shape usually other than round. (*n.*) A tool with serrated edges pushed or pulled through a hole to enlarge it to a required shape.

buff (*v.*)   To polish with abrasive on a cloth wheel or other soft carrier.

burnish (*v.*)   To smooth or polish by a rolling or sliding tool under pressure.

bushing (*n.*)   A removable sleeve or liner for a bearing; also a guide for a tool in a jig or fixture.

carburize (*v.*)   To prepare a low-carbon steel for heat-treatment by packing in a box with carbonizing material, such as wood charcoal, and heating to about 2000°F for several hours, then allowing to cool slowly.

caseharden (*v.*)   To harden the surface of carburized steel by heating to critical temperature and quenching, as in an oil or lead bath.

castellate (*v.*)   To form into a shape resembling a castle battlement, as castellated nut. Often applied to a shaft with multiple integral keys milled on it.

chamfer (*v.*)   To bevel a sharp external edge. (*n.*) A beveled edge.

Boss

Bushing

Chamfer

Counterbore

Countersink

Fillet

Flange

Kerf

chase (*v.*)　To cut threads in a lathe, as distinguished from cutting threads with a die. (*n.*) A slot or groove.

chill (*v.*)　To harden the surface of cast iron by sudden cooling against a metal mold.

chip (*v.*)　To cut or clean with a chisel.

coin (*v.*)　To stamp and form a metal piece in one operation, usually with a surface design.

cold-work (*v.*)　To deform metal stock by hammering, forming, drawing, etc., while the metal is at ordinary room temperature.

color-harden (*v.*)　To caseharden to a very shallow depth, chiefly for appearance.

core (*v.*)　To form the hollow part of a casting, using a solid form made of sand, shaped in a core box, baked, and placed in the mold. After cooling, the core is easily broken up, leaving the casting hollow.

counterbore (*v.*)　To enlarge a hole to a given depth. (*n.*) 1. The cylindrical enlargement of the end of a drilled or bored hole. 2. A cutting tool for counterboring, having a piloted end the size of the drilled hole.

countersink (*v.*)　To form a depression to fit the conic head of a screw or the thickness of a plate so that the face will be level with the surface. (*n.*) A conic tool for countersinking.

crown (*n.*)　Angular or rounded contour, as on the face of a pulley.

die (*n.*)　1. One of a pair of hardened metal blocks for forming, impressing, or cutting out a desired shape. 2 (thread). A tool for cutting external threads. Opposite of *tap*.

die casting (*n.*)　A very accurate and smooth casting made by pouring a molten alloy (or composition, as Bakelite) usually under pressure into a metal mold or die. Distinguished from a casting made in sand.

die stamping (*n.*)　A piece, usually of sheet metal, formed or cut out by a die.

draw (*v.*)　1. To form by a distorting or stretching process. 2. To temper steel by gradual or intermittent quenching.

drill (*v.*)　To sink a hole with a drill, usually a twist drill. (*n.*) A pointed cutting tool rotated under pressure.

drop forging (*n.*)　A wrought piece formed hot between dies under a drop hammer, or by pressure.

face (*v.*)　To machine a flat surface perpendicular to the axis of rotation on a lathe. Distinguished from *turn*.

feather (*n.*)　A flat sliding key, usually fastened to the hub.

fettle (*v.*)　To remove fins and smooth the corners on unfired ceramic products.

file (*v.*)　To finish or trim with a file.

fillet (*n.*)　A rounded filling of the internal angle between two surfaces.

fin (*n.*)　A thin projecting rib. Also, excess ridge of material.

fit (*n.*)　The kind of contact between two machined surfaces. 1. *Drive, force,* or *press:* When the shaft is slightly larger than the hole and must be forced in with sledge or power press. 2. *Shrink:* When the shaft is slightly larger than the hole, the piece containing the hole is heated, thereby expanding the hole sufficiently to slip over the shaft. On cooling, the shaft will be seized firmly if the fit allowances have been correctly proportioned. 3. *Running* or *sliding:* When sufficient allowance has been made between sizes of shaft and hole to allow free running without seizing or heating. 4. *Wringing:* When the allowance is smaller than a running fit and the shaft will enter the hole by twisting it by hand.

flange (*n.*)　A projecting rim or edge for fastening or stiffening.

forge (*v.*)　To shape metal while hot and plastic by a hammering or forcing process either by hand or by machine.

galvanize (*v.*)　To treat with a bath of lead and zinc to prevent rusting.

graduate (*v.*)　To divide a scale or dial into regular spaces.

grind (*v.*)　To finish or polish a surface by means of an abrasive wheel.

harden (*v.*)　To heat hardenable steel above critical temperature and quench in bath.

hot-work (*v.*)　To deform metal stock by hammering, forming, drawing, etc., while the metal is heated to a plastic state.

kerf (*n.*)　The channel or groove cut by a saw or other tool.

key (*n.*)   A small block or wedge inserted between shaft and hub to prevent circumferential movement.

keyway, key seat (*n.*)   A groove or slot cut to fit a key. A key fits into a key seat and slides in a keyway.

knurl (*v.*)   To roughen or indent a turned surface, as a knob or handle.

lap (*n.*)   A piece of soft metal, wood, or leather charged with abrasive material, used for obtaining an accurate finish. (*v.*) To finish by lapping.

lug (*n.*)   A projecting "ear," usually rectangular in cross section. Distinguished from *boss*.

malleable casting (*n.*)   An ordinary casting toughened by annealing. Applicable to small castings with uniform metal thicknesses.

mill (*v.*)   To machine with rotating toothed cutters on a milling machine.

neck (*v.*)   To cut a groove around a shaft, usually near the end or at a change in diameter. (*n.*) A portion reduced in diameter between the ends of a shaft.

normalize (*v.*)   To remove internal stresses by heating a metal piece to its critical temperature and allowing to cool very slowly.

pack-harden (*v.*)   To carburize and case-harden.

pad (*n.*)   A shallow projection. Distinguished from *boss* by shape or size.

peen (*v.*)   To stretch, rivet, or clinch over by strokes with the peen of a hammer. (*n.*) The end of a hammer head opposite the face, as *ball peen*.

pickle (*v.*)   To clean castings or forgings in a hot weak sulfuric acid bath.

plane (*v.*)   To machine work on a planer having a fixed tool and reciprocating bed.

planish (*v.*)   To finish sheet metal by hammering with polished-faced hammers.

plate (*v.*)   The electrochemical coating of a metal piece with a different metal.

polish (*v.*)   To make smooth or lustrous by friction with a very fine abrasive.

profile (*v.*)   To machine an outline with a rotary cutter usually controlled by a master cam or die.

punch (*v.*)   To perforate by pressing a non-rotating tool through the work.

ream (*v.*)   To finish a drilled or punched hole very accurately with a rotating fluted tool of the required diameter.

relief (*n.*)   The amount one plane surface of a piece is set below or above another plane, usually for clearance or for economy in machining.

rivet (*v.*)   1. To fasten with rivets. 2. To batter or upset the headless end of a pin used as a permanent fastening.

round (*n.*)   A rounded exterior corner between two surfaces. Compare with *fillet*.

sandblast (*v.*)   To clean castings or forgings by means of sand driven through a nozzle by compressed air.

shape (*v.*)   To machine with a shaper, a machine tool differing from a planer in that the work is stationary and the tool reciprocating.

shear (*v.*)   To cut off sheet or bar metal between two blades.

sherardize (*v.*)   To galvanize with zinc by a dry heating process.

shim (*n.*)   A thin spacer of sheet metal used for adjusting.

shoulder (*n.*)   A plane surface on a shaft, normal to the axis and formed by a difference in diameter.

spin (*v.*)   To shape sheet metal by forcing it against a form as it revolves.

spline (*n.*)   A long keyway. Sometimes also a flat key.

spot-face (*v.*)   To finish a round spot on a rough surface, usually around a drilled hole, to give a good seat to a screw or bolthead, cut, usually 1/16 in. deep, by a rotating milling cutter.

spot-weld (*v.*)   To weld in spots by means of the heat of resistance to an electric current. Not applicable to sheet copper or brass.

steel casting (*n.*)   Material used in machine construction. It is ordinary cast iron into which varying amounts of scrap steel have been added in the melting.

swage (*v.*)   To shape metal by hammering or pressure with the aid of a form or anvil called a "swage block."

Keyway

Key and seat

Lug

Neck

Pad

Round

Spline

Spot-face

sweat (*v.*)   To join metal pieces by clamping together with solder between and applying heat.

tack-weld (*v.*)   To join at the edge by welding in short intermittent sections.

tap (*v.*)   To cut threads in a hole with a rotating tool called a "tap," having threads on it and fluted to give cutting edges.

temper (*v.*)   To change the physical characteristics of hardened steel by reheating to a temperature below the critical point and allowing to cool.

template, templet (*n.*)   A flat pattern for laying out shapes, location of holes, etc.

trepan (*v.*)   To cut an outside annular groove around a hole.

tumble (*v.*)   To clean, smooth, or polish castings or forgings in a rotating barrel or drum by friction with each other, assisted by added mediums, as scraps, "jacks," balls, sawdust, etc.

turn (*v.*)   To machine on a lathe. Distinguished from *face*.

undercut (*v.*)   To cut, leaving an overhanging edge. (*n.*) A cut having inwardly sloping sides.

upset (*v.*)   To forge a larger diameter or shoulder on a bar.

weld (*v.*)   To join two pieces by heating them to the fusing point and pressing or hammering together.

Trepan

Undercut

PART B. STRUCTURAL TERMS

bar   Square or round rod; also flat steel up to 6 in. in width.

batten plate   A small plate used to hold two parts in their proper position when made up as one member.

batter   A deviation from the vertical in upright members.

bay   The distance between two trusses or transverse bents.

beam   A horizontal member forming part of the frame of a building or structure.

bearing plate   A steel plate, usually at the base of a column, used to distribute a load over a larger area.

bent   A vertical framework usually consisting of a truss or beam supported at the ends on columns.

brace   A diagonal member used to stiffen a framework.

buckle plate   A flat plate with dished depression pressed into it to give transverse strength.

built-up member   A member built from standard shapes to give one single stronger member.

camber   Slight upward curve given to trusses and girders to avoid effect of sag.

cantilever   A beam, girder, or truss overhanging one or both supports.

chord   The principal member of a truss on either the top or bottom.

clearance   Rivet driving clearance is distance from center of rivet to obstruction. Erection clearance is amount of space left between members for ease in assembly.

clevis   U-shaped shackle for connecting a rod to a pin.

clip angle   A small angle used for fastening various members together.

column   A vertical compression member.

cope   To cut out top or bottom of flanges and web so that one member will frame into another.

coping   A projecting top course of concrete or stone.

counters   Diagonal members in a truss to provide for reversal of shear due to live load.

cover plate   A plate used in building up flanges, in a built-up member, to give greater strength and area or for protection.

crimp   To offset the end of a stiffener to fit over the leg of an angle.

diagonals   Diagonal members used for stiffening and wind bracing.

dowel   An iron or wooden pin extending into, but not through, two timbers to connect them.

driftpin   A tapered steel pin used to bring rivet holes fair in assembling steel work.

edge distance   The distance from center of rivet to edge of plate or flange.

fabricate   To cut, punch, and subassemble members in the shop.

fillers Either plate or ring fills used to take up space in riveting two members where a gusset is not used.

flange The projecting portion of a beam, channel, or column.

gage line The center line for rivet holes.

gin pole A guyed mast with block at the top for hoisting.

girder A horizontal member, either single or built up, acting as a principal beam.

girt A beam usually bolted to columns to support the side covering or serve as window lintels.

gusset plate A plate used to connect various members, such as in a truss.

hip The intersection between two sloping surfaces forming an exterior angle.

knee brace A corner brace used to prevent angular movement.

lacing or lattice bars Bars used diagonally to space and stiffen two parallel members, such as in a built-up column.

laterals Members used to prevent lateral deflection.

lintel A horizontal member used to carry a wall over an opening.

louvers Metal slats either movable or fixed, as in a monitor ventilator.

monitor ventilator A framework that carries fixed or movable louvers at the top of the roof.

panel The space between adjacent floor supports or purlins in a roof.

pitch Center distance between rivets parallel to axis of member. Also, for roofs, the ratio of rise to span.

plate Flat steel over 6 in. in width and ¼ in. or more in thickness.

purlins Horizontal members extending between trusses, used as beams for supporting the roof.

rafters Beams or truss members supporting the purlins.

sag ties Tie rods between purlins in the plane of the roof to carry the component of the roof load parallel to the roof.

separator Either a cast-iron spacer or wrought-iron pipe on a bolt for the purpose of holding members a fixed distance apart.

sheet Flat steel over 6 in. in width and less than ¼ in. in thickness.

shim A thin piece of wood or steel placed under a member to bring it to a desired elevation.

sleeve nut A long nut with right and left threads for connecting two rods to make an adjustable member.

span Distance between centers of supports of a truss, beam, or girder.

splice A longitudinal connection between the parts of a continuous member.

stiffener Angle, plate, or channel riveted to a member to prevent buckling.

stringer A longitudinal member used to support loads directly.

strut A compression member in a framework.

truss A rigid framework for carrying loads, formed in a series of triangles.

turnbuckle A coupling, threaded right and left or swiveled on one end, for adjustably connecting two rods.

valley The intersection between two sloping surfaces, forming a reentrant angle.

web The part of a channel, I beam, or girder between the flanges.

PART C. ARCHITECTURAL TERMS

apron The finished board placed against the wall surface, immediately below a window stool.

ashlar Thin, squared, and dressed stone facing of a masonry wall.

backing The inner portion of a wall; that which is used behind the facing.

batten A strip of wood used for nailing across two other pieces of wood to hold them together and cover a crack.

batter boards Boards set up at the corners of a proposed building from which the lines marking off the walls are stretched.

bearing wall A wall that supports loads other than its own weight.

bond The joining together of building materials to ensure solidity.

bridging The braces or system of bracing used between joists or other structural members to stiffen them and to distribute the load.

centering   A substructure of temporary nature, usually of timber or planks, on which a masonry arch or vault is built.

coffer   An ornamental panel deeply recessed, usually in a dome or portico ceiling.

corbel   A bracket formed on a wall by building out successive courses of masonry.

curtain wall   A wall that carries no building load other than its own weight.

fenestration   The arrangement and proportioning of window and door openings.

flashing   The sheet metal built into the joints of a wall, or covering the valleys, ridges, and hips of a roof for the purpose of preventing leakage.

footing   A course or series of courses projecting at the base of a wall for the purpose of distributing the load from above over a greater area, thereby preventing excessive settlement.

furring   The application of thin wood, metal, or other building material to a wall, beam, ceiling, or the like to level a surface for lathing, boarding, etc., or to make an air space within a wall.

glazing   The act of furnishing or fitting with glass.

ground   Strips of wood, flush with the plastering, to which moldings, etc., are attached. Grounds are usually installed first and the plastering floated flush with them.

grout   A thin mortar used for filling up spaces where heavier mortar will not penetrate.

head   The horizontal piece forming the top of a wall opening, as a door or window.

hip   The intersection of two roof surfaces, which form on the plan an external angle.

jamb   The vertical piece forming the side of a wall opening.

lintel   The horizontal structural member that supports the wall over an opening.

millwork   The finish woodwork, machined and in some cases partly assembled at the mill.

miter   To match together, as two pieces of molding, on a line bisecting the angle of junction.

mullion   A vertical division of a window opening.

muntin   The thin members that separate the individual lights of glass in a window frame.

party wall   A division wall common to two adjacent pieces of property.

plate   A horizontal member that carries other structural members; usually the top timber of a wall that carries the roof trusses or rafters directly.

rail   A horizontal piece in a frame or paneling.

return   The continuation in a different direction, most often at right angles, of the face of a building or any member, as a colonnade or molding; applied to the shorter in contradistinction to the longer.

reveal   The side of a wall opening; the whole thickness of the wall; the jamb.

riser   The upright piece of a step, from tread to tread.

saddle   A small double-sloping roof to carry water away from behind chimneys, etc.

scratch coat   The first coat in plastering, roughened by scratching or scoring so that the next coat will firmly adhere to it.

screeds   A strip of plaster of the thickness proposed for the work, applied to the wall at intervals of 4 or 5 ft, to serve as guides.

shoring   A prop, as a timber, placed against the side of a structure; a prop placed beneath anything, as a beam, to prevent sinking or sagging.

sill   The horizontal piece, as a timber, which forms the lowest member of a frame.

sleepers   The timbers laid on a firm foundation to carry and secure the superstructure.

soffit   The underside of subordinate parts and members of buildings, such as staircases, beams, arches, etc.

stile   A vertical piece in a frame or paneling.

stool   The narrow shelf fitted on the inside of a window against the actual sill.

threshold   The stone, wood, or metal piece that lies directly under a door.

trap   A water seal in a sewage system to prevent sewer gas from entering the building.

tread The upper horizontal piece of a step, on which the foot is placed.

valley The intersection of two roof surfaces which form, on the plan, a reentrant angle.

PART D. WELDING TERMS

air-acetylene welding A gas-welding process in which coalescence is produced by heating with a gas flame or flames obtained from the combustion of acetylene with air, without the application of pressure and with or without the use of filler metal.

arc cutting A group of cutting processes in which the severing of metals is effected by melting with the heat of an arc between an electrode and the base metal.

arc welding A group of welding processes in which coalescence is produced by heating with an electric arc or arcs, with or without the application of pressure and with or without the use of filler metal.

As-welded The condition of weld metal, welded joints, and weldments after welding prior to any subsequent thermal or mechanical treatment.

atomic-hydrogen welding An arc-welding process in which coalescence is produced by heating with an electric arc maintained between two metal electrodes in an atmosphere of hydrogen. Shielding is obtained from the hydrogen. Pressure may or may not be used, and filler metal may or may not be used.

automatic welding Welding with equipment which performs the entire welding operation without constant observation and adjustment of the controls by an operator. The equipment may or may not perform the loading and unloading of the work.

axis of a weld A line through the length of a weld, perpendicular to the cross section at its center of gravity.

backing Material (metal, weld metal, asbestos, carbon, granular flux, etc.) backing up the joint during welding to facilitate obtaining a sound weld at the root.

bevel A type of edge preparation.

braze A weld in which coalescence is produced by heating to suitable temperatures above 800°F and by using a nonferrous filler metal having a melting point below that of the base metals. The filler metal is distributed between the closely fitted surfaces of the joint by capillary attraction.

butt joint A joint between two members lying approximately in the same plane.

coalesce To unite or merge into a single body or mass. Fusion.

die welding A forge-welding process in which coalescence is produced by heating in a furnace and by applying pressure by means of dies.

edge joint A joint between the edges of two or more parallel or nearly parallel members.

filler metal Metal to be added in making a weld.

fillet weld A weld of approximately triangular cross section joining two surfaces approximately at right angles to each other in a lap joint, tee joint, or corner joint.

forge welding A group of welding processes in which coalescence is produced by heating in a forge or other furnace and by applying pressure or blows.

fusion The melting together of filler metal and base metal, or of base metal only, which results in coalescence.

gas welding A group of welding processes in which coalescence is produced by heating with a gas flame or flames, with or without the application of pressure, and with or without the use of filler metal.

groove weld A weld made in the groove between two members to be joined. The standard types of groove welds are: square-groove weld; single-V-groove weld; single-bevel-groove weld; single-U-groove weld; single-J-groove weld; double-V-groove weld; double-bevel-groove weld; double-U-groove weld; double-J-groove weld.

hammer welding A forge-welding process in which coalescence is produced by heating in a forge or other furnace and by applying pressure by means of hammer blows.

intermittent welding Welding in which the

continuity is broken by recurring unwelded spaces.

joint penetration   The minimum depth a groove weld extends from its face into a joint, exclusive of reinforcement.

kerf   The space from which metal has been removed by a cutting process.

lap joint   A joint between two overlapping members.

oxy-acetylene welding   A gas-welding process in which coalescence is produced by heating with a gas flame or flames obtained from a combustion of acetylene with oxygen, with or without the application of pressure and with or without the use of filler metal.

peening   The mechanical working of metals by means of hammer blows.

plug weld   A circular weld made by either arc or gas welding through one member of a lap or tee joint joining that member to the other. The weld may or may not be made through a hole in the first member.

pressure welding   Any welding process or method in which pressure is used to complete the weld.

projection welding   A resistance-welding process in which coalescence is produced by the heat obtained from resistance to the flow of electric current through the work parts held together under pressure by electrodes.

root opening   The separation between the members to be joined, at the root of the joint.

seam weld   A weld consisting of a series of overlapping spot welds, made by seam welding or spot welding.

slot weld   A weld made in an elongated hole in one member of a lap or tee joint joining that member to the portion of the surface of the other member which is exposed through the hole.

spot welding   A resistance-welding process in which coalescence is produced by the heat obtained from resistance to the flow of electric current through the work parts, which are held together under pressure by electrodes.

tack weld   A weld made to hold parts of a weldment in proper alignment until the final welds are made.

tee joint   A joint between two members located approximately at right angles to each other in the form of a T.

upset welding   A resistance-welding process in which coalescence is produced, simultaneously over the entire area of abutting surfaces or progressively along a joint, by the heat obtained from resistance to the flow of electric current through the area of contact of those surfaces. Pressure is applied before heating is started and is maintained throughout the heating period.

Bibliography of Allied Subjects

The following classified list is given to supplement this book, whose scope as a general treatise on engineering drawing permits only the mention or brief explanation of some subjects.

AERONAUTICAL DRAFTING AND DESIGN

Anderson, Newton, H.: "Aircraft Layout and Detail Design," 2d ed., McGraw-Hill, New York, 1946.

ARCHITECTURAL DRAWING

Crane, T.: "Architectural Construction," 2d ed., Wiley, New York, 1956.

Kenney, Joseph E., and John P. McGrail: "Architectural Drawing for the Building Trades," McGraw-Hill, New York, 1949.

Morgan, Sherley W.: "Architectural Drawing," McGraw-Hill, New York, 1950.

Ramsey, C. G., and H. R. Sleeper: "Architectural Graphic Standards," 5th ed., Wiley, New York, 1956.

Saylor, H. H.: "Dictionary of Architecture," Wiley, New York, 1952.

Sleeper, H. R.: "Architectural Specifications," Wiley, New York, 1940.

DESCRIPTIVE GEOMETRY

Grant, Hiram E.: "Practical Descriptive Geometry," McGraw-Hill, New York, 1952.

Hood, George J., and Albert S. Palmerlee: "Geometry of Engineering Drawing," 5th ed., McGraw-Hill, New York, 1969.

Johnson, L. O., and I. Wladaver: "Elements of Descriptive Geometry," Prentice-Hall, Englewood Cliffs, N.J., 1953.

Paré, E. G., R. O. Loving, and I. L. Hill: "Descriptive Geometry," 2d ed., Macmillan, New York, 1952.

Rowe, C. E., and James Dorr McFarland: "Engineering Descriptive Geometry," 3d ed., Van Nostrand, Princeton, N.J., 1961.

Shupe, Hollie W., and Paul E. Machovina: "A Manual of Engineering Geometry and Graphics for Students and Draftsmen," McGraw-Hill, New York, 1956.

Slaby, S. M.: "Fundamentals of Three-Dimensional Descriptive Geometry," Harcourt Brace, New York, 1968.

Street, W. E.: "Technical Descriptive Geometry," 2d ed., Van Nostrand, Princeton, N.J., 1966.

Warner, Frank M., and Matthew McNeary, "Applied Descriptive Geometry," 5th ed., McGraw-Hill, New York, 1959.

Watts, Earle F., and John T. Rule: "Descriptive Geometry," Prentice-Hall, Englewood Cliffs, N.J., 1946.

Wellman, B. Leighton: "Technical Descriptive Geometry," 2d ed., McGraw-Hill, New York, 1957.

DRAWING-INSTRUMENT CATALOGUES

Theo. Alteneder and Sons, Philadelphia.

Eugene Dietzgen Co., Chicago.

Gramercy Guild Group, Inc., Denver, Colo.

Keuffel & Esser Co., Hoboken, N.J.

The Frederick Post Co., Chicago.

V and E Manufacturing Co., Pasadena, Calif.

ELECTRICAL DRAFTING

Baer, C. J.: "Electrical and Electronic Drawing," McGraw-Hill, New York, 1960.

Bishop, Calvin C., C. T. Gilliam, and Associates: "Electrical Drafting and Design," 3d ed., McGraw-Hill, New York, 1952.

Carini, L. F. B.: "Drafting for Electronics," McGraw-Hill, New York, 1946.

ENGINEERING GRAPHICS

Earle, J. H.: "Engineering Design Graphics," Addison-Wesley, Reading, Mass., 1969.

French, Thomas E., and Charles J. Vierck: "Fundamentals of Engineering Drawing," 2d ed., McGraw-Hill, New York, 1966.

French, Thomas E., and Charles J. Vierck: "Graphic Science," McGraw-Hill, New York, 1958.

French, Thomas E., and Charles J. Vierck: "A Manual of Engineering Drawing for Students and Draftsmen," 10th ed., McGraw-Hill, New York, 1966.

Geisecke, F. E., and others: "Engineering Graphics," Macmillan, New York, 1969.

Giesecke, F. E., A. Mitchell, and H. C. Spencer: "Technical Drawing," 4th ed., Macmillan, New York, 1959.

Healy, W. L., and A. H. Rau: "Simplified Drafting Practice," Wiley, New York, 1953.

Hoelscher, R. P., and C. H. Springer: "Engineering Drawing and Geometry," 2d ed., Wiley, New York, 1961.

Levens, A. S.: "Graphics with an Introduction to Conceptual Design," Wiley, New York, 1962.

Luzadder, W. J.: "Basic Graphics for Design," 2d ed., Prentice-Hall, Englewood Cliffs, N.J., 1968.

Zozzora, Frank: "Engineering Drawing," 2d ed., McGraw-Hill, New York, 1958.

ENGINEERING-GRAPHICS PROBLEM SHEETS

Cooper, Charles D., and Paul E. Machovina: "Engineering Drawing Problems," Series III, 11 × 17, McGraw-Hill, New York, 1960.

Higbee, F. G., and J. M. Russ: "Engineering Drawing Problems," 8½ × 11 in., Wiley, New York, 1955.

Levens, A. S., and A. E. Edstrom: "Problems in Engineering Graphics," Series VI, 8½ × 11 in., McGraw-Hill, New York, 1969.

Vierck, Charles J., and R. I. Hang: "Fundamental Engineering Drawing Problems," 8½ × 11 in., McGraw-Hill, New York, 1960.

Vierck, Charles, J., and R. I. Hang: "Engineering Drawing Problems," 8½ × 11 in., McGraw-Hill, New York, 1960.

Vierck, Charles J., and R. I. Hang: "Graphic Science Problems," 2d ed., 8½ × 11 in., McGraw-Hill, New York, 1963.

GRAPHIC SOLUTIONS

Douglass, Raymond D., and Douglas P. Adams: "Elements of Nomography," McGraw-Hill, New York, 1947.

Levens, A. S.: "Nomography," 2d ed., Wiley, New York, 1959.

Lipka, J.: "Graphical and Mechanical Computation," Wiley, New York, 1918.

HANDBOOKS

A great many handbooks, with tables, formulas, and information, are published for the different branches of the engineering profession, and are useful for ready reference. Handbook formulas and figures should of course be used only with an understanding of the principles upon which they are based. Among the best-known handbooks are the following, alphabetized by title:

"Chemical Engineers' Handbook," 4th ed., Robert H. Perry (ed.), McGraw-Hill, New York, 1963.

"Civil Engineering Handbook," 4th ed., by L. C. Urquhart, Porter, Urquhart, McCreary, and O'Brien, McGraw-Hill, New York, 1959.

"Cutting of Metals," American Society of Mechanical Engineers, New York, 1945.

"Definitions of Occupational Specialties in Engineering," American Society of Mechanical Engineers, New York, 1952.

"Design Data and Methods—Applied Mechanics," American Society of Mehanical Engineers, New York, 1953.

"Dynamics of Automatic Controls," American Society of Mechanical Engineers, New York, 1948.

"Engineering Tables," American Society of Mechancial Engineers, New York, 1956.

"Frequency Response," American Society of Mechanical Engineers, New York, 1956.

"General Engineering Handbook," 2d ed., Charles Edward O'Rourke (ed.), McGraw-Hill, New York, 1940.

"Glossary of Terms in Nuclear Science and Technology," American Society of Mechanical Engineers, New York, 1957.

"Machinery's Handbook," 17th ed., The Industrial Press, New York, 1964.

"Manual on Cutting Metals," American Society of Mechanical Engineers, New York, 1952.

"Manual of Standard Practice for Detailing Reinforced Concrete Structures," American Concrete Institute, Detroit, Mich., 1956.

"Mechanical Engineers' Handbook," 6th ed., Lionel S. Marks (ed.), McGraw-Hill, New York, 1958.

"Mechanical Engineers' Handbook," 12th ed., William Kent (ed.), Wiley, New York, 1950.

"Metals Engineering—Design," 2d ed., American Society of Mechanical Engineers, New York, 1965.

"Metals Properties," American Society of Mechanical Engineers, New York, 1954.

"New American Machinists' Handbook," Rupert Le Grand (ed.), McGraw-Hill, New York, 1955.

"Operation and Flow Process Charts," American Society of Mechanical Engineers, New York, 1949.

"Piping Handbook," 4th ed., by Sabin Crocker, McGraw-Hill, New York, 1945.

"Plant Layout Templates and Models," American Society of Mechanical Engineers, New York, 1949.

"Riveted Joints," American Society of Mechanical Engineers, New York, 1945.

"SAE Handbook," Society of Automotive Engineers, New York, yearly.

"Shock and Vibration Instrumentation," American Society of Mechanical Engineers, New York, 1956.

"Standard Handbook for Electrical Engineers," 9th ed., Archer E. Knowlton (ed.), McGraw-Hill, New York, 1957.

"Steel Castings Handbook," Steel Founders Society of America, Cleveland, Ohio, 1956.

"Steel Construction," American Institute of Steel Construction, New York, 1956.

"Structural Shop Drafting," American Institute of Steel Construction, New York, 1950.

"Tool Engineers' Handbook," 2d ed., Frank W. Wilson (ed.), McGraw-Hill, New York, 1959.

ILLUSTRATION

Hoelscher, Randolph Philip, Clifford Harry Springer, and Richard F. Pohle: "Industrial Production Illustration," 2d ed., McGraw-Hill, New York, 1946.

KINEMATICS AND MACHINE DESIGN

Black, P. H., and O. Eugene Adams, Jr.: "Machine Design," 3d ed., McGraw Hill, New York, 1968.

Faires, V. M.: "Design of Machine Elements," 3d ed., Macmillan, New York, 1955.

Grant, H. E.: "Jigs and Fixtures," McGraw-Hill, New York, 1967.

Guillet, G. L.: "Kinematics of Machines," 5th ed., Willey, New York, 1950.

Ham, C. W., E. J. Crane, and W. L. Rogers: "Mechanics of Machinery," 4th ed., McGraw-Hill, New York, 1958.

Keown, Robert McArdle, and Virgil Moring Faires: "Mechanism," 5th ed., McGraw-Hill, New York, 1960.

Schwamb, Peter, and others: "Elements of Mechanism," Wiley, New York, 1954.

Shigley, J. E.: "Kinematic Analysis of Mechanisms," McGraw-Hill, New York, 1969.

Shigley, J. E.: "Mechanical Engineering Design," McGraw-Hill, New York, 1963.

Vallance, Alex, and Venton L. Doughtie: "Design of Machine Members," 4th ed., McGraw-Hill, New York, 1964.

LETTERING

French, Thomas E., and W. D. Turnbull: "Lessons in Lettering," McGraw-Hill, New York, 1950.

Grant, H. E.: "Engineering and Architectural Lettering," McGraw-Hill, New York, 1960.

MAP AND TOPOGRAPHIC DRAWING

Sloane, Roscoe C., and John M. Montz: "Elements of Topographic Drawing," 2d ed., McGraw-Hill, New York, 1943.

PERSPECTIVE

Lawson, Philip J.: "Practical Perspective Drawing," McGraw-Hill, New York, 1943.

PIPING

See Handbooks, as well as the following:

"Catalogue," Crane Co., Chicago.

"Catalogue," Walworth Company, New York.

Crocker, Sabin: "Piping Handbook," 4th ed., McGraw-Hill, New York, 1945.

Plum, S.: "Plumbing Practice and Design," Wiley, New York, 1943.

SHOP PRACTICE AND TOOLS

See Handbooks, as well as the following:

Boston, O. W.: "Metal Processing," 2d ed., Wiley, New York, 1951.

Burghardt, Henry D., Aaron Axelrod, and James Anderson: "Machine Tool Operation," pt. I, 5th ed., 1959; pt. II, 4th ed., 1960, McGraw-Hill, New York.

Colvin, Fred H., and Lucian L. Haas: "Jigs and Fixtures," 5th ed., McGraw-Hill, New York, 1948.

Hine, Charles R.: "Machine Tools for Engineers," 2d ed., McGraw-Hill, New York, 1959.

Schaller, Gilbert S.: "Engineering Manufacturing Methods," 2d ed., McGraw-Hill, New York, 1959.

STRUCTURAL DRAWING AND DESIGN

See Handbooks, as well as the following:

Bishop, C. T.: "Structural Drafting," Wiley, New York, 1941.

Shedd and Vawter: "Theory of Simple Structures," 2d ed., Wiley, New York, 1941.

Urquhart, L. C., and C. E. O'Rourke: "Design of Steel Structures," McGraw-Hill, New York, 1930.

Urquhart, Leonard C., Charles Edward O'Rourke, George Winter, and A. H. Nilson: "Design of Concrete Structures," 7th ed., McGraw-Hill, New York, 1964.

AMERICAN NATIONAL STANDARDS

The American National Standards Institute, Inc., (ANSI) is working continually on standardization projects. Of its many publications, the following Standards relating to the subjects in this book are now available. A complete list of American National Standards will be sent by the Institute on application to its offices, 1430 Broadway, New York, N.Y. 10018.

AMERICAN NATIONAL STANDARD SAFETY CODES

Code for pressure piping, B31.10—1967

Gas-transmission and distribution piping systems, B31.8—1968

Jacks, B30.1—1952

Mechanical power-transmission apparatus, B15.1—1958

Scheme for identification of piping systems, A13.1—1956

ASME BOILER AND PRESSURE-VESSEL CODES

Material specifications, 1965

Power boilers, 1965

Welding qualifications, 1965

BOLTS, NUTS, RIVETS, AND SCREWS

Hexagonal- and slotted-head cap screws, square-head setscrews, slotted headless setscrews, B18.6.2—1956

High-strength, high-temperature internal wrenching bolts, B18.8—1958

Large rivets, B18.4—1960

Plow bolts, B18.9—1958

Round-head bolts, B18.5—1959

Slotted- and recessed-head wood screws, B18.6.1—1961

Small solid rivets, B18.1—1965

Socket-head cap screws and socket setscrews, B18.3—1961

Square and hexagonal bolts and nuts and lag bolts, B18.2.1—1965

Track bolts and nuts, B18.10—1963

DRAFTING, CHARTS, AND SYMBOLS

Abbreviations for scientific and engineering terms, Z10.1—1941—to be revised as Y1

Abbreviations for use on drawings, Z32.13—1950—to be revised as Y1

Drafting Manual, Y14

    Size and Format, Y14.1—1957

    Line Conventions, Sectioning, and Lettering, Y14.2—1957

    Projections, Y14.3—1957

    Pictorial Drawings, Y14.4—1957

    Dimensioning and Tolerancing for Engineering Drawings, Y14.5—1966

    Screw Threads, Y14.6—1957

    Gears, Splines, and Serrations, Y14.7—1958

    Forging, Y14.9—1958

    Metal Stampings, Y14.10—1959

    Plastics, Y14.11—1958

    Mechanical Assemblies, Y14.14—1961

    Electrical and Electronics Diagrams, Y14.15—1966

    Fluid Power Diagrams, Y14.17—1966

Drawings and drafting-room practice, Z14.1—1946—to be revised as Y14

Graphical symbols for heating, ventilating, and air conditioning, Z32.2.4—1953—to be revised as Y32

Graphical symbols for heat-power apparatus, Z32.2.6—1956—to be revised as Y32

Graphical symbols for pipe fittings, valves, and piping, Z32.2.3—1953 to be revised as Y32

Graphical symbols for plumbing, Y32.4—1955

Graphical symbols for railway use, Y32.7—1957

Graphical symbols for welding and instructions for their use, Y32.3—1959

A guide for preparing technical illustrations for publications and projection, Y15.1—1959

Letters symbols for acoustics, Y10.11—1959

Letter symbols for aeronautical sciences, Y10.7—1954

Letter symbols for chemical engineering, Y10.12—1955

Letter symbols for heat and thermodynamics, including heat flow, Y10.4—1957

Letter symbols for hydraulics, Y10.2—1958

Letter symbols for mechanics of solid bodies, Y10.3—1968

Letter symbols for meteorology, Y10.10—1953

Letter symbols for physics, Z10.6—1948—to be revised as Y10

Letter symbols for radio, Y10.5—1968

Letter symbols for structural analysis, Y10.8—1962

Time series charts, Y15.2—1960

ELECTRICAL DRAWING

Electrical Diagrams Y14.15—1966

Graphical Electrical Symbols for Architectural Plans, Y32.9—1962

Graphical Symbols for Electrical Diagrams, Y32.2—1967

Letter Symbols for Electrical Quantities, Y10.5—1968

GEAR DESIGN, DIMENSIONS, AND INSPECTION

Design for fine-pitch worm gearing, B6.9—1962

Fine-pitch straight bevel gears, B6.8—1950

Nomenclature for gear-tooth wear and failure, B6.12—1964

Spur-gear tooth form, B6.1—1968

System for straight bevel gears, B6.13—1965

Twenty-degree involute fine-pitch system for spur and helical gears, B6.7—1967

MISCELLANEOUS STANDARDS

Indicating pressure and vacuum gages, B40.1—1968

Lock washers, B27.1—1965

Plain washers, B27.2—1965

Preferred thickness for uncoated, thin, flat metals, B32.1—1968

Shaft coupling, B49.1—1967

Surface roughness, waviness, and lay, B46.1—1962

Woodruff keys, keyslots, and cutters, B17.2—1967

PIPE, PIPE FITTINGS, AND THREADS

Brass fittings for flared copper tubes, B16.26—1967

Brass or bronze flanges and flanged fittings—150 and 300 lb, B16.24—1962

Brass or bronze screwed fittings—125 lb, B16.15—1964

Brass or bronze screwed fittings—250 lb, B16.15—1964

Butt-welding ends, B16.25—1964

Cast-brass solder-joint drainage fittings, B16.23—1960

Cast-brass solder-joint fittings, B16.18—1963

CI pipe flanges and flanged fittings, 25-psi, B16b2—1952; class 125, B16.1—1960; class 250, B16.2—1960; 800-lb hydraulic pressure, B16b1—1952; class 300-lb refrigerant, B16.16—1952

CI screwed drainage fittings, B16.12—1965

CI screwed fittings, 125- and 250-lb, B16.4—1963

CI soil pipe and fittings, A112.5.1—1968

Face to face dimensions of ferrous flanged and welding end valves, B16.10—1957

Ferrous plugs, bushings, and locknuts with pipe threads, B16.14—1953

Malleable-iron screwed fittings, 150-lb, B16.3—1963

Malleable-iron screwed fittings, 300-lb, B16.3—1963

National plumbing code, A40.8—1955

Nonmetallic gaskets for pipe flanges, B16.21 1962

Pipe threads, B2.1—1960

Ring-joint gaskets and grooves for steel pipe flanges, B16.20—1963

Stainless-steel pipe, B36.19—1957

Steel butt-welding fittings, B16.9—1964

Steel pipe flanges and flanged fittings, 150-, 300-, 400-, 600-, 900-, 1,500-, and 2,500-lb, B16.5—1961

Steel-socket welding fittings, B16.11—1952

Threaded cast-iron pipe for drainage, vent, and waste services, A40.5—1943

Wrought-copper and wrought-bronze solder-joint fittings, B16.22—1963

Wrought-steel and wrought-iron pipe, B36.10—1959

SMALL TOOLS AND MACHINE-TOOL ELEMENTS

Acme screw threads, B1.5—1952

Buttress screw threads, B1.9—1953

Chucks and chuck jaws, B5.8—1959

Hose-coupling screw threads, B33.1—1947

Involute serrations, B5.15—1960

Involute splines, B5.15—1960

Jig bushings, B5.6—1962

Knurling, B5.30—1958

Machine tapers, B5.10—1963

Milling cutters, B5.3—1960

Nomenclature, definitions, and letter symbols for screw threads, B1.7—1953

Preferred limits and fits for cylindrical parts, B4.1—1955

Reamers, B5.14—1959

Screw thread gages and gaging, B1.2—1951

Stub Acme screw threads, B1.8—1952

Taps—cut and ground threads, B5.4—1959

T slots and their bolts, nuts, tongues, and cutters, B5.1—1949

Twist drills, B94.11—1967

Unified and American screw threads standard, B1.1—1960

STANDARDS UNDER DEVELOPMENT

Abbreviations—for use in text

Drafting standards manual—castings, die castings, helical and flat springs, hydraulic and pneumatic diagrams, schematic wiring and diagrams, structural drafting

Fluid meters—theory and application

Gears—inspection of coarse-pitch spur and helical gears

Screws and screw threads—microscope-objective threads, surveying-instrument mounting threads, national miniature screw threads, "trial" class 5 interference-fit thread

Small tools—inserted-blade milling-cutter bodies, driving and spindle ends for portable electric tools

Symbols—miscellaneous

Washers—precision

PUBLICATIONS OF
NATIONAL SOCIETIES

The national engineering organizations publish a wide variety of manuals, standards, handbooks, and pamphlets. Information concerning these publications is available directly from the societies. The following is a selected list of American organizations:

Aerospace Industries Assn. of America, 1725 Desales St. NW, Washington, D.C. 20036

Air Conditioning and Refrigeration Institute, 1815 North Fort Myer Drive, Arlington, Va.

American Association for the Advancement of Science (AAAS), 1515 Massachusetts Ave. NW, Washington 5, D.C.

American Association of Engineers (AAE), 8 South Michigan Ave., Chicago 3, Ill.

American Association of Petroleum Geologists, Inc. (AAPG), P.O. Box 979, Tulsa 1, Okla.

American Association of University Professors, 1785 Massachusetts Ave. NW, Washington 6, D.C.

American Ceramic Society (ACerS), 4055 North High St., Columbus 14, Ohio

American Chemical Society (ACS), ACS Bldg., 1155 16th St. NW, Washington 6, D.C.

American Concrete Institute (ACI), P.O. Box 4754, Redford Station, Detroit 19, Mich.

American Gas Association (AGA), 605 Third Ave., New York, N.Y. 10016

American Inst. of Aeronautics and Astronautics (AIAA) 1290 Ave. of the Americas, New York, N.Y. 10019

American Institute of Chemical Engineers (AIChE), 345 East 47th St., New York, N.Y. 10017

American Institute of Consulting Engineers (AICE), 345 East 47th St., New York, N.Y. 10017

American Institute of Mining and Metallurgical, and Petroleum Engineers, Inc. (AIME), 345 East 47th St., New York, N.Y. 10017

American Institute of Steel Construction, Inc. (AISC), 101 Park Ave., New York 17, N.Y.

American Mining Congress, Ring Bldg., Washington 6, D.C.

American National Standards Institute, Inc. (ANSI), 1430 Broadway, New York, N.Y. 10018

American Petroleum Institute (API), 1271 Ave. of the Americas, New York, N.Y. 10020

American Society of Engineering Education (ASEE), University of Illinois, Urbana, Ill.

American Society of Metals (ASM), Metals Park, Ohio

American Society for Quality Control (ASQC), 161 West Wisconsin Ave., Milwaukee 3, Wis.

American Society for Testing and Materials (ASTM), 1916 Race St., Philadelphia 3, Pa.

American Society of Agricultural Engineers (ASAE), 420 Main St., St. Joseph, Mich.

American Society of Civil Engineers (ASCE), 345 East 47th St., New York, N.Y. 10017

American Society of Heating, Refrigerating, and Air-conditioning Engineers (ASHRAE), 345 East 47th St., New York, N.Y. 10017

American Society of Lubrication Engineers, 838 Busse Highway, Park Ridge, Ill. 60068

American Society of Mechanical Engineers (ASME), 345 East 47th St., New York, N.Y.   10017

American Society of Photogrammetry, 44 Leesburg Pike, Falls Church, Va.

American Society of Safety Engineers, 5 N. Wabash Ave., Chicago 2, Ill.

American Society of Tool and Manufacturing Engineers, 10700 Puritan Ave., Detroit 38, Mich.

American Welding Society (AWS), 345 East 47th St., New York, N.Y.   10017

Asphalt Institute, Asphalt Institute Bldg., College Park, Md.

Association of Iron and Steel Engineers (AISE), 1010 Empire Bldg., Pittsburgh 22, Pa.

Concrete Pipe Association, 228 North LaSalle St., Chicago 1, Ill.

Electrochemical Society, Inc., The, 30 East 42nd St., New York, N.Y.   10017

Federation of American Scientists (FAS), 1700 K St., NW, Washington, D.C.   20036

Highway Research Board, 2101 Constitution Ave. NW, Washington 25, D.C.

Illuminating Engineering Society, 345 East 47th St., New York, N.Y.   10017

Industrial Management Society (IMS), 330 South Wells St., Chicago 6, Ill.

Industrial Research Institute, Inc., 100 Park Ave., New York 17, N.Y.

Institute of Electrical and Electronics Engineers (IEEE), 345 East 47th St., New York, N.Y.   10017

Mining and Metallurgical Society of America (MMSA), 11 Broadway, New York 4, N.Y.

National Aeronautic Association (NAA), 1025 Connecticut Ave. NW, Washington 6, D.C.

National Institute of Ceramic Engineers, The, 4055 North High St., Columbus 14, Ohio

National Society of Professional Engineers (NSPE), 2029 K St., NW, Washington 6, D.C.

Society of Automotive Engineers (SAE), 485 Lexington Ave., New York 17, N.Y.

APPENDIX **A**

Lettering

OUTLINED COMMERCIAL GOTHIC. In Chap. 4, the so-called "Gothic" letter was considered only as a single-stroke letter. For sizes larger than say ⅝ in., or for boldface letters, it is drawn in outline and filled in solid. For a given size, this letter is readable at a greater distance than any other style; hence it is used where legibility is the principal requirement. The stems may be one-tenth to one-fifth of the height, and care must be taken to keep them uniform in width at every point on the letter. In inking a penciled outline, keep the *outside* of the ink line on the pencil line (Fig. A-1) or the letter will be heavier than expected.

The general order and direction of penciling large commercial Gothic letters is similar to that for the single-stroke letter but with two strokes made in place of one, as shown in typical examples in Fig. A-2. Free ends, such as on *C, G,* and *S,* are cut off perpendicular to the stem. The stiffness of plain letters is sometimes relieved by finishing the ends with a slight spur, as in

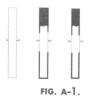

FIG. A-1.

FIG. A-2. Typical construction for large commercial Gothic.

A17

ABCDEFGHIJ
KLMNOPQRS
TUVWXYZ &

FIG. A-3.   Compressed commercial Gothic.

Fig. A-3. The complete alphabet in outline, with stems one-sixth of the height, is given in Fig. A-4. The same scale of widths may be used for drawing lighter-face letters. Figure A-3 illustrates a commercial Gothic alphabet compressed to two-thirds the normal width. In this figure the stems are drawn one-seventh of the height, but the scale is given in sixths, as in Fig. A-4.

THE ROMAN LETTER.   The Roman letter is the parent of all the styles that are in use today. Although there are many variations of it, the three general forms

FIG. A-4.   Large commercial Gothic construction.

are: (1) early or classic, (2) Renaissance, and (3) Modern. The first two are very similar in effect, and the general term "Old Roman" is used for both.

The Roman letter is composed of two weights of lines, corresponding to the downstroke and the upstroke of a broad reed pen, with which it was originally written. It is an inexcusable fault to shade a Roman letter on the wrong stroke.

Rule for shading. All horizontal strokes are light. All vertical strokes are heavy except in *M, N,* and *U.* To determine the heavy stroke in letters containing slanting sides, trace the shape of the letter from left to right in one stroke and note which lines were made downward. Figure A-5 is an Old Roman alphabet with the width of the body stroke one-tenth of the height of the letter and the light lines slightly over one-half this width. For inscriptions and

FIG. A-5. Old Roman capitals.

abcdefghijklmn
opqrstuvwxyz

FIG. A-6. Old Roman lower case.

titles, capitals are generally used, but sometimes lower case is needed; the examples given in Fig. A-6 are drawn with waist line six-tenths high and the width of the stems one-twelfth of capital height.

Old Roman is the architect's general-purpose letter. A single-stroke adaptation (Fig. A-7) is generally used on architectural drawings.

MODERN ROMAN. Civil engineers in particular must be familiar with Modern Roman, as it is the standard letter for titles of finished maps and the names of civil divisions, such as countries and cities. It is a difficult letter to draw and

can be mastered only by careful attention to details. The heavy or "body" strokes are one-sixth to one-eighth the height of the letter. Those in Fig. A-8 are one-seventh the height of the letter. A paper scale made by dividing the height into seven parts will aid in penciling.

Modern lower case (Fig. A-9) is used on maps for names of towns and villages. Notice the difference in the serifs of Figs. A-9 and A-6.

The order and direction of strokes used in drawing Modern Roman letters are illustrated in typical letters in Fig. A-10. The serifs on the ends of the strokes extend one space on each side

FIG. A-7. Single stroke Roman and italic.

ABCDEFGHIJKLMNOPQRS
TUVWXYZ& 1234567890
abcdefghijklmnopqrstuvwxyz
Compressed Italic for Limited Space
Sans-serif for Speed & Simplicity

FIG. A-8. Modern Roman capitals.

FIG. A-9. Modern Roman lower case.

FIG. A-10. Modern Roman construction.

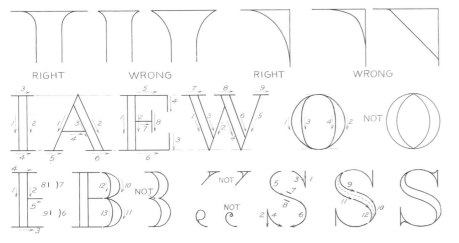

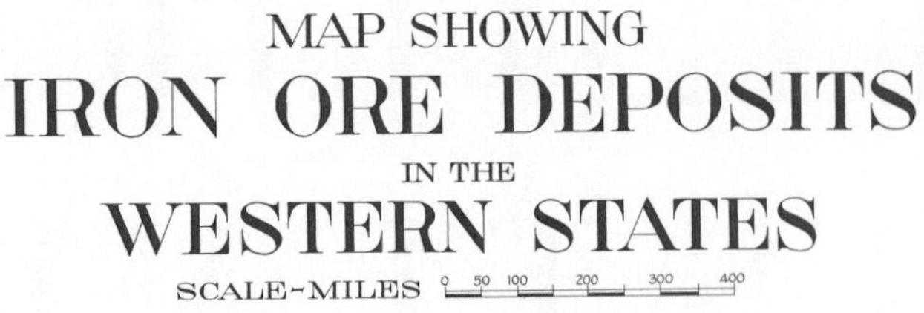

MAP SHOWING
IRON ORE DEPOSITS
IN THE
WESTERN STATES
SCALE-MILES   0 50 100   200   300   400

FIG. A-11. A Roman-letter title.

and are joined to the main stroke by small fillets. The curved letters are flattened slightly on their diagonals. A title in Roman letters is illustrated in Fig. A-11.

The Roman letter may be extended or compressed, as shown in Fig. A-12. For extended or compressed letters, a scale for widths would be longer or shorter than the normal scale. The compressed letters in Fig. A-12 are made with a scale three-fourths the height divided into sevenths.

INCLINED ROMAN.   Inclined letters are used for water features on maps. An alphabet of inclined Roman made to the same proportions as the vertical in Fig. A-8 is shown in Fig. A-13. The slope may be 65° to 75°. Those shown are inclined 2 to 5. The lower-case letters in this figure are known as stump letters. For small sizes, lines are made with one stroke of a fine flexible pen;

for larger sizes they are drawn and filled in.

THE PROPORTIONAL METHOD.   Because of the varying widths of Roman letters, it is sometimes difficult to space a word or line to a given length by counting letters. Figure A-14 illustrates the method of spacing by the principle of similar triangles. Suppose it is necessary to put the word "ROMAN" on the line to the length ab. Draw line ac from a at any angle, say 30°, and a second line de parallel to it; then sketch the word in this space, starting at a and spacing each letter with reference to the one before it, allowing the word to end where it will. Connect the end of the last letter, at c, with b, and draw lines parallel to cb from each letter, thus dividing ab proportionately. Obtain the height bf from ce by the construction shown. Then sketch the word in its final position.

THE GREEK ALPHABET.   While Greek is not a required subject in most engineering curricula, the engineer often uses letters of the Greek alphabet, both capitals and lower case, as symbols and reference letters. He should therefore be able to draw them readily and to read them without hesitation.

FIG. A-12. Modern Roman, extended and compressed.

EXTENDED ROMAN
BCGHJKLPQSUVW
COMPRESSED ROMAN-BHKTWG

*A B C D E F G H I J K L M N
O P Q R S T U V W X Y Z & a b
c d e f g h i j k l m n o p q r s t u v ᵒʳ V w ᵒʳ W
x y ᵒʳ y z 1 2 3 4 5 6 7 8 9 0*

FIG. A-13. Inclined Roman and stump letters.

There is variety in Greek alphabets, just as there is in Roman alphabets. The alphabet given in Fig. A-15 is clearly legible, and has accented and unaccented strokes in the capitals which follow closely the rules for shading Roman letters. The lower case has good historical precedent in form, shading, and comparative size.

When Greek letters are used in equations and formulas, the letters are made in a single stroke by simply following the letter shape without any attempt at shading. For display purposes and when shading is desirable for legibility, the letters are outlined and filled in by the method described for outlined commercial Gothic.

FIG. A-14. Proportional method.

Aα	Bβ	Γγ	Δδ	Eε	Zζ	Hη	Θϑ
ALPHA	BETA	GAMMA	DELTA	EPSILON	ZETA	ETA	THETA

Iι	Kκ	Λλ	Mμ	Nν	Ξξ	Oo	Ππ
IOTA	KAPPA	LAMBDA	MU	NU	XI	OMICRON	PI

Pρ	Σσ	Tτ	Yυ	Φφ	Xχ	Ψψ	Ωω
RHO	SIGMA	TAU	UPSILON	PHI	CHI	PSI	OMEGA

FIG. A-15. The Greek alphabet.

The slide rule is a graphic instrument for making mathematical calculations. Because the instrument is *graphic,* and also because its use is common in all engineering work, the following pictorial guide to its use is given.

The slide rule is based on the well-known mathematical relationships of logarithms of numbers. For example, the equation for the multiplication of two factors, $A \times B = C$, when written logarithmically becomes: $\log A + \log B = \log C$. Thus, to multiply, logarithms are *added* and, conversely, to divide, logarithms are subtracted. Slide-rule scales are arranged in such a way that the addition and subtraction of logarithms is accomplished *graphically.*

It is beyond our scope here to give a complete discussion of slide-rule use. The pictorial examples are intended only for quick, easy visual reference. Complete discussions on the theory and use of slide rules are given in manuals prepared especially for the slide rule (see Bibliography).

Because slide-rule settings of values and the answers depend upon reading a graphic scale, results are not absolutely accurate. However, the instrument is unrivaled as an inexpensive, portable, and efficient device for calculation whenever absolute accuracy is not essential.

MULTIPLICATION OF TWO VALUES (C AND D SCALES)

$A \times B = R$

Set A on D scale with index of C scale (Fig. B-1). Set B on C scale with hairline of glass slide. Read answer R on D scale at hairline. Example shown:

$$1.375 \times 1.962 = 2.697$$

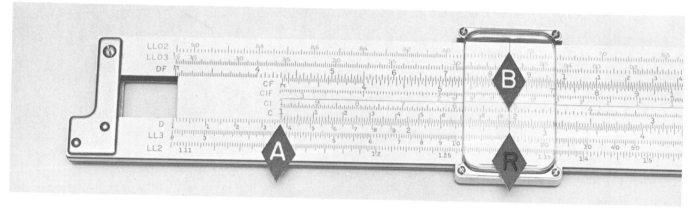

FIG. B-1.

DIVISION OF TWO VALUES (C AND D SCALES)

$\dfrac{A}{B} = C$

Set A on D scale with hairline (Fig. B-2). Set B on C scale under hairline.

Read answer R on D scale at index of C scale. Example shown:

$$\frac{2.70}{1.962} = 1.375$$

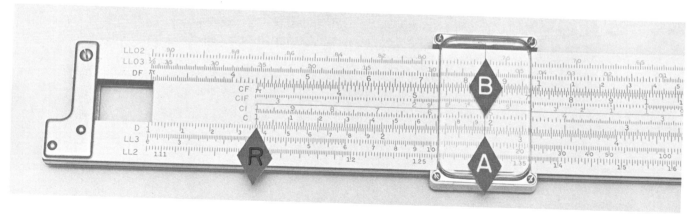

FIG. B-2.

PROPORTION (C AND D SCALES)

$$\frac{A}{B} = \frac{C}{D} = \frac{E}{F}$$

Set A on D scale and B on C scale opposite each other by using the hairline (Fig. B-3). Then any other combination in the same proportion is had by moving the hairline and reading both values on C and D scales. Example shown:

$$\frac{A}{B} = \frac{2.0}{1.5}, \frac{C}{D} = \frac{1.4}{1.05}, \frac{E}{F} = \frac{2.7}{2.025}$$

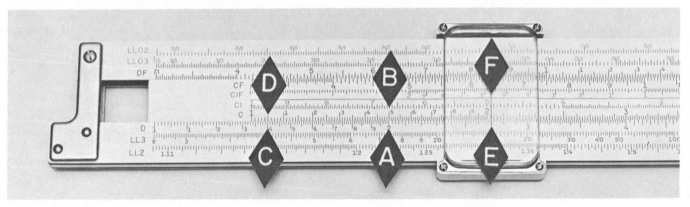

FIG. B-3.

SUCCESSIVE MULTIPLICATION OF ONE VALUE BY SEVERAL OTHERS (C AND D SCALES)

$A \times B = R$
$A \times C = S$
$A \times D = T$

Set A on D scale with index of C scale (Fig. B-4). Then set B, C, and D with hairline on C scale and read answers on D scale at R, S, and T under hairline. Example shown:

$2.4 \times 1.8 = 4.32$ (R)
$2.4 \times 2.5 = 6.0$ (S)
$2.4 \times 3.0 = 7.2$ (T)

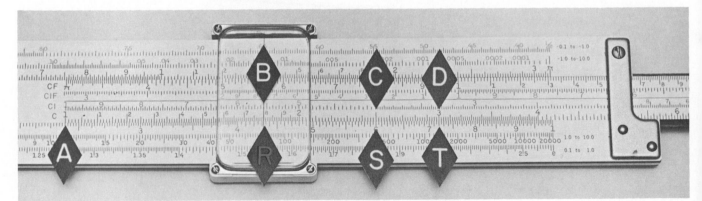

FIG. B-4.

SUCCESSIVE DIVISION OF ONE VALUE BY SEVERAL OTHERS (D AND CI SCALES)

$$\frac{A}{B} = R$$

$$\frac{A}{C} = S$$

$$\frac{A}{D} = T$$

Set A on D scale with index (right) of CI scale (Fig. B-5). The CI scale is the same as the C scale, but inverted. Then set B, C, and D with hairline on CI scale and read answers under hairline on D scale. Example shown:

$$\frac{7.0}{2} = 3.5 \ (R) \quad \frac{7.0}{3.0} = 2.33 \ (S)$$

$$\frac{7.0}{4.0} = 1.75 \ (T)$$

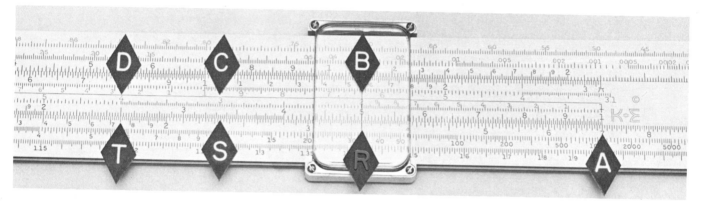

FIG. B-5.

MULTIPLICATION BY USING THE CF AND DF SCALES

The "folded" scales, CF and DF, are used whenever a value on the C scale falls beyond the D scale. In the example shown, value B on the C scale cannot be set. Therefore, using the CF and DF scales:

$$A \times C = R$$

Set A on D scale with index of C scale (Fig. B-6). CF and DF scales *have moved in exactly the same proportion as* C scale relative to D scale. Therefore, when value B falls off end of C scale, set C on CF scale and read answer on DF scale under hairline. Example shown:

$$3.1 \times 4.5 = 13.95$$

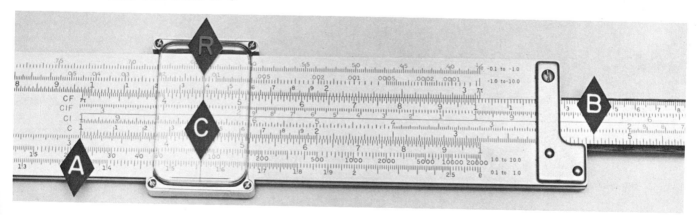

FIG. B-6.

DIVISION BY USING THE CIF SCALE

The "folded and inverted" scale, CIF, is a folded scale to augment the CI scale. In successive division, using the CI scale, some values will be off the end of the scale. The CIF scale can then be used:

$$\frac{A}{B} = R \text{ or } \frac{A}{C} = S$$

Set A on D scale with hairline (Fig. B-7). Set index of CIF scale under hairline. Then $\frac{A}{B} = R$, and $\frac{A}{C} = S$. Answer is read on D scale. Example shown:

$$\frac{2.0}{8.0} = 0.25 \ (R)$$

$$\frac{2.0}{5.0} = 0.40 \ (S)$$

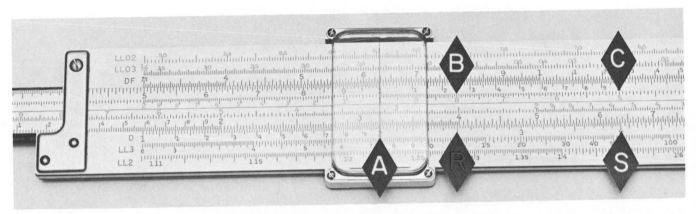

FIG. B-7.

MULTIPLICATION OF THREE VALUES (D AND CI SCALES)

$$A \times B \times C = S$$

Set A on D scale, using hairline (Fig. B-8). Set B on CI scale under hairline. The answer of this operation $(A \times B)$ can then be read at index of C scale at

R on D scale. The third value C, now set on C scale, gives answer of $A \times B \times C$ at S on D scale. Example shown:

$$2.5 \times 2 \times 3.6 = 18.0$$

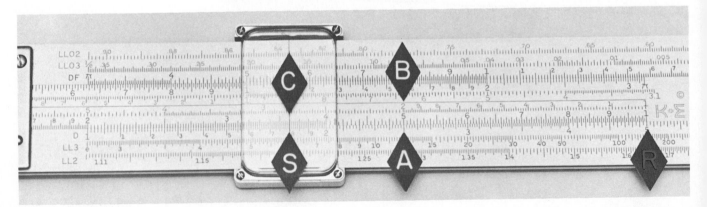

FIG. B-8.

COMBINED MULTIPLICATION AND DIVISION (D AND CI SCALES)

$$\frac{A \times B}{C} = S$$

Set A on D scale with hairline (Fig. B-9). Set B on CI scale under hairline. The answer of $A \times B$ is at index of CI scale at R on D scale. Then the third value C, on CI scale, gives answer of $\frac{A \times B}{C}$ at S on D scale. Example shown:

$$\frac{1.5 \times 2.0}{15.0} = 0.20$$

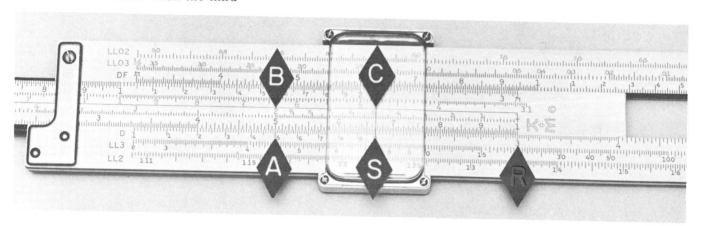

FIG. B-9.

COMBINED MULTIPLICATION AND DIVISION (C, D, AND CI SCALES)

$$\frac{A}{B \times C} = S$$

Set A on D scale with hairline (Fig. B-10). Set B on C scale under hairline. The answer of $\frac{A}{B}$ is at index of CI scale at R on D scale. Then the third value C, on the CI scale, gives the answer of $\frac{A}{B \times C}$ at S on D scale. Example shown:

$$\frac{3.0}{2.0 \times 7.0} = 0.214$$

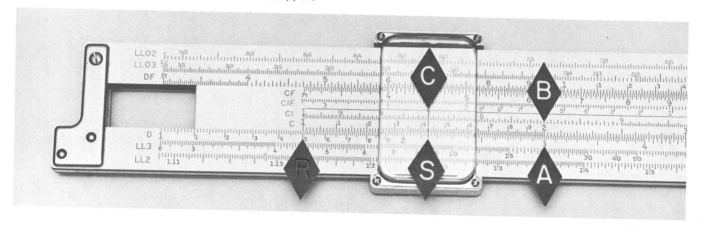

FIG. B-10.

COMBINED MULTIPLICATION AND DIVISION (C, D, CF, DF, AND CIF SCALES)

$$\frac{A}{B \times C} = S$$

Sometimes in combined multiplication and division, values needed will be inaccessible on a scale. To illustrate, set A on D scale with hairline (Fig. B-11). Set B on C scale under hairline. Then the answer of $\frac{A}{B}$ is at index of C scale at

R on D scale. If C is a value that cannot be set on CI scale, set C on CIF scale and read answer at S on DF scale. To prove this, note that CF scale has moved in exactly the same relationship to DF scale as C scale has moved in relation to D scale. Example shown:

$$\frac{15.0}{4.0 \times 6.0} = 0.625$$

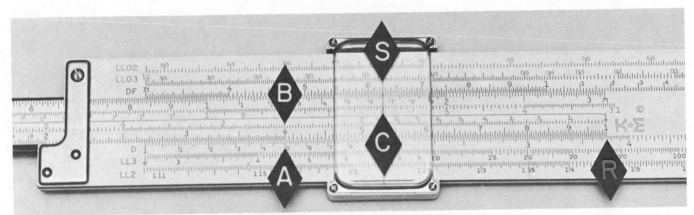

FIG. B-11.

SQUARES AND SQUARE ROOTS (D AND A SCALES)

$$R^2 = A \text{ and } \sqrt{A} = R$$

The A scale is plotted as the square of the D scale.

To determine $R^2 = A$, set R on D scale and read square on A scale (Fig. B-12). Example shown:

$$2.0^2 = 4.0$$

To determine $\sqrt{A} = R$, set A on A scale and read square root on D scale. Example shown:

$$\sqrt{4.0} = 2.0$$

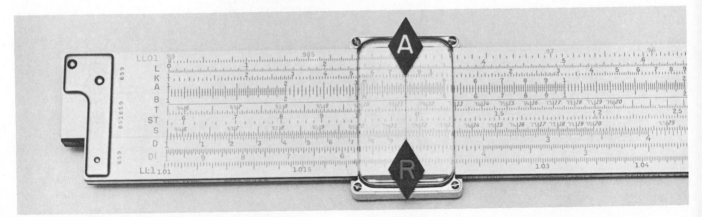

FIG. B-12.

CUBES AND CUBE ROOTS (D AND K SCALES)

$A^3 = R$ and $\sqrt[3]{R} = A$

The K scale is plotted as the cube of the D scale.

To determine $A^3 = R$, set A on D scale and read cube on K scale (Fig. B-13). Example shown:

$2.0^3 = 8.0$

To determine $\sqrt[3]{R} = A$, set R on K scale and read cube root on D scale. Example shown:

$\sqrt[3]{8.0} = 2.0$

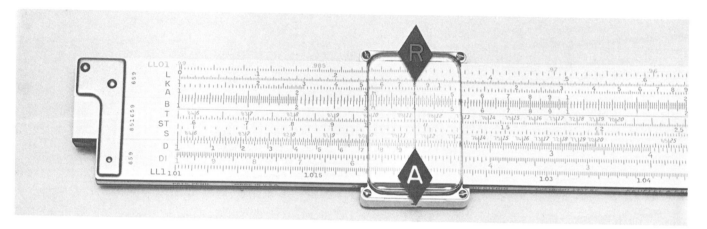

FIG. B-13.

USE OF THE A AND B SCALES

The A and B scales can be used to multiply and divide, and are useful for performing these operations *after* a square has been obtained, *or* if the square root is needed *after* multiplication or division.

$A^2 \times B = S$

Set A on D scale (Fig. B-14). A^2 can then be read on the A scale at R. Set B on B scale with hairline. The answer S is under hairline on A scale. Example shown:

$2.0^2 \times 4.0 = 16.0$

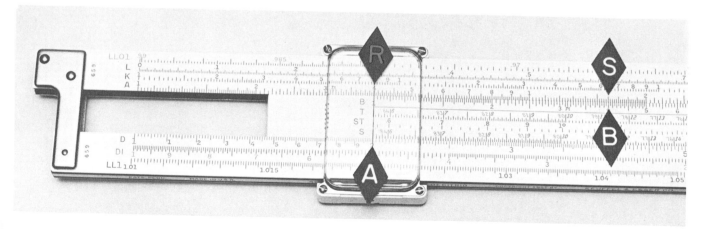

FIG. B-14.

MATHEMATICAL VALUE OF SINE OR TANGENT (ST SCALE)

sin A (or tan A) = R

The values of sines and tangents from zero degrees up to about 5½ degrees are identical for the accuracy with which the scales can be read.

Index the ST scale with the D scale (Fig. B-15). Set angle (A) on ST scale with hairline and read mathematical value (R) on D scale under hairline. Example shown:

sin (or tan) 1.5° = 0.0262

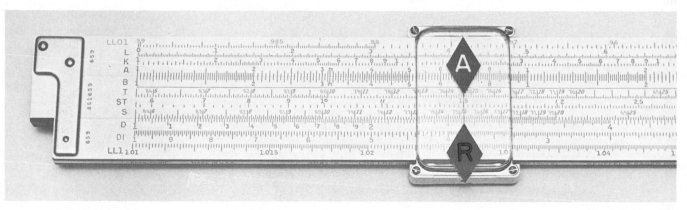

FIG. B-15.

MATHEMATICAL VALUE OF SINE (S SCALE)

sin A = R

Index S scale with D scale (Fig. B-16). Set angle (degrees) (A) on S scale with hairline and read mathematical value (R) on D scale under hairline. The cosine (degrees) is printed on most rules on the S scale in red. Example shown:

sin 15° = 0.2588
cos 75° = 0.2588

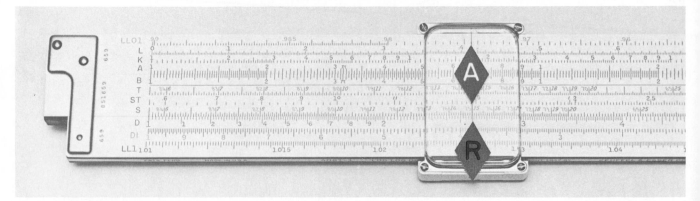

FIG. B-16.

ANGLE OF SINE, CORRESPONDING TO MATHEMATICAL VALUE (S SCALE)

A (sin) = R (angle in degrees)

Index S scale with D scale (Fig. B-17). Set A on D scale with hairline. Read angle in degrees (R) on S scale under hairline. Example shown:

sin = 0.176 = 10.16°

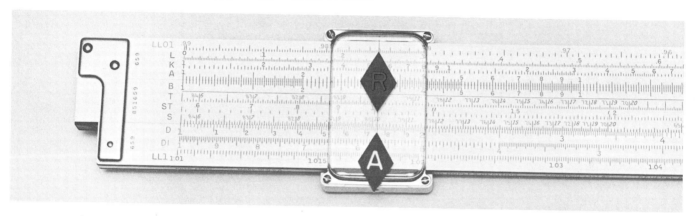

FIG. B-17.

MATHEMATICAL VALUE OF TANGENT (T SCALE) UP TO 45°

tan $A = R$

Index T scale with D scale (Fig. B-18). Set A, angle in degrees, on T scale with hairline. Read mathematical value of tangent (R) on D scale under hairline. Example shown:

tan 10° = 0.176

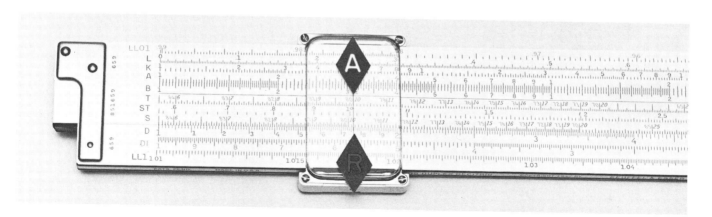

FIG. B-18.

MATHEMATICAL VALUE OF TANGENT (T SCALE) FROM 45° UP

tan $A = R$

Index T scale with DI scale—inverted D scale (Fig. B-19). On most rules, the T scale above 45° and the DI scale are printed in red. Set angle in degrees (A) on T scale with hairline. Read mathematical value (R) on DI scale under hairline. Example shown:

tan 75° = 3.74

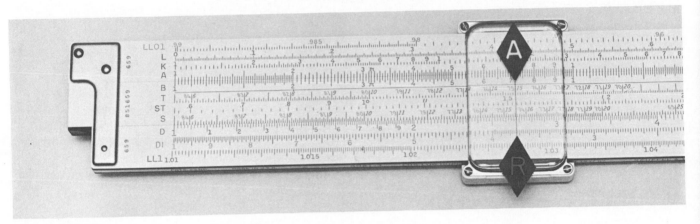

FIG. B-19.

MULTIPLICATION WITH THE TRIGONOMETRIC SCALES (ST SCALE)

$A \sin B = R$

Set A on D scale with index of ST scale (Fig. B-20). Set angle in degrees (B), corresponding to mathematical value of a sine or tangent, with hairline on ST scale. Read answer at R on D scale. Example shown:

2 sin (tan) 1° = 0.0350

The S and T scales are employed for multiplication in the same manner.

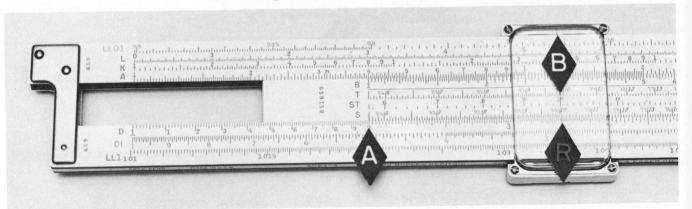

FIG. B-20.

DIVISION WITH THE TRIGONOMETRIC SCALES (S SCALE)

$$\frac{A}{\sin B} = R$$

Set A on D scale with hairline (Fig. B-21). Set angle in degrees (B), corresponding to mathematical value of the sine, on S scale, under hairline. Read answer R, at index of S scale on D scale. Example shown:

$$\frac{3.24}{\sin 11°} = 17.0$$

The ST and T scales are employed for division in the same manner.

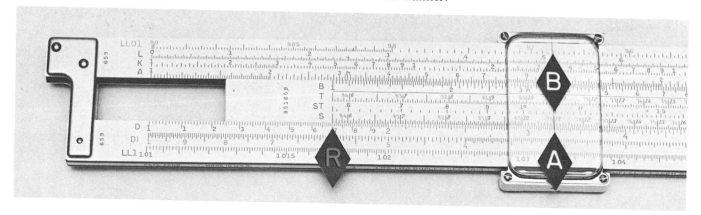

FIG. B-21.

LOGARITHMS (L SCALE)

$$\log A = R$$

Set A with hairline on D scale (Fig. B-22). Read logarithm, mantissa only, (R) under hairline on L scale. Example shown:

$$\log 2.10 = 0.322$$

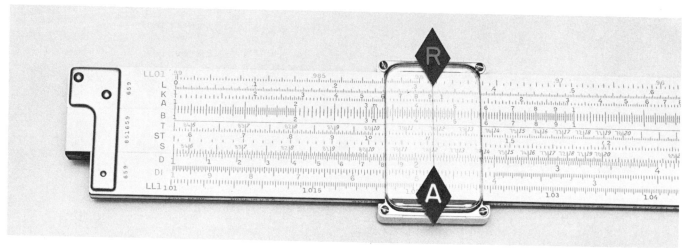

FIG. B-22.

ANTILOGARITHMS (L SCALE)

$A = \log R$

Set logarithms, mantissa only, (A) with hairline on L scale (Fig. B-23).

Read antilog (R) under hairline on D scale. Example shown:

$0.330 = \log 2.14$

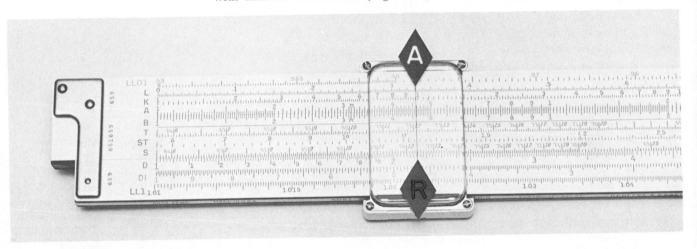

FIG. B-23.

POWERS (LL SCALES)

$A^B = R$

Set A with hairline on LL scale (depending upon the value) and match index of C scale under hairline (Fig.

B-24). Set power B with hairline on C scale. Read answer on LL scale at R. Example shown:

$6.0^{1.75} = 23.0$

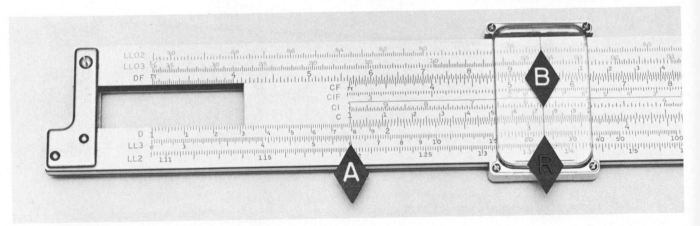

FIG. B-24.

THE LL SCALES

The LL scales run continuously, for example, LL2 ends at e at the right index, and LL3 begins with e at the left index (Fig. B-25). Depending on the value set, and the power, the answer *may* be on the next scale in sequence.

$$A^B = R$$

Set as in previous example, but if left index of the C scale is used and value of the power is then beyond range of scale, change to right index and answer will appear on *next* LL scale. Example shown:

$$2.0^4 = 16.0$$

(The value 2.0 is set on LL2 and 16.0 is read on LL3.) The LL01, LL02 and LL03 scales are for numbers less than 1.0. Note that these scales are inverted.

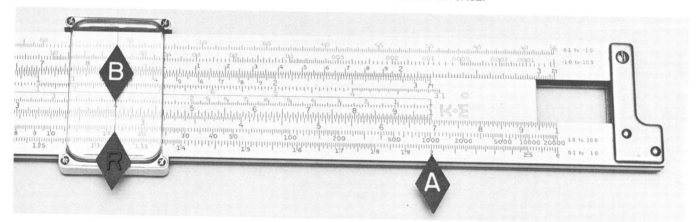

FIG. B-25.

ROOTS (LL SCALES)

$$(A)^{1/B} = R$$

Set A with hairline on LL scale (depending upon the value) and set root (B), exponential denominator, on C scale under hairline (Fig. B-26). Read answer on LL scale at R. Example shown:

$$49.0^{1/2} = 7.0$$

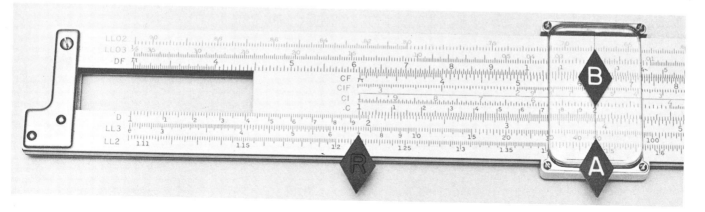

FIG. B-26.

Selected Mathematical Values

$\pi =$	3.141593
$2\pi =$	6.283185
$3\pi =$	9.424778
$4\pi =$	12.566371
$\dfrac{\pi}{2} =$	1.570796
$\dfrac{\pi}{3} =$	1.047198
$\dfrac{\pi}{4} =$	0.785398
$\pi^2 =$	9.869604
$\pi^3 =$	31.006277
$\sqrt{\pi} =$	1.772454
$\sqrt[3]{\pi} =$	1.464592
$\log_e \pi* =$	1.144730
$\dfrac{1}{\pi} =$	0.318310
$\dfrac{1}{\pi^2} =$	0.101321
$\dfrac{1}{\sqrt{\pi}} =$	0.564190
$\log_{10} \pi =$	0.497150
$\dfrac{1}{e} =$	0.367879
$\sqrt{2} =$	1.414214
$\sqrt{3} =$	1.732055
$\dfrac{\pi}{\sqrt{g}} =$	0.55399
$\dfrac{1}{\sqrt{g}} =$	0.17634
$\sqrt{2g} =$	8.01998
$\dfrac{1}{2g} =$	0.01555
$g^2 =$	1034.266
$2g =$	64.32
$g =$	32.16

*$e = 2.718282$

Inch-Metric Tolerance Equivalents‡

Conversion of Tolerances

Drawing usage†		Reference data	
Decimal inch	Millimeter	Difference between decimal inch and millimeter—Drawing usage (Inches)	Millimeter equivalent of decimal inch tolerance
0.0001	0.0025	−0.00000157	0.00254
0.0002	0.005	−0.00000314	0.00508
0.0003	0.008	+0.00001496	0.00762
0.0004	0.010	−0.00000629	0.01016
0.0005	0.013	+0.00001181	0.01270
0.0006	0.015	−0.00000944	0.01524
0.0007	0.018	+0.00000866	0.01778
0.0008	0.020	−0.00001259	0.02032
0.0009	0.023	+0.00000551	0.02286
0.001	0.025	−0.00001574	0.0254
0.0015	0.038	−0.00000393	0.0381
0.002	0.05	−0.00003149	0.0508
0.0025	0.06	−0.00013780	0.0635
0.003	0.08	+0.00014960	0.0762
0.004	0.10	−0.00006299	0.1016
0.005	0.13	+0.00011811	0.1270
0.006	0.15	−0.00009448	0.1524
0.007	0.18	+0.00008661	0.1778
0.008	0.20	−0.00012598	0.2032
0.009	0.23	+0.00005511	0.2286
0.010	0.25	−0.00015749	0.254
0.015	0.38	−0.00003938	0.381
0.02	0.5	−0.00031497	0.508
0.03	0.8	+0.00149606	0.762
0.04	1.0	−0.00062993	1.016
0.06	1.5	−0.00094489	1.524
0.08	2.0	−0.00125985	2.032
0.12	3.0	−0.00188977	3.048

† The conversions in these columns apply to tolerances only.
‡ Adapted from the SAE Aero-Space Drawing Standard (Revised Oct. 1967).

Decimal Equivalents of Inch Fractions

Fraction	Equiv.	Fraction	Equiv.	Fraction	Equiv.	Fraction	Equiv.
$\frac{1}{64}$	0.015625	$\frac{17}{64}$	0.265625	$\frac{33}{64}$	0.515625	$\frac{49}{64}$	0.765625
$\frac{1}{32}$	0.03125	$\frac{9}{32}$	0.28125	$\frac{17}{32}$	0.53125	$\frac{25}{32}$	0.78125
$\frac{3}{64}$	0.046875	$\frac{19}{64}$	0.296875	$\frac{35}{64}$	0.546875	$\frac{51}{64}$	0.796875
$\frac{1}{16}$	0.0625	$\frac{5}{16}$	0.3125	$\frac{9}{16}$	0.5625	$\frac{13}{16}$	0.8125
$\frac{5}{64}$	0.078125	$\frac{21}{64}$	0.328125	$\frac{37}{64}$	0.578125	$\frac{53}{64}$	0.828125
$\frac{3}{32}$	0.09375	$\frac{11}{32}$	0.34375	$\frac{19}{32}$	0.59375	$\frac{27}{32}$	0.84375
$\frac{7}{64}$	0.109375	$\frac{23}{64}$	0.359375	$\frac{39}{64}$	0.609375	$\frac{55}{64}$	0.859375
$\frac{1}{8}$	0.1250	$\frac{3}{8}$	0.3750	$\frac{5}{8}$	0.6250	$\frac{7}{8}$	0.8750
$\frac{9}{64}$	0.140625	$\frac{25}{64}$	0.390625	$\frac{41}{64}$	0.640625	$\frac{57}{64}$	0.890625
$\frac{5}{32}$	0.15625	$\frac{13}{32}$	0.40625	$\frac{21}{32}$	0.65625	$\frac{29}{32}$	0.90625
$\frac{11}{64}$	0.171875	$\frac{27}{64}$	0.421875	$\frac{43}{64}$	0.671875	$\frac{59}{64}$	0.921875
$\frac{3}{16}$	0.1875	$\frac{7}{16}$	0.4375	$\frac{11}{16}$	0.6875	$\frac{15}{16}$	0.9375
$\frac{13}{64}$	0.203125	$\frac{29}{64}$	0.453125	$\frac{45}{64}$	0.703125	$\frac{61}{64}$	0.953125
$\frac{7}{32}$	0.21875	$\frac{15}{32}$	0.46875	$\frac{23}{32}$	0.71875	$\frac{31}{32}$	0.96875
$\frac{15}{64}$	0.234375	$\frac{31}{64}$	0.484375	$\frac{47}{64}$	0.734375	$\frac{63}{64}$	0.984375
$\frac{1}{4}$	0.2500	$\frac{1}{2}$	0.5000	$\frac{3}{4}$	0.7500	1	1.0000

Metric Equivalents

Mm	In.*	Mm	In.	In.	Mm †	In.	Mm
1 = 0.0394		17 = 0.6693		$\frac{1}{32}$ = 0.794		$\frac{17}{32}$ = 13.493	
2 = 0.0787		18 = 0.7087		$\frac{1}{16}$ = 1.587		$\frac{9}{16}$ = 14.287	
3 = 0.1181		19 = 0.7480		$\frac{3}{32}$ = 2.381		$\frac{19}{32}$ = 15.081	
4 = 0.1575		20 = 0.7874		$\frac{1}{8}$ = 3.175		$\frac{5}{8}$ = 15.875	
5 = 0.1969		21 = 0.8268		$\frac{5}{32}$ = 3.968		$\frac{21}{32}$ = 16.668	
6 = 0.2362		22 = 0.8662		$\frac{3}{16}$ = 4.762		$\frac{11}{16}$ = 17.462	
7 = 0.2756		23 = 0.9055		$\frac{7}{32}$ = 5.556		$\frac{23}{32}$ = 18.256	
8 = 0.3150		24 = 0.9449		$\frac{1}{4}$ = 6.349		$\frac{3}{4}$ = 19.050	
9 = 0.3543		25 = 0.9843		$\frac{9}{32}$ = 7.144		$\frac{25}{32}$ = 19.843	
10 = 0.3937		26 = 1.0236		$\frac{5}{16}$ = 7.937		$\frac{13}{16}$ = 20.637	
11 = 0.4331		27 = 1.0630		$\frac{11}{32}$ = 8.731		$\frac{27}{32}$ = 21.431	
12 = 0.4724		28 = 1.1024		$\frac{3}{8}$ = 9.525		$\frac{7}{8}$ = 22.225	
13 = 0.5118		29 = 1.1418		$\frac{13}{32}$ = 10.319		$\frac{29}{32}$ = 23.018	
14 = 0.5512		30 = 1.1811		$\frac{7}{16}$ = 11.112		$\frac{15}{16}$ = 23.812	
15 = 0.5906		31 = 1.2205		$\frac{15}{32}$ = 11.906		$\frac{31}{32}$ = 24.606	
16 = 0.6299		32 = 1.2599		$\frac{1}{2}$ = 12.699		1 = 25.400	

* Calculated to *nearest* fourth decimal place.
† Calculated to *nearest* third decimal place.

Logarithms of Numbers

10	0	1	2	3	4	5	6	7	8	9
10	0000	0043	0086	0128	0170	0212	0253	0294	0334	0374
11	0414	0453	0492	0531	0569	0607	0645	0682	0719	0755
12	0792	0828	0864	0899	0934	0969	1004	1038	1072	1106
13	1139	1173	1206	1239	1271	1303	1335	1367	1399	1430
14	1461	1492	1523	1553	1584	1614	1644	1673	1703	1732
15	1761	1790	1818	1847	1875	1903	1931	1959	1987	2014
16	2041	2068	2095	2122	2148	2175	2201	2227	2253	2279
17	2304	2330	2355	2380	2405	2430	2455	2480	2504	2529
18	2553	2577	2601	2625	2648	2672	2695	2718	2742	2765
19	2788	2810	2833	2856	2878	2900	2923	2945	2967	2989
20	3010	3032	3054	3075	3096	3118	3139	3160	3181	3201
21	3222	3243	3263	3284	3304	3324	3345	3365	3385	3404
22	3424	3444	3464	3483	3502	3522	3541	3560	3579	3598
23	3617	3636	3655	3674	3692	3711	3729	3747	3766	3784
24	3802	3820	3838	3856	3874	3892	3909	3927	3945	3962
25	3979	3997	4014	4031	4048	4065	4082	4099	4116	4133
26	4150	4166	4183	4200	4216	4232	4249	4265	4281	4298
27	4314	4330	4346	4362	4378	4393	4409	4425	4440	4456
28	4472	4487	4502	4518	4533	4548	4564	4579	4594	4609
29	4624	4639	4654	4669	4683	4698	4713	4728	4742	4757
30	4771	4786	4800	4814	4829	4843	4857	4871	4886	4900
31	4914	4928	4942	4955	4969	4983	4997	5011	5024	5038
32	5051	5065	5079	5092	5105	5119	5132	5145	5159	5172
33	5185	5198	5211	5224	5237	5250	5263	5276	5289	5302
34	5315	5328	5340	5353	5366	5378	5391	5403	5416	5428
35	5441	5453	5465	5478	5490	5502	5514	5527	5539	5551
36	5563	5575	5587	5599	5611	5623	5635	5647	5658	5670
37	5682	5694	5705	5717	5729	5740	5752	5763	5775	5786
38	5798	5809	5821	5832	5843	5855	5866	5877	5888	5899
39	5911	5922	5933	5944	5955	5966	5977	5988	5999	6010
40	6021	6031	6042	6053	6064	6075	6085	6096	6107	6117
41	6128	6138	6149	6160	6170	6180	6191	6201	6212	6222
42	6232	6243	6253	6263	6274	6284	6294	6304	6314	6325
43	6335	6345	6355	6365	6375	6385	6395	6405	6415	6425
44	6435	6444	6454	6464	6474	6484	6493	6503	6513	6522
45	6532	6542	6551	6561	6571	6580	6590	6599	6609	6618
46	6628	6637	6646	6656	6665	6675	6684	6693	6702	6712
47	6721	6730	6739	6749	6758	6767	6776	6785	6794	6803
48	6812	6821	6830	6839	6848	6857	6866	6875	6884	6893
49	6902	6911	6920	6928	6937	6946	6955	6964	6972	6981
50	6990	6998	7007	7016	7024	7033	7042	7050	7059	7067
51	7076	7084	7093	7101	7110	7118	7126	7135	7143	7152
52	7160	7168	7177	7185	7193	7202	7210	7218	7226	7235
53	7243	7251	7259	7267	7275	7284	7292	7300	7308	7316
54	7324	7332	7340	7348	7356	7364	7372	7380	7388	7396

Logarithms of Numbers (Cont.)

55	0	1	2	3	4	5	6	7	8	9
55	7404	7412	7419	7427	7435	7443	7451	7459	7466	7474
56	7482	7490	7497	7505	7513	7520	7528	7536	7543	7551
57	7559	7566	7574	7582	7589	7597	7604	7612	7619	7627
58	7634	7642	7649	7657	7664	7672	7679	7686	7694	7701
59	7709	7716	7723	7731	7738	7745	7752	7760	7767	7774
60	7782	7789	7796	7803	7810	7818	7825	7832	7839	7846
61	7853	7860	7868	7875	7882	7889	7896	7903	7910	7917
62	7924	7931	7938	7945	7952	7959	7966	7973	7980	7987
63	7993	8000	8007	8014	8021	8028	8035	8041	8048	8055
64	8062	8069	8075	8082	8089	8096	8102	8109	8116	8122
65	8129	8136	8142	8149	8156	8162	8169	8176	8182	8189
66	8195	8202	8209	8215	8222	8228	8235	8241	8248	8254
67	8261	8267	8274	8280	8287	8293	8299	8306	8312	8319
68	8325	8331	8338	8344	8351	8357	8363	8370	8376	8382
69	8388	8395	8401	8407	8414	8420	8426	8432	8439	8445
70	8451	8457	8463	8470	8476	8482	8488	8494	8500	8506
71	8513	8519	8525	8531	8537	8543	8549	8555	8561	8567
72	8573	8579	8585	8591	8597	8603	8609	8615	8621	8627
73	8633	8639	8645	8651	8657	8663	8669	8675	8681	8686
74	8692	8698	8704	8710	8716	8722	8727	8733	8739	8745
75	8751	8756	8762	8768	8774	8779	8785	8791	8797	8802
76	8808	8814	8820	8825	8831	8837	8842	8848	8854	8859
77	8865	8871	8876	8882	8887	8893	8899	8904	8910	8915
78	8921	8927	8932	8938	8943	8949	8954	8960	8965	8971
79	8976	8982	8987	8993	8998	9004	9009	9015	9020	9025
80	9031	9036	9042	9047	9053	9058	9063	9069	9074	9079
81	9085	9090	9096	9101	9106	9112	9117	9122	9128	9133
82	9138	9143	9149	9154	9159	9165	9170	9175	9180	9186
83	9191	9196	9201	9206	9212	9217	9222	9227	9232	9238
84	9243	9248	9253	9258	9263	9269	9274	9279	9284	9289
85	9294	9299	9304	9309	9315	9320	9325	9330	9335	9340
86	9345	9350	9355	9360	9365	9370	9375	9380	9385	9390
87	9395	9400	9405	9410	9415	9420	9425	9430	9435	9440
88	9445	9450	9455	9460	9465	9469	9474	9479	9484	9489
89	9494	9499	9504	9509	9513	9518	9523	9528	9533	9538
90	9542	9547	9552	9557	9562	9566	9571	9576	9581	9586
91	9590	9595	9600	9605	9609	9614	9619	9624	9628	9633
92	9638	9643	9647	9652	9657	9661	9666	9671	9675	9680
93	9685	9689	9694	9699	9703	9708	9713	9717	9722	9727
94	9731	9736	9741	9745	9750	9754	9759	9763	9768	9773
95	9777	9782	9786	9791	9795	9800	9805	9809	9814	9818
96	9823	9827	9832	9836	9841	9845	9850	9854	9859	9863
97	9868	9872	9877	9881	9886	9890	9894	9899	9903	9908
98	9912	9917	9921	9926	9930	9934	9939	9943	9948	9952
99	9956	9961	9965	9969	9974	9978	9983	9987	9991	9996

Trigonometric Functions

Angle	Sine		Cosine		Tangent		Cotangent		Angle
	Nat.	Log.	Nat.	Log.	Nat.	Log.	Nat.	Log.	
0° 00′	.0000	∞	1.0000	0.0000	.0000	∞	∞	∞	90° 00′
10	.0029	7.4637	1.0000	0000	.0029	7.4637	343.77	2.5363	50
20	.0058	7648	1.0000	0000	.0058	7648	171.89	2352	40
30	.0087	9408	1.0000	0000	.0087	9409	114.59	0591	30
40	.0116	8.0658	.9999	0000	.0116	8.0658	85.940	1.9342	20
50	.0145	1627	.9999	0000	.0145	1627	68.750	8373	10
1° 00′	.0175	8.2419	.9998	9.9999	.0175	8.2419	57.290	1.7581	89° 00′
10	.0204	3088	.9998	9999	.0204	3089	49.104	6911	50
20	.0233	3668	.9997	9999	.0233	3669	42.964	6331	40
30	.0262	4179	.9997	9999	.0262	4181	38.188	5819	30
40	.0291	4637	.9996	9998	.0291	4638	34.368	5362	20
50	.0320	5050	.9995	9998	.0320	5053	31.242	4947	10
2° 00′	.0349	8.5428	.9994	9.9997	.0349	8.5431	28.636	1.4569	88° 00′
10	.0378	5776	.9993	9997	.0378	5779	26.432	4221	50
20	.0407	6097	.9992	9996	.0407	6101	24.542	3899	40
30	.0436	6397	.9990	9996	.0437	6401	22.904	3599	30
40	.0465	6677	.9989	9995	.0466	6682	21.470	3318	20
50	.0494	6940	.9988	9995	.0495	6945	20.206	3055	10
3° 00′	.0523	8.7188	.9986	9.9994	.0524	8.7194	19.081	1.2806	87° 00′
10	.0552	7423	.9985	9993	.0553	7429	18.075	2571	50
20	.0581	7645	.9983	9993	.0582	7652	17.169	2348	40
30	.0610	7857	.9981	9992	.0612	7865	16.350	2135	30
40	.0640	8059	.9980	9991	.0641	8067	15.605	1933	20
50	.0669	8251	.9978	9990	.0670	8261	14.924	1739	10
4° 00′	.0698	8.8436	.9976	9.9989	.0699	8.8446	14.301	1.1554	86° 00′
10	.0727	8613	.9974	9989	.0729	8624	13.727	1376	50
20	.0756	8783	.9971	9988	.0758	8795	13.197	1205	40
30	.0785	8946	.9969	9987	.0787	8960	12.706	1040	30
40	.0814	9104	.9967	9986	.0816	9118	12.251	0882	20
50	.0843	9256	.9964	9985	.0846	9272	11.826	0728	10
5° 00′	.0872	8.9403	.9962	9.9983	.0875	8.9420	11.430	1.0580	85° 00′
10	.0901	9545	.9959	9982	.0904	9563	11.059	0437	50
20	.0929	9682	.9957	9981	.0934	9701	10.712	0299	40
30	.0958	9816	.9954	9980	.0963	9836	10.385	0164	30
40	.0987	9945	.9951	9979	.0992	9966	10.078	0034	20
50	.1016	9.0070	.9948	9977	.1022	9.0093	9.7882	0.9907	10
6° 00′	.1045	9.0192	.9945	9.9976	.1051	9.0216	9.5144	0.9784	84° 00′
10	.1074	0311	.9942	9975	.1080	0336	9.2553	9664	50
20	.1103	0426	.9939	9973	.1110	0453	9.0098	9547	40
30	.1132	0539	.9936	9972	.1139	0567	8.7769	9433	30
40	.1161	0648	.9932	9971	.1169	0678	8.5555	9322	20
50	.1190	0755	.9929	9969	.1198	0786	8.3450	9214	10
7° 00′	.1219	9.0859	.9925	9.9968	.1228	9.0891	8.1443	0.9109	83° 00′
10	.1248	0961	.9922	9966	.1257	0995	7.9530	9005	50
20	.1276	1060	.9918	9964	.1287	1096	7.7704	8904	40
	Nat.	Log.	Nat.	Log.	Nat.	Log.	Nat.	Log.	
Angle	Cosine		Sine		Cotangent		Tangent		Angle

Trigonometric Functions (*Cont.*)

Angle	Sine Nat.	Sine Log.	Cosine Nat.	Cosine Log.	Tangent Nat.	Tangent Log.	Cotangent Nat.	Cotangent Log.	Angle
30	.1305	1157	.9914	9963	.1317	1194	7.5958	8806	30
40	.1334	1252	.9911	9961	.1346	1291	7.4287	8709	20
50	.1363	1345	.9907	9959	.1376	1385	7.2687	8615	10
8° 00′	.1392	9.1436	.9903	9.9958	.1405	9.1478	7.1154	0.8522	82° 00′
10	.1421	1525	.9899	9956	.1435	1569	6.9682	8431	50
20	.1449	1612	.9894	9954	.1465	1658	6.8269	8342	40
30	.1478	1697	.9890	9952	.1495	1745	6.6912	8255	30
40	.1507	1781	.9886	9950	.1524	1831	6.5606	8169	20
50	.1536	1863	.9881	9948	.1554	1915	6.4348	8085	10
9° 00′	.1564	9.1943	.9877	9.9946	.1584	9.1997	6.3138	0.8003	81° 00′
10	.1593	2022	.9872	9944	.1614	2078	6.1970	7922	50
20	.1622	2100	.9868	9942	.1644	2158	6.0844	7842	40
30	.1650	2176	.9863	9940	.1673	2236	5.9758	7764	30
40	.1679	2251	.9858	9938	.1703	2313	5.8708	7687	20
50	.1708	2324	.9853	9936	.1733	2389	5.7694	7611	10
10° 00′	.1736	9.2397	.9848	9.9934	.1763	9.2463	5.6713	0.7537	80° 00′
10	.1765	2468	.9843	9931	.1793	2536	5.5764	7464	50
20	.1794	2538	.9838	9929	.1823	2609	5.4845	7391	40
30	.1822	2606	.9833	9927	.1853	2680	5.3955	7320	30
40	.1851	2674	.9827	9924	.1883	2750	5.3093	7250	20
50	.1880	2740	.9822	9922	.1914	2819	5.2257	7181	10
11° 00′	.1908	9.2806	.9816	9.9919	.1944	9.2887	5.1446	0.7113	79° 00′
10	.1937	2870	.9811	9917	.1974	2953	5.0658	7047	50
20	.1965	2934	.9805	9914	.2004	3020	4.9894	6980	40
30	.1994	2997	.9799	9912	.2035	3085	4.9152	6915	30
40	.2022	3058	.9793	9909	.2065	3149	4.8430	6851	20
50	.2051	3119	.9787	9907	.2095	3212	4.7729	6788	10
12° 00′	.2079	9.3179	.9781	9.9904	.2126	9.3275	4.7046	0.6725	78° 00′
10	.2108	3238	.9775	9901	.2156	3336	4.6382	6664	50
20	.2136	3296	.9769	9899	.2186	3397	4.5736	6603	40
30	.2164	3353	.9763	9896	.2217	3458	4.5107	6542	30
40	.2193	3410	.9757	9893	.2247	3517	4.4494	6483	20
50	.2221	3466	.9750	9890	.2278	3576	4.3897	6424	10
13° 00′	.2250	9.3521	.9744	9.9887	.2309	9.3634	4.3315	0.6366	77° 00′
10	.2278	3575	.9737	9884	.2339	3691	4.2747	6309	50
20	.2306	3629	.9730	9881	.2370	3748	4.2193	6252	40
30	.2334	3682	.9724	9878	.2401	3804	4.1653	6196	30
40	.2363	3734	.9717	9875	.2432	3859	4.1126	6141	20
50	.2391	3786	.9710	9872	.2462	3914	4.0611	6086	10
14° 00′	.2419	9.3837	.9703	9.9869	.2493	9.3968	4.0108	0.6032	76° 00′
10	.2447	3887	.9696	9866	.2524	4021	3.9617	5979	50
20	.2476	3937	.9689	9863	.2555	4074	3.9136	5926	40
30	.2504	3986	.9681	9859	.2586	4127	3.8667	5873	30
40	.2532	4035	.9674	9856	.2617	4178	3.8208	5822	20
50	.2560	4083	.9667	9853	.2648	4230	3.7760	5770	10
	Nat.	Log.	Nat.	Log.	Nat.	Log.	Nat.	Log.	

Angle	Cosine		Sine		Cotangent		Tangent		Angle

Trigonometric Functions (*Cont.*)

Angle	Sine		Cosine		Tangent		Cotangent		Angle
	Nat.	Log.	Nat.	Log.	Nat.	Log.	Nat.	Log.	
15° 00′	.2588	9.4130	.9659	9.9849	.2679	9.4281	3.7321	0.5719	75° 00′
10	.2616	4177	.9652	9846	.2711	4331	3.6891	5669	50
20	.2644	4223	.9644	9843	.2742	4381	3.6470	5619	40
30	.2672	4269	.9636	9839	.2773	4430	3.6059	5570	30
40	.2700	4314	.9628	9836	.2805	4479	3.5656	5521	20
50	.2728	4359	.9621	9832	.2836	4527	3.5261	5473	10
16° 00′	.2756	9.4403	.9613	9.9828	.2867	9.4575	3.4874	0.5425	74° 00′
10	.2784	4447	.9605	9825	.2899	4622	3.4495	5378	50
20	.2812	4491	.9596	9821	.2931	4669	3.4124	5331	40
30	.2840	4533	.9588	9817	.2962	4716	3.3759	5284	30
40	.2868	4576	.9580	9814	.2994	4762	3.3402	5238	20
50	.2896	4618	.9572	9810	.3026	4808	3.3052	5192	10
17° 00′	.2924	9.4659	.9563	9.9806	.3057	9.4853	3.2709	0.5147	73° 00′
10	.2952	4700	.9555	9802	.3089	4898	3.2371	5102	50
20	.2979	4741	.9546	9798	.3121	4943	3.2041	5057	40
30	.3007	4781	.9537	9794	.3153	4987	3.1716	5013	30
40	.3035	4821	.9528	9790	.3185	5031	3.1397	4969	20
50	.3062	4861	.9520	9786	.3217	5075	3.1084	4925	10
18° 00′	.3090	9.4900	.9511	9.9782	.3249	9.5118	3.0777	0.4882	72° 00′
10	.3118	4939	.9502	9778	.3281	5161	3.0475	4839	50
20	.3145	4977	.9492	9774	.3314	5203	3.0178	4797	40
30	.3173	5015	.9483	9770	.3346	5245	2.9887	4755	30
40	.3201	5052	.9474	9765	.3378	5287	2.9600	4713	20
50	.3228	5090	.9465	9761	.3411	5329	2.9319	4671	10
19° 00′	.3256	9.5126	.9455	9.9757	.3443	9.5370	2.9042	0.4630	71° 00′
10	.3283	5163	.9446	9752	.3476	5411	2.8770	4589	50
20	.3311	5199	.9436	9748	.3508	5451	2.8502	4549	40
30	.3338	5235	.9426	9743	.3541	5491	2.8239	4509	30
40	.3365	5270	.9417	9739	.3574	5531	2.7980	4469	20
50	.3393	5306	.9407	9734	.3607	5571	2.7725	4429	10
20° 00′	.3420	9.5341	.9397	9.9730	.3640	9.5611	2.7475	0.4389	70° 00′
10	.3448	5375	.9387	9725	.3673	5650	2.7228	4350	50
20	.3475	5409	.9377	9721	.3706	5689	2.6985	4311	40
30	.3502	5443	.9367	9716	.3739	5727	2.6746	4273	30
40	.3529	5477	.9356	9711	.3772	5766	2.6511	4234	20
50	.3557	5510	.9346	9706	.3805	5804	2.6279	4196	10
21° 00′	.3584	9.5543	.9336	9.9702	.3839	9.5842	2.6051	0.4158	69° 00′
10	.3611	5576	.9325	9697	.3872	5879	2.5826	4121	50
20	.3638	5609	.9315	9692	.3906	5917	2.5605	4083	40
30	.3665	5641	.9304	9687	.3939	5954	2.5386	4046	30
40	.3692	5673	.9293	9682	.3973	5991	2.5172	4009	20
50	.3719	5704	.9283	9677	.4006	6028	2.4960	3972	10
22° 00′	.3746	9.5736	.9272	9.9672	.4040	9.6064	2.4751	0.3936	68° 00′
10	.3773	5767	.9261	9667	.4074	6100	2.4545	3900	50
20	.3800	5798	.9250	9661	.4108	6136	2.4342	3864	40
	Nat.	Log.	Nat.	Log.	Nat.	Log.	Nat.	Log.	
Angle	Cosine		Sine		Cotangent		Tangent		Angle

Trigonometric Functions (Cont.)

Angle	Sine		Cosine		Tangent		Cotangent		Angle
	Nat.	Log.	Nat.	Log.	Nat.	Log.	Nat.	Log.	
30	.3827	5828	.9239	9656	.4142	6172	2.4142	3828	30
40	.3854	5859	.9228	9651	.4176	6208	2.3945	3792	20
50	.3881	5889	.9216	9646	.4210	6243	2.3750	3757	10
23° 00′	.3907	9.5919	.9205	9.9640	4245	9.6279	2.3559	0.3721	67° 00′
10	.3934	5948	.9194	9635	.4279	6314	2.3369	3686	50
20	.3961	5978	.9182	9629	.4314	6348	2.3183	3652	40
30	.3987	6007	.9171	9624	.4348	6383	2.2998	3617	30
40	.4014	6036	.9159	9618	.4383	6417	2.2817	3583	20
50	.4041	6065	.9147	9613	.4417	6452	2.2637	3548	10
24° 00′	.4067	9.6093	.9135	9.9607	.4452	9.6486	2.2460	0.3514	66° 00′
10	.4094	6121	.9124	9602	.4487	6520	2.2286	3480	50
20	.4120	6149	.9112	9596	.4522	6553	2.2113	3447	40
30	.4147	6177	.9100	9590	.4557	6587	2.1943	3413	30
40	.4173	6205	.9088	9584	.4592	6620	2.1775	3380	20
50	.4200	6232	.9075	9579	.4628	6654	2.1609	3346	10
25° 00′	.4226	9.6259	.9063	9.9573	.4663	9.6687	2.1445	0.3313	65° 00′
10	.4253	6286	.9051	9567	.4699	6720	2.1283	3280	50
20	.4279	6313	.9038	9561	.4734	6752	2.1123	3248	40
30	.4305	6340	.9026	9555	.4770	6785	2.0965	3215	30
40	.4331	6366	.9013	9549	.4806	6817	2.0809	3183	20
50	.4358	6392	.9001	9543	.4841	6850	2.0655	3150	10
26° 00′	.4384	9.6418	.8988	9.9537	.4877	9.6882	2.0503	0.3118	64° 00′
10	.4410	6444	.8975	9530	.4913	6914	2.0353	3086	50
20	.4436	6470	.8962	9524	.4950	6946	2.0204	3054	40
30	.4462	6495	.8949	9518	.4986	6977	2.0057	3023	30
40	.4488	6521	.8936	9512	.5022	7009	1.9912	2991	20
50	.4514	6546	.8923	9505	.5059	7040	1.9768	2960	10
27° 00′	.4540	9.6570	.8910	9.9499	.5095	9.7072	1.9626	0.2928	63° 00′
10	.4566	6595	.8897	9492	.5132	7103	1.9486	2897	50
20	.4592	6620	.8884	9486	.5169	7134	1.9347	2866	40
30	.4617	6644	.8870	9479	.5206	7165	1.9210	2835	30
40	.4643	6668	.8857	9473	.5243	7196	1.9074	2804	20
50	.4669	6692	.8843	9466	.5280	7226	1.8940	2774	10
28° 00′	.4695	9.6716	.8829	9.9459	.5317	9.7257	1.8807	0.2743	62° 00′
10	.4720	6740	.8816	9453	.5354	7287	1.8676	2713	50
20	.4746	6763	.8802	9446	.5392	7317	1.8546	2683	40
30	.4772	6787	.8788	9439	.5430	7348	1.8418	2652	30
40	.4797	6810	.8774	9432	.5467	7378	1.8291	2622	20
50	.4823	6833	.8760	9425	.5505	7408	1.8165	2592	10
29° 00′	.4848	9.6856	.8746	9.9418	.5543	9.7438	1.8040	0.2562	61° 00′
10	.4874	6878	.8732	9411	.5581	7467	1.7917	2533	50
20	.4899	6901	.8718	9404	.5619	7497	1.7796	2503	40
30	.4924	6923	.8704	9397	.5658	7526	1.7675	2474	30
40	.4950	6946	.8689	9390	.5696	7556	1.7556	2444	20
50	.4975	6968	.8675	9383	.5735	7585	1.7437	2415	10
	Nat.	Log.	Nat.	Log.	Nat.	Log.	Nat.	Log.	
Angle	Cosine		Sine		Cotangent		Tangent		Angle

Trigonometric Functions (Cont.)

Angle	Sine		Cosine		Tangent		Cotangent		Angle
	Nat.	Log.	Nat.	Log.	Nat.	Log.	Nat.	Log.	
30° 00′	.5000	9.6990	.8660	9.9375	.5774	9.7614	1.7321	0.2386	60° 00′
10	.5025	7012	.8646	9368	.5812	7644	1.7205	2356	50
20	.5050	7033	.8631	9361	.5851	7673	1.7090	2327	40
30	.5075	7055	.8616	9353	.5890	7701	1.6977	2299	30
40	.5100	7076	.8601	9346	.5930	7730	1.6864	2270	20
50	.5125	7097	.8587	9338	.5969	7759	1.6753	2241	10
31° 00′	.5150	9.7118	.8572	9.9331	.6009	9.7788	1.6643	0.2212	59° 00′
10	.5175	7139	.8557	9323	.6048	7816	1.6534	2184	50
20	.5200	7160	.8542	9315	.6088	7845	1.6426	2155	40
30	.5225	7181	.8526	9308	.6128	7873	1.6319	2127	30
40	.5250	7201	.8511	9300	.6168	7902	1.6212	2098	20
50	.5275	7222	.8496	9292	.6208	7930	1.6107	2070	10
32° 00′	.5299	9.7242	.8480	9.9284	.6249	9.7958	1.6003	0.2042	58° 00′
10	.5324	7262	.8465	9276	.6289	7986	1.5900	2014	50
20	.5348	7282	.8450	9268	.6330	8014	1.5798	1986	40
30	.5373	7302	.8434	9260	.6371	8042	1.5697	1958	30
40	.5398	7322	.8418	9252	.6412	8070	1.5597	1930	20
50	.5422	7342	.8403	9244	.6453	8097	1.5497	1903	10
33° 00′	.5446	9.7361	.8387	9.9236	.6494	9.8125	1.5399	0.1875	57° 00′
10	.5471	7380	.8371	9228	.6536	8153	1.5301	1847	50
20	.5495	7400	.8355	9219	.6577	8180	1.5204	1820	40
30	.5519	7419	.8339	9211	.6619	8208	1.5108	1792	30
40	.5544	7438	.8323	9203	.6661	8235	1.5013	1765	20
50	.5568	7457	.8307	9194	.6703	8263	1.4919	1737	10
34° 00′	.5592	9.7476	.8290	9.9186	.6745	9.8290	1.4826	0.1710	56° 00′
10	.5616	7494	.8274	9177	.6787	8317	1.4733	1683	50
20	.5640	7513	.8258	9169	.6830	8344	1.4641	1656	40
30	.5664	7531	.8241	9160	.6873	8371	1.4550	1629	30
40	.5688	7550	.8225	9151	.6916	8398	1.4460	1602	20
50	.5712	7568	.8208	9142	.6959	8425	1.4370	1575	10
35° 00′	.5736	9.7586	.8192	9.9134	.7002	9.8452	1.4281	0.1548	55° 00′
10	.5760	7604	.8175	9125	.7046	8479	1.4193	1521	50
20	.5783	7622	.8158	9116	.7089	8506	1.4106	1494	40
30	.5807	7640	.8141	9107	.7133	8533	1.4019	1467	30
40	.5831	7657	.8124	9098	.7177	8559	1.3934	1441	20
50	.5854	7675	.8107	9089	.7221	8586	1.3848	1414	10
36° 00′	.5878	9.7692	.8090	9.9080	.7265	9.8613	1.3764	0.1387	54° 00′
10	.5901	7710	.8073	9070	.7310	8639	1.3680	1361	50
20	.5925	7727	.8056	9061	.7355	8666	1.3597	1334	40
30	.5948	7744	.8039	9052	.7400	8692	1.3514	1308	30
40	.5972	7761	.8021	9042	.7445	8718	1.3432	1282	20
50	.5995	7778	.8004	9033	.7490	8745	1.3351	1255	10
37° 00′	.6018	9.7795	.7986	9.9023	.7536	9.8771	1.3270	0.1229	53° 00′
10	.6041	7811	.7969	9014	.7581	8797	1.3190	1203	50
20	.6065	7828	.7951	9004	.7627	8824	1.3111	1176	40
	Nat.	Log.	Nat.	Log.	Nat.	Log.	Nat.	Log.	
Angle	Cosine		Sine		Cotangent		Tangent		Angle

Trigonometric Functions (*Cont.*)

Angle	Sine		Cosine		Tangent		Cotangent		Angle
	Nat.	Log.	Nat.	Log.	Nat.	Log.	Nat.	Log.	
30	.6088	7844	.7934	8995	.7673	8850	1.3032	1150	30
40	.6111	7861	.7916	8985	.7720	8876	1.2954	1124	20
50	.6134	7877	.7898	8975	.7766	8902	1.2876	1098	10
38° 00′	.6157	9.7893	.7880	9.8965	.7813	9.8928	1.2799	0.1072	52° 00′
10	.6180	7910	.7862	8955	.7860	8954	1.2723	1046	50
20	.6202	7926	.7844	8945	.7907	8980	1.2647	1020	40
30	.6225	7941	.7826	8935	.7954	9006	1.2572	0994	30
40	.6248	7957	.7808	8925	.8002	9032	1.2497	0968	20
50	.6271	7973	.7790	8915	.8050	9058	1.2423	0942	10
39° 00′	.6293	9.7989	.7771	9.8905	.8098	9.9084	1.2349	0.0916	51° 00′
10	.6316	8004	.7753	8895	.8146	9110	1.2276	0890	50
20	.6338	8020	.7735	8884	.8195	9135	1.2203	0865	40
30	.6361	8035	.7716	8874	.8243	9161	1.2131	0839	30
40	.6383	8050	.7698	8864	.8292	9187	1.2059	0813	20
50	.6406	8066	.7679	8853	.8342	9212	1.1988	0788	10
40° 00′	.6428	9.8081	.7660	9.8843	.8391	9.9238	1.1918	0.0762	50° 00′
10	.6450	8096	.7642	8832	.8441	9264	1.1847	0736	50
20	.6472	8111	.7623	8821	.8491	9289	1.1778	0711	40
30	.6494	8125	.7604	8810	.8541	9315	1.1708	0685	30
40	.6517	8140	.7585	8800	.8591	9341	1.1640	0659	20
50	.6539	8155	.7566	8789	.8642	9366	1.1571	0634	10
41° 00′	.6561	9.8169	.7547	9.8778	.8693	9.9392	1.1504	0.0608	49° 00′
10	.6583	8184	.7528	8767	.8744	9417	1.1436	0583	50
20	.6604	8198	.7509	8756	.8796	9443	1.1369	0557	40
30	.6626	8213	.7490	8745	.8847	9468	1.1303	0532	30
40	.6648	8227	.7470	8733	.8899	9494	1.1237	0506	20
50	.6670	8241	.7451	8722	.8952	9519	1.1171	0481	10
42° 00′	.6691	9.8255	.7431	9.8711	.9004	9.9544	1.1106	0.0456	48° 00′
10	.6713	8269	.7412	8699	.9057	9570	1.1041	0430	50
20	.6734	8283	.7392	8688	.9110	9595	1.0977	0405	40
30	.6756	8297	.7373	8676	.9163	9621	1.0913	0379	30
40	.6777	8311	.7353	8665	.9217	9646	1.0850	0354	20
50	.6799	8324	.7333	8653	.9271	9671	1.0786	0329	10
43° 00′	.6820	9.8338	.7314	9.8641	.9325	9.9697	1.0724	0.0303	47° 00′
10	.6841	8351	.7294	8629	.9380	9722	1.0661	0278	50
20	.6862	8365	.7274	8618	.9435	9747	1.0599	0253	40
30	.6884	8378	.7254	8606	.9490	9772	1.0538	0228	30
40	.6905	8391	.7234	8594	.9545	9798	1.0477	0202	20
50	.6926	8405	.7214	8582	.9601	9823	1.0416	0177	10
44° 00′	.6947	9.8418	.7193	9.8569	.9657	9.9848	1.0355	0.0152	46° 00′
10	.6967	8431	.7173	8557	.9713	9874	1.0295	0126	50
20	.6988	8444	.7153	8545	.9770	9899	1.0235	0101	40
30	.7009	8457	.7133	8532	.9827	9924	1.0176	0076	30
40	.7030	8469	.7112	8520	.9884	9949	1.0117	0051	20
50	.7050	8482	.7092	8507	.9942	9975	1.0058	0025	10
45° 00′	.7071	9.8495	.7071	9.8495	1.0000	0.0000	1.0000	0.0000	45° 00′
	Nat.	Log.	Nat.	Log.	Nat.	Log.	Nat.	Log	
Angle	Cosine		Sine		Cotangent		Tangent		Angle

A48

Length of Chord for Circle Arcs of 1-in. Radius

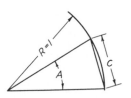

°	0′	10′	20′	30′	40′	50′
0	0.0000	0.0029	0.0058	0.0087	0.0116	0.0145
1	0.0175	0.0204	0.0233	0.0262	0.0291	0.0320
2	0.0349	0.0378	0.0407	0.0436	0.0465	0.0494
3	0.0524	0.0553	0.0582	0.0611	0.0640	0.0669
4	0.0698	0.0727	0.0756	0.0785	0.0814	0.0843
5	0.0872	0.0901	0.0931	0.0960	0.0989	0.1018
6	0.1047	0.1076	0.1105	0.1134	0.1163	0.1192
7	0.1221	0.1250	0.1279	0.1308	0.1337	0.1366
8	0.1395	0.1424	0.1453	0.1482	0.1511	0.1540
9	0.1569	0.1598	0.1627	0.1656	0.1685	0.1714
10	0.1743	0.1772	0.1801	0.1830	0.1859	0.1888
11	0.1917	0.1946	0.1975	0.2004	0.2033	0.2062
12	0.2091	0.2119	0.2148	0.2177	0.2206	0.2235
13	0.2264	0.2293	0.2322	0.2351	0.2380	0.2409
14	0.2437	0.2466	0.2495	0.2524	0.2553	0.2582
15	0.2611	0.2639	0.2668	0.2697	0.2726	0.2755
16	0.2783	0.2812	0.2841	0.2870	0.2899	0.2927
17	0.2956	0.2985	0.3014	0.3042	0.3071	0.3100
18	0.3129	0.3157	0.3186	0.3215	0.3244	0.3272
19	0.3301	0.3330	0.3358	0.3387	0.3416	0.3444
20	0.3473	0.3502	0.3530	0.3559	0.3587	0.3616
21	0.3645	0.3673	0.3702	0.3730	0.3759	0.3788
22	0.3816	0.3845	0.3873	0.3902	0.3930	0.3959
23	0.3987	0.4016	0.4044	0.4073	0.4101	0.4130
24	0.4158	0.4187	0.4215	0.4244	0.4272	0.4300
25	0.4329	0.4357	0.4386	0.4414	0.4442	0.4471
26	0.4499	0.4527	0.4556	0.4584	0.4612	0.4641
27	0.4669	0.4697	0.4725	0.4754	0.4782	0.4810
28	0.4838	0.4867	0.4895	0.4923	0.4951	0.4979
29	0.5008	0.5036	0.5064	0.5092	0.5120	0.5148
30	0.5176	0.5204	0.5233	0.5261	0.5289	0.5317
31	0.5345	0.5373	0.5401	0.5429	0.5457	0.5485
32	0.5513	0.5541	0.5569	0.5597	0.5625	0.5652
33	0.5680	0.5708	0.5736	0.5764	0.5792	0.5820
34	0.5847	0.5875	0.5903	0.5931	0.5959	0.5986
35	0.6014	0.6042	0.6070	0.6097	0.6125	0.6153
36	0.6180	0.6208	0.6236	0.6263	0.6291	0.6319
37	0.6346	0.6374	0.6401	0.6429	0.6456	0.6484
38	0.6511	0.6539	0.6566	0.6594	0.6621	0.6649
39	0.6676	0.6704	0.6731	0.6758	0.6786	0.6813
40	0.6840	0.6868	0.6895	0.6922	0.6950	0.6977
41	0.7004	0.7031	0.7059	0.7086	0.7113	0.7140
42	0.7167	0.7195	0.7222	0.7249	0.7276	0.7303
43	0.7330	0.7357	0.7384	0.7411	0.7438	0.7465
44	0.7492	0.7519	0.7546	0.7573	0.7600	0.7627
45 *	0.7654	0.7681	0.7707	0.7734	0.7761	0.7788

* For angles between 45° and 90°, draw 90° angle and lay off complement from 90° line.

Conversions of Weights and Measures

Given	Multiply by	To obtain
Absolute temperature (abs temp), centigrade	1.0	degrees Centigrade $+273.160 \pm .010$
Absolute temperature, Fahrenheit	1.0	degrees Fahrenheit $+491.2$
Acceleration by gravity	980.665	centimeters per second
Acceleration by gravity	32.16	feet per second
Acres	0.4047	hectares
Acres	10.0	square chains
Acres	43,560.0	square feet
Acre	0.00156	square miles
Ares	100.0	centiares
Ares	119.6	square yards
Atmospheres (atm)	29.921	inches of mercury
Atmospheres	33.934	feet of water
Atmospheres	1.033228	kilograms per square centimeter
Atmospheres	14.6959	pounds per square inch
British thermal units (Btu)	0.252	calories
British thermal units	778.0	foot-pounds
British thermal units	1,054.86	watt-seconds
Bushels (bu), imperial	1.032	bushels, U.S.
Bushels, imperial	1.2837	cubic feet
Bushels, imperial	2,218.19	cubic inches
Bushels, imperial	8.0	gallons, imperial
Bushels, imperial	36.368	liters
Bushels, U.S.	0.968	bushels, imperial
Bushels, U.S.	1.2445	cubic feet
Bushels, U.S.	2,150.42	cubic inches
Bushels, U.S.	35.2393	liters
Bushels, U.S.	4.0	pecks
Bushels, U.S.	64.0	pints, dry
Bushels, U.S.	32.0	quarts, dry
Calories (cal)	3.9682	British thermal units
Calories	3,088.4	foot-pounds
Carats	3.086	grains
Carats	200.0	milligrams
Centiares	1,549.997	square inches
Centiares	1.0	square meters
Centigrade, degrees (°C)	$\frac{9}{5}$°C $+ 32$	Fahrenheit, degrees
Centigrams (cg)	0.1543	grains
Centigrams	0.01	grams
Centiliters (cl)	0.01	liters
Centiliters	0.0338	ounces, fluid

Conversions of Weights and Measures (*Cont.*)

Given	Multiply by	To obtain
Centimeters (cm)	0.0328	feet
Centimeters	0.3937	inches
Centimeters	0.01	meters
Chains	0.10000	furlongs
Chains	0.01250	miles, statute
Chains	100.0	links
Circle (angular)	360.0	degrees
Circular inch (cir in.)	1.0	area of a 1-in.-diameter circle
Circular inches	1,000,000.0	circular mils
Circular inches	0.7854	square inches
Circular mil	1.0	area of a 0.001-in.-diameter circle
Circular mils	0.0000001	circular inches
Circumference of the earth at the equator	21,600.0	miles, nautical
Circumference of the earth at the equator	24,874.5	miles, statute
Cord (cd), of wood, (4 × 4 × 8)	128.0	cubic feet
Cubic centimeters (cu cm)	0.00003531	cubic feet
Cubic centimeters	0.06102	cubic inches
Cubic centimeters	0.0010	liters
Cubic centimeters	0.0000010	cubic meter
Cubic decimeters	1,000.0	cubic centimeters
Cubic decimeters	61.02	cubic inches
Cubic feet (cu ft)	0.7790	bushels, imperial
Cubic feet	0.80290	bushels, U.S.
Cubic feet	0.00781	cords, of wood
Cubic feet	28,317.08	cubic centimeters
Cubic feet	1,728.0	cubic inches
Cubic feet	0.0283	cubic meters
Cubic feet	0.0370	cubic yards
Cubic feet	7.4805	gallons, U.S.
Cubic feet	28.3163	liters
Cubic feet	0.04040	perch, of masonry
Cubic feet of water at 39.1 degrees Fahrenheit (°F)	28.3156	kilograms
Cubic feet of water at 39.1 degrees Fahrenheit	62.4245	pounds
Cubic inches (cu in.)	0.00045	bushels, imperial
Cubic inches	0.00046	bushels, U.S.
Cubic inches	16.3872	cubic centimeters
Cubic inches	0.00058	cubic feet
Cubic inches	0.000016	cubic meters
Cubic inches	0.0000214	cubic yards
Cubic inches	0.0036	gallons, imperial

Conversions of Weights and Measures (Cont.)

Given	Multiply by	To obtain
Cubic inches	0.00432	gallons, U.S.
Cubic inches	0.0164	liters
Cubic inches	0.00186	pecks
Cubic inches	0.02976	pints, dry
Cubic inches	0.0346	pints, liquid
Cubic inches	0.01488	quarts, dry
Cubic inches	0.0173	quarts, liquid
Cubic meters (cu m or m³)	1,000,000.0	cubic centimeters
Cubic meters	35.3133	cubic feet
Cubic meters	61,023.3753	cubic inches
Cubic meters	1.3079	cubic yards
Cubic meters	264.170	gallons, U.S.
Cubic millimeters (cu mm or mm³)	0.001	cubic centimeters
Cubic millimeters	0.00006	cubic inches
Cubic yards (cu yd)	27.0	cubic feet
Cubic yards	46,656.0	cubic inches
Cubic yards	0.7646	cubic meters
Decigrams	1.5432	grains
Decigrams	0.1	grams
Decimeters	3.937	inches
Decimeters	0.01	meters
Deciliter	0.338	ounces, fluid
Decagrams	10.0	grams
Decagrams	0.3527	ounces, avoirdupois
Decaliters	0.284	bushels, U.S.
Decaliters	2.64	gallons, U.S.
Decaliters	10.0	liters
Decameters	393.7	inches
Decameters	10.0	meters
Decileters	0.1	liters
Degrees (deg or °)	60.0	minutes
Degrees (arc)	0.0175	radians
Degrees (at the equator)	60.0	miles, nautical
Degrees (at the equator)	69.168	miles, statute
Dozens (doz)	12.0	units
Drams (dr), apothecaries	60.0	grains
Drams, apothecaries	3.543	grams
Drams, apothecaries	3.0	scruples
Drams, avoirdupois	27.344	grains
Drams, avoirdupois	1.772	grams
Drams, avoirdupois	0.0625	ounces, avoirdupois
Drams, fluid	0.2256	cubic inches
Drams, fluid	3.6966	milliliters

Conversions of Weights and Measures (*Cont.*)

Given	Multiply by	To obtain
Drams, fluid	60.0	minims
Drams, fluid	0.125	ounces, U.S. fluid
Dynes	0.00102	grams
Ergs	1.0	dyne-centimeters
Fahrenheit	$\dfrac{5(°F-32)}{9}$	centigrade, degrees
Fathoms	6.0	feet
Fathoms	1.8288	meters
Fathoms	2.0	yards
Feet (ft)	30.4801	centimeters
Feet	0.16667	fathom
Feet	12.0	inches
Feet	0.66000	links
Feet	0.3048	meters
Feet	0.000189	miles
Feet	0.0001645	miles, nautical
Feet	0.06061	rods
Feet	0.3333	yards
Feet of water at 62 degrees Fahrenheit	304.442	kilograms per square meter
Feet of water at 62 degrees Fahrenheit	62.355	pounds per square foot
Feet of water at 62 degrees Fahrenheit	0.4334	pounds per square inch
Feet per second (fps)	0.5921	knots
Feet per second	0.6816	miles per hour
Foot-pounds (ft-lb)	0.00129	British thermal units
Foot-pounds	0.00032	calories
Foot-pounds	0.13835	meter-kilograms
Foot-pounds per minute	0.000003	horsepower
Foot-pounds per second	0.000018	horsepower
Furlongs	10.0	chains
Furlongs	660.0	feet
Furlongs	201.17	meters
Furlongs	0.12500	miles, statute
Furlongs	220.0	yards
Gallons (gal), imperial	0.125	bushels, imperial
Gallons, imperial	277.4176	cubic inches
Gallons, imperial	1.2009	gallons, U.S.
Gallons, imperial	4.54607	liters
Gallons, U.S.	0.1337	cubic feet
Gallons, U.S.	231.0	cubic inches
Gallons, U.S.	0.0038	cubic meters
Gallons, U.S.	0.8327	gallons, imperial
Gallons, U.S.	3.7878	liters

Conversions of Weights and Measures (*Cont.*)

Given	Multiply by	To obtain
Gallons, U.S.	128.0	ounces, U.S. fluid
Gallons, U.S., water	8.5	pounds
Gills	0.25	pints, liquid
Grains	0.0366	drams, avoirdupois
Grains	0.0648	grams
Grains	64.7989	milligrams
Grains	0.00229	ounces, avoirdupois
Grains	0.00208	ounces, troy and apothecaries'
Grains	0.00014	pounds, avoirdupois
Grains	0.00017	pounds, troy and apothecaries'
Grams (g)	981	dynes
Grams	15.4475	grains
Grams	0.0010	kilograms
Grams	1,000.0	milligrams
Grams	0.0353	ounces, avoirdupois
Grams	0.0022	pounds, avoirdupois
Grams per cubic centimeter	1,000.0	kilograms per cubic meter
Grams per cubic centimeter	62.4	pounds per cubic foot
Grams per cubic centimeter	0.03613	pounds per cubic inch
Gross	12.0	dozen
Gross, great	12.0	gross
Hands	4.0	inches
Hectares (ha)	100.0	ares
Hectograms	100.0	grams
Hectograms	3.5274	ounces, avoirdupois
Hectoliters	26.417	gallons
Hectoliters	100.0	liters
Hectometers	328.083	feet
Hectometers	100.0	meters
Horsepower (hp)	76.042	kilogram-meters per second
Horsepower	550.0	foot-pounds per second
Horsepower	33,000.0	foot-pounds per minute
Horsepower	1.0139	metric horsepower
Horsepower	746.0	watts per minute
Horsepower, metric	0.9862	horsepower
Horsepower, metric	32,550.0	foot-pounds per minute
Horsepower, metric	542.5	foot-pounds per second
Horsepower, metric	75.0	kilogram meters per second
Inches (in.)	2.5400	centimeters
Inches	0.08333	feet
Inches	0.25000	hands
Inches	0.12626	links

Conversions of Weights and Measures (Cont.)

Given	Multiply by	To obtain
Inches	0.0254	meters
Inches	1,000.0	mils
Inches	0.11111	spans
Inches	0.02778	yards
Inches of mercury	1.1341	feet of water
Inches of mercury	34.542	grams per square centimeter
Inches of mercury	13.6092	inches of water
Inches of mercury	0.49115	pounds per square inch
Inches of water	2.537	grams per square centimeter
Inches of water	0.07347	inches of mercury
Inches of water	5.1052	pounds per square foot
Kilocycles	1,000.0	cycles per second
Kilogram-meters (kg-m)	7.2330	pound-feet
Kilogram-meters per second	0.01305	horsepower
Kilogram-meters per second	0.01333	horsepower, metric
Kilograms (kg)	15,432.36	grains
Kilograms	1,000.0	grams
Kilograms	35.2740	ounces, avoirdupois
Kilograms	2.2046	pounds, avoirdupois
Kilograms	0.00110	tons
Kilograms	0.00098	tons, long
Kilograms	0.001	tons, metric
Kilograms per cubic meter (kg per cu m or kg/m³)	0.06243	pounds per cubic foot
Kilograms per meter	0.6721	pounds per foot
Kilograms per square centimeter	14.22	pounds per square inch
Kilograms per square meter	0.2048	pounds per square inch
Kilograms per square meter	0.00142	pounds per square inch
Kiloliters (kl)	1,000.0	liters
Kilometers (km)	3,280.8330	feet
Kilometers	1,000.0	meters
Kilometers	0.5396	miles, nautical
Kilometers	0.6214	miles, statute
Kilometers per hour	0.5396	knots
Kilometers per hour	0.62138	miles per hour
Kilowatts (kw)	0.04426	foot-pounds per minute
Kilowatt-hours (kwhr)	3,412.75	British thermal units per hour
Kilowatt-hours	1.3414	horsepower hours
Knots	1.6889	feet per second
Knots	1.8532	kilometers per hour
Knots	0.5148	meters per second
Knots	1.1516	miles per hour
Knots	1.0	nautical miles per hour

Conversions of Weights and Measures (Cont.)

Given	Multiply by	To obtain
Leagues, land	4.83	kilometers
Leagues, land	2.6050	miles, nautical
Leagues, land	3.0	miles, statute
Leagues, marine	5.56	kilometers
Leagues, marine	3.0	miles, nautical
Leagues, marine	3.45	miles, statute
Links	0.01	chains
Links	0.66	feet
Links	7.92	inches
Links	0.04	rods
Links	0.22	yards
Liters (l)	0.0284	bushels, U.S.
Liters	1,000.0	cubic centimeters
Liters	0.035313	cubic feet
Liters	61.02398	cubic inches
Liters	0.2199	gallons, imperial
Liters	0.2641	gallons, U.S.
Liters	0.1135	pecks
Liters	0.9081	quarts, dry
Liters	1.0567	quarts, liquid
Long tons	2,240.0	pounds, avoirdupois
Megacycles	1,000,000.0	cycles per second
Megameters	100,000.0	meters
Meters (m)	0.5468	fathoms
Meters	3.2808	feet
Meters	39.370	inches
Meters	0.000541	miles, nautical
Meters	0.000622	miles, U.S.
Meters	1.0936	yards
Meter-kilograms (m-kg)	7.2330	foot-pounds
Meters per second	1.9425	knots
Meters per second	2.2369	miles per hour
Microns (μ)	0.000039	inches
Microns	0.000001	meters
Microns	0.03937	mils
Miles, nautical	6,080.20	feet
Miles, nautical	1.85325	kilometers
Miles, nautical	0.33333	leagues, marine
Miles, nautical	1,853.2486	meters
Miles, nautical	1.1516	miles, statute
Miles, statute	80.0	chains
Miles, statute	5,280.0	feet
Miles, statute	8.0	furlongs

Conversions of Weights and Measures (Cont.)

Given	Multiply by	To obtain
Miles, statute	1.6093	kilometers
Miles, statute	0.33333	leagues, land
Miles, statute	1,609.35	meters
Miles, statute	0.86836	miles, nautical
Miles, statute	1,760.0	yards
Miles per hour (mph)	1.4667	feet per second
Miles per hour	1.6093	kilometers per hour
Miles per hour	0.8684	knots
Miles per hour	0.4470	meters per second
Milligrams (mg)	0.01543	grains
Milligrams	0.001	grams
Milliliters (ml)	0.2705	drams, fluid
Milliliters	0.001	liters
Milliliters	0.0338	ounces, fluid
Millimeters (mm)	0.03937	inches
Millimeters	0.001	meters
Millimeters	1,000.0	microns
Millimeters	39.37	mils
Mils	0.001	inches
Mils	25.4001	microns
Mils	0.0254	millimeters
Minims	0.01667	drams, fluid
Minutes (min)	60.0	seconds
Myriagrams	10,000.0	grams
Myriameters	10,000.0	meters
Ounces (oz), apothecaries'	8.0	drams, apothecaries'
Ounces, avoirdupois	16.0	drams, avoirdupois
Ounces, avoirdupois	437.5	grains
Ounces, avoirdupois	28.3495	grams
Ounces, avoirdupois	1.0971	ounces, troy and apothecaries'
Ounces, avoirdupois	0.0625	pounds, avoirdupois
Ounces, British fluid	28.382	cubic centimeters
Ounces, British fluid	1.732	cubic inches
Ounces, fluid	29.57	milliliters
Ounces, troy	20.0	pennyweights
Ounces, troy and apothecaries'	480.0	grains
Ounces, troy and apothecaries'	31.10348	grams
Ounces, troy and apothecaries'	0.91149	ounces, avoirdupois
Ounces, U.S. fluid	1.805	cubic inches
Ounces, U.S. fluid	8.0	drams, fluid
Ounces, U.S. fluid	0.00781	gallons, U.S.
Ounces, U.S. fluid	0.0296	liters
Pecks (pk)	0.25	bushel, U.S.

Conversions of Weights and Measures (*Cont.*)

Given	Multiply by	To obtain
Pecks	537.61	cubic inches
Pecks	8.8096	liters
Pecks	8.0	quarts, dry
Pennyweights (dwt)	24.0	grains
Perch (of masonry)	24.75	cubic feet
Pints (pt), dry	0.015625	bushels, U.S.
Pints, dry	33.60	cubic inches
Pints, dry	0.5506	liters
Pints, dry	0.0625	pecks
Pints, dry	0.5	quarts, dry
Pints, liquid	28.875	cubic inches
Pints, liquid	4.0	gills
Pints, liquid	0.4732	liters
Poundals	0.03113	pounds, avoirdupois
Pounds (lb), avoirdupois	0.0160	cubic feet of water
Pounds, avoirdupois	7,000.0	grains
Pounds, avoirdupois	453.5924	grams
Pounds, avoirdupois	16.0	ounces, avoirdupois
Pounds, avoirdupois	32.1740	poundals
Pounds, avoirdupois	0.0311	slugs
Pounds, avoirdupois	0.00045	tons, long
Pounds, avoirdupois	0.0005	tons, short
Pound-feet (lb-ft)	0.1383	kilogram-meters
Pounds per cubic foot (lb per cu ft)	0.01602	grams per cubic centimeter
Pounds per cubic foot	16.0184	kilograms per cubic meter
Pounds per cubic foot	0.00058	pounds per cubic inch
Pounds per foot	1.4882	kilograms per meter
Pounds per square foot (psf)	0.1922	inches of water
Pounds per square foot	4.8824	kilograms per square meter
Pounds per square foot	0.00694	pounds per square inch
Pounds per square inch (psi)	0.0680	atmospheres
Pounds per square inch	2.3066	feet of water
Pounds per square inch	70.3067	grams per square centimeter
Pounds per square inch	27.7	inches of water
Pounds per square inch	2.0360	inches of mercury
Pounds per square inch	703.0669	kilograms per square meter
Pounds per square inch	144.0	pounds per square foot
Pounds, troy and apothecaries'	5,760.0	grains
Pounds, troy and apothecaries'	0.37324	kilograms
Pounds, troy and apothecaries'	12.0	ounces, troy and apothecaries'
Pounds, troy and apothecaries'	0.8229	pounds, avoirdupois
Quadrants	90.0	degrees
Quarts (qt), dry, imperial	1.032	quarts, dry, U.S.

Conversions of Weights and Measures (*Cont.*)

Given	Multiply by	To obtain
Quarts, dry, U.S.	1.1012	liters
Quarts, dry, U.S.	0.125	pecks
Quarts, dry, U.S.	2.0	pints, dry
Quarts, dry, U.S.	0.968	quarts, dry, imperial
Quarts, dry, U.S.	0.03125	bushel, U.S.
Quarts, dry, U.S.	67.2	cubic inches
Quarts, liquid	57.75	cubic inches
Quarts, liquid	0.94636	liters
Quintals	100,000.0	grams
Quintals	220.46	pounds, avoirdupois
Quire	24.0	sheets
Radians	57.2958	degrees, arc
Radians	3,437.7468	minutes, arc
Radians	0.1591	revolutions
Radians per second	9.4460	revolutions per minute
Ream	480.0	sheets
Ream, printing paper	500.0	sheets
Revolutions	6.2832	radians
Revolutions per minute (rpm)	0.1059	radians per second
Rods	0.25	chains
Rods	16.5	feet
Rods	40.0	furlongs
Rods	25.0	links
Rods	5.029	meters
Rods	5.5	yards
Score	20.0	units
Scruples	20.0	grains
Seconds	0.01667	minutes
Slugs	32.1740	pounds
Spans	9.0	inches
Square centimeters (sq cm or cm²)	0.001076	square feet
Square centimeters	0.1550	square inches
Square centimeters	100.0	square millimeters
Square chains	0.1	acres
Square chains	4,356.0	square feet
Square chains	404.7	square meters
Square chains	0.00016	square miles
Square chains	16.0	square rods
Square chains	484.0	square yards
Square decameters	100.0	square meters
Square decimeters	0.01	square meters
Square feet (sq ft)	0.000022988	acres

Conversions of Weights and Measures (*Cont.*)

Given	Multiply by	To obtain
Square feet	929.0341	square centimeters
Square feet	0.00023	square chains
Square feet	144.0	square inches
Square feet	0.0929	square meters
Square feet	0.00368	square rods
Square feet	0.11111	square yards
Square hectometers	10,000.0	square meters
Square inches (sq in.)	1.27324	circular inches
Square inches	6.4516	square centimeters
Square inches	0.00694	square feet
Square inches	645.1625	square millimeters
Square inches	0.00077	square yards
Square kilometers (sq km or km²)	100.0	hectares
Square kilometers	1,000,000.0	square meters
Square kilometers	0.3861	square miles
Square links	0.4356	square feet
Square links	0.0405	square meters
Square links	0.00160	square rods
Square links	0.04840	square yards
Square meters (sq m or m²)	1.0	centiares
Square meters	10.7639	square feet
Square meters	1.1960	square yards
Square miles	2.590	square kilometers
Square miles	640.0	acres
Square miles	6,400.0	square chains
Square millimeters (sq mm or mm²)	0.00155	square inches
Square millimeters	0.000001	square meters
Square rods	0.06250	square chains
Square rods	272.25	square feet
Square rods	625.0	square links
Square rods	25.29	square meters
Square rods	30.25	square yards
Square yards	0.00207	square chains
Square yards	9.0	square feet
Square yards	1,296.0	square inches
Square yards	20.66116	square links
Square yards	0.83613	square meters
Square yards	0.03306	square rods
Tons, long	1,016.0470	kilograms
Tons, long	2,240.0	pounds, avoirdupois
Tons, metric	1,000.0	kilograms
Tons, metric	2,204.62	pounds, avoirdupois
Tons, metric	10.0	quintals

Conversions of Weights and Measures (Cont.)

Given	Multiply by	To obtain
Tons, register	100.0	cubic feet
Tons, shipping, British	32.719	bushels, imperial
Tons, shipping, British	32.700	bushels, U.S.
Tons, shipping, British	42.0	cubic feet
Tons, shipping, U.S.	31.16	bushels, imperial
Tons, shipping, U.S.	32.143	bushels, U.S.
Tons, shipping, U.S.	40.0	cubic feet
Tons, short	907.18	kilograms
Tons, short	2,000.0	pounds, avoirdupois
Watts (w)	10,000,000.0	ergs per second
Yards (yd)	0.04545	chains
Yards	0.50000	fathoms
Yards	3.0	feet
Yards	0.004545	furlongs
Yards	36.0	inches
Yards	0.22000	links
Yards	0.9144	meters
Yards	0.000569	miles, statute
Yards	0.18182	rods

Standard Parts, Sizes, Symbols, and Abbreviations

American Standard Unified and American Thread Series[a]

Threads per inch for coarse, fine, extra-fine, 8-thread, 12-thread, and 16-thread series [b] [tap-drill sizes for approximately 75 per cent depth of thread (not American Standard)]

Nominal size (basic major diam.)	Coarse-thd. series UNC and NC[c] in classes 1A, 1B, 2A, 2B, 3A, 3B, 2, 3		Fine-thd. series UNF and NF[c] in classes 1A, 1B, 2A, 2B, 3A, 3B, 2, 3		Extra-fine thd. series UNEF and NEF[d] in classes 2A, 2B, 2, 3		8-thd. series 8N[c] in classes 2A, 2B, 2, 3		12-thd. series 12UN and 12N[d] in classes 2A, 2B, 2, 3		16-thd. series 16UN and 16N[d] in classes 2A, 2B, 2, 3	
	Thd. /in.	Tap drill	Thd. /in.	Tap drill	Thd. /in.	Tap drill	Thd. /in.	Tap drill	Thd. /in.	Tap drill	Thd. /in.	Tap drill
0(0.060)	....	.....	80	3/64								
1(0.073)	64	No. 53	72	No. 53								
2(0.086)	56	No. 50	64	No. 50								
3(0.099)	48	No. 47	56	No. 45								
4(0.112)	40	No. 43	48	No. 42								
5(0.125)	40	No. 38	44	No. 37								
6(0.138)	32	No. 36	40	No. 33								
8(0.164)	32	No. 29	36	No. 29								
10(0.190)	24	No. 25	32	No. 21								
12(0.216)	24	No. 16	28	No. 14	32	No. 13						
1/4	20	No. 7	28	No. 3	32	7/32						
5/16	18	Let. F	24	Let. I	32	9/32						
3/8	16	5/16	24	Let. Q	32	11/32						
7/16	14	Let. U	20	25/64	28	13/32						
1/2	13	27/64	20	29/64	28	15/32	..	....	12	27/64		
9/16	12	31/64	18	33/64	24	33/64	..	....	12	31/64		
5/8	11	17/32	18	37/64	24	37/64	..	....	12	35/64		
11/16	....	.....	..	.....	24	41/64	..	....	12	39/64		
3/4	10	21/32	16	11/16	20	45/64	..	....	12	43/64	16	11/16
13/16	....	.....	..	.....	20	49/64	..	....	12	47/64	16	3/4
7/8	9	49/64	14	13/16	20	53/64	..	....	12	51/64	16	13/16
15/16	....	.....	..	.....	20	57/64	..	....	12	55/64	16	7/8
1	....	.....	14	15/16	..	.....	8	7/8				
1	8	7/8	12	59/64	20	61/64	..	....	12	59/64	16	15/16
1 1/16	....	.....	..	.....	18	1	..	....	12	63/64	16	1
1 1/8	7	63/64	12	1 3/64	18	1 5/64	8	1	12	1 3/64	16	1 1/16
1 3/16	....	.....	..	.....	18	1 9/64	..	....	12	1 7/64	16	1 1/8
1 1/4	7	1 7/64	12	1 11/64	18	1 3/16	8	1 1/8	12	1 11/64	16	1 3/16
1 5/16	....	.....	..	.....	18	1 17/64	..	....	12	1 15/64	16	1 1/4
1 3/8	6	1 7/32	12	1 19/64	18	1 5/16	8	1 1/4	12	1 19/64	16	1 5/16
1 7/16	....	.....	..	.....	18	1 3/8	..	....	12	1 23/64	16	1 3/8
1 1/2	6	1 11/32	12	1 27/64	18	1 7/16	8	1 3/8	12	1 27/64	16	1 7/16
1 9/16	....	.....	..	.....	18	1 1/2	..	....			16	1 1/2
1 5/8	....	.....	..	.....	18	1 9/16	8	1 1/2	12	1 35/64	16	1 9/16
1 11/16	....	.....	..	.....	18	1 5/8	..	....			16	1 5/8

American Standard Unified and American Thread Series (*Cont.*)

Nominal size (basic major diam.)	Coarse-thd. series UNC and NC[c] in classes 1A, 1B, 2A, 2B, 3A, 3B, 2, 3		Fine-thd. series UNF and NF[c] in classes 1A, 1B, 2A, 2B, 3A, 3B, 2, 3		Extra-fine thd. series UNEF and NEF[d] in classes 2A, 2B, 2, 3		8-thd. series 8N[c] in classes 2A, 2B, 2, 3		12-thd. series 12UN and 12N[d] in classes 2A, 2B, 2, 3		16-thd. series 16UN and 16N[d] in classes 2A, 2B, 2, 3	
	Thd. /in.	Tap drill	Thd. /in.	Tap drill	Thd. /in.	Tap drill	Thd. /in.	Tap drill	Thd. /in.	Tap drill	Thd. /in.	Tap drill
$1\frac{3}{4}$	5	$1\frac{9}{16}$	..	.....	16	$1\frac{11}{16}$	8[e]	$1\frac{5}{8}$	12	$1\frac{43}{64}$	16	$1\frac{11}{16}$
$1\frac{13}{16}$	....	.....	..	.....	..	.....	..	.....	..	.....	16	$1\frac{3}{4}$
$1\frac{7}{8}$	....	.....	..	.....	..	.....	8	$1\frac{3}{4}$	12	$1\frac{51}{64}$	16	$1\frac{13}{16}$
$1\frac{15}{16}$	....	.....	..	.....	..	.....	..	.....	..	.....	16	$1\frac{7}{8}$
2	$4\frac{1}{2}$	$1\frac{25}{32}$	..	.....	16	$1\frac{15}{16}$	8[e]	$1\frac{7}{8}$	12	$1\frac{59}{64}$	16	$1\frac{15}{16}$
$2\frac{1}{16}$	....	.....	..	.....	..	.....	..	.....	..	.....	16	2
$2\frac{1}{8}$	....	.....	..	.....	..	.....	8	2	12	$2\frac{3}{64}$	16	$2\frac{1}{16}$
$2\frac{3}{16}$	....	.....	..	.....	..	.....	..	.....	..	.....	16	$2\frac{1}{8}$
$2\frac{1}{4}$	$4\frac{1}{2}$	$2\frac{1}{32}$	..	.....	..	.....	8[e]	$2\frac{1}{8}$	12	$2\frac{11}{64}$	16	$2\frac{3}{16}$
$2\frac{5}{16}$	....	.....	..	.....	..	.....	..	.....	..	.....	16	$2\frac{1}{4}$
$2\frac{3}{8}$	....	.....	..	.....	..	.....	..	.....	12	$2\frac{19}{64}$	16	$2\frac{5}{16}$
$2\frac{7}{16}$	....	.....	..	.....	..	.....	..	.....	..	.....	16	$2\frac{3}{8}$
$2\frac{1}{2}$	4	$2\frac{1}{4}$	..	.....	..	.....	8[e]	$2\frac{3}{8}$	12	$2\frac{27}{64}$	16	$2\frac{7}{16}$
$2\frac{5}{8}$	....	.....	..	.....	..	.....	..	.....	12	$2\frac{35}{64}$	16	$2\frac{9}{16}$
$2\frac{3}{4}$	4	$2\frac{1}{2}$	..	.....	..	.....	8[e]	$2\frac{5}{8}$	12	$2\frac{43}{64}$	16	$2\frac{11}{16}$
$2\frac{7}{8}$	....	.....	..	.....	..	.....	..	.....	12	$2\frac{51}{64}$	16	$2\frac{13}{16}$
3	4	$2\frac{3}{4}$	..	.....	..	.....	8[e]	$2\frac{7}{8}$	12	$2\frac{59}{64}$	16	$2\frac{15}{16}$
$3\frac{1}{8}$	....	.....	..	.....	..	.....	..	.....	12	$3\frac{3}{64}$	16	$3\frac{1}{16}$
$3\frac{1}{4}$	4	3	..	.....	..	.....	8[e]	$3\frac{1}{8}$	12	$3\frac{11}{64}$	16	$3\frac{3}{16}$
$3\frac{3}{8}$	....	.....	..	.....	..	.....	..	.....	12	$3\frac{19}{64}$	16	$3\frac{5}{16}$
$3\frac{1}{2}$	4	$3\frac{1}{4}$	..	.....	..	.....	8[e]	$3\frac{3}{8}$	12	$3\frac{27}{64}$	16	$3\frac{7}{16}$
$3\frac{5}{8}$	....	.....	..	.....	..	.....	..	.....	12	$3\frac{35}{64}$	16	$3\frac{9}{16}$
$3\frac{3}{4}$	4	$3\frac{1}{2}$	..	.....	..	.....	8[e]	$3\frac{5}{8}$	12	$3\frac{43}{64}$	16	$3\frac{11}{16}$
$3\frac{7}{8}$	....	.....	..	.....	..	.....	..	.....	12	$3\frac{51}{64}$	16	$3\frac{13}{16}$
4	4	$3\frac{3}{4}$	..	.....	..	.....	8[e]	$3\frac{7}{8}$	12	$3\frac{59}{64}$	16	$3\frac{15}{16}$
$4\frac{1}{4}$	....	.....	..	.....	..	.....	8[e]	$4\frac{1}{8}$	12	$4\frac{11}{64}$	16	$4\frac{3}{16}$
$4\frac{1}{2}$	....	.....	..	.....	..	.....	8[e]	$4\frac{3}{8}$	12	$4\frac{27}{64}$	16	$4\frac{7}{16}$
$4\frac{3}{4}$	....	.....	..	.....	..	.....	8[e]	$4\frac{5}{8}$	12	$4\frac{43}{64}$	16	$4\frac{11}{16}$
5	....	.....	..	.....	..	.....	8[e]	$4\frac{7}{8}$	12	$4\frac{59}{64}$	16	$4\frac{15}{16}$
$5\frac{1}{4}$	....	.....	..	.....	..	.....	8[e]	$5\frac{1}{8}$	12	$5\frac{11}{64}$	16	$5\frac{3}{16}$
$5\frac{1}{2}$	....	.....	..	.....	..	.....	8[e]	$5\frac{3}{8}$	12	$5\frac{27}{64}$	16	$5\frac{7}{16}$
$5\frac{3}{4}$	....	.....	..	.....	..	.....	8[e]	$5\frac{5}{8}$	12	$5\frac{43}{64}$	16	$5\frac{11}{16}$
6	....	.....	..	.....	..	.....	8[e]	$5\frac{7}{8}$	12	$5\frac{59}{64}$	16	$5\frac{15}{16}$

[a] ASA B1.1—1960. Dimensions are in inches.
[b] Bold type indicates unified combinations.
[c] Limits of size for classes are based on a length of engagement equal to the nominal diameter.
[d] Limits of size for classes are based on a length of engagement equal to nine times the pitch.
[e] These sizes, with specified limits of size, based on a length of engagement of 9 threads in classes 2A and 2B, are designated UN.

Note. If a thread is in both the 8-, 12-, or 16-thread series and the coarse, fine, or extra-fine-thread series, the symbols and tolerances of the latter series apply.

American Standard Square and Hexagon Bolts* and Hexagon Cap Screws †

Nominal size (basic major diam.)	Regular bolts			Heavy bolts		
	Width across flats W, sq.‡ and hex.	Height H		Width across flats W	Height H	
		Unfaced sq. and hex.	Semifin. hex., fin. hex., and hex. screw		Unfaced hex.	Semifin. hex. and fin. hex.
1/4	3/8(sq.), 7/16(hex.)	11/64	5/32			
5/16	1/2	7/32	13/64			
3/8	9/16	1/4	15/64			
7/16	5/8	19/64	9/32			
1/2	3/4	11/32	5/16	7/8	7/16	13/32
9/16	13/16	25/64	23/64	15/16	15/32	7/16
5/8	15/16	27/64	25/64	1 1/16	17/32	1/2
3/4	1 1/8	1/2	15/32	1 1/4	5/8	19/32
7/8	1 5/16	37/64	35/64	1 7/16	23/32	11/16
1	1 1/2	43/64	39/64	1 5/8	13/16	3/4
1 1/8	1 11/16	3/4	1 1/16	1 13/16	29/32	27/32
1 1/4	1 7/8	27/32	25/32	2	1	15/16
1 3/8	2 1/16	29/32	27/32	2 3/16	1 3/32	1 1/32
1 1/2	2 1/4	1	15/16	2 3/8	1 3/16	1 1/8
1 5/8	2 7/16	1 1/16	1	2 9/16	1 9/32	1 7/32
1 3/4	2 5/8	1 5/32	1 3/32	2 3/4	1 3/8	1 5/16
1 7/8	2 13/16	1 7/32	1 5/32	2 15/16	1 15/32	1 13/32
2	3	1 11/32	1 7/32	3 1/8	1 9/16	1 7/16
2 1/4	3 3/8	1 1/2	1 3/8	3 1/2	1 3/4	1 5/8
2 1/2	3 3/4	1 21/32	1 17/32	3 7/8	1 15/16	1 13/16
2 3/4	4 1/8	1 13/16	1 11/16	4 1/4	2 1/8	2
3	4 1/2	2	1 7/8	4 5/8	2 5/16	2 3/16
3 1/4	4 7/8	2 3/16	2			
3 1/2	5 1/4	2 5/16	2 1/8			
3 3/4	5 5/8	2 1/2	2 5/16			
4	6	2 11/16	2 1/2			

* ASA B18.2—1960. All dimensions in inches.

† ASA B18.6.2—1956. Hexagon-head cap screw in sizes 1/4 to 1 1/2 only.

‡ Square bolts in (nominal) sizes 1/4 to 1 5/8 only.

For bolt-length increments, see table, page 720. Threads are coarse series, class 2A, except for finished hexagon bolt and hexagon cap screw, which are coarse, fine, or 8-pitch, class 2A. Minimum thread length: $2D + 1/4$ in. for bolts 6 in. or less in length; $2D + 1/2$ in. for bolts over 6 in. in length; bolts too short for formula, thread entire length.

American Standard Square and Hexagon Nuts*

Columns are grouped as: **Reg. nuts** (Width across flats W; Thickness T) · **Heavy nuts** (Width across flats W; Thickness T; Slot) · **Reg. sq. nuts** (Width across flats W; Thickness T).

Nominal size (basic major diam.)	Reg. nuts — Width across flats W	Reg. hex.	Reg. hex. jam	Semifin. and fin. hex. and hex. slotted	Semifin. and fin. hex. jam	Semifin. hex. thick, thick slotted,† and castle	Heavy — Width across flats W	Reg. sq. and hex.	Reg. hex. jam	Semifin. hex. and hex. slotted	Semifin. hex. jam	Slot Width	Slot Depth	Reg. sq. nuts — Width across flats W	Thickness T
1/4	7/16	.....	....	7/32	5/32	9/32	1/2	1/4	3/16	15/64	11/64	5/64	3/32	7/16	7/32
5/16	1/2	.....	....	17/64	3/16	21/64	9/16	5/16	7/32	19/64	13/64	3/32	3/32	9/16	17/64
3/8	9/16	.....	....	21/64	7/32	13/32	11/16	3/8	1/4	23/64	15/64	1/8	1/8	5/8	21/64
7/16	11/16	.....	....	3/8	1/4	29/64	3/4	7/16	9/32	27/64	17/64	1/8	5/32	3/4	3/8
1/2	3/4	.....	....	7/16	5/16	9/16	7/8	1/2	5/16	31/64	19/64	5/32	5/32	13/16	7/16
9/16	7/8	.....	....	31/64	5/16	39/64	15/16			35/64	21/64	5/32	3/16		
5/8	15/16	.....	....	35/64	3/8	23/32	1 1/16	5/8	3/8	39/64	23/64	3/16	7/32	1	35/64
3/4	1 1/8	21/32	7/16	41/64	27/64	13/16	1 1/4	3/4	7/16	47/64	27/64	3/16	1/4	1 1/8	21/32
7/8	1 5/16	49/64	1/2	3/4	31/64	29/32	1 7/16	7/8	1/2	55/64	31/64	3/16	1/4	1 5/16	49/64
1	1 1/2	7/8	9/16	55/64	35/64	1	1 5/8	1	9/16	63/64	35/64	1/4	9/32	1 1/2	7/8
1 1/8	1 11/16	1	5/8	31/32	39/64	1 5/32	1 13/16	1 1/8	5/8	1 7/64	39/64	1/4	11/32	1 11/16	1
1 1/4	1 7/8	1 3/32	3/4	1 1/16	23/32	1 1/4	2	1 1/4	3/4	1 7/32	23/32	5/16	3/8	1 7/8	1 3/32
1 3/8	2 1/16	1 13/64	13/16	1 11/64	25/32	1 3/8	2 3/16	1 3/8	13/16	1 11/32	25/32	5/16	3/8	2 1/16	1 13/64
1 1/2	2 1/4	1 5/16	7/8	1 9/32	27/32	1 1/2	2 3/8	1 1/2	7/8	1 15/32	27/32	3/8	7/16	2 1/4	1 5/16
1 5/8	2 7/16	.....	....	1 25/64	29/32	.....	2 9/16	.....	.....	1 19/32	29/32	3/8	7/16		
1 3/4	2 5/8	.....	....	1 1/2	31/32	.....	2 3/4	1 3/4	1	1 23/32	31/32	7/16	1/2		
1 7/8	2 13/16	.....	....	1 39/64	1 1/32	.....	2 15/16	.....	.....	1 27/32	1 1/32	7/16	9/16		
2	3	.....	....	1 23/32	1 3/32	.....	3 1/8	2	1 1/8	1 31/32	1 3/32	7/16	9/16		
2 1/4	3 3/8	.....	....	1 59/64	1 13/64	.....	3 1/2	2 1/4	1 1/4	2 3/64	1 13/64	7/16	9/16		
2 1/2	3 3/4	.....	....	2 9/64	1 29/64	.....	3 7/8	2 1/2	1 1/2	2 29/64	1 29/64	9/16	11/16		
2 3/4	4 1/8	.....	....	2 23/64	1 37/64	.....	4 1/4	2 3/4	1 5/8	2 45/64	1 37/64	9/16	11/16		
3	4 1/2	.....	....	2 37/64	1 45/64	.....	4 5/8	3	1 3/4	2 61/64	1 45/64	9/16	11/16		
3 1/4	.....	.....	....	.....	.....	.....	5	3 1/4	1 7/8	3 3/16	1 13/16	5/8	3/4		
3 1/2	.....	.....	....	.....	.....	.....	5 3/8	3 1/2	2	3 7/16	1 15/16	5/8	3/4		
3 3/4	.....	.....	....	.....	.....	.....	5 3/4	3 3/4	2 1/8	3 11/16	2 1/16	5/8	3/4		
4	.....	.....	....	.....	.....	.....	6 1/8	4	2 1/4	3 15/16	2 3/16	5/8	3/4		

* ASA B18.2—1960.

† Slot dimensions for regular slotted nuts are same as for heavy slotted nuts.

Thread. Regular and heavy nuts: coarse series, class 2B; finished and semifinished nuts, regular and heavy (all): coarse, fine, or 8-pitch series, class 2B; thick nuts: coarse or fine series, class 2B.

Sizes of Numbered and Lettered Drills

No.	Size	No.	Size	No.	Size	Letter	Size
80	0.0135	53	0.0595	26	0.1470	*A*	0.2340
79	0.0145	52	0.0635	25	0.1495	*B*	0.2380
78	0.0160	51	0.0670	24	0.1520	*C*	0.2420
77	0.0180	50	0.0700	23	0.1540	*D*	0.2460
76	0.0200	49	0.0730	22	0.1570	*E*	0.2500
75	0.0210	48	0.0760	21	0.1590	*F*	0.2570
74	0.0225	47	0.0785	20	0.1610	*G*	0.2610
73	0.0240	46	0.0810	19	0.1660	*H*	0.2660
72	0.0250	45	0.0820	18	0.1695	*I*	0.2720
71	0.0260	44	0.0860	17	0.1730	*J*	0.2770
70	0.0280	43	0.0890	16	0.1770	*K*	0.2810
69	0.0292	42	0.0935	15	0.1800	*L*	0.2900
68	0.0310	41	0.0960	14	0.1820	*M*	0.2950
67	0.0320	40	0.0980	13	0.1850	*N*	0.3020
66	0.0330	39	0.0995	12	0.1890	*O*	0.3160
65	0.0350	38	0.1015	11	0.1910	*P*	0.3230
64	0.0360	37	0.1040	10	0.1935	*Q*	0.3320
63	0.0370	36	0.1065	9	0.1960	*R*	0.3390
62	0.0380	35	0.1100	8	0.1990	*S*	0.3480
61	0.0390	34	0.1110	7	0.2010	*T*	0.3580
60	0.0400	33	0.1130	6	0.2040	*U*	0.3680
59	0.0410	32	0.1160	5	0.2055	*V*	0.3770
58	0.0420	31	0.1200	4	0.2090	*W*	0.3860
57	0.0430	30	0.1285	3	0.2130	*X*	0.3970
56	0.0465	29	0.1360	2	0.2210	*Y*	0.4040
55	0.0520	28	0.1405	1	0.2280	*Z*	0.4130
54	0.0550	27	0.1440				

Acme and Stub Acme Threads*

ASA-preferred diameter-pitch combinations

Nominal (major) diam.	Threads/in.	Nominal (major) diam.	Threads/in.	Nominal (major) diam.	Threads/in.	Nominal (major) diam.	Threads/in.
1/4	16	3/4	6	1 1/2	4	3	2
5/16	14	7/8	6	1 3/4	4	3 1/2	2
3/8	12	1	5	2	4	4	2
7/16	12	1 1/8	5	2 1/4	3	4 1/2	2
1/2	10	1 1/4	5	2 1/2	3	5	2
5/8	8	1 3/8	4	2 3/4	3		

Buttress Threads*

Recommended diam., in.	Assoc. threads/in.
1/2, 9/16, 5/8, 11/16	20, 16, 12
3/4, 7/8, 1	16, 12, 10
1 1/8, 1 1/4, 1 3/8, 1 1/2	16, 12, 10, 8, 6
1 3/4, 2, 2 1/4, 2 1/2, 2 3/4, 3, 3 1/2, 4	16, 12, 10, 8, 6, 5, 4
4 1/2, 5, 5 1/2, 6	12, 10, 8, 6, 5, 4, 3
7, 8, 9, 10	10, 8, 6, 5, 4, 3, 2 1/2, 2
11, 12, 14, 16	10, 8, 6, 5, 4, 3, 2 1/2, 2, 1 1/2, 1 1/4
18, 20, 22, 24	8, 6, 5, 4, 3, 2 1/2, 2, 1 1/2, 1 1/4, 1

* ASA B1.5—1952 and B1.9—1953. Diameters in inches.

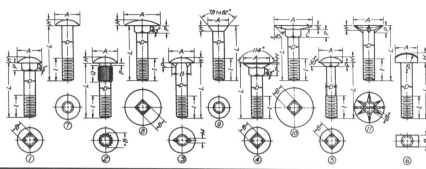

American Standard Round-head Bolts[a]

Proportions for drawing purposes

Fastener name		Nominal diam.[b] (basic major diam.)	A	H	P or M	B	
Carriage bolts	Round-head square-neck bolt[c]	No. 10, ¼″ to ½″ by (¹⁄₁₆″), ⅝″ to 1″ by (⅛″)	$2D + \frac{1}{16}$	$\frac{D}{2}$	$\frac{D}{2}$	D	
	Round-head ribbed-neck bolt[d]	No. 10, ¼″ to ½″ by (¹⁄₁₆″), ⅝″ and ¾″	$2D + \frac{1}{16}$	$\frac{D}{2}$	$\frac{1}{16}$	$D + \frac{1}{16}$	$Q \begin{cases} \text{³⁄₁₆″ for } L = \text{⅞″ or less} \\ \text{⁵⁄₁₆″ for } L = 1\text{″ and } 1\text{⅛″} \\ \text{½″ for } L = 1\text{¼″ or more} \end{cases}$
	Round-head fin.-neck bolt[c]	No. 10, ¼″ to ½″ by (¹⁄₁₆″)	$2D + \frac{1}{16}$	$\frac{D}{2}$	$\frac{3}{8}D$	$1\frac{1}{2}D + \frac{1}{16}$	
	114° countersunk square-neck bolt[c]	No. 10, ¼″ to ½″ by (¹⁄₁₆″), ⅝″ and ¾″	$2D + \frac{1}{8}$	$\frac{1}{32}$	$D + \frac{1}{32}$	D	
Round-head short square-neck bolt[e]		¼″ to ½″ by (¹⁄₁₆″), ⅝″ and ¾″	$2D + \frac{1}{16}$	$\frac{D}{2}$	$\frac{D}{4} + \frac{1}{32}$	D	
T-head bolt[d]		¼″ to ½″ by (¹⁄₁₆″), ⅝″ to 1″ by (⅛″)	$2D$	$\frac{7}{8}D$	$1\frac{5}{8}D$	D	
Round-head bolt[c] (buttonhead bolt)		No. 10, ¼″ to ½″ by (¹⁄₁₆″), ⅝″ to 1″ by (⅛″)	$2D + \frac{1}{16}$	$\frac{D}{2}$			
Step bolt[c]		No. 10, ¼″ to ½″ by (¹⁄₁₆″)	$3D + \frac{1}{16}$	$\frac{D}{2}$	$\frac{D}{2}$	D	
Countersunk bolt[c] (may be slotted if so specified)		¼″ to ½″ by (¹⁄₁₆″), ⅝″ to 1½″ by (⅛″)	$1.8D$	Obtain by projection			
Elevator bolt, flat head, countersunk[c]		No. 10, ¼″ to ½″ by (¹⁄₁₆″)	$2\frac{1}{2}D + \frac{5}{16}$	$\frac{D}{3}$	$\frac{D}{2} + \frac{1}{16}$	D	Angle $C = 16D + 5°$ (approx.)
Elevator bolt, ribbed head[d] (slotted or unslotted as specified)		¼″, ⁵⁄₁₆″, ⅜″	$2D + \frac{1}{16}$	$\frac{D}{2} - \frac{1}{32}$	$\frac{D}{2} + \frac{3}{64}$	$\frac{D}{8} + \frac{1}{16}$	

[a] The proportions in this table are in some instances approximate and are intended for drawing purposes only. For exact dimensions see ASA B18.5—1959, from which this table was compiled. Dimensions are in inches.

[b] Fractions in parentheses show diameter increments, *e.g.*, ¼ in. to ½ in. by (¹⁄₁₆ in.) includes the diameters ¼ in., ⁵⁄₁₆ in., ⅜ in., ⁷⁄₁₆ in., and ½ in.

Threads are coarse series, class 2A.

Minimum thread length l: $2D + ¼$ in. for bolts 6 in. or less in length; $2D + ½$ in. for bolts over 6 in. in length.

For bolt length increments see table page 720.

[c] Full-size body bolts furnished unless undersize body is specified.

[d] Only full-size body bolts furnished.

[e] Undersize body bolts furnished unless full-size body is specified.

Bolt-length Increments*

Bolt diameter	¼	⁵⁄₁₆	⅜	⁷⁄₁₆	½	⅝	¾	⅞	1
Length increments ¼	¾–3	¾–4	¾–6	1–3	1–6	1–6	1–6	1–4½	
½	3–4	4–5	6–9	3–6	6–13	6–10	6–15	4½–6	3–6
1	4–5	....	9–12	6–8	13–24	10–22	15–24	6–20	6–12
2	....	....	.....	...	.....	22–30	24–30	20–30	12–30

* Compiled from manufacturers' catalogues.

Example. ¼-in. bolt lengths increase by ¼-in. increments from ¾- to 3-in. length. ½-in. bolt lengths increase by ½-in. increments from 6- to 13-in. length. 1-in. bolt lengths increase by 2-in. increments from 12- to 30-in. length.

American Standard Cap Screws[a]—Socket[b] and Slotted Heads[c]

For hexagon-head screws, see page A64.

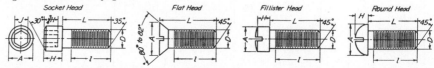

Nominal diam.	Socket head[d]			Flat head[e]	Fillister head[e]		Round head[e]	
	A	*H*	*J*	*A*	*A*	*H*	*A*	*H*
0	0.096	0.060	0.050					
1	0.118	0.073	0.050					
2	0.140	0.086	¹⁄₁₆					
3	0.161	0.099	⁵⁄₆₄					
4	0.183	0.112	⁵⁄₆₄					
5	0.205	0.125	³⁄₃₂					
6	0.226	0.138	³⁄₃₂					
8	0.270	0.164	⅛					
10	⁵⁄₁₆	0.190	⁵⁄₃₂					
12	¹¹⁄₃₂	0.216	⁵⁄₃₂					
¼	⅜	¼	³⁄₁₆	½	⅜	¹¹⁄₆₄	⁷⁄₁₆	³⁄₁₆
⁵⁄₁₆	⁷⁄₁₆	⁵⁄₁₆	⁷⁄₃₂	⅝	⁷⁄₁₆	¹³⁄₆₄	⁹⁄₁₆	¹⁵⁄₆₄
⅜	⁹⁄₁₆	⅜	⁵⁄₁₆	¾	⁹⁄₁₆	¼	⅝	¹⁷⁄₆₄
⁷⁄₁₆	⅝	⁷⁄₁₆	⁵⁄₁₆	¹³⁄₁₆	⅝	¹⁹⁄₆₄	¾	⁵⁄₁₆
½	¾	½	⅜	⅞	¾	²¹⁄₆₄	¹³⁄₁₆	¹¹⁄₃₂
⁹⁄₁₆	¹³⁄₁₆	⁹⁄₁₆	⅜	1	¹³⁄₁₆	⅜	¹⁵⁄₁₆	¹³⁄₃₂
⅝	⅞	⅝	½	1 ⅛	⅞	²⁷⁄₆₄	1	⁷⁄₁₆
¾	1	¾	⁹⁄₁₆	1 ⅜	1	½	1 ¼	¹⁷⁄₃₂
⅞	1 ⅛	⅞	⁹⁄₁₆	1 ⅝	1 ⅛	¹⁹⁄₃₂		
1	1 ⁵⁄₁₆	1	⅝	1 ⅞	1 ⁵⁄₁₆	²¹⁄₃₂		
1⅛	1 ½	1⅛	¾					
1¼	1 ¾	1¼	¾					
1⅜	1 ⅞	1⅜	¾					
1½	2	1½	1					

[a] Dimensions in inches.

[b] ASA B18.3—1961.

[c] ASA B18.6.2—1956.

[d] Thread coarse or fine, class 3A. Thread length *l*: coarse thread, $2D + ½$ in.; fine thread, $1½D + ½$ in.

[e] Thread coarse, fine, or 8-pitch, class 2A. Thread length *l*: $2D + ¼$ in.

Slot proportions vary with size of screw; draw to look well. All body-length increments for screw lengths ¼ in. to 1 in. = ⅛ in., for screw lengths 1 in. to 4 in. = ¼ in., for screw lengths 4 in. to 6 in. = ½ in.

American Standard Machine Screws*

Heads may be slotted or recessed

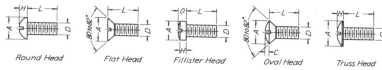

Round Head   Flat Head   Fillister Head   Oval Head   Truss Head

Nominal diam.	Round head		Flat head	Fillister head			Oval head		Truss head	
	A	H	A	A	H	O	A	C	A	H
0	0.113	0.053	0.119	0.096	0.045	0.059	0.119	0.021		
1	0.138	0.061	0.146	0.118	0.053	0.071	0.146	0.025	0.194	0.053
2	0.162	0.069	0.172	0.140	0.062	0.083	0.172	0.029	0.226	0.061
3	0.187	0.078	0.199	0.161	0.070	0.095	0.199	0.033	0.257	0.069
4	0.211	0.086	0.225	0.183	0.079	0.107	0.225	0.037	0.289	0.078
5	0.236	0.095	0.252	0.205	0.088	0.120	0.252	0.041	0.321	0.086
6	0.260	0.103	0.279	0.226	0.096	0.132	0.279	0.045	0.352	0.094
8	0.309	0.120	0.332	0.270	0.113	0.156	0.332	0.052	0.384	0.102
10	0.359	0.137	0.385	0.313	0.130	0.180	0.385	0.060	0.448	0.118
12	0.408	0.153	0.438	0.357	0.148	0.205	0.438	0.068	0.511	0.134
$\frac{1}{4}$	0.472	0.175	0.507	0.414	0.170	0.237	0.507	0.079	0.573	0.150
$\frac{5}{16}$	0.590	0.216	0.635	0.518	0.211	0.295	0.635	0.099	0.698	0.183
$\frac{3}{8}$	0.708	0.256	0.762	0.622	0.253	0.355	0.762	0.117	0.823	0.215
$\frac{7}{16}$	0.750	0.328	0.812	0.625	0.265	0.368	0.812	0.122	0.948	0.248
$\frac{1}{2}$	0.813	0.355	0.875	0.750	0.297	0.412	0.875	0.131	1.073	0.280
$\frac{9}{16}$	0.938	0.410	1.000	0.812	0.336	0.466	1.000	0.150	1.198	0.312
$\frac{5}{8}$	1.000	0.438	1.125	0.875	0.375	0.521	1.125	0.169	1.323	0.345
$\frac{3}{4}$	1.250	0.547	1.375	1.000	0.441	0.612	1.375	0.206	1.573	0.410

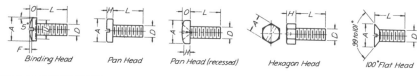

Binding Head   Pan Head   Pan Head (recessed)   Hexagon Head   100° Flat Head

Nominal diam.	Binding head				Pan head			Hexagon head		100° flat head
	A	O	F	U	A	H	O	A	H	A
2	0.181	0.046	0.018	0.141	0.167	0.053	0.062	0.125	0.050	
3	0.208	0.054	0.022	0.162	0.193	0.060	0.071	0.187	0.055	
4	0.235	0.063	0.025	0.184	0.219	0.068	0.080	0.187	0.060	0.225
5	0.263	0.071	0.029	0.205	0.245	0.075	0.089	0.187	0.070	
6	0.290	0.080	0.032	0.226	0.270	0.082	0.097	0.250	0.080	0.279
8	0.344	0.097	0.039	0.269	0.322	0.096	0.115	0.250	0.110	0.332
10	0.399	0.114	0.045	0.312	0.373	0.110	0.133	0.312	0.120	0.385
12	0.454	0.130	0.052	0.354	0.425	0.125	0.151	0.312	0.155	
$\frac{1}{4}$	0.513	0.153	0.061	0.410	0.492	0.144	0.175	0.375	0.190	0.507
$\frac{5}{16}$	0.641	0.193	0.077	0.513	0.615	0.178	0.218	0.500	0.230	0.635
$\frac{3}{8}$	0.769	0.234	0.094	0.615	0.740	0.212	0.261	0.562	0.295	0.762

* ASA B18.6.3—1962. Dimensions given are maximum values, all in inches.
Thread length: screws 2 in. long or less, thread entire length; screws over 2 in. long, thread length $l = 1\frac{3}{4}$ in. Threads are coarse or fine series, class 2. Heads may be slotted or recessed as specified, excepting hexagon form, which is plain or may be slotted if so specified. Slot and recess proportions vary with size of fastener; draw to look well.

American Standard Machine-screw* and Stove-bolt† Nuts‡

Nominal size	0	1	2	3	4	5	6	8	10	12	1/4	5/16	3/8
"W"	5/32	5/32	3/16	3/16	1/4	5/16	5/16	11/32	3/8	7/16	7/16	9/16	5/8
"T"	3/64	3/64	1/16	1/16	3/32	7/64	7/64	1/8	1/8	5/32	3/16	7/32	1/4

* Machine-screw nuts are hexagonal and square.

† Stove-bolt nuts are square.

‡ ASA B18.6.3—1962. Dimensions are in inches.

Thread is coarse series for square nuts and coarse or fine series for hexagon nuts; class 2B.

American Standard Hexagon Socket,* Slotted Headless,† and Square-head‡ Setscrews

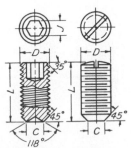

Cup Point   Flat Point

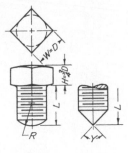

Oval Point   Cone Point

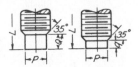

Full Dog Point   Half Dog Point

(All six point types are available in all three head types)

Diam. D	Cup and flat-point diam. C	Oval-point radius R	Cone-point angle Y — 118° for these lengths and shorter	90° for these lengths and longer	Full and half dog points — Diam. P	Length Full Q	Half q	Socket width J
5	1/16	3/32	1/8	3/16	0.083	0.06	0.03	1/16
6	0.069	7/64	1/8	3/16	0.092	0.07	0.03	1/16
8	5/64	1/8	3/16	1/4	0.109	0.08	0.04	5/64
10	3/32	9/64	3/16	1/4	0.127	0.09	0.04	3/32
12	7/64	5/32	3/16	1/4	0.144	0.11	0.06	3/32
1/4	1/8	3/16	1/4	5/16	5/32	1/8	1/16	1/8
5/16	11/64	15/64	5/16	3/8	13/64	5/32	5/64	5/32
3/8	13/64	9/32	3/8	7/16	1/4	3/16	3/32	3/16
7/16	15/64	21/64	7/16	1/2	19/64	7/32	7/64	1/4
1/2	9/32	3/8	1/2	9/16	11/32	1/4	1/8	1/4
9/16	5/16	27/64	9/16	5/8	25/64	9/32	9/64	1/4
5/8	23/64	15/32	5/8	3/4	15/32	5/16	5/32	5/16
3/4	7/16	9/16	3/4	7/8	9/16	3/8	3/16	3/8
7/8	33/64	21/32	7/8	1	21/32	7/16	7/32	1/2
1	19/32	3/4	1	1 1/8	3/4	1/2	1/4	9/16
1 1/8	43/64	27/32	1 1/8	1 1/4	27/32	9/16	9/32	9/16
1 1/4	3/4	15/16	1 1/4	1 1/2	15/16	5/8	5/16	5/8
1 3/8	53/64	1 1/32	1 3/8	1 5/8	1 1/32	11/16	11/32	5/8
1 1/2	29/32	1 1/8	1 1/2	1 3/4	1 1/8	3/4	3/8	3/4
1 3/4	1 1/16	1 5/16	1 3/4	2	1 5/16	7/8	7/16	1
2	1 7/32	1 1/2	2	2 1/4	1 1/2	1	1/2	1

* ASA B18.3—1961. Dimensions are in inches. Threads coarse or fine, class 3A. Length increments: 1/4 in. to 5/8 in. by (1/16 in.); 5/8 in. to 1 in. by (1/8 in.); 1 in. to 4 in. by (1/4 in.); 4 in. to 6 in. by (1/2 in.). Fractions in parentheses show length increments; for example, 5/8 in. to 1 in. by (1/8 in.) includes the lengths 5/8 in., 3/4 in., 7/8 in., and 1 in.

† ASA B18.6.2—1956. Threads coarse or fine, class 2A. Slotted headless screws standardized in sizes No. 5 to 3/4 in. only. Slot proportions vary with diameter. Draw to look well.

‡ ASA B18.6.2—1956. Threads coarse, fine, or 8-pitch, class 2A. Square-head setscrews standardized in sizes No. 10 to 1 1/2 in. only.

American Standard Socket-head Shoulder Screws[a]

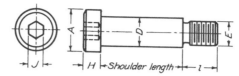

Shoulder diameter D			Head[b]			Thread		Shoulder lengths[d]
Nominal	Max.	Min.	Diam. A	Height H	Hexagon[c] J	Specification E	Length I	
¼	0.2480	0.2460	⅜	3/16	⅛	10-24NC-3	⅜	¾–2½
5/16	0.3105	0.3085	7/16	7/32	5/32	¼-20NC-3	7/16	1 –3
⅜	0.3730	0.3710	9/16	¼	3/16	5/16-18NC-3	½	1 –4
½	0.4980	0.4960	¾	5/16	¼	⅜-16NC-3	⅝	1¼–5
⅝	0.6230	0.6210	⅞	⅜	5/16	½-13NC-3	¾	1½–6
¾	0.7480	0.7460	1	½	⅜	⅝-11NC-3	⅞	1½–8
1	0.9980	0.9960	15/16	⅝	½	¾-10NC-3	1	1½–8
1¼	1.2480	1.2460	1¾	¾	⅝	⅞-9NC-3	1⅛	1½–8

[a] ASA B18.3—1961. Dimensions are in inches.
[b] Head chamfer is 30°.
[c] Socket depth = ¾H.
[d] Shoulder-length increments: shoulder lengths from ¾ in. to 1 in., ⅛-in. intervals; shoulder lengths from 1 in. to 5 in., ¼-in. intervals; shoulder lengths from 5 in. to 7 in., ½-in. intervals; shoulder lengths from 7 in. to 8 in., 1-in. intervals. Shoulder-length tolerance ±0.005.

American Standard Wood Screws*

Nominal size	Basic diam. of screw D	No. of threads per in.†	Slot width ‡ J (all heads)	Round head		Flat head	Oval head	
				A	H	A	A	C
0	0.060	32	0.023	0.113	0.053	0.119	0.119	0.021
1	0.073	28	0.026	0.138	0.061	0.146	0.146	0.025
2	0.086	26	0.031	0.162	0.069	0.172	0.172	0.029
3	0.099	24	0.035	0.187	0.078	0.199	0.199	0.033
4	0.112	22	0.039	0.211	0.086	0.225	0.225	0.037
5	0.125	20	0.043	0.236	0.095	0.252	0.252	0.041
6	0.138	18	0.048	0.260	0.103	0.279	0.279	0.045
7	0.151	16	0.048	0.285	0.111	0.305	0.305	0.049
8	0.164	15	0.054	0.309	0.120	0.332	0.332	0.052
9	0.177	14	0.054	0.334	0.128	0.358	0.358	0.056
10	0.190	13	0.060	0.359	0.137	0.385	0.385	0.060
12	0.216	11	0.067	0.408	0.153	0.438	0.438	0.068
14	0.242	10	0.075	0.457	0.170	0.491	0.491	0.076
16	0.268	9	0.075	0.506	0.187	0.544	0.544	0.084
18	0.294	8	0.084	0.555	0.204	0.597	0.597	0.092
20	0.320	8	0.084	0.604	0.220	0.650	0.650	0.100
24	0.372	7	0.094	0.702	0.254	0.756	0.756	0.116

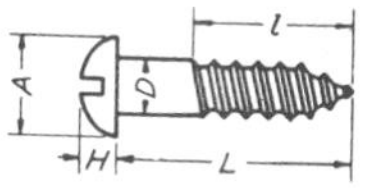

Round Head

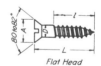

Flat Head

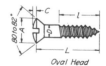

Oval Head

* ASA B18.6.1—1961. Dimensions given are maximum values, all in inches. Heads may be slotted or recessed as specified.

† Thread length $l = \frac{2}{3}L$.

‡ Slot depths and recesses vary with type and size of screw; draw to look well.

Small Rivets*

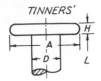

TINNERS'

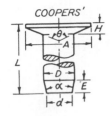

COOPERS'

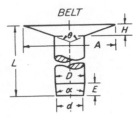

BELT

Tinner's			Cooper's			Belt		
Size No.†	D Diam. body	L Length	Size No.	D Diam. body	L Length	Size No.‡	D Diam. body	L Length
8 oz	0.089	0.16	1 lb	0.109	0.219	7	0.180	From 3/8 to 3/4 by 1/8" increments
12	0.105	0.19	1½	0.127	0.256	8	0.165	
1 lb	0.111	0.20	2	0.141	0.292	9	0.148	
1½	0.130	0.23	2½	0.148	0.325	10	0.134	
2	0.144	0.27	3	0.156	0.358	11	0.120	
2½	0.148	0.28	4	0.165	0.392	12	0.109	
3	0.160	0.31	6	0.203	0.466	13	0.095	
4	0.176	0.34	8	0.238	0.571			
6	0.203	0.39	10	0.250	0.606			
8	0.224	0.44	12	0.259	0.608			
10	0.238	0.47	14	0.271	0.643			
12	0.259	0.50	16	0.281	0.677			
14	0.284	0.52						
16	0.300	0.53						

Approx. proportions: (Tinner's)

$A = 2.25 \times D$

$H = 0.30 \times D$

Approx. proportions: (Cooper's)

$A = 2.25 \times D, \quad d = 0.90 \times D$

$E = 0.40 \times D, \quad H = 0.30 \times D$

Included $\angle \theta = 144°$

$\angle \alpha = 18°$

Approx. proportions: (Belt)

$A = 2.8 \times D, \quad d = 0.9 \times D$

$E = 0.4 \times D, \quad H = 0.3 \times D$

Tolerances on the nominal diameter:

$+0.002$

-0.004

Finished rivets shall be free from injurious defects.

* ASA B18.1—1955. All dimensions given in inches.
† Size numbers refer to the Trade Name or weight of 1,000 rivets.
‡ Size number refers to the Stubs iron-wire gage number of the stock used in the body of the rivet.

Dimensions of Standard Gib-head Keys, Square and Flat

Approved by ASA *

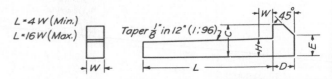

$L = 4W$ (Min.)
$L = 16W$ (Max.)

Taper $\frac{1}{8}$" in 12" (1:96)

Diameters of shafts	Square type					Flat type				
	Key		Gib head			Key		Gib head		
	W	H	C	D	E	W	H	C	D	E
½ – 9/16	1/8	1/8	1/4	7/32	5/32	1/8	3/32	3/16	1/8	1/8
5/8 – 7/8	3/16	3/16	5/16	9/32	7/32	3/16	1/8	1/4	3/16	5/32
15/16-1¼	1/4	1/4	7/16	11/32	11/32	1/4	3/16	5/16	1/4	3/16
1 5/16-1⅜	5/16	5/16	9/16	13/32	13/32	5/16	1/4	3/8	5/16	1/4
1 7/16-1¾	3/8	3/8	11/16	15/32	15/32	3/8	1/4	7/16	3/8	5/16
1 13/16-2¼	1/2	1/2	7/8	19/32	5/8	1/2	3/8	5/8	1/2	7/16
2 5/16-2¾	5/8	5/8	1 1/16	23/32	3/4	5/8	7/16	3/4	5/8	1/2
2 7/8 -3¼	3/4	3/4	1 1/4	7/8	7/8	3/4	1/2	7/8	3/4	5/8
3 3/8 -3¾	7/8	7/8	1 1/2	1	1	7/8	5/8	1 1/16	7/8	3/4
3 7/8 -4½	1	1	1 3/4	1 3/16	1 3/16	1	3/4	1 1/4	1	13/16
4 3/4 -5½	1 1/4	1 1/4	2	1 7/16	1 7/16	1 1/4	7/8	1 1/2	1 1/4	1
5 3/4 -6	1 1/2	1 1/2	2 1/2	1 3/4	1 3/4	1 1/2	1	1 3/4	1 1/2	1 1/4

A72

* ASA B17.1— 1964. Dimensions in inches.

Widths and Heights of Standard Square- and Flat-stock Keys with Corresponding Shaft Diameters*

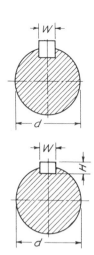

Shaft diam. d (inclusive)	Square-stock keys W	Flat-stock keys, $W \times H$	Shaft diam. d (inclusive)	Square-stock keys W	Flat-stock keys, $W \times H$
½ – 9⁄16	⅛	⅛ × 3⁄32	2⅞–3¼	¾	¾ × ½
⅝ – ⅞	3⁄16	3⁄16 × ⅛	3⅜–3¾	⅞	⅞ × ⅝
15⁄16–1¼	¼	¼ × 3⁄16	3⅞–4½	1	1 × ¾
1 5⁄16–1⅜	5⁄16	5⁄16 × ¼			
1 7⁄16–1¾	⅜	⅜ × ¼	4¾–5½	1¼	1¼ × ⅞
1 13⁄16–2¼	½	½ × ⅜	5¾–6	1½	1½ × 1
2 5⁄16–2¾	⅝	⅝ × 7⁄16			

* Compiled from manufacturers' catalogues.

Woodruff-key Dimensions

Key* No.	Nominal size $A \times B$	Max. width of key A	Max. diam. of key B	Max. height of key C	Max. height of key D	Distance below center E
204	1⁄16 × ½	0.0635	0.500	0.203	0.194	3⁄64
304	3⁄32 × ½	0.0948	0.500	0.203	0.194	3⁄64
305	3⁄32 × ⅝	0.0948	0.625	0.250	0.240	1⁄16
404	⅛ × ½	0.1260	0.500	0.203	0.194	3⁄64
405	⅛ × ⅝	0.1260	0.625	0.250	0.240	1⁄16
406	⅛ × ¾	0.1260	0.750	0.313	0.303	1⁄16
505	5⁄32 × ⅝	0.1573	0.625	0.250	0.240	1⁄16
506	5⁄32 × ¾	0.1573	0.750	0.313	0.303	1⁄16
507	5⁄32 × ⅞	0.1573	0.875	0.375	0.365	1⁄16
606	3⁄16 × ¾	0.1885	0.750	0.313	0.303	1⁄16
607	3⁄16 × ⅞	0.1885	0.875	0.375	0.365	1⁄16
608	3⁄16 × 1	0.1885	1.000	0.438	0.428	1⁄16
609	3⁄16 × 1⅛	0.1885	1.125	0.484	0.475	5⁄64
807	¼ × ⅞	0.2510	0.875	0.375	0.365	1⁄16
808	¼ × 1	0.2510	1.000	0.438	0.428	1⁄16
809	¼ × 1⅛	0.2510	1.125	0.484	0.475	5⁄64
810	¼ × 1¼	0.2510	1.250	0.547	0.537	5⁄64
811	¼ × 1⅜	0.2510	1.375	0.594	0.584	3⁄32
812	¼ × 1½	0.2510	1.500	0.641	0.631	7⁄64
1008	5⁄16 × 1	0.3135	1.000	0.438	0.428	1⁄16
1009	5⁄16 × 1⅛	0.3135	1.125	0.484	0.475	5⁄64
1010	5⁄16 × 1¼	0.3135	1.250	0.547	0.537	5⁄64
1011	5⁄16 × 1⅜	0.3135	1.375	0.594	0.584	3⁄32
1012	5⁄16 × 1½	0.3135	1.500	0.641	0.631	7⁄64
1210	⅜ × 1¼	0.3760	1.250	0.547	0.537	5⁄64
1211	⅜ × 1⅜	0.3760	1.375	0.594	0.584	3⁄32
1212	⅜ × 1½	0.3760	1.500	0.641	0.631	7⁄64

* Dimensions in inches. Key numbers indicate the nominal key dimensions. The last two digits give the nominal diameter B in eighths of an inch, and the digits preceding the last two give the nominal width A in thirty-seconds of an inch. Thus 204 indicates a key 2⁄32 by 4⁄8, or 1⁄16 by ½ in.

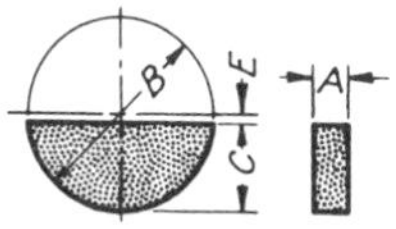

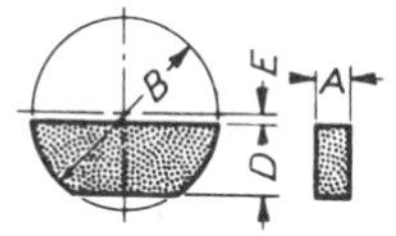

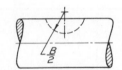

Woodruff-key-seat Dimensions

Key* No.	Nominal size	Key slot			
		Width W		Depth H	
		Max.	Min.	Max.	Min.
204	¹⁄₁₆ × ¹⁄₂	0.0630	0.0615	0.1718	0.1668
304	³⁄₃₂ × ¹⁄₂	0.0943	0.0928	0.1561	0.1511
305	³⁄₃₂ × ⁵⁄₈	0.0943	0 0928	0.2031	0.1981
404	¹⁄₈ × ¹⁄₂	0.1255	0.1240	0.1405	0.1355
405	¹⁄₈ × ⁵⁄₈	0.1255	0.1240	0.1875	0.1825
406	¹⁄₈ × ³⁄₄	0.1255	0.1240	0.2505	0.2455
505	⁵⁄₃₂ × ⁵⁄₈	0.1568	0.1553	0.1719	0.1669
506	⁵⁄₃₂ × ³⁄₄	0.1568	0.1553	0.2349	0.2299
507	⁵⁄₃₂ × ⁷⁄₈	0.1568	0.1553	0.2969	0.2919
606	³⁄₁₆ × ³⁄₄	0.1880	0.1863	0.2193	0.2143
607	³⁄₁₆ × ⁷⁄₈	0.1880	0.1863	0.2813	0.2763
608	³⁄₁₆ × 1	0.1880	0.1863	0.3443	0.3393
609	³⁄₁₆ × 1¹⁄₈	0.1880	0.1863	0.3903	0.3853
807	¹⁄₄ × ⁷⁄₈	0.2505	0.2487	0.2500	0.2450
808	¹⁄₄ × 1	0.2505	0.2487	0.3130	0.3080
809	¹⁄₄ × 1¹⁄₈	0.2505	0.2487	0.3590	0.3540
810	¹⁄₄ × 1¹⁄₄	0.2505	0.2487	0.4220	0.4170
811	¹⁄₄ × 1³⁄₈	0.2505	0.2487	0.4690	0.4640
812	¹⁄₄ × 1¹⁄₂	0.2505	0.2487	0.5160	0.5110
1008	⁵⁄₁₆ × 1	0.3130	0.3111	0.2818	0.2768
1009	⁵⁄₁₆ × 1¹⁄₈	0.3130	0.3111	0.3278	0.3228
1010	⁵⁄₁₆ × 1¹⁄₄	0.3130	0.3111	0.3908	0.3858
1011	⁵⁄₁₆ × 1³⁄₈	0.3130	0.3111	0.4378	0.4328
1012	⁵⁄₁₆ × 1¹⁄₂	0.3130	0.3111	0.4848	0.4798
1210	³⁄₈ × 1¹⁄₄	0.3755	0.3735	0.3595	0.3545
1211	³⁄₈ × 1³⁄₈	0.3755	0.3735	0.4060	0.4015
1212	³⁄₈ × 1¹⁄₂	0.3755	0.3735	0.4535	0.4485

* Dimensions in inches. Key numbers indicate the nominal key dimensions. The last two digits give the nominal diameter B in eighths of an inch, and the digits preceding the last two give the nominal width A in thirty-seconds of an inch. Thus 204 indicates a key ²⁄₃₂ by ⁴⁄₈, or ¹⁄₁₆ by ¹⁄₂ in.

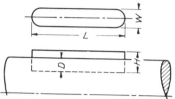

Dimensions of Pratt and Whitney Keys

Key No.	L	W	H	D	Key No.	L	W	H	D
1	1/2	1/16	3/32	1/16	22	1 3/8	1/4	3/8	1/4
2	1/2	3/32	9/64	3/32	23	1 3/8	5/16	15/32	5/16
3	1/2	1/8	3/16	1/8	F	1 3/8	3/8	9/16	3/8
4	5/8	3/32	9/64	3/32	24	1 1/2	1/4	3/8	1/4
5	5/8	1/8	3/16	1/8	25	1 1/2	5/16	15/32	5/16
6	5/8	5/32	15/64	5/32	G	1 1/2	3/8	9/16	3/8
7	3/4	1/8	3/16	1/8	51	1 3/4	1/4	3/8	1/4
8	3/4	5/32	15/64	5/32	52	1 3/4	5/16	15/32	5/16
9	3/4	3/16	9/32	3/16	53	1 3/4	3/8	9/16	3/8
10	7/8	5/32	15/64	5/32	26	2	3/16	9/32	3/16
11	7/8	3/16	9/32	3/16	27	2	1/4	3/8	1/4
12	7/8	7/32	21/64	7/32	28	2	5/16	15/32	5/16
A	7/8	1/4	3/8	1/4	29	2	3/8	9/16	3/8
13	1	3/16	9/32	3/16	54	2 1/4	1/4	3/8	1/4
14	1	7/32	21/64	7/32	55	2 1/4	5/16	15/16	5/16
15	1	1/4	3/8	1/4	56	2 1/4	3/8	9/16	3/8
B	1	5/16	15/32	5/16	57	2 1/4	7/16	21/32	7/16
16	1 1/8	3/16	9/32	3/16	58	2 1/2	5/16	15/32	5/16
17	1 1/8	7/32	21/64	7/32	59	2 1/2	3/8	9/16	3/8
18	1 1/8	1/4	3/8	1/4	60	2 1/2	7/16	21/32	7/16
C	1 1/8	5/16	15/32	5/16	61	2 1/2	1/2	3/4	1/2
19	1 1/4	3/16	9/32	3/16	30	3	3/8	9/16	3/8
20	1 1/4	7/32	21/64	7/32	31	3	7/16	21/32	7/16
21	1 1/4	1/4	3/8	1/4	32	3	1/2	3/4	1/2
D	1 1/4	5/16	15/32	5/16	33	3	9/16	27/32	9/16
E	1 1/4	3/8	9/16	3/8	34	3	5/8	15/16	5/8

Dimensions in inches. Key is 2/3 in shaft; 1/3 in hub. Keys are 0.001 in. oversize in width to ensure proper fitting in keyway. Keyway size: width = W; depth = $H - D$. Length L should never be less than $2W$.

American Standard Plain Washers*

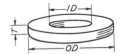

Size	Light			Medium			Heavy			Extra heavy		
	ID	OD	Thickness	ID	OD	Thickness	ID	OD	Thickness	ID	OD	Thickness
0	5/64	3/16	0.020									
1	3/32	7/32	0.020									
2	3/32	1/4	0.020									
3	1/8	1/4	0.022									
4	1/8	1/4	0.022	1/8	5/16	0.032						
5	5/32	5/16	0.035	5/32	3/8	0.049						
6	5/32	5/16	0.035	5/32	3/8	0.049						
7	11/64	13/32	0.049	3/16	3/8	0.049						
8	3/16	3/8	0.049	3/16	7/16	0.049						
9	13/64	15/32	0.049	7/32	1/2	0.049						
3/16	7/32	7/16	0.049	7/32	1/2	0.049	1/4	9/16	0.049			
10	7/32	7/16	0.049	1/4	9/16	0.049	1/4	9/16	0.065			
11	15/64	17/32	0.049	1/4	9/16	0.049	1/4	9/16	0.065			
12	1/4	1/2	0.049	1/4	9/16	0.049	1/4	9/16	0.065			
14	17/64	5/8	0.049	5/16	3/4	0.065	5/16	7/8	0.065			
1/4	9/32	5/8	0.065	5/16	3/4	0.065	5/16	3/4	0.065	5/16	7/8	0.065
16	9/32	5/8	0.065	5/16	3/4	0.065	5/16	7/8	0.065	5/16	7/8	0.065
18	5/16	3/4	0.065	3/8	3/4	0.065	3/8	7/8	0.083	3/8	1 1/8	0.065
5/16	11/32	11/16	0.065	3/8	3/4	0.065	3/8	7/8	0.083	3/8	1 1/8	0.065
20	11/32	11/16	0.065	3/8	3/4	0.065	3/8	7/8	0.083	3/8	1 1/8	0.065
24	13/32	13/16	0.065	7/16	7/8	0.083	7/16	1	0.083	7/16	1 3/8	0.083
3/8	13/32	13/16	0.065	7/16	7/8	0.083	7/16	1	0.083	7/16	1 3/8	0.083
7/16	15/32	59/64	0.065	1/2	1 1/8	0.083	1/2	1 1/4	0.083	1/2	1 5/8	0.083
1/2	17/32	1 1/16	0.095	9/16	1 1/4	0.109	9/16	1 3/8	0.109	9/16	1 7/8	0.109
9/16	19/32	1 3/16	0.095	5/8	1 3/8	0.109	5/8	1 1/2	0.109	5/8	2 1/8	0.134
5/8	21/32	1 5/16	0.095	11/16	1 1/2	0.134	11/16	1 3/4	0.134	11/16	2 3/8	0.165
3/4	13/16	1 1/2	0.134	13/16	1 3/4	0.148	13/16	2	0.148	13/16	2 7/8	0.165
7/8	15/16	1 3/4	0.134	15/16	2	0.165	15/16	2 1/4	0.165	15/16	3 3/8	0.180
1	1 1/16	2	0.134	1 1/16	2 1/4	0.165	1 1/16	2 1/2	0.165	1 1/16	3 7/8	0.238
1 1/8	.....	.....	.....	1 3/16	2 1/2	0.165	1 1/4	2 3/4	0.165			
1 1/4	.....	.....	.....	1 5/16	2 3/4	0.165	1 3/8	3	0.165			
1 3/8	.....	.....	.....	1 7/16	3	0.180	1 1/2	3 1/4	0.180			
1 1/2	.....	.....	.....	1 9/16	3 1/4	0.180	1 5/8	3 1/2	0.180			
1 5/8	.....	.....	.....	1 11/16	3 1/2	0.180	1 3/4	3 3/4	0.180			
1 3/4	.....	.....	.....	1 13/16	3 3/4	0.180	1 7/8	4	0.180			
1 7/8	.....	.....	.....	1 15/16	4	0.180	2	4 1/4	0.180			
2	.....	.....	.....	2 1/16	4 1/4	0.180	2 1/8	4 1/2	0.180			
2 1/4	.....	.....	.....	.....	....	.....	2 3/8	4 3/4	0.220			
2 1/2	.....	.....	.....	.....	....	.....	2 5/8	5	0.238			
2 3/4	.....	.....	.....	.....	....	.....	2 7/8	5 1/4	0.259			
3	.....	.....	.....	.....	....	.....	3 1/8	5 1/2	0.284			

* ASA B27.2—1958. All dimensions in inches.

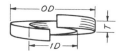

American Standard Lock Washers*

Nominal size	Inside diam., min.	Light		Medium		Heavy		Extra heavy	
		Min. thickness	Outside diam., max.	Min. thickness	Outside diam., max.	Min. thickness	Outside diam., max.	Min. thickness	Outside diam., max.
0.086 (No. 2)	0.088	0.015	0.165	0.020	0.175	0.025	0.185	0.027	0.211
0.099 (No. 3)	0.102	0.020	0.188	0.025	0.198	0.031	0.212	0.034	0.242
0.112 (No. 4)	0.115	0.020	0.202	0.025	0.212	0.031	0.226	0.034	0.256
0.125 (No. 5)	0.128	0.025	0.225	0.031	0.239	0.040	0.255	0.045	0.303
0.138 (No. 6)	0.141	0.025	0.239	0.031	0.253	0.040	0.269	0.045	0.317
0.164 (No. 8)	0.168	0.031	0.280	0.040	0.296	0.047	0.310	0.057	0.378
0.190 (No. 10)	0.194	0.040	0.323	0.047	0.337	0.056	0.353	0.068	0.437
0.216 (No. 12)	0.221	0.047	0.364	0.056	0.380	0.063	0.394	0.080	0.500
$\frac{1}{4}$	0.255	0.047	0.489	0.062	0.493	0.077	0.495	0.084	0.539
$\frac{5}{16}$	0.319	0.056	0.575	0.078	0.591	0.097	0.601	0.108	0.627
$\frac{3}{8}$	0.382	0.070	0.678	0.094	0.688	0.115	0.696	0.123	0.746
$\frac{7}{16}$	0.446	0.085	0.780	0.109	0.784	0.133	0.792	0.143	0.844
$\frac{1}{2}$	0.509	0.099	0.877	0.125	0.879	0.151	0.889	0.162	0.945
$\frac{9}{16}$	0.573	0.113	0.975	0.141	0.979	0.170	0.989	0.182	1.049
$\frac{5}{8}$	0.636	0.126	1.082	0.156	1.086	0.189	1.100	0.202	1.164
$\frac{11}{16}$	0.700	0.138	1.178	0.172	1.184	0.207	1.200	0.221	1.266
$\frac{3}{4}$	0.763	0.153	1.277	0.188	1.279	0.226	1.299	0.241	1.369
$\frac{13}{16}$	0.827	0.168	1.375	0.203	1.377	0.246	1.401	0.261	1.473
$\frac{7}{8}$	0.890	0.179	1.470	0.219	1.474	0.266	1.504	0.285	1.586
$\frac{15}{16}$	0.954	0.191	1.562	0.234	1.570	0.284	1.604	0.308	1.698
1	1.017	0.202	1.656	0.250	1.672	0.306	1.716	0.330	1.810
1 $\frac{1}{16}$	1.081	0.213	1.746	0.266	1.768	0.326	1.820	0.352	1.922
1 $\frac{1}{8}$	1.144	0.224	1.837	0.281	1.865	0.345	1.921	0.375	2.031
1 $\frac{3}{16}$	1.208	0.234	1.923	0.297	1.963	0.364	2.021	0.396	2.137
1 $\frac{1}{4}$	1.271	0.244	2.012	0.312	2.058	0.384	2.126	0.417	2.244
1 $\frac{5}{16}$	1.335	0.254	2.098	0.328	2.156	0.403	2.226	0.438	2.350
1 $\frac{3}{8}$	1.398	0.264	2.183	0.344	2.253	0.422	2.325	0.458	2.453
1 $\frac{7}{16}$	1.462	0.273	2.269	0.359	2.349	0.440	2.421	0.478	2.555
1 $\frac{1}{2}$	1.525	0.282	2.352	0.375	2.446	0.458	2.518	0.496	2.654

* ASA B27.1— 1958. All dimensions in inches.

Tapers. Taper means the difference in diameter or width in 1 ft of length; see figure below. *Taper pins*, much used for fastening cylindrical parts and for doweling, have a standard taper of ¼ in. per ft.

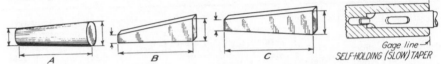

SELF-HOLDING (SLOW) TAPER

Machine tapers. The American Standard for self-holding (slow) machine tapers is designed to replace the various former standards. The table below shows its derivation. Detailed dimensions and tolerances for taper tool shanks and taper sockets will be found in ASA B5.10—1963.

Dimensions of Taper Pins

Taper ¼ in. per ft

Size No.	Diam., large end	Drill size for reamer	Max. length
000000	0.072	53	⅝
00000	0.092	47	⅝
0000	0.108	42	¾
000	0.125	37	¾
00	0.147	31	1
0	0.156	28	1
1	0.172	25	1¼
2	0.193	19	1½
3	0.219	12	1¾
4	0.250	3	2
5	0.289	¼	2¼
6	0.341	⁹⁄₃₂	3¼
7	0.409	¹¹⁄₃₂	3¾
8	0.492	¹³⁄₃₂	4½
9	0.591	³¹⁄₆₄	5¼
10	0.706	¹⁹⁄₃₂	6
11	0.857	²³⁄₃₂	7¼
12	1.013	⁵⁵⁄₆₄	8¾
13	1.233	1 ¹⁄₆₄	10¾

All dimensions in inches.

American Standard Machine Tapers,* Self-holding (Slow) Taper Series

Basic dimensions

Origin of series	No. of taper	Taper /ft	Diam. at gage line	Means of driving and holding
Brown and Sharpe taper series		0.239	0.500	0.239	Tongue drive with shank held in by friction
		0.299	0.500	0.299	
		0.375	0.500	0.375	
Morse taper series	1	0.600	0.475	Tongue drive with shank held in by key
	2	0.600	0.700	
	3	0.602	0.938	
	4	0.623	1.231	
	4½	0.623	1.500	
	5	0.630	1.748	
¾-in./ft taper series	200	0.750	2.000	Key drive with shank held in by key
	250	0.750	2.500	
	300	0.750	3.000	
	350	0.750	3.500	
	400	0.750	4.000	Key drive with shank held in by drawbolt
	500	0.750	5.000	
	600	0.750	6.000	
	800	0.750	8.000	
	1,000	0.750	10.000	
	1,200	0.750	12.000	

* ASA B5.10—1963. All dimensions in inches.

Wire and Sheet-metal Gages

Dimensions in decimal parts of an inch

No. of gage	American or Brown and Sharpe[a]	Washburn & Moen or American Steel & Wire Co.[b]	Birmingham or Stubs iron wire[c]	Music wire[d]	Imperial wire gage[e]	U.S. Std. for plate[f]
0000000	. . . . .	0.4900	. . . .	. . . . .	0.5000	0.5000
000000	0.5800	0.4615	. . . . .	0.004	0.4640	0.4688
00000	0.5165	0.4305	0.500	0.005	0.4320	0.4375
0000	0.4600	0.3938	0.454	0.006	0.4000	0.4063
000	0.4096	0.3625	0.425	0.007	0.3720	0.3750
00	0.3648	0.3310	0.380	0.008	0.3480	0.3438
0	0.3249	0.3065	0.340	0.009	0.3240	0.3125
1	0.2893	0.2830	0.300	0.010	0.3000	0.2813
2	0.2576	0.2625	0.284	0.011	0.2760	0.2656
3	0.2294	0.2437	0.259	0.012	0.2520	0.2500
4	0.2043	0.2253	0.238	0.013	0.2320	0.2344
5	0.1819	0.2070	0.220	0.014	0.2120	0.2188
6	0.1620	0.1920	0.203	0.016	0.1920	0.2031
7	0.1443	0.1770	0.180	0.018	0.1760	0.1875
8	0.1285	0.1620	0.165	0.020	0.1600	0.1719
9	0.1144	0.1483	0.148	0.022	0.1440	0.1563
10	0.1019	0.1350	0.134	0.024	0.1280	0.1406
11	0.0907	0.1205	0.120	0.026	0.1160	0.1250
12	0.0808	0.1055	0.109	0.029	0.1040	0.1094
13	0.0720	0.0915	0.095	0.031	0.0920	0.0938
14	0.0641	0.0800	0.083	0.033	0.0800	0.0781
15	0.0571	0.0720	0.072	0.035	0.0720	0.0703
16	0.0508	0.0625	0.065	0.037	0.0640	0.0625
17	0.0453	0.0540	0.058	0.039	0.0560	0.0563
18	0.0403	0.0475	0.049	0.041	0.0480	0.0500
19	0.0359	0.0410	0.042	0.043	0.0400	0.0438
20	0.0320	0.0348	0.035	0.045	0.0360	0.0375
21	0.0285	0.0317	0.032	0.047	0.0320	0.0344
22	0.0253	0.0286	0.028	0.049	0.0280	0.0313
23	0.0226	0.0258	0.025	0.051	0.0240	0.0281
24	0.0201	0.0230	0.022	0.055	0.0220	0.0250
25	0.0179	0.0204	0.020	0.059	0.0200	0.0219
26	0.0159	0.0181	0.018	0.063	0.0180	0.0188
27	0.0142	0.0173	0.016	0.067	0.0164	0.0172
28	0.0126	0.0162	0.014	0.071	0.0148	0.0156
29	0.0113	0.0150	0.013	0.075	0.0136	0.0141
30	0.0100	0.0140	0.012	0.080	0.0124	0.0125
31	0.0089	0.0132	0.010	0.085	0.0116	0.0109
32	0.0080	0.0128	0.009	0.090	0.0108	0.0102
33	0.0071	0.0118	0.008	0.095	0.0100	0.0094
34	0.0063	0.0104	0.007	0.100	0.0092	0.0086
35	0.0056	0.0095	0.005	0.106	0.0084	0.0078
36	0.0050	0.0090	0.004	0.112	0.0076	0.0070
37	0.0045	0.0085	. . . . .	0.118	0.0068	0.0066
38	0.0040	0.0080	. . . . .	0.124	0.0060	0.0063
39	0.0035	0.0075	. . . . .	0.130	0.0052	
40	0.0031	0.0070	. . . . .	0.138	0.0048	

[a] Recognized standard in the United States for wire and sheet metal of copper and other metals except steel and iron.

[b] Recognized standard for steel and iron wire. Called the "U.S. steel wire gage."

[c] Formerly much used, now nearly obsolete.

[d] American Steel & Wire Co.'s music wire gage. Recommended by U.S. Bureau of Standards.

[e] Official British Standard.

[f] Legalized U.S. Standard for iron and steel plate, although plate is now always specified by its thickness in decimals of an inch.

Preferred thicknesses for uncoated thin flat metals (under 0.250 in.): ASA B32.1—1959 gives recommended sizes for sheets.

Preferred Basic Sizes for Cylindrical Fits*

...	0.0100	...	...	...	0.80	5½	5.5000	5.5
...	0.0125	...	⅞	0.8750	...	5¾	5.7500	5.75
1/64	0.015625	...	...	...	0.90	6	6.0000	6.0
...	0.0200	...	1	1.0000	1.0	6½	6.5000	6.5
...	0.0250	...	...	...	1.1	7	7.0000	7.0
1/32	0.03125	...	1⅛	1.1250	...	7½	7.5000	7.5
...	0.0400	0.04	...	...	...	8	8.0000	8.0
...	0.0500	...	1¼	1.2500	1.25	8½	8.5000	8.5
...	...	0.06	1⅜	1.3750	...	9	9.0000	9.0
1/16	0.0625	...	...	...	1.40	9½	9.5000	9.5
...	0.0800	...	1½	1.5000	1.50	10	10.0000	10.0
3/32	0.09375	...	1⅝	1.6250	...	10½	10.5000	10.5
...	0.1000	0.10	1¾	1.7500	1.75	11	11.0000	11.0
1/8	0.1250	...	1⅞	1.8750	...	11½	11.5000	11.5
...	...	0.15	2	2.0000	2.0	12	12.0000	12.0
5/32	0.15625	...	2⅛	2.1250	...	12½	12.5000	12.5
3/16	0.1875	...	2¼	2.2500	2.25	13	13.0000	13.0
...	...	0.20	2⅜	2.3750	...	13½	13.5000	13.5
1/4	0.2500	0.25	2½	2.5000	2.5	14	14.0000	14.0
...	...	0.30	2⅝	2.6250	...	14½	14.5000	14.5
5/16	0.3125	...	2¾	2.7500	2.75	15	15.0000	15.0
...	...	0.35	2⅞	2.8750	...	15½	15.5000	15.5
3/8	0.3750	...	3	3.0000	3.0	16	16.0000	16.0
...	...	0.40	3¼	3.2500	3.25	16½	16.5000	16.5
7/16	0.4375	...	3½	3.5000	3.5	17	17.0000	17.0
1/2	0.5000	0.50	3¾	3.7500	3.75	17½	17.5000	17.5
9/16	0.5625	...	4	4.0000	4.0	18	18.0000	18.0
...	...	0.60	4¼	4.2500	4.25	18½	18.5000	18.5
5/8	0.6250	...	4½	4.5000	4.5	19	19.0000	19.0
11/16	0.6875	...	4¾	4.7500	4.75	19½	19.5000	19.5
...	...	0.70	5	5 0000	5.0	20	20.0000	20.0
3/4	0.7500	0.75	5¼	5.2500	5.25	20½	20.5000	...
						21	21.0000	...

* Adapted from ASA B4.1—1955

Table 1. Running and Sliding Fits

(THOUSANDTHS)

Nominal size, in.	Class RC 1 Clearance	Std. lim. Hole	Shaft	Class RC 2 Clearance	Std. lim. Hole	Shaft	Class RC 3 Clearance	Std. lim. Hole	Shaft	Class RC 4 Clearance	Std. lim. Hole	Shaft
0.04–0.12	0.1	+0.2	-0.1	0.1	+0.25	-0.1	0.3	+0.25	-0.3	0.3	+0.4	-0.3
	0.45	0	-0.25	0.55	0	-0.3	0.8	0	-0.55	1.1	0	-0.7
0.12–0.24	0.15	+0.2	-0.15	0.15	+0.3	-0.15	0.4	+0.3	-0.4	0.4	+0.5	-0.4
	0.5	0	-0.3	0.65	0	-0.35	1.0	0	-0.7	1.4	0	-0.9
0.24–0.40	0.2	+0.25	-0.2	0.2	+0.4	-0.2	0.5	+0.4	-0.5	0.5	+0.6	-0.5
	0.6	0	-0.35	0.85	0	-0.45	1.3	0	-0.9	1.7	0	-1.1
0.40–0.71	0.25	+0.3	-0.25	0.25	+0.4	-0.25	0.6	+0.4	-0.6	0.6	+0.7	-0.6
	0.75	0	-0.45	0.95	0	-0.55	1.4	0	-1.0	2.0	0	-1.3
0.71–1.19	0.3	+0.4	-0.3	0.3	+0.5	-0.3	0.8	+0.5	-0.8	0.8	+0.8	-0.8
	0.95	0	-0.55	1.2	0	-0.7	1.8	0	-1.3	2.4	0	-1.6
1.19–1.97	0.4	+0.4	-0.4	0.4	+0.6	-0.4	1.0	+0.6	-1.0	1.0	+1.0	-1.0
	1.1	0	-0.7	1.4	0	-0.8	2.2	0	-1.6	3.0	0	-2.0
1.97–3.15	0.4	+0.5	-0.4	0.4	+0.7	-0.4	1.2	+0.7	-1.2	1.2	+1.2	-1.2
	1.2	0	-0.7	1.6	0	-0.9	2.6	0	-1.9	3.6	0	-2.4
3.15–4.73	0.5	+0.6	-0.5	0.5	+0.9	-0.5	1.4	+0.9	-1.4	1.4	+1.4	-1.4
	1.5	0	-0.9	2.0	0	-1.1	3.2	0	-2.3	4.2	0	-2.8
4.73–7.09	0.6	+0.7	-0.6	0.6	+1.0	-0.6	1.6	+1.0	-1.6	1.6	+1.6	-1.6
	1.8	0	-1.1	2.3	0	-1.3	3.6	0	-2.6	4.8	0	-3.2

Nominal size, in.	Class RC 5			Class RC 6			Class RC 7			Class RC 8			Class RC 9		
0.04–0.12	0.6	+0.4	-0.6	0.6	+0.6	-0.6	1.0	+1.0	-1.0	2.5	+1.6	-2.5	4.0	+2.5	-4.0
	1.4	0	-1.0	1.8	0	-1.2	2.6	0	-1.6	5.1	0	-3.5	8.1	0	-5.6
0.12–0.24	0.8	+0.5	-0.8	0.8	+0.7	-0.8	1.2	+1.2	-1.2	2.8	+1.8	-2.8	4.5	+3.0	-4.5
	1.8	0	-1.3	2.2	0	-1.5	3.1	0	-1.9	5.8	0	-4.0	9.0	0	-6.0
0.24–0.40	1.0	+0.6	-1.0	1.0	+0.9	-1.0	1.6	+1.4	-1.6	3.0	+2.2	-3.0	5.0	+3.5	-5.0
	2.2	0	-1.6	2.8	0	-1.9	3.9	0	-2.5	6.6	0	-4.4	10.7	0	-7.2
0.40–0.71	1.2	+0.7	-1.2	1.2	+1.0	-1.2	2.0	+1.6	-2.0	3.5	+2.8	-3.5	6.0	+4.0	-6.0
	2.6	0	-1.9	3.2	0	-2.2	4.6	0	-3.0	7.9	0	-5.1	12.8	0	-8.8
0.71–1.19	1.6	+0.8	-1.6	1.6	+1.2	-1.6	2.5	+2.0	-2.5	4.5	+3.5	-4.5	7.0	+5.0	-7.0
	3.2	0	-2.4	4.0	0	-2.8	5.7	0	-3.7	10.0	0	-6.5	15.5	0	-10.5
1.19–1.97	2.0	+1.0	-2.0	2.0	+1.6	-2.0	3.0	+2.5	-3.0	5.0	+4.0	-5.0	8.0	+6.0	-8.0
	4.0	0	-3.0	5.2	0	-3.6	7.1	0	-4.6	11.5	0	-7.5	18.0	0	-12.0
1.97–3.15	2.5	+1.2	-2.5	2.5	+1.8	-2.5	4.0	+3.0	-4.0	6.0	+4.5	-6.0	9.0	+7.0	-9.0
	4.9	0	-3.7	6.1	0	-4.3	8.8	0	-5.8	13.5	0	-9.0	20.5	0	-13.5
3.15–4.73	3.0	+1.4	-3.0	3.0	+2.2	-3.0	5.0	+3.5	-5.0	7.0	+5.0	-7.0	10.0	+9.0	-10.0
	5.8	0	-4.4	7.4	0	-5.2	10.7	0	-7.2	15.5	0	-10.5	24.0	0	-15.0
4.73–7.09	3.5	+1.6	-3.5	3.5	+2.5	-3.5	6.0	+4.0	-6.0	8.0	+6.0	-8.0	12.0	+10.0	-12.0
	6.7	0	-5.1	8.5	0	-6.0	12.5	0	-8.5	18.0	0	-12.0	28.0	0	-18.0

Table 2. Clearance Locational Fits

Nominal size, in.	Class LC 1			Class LC 2			Class LC 3			Class LC 4			Class LC 5		
0.04–0.12	0	+0.25	+0	0	+0.4	+0	0	+0.6	+0	0	+1.0	+0	0.1	+0.4	-0.1
	0.45	-0	-0.2	0.65	-0	-0.25	1	-0	-0.4	2.0	-0	-1.0	0.75	-0	-0.35
0.12–0.24	0	+0.3	+0	0	+0.5	+0	0	+0.7	+0	0	+1.2	+0	0.15	+0.5	-0.15
	0.5	-0	-0.2	0.8	-0	-0.3	1.2	-0	-0.5	2.4	-0	-1.2	0.95	-0	-0.45
0.24–0.40	0	+0.4	+0	0	+0.6	+0	0	+0.9	+0	0	+1.4	+0	0.2	+0.6	-0.2
	0.65	-0	-0.25	1.0	-0	-0.4	1.5	-0	-0.6	2.8	-0	-1.4	1.2	-0	-0.6
0.40–0.71	0	+0.4	+0	0	+0.7	+0	0	+1.0	+0	0	+1.6	+0	0.25	+0.7	-0.25
	0.7	-0	-0.3	1.1	-0	-0.4	1.7	-0	-0.7	3.2	-0	-1.6	1.35	-0	-0.65
0.71–1.19	0	+0.5	+0	0	+0.8	+0	0	+1.2	+0	0	+2.0	+0	0.3	+0.8	-0.3
	0.9	-0	-0.4	1.3	-0	-0.5	2	-0	-0.8	4	-0	-2.0	1.6	-0	-0.8
1.19–1.97	0	+0.6	+0	0	+1.0	+0	0	+1.6	+0	0	+2.5	+0	0.4	+1.0	-0.4
	1.0	-0	-0.4	1.6	-0	-0.6	2.6	-0	-1	5	-0	-2.5	2.0	-0	-1.0
1.97–3.15	0	+0.7	+0	0	+1.2	+0	0	+1.8	+0	0	+3	+0	0.4	+1.2	-0.4
	1.2	-0	-0.5	1.9	-0	-0.7	3	-0	-1.2	6	-0	-3	2.3	-0	-1.1
3.15–4.73	0	+0.9	+0	0	+1.4	+0	0	+2.2	+0	0	+3.5	+0	0.5	+1.4	-0.5
	1.5	-0	-0.6	2.3	-0	-0.9	3.6	-0	-1.4	7	-0	-3.5	2.8	-0	-1.4
4.73–7.09	0	+1.0	+0	0	+1.6	+0	0	+2.5	+0	0	+4	+0	0.6	+1.6	-0.6
	1.7	-0	-0.7	2.6	-0	-1.0	4.1	-0	-1.6	8	-0	-4	3.2	-0	-1.6

Nominal size, in.	Class LC 6			Class LC 7			Class LC 8			Class LC 9			Class LC 10			Class LC 11		
0.04–0.12	0.3	+0.6	-0.3	0.6	+1.0	-0.6	1.0	+1.6	-1.0	2.5	+2.5	-2.5	4	+4	-4	5	+6	-5
	1.5	-0	-0.9	2.6	-0	-1.6	3.6	-0	-2.0	7.5	-0	-5.0	12	-0	-8	17	-0	-11
0.12–0.24	0.4	+0.7	-0.4	0.8	+1.2	-0.8	1.2	+1.8	-1.2	2.8	+3.0	-2.8	4.5	+5	-4.5	6	+7	-6
	1.8	-0	-1.1	3.2	-0	-2.0	4.2	-0	-2.4	8.8	-0	-5.8	14.5	-0	-9.5	20	-0	-13
0.24–0.40	0.5	+0.9	-0.5	1.0	+1.4	-1.0	1.6	+2.2	-1.6	3.0	+3.5	-3.0	5	+6	-5	7	+9	-7
	2.3	-0	-1.4	3.8	-0	-2.4	5.2	-0	-3.0	10.0	-0	-6.5	17	-0	-11	25	-0	-16
0.40–0.71	0.6	+1.0	-0.6	1.2	+1.6	-1.2	2.0	+2.8	-2.0	3.5	+4.0	-3.5	6	+7	-6	8	+10	-8
	2.6	-0	-1.6	4.4	-0	-2.8	6.4	-0	-3.6	11.5	-0	-7.5	20	-0	-13	28	-0	-18
0.71–1.19	0.8	+1.2	-0.8	1.6	+2.0	-1.6	2.5	+3.5	-2.5	4.5	+5.0	-4.5	7	+8	-7	10	+12	-10
	3.2	-0	-2.0	5.6	-0	-3.6	8.0	-0	-4.5	14.5	-0	-9.5	23	-0	-15	34	-0	-22
1.19–1.97	1.0	+1.6	-1.0	2.0	+2.5	-2.0	3.0	+4.0	-3.0	5	+6	-5	8	+10	-8	12	+16	-12
	4.2	-0	-2.6	7.0	-0	-4.5	9.5	-0	-5.5	17	-0	-11	28	-0	-18	44	-0	-28
1.97–3.15	1.2	+1.8	-1.2	2.5	+3.0	-2.5	4.0	+4.5	-4.0	6	+7	-6	10	+12	-10	14	+18	-14
	4.8	-0	-3.0	8.5	-0	-5.5	11.5	-0	-7.0	20	-0	-13	34	-0	-22	50	-0	-32
3.15–4.73	1.4	+2.2	-1.4	3.0	+3.5	-3.0	5.0	+5.0	-5.0	7	+9	-7	11	+14	-11	16	+22	-16
	5.8	-0	-3.6	10.0	-0	-6.5	13.5	-0	-8.5	25	-0	-16	39	-0	-25	60	-0	-38
4.73–7.09	1.6	+2.5	-1.6	3.5	+4.0	-3.5	6	+6	-6	8	+10	-8	12	+16	-12	18	+25	-18
	6.6	-0	-4.1	11.5	-0	-7.5	16	-0	-10	28	-0	-18	44	-0	-28	68	-0	-43

* Adapted from ASA B4.1—1955. Limits for hole and shaft are applied algebraically to basic size to obtain limits of size for parts. Data in boldface in accordance with ABC agreements.

Table 3. Transition Locational Fits

Nominal size, in.	Class LT 1 Fit†	Hole	Shaft	Class LT 2 Fit	Hole	Shaft	Class LT 3 Fit	Hole	Shaft	Class LT 4 Fit	Hole	Shaft	Class LT 6 Fit	Hole	Shaft	Class LT 7 Fit	Hole	Shaft
0.04–0.12	−0.15	+0.4	+0.15	−0.3	+0.6	+0.3							−0.55	+0.6	+0.55	−0.5	+0.4	+0.5
	+0.5	−0	−0.1	+0.7	−0	−0.1							+0.45	−0	+0.15	+0.15	−0	+0.25
0.12–0.24	−0.2	+0.5	+0.2	−0.4	+0.7	+0.4							−0.7	+0.7	+0.7	−0.6	+0.5	+0.6
	+0.6	−0	−0.1	+0.8	−0	−0.1							+0.5	−0	+0.2	+0.2	−0	+0.3
0.24–0.40	−0.3	+0.6	+0.3	−0.4	+0.9	+0.4	−0.5	+0.6	+0.5	−0.7	+0.9	+0.7	−0.8	+0.9	+0.8	−0.8	+0.6	+0.8
	+0.7	−0	−0.1	+1.1	−0	−0.2	+0.5	−0	+0.1	+0.8	−0	+0.1	+0.7	−0	+0.2	−0.2	−0	+0.4
0 40–0.71	−0.3	+0.7	+0.3	−0.5	+1.0	+0.5	−0.5	+0.7	+0.5	−0.8	+1.0	+0.8	−1.0	+1.0	+1.0	−0.9	+0.7	+0.9
	+0.8	−0	−0.1	+1.2	−0	−0.2	+0.6	−0	+0.1	+0.9	−0	+0.1	+0.7	−0	+0.3	+0.2	−0	+0.5
0.71–1.19	−0.3	+0.8	+0.3	−0.5	+1.2	+0.5	−0.6	+0.8	+0.6	−0.9	+1.2	+0.9	−1.1	+1.2	+1.1	−1.1	+0.8	+1.1
	+1.0	−0	−0.2	+1.5	−0	−0.3	+0.7	−0	+0.1	+0.9	−0	+0.1	+0.9	−0	+0.3	+0.2	−0	+0.6
1.19–1.97	−0.4	+1.0	+0.4	−0.6	+1.6	+0.6	−0.7	+1.0	+0.7	−1.1	+1.6	+1.1	−1.4	+1.6	+1.4	−1.3	+1.0	+1.3
	+1.2	−0	−0.2	+2.0	−0	−0.4	+0.9	−0	+0.1	+1.5	−0	+0.1	+1.2	−0	+0.4	+0.3	−0	+0.7
1.97–3.15	−0.4	+1.2	+0.4	−0.7	+1.8	+0.7	−0.8	+1.2	+0.8	−1.3	+1.8	+1.3	−1.7	+1.8	+1.7	−1.5	+1.2	+1.5
	+1.5	−0	−0.3	+2.3	−0	−0.5	+1.1	−0	+0.1	+1.7	−0	+0.1	+1.3	−0	+0.5	+0.4	−0	+0.8
3.15–4.73	−0.5	+1.4	+0.5	−0.8	+2.2	+0.8	−1.0	+1.4	+1.0	−1.5	+2.2	+1.5	−1.9	+2.2	+1.9	−1.9	+1.4	+1.9
	+1.8	−0	−0.4	+2.8	−0	−0.6	+1.3	−0	+0.1	+2.1	−0	+0.1	+1.7	−0	+0.5	+0.4	−0	+1.0
4.73–7.09	−0.6	+1.6	+0.6	−0.9	+2.5	+0.9	−1.1	+1.6	+1.1	−1.7	+2.5	+1.7	−2.2	+2.5	+2.2	−2.2	+1.6	+2.2
	+2.0	−0	−0.4	+3.2	−0	−0.7	+1.5	−0	+0.1	+2.4	−0	+0.1	+1.9	−0	+0.6	+0.4	−0	+1.2

† "Fit" represents the maximum interference (minus values) and the maximum clearance (plus values).

Table 4. Interference Locational Fits

Nominal size, in.	Class LN 2 Interference	Hole	Shaft	Class LN 3 Interference	Hole	Shaft
0.04–0.12	0	+0.4	+0.65	0.1	+0.4	+0.75
	0.65	−0	+0.4	0.75	−0	+0.5
0.12–0.24	0	+0.5	+0.8	0.1	+0.5	+0.9
	0.8	−0	+0.5	0.9	−0	+0.6
0.24–0.40	0	+0.6	+1.0	0.2	+0.6	+1.2
	1.0	−0	+0.6	1.2	−0	+0.8
0.40–0.71	0	+0.7	+1.1	0.3	+0.7	+1.4
	1.1	−0	+0.7	1.4	−0	+1.0
0.71–1.19	0	+0.8	+1.3	0.4	+0.8	+1.7
	1.3	−0	+0.8	1.7	−0	+1.2
1.19–1.97	0	+1.0	+1.6	0.4	+1.0	+2.0
	1.6	−0	+1.0	2.0	−0	+1.4
1.97–3.15	0.2	+1.2	+2.1	0.4	+1.2	+2.3
	2.1	−0	+1.4	2.3	−0	+1.6
3.15–4.73	0.2	+1.4	+2.5	0.6	+1.4	+2.9
	2.5	−0	+1.6	2.9	−0	+2.0
4.73–7.09	0.2	+1.6	+2.8	0.9	+1.6	+3.5
	2.8	−0	+1.8	3.5	−0	+2.5

Table 5. Force and Shrink Fits

Nominal size	Class FN 1	Hole	Shaft	Class FN 2	Hole	Shaft	Class FN 3	Hole	Shaft	Class FN 4	Hole	Shaft	Class FN 5	Hole	Shaft
0.04–0.12	0.05	+0.25	+0.5	0.2	+0.4	+0.85				0.3	+0.4	+0.95	0.5	+0.4	+1.3
	0.5	−0	+0.3	0.85	−0	+0.6				0.95	−0	+0.7	1.3	−0	+0.9
0.12–0.24	0.1	+0.3	+0.6	0.2	+0.5	+1.0				0.4	+0.5	+1.2	0.7	+0.5	+1.7
	0.6	−0	+0.4	1.0	−0	+0.7				1.2	−0	+0.9	1.7	−0	+1.2
0.24–0.40	0.1	+0.4	+0.75	0.4	+0.6	+1.4				0.6	+0.6	+1.6	0.8	+0.6	+2.0
	0.75	−0	+0.5	1.4	−0	+1.0				1.6	−0	+1.2	2.0	−0	+1.4
0.40–0.56	0.1	+0.4	+0.8	0.5	+0.7	+1.6				0.7	+0.7	+1.8	0.9	+0.7	+2.3
	0.8	−0	+0.5	1.6	−0	+1.2				1.8	−0	+1.4	2.3	−0	+1.6
0.56–0.71	0.2	+0.4	+0.9	0.5	+0.7	+1.6				0.7	+0.7	+1.8	1.1	+0.7	+2.5
	0.9	−0	+0.6	1.6	−0	+1.2				1.8	−0	+1.4	2.5	−0	+1.8
0.71–0.95	0.2	+0.5	+1.1	0.6	+0.8	+1.9				0.8	+0.8	+2.1	1.4	+0.8	+3.0
	1.1	−0	+0.7	1.9	−0	+1.4				2.1	−0	+1.6	3.0	−0	+2.2
0.95–1.19	0.3	+0.5	+1.2	0.6	+0.8	+1.9	0.8	+0.8	+2.1	1.0	+0.8	+2.3	1.7	+0.8	+3.3
	1.2	−0	+0.8	1.9	−0	+1.4	2.1	−0	+1.6	2.3	−0	+1.8	3.3	−0	+2.5
1.19–1.58	0.3	+0.6	+1.3	0.8	+1.0	+2.4	1.0	+1.0	+2.6	1.5	+1.0	+3.1	2.0	+1.0	+4.0
	1.3	−0	+0.9	2.4	−0	+1.8	2.6	−0	+2.0	3.1	−0	+2.5	4.0	−0	+3.0
1.58–1.97	0.4	+0.6	+1.4	0.8	+1.0	+2.4	1.2	+1.0	+2.8	1.8	+1.0	+3.4	3.0	+1.0	+5.0
	1.4	−0	+1.0	2.4	−0	+1.8	2.8	−0	+2.2	3.4	−0	+2.8	5.0	−0	+4.0
1.97–2.56	0.6	+0.7	+1.8	0.8	+1.2	+2.7	1.3	+1.2	+3.2	2.3	+1.2	+4.2	3.8	+1.2	+6.2
	1.8	−0	+1.3	2.7	−0	+2.0	3.2	−0	+2.5	4.2	−0	+3.5	6.2	−0	+5.0
2.56–3.15	0.7	+0.7	+1.9	1.0	+1.2	+2.9	1.8	+1.2	+3.7	2.8	+1.2	+4.7	4.8	+1.2	+7.2
	1.9	−0	+1.4	2.9	−0	+2.2	3.7	−0	+3.0	4.7	−0	+4.0	7.2	−0	+6.0
3.15–3.94	0.9	+0.9	+2.4	1.4	+1.4	+3.7	2.1	+1.4	+4.4	3.6	+1.4	+5.9	5.6	+1.4	+8.4
	2.4	−0	+1.8	3.7	−0	+2.8	4.4	−0	+3.5	5.9	−0	+5.0	8.4	−0	+7.0
3.94–4.73	1.1	+0.9	+2.6	1.6	+1.4	+3.9	2.6	+1.4	+4.9	4.6	+1.4	+6.9	6.6	+1.4	+9.4
	2.6	−0	+2.0	3.9	−0	+3.0	4.9	−0	+4.0	6.9	−0	+6.0	9.4	−0	+8.0
4.73–5.52	1.2	+1.0	+2.9	1.9	+1.6	+4.5	3.4	+1.6	+6.0	5.4	+1.6	+8.0	8.4	+1.6	+11.6
	2.9	−0	+2.2	4.5	−0	+3.5	6.0	−0	+5.0	8.0	−0	+7.0	11.6	−0	+10.0
5.52–6.30	1.5	+1.0	+3.2	2.4	+1.6	+5.0	3.4	+1.6	+6.0	5.4	+1.6	+8.0	10.4	+1.6	+13.6
	3.2	−0	+2.5	5.0	−0	+4.0	6.0	−0	+5.0	8.0	−0	+7.0	13.6	−0	+12.0
6.30–7.09	1.8	+1.0	+3.5	2.9	+1.6	+5.5	4.4	+1.6	+7.0	6.4	+1.6	+9.0	10.4	+1.6	+13.6
	3.5	−0	+2.8	5.5	−0	+4.5	7.0	−0	+6.0	9.0	−0	+8.0	13.6	−0	+12.0

American Standard Pipe[a, b]

Welded wrought iron

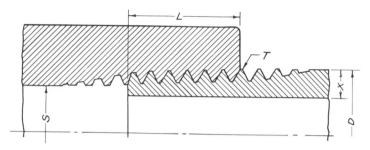

Nominal pipe size	Actual outside diam. D	Tap-drill size S	Thd. /in. T	Distance pipe enters fittings L	Wall thickness X			Weight, lb/ft[f]		
					Standard 40[c]	Extra strong 80[d]	Double extra strong[e]	Standard 40[c]	Extra strong 80[d]	Double extra strong[e]
1/8	0.405	11/32	27	3/16	0.070	0.098	....	0.25	0.32	
1/4	0.540	7/16	18	9/32	0.090	0.122	....	0.43	0.54	
3/8	0.675	37/64	18	19/64	0.093	0.129	....	0.57	0.74	
1/2	0.840	23/32	14	3/8	0.111	0.151	0.307	0.86	1.09	1.714
3/4	1.050	59/64	14	13/32	0.115	0.157	0.318	1.14	1.48	2.440
1	1.315	1 5/32	11½	½	0.136	0.183	0.369	1.68	2.18	3.659
1¼	1.660	1 ½	11½	35/64	0.143	0.195	0.393	2.28	3.00	5.214
1½	1.900	1 47/64	11½	9/16	0.148	0.204	0.411	2.72	3.64	6.408
2	2.375	2 7/32	11½	37/64	0.158	0.223	0.447	3.66	5.03	9.029
2½	2.875	2 5/8	8	7/8	0.208	0.282	0.565	5.80	7.67	13.695
3	3.5	3 ¼	8	15/16	0.221	0.306	0.615	7.58	10.3	18.583
3½	4.0	3 ¾	8	1	0.231	0.325	....	9.11	12.5	
4	4.5	4 ¼	8	1 1/16	0.242	0.344	0.690	10.8	15.0	27.451
5	5.563	5 5/16	8	1 5/32	0.263	0.383	0.768	14.7	20.8	38.552
6	6.625	6 5/16	8	1 ¼	0.286	0.441	0.884	19.0	28.6	53.160
8	8.625	.....	8	1 15/32	0.329	0.510	0.895	28.6	43.4	72.424
10	10.75	.....	8	1 43/64	0.372	0.606	....	40.5	64.4	
12	12.75	.....	8	1 7/8	0.414	0.702	....	53.6	88.6	
14 OD	14.0	.....	8	2	0.437	0.750	....	62.2	104.	
16 OD	16.0	.....	8	2 13/64	0.500	....	....	82.2		
18 OD	18.0	.....	8	2 13/32	0.562	....	....	103.		
20 OD	20.0	.....	8	2 19/32	0.562	....	....	115.		
24 OD	24.0	.....	8	3						

[a] For welded and seamless steel pipe. See ASA B36.10—1959. Dimensions in inches.

[b] A pipe size may be designated by giving the nominal pipe size and wall thickness or by giving the nominal pipe size and weight per linear foot.

[c] Refers to American Standard schedule numbers, approximate values for the expression $1,000 \times P/S$. Schedule 40—standard weight.

[d] Schedule 80—extra strong.

[e] Not American Standard, but commercially available in both wrought iron and steel.

[f] Plain ends.

American Standard 150-lb Malleable-iron Screwed Fittings[a]

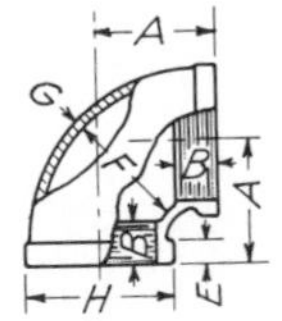

90° ELBOW

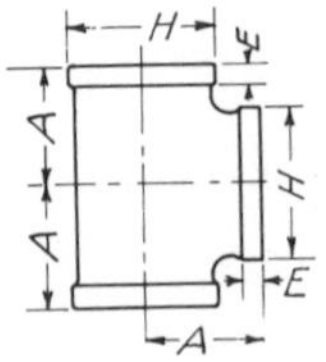

TEE

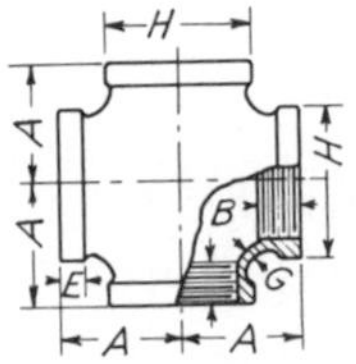

CROSS

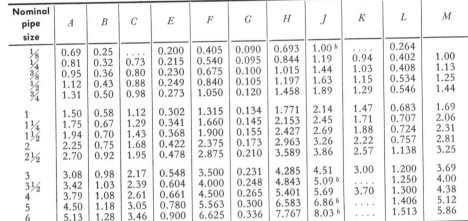

Nominal pipe size	A	B	C	E	F	G	H	J	K	L	M
1/8	0.69	0.25	....	0.200	0.405	0.090	0.693	1.00[b]	....	0.264	
1/4	0.81	0.32	0.73	0.215	0.540	0.095	0.844	1.19	0.94	0.402	1.00
3/8	0.95	0.36	0.80	0.230	0.675	0.100	1.015	1.44	1.03	0.408	1.13
1/2	1.12	0.43	0.88	0.249	0.840	0.105	1.197	1.63	1.15	0.534	1.25
3/4	1.31	0.50	0.98	0.273	1.050	0.120	1.458	1.89	1.29	0.546	1.44
1	1.50	0.58	1.12	0.302	1.315	0.134	1.771	2.14	1.47	0.683	1.69
1 1/4	1.75	0.67	1.29	0.341	1.660	0.145	2.153	2.45	1.71	0.707	2.06
1 1/2	1.94	0.70	1.43	0.368	1.900	0.155	2.427	2.69	1.88	0.724	2.31
2	2.25	0.75	1.68	0.422	2.375	0.173	2.963	3.26	2.22	0.757	2.81
2 1/2	2.70	0.92	1.95	0.478	2.875	0.210	3.589	3.86	2.57	1.138	3.25
3	3.08	0.98	2.17	0.548	3.500	0.231	4.285	4.51	3.00	1.200	3.69
3 1/2	3.42	1.03	2.39	0.604	4.000	0.248	4.843	5.09[b]	....	1.250	4.00
4	3.79	1.08	2.61	0.661	4.500	0.265	5.401	5.69	3.70	1.300	4.38
5	4.50	1.18	3.05	0.780	5.563	0.300	6.583	6.86[b]	....	1.406	5.12
6	5.13	1.28	3.46	0.900	6.625	0.336	7.767	8.03[b]	....	1.513	5.86

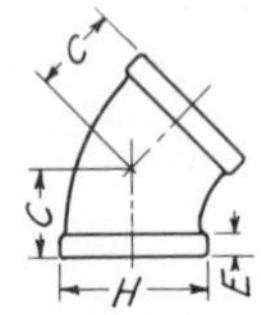

45° ELL

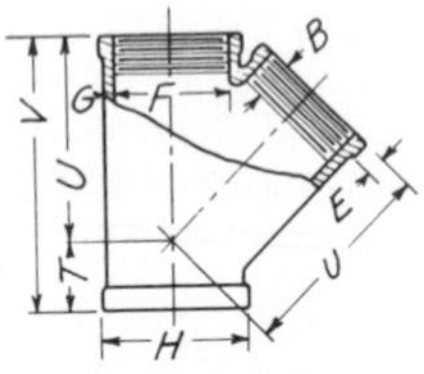

Y BRANCH

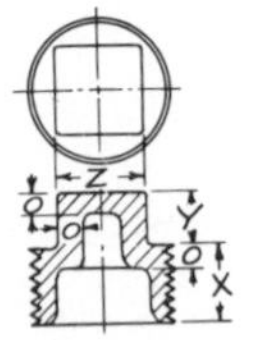

PLUG

Nominal pipe size	N	P	T	U	V	W	X	Y	Z[c]	O[d]	Thickness of ribs on caps, couplings
1/8	0.20	....	....	....	....	0.96	0.37	0.24	9/32	....	0.090
1/4	0.26	....	....	....	....	1.06	0.44	0.28	3/8	....	0.095
3/8	0.37	....	0.50	1.43	1.93	1.16	0.48	0.31	7/16	....	0.100
1/2	0.51	0.87	0.61	1.71	2.32	1.34	0.56	0.38	9/16	0.16	0.105
3/4	0.69	0.97	0.72	2.05	2.77	1.52	0.63	0.44	5/8	0.18	0.120
1	0.91	1.16	0.85	2.43	3.28	1.67	0.75	0.50	13/16	0.20	0.134
1 1/4	1.19	1.28	1.02	2.92	3.94	1.93	0.80	0.56	15/16	0.22	0.145
1 1/2	1.39	1.33	1.10	3.28	4.38	2.15	0.83	0.62	1 1/8	0.24	0.155
2	1.79	1.45	1.24	3.93	5.17	2.53	0.88	0.68	1 5/16	0.26	0.173
2 1/2	2.20	1.70	1.52	4.73	6.25	2.88	1.07	0.74	1 1/2	0.29	0.210
3	2.78	1.80	1.71	5.55	7.26	3.18	1.13	0.80	1 11/16	0.31	0.231
3 1/2	3.24	1.90	....	....	....	3.43	1.18	0.86	1 7/8	0.34	0.248
4	3.70	2.08	2.01	6.97	8.98	3.69	1.22	1.00	2 1/8	0.37	0.265
5	4.69	2.32	....	....	....	....	1.31	1.00	2 5/16	0.46	0.300
6	5.67	2.55	....	....	....	....	1.40	1.25	2 1/2	0.52	0.336

[a] ASA B16.3—1963. Street tee not made in 1/8-in. size. Dimensions in inches. Left-hand couplings have four or more ribs. Right-hand couplings have two ribs. [b] Street ell only.

[c] These dimensions are the nominal size of wrench (ASA B18.2—1960). Square-head plugs are designed to fit these wrenches.

[d] Solid plugs are provided in sizes 1/8 to 3 1/2 in. inclusive; cored plugs 1/2 to 3 1/2 in. inclusive. Cored plugs have min. metal thickness at all points equal to dimension O except at the end of thread.

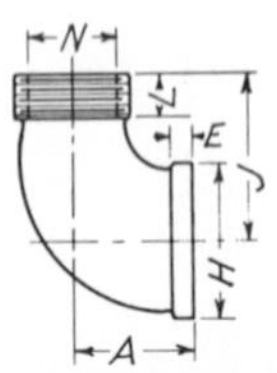

90° STREET ELBOW

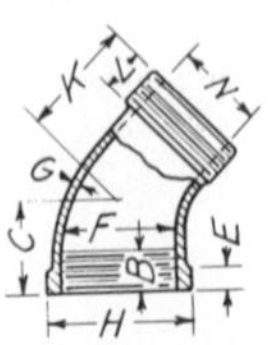

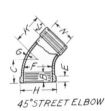

45° STREET ELBOW

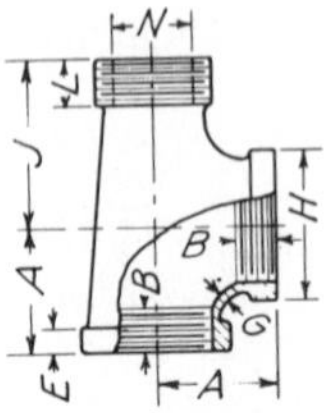

STREET TEE

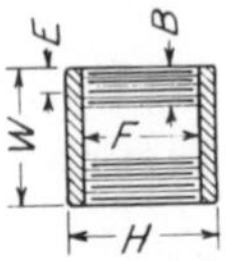

COUPLING

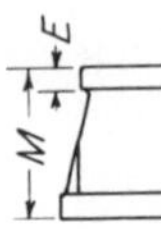

REDUCING COUPLING

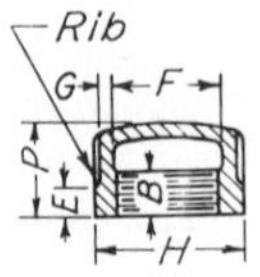

CAP

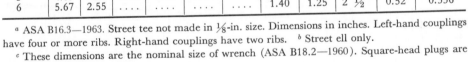

American Standard 150-lb Malleable-iron Screwed Fittings: Dimensions of Close-, Medium-, and Open-pattern Return Bends*†

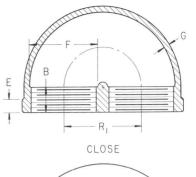

CLOSE

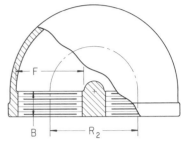

MEDIUM

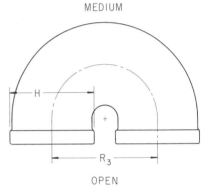

OPEN

Nominal pipe size	Length of thread, min. B	Width of band, min. E	Inside diam. of fittings F		Metal thickness ‡ G	Outside diam. of band, min. H	Center to center (close pattern) R_1	Center to center (medium pattern) R_2	Center to center (open pattern) R_3
			Max.	Min.					
½	0.43	0.249	0.840	0.897	0.116	1.197	1.000	1.250	1.50
¾	0.50	0.273	1.050	1.107	0.133	1.458	1.250	1.500	2.00
1	0.58	0.302	1.315	1.385	0.150	1.771	1.500	1.875	2.50
1¼	0.67	0.341	1.660	1.730	0.165	2.153	1.750	2.250	3.00
1½	0.70	0.368	1.900	1.970	0.178	2.427	2.188	2.500	3.50
2	0.75	0.422	2.375	2.445	0.201	2.963	2.625	3.000	4.00
2½	0.92	0.478	2.875	2.975	0.244	3.589	. . . .	. . . .	4.50
3	0.98	0.548	3.500	3.600	0.272	4.285	. . . .	. . . .	5.00
4	1.08	0.661	4.500	4.600	0.315	5.401	. . . .	. . . .	6.00

All dimensions given in inches.

* Adapted from ASA B16.3—1963.

† It is permissible to furnish close-pattern return bends not banded. Close-pattern return bends will not make up parallel coils, as the distance center to center of two adjacent bends is greater than the center to center of openings of a single bend.

‡ Patterns shall be designed to produce castings of metal thicknesses given in the table. Metal thickness at no point shall be less than 90 per cent of the thickness given in the table.

American Standard Cast-iron Screwed Fittings*

For maximum working saturated steam pressure of 125 and 250 lb per sq in.

Nominal pipe size	A	B min.	C	E min.	F		G min.	H min.
					Min.	Max.		
¼	0.81	0.32	0.73	0.38	0.540	0.584	0.110	0.93
⅜	0.95	0.36	0.80	0.44	0.675	0.719	0.120	1.12
½	1.12	0.43	0.88	0.50	0.840	0.897	0.130	1.34
¾	1.31	0.50	0.98	0.56	1.050	1.107	0.155	1.63
1	1.50	0.58	1.12	0.62	1.315	1.385	0.170	1.95
1¼	1.75	0.67	1.29	0.69	1.660	1.730	0.185	2.39
1½	1.94	0.70	1.43	0.75	1.900	1.970	0.200	2.68
2	2.25	0.75	1.68	0.84	2.375	2.445	0.220	3.28
2½	2.70	0.92	1.95	0.94	2.875	2.975	0.240	3.86
3	3.08	0.98	2.17	1.00	3.500	3.600	0.260	4.62
3½	3.42	1.03	2.39	1.06	4.000	4.100	0.280	5.20
4	3.79	1.08	2.61	1.12	4.500	4.600	0.310	5.79
5	4.50	1.18	3.05	1.18	5.563	5.663	0.380	7.05
6	5.13	1.28	3.46	1.28	6.625	6.725	0.430	8.28
8	6.56	1.47	4.28	1.47	8.625	8.725	0.550	10.63
10	8.08	1.68	5.16	1.68	10.750	10.850	0.690	13.12
12	9.50	1.88	5.97	1.88	12.750	12.850	0.800	15.47

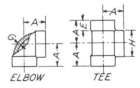

ELBOW   TEE

CROSS

45°ELBOW

* ASA B16.4—1963. Dimensions in inches.

Globe, Angle-globe, and Gate Valves*

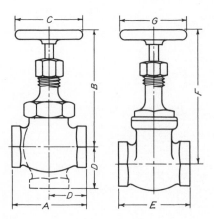

Size	A (globe only)	B (open)	C	D (angle only)	E	F (open)	G
1/8	2	4	1¾	1			
1/4	2	4	1¾	1	1⅞	5⅛	1¾
3/8	2¼	4½	2	1⅛	2	5⅛	1¾
1/2	2¾	5¼	2½	1¼	2⅛	5½	2
3/4	3³⁄₁₆	6	2¾	1½	2⅜	6⅝	2½
1	3¾	6¾	3	1¾	2⅞	7⅞	2¾
1¼	4¼	7¼	3⅝	2	3¼	9½	3
1½	4¾	8¼	4	2¼	3½	10⅞	3⅝
2	5¾	9½	4¾	2¾	3⅞	13⅛	4
2½	6¾	11	6	3¼	4½	15⅜	4¾
3	8	12¼	7	3¾	5	17⅞	5⅜

* Dimensions in inches and compiled from manufacturers' catalogues for drawing purposes.

Lengths of Pipe Nipples*

Size	Length Close	Length Short	Size	Length Close	Length Short	Size	Length Close	Length Short	Size	Length Close	Length Short
1/8	¾	1½	1/2	1⅛	1½	1¼	1⅝	2½	2½	2½	3
1/4	⅞	1½	3/4	1⅜	2	1½	1¾	2½	3	2⅝	3
3/8	1	1½	1	1½	2	2	2	2½			

* Compiled from manufacturers' catalogues. Dimensions in inches.

Long-nipple lengths: from short-nipple lengths to 6 in. in ½ in. increments; from 6 in. nipple lengths to 12 in. in 1 in. increments; from 12 in. nipple lengths to 24 in. in 2 in. increments.

Pipe Bushings*

Dimensions of outside-head, inside-head, and face bushings in inches

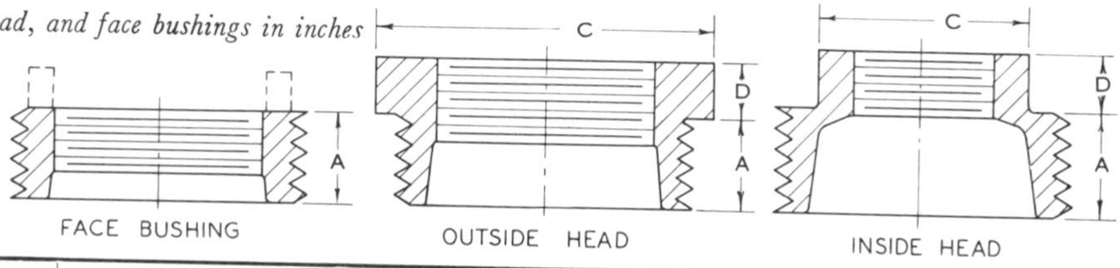

FACE BUSHING   OUTSIDE HEAD   INSIDE HEAD

Size	Length of external thread,† min., A	Height of head, min., D	Width of head,‡ min., C — Outside	Width of head,‡ min., C — Inside	Size	Length of external thread,‡ min., A	Height of head, min., D	Width of head,† min., C — Outside	Width of head,† min., C — Inside
¼ × ⅛	0.44	0.14	0.64		1½ × ¼	0.83	0.37	....	1.12
⅜ × ¼	0.48	0.16	0.68		2 × 1½	0.88	0.34	2.48	
⅜ × ⅛	0.48	0.16	0.68		2 × 1¼	0.88	0.34	2.48	
½ × ⅜	0.56	0.19	0.87		2 × 1	0.88	0.41	....	1.95
½ × ¼	0.56	0.19	0.87		2 × ¾	0.88	0.41	....	1.63
½ × ⅛	0.56	0.19	0.87		2 × ½	0.88	0.41	....	1.34
¾ × ½	0.63	0.22	1.15		2 × ⅜	0.88	0.41	....	1.12
¾ × ⅜	0.63	0.22	1.15		2 × ¼	0.88	0.41	....	1.12
¾ × ¼	0.63	0.22	1.15		2½ × 2	1.07	0.37	2.98	
¾ × ⅛	0.63	0.22	1.15		2½ × 1½	1.07	0.44	2.68	
1 × ¾	0.75	0.25	1.42		2½ × 1¼	1.07	0.44	....	2.39
1 × ½	0.75	0.25	1.42		2½ × 1	1.07	0.44	....	1.95
1 × ⅜	0.75	0.30	....	1.12	2½ × ¾	1.07	0.44	....	1.63
1 × ¼	0.75	0.30	....	1.12	2½ × ½	1.07	0.44	....	1.34
1 × ⅛	0.75	0.30	....	1.12	3 × 2½	1.13	0.40	3.86	
1¼ × 1	0.80	0.28	1.76		3 × 2	1.13	0.48	3.28	
1¼ × ¾	0.80	0.28	1.76		3 × 1½	1.13	0.48	....	2.68
1¼ × ½	0.80	0.34	....	1.34	3 × 1¼	1.13	0.48	....	2.39
1¼ × ⅜	0.80	0.34	....	1.12	3 × 1	1.13	0.48	....	1.95
1¼ × ¼	0.80	0.34	....	1.12	3 × ¾	1.13	0.48	....	1.63
1½ × 1¼	0.83	0.31	2.00		3 × ½	1.13	0.48	....	1.34
1½ × 1	0.83	0.31	2.00						
1½ × ¾	0.83	0.37	....	1.63					
1½ × ½	0.83	0.37	....	1.34					
1½ × ⅜	0.83	0.37	....	1.12					

  * ASA B16.14—1953.

  † In the case of outside-head bushings, length A includes provisions for imperfect threads.

  ‡ Heads of bushings shall be hexagonal or octagonal, except that on the larger sizes of outside-head bushings the heads may be made round with lugs instead of hexagonal or octagonal.

American Standard Cast-iron Pipe Flanges and Flanged Fittings*

For maximum working saturated steam pressure of 125 lb per sq in. (gage)

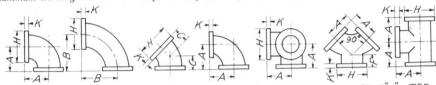

90° ELL LONG RAD ELL 45° ELL REDUCING ELL SIDE OUTLET ELL TRUE "Y" TEE

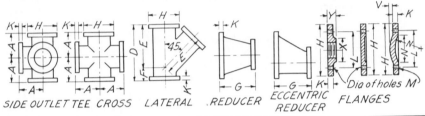

SIDE OUTLET TEE CROSS LATERAL REDUCER ECCENTRIC REDUCER FLANGES

Nominal pipe size N	A	B	C	D	E	F	G	H	K min.
1	$3\frac{1}{2}$	5	$1\frac{3}{4}$	$7\frac{1}{2}$	$5\frac{3}{4}$	$1\frac{3}{4}$	....	$4\frac{1}{4}$	$\frac{7}{16}$
$1\frac{1}{4}$	$3\frac{3}{4}$	$5\frac{1}{2}$	2	8	$6\frac{1}{4}$	$1\frac{3}{4}$	....	$4\frac{5}{8}$	$\frac{1}{2}$
$1\frac{1}{2}$	4	6	$2\frac{1}{4}$	9	7	2	....	5	$\frac{9}{16}$
2	$4\frac{1}{2}$	$6\frac{1}{2}$	$2\frac{1}{2}$	$10\frac{1}{2}$	8	$2\frac{1}{2}$	5	6	$\frac{5}{8}$
$2\frac{1}{2}$	5	7	3	12	$9\frac{1}{2}$	$2\frac{1}{2}$	$5\frac{1}{2}$	7	$\frac{11}{16}$
3	$5\frac{1}{2}$	$7\frac{3}{4}$	3	13	10	3	6	$7\frac{1}{2}$	$\frac{3}{4}$
$3\frac{1}{2}$	6	$8\frac{1}{2}$	$3\frac{1}{2}$	$14\frac{1}{2}$	$11\frac{1}{2}$	3	$6\frac{1}{2}$	$8\frac{1}{2}$	$\frac{13}{16}$
4	$6\frac{1}{2}$	9	4	15	12	3	7	9	$\frac{15}{16}$
5	$7\frac{1}{2}$	$10\frac{1}{4}$	$4\frac{1}{2}$	17	$13\frac{1}{2}$	$3\frac{1}{2}$	8	10	$\frac{15}{16}$
6	8	$11\frac{1}{2}$	5	18	$14\frac{1}{2}$	$3\frac{1}{2}$	9	11	1
8	9	14	$5\frac{1}{2}$	22	$17\frac{1}{2}$	$4\frac{1}{2}$	11	$13\frac{1}{2}$	$1\frac{1}{8}$
10	11	$16\frac{1}{2}$	$6\frac{1}{2}$	$25\frac{1}{2}$	$20\frac{1}{2}$	5	12	16	$1\frac{3}{16}$
12	12	19	$7\frac{1}{2}$	30	$24\frac{1}{2}$	$5\frac{1}{2}$	14	19	$1\frac{1}{4}$

Nominal pipe size N	L	M	No. of bolts	Diam. of bolts	Length of bolts	X min.	Y min.	Wall thickness	V
1	$3\frac{1}{8}$	$\frac{5}{8}$	4	$\frac{1}{2}$	$1\frac{3}{4}$	$1\frac{15}{16}$	$1\frac{1}{16}$	$\frac{5}{16}$	$\frac{3}{8}$
$1\frac{1}{4}$	$3\frac{1}{2}$	$\frac{5}{8}$	4	$\frac{1}{2}$	2	$2\frac{5}{16}$	$1\frac{3}{16}$	$\frac{5}{16}$	$\frac{7}{16}$
$1\frac{1}{2}$	$3\frac{7}{8}$	$\frac{5}{8}$	4	$\frac{1}{2}$	2	$2\frac{9}{16}$	$\frac{7}{8}$	$\frac{5}{16}$	$\frac{1}{2}$
2	$4\frac{3}{4}$	$\frac{3}{4}$	4	$\frac{5}{8}$	$2\frac{1}{4}$	$3\frac{1}{16}$	1	$\frac{5}{16}$	$\frac{9}{16}$
$2\frac{1}{2}$	$5\frac{1}{2}$	$\frac{3}{4}$	4	$\frac{5}{8}$	$2\frac{1}{2}$	$3\frac{9}{16}$	$1\frac{1}{8}$	$\frac{5}{16}$	$\frac{5}{8}$
3	6	$\frac{3}{4}$	4	$\frac{5}{8}$	$2\frac{1}{2}$	$4\frac{1}{4}$	$1\frac{3}{16}$	$\frac{3}{8}$	$\frac{11}{16}$
$3\frac{1}{2}$	7	$\frac{3}{4}$	8	$\frac{5}{8}$	$2\frac{3}{4}$	$4\frac{13}{16}$	$1\frac{1}{4}$	$\frac{7}{16}$	$\frac{3}{4}$
4	$7\frac{1}{2}$	$\frac{3}{4}$	8	$\frac{5}{8}$	3	$5\frac{5}{16}$	$1\frac{5}{16}$	$\frac{1}{2}$	$\frac{7}{8}$
5	$8\frac{1}{2}$	$\frac{7}{8}$	8	$\frac{3}{4}$	3	$6\frac{7}{16}$	$1\frac{7}{16}$	$\frac{1}{2}$	$\frac{7}{8}$
6	$9\frac{1}{2}$	$\frac{7}{8}$	8	$\frac{3}{4}$	$3\frac{1}{4}$	$7\frac{9}{16}$	$1\frac{9}{16}$	$\frac{9}{16}$	$\frac{15}{16}$
8	$11\frac{3}{4}$	$\frac{7}{8}$	8	$\frac{3}{4}$	$3\frac{1}{2}$	$9\frac{11}{16}$	$1\frac{3}{4}$	$\frac{5}{8}$	$1\frac{1}{16}$
10	$14\frac{1}{4}$	1	12	$\frac{7}{8}$	$3\frac{3}{4}$	$11\frac{15}{16}$	$1\frac{15}{16}$	$\frac{3}{4}$	$1\frac{1}{8}$
12	17	1	12	$\frac{7}{8}$	$3\frac{3}{4}$	$14\frac{1}{16}$	$2\frac{3}{16}$	$1\frac{3}{16}$	

* ASA B16.1—1960. Dimensions in inches.

Lengths of Malleable-iron Unions*

Ground joint

Nominal size	$\frac{1}{8}$	$\frac{1}{4}$	$\frac{3}{8}$	$\frac{1}{2}$	$\frac{3}{4}$	1	$1\frac{1}{4}$	$1\frac{1}{2}$	2	$2\frac{1}{2}$	3
End to end	$1\frac{1}{2}$	$1\frac{9}{16}$	$1\frac{5}{8}$	$1\frac{13}{16}$	$2\frac{1}{16}$	$2\frac{1}{4}$	$2\frac{1}{2}$	$2\frac{5}{8}$	3	$3\frac{9}{16}$	$3\frac{15}{16}$

* Compiled from manufacturers' catalogues. Dimensions in inches.

American Standard Steel Butt-welding Fittings*, †

Elbows, tees, caps, and stub ends

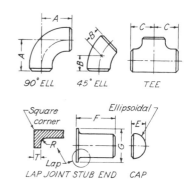

90° ELL   45° ELL   TEE

Square corner — Ellipsoidal

LAP JOINT STUB END   CAP

Nominal pipe size	Outside diam. at bevel	Center to end			Welding caps E	Lapped-joint stub ends		
		90° welding elbow A	45° welding elbow B	Of run, welding tee C		Lengths F	Radius of fillet R	Diameter of lap G
1	1.310	$1\frac{1}{2}$	$\frac{7}{8}$	$1\frac{1}{2}$	$1\frac{1}{2}$	4	$\frac{1}{8}$	2
$1\frac{1}{4}$	1.660	$1\frac{7}{8}$	1	$1\frac{7}{8}$	$1\frac{1}{2}$	4	$\frac{3}{16}$	$2\frac{1}{2}$
$1\frac{1}{2}$	1.900	$2\frac{1}{4}$	$1\frac{1}{8}$	$2\frac{1}{4}$	$1\frac{1}{2}$	4	$\frac{1}{4}$	$2\frac{7}{8}$
2	2.375	3	$1\frac{3}{8}$	$2\frac{1}{2}$	$1\frac{1}{2}$	6	$\frac{5}{16}$	$3\frac{5}{8}$
$2\frac{1}{2}$	2.875	$3\frac{3}{4}$	$1\frac{3}{4}$	3	$1\frac{1}{2}$	6	$\frac{5}{16}$	$4\frac{1}{8}$
3	3.500	$4\frac{1}{2}$	2	$3\frac{3}{8}$	2	6	$\frac{3}{8}$	5
$3\frac{1}{2}$	4.000	$5\frac{1}{4}$	$2\frac{1}{4}$	$3\frac{3}{4}$	$2\frac{1}{2}$	6	$\frac{3}{8}$	$5\frac{1}{2}$
4	4.500	6	$2\frac{1}{2}$	$4\frac{1}{8}$	$2\frac{1}{2}$	6	$\frac{7}{16}$	$6\frac{3}{16}$

Butt-welding reducers

CONCENTRIC REDUCER

ECCENTRIC REDUCER

Nominal pipe size	Outside diam. at bevel		End to end H	Nominal pipe size	Outside diam. at bevel		End to end H
	Large end	Small end			Large end	Small end	
1 × $\frac{3}{4}$	1.315	1.050	2	3 × $2\frac{1}{2}$	3.500	2.875	$3\frac{1}{2}$
1 × $\frac{1}{2}$		0.840		3 × 2		2.375	
1 × $\frac{3}{8}$		0.675		3 × $1\frac{1}{2}$		1.900	
				3 × $1\frac{1}{4}$		1.660	
$1\frac{1}{4}$ × 1	1.660	1.315	2	$3\frac{1}{2}$ × 3	4.000	3.500	4
$1\frac{1}{4}$ × $\frac{3}{4}$		1.050		$3\frac{1}{2}$ × $2\frac{1}{2}$		2.875	
$1\frac{1}{4}$ × $\frac{1}{2}$		0.840		$3\frac{1}{2}$ × 2		2.375	
				$3\frac{1}{2}$ × $1\frac{1}{2}$		1.900	
$1\frac{1}{2}$ × $1\frac{1}{4}$	1.900	1.660	$2\frac{1}{2}$	$3\frac{1}{2}$ × $1\frac{1}{4}$		1.660	
$1\frac{1}{2}$ × 1		1.315		4 × $3\frac{1}{2}$	4.500	4.000	4
$1\frac{1}{2}$ × $\frac{3}{4}$		1.050		4 × 3		3.500	
$1\frac{1}{2}$ × $\frac{1}{2}$		0.840		4 × $2\frac{1}{2}$		2.875	
2 × $1\frac{1}{2}$	2.375	1.900	3	4 × 2		2.375	
2 × $1\frac{1}{4}$		1.660		4 × $1\frac{1}{2}$		1.900	
2 × 1		1.315		5 × 4	5.563	4.500	5
2 × $\frac{3}{4}$		1.050		5 × $3\frac{1}{2}$		4.000	
$2\frac{1}{2}$ × 2	2.875	2.375	$3\frac{1}{2}$	5 × 3		3.500	
$2\frac{1}{2}$ × $1\frac{1}{2}$		1.900		5 × $2\frac{1}{2}$		2.875	
$2\frac{1}{2}$ × $1\frac{1}{4}$		1.660					
$2\frac{1}{2}$ × 1		1.315					

* For larger sizes, see ASA B16.3—1963.
† ASA B16.9— 1964. Dimensions in inches.

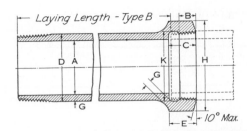

Laying Length - Type B

Threaded Cast-iron Pipe*

Dimension of pipe and drainage hubs

Pipe size	Pipe			Drainage hubs					Nominal weights	
	Nominal diam.		Wall thick- ness, min.,	Thread length*	Diam. of groove, max.,	End to shoulder †	Min. band		Type A and barrel of type B per foot	Addi- tional weight of hubs for type B
	Outside *D*	Inside *A*	*G*	*B*	*K*	*C*	Diam. *H*	Length *E*		
1¼	1.66	1.23	0.187	0.42	1.73	0.71	2.39	0.71	3.033	0.60
1½	1.90	1.45	0.195	0.42	1.97	0.72	2.68	0.72	3.666	0.90
2	2.38	1.89	0.211	0.43	2.44	0.76	3.28	0.76	5.041	1.00
2½	2.88	2.32	0.241	0.68	2.97	1.14	3.86	1.14	7.032	1.35
3	3.50	2.90	0.263	0.76	3.60	1.20	4.62	1.20	9.410	2.80
4	4.50	3.83	0.294	0.84	4.60	1.30	5.79	1.30	13.751	3.48
5	5.56	4.81	0.328	0.93	5.66	1.41	7.05	1.41	19.069	5.00
6	6.63	5.76	0.378	0.95	6.72	1.51	8.28	1.51	26.223	6.60
8	8.63	7.63	0.438	1.06	8.72	1.71	10.63	1.71	39.820	10.00
10	10.75	9.75	0.438	1.21	10.85	1.92	13.12	1.93	50.234	
12	12.75	11.75	0.438	1.36	12.85	2.12	15.47	2.13	60.036	

* ASA A40.5—1943. All dimensions are given in inches, except where otherwise stated. Type *A* has external threads both ends. Type *B* as shown.

† The length of thread *B* and the end to shoulder *C* shall not vary from the dimensions shown by more than plus or minus the equivalent of the pitch of one thread.

American Standard Class-125 Cast-iron and 150-lb Steel Valves: Valves with Class-125 or 150-lb End Flanges, or with Welding Ends—Face-to-face and End-to-end Dimensions[a]

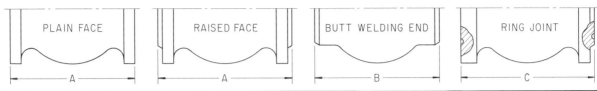

	Class-125 cast iron								150-lb steel							
	Flanged end—plain face								Flanged end (1/16 in. raised face) and welding end							
Nominal valve size	Gate		Plug			Globe and lift check	Swing check[b]	Control	Gate				Plug			
	Solid wedge	Double disc	Short pattern	Regular	Venturi				Solid wedge	Double disc	Solid wedge	Double disc	Short pattern	Regular	Venturi	Round port full bore
	A	A	A	A	A	A	A	A	A	A	B	B	A	A	A	A
¼	...	...	...	...	...	...	...	...	4	4	4	4	...	...	...	...
⅜	...	...	...	...	...	...	...	...	4	4	4	4	...	...	...	...
½	...	...	...	...	...	...	...	...	4¼	4¼	4¼	4¼	...	...	...	...
¾	...	...	...	...	...	...	...	...	4⅝	4⅝	4⅝	4⅝	...	...	...	...
1	...	...	5½	5½	...	...	...	7¼	5	5	5	5	5½	...	...	7
1¼	...	...	...	6½	...	...	...	...	5½	5½	5½	5½	...	...	...	...
1½	...	...	6½	6½	...	...	...	8¾	6½	6½	6½	6½	6½	...	...	8¾
2	7	7	7	7½	...	8	8	10	7	7	8½	8½	7	...	...	10½
2½	7½	7½	7½	8¼	...	8½	8½	10⅞	7½	7½	9½	9½	7½	...	...	11¾
3	8	8	8	9	...	9½	9½	11¾	8	8	11⅛	11⅛	8	...	...	13½
3½	8½	8½	...	...	...	...	...	...	...	...	...	...	...	...	...	...
4	9	9	9	9	...	11½	11½	13⅞	9	9	12	12	9	...	...	17
5	10	10	10	14	...	13	13	...	10	10	15	15	...	...	...	...
6	10½	10½	10½	15½	15½	14	14	17¾	10½	10½	15⅞	15⅞	10½	15½	...	21
8	11½	11½	11½	18	18	19½	19½	21⅜	11½	11½	16½	16½	11½	18	...	25

150-lb steel

	Flanged end (1/16 in. raised face) and welding end				Flanged end (ring joint)							
Nominal valve size	Globe and lift check	Swing check	"Y" pattern globe	Control	Gate		Plug			Round port full bore	Globe and lift check	Swing check
					Solid wedge	Double disc	Short pattern	Regular	Venturi			
	A & B	A & B	A & B	A	C	C	C	C	C	C	C	C
¼	4	4	...	...	...	...	...	...	...	...	...	...
⅜	4	4	...	...	...	...	...	...	...	...	...	...
½	4¼	4¼	5½	...	4 11/16	4 11/16	...	...	...	...	4 11/16	4 11/16
¾	4⅝	4⅝	6	...	5⅛	5⅛	...	...	...	...	5⅛	5⅛
1	5	5	6½	7¼	5½	5½	6	...	...	7½	5½	5½
1¼	5½	5½	7¼	...	6	6	...	...	...	...	6	6
1½	6½	6½	8	8¾	7	7	7	...	...	9¼	7	7
2	8	8	9	10	7½	7½	7½	...	...	11	8½	8½
2½	8½	8½	11	10⅞	8	8	8	...	...	12¼	9	9
3	9½	9½	12½	11¾	8½	8½	8½	...	...	14	...	10
3½	...	...	...	...	...	...	...	...	...	...	...	...
4	11½	11½	14½	13⅞	9½	9½	9½	...	...	17½	12	12
5	14	13	...	...	10½	10½	...	...	...	...	14½	13½
6	16	14	18½	17¾	11	11	11	16	...	21½	16½	14½
8	19½	19½	23½	21⅜	12	12	12	18½	...	25½	20	20

[a] Adapted from ASA B16.10—1957. API Standards 6D and 600 conform to the dimensions shown for corresponding sizes, valve type and flange class or welding end.

[b] These dimensions are not intended to cover the type of check valve having the seat angle at approximately 45 deg to the run of the valve or the "Underwriter Pattern" or other patterns where large clearances are required.

Beam Connections

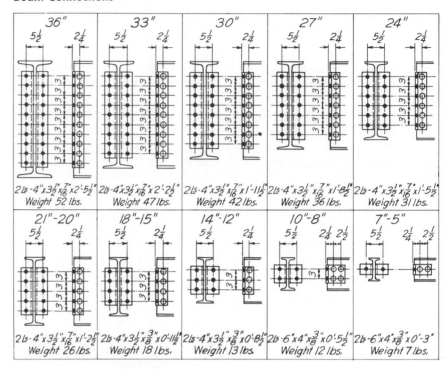

36"	33"	30"	27"	24"
2 ls -4"x3½"x⁷⁄₁₆"x2'-5½"	2 ls -4"x3½"x⁷⁄₁₆"x2'-2½"	2 ls -4"x3½"x⁷⁄₁₆"x1'-11½"	2 ls -4"x3½"x⁷⁄₁₆"x1'-8½"	2 ls -4"x3½"x⁷⁄₁₆"x1'-5½"
Weight 52 lbs.	Weight 47 lbs.	Weight 42 lbs.	Weight 36 lbs.	Weight 31 lbs.

21"-20"	18"-15"	14"-12"	10"-8"	7"-5"
2 ls -4"x3½"x⁷⁄₁₆"x1'-2½"	2 ls -4"x3½"x³⁄₈"x0'-11½"	2 ls -4"x3½"x³⁄₈"x0'-8½"	2 ls -6"x4"x³⁄₈"x0'-5½"	2 ls -6"x4"x³⁄₈"x0'-3"
Weight 26 lbs.	Weight 18 lbs.	Weight 13 lbs.	Weight 12 lbs.	Weight 7 lbs.

Driving Clearances for Riveting

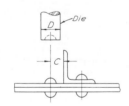

	Diam. of rivet								
	$\frac{1}{2}$	$\frac{5}{8}$	$\frac{3}{4}$	$\frac{7}{8}$	1	$1\frac{1}{8}$	$1\frac{1}{4}$	$1\frac{3}{8}$	$1\frac{1}{2}$
D	$1\frac{3}{4}$	2	$2\frac{1}{4}$	$2\frac{1}{2}$	$2\frac{3}{4}$	3	$3\frac{1}{4}$	$3\frac{1}{2}$	$3\frac{3}{4}$
C	1	$1\frac{1}{8}$	$1\frac{1}{4}$	$1\frac{3}{8}$	$1\frac{1}{2}$	$1\frac{5}{8}$	$1\frac{3}{4}$	$1\frac{7}{8}$	2

Dimensions in inches.

Gage and Maximum Rivet Size for Angles

Leg	8	7	6	5	4	$3\frac{1}{2}$	3	$2\frac{1}{2}$	2	$1\frac{3}{4}$	$1\frac{1}{2}$	$1\frac{3}{8}$	$1\frac{1}{4}$	1
g	$4\frac{1}{2}$	4	$3\frac{1}{2}$	3	$2\frac{1}{2}$	2	$1\frac{3}{4}$	$1\frac{3}{8}$	$1\frac{1}{8}$	1	$\frac{7}{8}$	$\frac{7}{8}$	$\frac{3}{4}$	$\frac{5}{8}$
g_1	3	$2\frac{1}{2}$	$2\frac{1}{4}$	2										
g_2	3	3	$2\frac{1}{2}$	$1\frac{3}{4}$										
Max. rivet	$1\frac{1}{8}$	$1\frac{1}{8}$	1	1	$\frac{7}{8}$	$\frac{7}{8}$	$\frac{7}{8}$	$\frac{3}{4}$	$\frac{5}{8}$	$\frac{1}{2}$	$\frac{3}{8}$	$\frac{3}{8}$	$\frac{3}{8}$	$\frac{1}{4}$

Dimensions in inches.

Selected Structural Shapes*

Dimensions for detailing

Name	Depth of section, in.	Weight per foot, lb	Flange Width, in.	Flange Mean thickness, in.	Web Thickness, in.	Web Half thickness, in.	T, in.	k, in.	g_1, in.	c, in.	Grip, in.	Max. flange rivet, in.	Usual gage g, in.	Clearance m
Channels 18	58.0	4¼	⅝	11/16	⅜	15⅜	1 5/16	2¾	¾	⅝	1	2½	
15	40.0	3½	⅝	9/16	¼	12⅜	1 5/16	2¾	⅝	⅝	1	2	
12	30.0	3⅛	½	½	¼	9⅞	1 1/16	2½	9/16	½	⅞	1¾	
10	15.3	2⅝	7/16	¼	⅛	8⅛	15/16	2½	5/16	7/16	¾	1½	
9	13.4	2⅜	7/16	¼	⅛	7¼	⅞	2½	5/16	⅜	¾	1⅜	
8	18.75	2½	⅜	½	¼	6⅜	13/16	2¼	9/16	⅜	¾	1½	
7	12.25	2¼	⅜	5/16	3/16	5⅜	13/16	2	⅜	⅜	⅝	1¼	
6	10.5	2	⅜	5/16	3/16	4½	¾	2	⅜	⅜	⅝	1⅛	
5	9.0	1⅞	5/16	5/16	3/16	3⅝	11/16	2	⅜	5/16	½	1⅛	
4	7.25	1¾	5/16	5/16	3/16	2¾	⅝	2	⅜	5/16	½	1	
3	6.0	1⅝	¼	⅜	3/16	1¾	⅝	...	7/16	5/16	½	⅞	
WF shapes 21†(21¼)	127	13	1	9/16	5/16	17¾	1 ¾	3	⅜	.....		5½	25
16 (16⅜)	96	11½	⅞	9/16	5/16	13⅛	1 ⅝	2¾	⅜	.....		5½	20
14 (14⅛)	84	12	¾	7/16	¼	11⅜	1 ⅜	2¾	5/16	.....		5½	18⅝
14 (13¾)	48	8	9/16	⅜	3/16	11⅜	1 3/16	2½	¼	.....		5½	16
12 (12¼)	50	8⅛	⅝	⅜	3/16	9¾	1 ¼	2½	¼			5½	14⅝
10 (10)	49	10	9/16	⅜	3/16	7⅞	1 1/16	2½	¼			5½	14⅛
10 (9¾)	33	8	7/16	5/16	3/16	7⅞	15/16	2¼	¼			5½	12⅝
8 (8)	28	6½	7/16	5/16	⅛	6⅜	13/16	2¼	3/16			3½	10½
Beams 24	120.0	8	1 ⅛	13/16	7/16	20⅛	1 15/16	3¼	½	1 ⅛	1	4	
20	85.0	7	15/16	11/16	5/16	16½	1 ¾	3¼	⅜	⅞	1	4	
18	70.0	6¼	11/16	¾	⅜	15¼	1 ⅜	2¾	7/16	11/16	⅞	3½	
15	50.0	5⅝	⅝	9/16	5/16	12½	1 ¼	2¾	⅜	9/16	¾	3½	
12	31.8	5	9/16	⅜	3/16	9¾	1 ⅛	2½	¼	½	¾	3	
10	35.0	5	½	⅝	5/16	8	1	2½	⅜	½	¾	2¾	
8	23.0	4⅛	7/16	7/16	¼	6¼	⅞	2¼	5/16	7/16	¾	2¼	
7	20.0	3⅞	⅜	7/16	¼	5⅜	13/16	2	5/16	⅜	⅝	2¼	
6	17.25	3⅝	⅜	½	¼	4½	¾	2	5/16	⅜	⅝	2	
5	10.0	3	5/16	¼	⅛	3⅝	11/16	2	3/16	5/16	½	1¾	
4	9.5	2¾	5/16	5/16	3/16	2¾	⅝	2	¼	5/16	½	1½	
3	7.5	2½	¼	⅜	3/16	1⅞	9/16	...	¼	¼	⅜	1½	

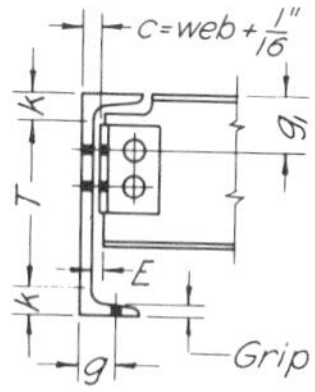

CHANNEL

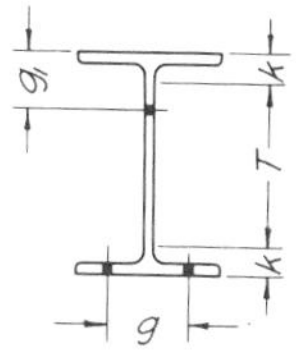

WF SHAPE

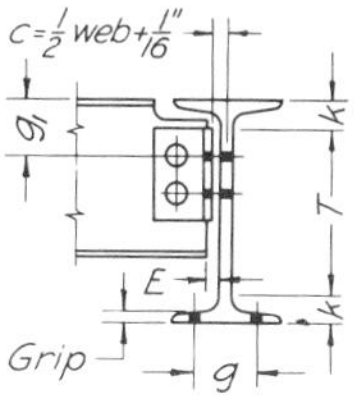

BEAM

* From Steel Construction Handbook.

† Nominal depth; ( ) indicates actual depth.

Standard Jig Bushings*

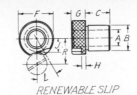

RENEWABLE SLIP

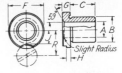

RENEWABLE FIXED

LINER
(used with Renewable
Type bushings)

					Renewable Slip Type and Renewable Fixed Type								Liners		
Slip type Hole size A	Fixed type Hole size A	Tolerance on hole	Body diameter limits B	Lengths available C	Head dimensions F	G Slip type	G Fixed type	H	J	L	R	Lock screw no.	Hole limits A	OD limits B	Lengths
0.052 to 0.089	0.055 to 0.089	+0.0004 +0.0001	0.3125 / 0.3123	5/16, 1/2, 3/4, 1	35/64	3/8	1/4	1/8	1 1/64	65°	1/2		0.3126 / 0.3129	0.5017 / 0.5014	
0.0935 to 0.1562	0.0935 to 0.1562			5/16, 1/2, 3/4, 1											
0.1406 to 0.3437	0.1570 to 0.3125	Incl 1/4 +0.0004 +0.0001 Over 1/4 +0.0005 +0.0001	0.5000 / 0.4998	5/16, 1/2, 3/4, 1, 1 3/8, 1 3/4	5 1/64	7/16	1/4	1/8	1 9/64	65°	5/8	1	0.5002 / 0.5005	0.7518 / 0.7515	
0.2812 to 0.5312	0.3160 to 0.5000	+0.0005 +0.0001	0.7500 / 0.7498	1/2, 3/8, 1, 1 3/8, 1 3/4, 2 1/8	1 3/64	7/16	1/4	1/8	2 7/64	50°	3/4		0.7503 / 0.7506	1.0015 / 1.0018	
0.4687 to 0.7812	0.5156 to 0.750		1.0000 / 0.9998	3/4, 1, 1 3/8, 1 3/4, 2 1/8, 2 1/2	1 27/64	7/16	3/8	3/16	1 9/32	35°	59/64	2	1.0004 / 1.0007	1.3772 / 1.3768	
0.7817 to 1.0312	0.7656 to 1.0000	+0.0006 +0.0002	1.3750 / 1.3747	3/4, 1, 1 3/8, 1 3/4, 2 1/8, 2 1/2	1 51/64	7/16	3/8	3/16	2 5/32	30°	1 7/64		1.3756 / 1.3760	1.7523 / 1.7519	
0.9687 to 1.4062	1.0156 to 1.3750		1.7500 / 1.7497	1, 1 3/8, 1 3/4, 2 1/8, 2 1/2, 3	2 19/64	5/8	3/8	3/16	1	30°	1 25/64	3	1.7508 / 1.7512	2.2521 / 2.2525	
1.3437 to 1.7812	1.3906 to 1.750	Incl 1 1/2 +0.0006 +0.0002 Over 1 1/2 +0.0007 +0.0003	2.2500 / 2.2496	1, 1 3/8, 1 3/4, 2 1/8, 2 1/2, 3	2 51/64	5/8	3/8	3/16	1 1/4	25°	1 41/64		2.2510 / 2.2515	2.7526 / 2.7522	

Liners Lengths column (spanning all rows): Same as the bushing

Dimensions in inches.
*ASA B5.6— 1962.
Head design in accordance with manufacturer's practice; slip type usually knurled.

Lock Screws

Screw No.	A	B	C	D	E	F	ASA thd
1	5/8	3/8	5/8	1/16	1/4	.138 .132	5/16–18
2	7/8	3/8	5/8	3/32	3/8	.200 .194	5/16–18
3	1	7/16	3/4	1/8	3/8	.200 .194	3/8–16

Standard Jig Bushings (*Cont.*)

Press-fit Headless and Press-fit Head Types

Hole size *A*	Tolerance on hole	OD limits *B*	Lengths available *C*	Head type dimension *F*	Head type dimension *G*
0.055 to 0.0995	+0.0004 +0.0001	0.2046 / 0.2043	5/16, 1/2	19/64	3/32
0.1015 to 0.1360		0.2516 / 0.2513	5/16, 1/2	23/64	3/32
0.1405 to 0.1875		0.3141 / 0.3138	5/16, 1/2 3/4, 1	27/64	1/8
0.1890 to 0.2500		0.4078 / 0.4075	5/16, 1/2 3/4, 1 1 3/8, 1 3/4	1/2	5/32
0.2570 to 0.3125	+0.0005 +0.0001	0.5017 / 0.5014		39/64	7/32
0.316 to 0.4219		0.6267 / 0.6264	1/2, 3/4 1, 1 3/8 1 3/4, 2 1/8	51/64	7/32
0.4375 to 0.500		0.7518 / 0.7515		59/64	7/32
0.5156 to 0.625		0.8768 / 0.8765	3/4, 1	1 7/64	1/4
0.6406 to 0.7500		1.0018 / 1.0015	1 3/8, 1 3/4	1 15/64	5/16
0.7656 to 1.0000	+0.0006 +0.0002	1.3772 / 1.3768	2 1/8, 2 1/2	1 39/64	3/8
1.0156 to 1.3750		1.7523 / 1.7519	1, 1 3/8 1 3/4, 2 1/8 2 1/2, 3	1 63/64	3/8
1.3906 to 1.7500	Incl 1 1/2 +0.0006 +0.0002 Over 1 1/2 +0.0007 +0.0003	2.2525 / 2.2521		2 31/64	3/8

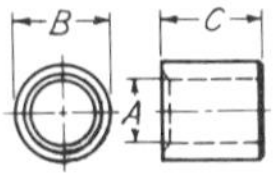

B
C
A

PRESS FIT
HEADLESS TYPE

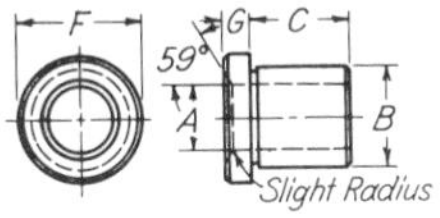

F
G
C
59°
A
B
Slight Radius

PRESS FIT
HEAD TYPE

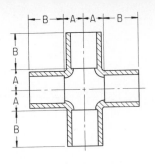

CROSS

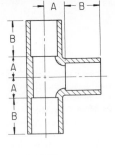

TEE

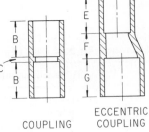

COUPLING ECCENTRIC COUPLING

90° ELL 45° ELL

American Standard Brass Solder-joint Fittings*

Tubing size	A	B	C	D	Reducing size	F	E	G
3/8	5/16	11/16	3/16	1/8	3/4 × 1/2	5/8	1	13/16
1/2	7/16	13/16	3/16	1/8	1 × 3/4	11/16	11/16	1
3/4	9/16	1	1/4	1/8	1 × 1/2	1/2	11/16	13/16
1	3/4	11/16	5/16	1/8	2 × 1 1/2	1 1/8	1 3/8	1 3/16
1 1/2	1	1 3/16	1/2	1/8	2 1/2 × 2	1 3/16	1 5/8	1 3/8
2	1 1/4	1 3/8	9/16	3/16	2 1/2 × 1 1/2	15/16	1 5/8	1 3/16
2 1/2	1 1/2	1 5/8	5/8	3/16	3 × 2 1/2	1 1/4	1 7/8	1 5/8
3	1 3/4	1 7/8	3/4	3/16	3 1/2 × 3	1 1/8	2 1/16	1 7/8
3 1/2	2	2 1/16	7/8	3/16	3 1/2 × 2 1/2	1 5/16	2 1/16	1 5/8
4	2 1/4	2 1/4	15/16	1/4	4 × 3 1/2	1 3/16	2 1/4	2 1/16

* Adapted from ASA B16.18— 1963.

SAE STANDARD COTTER PINS

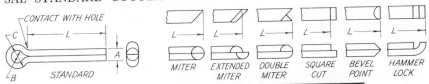

MITER EXTENDED MITER DOUBLE MITER SQUARE CUT BEVEL POINT HAMMER LOCK

CONTACT WITH HOLE STANDARD

Pin diameter A			Eye diameter, min.		Recommended hole diam., drill size
Nominal	Max.	Min.	Inside B	Outside C	
1/32 (0.031)	0.032	0.028	1/32	1/16	3/64 (0.0469)
3/64 (0.047)	0.048	0.044	3/64	3/32	1/16 (0.0625)
1/16 (0.062)	0.060	0.056	1/16	1/8	5/64 (0.0781)
5/64 (0.078)	0.076	0.072	5/64	5/32	3/32 (0.0937)
3/32 (0.094)	0.090	0.086	3/32	3/16	7/64 (0.1094)
1/8 (0.125)	0.120	0.116	1/8	1/4	9/64 (0.1406)
5/32 (0.156)	0.150	0.146	5/32	5/16	11/64 (0.1719)
3/16 (0.188)	0.176	0.172	3/16	3/8	13/64 (0.2031)
7/32 (0.219)	0.207	0.202	7/32	7/16	15/64 (0.2344)
1/4 (0.250)	0.225	0.220	1/4	1/2	17/64 (0.2656)
5/16 (0.312)	0.280	0.275	5/16	5/8	5/16 (0.3125)
3/8 (0.375)	0.335	0.329	3/8	3/4	3/8 (0.3750)
1/2 (0.500)	0.473	0.467	1/2	1	1/2 (0.5000)

American Standard Graphic Symbols for Piping and Heating*

PIPING					
Piping, General		(Lettered with name of material conveyed)			
Non-intersecting Pipes					
(To differentiate lines of piping on a drawing the following symbols may be used.)					

Air	Cold Water	Steam
Gas	Hot Water	Condensate
Oil	Vacuum	Refrigerant

PIPE FITTINGS AND VALVES					
	Flanged	Screwed	Bell and Spigot	Welded	Soldered
Joint					
Elbow—90 deg					
Elbow—45 deg					
Elbow—Turned Up					
Elbow—Turned Down					
Elbow—Long Radius					
Side Outlet Elbow Outlet Down					
Side Outlet Elbow Outlet Up					
Base Elbow					
Double Branch Elbow					
Reducing Elbow					
Reducer					
Eccentric Reducer					
Tee-Outlet Up					
Tee-Outlet Down					
Tee					
Side Outlet Tee Outlet Up					
Side Outlet Tee Outlet Down					
Single Sweep Tee					
Double Sweep Tee					
Cross					
Lateral					
Gate Valve					

* ASA Y32.2.3—1953.

Symbols for Piping and Heating (*Cont.*)

PIPING

	Flanged	Screwed	Bell and Spigot	Welded	Soldered
Globe Valve					
Angle Globe Valve					
Angle Gate Valve					
Check Valve					
Angle Check Valve					
Stop Cock					
Safety Valve					
Quick Opening Valve					
Float Operating Valve					
Motor Operated Gate Valve					
Motor Operated Globe Valve					
Expansion Joint Flanged					
Reducing Flange					
Union	(See Joint)				
Sleeve					
Bushing					

HEATING AND VENTILATING

Lock and Shield Valve		Tube Radiator	(Plan) (Elev.)	Exhaust Duct, Section
Reducing Valve		Wall Radiator	(Plan) (Elev.)	Butterfly Damper (Plan or Elev.) (Elev. or Plan)
Diaphragm Valve		Pipe Coil	(Plan) (Elev.)	Deflecting Damper Rectangular Pipe
Thermostat	(T)	Indirect Radiator	(Plan) (Elev.)	Vanes
Radiator Trap	(Plan) (Elev.)	Supply Duct, Section		Air Supply Outlet
				Exhaust Inlet

HEAT-POWER APPARATUS

Flue Gas Reheater (Intermediate Superheater)		Steam Turbine	Automatic By-pass Valve
Steam Generator (Boiler)		Condensing Turbine	Automatic Valve Operated by Governor
Live Steam Superheater		Open Tank	Pumps Air Service Boiler Feed Condensate Circulating Water Reciprocating
Feed Heater With Air Outlet		Closed Tank	
Surface Condenser		Automatic Reducing Valve	Dynamic Pump (Air Ejector)

American Standard Plumbing Symbols*

Corner Bath	Recessed Bath	Roll Rim Bath	S B — Sitz Bath
F B — Foot Bath	B — Bidet	Shower Stall	Shower Head (Plan) (Elev.)
Overhead Gang Shower (Plan) (Elev.)	M L — Manicure Lavatory / Medical Lavatory	LAV — Corner Lavatory	W L — Wall Lavatory
DENTAL LAV — Dental Lavatory	S — Plain Kitchen Sink	Kitchen Sink R&L Drain Board	P L — Pedestal Lavatory
Kitchen Sink L.H. Drain Board	Combination Sink and Dishwasher	S & T — Combination Sink and Laundry Tray	S S — Service Sink
L T — Laundry Tray	Wash Sink (Wall Type)	Water Closet (No Tank)	Wash Sink
Water Closet (Low Tank)	Urinal (Pedestal Type)	Urinal (Corner Type)	Urinal (Wall Type)
DF — Drinking Fountain (Pedestal Type)	DF — Drinking Fountain (Wall Type)	Urinal (Stall Type)	T U — Urinal (Trough Type)

DF — Drinking Fountain (Trough Type)	HW T — Hot Water Tank	WH — Water Heater	M — Meter	HR — Hose Rack
Vacuum Outlet	HB — Hose Bib	G — Gas Outlet	D — Drain	G — Grease Separator
O — Oil Separator	C O — Cleanout	Garage Drain	Floor Drain With Backwater Valve	Roof Sump

* ASA Y32.4—1955.

Wiring Symbols for Architecture

Ceiling Outlet	Branch Circuit, Run Exposed ─────
" " for Extensions	Run Concealed Under Floor ─ ─ ─
" Lamp Receptacle, Specifications	" " " Floor Above ────
to describe type, as Key, Keyless or Pull Chain	Feeder Run Exposed ─────
Ceiling Fan Outlet	Run Concealed Under Floor ─ ─ ─
Pull Switch	" " " Floor Above ────
Drop Cord	Telephone, Interior ◁, Public
Wall Bracket	Clock, Secondary ◔, Master
" Outlet for Extensions	Time Stamp
" Lamp Receptacle, as specified	Electric Door Opener
" Fan Outlet	Local Fire Alarm Gong
Single Convenience Outlet	City Fire Alarm Station
Double " " "	Local " " "
Junction Box	Fire Alarm Central Station
Special Purpose Outlets	Speaking Tube
Lighting, Heating and Power	Nurse's Signal Plug
as described in specifications	Maid's Plug
Exit Light	Horn Outlet
Floor Outlet	District Messenger Call
Floor Elbow O^E, Floor Tee O^T	Watchman Station
Local Switch, Single Pole S^1	Watchman Central Station Detector
Double Pole S^2, 3-Way S^3, 4-Way S^4	Public Telephone-P.B.X. Switchboard
Automatic Door Switch S^D	Interior Telephone Central Switchboard
Key Push Button Switch S^K	Interconnection Cabinet
Electrolier Switch S^E	Telephone Cabinet
Push Button Switch and Pilot S^P	Telegraph "
Remote Control Push Button Switch S^R	Special Outlet for Signal System as Specified
Tank Switch T.S.	Battery ||||||||
Motor ⊖, Motor Controller M.C	Signal Wires in Conduit Under Floor ───
Lighting Panel	" " " " " Floor Above ───
Power Panel	This Character Marked on Tap Circuits Indicates
Heating Panel	2 No. 14 Conductors in $\frac{1}{2}$" Conduit ‖
Pull Box	3 " 14 " " $\frac{1}{2}$" " ‖‖
Cable Supporting Box	4 " 14 " " $\frac{3}{4}$" $\left(\text{Unless}\atop\text{Marked }\frac{1}{2}\text{"}\right)$ ‖‖
Meter	5 " 14 " " $\frac{3}{4}$" ‖‖‖
Transformer	6 " 14 " " 1" " $\left(\text{Unless}\atop\text{Marked }\frac{3}{4}\text{"}\right)$ ‖‖‖
Push Button	7 " 14 " " 1" " ‖‖‖
Pole Line	8 " 14 " " 1" " ‖‖‖‖
Buzzer ☐, Bell	(Radio Outlet)
Annunciator	(Public Speaker Outlet)

American Standard Graphic Symbols for Electrical Diagrams*

Single-line symbols are shown at the left, complete symbols at the right, and symbols for both purposes are centered in each column.

Listing is alphabetical.

ADJUSTABLE
CONTINUOUSLY ADJUSTABLE (Variable)
The shaft of the arrow is drawn at about 45 degrees across the body of the symbol.

AMPLIFIER
See also MACHINE, ROTATING

General
The triangle is pointed in the direction of transmission.
Amplifier type may be indicated in the triangle by words, standard abbreviations, or a letter combination from the following list.

BDG	Bridging	MON	Monitoring
BST	Booster	PGM	Program
CMP	Compression	PRE	Preliminary
DC	Direct Current	PWR	Power
EXP	Expansion	TRQ	Torque
LIM	Limiting		

Applications

Booster amplifier with two inputs

Monitoring amplifier with two outputs

Amplifier with associated power supply

ANTENNA

General
Types or functions may be indicated by words or abbreviations adjacent to the symbol.

Dipole

ARRESTER (Electric Surge, Lightning, etc.)
GAP

General

Carbon block
The sides of the rectangle are to be approximately in the ratio of 1 to 2 and the space between rectangles shall be approximately equal to the width of a rectangle.

Electrolytic or aluminum cell
This symbol is not composed of arrowheads.

Protective gap
These arrowheads shall not be filled.

Sphere gap

Multigap, general

ATTENUATOR
See also PAD

General

Balanced, general

Unbalanced, general

BATTERY
The long line is always positive, but polarity may be indicated in addition.
Example:

Generalized direct-current source

BREAKER, CIRCUIT
If it is desired to show the condition causing the breaker to trip, the relay-protective-function symbols   may be used alongside the breaker symbol.

General
Note 1—Use appropriate number of single-line diagram symbols.

SEE NOTE 1

Air or, if distinction is needed, for alternating-current circuit breaker rated at 1,500 volts or less and for direct-current circuit breaker.

SEE NOTE 1

CAPACITOR
See also TERMINATION

General
If it is necessary to identify the capacitor electrodes, the curved element shall represent the outside electrode in fixed paper-dielectric and ceramic-dielectric capacitors, the negative electrode in electrolytic capacitors, the moving element in adjustable and variable capacitors, and the low-potential element in feed-through capacitors.

Application: shielded capacitor

Application: adjustable or variable capacitor

If it is necessary to identify trimmer capacitors, the letter T should appear adjacent to the symbol.

Application: adjustable or variable capacitors with mechanical linkage of units

Shunt capacitor

Feed-through capacitor (with terminals shown on feed-through element)
Commonly used for bypassing high-frequency currents to chassis.

Application: feed-through capacitor between 2 inductors with third lead connected to chassis

CELL, PHOTOSENSITIVE (Semiconductor)

λ indicates that the primary characteristic of the element within the circle is designed to vary under the influence of light.

Asymmetrical photoconductive transducer (resistive)
This arrowhead shall be solid.

Symmetrical photoconductive transducer; selenium cell

CHASSIS
FRAME
See also GROUND
The chassis or frame is not necessarily at ground potential.

COIL, BLOWOUT

COIL, OPERATING
See also INDUCTOR; WINDING

Note 3—The asterisk is not a part of the symbol. Always replace the asterisk by a device designation.

* SEE NOTE 3

CONNECTION, MECHANICAL –
MECHANICAL INTERLOCK
The preferred location of the mechanical connection is as shown in the various applications, but other locations may be equally acceptable.

Mechanical connection (*short dashes*)

- - - - -

---

* Adapted from ASA Y32.2—1962.

Symbols for Electrical Diagrams (*Cont.*)

Mechanical connection or interlock with fulcrum (*short dashes*)

Mechanical interlock, other

INDICATE BY A NOTE

CONNECTOR
DISCONNECTING DEVICE
The connector symbol is not an arrowhead. It is larger and the lines are drawn at a 90-degree angle.

Female contact

Male contact

Connector assembly, movable or stationary portion; jack, plug, or receptacle

Note 4—Use appropriate number of contact symbols.

OR   SEE NOTE 4

Commonly used for a jack or receptacle (usually stationary)

SEE NOTE 4 OR

Commonly used for a plug (usually movable)

SEE NOTE 4 OR

Separable connectors (engaged)

SEE NOTE 4 OR

Application: engaged 4-conductor connectors; the plug has 1 male and 3 female contacts

OR

Communication switchboard-type connector

2-conductor (jack)

2-conductor (plug)

Jacks with circuit normalled through one way

Jacks with circuit normalled through both ways

Jacks in multiple, one set with circuit normalled through both ways

Connectors of the type commonly used for power-supply purposes (convenience outlets and mating connectors)

Female contact

Male contact

2-conductor nonpolarized connector with female contacts

2-conductor nonpolarized connector with male contacts

2-conductor polarized connector with female contacts

2-conductor polarized connector with male contacts

3-conductor polarized connector with female contacts

3-conductor polarized connector with male contacts

4-conductor polarized connector with female contacts

4-conductor polarized connector with male contacts

Test blocks

Female portion with short-circuiting bar (with terminals shown)

Male portion (with terminals shown)

CONTACT, ELECTRIC
For build-ups or forms using electric contacts, see applications under CONNECTOR

Fixed contact

Fixed contact for jack, key, relay, etc.

→ OR ⌐• OR ⇁

Fixed contact for switch

○ OR →

Fixed contact for momentary switch
See SWITCH

Sleeve

‖ OR ‖ OR ⌐

Moving contact

Adjustable or sliding contact for resistor, inductor, etc.

→ OR ⌐

Locking

Nonlocking

Closed contact (break)

⊬ OR

Open contact (make)

OR

Transfer

OR

Make-before-break

Application: open contact with time closing (TC or TDC) feature

TC OR TDC

Application: closed contact with time opening (TO or TDO) feature

TO OR TDO

Time sequential closing

OR

COUPLER, DIRECTIONAL
Commonly used in coaxial and waveguide diagrams.

The arrows indicate the direction of power flow.

Number of coupling paths, type of coupling, and transmission loss may be indicated.

General

Symbols for Electrical Diagrams (Cont.)

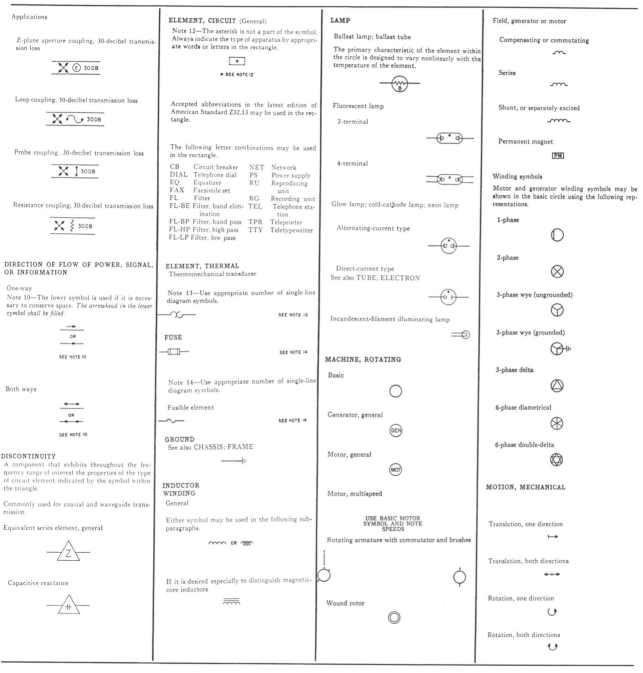

Applications

E-plane aperture coupling, 30-decibel transmission loss

Loop coupling, 30-decibel transmission loss

Probe coupling, 30-decibel transmission loss

Resistance coupling, 30-decibel transmission loss

DIRECTION OF FLOW OF POWER, SIGNAL, OR INFORMATION

One-way

Note 10—The lower symbol is used if it is necessary to conserve space. *The arrowhead in the lower symbol shall be filled.*

OR

SEE NOTE 10

Both ways

OR

SEE NOTE 10

DISCONTINUITY

A component that exhibits throughout the frequency range of interest the properties of the type of circuit element indicated by the symbol within the triangle.

Commonly used for coaxial and waveguide transmission.

Equivalent series element, general

Capacitive reactance

ELEMENT, CIRCUIT (General)

Note 12—The asterisk is not a part of the symbol. Always indicate the type of apparatus by appropriate words or letters in the rectangle.

* SEE NOTE 12

Accepted abbreviations in the latest edition of American Standard Z32.13 may be used in the rectangle.

The following letter combinations may be used in the rectangle.

CB   Circuit breaker   NET   Network
DIAL   Telephone dial   PS   Power supply
EQ   Equalizer   RU   Reproducing
FAX   Facsimile set   unit
FL   Filter   RG   Recording unit
FL-BE Filter, band elim- TEL   Telephone sta-
             ination   tion
FL-BP Filter, band pass TPR   Teleprinter
FL-HP Filter, high pass   TTY   Teletypewriter
FL-LP Filter, low pass

ELEMENT, THERMAL
Thermomechanical transducer

Note 13—Use appropriate number of single-line diagram symbols.

SEE NOTE 13

FUSE

SEE NOTE 14

Note 14—Use appropriate number of single-line diagram symbols.

Fusible element

SEE NOTE 14

GROUND
See also CHASSIS; FRAME

INDUCTOR WINDING
General

Either symbol may be used in the following subparagraphs.

OR

If it is desired especially to distinguish magnetic-core inductors

LAMP

Ballast lamp; ballast tube

The primary characteristic of the element within the circle is designed to vary nonlinearly with the temperature of the element.

Fluorescent lamp

2-terminal

4-terminal

Glow lamp; cold-cathode lamp; neon lamp

Alternating-current type

Direct-current type
See also TUBE, ELECTRON

Incandescent-filament illuminating lamp

MACHINE, ROTATING

Basic

Generator, general

Motor, general

Motor, multispeed

USE BASIC MOTOR SYMBOL AND NOTE SPEEDS

Rotating armature with commutator and brushes

Wound rotor

Field, generator or motor

Compensating or commutating

Series

Shunt, or separately excited

Permanent magnet

Winding symbols

Motor and generator winding symbols may be shown in the basic circle using the following representations.

1-phase

2-phase

3-phase wye (ungrounded)

3-phase wye (grounded)

3-phase delta

6-phase diametrical

6-phase double-delta

MOTION, MECHANICAL

Translation, one direction

Translation, both directions

Rotation, one direction

Rotation, both directions

Symbols for Electrical Diagrams (*Cont.*)

NETWORK

General

OSCILLATOR
GENERALIZED ALTERNATING-CURRENT SOURCE

PAD

See also ATTENUATOR

General

Balanced, general

Unbalanced, general

PATH, TRANSMISSION

Air or space path

Dielectric path other than air

Commonly used for coaxial and waveguide transmission.

DIEL

Crossing of paths or conductors not connected
The crossing is not necessarily at a 90-degree angle.

Junction of paths or conductors

Junction (if desired)

Application: junction of different-size cables

Junction of connected paths, conductors, or wires

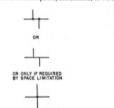

OR

OR ONLY IF REQUIRED
BY SPACE LIMITATION

RELAY

See also CONTACT

Fundamental symbols for contacts, mechanical connections, coils, etc., are the basis of relay symbols and should be used to represent relays on complete diagrams.

Basic

Relay coil

Note 21—The asterisk is not a part of the symbol. Always replace the asterisk by a device designation.

⊛ OR ⋛ OR ✛

* SEE NOTE 21

Application: 2-pole double-make

RESISTOR

Note 22—The asterisk is not a part of the symbol. Always add identification within or adjacent to the rectangle.

General

—∿— OR —□—

* SEE NOTE 22

Tapped resistor

* SEE NOTE 22

Application: with adjustable contact

* SEE NOTE 22

Application: adjustable or continuously adjustable (variable) resistor

* SEE NOTE 22

Heating resistor

—∿— OR —□—

* SEE NOTE 22

SWITCH

Fundamental symbols for contacts, mechanical connections, etc., may be used for switch symbols.

The standard method of showing switches is in a position with no operating force applied. For switches that may be in any one of two or more positions with no operating force applied and for switches actuated by some mechanical device (as in air-pressure, liquid-level, rate-of-flow, etc., switches), a clarifying note may be necessary to explain the point at which the switch functions.

Single throw, general

Double throw, general

Application: 2-pole double-throw switch with terminals shown

Knife switch, general

Switch, nonlocking; momentary or spring return

The symbols to the left are commonly used for spring buildups in key switches, relays, and jacks.

The symbols to the right are commonly used for toggle switches.

Circuit closing (make)

Circuit opening (break)

Switch, locking

The symbols to the left are commonly used for spring buildups in key switches, relays, and jacks.

The symbols to the right are commonly used for toggle switches.

Circuit closing (make)

Circuit opening (break)

Transfer, 2-position

TERMINAL, CIRCUIT

Terminal board or terminal strip with 4 terminals shown; group of 4 terminals

Number and arrangement as convenient.

TRANSFORMER

General

Either winding symbol may be used.

Additional windings may be shown or indicated by a note.

For power transformers, use polarity marking H_1, X_1, etc., from American Standard C6.1.

In coaxial and waveguide circuits, this symbol will represent a taper or step transformer without mode change.

 OR

If it is desired especially to distinguish a magnetic-core transformer

TUBE, ELECTRON

Tube-component symbols are shown first. These are followed by typical applications showing the use of these specific symbols in the various classes of devices such as thermionic, cold-cathode, and photoemissive tubes of varying structures and combinations of elements (triodes, pentodes, cathode-ray tubes, magnetrons, etc.).

Lines outside of the envelope are not part of the symbol but are electrical connections thereto.

Connections between the external circuit and electron tube symbols within the envelope may be located as required to simplify the diagram.

Emitting electrode

Directly heated (filamentary) cathode
Note—Leads may be connected in any convenient manner to ends of the ∧ provided the identity of the ∧ is retained.

∧

Indirectly heated cathode
Lead may be connected to either extreme end of the ⌐ or, if required, to both ends, in any convenient manner.

Cold cathode (including ionically heated cathode)

—○

Photocathode

—⟨

Pool cathode

Ionically heated cathode with provision for supplementary heating

8

Symbols for Electrical Diagrams (*Cont.*)

Controlling electrode

Grid (including beam-confining or beam-forming electrodes)

Deflecting electrodes (used in pairs); reflecting or repelling electrode (used in velocity-modulated tube)

Ignitor (in pool tubes) (should extend into pool) Starter (in gas tubes)

Excitor (contactor type)

Collecting electrode

Anode or plate (including collecting electrode and fluorescent target)

Target or X-ray anode
Drawn at about a 45-degree angle.

Collecting and emitting electrode

Dynode

Alternately collecting and emitting

Composite anode-photocathode

Composite anode-cold cathode

Composite anode-ionically heated cathode with provision for supplementary heating

Heater

Envelope (shell)

The general envelope symbol identifies the envelope or enclosure regardless of evacuation or pressure. When used with electron-tube component symbols, the general envelope symbol indicates a vacuum enclosure unless otherwise specified. A gas-filled electron device may be indicated by a dot within the envelope symbol.

General

Split envelope
If necessary, envelope may be split.

Gas-filled
The dot may be located as convenient.

Shield

This is understood to shield against electric fields unless otherwise noted.

Any shield against electric fields that is within the envelope and that is connected to an independent terminal

Outside envelope of X-ray tube

Coupling by loop (electromagnetic type)
Coupling loop may be shown inside or outside envelope as desired, but if inside it should be shown grounded.

Resonators (cavity type)

Single-cavity envelope and grid-type associated electrodes

Double-cavity envelope and grid-type associated electrodes

Multicavity magnetron anode and envelope

Associated parts of a circuit, such as focusing coils, deflecting coils, field coils, etc., are not a part of the tube symbol but may be added to the circuit in the form of standard symbols. For example, resonant-type magnetron with permanent magnet may be shown:

External and internal shields, whether integral parts of tubes or not, shall be omitted from the circuit diagram unless the circuit diagram requires their inclusion.

In line with standard drafting practice, straight-line crossovers are recommended.

Typical applications

Triode with directly heated filamentary cathode and envelope connection to base terminal

Equipotential-cathode pentode showing use of elongated envelope

---

Typical wiring figure
This figure illustrates how tube symbols may be placed in any convenient position in a circuit.

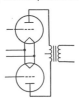

For tubes with keyed bases
Explanatory word and arrow are not a part of the symbol shown.

For tubes with bayonets, bosses, and other reference points

Base terminals
Explanatory words and arrows are not a part of the symbol.

Envelope terminals
Explanatory words and arrows are not a part of the symbol.

Applications

Triode with indirectly heated cathode and envelope connected to base terminal

Triode-heptode with rigid envelope connection

Transistor Symbols (MIL-STD-15-1A, 22 May 1963)

PNP transistor   NPN transistor

Symbols for Materials (Exterior)

Brick

Stone

Transparent Material
Glass. Celluloid. Etc.

Wood

Symbols for Materials (Section)

Cast Iron

Steel

Bronze, Brass, Copper
and Composition

White Metal, Zinc,
Lead, Babbitt & Alloys

Aluminum

(Show solid for narrow sections)
Electric Insulation, Mica,
Fibre, Vulcanite, Bakelite, Etc.

Sound or Heat Insulation
Cork, Asbestos, Packing, Etc.

Flexible Material
Fabric, Rubber, Etc.

Fire Brick and
Refractory Material

Concrete

Brick or Stone
Masonry

Marble, Slate, Glass,
Porcelain, Etc.

Earth

Rock

Sand

Water & Other Liquids

Weights of Materials

Metals	lb/cu in.	Wood	lb/cu in.
Aluminum alloy, cast	0.099	Ash	0.024
Aluminum, cast	0.094	Balsa	0.0058
Aluminum, wrought	0.097	Cedar	0.017
Babbitt metal	0.267	Cork	0.009
Brass, cast or rolled	0.303–0.313	Hickory	0.0295
Brass, drawn	0.323	Maple	0.025
Bronze, aluminum cast	0.277	Oak (white)	0.028
Bronze, phosphor	0.315–0.321	Pine (white)	0.015
Chromium	0.256	Pine (yellow)	0.025
Copper, cast	0.311	Poplar	0.018
Copper, rolled, drawn or wire	0.322	Walnut (black)	0.023
Dowmetal *A*	0.065	**Miscellaneous materials**	**lb/ cu ft**
Duralumin	0.101	Asbestos	175
Gold	0.697	Bakelite	79.5
Iron, cast	0.260	Brick, common	112
Iron, wrought	0.283	Brick, fire	144
Lead	0.411	Celluloid	86.4
Magnesium	0.063	Earth, packed	100
Mercury	0.491	Fiber	89.9
Monel metal	0.323	Glass	163
Silver	0.379	Gravel	109
Steel, cast or rolled	0.274–0.281	Limestone	163
Steel, tool	0.272	Plexiglass	74.3
Tin	0.263	Sandstone	144
Zinc	0.258	Water	62.4

ABBREVIATIONS FOR USE ON DRAWINGS

Abbreviations are shortened forms of words or expressions and their use on drawings is entirely for the purpose of conserving space and drafting time. Since they must be interpreted by shopmen, assemblers, construction men, and others, abbreviations should not be used where the meaning may not be clear. In case of doubt, spell out. Only words that are abbreviated on drawings are included in this list, which is selected from the more complete list given in the SAE Aerospace-Automotive Drawing Standards (Section Z.1)

The same abbreviation is used for all forms of a given word. Periods are used only to avoid misinterpretation of an abbreviation. Spaces between letters are for clarity only; the abbreviation of word combinations or phrases is sometimes spaced. The use of hyphens and slant bars has been avoided where practicable. Upper-case letters are used for abbreviations. Subscripts are not used in abbreviations. Whenever a special abbreviation is used (one not appearing in the SAE Aerospace-Automotive standard), it should be explained in a table on the drawing. For metals, chemicals, formulas, and equations, the abbreviations, symbols, and rules in general use and established by long acceptance are employed.

Abbreviations for colors and a partial list of chemical symbols are given after the general abbreviations.

Word	Abbreviation	Word	Abbreviation
Abbreviate	ABBR	American Wire Gage	AWG
Absolute	ABS	Ammeter	AM
Accelerate	ACCEL	Amount	AMT
Acceleration due to gravity	G	Ampere	AMP
Access panel	AP	Ampere hour	AMP HR
Accessory	ACCESS.	Amplifier	AMPL
Actual	ACT.	Anneal	ANL
Adapter	ADPT	Antenna	ANT.
Addendum	ADD.	Apparatus	APP
Adjust	ADJ	Approved	APPD
Advance	ADV	Approximate	APPROX
After	AFT.	Arc weld	ARC/W
Aggregate	AGGR	Area	A
Aileron	AIL	Armature	ARM.
Air-break switch	ABS	Arrange	ARR.
Air-circuit breaker	ACB	Arrester	ARR.
Aircraft	ACFT	Asbestos	ASB
Airplane	APL	Assemble	ASSEM
Airtight	AT	Assembly	ASSY
Alarm	ALM	Atomic	AT
Allowance	ALLOW	Attach	ATT
Alloy	ALY	Audio-frequency	AF
Alteration	ALT	Automatic	AUTO
Alternate	ALT	Auto-transformer	AUTO TR
Alternating current	AC	Auxiliary	AUX
Alternator	ALT	Average	AVG
Altitude	ALT		
Aluminum	AL	Babbitt	BAB
American Standard	AMER STD	Back to back	B to B

Word	Abbreviation	Word	Abbreviation
Baffle	BAF	Cast (used with other materials)	C
Balance	BAL	Cast iron	CI
Ball bearing	BB	Cast-iron pipe	CIP
Base line	BL	Cast steel	CS
Base plate	BP	Casting	CSTG
Battery	BAT.	Castle nut	CAS NUT
Bearing	BRG	Cement	CEM
Bent	BT	Center	CTR
Between	BET.	Center line	CL
Between centers	BC	Center to center	C to C
Between perpendiculars	BP	Centering	CTR
Bevel	BEV	Centigrade	C
Bill of material	B/M	Centigram	CG
Birmingham Wire Gage	BWG	Centiliter	CL
Blank	BLK	Centimeter	CM
Block	BLK	Centrifugal	CENT.
Blueprint	BP	Centrifugal force	CF
Bolt circle	BC	Ceramic	CER
Bottom	BOT	Chain	CH
Bottom chord	BC	Chamfer	CHAM
Brake	BK	Change	CHG
Brass	BRS	Change notice	CN
Brazing	BRZG	Change order	CO
Break	BRK	Channel	CHAN
Breaker	BKR	Check	CHK
Brinnell hardness	BH	Check valve	CV
British Standard	BR STD	Chemical	CHEM
British thermal units	BTU	Chord	CHD
Broach	BRO	Chrome molybdenum	CR MOLY
Bronze	BRZ	Chromium plate	CR PL
Brown & Sharp	B&S	Chrome vanadium	CR VAN
Brush	BR	Circle	CIR
Burnish	BNH	Circuit	CKT
Bushing	BUSH.	Circular	CIR
Bypass	BYP	Circular pitch	CP
		Circulate	CIRC
Cadmium plate	CD PL	Circumference	CIRC
Calculate	CALC	Clamp	CLP
Calibrate	CAL	Class	CL
Calking	CLKG	Clear	CLR
Capacitor	CAP	Clearance	CL
Capacity	CAP	Clockwise	CW
Cap screw	CAP. SCR	Closing	CL
Carburize	CARB	Clutch	CL
Caseharden	CH	Coated	CTD
Casing	CSG	Coaxial	COAX

Word	Abbreviation	Word	Abbreviation
Coefficient	COEF	Counterbore	CBORE
Cold drawn	CD	Counterdrill	CDRILL
Cold-drawn steel	CDS	Counterpunch	CPUNCH
Cold rolled	CR	Countersink	CSK
Cold-rolled steel	CRS	Countersink other side	CSK-O
Column	COL	Coupling	CPLG
Combination	COMB.	Cover	COV
Combustion	COMB	Crank	CRK
Communication	COMM	Cross connection	XCONN
Commutator	COMM	Cross section	XSECT
Complete	COMPL	Cubic	CU
Composite	CX	Current	CUR
Composition	COMP	Cyanide	CYN
Compressor	COMPR	Cycle	CY
Concentric	CONC	Cycles per minute	CPM
Concrete	CONC	Cycles per second	CPS
Condition	COND	Cylinder	CYL
Conduct	COND		
Conductor	COND	Decibel	DB
Conduit	CND	Decimal	DEC
Connect	CONN	Dedendum	DED
Constant	CONST	Deep drawn	DD
Contact	CONT	Deflect	DEFL
Container	CNTR	Degree	(°) DEG
Continue	CONT	Density	D
Continuous wave	CW	Describe	DESCR
Contract	CONT	Design	DSGN
Contractor	CONTR	Designation	DESIG
Control	CONT	Detail	DET
Control relay	CR	Detector	DET
Control switch	CS	Detonator	DET
Controller	CONT	Develop	DEV
Convert	CONV	Diagonal	DIAG
Conveyor	CNVR	Diagram	DIAG
Cooled	CLD	Diameter	DIA
Copper oxide	CUO	Diametral pitch	DP
Copper plate	COP. PL	Diaphragm	DIAPH
Cord	CD	Differential	DIFF
Correct	CORR	Dimension	DIM.
Corrosion resistant	CRE	Diode	DIO
Corrosion-resistant steel	CRES	Direct current	DC
Corrugate	CORR	Directional	DIR
Cotter	COT	Discharge	DISCH
Counter	CTR	Disconnect	DISC.
Counterclockwise	CCW	Distance	DIST
Counterbalance	CBAL	Distribute	DISTR

Word	Abbreviation	Word	Abbreviation
Ditto	DO.	Fahrenheit	F
Double	DBL	Fairing	FAIR.
Dovetail	DVTL	Farad	F
Dowel	DWL	Far side	FS
Down	DN	Feed	FD
Drafting	DFTG	Feeder	FDR
Draftsman	DFTSMN	Feet	(′) FT
Drain	DR	Feet per minute	FPM
Drawing	DWG	Feet per second	FPS
Drawing list	DL	Female	FEM
Drill	DR	Fiber	FBR
Drill rod	DR	Field	FLD
Drive	DR	Figure	FIG.
Drive fit	DF	Filament	FIL
Drop	D	Fillet	FIL
Drop forge	DF	Filling	FILL.
Duplex	DX	Fillister	FIL
Duplicate	DUP	Filter	FLT
Dynamic	DYN	Finish	FIN.
Dynamo	DYN	Finish all over	FAO
		Fireproof	FPRF
Each	EA	Fitting	FTG
Eccentric	ECC	Fixture	FIX.
Effective	EFF	Flange	FLG
Electric	ELEC	Flashing	FL
Elevation	EL	Flat	F
Enclose	ENCL	Flat head	FH
End to end	E to E	Flexible	FLEX.
Envelope	ENV	Float	FLT
Equal	EQ	Floor	FL
Equation	EQ	Fluid	FL
Equipment	EQUIP.	Fluorescent	FLUOR
Equivalent	EQUIV	Flush	FL
Estimate	EST	Focus	FOC
Evaporate	EVAP	Foot	(′) FT
Excavate	EXC	Force	F
Exhaust	EXH	Forging	FORG
Expand	EXP	Forward	FWD
Exterior	EXT	Foundation	FDN
External	EXT	Foundry	FDRY
Extra heavy	X HVY	Fractional	FRAC
Extra strong	X STR	Frame	FR
Extrude	EXTR	Freezing point	FP
		Frequency	FREQ
Fabricate	FAB	Frequency, high	HF
Face to face	F to F	Frequency, low	LF

Word	Abbreviation	Word	Abbreviation
Frequency, medium	MF	Harden	HDN
Frequency modulation	FM	Hardware	HDW
Frequency, super high	SHF	Head	HD
Frequency, ultra high	UHF	Headless	HDLS
Frequency, very high	VHF	Heat	HT
Frequency, very low	VLF	Heat treat	HT TR
Friction horsepower	FHP	Heater	HTR
From below	FR BEL	Heavy	HVY
Front	FR	Height	HGT
Fuel	F	Henry	H
Furnish	FURN	Hexagon	HEX
Fusible	FSBL	High	H
Fusion point	FNP	High frequency	HF
		High point	H PT
Gage or Gauge	GA	High pressure	HP
Gallon	GAL	High speed	HS
Galvanize	GALV	High-speed steel	HSS
Galvanized iron	GI	High tension	HT
Galvanized steel	GS	High voltage	HV
Galvanized steel wire rope	GSWR	Highway	HWY
Gas	G	Holder	HLR
Gasket	GSKT	Hollow	HOL
Gasoline	GASO	Horizontal	HOR
General	GEN	Horsepower	HP
Glaze	GL	Hot rolled	HR
Government	GOVT	Hot-rolled steel	HRS
Government furnished equipment	GFE	Hour	HR
Governor	GOV	Hydraulic	HYD
Grade	GR		
Graduation	GRAD	Identify	IDENT
Gram	G	Ignition	IGN
Graphic	GRAPH.	Illuminate	ILLUM
Graphite	GPH	Illustrate	ILLUS
Grating	GRTG	Impact	IMP
Gravity	G	Impedance	IMP.
Grid	G	Inch	(") IN.
Grind	GRD	Inches per second	IPS
Groove	GRV	Include	INCL
Ground	GRD	Increase	INCR
		Indicate	IND
Half hard	½H	Inductance or induction	IND
Half round	½RD	Industrial	IND
Handle	HDL	Information	INFO
Hanger	HGR	Injection	INJ
Hard	H	Inlet	IN
Hard-drawn	HD	Inspect	INSP

Word	Abbreviation	Word	Abbreviation
Install	INSTL	Lacquer	LAQ
Instantaneous	INST	Laminate	LAM
Instruct	INST	Lateral	LAT
Instrument	INST	Lead-coated metal	LCM
Insulate	INS	Lead covered	LC
Interchangeable	INTCHG	Leading edge	LE
Interior	INT	Left	L
Interlock	INTLK	Left hand	LH
Intermediate	INTER	Length	LG
Intermittent	INTMT	Length over all	LOA
Internal	INT	Letter	LTR
Interrupt	INTER	Light	LT
Interrupted continuous wave	ICW	Limit	LIM
Interruptions per minute	IPM	Line	L
Interruptions per second	IPS	Linear	LIN
Intersect	INT	Link	LK
Inverse	INV	Liquid	LIQ
Invert	INV	Liter	L
Iron	I	Locate	LOC
Iron-pipe size	IPS	Long	LG
Irregular	IRREG	Longitude	LONG.
Issue	ISS	Low explosive	LE
		Low frequency	LF
Jack	J	Low pressure	LP
Job order	JO	Low tension	LT
Joint	JT	Low voltage	LV
Junction	JCT	Low speed	LS
		Low torque	LT
Kelvin	K	Lubricate	LUB
Key	K	Lubricating oil	LO
Keyseat	KST	Lumen	L
Keyway	KWY	Lumens per watt	LPW
Kilo	K		
Kilocycle	KC	Machine	MACH
Kilocycles per second	KC	Magnet	MAG
Kilogram	KG	Main	MN
Kiloliter	KL	Male and female	M&F
Kilometer	KM	Malleable	MALL
Kilovolt	KV	Malleable iron	MI
Kilovolt-ampere	KVA	Manual	MAN.
Kilovolt-ampere hour	KVAH	Manufacture	MFR
Kilowatt	KW	Manufactured	MFD
Kilowatt-hour	KWH	Manufacturing	MFG
Kip (1000 lb)	K	Material	MATL
Knots	KN	Material list	ML
		Maximum	MAX
Laboratory	LAB		

Word	Abbreviation	Word	Abbreviation
Maximum working pressure	MWP	Mounted	MTD
Mean effective pressure	MEP	Mounting	MTG
Mechanical	MECH	Multiple	MULT
Mechanism	MECH	Multiple contact	MC
Medium	MED		
Mega	M	National	NATL
Megacycles	MC	Natural	NAT
Megawatt	MW	Near face	NF
Megohm	MEG	Near side	NS
Melting point	MP	Negative	NEG
Metal	MET.	Network	NET
Meter (instrument or measure		Neutral	NEUT
of length)	M	Nickel-silver	NI-SIL
Micro	μ or U	Nipple	NIP.
Microampere	μA or UA	Nominal	NOM
Microfarad	μF or UF	Normal	NOR
Microhenry	μH or UH	Normally closed	NC
Micro-inch-root-mean square	μ-IN-RMS or	Normally open	NO
	U-IN-RMS	Not to scale	NTS
Micrometer	MIC	Number	NO.
Micron	μ or U		
Microvolt	μV or UV	Obsolete	OBS
Microwatt	μW or UW	Octagon	OCT
Miles	MI	Ohm	Ω
Miles per gallon	MPG	Oil-circuit breaker	OCB
Miles per hour	MPH	Oil insulated	OI
Milli	M	Oil switch	OS
Milliampere	MA.	On center	OC
Milligram	MG	One pole	1 P
Millihenry	MH	Opening	OPNG
Millimeter	MM	Operate	OPR
Milliseconds	MS	Opposite	OPP
Millivolt	MV	Optical	OPT
Milliwatt	MW	Ordnance	ORD
Minimum	MIN	Orifice	ORF
Minute	(') MIN	Original	ORIG
Miscellaneous	MISC	Oscillate	OSC
Mixture	MIX.	Ounce	OZ
Model	MOD	Out to Out	O to O
Modify	MOD	Outlet	OUT.
Modulated continuous wave	MCW	Output	OUT.
Modulator	MOD	Outside diameter	OD
Molecular weight	MOL WT	Outside face	OF
Monument	MON	Outside radius	OR
Morse taper	MOR T	Over-all	OA
Motor	MOT	Overhead	OVHD

Word	Abbreviation	Word	Abbreviation
Overload	OVLD	Pounds per cubic foot	PCF
Overvoltage	OVV	Pounds per square foot	PSF
Oxidized	OXD	Pounds per square inch	PSI
		Pounds per square inch absolute	PSIA
Pack	PK	Power	PWR
Packing	PKG	Power amplifier	PA
Painted	PTD	Power directional relay	PDR
Pair	PR	Power factor	PF
Panel	PNL	Preamplifier	PREAMP
Parallel	PAR.	Precast	PRCST
Part	PT	Prefabricated	PREFAB
Pattern	PATT	Preferred	PFD
Perforate	PERF	Premolded	PRMLD
Permanent	PERM	Prepare	PREP
Permanent magnet	PM	Press	PRS
Perpendicular	PERP	Pressure	PRESS.
Phase	PH	Pressure angle	PA.
Phosphor bronze	PH BRZ	Primary	PRI
Photograph	PHOTO	Process	PROC
Physical	PHYS	Production	PROD
Piece	PC	Profile	PF
Piece mark	PC MK	Project	PROJ
Pierce	PRC	Punch	PCH
Pipe Tap	PT	Purchase	PUR
Pitch	P	Push-pull	P-P
Pitch circle	PC		
Pitch diameter	PD	Quadrant	QUAD
Plastic	PLSTC	Quality	QUAL
Plate	PL	Quantity	QTY
Plotting	PLOT.	Quart	QT
Pneumatic	PNEU	Quarter	QTR
Point	PT	Quarter hard	¼ H
Point of compound curve	PCC	Quarter round	¼ RD
Point of curve	PC	Quartz	QTZ
Point of intersection	PI		
Point of reverse curve	PRC	Radial	RAD
Point of switch	PS	Radio frequency	RF
Point of tangent	PT	Radius	R
Polar	POL	Reactive	REAC
Pole	P	Reactive kilovolt-ampere	KVAR
Polish	POL	Reactive volt-ampere	VAR
Port	P	Reactive voltmeter	RVM
Position	POS	Reactor	REAC
Positive	POS	Ream	RM
Potential	POT.	Reassemble	REASM
Pound	LB	Received	RECD

Word	Abbreviation	Word	Abbreviation
Receiver	REC	Saddle	SDL
Receptacle	RECP	Safe working pressure	SWP
Recriprocate	RECIP	Safety	SAF
Recirculate	RECIRC	Sand blast	SD BL
Reclosing	RECL	Saturate	SAT.
Record	REC	Schedule	SCH
Rectangle	RECT	Schematic	SCHEM
Rectifier	RECT	Scleroscope hardness	SH
Reduce	RED.	Screen	SCRN
Reference	REF	Screw	SCR
Reference line	REF L	Second	SEC
Regulator	REG	Section	SECT
Reinforce	REINF	Segment	SEG
Relay	REL	Select	SEL
Release	REL	Semifinished	SF
Relief	REL	Semifixed	SFXD
Remove	REM	Semisteel	SS
Repair	REP	Separate	SEP
Replace	REPL	Sequence	SEQ
Reproduce	REPRO	Serial	SER
Require	REQ	Series	SER
Required	REQD	Serrate	SERR
Resistance	RES	Service	SERV
Resistor	RES	Set screw	SS
Retainer	RET.	Shaft	SFT
Retard	RET.	Shield	SHLD
Return	RET.	Shipment	SHPT
Reverse	REV	Shop order	SO
Revise	REV	Short wave	SW
Revolution	REV	Shunt	SH
Revolutions per minute	RPM	Side	S
Revolutions per second	RPS	Signal	SIG
Rheostat	RHEO	Sink	SK
Right	R	Sketch	SK
Right hand	RH	Sleeve	SLV
Ring	R	Slide	SL
Rivet	RIV	Slotted	SLOT.
Rockwell hardness	RH	Small	SM
Roller bearing	RB	Smoke	SMK
Root diameter	RD	Smokeless	SMKLS
Root mean square	RMS	Socket	SOC
Rotary	ROT.	Soft	S
Rotate	ROT.	Solder	SLD
Rough	RGH	Solenoid	SOL
Round	RD	Sound	SND
Rubber	RUB.	South	S

Word	Abbreviation	Word	Abbreviation
Space	SP	Tangent	TAN.
Spare	SP	Taper	TPR
Speaker	SPKR	Technical	TECH
Special	SPL	Tee	T
Specific	SP	Teeth per inch	TPI
Specific gravity	SP GR	Television	TV
Specific heat	SP HT	Temperature	TEMP
Specification	SPEC	Template	TEMP
Speed	SP	Tensile strength	TS
Spherical	SPHER	Tension	TENS.
Spindle	SPDL	Terminal	TERM.
Split phase	SP PH	Terminal board	TB
Spot-faced	SF	That is	IE
Spring	SPG	Theoretical	THEO
Square	SQ	Thermal	THRM
Stabilize	STAB	Thermostat	THERMO
Stainless	STN	Thick	THK
Standard	STD	Thousand	M
Static pressure	SP	Thread	THD
Station	STA	Throttle	THROT
Stationary	STA	Through	THRU
Steel	STL	Time	T
Stiffener	STIFF.	Time delay	TD
Stock	STK	Time-delay closing	TDC
Storage	STG	Time-delay opening	TDO
Straight	STR	Tinned	TD
Strip	STR	Tobin bronze	TOB BRZ
Structural	STR	Toggle	TGL
Substitute	SUB	Tolerance	TOL
Suction	SUCT	Tongue and groove	T&G
Summary	SUM.	Tool steel	TS
Supervise	SUPV	Tooth	T
Supply	SUP	Total	TOT
Surface	SUR	Total indicator reading	TIR
Survey	SURV	Trace	TR
Switch	SW	Tracer	TCR
Symbol	SYM	Transfer	TRANS
Symmetrical	SYM	Transformer	TRANS
Synchronous	SYN	Transmission	XMSN
Synthetic	SYN	Transmitter	XMTR
System	SYS	Transmitting	XMTG
		Transportation	TRANS
Tabulate	TAB.	Transverse	TRANSV
Tachometer	TACH	Trimmer	TRIM.
Tandem	TDM	Triode	TRI

Word	Abbreviation	Word	Abbreviation
True air speed	TAS	Voltmeter	VM
Truss	T	Volts per mil	VPM
Tubing	TUB	Volume	VOL
Tuned radio frequency	TRF		
Turbine	TURB	Washer	WASH
Typical	TYP	Water	W
		Water line	WL
Ultimate	ULT	Watertight	WT
Ultra-high frequency	UHF	Watt	W
Under voltage	UV	Watt-hour	WHR
Unit	U	Watt-hour meter	WHM
United States Gage	USG	Wattmeter	WM
United States Standard	USS	Weight	WT
Universal	UNIV	West	W
		Wet bulb	WB
Vacuum	VAC	Width	W
Vacuum tube	VT	Wind	WD
Valve	V	Winding	WDG
Vapor proof	VAP PRF	Wire	W
Variable	VAR	With	W/
Variable-frequency oscillator	VFO	With equipment and	
Velocity	V	spare parts	W/E&SP
Ventilate	VENT.	Without	W/O
Versed sine	VERS	Without equipment and	
Versus	VS	spare parts	W/O E&SP
Vertical	VERT	Wood	WD
Very-high frequency	VHF	Woodruff	WDF
Very-low frequency	VLF	Working point	WP
Video-frequency	VDF	Working pressure	WP
Vibrate	VIB	Wrought	WRT
Viscosity	VISC	Wrought iron	WI
Vitreous	VIT	Yard	YD
Voice frequency	VF	Year	YR
Volt	V	Yield point	YP
Volt-ampere	VA	Yield strength	YS

Abbreviations for Colors

Amber	AMB	Green	GRN
Black	BLK	Orange	ORN
Blue	BLU	White	WHT
Brown	BRN	Yellow	YEL

Partial List of Chemical Symbols

Word	Abbreviation	Word	Abbreviation
Aluminum	Al	Molybdenum	Mo
Antimony (stibium)	Sb	Neon	Ne
Barium	Ba	Nickel	Ni
Beryllium	Be	Nitrogen	N
Bismuth	Bi	Oxygen	O
Boron	B	Phosphorus	P
Bromine	Br	Platinum	Pt
Cadmium	Cd	Potassium (kalium)	K
Calcium	Ca	Radium	Ra
Carbon	C	Rhodium	Rh
Chlorine	Cl	Ruthenium	Ru
Chromium	Cr	Selenium	Se
Cobalt	Co	Silicon	Si
Copper	Cu	Silver (argentum)	Ag
Fluorine	F	Sodium (natrium)	Na
Gold (aurium)	Au	Strontium	Sr
Helium	He	Sulfur	S
Hydrogen	H	Tantalum	Ta
Indium	In	Tellurium	Te
Iodine	I	Thallium	Tl
Iridium	Ir	Tin (stannum)	Sn
Iron (ferrum)	Fe	Titanium	Ti
Lead (plumbum)	Pb	Tungsten (wolframium)	W
Lithium	Li	Uranium	U
Magnesium	Mg	Vanadium	V
Manganese	Mn	Zinc	Zn
Mercury (hydrargyrum)	Hg	Zirconium	Zr

SUPPLY CATALOGUES AND TECHNICAL MANUALS

The following compilation shows representative pages from suppliers' and manufacturers' catalogues and technical manuals. These publications offer varied technical information, engineering specifications, and design data in many fields, material which is of great value both to students and to practicing engineers, designers, draftsmen, architects, and builders. In addition to their first-line role as sources of technical information and data, these publications exemplify interesting solutions to the graphic design problems involved in presenting large amounts of detail in readable form.

The student should take every opportunity to start and maintain a collection of such catalogues and manuals. He will find it a valuable addition to his technical library.

Blind riveting is easier when you follow these simple
TIPS ON INSTALLATION

BEFORE YOU START THE JOB

Measure your total material thickness. Select the correct grip length rivet from the tables on the next three pages by comparing your sheet thickness with the min. and max. grips shown in the column headed GRIP LENGTH.

IN METAL

GRIP LENGTH = Total thickness of sheets to be fastened

IN WOOD

USE "L" DIMENSION (length under head) instead of grip length. L = M (thickness of metal) + D (hole depth in wood.)

DRILL A HOLE

Select drill size according to your drilling method (hand or jig drilling)

RIVET DIA.	JIG DRILLING					HAND DRILLING				
	$\frac{1}{8}$	$\frac{5}{32}$	$\frac{3}{16}$	$\frac{1}{4}$	$\frac{5}{16}$	$\frac{1}{8}$	$\frac{5}{32}$	$\frac{3}{16}$	$\frac{1}{4}$	$\frac{5}{16}$
DRILL SIZE	30	20	11	F	P	$\frac{1}{8}$	$\frac{5}{32}$	$\frac{3}{16}$	$\frac{1}{4}$	$\frac{5}{16}$
HOLE DIA.	.128	.161	.191	.257	.323					

INSERT A RIVET

seat head firmly against outer surface

HIT THE PIN

Drive pin flush with rivet head

Expanding prongs clinch sheets tightly, eliminating gaps.

Metal and wood pulled tightly together. Nothing protrudes through wood.

 **SOUTHCO** ® **STEEL DRIVE RIVETS**

SEE PAGE 3 FOR INSTALLATION DATA

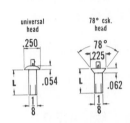

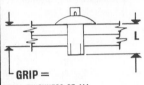

USE THESE COLUMNS
FIRST TO LOCATE
YOUR CORRECT

GRIP LENGTH

GRIP =
TOTAL THICKNESS OF ALL
SHEETS FASTENED TOGETHER

1/8" DIA.
PART NUMBERS

length under head L	UNIVERSAL HEAD	78° CSK. HEAD
5/32	38-404-01-93*	
5/32	38-104-02-93	
3/16	38-104-03-93	38-604-03-93‡
7/32	38-104-04-93	38-604-04-93
1/4	38-104-05-93	38-604-05-93
9/32	38-104-06-93	38-604-06-93
5/16	38-104-07-93	38-604-07-93
11/32	38-104-08-93	38-604-08-93
3/8	38-104-09-93	38-604-09-93
13/32	38-104-10-93	38-604-10-93
7/16	38-104-11-93	38-604-11-93
15/32	38-104-12-93	38-604-12-93
1/2	38-104-13-93	38-604-13-93

* SPECIAL CONE HEAD

‡ L = 7/32"

3/16" DIA.
PART NUMBERS

length under head L	UNIVERSAL HEAD	78° CSK. HEAD	FULL BRAZIER HEAD
7/32			38-206-02-91
7/32	38-106-03-91		38-206-03-91
1/4	38-106-04-91		38-206-04-91
9/32	38-106-05-91		38-206-05-91
5/16	38-106-06-91	38-606-06-91	38-206-06-91
11/32	38-106-07-91	38-606-07-91	38-206-07-91
3/8	38-106-08-91	38-606-08-91	38-206-08-91
13/32	38-106-09-91	38-606-09-91	38-206-09-91
7/16	38-106-10-91	38-606-10-91	38-206-10-91
15/32	38-106-11-91	38-606-11-91	
1/2	38-106-12-91	38-606-12-91	
17/32	38-106-13-91	38-606-13-91	38-206-13-91
9/16	38-106-14-91	38-606-14-91	
19/32	38-106-15-91	38-606-15-91	
5/8	38-106-16-91	38-606-16-91	38-206-16-91
21/32	38-106-17-91	38-606-17-91	
11/16	38-106-18-91	38-606-18-91	
23/32	38-106-19-91	38-606-19-91	
3/4	38-106-20-91	38-606-20-91	38-206-20-91

MINIMUM GRIP	NOMINAL GRIP	MAXIMUM GRIP
.015	1/32	.046
.046	1/16	.078
.078	3/32	.109
.109	1/8	.140
.140	5/32	.171
.171	3/16	.203
.203	7/32	.234
.234	1/4	.265
.265	9/32	.296
.296	5/16	.328
.328	11/32	.359
.359	3/8	.390
.390	13/32	.421
.421	7/16	.453
.453	15/32	.484
.484	1/2	.515
.515	17/32	.546
.546	9/16	.578
.578	19/32	.609
.609	5/8	.640

New: handy kit for experimental & short run jobs.

DRIVE RIVET SHOP ASSORTMENT

Contains approximately 1,000 Aluminum Drive Rivets, 3/16" & 1/4" diameter, with Full Brazier Heads. Grip lengths are carefully selected to handle the fastening of almost every common sheet thickness.

The package is a permanent metal-edge kit with refillable inner compartments. Complete instructions for drive riveting are a part of the box itself.

Part No. 38-88-101-10

MATERIAL

Steel, cadmium plated. 1/8 dia. rivets have stainless steel pins. 3/16 & 1/4 dia. rivets have carbon steel pins*, cad. plated

*Stainless steel pins may be substituted at Manufacturer's option.

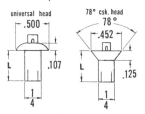

universal head .500

78° csk. head 78° .452 .107 .125

1 4

1/4" DIA.
PART NUMBERS

length under head L	UNIVERSAL HEAD	78° CSK. HEAD
7/32	38-108-03-91	
1/4	38-108-04-91	
9/32	38-108-05-91	
5/16	38-108-06-91	38-608-06-91
11/32	38-108-07-91	38-608-07-91
3/8	38-108-08-91	38-608-08-91
13/32	38-108-09-91	38-608-09-91
7/16	38-108-10-91	38-608-10-91
15/32	38-108-11-91	38-608-11-91
1/2	38-108-12-91	38-608-12-91
17/32	38-108-13-91	38-608-13-91
9/16	38-108-14-91	38-608-14-91
19/32	38-108-15-91	38-608-15-91
5/8	38-108-16-91	38-608-16-91
21/32	38-108-17-91	38-608-17-91
11/16	38-108-18-91	38-608-18-91
23/32	38-108-19-91	38-608-19-91
3/4	38-108-20-91	38-608-20-91

New . . . Larger diameter Steel Drive Rivets

SEE PAGE 3 FOR INSTALLATION DATA

USE THESE COLUMNS FIRST TO LOCATE YOUR CORRECT

GRIP LENGTH

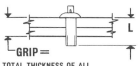

GRIP =

TOTAL THICKNESS OF ALL SHEETS FASTENED TOGETHER

MINIMUM GRIP	NOMINAL GRIP	MAXIMUM GRIP
.094	1/8	.156
.157	3/16	.218
.219	1/4	.281
.282	5/16	.343
.344	3/8	.406
.407	7/16	.468
.469	1/2	.531
.532	9/16	.593
.594	5/8	.656
.657	11/16	.718
.719	3/4	.781
.782	13/16	.843
.844	7/8	.906
.907	15/16	.968
.969	1	1.031

universal head

.625 .138

5 16

5/16" DIA.
PART NUMBER

length under head L	UNIVERSAL HEAD
5/16	38-110-04-91
3/8	38-110-06-91
7/16	38-110-08-91
1/2	38-110-10-91
9/16	38-110-12-91
5/8	38-110-14-91
11/16	38-110-16-91
3/4	38-110-18-91
13/16	38-110-20-91
7/8	38-110-22-91
15/16	38-110-24-91
1"	38-110-26-91
1-1/16	38-110-28-91
1-1/8	38-110-30-91
1-3/16	38-110-32-91

MATERIAL — RIVET and PIN
Steel, cadmium plated

Repair Truck Bodies in Minutes with RIVETPATCH™

Each Kit contains an aircraft type, Alclad Aluminum patch with formed edges, rounded corners, pilot holes. Sealant, Drive Rivets and instructions included. Only a drill and hammer needed to do a professional job in ten minutes!

4 sizes available: 3 x 5 (Part 38-99-337-11), 5 x 8 (Part 38-99-338-11), 8 x 11 5/8 (Part 38-99-339-11), and 11 5/8 x 24 (Part 38-99-353-11).

For Rivet Dia.	PART NUMBERS		
	Rivet Set Tools	100° Countersinks	Southco Rivet Selectors
1/8	29-1-504-10	29-13-101-11	29-12-101-23
5/32	29-1-505-10		
3/16	29-1-506-10	29-13-102-11	
1/4	29-1-508-10		

OPTIONAL TOOLS AND ACCESSORIES

 **SOUTHCO** ® # ALUMINUM

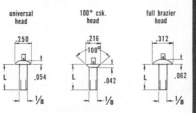

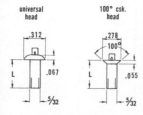

GRIP LENGTH

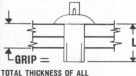

GRIP = **TOTAL THICKNESS OF ALL SHEETS FASTENED TOGETHER**

1/8" DIA.
PART NUMBERS

5/32" DIA.
PART NUMBERS

length under head L	UNIVERSAL HEAD	100° CSK. HEAD	FULL BRAZIER HEAD	length under head L	UNIVERSAL HEAD	100° CSK. HEAD	MINIMUM GRIP	NOMINAL GRIP	MAXIMUM GRIP
5/32	38-404-01-13*			3/16	38-105-01-13		.015	1/32	.046
5/32	38-104-02-13			3/16	38-105-02-13		.046	1/16	.078
3/16	38-104-03-13	38-504-03-13‡	38-204-03-13	7/32	38-105-03-13		.078	3/32	.109
7/32	38-104-04-13	38-504-04-13	38-204-04-13	1/4	38-105-04-13	38-505-04-13	.109	1/8	.140
1/4	38-104-05-13	38-504-05-13	38-204-05-13	9/32	38-105-05-13	38-505-05-13	.140	5/32	.171
9/32	38-104-06-13	38-504-06-13	38-204-06-13	5/16	38-105-06-13	38-505-06-13	.171	3/16	.203
5/16	38-104-07-13	38-504-07-13	38-204-07-13	11/32	38-105-07-13	38-505-07-13	.203	7/32	.234
11/32	38-104-08-13	38-504-08-13		3/8	38-105-08-13	38-505-08-13	.234	1/4	.265
3/8	38-104-09-13	38-504-09-13		13/32	38-105-09-13	38-505-09-13	.265	9/32	.296
13/32	38-104-10-13	38-504-10-13		7/16	38-105-10-13	38-505-10-13	.296	5/16	.328
7/16	38-104-11-13	38-504-11-13		15/32	38-105-11-13	38-505-11-13	.328	11/32	.359
15/32	38-104-12-13	38-504-12-13	38-204-12-13	1/2	38-105-12-13	38-505-12-13	.359	3/8	.390
1/2	38-104-13-13	38-504-13-13		17/32	38-105-13-13	38-505-13-13	.390	13/32	.421
17/32	38-104-14-13			9/16	38-105-14-13	38-505-14-13	.421	7/16	.453
				19/32	38-105-15-13	38-505-15-13	.453	15/32	.484
	* SPECIAL CONE HEAD		‡ L = 7/32"	5/8	38-105-16-13	38-505-16-13	.484	1/2	.515
				21/32	38-105-17-13	38-505-17-13	.515	17/32	.546
				11/16	38-105-18-13	38-505-18-13	.546	9/16	.578
				23/32	38-105-19-13	38-505-19-13	.578	19/32	.609
23/32	38-104-20-13			3/4	38-105-20-13	38-505-20-13	.609	5/8	.640
							.671	11/16	.703
							.734	3/4	.765
							.796	13/16	.828
							.859	7/8	.890
							.921	15/16	.953
							.984	1	1.015

ALUMINUM
EXTRA LONG
RIVETS FOR METAL OR MASONRY
(Head dimensions same as on page 5)

Subtract ⅛" from "L" to determine grip

length under head L	3/16" DIA. FULL BRAZIER HEAD	1/4" DIA. FULL BRAZIER HEAD	1/4" DIA. 100° CSK. HEAD
1⅛	38-206-32-13	38-208-32-13	38-508-32-13
1¼		38-208-36-13	
1⁵⁄₁₆		38-208-38-13	
1⅜		38-208-40-13	
1⁷⁄₁₆		38-208-42-13	
1½		38-208-44-13	38-508-44-13
1⁹⁄₁₆		38-208-46-13	
1⅝		38-208-48-13	
1¾		38-208-52-13	38-508-52-13

DRIVE RIVETS

**2117-T4 ALUMINUM RIVET BODY WITH
300 SERIES STAINLESS STEEL PINS.**

(Aluminum rivets of other alloys, and pins of aluminum available on special request)

SEE PAGE 3 FOR INSTALLATION DATA

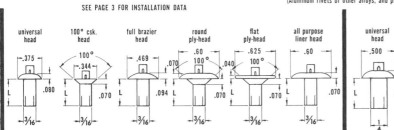

3/16" DIA.
PART NUMBERS

length under head L *	UNIVERSAL HEAD	100° CSK. HEAD	FULL BRAZIER HEAD	ROUND PLY-HEAD®	FLAT PLY-HEAD®	All Purpose LINER HEAD
7/32	38-106-02-13		38-206-02-13			
7/32	38-106-03-13		38-206-03-13			38-99-269-03
1/4	38-106-04-13		38-206-04-13			38-99-269-04
9/32	38-106-05-13		38-206-05-13			38-99-269-05
5/16	38-106-06-13	38-506-06-13	38-206-06-13			38-99-269-06
11/32	38-106-07-13	38-506-07-13	38-206-07-13			38-99-269-07
3/8	38-106-08-13	38-506-08-13	38-206-08-13	38-906-08-13		38-99-269-08
13/32	38-106-09-13	38-506-09-13	38-206-09-13	38-906-09-13		38-99-269-09
7/16	38-106-10-13	38-506-10-13	38-206-10-13	38-906-10-13	38-806-10-13	38-99-269-10
15/32	38-106-11-13	38-506-11-13	38-206-11-13	38-906-11-13		38-99-269-11
1/2	38-106-12-13	38-506-12-13	38-206-12-13	38-906-12-13	38-806-12-13	38-99-269-12
17/32	38-106-13-13	38-506-13-13	38-206-13-13		38-806-13-13	38-99-269-13
9/16	38-106-14-13	38-506-14-13	38-206-14-13	38-906-14-13	38-806-14-13	38-99-269-14
19/32	38-106-15-13	38-506-15-13	38-206-15-13			
5/8	38-106-16-13	38-506-16-13	38-206-16-13	38-906-16-13	38-806-16-13	38-99-269-16
21/32	38-106-17-13	38-506-17-13	38-206-17-13			
11/16	38-106-18-13	38-506-18-13	38-206-18-13	38-906-18-13	38-806-18-13	38-99-269-18
23/32	38-106-19-13	38-506-19-13	38-206-19-13			
3/4	38-106-20-13	38-506-20-13	38-206-20-13	38-906-20-13	38-806-20-13	38-99-269-20
13/16	38-106-22-13		38-206-22-13			
7/8	38-106-24-13		38-206-24-13			38-99-269-24
15/16	38-106-26-13		38-206-26-13			
1	38-106-28-13	38-506-28-13	38-206-28-13			38-99-269-28
1-1/16	38-106-30-13		38-206-30-13			
1-1/8	38-106-32-13		38-206-32-13			

1/4" DIA.
PART NUMBERS

length under head L *	UNIVERSAL HEAD	100° CSK. HEAD	FULL BRAZIER HEAD
7/32	38-108-02-13		
7/32	38-108-03-13		38-208-03-13
1/4	38-108-04-13		38-208-04-13
9/32	38-108-05-13		38-208-05-13
5/16	38-108-06-13	38-508-06-13	38-208-06-13
11/32	38-108-07-13	38-508-07-13	38-208-07-13
3/8	38-108-08-13	38-508-08-13	38-208-08-13
13/32	38-108-09-13	38-508-09-13	38-208-09-13
7/16	38-108-10-13	38-508-10-13	38-208-10-13
15/32	38-108-11-13	38-508-11-13	38-208-11-13
1/2	38-108-12-13	38-508-12-13	38-208-12-13
17/32	38-108-13-13	38-508-13-13	38-208-13-13
9/16	38-108-14-13	38-508-14-13	38-208-14-13
19/32	38-108-15-13	38-508-15-13	38-208-15-13
5/8	38-108-16-13	38-508-16-13	38-208-16-13
21/32	38-108-17-13	38-508-17-13	38-208-17-13
11/16	38-108-18-13	38-508-18-13	38-208-18-13
23/32	38-108-19-13	38-508-19-13	38-208-19-13
3/4	38-108-20-13	38-508-20-13	38-208-20-13
13/16	38-108-22-13	38-508-22-13	38-208-22-13
27/32			38-208-23-13
7/8	38-108-24-13	38-508-24-13	38-208-24-13
15/16	38-108-26-13	38-508-26-13	38-208-26-13
1	38-108-28-13	38-508-28-13	38-208-28-13
1-1/16	38-108-30-13	38-508-30-13	38-208-30-13
1-1/8	38-108-32-13	38-508-32-13	38-208-32-13

*NOTE: The L dimension (length under head) is of importance only as a means of dimensional description. This dimension is undergoing modification in some of our rivets. In cases where actual shank length differs from that given in the L column above, a note both inside the rivet package and on its label gives corrected information. The grip length of the rivet is not affected by shank length modification.

PALNUT® Self-Threading Nuts

SPECIFIC ADVANTAGES OF OTHER TYPES

Regular Type

This is the lowest-cost PALNUT Self-threading Nut. Especially adapted to assemblies where available space is at a premium. Uses shorter studs. Competitive with push types, yet assembles fast and assures better, tighter assemblies. Shape of nut makes it possible to assemble with internal wrench. (See wrench illustration below).

Acorn Type

All the cost and assembly advantages of the PALNUT Self-threading principle are gained in this decorative, crowned nut. It covers up the ends of studs for pleasing appearance and protection against scratching.

EASY, FAST ASSEMBLY

PALNUT Self-threading Nuts are formed to standard hex shape. They may be fastened with any standard tools, manual or power. *However, by using the PALNUT Magnetic Socket Wrench, which fits all standard tools, greater convenience and higher-speed assembly are obtained.*

Power Tool Assembly

Air or electric tools, equipped with the PALNUT Magnetic Socket Wrench, permit starting, running on and tightening in one simple, fast operation.

PALNUT Magnetic Socket Wrench

PALNUT Internal Hex Wrench

Manual Assembly

PALNUT Self-threading Nuts may be applied with hand tools, but power tools are recommended for production runs. The PALNUT Magnetic Socket Wrench facilitates manual assembly.

Write for Bulletin WR-516 giving full details on PALNUT Wrenches and Tools

STUD INFORMATION

Studs of any malleable material may be used, including zinc or aluminum die cast, steel, brass or aluminum wire and high tensile plastic materials.

Tolerance on stud diameter ±0.003"

Permissible tolerance on stud diameter is plus or minus 0.003". Tapered studs should be within this tolerance at the point where the nut grips the stud at completion of assembly. (See illustration).

PALNUT Self-threading Nuts will perform satisfactorily on blunt end studs or wire, but a 1/32" x 45° chamfered end is preferred for easier starting. Full data on stud specifications is available on request.

TORQUE-TENSILE DATA

Recommended assembly torque and resulting stud tension for each Self-Threading Nut is shown on page 7. The nominal torque figures given can be used for preliminary adjustment of power tools.

Power tools with ratcheting (slip) type clutch or the "one shot" quick-breaking type clutch may be used. For Self-Threaders with Sealer we specifically recommend power tools with the ratcheting type clutch.

Where assembly conditions deviate from the normal, a downward or upward revision of the recommended assembly torque setting on the power tool clutch may be necessary to meet the current conditions. Examples given below.

1. Dry, flat, non-slippery surfaces and stud diameters on the high side of the tolerance will require higher assembly torque.
2. Irregular, slippery surfaces and stud diameters on the low side of the tolerance will require lower assembly torque.

PALNUT® Self-Threading Nuts

DIMENSIONS AND TORQUE-TENSILE DATA

| **WASHER TYPE** | **WASHER TYPE** with SEALER (See Sealer Information on Page 5) | **WASHER TYPE** STYLE SG | **REGULAR TYPE** | **ACORN TYPE** |

Type	Stud Size	PALNUT Part No.	Hex Width "W"	PALNUT Height "H"	Washer Diameter "D"	Teeth Depth "T"	Net Wgt. Lbs./M Pieces	TORQUE-TENSILE DATA (See page 6 for details)			
								ON ZINC DIE CAST STUDS		ON STEEL STUDS	
								Recommended Torque (Inch Lbs.)	Stud Tension Lbs.	Recommended Torque (Inch Lbs.)	Stud Tension (Lbs.)
WASHER TYPE	1/8"	SD125007	5/16	.186"	7/16"		1.2	15	90	26	130
	1/8	SD125085	5/16	.194	17/32		1.5	20	80	30	110
	5/32	SD156009	11/32	.212	9/16		1.9	30	100	45	240
	3/16	SD188008	3/8	.217	1/2		1.7	38	210	50	330
	3/16	SD188009	3/8	.225	9/16		2.0	42	180	55	300
	3/16	SD188010	3/8	.235	5/8		2.3	46	160	60	280
	1/4	SD250095	7/16	.232	19/32		2.5	65	260	95	370
	1/4	SD250011	7/16	.247	11/16		3.1	75	240	90	340
WASHER TYPE STYLE SG	1/8	SG125085	5/16	.194	17/32	.013"	1.5	20	80	32	110
	3/16	SG188008	3/8	.207	1/2	.013	1.6	38	210	55	330
	3/16	SG188010	3/8	.235	5/8	.013	2.3	46	160	60	280
	1/4	SG250095	7/16	.219	19/32	.015	2.4	65	260	95	370
REGULAR TYPE	3/32	SR094005	5/16	.100			0.7	5	40	8	80
	1/8	SR125004	1/4	.088			0.4	8	50	10	110
	1/8	SR125	5/16	.100			0.7	11	65	16	130
	1/8	SR125009	9/16	.114			2.0	18	90	30	190
	5/32	SR156	11/32	.110			0.9	18	100	30	250
	3/16	SR188006	3/8	.116			1.1	26	140	32	280
	3/16	SR188	1/2	.129			2.1	30	140	38	250
TYPE ACORN	1/8	SC125	5/16	.265			1.6	11	65	18	130
	1/8	SC125006	3/8	.324			2.2	14	80	25	160
	1/8	SC125007	7/16	.372			3.2	16	90	28	210
	3/16	SC188	7/16	.380			3.7	26	140	45	320
	3/16	SC188008	1/2	.437				30	140	55	350
	3/16	SC188009	9/16	.474			6.3	32	140	65	400
	1/4	SC250009	9/16	.484				53	180	77	500

Standard Finish: Cadmium.* Material: Carbon Spring Steel. Optional Finishes: Phosphate, and Mechanical Zinc plus Chromate. (Except Acorn Type)
*Cadmium Plated PALNUT Self-Threading Nuts are usually colored yellow to differentiate them from PALNUT Lock Nuts. An exception is the Acorn Type which is plated with bright cadmium for appearance.

WRITE FOR FREE SAMPLES, STATING TYPE, SIZE AND APPLICATION

Detailed information can be supplied on recommended assembly
torques, stud tension, stud dimensions and types of sealers.

PUSHNUT® FASTENERS—FLAT ROUND TYPE

USER ADVANTAGES

Flat Round PUSHNUT Fasteners provide the advantages common to push-on type fasteners generally, which are made by several manufacturers. These include ● Exceptionally fast assembly ● Elimination of more expensive screws and nuts, washers or retaining rings ● Elimination of costly threading, hole drilling or annular grooving.

Compared with push-on nuts generally, Flat Round PUSHNUT Fasteners offer these *specific advantages*

SUPERIOR GRIP Means less slippage   **GREATER HOLDING POWER** Means higher axial load strength
The number, shape, length and angularity of teeth in each part represent a carefully-designed balance between relative ease of assembly and ultimate strength. Steel thickness and relation of outside diameter to stud size are also part of this "balanced design".

LOWER COST Production in large quantities on ultra-modern equipment, plus advanced finishing techniques, assure a per-thousand cost that is invariably below competitive designs.

STUD RECOMMENDATIONS

DIAMETER TOLERANCE: + .002″ − .003″, INCLUDING PLATING. Chamfered (45°) stud ends are preferred, but if cut or sheared from longer rod or wire, square ends should be free of burrs or mushrooming.

STUD MATERIALS: May be mild steel, aluminum, die cast zinc, or other malleable materials.

Subject to verification by your own tests, Style PV parts, and Styles PS and PD parts in the thinner gauges, are likely to perform satisfactorily on plastics having good tensile strength and toughness.

STUD FINISHES: Steel studs—any commercial finish is satisfactory, except nickel or chrome plating.
Die cast zinc—any finish is satisfactory, except nickel-chrome plating should not exceed .003″ maximum thickness.

STUD HARDNESS: See comments under PERFORMANCE DATA.

PERFORMANCE DATA

Push-on Force and Removal Resistance values are "averages" obtained when parts are applied to low carbon, cold drawn steel rod of hardness not exceeding 78 on Rockwell 30T scale (this is corrected reading allowing for curvature error on round rod).

PUSHNUT PART NO.	PUSH-ON FORCE LBS.	REMOV. RESIST. LBS.	PUSHNUT PART NO.	PUSH-ON FORCE LBS.	REMOV. RESIST. LBS.	PUSHNUT PART NO.	PUSH-ON FORCE LBS.	REMOV. RESIST. LBS
PS062032	20	100	PZ001514	130	600	PR375010	50	400
PS094032	25	150	PS240085	30	600	PS375312	50	650
PS125306	10	100	PS250385	25	400	PS375612	70	800
PS125006	20	250	PS250085	45	650	PS375012	85	1000
PD156307	10	250	PV250015	10	140	PV375015	15	450
PD156007	20	300	PR312075	40	300	PS438014	70	1400
PS188307	10	250	PS312310	30	650	PV438014	20	600
PS188007	25	420	PS312010	50	900	PS500016	160	2000
PD219385	20	300	PV312015	15	300			

NOTE: Application of PUSHNUT Fasteners to studs or rods exceeding specified size tolerances, or maximum hardness, can result in considerable variation in REMOVAL RESISTANCE values. Nevertheless, careful pre-testing may show the resulting strength is still more than adequate, depending on degree of performance needed.

PUSHNUT® FASTENERS—FLAT ROUND TYPE

AVAILABLE SIZES AND STYLES

STUD DIAM.	PUSHNUT PART NO.	DES #	STEEL THICK.	TOTAL HEIGHT H	WASH. DIAM.		WGT. LBS/M.
					INSIDE F	OUTSIDE D	
.062″ (1/16″)	PS062032	3	.009″	.038″	.142″	.195″	0.09
.094″ (3/32″)	PS094032	3	.009″	.038″	.142″	.194″	0.09
.125″ (1/8″)	PS125306	1	.009″	.045″	.228″	3/8″	0.3
	PS125006	1	.013″	.052″	.228″	3/8″	0.4
.156″ (5/32″)	PD156307	2	.010″	.047″	.320″	7/16″	0.4
	PD156007	2	.013″	.058″	.320″	7/16″	0.5
.188″ (3/16″)	PS188307	2	.010″	.056″	.320″	7/16″	0.4
	PS188007	2	.015″	.064″	.320″	7/16″	0.5
.219″ (7/32″)	PD219385	2	.012″	.067″	.388″	17/32″	0.7
.237″	PZ001514	2	.021″	.050″	.420″	3/4″	2.5
.240″	PS240085	2	.017″	.069″	.388″	17/32″	0.9
.250″ (1/4″)	PS250385	2	.012″	.057″	.388″	17/32″	0.6
	PS250085	2	.017″	.066″	.388″	17/32″	1.0
	PV250015		.015″	.083″	.750″	15/16″	2.5
.312″ (5/16″)	PR312075		.013″	.040″	.385″	15/32″	0.35
	PS312310	2	.015″	.059″	.456″	5/8″	1.1
	PS312010	2	.021″	.070″	.456″	5/8″	1.5
	PV312015		.015″	.097″	.750″	15/16″	2.7
.375″ (3/8″)	PR375010		.015″	.056″	.500″	5/8″	0.87
	PS375312	2	.017″	.061″	.546″	3/4″	1.7
	PS375612	2	.021″	.068″	.546″	3/4″	2.1
	PS375012	2	.027″	.081″	.546″	3/4″	2.8
	PV375015		.015″	.093″	.750″	15/16″	2.5
.438″ (7/16″)	PS438014	2	.030″	.097″	.638″	7/8″	4.1
	PV438015		.015″	.075″	.750″	15/16″	2.5
.500″ (1/2″)	PS500016	2	.035″	.112″	.730″	1″	6.4

DESIGN 1 STYLE PS

DESIGN 2 STYLE PS

STYLE PD AND PART PZ001514

DESIGN 3 STYLE PS

STYLE PV

PART PR312075

PART PR375010

MATERIALS: Spring Steel (some parts available in stainless steel on special order).

FINISHES: Mechanical Zinc, Cadmium or Electro-Zinc (see note), Phosphate and Oil, Plain. Other finishes on special order.

NOTE: Style PS and PD parts, and part PZ001514, are not available with Cadmium, Electro-Zinc or any other electroplated finish.

For aluminum, and some plastic studs, or wooden dowels, Style PV, Styles PS and PD in the thinner gauges, or Style PR parts are recommended.

RIVNUT ENGINEERING DATA
PREPARATION PROCEDURES

FOR FLAT HEAD INSTALLATION

Flat head Rivnuts require only a punched or drilled hole of the proper size for their installation. Use a lead drill if desired and follow with a sharp finish drill held at right angles to the work. Always see that dirt or metal particles are removed from between metal sheets and burrs removed wherever possible. Sheets should be clamped or pressed into contact to reduce air gap to a minimum.

FOR MACHINE COUNTERSINK INSTALLATION

Machine countersinking can be used only in metal thicker than the head thickness of the Rivnut. A precision hole and countersink can best be obtained by following these simple steps:

1. Drill undersized hole with lead drill

2. Countersink

3. Drill correct diameter hole with sharp finish drill

4. If keyed Rivnut is to be used cut keyway with key cutter tool or by the use of a guided drill

5. Install Rivnut

FOR DIMPLE COUNTERSINK INSTALLATION

Metal thinner than Rivnut head thickness requires a dimple countersink.

The ideal bulge on any Rivnut application will always be formed against a flat under surface. The bell-mouth that results from ordinary dimpling will not permit proper formation of the bulge. Rivnuts upset against the sharp edge will form a weak bulge, a spread shank, or possibly shear.

To provide a flat surface in the dimpling operation, a ledge at the bottom of the dimpling die can be used. The "flat" on the dimple will save costly deburring before dimpling and enables the Rivnut bulge to form normally, providing maximum strength.

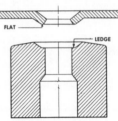

Dimple or press countersink hole. Note ledge at bottom of dimpling die

---

FOR KEYED RIVNUTS

Keyways can be cut with a B.F.Goodrich Key Cutter tool. Standard tool will cut 3/32" aluminum, 1/16" mild steel, 1/32" stainless steel. To cut keyways in metal too thick for this tool, use a small, round file or guided drill.

TORQUE WITHOUT KEYS

A hexagonal hole with a keyless Rivnut is an excellent substitute for keyed Rivnuts and eliminates the need to match the key to the keyway. This type installation offers torque resistance approximating that of keyed Rivnuts.

HOW TO REMOVE RIVNUTS

Should it be necessary to remove an installed Rivnut, it can be drilled out by using the same size drill as used for the original hole. Drill through the head of the Rivnut and then punch out the shank. The counterbore will act as a guide for the drill. The same size Rivnut can then be installed in the same hole.

ADJUSTING ANVIL TO SUIT RIVNUT LENGTH

Rivnut threads may be deformed or stripped if the pull-up stud does not engage all threads in the Rivnut. Speed Headers and all power tools have pull-up studs or anvils which can be adjusted easily to suit the Rivnut blank length. The following sketches demonstrate proper relation between face of anvil and end of pull-up stud.

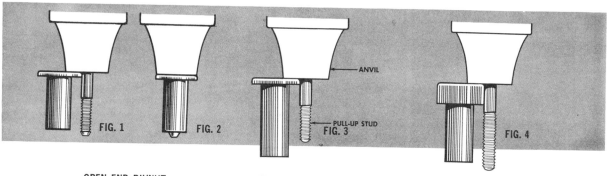

FIG. 1   FIG. 2   ANVIL   PULL-UP STUD   FIG. 3   FIG. 4

OPEN END RIVNUT

Point of the pull-up stud should extend just beyond the end of the Rivnut, as in Fig. 1. Fig. 2 shows Rivnut head tight against anvil, ready for upset.

CLOSED END RIVNUT

Thread Rivnut on pull-up stud all the way to bottom of threads. Back Rivnut off one complete turn, then adjust anvil so it contacts Rivnut head, as in Fig. 3.

FILLISTER HEAD RIVNUT

Adjust stud to same reference points as conventional types.

FINDING GRIP RANGE

GRIP RANGE

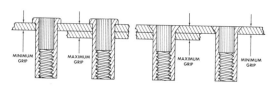

MINIMUM GRIP   MAXIMUM GRIP   MAXIMUM GRIP   MINIMUM GRIP

MEASURING "GRIP"

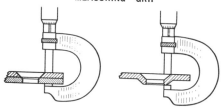

Maximum grip (above) represents the greatest material thickness in which a specific Rivnut should be properly installed. Minimum grip represents material of least thickness in which a specific Rivnut can be properly installed.

"Grip Range" is that area between maximum and minimum —the zone of thickness best suited to the installation of a specific Rivnut.

The grip ranges for various Rivnuts can be found on pages 8 and 9.

IMPORTANT: When material thickness (grip) approaches minimum or maximum for a given size Rivnut, a trial installation should be made.

In order to select the correct Rivnut, physical measurements must be made. When installing flat head Rivnuts in a surface installation or countersunk types in machine countersunk holes, "grip" is the same as metal thickness (left above).

For dimpled or press countersunk holes, "grip" is the measurement from the metal surface to the underside of the dimpled hole (right above).

IMPORTANT: Measurements should include air gaps, paint and any burrs which cannot be removed.

RIVNUT ENGINEERING DATA—FLAT HEAD

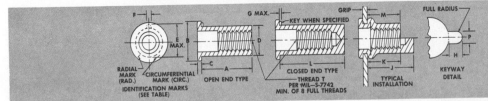

First No. of Type No.	Thread Size*	B ±.015	C Nom.	D +.000 −.004	E Max.	F +.005 −.000	G Max.	Install Drill Size (Ref.)	Install Hole Size Min.	Install Hole Size Max.	Keyway Dimensions P+.003 −.000	Keyway Dimensions H
4	≠ 4-40 UNC-3B	.270	.025	.155	.198	.054	.023	5/32	.155	.157	.062	.046-.048
6	≠ 6-32 UNC-3B	.325	.032	.189	.240	.054	.023	≠ 12	.189	.193	.062	.056-.058
8	≠ 8-32 UNC-3B	.357	.032	.221	.271	.054	.023	≠ 2	.221	.226	.062	.056-.058
10	≠10-32 UNF-3B	.406	.038	.250	.302	.054	.023	E	.250	.256	.062	.056-.058
25	¼-20 UNC-3B	.475	.058	.332	.382	.054	.035	Q	.332	.338	.062	.056-.058
31	5/16-18 UNC-3B	.665	.062	.413	.505	.120	.040	Z	.413	.423	.128	.097-.102
37	⅜-16 UNC-3B	.781	.088	.490	.597	.120	.040	12.5 MM	.490	.500	.128	.110-.115
50	½-13 UNC-3B	1.000	.125	.640	.772	.151	.040	41/64	.640	.650	.159	.135-.140

*Both UNC and UNF threads are available in No. 10 and larger thread sizes.

CODE: Diameter and grip range as tabulated. First letter of type number indicates material and finish: "A" for aluminum alloy, "S" for C-1108 or C-1110 steel, "SS" for Type 430 corrosion resistant steel, "CH" for heat treated C-4037 steel and "BR" for brass. Letter between dash numbers indicate type "—" for keyless open end, "K" for keyed open end, "B" for keyless closed end, "KB" for keyed closed end.

EXAMPLES: A25K80 = Aluminum alloy keyed open end ¼-20   SS6KB200 = Corrosion resistant steel keyed closed end No. internal thread .020 to .080 grip range.   6-32 internal thread .160 to .200 grip range.

WEIGHTS — For Brass Rivnuts multiply weight of aluminum Rivnuts by 3.31. Weights for "CH" Rivnuts (C-4037 steel) and "SS" Rivnuts (Type 430 corrosion resistant steel) same as for "S" Rivnuts.

TYPE NUMBER	GRIP RANGE	IDENT. MARK	OPEN END KEYED AND KEYLESS A ±.015	OPEN END M REF.	OPEN END Wt. ALUM.	OPEN END Wt. STEEL	CLOSED END KEYLESS L ±.015	CLOSED END J REF.	CLOSED END K REF.	CLOSED END Wt. ALUM.	CLOSED END Wt. STEEL	CLOSED END KEYED L ±.015	CLOSED END J REF.	CLOSED END K REF.	CLOSED END Wt. ALUM.	CLOSED END Wt. STEEL
4-60	.010-.060	Blank	.345	.230	.4	1.3	.500	.385	.230	.6	1.9	.500	.385	.230	.6	1.9
4-85	.060-.085	1-Rad.	.370	.230	.4	1.4	.525	.385	.230	.7	2.0	.525	.385	.230	.7	2.0
4-110	.085-.110	2-Rad.	.400	.230	.5	1.4	.555	.390	.230	.7	2.0	.555	.390	.230	.7	2.1
4-135	.110-.135	3-Rad.	.425	.230	.5	1.5	.580	.385	.230	.7	2.1	.580	.385	.230	.7	2.1
4-160	.135-.160	4-Rad.	.450	.230	.5	1.5	.605	.385	.230	.7	2.1	.605	.385	.230	.7	2.1
4-185	.160-.185	5-Rad.	.480	.230	.5	1.6	.635	.385	.230	.7	2.2	.635	.385	.230	.7	2.2
6-75	.010-.075	1-Rad.	.438	.300	.8	2.4	.625	.490	.305	1.2	3.5	.750	.615	.405	1.4	4.1
6-120	.075-.120	3-Rad.	.500	.315	.9	2.6	.625	.440	.255	1.1	3.4	.750	.565	.355	1.3	4.0
6-160	.120-.160	5-Rad.	.500	.270	.9	2.6	.750	.520	.260	1.3	4.0	.750	.520	.310	1.3	4.0
6-200	.160-.200	1-Circ.	.562	.290	.9	2.8	.750	.480	.260	1.3	3.9	.750	.480	.260	1.3	3.9
6-240	.200-.240	2-Circ.	.625	.310	1.0	3.0	.750	.435	.260	1.3	3.8	.750	.435	.260	1.3	3.8
6-280	.240-.280	3-Circ.	.687	.330	1.1	3.3	.812	.455	.265	1.3	4.1	.812	.455	.265	1.3	4.1
8-75	.010-.075	1-Rad.	.438	.300	1.0	3.0	.625	.490	.305	1.5	4.5	.750	.615	.405	1.7	5.2
8-120	.075-.120	3-Rad.	.500	.315	1.1	3.3	.625	.440	.255	1.4	4.4	.750	.565	.310	1.7	5.1
8-160	.120-.160	5-Rad.	.500	.270	1.1	3.2	.750	.520	.260	1.7	5.1	.750	.475	.265	1.6	5.0
8-200	.160-.200	1-Circ.	.625	.350	1.3	3.9	.750	.475	.265	1.6	5.0	.875	.555	.310	1.9	5.6
8-240	.200-.240	2-Circ.	.625	.305	1.2	3.8	.875	.555	.310	1.9	5.6	.875	.555	.310	1.9	5.6
8-280	.240-.280	3-Circ.	.687	.340	1.3	4.1	.875	.530	.290	1.8	5.6	.875	.530	.290	1.8	5.6
10-80	.010-.080	Blank	.531	.380	1.5	4.5	.781	.630	.380	2.3	6.8	.781	.630	.380	2.3	6.8
10-130	.080-.130	1-Rad.	.594	.390	1.6	4.9	.843	.640	.390	2.4	7.2	.843	.640	.390	2.4	7.2
10-180	.130-.180	2-Rad.	.641	.390	1.7	5.1	.891	.640	.390	2.4	7.4	.891	.640	.390	2.4	7.4
10-230	.180-.230	3-Rad.	.703	.395	1.8	5.4	.953	.645	.395	2.6	7.8	.953	.645	.395	2.6	7.8
10-280	.230-.280	4-Rad.	.750	.395	1.9	5.7	1.000	.645	.395	2.6	8.0	1.000	.645	.395	2.6	8.0
10-330	.280-.330	5-Rad.	.797	.385	1.9	5.9	1.047	.630	.385	2.7	8.2	1.047	.630	.385	2.7	8.2
25-80	.020-.080	Blank	.625	.450	3.2	9.7	.937	.760	.440	4.9	15.1	.937	.760	.440	5.0	15.1
25-140	.080-.140	1-Rad.	.687	.450	3.4	10.3	1.000	.760	.440	5.1	15.7	1.000	.760	.440	5.1	15.7
25-200	.140-.200	2-Rad.	.750	.450	3.6	10.9	1.062	.760	.440	5.3	16.2	1.062	.760	.440	5.3	16.3
25-260	.200-.260	3-Rad.	.812	.445	3.8	11.5	1.125	.755	.445	5.5	16.8	1.125	.755	.445	5.5	16.8
25-320	.260-.320	4-Rad.	.875	.445	3.9	12.0	1.187	.755	.445	5.7	17.4	1.187	.755	.445	5.7	17.4
25-380	.320-.380	5-Rad.	.937	.445	4.1	12.6	1.250	.755	.445	5.9	18.0	1.250	.755	.445	5.9	18.0
31-125	.030-.125	Blank	.750	.505	6.0	18.2	1.187	.940	.550	9.6	29.1	1.187	.940	.550	9.6	29.2
31-200	.125-.200	1-Rad.	.875	.555	6.7	20.3	1.281	.960	.555	10.1	30.6	1.281	.960	.560	10.1	30.7
31-275	.200-.275	2-Rad.	.937	.540	6.9	21.1	1.343	.950	.560	10.3	31.4	1.343	.950	.560	10.3	31.5
31-350	.275-.350	3-Rad.	1.032	.560	7.4	22.6	1.437	.965	.570	10.8	32.9	1.437	.965	.570	10.8	32.9
31-425	.350-.425	4-Rad.	1.125	.580	7.9	24.0	1.531	.985	.575	11.3	34.3	1.531	.985	.575	11.3	34.4
31-500	.425-.500	5-Rad.	1.187	.565	8.2	24.9	1.593	.975	.580	11.5	35.1	1.593	.975	.580	11.6	35.2
37-115	.030-.115	Blank	.844	.585	9.7	29.7	1.281	1.020	.660	14.8	45.0	1.281	1.020	.660	14.8	45.1
37-200	.115-.200	1-Rad.	.938	.595	10.3	31.4	1.375	1.030	.670	15.4	46.8	1.375	1.030	.670	15.4	46.9
37-285	.200-.285	2-Rad.	1.031	.605	10.9	33.2	1.468	1.040	.680	15.9	48.5	1.468	1.040	.680	16.0	48.6
37-370	.285-.370	3-Rad.	1.125	.615	11.5	34.9	1.562	1.050	.690	16.5	50.3	1.562	1.050	.690	16.5	50.4
37-455	.370-.455	4-Rad.	1.218	.630	12.0	36.7	1.656	1.065	.710	17.1	52.1	1.656	1.065	.710	17.2	52.2
37-540	.455-.540	5-Rad.	1.312	.640	12.6	38.5	1.750	1.075	.715	17.7	53.8	1.750	1.075	.715	17.7	53.9
50-145	.025-.145	Blank	1.062	.730	20.8	63.5	1.656	1.325	.855	31.9	97.3	1.656	1.325	.855	32.0	97.5
50-265	.145-.265	1-Rad.	1.188	.735	22.2	67.5	1.781	1.330	.865	33.2	101.3	1.781	1.330	.865	33.3	101.4
50-385	.265-.385	2-Rad.	1.312	.740	23.4	71.4	1.906	1.335	.875	34.5	105.1	1.906	1.335	.875	34.5	105.2
50-505	.385-.505	3-Rad.	1.453	.765	24.9	76.0	2.156	1.465	.895	37.8	115.1	2.156	1.465	.895	37.8	115.3
50-625	.505-.625	4-Rad.	1.578	.770	26.2	80.0	2.297	1.485	.905	39.3	119.9	2.297	1.485	.905	39.4	120.0
50-745	.625-.745	5-Rad.	1.719	.790	27.8	84.6	2.438	1.510	.920	40.9	124.5	2.438	1.510	.920	40.9	124.6

RIVNUT ENGINEERING DATA—COUNTERSUNK HEAD

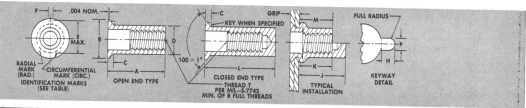

First No. of Type No.	Thread Size*	B Ref.	C Max.	D +.000 −.004	E Max.	F +.005 −.000	Install Drill Size (Ref.)	Install Hole Size Min.	Install Hole Size Max.	Keyway Dimensions P+.003 −.000	Keyway Dimensions H
4	# 4-40 UNC-3B	.263	.051	.155	.198	.054	5/32	.155	.157	.062	.046-.048
6	# 6-32 UNC-3B	.323	.063	.189	.240	.054	#12	.189	.193	.062	.056-.058
8	# 8-32 UNC-3B	.355	.063	.221	.271	.054	# 2	.221	.226	.062	.056-.058
10	#10-32 UNF-3B	.391	.065	.250	.302	.054	E	.250	.256	.062	.056-.058
25	¼-20 UNC-3B	.529	.089	.332	.382	.054	Q	.332	.338	.062	.056-.058
31	5/16-18 UNC-3B	.656	.104	.413	.505	.120	Z	.413	.423	.062	.056-.058
37	3/8-16 UNC-3B	.770	.124	.490	.597	.120	12.5 MM	.490	.500	.128	.097-.102
50	½-13 UNC-3B	.990	.154	.640	.772	.151	41/64	.640	.650	.159	.135-.140

*Both UNC and UNF threads are available in No. 10 and larger thread sizes.

CODE: Diameter and grip range as tabulated. First letter of type number indicates material and finish: "A" for aluminum alloy, "S" for C-1108 or C-1110 steel, "SS" for Type 430 corrosion resistant steel, "CH" for heat treated C-4037 steel and "BR" for brass. Letter between dash numbers indicate type "—" for keyless open end, "K" for keyed open end, "B" for keyless closed end, "KB" for keyed closed end.

EXAMPLES: A25K151 = Aluminum alloy keyed open end ¼-20 internal thread .089 to .151 grip range. SS6KB241 = Corrosion resistant steel keyed closed end No. 6-32 internal thread .201 to .241 grip range.

WEIGHTS — For Brass Rivnuts multiply weight of aluminum Rivnuts by 3.31. Weights for "CH" Rivnuts (C-4037 steel) and "SS" Rivnuts (Type 430 corrosion resistant steel) same as for "S" Rivnuts.

TYPE NUMBER	GRIP RANGE	IDENT. MARK	OPEN END KEYED AND KEYLESS A ±.015	M REF.	Wt. ALUM.	Wt. STEEL	CLOSED END KEYLESS L ±.015	J REF.	K REF.	Wt. ALUM.	Wt. STEEL	CLOSED END KEYED L ±.015	J REF.	K REF.	Wt. ALUM.	Wt. STEEL
4-81	.050-.081	Blank	.370	.235	.4	1.3	.525	.390	.235	.6	1.9	.525	.390	.235	.6	1.9
4-106	.081-.106	1-Rad.	.395	.235	.4	1.3	.550	.390	.235	.6	1.9	.550	.390	.235	.6	1.9
4-131	.106-.131	2-Rad.	.420	.235	.4	1.4	.575	.390	.235	.7	2.0	.575	.390	.235	.7	2.0
4-156	.131-.156	3-Rad.	.450	.235	.5	1.4	.600	.390	.235	.7	2.0	.600	.390	.235	.7	2.0
4-181	.156-.181	4-Rad.	.475	.235	.5	1.5	.625	.390	.235	.7	2.1	.625	.390	.235	.7	2.1
4-206	.181-.206	5-Rad.	.500	.235	.5	1.5	.650	.390	.235	.7	2.1	.650	.390	.235	.7	2.1
6-106	.065-.106	Blank	.500	.325	.8	2.5	.687	.510	.325	1.2	3.6	.812	.635	.425	1.4	4.2
6-161	.106-.161	2-Rad.	.500	.280	.8	2.4	.687	.465	.280	1.2	3.5	.812	.590	.380	1.3	4.1
6-201	.161-.201	4-Rad.	.562	.295	.9	2.6	.687	.420	.260	1.1	3.4	.812	.545	.335	1.3	4.0
6-241	.201-.241	1-Circ.	.625	.315	.9	2.9	.812	.505	.295	1.3	4.0	.812	.505	.295	1.3	4.0
6-281	.241-.281	2-Circ.	.625	.270	.9	2.8	.812	.465	.265	1.3	3.9	.812	.465	.265	1.3	3.9
6-321	.281-.321	3-Circ.	.687	.290	1.0	3.0	.844	.455	.265	1.3	4.0	.844	.455	.265	1.3	4.0
8-106	.065-.106	Blank	.500	.325	1.0	3.1	.687	.510	.325	1.5	4.6	.812	.635	.425	1.8	5.4
8-161	.106-.161	2-Rad.	.500	.280	1.0	3.0	.687	.465	.280	1.5	4.5	.812	.590	.380	1.7	5.3
8-201	.161-.201	4-Rad.	.562	.290	1.1	3.3	.687	.415	.255	1.4	4.4	.812	.540	.330	1.7	5.2
8-241	.201-.241	1-Circ.	.625	.310	1.2	3.6	.875	.560	.290	1.8	5.5	.875	.560	.290	1.8	5.5
8-281	.241-.281	2-Circ.	.687	.325	1.1	3.2	.875	.515	.290	1.8	5.4	.875	.515	.290	1.8	5.4
8-321	.281-.321	3-Circ.	.687	.295	1.2	3.8	.875	.485	.300	1.7	5.2	.875	.485	.300	1.7	5.2
10-116	.065-.116	Blank	.578	.395	1.4	4.3	.828	.645	.395	2.2	6.7	.828	.645	.395	2.2	6.7
10-166	.116-.166	1-Rad.	.625	.385	1.5	4.6	.875	.635	.385	2.3	6.9	.875	.635	.385	2.3	6.9
10-216	.166-.216	2-Rad.	.687	.400	1.6	4.9	.938	.650	.400	2.4	7.2	.938	.650	.400	2.4	7.2
10-266	.216-.266	3-Rad.	.734	.390	1.7	5.1	.984	.640	.390	2.5	7.5	.984	.640	.390	2.5	7.5
10-316	.266-.316	4-Rad.	.781	.385	1.8	5.4	1.031	.635	.385	2.5	7.7	1.031	.635	.385	2.5	7.7
10-366	.316-.366	5-Rad.	.844	.400	1.9	5.7	1.094	.650	.400	2.6	8.0	1.094	.650	.400	2.6	8.0
25-151	.089-.151	Blank	.687	.440	3.2	9.8	1.000	.750	.435	5.0	15.1	1.000	.750	.435	5.0	15.1
25-211	.151-.211	1-Rad.	.750	.440	3.4	10.3	1.062	.750	.435	5.2	15.7	1.062	.750	.435	5.2	15.7
25-271	.211-.271	2-Rad.	.812	.440	3.6	10.9	1.125	.750	.435	5.4	16.3	1.125	.750	.435	5.4	16.3
25-331	.271-.331	3-Rad.	.875	.435	3.8	11.5	1.187	.750	.435	5.5	16.9	1.187	.750	.435	5.5	16.9
25-391	.331-.391	4-Rad.	.937	.435	4.0	12.1	1.250	.750	.435	5.7	17.5	1.250	.750	.435	5.7	17.5
25-451	.391-.451	5-Rad.	1.000	.445	4.2	12.7	1.312	.760	.445	5.9	18.1	1.312	.760	.445	5.9	18.1
31-181	.106-.181	Blank	.844	.540	5.9	17.8	1.218	.915	.540	9.0	27.5	1.218	.915	.540	9.0	27.5
31-256	.181-.256	1-Rad.	.937	.560	6.3	19.3	1.312	.935	.560	9.5	28.9	1.312	.935	.560	9.5	29.0
31-331	.256-.331	2-Rad.	1.000	.550	6.6	20.1	1.406	.955	.550	10.0	30.4	1.406	.955	.550	10.0	30.5
31-406	.331-.406	3-Rad.	1.093	.565	7.1	21.5	1.468	.940	.565	10.2	31.1	1.468	.940	.565	10.2	31.2
31-481	.406-.481	4-Rad.	1.156	.555	7.3	22.3	1.562	.960	.555	10.7	32.6	1.562	.960	.555	10.8	32.7
31-556	.481-.556	5-Rad.	1.250	.575	7.8	23.7	1.625	.950	.575	10.9	33.3	1.625	.950	.575	11.0	33.4
37-211	.125-.211	Blank	.938	.580	8.9	27.0	1.375	1.020	.655	13.9	42.3	1.375	1.020	.655	13.9	42.4
37-296	.211-.296	1-Rad.	1.031	.590	9.4	28.7	1.468	1.030	.655	14.5	44.1	1.468	1.030	.655	14.5	44.1
37-381	.296-.381	2-Rad.	1.125	.600	10.0	30.5	1.562	1.040	.675	15.0	45.8	1.562	1.040	.675	15.1	45.9
37-466	.381-.466	3-Rad.	1.219	.615	10.6	32.3	1.656	1.050	.690	15.6	47.6	1.656	1.050	.690	15.7	47.7
37-551	.466-.551	4-Rad.	1.312	.625	11.2	34.0	1.750	1.065	.705	16.2	49.4	1.750	1.065	.705	16.2	49.5
37-636	.551-.636	5-Rad.	1.422	.650	11.9	36.2	1.859	1.090	.715	16.9	51.6	1.859	1.090	.715	17.0	51.7
50-276	.156-.276	Blank	1.188	.725	18.4	56.1	1.781	1.320	.850	29.5	89.9	1.781	1.320	.850	29.5	90.0
50-396	.276-.396	1-Rad.	1.312	.730	19.7	60.0	1.906	1.325	.865	30.8	93.7	1.906	1.325	.865	30.8	93.9
50-516	.396-.516	2-Rad.	1.438	.735	21.0	63.9	2.031	1.330	.880	32.0	97.6	2.031	1.330	.880	32.1	97.7
50-636	.516-.636	3-Rad.	1.578	.750	22.5	68.5	2.172	1.350	.890	33.6	102.3	2.172	1.350	.890	33.6	102.4
50-756	.636-.756	4-Rad.	1.718	.765	24.0	73.1	2.312	1.360	.900	35.1	106.9	2.312	1.360	.900	35.1	107.0
50-876	.756-.876	5-Rad.	1.843	.780	25.3	77.1	2.437	1.375	.930	36.3	110.8	2.437	1.375	.930	36.4	110.9

GENERAL DESIGN
for Utilizing the unique,

DOUBLE SHEAR STRENGTH will be the determining factor in specifying the Rollpin size for a given stress in numerous applications. These values, for carbon steel and corrosion resistant steel Rollpins, are given in the table on Pages 14 and 16.

In soft metals ultimate failure depends more upon the strength of the hole material than upon shear strength of the Rollpin. Under increased load, hole edges are deformed by compressive forces. At ultimate loads the soft material may be expected to fail before the Rollpin.

In many cases, particularly with smaller mechanisms, the choice of Rollpin sizes will be influenced by space considerations and by general proportions of related members. Recommended practices are given in the accompanying tables.

As with other types of pins, good Rollpin design practice is to avoid conditions where the direction of vibration parallels the axis of the pin. For most applications the Rollpin's capacity to withstand the loosening effects of vibration can be consistently relied upon; however, unusual conditions can result in an axial vibration component that should be carefully evaluated. In such instances accelerated vibration tests should be made of prototypes of the proposed design. ESNA will be glad to provide sample Rollpins for such tests.

EFFECT OF GAP ORIENTATION ON ROLLPIN SHEAR STRENGTH

Data obtained in tests made to determine the effect of gap orientation on Rollpin shear strength revealed that random slot positioning is satisfactory for all but the most extreme Rollpin applications. For special applications maximum shear strength is assured by inserting the Rollpin so the gap is in line with the direction of the load.

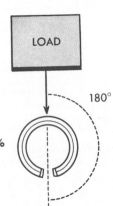

LOAD 90°

SHEAR VALUE — 100%

LOAD 180°

SHEAR VALUE — 106%

Double shear strength figures listed on Page 14 are based on tests made in accordance with Spec. MIL-P-10971 with pins in 90° position fastened in hardened steel fixtures.

RECOMMENDED ROLLPIN SIZES FOR VARIOUS SHAFT DIAMETERS

When used as a Transverse Pin

When used as a Longitudinal Key

When used as a Replacement for Taper Pins

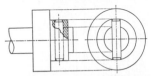

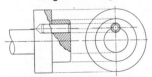

D Shaft Diameter Inches	d Rollpin Nominal Diameter, Inches	Rollpin Size Number
3/16	1/16	062
7/32	5/64	078
1/4	3/32	094
5/16-3/8	1/8	125
7/16-1/2	5/32	156
9/16 & 5/8	3/16	187
11/16 & 3/4	7/32	219
13/16	1/4	250
7/8	5/16	312
1	3/8	375
1-1/4	7/16	437
1-1/2	1/2	500

D Shaft Diameter, Inches	d Rollpin Nominal Diameter, Inches	Rollpin Size Number
1/4	1/16	062
5/16	5/64	078
3/8	3/32	094
7/16-1/2	1/8	125
9/16-5/8	5/32	156
11/16-3/4	3/16	187
7/8	7/32	219
15/16-1	1/4	250
1-1/4	5/16	312
1-3/8	3/8	375
1-1/2 - 1-5/8	7/16	437
2	1/2	500

EQUIVALENT TAPER PINS

Taper Pin Number	Equivalent Rollpin	
	Nominal Diameter, Inches	Rollpin Size Number
7/0	1/16	062
6/0	5/64	078
5/0	3/32	094
4/0	1/8	125
3/0	1/8	125
2/0	5/32	156
0	5/32	156
1	3/16	187
2	3/16	187
3	7/32	219
4	1/4	250
5	5/16	312
6	3/8	375
7	7/16	437
8	1/2	500

PRINCIPLES

inherent ROLLPIN advantages

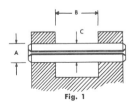

Fig. 1

Because of the inherent flexibility of the Rollpin it has found wide acceptance as a clevis joint pin. It is recommended, for greater bearing area, that the Rollpin be held by the outer members of the clevis (Fig. 1). However, the design may require that the inner member of the clevis (Fig. 2) be used to retain the pin. This alternate technique will also provide satisfactory performance results. The table below gives the average Rollpin spring back data relative to the span length.

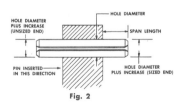

Fig. 2

BLACK — Minimum Hole | **Fig. 1** | RED — Maximum Hole

NOMINAL ROLLPIN DIAMETER	(A) HOLE DIAMETER	C — Rollpin Diameter at Center of Clevis Span — Thousandths / B — Span Length — Inches													
		1/8	1/4	3/8	1/2	5/8	3/4	7/8	1	1¼	1½	1¾	2	2½	3
.062	.062	.063	.065	.065	.065	.065									
	.065	.066	.067	.067	.067	.067	.067								
.078	.078	.079	.079	.079	.079	.079	.079								
	.081	.083	.084	.084	.084	.084	.084								
.094	.094	.096	.097	.098	.098	.098	.098								
	.097	.097	.097	.099	.099	.099	.099	.099							
.125	.125	.127	.129	.129	.130	.130	.130	.131	.131						
	.129	.129	.130	.130	.130	.131	.131	.131	.131						
.156	.156	.158	.159	.160	.161	.162	.162	.163	.163	.163	.163				
	.160	.160	.161	.161	.162	.162	.162	.163	.163	.163	.163				
.187	.187	.188	.189	.190	.191	.192	.193	.194	.195	.195	.195	.195	.195		
	.192	.192	.193	.193	.194	.194	.194	.195	.195	.195	.195	.195	.195		
.219	.219	.220	.221	.222	.223	.223	.224	.225	.225	.226	.226	.226	.226		
	.224	.224	.225	.225	.225	.225	.226	.226	.226	.226	.226	.226	.226		
.250	.250	.252	.254	.255	.256	.256	.257	.258	.258	.259	.260	.260	.260		
	.256	.257	.258	.258	.259	.259	.260	.260	.260	.260	.260	.260	.260		
.312	.312	.313	.313	.313	.314	.315	.315	.316	.317	.317	.318	.319	.320	.321	.321
	.318	.319	.319	.319	.319	.319	.319	.320	.320	.320	.320	.320	.321	.321	.321
.375	.375	.376	.376	.376	.376	.377	.378	.379	.380	.382	.383	.384	.384	.385	.385
	.382	.383	.383	.383	.383	.383	.383	.384	.384	.384	.384	.385	.385	.385	.385
.500	.500	.501	.502	.502	.503	.504	.504	.505	.506	.507	.508	.510	.512	.514	.514
	.510	.511	.511	.511	.512	.512	.512	.512	.513	.513	.513	.514	.514	.514	.514

Black-unsized end | **Fig. 2** | Red-Sized end

(Each cell shows black-unsized value / red-sized value)

		1/8	1/4	3/8	1/2	5/8	3/4	7/8	1	1¼	1½	2
.062	.062	.066 / .063	.068 / .064	.068 / .064	.068 / .064	.068 / .064	.068 / .064					
	.065	.067 / .066	.067 / .067	.067 / .067	.067 / .067	.067 / .067	.067 / .067					
.078	.078	.081 / .080	.083 / .080	.083 / .080	.083 / .080	.083 / .080	.083 / .080					
	.081	.083 / .083	.084 / .083	.084 / .083	.084 / .083	.084 / .083	.084 / .083					
.094	.094	.098 / .095	.100 / .097	.101 / .098	.101 / .098	.101 / .098	.101 / .098					
	.097	.099 / .098	.101 / .099	.101 / .099	.101 / .099	.101 / .099	.101 / .099					
.125	.125	.128 / .126	.130 / .127	.131 / .127	.131 / .128	.132 / .128	.132 / .128					
	.129	.130 / .130	.131 / .131	.131 / .131	.132 / .132	.132 / .132	.132 / .132					
.156	.156	.160 / .159	.161 / .159	.161 / .160	.161 / .160	.162 / .160	.162 / .161	.163 / .161	.163 / .161			
	.160	.162 / .162	.163 / .163	.163 / .163	.163 / .163	.163 / .163	.163 / .163	.163 / .163	.163 / .163			
.187	.187	.190 / .188	.192 / .189	.194 / .190	.195 / .191	.195 / .191	.195 / .191	.195 / .191	.195 / .191			
	.192	.194 / .193	.195 / .194	.195 / .194	.195 / .195	.195 / .195	.195 / .195	.195 / .195	.195 / .195			
.219	.219	.223 / .221	.225 / .222	.226 / .224	.227 / .225	.227 / .225	.228 / .226	.228 / .226	.228 / .226			
	.224	.225 / .225	.226 / .226	.227 / .226	.227 / .227	.227 / .227	.227 / .227	.227 / .227	.227 / .227			
.250	.250	.252 / .251	.253 / .252	.255 / .253	.257 / .254	.258 / .255	.258 / .255	.258 / .256	.259 / .256	.259 / .256	.259 / .256	.259
	.256	.257 / .257	.258 / .258	.259 / .259	.259 / .259	.260 / .259	.260 / .260	.260 / .260	.260 / .260	.260 / .260	.260 / .260	.260
.312	.312	.316 / .314	.319 / .316	.320 / .318	.322 / .319	.323 / .320	.324 / .320	.325 / .321	.325 / .321	.325 / .321	.325 / .321	.325
	.318	.319 / .319	.322 / .320	.323 / .321	.324 / .321	.324 / .322	.325 / .322	.325 / .322	.325 / .322	.325 / .322	.325 / .322	.325
.375	.375	.378 / .376	.380 / .378	.384 / .380	.385 / .381	.386 / .383	.387 / .384	.388 / .385	.388 / .385	.389 / .385	.389 / .385	.389 / .385
	.382	.384 / .383	.385 / .384	.386 / .385	.386 / .385	.387 / .386	.387 / .386	.388 / .387	.388 / .387	.389 / .387	.389 / .387	.389 / .387
.500	.500	.502 / .502	.503 / .502	.505 / .504	.506 / .505	.508 / .506	.509 / .507	.511 / .508	.512 / .509	.513 / .510	.514 / .510	.515 / .511
	.510	.511 / .511	.512 / .512	.513 / .513	.514 / .514	.514 / .514	.514 / .514	.515 / .515	.515 / .515	.515 / .515	.515 / .515	.515 / .515

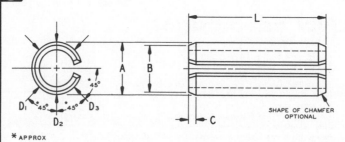

ESNA – FASTENER DIVISION

SHAPE OF CHAMFER OPTIONAL

* APPROX

TOLERANCE ON SPECIFIED LENGTH "L"
0.187 TO 1.000 ±.015
1.001 TO 2.000 ±.020
2.001 TO 3.000 ±.025
3.001 TO 4.000 ±.030
4.001 & ABOVE ±.035

A			B	C		STOCK THICKNESS	RECOMMENDED HOLE SIZE		MINIMUM DOUBLE SHEAR STRENGTH POUNDS
NOMINAL	MAXIMUM (GO RING GAGE)	MINIMUM 1/3(D₁+D₂+D₃)	MAX	MIN	MAX		MIN	MAX	
.062	.069	.066	.059	.007	.028	.012	.062	.065	425
.078	.086	.083	.075	.008	.032	.018	.078	.081	650
.094	.103	.099	.091	.008	.038	.022	.094	.097	1,000
.125	.135	.131	.122	.008	.044	.028	.125	.129	2,100
.140	.149	.145	.137	.008	.044	.028	.140	.144	2,200
.156	.167	.162	.151	.010	.048	.032	.156	.160	3,000
.187	.199	.194	.182	.011	.055	.040	.187	.192	4,400
.219	.232	.226	.214	.011	.065	.048	.219	.224	5,700
.250	.264	.258	.245	.012	.065	.048	.250	.256	7,700
.312	.328	.321	.306	.014	.080	.062	.312	.318	11,500
.375	.392	.385	.368	.016	.095	.077	.375	.382	17,600
.437	.456	.448	.430	.017	.095	.077	.437	.445	20,000
.500	.521	.513	.485	.025	.110	.094	.500	.510	25,800

CODE: PARTS ARE IDENTIFIED BY A SERIES OF DASH NUMBERS IN ACCORDANCE WITH THE EXAMPLE SHOWN BELOW.

EXAMPLE: 5 9 - 028 - 125 - 0750 = ROLLPIN, .125 DIA., .028 WALL, 3/4 LONG, PLAIN CARBON STEEL.

THIRD DASH NUMBER INDICATES LENGTH IN THOUSANDTHS OF AN INCH. PREFIX "O" IF LESS THAN ONE INCH.

SECOND DASH NUMBER INDICATES NOMINAL DIAMETER IN THOUSANDTHS OF AN INCH AND IS DETERMINED FROM "A-NOMINAL" COLUMN IN TABULATION ABOVE.

FIRST DASH NUMBER INDICATES WALL THICKNESS IN THOUSANDTHS OF AN INCH AND IS DETERMINED FROM "STOCK THICKNESS" COLUMN IN TABULATION ABOVE.

SECOND DIGIT INDICATES FINISH:
9 = PLAIN.
⑦ 3 = PHOSPHATE COATING, MIL SPEC MIL-C-16232(N Ord) TYPE Z.
2 = CADMIUM PLATE, FEDERAL SPEC QQ-P-416, TYPE 1, CLASS 3.
1 = ZINC PLATE, FEDERAL SPEC QQ-Z-325, TYPE 1, CLASS 3.

FIRST DIGIT INDICATES MATERIAL:
5 = HIGH CARBON STEEL.

FINISH: CARBON STEEL PINS ARE NORMALLY FURNISHED WITH A BLACK OILED FINISH.

HARDNESS: ROCKWELL "C" 46-53 OR EQUIVALENT.

ISSUED: 20 APR 50 REVISED: ⑦9 JAN 62

PERFORMANCE SPECIFICATION	ROLLPIN	RP-A
ESNA SPEC 401 (SEE NOTE: 1)	HIGH CARBON STEEL	PAGE 1 OF 2

PRINCIPLES

inherent ROLLPIN advantages

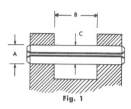

Fig. 1

Because of the inherent flexibility of the Rollpin it has found wide acceptance as a clevis joint pin. It is recommended, for greater bearing area, that the Rollpin be held by the outer members of the clevis (Fig. 1). However, the design may require that the inner member of the clevis (Fig. 2) be used to retain the pin. This alternate technique will also provide satisfactory performance results. The table below gives the average Rollpin spring back data relative to the span length.

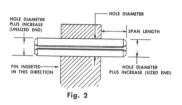

Fig. 2

BLACK — Minimum Hole   Fig. 1   RED — Maximum Hole

C — Rollpin Diameter at Center of Clevis Span —Thousandths
B — Span Length — Inches

NOMINAL ROLLPIN DIAMETER	(A) HOLE DIAMETER	1/8	1/4	3/8	1/2	5/8	3/4	7/8	1	1¼	1½	1¾	2	2½	3
.062	.062	.063	.065	.065	.065	.065									
	.065	.066	.067	.067	.067	.067									
.078	.078	.079	.079	.079	.079	.079	.079								
	.081	.083	.084	.084	.084	.084	.084								
.094	.094	.096	.097	.098	.098	.098	.098								
	.097	.097	.099	.099	.099	.099	.099								
.125	.125	.127	.129	.129	.130	.130	.130	.131	.131						
	.129	.129	.130	.130	.130	.131	.131	.131	.131						
.156	.156	.158	.159	.160	.161	.162	.162	.163	.163	.163	.163				
	.160	.160	.161	.161	.162	.162	.162	.163	.163	.163	.163				
.187	.187	.188	.189	.190	.191	.192	.193	.194	.195	.195	.195	.195	.195		
	.192	.192	.193	.193	.194	.194	.194	.195	.195	.195	.195	.195	.195		
.219	.219	.220	.221	.222	.223	.223	.224	.225	.225	.226	.226	.226	.226		
	.224	.224	.225	.225	.225	.225	.226	.226	.226	.226	.226	.226	.226		
.250	.250	.252	.254	.255	.256	.256	.257	.258	.258	.259	.260	.260	.260		
	.256	.257	.258	.258	.259	.259	.260	.260	.260	.260	.260	.260	.260		
.312	.312	.313	.313	.313	.314	.315	.315	.316	.317	.317	.318	.319	.320	.321	.321
	.318	.319	.319	.319	.319	.319	.319	.320	.320	.320	.320	.320	.321	.321	.321
.375	.375	.376	.376	.376	.376	.377	.378	.379	.380	.382	.383	.384	.384	.385	.385
	.382	.383	.383	.383	.383	.383	.383	.384	.384	.384	.384	.385	.385	.385	.385
.500	.500	.501	.502	.502	.503	.504	.504	.505	.506	.507	.508	.510	.512	.514	.514
	.510	.511	.511	.511	.512	.512	.512	.512	.513	.513	.513	.514	.514	.514	.514

Black-unsized end   Fig. 2   Red-Sized end

(Each span cell shows two values: Black-unsized end / Red-Sized end. Each nominal has a minimum-hole row and a maximum-hole row.)

Nominal	Hole	1/8	1/4	3/8	1/2	5/8	3/4	7/8	1	1¼	1½	2
.062	.062	.066 .063	.068 .064	.068 .064	.068 .064	.068 .064	.068 .064					
	.065	.067 .066	.067 .067	.067 .067	.067 .067	.067 .067	.067 .067					
.078	.078	.081 .080	.083 .080	.083 .080	.083 .080	.083 .080	.083 .080					
	.081	.083 .083	.084 .083	.084 .083	.084 .083	.084 .083	.084 .083					
.094	.094	.098 .095	.100 .097	.101 .098	.101 .098	.101 .098	.101 .098					
	.097	.099 .098	.101 .099	.101 .099	.101 .099	.101 .099	.101 .099					
.125	.125	.128 .126	.130 .127	.131 .127	.131 .128	.132 .128	.132 .128					
	.129	.130 .130	.131 .131	.131 .131	.132 .132	.132 .132	.132 .132					
.156	.156	.160 .159	.161 .159	.161 .160	.161 .160	.162 .160	.162 .161	.163 .161	.163 .161			
	.160	.162 .162	.163 .163	.163 .163	.163 .163	.163 .163	.163 .163	.163 .163	.163 .163			
.187	.187	.190 .188	.192 .189	.194 .190	.195 .191	.195 .191	.195 .191	.195 .191	.195 .191			
	.192	.194 .193	.195 .194	.195 .194	.195 .195	.195 .195	.195 .195	.195 .195	.195 .195			
.219	.219	.223 .221	.225 .222	.226 .224	.227 .225	.227 .225	.228 .226	.228 .226	.228 .226			
	.224	.225 .225	.226 .226	.227 .226	.227 .227	.227 .227	.227 .227	.227 .227	.227 .227			
.250	.250	.252 .251	.253 .252	.255 .253	.257 .254	.258 .255	.258 .255	.258 .256	.259 .256	.259 .256	.259 .256	.259
	.256	.257 .257	.258 .258	.259 .259	.259 .259	.260 .259	.260 .260	.260 .260	.260 .260	.260 .260	.260 .260	.260
.312	.312	.316 .314	.319 .316	.320 .318	.322 .319	.323 .320	.324 .321	.325 .321	.325 .321	.325 .321	.325 .321	.325
	.318	.320 .319	.322 .320	.323 .321	.324 .321	.324 .322	.325 .322	.325 .322	.325 .322	.325 .322	.325 .322	.325
.375	.375	.378 .376	.380 .378	.384 .380	.385 .381	.386 .383	.387 .384	.388 .385	.388 .385	.389 .385	.389 .385	.389 .385
	.382	.384 .383	.384 .384	.386 .385	.386 .385	.387 .386	.387 .386	.388 .387	.388 .387	.389 .387	.389 .387	.389 .387
.500	.500	.502 .502	.503 .502	.505 .504	.506 .505	.508 .506	.509 .507	.511 .508	.512 509	.513 .510	.514 .510	.515 .511
	.510	.511 .511	.512 .512	.513 .513	.514 .514	.514 .514	.514 .514	.515 .515	.515 .515	.515 .515	.515 .515	.515 .515

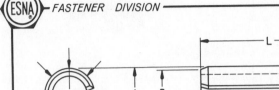

ESNA — FASTENER DIVISION

TOLERANCE ON SPECIFIED
LENGTH "L"
0.187 TO 1.000 ±.015
1.001 TO 2.000 ±.020
2.001 TO 3.000 ±.025
3.001 TO 4.000 ±.030
4.001 & ABOVE ±.035

SHAPE OF CHAMFER
OPTIONAL

* APPROX

| NOMINAL | A | | B | C | | STOCK THICKNESS | RECOMMENDED HOLE SIZE | | MINIMUM DOUBLE SHEAR STRENGTH POUNDS |
	MAXIMUM (GO RING GAGE)	MINIMUM $1/3(D_1+D_2+D_3)$	MAX	MIN	MAX		MIN	MAX	
.062	.069	.066	.059	.007	.028	.012	.062	.065	425
.078	.086	.083	.075	.008	.032	.018	.078	.081	650
.094	.103	.099	.091	.008	.038	.022	.094	.097	1,000
.125	.135	.131	.122	.008	.044	.028	.125	.129	2,100
.140	.149	.145	.137	.008	.044	.028	.140	.144	2,200
.156	.167	.162	.151	.010	.048	.032	.156	.160	3,000
.187	.199	.194	.182	.011	.055	.040	.187	.192	4,400
.219	.232	.226	.214	.011	.065	.048	.219	.224	5,700
.250	.264	.258	.245	.012	.065	.048	.250	.256	7,700
.312	.328	.321	.306	.014	.080	.062	.312	.318	11,500
.375	.392	.385	.368	.016	.095	.077	.375	.382	17,600
.437	.456	.448	.430	.017	.095	.077	.437	.445	20,000
.500	.521	.513	.485	.025	.110	.094	.500	.510	25,800

CODE: PARTS ARE IDENTIFIED BY A SERIES OF DASH NUMBERS IN ACCORDANCE WITH THE EXAMPLE SHOWN BELOW.

EXAMPLE: 5 9 - 028 - 125 - 0750 = ROLLPIN, .125 DIA., .028 WALL, 3/4 LONG, PLAIN CARBON STEEL.

THIRD DASH NUMBER INDICATES LENGTH IN THOUSANDTHS OF AN INCH.
PREFIX "O" IF LESS THAN ONE INCH.

SECOND DASH NUMBER INDICATES NOMINAL DIAMETER IN THOUSANDTHS OF AN INCH AND IS DETERMINED FROM "A-NOMINAL" COLUMN IN TABULATION ABOVE.

FIRST DASH NUMBER INDICATES WALL THICKNESS IN THOUSANDTHS OF AN INCH AND IS DETERMINED FROM "STOCK THICKNESS" COLUMN IN TABULATION ABOVE.

SECOND DIGIT INDICATES FINISH:
9 = PLAIN.
(7) 3 = PHOSPHATE COATING, MIL SPEC MIL-C-16232(N Ord) TYPE Z.
2 = CADMIUM PLATE, FEDERAL SPEC QQ-P-416, TYPE 1, CLASS 3.
1 = ZINC PLATE, FEDERAL SPEC QQ-Z-325, TYPE 1, CLASS 3.

FIRST DIGIT INDICATES MATERIAL:
5 = HIGH CARBON STEEL.

FINISH: CARBON STEEL PINS ARE NORMALLY FURNISHED WITH A BLACK OILED FINISH.

HARDNESS: ROCKWELL "C" 46-53 OR EQUIVALENT.

ISSUED: 20 APR 50 REVISED: (7) 9 JAN 62

PERFORMANCE SPECIFICATION	ROLLPIN	RP-A
ESNA SPEC 401 (SEE NOTE: 1)	HIGH CARBON STEEL	PAGE 1 OF 2

ELASTIC STOP NUT CORPORATION OF AMERICA, 2330 VAUXHALL ROAD, UNION, NEW JERSEY.

— FASTENER DIVISION ————————————————

NOTE 1. CARBON STEEL ROLLPINS MEET THE REQUIREMENTS OF THE FOLLOWING:
SPECIFICATIONS: MIL-P-10971, AMS 7205.
STANDARDS: ARMY ORDNANCE DRAWINGS BFSX2 AND BFSX2.1
NAVY DRAWINGS NAVORD OSTD 600, PAGES 5-6.11 TO 5-6.13
MS9047(ASG), MS9048(ASG), MSI6562, NAS561

PLAIN CARBON STEEL ROLLPIN AVAILABILITY
NOMINAL DIAMETER

```
LENGTH    .062  .078  .094  .125  .140  .156  .187  .219  .250  .312  .375  .437  .500
0.125"...  *
0.187 ...  *     *     *
0.250 ...  *     *     *     *     Δ     *
0.312 ...  *     *     *     *     Δ     *     *
0.375 ...  *     *     *     *     Δ     *     *     *     *
0.437 ...  *     *     *     *     Δ     *     *     *     *     *
0.500 ...  *     *     *     *     Δ     *     *     *     *     *     *
0.562 ...  *     *     *     *     Δ     *     *     *     *     *     *
0.625 ...  *     *     *     *     Δ     *     *     *     *     Δ     *
0.687 ...  *     *     *     *     Δ     *     *     *     *     Δ     Δ
0.750 ...  *     *     *     *     *     *     *     *     *     *     *     Δ     *
0.812 ...  *     *     *     *     *     *     *     *     *     *     Δ     Δ     Δ
0.875 ...  *     *     *     *     *     *     *     *     *     *     Δ     *
0.937 ...  *     *     *     *     *     *     *     *     *     *     Δ     Δ
1.000 ...  *     *     *     *     *     *     *     *     *     *     *     *
1.125 ...  *     *     *     *     *     *     *     *     *     *     Δ     *
1.250 ...  Δ     *     *     *     *     *     *     *     *     *     *     *
1.375 ...  *     *     *     *     *     *     *     *     *     *     Δ     *
1.500 ...        *     *     *     Δ     *     *     *     *     *     *     *
1.625 ...        Δ     Δ     *     Δ     *     *     *     *     *     *     *
1.750 ...        Δ     Δ     *     Δ     *     *     *     *     *     *     *
1.875 ...        Δ     Δ     Δ     Δ     *     *     *     *     *     Δ     *
2.000 ...        Δ     Δ     *     Δ     *     *     *     *     *     *     *
2.250 ...              *     Δ     *     *     *     *     *     *     *     *
2.500 ...              Δ     Δ     *     *     *     *     *     *     *     *
2.750 ...                    *     Δ     Δ     *     *     *     *     *
3.000 ...                          Δ     Δ     Δ     *     *     *     *     *
3.250 ...                          Δ     Δ     *     *     *     *     Δ     *
3.500 ...                          Δ     Δ     *     *     *     *     *
3.750 ...                          Δ     Δ     Δ     Δ     *     *     Δ     *
4.000 ...                          Δ     Δ     Δ     *     *     *     *     *
4.250 ...                          Δ     Δ     Δ     Δ     Δ     Δ     Δ     Δ
4.500 ...                          Δ     Δ     Δ     Δ     Δ     Δ     Δ     *
4.750 ...                          Δ     Δ     Δ     Δ     Δ     Δ     Δ     Δ
5.000 ...                          Δ     Δ     Δ     Δ     *     Δ     *
5.250 ...                                                  Δ     Δ     Δ
5.500 ...                                                  Δ     Δ     Δ
```

ESNA AVAILABILITY CODE:
* - STANDARD PARTS NORMALLY CARRIED IN STOCK.
Δ - STANDARD PARTS NOT ALWAYS CARRIED IN INVENTORY AND ON WHICH IT MAY BE NECESSARY TO REQUIRE MINIMUM ECONOMICAL RUNS.

IN ADDITION TO THE STOCK LENGTHS APPEARING IN THIS TABLE, ROLLPINS LESS THAN 1" LONG CAN BE MADE AVAILABLE IN LENGTH INCREMENTS OF 1/32". ROLLPINS LONGER THAN 1" CAN BE MADE AVAILABLE IN LENGTH INCREMENTS OF 1/16", BUT IN BOTH CASES SUCH PARTS ARE NON-STOCK ITEMS AND MUST BE MADE TO ORDER. ROLLPINS OF SPECIAL DECIMAL LENGTHS ARE SUBJECT TO SPECIAL ORDER REQUIREMENTS.

ISSUED: 20 APR 50 REVISED: (7) 9 JAN 62

PERFORMANCE SPECIFICATION	ROLLPIN	RP-A
ESNA SPEC 401 (SEE NOTE: 1)	HIGH CARBON STEEL	PAGE 2 OF 2

ELASTIC STOP NUT CORPORATION OF AMERICA, 2330 VAUXHALL ROAD, UNION, NEW JERSEY.

BASIC
internal series
N5000

WALDES
TRUARC
RETAINING
RINGS

U.S. Pat. No. 2,861,824

See Fig. 2, Page 27

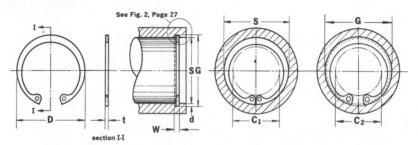

section I-I

● Sizes identified by this symbol
are available in tape-wrapped
Rol-Pak ® cartridges.

HOUSING DIA.				TRUARC RING DIMENSIONS					GROOVE DIMENSIONS					APPLICATION DATA			
			MIL-R-21248 MS 16625 NAS 669 **INTERNAL SERIES N5000**	Thickness t applies only to unplated rings. For **plated** and **stainless steel** (Type H) rings, add .002" to the listed maximum thickness. Maximum ring thickness will be at least .0002" less than the listed minimum groove width (**W**).					T.I.R. (total indicator reading) is the maximum allowable deviation of concentricity between groove and housing.					CLEARANCE DIAMETER		ALLOW. THRUST LOAD (lbs.) Sharp Corner Abutment	
								Approx. weight per 1000 pieces					Nominal groove depth	When sprung into housing S	When sprung into groove G	RINGS Safety factor = 4 Important! See Page 19	GROOVES Safety factor = 2 Important! See Page 19
Dec. equiv. inch	Approx. fract. equiv. inch	Approx. mm.	size—no.	FREE DIA.		THICKNESS			DIAMETER		WIDTH						
S	S	S		D	tol.	t	tol.	lbs.	G	tol.	W	tol.	d	C₁	C₂	Pᵣ	P_g
.250	¼	6.4	● N5000-25	.280		.015		.08	.268	±.001 .0015	.018	+.002	.009	.115	.133	420	190
.312	5⁄16	7.9	● N5000-31	.346		.015		.11	.330	±T.I.R.	.018	−.000	.009	.173	.191	530	240
.375	⅜	9.5	● N5000-37	.415		.025		.25	.397	±.002	.029		.011	.204	.226	1050	350
.438	7⁄16	11.1	● N5000-43	.482		.025		.37	.461	.002	.029		.012	.23	.254	1220	440
.453	29⁄64	11.5	● N5000-45	.498		.025		.43	.477	T.I.R.	.029		.012	.25	.274	1280	460
.500	½	12.7	● N5000-50	.548	+.010 −.005	.035		.70	.530		.039		.015	.26	.29	1980	510
.512	—	13.0	● N5000-51	.560		.035		.77	.542	±.002 .004 T.I.R.	.039		.015	.27	.30	2030	520
.562	9⁄16	14.3	● N5000-56	.620		.035		.86	.596		.039		.017	.275	.305	2220	710
.625	⅝	15.9	● N5000-62	.694		.035		1.0	.665		.039		.020	.34	.38	2470	1050
.688	11⁄16	17.5	● N5000-68	.763		.035		1.2	.732		.039	+.003 −.000	.022	.40	.44	2700	1280
.750	¾	19.0	● N5000-75	.831		.035		1.3	.796		.039		.023	.45	.49	3000	1460
.777	—	19.7	● N5000-77	.859		.042		1.7	.825		.046		.024	.475	.52	4550	1580
.812	13⁄16	20.6	● N5000-81	.901		.042		1.9	.862		.046		.025	.49	.54	4800	1710
.866	—	22.0	● N5000-86	.961		.042		2.0	.920		.046		.027	.54	.59	5100	1980
.875	⅞	22.2	● N5000-87	.971	+.015 −.010	.042	±.002	2.1	.931	±.003 .004 T.I.R.	.046		.028	.545	.60	5150	2080
.901	—	22.9	● N5000-90	1.000		.042		2.2	.959		.046		.029	.565	.62	5350	2200
.938	15⁄16	23.8	● N5000-93	1.041		.042		2.4	1.000		.046		.031	.61	.67	5600	2450
1.000	1	25.4	● N5000-100	1.111		.042		2.7	1.066		.046		.033	.665	.73	5950	2800
1.023	—	26.0	● N5000-102	1.136		.042		2.8	1.091		.046		.034	.69	.755	6050	3000
1.062	1 1⁄16	27.0	● N5000-106	1.180		.050		3.7	1.130		.056		.034	.685	.75	7450	3050
1.125	1⅛	28.6	● N5000-112	1.249		.050		4.0	1.197		.056		.036	.745	.815	7900	3400
1.181	—	30.0	● N5000-118	1.319		.050		4.3	1.255		.056		.037	.79	.86	8400	3700
1.188	1 3⁄16	30.2	● N5000-118	1.319		.050		4.3	1.262		.056		.037	.80	.87	8400	3700
1.250	1¼	31.7	● N5000-125	1.388		.050		4.8	1.330		.056		.040	.875	.955	8800	4250
1.259	—	32.0	● N5000-125	1.388	+.025 −.020	.050		4.8	1.339		.056		.040	.885	.965	8800	4250
1.312	1 5⁄16	33.3	● N5000-131	1.456		.050		5.0	1.396		.056		.042	.93	1.01	9300	4700
1.375	1⅜	34.9	● N5000-137	1.526		.050		5.1	1.461	±.004 .005 T.I.R.	.056		.043	.99	1.07	9700	5050
1.378	—	35.0	● N5000-137	1.526		.050		5.1	1.464		.056	+.004 −.000	.043	.99	1.07	9700	5050
1.438	1 7⁄16	36.5	● N5000-143	1.596		.050		5.8	1.528		.056		.045	1.06	1.15	10200	5500
1.456	—	37.0	● N5000-145	1.616		.050		6.4	1.548		.056		.046	1.08	1.17	10300	5700
1.500	1½	38.1	● N5000-150	1.660		.050		6.5	1.594		.056		.047	1.12	1.21	10550	6000
1.562	1 9⁄16	39.7	● N5000-156	1.734		.062		8.1	1.658		.068		.048	1.14	1.23	13700	6350
1.575	—	40.0	● N5000-156	1.734	+.035 −.025	.062	±.003	8.1	1.671	±.005 .005 T.I.R.	.068		.048	1.15	1.24	13700	6350
1.625	1⅝	41.3	● N5000-162	1.804		.062		10.0	1.725		.068		.050	1.15	1.25	14200	6900
1.653	—	42.0	● N5000-165	1.835		.062		10.4	1.755		.068		.051	1.17	1.27	14500	7200
1.688	1 11⁄16	42.9	● N5000-168	1.874		.062		10.8	1.792		.068		.052	1.21	1.31	14800	7450

Additional sizes appear on Pages 28 and 30

WALDES **TRUARC** RETAINING RINGS

BASIC *internal series* **N5000**

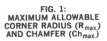

FIG. 1:
MAXIMUM ALLOWABLE
CORNER RADIUS (R_max.)
AND CHAMFER (Ch_max.)

R_max.

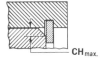

CH_max.

FIG. 2:
ENLARGED DETAIL
OF GROOVE PROFILE
AND EDGE MARGIN (Z)

MAXIMUM BOTTOM RADII	
Ring Size	R
·25 thru ·100	.005
·102 thru ·1000	.010

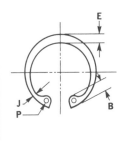

FIG. 3:
SUPPLEMENTARY
RING DIMENSIONS

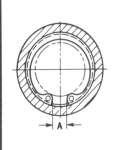

FIG. 4:
MINIMUM GAP WIDTH
(Ring installed in groove)

	SUPPLEMENTARY APPLICATION DATA				SUPPLEMENTARY RING DIMENSIONS							
INTERNAL SERIES **N5000**	Maximum allowable corner radii and chamfers of retained parts (Fig. 1). See Page 21.		Allowable assembly load with R_max. or Ch_max.	Edge margin (Fig. 2) See Page 19	LUG		LARGE SECTION		SMALL SECTION		HOLE DIAMETER		MIN. GAP WIDTH (Fig. 4) Ring installed in groove
size—no.	R_max.	Ch_max.	P'_r (lbs.)	Z	B	tol.	E	tol.	J	tol.	P	tol.	A
• N5000-25	.011	.0085	190	.027	.065		.025	±.002	.015	±.002	.031		.047
• N5000-31	.016	.013	190	.027	.066		.033		.018		.031		.055
• N5000-37	.023	.018	530	.033	.082		.040		.028		.041		.063
• N5000-43	.027	.021	530	.036	.098	±.003	.049	±.003	.029	±.003	.041		.063
• N5000-45	.027	.021	530	.036	.098		.050		.030		.047		.071
• N5000-50	.027	.021	1100	.045	.114		.053		.035		.047		.090
• N5000-51	.027	.021	1100	.045	.114		.053		.035		.047		.092
• N5000-56	.027	.021	1100	.051	.132		.053		.035		.047		.095
• N5000-62	.027	.021	1100	.060	.132		.060	±.004	.035	±.004	.062		.104
• N5000-68	.027	.021	1100	.066	.132		.063		.036		.062	+.010 −.002	.118
• N5000-75	.032	.025	1100	.069	.142		.070		.040		.062		.143
• N5000-77	.035	.028	1650	.072	.146		.074		.044		.062		.145
• N5000-81	.035	.028	1650	.075	.155		.077		.044		.062		.153
• N5000-86	.035	.028	1650	.081	.155		.081		.045		.062		.172
• N5000-87	.035	.028	1650	.084	.155		.084	±.005	.045	±.005	.062		.179
• N5000-90	.038	.030	1650	.087	.155		.087		.047		.062		.188
• N5000-93	.038	.030	1650	.093	.155		.091		.050		.062		.200
• N5000-100	.042	.034	2400	.099	.155		.104		.052		.062		.212
• N5000-102	.042	.034	2400	.102	.155		.106		.054		.062		.220
• N5000-106	.044	.035	2400	.102	.180		.110		.055		.078		.213
• N5000-112	.047	.036	2400	.108	.180	±.005	.116		.057		.078		.232
(S=1.181) • N5000-118	.047	.036	2400	.111	.180		.120		.058		.078		.226
(S=1.188) • N5000-118	.047	.036	2400	.111	.180		.120		.058		.078		.245
(S=1.250) • N5000-125	.048	.038	2400	.120	.180		.124		.062		.078		.265
(S=1.259) • N5000-125	.048	.038	2400	.120	.180		.124	±.006	.062	±.006	.078		.290
• N5000-131	.048	.038	2400	.126	.180		.130		.062		.078		.284
(S=1.375) • N5000-137	.048	.038	2400	.129	.180		.130		.063		.078	+.015 −.002	.297
(S=1.378) • N5000-137	.048	.038	2400	.129	.180		.130		.063		.078		.305
• N5000-143	.048	.038	2400	.135	.180		.133		.065		.078		.313
• N5000-145	.048	.038	2400	.138	.180		.133		.065		.078		.320
• N5000-150	.048	.038	2400	.141	.180		.133		.066		.078		.340
(S=1.562) • N5000-156	.064	.050	3900	.144	.202		.157		.078		.078		.338
(S=1.575) • N5000-156	.064	.050	3900	.144	.202		.157		.078		.078		.374
• N5000-162	.064	.050	3900	.150	.227		.164	±.007	.082	±.007	.078		.339
• N5000-165	.064	.050	3900	.153	.227		.167		.083		.078		.348
• N5000-168	.064	.050	3900	.156	.227		.170		.085		.078		.357

BASIC *internal series* **N5000** (Continued)

WALDES TRUARC RETAINING RINGS

U. S. Pat. No. 2,861,824

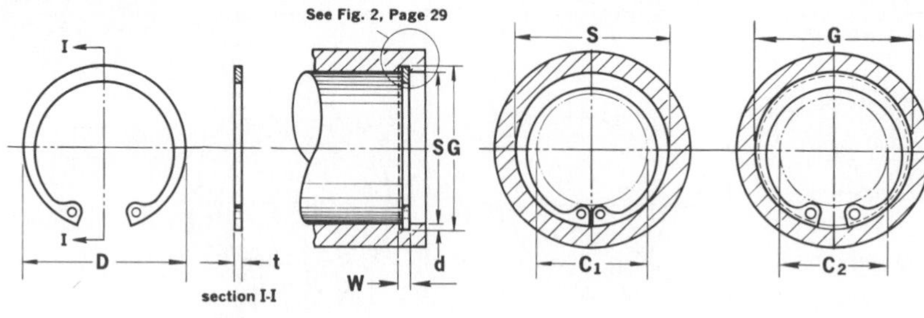

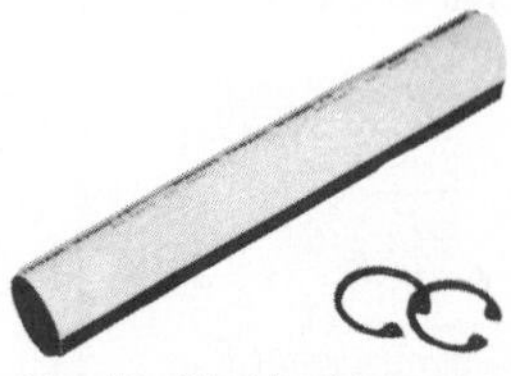

• Sizes identified by this symbol are available in tape-wrapped **Rol-Pak®** cartridges.

HOUSING DIA. Dec. equiv. inch	HOUSING DIA. Approx. fract. equiv. inch	HOUSING DIA. Approx. mm.	MIL-R-21248 MS 16625 NAS 669 INTERNAL SERIES N5000	TRUARC RING DIMENSIONS: FREE DIA.		THICKNESS		Approx. weight per 1000 pieces	GROOVE DIMENSIONS: DIAMETER		WIDTH		Nominal groove depth	CLEARANCE DIAMETER: When sprung into housing S	CLEARANCE DIAMETER: When sprung into groove G	ALLOW. THRUST LOAD (lbs.) Sharp Corner Abutment: RINGS Safety factor = 4 Important! See Page 19	GROOVES Safety factor = 2 Important! See Page 19
S	S	S	size—no.	D	tol.	t	tol.	lbs.	G	tol.	W	tol.	d	C_1	C_2	P_r	P_g
1.750	1 3/4	44.4	• N5000-175	1.942	+.035 −.025	.062	±.003	10.3	1.858	±.005 .005 T.I.R.	.068	+.004 −.000	.054	1.26	1.36	15350	8050
1.812	1 13/16	46.0	• N5000-181	2.012		.062		11.5	1.922		.068		.055	1.32	1.43	15900	8450
1.850	—	47.0	• N5000-185	2.054		.062		12.8	1.962		.068		.056	1.36	1.47	16200	8750
1.875	1 7/8	47.6	• N5000-187	2.072		.062		12.8	1.989		.068		.057	1.39	1.50	16450	9050
1.938	1 15/16	49.2	• N5000-193	2.141		.062		13.3	2.056		.068		.059	1.45	1.56	17000	9700
2.000	2	50.8	• N5000-200	2.210		.062		14.0	2.122		.068		.061	1.50	1.62	17500	10300
2.047	—	52.0	N5000-206	2.280	+.040 −.030	.078		18.0	2.171	±.006 .006 T.I.R.	.086	+.005 −.000	.062	1.52	1.64	22750	10850
2.062	2 1/16	52.4	N5000-206	2.280		.078		18.0	2.186		.086		.062	1.54	1.66	22750	10850
2.125	2 1/8	54.0	N5000-212	2.350		.078		19.4	2.251		.086		.063	1.58	1.70	23400	11350
2.165	—	55.0	N5000-218	2.415		.078		19.6	2.295		.086		.065	1.61	1.74	24100	12050
2.188	2 3/16	55.6	N5000-218	2.415		.078		19.6	2.318		.086		.065	1.64	1.77	24100	12050
2.250	2 1/4	57.1	N5000-225	2.490		.078		21.8	2.382		.086		.066	1.69	1.82	24850	12600
2.312	2 5/16	58.7	N5000-231	2.560		.078		22.6	2.450		.086		.069	1.75	1.88	25450	13550
2.375	2 3/8	60.3	N5000-237	2.630		.078		23.2	2.517		.086		.071	1.81	1.95	26150	14300
2.440	2 7/16	62.0	N5000-244	2.702		.078		25.4	2.584		.086		.072	1.86	2.00	26900	14900
2.500	2 1/2	63.5	N5000-250	2.775		.078		25.5	2.648		.086		.074	1.91	2.05	27600	15650
2.531	2 17/32	64.3	N5000-250	2.775		.078		25.5	2.681		.086		.075	1.94	2.09	27600	15650
2.562	2 9/16	65.1	N5000-256	2.844		.093		34.0	2.714		.103		.076	1.95	2.10	33700	16500
2.625	2 5/8	66.7	N5000-262	2.910		.093		34.5	2.781		.103		.078	2.02	2.17	34550	17350
2.677	—	68.0	N5000-268	2.980		.093		35.0	2.837		.103		.080	2.05	2.21	35400	18250
2.688	2 11/16	68.3	N5000-268	2.980		.093		35.0	2.848		.103		.080	2.06	2.22	35400	18250
2.750	2 3/4	69.8	N5000-275	3.050		.093		35.5	2.914		.103		.082	2.12	2.28	36100	19200
2.812	2 13/16	71.4	N5000-281	3.121		.093		36.0	2.980		.103		.084	2.18	2.34	36950	20050
2.835	—	72.0	N5000-281	3.121		.093		36.0	3.006		.103		.085	2.21	2.38	36950	20050
2.875	2 7/8	73.0	N5000-287	3.191		.093		41.0	3.051		.103		.088	2.22	2.39	37800	21500
2.953	—	75.0	N5000-300	3.325		.093		42.5	3.135		.103		.091	2.30	2.48	39500	23150
3.000	3	76.2	N5000-300	3.325		.093		42.5	3.182		.103		.091	2.35	2.53	39500	23150
3.062	3 1/16	77.8	N5000-306	3.418	±.055	.109		53.0	3.248		.120		.093	2.41	2.59	47100	24100
3.125	3 1/8	79.4	N5000-312	3.488		.109		56.0	3.315		.120		.095	2.47	2.66	48100	25200
3.149	—	80.0	N5000-315	3.523		.109		57.0	3.341		.120		.096	2.49	2.68	48600	25700
3.156	3 5/32	80.2	N5000-315	3.523		.109		57.0	3.348		.120		.096	2.50	2.69	48600	25700
3.250	3 1/4	82.5	N5000-325	3.623		.109		60.0	3.446		.120		.098	2.54	2.73	50000	27000
3.346	3 11/32	85.0	N5000-334	3.734		.109		65.0	3.546		.120		.100	2.63	2.83	51600	28300
3.469	3 15/32	88.1	N5000-347	3.857		.109		69.0	3.675		.120		.103	2.76	2.96	53400	30200
3.500	3 1/2	88.9	N5000-350	3.890		.109		71.0	3.710		.120		.105	2.79	3.00	53900	31200
3.543	—	90.0	N5000-354	3.936		.109		72.0	3.755		.120		.106	2.83	3.04	54600	31800
3.562	3 9/16	90.5	N5000-354	3.936		.109		72.0	3.776		.120		.107	2.85	3.06	54600	31800

Thickness **t** applies only to **unplated** rings. For **plated** and **stainless steel** (Type H) rings, add .002" to the listed maximum thickness. Maximum ring thickness will be at least .0002" **less** than the listed minimum groove width (**W**).

T.I.R. (total indicator reading) is the maximum allowable deviation of concentricity between groove and housing.

Additional sizes appear on Pages 26 and 30

WALDES **TRUARC** RETAINING RINGS

BASIC *internal series* **N5000** (Continued)

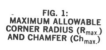

FIG. 1:
MAXIMUM ALLOWABLE
CORNER RADIUS ($R_{max.}$)
AND CHAMFER ($Ch_{max.}$)

$R_{max.}$

$CH_{max.}$

FIG. 2:
ENLARGED DETAIL
OF GROOVE PROFILE
AND EDGE MARGIN (Z)

MAXIMUM BOTTOM RADII	
Ring Size	R
-25 thru -100	.005
-102 thru -1000	.010

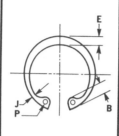

FIG. 3:
SUPPLEMENTARY
RING DIMENSIONS

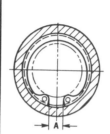

FIG 4:
MINIMUM GAP WIDTH
(Ring installed in groove)

FIG. 5:
LUG DESIGN:
SIZES -206 THRU -275
AND -300 THRU -1000

INTERNAL SERIES N5000 size—no.	Maximum allowable corner radii and chamfers of retained parts (Fig. 1). See Page 21. $R_{max.}$	$Ch_{max.}$	Allowable assembly load with $R_{max.}$ or $Ch_{max.}$ P'_r(lbs.)	Edge margin (Fig. 2) See Page 19 Z	LUG B	tol.	LARGE SECTION E	tol.	SMALL SECTION J	tol.	HOLE DIAMETER P	tol.	MIN. GAP WIDTH (Fig. 4) Ring installed in groove A
• N5000-175	.064	.050	3900	.162	.234		.171		.083		.078		.372
• N5000-181	.064	.050	3900	.165	.234		.170		.084		.093		.382
• N5000-185	.064	.050	3900	.168	.234		.170		.085		.093		.392
• N5000-187	.064	.050	3900	.171	.234		.170		.085		.093		.420
• N5000-193	.064	.050	3900	.177	.234		.170		.085		.093		.438
• N5000-200	.064	.050	3900	.183	.240		.170		.085		.093		.453
(S=2.047) N5000-206	.076	.061	6200	.186	.250		.186		.091		.093		.428
(S=2.062) N5000-206	.078	.062	6200	.186	.250		.186		.091		.093		.468
N5000-212	.078	.062	6200	.189	.260		.195		.096		.093		.460
(S=2.165) N5000-218	.078	.062	6200	.195	.264		.199		.098		.093		.439
(S=2.188) N5000-218	.078	.062	6200	.195	.264		.199		.098		.093		.489
N5000-225	.078	.062	6200	.198	.270		.203		.099		.093		.478
N5000-231	.078	.062	6200	.207	.270		.206		.100		.093		.486
N5000-237	.078	.062	6200	.213	.270	±.005	.207	±.007	.102	±.007	.093		.504
N5000-244	.078	.062	6200	.216	.280		.209		.103		.110		.518
(S=2.500) N5000-250	.078	.062	6200	.222	.280		.210		.103		.110		.532
(S=2.531) N5000-250	.078	.062	6200	.225	.280		.210		.103		.110		.597
N5000-256	.088	.070	9000	.228	.290		.222		.109		.110		.540
N5000-262	.088	.070	9000	.234	.290		.226		.111		.110	+.015	.558
(S=2.677) N5000-268	.090	.072	9000	.240	.300		.230		.113		.110	−.002	.539
(S=2.688) N5000-268	.090	.072	9000	.240	.300		.230		.113		.110		.568
N5000-275	.092	.074	9000	.246	.300		.234		.115		.110		.590
(S=2.812) N5000-281	.088	.070	9000	.252	.300		.230		.115		.110		.615
(S=2.835) N5000-281	.088	.070	9000	.255	.300		.230		.115		.110		.676
N5000-287	.092	.074	9000	.264	.310		.240		.120		.110		.626
(S=2.953) N5000-300	.092	.074	9000	.273	.310		.250		.122		.110		.619
(S=3.000) N5000-300	.092	.074	9000	.273	.310		.250		.122		.110		.738
N5000-306	.097	.078	12000	.279	.310		.254		.126		.125		.651
N5000-312	.099	.079	12000	.285	.310		.259		.129		.125		.655
(S=3.149) N5000-315	.100	.080	12000	.288	.310		.262		.129		.125		.650
(S=3.156) N5000-315	.100	.080	12000	.288	.310		.262		.129		.125		.669
N5000-325	.104	.083	12000	.294	.342		.269		.135		.125		.698
N5000-334	.108	.086	12000	.300	.342	±.008	.276	±.008	.140	±.008	.125		.705
N5000-347	.108	.086	12000	.309	.342		.286		.144		.125		.763
N5000-350	.110	.088	12000	.315	.342		.289		.142		.125		.774
(S=3.543) N5000-354	.110	.088	12000	.318	.342		.292		.142		.125		.788
(S=3.562) N5000-354	.110	.088	12000	.321	.342		.292		.142		.125		.842

SUPPLEMENTARY APPLICATION DATA | SUPPLEMENTARY RING DIMENSIONS

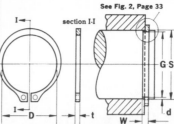

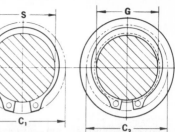

BASIC external series 5100

WALDES TRUARC RETAINING RINGS

See Fig. 2, Page 33

section I-I

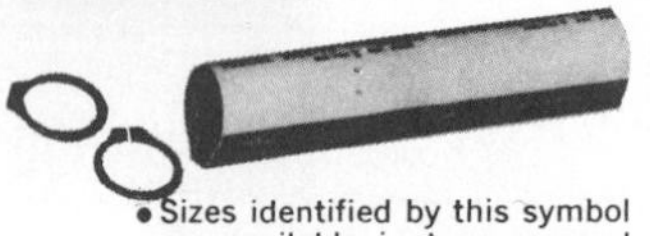

● Sizes identified by this symbol are available in tape-wrapped Rol-Pak® cartridges

SHAFT DIAMETER			MIL-R-21248 MS 16624 NAS 670 EXTERNAL SERIES 5100	TRUARC RING DIMENSIONS				Approx. weight per 1000 pieces	GROOVE DIMENSIONS					APPLICATION DATA			
				Thickness **t** applies only to un-plated rings. For **plated** and **stainless steel** (Type H) rings, add .002" to the listed maximum thickness. Maximum ring thickness will be at least .0002" less than the listed minimum groove width (**W**).					T.I.R. (total indicator reading) is the maximum allowable deviation of concentricity between groove and shaft.					CLEARANCE DIAMETER		ALLOW. THRUST LOAD (lbs.) Sharp Corner Abutment	
Dec. equiv. inch	Approx fract. equiv. inch	Approx. mm	size — no.	FREE DIA.		THICKNESS			DIAMETER		WIDTH		Nominal groove depth	When sprung over shaft	When sprung into groove	RINGS Safety factor = 4 Important! See Page 19	GROOVES Safety factor = 2 Important! See Page 19
S	S	S		D	tol.	t	tol.	lbs.	G	tol.	W	tol.	d	C₁	C₂	Pᵣ	P_g
.125	⅛	3.2	5100-12	.112		.010	±.001	.018	.117		.012		.004	.222	.214	110	35
.156	5⁄32	4.0	5100-15	.142		.010		.037	.146		.012		.005	.270	.260	130	55
.188	3⁄16	4.8	5100-18	.168	+.002 −.004	.015		.059	.175	±.0015 .0015 T.I.R.	.018	+.002 −.000	.006	.298	.286	240	80
.197	---	5.0	5100-19	.179		.015		.063	.185		.018		.006	.319	.307	250	85
.219	7⁄32	5.6	5100-21	.196		.015		.074	.205		.018		.007	.338	.324	280	110
.236	15⁄64	6.0	5100-23	.215		.015		.086	.222		.018		.007	.355	.341	310	120
.250	¼	6.4	●5100-25	.225		.025		.21	.230		.029		.010	.45	.43	590	175
.276	---	7.0	5100-27	.250		.025		.23	.255		.029		.010	.48	.46	650	195
.281	9⁄32	7.1	●5100-28	.256		.025		.24	.261		.029		.010	.49	.47	660	200
.312	5⁄16	7.9	●5100-31	.281		.025		.27	.290		.029		.011	.54	.52	740	240
.344	11⁄32	8.7	5100-34	.309		.025		.31	.321	±.002 .002 T.I.R.	.029		.011	.57	.55	800	265
.354	---	9.0	5100-35	.320		.025		.35	.330		.029		.012	.59	.57	820	300
.375	⅜	9.5	●5100-37	.338	+.002 −.005	.025		.39	.352		.029		.012	.61	.59	870	320
.394	---	10.0	5100-39	.354		.025		.42	.369		.029		.012	.62	.60	940	335
.406	13⁄32	10.3	5100-40	.366		.025		.43	.382		.029		.012	.63	.61	950	350
.438	7⁄16	11.1	●5100-43	.395		.025		.50	.412		.029		.013	.66	.64	1020	400
.469	15⁄32	11.9	5100-46	.428		.025		.54	.443		.029		.013	.68	.66	1100	450
.500	½	12.7	●5100-50	.461		.035		.91	.468	±.002 .004 T.I.R.	.039		.016	.77	.74	1650	550
.551	---	14.0	5100-55	.509		.035		.90	.519		.039		.016	.81	.78	1800	600
.562	9⁄16	14.3	●5100-56	.521		.035		1.1	.530		.039	+.003 −.000	.016	.82	.79	1850	650
.594	19⁄32	15.1	5100-59	.550		.035	±.002	1.2	.559		.039		.017	.86	.83	1950	750
.625	⅝	15.9	●5100-62	.579		.035		1.3	.588		.039		.018	.90	.87	2060	800
.669	---	17.0	5100-66	.621		.035		1.4	.629		.039		.020	.93	.89	2200	950
.672	43⁄64	17.1	5100-66	.621		.035		1.4	.631		.039		.020	.93	.89	2200	950
.688	11⁄16	17.5	●5100-68	.635	+.005 −.010	.042		1.8	.646	±.003 .004 T.I.R.	.046		.021	1.01	.97	3400	1000
.750	¾	19.0	●5100-75	.693		.042		2.1	.704		.046		.023	1.09	1.05	3700	1200
.781	25⁄32	19.8	5100-78	.722		.042		2.2	.733		.046		.024	1.12	1.08	3900	1300
.812	13⁄16	20.6	5100-81	.751		.042		2.5	.762		.046		.025	1.15	1.10	4000	1450
.875	⅞	22.2	5100-87	.810		.042		2.8	.821		.046		.027	1.21	1.16	4300	1650
.938	15⁄16	23.8	5100-93	.867		.042		3.1	.882		.046		.028	1.34	1.29	4650	1850
.984	63⁄64	25.0	5100-98	.910		.042		3.5	.926		.046		.029	1.39	1.34	4850	2000
1.000	1	25.4	5100-100	.925		.042		3.6	.940		.046		.030	1.41	1.35	4950	2100
1.023	---	26.0	5100-102	.946		.042		3.9	.961		.046		.031	1.43	1.37	5050	2250
1.062	1 1⁄16	27.0	5100-106	.982		.050		4.8	.998		.056		.032	1.50	1.44	6200	2400
1.125	1⅛	28.6	5100-112	1.041		.050		5.1	1.059		.056		.033	1.55	1.49	6600	2600
1.188	1 3⁄16	30.2	5100-118	1.098		.050		5.6	1.118		.056		.035	1.61	1.54	7000	2950
1.250	1¼	31.7	5100-125	1.156	+.010 −.015	.050		5.9	1.176	±.004 .005 T.I.R	.056		.037	1.69	1.62	7350	3250
1.312	1 5⁄16	33.3	5100-131	1.214		.050		6.8	1.232		.056		.040	1.75	1.67	7750	3700
1.375	1⅜	34.9	5100-137	1.272		.050		7.2	1.291		.056		.042	1.80	1.72	8100	4100
1.438	1 7⁄16	36.5	5100-143	1.333		.050		8.1	1.350		.056		.044	1.87	1.79	8500	4500
1.500	1½	38.1	5100-150	1.387		.050		9.0	1.406		.056	+.004 −.000	.047	1.99	1.90	8800	5000
1.562	1 9⁄16	39.7	5100-156	1.446		.062		12.4	1.468		.068		.047	2.10	2.01	11400	5200
1.625	1⅝	41.3	5100-162	1.503		.062		13.2	1.529		.068		.048	2.17	2.08	11850	5500
1.688	1 11⁄16	42.9	5100-168	1.560		.062		14.8	1.589		.068		.049	2.24	2.15	12350	5850
1.750	1¾	44.4	5100-175	1.618		.062		15.3	1.650	±.005 .005 T.I.R.	.068		.050	2.31	2.21	12800	6200
1.772	---	45.0	5100-177	1.637	+.013 −.020	.062	±.003	15.4	1.669		.068		.051	2.33	2.23	12950	6400
1.812	1 13⁄16	46.0	5100-181	1.675		.062		16.2	1.708		.068		.052	2.38	2.28	13250	6650
1.875	1⅞	47.6	5100-187	1.735		.062		17.3	1.769		.068		.053	2.44	2.34	13700	7000
1.969	1 31⁄32	50.0	5100-196	1.819		.062		18.0	1.857		.068		.056	2.54	2.43	14350	7800
2.000	2	50.8	5100-200	1.850		.062		19.0	1.886		.068		.057	2.55	2.44	14600	8050

A140

(For continuation of sizes, see Page 34)

TRUARC RETAINING RINGS DIVISION

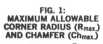

FIG. 1:
MAXIMUM ALLOWABLE
CORNER RADIUS (R_max.)
AND CHAMFER (Ch_max.)

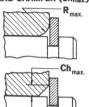

FIG. 2:
ENLARGED DETAIL
OF GROOVE PROFILE
AND EDGE MARGIN (Z)

MAXIMUM BOTTOM RADII	
Ring size	R
-12 thru -23	Sharp corners
-25 thru -35	.003
-37 thru -100	.005
-102 thru -200	.010

FIG. 3:
SUPPLEMENTARY
RING DIMENSIONS

FIG. 4:
MAXIMUM
GAGING DIAMETER
(Ring installed in groove)

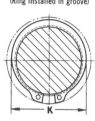

FIG. 5:
LUG DESIGN
Sizes -12 thru -23

SUPPLEMENTARY APPLICATION DATA						SUPPLEMENTARY RING DIMENSIONS								
EXTERNAL SERIES **5100**	Max. allow. corner radii and chamfers of retained parts. (Fig. 1). See Pg. 21		Allow. assembly load with R_max. or Ch_max.	Edge margin (Fig. 2) See Page 19	Safe rotational speeds	(Fig. 3)								MAX. GAGING DIA. Ring installed in groove (Fig. 4)
						LUG		LARGE SECTION		SMALL SECTION		HOLE DIAMETER		
size — no.	R_max.	Ch_max.	P′ (lbs.)	Z	rpm	B	tol.	E	tol.	J	tol.	P	tol.	K
5100-12	.010	.006	45	.012	80000	.046		.018	±.0015	.011	±.0015	.026		.148
5100-15	.015	.009	45	.015	80000	.054		.026		.016		.026		.189
5100-18	.014	.0085	105	.018	80000	.050	±.002	.025		.016		.025		.218
5100-19	.0145	.009	105	.018	80000	.056		.026	±.002	.016	±.002	.026		.229
5100-21	.015	.009	105	.021	80000	.056		.028		.017		.026		.252
5100-23	.0165	.010	105	.021	80000	.056		.030		.019		.026		.272
• 5100-25	.018	.011	470	.030	80000	.080		.035		.025		.041		.290
5100-27	.0175	.0105	470	.031	76000	.081		.035		.024		.041		.315
• 5100-28	.020	.012	470	.030	74000	.080		.038		.0255		.041		.326
• 5100-31	.020	.012	470	.033	70000	.087		.040		.026		.041		.357
5100-34	.021	.0125	470	.033	64000	.087		.042		.0265		.041		.390
5100-35	.023	.014	470	.036	62000	.087		.046	±.003	.029	±.003	.041		.405
• 5100-37	.026	.0155	470	.036	60000	.088		.050		.0305		.041		.433
5100-39	.027	.016	470	.037	56500	.087		.052		.031		.041		.452
5100-40	.0285	.017	470	.036	55000	.087	±.003	.054		.033		.041	+.010 −.002	.468
• 5100-43	.029	.0175	470	.039	50000	.088		.055		.033		.041		.501
5100-46	.031	.018	470	.039	42000	.088		.060		.035		.041		.540
• 5100-50	.034	.020	910	.048	40000	.108		.065		.040		.047		.574
5100-55	.027	.0165	910	.048	36000	.108		.053		.036		.047		.611
• 5100-56	.038	.023	910	.048	35000	.108		.072		.041		.047		.644
5100-59	.0395	.0235	910	.052	32000	.109		.076	±.004	.043	±.004	.047		.680
• 5100-62	.0415	.025	910	.055	30000	.110		.080		.045		.047		.715
(S=.669) 5100-66	.040	.024	910	.060	29000	.110		.082		.043		.047		.756
(S=.672) 5100-66	.040	.024	910	.060	29000	.110		.082		.043		.047		.758
• 5100-68	.042	.025	1340	.063	28000	.136		.084		.048		.052		.779
• 5100-75	.046	.0275	1340	.069	26500	.136		.092		.051		.052		.850
5100-78	.047	.028	1340	.072	25500	.136		.094		.052		.052		.883
5100-81	.047	.028	1340	.075	24500	.136		.096		.054		.052		.914
5100-87	.051	.0305	1340	.081	23000	.137		.104	±.005	.057	±.005	.052		.987
5100-93	.055	.033	1340	.084	21500	.166		.110		.063		.078		1.054
5100-98	.056	.0335	1340	.087	20500	.167		.114		.0645		.078		1.106
5100-100	.057	.034	1340	.090	20000	.167		.116		.065		.078		1.122
5100-102	.058	.035	1340	.093	19500	.168		.118		.066		.078		1.147
5100-106	.060	.036	1950	.096	19000	.181		.122		.069		.078		1.192
5100-112	.063	.038	1950	.099	18800	.182		.128		.071		.078		1.261
5100-118	.064	.0385	1950	.105	18000	.182	±.004	.132		.072		.078		1.325
5100-125	.068	.041	1950	.111	17000	.183		.140		.076		.078		1.396
5100-131	.068	.041	1950	.120	16500	.183		.146		.0765		.078		1.458
5100-137	.072	.043	1950	.126	16000	.184		.152		.082		.078		1.529
5100-143	.076	.045	1950	.132	15000	.184		.160		.086		.078	+.015 −.002	1.600
5100-150	.079	.047	1950	.141	14800	.214		.168		.091		.120		1.668
5100-156	.082	.049	3000	.141	14000	.235		.172	±.006	.093	±.006	.125		1.740
5100-162	.087	.052	3000	.144	13200	.235		.180		.097		.125		1.812
5100-168	.090	.054	3000	.148	13000	.235		.184		.099		.125		1.877
5100-175	.091	.054	3000	.150	12200	.237		.188		.101		.125		1.945
5100-177	.092	.055	3000	.154	11700	.237		.190		.102		.125		1.967
5100-181	.092	.055	3000	.156	11500	.238		.192		.102		.125		2.010
5100-187	.094	.056	3000	.159	11000	.239		.196		.104		.125		2.076
5100-196	.094	.056	3000	.168	10500	.245		.200		.106		.125		2.170
5100-200	.096	.057	3000	.171	10000	.239		.204		.108		.125		2.205

WALDES KOHINOOR, INC. • LONG ISLAND CITY 1, N.Y.

A141

E-RING *external series* **5133** X5133 • Y5133 — **WALDES TRUARC RETAINING RINGS**

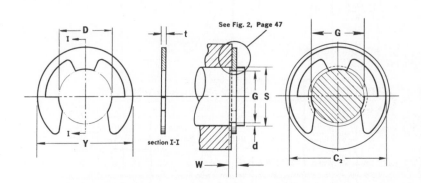

See Fig. 2, Page 47

section I-I

• Sizes identified by this symbol are available in tape-wrapped **Rol-Pak®** cartridges for use with Truarc Applicators, Dispensers and other assembly tools

SHAFT DIA.			MIL-R-21248 MS 16633 **EXTERNAL SERIES 5133** X5133 Y5133	TRUARC RING DIMENSIONS					GROOVE DIMENSIONS					APPLICATION DATA			
				Thickness t applies only to unplated rings. For plated and stainless steel (Type H) rings, add .002″ to the listed maximum thickness. Maximum ring thickness will be at least .0002″ less than the listed minimum groove width (W).					T.I.R. (total indicator reading) is the maximum allowable deviation of concentricity between groove and shaft.						CLEARANCE DIAMETER		ALLOW. THRUST LOAD (lbs.) Sharp Corner Abutment
																	RINGS Safety factor=3	GROOVES Safety factor=2
Dec. equiv. inch	Approx. fract. equiv. inch	Approx. mm.	size—no.	FREE DIA.		THICKNESS		Approx. weight per 1000 pieces	DIAMETER		WIDTH		Nominal groove depth	Free outside dia. (REF.)	When sprung into groove G	Important! See Page 19	Important! See Page 19
S	S	S		D	tol.	t	tol.	lbs.	G	tol.	W	tol.	d	Y	C_2	P_r	P_g
.040	—	1.0	X5133-4	.025	+.001 −.003	.010	±.001	.009	.026	+.002 −.000 .0015 T.I.R.	.012	+.002 −.000	.007	.079	.090	13	6
.062	1/16	1.6	• X5133-6	.051		.010		.028	.052		.012		.005	.140	.150	20	7
.062	1/16	1.6	• Y5133-6	.051		.020	±.002	.094	.052		.023		.005	.187	.200	40	7
.062	1/16	1.6	• 5133-6	.051		.010	±.001	.030	.052		.012		.005	.156	.165	20	7
.094	3/32	2.4	• X5133-9	.069	±.002 .003	.015		.10	.074		.018		.010	.230	.245	45	20
.094	3/32	2.4	• 5133-9	.073		.015		.058	.074		.018		.010	.187	.200	45	20
.110	7/64	2.8	• X5133-11	.076		.015		.31	.079		.018		.015	.375	.390	60	40
.125	1/8	3.2	• 5133-12	.094		.015		.087	.095		.018		.015	.230	.240	65	45
.140	9/64	3.6	• X5133-14	.100		.015		.060	.102		.018		.019	.203	.215	75	60
.140	9/64	3.6	• Y5133-14	.108		.015		.10	.110		.018		.015	.250	.265	75	45
.140	9/64	3.6	• 5133-14	.102	+.001 −.003	.025		.21	.105	+.002 −.000 .002 T.I.R.	.029		.017	.270	.285	170	60
.156	5/32	4.0	• 5133-15	.114		.025		.21	.116		.029		.020	.282	.295	175	75
.172	11/64	4.4	• X5133-17	.125		.025		.24	.127		.029		.022	.312	.325	180	90
.188	3/16	4.8	• X5133-18	.122		.025		.45	.125		.029		.031	.375	.39	200	135
.188	3/16	4.8	• 5133-18	.145		.025		.29	.147		.029		.020	.335	.35	190	90
.219	7/32	5.6	• X5133-21	.185		.025	±.002	.47	.188		.029	+.003 −.000	.015	.437	.45	225	75
.250	1/4	6.3	• 5133-25	.207		.025		.76	.210		.029		.020	.527	.54	255	115
.312	5/16	7.9	• X5133-31	.243		.025		.57	.250		.029		.031	.500	.52	325	225
.375	3/8	9.5	• 5133-37	.300	+.002 −.004	.035		1.5	.303		.039		.036	.660	.68	690	315
.438	7/16	11.1	• 5133-43	.337		.035		1.5	.343		.039		.047	.687	.71	830	480
.438	7/16	11.1	• X5133-43	.375		.035		1.0	.380	+.003 −.000 .004 T.I.R.	.039		.029	.600	.62	800	280
.500	1/2	12.7	• 5133-50	.392		.042		2.5	.396		.046		.052	.800	.82	1110	600
.625	5/8	15.9	• 5133-62	.480		.042		3.2	.485		.046		.070	.940	.96	1420	1050
.744	—	18.9	X5133-74	.616		.050		4.3	.625		.056		.059	1.000	1.02	1900	1050
.750	3/4	19.0	X5133-74	.616	+.003 −.005	.050		4.3	.625		.056		.062	1.000	1.02	1950	1100
.750	3/4	19.0	• 5133-75	.574		.050		5.8	.580		.056		.085	1.120	1.14	2000	1500
.875	7/8	22.2	5133-87	.668		.050		7.6	.675		.056		.100	1.300	1.32	2350	2050
.984	63/64	25.0	X5133-98	.822		.050		9.2	.835		.056		.074	1.500	1.53	2600	1750
1.000	1	25.4	X5133-98	.822		.050		9.2	.835		.056		.082	1.500	1.53	2650	1900
1.188	1 3/16	30.2	X5133-118	1.066	+.006 −.010	.062	±.003	11.3	1.079	+.005 −.000 .005 T.I.R.	.068	+.004 −.000	.054	1.626	1.67	3450	1500
1.375	1 3/8	34.9	X5133-137	1.213		.062		15.4	1.230		.068		.072	1.875	1.92	4100	2350

WALDES **TRUARC** RETAINING RINGS

E-RING
external series
5133
X5133 • Y5133

FIG. 1:
MAXIMUM ALLOWABLE
CORNER RADIUS (R_{max.})
AND CHAMFER (Ch_{max.})

FIG. 2:
ENLARGED DETAIL
OF GROOVE PROFILE
AND EDGE MARGIN (Z)

MAXIMUM BOTTOM RADII	
Ring size	**R**
X-4 thru -6	Sharp Corners
X-9 thru -25	.005
X-31 thru X-43	.010
-50 thru X-137	.015

SUPPLEMENTARY APPLICATION DATA

EXTERNAL SERIES **5133** X5133 Y5133	Maximum allowable corner radii and chamfers of retained parts (Fig. 1). See Page 21.		Allow. assembly load with R_{max.} or Ch_{max.}	Edge margin (Fig. 2) See Page 19	Safe rotational speeds
size—no.	$R_{max.}$	$Ch_{max.}$	$P'_{r(lbs.)}$	Z	rpm
X5133-4	.015	.010	13	.014	40000
• X5133-6	.030	.020	20	.010	40000
• Y5133-6	.035	.025	40	.010	40000
• 5133-6	.030	.020	20	.010	40000
• X5133-9	.053	.040	45	.020	36000
• 5133-9	.040	.030	45	.020	36000
• X5133-11	.080	.060	60	.030	35000
• 5133-12	.040	.030	65	.030	35000
• X5133-14	.029	.022	75	.038	32000
• Y5133-14	.040	.030	75	.030	32000
• 5133-14	.060	.045	170	.034	32000
• 5133-15	.060	.045	175	.040	31000
• X5133-17	.060	.045	180	.044	30000
• X5133-18	.060	.045	200	.062	30000
• 5133-18	.060	.045	190	.040	30000
• X5133-21	.060	.045	225	.030	26000
• 5133-25	.060	.045	255	.040	25000
• X5133-31	.060	.045	325	.062	22000
• 5133-37	.065	.050	690	.072	20000
• 5133-43	.065	.050	830	.094	16500
• X5133-43	.050	.035	800	.058	16500
• 5133-50	.080	.060	1110	.104	14000
• 5133-62	.080	.060	1420	.140	12000
X5133-74	.060	.045	1900	.118	11000
X5133-74	.057	.042	1900	.124	11000
• 5133-75	.085	.065	2000	.170	10500
5133-87	.085	.065	2350	.200	9000
X5133-98	.085	.065	2700	.148	6500
X5133-98	.077	.057	2700	.164	6500
X5133-118	.090	.070	3450	.108	5500
X5133-137	.090	.070	4100	.144	4000

Index